THE MYSTERY
⇒≫|⇐ OF THE |≫⇐
BLUE TRAIN

AGATHA CHRISTIE

THE MYSTERY OF THE BLUE TRAIN

PAGE CLASSICS

ISBN: 978-1-64833-742-0

First published 1928
Published by Page Publications 2024

Printed in China

Contents

1.	The Man with the White Hair	1
2.	M. le Marquis	6
3.	Heart of Fire	11
4.	In Curzon Street	16
5.	A Useful Gentleman	23
6.	Mirelle	33
7.	Letters	39
8.	Lady Tamplin Writes a Letter	47
9.	An Offer Refused	55
10.	On the Blue Train	61
11.	Murder	72
12.	At the Villa Marguerite	84
13.	Van Aldin Gets a Telegram	91
14.	Ada Mason's Story	96
15.	The Comte de la Roche	101
16.	Poirot Discusses the Case	108
17.	An Aristocratic Gentleman	115
18.	Derek Lunches	124
19.	An Unexpected Visitor	128
20.	Katherine Makes a Friend	136

21.	At the Tennis	142
22.	M. Papopolous Breakfasts	152
23.	A New Theory	158
24.	Poirot Gives Advice	162
25.	Defiance	168
26.	A Warning	175
27.	Interview with Mirelle	183
28.	Poirot Plays the Squirrel	194
29.	A Letter From Home	204
30.	Miss Viner Gives Judgment	214
31.	Mr. Aarons Lunches	222
32.	Katherine and Poirot Compare Notes	226
33.	A New Theory	232
34.	The Blue Train Again	236
35.	Explanations	241
36.	By the Sea	251

ONE

The Man with the White Hair

It was close on midnight when a man crossed the Place de la Concorde. In spite of the handsome fur coat which garbed his meagre form, there was something essentially weak and paltry about him.

A little man with a face like a rat. A man, one would say, who could never play a conspicuous part, or rise to prominence in any sphere. And yet, in leaping to such a conclusion, an onlooker would have been wrong. For this man, negligible and inconspicuous as he seemed, played a prominent part in the destiny of the world. In an Empire where rats ruled, he was the king of the rats.

Even now, an Embassy awaited his return. But he had business to do first—business of which the Embassy was not officially cognizant. His face gleamed white and sharp in the moonlight. There was the least hint of a curve in the thin nose. His father had been a Polish Jew, a journeyman tailor. It was business such as his father would have loved that took him abroad to-night.

He came to the Seine, crossed it, and entered one of the less reputable quarters of Paris. Here he stopped before a tall, dilapidated house and made his way up to an apartment on the fourth floor. He had barely time to knock before the door was opened by a woman who had evidently been awaiting his arrival. She gave him no greeting, but helped him off with his overcoat and then led the way into the tawdrily furnished sitting-room. The electric light

1

was shaded with dirty pink festoons and it softened, but could not disguise, the girl's face with its mask of crude paint. Could not disguise, either, the broad Mongolian cast of her countenance. There was no doubt of Olga Demiroff's profession, nor of her nationality.

"All is well, little one?"

"All is well, Boris Ivanovitch."

He nodded murmuring: "I do not think I have been followed."

But there was anxiety in his tone. He went to the window, drawing the curtains aside slightly, and peering carefully out. He started away violently.

"There are two men—on the opposite pavement. It looks to me—" He broke off and began gnawing at his nails—a habit he had when anxious.

The Russian girl was shaking her head with a slow, reassuring action.

"They were here before you came."

"All the same, it looks to me as though they were watching this house."

"Possibly," she admitted indifferently.

"But then—"

"What of it? Even if they *know*—it will not be *you* they will follow from here."

A thin, cruel smile came to his lips.

"No," he admitted, "that is true."

He mused for a minute or two and then observed:

"This damned American—he can look after himself as well as anybody."

"I suppose so."

He went again to the window.

"Tough customers," he muttered, with a chuckle. "Known to the police, I fear. Well, well, I wish Brother Apache good hunting."

Olga Demiroff shook her head.

"If the American is the kind of man they say he is, it will take more than a couple of cowardly apaches to get the better of him."

2

She paused. "I wonder—"

"Well?"

"Nothing. Only twice this evening a man has passed along this street—a man with white hair."

"What of it?"

"This. As he passed those two men, he dropped his glove. One of them picked it up and returned it to him. A thread-bare device."

"You mean—that the white-haired man is—their employer?"

"Something of the kind."

The Russian looked alarmed and uneasy.

"You are sure—the parcel is safe? It has not been tampered with? There has been too much talk ... much too much talk."

He gnawed his nails again.

"Judge for yourself."

She bent to the fireplace, deftly removing the coals. Underneath, from amongst the crumpled balls of newspaper, she selected from the very middle an oblong package wrapped round with grimy newspaper, and handed it to the man.

"Ingenious," he said, with a nod of approval.

"The apartment has been searched twice. The mattress on my bed was ripped open."

"It is as I said," he muttered. "There has been too much talk. This haggling over the price—it was a mistake."

He had unwrapped the newspaper. Inside was a small brown paper parcel. This in turn he unwrapped, verified the contents, and quickly wrapped it up once more. As he did so, an electric bell rang sharply.

"The American is punctual," said Olga, with a glance at the clock.

She left the room. In a minute she returned ushering in a stranger, a big, broad-shouldered man whose transatlantic origin was evident. His keen glance went from one to the other.

"M. Krassnine?" he inquired politely.

"I am he," said Boris. "I must apologize for—for the

unconventionality of this meeting-place. But secrecy is urgent. I—I cannot afford to be connected with this business in any way."

"Is that so?" said the American politely.

"I have your word, have I not, that no details of this transaction will be made public? That is one of the conditions of—sale."

The American nodded.

"That has already been agreed upon," he said indifferently. "Now, perhaps, you will produce the goods."

"You have the money—in notes?"

"Yes," replied the other.

He did not, however, make any attempt to produce it. After a moment's hesitation, Krassnine gestured towards the small parcel on the table.

The American took it up and unrolled the wrapping paper. The contents he took over to a small electric lamp and submitted them to a very thorough examination. Satisfied, he drew from his pocket a thick leather wallet and extracted from it a wad of notes. These he handed to the Russian, who counted them carefully.

"All right?"

"I thank you, Monsieur. Everything is correct."

"Ah!" said the other. He slipped the brown paper parcel negligently into his pocket. He bowed to Olga. "Good evening, Mademoiselle. Good evening, M. Krassnine."

He went out shutting the door behind him. The eyes of the two in the room met. The man passed his tongue over his dry lips.

"I wonder—will he ever get back to his hotel?" he muttered.

By common accord, they both turned to the window. They were just in time to see the American emerge into the street below. He turned to the left and marched along at a good pace without once turning his head. Two shadows stole from a doorway and followed noiselessly. Pursuers and pursued vanished into the night. Olga Demiroff spoke.

"He will get back safely," she said. "You need not fear—or hope—whichever it is."

"Why do you think he will be safe?" asked Krassnine curiously.

"A man who has made as much money as he has could not possibly be a fool," said Olga. "And talking of money—"

She looked significantly at Krassnine.

"Eh?"

"My share, Boris Ivanovitch."

With some reluctance, Krassnine handed over two of the notes. She nodded her thanks, with a complete lack of emotion, and tucked them away in her stocking.

"That is good," she remarked, with satisfaction.

He looked at her curiously.

"You have no regrets, Olga Vassilovna?"

"Regrets? For what?"

"For what has been in your keeping. There are women—most women, I believe, who go mad over such things."

She nodded reflectively.

"Yes, you speak truth there. Most women have that madness. I—have not. I wonder now—" She broke off.

"Well?" asked the other curiously.

"The American will be safe with them—yes, I am sure of that. But afterwards—"

"Eh? What are you thinking of?"

"He will give them, of course, to some woman," said Olga thoughtfully. "I wonder what will happen then...."

She shook herself impatiently and went over to the window. Suddenly she uttered an exclamation and called to her companion.

"See, he is going down the street now—the man I mean."

They both gazed down together. A slim, elegant figure was progressing along at a leisurely pace. He wore an opera hat and a cloak. As he passed a street lamp, the light illumined a thatch of thick white hair.

TWO

M. le Marquis

The man with the white hair continued on his course, unhurried, and seemingly indifferent to his surroundings. He took a side turning to the right and another one to the left. Now and then he hummed a little air to himself.

Suddenly he stopped dead and listened intently. He had heard a certain sound. It might have been the bursting of a tyre or it might have been—a shot. A curious smile played round his lips for a minute. Then he resumed his leisurely walk.

On turning a corner he came upon a scene of some activity. A representative of the law was making notes in a pocket-book, and one or two late passers-by had collected on the spot. To one of these the man with the white hair made a polite request for information.

"Something has been happening, yes?"

"*Mais oui*, Monsieur. Two apaches set upon an elderly American gentleman."

"They did him no injury?"

"No, indeed." The man laughed. "The American, he had a revolver in his pocket, and before they could attack him, he fired shots so closely round them that they took alarm and fled. The police, as usual, arrived too late."

"Ah!" said the inquirer.

He displayed no emotion of any kind.

Placidly and unconcernedly he resumed his nocturnal strolling. Presently he crossed the Seine and came into the richer areas of the city. It was some twenty minutes later that he came to a stop before a certain house in a quiet but aristocratic thoroughfare.

The shop, for shop it was, was a restrained and unpretentious one. D. Papopolous, dealer in antiques, was so known to fame that he needed no advertisement, and indeed most of his business was not done over a counter. M. Papopolous had a very handsome apartment of his own overlooking the Champs Élysées, and it might reasonably be supposed that he would have been found there and not at his place of business at such an hour, but the man with the white hair seemed confident of success as he pressed the obscurely placed bell, having first given a quick glance up and down the deserted street.

His confidence was not misplaced. The door opened and a man stood in the aperture. He wore gold rings in his ears and was of a swarthy cast of countenance.

"Good evening," said the stranger. "Your master is within?"

"The master is here, but he does not see chance visitors at this time of night," growled the other.

"I think he will see me. Tell him that his friend M. le Marquis is here."

The man opened the door a little wider and allowed the visitor to enter.

The man who gave his name as M. le Marquis had shielded his face with his hand as he spoke. When the man-servant returned with the information that M. Papopolous would be pleased to receive the visitor a further change had taken place in the stranger's appearance. The man-servant must have been very unobservant or very well trained for he betrayed no surprise at the small black satin mask which hid the other's features. Leading the way to a door at the end of the hall, he opened it and announced in a respectful murmur: *"M. le Marquis."*

The figure which rose to receive this strange guest was an

imposing one. There was something venerable and patriarchal about M. Papopolous. He had a high domed forehead and a beautiful white beard. His manner had in it something ecclesiastical and benign.

"My dear friend," said M. Papopolous.

He spoke in French and his tones were rich and unctuous.

"I must apologize," said the visitor, "for the lateness of the hour."

"Not at all. Not at all," said M. Papopolous—"an interesting time of night. You have had, perhaps, an interesting evening?"

"Not personally," said M. le Marquis.

"Not personally," repeated M. Papopolous, "no, no, of course not. And there is news, eh?"

He cast a sharp glance sideways at the other, a glance that was not ecclesiastical or benign in the least.

"There is no news. The attempt failed. I hardly expected anything else."

"Quite so," said M. Papopolous; "anything crude—"

He waved his hand to express his intense distaste for crudity in any form. There was indeed nothing crude about M. Papopolous nor about the goods he handled. He was well known in most European courts, and kings called him Demetrius in a friendly manner. He had the reputation for the most exquisite discretion. That, together with the nobility of his aspect, had carried him through several very questionable transactions.

"The direct attack—" said M. Papopolous. He shook his head. "It answers sometimes—but very seldom."

The other shrugged his shoulders.

"It saves time," he remarked, "and to fail costs nothing—or next to nothing. The other plan—will not fail."

"Ah," said M. Papopolous, looking at him keenly.

The other nodded slowly.

"I have great confidence in your—er—reputation," said the antique dealer.

M. le Marquis smiled gently.

"I think I may say," he murmured, "that your confidence will not be misplaced."

"You have unique opportunities," said the other, with a note of envy in his voice.

"I make them," said M. le Marquis.

He rose and took up the cloak which he had thrown carelessly on the back of a chair.

"I will keep you informed, M. Papopolous, through the usual channels, but there must be no hitch in your arrangements."

M. Papopolous was pained.

"There is *never* a hitch in my arrangements," he complained.

The other smiled, and without any further word of adieu he left the room, closing the door behind him.

M. Papopolous remained in thought for a moment stroking his venerable white beard, and then moved across to a second door which opened inwards. As he turned the handle, a young woman, who only too clearly had been leaning against it with her ear to the keyhole, stumbled headlong into the room. M. Papopolous displayed neither surprise nor concern. It was evidently all quite natural to him.

"Well, Zia?" he asked.

"I did not hear him go," explained Zia.

She was a handsome young woman, built on Junoesque lines, with dark flashing eyes and such a general air of resemblance to M. Papopolous that it was easy to see they were father and daughter.

"It is annoying," she continued vexedly, "that one cannot see through a keyhole and hear through it at the same time."

"It has often annoyed me," said M. Papopolous, with great simplicity.

"So that is M. le Marquis," said Zia slowly. "Does he always wear a mask, father?"

"Always."

There was a pause.

"It is the rubies, I suppose?" asked Zia.

Her father nodded.

"What do you think, my little one?" he inquired, with a hint of amusement in his beady black eyes.

"Of M. le Marquis?"

"Yes."

"I think," said Zia slowly, "that it is a very rare thing to find a well-bred Englishman who speaks French as well as that."

"Ah," said M. Papopolous, "so that is what you think."

As usual, he did not commit himself, but he regarded Zia with benign approval.

"I thought, too," said Zia, "that his head was an odd shape."

"Massive," said her father—"a trifle massive. But then that effect is always created by a wig."

They both looked at each other and smiled.

THREE

Heart of Fire

Rufus Van Aldin passed through the revolving doors of the Savoy, and walked to the reception desk. The desk clerk smiled a respectful greeting.

"Pleased to see you back again, Mr. Van Aldin," he said.

The American millionaire nodded his head in a casual greeting.

"Everything all right?" he asked.

"Yes, sir. Major Knighton is upstairs in the suite now."

Van Aldin nodded again.

"Any mail?" he vouchsafed.

"They have all been sent up, Mr. Van Aldin. Oh! wait a minute."

He dived into a pigeon hole, and produced a letter.

"Just come this minute," he explained.

Rufus Van Aldin took the letter from him, and as he saw the handwriting, a woman's flowing hand, his face was suddenly transformed. The harsh contours of it softened, and the hard line of his mouth relaxed. He looked a different man. He walked across to the lift with the letter in his hand and the smile still on his lips.

In the drawing-room of his suite, a young man was sitting at a desk nimbly sorting correspondence with the ease born of long practice. He sprang up as Van Aldin entered.

"Hallo, Knighton!"

"Glad to see you back, sir. Had a good time?"

"So-so!" said the millionaire unemotionally. "Paris is rather a one-horse city nowadays. Still—I got what I went over for."

He smiled to himself rather grimly.

"You usually do, I believe," said the secretary, laughing.

"That's so," agreed the other.

He spoke in a matter-of-fact manner, as one stating a well-known fact. Throwing off his heavy overcoat, he advanced to the desk.

"Anything urgent?"

"I don't think so, sir. Mostly the usual stuff. I have not quite finished sorting it out."

Van Aldin nodded briefly. He was a man who seldom expressed either blame or praise. His methods with those he employed were simple; he gave them a fair trial and dismissed promptly those who were inefficient. His selections of people were unconventional. Knighton, for instance, he had met casually at a Swiss resort two months previously. He had approved of the fellow, looked up his war record, and found in it the explanation of the limp with which he walked. Knighton had made no secret of the fact that he was looking for a job, and indeed diffidently asked the millionaire if he knew of any available post. Van Aldin remembered, with a grim smile of amusement, the young man's complete astonishment when he had been offered the post of secretary to the great man himself.

"But—but I have no experience of business," he had stammered.

"That doesn't matter a cuss," Van Aldin had replied. "I have got three secretaries already to attend to that kind of thing. But I am likely to be in England for the next six months, and I want an Englishman who—well, knows the ropes—and can attend to the social side of things for me."

So far, Van Aldin had found his judgment confirmed. Knighton had proved quick, intelligent, and resourceful, and he had a distinct charm of manner.

The secretary indicated three or four letters placed by themselves on the top of the desk.

"It might perhaps be as well, sir, if you glanced at these," he suggested. "The top one is about the Colton agreement—"

But Rufus Van Aldin held up a protesting hand.

"I am not going to look at a durned thing to-night," he declared. "They can all wait till the morning. Except this one," he added, looking down at the letter he held in his hand. And again that strange transforming smile stole over his face.

Richard Knighton smiled sympathetically.

"Mrs. Kettering?" he murmured. "She rang up yesterday and to-day. She seems very anxious to see you at once, sir."

"Does she, now!"

The smile faded from the millionaire's face. He ripped open the envelope which he held in his hand and took out the enclosed sheet. As he read it his face darkened, his mouth set grimly in the line which Wall Street knew so well, and his brows knit themselves ominously. Knighton turned tactfully away, and went on opening letters and sorting them. A muttered oath escaped the millionaire, and his clenched fist hit the table sharply.

"I'll not stand for this," he muttered to himself. "Poor little girl, it's a good thing she has her old father behind her."

He walked up and down the room for some minutes, his brows drawn together in a scowl. Knighton still bent assiduously over the desk. Suddenly Van Aldin came to an abrupt halt. He took up his overcoat from the chair where he had thrown it.

"Are you going out again, sir?"

"Yes; I'm going round to see my daughter."

"If Colton's people ring up—"

"Tell them to go to the devil," said Van Aldin.

"Very well," said the secretary unemotionally.

Van Aldin had his overcoat on by now. Cramming his hat upon his head, he went towards the door. He paused with his hand upon the handle.

"You are a good fellow, Knighton," he said. "You don't worry me when I am rattled."

Knighton smiled a little, but made no reply.

"Ruth is my only child," said Van Aldin, "and there is no one on this earth who knows quite what she means to me."

A faint smile irradiated his face. He slipped his hand into his pocket.

"Care to see something, Knighton?"

He came back towards the secretary.

From his pocket he drew out a parcel carelessly wrapped in brown paper. He tossed off the wrapping and disclosed a big, shabby, red velvet case. In the centre of it were some twisted initials surmounted by a crown. He snapped the case open, and the secretary drew in his breath sharply. Against the slightly dingy white of the interior, the stones glowed like blood.

"My God! sir," said Knighton. "Are they—are they real?"

Van Aldin laughed a quiet little cackle of amusement.

"I don't wonder at your asking that. Amongst these rubies are the three largest in the world. Catherine of Russia wore them, Knighton. That centre one there is known as Heart of Fire. It's perfect—not a flaw in it."

"But," the secretary murmured, "they must be worth a fortune."

"Four or five hundred thousand dollars," said Van Aldin nonchalantly, "and that is apart from the historical interest."

"And you carry them about—like that, loose in your pocket?"

Van Aldin laughed amusedly.

"I guess so. You see, they are my little present for Ruthie."

The secretary smiled discreetly.

"I can understand now Mrs. Kettering's anxiety over the telephone," he murmured.

But Van Aldin shook his head. The hard look returned to his face.

"You are wrong there," he said. "She doesn't know about these;

they are my little surprise for her."

He shut the case, and began slowly to wrap it up again.

"It's a hard thing, Knighton," he said, "how little one can do for those one loves. I can buy a good portion of the earth for Ruth, if it would be any use to her, but it isn't. I can hang these things round her neck and give her a moment or two's pleasure, maybe, but—"

He shook his head.

"When a woman is not happy in her home—"

He left the sentence unfinished. The secretary nodded discreetly. He knew, none better, the reputation of the Hon. Derek Kettering. Van Aldin sighed. Slipping the parcel back in his coat pocket, he nodded to Knighton and left the room.

FOUR
In Curzon Street

The Hon. Mrs. Derek Kettering lived in Curzon Street. The butler who opened the door recognized Rufus Van Aldin at once and permitted himself a discreet smile of greeting. He led the way upstairs to the big double drawing-room on the first floor.

A woman who was sitting by the window started up with a cry.

"Why, Dad, if that isn't too good for anything! I've been telephoning Major Knighton all day to try and get hold of you, but he couldn't say for sure when you were expected back."

Ruth Kettering was twenty-eight years of age. Without being beautiful, or in the real sense of the word even pretty, she was striking looking because of her colouring. Van Aldin had been called Carrots and Ginger in his time, and Ruth's hair was almost pure auburn. With it went dark eyes and very black lashes—the effect somewhat enhanced by art. She was tall and slender, and moved well. At a careless glance it was the face of a Raphael Madonna. Only if one looked closely did one perceive the same line of jaw and chin as in Van Aldin's face, bespeaking the same hardness and determination. It suited the man, but suited the woman less well. From her childhood upward Ruth Van Aldin had been accustomed to having her own way, and anyone who had ever stood up against her soon realized that Rufus Van Aldin's daughter never gave in.

"Knighton told me you'd 'phoned him," said Van Aldin. "I only got back from Paris half an hour ago. What's all this about Derek?"

Ruth Kettering flushed angrily.

"It's unspeakable. It's beyond all limits," she cried. "He—he doesn't seem to listen to anything I say."

There was bewilderment as well as anger in her voice.

"He'll listen to me," said the millionaire grimly.

Ruth went on.

"I've hardly seen him for the last month. He goes about everywhere with that woman."

"With what woman?"

"Mirelle. She dances at the Parthenon, you know."

Van Aldin nodded.

"I was down at Leconbury last week. I—I spoke to Lord Leconbury. He was awfully sweet to me, sympathized entirely. He said he'd give Derek a good talking to."

"Ah!" said Van Aldin.

"What do you mean by 'Ah!', Dad?"

"Just what you think I mean, Ruthie. Poor old Leconbury is a wash-out. Of course he sympathized with you, of course he tried to soothe you down. Having got his son and heir married to the daughter of one of the richest men in the States, he naturally doesn't want to mess the thing up. But he's got one foot in the grave already, everyone knows that, and anything he may say will cut darned little ice with Derek."

"Can't *you* do anything, Dad?" urged Ruth, after a minute or two.

"I might," said the millionaire. He waited a second reflectively, and then went on. "There are several things I might do, but there's only one that will be any real good. How much pluck have you got, Ruthie?"

She stared at him. He nodded back at her.

"I mean just what I say. Have you got the grit to admit to all the world that you've made a mistake? There's only one way out of this mess, Ruthie. Cut your losses and start afresh."

"You mean—"

"Divorce."

"Divorce!"

Van Aldin smiled drily.

"You say that word, Ruth, as though you'd never heard it before. And yet your friends are doing it all round you every day."

"Oh! I know that. But—"

She stopped, biting her lip. Her father nodded comprehendingly.

"I know, Ruth. You're like me, you can't bear to let go. But I've learnt, and you've got to learn, that there are times when it's the only way. I might find ways of whistling Derek back to you, but it would all come to the same in the end. *He's no good*, Ruth; he's rotten through and through. And mind you, I blame myself for ever letting you marry him. But you were kind of set on having him, and he seemed in earnest about turning over a new leaf—and well, I'd crossed you once, honey...."

He did not look at her as he said the last words. Had he done so, he might have seen the swift colour that came up in her face.

"You did," she said in a hard voice.

"I was too darned softhearted to do it a second time. I can't tell you how I wish I had, though. You've led a poor kind of life for the last few years, Ruth."

"It has not been very—agreeable," agreed Mrs. Kettering.

"That's why I say to you that this thing has got to *stop!*" He brought his hand down with a bang on the table. "You may have a hankering after the fellow still. *Cut it out*. Face facts. Derek Kettering married you for your money. That's all there is to it. Get rid of him, Ruth."

Ruth Kettering looked down at the ground for some moments, then she said, without raising her head:

"Supposing he doesn't consent?"

Van Aldin looked at her in astonishment.

18

"He won't have a say in the matter."

She flushed and bit her lip.

"No—no—of course not. I only meant—"

She stopped. Her father eyed her keenly.

"What did you mean?"

"I meant—" She paused, choosing her words carefully. "He mayn't take it lying down."

The millionaire's chin shot out grimly.

"You mean he'll fight the case? Let him! But, as a matter of fact, you're wrong. He won't fight. Any solicitor he consults will tell him he hasn't a leg to stand upon."

"You don't think"—she hesitated—"I mean—out of sheer spite against me—he might, try to make it awkward?"

Her father looked at her in some astonishment.

"Fight the case, you mean?"

He shook his head.

"Very unlikely. You see, he would have to have something to go upon."

Mrs. Kettering did not answer. Van Aldin looked at her sharply.

"Come, Ruth, out with it. There's something troubling you— what is it?"

"Nothing, nothing at all."

But her voice was unconvincing.

"You are dreading the publicity, eh? Is that it? You leave it to me. I'll put the whole thing through so smoothly that there will be no fuss at all."

"Very well, Dad, if you really think it's the best thing to be done."

"Got a fancy for the fellow still, Ruth? Is that it?"

"No."

The word came with no uncertain emphasis. Van Aldin seemed satisfied. He patted his daughter on the shoulder.

"It will be all right, little girl. Don't you worry any. Now let's forget all about this. I have brought you a present from Paris."

"For me? Something very nice?"

"I hope you'll think so," said Van Aldin, smiling.

He took the parcel from his coat pocket and handed it to her. She unwrapped it eagerly, and snapped open the case. A long-drawn "Oh!" came from her lips. Ruth Kettering loved jewels—always had done so.

"Dad, how—how wonderful!"

"Rather in a class by themselves, aren't they?" said the millionaire, with satisfaction. "You like them, eh?"

"Like them? Dad, they're unique. How did you get hold of them?"

Van Aldin smiled.

"Ah! that's my secret. They had to be bought privately, of course. They are rather well known. See that big stone in the middle? You have heard of it, maybe; that's the historic 'Heart of Fire.'"

"Heart of Fire!" repeated Mrs. Kettering.

She had taken the stones from the case and was holding them against her breast. The millionaire watched her. He was thinking of the series of women who had worn the jewels. The heartaches, the despairs, the jealousies. "Heart of Fire," like all famous stones, had left behind it a trail of tragedy and violence. Held in Ruth Kettering's assured hand, it seemed to lose its potency of evil. With her cool, equable poise, this woman of the western world seemed a negation to tragedy or heart-burnings. Ruth returned the stones to their case; then, jumping up, she flung her arms round her father's neck.

"Thank you, thank you, thank you, Dad! They are wonderful! You do give me the most marvellous presents always."

"That's all right," said Van Aldin, patting her shoulder. "You are all I have, you know, Ruthie."

"You will stay to dinner, won't you, father?"

"I don't think so. You were going out, weren't you?"

"Yes, but I can easily put that off. Nothing very exciting."

"No," said Van Aldin. "Keep your engagement. I have got a good deal to attend to. See you to-morrow, my dear. Perhaps if I 'phone you, we can meet at Galbraiths'?"

Messrs. Galbraith, Galbraith, Cuthbertson, & Galbraith were Van Aldin's London solicitors.

"Very well, Dad." She hesitated. "I suppose it—this—won't keep me from going to the Riviera?"

"When are you off?"

"On the fourteenth."

"Oh, that will be all right. These things take a long time to mature. By the way, Ruth, I shouldn't take those rubies abroad if I were you. Leave them at the bank."

Mrs. Kettering nodded.

"We don't want to have you robbed and murdered for the sake of 'Heart of Fire,'" said the millionaire jocosely.

"And yet you carried it about in your pocket loose," retorted his daughter, smiling.

"Yes—"

Something, some hesitation, caught her attention.

"What is it, Dad?"

"Nothing." He smiled. "Thinking of a little adventure of mine in Paris."

"An adventure?"

"Yes, the night I bought these things."

He made a gesture towards the jewel case.

"Oh, do tell me."

"Nothing to tell, Ruthie. Some apache fellows got a bit fresh and I shot at them and they got off. That's all."

She looked at him with some pride.

"You're a tough proposition, Dad."

"You bet I am, Ruthie."

He kissed her affectionately and departed. On arriving back at the Savoy, he gave a curt order to Knighton.

"Get hold of a man called Goby; you'll find his address in my private book. He's to be here to-morrow morning at half-past nine."

"Yes, sir."

"I also want to see Mr. Kettering. Run him to earth for me if you can. Try his Club—at any rate, get hold of him somehow, and arrange for me to see him here to-morrow morning. Better make it latish, about twelve. His sort aren't early risers."

The secretary nodded in comprehension of these instructions. Van Aldin gave himself into the hands of his valet. His bath was prepared, and as he lay luxuriating in the hot water, his mind went back over the conversation with his daughter. On the whole he was well satisfied. His keen mind had long since accepted the fact that divorce was the only possible way out. Ruth had agreed to the proposed solution with more readiness than he had hoped for. Yet, in spite of her acquiescence, he was left with a vague sense of uneasiness. Something about her manner, he felt, had not been quite natural. He frowned to himself.

"Maybe I'm fanciful," he muttered, "and yet—I bet there's something she has not told me."

FIVE

A Useful Gentleman

Rufus Van Aldin had just finished the sparse breakfast of coffee and dry toast, which was all he ever allowed himself, when Knighton entered the room.

"Mr. Goby is below, sir, waiting to see you."

The millionaire glanced at the clock. It was just half-past nine.

"All right," he said curtly. "He can come up."

A minute or two later, Mr. Goby entered the room. He was a small, elderly man, shabbily dressed, with eyes that looked carefully all round the room, and never at the person he was addressing.

"Good morning, Goby," said the millionaire. "Take a chair."

"Thank you, Mr. Van Aldin."

Mr. Goby sat down with his hands on his knees, and gazed earnestly at the radiator.

"I have got a job for you."

"Yes, Mr. Van Aldin?"

"My daughter is married to the Hon. Derek Kettering, as you may perhaps know."

Mr. Goby transferred his gaze from the radiator to the left-hand drawer of the desk, and permitted a deprecating smile to pass over his face. Mr. Goby knew a great many things, but he always hated to admit the fact.

"By my advice, she is about to file a petition for divorce. That, of course, is a solicitor's business. But, for private reasons, I want the fullest and most complete information."

Mr. Goby looked at the cornice and murmured:

"About Mr. Kettering?"

"About Mr. Kettering."

"Very good, sir."

Mr. Goby rose to his feet.

"When will you have it ready for me?"

"Are you in a hurry, sir?"

"I'm always in a hurry," said the millionaire.

Mr. Goby smiled understandingly at the fender.

"Shall we say two o'clock this afternoon, sir?" he asked.

"Excellent," approved the other. "Good morning, Goby."

"Good morning, Mr. Van Aldin."

"That's a very useful man," said the millionaire as Goby went out and his secretary came in. "In his own line he's a specialist."

"What is his line?"

"Information. Give him twenty-four hours and he would lay the private life of the Archbishop of Canterbury bare for you."

"A useful sort of chap," said Knighton, with a smile.

"He has been useful to me once or twice," said Van Aldin. "Now then, Knighton, I'm ready for work."

The next few hours saw a vast quantity of business rapidly transacted. It was half-past twelve when the telephone bell rang, and Mr. Van Aldin was informed that Mr. Kettering had called. Knighton looked at Van Aldin, and interpreted his brief nod.

"Ask Mr. Kettering to come up, please."

The secretary gathered up his papers and departed. He and the visitor passed each other in the doorway, and Derek Kettering stood aside to let the other go out. Then he came in, shutting the door behind him.

"Good morning, sir. You are very anxious to see me, I hear."

The lazy voice with its slightly ironic inflection roused memories in Van Aldin. There was charm in it—there had always been charm in it. He looked piercingly at his son-in-law. Derek

Kettering was thirty-four, lean of build, with a dark, narrow face, which had even now something indescribably boyish in it.

"Come in," said Van Aldin curtly. "Sit down."

Kettering flung himself lightly into an arm-chair. He looked at his father-in-law with a kind of tolerant amusement.

"Not seen you for a long time, sir," he remarked pleasantly. "About two years, I should say. Seen Ruth yet?"

"I saw her last night," said Van Aldin.

"Looking very fit, isn't she?" said the other lightly.

"I didn't know you had had much opportunity of judging," said Van Aldin drily.

Derek Kettering raised his eyebrows.

"Oh, we sometimes meet at the same night club, you know," he said airily.

"I am not going to beat about the bush," Van Aldin said curtly. "I have advised Ruth to file a petition for divorce."

Derek Kettering seemed unmoved.

"How drastic!" he murmured. "Do you mind if I smoke, sir?"

He lit a cigarette, and puffed out a cloud of smoke as he added nonchalantly:

"And what did Ruth say?"

"Ruth proposes to take my advice," said her father.

"Does she really?"

"Is that all you have got to say?" demanded Van Aldin sharply.

Kettering flicked his ash into the grate.

"I think, you know," he said, with a detached air, "that she's making a great mistake."

"From your point of view she doubtless is," said Van Aldin grimly.

"Oh, come now," said the other; "don't let's be personal. I really wasn't thinking of myself at the moment. I was thinking of Ruth. You know my poor old Governor really can't last much longer; all the doctors say so. Ruth had better give it a couple more years, then I shall be Lord Leconbury, and she can be châtelaine

25

of Leconbury, which is what she married me for."

"I won't have any of your darned impudence," roared Van Aldin.

Derek Kettering smiled at him quite unmoved.

"I agree with you. It's an obsolete idea," he said. "There's nothing in a title nowadays. Still, Leconbury is a very fine old place, and, after all, we are one of the oldest families in England. It will be very annoying for Ruth if she divorces me to find me marrying again, and some other woman queening it at Leconbury instead of her."

"I am serious, young man," said Van Aldin.

"Oh, so am I," said Kettering. "I am in very low water financially; it will put me in a nasty hole if Ruth divorces me, and, after all, if she has stood it for ten years, why not stand it a little longer? I give you my word of honour that the old man can't possibly last out another eighteen months, and, as I said before, it's a pity Ruth shouldn't get what she married me for."

"You suggest that my daughter married you for your title and position?"

Derek Kettering laughed a laugh that was not all amusement.

"You don't think it was a question of a love match?" he asked.

"I know," said Van Aldin slowly, "that you spoke very differently in Paris ten years ago."

"Did I? Perhaps I did. Ruth was very beautiful, you know— rather like an angel or a saint, or something that had stepped down from a niche in a church. I had fine ideas, I remember, of turning over a new leaf, of settling down and living up to the highest traditions of English home-life with a beautiful wife who loved me."

He laughed again, rather more discordantly.

"But you don't believe that, I suppose?" he said.

"I have no doubt at all that you married Ruth for her money," said Van Aldin unemotionally.

"And that she married me for love?" asked the other ironically.

"Certainly," said Van Aldin.

Derek Kettering stared at him for a minute or two, then he nodded reflectively.

"I see you believe that," he said. "So did I at the time. I can assure you, my dear father-in-law, I was very soon undeceived."

"I don't know what you are getting at," said Van Aldin, "and I don't care. You have treated Ruth darned badly."

"Oh, I have," agreed Kettering lightly, "but she's tough, you know. She's your daughter. Underneath the pink-and-white soft-ness of her she's as hard as granite. You have always been known as a hard man, so I have been told, but Ruth is harder than you are. You, at any rate, love one person better than yourself. Ruth never has and never will."

"That is enough," said Van Aldin. "I asked you here so that I could tell you fair and square what I meant to do. My girl has got to have some happiness, and remember this, I am behind her."

Derek Kettering got up and stood by the mantelpiece. He tossed away his cigarette. When he spoke, his voice was very quiet.

"What exactly do you mean by that, I wonder?" he said.

"I mean," said Van Aldin, "that you had better not try to defend the case."

"Oh," said Kettering. "Is that a threat?"

"You can take it any way you please," said Van Aldin.

Kettering drew a chair up to the table. He sat down fronting the millionaire.

"And supposing," he said softly, "that, just for argument's sake, I did defend the case?"

Van Aldin shrugged his shoulders.

"You have not got a leg to stand upon, you young fool. Ask your solicitors, they will soon tell you. Your conduct has been notorious, the talk of London."

"Ruth has been kicking up a row about Mirelle, I suppose. Very foolish of her. I don't interfere with her friends."

"What do you mean?" said Van Aldin sharply.

Derek Kettering laughed.

27

"I see you don't know everything sir," he said. "You are, perhaps naturally, prejudiced."

He took up his hat and stick and moved towards the door.

"Giving advice is not much in my line." He delivered his final thrust. "But, in this case, I should advise most strongly perfect frankness between father and daughter."

He passed quickly out of the room and shut the door behind him just as the millionaire sprang up.

"Now, what the hell did he mean by that?" said Van Aldin as he sank back into his chair again.

All his uneasiness returned in full force. There was something here that he had not yet got to the bottom of. The telephone was by his elbow; he seized it, and asked for the number of his daughter's house.

"Hallo! Hallo! Is that Mayfair 81907? Mrs. Kettering in? Oh, she's out, is she? Yes, out to lunch. What time will she be in? You don't know? Oh, very good; no, there's no message."

He slammed the receiver down again angrily. At two o'clock he was pacing the floor of his room waiting expectantly for Goby. The latter was ushered in at ten minutes past two.

"Well?" barked the millionaire sharply.

But little Mr. Goby was not to be hurried. He sat down at the table, produced a very shabby pocket-book, and proceeded to read from it in a monotonous voice. The millionaire listened attentively, with an increasing satisfaction. Goby came to a full stop, and looked attentively at the wastepaper-basket.

"Um!" said Van Aldin. "That seems pretty definite. The case will go through like winking. The hotel evidence is all right, I suppose?"

"Cast iron," said Mr. Goby, and looked malevolently at a gilt arm-chair.

"And financially he's in very low water. He's trying to raise a loan now, you say? Has already raised practically all he can upon his expectations from his father. Once the news of the divorce gets about, he won't be able to raise another cent, and not only that, his obligations can be bought up and pressure can be put upon him from that quarter. We have got him, Goby; we have got him in a cleft stick."

He hit the table a bang with his fist. His face was grim and triumphant.

"The information," said Mr. Goby in a thin voice, "seems satisfactory."

"I have got to go round to Curzon Street now," said the millionaire. "I am much obliged to you, Goby. You are the goods all right."

A pale smile of gratification showed itself on the little man's face.

"Thank you, Mr. Van Aldin," he said; "I try to do my best."

Van Aldin did not go direct to Curzon Street. He went first to the City, where he had two interviews which added to his satisfaction. From there he took the tube to Down Street. As he was walking along Curzon Street, a figure came out of No. 160, and turned up the street towards him, so that they passed each other on the pavement. For a moment, the millionaire had fancied it might be Derek Kettering himself; the height and build were not unlike. But as they came face to face, he saw that the man was a stranger to him. At least—no, not a stranger; his face awoke some call of recognition in the millionaire's mind, and it was associated definitely with something unpleasant. He cudgelled his brains in vain, but the thing eluded him. He went on, shaking his head irritably. He hated to be baffled.

Ruth Kettering was clearly expecting him. She ran to him and kissed him when he entered.

"Well, Dad, how are things going?"

"Very well," said Van Aldin; "but I have got a word or two to say to you, Ruth."

Almost insensibly he felt the change in her; something shrewd and watchful replaced the impulsiveness of her greeting. She sat down in a big arm-chair.

"Well, Dad?" she asked. "What is it?"

"I saw your husband this morning," said Van Aldin.

"You saw Derek?"

"I did. He said a lot of things, most of which were darned cheek. Just as he was leaving, he said something that I didn't understand. He advised me to be sure that there was perfect frankness between father and daughter. What did he mean by that, Ruthie?"

Mrs. Kettering moved a little in her chair.

"I—I don't know, Dad. How should I?"

"Of course you know," said Van Aldin. "He said something else, about his having his friends and not interfering with yours. What did he mean by that?"

"I don't know," said Ruth Kettering again.

Van Aldin sat down. His mouth set itself in a grim line.

"See here, Ruth. I am not going into this with my eyes closed. I am not at all sure that that husband of yours doesn't mean to make trouble. Now, he can't do it, I am sure of that. I have got the means to silence him, to shut his mouth for good and all, but I have got to know if there's any need to use those means. What did he mean by your having your own friends?"

Mrs. Kettering shrugged her shoulders.

"I have got lots of friends," she said uncertainly. "I don't know what he meant, I am sure."

"You do," said Van Aldin.

He was speaking now as he might have spoken to a business adversary.

"I will put it plainer. Who is the man?"

"What man?"

"*The* man. That's what Derek was driving at. Some special man who is a friend of yours. You needn't worry, honey, I know there is nothing in it, but we have got to look at everything as it might appear to the Court. They can twist these things about a good deal, you know. I want to know who the man is, and just how friendly you have been with him."

Ruth didn't answer. Her hands were kneading themselves together in intense nervous absorption.

"Come, honey," said Van Aldin in a softer voice. "Don't be afraid of your old Dad. I was not too harsh, was I, even that time in Paris?—By gosh!"

He stopped, thunderstruck.

"That's who it was," he murmured to himself. "I thought I knew his face."

"What are you talking about, Dad? I don't understand."

The millionaire strode across to her and took her firmly by the wrist.

"See here, Ruth, have you been seeing that fellow again?"

"What fellow?"

"The one we had all that fuss about years ago. You know who I mean well enough."

"You mean"—she hesitated—"you mean the Comte de la Roche?"

"Comte de la Roche!" snorted Van Aldin. "I told you at the time that the man was no better than a swindler. You had entangled yourself with him then very deeply, but I got you out of his clutches."

"Yes, you did," said Ruth bitterly. "And I married Derek Kettering."

"You wanted to," said the millionaire sharply.

She shrugged her shoulders.

"And now," said Van Aldin slowly, "you have been seeing him again—after all I told you. He has been in the house to-day. I met him outside, and couldn't place him for the moment."

Ruth Kettering had recovered her composure.

"I want to tell you one thing, Dad; you are wrong about Armand—the Comte de la Roche, I mean. Oh, I know there were several regrettable incidents in his youth—he has told me about them; but—well, he has cared for me always. It broke his heart when you parted us in Paris, and now—"

She was interrupted by the snort of indignation her father gave.

"So you fell for that stuff, did you? You, a daughter of mine! My God!"

He threw up his hands.

"That women can be such darned fools!"

SIX

Mirelle

Derek Kettering emerged from Van Aldin's suite so precipitantly that he collided with a lady passing across the corridor. He apologized, and she accepted his apologies with a smiling reassurance and passed on, leaving with him a pleasant impression of a soothing personality and rather fine grey eyes.

For all his nonchalance, his interview with his father-in-law had shaken him more than he cared to show. He had a solitary lunch, and after it, frowning to himself a little, he went around to the sumptuous flat that housed the lady known as Mirelle. A trim Frenchwoman received him with smiles.

"But enter then, Monsieur. Madame reposes herself."

He was ushered into the long room with its Eastern setting which he knew so well. Mirelle was lying on the divan, supported by an incredible number of cushions, all in varying shades of amber, to harmonize with the yellow ochre of her complexion. The dancer was a beautifully made woman, and if her face, beneath its mask of yellow, was in truth somewhat haggard, it had a bizarre charm of its own, and her orange lips smiled invitingly at Derek Kettering.

He kissed her, and flung himself into a chair.

"What have you been doing with yourself? Just got up, I suppose?"

The orange mouth widened into a long smile.

"No," said the dancer. "I have been at work."

She flung out a long, pale hand towards the piano, which was littered with untidy music scores.

"Ambrose has been here. He has been playing me the new Opera."

Kettering nodded without paying much attention. He was profoundly uninterested in Claud Ambrose and the latter's operatic setting of Ibsen's *Peer Gynt*. So was Mirelle, for that matter, regarding it merely as a unique opportunity for her own presentation as Anitra.

"It is a marvellous dance," she murmured. "I shall put all the passion of the desert into it. I shall dance hung over with jewels—ah! and, by the way, *mon ami*, there is a pearl that I saw yesterday in Bond Street—a black pearl."

She paused, looking at him invitingly.

"My dear girl," said Kettering, "it's no use talking of black pearls to me. At the present minute, as far as I am concerned, the fat is in the fire."

She was quick to respond to his tone. She sat up, her big black eyes widening.

"What is that you say, Dereek? What has happened?"

"My esteemed father-in-law," said Kettering, "is preparing to go off the deep-end."

"Eh?"

"In other words, he wants Ruth to divorce me."

"How stupid!" said Mirelle. "Why should she want to divorce you?"

Derek Kettering grinned.

"Mainly because of you, *chérie*!" he said.

Mirelle shrugged her shoulders.

"That is foolish," she observed in a matter-of-fact voice.

"Very foolish," agreed Derek.

"What are you going to do about it?" demanded Mirelle.

"My dear girl, what can I do? On the one side, the man with

34

unlimited money; on the other side, the man with unlimited debts. There is no question as to who will come out on top."

"They are extraordinary, these Americans," commented Mirelle. "It is not as though your wife were fond of you."

"Well," said Derek, "what are we going to do about it?"

She looked at him inquiringly. He came over and took both her hands in his.

"Are you going to stick to me?"

"What do you mean? After—"

"Yes," said Kettering. "After, when the creditors come down like wolves on the fold. I am damned fond of you, Mirelle; are you going to let me down?"

She pulled her hands away from him.

"You know I adore you, Dereek."

He caught the note of evasion in her voice.

"So that's that, is it? The rats will leave the sinking ship."

"Ah, Dereek!"

"Out with it," he said violently. "You will fling me over; is that it?"

She shrugged her shoulders.

"I am fond of you, *mon ami*—indeed I am fond of you. You are very charming—*un beau garçon*, but *ce n'est pas pratique*."

"You are a rich man's luxury, eh? Is that it?"

"If you like to put it that way."

She leaned back on the cushions, her head flung back.

"All the same, I am fond of you, Dereek."

He went over to the window and stood there some time looking out, with his back to her. Presently the dancer raised herself on her elbow and stared at him curiously.

"What are you thinking of, *mon ami*?"

He grinned at her over his shoulder, a curious grin, that made her vaguely uneasy.

"As it happened, I was thinking of a woman, my dear."

"A woman, eh?"

Mirelle pounced on something that she could understand.

"You are thinking of some other woman, is that it?"

"Oh, you needn't worry; it is purely a fancy portrait. 'Portrait of a lady with grey eyes.'"

Mirelle said sharply, "When did you meet her?"

Derek Kettering laughed, and his laughter had a mocking, ironical sound.

"I ran into the lady in the corridor of the Savoy Hotel."

"Well! What did she say?"

"As far as I can remember, I said, 'I beg your pardon,' and she said, 'It doesn't matter,' or words to that effect."

"And then?" persisted the dancer.

Kettering shrugged his shoulders.

"And then—nothing. That was the end of the incident."

"I don't understand a word of what you are talking about," declared the dancer.

"Portrait of a lady with grey eyes," murmured Derek reflectively. "Just as well I am never likely to meet her again."

"Why?"

"She might bring me bad luck. Women do."

Mirelle slipped quickly from her couch, and came across to him, laying one long, snake-like arm round his neck.

"You are foolish, Dereek," she murmured. "You are very foolish. You are *beau garçon*, and I adore you, but I am not made to be poor—no, decidedly I am not made to be poor. Now listen to me; everything is very simple. You must make it up with your wife."

"I am afraid that's not going to be actually in the sphere of practical politics," said Derek drily.

"How do you say? I do not understand."

"Van Aldin, my dear, is not taking any. He is the kind of man who makes up his mind and sticks to it."

"I have heard of him," nodded the dancer. "He is very rich, is he not? Almost the richest man in America. A few days ago, in Paris, he bought the most wonderful ruby in the world—'Heart of Fire' it is called."

Kettering did not answer. The dancer went on musingly:

"It is a wonderful stone—a stone that should belong to a woman like me. I love jewels, Dereek; they say something to me. Ah! to wear a ruby like 'Heart of Fire.'"

She gave a little sigh, and then became practical once more.

"You don't understand these things, Dereek; you are only a man. Van Aldin will give these rubies to his daughter, I suppose. Is she his only child?"

"Yes."

"Then when he dies, she will inherit all his money. She will be a rich woman."

"She is a rich woman already," said Kettering drily. "He settled a couple of millions on her at her marriage."

"A couple of millions! But that is immense. And if she died suddenly, eh? That would all come to you?"

"As things stand at present," said Kettering slowly, "it would. As far as I know she has not made a will."

"*Mon Dieu!*" said the dancer. "If she were to die, what a solution that would be."

There was a moment's pause, and then Derek Kettering laughed outright.

"I like your simple, practical mind, Mirelle, but I am afraid what you desire won't come to pass. My wife is an extremely healthy person."

"*Eh, bien!*" said Mirelle; "there are accidents."

He looked at her sharply but did not answer.

She went on.

"But you are right, *mon ami*, we must not dwell on possibilities. See now, my little Dereek, there must be no more talk of this divorce. Your wife must give up the idea."

"And if she won't?"

The dancer's eyes narrowed to slits.

"I think she will, my friend. She is one of those who would

not like the publicity. There are one or two pretty stories that she would not like her friends to read in the newspapers."

"What do you mean?" asked Kettering sharply.

Mirelle laughed, her head thrown back.

"*Parbleu!* I mean the gentleman who calls himself the Comte de la Roche. I know all about him. I am Parisienne, you remember. He was her lover before she married you, was he not?"

Kettering took her sharply by the shoulders.

"That is a damned lie," he said, "and please remember that, after all, you are speaking of my wife."

Mirelle was a little sobered.

"You are extraordinary, you English," she complained. "All the same, I dare say that you may be right. The Americans are so cold, are they not? But you will permit me to say, *mon ami*, that she was *in love with him* before she married you, and her father stepped in and sent the Comte about his business. And the little Mademoiselle, she wept many tears! But she obeyed. Still, you must know as well as I do, Dereek, that it is a very different story now. She sees him nearly every day, and on the fourteenth she goes to Paris to meet him."

"How do you know all this?" demanded Kettering.

"Me? I have friends in Paris, my dear Dereek, who know the Comte intimately. It is all arranged. She is going to the Riviera, so she says, but in reality the Comte meets her in Paris and—who knows! Yes, yes, you can take my word for it, it is all arranged."

Derek Kettering stood motionless.

"You see," purred the dancer, "if you are clever, you have her in the hollow of your hand. You can make things very awkward for her."

"Oh, for God's sake be quiet," cried Kettering. "Shut your cursed mouth!"

Mirelle flung herself down again on the divan with a laugh. Kettering caught up his hat and coat and left the flat, banging the door violently. And still the dancer sat on the divan and laughed softly to herself. She was not displeased with her work.

SEVEN
Letters

*M*rs. Samuel Harfield presents her compliments to Miss
Katherine Grey and wishes to point out that under the
circumstances Miss Grey may not be aware—"

Mrs. Harfield, having written so far fluently, came to a dead
stop, held up by what has proved an insuperable difficulty to many
other people—namely, the difficulty of expressing oneself fluently
in the third person.

After a minute or two of hesitation, Mrs. Harfield tore up the
sheet of notepaper and started afresh.

*"Dear Miss Grey—Whilst fully appreciating the adequate way
you discharged your duties to my Cousin Jane (whose recent death
has indeed been a severe blow to us all), I cannot but feel—"*

Again Mrs. Harfield came to a stop. Once more the letter was
consigned to the wastepaper-basket. It was not until four false
starts had been made that Mrs. Harfield at last produced an epistle
that satisfied her. It was duly sealed and stamped and addressed
to Miss Katherine Grey, Little Crampton, St. Mary Mead, Kent,
and it lay beside that lady's plate on the following morning at
breakfast-time in company with a more important looking communication in a long blue envelope.

Katherine Grey opened Mrs. Harfield's letter first. The finished production ran as follows:

"Dear Miss Grey—My husband and I wish to express our thanks to you for your services to my poor cousin, Jane. Her death has been a great blow to us, though we were, of course, aware that her mind has been failing for some time past. I understand that her latter testamentary dispositions have been of a most peculiar character, and they would not hold good, of course, in any court of law. I have no doubt that, with your usual good sense, you have already realized this fact. If these matters can be arranged privately it is always so much better, my husband says. We shall be pleased to recommend you most highly for a similar post and hope that you will also accept a small present. Believe me, dear Miss Grey, Yours cordially,

"Mary Anne Harfield."

Katherine Grey read the letter through, smiled a little, and read it a second time. Her face as she laid the letter down after the second reading was distinctly amused. Then she took up the second letter. After one brief perusal she laid it down and stared very straight in front of her. This time she did not smile. Indeed, it would have been hard for anyone watching her to guess what emotions lay behind that quiet, reflective gaze.

Katherine Grey was thirty-three. She came of good family, but her father had lost all his money, and Katherine had had to work for her living from an early age. She had been just twenty-three when she had come to old Mrs. Harfield as companion.

It was generally recognized that old Mrs. Harfield was "difficult." Companions came and went with startling rapidity. They arrived full of hope and they usually left in tears. But from the moment Katherine Grey set foot in Little Crampton, ten years ago, perfect peace had reigned. No one knows how these things come about. Snake-charmers, they say, are born, not made. Katherine Grey was born with the power of managing old ladies, dogs, and small boys, and she did it without any apparent sense of strain.

At twenty-three she had been a quiet girl with beautiful eyes. At thirty-three she was a quiet woman, with those same grey eyes, shining steadily out on the world with a kind of happy serenity that nothing could shake. Moreover, she had been born with, and still possessed, a sense of humour.

As she sat at the breakfast-table, staring in front of her, there was a ring at the bell, accompanied by a very energetic rat-a-tat-tat at the knocker. In another minute the little maid-servant opened the door and announced rather breathlessly:

"Dr. Harrison."

The big, middle-aged doctor came bustling in with the energy and breeziness that had been foreshadowed by his onslaught on the knocker.

"Good morning, Miss Grey."

"Good morning, Dr. Harrison."

"I dropped in early," began the doctor, "in case you should have heard from one of those Harfield cousins. Mrs. Samuel, she calls herself—a perfectly poisonous person."

Without a word, Katherine picked up Mrs. Harfield's letter from the table and gave it to him. With a good deal of amusement she watched his perusal of it, the drawing together of the bushy eyebrows, the snorts and grunts of violent disapproval. He dashed it down again on the table.

"Perfectly monstrous," he fumed. "Don't you let it worry you, my dear. They're talking through their hat. Mrs. Harfield's intellect was as good as yours or mine and you won't get anyone to say the contrary. They wouldn't have a leg to stand upon, and they know it. All that talk of taking it into court is pure bluff. Hence, this attempt to get round you in a hole-and-corner way. And look here, my dear, don't let them get round you with soft soap either. Don't get fancying it's your duty to hand over the cash, or any tomfoolery of conscientious scruples."

"I'm afraid it hasn't occurred to me to have scruples," said Katherine. "All these people are distant relatives of Mrs. Harfield's husband, and they never came near her or took any notice of her in her lifetime."

"You're a sensible woman," said the doctor. "I know, none better, that you've had a hard life of it for the last ten years. You're fully entitled to enjoy the old lady's savings, such as they were."

Katherine smiled thoughtfully.

"Such as they were," she repeated. "You've no idea of the amount, doctor?"

"Well—enough to bring in five hundred a year or so, I suppose."

Katherine nodded.

"That's what I thought," she said. "Now read this."

She handed him the letter she had taken from the long blue envelope. The doctor read and uttered an exclamation of utter astonishment.

"Impossible," he muttered. "Impossible."

"She was one of the original shareholders in Mortaulds. Forty years ago she must have had an income of eight or ten thousand a year. She has never, I am sure, spent more than four hundred a year. She was always terribly careful about money. I always believed that she was obliged to be careful about every penny."

"And all the time the income has accumulated at compound interest. My dear, you're going to be a very rich woman."

Katherine Grey nodded.

"Yes," she said, "I am."

She spoke in a detached, impersonal tone, as though she were looking at the situation from outside.

"Well," said the doctor, preparing to depart, "you have all my congratulations." He flicked Mrs. Samuel Harfield's letter with his thumb. "Don't worry about that woman and her odious letter."

"It really isn't an odious letter," said Miss Grey tolerantly. "Under the circumstances, I think it's really quite a natural thing to do."

"I have the gravest suspicions of you sometimes," said the doctor.

"Why?"

"The things that you find perfectly natural."

Katherine Grey laughed.

Doctor Harrison retailed the great news to his wife at lunch-time. She was very excited about it.

"Fancy old Mrs. Harfield—with all that money. I'm glad she left it to Katherine Grey. That girl's a saint."

The doctor made a wry face.

"Saints I always imagine must have been difficult people. Katherine Grey is too human for a saint."

"She's a saint with a sense of humour," said the doctor's wife, twinkling. "And, though I don't suppose you've ever noticed the fact, she's extremely good looking."

"Katherine Grey?" The doctor was honestly surprised. "She's got very nice eyes, I know."

"Oh, you men!" cried his wife. "Blind as bats. Katherine's got all the makings of a beauty in her. All she wants is clothes!"

"Clothes? What's wrong with her clothes? She always looks very nice."

Mrs. Harrison gave an exasperated sigh, and the doctor rose preparatory to starting on his rounds.

"You might look in on her, Polly," he suggested.

"I'm going to," said Mrs. Harrison promptly.

She made her call about three o'clock.

"My dear, I'm so glad," she said warmly, as she squeezed Katherine's hand. "And everyone in the village will be glad too."

"It's very nice of you to come and tell me," said Katherine. "I hoped you would come in because I wanted to ask about Johnnie."

"Oh! Johnnie. Well—"

Johnnie was Mrs. Harrison's youngest son. In another minute she was off, retailing a long history in which Johnnie's adenoids and tonsils bulked largely. Katherine listened sympathetically. Habits die hard. Listening had been her portion for ten years now. "My dear, I wonder if I ever told you about that naval ball at Portsmouth? When Lord Charles admired my gown?" And composedly, kindly, Katherine would reply: "I rather think you have, Mrs. Harfield, but I've forgotten about it. Won't you tell it me again?" And then the old lady would start off full swing, with numerous details. And half of Katherine's mind would be listening, saying the right things mechanically when the old lady paused....

Now, with that same curious feeling of duality to which she was accustomed, she listened to Mrs. Harrison.

At the end of half an hour, the latter recalled herself suddenly.

"I've been talking about myself all this time," she exclaimed. "And I came here to talk about you and your plans."

"I don't know that I've got any yet."

"My dear—you're not going to stay on *here*."

Katherine smiled at the horror in the other's tone.

"No; I think I want to travel. I've never seen much of the world, you know."

"I should think not. It must have been an awful life for you cooped up here all these years."

"I don't know," said Katherine. "It gave me a lot of freedom."

She caught the other's gasp, and reddened a little.

"It must sound foolish—saying that. Of course, I hadn't much freedom in the downright physical sense—"

"I should think not," breathed Mrs. Harrison, remembering that Katherine had seldom had that useful thing—a "day off."

"But, in a way, being tied physically gives you lots of scope mentally. You're always free to think. I've had a lovely feeling always of mental freedom."

Mrs. Harrison shook her head.

"I can't understand that."

"Oh! you would if you'd been in my place. But, all the same, I feel I want a change. I want—well, I want things to happen. Oh! not to me—I don't mean that. But to be in the midst of things, exciting things—even if I'm only the looker-on. You know, things don't happen in St. Mary Mead."

44

"They don't indeed," said Mrs. Harrison, with fervour.

"I shall go to London first," said Katherine. "I have to see the solicitors, anyway. After that, I shall go abroad, I think."

"Very nice."

"But, of course, first of all——"

"Yes?"

"I must get some clothes."

"Exactly what I said to Arthur this morning," cried the doctor's wife. "You know, Katherine, you could look positively beautiful if you tried."

Miss Grey laughed unaffectedly.

"Oh! I don't think you could ever make a beauty out of me," she said sincerely. "But I shall enjoy having some really good clothes. I'm afraid I'm talking about myself an awful lot."

Mrs. Harrison looked at her shrewdly.

"It must be quite a novel experience for you," she said drily.

Katherine went to say good-bye to old Miss Viner before leaving the village. Miss Viner was two years older than Mrs. Harfield, and her mind was mainly taken with her own success in outliving her dead friend.

"You wouldn't have thought I'd have outlasted Jane Harfield, would you?" she demanded triumphantly of Katherine. "We were at school together, she and I. And here we are, she taken, and I left. Who would have thought it?"

"You've always eaten brown bread for supper, haven't you?" murmured Katherine mechanically.

"Fancy your remembering that, my dear. Yes; if Jane Harfield had had a slice of brown bread every evening and taken a little stimulant with her meals she might be here to-day."

The old lady paused, nodding her head triumphantly, then added in sudden remembrance:

"And so you've come into a lot of money, I hear? Well, well. Take care of it. And you're going up to London to have a good time? Don't think you'll get married, though, my dear, because you won't. You're not the kind to attract the men. And, besides, you're getting on. How old are you now?"

"Thirty-three," Katherine told her.

"Well," remarked Miss Viner doubtfully, "that's not so very bad. You've lost your first freshness, of course."

"I'm afraid so," said Katherine, much entertained.

"But you're a very nice girl," said Miss Viner kindly. "And I'm sure there's many a man might do worse than take you for a wife instead of one of these flibbertigibbets running about nowadays showing more of their legs than the Creator ever intended them to. Good-bye, my dear, and I hope you'll enjoy yourself, but things are seldom what they seem in this life."

Heartened by these prophecies, Katherine took her departure. Half the village came to see her off at the station, including the little maid of all work, Alice, who brought a stiff wired nosegay and cried openly.

"There ain't a many like her," sobbed Alice when the train had finally departed. "I'm sure when Charlie went back on me with that girl from the Dairy, nobody could have been kinder than Miss Grey was, and though particular about the brasses and the dust, she was always one to notice when you'd give a thing an extra rub. Cut myself in little pieces for her, I would, any day. A real lady, that's what I call her."

Such was Katherine's departure from St. Mary Mead.

EIGHT
Lady Tamplin Writes a Letter

W ell," said Lady Tamplin, "well."

She laid down the continental *Daily Mail* and stared out across the blue waters of the Mediterranean. A branch of golden mimosa, hanging just above her head, made an effective frame for a very charming picture. A golden-haired, blue-eyed lady in a very becoming negligee. That the golden hair owed something to art, as did the pink-and-white complexion, was undeniable, but the blue of the eyes was Nature's gift, and at forty-four Lady Tamplin could still rank as a beauty.

Charming as she looked, Lady Tamplin was, for once, not thinking of herself. That is to say, she was not thinking of her appearance. She was intent on graver matters.

Lady Tamplin was a well-known figure on the Riviera, and her parties at the Villa Marguerite were justly celebrated. She was a woman of considerable experience, and had had four husbands. The first had been merely an indiscretion, and so was seldom referred to by the lady. He had had the good sense to die with commendable promptitude, and his widow thereupon espoused a rich manufacturer of buttons. He too had departed for another sphere after three years of married life—it was said after a congenial evening with some boon companions. After him came Viscount Tamplin, who had placed Rosalie securely on those heights where she wished to tread. She had retained her title when she married

47

for a fourth time. This fourth venture had been undertaken for pure pleasure. Mr. Charles Evans, an extremely good-looking young man of twenty-seven, with delightful manners, a keen love of sport, and an appreciation of this world's goods, had no money of his own whatsoever.

Lady Tamplin was very pleased and satisfied with life generally, but she had occasional faint preoccupations about money. The button manufacturer had left his widow a considerable fortune, but, as Lady Tamplin was wont to say, "what with one thing and another—" (one thing being the depreciation of stocks owing to the War, and the other the extravagances of the late Lord Tamplin). She was still comfortably off. But to be merely comfortably off is hardly satisfactory to one of Rosalie Tamplin's temperament.

So, on this particular January morning, she opened her blue eyes extremely wide as she read a certain item of news and uttered that non-committal monosyllable "Well." The only other occupant of the balcony was her daughter, the Hon. Lenox Tamplin. A daughter such as Lenox was a sad thorn in Lady Tamplin's side, a girl with no kind of tact, who actually looked older than her age, and whose peculiar sardonic form of humour was, to say the least of it, uncomfortable.

"Darling," said Lady Tamplin, "just fancy."

"What is it?"

Lady Tamplin picked up the *Daily Mail*, handed it to her daughter, and indicated with an agitated fore finger the paragraph of interest.

Lenox read it without any of the signs of agitation shown by her mother. She handed back the paper.

"What about it?" she asked. "It is the sort of thing that is always happening. Cheese-paring old women are always dying in villages and leaving fortunes of millions to their humble companions."

"Yes, dear, I know," said her mother, "and I dare say the fortune is not anything like as large as they say it is; newspapers are so inaccurate. But even if you cut it down by half—"

"Well," said Lenox, "it has not been left to us."

"Not exactly, dear," said Lady Tamplin; "but this girl, this Katherine Grey, is actually a cousin of mine. One of the Worcestershire Greys, the Edgeworth lot. My very own cousin! Fancy!"

"Ah-ha," said Lenox.

"And I was wondering—" said her mother.

"What there was in it for us," finished Lenox, with that sideways smile that her mother always found difficult to understand.

"Oh, darling," said Lady Tamplin, on a faint note of reproach.

It was very faint, because Rosalie Tamplin was used to her daughter's outspokenness and to what she called Lenox's uncomfortable way of putting things.

"I was wondering," said Lady Tamplin, again drawing her artistically pencilled brows together, "whether—oh, good morning, Chubby darling; are you going to play tennis? How nice!"

Chubby, thus addressed, smiled kindly at her, remarked perfunctorily, "How topping you look in that peach-coloured thing," and drifted past them and down the steps.

"The dear thing," said Lady Tamplin, looking affectionately after her husband. "Let me see, what was I saying? Ah!" She switched her mind back to business once more. "I was wondering—"

"Oh, for God's sake get on with it. That is the third time you have said that."

"Well, dear," said Lady Tamplin, "I was thinking that it would be very nice if I wrote to dear Katherine and suggested that she should pay us a little visit out here. Naturally, she is quite out of touch with Society. It would be nicer for her to be launched by one of her own people. An advantage for her and an advantage for us."

"How much do you think you would get her to cough up?" asked Lenox.

Her mother looked at her reproachfully and murmured:

"We should have to come to some financial arrangement, of

course. What with one thing and another—the War—your poor father—"

"And Chubby now," said Lenox. "He is an expensive luxury if you like."

"She was a nice girl as I remember her," murmured Lady Tamplin, pursuing her own line of thought—"quiet, never wanted to shove herself forward, not a beauty, and never a man-hunter."

"She will leave Chubby alone, then?" said Lenox.

Lady Tamplin looked at her in protest. "Chubby would never—" she began.

"No," said Lenox, "I don't believe he would; he knows a jolly sight too well which way his bread is buttered."

"Darling," said Lady Tamplin, "you have such a coarse way of putting things."

"Sorry," said Lenox.

Lady Tamplin gathered up the *Daily Mail* and her negligee, a vanity-bag, and various odd letters.

"I shall write to dear Katherine at once," she said, "and remind her of the dear old days at Edgeworth."

She went into the house, a light of purpose shining in her eyes.

Unlike Mrs. Samuel Harfield, correspondence flowed easily from her pen. She covered four sheets without pause or effort, and on re-reading it found no occasion to alter a word.

Katherine received it on the morning of her arrival in London. Whether she read between the lines of it or not is another matter. She put it in her handbag and started out to keep the appointment she had made with Mrs. Harfield's lawyers.

The firm was an old-established one in Lincoln's Inn Fields, and after a few minutes' delay Katherine was shown into the presence of the senior partner, a kindly, elderly man with shrewd blue eyes and a fatherly manner.

They discussed Mrs. Harfield's will and various legal matters for some minutes, then Katherine handed the lawyer Mrs. Samuel's letter.

"I had better show you this, I suppose," she said, "though it is really rather ridiculous."

He read it with a slight smile.

"Rather a crude attempt, Miss Grey. I need hardly tell you, I suppose, that these people have no claim of any kind upon the estate, and if they endeavour to contest the will no court will uphold them."

"I thought as much."

"Human nature is not always very wise. In Mrs. Samuel Harfield's place, I should have been more inclined to make an appeal to your generosity."

"That is one of the things I wanted to speak to you about. I should like a certain sum to go to these people."

"There is no obligation."

"I know that."

"And they will not take it in the spirit it is meant. They will probably regard it as an attempt to pay them off, though they will not refuse it on that account."

"I can see that, and it can't be helped."

"I should advise you, Miss Grey, to put that idea out of your head."

Katherine shook her head. "You are quite right, I know, but I should like it done all the same."

"They will grab at the money and abuse you all the more afterwards."

"Well," said Katherine, "let them if they like. We all have our own ways of enjoying ourselves. They were, after all, Mrs. Harfield's only relatives, and though they despised her as a poor relation and paid no attention to her when she was alive, it seems to me unfair that they should be cut off with nothing."

She carried her point, though the lawyer was still unwilling, and she presently went out into the streets of London with a comfortable assurance that she could spend money freely and make what plans she liked for the future. Her first action was to visit the establishment of a famous dressmaker.

A slim, elderly Frenchwoman, rather like a dreaming duchess, received her, and Katherine spoke with a certain *naïveté*.

"I want, if I may, to put myself in your hands. I have been very poor all my life and know nothing about clothes, but now I have come into some money and want to look really well dressed."

The Frenchwoman was charmed. She had an artist's temperament, which had been soured earlier in the morning by a visit from an Argentine meat queen, who had insisted on having those models least suited to her flamboyant type of beauty. She scrutinized Katherine with keen, clever eyes. "Yes—yes, it will be a pleasure. Mademoiselle has a very good figure; for her the simple lines will be best. She is also *très anglaise*. Some people it would offend them if I said that, but Mademoiselle, no. *Une belle Anglaise*, there is no style more delightful."

The demeanour of a dreaming duchess was suddenly put off. She screamed out directions to various mannequins. "Clothilde, Virginie, quickly, my little ones, the little *tailleur gris clair* and the *robe de soirée 'soupir d'automne.'* Marcelle, my child, the little mimosa suit of crêpe de chine."

It was a charming morning. Marcelle, Clothilde, Virginie, bored and scornful, passed slowly round, squirming and wriggling in the time-honoured fashion of mannequins. The Duchess stood by Katherine and made entries in a small notebook.

"An excellent choice, Mademoiselle. Mademoiselle has great *goût*. Yes, indeed. Mademoiselle cannot do better than those little suits if she is going to the Riviera, as I suppose, this winter."

"Let me see that evening dress once more," said Katherine—"the pinky mauve one."

Virginie appeared, circling slowly.

"That is the prettiest of all," said Katherine, as she surveyed the exquisite draperies of mauve and grey and blue. "What do you call it?"

"*Soupir d'automne*; yes, yes, that is truly the dress of Mademoiselle."

What was there in these words that came back to Katherine with a faint feeling of sadness after she had left the dressmaking establishment?

"'*Soupir d'automne; that is truly the dress of Mademoiselle.*'" Autumn, yes, it was autumn for her. She who had never known spring or summer, and would never know them now. Something she had lost never could be given to her again. These years of servitude in St. Mary Mead—and all the while life passing by.

"I am an idiot," said Katherine. "I am an idiot. What do I want? Why, I was more contented a month ago than I am now."

She drew out from her handbag the letter she had received that morning from Lady Tamplin. Katherine was no fool. She understood the *nuances* of that letter as well as anybody and the reason of Lady Tamplin's sudden show of affection towards a long-forgotten cousin was not lost upon her. It was for profit and not for pleasure that Lady Tamplin was so anxious for the company of her dear cousin. Well, why not? There would be profit on both sides.

"I will go," said Katherine.

She was walking down Piccadilly at the moment, and turned into Cook's to clinch the matter then and there. She had to wait for a few minutes. The man with whom the clerk was engaged was also going to the Riviera. Everyone, she felt, was going. Well, for the first time in her life, she, too, would be doing what "everybody did."

The man in front of her turned abruptly, and she stepped into his place. She made her demand to the clerk, but at the same time half of her mind was busy with something else. That man's face—in some vague way it was familiar to her. Where had she seen him before? Suddenly she remembered. It was in the Savoy outside her room that morning. She had collided with him in the passage. Rather an odd coincidence that she should run into him twice in a day. She glanced over her shoulder, rendered uneasy by something, she knew not what. The man was standing in the doorway looking back at her. A cold shiver passed over Katherine; she had a haunting sense of tragedy, of doom impending....

Then she shook the impression from her with her usual good sense and turned her whole attention to what the clerk was saying.

NINE
An Offer Refused

It was rarely that Derek Kettering allowed his temper to get the better of him. An easy-going insouciance was his chief characteristic, and it had stood him in good stead in more than one tight corner. Even now, by the time he had left Mirelle's flat, he had cooled down. He had need of coolness. The corner he was in now was a tighter one than he had ever been in before, and unforeseen factors had arisen with which, for the moment, he did not know how to deal.

He strolled along deep in thought. His brow was furrowed, and there was none of the easy, jaunty manner which sat so well upon him. Various possibilities floated through his mind. It might have been said of Derek Kettering that he was less of a fool than he looked. He saw several roads that he might take—one in particular. If he shrank from it, it was for the moment only. Desperate ills need desperate remedies. He had gauged his father-in-law correctly. A war between Derek Kettering and Rufus Van Aldin could end only one way. Derek damned money and the power of money vehemently to himself. He walked up St. James's Street, across Piccadilly, and strolled along it in the direction of Piccadilly Circus. As he passed the offices of Messrs. Thomas Cook & Sons his footsteps slackened. He walked on, however, still turning the matter over in his mind. Finally, he gave a brief nod of his head, turned sharply—so sharply as to collide with a couple of pedestrians who were following in his footsteps, and went back the way he had come. This time he did not pass Cook's, but went in. The office was comparatively empty, and he got attended to at once.

"I want to go to Nice next week. Will you give me particulars?"

"What date, sir?"

"The 14th. What is the best train?"

"Well, of course, *the* best train is what they call the 'Blue Train.' You avoid the tiresome Customs business at Calais."

Derek nodded. He knew all this, none better.

"The 14th," murmured the clerk; "that is rather soon. The Blue Train is nearly always all booked up."

"See if there is a berth left," said Derek. "If there is not—" He left the sentence unfinished, with a curious smile on his face.

The clerk disappeared for a few minutes, and presently returned.

"That is all right, sir; still three berths left. I will book you one of them. What name?"

"Pavett," said Derek. He gave the address of his rooms in Jermyn Street.

The clerk nodded, finished writing it down, wished Derek good morning politely, and turned his attention to the next client.

"I want to go to Nice—on the 14th. Isn't there a train called the Blue Train?"

Derek looked round sharply.

Coincidence—a strange coincidence. He remembered his own half-whimsical words to Mirelle, "*Portrait of a lady with grey eyes. I don't suppose I shall ever see her again.*" But he *had* seen her again, and, what was more, she proposed to travel to the Riviera on the same day as he did.

Just for a moment a shiver passed over him; in some ways he was superstitious. He had said, half-laughingly, that this woman might bring him bad luck. Suppose—suppose that should prove to be true. From the doorway he looked back at her as she stood talking to the clerk. For once his memory had not played him false. A lady—a lady in every sense of the word. Not very young, not singularly beautiful. But with something—grey eyes that might perhaps see too much. He knew as he went out of the door that in some way he was afraid of this woman. He had a sense of fatality.

He went back to his rooms in Jermyn Street and summoned his man.

"Take this cheque, Pavett, cash it first thing in the morning, and go around to Cook's in Piccadilly. They will have some tickets there booked in your name, pay for them, and bring them back."

"Very good, sir."

Pavett withdrew.

Derek strolled over to a side-table and picked up a handful of letters. They were of a type only too familiar. Bills, small bills and large bills, one and all pressing for payment. The tone of the demands was still polite. Derek knew how soon that polite tone would change if—if certain news became public property.

He flung himself moodily into a large, leather-covered chair. A damned hole—that was what he was in. Yes, a damned hole! And ways of getting out of that damned hole were not too promising.

Pavett appeared with a discreet cough.

"A gentleman to see you—sir—Major Knighton."

"Knighton, eh?"

Derek sat up, frowned, became suddenly alert. He said in a softer tone, almost to himself: "Knighton—I wonder what is in the wind now?"

"Shall I—er—show him in, sir?"

His master nodded. When Knighton entered the room he found a charming and genial host awaiting him.

"Very good of you to look me up," said Derek.

Knighton was nervous.

The other's keen eyes noticed that at once. The errand on which the secretary had come was clearly distasteful to him. He replied almost mechanically to Derek's easy flow of conversation.

AGATHA CHRISTIE

He declined a drink, and, if anything, his manner became stiffer than before. Derek appeared at last to notice it.

"Well," he said cheerfully, "what does my esteemed father-in-law want with me? You have come on his business, I take it?"

Knighton did not smile in reply.

"I have, yes," he said carefully. "I—I wish Mr. Van Aldin had chosen someone else."

Derek raised his eyebrows in mock dismay.

"Is it as bad as all that? I am not very thin skinned, I can assure you, Knighton."

"No," said Knighton; "but this—"

He paused.

Derek eyed him keenly.

"Go on, out with it," he said kindly. "I can imagine my dear father-in-law's errands might not always be pleasant ones."

Knighton cleared his throat. He spoke formally in tones that he strove to render free of embarrassment.

"I am directed by Mr. Van Aldin to make you a definite offer."

"An offer?" For a moment Derek showed his surprise. Knighton's opening words were clearly not what he had expected. He offered a cigarette to Knighton, lit one himself, and sank back in his chair, murmuring in a slightly sardonic voice:

"An offer? That sounds rather interesting."

"Shall I go on?"

"Please. You must forgive my surprise, but it seems to me that my dear father-in-law has rather climbed down since our chat this morning. And climbing down is not what one associates with strong men, Napoleons of finance, etc. It shows—I think it shows that he finds his position weaker than he thought it."

Knighton listened politely to the easy, mocking voice, but no sign of any kind showed itself on his rather stolid countenance. He waited until Derek had finished, and then he said quietly:

"I will state the proposition in the fewest possible words."

"Go on."

Knighton did not look at the other. His voice was curt and matter-of-fact.

"The matter is simply this. Mrs. Kettering, as you know, is about to file a petition for divorce. If the case goes undefended you will receive one hundred thousand on the day that the decree is made absolute."

Derek, in the act of lighting his cigarette, suddenly stopped dead.

"A hundred thousand!" he said sharply. "Dollars?"

"Pounds."

There was dead silence for at least two minutes. Kettering had his brows together thinking. A hundred thousand pounds. It meant Mirelle and a continuance of his pleasant, carefree life. It meant that Van Aldin knew something. Van Aldin did not pay for nothing. He got up and stood by the chimney-piece.

"And in the event of my refusing his handsome offer?" he asked, with a cold, ironical politeness.

Knighton made a deprecating gesture.

"I can assure you, Mr. Kettering," he said earnestly, "that it is with the utmost unwillingness that I came here with this message."

"That's all right," said Kettering. "Don't distress yourself; it's not your fault. Now then—I asked you a question, will you answer it?"

Knighton also rose. He spoke more reluctantly than before.

"In the event of your refusing this proposition," he said, "Mr. Van Aldin wished me to tell you in plain words that he proposes to break you. Just that."

Kettering raised his eyebrows, but he retained his light, amused manner.

"Well, well!" he said, "I suppose he can do it. I certainly should not be able to put up much of a fight against America's man of millions. A hundred thousand! If you are going to bribe a man there is nothing like doing it thoroughly. Supposing I were to tell you that for two hundred thousand I'd do what he wanted, what then?"

"I would take your message back to Mr. Van Aldin," said Knighton unemotionally. "Is that your answer?"

"No," said Derek; "funnily enough it is not. You can go back to my father-in-law and tell him to take himself and his bribes to hell. Is that clear?"

"Perfectly," said Knighton. He got up, hesitated, and then flushed. "I—you will allow me to say, Mr. Kettering, that I am glad you have answered as you have."

Derek did not reply. When the other had left the room he remained for a minute or two lost in thought. A curious smile came to his lips.

"And that is that," he said softly.

TEN

On the Blue Train

D ad!"

Mrs. Kettering started violently. Her nerves were not completely under control this morning. Very perfectly dressed in a long mink coat and a little hat of Chinese lacquer red, she had been walking along the crowded platform of Victoria deep in thought, and her father's sudden appearance and hearty greeting had an unlooked-for effect upon her.

"Why, Ruth, how you jumped!"

"I didn't expect to see you, I suppose, Dad. You said good-bye to me last night and said you had a conference this morning."

"So I have," said Van Aldin, "but you are more to me than any number of darned conferences. I came to take a last look at you, since I am not going to see you for some time."

"That is very sweet of you, Dad. I wish you were coming too."

"What would you say if I did?"

The remark was merely a joking one. He was surprised to see the quick colour flame in Ruth's cheeks. For a moment he almost thought he saw dismay flash out of her eyes. She laughed uncertainly and nervously.

"Just for a moment I really thought you meant it," she said.

"Would you have been pleased?"

"Of course." She spoke with exaggerated emphasis.

"Well," said Van Aldin, "that's good."

"It isn't really for very long, Dad," continued Ruth; "you know, you are coming out next month."

"Ah!" said Van Aldin unemotionally, "sometimes I guess I will go to one of these big guys in Harley Street and have him tell me that I need sunshine and change of air right away."

"Don't be so lazy," cried Ruth; "next month is ever so much nicer than this month out there. You have got all sorts of things you can't possibly leave just now."

"Well, that's so, I suppose," said Van Aldin, with a sigh. "You had better be getting on board this train of yours, Ruth. Where is your seat?"

Ruth Kettering looked vaguely up at the train. At the door of one of the Pullman cars a thin, tall woman dressed in black was standing—Ruth Kettering's maid. She drew aside as her mistress came up to her.

"I have put your dressing-case under your seat, Madam, in case you should need it. Shall I take the rugs, or will you require one?"

"No, no, I shan't want one. Better go and find your own seat now, Mason."

"Yes, Madam."

The maid departed.

Van Aldin entered the Pullman car with Ruth. She found her seat, and Van Aldin deposited various papers and magazines on the table in front of her. The seat opposite to her was already taken, and the American gave a cursory glance at its occupant. He had a fleeting impression of attractive grey eyes and a neat travelling costume. He indulged in a little more desultory conversation with Ruth, the kind of talk peculiar to those seeing other people off by train.

Presently, as whistles blew, he glanced at his watch.

"I had best be clearing out of here. Good-bye, my dear. Don't worry, I will attend to things."

"Oh, father!"

He turned back sharply. There had been something in Ruth's voice, something so entirely foreign to her usual manner, that he was startled. It was almost a cry of despair. She had made an impulsive movement towards him, but in another minute she was mistress of herself once more.

"Till next month," she said cheerfully.

Two minutes later the train started.

Ruth sat very still, biting her under lip and trying hard to keep the unaccustomed tears from her eyes. She felt a sudden sense of horrible desolation. There was a wild longing upon her to jump out of the train and to go back before it was too late. She, so calm, so self-assured, for the first time in her life felt like a leaf swept by the wind. If her father knew—what would he say?

Madness! Yes, just that, madness! For the first time in her life she was swept away by emotion, swept away to the point of doing a thing which even she knew to be incredibly foolish and reckless. She was enough Van Aldin's daughter to realize her own folly, and level headed enough to condemn her own action. But she was his daughter in another sense also. She had that same iron determination that would have what it wanted, and once it had made up its mind would not be balked. From her cradle she had been self-willed; the very circumstances of her life had developed that self-will in her. It drove her now remorselessly. Well, the die was cast. She must go through with it now.

She looked up, and her eyes met those of the woman sitting opposite. She had a sudden fancy that in some way this other woman had read her mind. She saw in those grey eyes understanding and—yes—compassion.

It was only a fleeting impression. The faces of both women hardened to well-bred impassiveness. Mrs. Kettering took up a magazine, and Katherine Grey looked out of the window and watched a seemingly endless vista of depressing streets and suburban houses.

Ruth found an increasing difficulty in fixing her mind on the printed page in front of her. In spite of herself, a thousand apprehensions preyed on her mind. What a fool she had been! What a fool she was! Like all cool and self-sufficient people, when she did lose her self-control she lost it thoroughly. It was too late.... Was it too late? Oh, for someone to speak to, for someone to advise her. She had never before had such a wish; she would have scorned the idea of relying on any judgment other than her own, but now—what was the matter with her? Panic. Yes, that would describe it best—panic. She, Ruth Kettering, was completely and utterly panic stricken.

She stole a covert glance at the figure opposite. If only she knew someone like that, some nice, cool, calm, sympathetic creature. That was the sort of person one could talk to. But you can't, of course, confide in a stranger. And Ruth smiled to herself a little at the idea. She picked up the magazine again. Really she must control herself. After all, she had thought all this out. She had decided of her own free will. What happiness had she ever had in her life up to now? She said to herself restlessly: "Why shouldn't I be happy? No one will ever know."

It seemed no time before Dover was reached. Ruth was a good sailor. She disliked the cold, and was glad to reach the shelter of the private cabin she had telegraphed for. Although she would not have admitted the fact, Ruth was in some ways superstitious. She was of the order of people to whom coincidence appeals. After disembarking at Calais and settling herself down with her maid in her double compartment in the Blue Train, she went along to the luncheon car. It was with a little shock of surprise that she found herself set down to a small table with, opposite her, the same woman who had been her *vis-à-vis* in the Pullman. A faint smile came to the lips of both women.

"This is quite a coincidence," said Mrs. Kettering.

"I know," said Katherine; "it is odd the way things happen."

A flying attendant shot up to them with the wonderful velocity always displayed by the Compagnie Internationale des

Wagons-Lits and deposited two cups of soup. By the time the omelette succeeded the soup they were chatting together in friendly fashion.

"It will be heavenly to get into the sunshine," sighed Ruth.

"I am sure it will be a wonderful feeling."

"You know the Riviera well?"

"No; this is my first visit."

"Fancy that."

"You go every year, I expect?"

"Practically. January and February in London are horrible."

"I have always lived in the country. They are not very inspiring months there either. Mostly mud."

"What made you suddenly decide to travel?"

"Money," said Katherine. "For ten years I have been a paid companion with just enough money of my own to buy myself strong country shoes; now I have been left what seems to me a fortune, though I dare say it would not seem so to you."

"Now I wonder why you say that—that it would not seem so to me."

Katherine laughed. "I don't really know. I suppose one forms impressions without thinking of it. I put you down in my own mind as one of the very rich of the earth. It was just an impression. I dare say I am wrong."

"No," said Ruth, "you are not wrong." She had suddenly become very grave. "I wish you would tell me what other impressions you formed about me?"

"I—"

Ruth swept on disregarding the other's embarrassment.

"Oh, please, don't be conventional. I want to know. As we left Victoria I looked across at you, and I had the sort of feeling that you—well, understood what was going on in my mind."

"I can assure you I am not a mind reader," said Katherine, smiling.

"No; but will you tell me, please, just what you thought."

Ruth's eagerness was so intense and so sincere that she carried her point.

"I will tell you if you like, but you must not think me impertinent. I thought that for some reason you were in great distress of mind, and I was sorry for you."

"You are right. You are quite right. I am in terrible trouble. I—I should like to tell you something about it, if I may."

"Oh, dear," Katherine thought to herself, "how extraordinarily alike the world seems to be everywhere! People were always telling me things in St. Mary Mead, and it is just the same thing here, and I don't really want to hear anybody's troubles!"

She replied politely:

"Do tell me."

They were just finishing their lunch. Ruth gulped down her coffee, rose from her seat, and quite oblivious of the fact that Katherine had not begun to sip her coffee, said: "Come to my compartment with me."

They were two single compartments with a communicating door between them. In the second of them a thin maid, whom Katherine had noticed at Victoria, was sitting very upright on the seat, clutching a big scarlet morocco case with the initials R. V. K. on it. Mrs. Kettering pulled the communicating door to and sank down on the seat. Katherine sat down beside her.

"I am in trouble and I don't know what to do. There is a man whom I am fond of—very fond of indeed. We cared for each other when we were young, and we were thrust apart most brutally and unjustly. Now we have come together again."

"Yes?"

"I—I am going to meet him now. Oh! I dare say you think it is all wrong, but you don't know the circumstances. My husband is impossible. He has treated me disgracefully."

"Yes," said Katherine again.

"What I feel so badly about is this. I have deceived my father— it was he who came to see me off at Victoria to-day. He wishes me to divorce my husband, and, of course, he has no idea—that I am going to meet this other man. He would think it extraordinarily foolish."

"Well, don't you think it is?"

"I—I suppose it is."

Ruth Kettering looked down at her hands; they were shaking violently.

"But I can't draw back now."

"Why not?"

"I—it is all arranged, and it would break his heart."

"Don't you believe it," said Katherine robustly; "hearts are pretty tough."

"He will think I have no courage, no strength of purpose."

"It seems to me an awfully silly thing that you are going to do," said Katherine. "I think you realize that yourself."

Ruth Kettering buried her face in her hands. "I don't know—I don't know. Ever since I left Victoria I have had a horrible feeling of something—something that is coming to me very soon—that I can't escape."

She clutched convulsively at Katherine's hand.

"You must think I am mad talking to you like this, but I tell you I know something horrible is going to happen."

"Don't think it," said Katherine; "try to pull yourself together. You could send your father a wire from Paris, if you like, and he would come to you at once."

The other brightened.

"Yes, I could do that. Dear old Dad. It is queer—but I never knew until to-day how terribly fond of him I am." She sat up and dried her eyes with a handkerchief. "I have been very foolish. Thank you so much for letting me talk to you. I don't know why I got into such a queer, hysterical state."

She got up. "I am quite all right now. I suppose, really, I just needed someone to talk to. I can't think now why I have been making such an absolute fool of myself."

Katherine got up too.

"I am so glad you feel better," she said, trying to make her voice sound as conventional as possible. She was only too well aware that the aftermath of confidences is embarrassment. She added tactfully:

"I must be going back to my own compartment."

She emerged into the corridor at the same time as the maid was also coming out from the next door. The latter looked towards Katherine, over her shoulder, and an expression of intense surprise showed itself on her face. Katherine turned also, but by that time whoever it was who had aroused the maid's interest had retreated into his or her compartment, and the corridor was empty. Katherine walked down it to regain her own place, which was in the next coach. As she passed the end compartment the door opened and a woman's face looked out for a moment and then pulled the door to sharply. It was a face not easily forgotten, as Katherine was to know when she saw it again. A beautiful face, oval and dark, very heavily made up in a bizarre fashion. Katherine had a feeling that she had seen it before somewhere.

She regained her own compartment without other adventure and sat for some time thinking of the confidence which had just been made to her. She wondered idly who the woman in the mink coat might be, wondered also how the end of her story would turn out.

"If I have stopped anyone from making an idiot of themselves, I suppose I have done good work," she thought to herself. "But who knows? That is the kind of woman who is hard-headed and egotistical all her life, and it might be good for her to do the other sort of thing for a change. Oh, well—I don't suppose I shall ever see her again. She certainly won't want to see *me* again. That is the worst of letting people tell you things. They never do."

She hoped that she would not be given the same place at dinner. She reflected, not without humour, that it might be awkward for both of them. Leaning back with her head against a cushion she felt tired and vaguely depressed. They had reached Paris, and the slow journey round the *ceinture*, with its interminable stops and waits, was very wearisome. When they arrived at the Gare de Lyon she was glad to get out and walk up and down the platform. The keen cold air was refreshing after the steam-heated train. She observed with a smile that her friend of the mink coat was solving the possible awkwardness of the dinner problem in her own way. A dinner basket was being handed up and received through the window by the maid.

When the train started once more, and dinner was announced by a violent ringing of bells, Katherine went along to it much relieved in mind. Her *vis-à-vis* to-night was of an entirely different kind—a small man, distinctly foreign in appearance, with a rigidly waxed moustache and an egg-shaped head which he carried rather on one side. Katherine had taken in a book to dinner with her. She found the little man's eyes fixed upon it with a kind of twinkling amusement.

"I see, Madame, that you have a *roman policier*. You are fond of such things?"

"They amuse me," Katherine admitted.

The little man nodded with the air of complete understanding.

"They have a good sale always, so I am told. Now why is that, eh, Mademoiselle? I ask it of you as a student of human nature—why should that be?"

Katherine felt more and more amused.

"Perhaps they give one the illusion of living an exciting life," she suggested.

He nodded gravely.

"Yes; there is something in that."

"Of course, one knows that such things don't really happen," Katherine was continuing, but he interrupted her sharply.

"Sometimes, Mademoiselle! Sometimes! I who speak to you—they have happened to *me*."

She threw him a quick, interested glance.

"Someday, who knows, *you* might be in the thick of things," he went on. "It is all chance."

"I don't think it is likely," said Katherine. "Nothing of that kind ever happens to me."

He leaned forward.

"Would you like it to?"

The question startled her, and she drew in her breath sharply.

"It is my fancy, perhaps," said the little man, as he dexterously polished one of the forks, "but I think that you have a yearning in you for interesting happenings. *Eh bien*, Mademoiselle, all through my life I have observed one thing—'All one wants one gets!' Who knows?" His face screwed itself up comically. "You may get more than you bargain for."

"Is that a prophecy?" asked Katherine, smiling as she rose from the table.

The little man shook his head.

"I never prophesy," he declared pompously. "It is true that I have the habit of being always right—but I do not boast of it. Good-night, Mademoiselle, and may you sleep well."

Katherine went back along the train amused and entertained by her little neighbour. She passed the open door of her friend's compartment and saw the conductor making up the bed. The lady in the mink coat was standing looking out of the window. The second compartment, as Katherine saw through the communicating door, was empty, with rugs and bags heaped up on the seat. The maid was not there.

Katherine found her own bed prepared, and since she was tired, she went to bed and switched off her light about half-past nine.

She woke with a sudden start; how much time had passed she did not know. Glancing at her watch, she found that it had stopped. A feeling of intense uneasiness pervaded her and grew stronger moment by moment. At last she got up, threw her dressing-gown round her shoulders, and stepped out into the corridor.

The whole train seemed wrapped in slumber. Katherine let down the window and sat by it for some minutes, drinking in the cool night air and trying vainly to calm her uneasy fears. She presently decided that she would go along to the end and ask the conductor for the right time so that she could set her watch. She found, however, that his little chair was vacant. She hesitated for a moment and then walked through into the next coach. She looked down the long, dim line of the corridor and saw, to her surprise, that a man was standing with his hand on the door of the compartment occupied by the lady in the mink coat. That is to say, she thought it was the compartment. Probably, however, she was mistaken. He stood there for a moment or two with his back to her, seeming uncertain and hesitating in his attitude. Then he slowly turned, and with an odd feeling of fatality, Katherine recognized him as the same man whom she had noticed twice before—once in the corridor of the Savoy hotel and once in Cook's offices. Then he opened the door of the compartment and passed in, drawing it to behind him.

An idea flashed across Katherine's mind. Could this be the man of whom the other woman had spoken—the man she was journeying to meet.

Then Katherine told herself that she was romancing. In all probability she had mistaken the compartment.

She went back to her own carriage. Five minutes later the train slackened speed. There was the long plaintive hiss of the Westinghouse brake, and a few minutes later the train came to a stop at Lyons.

ELEVEN
Murder

Katherine wakened the next morning to brilliant sunshine. She went along to breakfast early, but met none of her acquaintances of the day before. When she returned to her compartment it had just been restored to its day-time appearance by the conductor, a dark man with a drooping moustache and melancholy face.

"Madame is fortunate," he said; "the sun shines. It is always a great disappointment to passengers when they arrive on a grey morning."

"I should have been disappointed, certainly," said Katherine.

The man prepared to depart.

"We are rather late, Madame," he said. "I will let you know just before we get to Nice."

Katherine nodded. She sat by the window, entranced by the sunlit panorama. The palm trees, the deep blue of the sea, the bright yellow mimosa came with all the charm of novelty to the woman who for fourteen years had known only the drab winters of England.

When they arrived at Cannes, Katherine got out and walked up and down the platform. She was curious about the lady in the mink coat, and looked up at the windows of her compartment. The blinds were still drawn down—the only ones to be so on the whole train. Katherine wondered a little, and when she re-entered the train she passed along the corridor and noticed that these two compartments were still shuttered and closed. The lady of the mink coat was clearly no early riser.

Presently the conductor came to her and told her that in a few minutes the train would arrive at Nice. Katherine handed him a tip; the man thanked her, but still lingered. There was something odd about him. Katherine, who had at first wondered whether the tip had not been big enough, was now convinced that something far more serious was amiss. His face was of a sickly pallor, he was shaking all over, and looked as if he had been frightened out of his life. He was eyeing her in a curious manner. Presently he said abruptly: "Madame will excuse me, but is she expecting friends to meet her at Nice?"

"Probably," said Katherine. "Why?"

But the man merely shook his head and murmured something that Katherine could not catch and moved away, not reappearing until the train came to rest at the station, when he started handing her belongings down from the window.

Katherine stood for a moment or two on the platform rather at a loss, but a fair young man with an ingenuous face came up to her and said rather hesitatingly:

"Miss Grey, is it not?"

Katherine said that it was, and the young man beamed upon her seraphically and murmured:

"I am Chubby, you know—Lady Tamplin's husband. I expect she mentioned me, but perhaps she forgot. Have you got your *billet de bagages*? I lost mine when I came out this year, and you would not believe the fuss they made about it. Regular French red tape!"

Katherine produced it, and was just about to move off beside him when a very gentle and insidious voice murmured in her ear:

"A little moment, Madame, if you please."

Katherine turned to behold an individual who made up for insignificance of stature by a large quantity of gold lace and uniform. The individual explained. "There were certain formalities. Madame would perhaps be so kind as to accompany him. The

73

regulations of the police—" He threw up his arms. "Absurd, doubt-less, but there it was."

Mr. Chubby Evans listened with a very imperfect compre-hension, his French being of a limited order.

"So like the French," murmured Mr. Evans. He was one of those staunch patriotic Britons who, having made a portion of a foreign country their own, strongly resent the original inhabitants of it. "Always up to some silly dodge or other. They've never tackled people on the station before, though. This is something quite new. I suppose you'll have to go."

Katherine departed with her guide. Somewhat to her surprise, he led her towards a siding where a coach of the departed train had been shunted. He invited her to mount into this, and, preceding her down the corridor, held aside the door of one of the compart-ments. In it was a pompous-looking official personage, and with him a nondescript being who appeared to be a clerk. The pomp-ous-looking personage rose politely, bowed to Katherine, and said:

"You will excuse me, Madame, but there are certain formali-ties to be complied with. Madame speaks French, I trust?"

"Sufficiently, I think, Monsieur," replied Katherine in that language.

"That is good. Pray be seated, Madame. I am M. Caux, the Commissary of Police." He blew out his chest importantly, and Katherine tried to look sufficiently impressed.

"You wish to see my passport?" she inquired. "Here it is."

The Commissary eyed her keenly and gave a little grunt.

"Thank you, Madame," he said, taking the passport from her. He cleared his throat. "But what I really desire is a little information."

"Information?"

The Commissary nodded his head slowly.

"About a lady who has been a fellow-passenger of yours. You lunched with her yesterday."

"I am afraid I can't tell you anything about her. We fell into

74

conversation over our meal, but she is a complete stranger to me. I have never seen her before."

"And yet," said the Commissary sharply, "you returned to her compartment with her after lunch and sat talking for some time?"

"Yes," said Katherine; "that is true."

The Commissary seemed to expect her to say something more. He looked at her encouragingly.

"Yes, Madame?"

"Well, Monsieur?" said Katherine.

"You can, perhaps, give me some kind of idea of that conversation?"

"I could," said Katherine, "but at the moment I see no reason to do so."

In somewhat British fashion she felt annoyed. This foreign official seemed to her impertinent.

"No reason?" cried the Commissary. "Oh yes, Madame, I can assure you that there *is* a reason."

"Then perhaps you will give it to me."

The Commissary rubbed his chin thoughtfully for a minute or two without speaking.

"Madame," he said at last, "the reason is very simple. The lady in question was found dead in her compartment this morning."

"Dead!" gasped Katherine. "What was it—heart failure?"

"No," said the Commissary in a reflective, dreamy voice. "No—she was murdered."

"Murdered!" cried Katherine.

"So you see, Madame, why we are anxious for any information we can possibly get."

"But surely her maid—"

"The maid has disappeared."

"Oh!" Katherine paused to assemble her thoughts.

"Since the conductor had seen you talking with her in her compartment, he quite naturally reported the fact to the police, and that is why, Madame, we have detained you, in the hope of gaining some information."

"I am very sorry," said Katherine; "I don't even know her name."

"Her name is Kettering. That we know from her passport and from the labels on her luggage. If we—"

There was a knock on the compartment door. M. Caux frowned. He opened it about six inches.

"What is the matter?" he said peremptorily. "I cannot be disturbed."

The egg-shaped head of Katherine's dinner acquaintance showed itself in the aperture. On his face was a beaming smile.

"My name," he said, "is Hercule Poirot."

"Not," the Commissary stammered, "not *the* Hercule Poirot?"

"The same," said M. Poirot. "I remember meeting you once, M. Caux, at the *Sûreté* in Paris, though doubtless you have forgotten me?"

"Not at all, Monsieur, not at all," declared the Commissary heartily. "But enter, I pray of you. You know of this—"

"Yes, I know," said Hercule Poirot. "I came to see if I might be of any assistance?"

"We should be flattered," replied the Commissary promptly. "Let me present you, M. Poirot, to"—he consulted the passport he still held in his hand—"to Madame—er—Mademoiselle Grey."

Poirot smiled across at Katherine.

"It is strange, is it not," he murmured, "that my words should have come true so quickly?"

"Mademoiselle, alas! can tell us very little," said the Commissary.

"I have been explaining," said Katherine, "that this poor lady was a complete stranger to me."

Poirot nodded.

"But she talked to you, did she not?" he said gently. "You formed an impression—is it not so?"

"Yes," said Katherine thoughtfully. "I suppose I did."

"And that impression was—"

"Yes, Mademoiselle"—the Commissary jerked himself forward—"let us by all means have your impressions."

Katherine sat turning the whole thing over in her mind. She felt in a way as if she were betraying a confidence, but with that ugly word "Murder" ringing in her ears she dared not keep anything back. Too much might hang upon it. So, as nearly as she could, she repeated word for word the conversation she had had with the dead woman.

"That is interesting," said the Commissary, glancing at the other. "Eh, M. Poirot, that is interesting? Whether it has anything to do with the crime—" He left the sentence unfinished.

"I suppose it could not be suicide," said Katherine, rather doubtfully.

"No," said the Commissary, "it could not be suicide. She was strangled with a length of black cord."

"Oh!" Katherine shivered. M. Caux spread out his hands apologetically. "It is not nice—no. I think that our train robbers are more brutal than they are in your country."

"It is horrible."

"Yes, yes"—he was soothing and apologetic—"but you have great courage, Mademoiselle. At once, as soon as I saw you, I said to myself, 'Mademoiselle has great courage.' That is why I am going to ask you to do something more—something distressing, but I assure you very necessary."

Katherine looked at him apprehensively.

He spread out his hands apologetically.

"I am going to ask you, Mademoiselle, to be so good as to accompany me to the next compartment."

"Must I?" asked Katherine in a low voice.

"Someone must identify her," said the Commissary, "and since the maid has disappeared"—he coughed significantly—"you appear to be the person who has seen most of her since she joined the train."

"Very well," said Katherine quietly; "if it is necessary—"

She rose. Poirot gave her a little nod of approval.

"Mademoiselle is sensible," he said. "May I accompany you, M. Caux?"

"Enchanted, my dear M. Poirot."

They went out into the corridor, and M. Caux unlocked the door of the dead woman's compartment. The blinds on the far side had been drawn half-way up to admit light. The dead woman lay on the berth to their left, in so natural a posture that one could have thought her asleep. The bedclothes were drawn up over her, and her head was turned to the wall, so that only the red auburn curls showed. Very gently M. Caux laid a hand on her shoulder and turned the body back so that the face came into view. Katherine flinched a little and dug her nails into her palms. A heavy blow had disfigured the features almost beyond recognition. Poirot gave a sharp exclamation.

"When was that done, I wonder?" he demanded. "Before death or after?"

"The doctor says after," said M. Caux.

"Strange," said Poirot, drawing his brows together. He turned to Katherine. "Be brave, Mademoiselle; look at her well. Are you sure that this is the woman you talked to in the train yesterday?"

Katherine had good nerves. She steeled herself to look long and earnestly at the recumbent figure. Then she leaned forward and took up the dead woman's hand.

"I am quite sure," she replied at length. "The face is too disfigured to recognize, but the build and carriage and hair are exact, and besides I noticed *this*"—she pointed to a tiny mole on the dead woman's wrist—"while I was talking to her."

"*Bon*," approved Poirot. "You are an excellent witness, Mademoiselle. There is, then, no question as to the identity, but it is strange, all the same." He frowned down on the dead woman in perplexity.

M. Caux shrugged his shoulders.

"The murderer was carried away by rage, doubtless," he suggested.

"If she had been struck down, it would have been comprehensible," mused Poirot, "but the man who strangled her slipped up behind and caught her unawares. A little choke—a little gurgle—that is all that would be heard, and then afterwards—that smashing blow on her face. Now why? Did he hope that if the face were unrecognizable she might not be identified? Or did he hate her so much that he could not resist striking that blow even after she was dead?"

Katherine shuddered, and he turned at once to her kindly.

"You must not let me distress you, Mademoiselle," he said. "To you this is all very new and terrible. To me, alas! it is an old story. One moment, I pray of you both."

They stood against the door watching him as he went quickly round the compartment. He noted the dead woman's clothes neatly folded on the end of the berth, the big fur coat that hung from a hook, and the little red lacquer hat tossed up on the rack. Then he passed through into the adjoining compartment, that in which Katherine had seen the maid sitting. Here the berth had not been made up. Three or four rugs were piled loosely on the seat; there was a hat-box and a couple of suit-cases. He turned suddenly to Katherine.

"You were in here yesterday," he said. "Do you see anything changed, anything missing?"

Katherine looked carefully round both compartments.

"Yes," she said, "there is something missing—a scarlet morocco case. It had the initials 'R. V. K.' on it. It might have been a small dressing-case or a big jewel-case. When I saw it, the maid was holding it."

"Ah!" said Poirot.

"But, surely," said Katherine. "I—of course, I don't know anything about such things, but surely it is plain enough, if the maid and the jewel-case are missing?"

"You mean that it was the maid who was the thief? No, Mademoiselle; there is a very good reason against that."

"What?"

"The maid was left behind in Paris."

He turned to Poirot.

"I should like you to hear the conductor's story yourself," he murmured confidentially. "It is very suggestive."

"Mademoiselle would doubtless like to hear it also," said Poirot. "You do not object, Monsieur le Commissaire?"

"No," said the Commissary, who clearly did object very much. "No, certainly, M. Poirot, if you say so. You have finished here?"

"I think so. One little minute."

He had been turning over the rugs, and now he took one to the window and looked at it, picking something off it with his fingers.

"What is it?" demanded M. Caux sharply.

"Four auburn hairs." He bent over the dead woman. "Yes, they are from the head of Madame."

"And what of it? Do you attach importance to them?"

Poirot let the rug drop back on the seat.

"What is important? What is not? One cannot say at this stage. But we must note each little fact carefully."

They went back again into the first compartment, and in a minute or two the conductor of the carriage arrived to be questioned.

"Your name is Pierre Michel?" said the Commissary.

"Yes, Monsieur le Commissaire."

"I should like you to repeat to this gentleman"—he indicated Poirot—"the story that you told me as to what happened in Paris."

"Very good, Monsieur le Commissaire. It was after we had left the Gare de Lyon. I came along to make the beds, thinking that Madame would be at dinner, but she had a dinner basket in her compartment. She said to me that she had been obliged to leave her maid behind in Paris, so that I need make up only one berth. She took her dinner basket into the adjoining compartment, and sat there while I made up the bed; then she told me that she did not wish to be wakened early in the morning, that she liked to sleep on. I told her I quite understood, and she wished me 'good-night.'"

"You yourself did not go into the adjoining compartment?"

"No, Monsieur."

"Then you did not happen to notice if a scarlet morocco case was amongst the luggage there?"

"No, Monsieur, I did not."

"Would it have been possible for a man to have been concealed in the adjoining compartment?"

The conductor reflected.

"The door was half open," he said. "If a man had stood behind that door I should not have been able to see him, but he would, of course, have been perfectly visible to Madame when she went in there."

"Quite so," said Poirot. "Is there anything more you have to tell us?"

"I think that is all, Monsieur. I can remember nothing else."

"And now this morning?" prompted Poirot.

"As Madame had ordered, I did not disturb her. It was not until just before Cannes that I ventured to knock at the door. Getting no reply, I opened it. The lady appeared to be in her bed asleep. I took her by the shoulder to rouse her, and then—"

"And then you saw what had happened," volunteered Poirot. "*Très bien.* I think I know all I want to know."

"I hope, Monsieur le Commissaire, it is not that I have been guilty of any negligence," said the man piteously. "Such an affair to happen on the Blue Train! It is horrible."

"Console yourself," said the Commissary. "Everything will be done to keep the affair as quiet as possible, if only in the interests of justice. I cannot think you have been guilty of any negligence."

"And Monsieur le Commissaire will report as much to the Company?"

"But certainly, but certainly," said M. Caux impatiently. "That will do now."

The conductor withdrew.

"According to the medical evidence," said the Commissary, "the lady was probably dead before the train reached Lyons. Who then was the murderer? From Mademoiselle's story, it seems clear that somewhere on her journey she was to meet this man of whom she spoke. Her action in getting rid of the maid seems significant. Did the man join the train at Paris, and did she conceal him in the adjoining compartment? If so, they may have quarrelled, and he may have killed her in a fit of rage. That is one possibility. The other, and the more likely to my mind, is that her assailant was a train robber travelling on the train; that he stole along the corridor unseen by the conductor, killed her, and went off with the red morocco case, which doubtless contained jewels of some value. In all probability he left the train at Lyons, and we have already telegraphed to the station there for full particulars of anyone seen leaving the train."

"Or he might have come on to Nice," suggested Poirot.

"He might," agreed the Commissary, "but that would be a very bold course."

Poirot let a minute or two go by before speaking, and then he said:

"In the latter case you think the man was an ordinary train robber?"

The Commissary shrugged his shoulders.

"It depends. We must get hold of the maid. It is possible that she has the red morocco case with her. If so, then the man of whom she spoke to Mademoiselle may be concerned in the case, and the affair is a crime of passion. I myself think the solution of a train robber is the more probable. These bandits have become very bold of late."

Poirot looked suddenly across to Katherine.

"And you, Mademoiselle," he said, "you heard and saw nothing during the night?"

"Nothing," said Katherine.

Poirot turned to the Commissary.

"We need detain Mademoiselle no longer, I think," he suggested.

The latter nodded.

"She will leave us her address?" he said.

Katherine gave him the name of Lady Tamplin's villa. Poirot made her a little bow.

"You permit that I see you again, Mademoiselle?" he said. "Or have you so many friends that your time will be all taken up?"

"On the contrary," said Katherine, "I shall have plenty of leisure, and I shall be very pleased to see you again."

"Excellent," said Poirot, and gave her a little friendly nod. "This shall be a *'roman policier' à nous*. We will investigate this affair together."

TWELVE
At the Villa Marguerite

Then you were really in the thick of it all!" said Lady Tamplin enviously. "My dear, how thrilling!" She opened her china blue eyes very wide and gave a little sigh.

"A real murder," said Mr. Evans gloatingly.

"Of course Chubby had no idea of anything of the kind," went on Lady Tamplin; "he simply could *not* imagine why the police wanted you. My dear, what an opportunity! I think, you know—yes, I certainly think something might be made out of this."

A calculating look rather marred the ingenuousness of the blue eyes.

Katherine felt slightly uncomfortable. They were just finishing lunch, and she looked in turn at the three people sitting round the table. Lady Tamplin, full of practical schemes; Mr. Evans, beaming with naïve appreciation, and Lenox with a queer crooked smile on her dark face.

"Marvellous luck," murmured Chubby; "I wish I could have gone along with you—and seen—all the exhibits."

His tone was wistful and childlike.

Katherine said nothing. The police had laid no injunctions of secrecy upon her, and it was clearly impossible to suppress the bare facts or try to keep them from her hostess. But she did rather wish it had been possible to do so.

"Yes," said Lady Tamplin, coming suddenly out of her reverie, "I do think something might be done. A little account, you know, cleverly written up. An eye-witness, a feminine touch: *'How I chatted with the dead woman, little thinking—'* that sort of thing, you know."

"Rot!" said Lenox.

"You have no idea," said Lady Tamplin in a soft, wistful voice, "what newspapers will pay for a little titbit! Written, of course, by someone of really unimpeachable social position. You would not like to do it yourself, I dare say, Katherine dear, but just give me the bare bones of it, and *I* will manage the whole thing for you. Mr. de Haviland is a special friend of mine. We have a little understanding together. A most delightful man—not at all reporterish. How does the idea strike you, Katherine?"

"I would much prefer to do nothing of the kind," said Katherine bluntly.

Lady Tamplin was rather disconcerted at this uncompromising refusal. She sighed and turned to the elucidation of further details.

"A very striking-looking woman, you said? I wonder now who she could have been. You didn't hear her name?"

"It was mentioned," Katherine admitted, "but I can't remember it. You see, I was rather upset."

"I should think so," said Mr. Evans; "it must have been a beastly shock."

It is to be doubted whether, even if Katherine had remembered the name, she would have admitted the fact. Lady Tamplin's remorseless cross-examination was making her restive. Lenox, who was observant in her own way, noticed this, and offered to take Katherine upstairs to see her room. She left her there, remarking kindly before she went: "You mustn't mind Mother; she would make a few pennies' profit out of her dying grandmother if she could."

Lenox went down again to find her mother and her step-father discussing the newcomer.

"Presentable," said Lady Tamplin, "quite presentable. Her clothes are all right. That grey thing is the same model that Gladys

Cooper wore in *Palm Trees in Egypt.*"

"Have you noticed her eyes—what?" interposed Mr. Evans.

"Never mind her eyes, Chubby," said Lady Tamplin tartly; "we are discussing the things that really matter."

"Oh, quite," said Mr. Evans, and retired into his shell.

"She doesn't seem to me very—malleable," said Lady Tamplin, rather hesitating to choose the right word.

"She has all the instincts of a lady, as they say in books," said Lenox, with a grin.

"Narrow-minded," murmured Lady Tamplin. "Inevitable under the circumstances, I suppose."

"I expect you will do your best to broaden her," said Lenox, with a grin, "but you will have your work cut out. Just now, you noticed, she stuck down her fore feet and laid back her ears and refused to budge."

"Anyway," said Lady Tamplin hopefully, "she doesn't look to me at all mean. Some people, when they come into money, seem to attach undue importance to it."

"Oh, you'll easily touch her for what you want," said Lenox; "and, after all, that is all that matters, isn't it? That is what she is here for."

"She is my own cousin," said Lady Tamplin, with dignity.

"Cousin, eh?" said Mr. Evans, waking up again. "I suppose I call her Katherine, don't I?"

"It is of no importance at all what you call her, Chubby," said Lady Tamplin.

"Good," said Mr. Evans; "then I will. Do you suppose she plays tennis?" he added hopefully.

"Of course not," said Lady Tamplin. "She has been a companion, I tell you. Companions don't play tennis—or golf. They might possibly play golf-croquet, but I have always understood that they wind wool and wash dogs most of the day."

"O God!" said Mr. Evans; "do they really?"

Lenox drifted upstairs again to Katherine's room. "Can I help you?" she asked rather perfunctorily.

On Katherine's disclaimer, Lenox sat on the edge of the bed and stared thoughtfully at her guest.

"Why did you come?" she said at last. "To us, I mean. We're not your sort."

"Oh, I am anxious to get into Society."

"Don't be an ass," said Lenox promptly, detecting the flicker of a smile. "You know what I mean well enough. You are not a bit what I thought you would be. I say, you *have* got some decent clothes." She sighed. "Clothes are no good to me. I was born awkward. It's a pity, because I love them."

"I love them too," said Katherine, "but it has not been much use my loving them up to now. Do you think this is nice?"

She and Lenox discussed several models with artistic fervour.

"I like you," said Lenox suddenly. "I came up to warn you not to be taken in by Mother, but I think now that there is no need to do that. You are frightfully sincere and upright and all those queer things, but you are not a fool. Oh hell! what is it now?"

Lady Tamplin's voice was calling plaintively from the hall:

"Lenox, Derek has just rung up. He wants to come to dinner to-night. Will it be all right? I mean, we haven't got anything awkward, like quails, have we?"

Lenox reassured her and came back into Katherine's room. Her face looked brighter and less sullen.

"I'm glad old Derek is coming," she said; "you'll like him."

"Who is Derek?"

"He is Lord Leconbury's son, married a rich American woman. Women are simply potty about him."

"Why?"

"Oh, the usual reason—very good-looking and a regular bad lot. Every one goes off their head about him."

"Do you?"

"Sometimes I do," said Lenox, "and sometimes I think I would like to marry a nice curate and live in the country and grow things in frames." She paused a minute, and then added, "An Irish curate would be best, and then I should hunt."

After a minute or two she reverted to her former theme. "There is something queer about Derek. All that family are a bit potty—mad gamblers, you know. In the old days they used to gamble away their wives and their estates, and did most reckless things just for the love of it. Derek would have made a perfect highwayman—debonair and gay, just the right manner." She moved to the door. "Well, come down when you feel like it."

Left alone, Katherine gave herself up to thought. Just at present she felt thoroughly ill at ease and jarred by her surroundings. The shock of the discovery in the train and the reception of the news by her new friends jarred upon her susceptibilities. She thought long and earnestly about the murdered woman. She had been sorry for Ruth, but she could not honestly say that she had liked her. She had divined only too well the ruthless egoism that was the keynote of her personality, and it repelled her.

She had been amused and a trifle hurt by the other's cool dismissal of her when she had served her turn. That she had come to some decision, Katherine was quite certain, but she wondered now what that decision had been. Whatever it was, death had stepped in and made all decisions meaningless. Strange that it should have been so, and that a brutal crime should have been the ending of that fateful journey. But suddenly Katherine remembered a small fact that she ought, perhaps, to have told the police—a fact that had for the moment escaped her memory. Was it of any real importance? She had certainly thought that she had seen a man going into that particular compartment, but she realized that she might easily have been mistaken. It might have been the compartment next door, and certainly the man in question could be no train robber. She recalled him very clearly as she had seen him on those two previous occasions—once at the Savoy and once at Cook's office. No, doubtless she had been mistaken. He had not gone into the dead woman's compartment, and it was perhaps as well that she had said nothing to the police. She might have done incalculable harm by doing so.

She went down to join the others on the terrace outside. Through the branches of mimosa, she looked out over the blue of the Mediterranean, and, whilst listening with half an ear to Lady Tamplin's chatter, she was glad that she had come. This was better than St. Mary Mead.

That evening she put on the mauvy pink dress that went by the name of *soupir d'automne*, and after smiling at her reflection in the mirror, went downstairs with, for the first time in her life, a faint feeling of shyness.

Most of Lady Tamplin's guests had arrived, and since noise was the essential of Lady Tamplin's parties, the din was already terrific. Chubby rushed up to Katherine, pressed a cocktail upon her, and took her under his wing.

"Oh, here you are, Derek," cried Lady Tamplin, as the door opened to admit the last comer. "Now at last we can have something to eat. I am starving."

Katherine looked across the room. She was startled. So this—was Derek, and she realized that she was not surprised. She had always known that she would someday meet the man whom she had seen three times by such a curious chain of coincidences. She thought, too, that he recognized her. He paused abruptly in what he was saying to Lady Tamplin, and went on again as though with an effort. They all went into dinner, and Katherine found that he was placed beside her. He turned to her at once with a vivid smile.

"I knew I was going to meet you soon," he remarked, "but I never dreamt that it would be here. It had to be, you know. Once at the Savoy and once at Cook's—never twice without three times. Don't say you can't remember me or never noticed me. I insist upon your pretending that you noticed me, anyway."

"Oh, I did," said Katherine; "but this is not the third time. It is the fourth. I saw you on the Blue Train."

"On the Blue Train!" Something undefinable came over his

manner; she could not have said just what it was. It was as though he had received a check, a setback. Then he said carelessly:

"What was the rumpus this morning? Somebody had died, hadn't they?"

"Yes," said Katherine slowly; "somebody had died."

"You shouldn't die on a train," remarked Derek flippantly. "I believe it causes all sorts of legal and international complications, and it gives the train an excuse for being even later than usual."

"Mr. Kettering?" A stout American lady, who was sitting opposite, leaned forward and spoke to him with the deliberate intonation of her race. "Mr. Kettering, I do believe you have forgotten me, and I thought you such a perfectly lovely man."

Derek leaned forward, answering her, and Katherine sat almost dazed.

Kettering! That was the name, of course! She remembered it now—but what a strange, ironical situation! Here was this man whom she had seen go into his wife's compartment last night, who had left her alive and well, and now he was sitting at dinner, quite unconscious of the fate that had befallen her. Of that there was no doubt. He did not know.

A servant was leaning over Derek, handing him a note and murmuring in his ear. With a word of excuse to Lady Tamplin, he broke it open, and an expression of utter astonishment came over his face as he read; then he looked at his hostess.

"This is most extraordinary. I say, Rosalie, I am afraid I will have to leave you. The Prefect of Police wants to see me at once. I can't think what about."

"Your sins have found you out," remarked Lenox.

"They must have," said Derek; "probably some idiotic nonsense, but I suppose I shall have to push off to the Prefecture. How dare the old boy rout me out from dinner? It ought to be something deadly serious to justify that," and he laughed as he pushed back his chair and rose to leave the room.

THIRTEEN
Van Aldin Gets a Telegram

O n the afternoon of the 15th of February a thick yellow fog had settled down on London. Rufus Van Aldin was in his suite at the Savoy and was making the most of the atmospheric conditions by working double time. Knighton was overjoyed. He had found it difficult of late to get his employer to concentrate on the matters in hand. When he had ventured to urge certain courses, Van Aldin had put him off with a curt word. But now Van Aldin seemed to be throwing himself into work with redoubled energy, and the secretary made the most of his opportunities. Always tactful, he plied the spur so unobtrusively that Van Aldin never suspected it.

Yet in the middle of this absorption in business matters, one little fact lay at the back of Van Aldin's mind. A chance remark of Knighton's, uttered by the secretary in all unconsciousness, had given rise to it. It now festered unseen, gradually reaching further and further forward into Van Aldin's consciousness, until at last, in spite of himself, he had to yield to its insistence.

He listened to what Knighton was saying with his usual air of keen attention, but in reality not one word of it penetrated his mind. He nodded automatically, however, and the secretary turned to some other papers. As he was sorting them out, his employer spoke:

"Do you mind telling me that over again, Knighton?"

For a moment Knighton was at a loss.

"You mean about this, sir?" He held up a closely written Company report.

"No, no," said Van Aldin; "what you told me about seeing Ruth's maid in Paris last night. I can't make it out. You must have been mistaken."

"I can't have been mistaken, sir; I actually spoke to her."

"Well, tell me the whole thing again."

Knighton complied.

"I had fixed up the deal with Bartheimers," he explained, "and had gone back to the Ritz to pick up my traps preparatory to having dinner and catching the nine o'clock train from the Gare du Nord. At the reception desk I saw a woman whom I was quite sure was Mrs. Kettering's maid. I went up to her and asked if Mrs. Kettering was staying there."

"Yes, yes," said Van Aldin. "Of course. Naturally. And she told you that Ruth had gone on to the Riviera and had sent her to the Ritz to await further orders there?"

"Exactly that, sir."

"It is very odd," said Van Aldin. "Very odd, indeed, unless the woman had been impertinent or something of that kind."

"In that case," objected Knighton, "surely Mrs. Kettering would have paid her down a sum of money, and told her to go back to England. She would hardly have sent her to the Ritz."

"No," muttered the millionaire; "that's true."

He was about to say something further, but checked himself. He was fond of Knighton and liked and trusted him, but he could hardly discuss his daughter's private affairs with his secretary. He had already felt hurt by Ruth's lack of frankness, and this chance information which had come to him did nothing to allay his misgivings.

Why had Ruth got rid of her maid in Paris? What possible object or motive could she have had in so doing?

He reflected for a moment or two on the curious combination

of chance. How should it have occurred to Ruth, except as the wildest coincidence, that the first person that the maid should run across in Paris should be her father's secretary? Ah, but that was the way things happened. That was the way things got found out.

He winced at the last phrase; it had arisen with complete naturalness to his mind. Was there then "something to be found out"? He hated to put this question to himself; he had no doubt of the answer. The answer was—he was sure of it—Armand de la Roche.

It was bitter to Van Aldin that a daughter of his should be gulled by such a man, yet he was forced to admit that she was in good company—that other well-bred and intelligent women had succumbed just as easily to the Count's fascination. Men saw through him, women did not.

He sought now for a phrase that would allay any suspicion that his secretary might have felt.

"Ruth is always changing her mind about things at a moment's notice," he remarked, and then he added in a would-be careless tone: "The maid didn't give any—er—reason for this change of plan?"

Knighton was careful to make his voice as natural as possible as he replied:

"She said, sir, that Mrs. Kettering had met a friend unexpectedly."

"Is that so?"

The secretary's practised ears caught the note of strain underlying the seemingly casual tone.

"Oh, I see. Man or woman?"

"I think she said a man, sir."

Van Aldin nodded. His worst fears were being realized. He rose from his chair, and began pacing up and down the room, a habit of his when agitated. Unable to contain his feelings any longer, he burst forth:

"There is one thing no man can do, and that is to get a woman to listen to reason. Somehow or other, they don't seem to have any kind of *sense*. Talk of woman's instinct—why, it is well known all the world over that a woman is the surest mark for any rascally swindler. Not one in ten of them knows a scoundrel when she meets one; they can be preyed on by any good-looking fellow with a soft side to his tongue. If I had my way—"

He was interrupted. A page-boy entered with a telegram. Van Aldin tore it open, and his face went a sudden chalky white. He caught hold of the back of a chair to steady himself, and waved the page-boy from the room.

"What's the matter, sir?"

Knighton had risen in concern.

"Ruth!" said Van Aldin hoarsely.

"Mrs. Kettering?"

"Killed!"

"An accident to the train?"

Van Aldin shook his head.

"No. From this it seems she has been robbed as well. They don't use the word, Knighton, but my poor girl has been murdered."

"Oh, my God, sir!"

Van Aldin tapped the telegram with his forefinger.

"This is from the police at Nice. I must go out there by the first train."

Knighton was efficient as ever. He glanced at the clock.

"Five o'clock from Victoria, sir."

"That's right. You will come with me, Knighton. Tell my man, Archer, and pack your own things. See to everything here. I want to go round to Curzon Street."

The telephone rang sharply, and the secretary lifted the receiver.

"Yes; who is it?"

Then to Van Aldin.

"Mr. Goby, sir."

"Goby? I can't see him now. No—wait, we have plenty of

time. Tell them to send him up."

Van Aldin was a strong man. Already he had recovered that iron calm of his. Few people would have noticed anything amiss in his greeting to Mr. Goby.

"I am pressed for time, Goby. Got anything important to tell me?"

Mr. Goby coughed.

"The movements of Mr. Kettering, sir. You wished them reported to you."

"Yes—well?"

"Mr. Kettering, sir, left London for the Riviera yesterday morning."

"What?"

Something in his voice must have startled Mr. Goby. That worthy gentleman departed from his usual practice of never looking at the person to whom he was talking, and stole a fleeting glance at the millionaire.

"What train did he go on?" demanded Van Aldin.

"The Blue Train, sir."

Mr. Goby coughed again and spoke to the clock on the mantelpiece.

"Mademoiselle Mirelle, the dancer from the Parthenon, went by the same train."

FOURTEEN

Ada Mason's Story

I cannot repeat to you often enough, Monsieur, our horror, our consternation, and the deep sympathy we feel for you."

Thus M. Carrège, the Juge d'Instruction, addressed Van Aldin. M. Caux, the Commissary, made sympathetic noises in his throat. Van Aldin brushed away horror, consternation, and sympathy with an abrupt gesture. The scene was the Examining Magistrate's room at Nice. Besides M. Carrège, the Commissary, and Van Aldin, there was a further person in the room. It was that person who now spoke.

"M. Van Aldin," he said, "desires action—swift action."

"Ah!" cried the Commissary, "I have not yet presented you. M. Van Aldin, this is M. Hercule Poirot; you have doubtless heard of him. Although he has retired from his profession for some years now, his name is still a household word as one of the greatest living detectives."

"Pleased to meet you, M. Poirot," said Van Aldin, falling back mechanically on a formula that he had discarded some years ago. "You have retired from your profession?"

"That is so, Monsieur. Now I enjoy the world."

The little man made a grandiloquent gesture.

"M. Poirot happened to be travelling on the Blue Train," explained the Commissary, "and he has been so kind as to assist us out of his vast experience."

The millionaire looked at Poirot keenly. Then he said unexpectedly:

"I am a very rich man, M. Poirot. It is usually said that a rich man labours under the belief that he can buy everything and everyone. That is not true. I am a big man in my way, and one big man can ask a favour from another big man."

Poirot nodded a quick appreciation.

"That is very well said, M. Van Aldin. I place myself entirely at your service."

"Thank you," said Van Aldin. "I can only say call upon me at any time, and you will not find me ungrateful. And now, gentlemen, to business."

"I propose," said M. Carrège, "to interrogate the maid, Ada Mason. You have her here, I understand?"

"Yes," said Van Aldin. "We picked her up in Paris in passing through. She was very upset to hear of her mistress's death, but she tells her story coherently enough."

"We will have her in, then," said M. Carrège.

He rang the bell on his desk, and in a few minutes Ada Mason entered the room.

She was very neatly dressed in black, and the tip of her nose was red. She had exchanged her grey travelling gloves for a pair of black suède ones. She cast a look round the Examining Magistrate's office in some trepidation, and seemed relieved at the presence of her mistress's father. The Examining Magistrate prided himself on his geniality of manner, and did his best to put her at her ease. He was helped in this by Poirot, who acted as interpreter, and whose friendly manner was reassuring to the Englishwoman.

"Your name is Ada Mason; is that right?"

"Ada Beatrice I was christened, sir," said Mason primly.

"Just so. And we can understand, Mason, that this has all been very distressing."

"Oh, indeed it has, sir. I have been with many ladies and

always given satisfaction, I hope, and I never dreamt of anything of this kind happening in any situation where I was."

"No, no," said M. Carrège.

"Naturally I have read of such things, of course, in the Sunday papers. And then I always have understood that those foreign trains—" She suddenly checked her flow, remembering that the gentlemen who were speaking to her were of the same nationality as the trains.

"Now let us talk this affair over," said M. Carrège. "There was, I understand, no question of your staying in Paris when you started from London?"

"Oh no, sir. We were to go straight through to Nice."

"Have you ever been abroad with your mistress before?"

"No, sir. I had only been with her two months, you see."

"Did she seem quite as usual when starting on this journey?"

"She was worried like and a bit upset, and she was rather irritable and difficult to please."

M. Carrège nodded.

"Now then, Mason, what was the first you heard of your stopping in Paris?"

"It was at the place they call the Gare de Lyon, sir. My mistress was thinking of getting out and walking up and down the platform. She was just going out into the corridor when she gave a sudden exclamation, and came back into her compartment with a gentleman. She shut the door between her carriage and mine, so that I didn't see or hear anything, till she suddenly opened it again and told me that she had changed her plans. She gave me some money and told me to get out and go to the Ritz. They knew her well there, she said, and would give me a room. I was to wait there until I heard from her; she would wire me what she wanted me to do. I had just time to get my things together and jump out of the train before it started off. It was a rush."

"While Mrs. Kettering was telling you this, where was the gentleman?"

"He was standing in the other compartment, sir, looking out

of the window."

"Can you describe him to us?"

"Well, you see, sir, I hardly saw him. He had his back to me most of the time. He was a tall gentleman and dark; that's all I can say. He was dressed very like any other gentleman in a dark blue overcoat and a grey hat."

"Was he one of the passengers on the train?"

"I don't think so, sir; I took it that he had come to the station to see Mrs. Kettering in passing through. Of course he might have been one of the passengers; I never thought of that."

Mason seemed a little flurried by the suggestion.

"Ah!" M. Carrège passed lightly to another subject. "Your mistress later requested the conductor not to rouse her early in the morning. Was that a likely thing for her to do, do you think?"

"Oh yes, sir. The mistress never ate any breakfast and she didn't sleep well at nights, so that she liked sleeping on in the morning."

Again M. Carrège passed to another subject.

"Amongst the luggage there was a scarlet morocco case, was there not?" he asked. "Your mistress's jewel-case?"

"Yes, sir."

"Did you take that case to the Ritz?"

"*Me* take the mistress's jewel-case to the Ritz! Oh no, indeed, sir." Mason's tones were horrified.

"You left it behind you in the carriage?"

"Yes, sir."

"Had your mistress many jewels with her, do you know?"

"A fair amount, sir; made me a bit uneasy sometimes, I can tell you, with those nasty tales you hear of being robbed in foreign countries. They were insured, I know, but all the same it seemed a frightful risk. Why, the rubies alone, the mistress told me, were worth several hundred thousand pounds."

"The rubies! What rubies?" barked Van Aldin suddenly.

Mason turned to him.

"I think it was you who gave them to her, sir, not very long ago."

"My God!" cried Van Aldin. "You don't say she had those rubies with her? I told her to leave them at the Bank."

Mason gave once more the discreet cough which was apparently part of her stock-in-trade as a lady's maid. This time it expressed a good deal. It expressed far more clearly than words could have done, that Mason's mistress had been a lady who took her own way.

"Ruth must have been mad," muttered Van Aldin. "What on earth could have possessed her?"

M. Carrège in turn gave vent to a cough, again a cough of significance. It riveted Van Aldin's attention on him.

"For the moment," said M. Carrège, addressing Mason, "I think that is all. If you will go into the next room, Mademoiselle, they will read over to you the questions and answers, and you will sign accordingly."

Mason went out escorted by the clerk, and Van Aldin said immediately to the Magistrate:

"Well?"

M. Carrège opened a drawer in his desk, took out a letter, and handed it across to Van Aldin.

"This was found in Madame's handbag."

"Chère Amie" (the letter ran)—"I will obey you; I will be prudent, discreet—all those things that a lover most hates. Paris would perhaps have been unwise, but the Isles d'Or are far away from the world, and you may be assured that nothing will leak out. It is like you and your divine sympathy to be so interested in the work on famous jewels that I am writing. It will, indeed, be an extraordinary privilege to actually see and handle these historic rubies. I am devoting a special passage to 'Heart of Fire.' My wonderful one! Soon I will make up to you for all those sad years of separation and emptiness.—Your ever-adoring,

"Armand."

FIFTEEN
The Comte de la Roche

Van Aldin read the letter through in silence. His face turned a dull angry crimson. The men watching him saw the veins start out on his forehead, and his big hands clench themselves unconsciously. He handed back the letter without a word. M. Carrège was looking with close attention at his desk, M. Caux's eyes were fixed upon the ceiling, and M. Hercule Poirot was tenderly brushing a speck of dust from his coat sleeve. With the greatest tact they none of them looked at Van Aldin.

It was M. Carrège, mindful of his status and his duties, who tackled the unpleasant subject.

"Perhaps, Monsieur," he murmured, "you are aware by whom—er—this letter was written?"

"Yes, I know," said Van Aldin heavily.

"Ah?" said the Magistrate inquiringly.

"A scoundrel who calls himself the Comte de la Roche."

There was a pause; then M. Poirot leaned forward, straightened a ruler on the judge's desk, and addressed the millionaire directly.

"M. Van Aldin, we are all sensible, deeply sensible, of the pain it must give you to speak of these matters, but believe me, Monsieur, it is not the time for concealments. If justice is to be done, we must know everything. If you will reflect a little minute you will realize the truth of that clearly for yourself."

Van Aldin was silent for a moment or two, then almost reluctantly he nodded his head in agreement.

"You are quite right, M. Poirot," he said. "Painful as it is, I have no right to keep anything back."

The Commissary gave a sigh of relief, and the Examining Magistrate leaned back in his chair and adjusted a pince-nez on his long thin nose.

"Perhaps you will tell us in your own words, M. Van Aldin," he said, "all that you know of this gentleman."

"It began eleven or twelve years ago—in Paris. My daughter was a young girl then, full of foolish, romantic notions, like all young girls are. Unknown to me, she made the acquaintance of this Comte de la Roche. You have heard of him, perhaps?"

The Commissary and Poirot nodded in assent.

"He calls himself the Comte de la Roche," continued Van Aldin, "but I doubt if he has any right to the title."

"You would not have found his name in the *Almanach de Gotha*," agreed the Commissary.

"I discovered as much," said Van Aldin. "The man was a good-looking, plausible scoundrel, with a fatal fascination for women. Ruth was infatuated with him, but I soon put a stop to the whole affair. The man was no better than a common swindler."

"You are quite right," said the Commissary. "The Comte de la Roche is well known to us. If it were possible, we should have laid him by the heels before now, but *ma foi!* it is not easy; the fellow is cunning, his affairs are always conducted with ladies of high social position. If he obtains money from them under false pretences or as the fruit of blackmail, *eh bien!* naturally they will not prosecute. To look foolish in the eyes of the world, oh no, that would never do, and he has an extraordinary power over women."

"That is so," said the millionaire heavily. "Well, as I told you, I broke the affair up pretty sharply. I told Ruth exactly what he was, and she had, perforce, to believe me. About a year afterwards, she met her present husband and married him. As far as I knew, that was the end of the matter; but only a week ago, I discovered, to my amazement, that my daughter had resumed her acquaintance with the Comte de la Roche. She had been meeting him frequently in London and Paris. I remonstrated with her on her imprudence, for I may tell you gentlemen, that, on my insistence, she was preparing to bring a suit for divorce against her husband."

"That is interesting," murmured Poirot softly, his eyes on the ceiling.

Van Aldin looked at him sharply, and then went on.

"I pointed out to her the folly of continuing to see the Comte under the circumstances. I thought she agreed with me."

The Examining Magistrate coughed delicately.

"But according to this letter—" he began, and then stopped.

Van Aldin's jaw set itself squarely.

"I know. It's no good mincing matters. However unpleasant, we have got to face facts. It seems clear that Ruth had arranged to go to Paris and meet de la Roche there. After my warnings to her, however, she must have written to the Count suggesting a change of rendezvous."

"The Isles d'Or," said the Commissary thoughtfully, "are situated just opposite Hyères, a remote and idyllic spot."

Van Aldin nodded.

"My God! How could Ruth be such a fool?" he exclaimed bitterly. "All this talk about writing a book on jewels! Why, he must have been after the rubies from the first."

"There are some very famous rubies," said Poirot, "originally part of the Crown jewels of Russia; they are unique in character, and their value is almost fabulous. There has been a rumour that they have lately passed into the possession of an American. Are we right in concluding, Monsieur, that you were the purchaser?"

"Yes," said Van Aldin. "They came into my possession in Paris about ten days ago."

"Pardon me, Monsieur, but you have been negotiating for their purchase for some time?"

"A little over two months. Why?"

"These things become known," said Poirot. "There is always a pretty formidable crowd on the track of jewels such as these."

A spasm distorted the other's face.

"I remember," he said brokenly, "a joke I made to Ruth when I gave them to her. I told her not to take them to the Riviera with her, as I could not afford to have her robbed and murdered for the sake of the jewels. My God! the things one says—never dreaming or knowing they will come true."

There was a sympathetic silence, and then Poirot spoke in a detached manner.

"Let us arrange our facts with order and precision. According to our present theory, this is how they run. The Comte de la Roche knows of your purchase of these jewels. By an easy stratagem he induces Madame Kettering to bring the stones with her. He, then, is the man Mason saw in the train at Paris."

The other three nodded in agreement.

"Madame is surprised to see him, but she deals with the situation promptly. Mason is got out of the way; a dinner basket is ordered. We know from the conductor that he made up the berth for the first compartment, but he did not go into the second compartment, and that a man could quite well have been concealed from him. So far the Comte could have been hidden to a marvel. No one knows of his presence on the train except Madame; he has been careful that the maid did not see his face. All that she could say is that he was tall and dark. It is all most conveniently vague. They are alone—and the train rushes through the night. There would be no outcry, no struggle, for the man is, so she thinks, her lover."

He turned gently to Van Aldin.

"Death, Monsieur, must have been almost instantaneous. We will pass over that quickly. The Comte takes the jewel-case which lies ready to his hand. Shortly afterwards the train draws into Lyons."

M. Carrège nodded his approval.

"Precisely. The conductor without descends. It would be easy for our man to leave the train unseen; it would be easy to catch a train back to Paris or anywhere he pleases. And the crime would be put down as an ordinary train robbery. But for the letter found in Madame's bag, the Comte would not have been mentioned."

"It was an oversight on his part not to search that bag," declared the Commissary.

"Without doubt he thought she had destroyed that letter. It was—pardon me, Monsieur—it was an indiscretion of the first water to keep it."

"And yet," murmured Poirot, "it was an indiscretion the Comte might have foreseen."

"You mean?"

"I mean we are all agreed on one point, and that is that the Comte de la Roche knows one subject *à fond*: Women. How was it that, knowing women as he does, he did not foresee that Madame would have kept that letter?"

"Yes—yes," said the Examining Magistrate doubtfully, "there is something in what you say. But at such times, you understand, a man is not master of himself. He does not reason calmly. *Mon Dieu!*" he added, with feeling, "if our criminals kept their heads and acted with intelligence, how should we capture them?"

Poirot smiled to himself.

"It seems to me a clear case," said the other, "but a difficult one to prove. The Comte is a slippery customer, and unless the maid can identify him—"

"Which is most unlikely," said Poirot.

"True, true." The Examining Magistrate rubbed his chin. "It is going to be difficult."

"If he did indeed commit the crime—" began Poirot. M. Caux interrupted.

"If—you say *if*?"

"Yes, Monsieur le Juge, I say *if*."

The other looked at him sharply. "You are right," he said at last, "we go too fast. It is possible that the Comte may have an alibi. Then we should look foolish."

"*Ah, ça par exemple*," replied Poirot, "that is of no importance whatever. Naturally, if he committed the crime he will have an alibi. A man with the Comte's experience does not neglect to take precautions. No, I said *if* for a very different reason."

"And what was that?"

Poirot wagged an emphatic forefinger. "The psychology."

"Eh?" said the Commissary.

"The psychology is at fault. The Comte is a scoundrel—yes. The Comte is a swindler—yes. The Comte preys upon women—yes. He proposes to steal Madame's jewels—again yes. Is he the kind of man to commit murder? I say *no*! A man of the type of the Comte is always a coward; he takes no risks. He plays the safe, the mean, what the English call the low-down game; but murder, a hundred times no!" He shook his head in a dissatisfied manner.

The Examining Magistrate, however, did not seem disposed to agree with him.

"The day always comes when such gentry lose their heads and go too far," he observed sagely. "Doubtless that is the case here. Without wishing to disagree with you, M. Poirot—"

"It was only an opinion," Poirot hastened to explain. "The case is, of course, in your hands, and you will do what seems fit to you."

"I am satisfied in my own mind that the Comte de la Roche is the man we need to get hold of," said M. Carrège. "You agree with me, Monsieur le Commissaire?"

"Perfectly."

"And you, M. Van Aldin?"

"Yes," said the millionaire. "Yes; the man is a thorough-paced villain, no doubt about it."

"It will be difficult to lay hands on him, I am afraid," said the Magistrate, "but we will do our best. Telegraphed instructions shall go out at once."

"Permit me to assist you," said Poirot. "There need be no difficulty."

"Eh?"

The others stared at him. The little man smiled beamingly back at them.

"It is my business to know things," he explained. "The Comte is a man of intelligence. He is at present at a villa he has leased, the Villa Marina at Antibes."

SIXTEEN
Poirot Discusses the Case

Everybody looked respectfully at Poirot. Undoubtedly the little man had scored heavily. The Commissary laughed—on a rather hollow note.

"You teach us all our business," he cried. "M. Poirot knows more than the police."

Poirot gazed complacently at the ceiling, adopting a mock-modest air.

"What will you; it is my little hobby," he murmured, "to know things. Naturally I have the time to indulge it. I am not overburdened with affairs."

"Ah!" said the Commissary shaking his head portentously. "As for me—"

He made an exaggerated gesture to represent the cares that lay on his shoulders.

Poirot turned suddenly to Van Aldin.

"You agree, Monsieur, with this view? You feel certain that the Comte de la Roche is the murderer?"

"Why, it would seem so—yes, certainly."

Something guarded in the answer made the Examining Magistrate look at the American curiously. Van Aldin seemed aware of his scrutiny and made an effort as though to shake off some preoccupation.

"What about my son-in-law?" he asked. "You have acquainted him with the news? He is in Nice, I understand."

"Certainly, Monsieur." The Commissary hesitated, and then murmured very discreetly: "You are doubtless aware, M. Van Aldin, that M. Kettering was also one of the passengers on the Blue Train that night?"

The millionaire nodded.

"Heard it just before I left London," he vouchsafed laconically.

"He tells us," continued the Commissary, "that he had no idea his wife was travelling on the train."

"I bet he hadn't," said Van Aldin grimly. "It would have been rather a nasty shock to him if he'd come across her on it."

The three men looked at him questioningly.

"I'm not going to mince matters," said Van Aldin savagely. "No one knows what my poor girl has had to put up with. Derek Kettering wasn't alone. He had a lady with him."

"Ah?"

"Mirelle—the dancer."

M. Carrège and the Commissary looked at each other and nodded as though confirming some previous conversation. M. Carrège leaned back in his chair, joined his hands, and fixed his eyes on the ceiling.

"Ah!" he murmured again. "One wondered." He coughed. "One has heard rumours."

"The lady," said M. Caux, "is very notorious."

"And also," murmured Poirot softly, "very expensive."

Van Aldin had gone very red in the face. He leant forward and hit the table a bang with his fist.

"See here," he cried, "my son-in-law is a damned scoundrel!"

He glared at them, looking from one face to another.

"Oh, I know," he went on. "Good looks and a charming, easy manner. It took me in once upon a time. I suppose he pretended to be broken-hearted when you broke the news to him—that is, if he didn't know it already."

"Oh, it came as a complete surprise to him. He was overwhelmed."

"Darned young hypocrite," said Van Aldin. "Simulated great grief, I suppose?"

"N—no," said the Commissary cautiously. "I would not quite say that—eh, M. Carrège?"

The Magistrate brought the tips of his fingers together, and half closed his eyes.

"Shock, bewilderment, horror—these things, yes," he declared judicially. "Great sorrow—no—I should not say that."

Hercule Poirot spoke once more.

"Permit me to ask, M. Van Aldin, does M. Kettering benefit by the death of his wife?"

"He benefits to the tune of a couple of millions," said Van Aldin.

"Dollars?"

"Pounds. I settled that sum on Ruth absolutely on her marriage. She made no will and leaves no children, so the money will go to her husband."

"Whom she was on the point of divorcing," murmured Poirot. "Ah, yes—*précisément*."

The Commissary turned and looked sharply at him.

"Do you mean—" he began.

"I mean nothing," said Poirot. "I arrange the facts, that is all."

Van Aldin stared at him with awakening interest.

The little man rose to his feet.

"I do not think I can be of any further service to you, M. le Juge," he said politely, bowing to M. Carrège. "You will keep me informed of the course of events? It will be a kindness."

"But certainly—most certainly."

Van Aldin rose also.

"You don't want me any more at present?"

"No, Monsieur; we have all the information we need for the moment."

"Then I will walk a little way with M. Poirot. That is, if he does not object?"

"Enchanted, Monsieur," said the little man, with a bow.

Van Aldin lighted a large cigar, having first offered one to Poirot, who declined it and lit one of his own tiny cigarettes. A man of great strength of character, Van Aldin already appeared to be his everyday, normal self once more. After strolling along for a minute or two in silence, the millionaire spoke:

"I take it, M. Poirot, that you no longer exercise your profession?"

"That is so, Monsieur. I enjoy the world."

"Yet you are assisting the police in this affair?"

"Monsieur, if a doctor walks along the street and an accident happens, does he say, 'I have retired from my profession, I will continue my walk,' when there is someone bleeding to death at his feet? If I had been already in Nice, and the police had sent to me and asked me to assist them, I should have refused. But this affair, the good God thrust it upon me."

"You were on the spot," said Van Aldin thoughtfully. "You examined the compartment, did you not?"

Poirot nodded.

"Doubtless you found things that were, shall we say, suggestive to you?"

"Perhaps," said Poirot.

"I hope you see what I am leading up to?" said Van Aldin. "It seems to me that the case against this Comte de la Roche is perfectly clear, but I am not a fool. I have been watching you for this last hour or so, and I realize that for some reason of your own you don't agree with that theory?"

Poirot shrugged his shoulders.

"I may be wrong."

"So we come to the favour I want to ask you. Will you act in this matter for me?"

"For you personally?"

"That was my meaning."

Poirot was silent for a moment or two. Then he said:

"You realize what you are asking?"

"I guess so," said Van Aldin.

"Very well," said Poirot. "I accept. But in that case, I must have frank answers to my questions."

"Why, certainly. That is understood."

Poirot's manner changed. He became suddenly brusque and business-like.

"This question of a divorce," he said. "It was you who advised your daughter to bring the suit?"

"Yes."

"When?"

"About ten days ago. I had had a letter from her complaining of her husband's behaviour, and I put it to her very strongly that divorce was the only remedy."

"In what way did she complain of his behaviour?"

"He was being seen about with a *very* notorious lady—the one we have been speaking of—Mirelle."

"The dancer. Ah-ha! And Madame Kettering objected? Was she very devoted to her husband?"

"I would not say that," said Van Aldin, hesitating a little.

"It was not her heart that suffered, it was her pride—is that what you would say?"

"Yes, I suppose you might put it like that."

"I gather that the marriage had not been a happy one from the beginning?"

"Derek Kettering is rotten to the core," said Van Aldin. "He is incapable of making any woman happy."

"He is, as you say in England, a bad lot. That is right, is it not?"

Van Aldin nodded.

"*Très bien!* You advise Madame to seek a divorce, she agrees; you consult your solicitors. When does M. Kettering get news of what is in the wind?"

"I sent for him myself, and explained the course of action I proposed to take."

"And what did he say?" murmured Poirot softly.

Van Aldin's face darkened at the remembrance.

"He was infernally impudent."

"Excuse the question, Monsieur, but did he refer to the Comte de la Roche?"

"Not by name," growled the other unwillingly, "but he showed himself cognizant of the affair."

"What, if I may ask, was M. Kettering's financial position at the time?"

"How do you suppose I should know that?" asked Van Aldin, after a very brief hesitation.

"It seemed likely to me that you would inform yourself on that point."

"Well—you are quite right, I did. I discovered that Kettering was on the rocks."

"And now he has inherited two million pounds! *La vie*—it is a strange thing, is it not?"

Van Aldin looked at him sharply.

"What do you mean?"

"I moralize," said Poirot. "I reflect, I speak the philosophy. But to return to where we were. Surely M. Kettering did not propose to allow himself to be divorced without making a fight for it?"

Van Aldin did not answer for a minute or two, then he said:

"I don't exactly know what his intentions were."

"Did you hold any further communications with him?"

Again a slight pause, then Van Aldin said:

"No."

Poirot stopped dead, took off his hat, and held out his hand.

"I must wish you good-day, Monsieur. I can do nothing for you."

"What are you getting at?" demanded Van Aldin angrily.

"If you do not tell me the truth, I can do nothing."

"I don't know what you mean."

"I think you do. You may rest assured, M. Van Aldin, that I know how to be discreet."

"Very well, then," said the millionaire. "I'll admit that I was not speaking the truth just now. I *did* have further communication with my son-in-law."

"Yes?"

"To be exact, I sent my secretary, Major Knighton, to see him, with instructions to offer him the sum of one hundred thousand pounds in cash if the divorce went through undefended."

"A pretty sum of money," said Poirot appreciatively; "and the answer of Monsieur your son-in-law?"

"He sent back word that I could go to hell," replied the millionaire succinctly.

"Ah!" said Poirot.

He betrayed no emotion of any kind. At the moment he was engaged in methodically recording facts.

"Monsieur Kettering has told the police that he neither saw nor spoke to his wife on the journey from England. Are you inclined to believe that statement, Monsieur?"

"Yes, I am," said Van Aldin. "He would take particular pains to keep out of her way, I should say."

"Why?"

"Because he had got that woman with him."

"Mirelle?"

"Yes."

"How did you come to know that fact?"

"A man of mine, whom I had put on to watch him, reported to me that they had both left by that train."

"I see," said Poirot. "In that case, as you said before, he would not be likely to attempt to hold any communication with Madame Kettering."

The little man fell silent for some time. Van Aldin did not interrupt his meditation.

SEVENTEEN
An Aristocratic Gentleman

Y ou have been to the Riviera before, Georges?" said Poirot
to his valet the following morning.
George was an intensely English, rather wooden-faced
individual.

"Yes, sir. I was here two years ago when I was in the service
of Lord Edward Frampton."

"And to-day," murmured his master, "you are here with
Hercule Poirot. How one mounts in the world!"

The valet made no reply to this observation. After a suitable
pause he asked:

"The brown lounge suit, sir? The wind is somewhat chilly
to-day."

"There is a grease spot on the waistcoat," objected Poirot. "A
morceau of *filet de sole à la Jeannette* alighted there when I was
lunching at the Ritz last Tuesday."

"There is no spot there now, sir," said George reproachfully.
"I have removed it."

"*Très bien!*" said Poirot. "I am pleased with you, Georges."

"Thank you, sir."

There was a pause, and then Poirot murmured dreamily:

"Supposing, my good Georges, that you had been born in the
same social sphere as your late master, Lord Edward Frampton—
that, penniless yourself, you had married an extremely wealthy

wife, but that that wife proposed to divorce you, with excellent reasons, what would you do about it?"

"I should endeavour, sir," replied George, "to make her change her mind."

"By peaceful or by forcible methods?"

George looked shocked.

"You will excuse me, sir," he said, "but a gentleman of the aristocracy would not behave like a Whitechapel coster. He would not do anything low."

"Would he not, Georges? I wonder now. Well, perhaps you are right."

There was a knock on the door. George went to it and opened it a discreet inch or two. A low murmured colloquy went on, and then the valet returned to Poirot.

"A note, sir."

Poirot took it. It was from M. Caux, the Commissary of Police.

"We are about to interrogate the Comte de la Roche. The Juge d'Instruction begs that you will be present."

"Quickly, my suit, Georges! I must hasten myself."

A quarter of an hour later, spick and span in his brown suit, Poirot entered the Examining Magistrate's room. M. Caux was already there, and both he and M. Carrège greeted Poirot with polite *empressement*.

"The affair is somewhat discouraging," murmured M. Caux.

"It appears that the Comte arrived in Nice the day before the murder."

"If that is true, it will settle your affair nicely for you," responded Poirot.

M. Carrège cleared his throat.

"We must not accept this alibi without very cautious inquiry," he declared. He struck the bell upon the table with his hand.

In another minute a tall dark man, exquisitely dressed, with a somewhat haughty cast of countenance, entered the room. So very aristocratic-looking was the Count, that it would have seemed sheer heresy even to whisper that his father had been an obscure corn-chandler in Nantes—which, as a matter of fact, was the case. Looking at him, one would have been prepared to swear that innumerable ancestors of his must have perished by the guillotine in the French Revolution.

"I am here, gentlemen," said the Count haughtily. "May I ask why you wish to see me?"

"Pray be seated, Monsieur le Comte," said the Examining Magistrate politely. "It is the affair of the death of Madame Kettering that we are investigating."

"The death of Madame Kettering? I do not understand."

"You were—ahem!—acquainted with the lady, I believe, Monsieur le Comte?"

"Certainly I was acquainted with her. What has that to do with the matter?"

Sticking an eyeglass in his eye, he looked coldly round the room, his glance resting longest on Poirot, who was gazing at him with a kind of simple, innocent admiration which was most pleasing to the Count's vanity. M. Carrège leaned back in his chair and cleared his throat.

"You do not perhaps know, Monsieur le Comte"—he paused—"that Madame Kettering was murdered?"

"Murdered? *Mon Dieu*, how terrible!"

The surprise and the sorrow were excellently done—so well done, indeed, as to seem wholly natural.

"Madame Kettering was strangled between Paris and Lyons," continued M. Carrège, "and her jewels were stolen."

"It is iniquitous!" cried the Count warmly; "the police should do something about these train bandits. Nowadays no one is safe."

"In Madame's handbag," continued the Judge, "we found a letter to her from you. She had, it seemed, arranged to meet you?"

The Count shrugged his shoulders and spread out his hands.

"Of what use are concealments," he said frankly. "We are all men of the world. Privately and between ourselves, I admit the affair."

"You met her in Paris and travelled down with her, I believe?" said M. Carrège.

"That was the original arrangement, but by Madame's wish it was changed. I was to meet her at Hyères."

"You did not meet her on the train at the Gare de Lyon on the evening of the 14th?"

"On the contrary, I arrived in Nice on the morning of that day, so what you suggest is impossible."

"Quite so, quite so," said M. Carrège. "As a matter of form, you would perhaps give me an account of your movements during the evening and night of the 14th."

The Count reflected for a minute.

"I dined in Monte Carlo at the Café de Paris. Afterwards I went to the Le Sporting. I won a few thousand francs," he shrugged his shoulders. "I returned home at perhaps one o'clock."

"Pardon me, Monsieur, but how did you return home?"

"In my own two-seater car."

"No one was with you?"

"No one."

"You could produce witnesses in support of this statement?"

"Doubtless many of my friends saw me there that evening. I dined alone."

"Your servant admitted you on your return to your villa?"

"I let myself in with my own latch-key."

"Ah!" murmured the Magistrate.

Again he struck the bell on the table with his hand. The door opened, and a messenger appeared.

"Bring in the maid, Mason," said M. Carrège.

"Very good, Monsieur le Juge."

Ada Mason was brought in.

"Will you be so good, Mademoiselle, as to look at this gentleman. To the best of your ability was it he who entered your mistress's compartment in Paris?"

The woman looked long and searchingly at the Count, who was, Poirot fancied, rather uneasy under this scrutiny.

"I could not say, sir, I am sure," said Mason at last. "It might be and again it might not. Seeing as how I only saw his back, it's hard to say. I rather think it *was* the gentleman."

"But you are not sure?"

"No—o," said Mason unwillingly; "n—no, I am not sure."

"You have seen this gentleman before in Curzon Street?"

Mason shook her head.

"I should not be likely to see any visitors that come to Curzon Street," she explained, "unless they were staying in the house."

"Very well, that will do," said the Examining Magistrate sharply.

Evidently he was disappointed.

"One moment," said Poirot. "There is a question I would like to put to Mademoiselle, if I may?"

"Certainly, M. Poirot—certainly, by all means."

Poirot addressed himself to the maid.

"What happened to the tickets?"

"The tickets, sir?"

"Yes; the tickets from London to Nice. Did you or your mistress have them?"

"The mistress had her own Pullman ticket, sir; the others were in my charge."

"What happened to them?"

"I gave them to the conductor on the French train, sir; he said it was usual. I hope I did right, sir?"

"Oh, quite right, quite right. A mere matter of detail."

Both M. Caux and the Examining Magistrate looked at him curiously. Mason stood uncertainly for a minute or two, and then the Magistrate gave her a brief nod of dismissal, and she went out. Poirot scribbled something on a scrap of paper and handed it across to M. Carrège. The latter read it and his brow cleared.

"Well, gentlemen," demanded the Count haughtily, "am I to be detained further?"

"Assuredly not, assuredly not," M. Carrège hastened to say, with a great deal of amiability. "Everything is now cleared up as regards your own position in this affair. Naturally, in view of Madame's letter, we were bound to question you."

The Count rose, picked up his handsome stick from the corner, and, with rather a curt bow, left the room.

"And that is that," said M. Carrège. "You were quite right, M. Poirot—much better to let him feel he is not suspected. Two of my men will shadow him night and day, and at the same time we will go into the question of the alibi. It seems to me rather—er—a fluid one."

"Possibly," agreed Poirot thoughtfully.

"I asked M. Kettering to come here this morning," continued the Magistrate, "though really I doubt if we have much to ask him, but there are one or two suspicious circumstances——" He paused, rubbing his nose.

"Such as?" asked Poirot.

"Well"—the Magistrate coughed—"this lady with whom he is said to be travelling—Mademoiselle Mirelle. She is staying at one hotel and he at another. That strikes me—er—as rather odd."

"It looks," said M. Caux, "as though they were being careful."

"Exactly," said M. Carrège triumphantly; "and what should they have to be careful about?"

"An excess of caution is suspicious, eh?" said Poirot.

"*Précisément*."

"We might, I think," murmured Poirot, "ask M. Kettering one or two questions."

The Magistrate gave instructions. A moment or two later, Derek Kettering, debonair as ever, entered the room.

"Good morning, Monsieur," said the Judge politely.

"Good morning," said Derek Kettering curtly. "You sent for me. Has anything fresh turned up?"

"Pray sit down, Monsieur."

Derek took a seat and flung his hat and stick on the table.

"Well?" he asked impatiently.

"We have, so far, no fresh data," said M. Carrège cautiously.

"That's very interesting," said Derek drily. "Did you send for me here in order to tell me that?"

"We naturally thought, Monsieur, that you would like to be informed of the progress of the case," said the Magistrate severely.

"Even if the progress was non-existent."

"We also wished to ask you a few questions."

"Ask away."

"You are quite sure that you neither saw nor spoke with your wife on the train?"

"I've answered that already. I did not."

"You had, no doubt, your reasons."

Derek stared at him suspiciously.

"I—did—not—know—she—was—on—the—train," he explained, spacing his words elaborately, as though to someone dull of intellect.

"That is what you say, yes," murmured M. Carrège. A frown suffused Derek's face.

"I should like to know what you're driving at. Do you know what I think, M. Carrège?"

"What do you think, Monsieur?"

"I think the French police are vastly overrated. Surely you must have some data as to these gangs of train robbers. It's outrageous that such a thing could happen on a *train de luxe* like that, and that the French police should be helpless to deal with the matter."

"We are dealing with it, Monsieur, never fear."

"Madame Kettering, I understand, did not leave a will," interposed Poirot suddenly. His fingertips were joined together, and he was looking intently at the ceiling.

"I don't think she ever made one," said Kettering. "Why?"

121

"It is a very pretty little fortune that you inherit there," said Poirot—"a very pretty little fortune."

Although his eyes were still on the ceiling, he managed to see the dark flush that rose to Derek Kettering's face.

"What do you mean, and who are you?"

Poirot gently uncrossed his knees, withdrew his gaze from the ceiling, and looked the young man full in the face.

"My name is Hercule Poirot," he said quietly, "and I am probably the greatest detective in the world. You are quite sure that you did not see or speak to your wife on that train?"

"What are you getting at? Do you—do you mean to insinuate that I—I killed her?"

He laughed suddenly.

"I mustn't lose my temper; it's too palpably absurd. Why, if I killed her I should have had no need to steal her jewels, would I?"

"That is true," murmured Poirot, with a rather crestfallen air. "I did not think of that."

"If ever there were a clear case of murder and robbery, this is it," said Derek Kettering. "Poor Ruth, it was those damned rubies did for her. It must have got about she had them with her. There has been murder done for those same stones before now, I believe."

Poirot sat up suddenly in his chair. A very faint green light glowed in his eyes. He looked extraordinarily like a sleek, well-fed cat.

"One more question, M. Kettering," he said. "Will you give me the date when you last saw your wife?"

"Let me see," Kettering reflected. "It must have been—yes over three weeks ago. I am afraid I can't give you the date exactly."

"No matter," said Poirot drily; "that is all I wanted to know."

"Well," said Derek Kettering impatiently, "anything further?"

He looked towards M. Carrège. The latter sought inspiration from Poirot, and received it in a very faint shake of the head.

"No, M. Kettering," he said politely; "no, I do not think we need trouble you any further. I wish you good morning."

"Good morning," said Kettering. He went out, banging the door behind him.

Poirot leaned forward and spoke sharply, as soon as the young man was out of the room.

"Tell me," he said peremptorily, "when did you speak of these rubies to M. Kettering?"

"I have not spoken of them," said M. Carrège. "It was only yesterday afternoon that we learnt about them from M. Van Aldin."

"Yes; but there was a mention of them in the Comte's letter." M. Carrège looked pained.

"Naturally I did not speak of that letter to M. Kettering," he said in a shocked voice. "It would have been most indiscreet at the present juncture of affairs."

Poirot leaned forward and tapped the table.

"Then how did he know about them?" he demanded softly. "Madame could not have told him, for he has not seen her for three weeks. It seems unlikely that either M. Van Aldin or his secretary would have mentioned them; their interviews with him have been on entirely different lines, and there has not been any hint or reference to them in the newspapers."

He got up and took his hat and stick.

"And yet," he murmured to himself, "our gentleman knows all about them. I wonder now, yes, I wonder!"

EIGHTEEN
Derek Lunches

Derek Kettering went straight to the Negresco, where he ordered a couple of cocktails and disposed of them rapidly; then he stared moodily out over the dazzling blue sea. He noted the passers-by mechanically—a damned dull crowd, badly dressed, and painfully uninteresting; one hardly ever saw anything worth while nowadays. Then he corrected this last impression rapidly, as a woman placed herself at a table a little distance away from him. She was wearing a marvellous confection of orange and black, with a little hat that shaded her face. He ordered a third cocktail; again he stared out to sea, and then suddenly he started. A well-known perfume assailed his nostrils, and he looked up to see the orange-and-black lady standing beside him. He saw her face now, and recognized her. It was Mirelle. She was smiling that insolent, seductive smile he knew so well.

"Dereek!" she murmured. "You are pleased to see me, no?"

She dropped into a seat the other side of the table.

"But welcome me, then, stupid one," she mocked.

"This is an unexpected pleasure," said Derek. "When did you leave London?"

She shrugged her shoulders.

"A day or two ago."

"And the Parthenon?"

"I have, how do you say it?—given them the chuck!"

"Really?"

"You are not very amiable, Dereek."

"Do you expect me to be?"

Mirelle lit a cigarette and puffed at it for a few minutes before saying:

"You think, perhaps, that it is not prudent so soon?"

Derek stared at her, then he shrugged his shoulders, and remarked formally:

"You are lunching here?"

"*Mais oui.* I am lunching with you."

"I am extremely sorry," said Derek. "I have a very important engagement."

"*Mon Dieu!* But you men are like children," exclaimed the dancer. "But yes, it is the spoilt child that you act to me ever since that day in London when you flung yourself out of my flat, you sulk. Ah! *mais c'est inouï!*"

"My dear girl," said Derek, "I really don't know what you are talking about. We agreed in London that rats desert a sinking ship, that is all that there is to be said."

In spite of his careless words, his face looked haggard and strained. Mirelle leaned forward suddenly.

"You cannot deceive me," she murmured. "I know—I know what you have done for me."

He looked up at her sharply. Some undercurrent in her voice arrested his attention. She nodded her head at him.

"Ah! have no fear; I am discreet. You are magnificent! You have a superb courage, but, all the same, it was I who gave you the idea that day, when I said to you in London that accidents sometimes happened. And you are not in danger? The police do not suspect you?"

"What the devil—"

"Hush!"

She held up a slim olive hand with one big emerald on the little finger.

"You are right; I should not have spoken so in a public place. We will not speak of the matter again, but our troubles are ended; our life together will be wonderful—wonderful!"

Derek laughed suddenly—a harsh, disagreeable laugh.

"So the rats come back, do they? Two million makes a difference—of course it does. I ought to have known that." He laughed again. "You will help me to spend that two million, won't you, Mirelle? You know how, no woman better." He laughed again.

"Hush!" cried the dancer. "What is the matter with you, Dereek? See—people are turning to stare at you."

"Me? I will tell you what is the matter. I have finished with you, Mirelle. Do you hear? Finished!"

Mirelle did not take it as he expected her to do. She looked at him for a minute or two, and then she smiled softly.

"But what a child! You are angry—you are sore, and all because I am practical. Did I not always tell you that I adored you?"

She leaned forward.

"But I know you, Dereek. Look at me—see, it is Mirelle who speaks to you. You cannot live without her, you know it. I loved you before, I will love you a hundred times more now. I will make life wonderful for you—but wonderful. There is no one like Mirelle."

Her eyes burned into his. She saw him grow pale and draw in his breath, and she smiled to herself contentedly. She knew her own magic and power over men.

"That is settled," she said softly, and gave a little laugh. "And now, Dereek, will you give me lunch?"

"No."

He drew in his breath sharply and rose to his feet.

"I am sorry, but I told you—I have got an engagement."

"You are lunching with someone else? Bah! I don't believe it."

"I am lunching with that lady over there."

He crossed abruptly to where a lady in white had just come

up the steps. He addressed her a little breathlessly.

"Miss Grey, will you—will you have lunch with me? You met me at Lady Tamplin's, if you remember."

Katherine looked at him for a minute or two with those thoughtful grey eyes that said so much.

"Thank you," she said, after a moment's pause; "I should like to very much."

NINETEEN
An Unexpected Visitor

The Comte de la Roche had just finished *déjeuner*, consisting of an *omelette fines herbes*, an *entrecôte Béarnaise*, and a *Savarin au Rhum*. Wiping his fine black moustache delicately with his table napkin, the Comte rose from the table. He passed through the salon of the villa, noting with appreciation the few *objets d'art* which were carelessly scattered about. The Louis XV snuff-box, the satin shoe worn by Marie Antoinette, and the other historic trifles were part of the Comte's *mise en scène*. They were, he would explain to his fair visitors, heirlooms in his family. Passing through on to the terrace, the Comte looked out on the Mediterranean with an unseeing eye. He was in no mood for appreciating the beauties of scenery. A fully matured scheme had been rudely brought to naught, and his plans had to be cast afresh. Stretching himself out in a basket chair, a cigarette held between his white fingers, the Comte pondered deeply.

Presently Hippolyte, his man-servant, brought out coffee and a choice of liqueurs. The Comte selected some very fine old brandy.

As the man-servant was preparing to depart, the Comte arrested him with a slight gesture. Hippolyte stood respectfully to attention. His countenance was hardly a prepossessing one, but the correctitude of his demeanour went far to obliterate the fact.

He was now the picture of respectful attention.

"It is possible," said the Comte, "that in the course of the next few days various strangers may come to the house. They will endeavour to scrape acquaintance with you and with Marie. They will probably ask you various questions concerning me."

"Yes, Monsieur le Comte."

"Perhaps this has already happened?"

"No, Monsieur le Comte."

"There have been no strangers about the place? You are certain?"

"There has been no one, Monsieur le Comte."

"That is well," said the Comte drily; "nevertheless they will come—I am sure of it. They will ask questions."

Hippolyte looked at his master in intelligent anticipation.

The Comte spoke slowly, without looking at Hippolyte.

"As you know, I arrived here last Tuesday morning. If the police or any other inquirer should question you, do not forget that fact. I arrived on Tuesday, the 14th—not Wednesday, the 15th. You understand?"

"Perfectly, Monsieur le Comte."

"In an affair where a lady is concerned, it is always necessary to be discreet. I feel certain, Hippolyte, that you can be discreet."

"I can be discreet, Monsieur."

"And Marie?"

"Marie also. I will answer for her."

"That is well then," murmured the Comte.

When Hippolyte had withdrawn, the Comte sipped his black coffee with a reflective air. Occasionally he frowned, once he shook his head slightly, twice he nodded it. Into the midst of these cogitations came Hippolyte once more.

"A lady, Monsieur."

"A lady?"

The Comte was surprised. Not that a visit from a lady was an unusual thing at the Villa Marina, but at this particular moment the Comte could not think who the lady was likely to be.

"She is, I think, a lady not known to Monsieur," murmured the valet helpfully.

The Comte was more and more intrigued.

"Show her out here, Hippolyte," he commanded.

A moment later a marvellous vision in orange and black stepped out on the terrace, accompanied by a strong perfume of exotic blossoms.

"Monsieur le Comte de la Roche?"

"At your service, Mademoiselle," said the Comte, bowing.

"My name is Mirelle. You may have heard of me."

"Ah, indeed, Mademoiselle, but who has not been enchanted by the dancing of Mademoiselle Mirelle? Exquisite!"

The dancer acknowledged this compliment with a brief mechanical smile.

"My descent upon you is unceremonious," she began.

"But seat yourself, I beg of you, Mademoiselle," cried the Comte, bringing forward a chair.

Behind the gallantry of his manner he was observing her narrowly. There were very few things that the Comte did not know about women. True, his experience had not lain much in ladies of Mirelle's class, who were themselves predatory. He and the dancer were, in a sense, birds of a feather. His arts, the Comte knew, would be thrown away on Mirelle. She was a Parisienne, and a shrewd one. Nevertheless, there was one thing that the Comte could recognize infallibly when he saw it. He knew at once that he was in the presence of a very angry woman, and an angry woman, as the Comte was well aware, always says more than is prudent, and is occasionally a source of profit to a level-headed gentleman who keeps cool.

"It is most amiable of you, Mademoiselle, to honour my poor abode thus."

"We have mutual friends in Paris," said Mirelle. "I have heard of you from them, but I come to see you to-day for another reason.

I have heard of you since I came to Nice—in a different way, you understand."

"Ah?" said the Comte softly.

"I will be brutal," continued the dancer; "nevertheless, believe that I have your welfare at heart. They are saying in Nice, Monsieur le Comte, that you are the murderer of the English lady, Madame Kettering."

"I!—the murderer of Madame Kettering? Bah! But how absurd!"

He spoke more languidly than indignantly, knowing that he would thus provoke her further.

"But yes," she insisted; "it is as I tell you."

"It amuses people to talk," murmured the Comte indifferently. "It would be beneath me to take such wild accusations seriously."

"You do not understand." Mirelle bent forward, her dark eyes flashing. "It is not the idle talk of those in the streets. It is the police."

"The police—ah?"

The Comte sat up, alert once more.

Mirelle nodded her head vigorously several times.

"Yes, yes. You comprehend me—I have friends every where. The Prefect himself—" She left the sentence unfinished, with an eloquent shrug of the shoulders.

"Who is not indiscreet where a beautiful woman is concerned?" murmured the Count politely.

"The police believe that you killed Madame Kettering. But they are wrong."

"Certainly they are wrong," agreed the Comte easily.

"You say that, but you do not know the truth. I do."

The Comte looked at her curiously.

"You know who killed Madame Kettering? Is that what you would say, Mademoiselle?"

Mirelle nodded vehemently.

"Yes."

"Who was it?" asked the Comte sharply.

"Her husband." She bent nearer to the Comte, speaking in a low voice that vibrated with anger and excitement. "It was her husband who killed her."

The Comte leant back in his chair. His face was a mask.

"Let me ask you, Mademoiselle—how do you know this?"

"How do I know it?" Mirelle sprang to her feet, with a laugh. "He boasted of it beforehand. He was ruined, bankrupt, dishonoured. Only the death of his wife could save him. He told me so. He travelled on the same train—but she was not to know it. Why was that, I ask you? So that he might creep upon her in the night—Ah!"—she shut her eyes—"I can see it happening...."

The Count coughed.

"Perhaps—perhaps," he murmured. "But surely, Mademoiselle, in that case he would not steal the jewels?"

"The jewels!" breathed Mirelle. "The jewels. Ah! Those rubies...."

Her eyes grew misty, a far-away light in them. The Comte looked at her curiously, wondering for the hundredth time at the magical influence of precious stones on the female sex. He recalled her to practical matters.

"What do you want me to do, Mademoiselle?"

Mirelle became alert and business-like once more.

"Surely it is simple. You will go to the police. You will say to them that M. Kettering committed this crime."

"And if they do not believe me? If they ask for proof?" He was eyeing her closely.

Mirelle laughed softly, and drew her orange-and-black wrap closer round her.

"Send them to me, Monsieur le Comte," she said softly; "I will give them the proof they want."

Upon that she was gone, an impetuous whirlwind, her errand accomplished.

The Comte looked after her, his eyebrows delicately raised.

"She is in a fury," he murmured. "What has happened now to upset her? But she shows her hand too plainly. Does she really believe that Mr. Kettering killed his wife? She would like me to believe it. She would even like the police to believe it."

He smiled to himself. He had no intention whatsoever of going to the police. He saw various other possibilities, to judge by his smile, an agreeable vista of them.

Presently, however, his brow clouded. According to Mirelle, he was suspected by the police. That might be true or it might not. An angry woman of the type of the dancer was not likely to bother about the strict veracity of her statements. On the other hand, she might easily have obtained—inside information. In that case—his mouth set grimly—in that case he must take certain precautions.

He went into the house and questioned Hippolyte closely once more as to whether any strangers had been to the house. The valet was positive in his assurances that this was not the case. The Comte went up to his bedroom and crossed over to an old bureau that stood against the wall. He let down the lid of this, and his delicate fingers sought for a spring at the back of one of the pigeon-holes. A secret drawer flew out; in it was a small brown paper package. The Comte took this out and weighed it in his hand carefully for a minute or two. Raising his hand to his head, with a slight grimace he pulled out a single hair. This he placed on the lip of the drawer and shut it carefully. Still carrying the small parcel in his hand, he went downstairs and out of the house to the garage, where stood a scarlet two-seater car. Ten minutes later he had taken the road for Monte Carlo.

He spent a few hours at the Casino, then sauntered out into the town. Presently he re-entered the car and drove off in the direction of Mentone. Earlier in the afternoon he had noticed an inconspicuous grey car some little distance behind him. He noticed it again now. He smiled to himself. The road was climbing steadily upwards. The Comte's foot pressed hard on the accelerator. The little red car had been specially built to the Comte's design, and had a far more powerful engine than would have been suspected from its appearance. It shot ahead.

Presently he looked back and smiled; the grey car was following behind. Smothered in dust, the little red car leaped along the road. It was travelling now at a dangerous pace, but the Comte was a first-class driver. Now they were going down hill, twisting and curving unceasingly. Presently the car slackened speed, and finally came to a standstill before a Bureau de Poste. The Comte jumped out, lifted the lid of the tool chest, extracted the small brown paper parcel and hurried into the post office. Two minutes later he was driving once more in the direction of Mentone. When the grey car arrived there, the Comte was drinking English five o'clock tea on the terrace of one of the hotels.

Later, he drove back to Monte Carlo, dined there, and reached home once more at eleven o'clock. Hippolyte came out to meet him with a disturbed face.

"Ah! Monsieur le Comte has arrived. Monsieur le Comte did not telephone me, by any chance?"

The Comte shook his head.

"And yet at three o'clock I received a summons from Monsieur le Comte, to present myself to him at Nice, at the Negresco."

"Really," said the Comte; "and you went?"

"Certainly, Monsieur, but at the Negresco they knew nothing of Monsieur le Comte. He had not been there."

"Ah," said the Comte, "doubtless at that hour Marie was out doing her afternoon marketing?"

"That is so, Monsieur le Comte."

"Ah, well," said the Comte, "it is of no importance. A mistake."

He went upstairs, smiling to himself.

Once within his own room, he bolted his door and looked sharply round. Everything seemed as usual. He opened various drawers and cupboards. Then he nodded to himself. Things had been replaced almost exactly as he had left them, but not quite. It was evident that a very thorough search had been made.

He went over to the bureau and pressed the hidden spring. The drawer flew open, but the hair was no longer where he had placed it. He nodded his head several times.

"They are excellent, our French police," he murmured to himself—"excellent. Nothing escapes them."

TWENTY
Katherine Makes a Friend

On the following morning Katherine and Lenox were sitting on the terrace of the Villa Marguerite. Something in the nature of a friendship was springing up between them, despite the difference in age. But for Lenox, Katherine would have found life at the Villa Marguerite quite intolerable. The Kettering case was the topic of the moment. Lady Tamplin frankly exploited her guest's connection with the affair for all it was worth. The most persistent rebuffs that Katherine could administer quite failed to pierce Lady Tamplin's self-esteem. Lenox adopted a detached attitude, seemingly amused at her mother's manœuvres, and yet with a sympathetic understanding of Katherine's feelings. The situation was not helped by Chubby, whose naïve delight was unquenchable, and who introduced Katherine to all and sundry as:

"This is Miss Grey. You know that Blue Train business? She was in it up to the ears! Had a long talk with Ruth Kettering a few hours before the murder! Bit of luck for her, eh?"

A few remarks of this kind had provoked Katherine that morning to an unusually tart rejoinder, and when they were alone together Lenox observed in her slow drawl:

"Not used to exploitation, are you? You have a lot to learn, Katherine."

"I am sorry I lost my temper. I don't, as a rule."

"It is about time you learnt to blow off steam. Chubby is only an ass; there is no harm in him. Mother, of course, is trying, but you can lose your temper with her until Kingdom come, and it won't make any impression. She will open large, sad blue eyes at you and not care a bit."

Katherine made no reply to this filial observation, and Lenox presently went on:

"I am rather like Chubby. I delight in a good murder, and besides—well, knowing Derek makes a difference."

Katherine nodded.

"So you lunched with him yesterday," pursued Lenox reflectively. "Do you like him, Katherine?"

Katherine considered for a minute or two.

"I don't know," she said very slowly.

"He is very attractive."

"Yes, he is attractive."

"What don't you like about him?"

Katherine did not reply to the question, or at any rate not directly. "He spoke of his wife's death," she said. "He said he would not pretend that it had been anything but a bit of most marvellous luck for him."

"And that shocked you, I suppose," said Lenox. She paused, and then added in rather a queer tone of voice: "He likes you, Katherine."

"He gave me a very good lunch," said Katherine, smiling.

Lenox refused to be side-tracked.

"I saw it the night he came here," she said thoughtfully. "The way he looked at you; and you are not his usual type—just the opposite. Well, I suppose it is like religion—you get it at a certain age."

"Mademoiselle is wanted at the telephone," said Marie, appearing at the window of the salon. "M. Hercule Poirot desires to speak with her."

"More blood and thunder. Go on, Katherine; go and dally with your detective."

M. Hercule Poirot's voice came neat and precise in its intonation to Katherine's ear.

"That is Mademoiselle Grey who speaks? *Bon.* Mademoiselle, I have a word for you from M. Van Aldin, the father of Madame Kettering. He wishes very much to speak with you, either at the Villa Marguerite or at his hotel, whichever you prefer."

Katherine reflected for a moment, but she decided that for Van Aldin to come to the Villa Marguerite would be both painful and unnecessary. Lady Tamplin would have hailed his advent with far too much delight. She never lost a chance of cultivating millionaires. She told Poirot that she would much rather come to Nice.

"Excellent, Mademoiselle. I will call for you myself in an auto. Shall we say in about three-quarters of an hour?"

Punctually to the moment Poirot appeared. Katherine was waiting for him, and they drove off at once.

"Well, Mademoiselle, how goes it?"

She looked at his twinkling eyes, and was confirmed in her first impression that there was something very attractive about M. Hercule Poirot.

"This is our own Roman Policier, is it not?" said Poirot. "I made you the promise that we should study it together. And me, I always keep my promises."

"You are too kind," murmured Katherine.

"Ah, you mock yourself at me; but do you want to hear the developments of the case, or do you not?"

Katherine admitted that she did, and Poirot proceeded to sketch for her a thumbnail portrait of the Comte de la Roche.

"You think he killed her," said Katherine thoughtfully.

"That is the theory," said Poirot guardedly.

"Do you yourself believe that?"

"I did not say so. And you, Mademoiselle, what do you think?"

Katherine shook her head.

"How should I know? I don't know anything about those things, but I should say that—"

"Yes," said Poirot encouragingly.

"Well—from what you say the Count does not sound the kind of man who would actually kill anybody."

"Ah! Very good," cried Poirot, "you agree with me; that is just what I have said." He looked at her sharply. "But tell me, you have met Mr. Derek Kettering?"

"I met him at Lady Tamplin's, and I lunched with him yesterday."

"A *mauvais sujet*," said Poirot, shaking his head; "but *les femmes*—they like that, eh?"

He twinkled at Katherine and she laughed.

"He is the kind of man one would notice anywhere," continued Poirot. "Doubtless you observed him on the Blue Train?"

"Yes, I noticed him."

"In the restaurant car?"

"No. I didn't notice him at meals at all. I only saw him once— going into his wife's compartment."

Poirot nodded. "A strange business," he murmured. "I believe you said you were awake, Mademoiselle, and looked out of your window at Lyons? You saw no tall dark man such as the Comte de la Roche leave the train?"

Katherine shook her head. "I don't think I saw anyone at all," she said. "There was a youngish lad in a cap and overcoat who got out, but I don't think he was leaving the train, only walking up and down the platform. There was a fat Frenchman with a beard, in pyjamas and an overcoat, who wanted a cup of coffee. Otherwise, I think there were only the train attendants."

Poirot nodded his head several times. "It is like this, you see," he confided, "the Comte de la Roche has an alibi. An alibi, it is a very pestilential thing, and always open to the gravest suspicion. But here we are!"

AGATHA CHRISTIE

They went straight up to Van Aldin's suite, where they found Knighton. Poirot introduced him to Katherine. After a few commonplaces had been exchanged, Knighton said, "I will tell Mr. Van Aldin that Miss Grey is here."

He went through a second door into an adjoining room. There was a low murmur of voices, and then Van Aldin came into the room and advanced towards Katherine with outstretched hand, giving her at the same time a shrewd and penetrating glance.

"I am pleased to meet you, Miss Grey," he said simply. "I have been wanting very badly to hear what you can tell me about Ruth."

The quiet simplicity of the millionaire's manner appealed to Katherine strongly. She felt herself in the presence of a very genuine grief, the more real for its absence of outward sign.

He drew forward a chair.

"Sit here, will you, and just tell me all about it."

Poirot and Knighton retired discreetly into the other room, and Katherine and Van Aldin were left alone together. She found no difficulty in her task. Quite simply and naturally she related her conversation with Ruth Kettering, word for word as nearly as she could. He listened in silence, leaning back in his chair, with one hand shading his eyes. When she had finished he said quietly:

"Thank you, my dear."

They both sat silent for a minute or two. Katherine felt that words of sympathy would be out of place. When the millionaire spoke, it was in a different tone:

"I am very grateful to you, Miss Grey. I think you did something to ease my poor Ruth's mind in the last hours of her life. Now I want to ask you something. You know—M. Poirot will have told you—about the scoundrel that my poor girl had got herself mixed up with. He was the man of whom she spoke to you—the man she was going to meet. In your judgment do you think she might have changed her mind after her conversation with you? Do you think she meant to go back on her word?"

"I can't honestly tell you. She had certainly come to some

140

decision, and seemed more cheerful in consequence of it."

"She gave you no idea where she intended to meet the skunk—whether in Paris or at Hyères?"

Katherine shook her head.

"She said nothing as to that."

"Ah!" said Van Aldin thoughtfully, "and that is the important point. Well, time will show."

He got up and opened the door of the adjoining room. Poirot and Knighton came back.

Katherine declined the millionaire's invitation to lunch, and Knighton went down with her and saw her into the waiting car. He returned to find Poirot and Van Aldin deep in conversation.

"If we only knew," said the millionaire thoughtfully, "what decision Ruth came to. It might have been any of half a dozen. She might have meant to leave the train at Paris and cable to me. She may have meant to have gone on to the south of France and have an explanation with the Count there. We are in the dark— absolutely in the dark. But we have the maid's word for it that she was both startled and dismayed at the Count's appearance at the station in Paris. That was clearly not part of the preconceived plan. You agree with me, Knighton?"

The secretary started. "I beg your pardon, Mr. Van Aldin. I was not listening."

"Day-dreaming, eh?" said Van Aldin. "That's not like you. I believe that girl has bowled you over."

Knighton blushed.

"She is a remarkably nice girl," said Van Aldin thoughtfully, "very nice. Did you happen to notice her eyes?"

"Any man," said Knighton, "would be bound to notice her eyes."

TWENTY-ONE
At the Tennis

Several days had elapsed. Katherine had been for a walk by herself one morning, and came back to find Lenox grinning at her expectantly.

"Your young man has been ringing you up, Katherine!"

"Who do you call my young man?"

"A new one—Rufus Van Aldin's secretary. You seem to have made rather an impression there. You are becoming a serious breaker of hearts, Katherine. First Derek Kettering, and now this young Knighton. The funny thing is, that I remember him quite well. He was in Mother's War Hospital that she ran out here. I was only a kid of about eight at the time."

"Was he badly wounded?"

"Shot in the leg, if I remember rightly—rather a nasty business. I think the doctors messed it up a bit. They said he wouldn't limp or anything, but when he left here he was still completely dot and go one."

Lady Tamplin came out and joined them.

"Have you been telling Katherine about Major Knighton?" she asked. "Such a dear fellow! Just at first I didn't remember him—one had so many—but now it all comes back."

"He was a bit too unimportant to be remembered before," said Lenox. "Now that he is a secretary to an American millionaire, it is a very different matter."

"Darling!" said Lady Tamplin in her vague reproachful voice.

"What did Major Knighton ring up about?" inquired Katherine.

"He asked if you would like to go to the tennis this afternoon. If so, he would call for you in a car. Mother and I accepted for you with *empressement*. Whilst you dally with a millionaire's secretary, you might give me a chance with the millionaire, Katherine. He is about sixty, I suppose, so that he will be looking about for a nice sweet young thing like me."

"I should like to meet Mr. Van Aldin," said Lady Tamplin earnestly; "one has heard so much of him. Those fine rugged figures of the Western world"—she broke off—"so fascinating," she murmured.

"Major Knighton was very particular to say it was Mr. Van Aldin's invitation," said Lenox. "He said it so often that I began to smell a rat. You and Knighton would make a very nice pair, Katherine. Bless you, my children!"

Katherine laughed, and went upstairs to change her clothes.

Knighton arrived soon after lunch and endured manfully Lady Tamplin's transports of recognition.

When they were driving together towards Cannes he remarked to Katherine: "Lady Tamplin has changed wonderfully little."

"In manner or appearance?"

"Both. She must be, I suppose, well over forty, but she is a remarkably beautiful woman still."

"She is," agreed Katherine.

"I am very glad that you could come to-day," went on Knighton. "M. Poirot is going to be there also. What an extraordinary little man he is. Do you know him well, Miss Grey?"

Katherine shook her head. "I met him on the train on the way here. I was reading a detective novel, and I happened to say something about such things not happening in real life. Of course, I had no idea of who he was."

"He is a very remarkable person," said Knighton slowly, "and has done some very remarkable things. He has a kind of genius for going to the root of the matter, and right up to the end no one has any idea of what he is really thinking. I remember I was staying at a house in Yorkshire, and Lady Clanravon's jewels were stolen. It seemed at first to be a simple robbery, but it completely baffled the local police. I wanted them to call in Hercule Poirot, and said he was the only man who could help them, but they pinned their faith to Scotland Yard."

"And what happened?" said Katherine curiously.

"The jewels were never recovered," said Knighton drily.

"You really do believe in him?"

"I do indeed. The Comte de la Roche is a pretty wily customer. He has wriggled out of most things. But I think he has met his match in Hercule Poirot."

"The Comte de la Roche," said Katherine thoughtfully; "so you really think he did it?"

"Of course." Knighton looked at her in astonishment. "Don't you?"

"Oh yes," said Katherine hastily; "that is, I mean, if it was not just an ordinary train robbery."

"It might be, of course," agreed the other, "but it seems to me that the Comte de la Roche fits into this business particularly well."

"And yet he has an alibi."

"Oh, alibis!" Knighton laughed, his face broke into his attractive boyish smile.

"You confess that you read detective stories, Miss Grey. You must know that anyone who has a perfect alibi is always open to grave suspicion."

"Do you think that real life is like that?" asked Katherine, smiling.

"Why not? Fiction is founded on fact."

"But is rather superior to it," suggested Katherine.

"Perhaps. Anyway, if I was a criminal I should not like to have Hercule Poirot on my track."

"No more should I," said Katherine, and laughed.

They were met on arrival by Poirot. As the day was warm he was attired in a white duck suit, with a white camellia in his buttonhole.

"*Bon jour*, Mademoiselle," said Poirot. "I look very English, do I not?"

"You look wonderful," said Katherine tactfully.

"You mock yourself at me," said Poirot genially, "but no matter. Papa Poirot, he always laughs the last."

"Where is Mr. Van Aldin?" asked Knighton.

"He will meet us at our seats. To tell you the truth, my friend, he is not too well pleased with me. Oh, those Americans—the repose, the calm, they know it not! Mr. Van Aldin, he would that I fly myself in the pursuit of criminals through all the byways of Nice."

"I should have thought myself that it would not have been a bad plan," observed Knighton.

"You are wrong," said Poirot; "in these matters one needs not energy but finesse. At the tennis one meets everyone. That is so important. Ah, there is Mr. Kettering."

Derek came abruptly up to them. He looked reckless and angry, as though something had arisen to upset him. He and Knighton greeted each other with some frigidity. Poirot alone seemed unconscious of any sense of strain, and chatted pleasantly in a laudable attempt to put everyone at his ease. He paid little compliments.

"It is amazing, M. Kettering, how well you speak the French," he observed—"so well that you could be taken for a Frenchman if you chose. That is a very rare accomplishment among Englishmen."

"I wish I did," said Katherine. "I am only too well aware that my French is of a painfully British order."

They reached their seats and sat down, and almost immediately Knighton perceived his employer signaling to him from the other end of the court, and went off to speak to him.

"Me, I approve of that young man," said Poirot, sending a beaming smile after the departing secretary; "and you, Mademoiselle?"

"I like him very much."

"And you, M. Kettering?"

Some quick rejoinder was springing to Derek's lips, but he checked it as though something in the little Belgian's twinkling eyes had made him suddenly alert. He spoke carefully, choosing his words.

"Knighton is a very good fellow," he said.

Just for a moment Katherine fancied that Poirot looked disappointed.

"He is a great admirer of yours, M. Poirot," she said, and she related some of the things that Knighton had said. It amused her to see the little man plume himself like a bird, thrusting out his chest, and assuming an air of mock modesty that would have deceived no one.

"That reminds me, Mademoiselle," he said suddenly, "I have a little matter of business I have to speak to you about. When you were sitting talking to that poor lady in the train, I think you must have dropped a cigarette case."

Katherine looked rather astonished. "I don't think so," she said. Poirot drew from his pocket a cigarette case of soft blue leather, with the initial "K" on it in gold.

"No, that is not mine," Katherine said.

"Ah, a thousand apologies. It was doubtless Madame's own. 'K,' of course, stands for Kettering. We were doubtful, because she had another cigarette case in her bag, and it seemed odd that she should have two." He turned to Derek suddenly. "You do not know, I suppose, whether this was your wife's case or not?"

Derek seemed momentarily taken aback. He stammered a little in his reply: "I—I don't know. I suppose so."

"It is not yours by any chance?"

"Certainly not. If it were mine it would hardly have been in my wife's possession."

146

Poirot looked more ingenuous and childlike than ever.

"I thought perhaps you might have dropped it when you were in your wife's compartment," he explained guilelessly.

"I never was there. I have already told the police that a dozen times."

"A thousand pardons," said Poirot, with his most apologetic air. "It was Mademoiselle here who mentioned having seen you going in."

He stopped with an air of embarrassment.

Katherine looked at Derek. His face had gone rather white, but perhaps that was her fancy. His laugh, when it came, was natural enough.

"You made a mistake, Miss Grey," he said easily. "From what the police have told me, I gather that my own compartment was only a door or two away from that of my wife's—though I never suspected the fact at the time. You must have seen me going into my own compartment." He got up quickly as he saw Van Aldin and Knighton approaching.

"I'm going to leave you now," he announced. "I can't stand my father-in-law at any price."

Van Aldin greeted Katherine very courteously, but was clearly in a bad humour.

"You seem fond of watching tennis, M. Poirot," he growled.

"It is a pleasure to me, yes," cried Poirot placidly.

"It is as well you are in France," said Van Aldin. "We are made of sterner stuff in the States. Business comes before pleasure there."

Poirot did not take offence; indeed, he smiled gently and confidingly at the irate millionaire.

"Do not enrage yourself, I beg of you. Everyone has his own methods. Me, I have always found it a delightful and pleasing idea to combine business and pleasure together."

He glanced at the other two. They were deep in conversation, absorbed in each other. Poirot nodded his head in satisfaction, and then leant towards the millionaire, lowering his voice as he did so.

"It is not only for pleasure that I am here, M. Van Aldin. Observe just opposite us that tall old man—the one with the yellow face and the venerable beard."

"Well, what of him?"

"That," Poirot said, "is M. Papopolous."

"A Greek, eh?"

"As you say—a Greek. He is a dealer in antiques of world-wide reputation. He has a small shop in Paris, and he is suspected by the police of being something more."

"What?"

"A receiver of stolen goods, especially jewels. There is nothing as to the re-cutting and re-setting of gems that he does not know. He deals with the highest in Europe and with the lowest of the riff-raff of the underworld."

Van Aldin was looking at Poirot with suddenly awakened attention.

"Well?" he demanded, a new note in his voice.

"I ask myself," said Poirot, "I, Hercule Poirot"—he thumped himself dramatically on the chest—"ask myself *why is M. Papopolous suddenly come to Nice?*"

Van Aldin was impressed. For a moment he had doubted Poirot and suspected the little man of being past his job, a *poseur* only. Now, in a moment, he switched back to his original opinion. He looked straight at the little detective.

"I must apologize to you, M. Poirot."

Poirot waved the apology aside with an extravagant gesture.

"Bah!" he cried, "all that is of no importance. Now listen, M. Van Aldin; I have news for you."

The millionaire looked sharply at him, all his interest aroused. Poirot nodded.

"It is as I say. You will be interested. As you know, M. Van Aldin, the Comte de la Roche has been under surveillance ever since his interview with the Juge d'Instruction. The day after that, during his absence, the Villa Marina was searched by the police."

"Well," said Van Aldin, "did they find anything? I bet they didn't."

Poirot made him a little bow.

"Your acumen is not at fault, M. Van Aldin. They found nothing of an incriminating nature. It was not to be expected that they would. The Comte de la Roche, as your expressive idiom has it, was not born on the preceding day. He is an astute gentleman with great experience."

"Well, go on," growled Van Aldin.

"It may be, of course, that the Comte had nothing of a compromising nature to conceal. But we must not neglect the possibility. If, then, he has something to conceal, where is it? Not in his house—the police searched thoroughly. Not on his person, for he knows that he is liable to arrest at any minute. There remains—his car. As I say, he was under surveillance. He was followed on that day to Monte Carlo. From there he went by road to Mentone, driving himself. His car is a very powerful one, it outdistanced his pursuers, and for about a quarter of an hour they completely lost sight of him."

"And during that time you think he concealed something by the roadside?" asked Van Aldin, keenly interested.

"By the roadside, no. *Ça n'est pas pratique.* But listen now—me, I have made a little suggestion to M. Carrège. He is graciously pleased to approve of it. In each Bureau de Poste in the neighbourhood it has been seen to that there is someone who knows the Comte de la Roche by sight. Because, you see, Monsieur, the best way of hiding a thing is by sending it away by the post."

"Well?" demanded Van Aldin; his face was keenly alight with interest and expectation.

"Well—*voilà!*" With a dramatic flourish Poirot drew out from his pocket a loosely wrapped brown paper package from which the string had been removed.

"During that quarter of an hour's interval, our good gentleman mailed this."

"The address?" asked the other sharply.

Poirot nodded his head.

"Might have told us something, but unfortunately it does not. The package was addressed to one of these little newspaper shops in Paris where letters and parcels are kept until called for on payment of a small commission."

"Yes, but what is inside?" demanded Van Aldin impatiently.

Poirot unwrapped the brown paper and disclosed a square cardboard box. He looked round him.

"It is a good moment," he said quietly. "All eyes are on the tennis. Look, Monsieur!"

He lifted the lid of the box for the fraction of a second. An exclamation of utter astonishment came from the millionaire. His face turned as white as chalk.

"My God!" he breathed, "the rubies."

He sat for a minute as though dazed. Poirot restored the box to his pocket and beamed placidly. Then suddenly the millionaire seemed to come out of his trance; he leaned across to Poirot and wrung his hand so heartily that the little man winced with pain.

"This is great," said Van Aldin. "Great! You are the goods, M. Poirot. Once and for all, you are the goods."

"It is nothing," said Poirot modestly. "Order, method, being prepared for eventualities beforehand—that is all there is to it."

"And now, I suppose, the Comte de la Roche has been arrested?" continued Van Aldin eagerly.

"No," said Poirot.

A look of utter astonishment came over Van Aldin's face.

"But why? What more do you want?"

"The Comte's alibi is still unshaken."

"But that is nonsense."

"Yes," said Poirot; "I rather think it is nonsense, but unfortunately we have to prove it so."

"In the meantime he will slip through your fingers."

Poirot shook his head very energetically.

"No," he said, "he will not do that. The one thing the Comte cannot afford to sacrifice is his social position. At all costs he must stop and brazen it out."

Van Aldin was still dissatisfied.

"But I don't see—"

Poirot raised a hand. "Grant me a little moment, Monsieur. Me, I have a little idea. Many people have mocked themselves at the little ideas of Hercule Poirot—and they have been wrong."

"Well," said Van Aldin, "go ahead. What is this little idea?"

Poirot paused for a moment and then he said:

"I will call upon you at your hotel at eleven o'clock to-morrow morning. Until then, say nothing to anyone."

TWENTY-TWO
M. Papopolous Breakfasts

M. Papopolous was at breakfast. Opposite him sat his daughter, Zia.

There was a knock at the sitting-room door, and a chasseur entered with a card which he brought to Mr. Papopolous. The latter scrutinized it, raised his eyebrows, and passed it over to his daughter.

"Ah!" said M. Papopolous, scratching his left ear thoughtfully, "Hercule Poirot. I wonder now."

Father and daughter looked at each other.

"I saw him yesterday at the tennis," said M. Papopolous. "Zia, I hardly like this."

"He was very useful to you once," his daughter reminded him.

"That is true," acknowledged M. Papopolous; "also he has retired from active work, so I hear."

These interchanges between father and daughter had passed in their own language. Now M. Papopolous turned to the chasseur and said in French:

"*Faites monter ce monsieur.*"

A few minutes later Hercule Poirot, exquisitely attired, and swinging a cane with a jaunty air, entered the room.

"My dear M. Papopolous."

"My dear M. Poirot."

"And Mademoiselle Zia." Poirot swept her a low bow.

"You will excuse us going on with our breakfast," said M. Papopolous, pouring himself out another cup of coffee. "Your call is—ahem!—a little early."

"It is scandalous," said Poirot, "but see you, I am pressed."

"Ah!" murmured M. Papopolous, "you are on an affair then?"

"A very serious affair," said Poirot: "the death of Madame Kettering."

"Let me see," M. Papopolous looked innocently up at the ceiling, "that was the lady who died on the Blue Train, was it not? I saw a mention of it in the papers, but there was no suggestion of foul play."

"In the interests of justice," said Poirot, "it was thought best to suppress that fact."

There was a pause.

"And in what way can I assist you, M. Poirot?" asked the dealer politely.

"*Voilà*," said Poirot, "I shall come to the point." He took from his pocket the same box that he had displayed at Cannes, and opening it, he took out the rubies and pushed them across the table to Papopolous.

Although Poirot was watching him narrowly, not a muscle of the old man's face moved. He took up the jewels and examined them with a kind of detached interest, then he looked across at the detective inquiringly:

"Superb, are they not?" asked Poirot.

"Quite excellent," said M. Papopolous.

"How much should you say they are worth?"

The Greek's face quivered a little.

"Is it really necessary to tell you, M. Poirot?" he asked.

"You are shrewd, M. Papopolous. No, it is not. They are not, for instance, worth five hundred thousand dollars."

Papopolous laughed, and Poirot joined with him.

"As an imitation," said Papopolous, handing them back to Poirot, "they are, as I said, quite excellent. Would it be indiscreet to ask, M. Poirot, where you came across them?"

"Not at all," said Poirot; "I have no objection to telling an old friend like yourself. They were in the possession of the Comte de la Roche."

M. Papopolous' eyebrows lifted themselves eloquently.

"In-deed," he murmured.

Poirot leant forward and assumed his most innocent and beguiling air.

"M. Papopolous," he said, "I am going to lay my cards upon the table. The original of these jewels was stolen from Madame Kettering on the Blue Train. Now I will say to you first this: *I am not concerned with the recovery of these jewels. That is the affair of the police.* I am working not for the police but for M. Van Aldin. I want to lay hands on the man who killed Madame Kettering. I am interested in the jewels only in so far as they may lead me to the man. You understand?"

The last two words were uttered with great significance. M. Papopolous, his face quite unmoved, said quietly:

"Go on."

"It seems to me probable, Monsieur, that the jewels will change hands in Nice—may already have done so."

"Ah!" said M. Papopolous.

He sipped his coffee reflectively, and looked a shade more noble and patriarchal than usual.

"I say to myself," continued Poirot, with animation, "what good fortune! My old friend, M. Papopolous, is in Nice. He will aid me."

"And how do you think I can aid you?" inquired M. Papopolous coldly.

"I said to myself, without doubt M. Papopolous is in Nice on business."

"Not at all," said M. Papopolous, "I am here for my health—by the doctor's orders."

He coughed hollowly.

"I am desolated to hear it," replied Poirot, with somewhat insincere sympathy. "But to continue. When a Russian Grand Duke, an Austrian Archduchess, or an Italian Prince wish to dispose of their family jewels—to whom do they go? To M. Papopolous, is it not? He who is famous all over the world for the discretion with which he arranges these things."

The other bowed.

"You flatter me."

"It is a great thing, discretion," mused Poirot, and was rewarded by the fleeting smile which passed across the Greek's face. "I, too, can be discreet."

The eyes of the two men met.

Then Poirot went on speaking very slowly, and obviously picking his words with care.

"I say to myself, this: if these jewels have changed hands in Nice, M. Papopolous would have heard of it. He has knowledge of all that passes in the jewel world."

"Ah!" said M. Papopolous, and helped himself to a *croissant*.

"The police, you understand," said M. Poirot, "do not enter into the matter. It is a personal affair."

"One hears rumours," admitted M. Papopolous cautiously.

"Such as?" prompted Poirot.

"Is there any reason why I should pass them on?"

"Yes," said Poirot, "I think there is. You may remember, M. Papopolous, that seventeen years ago there was a certain article in your hands, left there as security by a very—er—Prominent Person. It was in your keeping and it unaccountably disappeared. You were, if I may use the English expression, in the soup."

His eyes came gently round to the girl. She had pushed her cup and plate aside, and with both elbows on the table and her chin resting on her hands was listening eagerly. Still keeping an eye on her he went on:

"I am in Paris at the time. You send for me. You place yourself in my hands. If I restore to you that—article, you say I shall earn your undying gratitude. *Eh bien!* I did restore it to you."

A long sigh came from M. Papopolous.

"It was the most unpleasant moment of my career," he murmured.

"Seventeen years is a long time," said Poirot thoughtfully, "but I believe that I am right in saying, Monsieur, that your race does not forget."

"A Greek?" murmured Papopolous, with an ironical smile.

"It was not as a Greek I meant," said Poirot.

There was a silence, and then the old man drew himself up proudly.

"You are right, M. Poirot," he said quietly. "I am a Jew. And, as you say, our race does not forget."

"You will aid me then?"

"As regards the jewels, Monsieur, I can do nothing."

The old man, as Poirot had done just now, picked his words carefully.

"I know nothing. I have heard nothing. But I can perhaps do you a good turn—that is, if you are interested in racing."

"Under certain circumstances I might be," said Poirot, eyeing him steadily.

"There is a horse running at Longchamps that would, I think, repay attention. I cannot say for certain, you understand; this news passed through so many hands."

He stopped, fixing Poirot with his eye, as though to make sure that the latter was comprehending him.

"Perfectly, perfectly," said Poirot, nodding.

"The name of the horse," said M. Papopolous, leaning back and joining the tips of his fingers together, "is the Marquis. I think, but I am not sure, that it is an English horse, eh, Zia?"

"I think so too," said the girl.

Poirot got up briskly.

"I thank you, Monsieur," he said. "It is a great thing to have what the English call a tip from the stable. Au revoir, Monsieur, and many thanks."

He turned to the girl.

"Au revoir, Mademoiselle Zia. It seems to me but yesterday that I saw you in Paris. One would say that two years had passed at most."

"There is a difference between sixteen and thirty-three," said Zia ruefully.

"Not in your case," declared Poirot gallantly. "You and your father will perhaps dine with me one night."

"We shall be delighted," replied Zia.

"Then we will arrange it," declared Poirot, "and now—*je me sauve.*"

Poirot walked along the street humming a little tune to himself. He twirled his stick with a jaunty air, once or twice he smiled to himself quietly. He turned into the first Bureau de Poste he came to and sent off a telegram. He took some time in wording it, but it was in code and he had to call upon his memory. It purported to deal with a missing scarf-pin, and was addressed to Inspector Japp, Scotland Yard.

Decoded, it was short and to the point. *"Wire me everything known about man whose soubriquet is the Marquis."*

TWENTY-THREE
A New Theory

It was exactly eleven o'clock when Poirot presented himself at Van Aldin's hotel. He found the millionaire alone.

"You are punctual, M. Poirot," he said, with a smile, as he rose to greet the detective.

"I am always punctual," said Poirot. "The exactitude—always do I observe it. Without order and method—"

He broke off. "Ah, but it is possible that I have said these things to you before. Let us come at once to the object of my visit."

"Your little idea?"

"Yes, my little idea." Poirot smiled.

"First of all, Monsieur. I should like to interview once more the maid, Ada Mason. She is here?"

"Yes, she's here."

"Ah!"

Van Aldin looked at him curiously. He rang the bell, and a messenger was dispatched to find Mason.

Poirot greeted her with his usual politeness, which was never without effect on that particular class.

"Good afternoon, Mademoiselle," he said cheerfully. "Be seated, will you not, if Monsieur permits."

"Yes, yes, sit down, my girl," said Van Aldin.

"Thank you, sir," said Mason primly, and she sat down on the extreme edge of a chair. She looked bonier and more acid than ever.

"I have come to ask you yet more questions," said Poirot. "We must get to the bottom of this affair. Always I return to the question of the man in the train. You have been shown the Comte de la Roche. You say that it is possible he was the man, but you are not sure."

"As I told you, sir, I never saw the gentleman's face. That is what makes it so difficult."

Poirot beamed and nodded.

"Precisely, exactly. I comprehend well the difficulty. Now, Mademoiselle, you have been in the service of Madame Kettering two months, you say. During that time, how often did you see your master?"

Mason reflected a minute or two, and then said:

"Only twice, sir."

"And was that near to, or far away?"

"Well once, sir, he came to Curzon Street. I was upstairs, and I looked over the banisters and saw him in the hall below. I was a bit curious like, you understand, knowing the way things—er— were." Mason finished up with her discreet cough.

"And the other time?"

"I was in the Park, sir, with Annie—one of the housemaids, sir, and she pointed out the master to me walking with a foreign lady."

Again Poirot nodded.

"Now listen, Mason, this man whom you saw in the carriage talking to your mistress at the Gare de Lyon, how do you know it was not your master?"

"The master, sir? Oh, I don't think it could have been."

"But you are not sure," Poirot persisted.

"Well—I never thought of it, sir."

Mason was clearly upset at the idea.

"You have heard that your master was also on the train. What more natural than that it should be he who came along the corridor."

"But the gentleman who was talking to the mistress must have come from outside, sir. He was dressed for the street. In an overcoat and soft hat."

"Just so, Mademoiselle, but reflect a minute. The train has just arrived at the Gare de Lyon. Many of the passengers promenade themselves upon the quay. Your mistress was about to do so, and for that purpose had doubtless put on her fur coat, eh?"

"Yes, sir," agreed Mason.

"Your master, then, does the same. The train is heated, but outside in the station it is cold. He puts on his overcoat and his hat and he walks along beside the train, and looking up at the lighted windows he suddenly sees Madame Kettering. Until then he has had no idea that she was on the train. Naturally, he mounts the carriage and goes to her compartment. She gives an exclamation of surprise at seeing him and quickly shuts the door between the two compartments since it is possible that their conversation may be of a private nature."

He leaned back in his chair and watched the suggestion slowly take effect. No one knew better than Hercule Poirot that the class to which Mason belongs cannot be hurried. He must give her time to get rid of her own preconceived ideas. At the end of three minutes she spoke:

"Well, of course, sir, it might be so. I never thought of it that way. The master is tall and dark, and just about that build. It was seeing the hat and coat that made me say it was a gentleman from outside. Yes, it might have been the master. I would not like to say either way, I am sure."

"Thank you very much, Mademoiselle. I shall not require you any further. Ah, just one thing more." He took from his pocket the cigarette case he had already shown to Katherine. "Is that your mistress's case?" he said to Mason.

"No, sir, it is not the mistress's—at least—"

She looked suddenly startled. An idea was clearly working its way to the forefront of her mind.

"Yes," said Poirot encouragingly.

"I think, sir—I can't be sure, but I think—it is a case that the mistress bought to give to the master."

"Ah," said Poirot in a non-committal manner.

"But whether she ever did give it to him or not, I can't say, of course."

"Precisely," said Poirot, "precisely. That is all, I think, Mademoiselle. I wish you good afternoon."

Ada Mason retired discreetly, closing the door noiselessly behind her.

Poirot looked across at Van Aldin, a faint smile upon his face. The millionaire looked thunderstruck.

"You think—you think it was Derek?" he queried, "but—everything points the other way. Why, the Count has actually been caught redhanded with the jewels on him."

"No."

"But you told me—"

"What did I tell you?"

"That story about the jewels. You showed them to me."

"No."

Van Aldin stared at him.

"You mean to say you didn't show them to me."

"No."

"Yesterday—at the tennis?"

"No."

"Are you crazy, M. Poirot, or am I?"

"Neither of us is crazy," said the detective. "You ask me a question; I answer it. You say have I not shown you the jewels yesterday? I reply—no. What I showed you, M. Van Aldin, was a first-class imitation, hardly to be distinguished except by an expert from the real ones."

TWENTY-FOUR

Poirot Gives Advice

It took the millionaire some few minutes to take the thing in. He stared at Poirot as though dumbfounded. The little Belgian nodded at him gently.

"Yes," he said, "it alters the position, does it not?"

"Imitation!"

He leaned forward.

"All along, M. Poirot, you have had this idea? All along this is what you have been driving at? You never believed that the Comte de la Roche was the murderer?"

"I have had doubts," said Poirot quietly. "I said as much to you. Robbery with violence and murder"—he shook his head energetically—"no, it is difficult to picture. It does not harmonize with the personality of the Comte de la Roche."

"But you believe that he meant to steal the rubies?"

"Certainly. There is no doubt as to that. See, I will recount to you the affair as I see it. The Comte knew of the rubies and he laid his plans accordingly. He made up a romantic story of a book he was writing, so as to induce your daughter to bring them with her. He provided himself with an exact duplicate. It is clear, is it not, that substitution is what he was after. Madame, your daughter, was not an expert on jewels. It would probably be a long time before she discovered what had occurred. When she did so—well—I do not think she would prosecute the Comte. Too

162

much would come out. He would have in his possession various letters of hers. Oh yes, a very safe scheme from the Comte's point of view—one that he has probably carried out before."

"It seems clear enough, yes," said Van Aldin musingly.

"It accords with the personality of the Comte de la Roche," said Poirot.

"Yes, but now—" Van Aldin looked searchingly at the other. "What actually happened? Tell me that, M. Poirot."

Poirot shrugged his shoulders.

"It is quite simple," he said; "someone stepped in ahead of the Comte."

There was a long pause.

Van Aldin seemed to be turning things over in his mind. When he spoke it was without beating about the bush.

"How long have you suspected my son-in-law, M. Poirot?"

"From the very first. He had the motive and the opportunity. Everyone took for granted that the man in Madame's compartment in Paris was the Comte de la Roche. I thought so, too. Then you happened to mention that you had once mistaken the Comte for your son-in-law. That told me that they were of the same height and build, and alike in colouring. It put some curious ideas in my head. The maid had only been with your daughter a short time. It was unlikely that she would know Mr. Kettering well by sight, since he had not been living in Curzon Street; also the man was careful to keep his face turned away."

"You believe he—murdered her," said Van Aldin hoarsely.

Poirot raised a hand quickly.

"No, no, I did not say that—but it is a possibility—a very strong possibility. He was in a tight corner, a very tight corner, threatened with ruin. This was the one way out."

"But why take the jewels?"

"To make the crime appear an ordinary one committed by train robbers. Otherwise suspicion might have fallen on him straight away."

"If that is so, what has he done with the rubies?"

"That remains to be seen. There are several possibilities. There is a man in Nice who may be able to help, the man I pointed out at the tennis."

He rose to his feet and Van Aldin rose also and laid his hand on the little man's shoulder. His voice when he spoke was harsh with emotion.

"Find Ruth's murderer for me," he said, "that is all I ask."

Poirot drew himself up.

"Leave it in the hands of Hercule Poirot," he said superbly; "have no fears. I will discover the truth."

He brushed a speck of fluff from his hat, smiled reassuringly at the millionaire, and left the room. Nevertheless, as he went down the stairs some of the confidence faded from his face.

"It is all very well," he murmured to himself, "but there are difficulties. Yes, there are great difficulties." As he was passing out of the hotel he came to a sudden halt. A car had drawn up in front of the door. In it was Katherine Grey, and Derek Kettering was standing beside it talking to her earnestly. A minute or two later the car drove off and Derek remained standing on the pavement looking after it. The expression on his face was an odd one. He gave a sudden impatient gesture of the shoulders, sighed deeply, and turned to find Hercule Poirot standing at his elbow. In spite of himself he started. The two men looked at each other. Poirot steadily and unwaveringly and Derek with a kind of light-hearted defiance. There was a sneer behind the easy mockery of his tone when he spoke, raising his eyebrows slightly as he did so.

"Rather a dear, isn't she?" he asked easily.

His manner was perfectly natural.

"Yes," said Poirot thoughtfully, "that describes Mademoiselle Katherine very well. It is very English, that phrase there, and Mademoiselle Katherine, she also is very English."

Derek remained perfectly still without answering.

"And yet she is *sympathique*, is it not so?"

"Yes," said Derek; "there are not many like her."

He spoke softly, almost as though to himself. Poirot nodded significantly. Then he leant towards the other and spoke in a different tone, a quiet, grave tone that was new to Derek Kettering.

"You will pardon an old man, Monsieur, if he says to you something that you may consider impertinent. There is one of your English proverbs that I would quote to you. It says that 'it is well to be off with the old love, before being on with the new.'"

Kettering turned on him angrily.

"What the devil do you mean?"

"You enrage yourself at me," said Poirot placidly. "I expected as much. As to what I mean—I mean, Monsieur, that there is a second car with a lady in it. If you turn your head you will see her."

Derek spun round. His face darkened with anger.

"Mirelle, damn her!" he muttered. "I will soon——"

Poirot arrested the movement he was about to make.

"Is it wise what you are about to do there?" he asked warningly. His eyes shone softly with a green light in them. But Derek was past noticing the warning signs. In his anger he was completely off his guard.

"I have broken with her utterly, and she knows it," cried Derek angrily.

"You have broken with her, yes, but has *she* broken with you?"

Derek gave a sudden harsh laugh.

"She won't break with two million pounds if she can help it," he murmured brutally; "trust Mirelle for that."

Poirot raised his eyebrows.

"You have the outlook cynical," he murmured.

"Have I?" There was no mirth in his sudden wide smile. "I have lived in the world long enough, M. Poirot, to know that all women are pretty much alike." His face softened suddenly. "All save one."

He met Poirot's gaze defiantly. A look of alertness crept into his eyes, then faded again. "That one," he said, and jerked his head in the direction of Cap Martin.

"Ah!" said Poirot.

This quiescence was well calculated to provoke the impetuous temperament of the other.

"I know what you are going to say," said Derek rapidly, "the kind of life I have led, the fact that I am not worthy of her. You will say that I have no right to think even of such a thing. You will say that it is not a case of giving a dog a bad name—I know that it is not decent to be speaking like this with my wife dead only a few days, and murdered at that."

He paused for breath, and Poirot took advantage of the pause to remark in his plaintive tone:

"But, indeed, I have not said anything at all."

"But you will."

"Eh?" said Poirot.

"You will say that I have no earthly chance of marrying Katherine."

"No," said Poirot, "I would not say that. Your reputation is bad, yes, but with women—never does that deter them. If you were a man of excellent character, of strict morality who had done nothing that he should not do, and—possibly everything that he should do—*eh bien!* then I should have grave doubts of your success. Moral worth, you understand, it is not romantic. It is appreciated, however, by widows."

Derek Kettering stared at him, then he swung round on his heel and went up to the waiting car.

Poirot looked after him with some interest. He saw the lovely vision lean out of the car and speak.

Derek Kettering did not stop. He lifted his hat and passed straight on.

"*Ça y est,*" said M. Hercule Poirot, "it is time, I think, that I return *chez moi.*"

He found the imperturbable George pressing trousers.

166

"A pleasant day, Georges, somewhat fatiguing, but not without interest," he said.

George received these remarks in his usual wooden fashion. "Indeed, sir."

"The personality of a criminal, Georges, is an interesting matter. Many murderers are men of great personal charm."

"I always heard, sir, that Dr. Crippen was a pleasant-spoken gentleman. And yet he cut up his wife like so much mincemeat."

"Your instances are always apt, Georges."

The valet did not reply, and at that moment the telephone rang. Poirot took up the receiver.

"'Allo—'allo—yes, yes, it is Hercule Poirot who speaks."

"This is Knighton. Will you hold the line a minute, M. Poirot? Mr. Van Aldin would like to speak to you."

There was a moment's pause, then the millionaire's voice came through.

"Is that you, M. Poirot? I just wanted to tell you that Mason came to me now of her own accord. She has been thinking it over, and she says that she is almost certain that the man at Paris was Derek Kettering. There was something familiar about him at the time, she says, but at the minute she could not place it. She seems pretty certain now."

"Ah," said Poirot, "thank you, M. Van Aldin. That advances us."

He replaced the receiver, and stood for a minute or two with a very curious smile on his face. George had to speak to him twice before obtaining an answer.

"Eh?" said Poirot. "What is that that you say to me?"

"Are you lunching here, sir, or are you going out?"

"Neither," said Poirot, "I shall go to bed and take a *tisane*. The expected has happened, and when the expected happens, it always causes me emotion."

TWENTY-FIVE

Defiance

As Derek Kettering passed the car, Mirelle leant out.

"Dereek—I must speak to you for a moment—"

But, lifting his hat, Derek passed straight on without stopping.

When he got back to his hotel, the concierge detached himself from his wooden pen and accosted him.

"A gentleman is waiting to see you, Monsieur."

"Who is it?" asked Derek.

"He did not give me his name, Monsieur, but he said his business with you was important, and that he would wait."

"Where is he?"

"In the little salon, Monsieur. He preferred it to the lounge he said, as being more private."

Derek nodded, and turned his steps in that direction.

The small salon was empty except for the visitor, who rose and bowed with easy foreign grace as Derek entered. As it chanced, Derek had seen the Comte de la Roche only once, but found no difficulty in recognizing that aristocratic nobleman, and he frowned angrily. Of all the consummate impertinence!

"The Comte de la Roche, is it not?" he said. "I am afraid you have wasted your time in coming here."

"I hope not," said the Comte agreeably. His white teeth glittered.

168

The Comte's charm of manner was usually wasted on his own sex. All men, without exception, disliked him heartily. Derek Kettering was already conscious of a distinct longing to kick the Count bodily out of the room. It was only the realization that scandal would be unfortunate just at present that restrained him. He marvelled anew that Ruth could have cared, as she certainly had, for this fellow. A bounder, and worse than a bounder. He looked with distaste at the Count's exquisitely manicured hands.

"I called," said the Comte, "on a little matter of business. It would be advisable, I think, for you to listen to me."

Again Derek felt strongly tempted to kick him out, but again he refrained. The hint of a threat was not lost upon him, but he interpreted it in his own way. There were various reasons why it would be better to hear what the Comte had to say.

He sat down and drummed impatiently with his fingers on the table.

"Well," he said sharply, "what is it?"

It was not the Comte's way to come out into the open at once.

"Allow me, Monsieur, to offer you my condolences on your recent bereavement."

"If I have any impertinence from you," said Derek quietly, "you go out by that window."

He nodded his head towards the window beside the Comte, and the latter moved uneasily.

"I will send my friends to you, Monsieur, if that is what you desire," he said haughtily.

Derek laughed.

"A duel, eh? My dear Count, I don't take you seriously enough for that. But I should take a good deal of pleasure in kicking you down the Promenade des Anglais."

The Comte was not at all anxious to take offence. He merely raised his eyebrows and murmured:

"The English are barbarians."

"Well," said Derek, "what is it you have to say to me?"

"I will be frank," said the Comte, "I will come immediately to the point. That will suit us both, will it not?"

Again he smiled in his agreeable fashion.

"Go on," said Derek curtly.

The Comte looked at the ceiling, joined the tips of his fingers together, and murmured softly:

"You have come into a lot of money, Monsieur."

"What the devil has that got to do with you?"

The Comte drew himself up.

"Monsieur, my name is tarnished! I am suspected—accused—of foul crime."

"The accusation does not come from me," said Derek coldly; "as an interested party I have not expressed any opinion."

"I am innocent," said the Comte, "I swear before heaven"—he raised his hand to heaven—"that I am innocent."

"M. Carrège is, I believe, the Juge d'Instruction in charge of the case," hinted Derek politely.

The Comte took no notice.

"Not only am I unjustly suspected of a crime that I did not commit, but I am also in serious need of money."

He coughed softly and suggestively.

Derek rose to his feet.

"I was waiting for that," he said softly; "you blackmailing brute! I will not give you a penny. My wife is dead, and no scandal that you can make can touch her now. She wrote you foolish letters, I dare say. If I were to buy them from you for a round sum at this minute, I am pretty certain that you would manage to keep one or two back; and I will tell you this, M. de la Roche, blackmailing is an ugly word both in England and in France. That is my answer to you. Good afternoon."

"One moment"—the Comte stretched out a hand as Derek was turning to leave the room. "You are mistaken, Monsieur. You are completely mistaken. I am, I hope, a 'gentleman.'" Derek laughed. "Any letters that a lady might write to me I should hold sacred." He flung back his head with a beautiful air of nobility. "The proposition that I was putting before you was of quite a different nature. I am, as I said, extremely short of money, and my conscience might impel me to go to the police with certain information."

Derek came slowly back into the room.

"What do you mean?"

The Comte's agreeable smile flashed forth once more.

"Surely it is not necessary to go into details," he purred. "Seek whom the crime benefits, they say, don't they? As I said just now, you have come into a lot of money lately."

Derek laughed.

"If that is all—" he said contemptuously.

But the Comte was shaking his head.

"But it is not all, my dear sir. I should not come to you unless I had much more precise and detailed information than that. It is not agreeable, Monsieur, to be arrested and tried for murder."

Derek came close up to him. His face expressed such furious anger that involuntarily the Comte drew back a pace or two.

"Are you threatening *me*?" the young man demanded angrily.

"You shall hear nothing more of the matter," the Comte assured him.

"Of all the colossal bluffs that I have ever struck—"

The Comte raised a white hand.

"You are wrong. It is not a bluff. To convince you I will tell you this. My information was obtained from a certain lady. It is she who holds the irrefutable proof that you committed the murder."

"She? Who?"

"Mademoiselle Mirelle."

Derek drew back as though struck.

"Mirelle," he muttered.

The Comte was quick to press what he took to be his advantage.

"A bagatelle of one hundred thousand francs," he said. "I ask no more."

171

"Eh?" said Derek absently.

"I was saying, Monsieur, that a bagatelle of one hundred thousand francs would satisfy my—conscience."

Derek seemed to recollect himself. He looked earnestly at the Comte.

"You would like my answer now?"

"If you please, Monsieur."

"Then here it is. You can go to the devil. See?"

Leaving the Comte too astonished to speak, Derek turned on his heel and swung out of the room.

Once out of the hotel he hailed a taxi and drove to Mirelle's hotel. On inquiring, he learned that the dancer had just come in. Derek gave the concierge his card.

"Take this up to Mademoiselle and ask if she will see me."

A very brief interval elapsed, and then Derek was bidden to follow a *chasseur*.

A wave of exotic perfume assailed Derek's nostrils as he stepped over the threshold of the dancer's apartments. The room was filled with carnations, orchids, and mimosa. Mirelle was standing by the window in a *peignoir* of foamy lace.

She came towards him, her hands outstretched.

"Dereek—you have come to me. I knew you would."

He put aside the clinging arms and looked down on her sternly.

"Why did you send the Comte de la Roche to me?"

She looked at him in astonishment, which he took to be genuine.

"I? Send the Comte de la Roche to you? But for what?"

"Apparently—for blackmail," said Derek grimly.

Again she stared. Then suddenly she smiled and nodded her head.

"Of course. It was to be expected. It is what he would do, *ce type là*. I might have known it. No, indeed, Dereek, I did not send him."

He looked at her piercingly, as though seeking to read her mind.

"I will tell you," said Mirelle. "I am ashamed, but I will tell you. The other day, you comprehend, I was mad with rage, quite mad—" she made an eloquent gesture. "My temperament, it is not a patient one. I want to be revenged on you, and so I go to the Comte de la Roche, and I tell him to go to the police and say so and so, and so and so. But have no fear, Dereek. Not completely did I lose my head; the proof rests with me alone. The police can do nothing without my word, you understand? And now—now?"

She nestled up close to him, looking up at him with melting eyes.

He thrust her roughly away from him. She stood there, her breast heaving, her eyes narrowing to a cat-like slit.

"Be careful, Dereek, be very careful. You have come back to me, have you not?"

"I shall never come back to you," said Derek steadily.

"Ah!"

More than ever the dancer looked like a cat. Her eyelids flickered.

"So there is another woman? The one with whom you lunched that day. Eh! am I right?"

"I intend to ask that lady to marry me. You might as well know."

"That prim Englishwoman! Do you think that I will support that for one moment? Ah, no." Her beautiful lithe body quivered. "Listen, Dereek, do you remember that conversation we had in London? You said the only thing that could save you was the death of your wife. You regretted that she was so healthy. Then the idea of an accident came to your brain. And more than an accident."

"I suppose," said Derek contemptuously, "that it was this conversation that you repeated to the Comte de la Roche."

Mirelle laughed.

"Am I a fool? Could the police do anything with a vague story

AGATHA CHRISTIE

like that? See—I will give you a last chance. You shall give up this Englishwoman. You shall return to me. And then, *chéri*, never, never will I breathe—"

"Breathe what?"

She laughed softly. "You thought no one saw you—"

"What do you mean?"

"As I say, you thought no one saw you—but *I* saw you, Dereek, *mon ami; I saw you coming out of the compartment of Madame your wife just before the train got into Lyons that night. And* I know more than that. I know that when you came out of her compartment she was dead."

He stared at her. Then, like a man in a dream he turned very slowly and went out of the room, swaying slightly as he walked.

174

TWENTY-SIX

A Warning

Aand so it is," said Poirot, "that we are the good friends and have no secrets from each other."

Katherine turned her head to look at him. There was something in his voice, some undercurrent of seriousness, which she had not heard before.

They were sitting in the gardens of Monte Carlo. Katherine had come over with her friends, and they had run into Knighton and Poirot almost immediately on arrival. Lady Tamplin had seized upon Knighton and had overwhelmed him with reminiscences, most of which Katherine had a faint suspicion were invented. They had moved away together, Lady Tamplin with her hand on the young man's arm. Knighton had thrown a couple of glances back over his shoulder, and Poirot's eyes twinkled a little as he saw them.

"Of course we are friends," said Katherine.

"From the beginning we have been sympathetic to each other," mused Poirot.

"When you told me that a 'Roman Policier' occurs in real life."

"And I was right, was I not?" he challenged her, with an emphatic forefinger. "Here we are, plunged in the middle of one. That is natural for me—it is my *métier*—but for you it is different. Yes," he added in a reflective tone, "for you it is different."

She looked sharply at him. It was as though he were warning

her, pointing out to her some menace that she had not seen.

"Why do you say that I am in the middle of it? It is true that I had that conversation with Mrs. Kettering just before she died, but now—now all that is over. I am not connected with the case any more."

"Ah, Mademoiselle, Mademoiselle, can we ever say, 'I have finished with this or that'?"

Katherine turned defiantly round to face him.

"What is it?" she asked. "You are trying to tell me something—to convey it to me rather. But I am not clever at taking hints. I would much rather that you said anything you have to say straight out."

Poirot looked at her sadly. "*Ah, mais c'est Anglais ça,*" he murmured, "everything in black and white, everything clear cut and well defined. But life, it is not like that, Mademoiselle. There are the things that are not yet, but which cast their shadow before."

He dabbed his brow with a very large silk pocket-handkerchief and murmured:

"Ah, but it is that I become poetical. Let us, as you say, speak only of facts. And, speaking of facts, tell me what you think of Major Knighton."

"I like him very much indeed," said Katherine warmly; "he is quite delightful."

Poirot sighed.

"What is the matter?" asked Katherine.

"You reply so heartily," said Poirot. "If you had said in an indifferent voice, 'Oh, quite nice,' *eh bien*, do you know I should have been better pleased."

Katherine did not answer. She felt slightly uncomfortable. Poirot went on dreamily:

"And yet, who knows? With *les femmes*, they have so many ways of concealing what they feel—and heartiness is perhaps as good a way as any other."

He sighed.

"I don't see—" began Katherine.

He interrupted her.

"You do not see why I am being so impertinent, Mademoiselle? I am an old man, and now and then—not very often—I come across someone whose welfare is dear to me. We are friends, Mademoiselle. You have said so yourself. And it is just this—I should like to see you happy."

Katherine stared very straight in front of her. She had a cretonne sunshade with her, and with its point she traced little designs in the gravel at her feet.

"I have asked you a question about Major Knighton, now I will ask you another. Do you like Mr. Derek Kettering?"

"I hardly know him," said Katherine.

"That is not an answer, that."

"I think it is."

He looked at her, struck by something in her tone. Then he nodded his head gravely and slowly.

"Perhaps you are right, Mademoiselle. See you, I who speak to you have seen much of the world, and I know that there are two things which are true. A good man may be ruined by his love for a bad woman—but the other way holds good also. A bad man may equally be ruined by his love for a good woman."

Katherine looked up sharply.

"When you say ruined—"

"I mean from his point of view. One must be wholehearted in crime as in everything else."

"You are trying to warn me," said Katherine in a low voice. "Against whom?"

"I cannot look into your heart, Mademoiselle; I do not think you would let me if I could. I will just say this. There are men who have a strange fascination for women."

"The Comte de la Roche," said Katherine, with a smile.

"There are others—more dangerous than the Comte de la Roche. They have qualities that appeal—recklessness, daring, audacity. You are fascinated, Mademoiselle; I see that, but I think that it is no more than that. I hope so. This man of whom I speak, the emotion he feels is genuine enough, but all the same—"

"Yes?"

He got up and stood looking down at her. Then he spoke, in a low, distinct voice:

"You could, perhaps, love a thief, Mademoiselle, *but not a murderer.*"

He wheeled sharply away on that and left her sitting there.

He heard the little gasp she gave and paid no attention. He had said what he meant to say. He left her there to digest that last unmistakable phrase.

Derek Kettering, coming out of the Casino into the sunshine, saw her sitting alone on the bench and joined her.

"I have been gambling," he said, with a light laugh, "gambling unsuccessfully. I have lost everything—everything, that is, that I have with me."

Katherine looked at him with a troubled face. She was aware at once of something new in his manner, some hidden excitement that betrayed itself in a hundred different infinitesimal signs.

"I should think you were always a gambler. The spirit of gambling appeals to you."

"Every day and in every way a gambler? You are about right. Don't *you* find something stimulating in it? To risk all on one throw—there is nothing like it."

Calm and stolid as she believed herself to be, Katherine felt a faint answering thrill.

"I want to talk to you," went on Derek, "and who knows when I may have another opportunity? There is an idea going about that I murdered my wife—no, please don't interrupt. It is absurd, of course." He paused for a minute or two, then went on, speaking more deliberately. "In dealing with the police and Local Authorities here I have had to pretend to—well—a certain decency. I prefer not to pretend with you. I meant to marry money.

I was on the lookout for money when I first met Ruth Van Aldin. She had the look of a slim Madonna about her, and I—well—I made all sorts of good resolutions—and was bitterly disillusioned. My wife was in love with another man when she married me. She never cared for me in the least. Oh, I am not complaining; the thing was a perfectly respectable bargain. She wanted Leconbury and I wanted money. The trouble arose simply through Ruth's American blood. Without caring a pin for me, she would have liked me to be continually dancing attendance. Time and again she as good as told me that she had bought me and that I belonged to her. The result was that I behaved abominably to her. My father-in-law will tell you that, and he is quite right. At the time of Ruth's death, I was faced with absolute disaster." He laughed suddenly. "One *is* faced with absolute disaster when one is up against a man like Rufus Van Aldin."

"And then?" asked Katherine in a low voice.

"And then," Derek shrugged his shoulders, "Ruth was murdered—very providentially."

He laughed, and the sound of his laugh hurt Katherine. She winced.

"Yes," said Derek, "that wasn't in very good taste. But it is quite true. Now I am going to tell you something more. From the very first moment I saw you I knew you were the only woman in the world for me. I was—afraid of you. I thought you might bring me bad luck."

"Bad luck?" said Katherine sharply.

He stared at her. "Why do you repeat it like that? What have you got in your mind?"

"I was thinking of things that people have said to me."

Derek grinned suddenly. "They will say a lot to you about me, my dear, and most of it will be true. Yes, and worse things too—things that I shall never tell you. I have been a gambler always—and I have taken some long odds. I shan't confess to you now or at any other time. The past is done with. There is one thing I do wish you to believe. I swear to you solemnly that I did not kill my wife."

He said the words earnestly enough, yet there was somehow a theatrical touch about them. He met her troubled gaze and went on:

"I know. I lied the other day. It *was* my wife's compartment I went into."

"Ah," said Katherine.

"It's difficult to explain just why I went in, but I'll try. I did it on an impulse. You see, I was more or less spying on my wife. I kept out of sight on the train. Mirelle had told me that my wife was meeting the Comte de la Roche in Paris. Well, as far as I had seen, that was not so. I felt ashamed, and I thought suddenly that it would be a good thing to have it out with her once and for all, so I pushed open the door and went in."

He paused.

"Yes," said Katherine gently.

"Ruth was lying on the bunk asleep—her face was turned away from me—I could see only the back of her head. I could have waked her up, of course. But suddenly I felt a reaction. What, after all, was there to say that we hadn't both of us said a hundred times before? She looked so peaceful lying there. I left the compartment as quietly as I could."

"Why lie about it to the police?" asked Katherine.

"Because I'm not a complete fool. I've realized from the beginning that, from the point of view of motive, I'm the ideal murderer. If I once admitted that I had been in her compartment just before she was murdered, I'd do for myself once and for all."

"I see."

Did she see? She could not have told herself. She was feeling the magnetic attraction of Derek's personality, but there was something in her that resisted, that held back....

"Katherine—"

"I—"

"You know that I care for you. Do—do you care for me?"

"I—I don't know."

Weakness there. Either she knew or she did not know. If—if only—

She cast a look round desperately as though seeking something that would help her. A soft colour rose in her cheeks as a tall fair man with a limp came hurrying along the path towards them—Major Knighton.

There was relief and an unexpected warmth in her voice as she greeted him.

Derek stood up scowling, his face black as a thundercloud.

"Lady Tamplin having a flutter?" he said easily. "I must join her and give her the benefit of my system."

He swung round on his heel and left them together. Katherine sat down again. Her heart was beating rapidly and unevenly, but as she sat there talking commonplaces to the quiet, rather shy man beside her, her self-command came back.

Then she realized with a shock that Knighton also was laying bare his heart, much as Derek had done, but in a very different manner.

He was shy and stammering. The words came haltingly with no eloquence to back them.

"From the first moment I saw you—I—I ought not to have spoken so soon—but Mr. Van Aldin may leave here any day, and I might not have another chance. I know you can't care for me so soon—that is impossible. I dare say it is presumption anyway on my part. I have private means, but not very much—no, please don't answer now. I know what your answer would be. But in case I went away suddenly I just wanted you to know—that I care."

She was shaken—touched. His manner was so gentle and appealing.

"There's one thing more. I just wanted to say that if—if you are ever in trouble, anything that I can do—"

He took her hand in his, held it tightly for a minute, then

dropped it and walked rapidly away towards the Casino without looking back.

Katherine sat perfectly still, looking after him. Derek Kettering—Richard Knighton—two men so different—so very different. There was something kind about Knighton, kind and trustworthy. As to Derek—

Then suddenly Katherine had a very curious sensation. She felt that she was no longer sitting alone on the seat in the Casino gardens, but that someone was standing beside her, and that that someone was the dead woman, Ruth Kettering. She had a further impression that Ruth wanted—badly—to tell her something. The impression was so curious, so vivid, that it could not be driven away. She felt absolutely certain that the spirit of Ruth Kettering was trying to convey something of vital importance to her. The impression faded. Katherine got up, trembling a little. What was it that Ruth Kettering had wanted so badly to say?

TWENTY-SEVEN
Interview with Mirelle

When Knighton left Katherine he went in search of Hercule Poirot, whom he found in the Rooms, jauntily placing the minimum stake on the even numbers. As Knighton joined him, the number thirty-three turned up, and Poirot's stake was swept away.

"Bad luck!" said Knighton; "are you going to stake again?"

Poirot shook his head.

"Not at present."

"Do you feel the fascination of gambling?" asked Knighton curiously.

"Not at roulette."

Knighton shot a swift glance at him. His own face became troubled. He spoke haltingly, with a touch of deference.

"I wonder, are you busy, M. Poirot? There is something I would like to ask you about."

"I am at your disposal. Shall we go outside? It is pleasant in the sunshine."

They strolled out together, and Knighton drew a deep breath.

"I love the Riviera," he said. "I came here first twelve years ago, during the War, when I was sent to Lady Tamplin's Hospital. It was like Paradise, coming from Flanders to this."

"It must have been," said Poirot.

"How long ago the War seems now!" mused Knighton.

They walked on in silence for some little way.

"You have something on your mind?" said Poirot.

Knighton looked at him in some surprise.

"You are quite right," he confessed. "I don't know how you knew it, though."

"It showed itself only too plainly," said Poirot drily.

"I did not know that I was so transparent."

"It is my business to observe the physiognomy," the little man explained, with dignity.

"I will tell you, M. Poirot. You have heard of this dancer woman—Mirelle?"

"She who is the *chère amie* of M. Derek Kettering?"

"Yes, that is the one; and, knowing this, you will understand that Mr. Van Aldin is naturally prejudiced against her. She wrote to him, asking for an interview. He told me to dictate a curt refusal, which of course I did. This morning she came to the hotel and sent up her card, saying that it was urgent and vital that she should see Mr. Van Aldin at once."

"You interest me," said Poirot.

"Mr. Van Aldin was furious. He told me what message to send down to her. I ventured to disagree with him. It seemed to me both likely and probable that this woman Mirelle might give us valuable information. We know that she was on the Blue Train, and she may have seen or heard something that it might be vital for us to know. Don't you agree with me, M. Poirot?"

"I do," said Poirot drily. "M. Van Aldin, if I may say so, behaved exceedingly foolishly."

"I am glad you take that view of the matter," said the secretary. "Now I am going to tell you something, M. Poirot. So strongly did I feel the unwisdom of Mr. Van Aldin's attitude that I went down privately and had an interview with the lady."

"*Eh bien?*"

"The difficulty was that she insisted on seeing Mr. Van Aldin himself. I softened his message as much as I possibly could. In fact—to be candid—I gave it in a very different form. I said that Mr. Van Aldin was too busy to see her at present, but that she might make any communication she wished to me. That, however, she could not bring herself to do, and she left without saying anything further. But I have a strong impression, M. Poirot, that that woman knows something."

"This is serious," said Poirot quietly. "You know where she is staying?"

"Yes." Knighton mentioned the name of the hotel.

"Good," said Poirot; "we will go there immediately."

The secretary looked doubtful.

"And Mr. Van Aldin?" he queried doubtfully.

"M. Van Aldin is an obstinate man," said Poirot drily. "I do not argue with obstinate men. I act in spite of them. We will go and see the lady immediately. I will tell her that you are empowered by M. Van Aldin to act for him, and you will guard yourself well from contradicting me."

Knighton still looked slightly doubtful, but Poirot took no notice of his hesitation.

At the hotel, they were told that Mademoiselle was in, and Poirot sent up both his and Knighton's cards, with "From Mr. Van Aldin" pencilled upon them.

Word came down that Mademoiselle Mirelle would receive them.

When they were ushered into the dancer's apartments, Poirot immediately took the lead.

"Mademoiselle," he murmured, bowing very low, "we are here on behalf of M. Van Aldin."

"Ah! And why did he not come himself?"

"He is indisposed," said Poirot mendaciously; "the Riviera throat, it has him in its grip, but me, I am empowered to act for him, as is Major Knighton, his secretary. Unless, of course, Mademoiselle would prefer to wait a fortnight or so."

If there was one thing of which Poirot was tolerably certain, it was that to a temperament such as Mirelle's the mere word "wait" was anathema.

"*Eh bien*, I will speak, Messieurs," she cried. "I have been patient. I have held my hand. And for what? That I should be insulted! Yes, insulted! Ah! Does he think to treat Mirelle like that? To throw her off like an old glove. I tell you never has a man tired of me. Always it is I who tire of them."

She paced up and down the room, her slender body trembling with rage. A small table impeded her free passage and she flung it from her into a corner, where it splintered against the wall.

"That is what I will do to him," she cried, "and that!"

Picking up a glass bowl filled with lilies she flung it into the grate, where it smashed into a hundred pieces.

Knighton was looking at her with cold British disapproval. He felt embarrassed and ill at ease. Poirot, on the other hand, with twinkling eyes was thoroughly enjoying the scene.

"Ah, it is magnificent!" he cried. "It can be seen—Madame has a temperament."

"I am an artist," said Mirelle; "every artist has a temperament. I told Dereek to beware, and he would not listen." She whirled round on Poirot suddenly. "It is true, is it not, that he wants to marry that English miss?"

Poirot coughed.

"*On m'a dit*," he murmured, "that he adores her passionately."

Mirelle came towards them.

"He murdered his wife," she screamed. "There—now you have it! He told me beforehand that he meant to do it. He had got to an *impasse*—zut! he took the easiest way out."

"You say that M. Kettering murdered his wife."

"Yes, yes, yes. Have I not told you so?"

"The police," murmured Poirot, "will need proof of that—er—statement."

"I tell you I saw him come out of her compartment that night on the train."

"When?" asked Poirot sharply.

"Just before the train reached Lyons."

"You will swear to that, Mademoiselle?"

It was a different Poirot who spoke now, sharp and decisive.

"Yes."

There was a moment's silence. Mirelle was panting, and her eyes, half defiant, half frightened, went from the face of one man to the other.

"This is a serious matter, Mademoiselle," said the detective. "You realize how serious?"

"Certainly I do."

"That is well," said Poirot. "Then you understand, Mademoiselle, that no time must be lost. You will, perhaps, accompany us immediately to the office of the Examining Magistrate."

Mirelle was taken aback. She hesitated, but, as Poirot had foreseen, she had no loophole for escape.

"Very well," she muttered. "I will fetch a coat."

Left alone together, Poirot and Knighton exchanged glances.

"It is necessary to act while—how do you say it?—the iron is hot," murmured Poirot. "She is temperamental; in an hour's time, maybe, she will repent, and she will wish to draw back. We must prevent that at all costs."

Mirelle reappeared, wrapped in a sand-coloured velvet wrap trimmed with leopard skin. She looked not altogether unlike a leopardess, tawny and dangerous. Her eyes still flashed with anger and determination.

They found M. Caux and the Examining Magistrate together. A few brief introductory words from Poirot, and Mademoiselle Mirelle was courteously entreated to tell her tale. This she did in much the same words as she had done to Knighton and Poirot, though with far more soberness of manner.

"This is an extraordinary story, Mademoiselle," said M. Carrège slowly. He leant back in his chair, adjusted his pince-nez, and looked keenly and searchingly at the dancer through them.

"You wish us to believe M. Kettering actually boasted of the crime to you beforehand?"

"Yes, yes. She was too healthy, he said. If she were to die it must be an accident—he would arrange it all."

"You are aware, Mademoiselle," said M. Carrège sternly, "that you are making yourself out to be an accessory before the fact?"

"Me? But not the least in the world, Monsieur. Not for a moment did I take that statement seriously. Ah no, indeed! I know men, Monsieur; they say many wild things. It would be an odd state of affairs if one were to take all they said *au pied de la lettre*."

The Examining Magistrate raised his eyebrows.

"We are to take it, then, that you regarded M. Kettering's threats as mere idle words? May I ask, Mademoiselle, what made you throw up your engagements in London and come out to the Riviera?"

Mirelle looked at him with melting black eyes.

"I wished to be with the man I loved," she said simply. "Was it so unnatural?"

Poirot interpolated a question gently.

"Was it, then, at M. Kettering's wish that you accompanied him to Nice?"

Mirelle seemed to find a little difficulty in answering this. She hesitated perceptibly before she spoke. When she did, it was with a haughty indifference of manner.

"In such matters I please myself, Monsieur," she said.

That the answer was not an answer at all was noted by all three men. They said nothing.

"When were you first convinced that M. Kettering had murdered his wife?"

"As I tell you, Monsieur, I saw M. Kettering come out of his wife's compartment just before the train drew into Lyons. There was a look on his face—ah! at the moment I could not understand it—a look haunted and terrible. I shall never forget it."

Her voice rose shrilly, and she flung out her arms in an extravagant gesture.

"Quite so," said M. Carrège.

"Afterwards, when I found that Madame Kettering was dead when the train left Lyons, then—then I knew!"

"And still—you did not go to the police, Mademoiselle," said the Commissary mildly.

Mirelle glanced at him superbly; she was clearly enjoying herself in the rôle she was playing.

"Shall I betray my lover?" she asked. "Ah no; do not ask a woman to do that."

"Yet now—" hinted M. Caux.

"Now it is different. He has betrayed me! Shall I suffer that in silence...?"

The Examining Magistrate checked her.

"Quite so, quite so," he murmured soothingly. "And now, Mademoiselle, perhaps you will read over the statement of what you have told us, see that it is correct, and sign it."

Mirelle wasted no time on the document.

"Yes, yes," she said, "it is correct." She rose to her feet. "You require me no longer, Messieurs?"

"At present, no, Mademoiselle."

"And Dereek will be arrested?"

"At once, Mademoiselle."

Mirelle laughed cruelly and drew her fur draperies closer about her.

"He should have thought of this before he insulted me," she cried.

"There is one little matter"—Poirot coughed apologetically—"just a matter of detail."

"Yes?"

"What makes you think Madame Kettering was dead when the train left Lyons?"

Mirelle stared.

"But she *was* dead."

"Was she?"

"Yes, of course. I—"

She came to an abrupt stop. Poirot was regarding her intently, and he saw the wary look that came into her eyes.

"I have been told so. Everybody says so."

"Oh," said Poirot, "I was not aware that the fact had been mentioned outside the Examining Magistrate's office."

Mirelle appeared somewhat discomposed.

"One hears those things," she said vaguely; "they get about. Somebody told me. I can't remember who it was."

She moved to the door. M. Caux sprang forward to open it for her, and as he did so, Poirot's voice rose gently once more.

"And the jewels? Pardon, Mademoiselle. Can you tell me anything about those?"

"The jewels? What jewels?"

"The rubies of Catherine the Great. Since you hear so much, you must have heard of them."

"I know nothing about any jewels," said Mirelle sharply.

She went out, closing the door behind her. M. Caux came back to his chair; the Examining Magistrate sighed.

"What a fury!" he said, "but *diablement chic*, I wonder if she is telling the truth? I think so."

"There is *some* truth in her story, certainly," said Poirot. "We have confirmation of it from Miss Grey. She was looking down the corridor a short time before the train reached Lyons and she saw M. Kettering go into his wife's compartment."

"The case against him seems quite clear," said the Commissary, sighing; "it is a thousand pities," he murmured.

"How do you mean?" asked Poirot.

"It has been the ambition of my life to lay the Comte de la Roche by the heels. This time, *ma foi*, I thought we had got him. This other—it is not nearly so satisfactory."

M. Carrège rubbed his nose.

"If anything goes wrong," he observed cautiously, "it will be most awkward. M. Kettering is of the aristocracy. It will get into the newspapers. If we have made a mistake—" He shrugged his shoulders forebodingly.

"The jewels now," said the Commissary, "what do you think he has done with them?"

"He took them for a plant, of course," said M. Carrège; "they must have been a great inconvenience to him and very awkward to dispose of."

Poirot smiled.

"I have an idea of my own about the jewels. Tell me, Messieurs, what do you know of a man called the Marquis?"

The Commissary leant forward excitedly.

"The Marquis," he said, "the Marquis? Do you think he is mixed up in this affair, M. Poirot?"

"I ask you what you know of him."

The Commissary made an expressive grimace.

"Not as much as we should like to," he observed ruefully. "He works behind the scenes, you understand. He has underlings who do his dirty work for him. But he is someone high up. That we are sure of. He does not come from the criminal classes."

"A Frenchman?"

"Y—es. At least we believe so. But we are not sure. He has worked in France, in England, in America. There was a series of robberies in Switzerland last autumn which were laid at his door. By all accounts he is a *grand seigneur*, speaking French and English with equal perfection and his origin is a mystery."

Poirot nodded and rose to take his departure.

"Can you tell us nothing more, M. Poirot," urged the Commissary.

"At present, no," said Poirot, "but I may have news awaiting me at my hotel."

M. Carrège looked uncomfortable. "If the Marquis is concerned in this—" he began, and then stopped.

"It upsets our ideas," complained M. Caux.

"It does not upset mine," said Poirot. "On the contrary, I think it agrees with them very well. Au revoir, Messieurs; if news of any importance comes to me I will communicate it to you immediately."

He walked back to his hotel with a grave face. In his absence a telegram had come to him. Taking a paper-cutter from his pocket, he slit it open. It was a long telegram, and he read it over twice before slowly putting it in his pocket. Upstairs, George was awaiting his master.

"I am fatigued, Georges, much fatigued. Will you order for me a small pot of chocolate?"

The chocolate was duly ordered and brought, and George set it at the little table at his master's elbow. As he was preparing to retire, Poirot spoke:

"I believe, Georges, that you have a good knowledge of the English aristocracy?" murmured Poirot.

George smiled apologetically.

"I think that I might say that I have, sir," he replied.

"I suppose that it is your opinion, Georges, that criminals are invariably drawn from the lower orders."

"Not always, sir. There was great trouble with one of the Duke of Devize's younger sons. He left Eton under a cloud, and after that he caused great anxiety on several occasions. The police would not accept the view that it was kleptomania. A very clever young gentleman, sir, but vicious through and through, if you take my meaning. His Grace shipped him to Australia, and I hear he was convicted out there under another name. Very odd, sir, but there it is. The young gentleman, I need hardly say, was not in want financially."

Poirot nodded his head slowly.

"Love of excitement," he murmured, "and a little kink in the brain somewhere. I wonder now—"

He drew out the telegram from his pocket and read it again.

"Then there was Lady Mary Fox's daughter," continued the

valet in a mood of reminiscence. "Swindled tradespeople some-thing shocking, she did. Very worrying to the best families, if I may say so, and there are many other queer cases I could mention."

"You have a wide experience, Georges," murmured Poirot. "I often wonder having lived so exclusively with titled families that you demean yourself by coming as a valet to me. I put it down to love of excitement on your part."

"Not exactly, sir," said George. "I happened to see in *Society Snippets* that you had been received at Buckingham Palace. That was just when I was looking for a new situation. His Majesty, so it said, had been most gracious and friendly and thought very highly of your abilities."

"Ah," said Poirot, "one always likes to know the reason for things."

He remained in thought for a few moments and then said:

"You rang up Mademoiselle Papopolous?"

"Yes, sir; she and her father will be pleased to dine with you to-night."

"Ah," said Poirot thoughtfully. He drank off his chocolate, set the cup and saucer neatly in the middle of the tray, and spoke gently, more to himself than to the valet.

"The squirrel, my good Georges, collects nuts. He stores them up in the autumn so that they may be of advantage to him later. To make a success of humanity, Georges, we must profit by the lessons of those below us in the animal kingdom. I have always done so. I have been the cat, watching at the mouse hole. I have been the good dog following up the scent, and not taking my nose from the trail. And also, my good Georges, I have been the squirrel. I have stored away the little fact here, the little fact there. I go now to my store and I take out one particular nut, a nut that I stored away—let me see, seventeen years ago. You follow me, Georges?"

"I should hardly have thought, sir," said George, "that nuts would have kept so long as that, though I know one can do won-ders with preserving bottles."

Poirot looked at him and smiled.

TWENTY-EIGHT
Poirot Plays the Squirrel

Poirot started to keep his dinner appointment with a margin of three-quarters of an hour to spare. He had an object in this. The car took him, not straight to Monte Carlo, but to Lady Tamplin's house at Cap Martin, where he asked for Miss Grey. The ladies were dressing and Poirot was shown into a small salon to wait, and here, after a lapse of three or four minutes, Lenox Tamplin came to him.

"Katherine is not quite ready yet," she said. "Can I give her a message, or would you rather wait until she comes down?"

Poirot looked at her thoughtfully. He was a minute or two in replying, as though something of great weight hung upon his decision. Apparently the answer to such a simple question mattered.

"No," he said at last, "no, I do not think it is necessary that I should wait to see Mademoiselle Katherine. I think, perhaps, that it is better that I should not. These things are sometimes difficult."

Lenox waited politely, her eyebrows slightly raised.

"I have a piece of news," continued Poirot. "You will, perhaps, tell your friend. M. Kettering was arrested to-night for the murder of his wife."

"You want me to tell Katherine that?" asked Lenox. She breathed rather hard, as though she had been running; her face, Poirot thought, looked white and strained—rather noticeably so.

"If you please, Mademoiselle."

194

"Why?" said Lenox. "Do you think Katherine will be upset? Do you think she cares?"

"I don't know, Mademoiselle," said Poirot. "See, I admit it frankly. As a rule I know everything, but in this case, I—well, I do not. You, perhaps, know better than I do."

"Yes," said Lenox, "I know—but I am not going to tell you all the same."

She paused for a minute or two, her dark brows drawn together in a frown.

"You believe he did it?" she said abruptly.

Poirot shrugged his shoulders.

"The police say so."

"Ah," said Lenox, "hedging, are you? So there is something to hedge about."

Again she was silent, frowning. Poirot said gently:

"You have known Derek Kettering a long time, have you not?"

"Off and on ever since I was a kid," said Lenox gruffly.

Poirot nodded his head several times without speaking.

With one of her brusque movements Lenox drew forward a chair and sat down on it, her elbows on the table and her face supported by her hands. Sitting thus, she looked directly across the table at Poirot.

"What have they got to go on?" she demanded. "Motive, I suppose. Probably came into money at her death."

"He came into two million."

"And if she had not died he would have been ruined?"

"Yes."

"But there must have been more than that," persisted Lenox. "He travelled by the same train, I know, but—that would not be enough to go on by itself."

"A cigarette case with the letter 'K' on it which did not belong to Mrs. Kettering was found in her carriage, and he was seen by two people entering and leaving the compartment just before the train got into Lyons."

195

"What two people?"

"Your friend Miss Grey was one of them. The other was Mademoiselle Mirelle, the dancer."

"And he, Derek, what has he got to say about it?" demanded Lenox sharply.

"He denies having entered his wife's compartment at all," said Poirot.

"Fool!" said Lenox crisply, frowning. "Just before Lyons, you say? Does nobody know when—when she died?"

"The doctors' evidence necessarily cannot be very definite," said Poirot; "they are inclined to think that death was unlikely to have occurred after leaving Lyons. And we know this much, that a few moments after leaving Lyons Mrs. Kettering was dead."

"How do you know that?"

Poirot was smiling rather oddly to himself.

"Someone else went into her compartment and found her dead."

"And they did not rouse the train?"

"No."

"Why was that?"

"Doubtless they had their reasons."

Lenox looked at him sharply.

"Do you know the reason?"

"I think so—yes."

Lenox sat still turning things over in her mind. Poirot watched her in silence. At last she looked up. A soft colour had come into her cheeks and her eyes were shining.

"You think someone on the train must have killed her, but that need not be so at all. What is to stop anyone swinging themselves on to the train when it stopped at Lyons? They could go straight to her compartment, strangle her, and take the rubies and drop off the train again without anyone being the wiser. She may have been actually killed while the train was in Lyons station. Then she would have been alive when Derek went in, and dead when the other person found her."

Poirot leant back in his chair. He drew a deep breath. He looked across at the girl and nodded his head three times, then he heaved a sigh.

"Mademoiselle," he said, "what you have said there is very just—very true. I was struggling in darkness, and you have shown me a light. There was a point that puzzled me and you have made it plain."

He got up.

"And Derek?" said Lenox.

"Who knows?" said Poirot, with a shrug of his shoulders. "But I will tell you this, Mademoiselle. I am not satisfied; no, I, Hercule Poirot, am not yet satisfied. It may be that this very night I shall learn something more. At least, I go to try."

"You are meeting someone?"

"Yes."

"Someone who knows something?"

"Someone who might know something. In these matters one must leave no stone unturned. Au revoir, Mademoiselle."

Lenox accompanied him to the door.

"Have I—helped?" she asked.

Poirot's face softened as he looked up at her standing on the doorstep above him.

"Yes, Mademoiselle, you have helped. If things are very dark, always remember that."

When the car had driven off he relapsed into a frowning absorption, but in his eyes was that faint green light which was always the precursor of the triumph to be.

He was a few minutes late at the rendezvous, and found that M. Papopolous and his daughter had arrived before him. His apologies were abject, and he outdid himself in politeness and small attentions. The Greek was looking particularly benign and noble this evening, a sorrowful patriarch of blameless life. Zia was looking handsome and good humoured. The dinner was a pleasant one.

Poirot was his best and most sparkling self. He told anecdotes, he made jokes, he paid graceful compliments to Zia Papopolous, and he told many interesting incidents of his career. The menu was a carefully selected one, and the wine was excellent.

At the close of dinner M. Papopolous inquired politely:

"And the tip I gave you? You have had your little flutter on the horse?"

"I am in communication with—er—my bookmaker," replied Poirot.

The eyes of the two men met.

"A well-known horse, eh?"

"No," said Poirot; "it is what our friends, the English, call a dark horse."

"Ah!" said M. Papopolous thoughtfully.

"Now we must step across to the Casino and have our little flutter at the roulette table," cried Poirot gaily.

At the Casino the party separated, Poirot devoting himself solely to Zia, whilst Papopolous himself drifted away.

Poirot was not fortunate, but Zia had a run of good luck, and had soon won a few thousand francs.

"It would be as well," she observed drily to Poirot, "if I stopped now."

Poirot's eyes twinkled.

"Superb!" he exclaimed. "You are the daughter of your father, Mademoiselle Zia. To know when to stop. Ah! that is the art."

He looked round the rooms.

"I cannot see your father anywhere about," he remarked carelessly. "I will fetch your cloak for you, Mademoiselle, and we will go out in the gardens."

He did not, however, go straight to the cloak-room. His sharp eyes had seen but a little while before the departure of M. Papopolous. He was anxious to know what had become of the wily Greek. He ran him to earth unexpectedly in the big entrance hall. He was standing by one of the pillars, talking to a lady who had just arrived. The lady was Mirelle.

Poirot sidled unostentatiously round the room. He arrived at the other side of the pillar, and unnoticed by the two who were talking together in an animated fashion—or rather, that is to say, the dancer was talking, Papopolous contributing an occasional monosyllable and a good many expressive gestures.

"I tell you I must have time," the dancer was saying. "If you give me time I will get the money."

"To wait"—the Greek shrugged his shoulders—"it is awkward."

"Only a very little while," pleaded the other. "Ah! but you must! A week—ten days—that is all I ask. You can be sure of your affair. The money will be forthcoming."

Papopolous shifted a little and looked round him uneasily—to find Poirot almost at his elbow with a beaming innocent face.

"*Ah! vous voilà*, M. Papopolous. I have been looking for you. It is permitted that I take Mademoiselle Zia for a little turn in the gardens? Good evening, Mademoiselle." He bowed very low to Mirelle. "A thousand pardons that I did not see you immediately."

The dancer accepted his greetings rather impatiently. She was clearly annoyed at the interruption of her *tête-à-tête*. Poirot was quick to take the hint. Papopolous had already murmured: "Certainly—but certainly," and Poirot withdrew forthwith.

He fetched Zia's cloak, and together they strolled out into the gardens.

"This is where the suicides take place," said Zia.

Poirot shrugged his shoulders. "So it is said. Men are foolish, are they not, Mademoiselle? To eat, to drink, to breathe the good air, it is a very pleasant thing, Mademoiselle. One is foolish to leave all that simply because one has no money—or because the heart aches. *L'amour*, it causes many fatalities, does it not?"

Zia laughed.

"You should not laugh at love, Mademoiselle," said Poirot, shaking an energetic forefinger at her. "You who are young and beautiful."

"Hardly that," said Zia; "you forget that I am thirty-three, M. Poirot. I am frank with you, because it is no good being otherwise. As you told my father, it is exactly seventeen years since you aided us in Paris that time."

"When I look at you, it seems much less," said Poirot gallantly. "You were then very much as you are now, Mademoiselle, a little thinner, a little paler, a little more serious. Sixteen years old and fresh from your pension. Not quite the *petite pensionnaire*, not quite a woman. You were very delicious, very charming, Mademoiselle Zia; others thought so too, without doubt."

"At sixteen," said Zia, "one is simple and a little fool."

"That may be," said Poirot, "yes, that well may be. At sixteen one is credulous, is one not? One believes what one is told."

If he saw the quick sideways glance that the girl shot at him, he pretended not to have done so. He continued dreamily: "It was a curious affair that, altogether. Your father, Mademoiselle, has never understood the true inwardness of it."

"No?"

"When he asked me for details, for explanations, I said to him thus: 'Without scandal, I have got back for you that which was lost. You must ask no questions.' Do you know, Mademoiselle, why I said these things?"

"I have no idea," said the girl coldly.

"It was because I had a soft spot in my heart for a little pensionnaire, so pale, so thin, so serious."

"I don't understand what you are talking about," cried Zia angrily.

"Do you not, Mademoiselle? Have you forgotten Antonio Pirezzio?"

He heard the quick intake of her breath—almost a gasp.

"He came to work as an assistant in the shop, but not thus could he have got hold of what he wanted. An assistant can lift his eyes to his master's daughter, can he not? If he is young and handsome with a glib tongue. And since they cannot make love all the time, they must occasionally talk of things that interest them both—such as that very interesting thing which was temporarily in M. Papopolous' possession. And since, as you say, Mademoiselle, the young are foolish and credulous, it was easy to believe him and to give him a sight of that particular thing, to show him where it was kept. And afterwards when it is gone—when the unbelievable catastrophe has happened. Alas! the poor little pensionnaire. What a terrible position she is in. She is frightened, the poor little one. To speak or not to speak? And then there comes along that excellent fellow, Hercule Poirot. Almost a miracle it must have been, the way things arranged themselves. The priceless heirlooms are restored and there are no awkward questions."

Zia turned on him fiercely.

"You have known all the time? Who told you? Was it—was it Antonio?"

Poirot shook his head.

"No one told me," he said quietly. "I guessed. It was a good guess, was it not, Mademoiselle? You see, unless you are good at guessing, it is not much use being a detective."

The girl walked along beside him for some minutes in silence. Then she said in a hard voice:

"Well, what are you going to do about it, are you going to tell my father?"

"No," said Poirot sharply. "Certainly not."

She looked at him curiously.

"You want something from me?"

"I want your help, Mademoiselle."

"What makes you think that I can help you?"

"I do not think so. I only hope so."

"And if I do not help you, then—you will tell my father?"

"But no, but no! Debarrass yourself of that idea, Mademoiselle. I am not a blackmailer. I do not hold your secret over your head and threaten you with it."

"If I refuse to help you—" began the girl slowly.

"Then you refuse, and that is that."

"Then why—" she stopped.

"Listen, and I will tell you why. Women, Mademoiselle, are generous. If they can render a service to one who has rendered a service to them, they will do it. I was generous once to you, Mademoiselle. When I might have spoken, I held my tongue."

There was another silence; then the girl said, "My father gave you a hint the other day."

"It was very kind of him."

"I do not think," said Zia slowly, "that there is anything that I can add to that."

If Poirot was disappointed he did not show it. Not a muscle of his face changed.

"*Eh bien!*" he said cheerfully, "then we must talk of other things."

And he proceeded to chat gaily. The girl was *distraite*, however, and her answers were mechanical and not always to the point. It was when they were approaching the Casino once more that she seemed to come to a decision.

"M. Poirot?"

"Yes, Mademoiselle?"

"I—I should like to help you if I could."

"You are very amiable, Mademoiselle—very amiable."

Again there was a pause. Poirot did not press her. He was quite content to wait and let her take her own time.

"Ah bah," said Zia, "after all, why should I not tell you? My father is cautious—always cautious in everything he says. But I know that with you it is not necessary. You have told us it is only the murderer you seek, and that you are not concerned over the jewels. I believe you. You were quite right when you guessed that we were in Nice because of the rubies. They have been handed over here according to plan. My father has them now. He gave you a hint the other day as to who our mysterious client was."

"The Marquis?" murmured Poirot softly.

"Yes, the Marquis."

"Have you ever seen the Marquis, Mademoiselle Zia?"

"Once," said the girl. "But not very well," she added. "It was through a keyhole."

"That always presents difficulties," said Poirot sympathetically, "but all the same you saw him. You would know him again?"

Zia shook her head.

"He wore a mask," she explained.

"Young or old?"

"He had white hair. It may have been a wig, it may not. It fitted very well. But I do not think he was old. His walk was young, and so was his voice."

"His voice?" said Poirot thoughtfully. "Ah, his voice! Would you know it again, Mademoiselle Zia?"

"I might," said the girl.

"You were interested in him, eh? It was that that took you to the keyhole."

Zia nodded.

"Yes, yes. I was curious. One had heard so much—he is not the ordinary thief—he is more like a figure of history or romance."

"Yes," said Poirot thoughtfully, "yes; perhaps so."

"But it is not this that I meant to tell you," said Zia. "It was just one other little fact that I thought might be—well—useful to you."

"Yes?" said Poirot encouragingly.

"The rubies, as I say, were handed over to my father here at Nice. I did not see the person who handed them over, but—"

"Yes?"

"I know one thing. *It was a woman.*"

TWENTY-NINE
A Letter From Home

*D*ear Katherine—Living among grand friends as you are doing now, I don't suppose you will care to hear any of our news; but as I always thought you were a sensible girl, perhaps you are a trifle less swollen-headed than I suppose. Everything goes on much the same here. There was great trouble about the new curate, who is scandalously high. In my view, he is neither more nor less than a Roman. Everybody has spoken to the Vicar about it, but you know what the Vicar is—all Christian charity and no proper spirit. I have had a lot of trouble with maids lately. That girl Annie was no good—skirts up to her knees and wouldn't wear sensible woollen stockings. Not one of them can bear being spoken to. I have had a lot of pain with my rheumatism one way and another, and Dr. Harris persuaded me to go and see a London specialist—a waste of three guineas and a railway fare, as I told him; but by waiting until Wednesday I managed to get a cheap return. The London doctor pulled a long face and talked all round about and never straight out, until I said to him, 'I'm a plain woman, Doctor, and I like things to be plainly stated. Is it cancer, or is it not?' And then, of course, he had to say it was. They say a year with care, and not too much pain, though I am sure I can bear pain as well as any other Christian woman. Life seems rather lonely at times, with most of my friends dead or gone before. I wish you were in St. Mary Mead, my dear, and that is a fact.

If you hadn't come into this money and gone off into grand society, I would have offered you double the salary poor Jane gave you to come and look after me; but there—there's no good wanting what we can't get. However, if things should go ill with you—and that is always possible. I have heard no end of tales of bogus noblemen marrying girls and getting hold of their money and then leaving them at the church door. I dare say you are too sensible for anything of the kind to happen to you, but one never knows; and never having had much attention of any kind it might easily go to your head now. So just in case, my dear, remember there is always a home for you here; and though a plain-spoken woman I am a warm-hearted one too.—Your affectionate old friend,

"Amelia Viner."

"P.S.—*I saw a mention of you in the paper with your cousin, Viscountess Tamplin, and I cut it out and put it with my cuttings. I prayed for you on Sunday that you might be kept from pride and vainglory.*"

Katherine read this characteristic epistle through twice, then she laid it down and stared out of her bedroom window across the blue waters of the Mediterranean. She felt a curious lump in her throat. A sudden wave of longing for St. Mary Mead swept over her. So full of familiar, everyday, stupid little things—and yet—home. She felt very inclined to lay her head down on her arms and indulge in a real good cry.

Lenox, coming in at the moment, saved her.

"Hello, Katherine," said Lenox. "I say—what is the matter?"

"Nothing," said Katherine, grabbing up Miss Viner's letter and thrusting it into her handbag.

"You looked rather queer," said Lenox. "I say—I hope you don't mind—I rang up your detective friend, M. Poirot, and asked him to lunch with us in Nice. I said you wanted to see him, as I thought he might not come for me."

"Did you want to see him then?" asked Katherine.

"Yes," said Lenox. "I have rather lost my heart to him. I never met a man before whose eyes were really green like a cat's."

"All right," said Katherine. She spoke listlessly. The last few days had been trying. Derek Kettering's arrest had been the topic of the hour, and the Blue Train Mystery had been thrashed out from every conceivable standpoint.

"I have ordered the car," said Lenox, "and I have told Mother some lie or other—unfortunately I can't remember exactly what; but it won't matter, as she never remembers. If she knew where we were going, she would want to come too, to pump M. Poirot."

The two girls arrived at the Negresco to find Poirot waiting.

He was full of Gallic politeness, and showered so many compliments upon the two girls that they were soon helpless with laughter; yet for all that the meal was not a gay one. Katherine was dreamy and distracted, and Lenox made bursts of conversation, interspersed by silences. As they were sitting on the terrace sipping their coffee she suddenly attacked Poirot bluntly.

"How are things going? You know what I mean?"

Poirot shrugged his shoulders. "They take their course," he said.

"And you are just letting them take their course?"

He looked at Lenox a little sadly.

"You are young, Mademoiselle, but there are three things that cannot be hurried—*le bon Dieu*, Nature, and old people."

"Nonsense!" said Lenox. "You are not old."

"Ah, it is pretty what you say there."

"Here is Major Knighton," said Lenox.

Katherine looked round quickly and then turned back again.

"He is with Mr. Van Aldin," continued Lenox. "There is something I want to ask Major Knighton about. I won't be a minute."

Left alone together, Poirot bent forward and murmured to Katherine:

"You are *distraite*, Mademoiselle; your thoughts, they are far away, are they not?"

"Just as far as England, no farther."

Guided by a sudden impulse, she took the letter she had received that morning and handed it across to him to read.

"That is the first word that has come to me from my old life; somehow or other—it hurts."

He read it through and then handed it back to her. "So you are going back to St. Mary Mead?" he said slowly.

"No, I am not," said Katherine; "why should I?"

"Ah," said Poirot, "it is my mistake. You will excuse me one little minute."

He strolled across to where Lenox Tamplin was talking to Van Aldin and Knighton. The American looked old and haggard. He greeted Poirot with a curt nod but without any other sign of animation.

As he turned to reply to some observation made by Lenox, Poirot drew Knighton aside.

"M. Van Aldin looks ill," he said.

"Do you wonder?" asked Knighton. "The scandal of Derek Kettering's arrest has about put the lid on things, as far as he is concerned. He is even regretting that he asked you to find out the truth."

"He should go back to England," said Poirot.

"We are going the day after to-morrow."

"That is good news," said Poirot.

He hesitated, and looked across the terrace to where Katherine was sitting.

"I wish," he murmured, "that you could tell Miss Grey that."

"Tell her what?"

"That you—I mean that M. Van Aldin is returning to England."

Knighton looked a little puzzled, but he readily crossed the terrace and joined Katherine.

Poirot saw him go with a satisfied nod of the head, and then joined Lenox and the American. After a minute or two they joined the others. Conversation was general for a few minutes, then the millionaire and his secretary departed. Poirot also prepared to take his departure.

"A thousand thanks for your hospitality, Mesdemoiselles," he cried; "it has been a most charming luncheon. *Ma foi*, I needed it!" He swelled out his chest and thumped it. "I am now a lion—a giant. Ah, Mademoiselle Katherine, you have not seen me as I can be. You have seen the gentle, the calm Hercule Poirot; but there is another Hercule Poirot. I go now to bully, to threaten, to strike terror into the hearts of those who listen to me."

He looked at them in a self-satisfied way, and they both appeared to be duly impressed, though Lenox was biting her under lip, and the corners of Katherine's mouth had a suspicious twitch.

"And I shall do it," he said gravely. "Oh yes, I shall succeed."

He had gone but a few steps when Katherine's voice made him turn.

"M. Poirot, I—I want to tell you. I think you were right in what you said. I am going back to England almost immediately."

Poirot stared at her very hard, and under the directness of his scrutiny she blushed.

"I see," he said gravely.

"I don't believe you do," said Katherine.

"I know more than you think, Mademoiselle," he said quietly.

He left her, with an odd little smile upon his lips. Entering a waiting car, he drove to Antibes.

Hippolyte, the Comte de la Roche's wooden-faced man-servant, was busy at the Villa Marina polishing his master's beautiful cut table glass. The Comte de la Roche himself had gone to Monte Carlo for the day. Chancing to look out of the window, Hippolyte espied a visitor walking briskly up to the hall door, a visitor of so uncommon a type that Hippolyte, experienced as he was, had some difficulty in placing him. Calling to his wife, Marie, who was busy in the kitchen, he drew her attention to what he called *ce type là*.

"It is not the police again?" said Marie anxiously.

"Look for yourself," said Hippolyte.

Marie looked.

"Certainly not the police," she declared. "I am glad."

"They have not really worried us much," said Hippolyte. "In fact, but for Monsieur le Comte's warning, I should never have guessed that stranger at the wine-shop to be what he was."

The hall bell pealed and Hippolyte, in a grave and decorous manner, went to open the door.

"M. le Comte, I regret to say, is not at home."

The little man with the large moustaches beamed placidly.

"I know that," he replied. "You are Hippolyte Flavelle, are you not?"

"Yes, Monsieur, that is my name."

"And you have a wife, Marie Flavelle?"

"Yes, Monsieur, but—"

"I desire to see you both," said the stranger, and he stepped nimbly past Hippolyte into the hall.

"Your wife is doubtless in the kitchen," he said. "I will go there."

Before Hippolyte could recover his breath, the other had selected the right door at the back of the hall and passed along the passage and into the kitchen, where Marie paused open-mouthed to stare at him.

"*Voilà*," said the stranger, and sank into a wooden arm-chair; "I am Hercule Poirot."

"Yes, Monsieur?"

"You do not know the name?"

"I have never heard it," said Hippolyte.

"Permit me to say that you have been badly educated. It is the name of one of the great ones of this world."

He sighed and folded his hands across his chest.

Hippolyte and Marie were staring at him uneasily. They were at a loss what to make of this unexpected and extremely strange visitor.

"Monsieur desires—" murmured Hippolyte mechanically.

"I desire to know why you have lied to the police."

"Monsieur!" cried Hippolyte; "I—lied to the police? Never have I done such a thing."

M. Poirot shook his head.

"You are wrong," he said; "you have done it on several occasions. Let me see." He took a small notebook from his pocket and consulted it. "Ah, yes; on seven occasions at least. I will recite them to you."

In a gentle unemotional voice he proceeded to outline the seven occasions.

Hippolyte was taken aback.

"But it is not of these past lapses that I wish to speak," continued Poirot, "only, my dear friend, do not get into the habit of thinking yourself too clever. I come now to the particular lie in which I am concerned—your statement that the Comte de la Roche arrived at this villa on the morning of 14th January."

"But that was no lie, Monsieur; that was the truth. Monsieur le Comte arrived here on the morning of Tuesday, the 14th. That is so, Marie, is it not?"

Marie assented eagerly.

"Ah, yes, that is quite right. I remember it perfectly."

"Ah," said Poirot, "and what did you give your good master for *déjeuner* that day?"

"I—" Marie paused, trying to collect herself.

"Odd," said Poirot, "how one remembers some things—and forgets others."

He leant forward and struck the table a blow with his fist; his eyes flashed with anger.

"Yes, yes, it is as I say. You tell your lies and you think nobody knows. But there are two people who know. Yes—two people. One is *le bon Dieu*—"

He raised a hand to heaven, and then settling himself back in his chair and shutting his eyelids, he murmured comfortably:

"And the other is Hercule Poirot."

"I assure you, Monsieur, you are completely mistaken. Monsieur le Comte left Paris on Monday night—"

"True," said Poirot—"by the Rapide. I do not know where he broke his journey. Perhaps you do not know that. What I do know is that he arrived here on Wednesday morning, and not on Tuesday morning."

"Monsieur is mistaken," said Marie stolidly.

Poirot rose to his feet.

"Then the law must take its course," he murmured. "A pity."

"What do you mean, Monsieur?" asked Marie, with a shade of uneasiness.

"You will be arrested and held as accomplices concerned in the murder of Mrs. Kettering, the English lady who was killed."

"Murder!"

The man's face had gone chalk white, his knees knocked together. Marie dropped the rolling-pin and began to weep.

"But it is impossible—impossible. I thought—"

"Since you stick to your story, there is nothing to be said. I think you are both foolish."

He was turning towards the door when an agitated voice arrested him.

"Monsieur, Monsieur, just a little moment. I—I had no idea that it was anything of this kind. I—I thought it was just a matter concerning a lady. There have been little awkwardnesses with the police over ladies before. But murder—that is very different."

"I have no patience with you," cried Poirot. He turned round on them and angrily shook his fist in Hippolyte's face. "Am I to stop here all day, arguing with a couple of imbeciles thus? It is the truth I want. If you will not give it to me, that is your look out. *For the last time, when did Monsieur le Comte arrive at the Villa Marina—Tuesday morning or Wednesday morning?*"

"Wednesday," gasped the man, and behind him Marie nodded confirmation.

Poirot regarded them for a minute or two, then inclined his head gravely.

"You are wise, my children," he said quietly. "Very nearly you were in serious trouble."

He left the Villa Marina, smiling to himself.

"One guess, confirmed," he murmured to himself. "Shall I take a chance on the other?"

It was six o'clock when the card of Monsieur Hercule Poirot was brought up to Mirelle. She stared at it for a moment or two, and then nodded. When Poirot entered, he found her walking up and down the room feverishly. She turned on him furiously.

"Well?" she cried. "Well? What is it now? Have you not tortured me enough, all of you? Have you not made me betray my poor Dereek? What more do you want?"

"Just one little question, Mademoiselle. After the train left Lyons, when you entered Mrs. Kettering's compartment—"

"What is that?"

Poirot looked at her with an air of mild reproach and began again.

"I say when you entered Mrs. Kettering's compartment—"

"I never did."

"And found her—"

"I never did."

"Ah, sacré!"

He turned on her in a rage and shouted at her, so that she cowered back before him.

"Will you lie to me? I tell you I know what happened as well as though I had been there. You went into her compartment and you found her dead. I tell you I know it. To lie to me is dangerous. Be careful, Mademoiselle Mirelle."

Her eyes wavered beneath his gaze and fell.

"I—I didn't—" she began uncertainly and stopped.

"There is only one thing about which I wonder," said Poirot—"I wonder, Mademoiselle, if you found what you were looking for or whether—"

"Whether what?"

"Or whether someone else had been before you."

"I will answer no more questions," screamed the dancer. She tore herself away from Poirot's restraining hand, and flinging herself down on the floor in a frenzy, she screamed and sobbed. A frightened maid came rushing in.

Hercule Poirot shrugged his shoulders, raised his eyebrows, and quietly left the room.

But he seemed satisfied.

THIRTY

Miss Viner Gives Judgment

Katherine looked out of Miss Viner's bedroom window. It was raining, not violently, but with a quiet, well-bred persistence. The window looked out on a strip of front garden with a path down to the gate and neat little flower-beds on either side, where later roses and pinks and blue hyacinths would bloom.

Miss Viner was lying in a large Victorian bedstead. A tray with the remains of breakfast had been pushed to one side and she was busy opening her correspondence and making various caustic comments upon it.

Katherine had an open letter in her hand and was reading it through for the second time. It was dated from the Ritz Hotel, Paris.

"Chère Mademoiselle Katherine" (it began)—*"I trust that you are in good health and that the return to the English winter has not proved too depressing. Me, I prosecute my inquiries with the utmost diligence. Do not think that it is the holiday that I take here. Very shortly I shall be in England, and I hope then to have the pleasure of meeting you once more. It shall be so, shall it not? On arrival in London I shall write to you. You remember that we are the colleagues in this affair? But indeed I think you know that very well.*

"Be assured, Mademoiselle, of my most respectful and devoted sentiments.

"Hercule Poirot."

Katherine frowned slightly. It was as though something in the letter puzzled and intrigued her.

"A choir boys' picnic indeed," came from Miss Viner. "Tommy Saunders and Albert Dykes ought to be left behind, and I shan't subscribe to it unless they are. What those two boys think they are doing in church on Sundays I don't know. Tommy sang, 'O God, make speed to save us,' and never opened his lips again, and if Albert Dykes wasn't sucking a mint humbug, my nose is not what it is and always has been."

"I know, they are awful," agreed Katherine.

She opened her second letter, and a sudden flush came to her cheeks. Miss Viner's voice in the room seemed to recede into the far distance.

When she came back to a sense of her surroundings Miss Viner was bringing a long speech to a triumphant termination.

"And I said to her, 'Not at all. As it happens, Miss Grey is Lady Tamplin's own cousin.' What do you think of that?"

"Were you fighting my battles for me? That was very sweet of you."

"You can put it that way if you like. There is nothing to me in a title. Vicar's wife or no vicar's wife, that woman is a cat. Hinting you had bought your way into Society."

"Perhaps she was not so very far wrong."

"And look at you," continued Miss Viner. "Have you come back a stuck-up fine lady, as well you might have done? No, there you are, as sensible as ever you were, with a pair of good Balbriggan stockings on and sensible shoes. I spoke to Ellen about it only yesterday. 'Ellen,' I said, 'you look at Miss Grey. She has been hobnobbing with some of the greatest in the land, and does she go about as you do with skirts up to her knees and silk stockings that ladder when you look at them, and the most ridiculous shoes that ever I set eyes on?'"

Katherine smiled a little to herself; it had apparently been worth while to conform to Miss Viner's prejudices. The old lady went on with increasing gusto.

"It has been a great relief to me that you have not had your head turned. Only the other day I was looking for my cuttings. I have several about Lady Tamplin and her War Hospital and what not, but I cannot lay my hand upon them. I wish you would look, my dear; your eyesight is better than mine. They are all in a box in the bureau drawer."

Katherine glanced down at the letter in her hand and was about to speak, but checked herself, and going over to the bureau found the box of cuttings and began to look over them. Since her return to St. Mary Mead her heart had gone out to Miss Viner in admiration of the old woman's stoicism and pluck. She felt that there was little she could do for her old friend, but she knew from experience how much those seemingly small trifles meant to old people.

"Here is one," she said presently. "'Viscountess Tamplin, who is running her villa at Nice as an Officers' Hospital, has just been the victim of a sensational robbery, her jewels having been stolen. Amongst them were some very famous emeralds, heirlooms of the Tamplin family.'"

"Probably paste," said Miss Viner; "a lot of these Society women's jewels are."

"Here is another," said Katherine. "A picture of her, 'A charming camera study of Viscountess Tamplin with her little daughter Lenox.'"

"Let me look," said Miss Viner. "You can't see much of the child's face, can you? But I dare say that is just as well. Things go by contraries in this world and beautiful mothers have hideous children. I dare say the photographer realized that to take the back of the child's head was the best thing he could do for her."

Katherine laughed.

"'One of the smartest hostesses on the Riviera this season is Viscountess Tamplin, who has a villa at Cap Martin. Her cousin, Miss Grey, who recently inherited a vast fortune in a most romantic manner, is staying with her there.'"

"That is the one I wanted," said Miss Viner. "I expect there has been a picture of you in one of the papers that I have missed; you know the kind of thing. Mrs. Somebody or other Jones-Williams, at the something or other Point-to-point, usually carrying a shooting-stick and having one foot lifted up in the air. It must be a trial to some of them to see what they look like."

Katherine did not answer. She was smoothing out the cutting with her finger, and her face had a puzzled, worried look. Then she drew the second letter out of its envelope and mastered its contents once more. She turned to her friend.

"Miss Viner? I wonder—there is a friend of mine, someone I met on the Riviera, who wants very much to come down and see me here?"

"A man," said Miss Viner.

"Yes."

"Who is he?"

"He is secretary to Mr. Van Aldin, the American millionaire."

"What is his name?"

"Knighton. Major Knighton."

"Hm—secretary to a millionaire. And wants to come down here. Now, Katherine, I am going to say something to you for your own good. You are a nice girl and a sensible girl, and though you have your head screwed on the right way about most things, every woman makes a fool of herself once in her life. Ten to one what this man is after is your money."

With a gesture she arrested Katherine's reply. "I have been waiting for something of this kind. What is a secretary to a millionaire? Nine times out of ten it is a young man who likes living soft. A young man with nice manners and a taste for luxury and no brains and no enterprise, and if there is anything that is a softer job than being a secretary to a millionaire it is marrying a rich woman for her money. I am not saying that you might not be some man's fancy. But you are not young, and though you have a very good complexion you are not a beauty, and what I say to you is, don't make a fool of yourself; but if you are determined to do so, do see that your money is properly tied up on yourself. There, now I have finished. What have you got to say?"

"Nothing," said Katherine; "but would you mind if he did come to see me?"

"I wash my hands of it," said Miss Viner. "I have done my duty, and whatever happens now is on your own head. Would you like him to lunch or to dinner? I dare say Ellen could manage dinner—that is, if she didn't lose her head."

"Lunch would be very nice," said Katherine. "It is awfully kind of you, Miss Viner. He asked me to ring him up, so I will do so and say that we shall be pleased if he will lunch with us. He will motor down from town."

"Ellen does a steak with grilled tomatoes pretty fairly," said Miss Viner. "She doesn't do it well, but she does it better than anything else. It is no good having a tart because she is heavy handed with pastry; but her little castle puddings are not bad, and I dare say you could find a nice piece of Stilton at Abbot's. I have always heard that gentlemen like a nice piece of Stilton, and there is a good deal of father's wine left, a bottle of sparkling Moselle, perhaps."

"Oh, no, Miss Viner; that is really not necessary."

"Nonsense, my child. No gentleman is happy unless he drinks something with his meal. There is some good prewar whisky if you think he would prefer that. Now do as I say and don't argue. The key of the wine-cellar is in the third drawer down in the dressing-table, in the second pair of stockings on the left-hand side."

Katherine went obediently to the spot indicated.

"The second pair, now mind," said Miss Viner. "The first pair has my diamond earrings and my filigree brooch in it."

"Oh," said Katherine, rather taken aback, "wouldn't you like them put in your jewel-case?"

Miss Viner gave vent to a terrific and prolonged snort.

"No, indeed! I have much too much sense for that sort of

thing, thank you. Dear, dear, I well remember how my poor father had a safe built in downstairs. Pleased as Punch he was with it, and he said to my mother, 'Now, Mary, you bring me your jewels in their case every night and I will lock them away for you.' My mother was a very tactful woman, and she knew that gentlemen like having their own way, and she brought him the jewel-case locked up just as he said.

"And one night burglars broke in, and of course—naturally— the first thing they went for was the safe! It would be, with my father talking up and down the village and bragging about it until you might have thought he kept all King Solomon's diamonds there. They made a clean sweep, got the tankards, the silver cups, and the presentation gold plate that my father had had presented to him, *and* the jewel-case."

She sighed reminiscently. "My father was in a great state over my mother's jewels. There was the Venetian set and some very fine cameos and some pale pink corals, and two diamond rings with quite large stones in them. And then, of course, she had to tell him that, being a sensible woman, she had kept her jewellery rolled up in a pair of corsets, and there it was still as safe as anything."

"And the jewel-case had been quite empty?"

"Oh no, dear," said Miss Viner, "it would have been too light a weight then. My mother was a very intelligent woman; she saw to that. She kept her buttons in the jewel-case, and a very handy place it was. Boot buttons in the top tray, trouser buttons in the second tray, and assorted buttons below. Curiously enough, my father was quite annoyed with her. He said he didn't like deceit. But I mustn't go chattering on; you want to go and ring up your friend, and mind you choose a nice piece of steak, and tell Ellen she is not to have holes in her stockings when she waits at lunch."

"Is her name Ellen or Helen, Miss Viner? I thought—"

Miss Viner closed her eyes.

"I can sound my h's, dear, as well as anyone, but Helen is *not* a suitable name for a servant. I don't know what the mothers in the lower classes are coming to nowadays."

The rain had cleared away when Knighton arrived at the cottage. The pale fitful sunshine shone down on it and burnished Katherine's head as she stood in the doorway to welcome him. He came up to her quickly, almost boyishly.

"I say, I hope you don't mind. I simply had to see you again soon. I hope the friend you are staying with does not mind."

"Come in and make friends with her," said Katherine. "She can be most alarming, but you will soon find that she has the softest heart in the world."

Miss Viner was enthroned majestically in the drawing-room, wearing a complete set of the cameos which had been so providentially preserved in the family. She greeted Knighton with dignity and an austere politeness which would have damped many men. Knighton, however, had a charm of manner which was not easily set aside, and after about ten minutes Miss Viner thawed perceptibly. Luncheon was a merry meal, and Ellen, or Helen, in a new pair of silk stockings devoid of ladders performed prodigies of waiting. Afterwards, Katherine and Knighton went for a walk and they came back to have tea *tête-à-tête*, since Miss Viner had gone to lie down.

When the car had finally driven off Katherine went slowly upstairs. A voice called her and she went in to Miss Viner's bedroom.

"Friend gone?"

"Yes. Thank you so much for letting me ask him down."

"No need to thank me. Do you think I am the sort of old curmudgeon who never will do anything for anybody?"

"I think you are a dear," said Katherine affectionately.

"Humph," said Miss Viner mollified.

As Katherine was leaving the room she called her back.

"Katherine?"

"Yes."

"I was wrong about that young man of yours. A man when

he is making up to anybody can be cordial and gallant and full of little attentions and altogether charming. But when a man is really in love he can't help looking like a sheep. Now, whenever that young man looked at you he looked like a sheep. I take back all I said this morning. It is genuine."

THIRTY-ONE
Mr. Aarons Lunches

"Ah!" said Mr. Joseph Aarons, appreciatively.

He took a long draught from his tankard, set it down with a sigh, wiped the froth from his lips, and beamed across the table at his host, Monsieur Hercule Poirot.

"Give me," said Mr. Aarons, "a good Porterhouse steak and a tankard of something worth drinking, and anyone can have your French fallals and whatnots, your ordoovres and your omelettes and your little bits of quail. Give me," he reiterated, "a Porterhouse steak."

Poirot, who had just complied with this request, smiled sympathetically.

"Not that there is much wrong with a steak and kidney pudding," continued Mr. Aarons. "Apple tart? Yes, I will take apple tart, thank you, Miss, and a jug of cream."

The meal proceeded. Finally, with a long sigh, Mr. Aarons laid down his spoon and fork preparatory to toying with some cheese before turning his mind to other matters.

"There was a little matter of business I think you said, Monsieur Poirot," he remarked. "Anything I can do to help you I am sure I shall be most happy."

"That is very kind of you," said Poirot. "I said to myself, 'If you want to know anything about the dramatic profession there is one person who knows all that is to be known and that is my old

222

friend, Mr. Joseph Aarons.'"

"And you don't say far wrong," said Mr. Aarons complacently; "whether it is past, present, or future, Joe Aarons is the man to come to."

"*Précisément.* Now I want to ask you, Monsieur Aarons, what you know about a young woman called Kidd."

"Kidd? Kitty Kidd?"

"Kitty Kidd."

"Pretty smart, she was. Male impersonator, song and a dance—That one?"

"That is the one."

"*Very* smart, she was. Made a good income. Never out of an engagement. Male impersonation mostly, but, as a matter of fact, you could not touch her as a character actress."

"So I have heard," said Poirot; "but she has not been appearing lately, has she?"

"No. Dropped right out of things. Went over to France and took up with some swell nobleman there. She quitted the stage then for good and all, I guess."

"How long ago was that?"

"Let me see. Three years ago. And she has been a loss—let me tell you that."

"She was clever?"

"Clever as a cartload of monkeys."

"You don't know the name of the man she became friends with in Paris?"

"He was a swell, I know that. A Count—or was it a Marquis? Now I come to think of it, I believe it was a Marquis."

"And you know nothing about her since?"

"Nothing. Never even run across her accidentally like. I bet she is tooling it round some of these foreign resorts. Being a Marquise to the life. You couldn't put one over on Kitty. She would give as good as she got any day."

"I see," said Poirot thoughtfully.

"I am sorry I can't tell you more, Monsieur Poirot," said the other. "I would like to be of use to you if I could. You did me a good turn once."

"Ah, but we are quits on that; you, too, did me a good turn."

"One good turn deserves another. Ha, ha!" said Mr. Aarons.

"Your profession must be a very interesting one," said Poirot.

"So-so," said Mr. Aarons non-committally. "Taking the rough with the smooth, it is all right. I don't do so badly at it, all things considered, but you have to keep your eyes skinned. Never know what the public will jump for next."

"Dancing has come very much to the fore in the last few years," murmured Poirot reflectively.

"I never saw anything in this Russian ballet, but people like it. Too highbrow for me."

"I met one dancer out on the Riviera—Mademoiselle Mirelle."

"Mirelle? She is hot stuff, by all accounts. There is always money going to back her—though, so far as that goes, the girl can dance; I have seen her, and I know what I am talking about. I never had much to do with her myself, but I hear she is a terror to deal with. Tempers and tantrums all the time."

"Yes," said Poirot thoughtfully; "yes, so I should imagine."

"Temperament!" said Mr. Aarons, "temperament! That is what they call it themselves. My missus was a dancer before she married me, but I am thankful to say she never had any temperament. You don't want temperament in the home, Monsieur Poirot."

"I agree with you, my friend; it is out of place there."

"A woman should be calm and sympathetic, and a good cook," said Mr. Aarons.

"Mirelle has not been long before the public, has she?" asked Poirot.

"About two and a half years, that is all," said Mr. Aarons. "Some French Duke started her. I hear now that she has taken up with the ex-Prime Minister of Greece. These are the chaps who manage to put money away quietly."

"That is news to me," said Poirot.

"Oh, she's not one to let the grass grow under her feet. They say that young Kettering murdered his wife on her account. I don't know, I am sure. Anyway, he is in prison, and she had to look round for herself, and pretty smart she has been about it. They say she is wearing a ruby the size of a pigeon's egg—not that I have ever seen a pigeon's egg myself, but that is what they always call it in works of fiction."

"A ruby the size of a pigeon's egg!" said Poirot. His eyes were green and cat-like. "How interesting!"

"I had it from a friend of mine," said Mr. Aarons. "But, for all I know, it may be coloured glass. They are all the same, these women—they never stop telling tall stories about their jewels. Mirelle goes about bragging that it has got a curse on it. 'Heart of Fire,' I think she calls it."

"But if I remember rightly," said Poirot, "the ruby that is named 'Heart of Fire' is the centre stone in a necklace."

"There you are! Didn't I tell you there is no end to the lies women will tell about their jewellery? This is a single stone, hung on a platinum chain round her neck; but, as I said before, ten to one it is a bit of coloured glass."

"No," said Poirot gently; "no—somehow I do not think it is coloured glass."

THIRTY-TWO

Katherine and Poirot Compare Notes

"You have changed, Mademoiselle," said Poirot suddenly. He and Katherine were seated opposite each other at a small table at the Savoy.

"Yes, you have changed," he continued.

"In what way?"

"Mademoiselle, these *nuances* are difficult to express."

"I am older."

"Yes, you are older. And by that I do not mean that the wrinkles and the crows' feet are coming. When I first saw you, Mademoiselle, you were a looker-on at life. You had the quiet, amused look of one who sits back in the stalls and watches the play."

"And now?"

"Now, you no longer watch. It is an absurd thing, perhaps, that I say here, but you have the wary look of a fighter who is playing a difficult game."

"My old lady is difficult sometimes," said Katherine, with a smile; "but I can assure you that I don't engage in deadly contests with her. You must go down and see her some day, Monsieur Poirot. I think you are one of the people who would appreciate her pluck and her spirit."

There was a silence while the waiter deftly served them with chicken *en casserole*. When he had departed, Poirot said:

"You have heard me speak of my friend Hastings?—he who said that I was a human oyster. *Eh bien*, Mademoiselle, I have met my match in you. You, far more than I, play a lone hand."

"Nonsense," said Katherine lightly.

"Never does Hercule Poirot talk nonsense. It is as I say."

Again there was a silence. Poirot broke it by inquiring:

"Have you seen any of our Riviera friends since you have been back, Mademoiselle?"

"I have seen something of Major Knighton."

"A-ha! Is that so?"

Something in Poirot's twinkling eyes made Katherine lower hers.

"So Mr. Van Aldin remains in London?"

"Yes."

"I must try to see him to-morrow or the next day."

"You have news for him?"

"What makes you think that?"

"I—wondered, that is all."

Poirot looked across at her with twinkling eyes.

"And now, Mademoiselle, there is much that you wish to ask me, I can see that. And why not? Is not the affair of the Blue Train our own 'Roman Policier'?"

"Yes, there are things I should like to ask you."

"*Eh bien?*"

Katherine looked up with a sudden air of resolution.

"What were you doing in Paris, Monsieur Poirot?"

Poirot smiled slightly.

"I made a call at the Russian Embassy."

"Oh."

"I see that that tells you nothing. But I will not be a human oyster. No, I will lay my cards on the table, which is assuredly a thing that oysters do not do. You suspect, do you not, that I am not satisfied with the case against Derek Kettering?"

"That is what I have been wondering. I thought, in Nice, that you had finished with the case."

"You do not say all that you mean, Mademoiselle. But I admit everything. It was I—my researches—which placed Derek Kettering where he is now. But for me the Examining Magistrate would still be vainly trying to fasten the crime on the Comte de la Roche. *Eh bien*, Mademoiselle, what I have done I do not regret. I have only one duty—to discover the truth, and that way led straight to Mr. Kettering. But did it end there? The police say yes, but I, Hercule Poirot, am not satisfied."

He broke off suddenly. "Tell me, Mademoiselle, have you heard from Mademoiselle Lenox lately?"

"One very short, scrappy letter. She is, I think, annoyed with me for coming back to England."

Poirot nodded.

"I had an interview with her the night that Monsieur Kettering was arrested. It was an interesting interview in more ways than one."

Again he fell silent, and Katherine did not interrupt his train of thought.

"Mademoiselle," he said at last, "I am now on delicate ground, yet I will say this to you. There is, I think, someone who loves Monsieur Kettering—correct me if I am wrong—and for her sake—well—for her sake I hope that I am right and the police are wrong. You know who that someone is?"

There was a pause, then Katherine said:

"Yes—I think I know."

Poirot leant across the table towards her.

"I am not satisfied, Mademoiselle; no, I am not satisfied. The facts, the main facts, led straight to Monsieur Kettering. But there is one thing that has been left out of account."

"And what is that?"

"The disfigured face of the victim. I have asked myself, Mademoiselle, a hundred times, 'Was Derek Kettering the kind of man who would deal that smashing blow after having committed the murder?' What end would it serve? What purpose would it accomplish? Was it a likely action for one of Monsieur Kettering's temperament? And, Mademoiselle, the answer to these questions is profoundly unsatisfactory. Again and again I go back to that one point—'why?' And the only things I have to help me to a solution of the problem are these."

He whipped out his pocket-book and extracted something from it which he held between his finger and thumb.

"Do you remember, Mademoiselle? You saw me take these hairs from the rug in the railway carriage."

Katherine leant forward, scrutinizing the hairs keenly.

Poirot nodded his head slowly several times.

"They suggest nothing to you, I see that, Mademoiselle. And yet—I think somehow that you see a good deal."

"I have had ideas," said Katherine slowly, "curious ideas. That is why I ask you what you were doing in Paris, Monsieur Poirot."

"When I wrote to you—"

"From the Ritz?"

A curious smile came over Poirot's face.

"Yes, as you say, from the Ritz. I am a luxurious person some-times—when a millionaire pays."

"The Russian Embassy," said Katherine, frowning. "No, I don't see where that comes in."

"It does not come in directly, Mademoiselle. I went there to get certain information. I saw a particular personage and I threat-ened him—yes, Mademoiselle, I, Hercule Poirot, threatened him."

"With the police?"

"No," said Poirot drily, "with the Press—a much more deadly weapon."

He looked at Katherine and she smiled at him, just shaking her head.

"Are you not just turning back into an oyster again, Monsieur Poirot?"

"No, no! I do not wish to make mysteries. See, I will tell you everything. I suspect this man of being the active party in the sale of the jewels of Monsieur Van Aldin. I tax him with it, and in the end I get the whole story out of him. I learn where the jewels were handed over, and I learn, too, of the man who paced up and down outside in the street—a man with a venerable head of white hair, but who walked with the light, springy step of a young man—and I give that man a name in my own mind—the name of 'Monsieur le Marquis.'"

"And now you have come to London to see Mr. Van Aldin?"

"Not entirely for that reason. I had other work to do. Since I have been in London I have seen two more people—a theatrical agent and a Harley Street doctor. From each of them I have got certain information. Put these things together, Mademoiselle, and see if you can make of them the same as I do."

"I?"

"Yes, you. I will tell you one thing, Mademoiselle. There has been a doubt all along in my mind as to whether the robbery and the murder were done by the same person. For a long time I was not sure—"

"And now?"

"And now I *know*."

There was a silence. Then Katherine lifted her head. Her eyes were shining.

"I am not clever like you, Monsieur Poirot. Half the things that you have been telling me don't seem to me to point anywhere at all. The ideas that came to me came from such an entirely different angle—"

"Ah, but that is always so," said Poirot quietly. "A mirror shows the truth, but everyone stands in a different place for looking into the mirror."

"My ideas may be absurd—they may be entirely different from yours, but—"

"Yes?"

"Tell me, does this help you at all?"

He took a newspaper cutting from her outstretched hand. He read it and, looking up, he nodded gravely.

"As I told you, Mademoiselle, one stands at a different angle for looking into the mirror, but it is the same mirror and the same things are reflected there."

Katherine got up. "I must rush," she said. "I have only just time to catch my train. Monsieur Poirot—"

"Yes, Mademoiselle."

"It—it mustn't be much longer, you understand. I—I can't go on much longer."

There was a break in her voice.

He patted her hand reassuringly.

"Courage, Mademoiselle, you must not fail now; the end is very near."

THIRTY-THREE
A New Theory

Monsieur Poirot wants to see you, sir."

"Damn the fellow!" said Van Aldin.

Knighton remained sympathetically silent.

Van Aldin got up from his chair and paced up and down.

"I suppose you have seen the cursed newspapers this morning?"

"I have glanced at them, sir."

"Still at it hammer and tongs?"

"I am afraid so, sir."

The millionaire sat down again and pressed his hand to his forehead.

"If I had had an idea of this," he groaned. "I wish to God I had never got that little Belgian to ferret out the truth. Find Ruth's murderer—that was all I thought about."

"You wouldn't have liked your son-in-law to go scot free?"

Van Aldin sighed.

"I would have preferred to take the law into my own hands."

"I don't think that would have been a very wise proceeding, sir."

"All the same—are you sure the fellow wants to see me?"

"Yes, Mr. Van Aldin. He is very urgent about it."

"Then I suppose he will have to. He can come along this morning if he likes."

It was a very fresh and debonair Poirot who was ushered in. He did not seem to see any lack of cordiality in the millionaire's manner, and chatted pleasantly about various trifles. He was in London, he explained, to see his doctor. He mentioned the name of an eminent surgeon.

"No, no, *pas la guerre*—a memory of my days in the police force, a bullet of a rascally Apache."

He touched his left shoulder and winced realistically.

"I always consider you a lucky man, Monsieur Van Aldin; you are not like our popular idea of American millionaires, martyrs to the dyspepsia."

"I am pretty tough," said Van Aldin. "I lead a very simple life, you know; plain fare and not too much of it."

"You have seen something of Miss Grey, have you not?" inquired Poirot, innocently turning to the secretary.

"I—yes; once or twice," said Knighton.

He blushed slightly and Van Aldin exclaimed in surprise:

"Funny you never mentioned to me that you had seen her, Knighton?"

"I didn't think you would be interested, sir."

"I like that girl very much," said Van Aldin.

"It is a thousand pities that she should have buried herself once more in St. Mary Mead," said Poirot.

"It is very fine of her," said Knighton hotly. "There are very few people who would bury themselves down there to look after a cantankerous old woman who has no earthly claim on her."

"I am silent," said Poirot, his eyes twinkling a little; "but all the same I say it is a pity. And now, Messieurs, let us come to business."

Both the other men looked at him in some surprise.

"You must not be shocked or alarmed at what I am about to say. Supposing, Monsieur Van Aldin, that, after all, Monsieur Derek Kettering did not murder his wife?"

"What?"

Both men stared at him in blank surprise.

"Supposing, I say, that Monsieur Kettering did not murder his wife?"

"Are you mad, Monsieur Poirot?"

It was Van Aldin who spoke.

"No," said Poirot, "I am not mad. I am eccentric, perhaps—at least certain people say so; but as regards my profession, I am very much, as one says, 'all there.' I ask you, Monsieur Van Aldin, whether you would be glad or sorry if what I tell you should be the case?"

Van Aldin stared at him.

"Naturally I should be glad," he said at last. "Is this an exercise in suppositions, Monsieur Poirot, or are there any facts behind it?"

Poirot looked at the ceiling.

"There is an off-chance," he said quietly, "that it might be the Comte de la Roche after all. At least I have succeeded in upsetting his alibi."

"How did you manage that?"

Poirot shrugged his shoulders modestly.

"I have my own methods. The exercise of a little tact, a little cleverness—and the thing is done."

"But the rubies," said Van Aldin, "these rubies that the Count had in his possession were false."

"And clearly he would not have committed the crime except for the rubies. But you are overlooking one point, Monsieur Van Aldin. Where the rubies were concerned, someone might have been before him."

"But this is an entirely new theory," cried Knighton.

"Do you really believe all this rigmarole, Monsieur Poirot?" demanded the millionaire.

"The thing is not proved," said Poirot quietly. "It is as yet only a theory, but I tell you this, Monsieur Van Aldin, the facts are worth investigating. You must come out with me to the south of France and go into the case on the spot."

"You really think this is necessary—that I should go, I mean."

"I thought it would be what you yourself would wish," said Poirot.

There was a hint of reproach in his tone which was not lost upon the other.

"Yes, yes, of course," he said. "When do you wish to start, Monsieur Poirot?"

"You are very busy at present, sir," murmured Knighton.

But the millionaire had now made up his mind, and he waved the other's objections aside.

"I guess this business comes first," he said. "All right, Monsieur Poirot, to-morrow. What train?"

"We will go, I think, by the Blue Train," said Poirot, and he smiled.

THIRTY-FOUR
The Blue Train Again

T he Millionaire's Train," as it is sometimes called, swung round a curve of line at what seemed a dangerous speed. Van Aldin, Knighton, and Poirot sat together in silence. Knighton and Van Aldin had two compartments connecting with each other, as Ruth Kettering and her maid had had on the fateful journey. Poirot's own compartment was further along the coach.

The journey was a painful one for Van Aldin, recalling as it did the most agonizing memories. Poirot and Knighton conversed occasionally in low tones without disturbing him.

When, however, the train had completed its slow journey round the *ceinture* and reached the Gare de Lyon, Poirot became suddenly galvanized into activity. Van Aldin realized that part of his object in travelling by the train had been to attempt to reconstruct the crime. Poirot himself acted every part. He was in turn the maid, hurriedly shut into her own compartment, Mrs. Kettering, recognizing her husband with surprise and a trace of anxiety, and Derek Kettering discovering that his wife was travelling on the train. He tested various possibilities, such as the best way for a person to conceal himself in the second compartment.

Then suddenly an idea seemed to strike him. He clutched at Van Aldin's arm.

"*Mon Dieu*, but that is something I have not thought of! We must break our journey in Paris. Quick, quick, let us alight at once."

Seizing suit-cases he hurried from the train. Van Aldin and Knighton, bewildered but obedient, followed him. Van Aldin having once formed his opinion of Poirot's ability was slow to part from it. At the barrier they were held up. Their tickets were in charge of the conductor of the train, a fact which all three of them had forgotten.

Poirot's explanations were rapid, fluent, and impassioned, but they produced no effect upon the stolid-faced official.

"Let us get quit of this," said Van Aldin abruptly. "I gather you are in a hurry, Monsieur Poirot. For God's sake pay the fares from Calais and let us get right on with whatever you have got in your mind."

But Poirot's flood of language had suddenly stopped dead, and he had the appearance of a man turned to stone. His arm, still outflung in an impassioned gesture, remained there as though stricken with paralysis.

"I have been an imbecile," he said simply. "*Ma foi*, I lose my head nowadays. Let us return and continue our journey quietly. With reasonable luck the train will not have gone."

They were only just in time, the train moving off as Knighton, the last of the three, swung himself and his suitcase on board.

The conductor remonstrated with them feelingly, and assisted them to carry their luggage back to their compartments. Van Aldin said nothing, but he was clearly disgusted at Poirot's extraordinary conduct. Alone with Knighton for a moment or two, he remarked:

"This is a wildgoose chase. The man has lost his grip on things. He has got brains up to a point, but any man who loses his head and scuttles round like a frightened rabbit is no earthly darned good."

Poirot came to them in a moment or two, full of abject apologies and clearly so crestfallen that harsh words would have been superfluous. Van Aldin received his apologies gravely, but managed to restrain himself from making acid comments.

They had dinner on the train, and afterwards, somewhat to

the surprise of the other two, Poirot suggested that they should all three set up in Van Aldin's compartment.

The millionaire looked at him curiously.

"Is there anything that you are keeping back from us, Monsieur Poirot?"

"I?" Poirot opened his eyes in innocent surprise. "But what an idea."

Van Aldin did not answer, but he was not satisfied. The conductor was told that he need not make up the beds. Any surprise he might have felt was obliterated by the largeness of the tip which Van Aldin handed to him. The three men sat in silence. Poirot fidgeted and seemed restless. Presently he turned to the secretary.

"Major Knighton, is the door of your compartment bolted? The door into the corridor, I mean."

"Yes; I bolted it myself just now."

"Are you sure?" said Poirot.

"I will go and make sure, if you like," said Knighton smiling.

"No, no, do not derange yourself. I will see for myself."

He passed through the connecting door and returned in a second or two, nodding his head.

"Yes, yes, it is as you said. You must pardon an old man's fussy ways."

He closed the connecting door and resumed his place in the right-hand corner.

The hours passed. The three men dozed fitfully, waking with uncomfortable starts. Probably never before had three people booked berths on the most luxurious train available, then declined to avail themselves of the accommodations they had paid for. Every now and then Poirot glanced at his watch, and then nodded his head and composed himself to slumber once more. On one occasion he rose from his seat and opened the connecting door, peered sharply into the adjoining compartment, and then returned to his seat, shaking his head.

"What is the matter?" whispered Knighton. "You are expecting something to happen, aren't you?"

"I have the nerves," confessed Poirot. "I am like the cat upon the hot tiles. Every little noise it makes me jump."

Knighton yawned.

"Of all the darned uncomfortable journeys," he murmured. "I suppose you know what you are playing at, Monsieur Poirot."

He composed himself to sleep as best he could. Both he and Van Aldin had succumbed to slumber, when Poirot, glancing for the fourteenth time at his watch, leant across and tapped the millionaire on the shoulder.

"Eh? What is it?"

"In five or ten minutes, Monsieur, we shall arrive at Lyons."

"My God!" Van Aldin's face looked white and haggard in the dim light. "Then it must have been about this time that poor Ruth was killed."

He sat staring straight in front of him. His lips twitched a little, his mind reverting back to the terrible tragedy that had saddened his life.

There was the usual long screaming sigh of the brake, and the train slackened speed and drew into Lyons. Van Aldin let down the window and leant out.

"If it wasn't Derek—if your new theory is correct, it is here that the man left the train?" he asked over his shoulder.

Rather to his surprise Poirot shook his head.

"No," he said thoughtfully, "no *man* left the train, but I think—yes, I think, a *woman* may have done so."

Knighton gave a gasp.

"A woman?" demanded Van Aldin sharply.

"Yes, a woman," said Poirot, nodding his head. "You may not remember, Monsieur Van Aldin, but Miss Grey in her evidence mentioned that a youth in a cap and overcoat descended on to the platform ostensibly to stretch his legs. Me, I think that that youth was most probably a woman."

"But who was she?"

Van Aldin's face expressed incredulity, but Poirot replied seriously and categorically.

"Her name—or the name under which she was known, for many years—is Kitty Kidd, but you, Monsieur Van Aldin, knew her by another name—*that of Ada Mason.*"

Knighton sprang to his feet.

"What?" he cried.

Poirot swung round to him.

"Ah!—before I forget it." He whipped something from a pocket and held it out.

"Permit me to offer you a cigarette—out of your own cigarette case. It was careless of you to drop it when you boarded the train on the *ceinture* at Paris."

Knighton stood staring at him as though stupefied. Then he made a movement, but Poirot flung up his hand in a warning gesture.

"No, don't move," he said in a silky voice; "the door into the next compartment is open, and you are being covered from there this minute. I unbolted the door into the corridor when we left Paris, and our friends the police were told to take their places there. As I expect you know, the French police want you rather urgently, Major Knighton—or shall we say—Monsieur le Marquis?"

THIRTY-FIVE
Explanations

"Explanations?"

Poirot smiled. He was sitting opposite the millionaire at a luncheon table in the latter's private suite at the Negresco. Facing him was a relieved but very puzzled man. Poirot leant back in his chair, lit one of his tiny cigarettes, and stared reflectively at the ceiling.

"Yes, I will give you explanations. It began with the one point that puzzled me. You know what that point was? *The disfigured face.* It is not an uncommon thing to find when investigating a crime and it rouses an immediate question, the question of identity. That naturally was the first thing that occurred to me. Was the dead woman really Mrs. Kettering? But that line led me nowhere, for Miss Grey's evidence was positive and very reliable, so I put that idea aside. The dead woman *was* Ruth Kettering."

"When did you first begin to suspect the maid?"

"Not for some time, but one peculiar little point drew my attention to her. The cigarette case found in the railway carriage and which she told us was one which Mrs. Kettering had given to her husband. Now that was, on the face of it, most improbable, seeing the terms that they were on. It awakened a doubt in my mind as to the general veracity of Ada Mason's statements. There was the rather suspicious fact to be taken into consideration, that she had only been with her mistress for two months. Certainly

241

it did not seem as if she could have had anything to do with the crime since she had been left behind in Paris and Mrs. Kettering had been seen alive by several people afterwards, but—"

Poirot leant forward. He raised an emphatic forefinger and wagged it with intense emphasis at Van Aldin.

"But I am a good detective. I suspect. There is nobody and nothing that I do not suspect. I believe nothing that I am told. I say to myself: how do we know that Ada Mason was left behind in Paris? And at first the answer to that question seemed completely satisfactory. There was the evidence of your secretary, Major Knighton, a complete outsider whose testimony might be supposed to be entirely impartial, and there was the dead woman's own words to the conductor on the train. But I put the latter point aside for the moment, because a very curious idea—an idea perhaps fantastic and impossible—was growing up in my mind. If by any outside chance it happened to be true, that particular piece of testimony was worthless.

"I concentrated on the chief stumbling-block to my theory, Major Knighton's statement that he saw Ada Mason at the Ritz after the Blue Train had left Paris. That seemed conclusive enough, but yet, on examining the facts carefully, I noted two things. First, that by a curious coincidence he, too, had been exactly two months in your service. Secondly, his initial letter was the same—'K.' Supposing—just supposing—that it was *his* cigarette case which had been found in the carriage. Then, if Ada Mason and he were working together, and she recognized it when we showed it to her, would she not act precisely as she had done? At first, taken aback, she quickly evolved a plausible theory that would agree with Mr. Kettering's guilt. *Bien entendu*, that was not the original idea. The Comte de la Roche was to be the scapegoat, though Ada Mason would not make her recognition of him too certain, in case he should be able to prove an alibi. Now, if you will cast your mind back to that time, you will remember a significant thing that happened. I suggested to Ada

Mason that the man she had seen was not the Comte de la Roche, but Derek Kettering. She seemed uncertain at the time, but after I had got back to my hotel you rang me up and told me that she had come to you and said that, on thinking it over, she was now quite convinced that the man in question *was* Mr. Kettering. I had been expecting something of the kind. There could be but one explanation of this sudden certainty on her part. After my leaving your hotel, she had had time to consult with somebody, and had received instructions which she acted upon. Who had given her these instructions? Major Knighton. And there was another very small point, which might mean nothing or might mean a great deal. In casual conversation Knighton had talked of a jewel robbery in Yorkshire in a house where he was staying. Perhaps a mere coincidence—perhaps another small link in the chain."

"But there is one thing I do not understand, Monsieur Poirot. I guess I must be dense or I would have seen it before now. Who was the man in the train at Paris? Derek Kettering or the Comte de la Roche?"

"That is the simplicity of the whole thing. *There was no man.* Ah—*mille tonnerres!*—do you not see the cleverness of it all? Whose word have we for it that there ever was a man there? Only Ada Mason's. And we believe in Ada Mason because of Knighton's evidence that she was left behind in Paris."

"But Ruth herself told the conductor that she had left her maid behind there," demurred Van Aldin.

"Ah! I am coming to that. We have Mrs. Kettering's own evidence there, but, on the other hand, we have not really got her evidence, because, Monsieur Van Aldin, a dead woman cannot give evidence. It is not *her* evidence, but the evidence of the conductor of the train—a very different affair altogether."

"So you think the man was lying?"

"No, no, not at all. He spoke what he thought to be the truth. But the woman who told him that she had left her maid in Paris was not Mrs. Kettering."

Van Aldin stared at him.

"Monsieur Van Aldin, Ruth Kettering was dead before the train arrived at the Gare de Lyon. It was Ada Mason, dressed in her mistress's very distinctive clothing, who purchased a dinner basket and who made that very necessary statement to the conductor."

"Impossible!"

"No, no, Monsieur Van Aldin; not impossible. *Les femmes*, they look so much alike nowadays that one identifies them more by their clothing than by their faces. Ada Mason was the same height as your daughter. Dressed in that very sumptuous fur coat and the little red lacquer hat jammed down over her eyes, with just a bunch of auburn curls showing over each ear, it was no wonder that the conductor was deceived. He had not previously spoken to Mrs. Kettering, you remember. True, he had seen the maid just for a moment when she handed him the tickets, but his impression had been merely that of a gaunt, black-clad female. If he had been an unusually intelligent man, he might have gone so far as to say that mistress and maid were not unlike, but it is extremely unlikely that he would even think that. And remember, Ada Mason, or Kitty Kidd, was an actress, able to change her appearance and tone of voice at a moment's notice. No, no; there was no danger of his recognizing the maid in the mistress's clothing, but there *was* the danger that when he came to discover the body he might realize it was not the woman he had talked to the night before. And now we see the reason for the disfigured face. The chief danger that Ada Mason ran was that Katherine Grey might visit her compartment after the train left Paris, and she provided against that difficulty by ordering a dinner basket and by locking herself in her compartment."

"But who killed Ruth—and when?"

"First, bear it in mind that the crime was planned and undertaken by the two of them—Knighton and Ada Mason, working together. Knighton was in Paris that day on your business. He boarded the train somewhere on its way round the *ceinture*. Mrs.

Kettering would be surprised, but she would be quite unsuspicious. Perhaps he draws her attention to something out the window, and as she turns to look he slips the cord round her neck—and the whole thing is over in a second or two. The door of the compartment is locked, and he and Ada Mason set to work. They strip off the dead woman's outer clothes. Mason and Knighton roll the body up in a rug and put it on the seat in the adjoining compartment amongst the bags and suit-cases. Knighton drops off the train, taking the jewel-case containing the rubies with him. Since the crime is not supposed to have been committed until nearly twelve hours later he is perfectly safe, and his evidence and the supposed Mrs. Kettering's words to the conductor will provide a perfect alibi for his accomplice.

"At the Gare de Lyon Ada Mason gets a dinner basket, and shutting herself into the toilet compartment she quickly changes into her mistress's clothes, adjusts two false bunches of auburn curls, and generally makes up to resemble her as closely as possible. When the conductor comes to make up the bed, she tells him the prepared story about having left her maid behind in Paris; and whilst he is making up the berth, she stands looking out of the window, so that her back is towards the corridor and people passing along there. That was a wise precaution, because, as we know, Miss Grey was one of those passing, and she, among others, was willing to swear that Mrs. Kettering was still alive at that hour."

"Go on," said Van Aldin.

"Before getting to Lyons, Ada Mason arranged her mistress's body in the bunk, folded up the dead woman's clothes neatly on the end of it, and herself changed into a man's clothes and prepared to leave the train. When Derek Kettering entered his wife's compartment, and, as he thought, saw her asleep in her berth, the scene had been set, and Ada Mason was hidden in the next compartment waiting for the moment to leave the train unobserved. As soon as the conductor had swung himself down on to the platform at Lyons, she follows, slouching along as though just taking a breath of air. At a moment when she is unobserved, she hurriedly crosses to the other platform, and takes the first train back to Paris and the Ritz Hotel. Her name has been registered there as taking a room the night before by one of Knighton's female accomplices. She has nothing to do but wait there placidly for your arrival. The jewels are not, and never have been, in her possession. No suspicion attaches to him, and, as your secretary, he brings them to Nice without the least fear of discovery. Their delivery there to Monsieur Papopolous is already arranged for and they are entrusted to Mason at the last moment to hand over to the Greek. Altogether a very neatly planned coup, as one would expect from a master of the game such as the Marquis."

"And you honestly mean that Richard Knighton is a well-known criminal, who has been at this business for years?"

Poirot nodded.

"One of the chief assets of the gentleman called the Marquis was his plausible, ingratiating manner. You fell a victim to his charm, Monsieur Van Aldin, when you engaged him as a secretary on such a slight acquaintanceship."

"I could have sworn that he never angled for the post," cried the millionaire.

"It was very astutely done—so astutely done that it deceived a man whose knowledge of other men is as great as yours is."

"I looked up his antecedents too. The fellow's record was excellent."

"Yes, yes; that was part of the game. As Richard Knighton his life was quite free from reproach. He was well born, well connected, did honourable service in the War, and seemed altogether above suspicion; but when I came to glean information about the mysterious Marquis, I found many points of similarity. Knighton spoke French like a Frenchman, he had been in America, France, and England at much the same time as the Marquis was operating. The Marquis was last heard of as engineering various jewel robberies in Switzerland, and it was in Switzerland that you had come across Major Knighton; and it was at precisely that time that the first rumours were going round of your being in treaty for the famous rubies."

"But why murder?" murmured Van Aldin brokenly. "Surely a clever thief could have stolen the jewels without running his head into a noose."

Poirot shook his head. "This is not the first murder that lies to the Marquis's charge. He is a killer by instinct; he believes, too, in leaving no evidence behind him. Dead men and women tell no tales.

"The Marquis had an intense passion for famous and historical jewels. He laid his plans far beforehand by installing himself as your secretary and getting his accomplice to obtain the situation of maid with your daughter, for whom he guessed the jewels were destined. And, though this was his matured and carefully thought-out plan, he did not scruple to attempt a shortcut by hiring a couple of Apaches to waylay you in Paris on the night you bought the jewels. That plan failed, which hardly surprised him, I think. This plan was, so he thought, completely safe. No possible suspicion could attach to Richard Knighton. But like all great men—and the Marquis was a great man—he had his weaknesses. He fell genuinely in love with Miss Grey, and suspecting her liking for Derek Kettering, he could not resist the temptation to saddle him with the crime when the opportunity presented itself. And now, Monsieur Van Aldin, I am going to tell you something very curious. Miss Grey is not a fanciful woman by any means, yet she firmly believes that she felt your daughter's presence beside her one day in the Casino Gardens at Monte Carlo, just after she had been having a long talk with Knighton. She was convinced, she says, that the dead woman was urgently trying to tell her something, and it suddenly came to her that what the dead woman was trying to say was that Knighton was her murderer! The idea seemed so fantastic at the time that Miss Grey spoke of it to no one. But she was so convinced of its truth that she acted on it—wild as it seemed. She did not discourage Knighton's advances, and she pretended to him that she was convinced of Derek Kettering's guilt."

"Extraordinary," said Van Aldin.

"Yes, it is very strange. One cannot explain these things. Oh, by the way, there is one little point that baffled me considerably. Your secretary has a decided limp—the result of a wound that he received in the War. Now the Marquis most decidedly did not limp. That was a stumbling-block. But Miss Lenox Tamplin happened to mention one day that Knighton's limp had been a surprise to the surgeons who had been in charge of the case in her mother's hospital. That suggested camouflage. When I was in London I went to the surgeon in question, and I got several technical details from him which confirmed me in that belief. I mentioned the name of that surgeon in Knighton's hearing the day before yesterday. The natural thing would have been for Knighton to mention that he had been attended by him during the War, but he said nothing—and that little point, if nothing else, gave me the last final assurance that my theory of the crime was correct. Miss Grey, too, provided me with a cutting, showing that there had been a robbery at Lady Tamplin's hospital during the time that Knighton had been there. She realized that I was on the same track as herself when I wrote to her from the Ritz in Paris.

"I had some trouble in my inquiries there, but I got what I wanted—evidence that Ada Mason arrived on the morning after the crime and not on the evening of the day before."

There was a long silence, then the millionaire stretched out a hand to Poirot across the table.

"I guess you know what this means to me, Monsieur Poirot," he said huskily. "I am sending you round a cheque in the morning, but no cheque in the world will express what I feel about what you have done for me. You are the goods, Monsieur Poirot. Every time, you are the goods."

Poirot rose to his feet; his chest swelled.

"I am only Hercule Poirot," he said modestly, "yet, as you say, in my own way I am a big man, even as you also are a big man. I am glad and happy to have been of service to you. Now I go to repair the damages caused by travel. Alas! my excellent Georges is not with me."

In the lounge of the hotel he encountered a friend—the venerable Monsieur Papopolous, his daughter Zia beside him.

"I thought you had left Nice, Monsieur Poirot," murmured the Greek as he took the detective's affectionately proffered hand.

"Business compelled me to return, my dear Monsieur Papopolous."

"Business?"

"Yes, business. And talking of business, I hope your health is better, my dear friend?"

"Much better. In fact, we are returning to Paris to-morrow."

"I am enchanted to hear such good news. You have not completely ruined the Greek ex-Minister, I hope."

"I?"

"I understand you sold him a very wonderful ruby which—strictly *entre nous*—is being worn by Mademoiselle Mirelle, the dancer?"

"Yes," murmured Monsieur Papopolous; "yes, that is so."

"A ruby not unlike the famous 'Heart of Fire'."

"It has points of resemblance, certainly," said the Greek casually.

"You have a wonderful hand with jewels, Monsieur Papopolous. I congratulate you. Mademoiselle Zia, I am desolate that you are returning to Paris so speedily. I had hoped to see some more of you now that my business is accomplished."

"Would one be indiscreet if one asked what that business was?" asked Monsieur Papopolous.

"Not at all, not at all. I have just succeeded in laying the Marquis by the heels."

A far-away look came over Monsieur Papopolous' noble countenance.

"The Marquis?" he murmured; "now why does that seem familiar to me? No—I cannot recall it."

"You would not, I am sure," said Poirot. "I refer to a very notable criminal and jewel robber. He has just been arrested for the murder of the English lady, Madame Kettering."

"Indeed? How interesting these things are!"

A polite exchange of farewells followed, and when Poirot was out of earshot, Monsieur Papopolous turned to his daughter.

"Zia," he said, with feeling, "that man is the devil!"

"I like him."

"I like him myself," admitted Monsieur Papopolous. "But he is the devil, all the same."

THIRTY-SIX

By the Sea

The mimosa was nearly over. The scent of it in the air was faintly unpleasant. There were pink geraniums twining along the balustrade of Lady Tamplin's villa, and masses of carnations below sent up a sweet, heavy perfume. The Mediterranean was at its bluest. Poirot sat on the terrace with Lenox Tamplin. He had just finished telling her the same story he had told to Van Aldin two days before. Lenox had listened to him with absorbed attention, her brows knitted and her eyes sombre.

When he had finished she said simply:

"And Derek?"

"He was released yesterday."

"And he has gone—where?"

"He left Nice last night."

"For St. Mary Mead?"

"Yes, for St. Mary Mead."

There was a pause.

"I was wrong about Katherine," said Lenox. "I thought she did not care."

"She is very reserved. She trusts no one."

"She might have trusted me," said Lenox, with a shade of bitterness.

"Yes," said Poirot gravely, "she might have trusted you. But Mademoiselle Katherine has spent a great deal of her life listening, and those who have listened do not find it easy to talk; they keep their sorrows and joys to themselves and tell no one."

"I was a fool," said Lenox; "I thought she really cared for Knighton. I ought to have known better. I suppose I thought so because—well, I hoped so."

Poirot took her hand and gave it a little friendly squeeze. "Courage, Mademoiselle," he said gently.

Lenox looked very straight out across the sea, and her face, in its ugly rigidity, had for the moment a tragic beauty.

"Oh, well," she said at last, "it would not have done. I am too young for Derek; he is like a kid that has never grown up. He wants the Madonna touch."

There was a long silence, then Lenox turned to him quickly and impulsively. "But I *did* help, Monsieur Poirot—at any rate I did help."

"Yes, Mademoiselle. It was you who gave me the first inkling of the truth when you said that the person who committed the crime need not have been on the train at all. Before that, I could not see how the thing had been done."

Lenox drew a deep breath.

"I am glad," she said; "at any rate—that is something."

From far behind them there came a long-drawn-out scream of an engine's whistle.

"That is that damned Blue Train," said Lenox. "Trains are relentless things, aren't they, Monsieur Poirot? People are murdered and die, but they go on just the same. I am talking nonsense, but you know what I mean."

"Yes, yes, I know. Life is like a train, Mademoiselle. It goes on. And it is a good thing that that is so."

"Why?"

"Because the train gets to its journey's end at last, and there is a proverb about that in your language, Mademoiselle."

"'Journeys end in lovers meeting.'" Lenox laughed. "That is not going to be true for me."

"Yes—yes, it is true. You are young, younger than you yourself know. Trust the train, Mademoiselle, for it is *le bon Dieu* who drives it."

The whistle of the engine came again.

"Trust the train, Mademoiselle," murmured Poirot again. "And trust Hercule Poirot. He knows."

THE
BIG FOUR

❋ AGATHA CHRISTIE ❋

❋ THE ❋
BIG FOUR

ISBN: 978-1-64833-751-2

First published 1927
Published by Page Publications 2024

Printed in China

Contents

1. The Unexpected Guest   1

2. The Man From The Asylum   10

3. We Hear More About Li Chang Yen   16

4. The Importance of A Leg of Mutton   26

5. Disappearance of A Scientist   34

6. The Woman on the Stairs   41

7. The Radium Thieves   50

8. In The House Of The Enemy   62

9. The Yellow Jasmine Mystery   74

10. We Investigate At Croftlands   81

11. A Chess Problem   89

12. The Baited Trap   105

13. The Mouse Walks In   114

14. The Peroxide Blonde   123

15. The Terrible Catastrophe   137

16. The Dying Chinaman   150

17. Number Four Wins A Trick   163

18. In The Felsenlabyrynth   173

ONE

The Unexpected Guest

I have met people who enjoy a channel crossing; men who can sit calmly in their deckchairs and, on arrival, wait until the boat is moored, then gather their belongings together without fuss and disembark. Personally, I can never manage this. From the moment I get on board I feel that the time is too short to settle down to anything. I move my suit-cases from one spot to another, and if I go down to the saloon for a meal, I bolt my food with an uneasy feeling that the boat may arrive unexpectedly whilst I am below. Perhaps all this is merely a legacy from one's short leaves in the war, when it seemed a matter of such importance to secure a place near the gangway, and to be amongst the first to disembark lest one should waste precious minutes of one's three or five days' leave.

On this particular July morning, as I stood by the rail and watched the white cliffs of Dover drawing nearer, I marvelled at the passengers who could sit calmly in their chairs and never even raise their eyes for the first sight of their native land. Yet perhaps their case was different from mine. Doubtless many of them had only crossed to Paris for the week-end, whereas I had spent the last year and a half on a ranch in the Argentine. I had prospered there, and my wife and I had both enjoyed the free and easy life of the South American continent, nevertheless it was with a lump

1

in my throat that I watched the familiar shore draw nearer and nearer.

I had landed in France two days before, transacted some necessary business, and was now *en route* for London. I should be there some months—time enough to look up old friends, and one old friend in particular. A little man with an egg-shaped head and green eyes—Hercule Poirot! I proposed to take him completely by surprise. My last letter from the Argentine had given no hint of my intended voyage—indeed, that had been decided upon hurriedly as a result of certain business complications—and I spent many amused moments picturing to myself his delight and stupefaction on beholding me.

He, I knew, was not likely to be far from his headquarters. The time when his cases had drawn him from one end of England to the other was past. His fame had spread, and no longer would he allow one case to absorb all his time. He aimed more and more, as time went on, at being considered a "consulting detective"—as much a specialist as a Harley Street physician. He had always scoffed at the popular idea of the human bloodhound who assumed wonderful disguises to track criminals, and who paused at every footprint to measure it.

"No, my friend Hastings," he would say; "we leave that to Giraud and his friends. Hercule Poirot's methods are his own. Order and method, and 'the little gray cells.' Sitting at ease in our own armchairs we see the things that these others overlook, and we do not jump to the conclusion like the worthy Japp."

No; there was little fear of finding Hercule Poirot far afield.

On arrival in London, I deposited my luggage at an hotel and drove straight on to the old address. What poignant memories it brought back to me! I hardly waited to greet my old landlady, but hurried up the stairs two at a time and rapped on Poirot's door.

"Enter, then," cried a familiar voice from within.

I strode in. Poirot stood facing me. In his arms he carried a small valise, which he dropped with a crash on beholding me.

"*Mon ami*, Hastings!" he cried. "*Mon ami*, Hastings!"

And, rushing forward, he enveloped me in a capacious embrace. Our conversation was incoherent and inconsequent. Ejaculations, eager questions, incomplete answers, messages from my wife, explanations as to my journey, were all jumbled up together.

"I suppose there's someone in my old rooms?" I asked at last, when we had calmed down somewhat. "I'd love to put up here again with you."

Poirot's face changed with startling suddenness.

"*Mon Dieu!* but what a *chance épouvantable*. Regard around you, my friend."

For the first time I took note of my surroundings. Against the wall stood a vast ark of a trunk of prehistoric design. Near to it were placed a number of suit-cases, ranged neatly in order of size from large to small. The inference was unmistakable.

"You are going away?"

"Yes."

"Where to?"

"South America."

"*What?*"

"Yes, it is a droll farce, is it not? It is to Rio I go, and every day I say to myself, I will write nothing in my letters—but oh! the surprise of the good Hastings when he beholds me!"

"But when are you going?"

Poirot looked at his watch.

"In an hour's time."

"I thought you always said nothing would induce you to make a long sea voyage?"

Poirot closed his eyes and shuddered.

"Speak not of it to me, my friend. My doctor, he assures me that one dies not of it—and it is for the one time only; you understand, that never—never shall I return."

He pushed me into a chair.

"Come, I will tell you how it all came about. Do you know who is the richest man in the world? Richer even than Rockefeller? Abe Ryland."

"The American Soap King?"

"Precisely. One of his secretaries approached me. There is some very considerable, as you would call it, hocus-pocus going on in connection with a big company in Rio. He wished me to investigate matters on the spot. I refused. I told him that if the facts were laid before me, I would give him my expert opinion. But that he professed himself unable to do. I was to be put in possession of the facts only on my arrival out there. Normally, that would have closed the matter. To dictate to Hercule Poirot is sheer impertinence. But the sum offered was so stupendous that for the first time in my life I was tempted by mere money. It was a compettence—a fortune! And there was a second attraction—*you*, my friend. For this last year and a half I have been a very lonely old man. I thought to myself, Why not? I am beginning to weary of this unending solving of foolish problems. I have achieved sufficient fame. Let me take this money and settle down somewhere near my old friend."

I was quite affected by this token of Poirot's regard.

"So I accepted," he continued, "and in an hour's time I must leave to catch the boat train. One of life's little ironies, is it not? But I will admit to you, Hastings, that had not the money offered been so big, I might have hesitated, for just lately I have begun a little investigation of my own. Tell me, what is commonly meant by the phrase, 'The Big Four'?"

"I suppose it had its origin at the Versailles Conference, and then there's the famous 'Big Four' in the film world, and the term is used by hosts of smaller fry."

"I see," said Poirot thoughtfully. "I have come across the phrase, you understand, under certain circumstances where none of those explanations would apply. It seems to refer to a gang of international criminals or something of that kind; only—"

"Only what?" I asked, as he hesitated.

"Only that I fancy that it is something on a large scale. Just a little idea of mine, nothing more. Ah, but I must complete my packing. The time advances."

"Don't go," I urged. "Cancel your passage and come out on the same boat with me."

Poirot drew himself up and glanced at me reproachfully.

"Ah, it is that you do not understand! I have passed my word, you comprehend—the word of Hercule Poirot. Nothing but a matter of life or death could detain me now."

"And that's not likely to occur," I murmured ruefully. "Unless at the eleventh hour 'the door opens and the unexpected guest comes in.'"

I quoted the old saw with a slight laugh, and then, in the pause that succeeded it, we both started as a sound came from the inner room.

"What's that?" I cried.

"Ma foi!" retorted Poirot. "It sounds very like your 'unexpected guest' in my bedroom."

"But how can anyone be in there? There's no door except into this room."

"Your memory is excellent, Hastings. Now for the deductions."

"The window! But it's a burglar then? He must have had a stiff climb of it—I should say it was almost impossible."

I had risen to my feet and was striding in the direction of the door when the sound of a fumbling at the handle from the other side arrested me.

The door swung slowly open. Framed in the doorway stood a man. He was coated from head to foot with dust and mud; his face was thin and emaciated. He stared at us for a moment, and then swayed and fell. Poirot hurried to his side, then he looked up and spoke to me.

"Brandy—quickly."

I dashed some brandy into a glass and brought it. Poirot

managed to administer a little, and together we raised him and carried him to the couch. In a few minutes he opened his eyes and looked round him with an almost vacant stare.

"What is it you want, monsieur?" said Poirot.

The man opened his lips and spoke in a queer mechanical voice.

"M. Hercule Poirot, 14 Farraway Street."

"Yes, yes; I am he."

The man did not seem to understand, and merely repeated in exactly the same tone:—

"M. Hercule Poirot, 14 Farraway Street."

Poirot tried him with several questions. Sometimes the man did not answer at all; sometimes he repeated the same phrase. Poirot made a sign to me to ring up on the telephone.

"Get Dr. Ridgeway to come round."

The doctor was in luckily; and as his house was only just round the corner, few minutes elapsed before he came bustling in.

"What's all this, eh?"

Poirot gave a brief explanation, and the doctor started examining our strange visitor, who seemed quite unconscious of his presence or ours.

"H'm!" said Dr. Ridgeway, when he had finished. "Curious case."

"Brain fever?" I suggested.

The doctor immediately snorted with contempt.

"Brain fever! Brain fever! No such thing as brain fever. An invention of novelists. No; the man's had a shock of some kind. He's come here under the force of a persistent idea—to find M. Hercule Poirot, 14 Farraway Street—and he repeats those words mechanically without in the least knowing what they mean."

"Aphasia?" I said eagerly.

This suggestion did not cause the doctor to snort quite as violently as my last one had done. He made no answer, but handed the man a sheet of paper and a pencil.

"Let's see what he'll do with that," he remarked.

The man did nothing with it for some moments, then he suddenly began to write feverishly. With equal suddenness he stopped and let both paper and pencil fall to the ground. The doctor picked it up, and shook his head.

"Nothing here. Only the figure 4 scrawled a dozen times, each one bigger than the last. Wants to write 14 Farraway Street, I expect. It's an interesting case—very interesting. Can you possibly keep him here until this afternoon? I'm due at the hospital now, but I'll come back this afternoon and make all arrangements about him. It's too interesting a case to be lost sight of."

I explained Poirot's departure and the fact that I proposed to accompany him to Southampton.

"That's all right. Leave the man here. He won't get into mischief. He's suffering from complete exhaustion. Will probably sleep for eight hours on end. I'll have a word with that excellent Mrs. Funnyface of yours, and tell her to keep an eye on him."

And Dr. Ridgeway bustled out with his usual celerity. Poirot hastily completed his packing, with one eye on the clock.

"The time, it marches with a rapidity unbelievable. Come now, Hastings, you cannot say that I have left you with nothing to do. A most sensational problem. The man from the unknown. Who is he? What is he? Ah, *sapristi*, but I would give two years of my life to have this boat go to-morrow instead of to-day. There is something here very curious—very interesting. But one must have time—*time*. It may be days—or even months—before he will be able to tell us what he came to tell."

"I'll do my best, Poirot," I assured him. "I'll try to be an efficient substitute."

"Ye-es."

His rejoinder struck me as being a shade doubtful. I picked up the sheet of paper.

"If I were writing a story," I said lightly, "I should weave this in with your latest idiosyncrasy and call it *The Mystery of the Big*

Four." I tapped the pencilled figures as I spoke.

And then I started, for our invalid, roused suddenly from his stupor, sat up in his chair and said clearly and distinctly:

"Li Chang Yen."

He had the look of a man suddenly awakened from sleep. Poirot made a sign to me not to speak. The man went on. He spoke in a clear, high voice, and something in his enunciation made me feel that he was quoting from some written report or lecture.

"Li Chang Yen may be regarded as representing the brains of the Big Four. He is the controlling and motive force. I have designated him, therefore, as Number One. Number Two is seldom mentioned by name. He is represented by an 'S' with two lines through it—the sign for a dollar; also by two stripes and a star. It may be conjectured, therefore, that he is an American subject, and that he represents the power of wealth. There seems no doubt that Number Three is a woman, and her nationality French. It is possible that she may be one of the sirens of the *demi-monde* but nothing is known definitely. Number Four—"

His voice faltered and broke. Poirot leant forward.

"Yes," he prompted eagerly. "Number Four?"

His eyes were fastened on the man's face. Some overmastering terror seemed to be gaining the day; the features were distorted and twisted.

"*The destroyer*," gasped the man. Then, with a final convulsive movement, he fell back in a dead faint.

"*Mon Dieu!*" whispered Poirot, "I was right then. I was right."

"You think—?"

He interrupted me.

"Carry him on to the bed in my room. I have not a minute to lose if I would catch my train. Not that I want to catch it. Oh, that I could miss it with a clear conscience! But I gave my word. Come, Hastings!"

Leaving our mysterious visitor in the charge of Mrs. Pearson, we drove away, and duly caught the train by the skin of our teeth.

Poirot was alternately silent and loquacious. He would sit staring out of the window like a man lost in a dream, apparently not hearing a word that I said to him. Then, reverting to animation suddenly, he would shower injunctions and commands upon me, and urge the necessity of constant marconigrams.

We had a long fit of silence just after we passed Woking. The train, of course, did not stop anywhere until Southampton; but just here it happened to be held up by a signal.

"Ah! *Sacré mille tonnerres!*" cried Poirot suddenly. "But I have been an imbecile. I see clearly at last. It is undoubtedly the blessed saints who stopped the train. Jump, Hastings, but jump, I tell you."

In an instant he had unfastened the carriage door, and jumped out on the line.

"Throw out the suit-cases and jump yourself."

I obeyed him. Just in time. As I alighted beside him, the train moved on.

"And now Poirot," I said, in some exasperation, "perhaps you will tell me what all this is about."

"It is, my friend, that I have seen the light."

"That," I said, "is very illuminating to me."

"It should be," said Poirot, "but I fear—I very much fear that it is not. If you can carry two of these valises, I think I can manage the rest."

TWO
The Man From The Asylum

Fortunately the train had stopped near a station. A short walk brought us to a garage where we were able to obtain a car, and half an hour later we were spinning rapidly back to London. Then, and not till then, did Poirot deign to satisfy my curiosity.

"You do not see? No more did I. But I see now. Hastings, *I was being got out of the way.*"

"What!"

"Yes. Very cleverly. Both the place and the method were chosen with great knowledge and acumen. They were afraid of me."

"Who were?"

"Those four geniuses who have banded themselves together to work outside the law. A Chinaman, an American, a Frenchwoman, and—another. Pray the good God we arrive back in time, Hastings."

"You think there is danger to our visitor?"

"I am sure of it."

Mrs. Pearson greeted us on arrival. Brushing aside her ecstasies of astonishment on beholding Poirot, we asked for information. It was reassuring. No one had called, and our guest had not made any sign.

With a sigh of relief we went up to the rooms. Poirot crossed the outer one and went through to the inner one. Then he called me, his voice strangely agitated.

"Hastings, he's dead."

I came running to join him. The man was lying as we had left him, but he was dead, and had been dead some time. I rushed out for a doctor. Ridgeway, I knew, would not have returned yet. I found one almost immediately, and brought him back with me.

"He's dead right enough, poor chap. Tramp you've been befriending, eh?"

"Something of the kind," said Poirot evasively. "What was the cause of death, doctor?"

"Hard to say. Might have been some kind of fit. There are signs of asphyxiation. No gas laid on, is there?"

"No, electric light—nothing else."

"And both windows wide open, too. Been dead about two hours, I should say. You'll notify the proper people, won't you?"

He took his departure. Poirot did some necessary telephoning. Finally, somewhat to my surprise, he rang up our old friend Inspector Japp, and asked him if he could possibly come round.

No sooner were these proceedings completed than Mrs. Pearson appeared, her eyes as round as saucers.

"There's a man here from 'Anwell—from the 'Sylum. Did you ever? Shall I show him up?"

We signified assent, and a big burly man in uniform was ushered in.

"'Morning, gentlemen," he said cheerfully. "I've got reason to believe you've got one of my birds here. Escaped last night, he did."

"He was here," said Poirot quietly.

"Not got away again, has he?" asked the keeper, with some concern.

"He is dead."

The man looked more relieved than otherwise.

"You don't say so. Well, I dare say it's best for all parties."

"Was he—dangerous?"

"'Omicidal, d'you mean? Oh, no. 'Armless enough. Persecution mania very acute. Full of secret societies from China that had got him shut up. They're all the same."

I shuddered.

"How long had he been shut up?" asked Poirot.

"A matter of two years now."

"I see," said Poirot quietly. "It never occurred to anybody that he might—be sane?"

The keeper permitted himself to laugh.

"If he was sane, what would he be doing in a lunatic asylum? They all *say* they're sane, you know."

Poirot said no more. He took the man in to see the body. The identification came immediately.

"That's him—right enough," said the keeper callously; "funny sort of bloke, ain't he? Well, gentlemen, I had best go off now and make arrangements under the circumstances. We won't trouble you with the corpse much longer. If there's an inquest, you will have to appear at it, I dare say. Good morning, sir."

With a rather uncouth bow he shambled out of the room.

A few minutes later Japp arrived. The Scotland Yard Inspector was jaunty and dapper as usual.

"Here I am Moosior Poirot. What can I do for you? Thought you were off to the coral strands of somewhere or other to-day?"

"My good Japp, I want to know if you have ever seen this man before."

He led Japp into the bedroom. The inspector stared down at the figure on the bed with a puzzled face.

"Let me see now—he seems sort of familiar—and I pride myself on my memory, too. Why, God bless my soul, it's Mayerling!"

"And who is—or was—Mayerling?"

"Secret Service chap—not one of our people. Went to Russia five years ago. Never heard of again. Always thought the Bolshies had done him in."

"It all fits in," said Poirot, when Japp had taken his leave, "except for the fact that he seems to have died a natural death."

He stood looking down on the motionless figure with a dissatisfied frown. A puff of wind set the window-curtains flying out, and he looked up sharply.

"I suppose you opened the windows when you laid him down on the bed, Hastings?"

"No, I didn't," I replied. "As far as I remember, they were shut."

Poirot lifted his head suddenly.

"Shut—and now they are open. What can that mean?"

"Somebody came in that way," I suggested.

"Possibly," agreed Poirot, but he spoke absently and without conviction. After a minute or two he said:

"That is not exactly the point I had in mind, Hastings. If only one window was open it would not intrigue me so much. It is both windows being open that strikes me as curious."

He hurried into the other room.

"The sitting-room window is open, too. That also we left shut. Ah!"

He bent over the dead man, examining the corners of the mouth minutely. Then he looked up suddenly.

"He has been gagged, Hastings. Gagged and then poisoned."

"Good heavens!" I exclaimed, shocked. "I suppose we shall find out all about it from the post-mortem."

"We shall find out nothing. He was killed by inhaling strong prussic acid. It was jammed right under his nose. Then the murderer went away again, first opening all the windows. Hydrocyanic acid is exceedingly volatile, but it has a pronounced smell of bitter almonds. With no trace of the smell to guide them, and no suspicion of foul play, death would be put down to some natural cause by the doctors. So this man was in the Secret Service, Hastings. And five years ago he disappeared in Russia."

"The last two years he's been in the Asylum," I said. "But what of the three years before that?"

Poirot shook his head, and then caught my arm.

"The clock, Hastings, look at the clock."

I followed his gaze to the mantelpiece. The clock had stopped at four o'clock.

"*Mon ami*, some one has tampered with it. It had still three days to run. It is an eight-day clock, you comprehend?"

"But what should they want to do that for? Some idea of a false scent by making the crime appear to have taken place at four o'clock?"

"No, no; rearrange your ideas, mon ami. Exercise your little gray cells. You are Mayerling. You hear something, perhaps—and you know well enough that your doom is sealed. You have just time to leave a sign. *Four* o'clock, Hastings. Number Four, the *destroyer*. Ah! an idea!"

He rushed into the other room and seized the telephone. He asked for Hanwell.

"You are the Asylum, yes? I understand there has been an escape to-day? What is that you say? A little moment, if you please. Will you repeat that? Ah! *parfaitement*."

He hung up the receiver, and turned to me.

"You heard, Hastings? *There has been no escape*."

"But the man who came—the keeper?" I said.

"I wonder—I very much wonder."

"You mean—?"

"Number Four—the destroyer."

I gazed at Poirot dumbfounded. A minute or two after, on recovering my voice, I said:—

"We shall know him again, anywhere, that's one thing. He was a man of very pronounced personality."

"Was he, *mon ami*? I think not. He was burly and bluff and red-faced, with a thick moustache and a hoarse voice. He will be none of those things by this time, and for the rest, he has nondescript eyes, nondescript ears, and a perfect set of false teeth. Identification is not such an easy matter as you seem to think. Next time—"

"You think there will be a next time?" I interrupted.

Poirot's face grew very grave.

"It is a duel to the death, *mon ami*. You and I on the one side, the Big Four on the other. They have won the first trick; but they have failed in their plan to get me out of the way, and in the future they have to reckon with Hercule Poirot!"

THREE
We Hear More About Li Chang Yen

For a day or two after our visit from the fake Asylum attendant I was in some hopes that he might return, and I refused to leave the flat even for a moment. As far as I could see, he had no reason to suspect that we had penetrated his disguise. He might, I thought, return and try to remove the body, but Poirot scoffed at my reasoning.

"*Mon ami*," he said, "if you wish you may wait in to put salt on the little bird's tail, but for me I do not waste my time so."

"Well then, Poirot," I argued, "why did he run the risk of coming at all. If he intended to return later for the body, I can see some point in his visit. He would at least be removing the evidence against himself; as it is, he does not seem to have gained anything."

Poirot shrugged his most Gallic shrug. "But you do not see with the eyes of Number Four, Hastings," he said. "You talk of evidence, but what evidence have we against him? True, we have a body, but we have no proof even that the man was murdered— prussic acid, when inhaled, leaves no trace. Again, we can find no one who saw any one enter the flat during our absence, and we have found out nothing about the movements of our late friend, Mayerling....

"No, Hastings, Number Four has left no trace, and he knows

it. His visit we may call a reconnaissance. Perhaps he wanted to make quite sure that Mayerling was dead, but more likely, I think, he came to see Hercule Poirot, and to have speech with the adversary whom alone he must fear."

Poirot's reasoning appeared to me typically egotistical, but I forbore to argue.

"And what about the inquest?" I asked. "I suppose you will explain things clearly there, and let the police have a full description of Number Four."

"And to what end? Can we produce anything to impress a coroner's jury of your solid Britishers? Is our description of Number Four of any value? No; we shall allow them to call it 'Accidental Death,' and may be, although I have not much hope, our clever murderer will pat himself on the back that he deceived Hercule Poirot in the first round."

Poirot was right as usual. We saw no more of the man from the asylum, and the inquest, at which I gave evidence, but which Poirot did not even attend, aroused no public interest.

As, in view of his intended trip to South America, Poirot had wound up his affairs before my arrival, he had at this time no cases on hand, but although he spent most of his time in the flat I could get little out of him. He remained buried in an armchair, and discouraged my attempts at conversation.

And then one morning, about a week after the murder, he asked me if I would care to accompany him on a visit he wished to make. I was pleased, for I felt he was making a mistake in trying to work things out so entirely on his own, and I wished to discuss the case with him. But I found he was not communicative. Even when I asked where we were going, he would not answer.

Poirot loves being mysterious. He will never part with a piece of information until the last possible moment. In this instance, having taken successively a 'bus and two trains, and arrived in the neighbourhood of one of London's most depressing southern suburbs, he consented at last to explain matters.

17

"We go, Hastings, to see the one man in England who knows most of the underground life of China."

"Indeed! Who is he?"

"A man you have never heard of—a Mr. John Ingles. To all intents and purposes, he is a retired Civil Servant of mediocre intellect, with a house full of Chinese curios with which he bores his friends and acquaintances. Nevertheless, I am assured by those who should know that the only man capable of giving me the information I seek is this same John Ingles."

A few moments more saw us ascending the steps of The Laurels, as Mr. Ingles's residence was called. Personally, I did not notice a laurel bush of any kind, so deduced that it had been named according to the usual obscure nomenclature of the suburbs.

We were admitted by an impassive-faced Chinese servant and ushered into the presence of his master. Mr. Ingles was a squarely-built man, somewhat yellow of countenance, with deep-set eyes that were oddly reflective in character. He rose to greet us, setting aside an open letter which he had held in his hand. He referred to it after his greeting.

"Sit down, won't you? Halsey tells me that you want some information and that I may be useful to you in the matter."

"That is so, monsieur. I ask of you if you have any knowledge of a man named Li Chang Yen?"

"That's rum—very rum indeed. How did you come to hear about the man?"

"You know him, then?"

"I've met him once. And I know something of him—not quite as much as I should like to. But it surprises me that anyone else in England should even have heard of him. He's a great man in his way—mandarin class and all that, you know—but that's not the crux of the matter. There's good reason to suppose that he's the man behind it all."

"Behind what?"

"Everything. The world-wide unrest, the labour troubles that beset every nation, and the revolutions that break out in some. There are people, not scaremongers, who know what they are talking about, and they say that there is a force behind the scenes which aims at nothing less than the disintegration of civilisation. In Russia, you know, there were many signs that Lenin and Trotsky were mere puppets whose every action was dictated by another's brain. I have no definite proof that would count with you, but I am quite convinced that this brain was Li Chang Yen's."

"Oh, come," I protested, "isn't that a bit farfetched? How would a Chinaman cut any ice in Russia?"

Poirot frowned at me irritably.

"For you, Hastings," he said, "everything is farfetched that comes not from your own imagination; for me, I agree with this gentleman. But continue, I pray, monsieur."

"What exactly he hopes to get out of it all I cannot pretend to say for certain," went on Mr. Ingles; "but I assume his disease is one that has attacked great brains from the time of Akbar and Alexander to Napoleon—a lust for power and personal supremacy. Up to modern times armed force was necessary for conquest, but in this century of unrest a man like Li Chang Yen can use other means. I have evidence that he has unlimited money behind him for bribery and propaganda, and there are signs that he controls some scientific force more powerful than the world has dreamed of."

Poirot was following Mr. Ingles's words with the closest attention.

"And in China?" he asked. "He moves there too?"

The other nodded in emphatic assent.

"There," he said, "although I can produce no proof that would count in a court of law, I speak from my own knowledge. I know personally every man who counts for anything in China to-day, and this I can tell you: the men who loom most largely in the public eye are men of little or no personality. They are marionettes who dance to the wires pulled by a master hand, and that hand is Li Chang Yen's. His is the controlling brain of the East to-day. We don't understand the East—we never shall; but Li Chang Yen is its moving spirit. Not that he comes out into the limelight—oh, not at all; he never moves from his palace in Pekin. But he pulls strings—that's it, pulls strings—and things happen far away."

"And is there no one to oppose him?" asked Poirot.

Mr. Ingles leant forward in his chair.

"Four men have tried in the last four years," he said slowly; "men of character, and honesty, and brain power. Any one of them might in time have interfered with his plans." He paused.

"Well?" I queried.

"Well, they are dead. One wrote an article, and mentioned Li Chang Yen's name in connection with the riots in Peking, and within two days he was stabbed in the street. His murderer was never caught. The offences of the other two were similar. In a speech or an article, or in conversation, each linked Li Chang Yen's name with rioting or revolution, and within a week of his indiscretion each was dead. One was poisoned; one died of cholera, an isolated case—not part of an epidemic; and one was found dead in his bed. The cause of the last death was never determined, but I was told by a doctor who saw the corpse that it was burnt and shrivelled as though a wave of electrical energy of incredible power had passed through it."

"And Li Chang Yen?" inquired Poirot. "Naturally nothing is traced to him, but there are signs, eh?"

Mr. Ingles shrugged.

"Oh, signs—yes, certainly. And once I found a man who would talk, a brilliant young Chinese chemist who was a protégé of Li Chang Yen's. He came to me one day, this chemist, and I could see that he was on the verge of a nervous breakdown. He hinted to me of experiments on which he'd been engaged in Li Chang Yen's palace under the mandarin's direction—experiments on coolies in which the most revolting disregard for human life and suffering had been shown. His nerve had completely broken, and he was in the most pitiable state of terror. I put him to bed in a top room of my own house, intending to question him the next day—and that, of course, was stupid of me."

"How did they get him?" demanded Poirot.

"That I shall never know. I woke that night to find my house in flames, and was lucky to escape with my life. Investigation showed that a fire of amazing intensity had broken out on the top floor, and the remains of my young chemist friend were charred to a cinder."

I could see from the earnestness with which he had been speaking that Mr. Ingles was a man mounted on his hobby horse, and evidently he, too, realised that he had been carried away, for he laughed apologetically.

"But, of course," he said, "I have no proofs, and you, like the others, will merely tell me that I have a bee in my bonnet."

"On the contrary," said Poirot quietly, "we have every reason to believe your story. We ourselves are more than a little interested in Li Chang Yen."

"Very odd your knowing about him. Didn't fancy a soul in England had ever heard of him. I'd rather like to know how you did come to hear of him—if it's not indiscreet."

"Not in the least, monsieur. A man took refuge in my rooms. He was suffering badly from shock, but he managed to tell us enough to interest us in this Li Chang Yen. He described four people—the Big Four—an organisation hitherto undreamed of. Number One is Li Chang Yen, Number Two is an unknown American, Number Three an equally unknown Frenchwoman, Number Four may be called the executive of the organisation—*the destroyer*. My informant died. Tell me, monsieur, is that phrase known to you at all? The Big Four."

"Not in connection with Li Chang Yen. No, I can't say it is. But I've heard it, or read it, just lately—and in some unusual connection too. Ah, I've got it."

He rose and went across to an inlaid lacquer cabinet—an exquisite thing, as even I could see. He returned with a letter in his hand.

21

"Here you are. Note from an old sea-faring man I ran against once in Shanghai. Hoary old reprobate—maudlin with drink by now, I should say. I took this to be the ravings of alcoholism."

He read it aloud:—

"Dear Sir,—You may not remember me, but you did me a good turn once in Shanghai. Do me another now. I must have money to get out of the country. I'm well hid here, I hope, but any day they may get me. The Big Four, I mean. It's life or death. I've plenty of money, but I daren't get at it, for fear of putting them wise. Send me a couple of hundred in notes. I'll repay it faithful—I swear to that.—Your servant, sir,

"Jonathan Whalley."

"Dated from Granite Bungalow, Hoppaton, Dartmoor. I'm afraid I regarded it as rather a crude method of relieving me of a couple of hundred which I can ill spare. If it's any use to you—"
He held it out.

"*Je vous remercie*, monsieur. I start for Hoppaton *à l'heure même.*"

"Dear me, this is very interesting. Supposing I come along too? Any objection?"

"I should be charmed to have your company, but we must start at once. We shall not reach Dartmoor until close on nightfall, as it is."

John Ingles did not delay us more than a couple of minutes, and soon we were in the train moving out of Paddington bound for the West Country. Hoppaton was a small village clustering in a hollow right on the fringe of the moorland. It was reached by a nine-mile drive from Moretonhamstead. It was about eight o'clock when we arrived; but as the month was July, the daylight was still abundant.

We drove into the narrow street of the village and then stopped to ask our way of an old rustic.

"Granite Bungalow," said the old man reflectively, "it be Granite Bungalow you do want? Eh?"

We assured him that this was what we did want.

The old man pointed to a small gray cottage at the end of the street.

"There be the Bungalow. Do yee want to see t'Inspector?"

"What Inspector?" asked Poirot sharply; "what do you mean?"

"Haven't yee heard about t'murder, then? A shocking business t'was seemingly. Pools of blood, they do say."

"*Mon Dieu!*" murmured Poirot. "This Inspector of yours, I must see him at once."

Five minutes later we were closeted with Inspector Meadows. The Inspector was inclined to be stiff at first, but at the magic name of Inspector Japp of Scotland Yard, he unbent.

"Yes, sir; murdered this morning. A shocking business. They 'phoned to Moreton, and I came out at once. Looked a mysterious thing to begin with. The old man—he was about seventy, you know, and fond of his glass, from all I hear—was lying on the floor of the living-room. There was a bruise on his head and his throat was cut from ear to ear. Blood all over the place, as you can understand. The woman who cooks for him, Betsy Andrews, she told us that her master had several little Chinese jade figures, that he'd told her were very valuable, and these had disappeared. That, of course, looked like assault and robbery; but there were all sorts of difficulties in the way of that solution. The old fellow had two people in the house; Betsy Andrews, who is a Hoppaton woman, and a rough kind of manservant, Robert Grant. Grant had gone to the farm to fetch the milk, which he does every day, and Betsy had stepped out to have a chat with a neighbour. She was only away twenty minutes—between ten and half-past—and the crime must have been done then. Grant returned to the house first. He went in by the back door, which was open—no one locks up doors round here—not in broad daylight, at all events—put the milk in the larder, and went into his own room to read the paper and have a smoke. Had no idea anything unusual had occurred—at least, that's what he says. Then Betsy comes in, goes into the living-room, sees what's happened, and lets out a screech to wake the dead. That's all fair and square. Someone got in whilst those two were out, and did the poor old man in. But it struck me at once that he must be a pretty cool customer. He'd have to come right up the village street, or creep through someone's back yard. Granite Bungalow has got houses all round it, as you can see. How was it that no one had seen him?"

The Inspector paused with a flourish.

"Aha, I perceive your point," said Poirot. "To continue?"

"Well, sir, fishy, I said to myself—fishy. And I began to look about me. Those jade figures, now. Would a common tramp ever suspect that they were valuable? Anyway, it was madness to try such a thing in broad daylight. Suppose the old man had yelled for help?"

"I suppose, Inspector," said Mr. Ingles, "that the bruise on the head was inflicted before death?"

"Quite right, sir. First knocked him silly, the murderer did, and then cut his throat. That's clear enough. But how the dickens did he come or go? They notice strangers quick enough in a little place like this. It came to me all at once—nobody did come. I took a good look round. It had rained the night before, and there were footprints clear enough going in and out of the kitchen. In the living-room there were two sets of footprints only (Betsy Andrews' stopped at the door)—Mr. Whalley's (he was wearing carpet slippers) and another man's. The other man had stepped in the blood-stains, and I traced his bloody footprints—I beg your pardon, sir."

"Not at all," said Mr. Ingles, with a faint smile; "the adjective is perfectly understood."

"I traced them to the kitchen—but not beyond. Point Number One. On the lintel of Robert Grant's door was a faint smear—a smear of blood. That's point Number Two. Point Number Three was when I got hold of Grant's boots—which he had taken off—and fitted them to the marks. That settled it. It was an inside job. I warned Grant and took him into custody; and what do you think I found packed away in his portmanteau? The little jade figures and a ticket-of-leave. Robert Grant was also Abraham Biggs, convicted for felony and housebreaking five years ago."

The Inspector paused triumphantly.

"What do you think of that, gentlemen?"

"I think," said Poirot, "that it appears a very clear case—of a surprising clearness, in fact. This Biggs, or Grant, he must be a man very foolish and uneducated, eh?"

"Oh, he is that—a rough, common sort of fellow. No idea of what a footprint may mean."

"Clearly he reads not the detective fiction! Well, Inspector, I congratulate you. We may look at the scene of the crime. Yes?"

"I'll take you there myself this minute. I'd like you to see those footprints."

"I, too, should like to see them. Yes, yes, very interesting, very ingenious."

We set out forthwith. Mr. Ingles and the Inspector forged ahead. I drew Poirot back a little so as to be able to speak to him out of the Inspector's hearing.

"What do you really think, Poirot. Is there more in this than meets the eye?"

"That is just the question, *mon ami*. Whalley says plainly enough in his letter that the Big Four are on his track, and we know, you and I, that the Big Four is no bogey for the children. Yet everything seems to say that this man Grant committed the crime. Why did he do so? For the sake of the little jade figures? Or is he an agent of the Big Four? I confess that this last seems more likely. However valuable the jade, a man of that class was not likely to realise the fact—at any rate, not to the point of committing murder for them. (That, *par exemple*, ought to have struck the Inspector.) He could have stolen the jade and made off with it instead of committing a brutal and quite purposeless murder. Ah, yes; I fear our Devonshire friend has not used his little gray cells. He has measured footprints, and has omitted to reflect and arrange his ideas with the necessary order and method."

FOUR

The Importance of A Leg of Mutton

T he inspector drew a key from his pocket and unlocked the door of Granite Bungalow. The day had been fine and dry, so our feet were not likely to leave any prints; nevertheless, we wiped them carefully on the mat before entering.

A woman came up out of the gloom and spoke to the Inspector, and he turned aside. Then he spoke over his shoulder.

"Have a good look round, Mr. Poirot, and see all there is to be seen. I'll be back in about ten minutes. By the way, here's Grant's boot. I brought it along with me for you to compare the impressions."

We went into the living-room, and the sound of the Inspector's footsteps died away outside. Ingles was attracted immediately by some Chinese curios on a table in the corner, and went over to examine them. He seemed to take no interest in Poirot's doings. I, on the other hand, watched him with breathless interest. The floor was covered with a dark-green linoleum which was ideal for showing up footprints. A door at the farther end led into the small kitchen. From there another door led into the scullery (where the back door was situated), and another into the bedroom which had been occupied by Robert Grant. Having explored the ground, Poirot commented upon it in a low running monologue.

26

"Here is where the body lay; that big dark stain and the splashes all around mark the spot. Traces of carpet slippers and 'number nine' boots, you observe, but all very confused. Then two sets of tracks leading to and from the kitchen; whoever the murderer was, he came in that way. You have the boot, Hastings? Give it to me." He compared it carefully with the prints. "Yes, both made by the same man, Robert Grant. He came in that way, killed the old man, and went back to the kitchen. He had stepped in the blood; see the stains he left as he went out? Nothing to be seen in the kitchen—all the village has been walking about in it. He went into his own room—no, first he went back again to the scene of the crime—was that to get the little jade figures? Or had he forgotten something that might incriminate him?"

"Perhaps he killed the old man the second time he went in?" I suggested.

"*Mais non*, you do not observe. On one of the outgoing foot-marks stained with blood there is superimposed an ingoing one. I wonder what he went back for—the little jade figures as an afterthought? It is all ridiculous—stupid."

"Well, he's given himself away pretty hopelessly."

"*N'est-ce pas?* I tell you, Hastings, it goes against reason. It offends my little gray cells. Let us go into his bedroom—ah, yes; there is the smear of blood on the lintel and just a trace of foot-marks—the blood-stained. Robert Grant's footmarks, and his only, near the body—Robert Grant the only man who went near the house. Yes, it must be so."

"What about the old woman?" I said suddenly. "She was in the house alone after Grant had gone for the milk. She might have killed him and then gone out. Her feet would leave no prints if she hadn't been outside."

"Very good, Hastings. I wondered whether that hypothesis would occur to you. I had already thought of it and rejected it. Betsy Andrews is a local woman, well-known hereabouts. She can have no connection with the Big Four; and, besides, old Whalley was a powerful fellow, by all accounts. This is a man's work—not a woman's."

"I suppose the Big Four couldn't have had some diabolical contrivance concealed in the ceiling—something which descended automatically and cut the old man's throat and was afterwards drawn up again?"

"Like Jacob's ladder? I know, Hastings, that you have an imagination of the most fertile—but I implore of you to keep it within bounds."

I subsided, abashed. Poirot continued to wander about, poking into rooms and cupboards with a profoundly dissatisfied expression on his face. Suddenly he uttered an excited yelp, reminiscent of a Pomeranian dog. I rushed to join him. He was standing in the larder in a dramatic attitude. In his hand he was brandishing a leg of mutton!

"My dear Poirot!" I cried. "What is the matter? Have you suddenly gone mad?"

"Regard, I pray you, this mutton. But regard it closely!"

I regarded it as closely as I could, but could see nothing unusual about it. It seemed to me a very ordinary leg of mutton. I said as much. Poirot threw me a withering glance.

"But do you not see this—and this—and this—"

He illustrated each "this" with a jab at the unoffending joint, dislodging small icicles as he did so.

Poirot had just accused me of being imaginative, but I now felt that he was far more wildly so than I had ever been. Did he seriously think these slivers of ice were crystals of a deadly poison? That was the only construction I could put upon his extraordinary agitation.

"It's frozen meat," I explained gently. "Imported, you know. New Zealand."

He stared at me for a moment or two and then broke into a strange laugh.

"How marvellous is my friend Hastings! He knows

everything—but everything! How do they say—Inquire Within Upon Everything. That is my friend Hastings."

He flung down the leg of mutton onto its dish again and left the larder. Then he looked through the window.

"Here comes our friend the Inspector. It is well. I have seen all I want to see here." He drummed on the table absent-mindedly, as though absorbed in calculation, and then asked suddenly, "What is the day of the week, *mon ami?*"

"Monday," I said, rather astonished. "What—?"

"Ah! Monday, is it? A bad day of the week. To commit a murder on a Monday is a mistake."

Passing back to the living-room, he tapped the glass on the wall and glanced at the thermometer.

"Set fair, and seventy degrees Fahrenheit. An orthodox English summer's day."

Ingles was still examining various pieces of Chinese pottery.

"You do not take much interest in this inquiry, monsieur?" said Poirot.

The other gave a slow smile.

"It's not my job, you see. I'm a connoisseur of some things, but not of this. So I just stand back and keep out of the way. I've learnt patience in the East."

The Inspector came bustling in, apologising for having been so long away. He insisted on taking us over most of the ground again, but finally we got away.

"I must appreciate your thousand politenesses, Inspector," said Poirot, as we were walking down the village street again. "There is just one more request I should like to put to you."

"You want to see the body, perhaps, sir?"

"Oh, dear me, no! I have not the least interest in the body. I want to see Robert Grant."

"You'll have to drive back with me to Moreton to see him, sir."

"Very well, I will do so. But I must see him and be able to speak to him alone."

The Inspector caressed his upper lip.

"Well, I don't know about that, sir."

"I assure you that if you can get through to Scotland Yard you will receive full authority."

"I've heard of you, of course, sir, and I know you've done us a good turn now and again. But it's very irregular."

"Nevertheless, it is necessary," said Poirot calmly. "It is necessary for this reason—Grant is not the murderer."

"What? Who is, then?"

"The murderer was, I should fancy, a youngish man. He drove up to Granite Bungalow in a trap, which he left outside. He went in, committed the murder, came out, and drove away again. He was bare-headed, and his clothing was slightly blood-stained."

"But—but the whole village would have seen him!"

"Not under certain circumstances."

"Not if it was dark, perhaps; but the crime was committed in broad daylight."

Poirot merely smiled.

"And the horse and trap, sir—how could you tell that? Any amount of wheeled vehicles have passed along outside. There's no mark of one in particular to be seen."

"Not with the eyes of the body, perhaps; but with the eyes of the mind, yes."

The Inspector touched his forehead significantly with a grin at me. I was utterly bewildered, but I had faith in Poirot. Further discussion ended in our all driving back to Moreton with the Inspector. Poirot and I were taken to Grant, but a constable was to be present during the interview. Poirot went straight to the point.

"Grant, I know you to be innocent of this crime. Relate to me in your own words exactly what happened."

The prisoner was a man of medium height, with a somewhat unpleasing cast of features. He looked a jailbird if ever a man did.

"Honest to God, I never did it," he whined. "Someone put those little glass figures amongst my traps. It was a frame-up, that's what it was. I went straight to my rooms when I came in, like I said. I never knew a thing till Betsy screeched out. S'welp me, God, I didn't."

Poirot rose.

"If you can't tell me the truth, that is the end of it."

"But, guv'nor—"

"You *did* go into the room—you *did* know your master was dead; and you were just preparing to make a bolt of it when the good Betsy made her terrible discovery."

The man stared at Poirot with a dropped jaw.

"Come now, is it not so? I tell you solemnly—on my word of honour—that to be frank now is your only chance."

"I'll risk it," said the man suddenly. "It was just as you say. I came in, and went straight to the master—and there he was, dead on the floor and blood all round. Then I got the wind up proper. They'd ferret out my record, and for a certainty they'd say it was me as had done him in. My only thought was to get away—at once—before he was found—"

"And the jade figures?"

The man hesitated.

"You see—"

"You took them by a kind of reversion to instinct, as it were? You had heard your master say that they were valuable, and you felt you might as well go the whole hog. That, I understand. Now, answer me this. Was it the second time that you went into the room that you took the figures?"

"I didn't go in a second time. Once was enough for me."

"You are sure of that?"

"Absolutely certain."

"Good. Now, when did you come out of prison?"

"Two months ago."

"How did you obtain this job?"

"Through one of them Prisoners' Help Societies. Bloke met me when I came out."

"What was he like?"

"Not exactly a parson, but looked like one. Soft black hat and mincing way of talking. Got a broken front tooth. Spectacled chap. Saunders his name was. Said he hoped I was repentant, and that he'd find me a good post. I went to old Whalley on his recommendation."

Poirot rose once more.

"I thank you. I know all now. Have patience." He paused in the doorway and added: "Saunders gave you a pair of boots, didn't he?"

Grant looked very astonished.

"Why, yes, he did. But how did you know?"

"It is my business to know things," said Poirot gravely.

After a word or two to the Inspector, the three of us went to the White Hart and discussed eggs and bacon and Devonshire cider.

"Any elucidations yet?" asked Ingles, with a smile.

"Yes, the case is clear enough now; but, see you, I shall have a good deal of difficulty in proving it. Whalley was killed by order of the Big Four—but not by Grant. A very clever man got Grant the post and deliberately planned to make him the scapegoat—an easy matter with Grant's prison record. He gave him a pair of boots, one of two duplicate pairs. The other he kept himself. It was all so simple. When Grant is out of the house, and Betsy is chatting in the village (which she probably did every day of her life), he drives up wearing the duplicate boots, enters the kitchen, goes through into the living-room, fells the old man with a blow, and then cuts his throat. Then he returns to the kitchen, removes the boots, puts on another pair, and, carrying the first pair, goes out to his trap and drives off again."

Ingles looked steadily at Poirot.

"There's a catch in it still. Why did nobody see him?"

"Ah! That is where the cleverness of Number Four, I am convinced, comes in. Everybody saw him—and yet nobody saw him. You see, he drove up in a butcher's cart!"

I uttered an exclamation.

"The leg of mutton?"

"Exactly, Hastings, the leg of mutton. Everybody swore that no one had been to Granite Bungalow that morning, but, nevertheless, I found in the larder a leg of mutton, still frozen. It was Monday, so the meat must have been delivered that morning; for if on Saturday, in this hot weather, it would not have remained frozen over Sunday. So some one *had* been to the Bungalow, and a man on whom a trace of blood here and there would attract no attention."

"Damned ingenious!" cried Ingles approvingly.

"Yes, he is clever, Number Four."

"As clever as Hercule Poirot?" I murmured.

My friend threw me a glance of dignified reproach.

"There are some jests that you should not permit yourself, Hastings," he said sententiously. "Have I not saved an innocent man from being sent to the gallows? That is enough for one day."

FIVE
Disappearance of A Scientist

Personally, I don't think that, even when a jury had acquit-ted Robert Grant, alias Biggs, of the murder of Jonathan Whalley, Inspector Meadows was entirely convinced of his innocence. The case which he had built up against Grant—the man's record, the jade which he had stolen, the boots which fitted the footprints so exactly—was to his matter-of-fact mind too com-plete to be easily upset; but Poirot, compelled much against his inclination to give evidence, convinced the jury. Two witnesses were produced who had seen a butcher's cart drive up to the bun-galow on that Monday morning, and the local butcher testified that his cart only called there on Wednesdays and Fridays.

A woman was actually found who, when questioned, remem-bered seeing the butcher's man leaving the bungalow, but she could furnish no useful description of him. The only impression he seemed to have left on her mind was that he was clean-shaven, of medium height, and looked exactly like a butcher's man. At this description Poirot shrugged his shoulders philosophically.

"It is as I tell you, Hastings," he said to me, after the trial. "He is an artist, this one. He disguises himself not with the false beard and the blue spectacles. He alters his features, yes; but that is the least part. For the time being he *is* the man he would be. He lives in his part."

Certainly I was compelled to admit that the man who had visited us from Hanwell had fitted in exactly with my idea of what an Asylum attendant should look like. I should never for a moment have dreamt of doubting that he was genuine.

It was all a little discouraging, and our experience on Dartmoor did not seem to have helped us at all. I said as much to Poirot, but he would not admit that we had gained nothing.

"We progress," he said; "we progress. At every contact with this man we learn a little of his mind and his methods. Of us and our plans he knows nothing."

"And there, Poirot," I protested, "he and I seem to be in the same boat. You don't seem to me to have any plans, you seem to sit and wait for him to do something."

Poirot smiled.

"Mon ami, you do not change. Always the same Hastings, who would be up and at their throats. Perhaps," he added, as a knock sounded on the door, "you have here your chance; it may be our friend who enters." And he laughed at my disappointment when Inspector Japp and another man entered the room.

"Good-evening, moosior," said the Inspector. "Allow me to introduce Captain Kent of the United States Secret Service."

Captain Kent was a tall, lean American, with a singularly impassive face which looked as though it had been carved out of wood.

"Pleased to meet you, gentlemen," he murmured, as he shook hands jerkily.

Poirot threw an extra log on the fire, and brought forward more easy-chairs. I brought out glasses and the whisky and soda. The captain took a deep draught, and expressed appreciation.

"Legislation in your country is still sound," he observed.

"And now to business," said Japp. "Moosior Poirot here made a certain request to me. He was interested in some concern that went by the name of the Big Four, and he asked me to let him know at any time if I came across a mention of it in my official line of business. I didn't take much stock in the matter, but I remembered what he said, and when the captain here came over with rather a curious story, I said at once, 'We'll go round to Moosior Poirot's.'"

Poirot looked across at Captain Kent, and the American took up the tale.

"You may remember reading, M. Poirot, that a number of torpedo boats and destroyers were sunk by being dashed upon the rocks off the American coast. It was just after the Japanese earthquake, and the explanation given was that the disaster was the result of a tidal wave. Now, a short time ago, a round-up was made of certain crooks and gunmen, and with them were captured some papers which put an entirely new face upon the matter. They appeared to refer to some organisation called the 'Big Four,' and gave an incomplete description of some powerful wireless installation—a concentration of wireless energy far beyond anything so far attempted, and capable of focusing a beam of great intensity upon some given spot. The claims made for this invention seemed manifestly absurd, but I turned them in to headquarters for what they were worth, and one of our highbrow professors got busy on them. Now it appears that one of your British scientists read a paper upon the subject before the British Association. His colleagues didn't think great shakes of it, by all accounts, thought it farfetched and fanciful, but your scientist stuck to his guns, and declared that he himself was on the eve of success in his experiments."

"*Eh, bien?*" demanded Poirot, with interest.

"It was suggested that I should come over here and get an interview with this gentleman. Quite a young fellow, he is, Halliday by name. He is the leading authority on the subject, and I was to get from him whether the thing suggested was anyway possible."

"And was it?" I asked eagerly.

"That's just what I don't know. I haven't seen Mr. Halliday— and I'm not likely to, by all accounts."

"The truth of the matter is," said Japp, shortly, "Halliday's disappeared."

"When?"

"Two months ago."

"Was his disappearance reported?"

"Of course it was. His wife came to us in a great state. We did what we could, but I knew all along it would be no good."

"Why not?"

"Never is—when a man disappears that way." Japp winked.

"What way?"

"Paris."

"So Halliday disappeared in Paris?"

"Yes. Went over there on scientific work—so he said. Of course, he'd have to say something like that. But you know what it means when a man disappears over there. Either it's Apache work, and that's the end of it—or else it's voluntary disappearance—and that's a great deal the commoner of the two, I can tell you. Gay Paree and all that, you know. Sick of home life. Halliday and his wife had had a tiff before he started, which all helps to make it a pretty clear case."

"I wonder," said Poirot thoughtfully.

The American was looking at him curiously.

"Say, mister," he drawled, "what's this Big Four idea?"

"The Big Four," said Poirot, "is an international organisation which has at its head a Chinaman. He is known as Number One. Number Two is an American. Number Three is a Frenchwoman. Number Four, the 'Destroyer,' is an Englishman."

"A Frenchwoman, eh?" The American whistled. "And Halliday disappeared in France. Maybe there's something in this. What's her name?"

"I don't know. I know nothing about her."

"But it's a mighty big proposition, eh?" suggested the other.

Poirot nodded, as he arranged the glasses in a neat row on the tray. His love of order was as great as ever.

"What was the idea in sinking those boats? Are the Big Four a German stunt?"

"The Big Four are for themselves—and for themselves only, M. le Capitaine. Their aim is world domination."

The American burst out laughing, but broke off at the sight of Poirot's serious face.

"You laugh, monsieur," said Poirot, shaking a finger at him. "You reflect not—you use not the little gray cells of the brain. Who are these men who send a portion of your navy to destruction simply as a trial of their power? For that was all it was, Monsieur, a test of this new force of magnetical attraction which they hold."

"Go on with you, moosior," said Japp good-humouredly. "I've read of super criminals many a time, but I've never come across them. Well, you've heard Captain Kent's story. Anything further I can do for you?"

"Yes, my good friend. You can give me the address of Mrs. Halliday—and also a few words of introduction to her if you will be so kind."

Thus it was that the following day saw us bound for Chetwynd Lodge, near the village of Chobham in Surrey.

Mrs. Halliday received us at once, a tall, fair woman, nervous and eager in manner. With her was her little girl, a beautiful child of five.

Poirot explained the purpose of our visit.

"Oh! Monsieur Poirot, I am so glad, so thankful. I have heard of you, of course. You will not be like these Scotland Yard people, who will not listen or try to understand. And the French Police are just as bad—worse, I think. They are all convinced that my husband has gone off with some other woman. But he wasn't like that! All he thought of in life was his work. Half our quarrels came from that. He cared for it more than he did for me."

"Englishmen, they are like that," said Poirot soothingly. "And if it is not work, it is the games, the sport. All those things they take *au grand sérieux*. Now, madame, recount to me exactly, in detail, and as methodically as you can, the exact circumstances of your husband's disappearance."

"My husband went to Paris on Thursday, the 20th of July. He was to meet and visit various people there connected with his work, amongst them Madame Olivier."

Poirot nodded at the mention of the famous French woman chemist, who had eclipsed even Madame Curie in the brilliance of her achievements. She had been decorated by the French Government, and was one of the most prominent personalities of the day.

"He arrived there in the evening and went at once to the Hotel Castiglione in the Rue de Castiglione. On the following morning, he had an appointment with Professor Bourgoneau, which he kept. His manner was normal and pleasant. The two men had a most interesting conversation, and it was arranged that he should witness some experiments in the professor's laboratory on the following day. He lunched alone at the Café Royal, went for a walk in the Bois, and then visited Madame Olivier at her house at Passy. There, also, his manner was perfectly normal. He left about six. Where he dined is not known, probably alone at some restaurant. He returned to the hotel about eleven o'clock and went straight up to his room, after inquiring if any letters had come for him. On the following morning, he walked out of the hotel, and has not been seen again."

"At what time did he leave the hotel? At the hour when he would normally leave it to keep his appointment at Professor Bourgoneau's laboratory?"

"We do not know. He was not remarked leaving the hotel. But no *petit déjeuner* was served to him, which seems to indicate that he went out early."

"Or he might, in fact, have gone out again after he came in the night before?"

"I do not think so. His bed had been slept in, and the night porter would have remembered any one going out at that hour."

"A very just observation, madame. We may take it, then, that he left early on the following morning—and that is reassuring from one point of view. He is not likely to have fallen a victim to any Apache assault at that hour. His baggage, now, was it all left behind?"

Mrs. Halliday seemed rather reluctant to answer, but at last she said:—-

"No—he must have taken one small suit-case with him."

"H'm," said Poirot thoughtfully, "I wonder where he was that evening. If we knew that, we should know a great deal. Whom did he meet?—there lies the mystery. Madame, myself I do not of necessity accept the view of the police; with them is it always 'Cherchez la femme.' Yet it is clear that something occurred that night to alter your husband's plans. You say he asked for letters on returning to the hotel. Did he receive any?"

"One only, and that must have been the one I wrote him on the day he left England."

Poirot remained sunk in thought for a full minute, then he rose briskly to his feet.

"Well, madame, the solution of the mystery lies in Paris, and to find it I myself journey to Paris on the instant."

"It is all a long time ago, monsieur."

"Yes, yes. Nevertheless, it is there that we must seek."

He turned to leave the room, but paused with his hand on the door.

"Tell me, madame, do you ever remember your husband mentioning the phrase, 'The Big Four'?"

"The Big Four," she repeated thoughtfully. "No, I can't say I do."

SIX

The Woman on the Stairs

That was all that could be elicited from Mrs. Halliday. We hurried back to London, and the following day saw us *en route* for the Continent. With rather a rueful smile, Poirot observed:

"This Big Four, they make me to bestir myself, *mon ami*. I run up and down, all over the ground, like our old friend 'the human foxhound.'"

"Perhaps you'll meet him in Paris," I said, knowing that he referred to a certain Giraud, one of the most trusted detectives of the Sureté, whom he had met on a previous occasion.

Poirot made a grimace. "I devoutly hope not. He loved me not, that one."

"Won't it be a very difficult task?" I asked. "To find out what an unknown Englishman did on an evening two months ago?"

"Very difficult, *mon ami*. But, as you know well, difficulties rejoice the heart of Hercule Poirot."

"You think the Big Four kidnapped him?"

Poirot nodded.

Our inquiries necessarily went over old ground, and we learnt little to add to what Mrs. Halliday had already told us. Poirot had a lengthy interview with Professor Bourgoneau, during which he sought to elicit whether Halliday had mentioned any plan of his

41

own for the evening, but we drew a complete blank.

Our next source of information was the famous Madame Olivier. I was quite excited as we mounted the steps of her villa at Passy. It has always seemed to me extraordinary that a woman should go so far in the scientific world. I should have thought a purely masculine brain was needed for such work.

The door was opened by a young lad of seventeen or there-abouts, who reminded me vaguely of an acolyte, so ritualistic was his manner. Poirot had taken the trouble to arrange our interview beforehand, as he knew Madame Olivier never received any one without an appointment, being immersed in research work most of the day.

We were shown into a small *salon*, and presently the mistress of the house came to us there. Madame Olivier was a very tall woman, her tallness accentuated by the long white overall she wore, and a coif like a nun's that shrouded her head. She had a long pale face, and wonderful dark eyes that burnt with a light almost fanatical. She looked more like a priestess of old than a modern Frenchwoman. One cheek was disfigured by a scar, and I remembered that her husband and co-worker had been killed in an explosion in the laboratory three years before, and that she herself had been terribly burned. Ever since then she had shut herself away from the world, and plunged with fiery energy into the work of scientific research. She received us with cold politeness.

"I have been interviewed by the police many times, messieurs. I think it hardly likely that I can help you, since I have not been able to help them."

"Madame, it is possible that I shall not ask you quite the same questions. To begin with, of what did you talk together, you and M. Halliday?"

She looked a trifle surprised.

"But of his work! His work—and also mine."

"Did he mention to you the theories he had embodied recently in his paper read before the British Association?"

"Certainly he did. It was chiefly of those we spoke."

"His ideas were somewhat fantastic, were they not?" asked Poirot carelessly.

"Some people have thought so. I do not agree."

"You considered them practicable?"

"Perfectly practicable. My own line of research has been somewhat similar, though not undertaken with the same end in view. I have been investigating the *gamma* rays emitted by the substance usually known as Radium C., a product of Radium emanation, and in doing so I have come across some very interesting magnetical phenomena. Indeed, I have a theory as to the actual nature of the force we call magnetism, but it is not yet time for my discoveries to be given to the world. Mr. Halliday's experiments and views were exceedingly interesting to me."

Poirot nodded. Then he asked a question which surprised me.

"Madame, where did you converse on these topics. In here?"

"No, monsieur. In the laboratory."

"May I see it?"

"Certainly."

She led the way to the door from which she had entered. It opened on a small passage. We passed through two doors and found ourselves in the big laboratory, with its array of beakers and crucibles and a hundred appliances of which I did not even know the names. There were two occupants, both busy with some experiment. Madame Olivier introduced them.

"Mademoiselle Claude, one of my assistants." A tall, serious-faced young girl bowed to us. "Monsieur Henri, an old and trusted friend."

The young man, short and dark, bowed jerkily.

Poirot looked round him. There were two other doors besides the one by which we had entered. One, madame explained, led into the garden, the other into a smaller chamber also devoted to research. Poirot took all this in, then declared himself ready to return to the salon.

43

"Madame, were you alone with M. Halliday during your interview?"

"Yes, monsieur. My two assistants were in the smaller room next door."

"Could your conversation be overheard—by them or any one else?"

Madame reflected, then shook her head.

"I do not think so. I am almost sure it could not. The doors were all shut."

"Could any one have been concealed in the room?"

"There is the big cupboard in the corner—but the idea is absurd."

"*Pas tout à fait*, madame. One thing more: did M. Halliday make any mention of his plans for the evening?"

"He said nothing whatever, monsieur."

"I thank you, madame, and I apologise for disturbing you. Pray do not trouble—we can find our way out."

We stepped out into the hall. A lady was just entering the front door as we did so. She ran quickly up the stairs, and I was left with an impression of the heavy mourning that denotes a French widow.

"A most unusual type of woman, that," remarked Poirot, as we walked away.

"Madame Olivier? Yes, she—"

"*Mais non*, not Madame Olivier. *Cela va sans dire!* There are not many geniuses of her stamp in the world. No, I referred to the other lady—the lady on the stairs."

"I didn't see her face," I said, staring. "And I hardly see how you could have done. She never looked at us."

"That is why I said she was an unusual type," said Poirot placidly. "A woman who enters her home—for I presume that it is her home since she enters with a key—and runs straight upstairs without even looking at two strange visitors in the hall to see who they are, is a *very* unusual type of woman—quite unnatural, in fact. *Mille tonnerres!* what is that?"

He dragged me back—just in time. A tree had crashed down on to the side walk, just missing us. Poirot stared at it, pale and upset.

"It was a near thing that! But clumsy, all the same—for I had no suspicion—at least hardly any suspicion. Yes, but for my quick eyes, the eyes of a cat, Hercule Poirot might now be crushed out of existence—a terrible calamity for the world. And you, too, *mon ami*—though that would not be such a national catastrophe."

"Thank you," I said coldly. "And what are we going to do now?"

"Do?" cried Poirot. "We are going to think. Yes, here and now, we are going to exercise our little gray cells. This M. Halliday now, was he really in Paris? Yes, for Professor Bourgoneau, who knows him, saw and spoke to him."

"What on earth are you driving at?" I cried.

"That was Friday morning. He was last seen at eleven Friday night—but *was* he seen then?"

"The porter—"

"A night porter—who had not previously seen Halliday. A man comes in, sufficiently like Halliday—-we may trust Number Four for that—asks for letters, goes upstairs, packs a small suit-case, and slips out the next morning. Nobody saw Halliday all that evening—no, because he was already in the hands of his enemies. Was it Halliday whom Madame Olivier received? Yes, for though she did not know him by sight, an imposter could hardly deceive her on her own special subject. He came here, he had his inter-view, he left. What happened next?"

Seizing me by the arm, Poirot was fairly dragging me back to the villa.

"Now, *mon ami*, imagine that it is the day after the disap-pearance, and that we are tracking footprints. You love footprints, do you not? See—here they go, a man's, Mr. Halliday's.... He turns to the right as we did, he walks briskly—ah! other footsteps

45

following behind—very quickly—small footsteps, a woman's. See, she catches him up—a slim young woman, in a widow's veil. 'Pardon, monsieur, Madame Olivier desires that I recall you.' He stops, he turns. Now where would the young woman take him? She does not wish to be seen walking with him. Is it coincidence that she catches up with him just where a narrow alleyway opens, dividing two gardens? She leads him down it. 'It is shorter this way, monsieur.' On the right is the garden of Madame Olivier's villa, on the left the garden of another villa—and from that garden, mark you, the tree fell—so nearly on us. Garden doors from both open on the alley. The ambush is there. Men pour out, overpower him, and carry him into the strange villa."

"Good gracious, Poirot," I cried, "are you pretending to see all this?"

"I see it with the eyes of the mind, *mon ami*. So, and only so, could it have happened. Come, let us go back to the house."

"You want to see Madame Olivier again?"

Poirot gave a curious smile.

"No, Hastings, I want to see the face of the lady on the stairs."

"Who do you think she is, a relation of Madame Olivier's?"

"More probably a secretary—and a secretary engaged not very long ago."

The same gentle acolyte opened the door to us.

"Can you tell me," said Poirot, "the name of the lady, the widow lady, who came in just now?"

"Madame Veroneau? Madame's secretary?"

"That is the lady. Would you be so kind as to ask her to speak to us for a moment."

The youth disappeared. He soon reappeared.

"I am sorry. Madame Veroneau must have gone out again."

"I think not," said Poirot quietly. "Will you give her my name, M. Hercule Poirot, and say that it is important I should see her at once, as I am just going to the Prefecture."

Again our messenger departed. This time the lady descended. She walked into the salon. We followed her. She turned and raised her veil. To my astonishment I recognised our old antagonist, the Countess Rossakoff, a Russian countess, who had engineered a particularly smart jewel robbery in London.

"As soon as I caught sight of you in the hall, I feared the worst," she observed plaintively.

"My dear Countess Rossakoff—"

She shook her head.

"Inez Veroneau now," she murmured. "A Spaniard, married to a Frenchman. What do you want of me, M. Poirot? You are a terrible man. You hunted me from London. Now, I suppose, you will tell our wonderful Madame Olivier about me, and hunt me from Paris? We poor Russians, we must live, you know."

"It is more serious than that, madame," said Poirot, watching her. "I propose to enter the villa next door, and release M. Halliday, if he is still alive. I know everything, you see."

I saw her sudden pallor. She bit her lip. Then she spoke with her usual decision.

"He is still alive—but he is not at the villa. Come, monsieur, I will make a bargain with you. Freedom for me—and M. Halliday, alive and well, for you."

"I accept," said Poirot. "I was about to propose the same bargain myself. By the way, are the Big Four your employers, madame?"

Again I saw that deathly pallor creep over her face, but she left his question unanswered.

Instead, "You permit me to telephone?" she asked, and crossing to the instrument she rang up a number. "The number of the villa," she explained, "where our friend is now imprisoned. You may give it to the police—the nest will be empty when they arrive. Ah! I am through. Is that you, André? It is I, Inez. The little Belgian knows all. Send Halliday to the hotel, and clear out."

She replaced the receiver, and came towards us, smiling.

"You will accompany us to the hotel, madame."

"Naturally. I expected that."

I got a taxi, and we drove off together. I could see by Poirot's face that he was perplexed. The thing was almost too easy. We arrived at the hotel. The porter came up to us.

"A gentleman has arrived. He is in your rooms. He seems very ill. A nurse came with him, but she has left."

"That is all right," said Poirot, "he is a friend of mine."

We went upstairs together. Sitting in a chair by the window was a haggard young fellow who looked in the last stages of exhaustion. Poirot went over to him.

"Are you John Halliday?" The man nodded. "Show me your left arm. John Halliday has a mole just below the left elbow."

The man stretched out his arm. The mole was there. Poirot bowed to the countess. She turned and left the room.

A glass of brandy revived Halliday somewhat.

"My God!" he muttered. "I have been through hell—hell.... Those fiends are devils incarnate. My wife, where is she? What does she think? They told me that she would believe—would believe—"

"She does not," said Poirot firmly. "Her faith in you has never wavered. She is waiting for you—she and the child."

"Thank God for that. I can hardly believe that I am free once more."

"Now that you are a little recovered, monsieur, I should like to hear the whole story from the beginning."

Halliday looked at him with an indescribable expression.

"I remember—nothing," he said.

"What?"

"Have you ever heard of the Big Four?"

"Something of them," said Poirot dryly.

"You do not know what I know. They have unlimited power. If I remain silent, I shall be safe—if I say one word—not only I, but my nearest and dearest will suffer unspeakable things. It is no good arguing with me. *I know*.... I remember—nothing."

And, getting up, he walked from the room.

• • • •

Poirot's face wore a baffled expression.

"So it is like that, is it?" he muttered. "The Big Four win again. What is that you are holding in your hand, Hastings?"

I handed it to him.

"The countess scribbled it before she left," I explained.

He read it.

"Au revoir.—I.V."

"Signed with her initials—I.V. Just a coincidence, perhaps, that they also stand for *Four*. I wonder, Hastings, I wonder."

SEVEN
The Radium Thieves

On the night of his release, Halliday slept in the room next to ours at the hotel, and all night long I heard him moaning and protesting in his sleep. Undoubtedly his experience in the villa had broken his nerve, and in the morning we failed completely to extract any information from him. He would only repeat his statement about the unlimited power at the disposal of the Big Four, and his assurance of the vengeance which would follow if he talked.

After lunch he departed to rejoin his wife in England, but Poirot and I remained behind in Paris. I was all for energetic proceedings of some kind or other, and Poirot's quiescence annoyed me.

"For Heaven's sake, Poirot," I urged, "let us be up and at them."

"Admirable, *mon ami*, admirable! Up where, and at whom? Be precise, I beg of you."

"At the Big Four, of course."

"*Cela va sans dire.* But how would you set about it?"

"The police," I hazarded doubtfully.

Poirot smiled.

"They would accuse us of romancing. We have nothing to go upon—nothing whatever. We must wait."

50

"Wait for what?"

"Wait for them to make a move. See now, in England you all comprehend and adore *la boxe*. If one man does not make a move, the other must, and by permitting the adversary to make the attack one learns something about him. That is our part—to let the other side make the attack."

"You think they will?" I said doubtfully.

"I have no doubt whatever of it. To begin with, see, they try to get me out of England. That fails. Then, in the Dartmoor affair, we step in and save their victim from the gallows. And yesterday, once again, we interfere with their plans. Assuredly, they will not leave the matter there."

As I reflected on this, there was a knock on the door. Without waiting for a reply, a man stepped into the room and closed the door behind him. He was a tall, thin man, with a slightly hooked nose and a sallow complexion. He wore an overcoat buttoned up to his chin, and a soft hat well pulled down over his eyes.

"Excuse me, gentlemen, for my somewhat unceremonious entry," he said in a soft voice, "but my business is of a rather unorthodox nature."

Smiling, he advanced to the table and sat down by it. I was about to spring up, but Poirot restrained me with a gesture.

"As you say, Monsieur, your entry is somewhat unceremonious. Will you kindly state your business?"

"My dear M. Poirot, it is very simple. You have been annoying my friends."

"In what way?"

"Come, come, Monsieur Poirot. You do not seriously ask me that? You know as well as I do."

"It depends, monsieur, upon who these friends of yours are."

Without a word, the man drew from his pocket a cigarette case, and, opening it, took out four cigarettes and tossed them on the table. Then he picked them up and returned them to his case, which he replaced in his pocket.

"Aha!" said Poirot, "so it is like that, is it? And what do your friends suggest?"

"They suggest, monsieur, that you should employ your talents—your very considerable talents—in the detection of legitimate crime—return to your former avocations, and solve the problems of London society ladies."

"A peaceful programme," said Poirot. "And supposing I do not agree?"

The man made an eloquent gesture.

"We should regret it, of course, exceedingly," he said. "So would all the friends and admirers of the great M. Hercule Poirot. But regrets, however poignant, do not bring a man to life again."

"Put very delicately," said Poirot, nodding his head. "And supposing I—accept?"

"In that case I am empowered to offer you—compensation."

He drew out a pocket-book, and threw ten notes on the table. They were for ten thousand francs each.

"That is merely as a guarantee of our good faith," he said. "Ten times that amount will be paid you."

"Good God," I cried, springing up, "you dare to think—!"

"Sit down, Hastings," said Poirot autocratically. "Subdue your so beautiful and honest nature and sit down. To you, monsieur, I will say this. What is to prevent me ringing up the police and giving you into their custody, whilst my friend here prevents you from escaping?"

"By all means do so if you think it advisable," said our visitor calmly.

"Oh! look here, Poirot," I cried. "I can't stand this. Ring up the police and have done with it."

Rising swiftly, I strode to the door and stood with my back against it.

"It seems the obvious course," murmured Poirot, as though debating with himself.

"But you distrust the obvious, eh?" said our visitor, smiling.

"Go on, Poirot," I urged.

"It will be your responsibility, *mon ami*."

As he lifted the receiver, the man made a sudden, cat-like jump at me. I was ready for him. In another minute we were locked together, staggering round the room. Suddenly I felt him slip and falter. I pressed my advantage. He went down before me. And then, in the very flush of victory, an extraordinary thing happened. I felt myself flying forwards. Head first, I crashed into the wall in a complicated heap. I was up in a minute, but the door was already closing behind my late adversary. I rushed to it and shook it, it was locked on the outside. I seized the telephone from Poirot.

"Is that the bureau? Stop a man who is coming out. A tall man, with a buttoned-up overcoat and a soft hat. He is wanted by the police."

Very few minutes elapsed before we heard a noise in the corridor outside. The key was turned and the door flung open. The manager himself stood in the doorway.

"The man—you have got him?" I cried.

"No, monsieur. No one has descended."

"You must have passed him."

"We have passed no one, monsieur. It is incredible that he can have escaped."

"You have passed some one, I think," said Poirot, in his gentle voice. "One of the hotel staff, perhaps?"

"Only a waiter carrying a tray, monsieur."

"Ah!" said Poirot, in a tone that spoke infinities.

"So that was why he wore his overcoat buttoned up to his chin," mused Poirot, when we had finally got rid of the excited hotel officials.

"I'm awfully sorry, Poirot," I murmured, rather crestfallen. "I thought I'd downed him all right."

"Yes, that was a Japanese trick, I fancy. Do not distress yourself, *mon ami*. All went according to plan—his plan. That is what I wanted."

"What's this?" I cried, pouncing on a brown object that lay on the floor.

It was a slim pocket-book of brown leather, and had evidently fallen from our visitor's pocket during his struggle with me. It contained two receipted bills in the name of M. Felix Laon, and a folded-up piece of paper which made my heart beat faster. It was a half sheet of note-paper on which a few words were scrawled in pencil but they were words of supreme importance.

"The next meeting of the council will be on Friday at 34 Rue des Echelles at 11 a.m."

It was signed with a big figure 4.

And to-day was Friday, and the clock on the mantelpiece showed the hour to be 10:30.

"My God, what a chance!" I cried. "Fate is playing into our hands. We must start at once—though. What stupendous luck."

"So that was why he came," murmured Poirot. "I see it all now."

"See what? Come on, Poirot, don't stay daydreaming there."

Poirot looked at me, and slowly shook his head, smiling as he did so.

"'Will you walk into my parlour, said the spider to the fly?' That is your little English nursery rhyme, is it not? No, no—they are subtle—but not so subtle as Hercule Poirot."

"What on earth are you driving at, Poirot?"

"My friend, I have been asking myself the reason of this morning's visit. Did our visitor really hope to succeed in bribing me? Or, alternatively, in frightening me into abandoning my task? It seemed hardly credible. Why, then, did he come? And now I see the whole plan—very neat—very pretty—the ostensible reason to bribe or frighten me—the necessary struggle which he took no pains to avoid, and which should make the dropped pocket-book natural and reasonable—and finally—the pitfall! Rue des Echelles, 11 a.m.? I think not, *mon ami*! One does not catch Hercule Poirot as easily as that."

"Good heavens," I gasped.

Poirot was frowning to himself.

"There is still one thing I do not understand."

"What is that?"

"The time, Hastings—the time. If they wanted to decoy me away, surely night time would be better? Why this early hour? Is it possible that something is about to happen this morning? Something which they are anxious Hercule Poirot should not know about?"

He shook his head.

"We shall see. Here I sit, *mon ami*. We do not stir out this morning. We await events here."

It was at half-past eleven exactly that the summons came. A *petit bleu*. Poirot tore it open, then handed it to me. It was from Madame Olivier, the world-famous scientist, whom we had visited yesterday in connection with the Halliday case. It asked us to come out to Passy at once.

We obeyed the summons without an instant's delay. Madame Olivier received us in the same small salon. I was struck anew with the wonderful power of this woman, with her long nun's face and burning eyes—this brilliant successor of Becquerel and the Curies. She came to the point at once.

"Messieurs, you interviewed me yesterday about the disappearance of M. Halliday. I now learn that you returned to the house a second time, and asked to see my secretary, Inez Veroneau. She left the house with you, and has not returned here since."

"Is that all, madame?"

"No, monsieur, it is not. Last night the laboratory was broken into, and several valuable papers and memoranda were stolen. The thieves had a try for something more precious still, but luckily they failed to open the big safe."

"Madame, these are the facts of the case. Your late secretary, Madame Veroneau, was really the Countess Rossakoff, an expert thief, and it was she who was responsible for the disappearance of M. Halliday. How long had she been with you?"

"Five months, monsieur. What you say amazes me."

"It is true, nevertheless. These papers, were they easy to find? Or do you think an inside knowledge was shown?"

"It is rather curious that the thieves knew exactly where to look. You think Inez—"

"Yes, I have no doubt that it was upon her information that they acted. But what is this precious thing that the thieves failed to find? Jewels?"

Madame Olivier shook her head with a faint smile.

"Something much more precious than that, monsieur." She looked round her, then bent forward, lowering her voice. "Radium, monsieur."

"Radium?"

"Yes, monsieur. I am now at the crux of my experiments. I possess a small portion of radium myself—more has been lent to me for the process I am at work upon. Small though the actual quantity is, it comprises a large amount of the world's stock and represents a value of millions of francs."

"And where is it?"

"In its leaden case in the big safe—the safe purposely appears to be of an old and worn-out pattern, but it is really a triumph of the safe-maker's art. That is probably why the thieves were unable to open it."

"How long are you keeping this radium in your possession?"

"Only for two days more, monsieur. Then my experiments will be concluded."

Poirot's eyes brightened.

"And Inez Veroneau is aware of the fact? Good—then our friends will come back. Not a word of me to any one, madame. But rest assured, I will save your radium for you. You have a key of the door leading from the laboratory to the garden?"

"Yes, monsieur. Here it is. I have a duplicate for myself. And here is the key of the garden door leading out into the alleyway between this villa and the next one."

"I thank you, madame. To-night, go to bed as usual, have no fears, and leave all to me. But not a word to any one—not to your two assistants—Mademoiselle Claude and Monsieur Henri, is it not?—particularly not a word to them."

Poirot left the villa rubbing his hands in great satisfaction.

"What are we going to do now?" I asked.

"Now, Hastings, we are about to leave Paris—for England."

"What?"

"We will pack our effects, have lunch, and drive to the Gare du Nord."

"But the radium?"

"I said we were going to leave for England—I did not say we were going to arrive there. Reflect a moment, Hastings. It is quite certain that we are being watched and followed. Our enemies must believe that we are going back to England, and they certainly will not believe that unless they see us get on board the train and start."

"Do you mean we are to slip off again at the last minute?"

"No, Hastings. Our enemies will be satisfied with nothing less than a *bona fide* departure."

"But the train doesn't stop until Calais?"

"It will stop if it is paid to do so."

"Oh, come now, Poirot—surely you can't pay an express to stop—they'd refuse."

"My dear friend, have you never remarked the little handle—the *signal d'arrêt*—penalty for improper use, 100 francs, I think?"

"Oh! you are going to pull that?"

"Or rather a friend of mine, Pierre Combeau, will do so. Then, while he is arguing with the guard, and making a big scene, and all the train is agog with interest, you and I will fade quietly away."

We duly carried out Poirot's plan. Pierre Combeau, an old crony of Poirot's, and who evidently knew my little friend's methods pretty well, fell in with the arrangements. The communication cord was pulled just as we got to the outskirts of Paris. Combeau "made a scene" in the most approved French fashion and Poirot and I were able to leave the train without any one being interested in our departure. Our first proceeding was to make a considerable change in our appearance. Poirot had brought the materials for this with him in a small case. Two loafers in dirty blue blouses were the result. We had dinner in an obscure hostelry, and started back to Paris afterwards.

It was close on eleven o'clock when we found ourselves once more in the neighbourhood of Madame Olivier's villa. We looked up and down the road before slipping into the alleyway. The whole place appeared to be perfectly deserted. One thing we could be quite certain of, no one was following us.

"I do not expect them to be here yet," whispered Poirot to me. "Possibly they may not come until to-morrow night, but they know perfectly well that there are only two nights on which the radium will be there."

Very cautiously we turned the key in the garden door. It opened noiselessly and we stepped into the garden.

And then, with complete unexpectedness, the blow fell. In a minute we were surrounded, gagged and bound. At least ten men must have been waiting for us. Resistance was useless. Like two helpless bundles we were lifted up and carried along. To my intense astonishment, they took us *towards* the house and not away from it. With a key they opened the door into the laboratory and carried us into it. One of the men stooped down before the big safe. The door of it swung open. I felt an unpleasant sensation down my spine. Were they going to bundle us into it, and leave us there to asphyxiate slowly?

However, to my amazement, I saw that from the inside of the safe steps led down beneath the floor. We were thrust down this narrow way and eventually came out into a big subterranean chamber. A woman stood there, tall and imposing, with a black velvet mask covering her face. She was clearly in command of the situation by her gestures of authority. The men slung us down on the floor and left us—alone with the mysterious creature in the mask. I had no doubt who she was. This was the unknown Frenchwoman—Number Three of the Big Four.

She knelt down beside us and removed the gags, but left us bound, then rising and facing us, with a sudden swift gesture she removed her mask.

It was Madame Olivier!

"M. Poirot," she said, in a low mocking tone. "The great, the wonderful, the unique M. Poirot. I sent a warning to you yesterday morning. You chose to disregard it—you thought you could pit your wits against US. And now, you are here!"

There was a cold malignity about her that froze me to the marrow. It was so at variance with the burning fire of her eyes. She was mad—mad—with the madness of genius!

Poirot said nothing. His jaw had dropped, and he was staring at her.

"Well," she said softly, "this is the end. WE cannot permit our plans to be interfered with. Have you any last request to make?"

Never before, or since, have I felt so near death. Poirot was magnificent. He neither flinched nor paled, just stared at her with unabated interest.

"Your psychology interests me enormously, madame," he said quietly. "It is a pity that I have so short a time to devote to studying it. Yes, I have a request to make. A condemned man is always allowed a last smoke, I believe. I have my cigarette case on me. If you would permit—" He looked down at his bonds.

"Ah, yes!" she laughed. "You would like me to untie your hands, would you not? You are clever, M. Hercule Poirot, I know that. I shall not untie your hands—but I will find you a cigarette."

She knelt down by him, extracted his cigarette case, took out a cigarette, and placed it between his lips.

"And now a match," she said, rising.

"It is not necessary, madame." Something in his voice startled me. She, too, was arrested.

"Do not move, I pray of you, madame. You will regret it if you do. Are you acquainted at all with the properties of cuare? The South American Indians use it as an arrow poison. A scratch with it means death. Some tribes use a little blow-pipe—I, too, have a little blow-pipe constructed so as to look exactly like a cigarette. I have only to blow.... Ah! you start. Do not move, madame. The mechanism of this cigarette is most ingenious. One blows—and a tiny dart resembling a fishbone flies through the air—to find its mark. You do not wish to die, madame. Therefore, I beg of you, release my friend Hastings from his bonds. I cannot use my hands, but I can turn my head—so—you are still covered, madame. Make no mistake, I beg of you."

Slowly, with shaking hands, and rage and hate convulsing her face, she bent down and did his bidding. I was free. Poirot's voice gave me instructions.

"Your bonds will now do for the lady, Hastings. That is right. Is she securely fastened? Then release me, I pray of you. It is a fortunate circumstance she sent away her henchmen. With a little luck we may hope to find the way out unobstructed."

In another minute, Poirot stood by my side. He bowed to the lady.

"Hercule Poirot is not killed so easily, madame. I wish you good-night."

The gag prevented her from replying, but the murderous gleam in her eyes frightened me. I hoped devoutly that we should never fall into her power again.

Three minutes later we were outside the villa, and hurriedly traversing the garden. The road outside was deserted, and we were soon clear of the neighbourhood.

Then Poirot broke out.

"I deserve all that that woman said to me. I am a triple imbecile, a miserable animal, thirty-six times an idiot. I was proud of myself for not falling into their trap. And it was not even meant as a trap—except exactly in the way in which I fell into it. They knew I would see through it—they counted on my seeing through it. This explains all—the ease with which they surrendered Halliday—everything. Madame Olivier was the ruling spirit—-Vera Rossakoff only her lieutenant. Madame needed Halliday's ideas—she herself had the necessary genius to supply the gaps that perplexed him. Yes, Hastings, we know now who Number Three is—the woman who is probably the greatest scientist in the world! Think of it. The brain of the East, the science of the West—and two others whose identities we do not yet know. But we must find out. To-morrow we will return to London and set about it."

"You are not going to denounce Madame Olivier to the police?"

"I should not be believed. That woman is one of the idols of France. And we can prove nothing. We are lucky if she does not denounce *us*."

"What?"

"Think of it. We are found at night upon the premises with keys in our possession which she will swear she never gave us. She surprises us at the safe, and we gag and bind her and make away. Have no illusions, Hastings. The boot is not upon the right leg—is that how you say it?"

EIGHT
In The House Of The Enemy

After our adventure in the villa at Passy we returned post haste to London. Several letters were awaiting Poirot. He read one of them with a curious smile, and then handed it to me.

"Read this, *mon ami*."

I turned first to the signature, "Abe Ryland," and recalled Poirot's words: "the richest man in the world." Mr. Ryland's letter was curt and incisive. He expressed himself as profoundly dissatisfied with the reasons Poirot had given for withdrawing from the South American proposition at the last moment.

"This gives one furiously to think, does it not?" said Poirot.

"I suppose it's only natural he should be a bit ratty."

"No, no, you comprehend not. Remember the words of Mayerling, the man who took refuge here—only to die by the hands of his enemies. 'Number Two is represented by an S with two lines through it—the sign for a dollar, also by two stripes and a star. It may be conjectured therefore that he is an American subject, and that he represents the power of wealth.' Add to those words the fact that Ryland offered me a huge sum to tempt me out of England—and—and what about it, Hastings?"

"You mean," I said, staring, "that you suspect Abe Ryland, the multi-millionaire, of being Number Two of the Big Four."

"Your bright intellect has grasped the idea, Hastings. Yes, I do. The tone in which you said multi-millionaire was eloquent—but let me impress upon you one fact—this thing is being run by men at the top—and Mr. Ryland has the reputation of being no beauty in his business dealings. An able, unscrupulous man, a man who has all the wealth that he needs, and is out for unlimited power."

There was undoubtedly something to be said for Poirot's view. I asked him when he had made up his mind definitely upon the point.

"That is just it. I am not sure. I cannot be sure. *Mon ami*, I would give anything to *know*. Let me but place Number Two definitely as Abe Ryland, and we draw nearer to our goal."

"He has just arrived in London, I see by this," I said, tapping the letter. "Shall you call upon him, and make your apologies in person?"

"I might do so."

Two days later, Poirot returned to our rooms in a state of boundless excitement. He grasped me by both hands in his most impulsive manner.

"My friend, an occasion stupendous, unprecedented, never to be repeated, has presented itself! But there is danger, grave danger. I should not even ask you to attempt it."

If Poirot was trying to frighten me, he was going the wrong way to work, and so I told him. Becoming less incoherent, he unfolded his plan.

It seemed that Ryland was looking for an English secretary, one with a good social manner and presence. It was Poirot's suggestion that I should apply for the post.

"I would do it, myself, *mon ami*," he explained apologetically. "But, see you, it is almost impossible for me to disguise myself in the needful manner. I speak the English very well—except when I am excited—but hardly so as to deceive the ear; and even though I were to sacrifice my moustaches, I doubt not but that I should still be recognisable as Hercule Poirot."

I doubted it also, and declared myself ready and willing to take up the part and penetrate into Ryland's household.

"Ten to one he won't engage me anyway," I remarked.

"Oh, yes, he will. I will arrange for you such testimonials as shall make him lick his lips. The Home Secretary himself shall recommend you."

This seemed to be carrying things a bit far, but Poirot waved aside my remonstrances.

"Oh, yes, he will do it. I investigated for him a little matter which might have caused a grave scandal. All was solved with discretion and delicacy, and now, as you would say, he perches upon my hand like the little bird and pecks the crumbs."

Our first step was to engage the services of an artist in "make up." He was a little man, with a quaint bird-like turn of the head, not unlike Poirot's own. He considered me some time in silence, and then fell to work. When I looked at myself in the glass half an hour afterwards, I was amazed. Special shoes caused me to stand at least two inches taller, and the coat I wore was arranged so as to give me a long, lank, weedy look. My eyebrows had been cunningly altered, giving a totally different expression to my face, I wore pads in my cheeks, and the deep tan of my face was a thing of the past. My moustache had gone, and a gold tooth was prominent on one side of my mouth.

"Your name," said Poirot, "is Arthur Neville. God guard you, my friend—for I fear that you go into perilous places."

It was with a beating heart that I presented myself at the Savoy, at an hour named by Mr. Ryland, and asked to see the great man.

After being kept waiting a minute or two, I was shown upstairs to his suite.

Ryland was sitting at a table. Spread out in front of him was a letter which I could see out of the tail of my eye was in the Home Secretary's handwriting. It was my first sight of the American millionaire, and, in spite of myself, I was impressed. He was tall and lean, with a jutting out chin and slightly hooked nose. His eyes glittered cold and gray behind penthouse brows. He had thick grizzled hair, and a long black cigar (without which, I learned later, he was never seen) protruded rakishly from the corner of his mouth.

"Siddown," he grunted.

I sat. He tapped the letter in front of him.

"According to this piece here, you're the goods all right, and I don't need to look further. Say, are you well up in the social matters?"

I said that I thought I could satisfy him in that respect.

"I mean to say, if I have a lot of dooks and earls and viscounts and suchlike down to the country place I've gotten, you'll be able to sort them out all right and put them where they should be round the dining table?"

"Oh! quite easily," I replied, smiling.

We exchanged a few more preliminaries, and then I found myself engaged. What Mr. Ryland wanted was a secretary conversant with English society, as he already had an American secretary and a stenographer with him.

Two days later I went down to Hatton Chase, the seat of the Duke of Loamshire, which the American millionaire had rented for a period of six months.

My duties gave me no difficulty whatever. At one period of my life I had been private secretary to a busy member of Parliament, so I was not called upon to assume a role unfamiliar to me. Mr. Ryland usually entertained a large party over the week-end, but the middle of the week was comparatively quiet. I saw very little of Mr. Appleby, the American secretary, but he seemed a pleasant, normal young American, very efficient in his work. Of Miss Martin, the stenographer, I saw rather more. She was a pretty girl of about twenty-three or four, with auburn hair and brown eyes that could look mischievous enough upon occasion, though they were usually cast demurely down. I had an idea that she both disliked and distrusted her employer, though, of course, she was careful never to hint at anything of the kind, but the time came when I was unexpectedly taken into her confidence.

I had, of course, carefully scrutinised all the members of the household. One or two of the servants had been newly engaged, one of the footmen, I think, and some of the housemaids. The butler, the housekeeper, and the chef were the duke's own staff, who had consented to remain on in the establishment. The housemaids I dismissed as unimportant; I scrutinised James, the second footman, very carefully; but it was clear that he was an under-footman and an under-footman only. He had, indeed, been engaged by the butler. A person of whom I was far more suspicious was Deaves, Ryland's valet, whom he had brought over from New York with him. An Englishman by birth, with an irreproachable manner, I yet harboured vague suspicions about him.

I had been at Hatton Chase three weeks, and not an incident of any kind had arisen which I could lay my finger on in support of our theory. There was no trace of the activities of the Big Four. Mr. Ryland was a man of overpowering force and personality, but I was coming to believe that Poirot had made a mistake when he associated him with that dread organisation. I even heard him mention Poirot in a casual way at dinner one night.

"Wonderful little man, they say. But he's a quitter. How do I know? I put him on a deal, and he turned me down the last minute. I'm not taking any more of your Monsieur Hercule Poirot."

It was at moments such as these that I felt my cheek pads most wearisome!

And then Miss Martin told me a rather curious story. Ryland had gone to London for the day, taking Appleby with him. Miss Martin and I were strolling together in the garden after tea. I liked the girl very much, she was so unaffected and so natural. I could see that there was something on her mind, and at last out it came.

"Do you know, Major Neville," she said, "I am really thinking of resigning my post here."

I looked somewhat astonished, and she went on hurriedly.

"Oh! I know it's a wonderful job to have got, in a way. I suppose most people would think me a fool to throw it up. But I can't stand abuse, Major Neville. To be sworn at like a trooper is more than I can bear. No gentleman would do such a thing."

"Has Ryland been swearing at you?"

She nodded.

"Of course, he's always rather irritable and short tempered. That one expects. It's all in the day's work. But to fly into such an absolute fury—over nothing at all. He really looked as though he could have murdered me! And, as I say, over nothing at all!"

"Tell me about it?" I said, keenly interested.

"As you know, I open all Mr. Ryland's letters. Some I hand on to Mr. Appleby, others I deal with myself, but I do all the preliminary sorting. Now there are certain letters that come, written on blue paper, and with a tiny 4 marked on the corner—I beg your pardon, did you speak?"

I had been unable to repress a stifled exclamation, but I hurriedly shook my head, and begged her to continue.

"Well, as I was saying, these letters come, and there are strict orders that they are never to be opened, but to be handed over to Mr. Ryland intact. And, of course, I always do so. But there was an unusually heavy mail yesterday morning, and I was opening the letters in a terrific hurry. By mistake I opened one of these letters. As soon as I saw what I had done, I took it to Mr. Ryland and explained. To my utter amazement he flew into the most awful rage. As I tell you, I was quite frightened."

"What was there in the letter, I wonder, to upset him so?"

"Absolutely nothing—that's just the curious part of it. I had read it before I discovered my mistake. It was quite short. I can still remember it word for word, and there was nothing in it that could possibly upset any one."

"You can repeat it, you say?" I encouraged her.

"Yes." She paused a minute and then repeated slowly, whilst I noted down the words unobtrusively, the following:—

"Dear Sir,—The essential thing now, I should say, is to see the property. If you insist on the quarry being included, then seventeen thousand seems reasonable. 11% commission too much, 4% is ample.

"Yours truly,

"Arthur Leversham."

Miss Martin went on:—

"Evidently about some property Mr. Ryland was thinking of buying. But really, I do feel that a man who can get into a rage over such a trifle is, well, dangerous. What do you think I ought to do, Major Neville? You've more experience of the world than I have."

I soothed the girl down, pointed out to her that Mr. Ryland had probably been suffering from the enemy of his race—dyspepsia. In the end I sent her away quite comforted. But I was not so easily satisfied myself. When the girl had gone, and I was alone, I took out my notebook, and ran over the letter which I had jotted down. What did it mean—this apparently innocent-sounding missive? Did it concern some business deal which Ryland was undertaking, and was he anxious that no details about it should leak out until it was carried through? That was a possible explanation. But I remembered the small figure 4 with which the envelopes were marked, and I felt that, at last, I was on the track of the thing we were seeking.

I puzzled over the letter all that evening, and most of the next day—and then suddenly the solution came to me. It was so simple, too. The figure 4 was the clue. Read every fourth word in the letter, and an entirely different message appeared. "Essential should see you quarry seventeen eleven four."

The solution of the figures was easy. Seventeen stood for the seventeenth of October—which was to-morrow, eleven was the time, and four was the signature—either referring to the mysterious Number Four himself—or else it was the "trade-mark" so to speak, of the Big Four. The quarry was also intelligible. There was a big disused quarry on the estate about half a mile from the house—a lonely spot, ideal for a secret meeting.

For a moment or two I was tempted to run the show myself. It would be such a feather in my cap, for once, to have the pleasure of crowing over Poirot.

But in the end I overcame the temptation. This was a big business—I had no right to play a lone hand, and perhaps jeopardise our chances of success. For the first time, we had stolen a march upon our enemies. We must make good this time—and, disguise the fact as I might, Poirot had the better brain of the two.

I wrote off post haste to him, laying the facts before him, and explaining how urgent it was that we should overhear what went on at the interview. If he liked to leave it to me, well and good, but I gave him detailed instructions how to reach the quarry from the station in case he should deem it wise to be present himself.

I took the letter down to the village and posted it myself. I had been able to communicate with Poirot throughout my stay, by the simple expedient of posting my letters myself, but we had agreed that he should not attempt to communicate with me in case my letters should be tampered with.

I was in a glow of excitement the following evening. No guests were staying in the house, and I was busy with Mr. Ryland in his study all the evening. I had foreseen that this would be the case, which was why I had had no hope of being able to meet Poirot at the station. I was, however, confident that I would be dismissed well before eleven o'clock.

Sure enough, just after ten-thirty, Mr. Ryland glanced at the clock, and announced that he was "through." I took the hint and retired discreetly. I went upstairs as though going to bed, but slipped quietly down a side staircase and let myself out into the garden, having taken the precaution to don a dark overcoat to hide my white shirt-front.

I had gone some way down the garden when I chanced to look over my shoulder. Mr. Ryland was just stepping out from his study window into the garden. He was starting to keep the appointment.

I redoubled my pace, so as to get a clear start. I arrived at the quarry somewhat out of breath. There seemed no one about, and I crawled into a thick tangle of bushes and awaited developments.

Ten minutes later, just on the stroke of eleven, Ryland stalked up, his hat over his eyes and the inevitable cigar in his mouth. He gave a quick look round, and then plunged into the hollows of the quarry below. Presently I heard a low murmur of voices come up to me. Evidently the other man—or men—whoever they were, had arrived first at the rendezvous. I crawled cautiously out of the bushes, and inch by inch, using the utmost precaution against noise, I wormed myself down the steep path. Only a boulder now separated me from the talking men. Secure in the blackness, I peeped round the edge of it and found myself facing the muzzle of a black, murderous-looking automatic!

"Hands up!" said Mr. Ryland succinctly. "I've been waiting for you."

He was seated in the shadow of the rock, so that I could not see his face, but the menace in his voice was unpleasant. Then I felt a ring of cold steel on the back of my neck, and Ryland lowered his own automatic.

"That's right, George," he drawled. "March him around here."

Raging inwardly, I was conducted to a spot in the shadows, where the unseen George (whom I suspected of being the impeccable Deaves), gagged and bound me securely.

Ryland spoke again in a tone which I had difficulty in recognising, so cold and menacing was it.

"This is going to be the end of you two. You've got in the way of the Big Four once too often. Ever heard of land slides? There was one about here two years ago. There's going to be another to-night. I've fixed that good and square. Say, that friend of yours doesn't keep his dates very punctually."

A wave of horror swept over me. Poirot! In another minute he would walk straight into the trap. And I was powerless to warn him. I could only pray that he had elected to leave the matter in my hands, and had remained in London. Surely, if he had been coming, he would have been here by now.

With every minute that passed, my hopes rose.

Suddenly they were dashed to pieces. I heard footsteps—cautious footsteps, but footsteps nevertheless. I writhed in impotent agony. They came down the path, paused, and then Poirot himself appeared, his head a little on one side, peering into the shadows.

I heard the growl of satisfaction Ryland gave as he raised the big automatic and shouted "Hands up." Deaves sprang forward as he did so, and took Poirot in the rear. The ambush was complete.

"Please to meet you, Mr. Hercule Poirot," said the American grimly.

Poirot's self-possession was marvellous. He did not turn a hair. But I saw his eyes searching in the shadows.

"My friend? He is here?"

"Yes, you are both in the trap—the trap of the Big Four."

He laughed.

"A trap?" queried Poirot.

"Say, haven't you tumbled to it yet?"

"I comprehend that there is a trap—yes," said Poirot gently. "But you are in error, monsieur. It is *you* who are in it—not I and my friend."

"What?" Ryland raised the big automatic, but I saw his gaze falter.

"If you fire, you commit murder watched by ten pairs of eyes, and you will be hanged for it. This place is surrounded—has been for the last hour—by Scotland Yard men. It is checkmate, Mr. Abe Ryland."

He uttered a curious whistle, and as though by magic, the place was alive with men. They seized Ryland and the valet and disarmed them. After speaking a few words to the officer in charge, Poirot took me by the arm, and led me away.

Once clear of the quarry he embraced me with vigour.

"You are alive—you are unhurt. It is magnificent. Often have

I blamed myself for letting you go."

"I'm perfectly all right," I said, disengaging myself. "But I'm just a bit fogged. You tumbled to their little scheme, did you?"

"But I was waiting for it! For what else did I permit you to go there? Your false name, your disguise, not for a moment was it intended to deceive!"

"What?" I cried. "You never told me."

"As I have frequently told you, Hastings, you have a nature so beautiful and so honest that unless you are yourself deceived, it is impossible for you to deceive others. Good, then, you are spotted from the first, and they do what I had counted on their doing—a mathematical certainty to any one who uses his gray cells properly—use you as a decoy. They set the girl on—By the way, *mon ami*, as an interesting fact psychologically, has she got red hair?"

"If you mean Miss Martin," I said coldly. "Her hair is a delicate shade of auburn, but—"

"They are *épatant*—these people! They have even studied your psychology. Oh! yes, my friend, Miss Martin was in the plot—very much so. She repeats the letter to you, together with her tale of Mr. Ryland's wrath, you write it down, you puzzle your brains—the cipher is nicely arranged, difficult, but not too difficult—you solve it, and you send for me."

"But what they do not know is that I am waiting for just this very thing to happen. I go post haste to Japp and arrange things. And so, as you see, all is triumph!"

I was not particularly pleased with Poirot, and I told him so. We went back to London on a milk train in the early hours of the morning, and a most uncomfortable journey it was.

I was just out of my bath and indulging in pleasurable thoughts of breakfast when I heard Japp's voice in the sitting-room. I threw on a bathrobe and hurried in.

"A pretty mare's nest you've got us into this time," Japp was saying. "It's too bad of you, M. Poirot. First time I've ever known you take a toss."

Poirot's face was a study. Japp went on.

"There were we, taking all this Black Hand stuff seriously—and all the time it was the footman."

"The footman?" I gasped.

"Yes, James, or whatever his name is. Seems he laid 'em a wager in the servants' hall that he could get taken for the old man by his nibs—that's you, Captain Hastings—and would hand him out a lot of spy stuff about a Big Four gang."

"Impossible!" I cried.

"Don't you believe it. I marched our gentleman straight to Hatton Chase, and there was the real Ryland in bed and asleep, and the butler and the cook and God knows how many of them to swear to the wager. Just a silly hoax—that's all it was—and the valet is with him."

"So that was why he kept in the shadow," murmured Poirot.

After Japp had gone we looked at each other.

"We *know*, Hastings," said Poirot at last. "Number Two of the Big Four is Abe Ryland. The masquerading on the part of the footman was to ensure a way of retreat in case of emergencies. And the footman—"

"Yes," I breathed.

"*Number Four*," said Poirot gravely.

NINE
The Yellow Jasmine Mystery

It was all very well for Poirot to say that we were acquiring information all the time and gaining an insight into our adversaries' minds—I felt myself that I required some more tangible success than this.

Since we had come into contact with the Big Four, they had committed two murders, abducted Halliday, and had been within an ace of killing Poirot and myself; whereas so far we had hardly scored a point in the game.

Poirot treated my complaints lightly.

"So far, Hastings," he said, "they laugh. That is true, but you have a proverb, have you not: 'He laughs best who laughs at the end'? And at the end, *mon ami*, you shall see.

"You must remember, too," he added, "that we deal with no ordinary criminal, but with the second greatest brain in the world."

I forbore to pander to his conceit by asking the obvious question. I knew the answer, at least I knew what Poirot's answer would be, and instead I tried without success to elicit some information as to what steps he was taking to track down the enemy. As usual he had kept me completely in the dark as to his movements, but I gathered that he was in touch with secret service agents in India, China, and Russia, and, from his occasional bursts of self-glorification, that he was at least progressing in his favourite game of gauging his enemy's mind.

He had abandoned his private practice almost entirely, and I know that at this time he refused some remarkably handsome fees. True, he would sometimes investigate cases which intrigued him, but he usually dropped them the moment he was convinced that they had no connection with the activities of the Big Four.

This attitude of his was remarkably profitable to our friend, Inspector Japp. Undeniably he gained much kudos for solving several problems in which his success was really due to a half-contemptuous hint from Poirot.

In return for such service Japp supplied full details of any case which he thought might interest the little Belgian, and when he was put in charge of what the newspaper called "The Yellow Jasmine Mystery," he wired Poirot, asking him whether he would care to come down and look into the case.

It was in response to this wire that, about a month after my adventure in Abe Ryland's house, we found ourselves alone in a railway compartment whirling away from the smoke and dust of London, bound for the little town of Market Handford in Worcestershire, the seat of the mystery.

Poirot leant back in his corner.

"And what exactly is your opinion of the affair, Hastings?"

I did not at once reply to his question; I felt the need of going warily.

"It all seems so complicated," I said cautiously.

"Does it not?" said Poirot delightedly.

"I suppose our rushing off like this is a pretty clear sign that you consider Mr. Paynter's death to be murder—not suicide or the result of an accident?"

"No, no; you misunderstand me, Hastings. Granting that Mr. Paynter died as the result of a particularly terrible accident, there are still a number of mysterious circumstances to be explained."

"That was what I meant when I said it was all so complicated."

"Let us go over all the main facts quietly and methodically.

Recount them to me, Hastings, in an orderly and lucid fashion."

I started forthwith, endeavouring to be as orderly and lucid as I could.

"We start," I said, "with Mr. Paynter. A man of fifty-five, rich, cultured, and somewhat of a globetrotter. For the last twelve years he has been little in England, but suddenly tiring of incessant travelling, he bought a small place in Worcestershire, near Market Handford, and prepared to settle down. His first action was to write to his only relative, a nephew, Gerald Paynter, the son of his younger brother, and to suggest to him that he should come and make his home at Croftlands (as the place is called) with his uncle. Gerald Paynter, who is an impecunious young artist, was glad enough to fall in with the arrangement, and had been living with his uncle for about seven months when the tragedy occurred."

"Your narrative style is masterly," murmured Poirot. "I say to myself, it is a book that talks, not my friend Hastings."

Paying no attention to Poirot, I went on, warming to the story.

"Mr. Paynter kept up a fair staff at Croftlands—six servants as well as his own Chinese body servant—Ah Ling."

"His Chinese servant, Ah Ling," murmured Poirot.

"On Tuesday last, Mr. Paynter complained of feeling unwell after dinner, and one of the servants was despatched to fetch the doctor. Mr. Paynter received the doctor in his study, having refused to go to bed. What passed between them was not then known, but before Doctor Quentin left, he asked to see the housekeeper, and mentioned that he had given Mr. Paynter a hypodermic injection as his heart was in a very weak state, recommended that he should not be disturbed, and then proceeded to ask some rather curious questions about the servants—how long they had been there, from whom they had come, etc.

"The housekeeper answered these questions as best she could, but was rather puzzled as to their purport. A terrible discovery was made on the following morning. One of the housemaids, on descending, was met by a sickening odour of burned flesh which seemed to come from her master's study. She tried the door, but it was locked on the inside. With the assistance of Gerald Paynter and the Chinaman that was soon broken in, but a terrible sight greeted them. Mr. Paynter had fallen forward into the gas fire, and his face and head were charred beyond recognition.

"Of course, at the moment, no suspicion was aroused as to its being anything but a ghastly accident. If blame attached to any one, it was to Doctor Quentin for giving his patient a narcotic and leaving him in such a dangerous position. And then a rather curious discovery was made.

"There was a newspaper on the floor, lying where it had slipped from the old man's knees. On turning it over, words were found to be scrawled across it, feebly traced in ink. A writing-table stood close to the chair in which Mr. Paynter had been sitting, and the forefinger of the victim's right hand was ink-stained up to the second joint. It was clear that, too weak to hold a pen, Mr. Paynter had dipped his finger in the ink-pot and managed to scrawl these two words across the surface of the newspaper he held—but the words themselves seemed utterly fantastic: *Yellow Jasmine*—just that and nothing more.

"Croftlands has a large quantity of yellow jasmine growing up its walls, and it was thought that this dying message had some reference to them, showing that the poor old man's mind was wandering. Of course, the newspapers, agog for anything out of the common, took up the story hotly, calling it the Mystery of the Yellow Jasmine—though in all probability the words are completely unimportant."

"They are unimportant, you say?" said Poirot. "Well, doubtless, since you say so, it must be so."

I regarded him dubiously, but I could detect no mockery in his eye.

"And then," I continued, "there came the excitements of the inquest."

"This is where you lick your lips, I perceive."

"There was a certain amount of feeling evidenced against Dr. Quentin. To begin with, he was not the regular doctor, only a locum, putting in a month's work, whilst Dr. Bolitho was away on a well-earned holiday. Then it was felt that his carelessness was the direct cause of the accident. But his evidence was little short of sensational. Mr. Paynter had been ailing in health ever since his arrival at Croftlands. Dr. Bolitho had attended him for some time, but when Dr. Quentin first saw his patient, he was mystified by some of the symptoms. He had only attended him once before the night when he was sent for after dinner. As soon as he was alone with Mr. Paynter, the latter had unfolded a surprising tale. To begin with, he was not feeling ill at all, he explained, but the taste of some curry that he had been eating at dinner had struck him as peculiar. Making an excuse to get rid of Ah Ling for a few minutes, he had turned the contents of his plate into a bowl, and he now handed it over to the doctor with injunctions to find out if there were really anything wrong with it.

"In spite of his statement that he was not feeling ill, the doctor noted that the shock of his suspicions had evidently affected him, and that his heart was feeling it. Accordingly he administered an injection—not of a narcotic, but of strychnine.

"That, I think, completes the case—except for *the* crux of the whole thing—the fact that the uneaten curry, duly analysed, was found to contain enough powdered opium to have killed two men!"

I paused.

"And your conclusions, Hastings?" asked Poirot quietly.

"It's difficult to say. It *might* be an accident—the fact that some one attempted to poison him the same night might be merely a coincidence."

"But you don't think so? You prefer to believe it—murder!"

"Don't you?"

"*Mon ami*, you and I do not reason in the same way. I am not trying to make up my mind between two opposite solutions—murder or accident—that will come when we have solved the other problem—the mystery of the 'Yellow Jasmine.' By the way, you have left out something there."

"You mean the two lines at right angles to each other faintly indicated under the words? I did not think they could be of any possible importance."

"What you think is always so important to yourself, Hastings. But let us pass from the mystery of the Yellow Jasmine to the Mystery of the Curry."

"I know. Who poisoned it? Why? There are a hundred questions one can ask. Ah Ling, of course, prepared it. But why should he wish to kill his master? Is he a member of a *tong*, or something like that. One reads of such things. The *tong* of the Yellow Jasmine, perhaps. Then there is Gerald Paynter."

I came to an abrupt pause.

"Yes," said Poirot, nodding his head. "There is Gerald Paynter, as you say. He is his uncle's heir. He was dining out that night, though."

"He might have got at some of the ingredients of the curry," I suggested. "And he would take care to be out, so as not to have to partake of the dish."

I think my reasoning rather impressed Poirot. He looked at me with a more respectful attention than he had given me so far.

"He returns late," I mused, pursuing a hypothetical case. "Sees the light in his uncle's study, enters, and, finding his plan has failed, thrusts the old man down into the fire."

"Mr. Paynter, who was a fairly hearty man of fifty-five, would not permit himself to be burnt to death without a struggle, Hastings. Such a reconstruction is not feasible."

"Well, Poirot," I cried, "we're nearly there, I fancy. Let us hear what you think?"

Poirot threw me a smile, swelled out his chest, and began in a pompous manner.

"Assuming murder, the question at once arises, why choose that particular method? I can think of only one reason—to confuse identity, the face being charred beyond recognition."

"What?" I cried. "You think—"

"A moment's patience, Hastings. I was going on to say that I examine that theory. Is there any ground for believing that the body is not that of Mr. Paynter? Is there any one else whose body it possibly could be? I examine these two questions and finally I answer them both in the negative."

"Oh!" I said, rather disappointed. "And then?"

Poirot's eyes twinkled a little.

"And then I say to myself, 'since there is here something that I do not understand, it would be well that I should investigate the matter. I must not permit myself to be wholly engrossed by the Big Four.' Ah! we are just arriving. My little clothes brush, where does it hide itself? Here it is—brush me down, I pray you, my friend, and then I will perform the same service for you."

"Yes," said Poirot thoughtfully, as he put away the brush, "one must not permit oneself to be obsessed by one idea. I have been in danger of that. Figure to yourself, my friend, that even here, in this case, I am in danger of it. Those two lines you mentioned, a downstroke and a line at right angles to it, what are they but the beginning of a 4?"

"Good gracious, Poirot," I cried, laughing.

"Is it not absurd? I see the hand of the Big Four everywhere. It is well to employ one's wits in a totally different *milieu*. Ah! there is Japp come to meet us."

We Investigate At Croftlands

The Scotland Yard Inspector was, indeed, waiting on the platform, and greeted us warmly.

"Well, Moosior Poirot, this is good. Thought you'd like to be let in on this. Tip-top mystery, isn't it?"

I read this aright as showing Japp to be completely puzzled and hoping to pick up a pointer from Poirot.

Japp had a car waiting, and we drove up in it to Croftlands. It was a square, white house, quite unpretentious, and covered with creepers, including the starry yellow jasmine. Japp looked up at it as we did.

"Must have been balmy to go writing that, poor old cove," he remarked. "Hallucinations, perhaps, and thought he was outside."

Poirot was smiling at him.

"Which was it, my good Japp?" he asked; "accident or murder?"

The Inspector seemed a little embarrassed by the question.

"Well, if it weren't for that curry business, I'd be for accident every time. There's no sense in holding a live man's head in the fire—why, he'd scream the house down."

"Ah!" said Poirot in a low voice. "Fool that I have been. Triple imbecile! You are a cleverer man than I am, Japp."

Japp was rather taken aback by the compliment—Poirot being usually given to exclusive self praise. He reddened and muttered something about there being a lot of doubt about that.

He led the way through the house to the room where the tragedy had occurred—Mr. Paynter's study. It was a wide, low room, with book-lined walls and big leather arm-chairs.

Poirot looked across at once to the window which gave upon a gravelled terrace.

"The window, it was unlatched?" he asked.

"That's the whole point, of course. When the doctor left this room, he merely closed the door behind him. The next morning it was found locked. Who locked it? Mr. Paynter? Ah Ling declares that the window was closed and bolted. Dr. Quentin, on the other hand, has an impression that it was closed, but not fastened, but he won't swear either way. If he could, it would make a great difference. If the man *was* murdered, some one entered the room either through the door or the window—if through the door, it was an inside job; if through the window, it might have been any one. First thing when they had broken the door down, they flung the window open, and the housemaid who did it thinks that it wasn't fastened, but she's a precious bad witness—will remember anything you ask her to!"

"What about the key?"

"There you are again. It was on the floor among the wreckage of the door. Might have fallen from the keyhole, might have been dropped there by one of the people who entered, might have been slipped underneath the door from the outside."

"In fact everything is 'might have been'?"

"You've hit it, Moosior Poirot. That's just what it is."

Poirot was looking round him, frowning unhappily.

"I cannot see light," he murmured. "Just now—-yes, I got a gleam, but now all is darkness once more. I have not the clue—the motive."

"Young Gerald Paynter had a pretty good motive," remarked Japp grimly. "He's been wild enough in his time, I can tell you. *And* extravagant. You know what artists are, too—no morals at all."

Poirot did not pay much attention to Japp's sweeping strictures on the artistic temperament. Instead he smiled knowingly.

"My good Japp, is it possible that you throw the mud in my eyes? I know well enough that it is the Chinaman you suspect. But you are so artful. You want me to help you—and yet you drag the red kipper across the trail."

Japp burst out laughing.

"That's you all over, Mr. Poirot. Yes, I'd bet on the Chink, I'll admit it now. It stands to reason that it was he who doctored the curry, and if he'd try once in an evening to get his master out of the way, he'd try twice."

"I wonder if he would," said Poirot softly.

"But it's the motive that beats me. Some heathen revenge or other, I suppose."

"I wonder," said Poirot again. "There has been no robbery? Nothing has disappeared? No jewellery, or money, or papers?"

"No—that is, not exactly."

I pricked up my ears; so did Poirot.

"There's been no robbery, I mean," explained Japp. "But the old boy was writing a book of some sort. We only knew about it this morning when there was a letter from the publishers asking about the manuscript. It was just completed, it seems. Young Paynter and I have searched high and low, but can't find a trace of it—he must have hidden it away somewhere."

Poirot's eyes were shining with the green light I knew so well.

"How was it called, this book?" he asked.

"*The Hidden Hand in China*, I think it was called."

"Aha!" said Poirot, with almost a gasp. Then he said quickly, "Let me see the Chinaman, Ah Ling."

The Chinaman was sent for and appeared, shuffling along, with his eyes cast down, and his pigtail swinging. His impassive face showed no trace of any kind of emotion.

"Ah Ling," said Poirot, "are you sorry your master is dead?"

"I welly sorry. He good master."

83

"You know who kill him?"

"I not know. I tell pleeceman if I know."

The questions and answers went on. With the same impassive face, Ah Ling described how he had made the curry. The cook had had nothing to do with it, he declared, no hand had touched it but his own. I wondered if he saw where his admission was leading him. He stuck to it too, that the window to the garden was bolted that evening. If it was open in the morning, his master must have opened it himself. At last Poirot dismissed him.

"That will do, Ah Ling." Just as the Chinaman had got to the door, Poirot recalled him. "And you know nothing, you say, of the Yellow Jasmine?"

"No, what should I know?"

"Nor yet of the sign that was written underneath it?"

Poirot leant forward as he spoke, and quickly traced something on the dust of a little table. I was near enough to see it before he rubbed it out. A down stroke, a line at right angles, and then a second line down which completed a big 4. The effect on the Chinaman was electrical. For one moment his face was a mask of terror. Then, as suddenly, it was impassive again, and repeating his grave disclaimer, he withdrew.

Japp departed in search of young Paynter, and Poirot and I were left alone together.

"The Big Four, Hastings," cried Poirot. "Once again, the Big Four. Paynter was a great traveller. In his book there was doubtless some vital information concerning the doings of Number One, Li Chang Yen, the head and brains of the Big Four."

"But who—how—"

"Hush, here they come."

Gerald Paynter was an amiable, rather weak-looking young man. He had a soft brown beard, and a peculiar flowing tie. He answered Poirot's questions readily enough.

"I dined out with some neighbours of ours, the Wycherlys," he explained. "What time did I get home? Oh, about eleven. I had a latch-key, you know. All the servants had gone to bed, and I naturally thought my uncle had done the same. As a matter of fact, I did think I caught sight of that soft-footed Chinese beggar Ah Ling just whisking round the corner of the hall, but I fancy I was mistaken."

"When did you last see your uncle, Mr. Paynter? I mean before you came to live with him."

"Oh! not since I was a kid of ten. He and his brother (my father) quarrelled, you know."

"But he found you again with very little trouble, did he not? In spite of all the years that had passed?"

"Yes, it was quite a bit of luck my seeing the lawyer's advertisement."

Poirot asked no more questions.

Our next move was to visit Dr. Quentin. His story was substantially the same as he had told at the inquest, and he had little to add to it. He received us in his surgery, having just come to the end of his consulting patients. He seemed an intelligent man. A certain primness of manner went well with his pince-nez, but I fancied that he would be thoroughly modern in his methods.

"I wish I could remember about the window," he said frankly. "But it's dangerous to think back, one becomes quite positive about something that never existed. That's psychology, isn't it, M. Poirot? You see, I've read all about your methods, and I may say I'm an enormous admirer of yours. No, I suppose it's pretty certain that the Chinaman put the powdered opium in the curry, but he'll never admit it, and we shall never know why. But holding a man down in a fire—that's not in keeping with our Chinese friend's character, it seems to me."

I commented on this last point to Poirot as we walked down the main street of Market Handford.

"Do you think he let a confederate in?" I asked. "By the way, I suppose Japp can be trusted to keep an eye on him?" (The Inspector had passed into the police station on some business or other.) "The emissaries of the Big Four are pretty spry."

"Japp is keeping an eye on both of them," said Poirot grimly. "They have been closely shadowed ever since the body was discovered."

"Well, at any rate *we* know that Gerald Paynter had nothing to do with it."

"You always know so much more than I do, Hastings, that it becomes quite fatiguing."

"You old fox," I laughed. "You never will commit yourself."

"To be honest, Hastings, the case is now quite clear to me— all but the words, *Yellow Jasmine*—and I am coming to agree with you that they have no bearing on the crime. In a case of this kind, you have got to make up your mind who is lying. I have done that. And yet—"

He suddenly darted from my side and entered an adjacent bookshop. He emerged a few minutes later, hugging a parcel. Then Japp rejoined us, and we all sought quarters at the inn.

I slept late the next morning. When I descended to the sitting-room reserved for us, I found Poirot already there, pacing up and down, his face contorted with agony.

"Do not converse with me," he cried, waving an agitated hand. "Not until I know that all is well—that the arrest is made. Ah! but my psychology has been weak. Hastings, if a man writes a dying message, it is because it is important. Every one has said—Yellow Jasmine? There is yellow jasmine growing up the house—it means nothing."

"Well, what does it mean? Just what it says. Listen." He held up a little book he was holding.

"My friend, it struck me that it would be well to inquire into the subject. What exactly is yellow jasmine? This little book has told me. Listen."

He read.

"'*Gelsemini Radix*. Yellow Jasmine. Composition: Alkaloids *gelseminine* $C_{22}H_{26}N_2O_3$, a potent poison acting like coniine;

gelsemine $C_{12}H_{14}NO_2$, acting like strychnine; *gelsemic acid*, etc. Gelsemium is a powerful depressant to the central nervous system. At a late stage in its action it paralyses the motor nerve endings, and in large doses causes giddiness and loss of muscular power. Death is due to paralysis of the respiratory centre.'

"You see, Hastings? At the beginning I had an inkling of the truth when Japp made his remark about a live man being forced into the fire. I realised then that it was a dead man who was burned."

"But why? What was the point?"

"My friend, if you were to shoot a man, or stab a man after he were dead, or even knock him on the head, it would be apparent that the injuries were inflicted after death. But with his head charred to a cinder, no one is going to hunt about for obscure causes of death, and a man who has apparently just escaped being poisoned at dinner, is not likely to be poisoned just afterwards. *Who* is lying, that is always the question? I decided to believe Ah Ling—"

"What!" I exclaimed.

"You are surprised, Hastings? Ah Ling knew of the existence of the Big Four, that was evident—so evident that it was clear he knew nothing of their association with the crime until that moment. Had he been the murderer, he would have been able to retain his impassive face perfectly. So I decided then, to believe Ah Ling, and I fixed my suspicions on Gerald Paynter. It seemed to me that Number Four would have found an impersonation of a long lost nephew very easy."

"What!" I cried. "Number Four?"

"No, Hastings, *not* Number Four. As soon as I had read up the subject of yellow jasmine, I saw the truth. In fact, it leapt to the eye."

"As always," I said coldly, "it doesn't leap to mine."

"Because you will not use your little gray cells. Who had a chance to tamper with the curry?"

"Ah Ling. No one else."

"No one else? *What about the doctor?*"

"But that was *afterwards*."

"Of course it was afterwards. There was no trace of powdered opium in the curry served to Mr. Paynter, but acting in obedience to the suspicions Dr. Quentin had aroused, the old man eats none of it, and preserves it to give to his medical attendant, whom he summons according to plan. Dr. Quentin arrives, takes charge of the curry, *and gives Mr. Paynter an injection*—of strychnine, he says, but really of yellow jasmine—a poisonous dose. When the drug begins to take effect, he departs, after unlatching the window. Then, in the night, he returns by the window, finds the manuscript, and shoves Mr. Paynter into the fire. He does not heed the newspaper that drops to the floor and is covered by the old man's body. Paynter knew what drug he had been given, and strove to accuse the Big Four of his murder. It is easy for Quentin to mix powdered opium with the curry before handing it over to be analysed. He gives his version of the conversation with the old man, and mentions the strychnine injection casually, in case the mark of the hypodermic needle is noticed. Suspicion at once is divided between accident and the guilt of Ah Ling owing to the poison in the curry."

"But Dr. Quentin cannot be Number Four?"

"I fancy he can. There is undoubtedly a real Dr. Quentin who is probably abroad somewhere. Number Four has simply masqueraded as him for a short time. The arrangements with Dr. Bolitho were all carried out by correspondence, the man who was to do locum originally having been taken ill at the last minute."

At that minute, Japp burst in, very red in the face.

"You have got him?" cried Poirot anxiously.

Japp shook his head, very out of breath.

"Bolitho came back from his holiday this morning—recalled by telegram. No one knows who sent it. The other man left last night. We'll catch him yet, though."

Poirot shook his head quietly.

"I think not," he said, and absent-mindedly he drew a big 4 on the table with a fork.

ELEVEN
A Chess Problem

Poirot and I often dined at a small restaurant in Soho. We were there one evening, when we observed a friend at an adjacent table. It was Inspector Japp, and as there was room at our table, he came and joined us. It was some time since either of us had seen him.

"Never do you stop in to see us nowadays," declared Poirot reproachfully. "Not since the affair of the Yellow Jasmine have we met, and that is nearly a month ago."

"I've been up north—that's why. How are things with you? Big Four still going strong—eh?"

Poirot shook a finger at him reproachfully.

"Ah! you mock yourself at me—but the Big Four—they exist."

"Oh! I don't doubt that—but they're not the hub of the universe, as you make out."

"My friend, you are very much mistaken. The greatest power for evil in the world to-day is this 'Big Four.' To what end they are tending, no one knows, but there has never been another such criminal organisation. The finest brain in China at the head of it, an American millionaire, and a French woman scientist as members, and for the fourth—"

Japp interrupted.

"I know—I know. Regular bee in your bonnet over it all. It's becoming your little mania, Moosior Poirot. Let's talk of something else for a change. Take any interest in chess?"

"I have played it, yes."

"Did you see that curious business yesterday? Match between two players of world-wide reputation, and one died during the game?"

"I saw a mention of it. Dr. Savaronoff, the Russian champion, was one of the players, and the other, who succumbed to heart failure, was the brilliant young American, Gilmour Wilson."

"Quite right. Savaronoff beat Rubenstein and became Russian champion some years ago. Wilson is said to be a second Capablanca."

"A very curious occurrence," mused Poirot. "If I mistake not, you have a particular interest in the matter?"

Japp gave a rather embarrassed laugh.

"You've hit it, Moosior Poirot. I'm puzzled. Wilson was sound as a bell—no trace of heart trouble. His death is quite inexplicable."

"You suspect Dr. Savaronoff of putting him out of the way?" I cried.

"Hardly that," said Japp dryly. "I don't think even a Russian would murder another man in order not to be beaten at chess—and anyway, from all I can make out, the boot was likely to be on the other leg. The doctor is supposed to be very hot stuff—second to Lasker they say he is."

Poirot nodded thoughtfully.

"Then what exactly is your little idea?" he asked. "Why should Wilson be poisoned? For, I assume, of course, that it is poison you suspect."

"Naturally. Heart failure means your heart stops beating—that's all there is to that. That's what a doctor says officially at the moment, but privately he tips us the wink that he's not satisfied."

"When is the autopsy to take place?"

"To-night. Wilson's death was extraordinarily sudden. He

seemed quite as usual and was actually moving one of the pieces when he suddenly fell forward—dead!"

"There are very few poisons would act in such a fashion," objected Poirot.

"I know. The autopsy will help us, I expect. But why should any one want Gilmour Wilson out of the way—that's what I'd like to know? Harmless unassuming young fellow. Just come over here from the States, and apparently hadn't an enemy in the world."

"It seems incredible," I mused.

"Not at all," said Poirot, smiling. "Japp has his theory, I can see."

"I have, Moosior Poirot. I don't believe the poison was meant for Wilson—it was meant for the other man."

"Savaronoff?"

"Yes. Savaronoff fell foul of the Bolsheviks at the outbreak of the Revolution. He was even reported killed. In reality he escaped, and for three years endured incredible hardships in the wilds of Siberia. His sufferings were so great that he is now a changed man. His friends and acquaintances declare they would hardly have recognised him. His hair is white, and his whole aspect that of a man terribly aged. He is a semi-invalid, and seldom goes out, living alone with a niece, Sonia Daviloff, and a Russian man-servant in a flat down Westminster way. It is possible that he still considers himself a marked man. Certainly he was very unwilling to agree to this chess contest. He refused several times point blank, and it was only when the newspapers took it up and began making a fuss about the 'unsportsmanlike refusal' that he gave in. Gilmour Wilson had gone on challenging him with real Yankee pertinacity, and in the end he got his way. Now I ask you, Moosior Poirot, why wasn't he willing? Because he didn't want attention drawn to him. Didn't want somebody or other to get on his track. That's my solution—Gilmour Wilson got pipped by mistake."

"There is no one who has any private reason to gain by Savaronoff's death?"

"Well, his niece, I suppose. He's recently come into an immense fortune. Left him by Madame Gospoja whose husband was a sugar profiteer under the old regime. They had an affair together once, I believe, and she refused steadfastly to credit the reports of his death."

"Where did the match take place?"

"In Savaronoff's own flat. He's an invalid, as I told you."

"Many people there to watch it?"

"At least a dozen—probably more."

Poirot made an expressive grimace.

"My poor Japp, your task is not an easy one."

"Once I know definitely that Wilson was poisoned, I can get on."

"Has it occurred to you that, in the meantime, supposing your assumption that Savaronoff was the intended victim to be correct, the murderer may try again?"

"Of course it has. Two men are watching Savaronoff's flat."

"That will be very useful if any one should call with a bomb under his arm," said Poirot dryly.

"You're getting interested, Moosior Poirot," said Japp, with a twinkle. "Care to come round to the mortuary and see Wilson's body before the doctors start on it? Who knows, his tie-pin may be askew, and that may give you a valuable clue that will solve the mystery."

"My dear Japp, all through dinner my fingers have been itching to rearrange your own tie-pin. You permit, yes? Ah! that is much more pleasing to the eye. Yes, by all means, let us go to the mortuary."

I could see that Poirot's attention was completely captivated by this new problem. It was so long since he had shown any interest over any outside case that I was quite rejoiced to see him back in his old form.

For my own part, I felt a deep pity as I looked down upon the motionless form and convulsed face of the hapless young

American who had come by his death in such a strange way. Poirot examined the body attentively. There was no mark on it anywhere, except a small scar on the left hand.

"And the doctor says that's a burn, not a cut," explained Japp.

Poirot's attention shifted to the contents of the dead man's pockets which a constable spread out for our inspection. There was nothing much—a handkerchief, keys, notecase filled with notes, and some unimportant letters. But one object standing by itself filled Poirot with interest.

"A chessman!" he exclaimed. "A white bishop. Was that in his pocket?"

"No, clasped in his hand. We had quite a difficulty to get it out of his fingers. It must be returned to Dr. Savaronoff sometime. It's part of a very beautiful set of carved ivory chessmen."

"Permit me to return it to him. It will make an excuse for my going there."

"Aha!" cried Japp. "So you want to come in on this case?"

"I admit it. So skilfully have you aroused my interest."

"That's fine. Got you away from your brooding. Captain Hastings is pleased, too, I can see."

"Quite right," I said, laughing.

Poirot turned back towards the body.

"No other little detail you can tell me about—him?" he asked.

"I don't think so."

"Not even—that he was left-handed?"

"You're a wizard, Moosior Poirot. How did you know that? He *was* left-handed. Not that it's anything to do with the case."

"Nothing whatever," agreed Poirot hastily, seeing that Japp was slightly ruffled. "My little joke—that was all. I like to play you the trick, see you."

We went out upon an amicable understanding.

The following morning saw us wending our way to Dr. Savaronoff's flat in Westminster.

"Sonia Daviloff," I mused. "It's a pretty name."

Poirot stopped, and threw me a look of despair.

"Always looking for romance! You are incorrigible. It would serve you right if Sonia Daviloff turned out to be our friend and enemy the Countess Vera Rossakoff."

At the mention of the countess, my face clouded over.

"Surely, Poirot, you don't suspect—"

"But, no, no. It was a joke! I have not the Big Four on the brain to that extent, whatever Japp may say."

The door of the flat was opened to us by a man-servant with a peculiarly wooden face. It seemed impossible to believe that that impassive countenance could ever display emotion.

Poirot presented a card on which Japp had scribbled a few words of introduction, and we were shown into a low, long room furnished with rich hangings and curios. One or two wonderful icons hung upon the walls, and exquisite Persian rugs lay upon the floor. A samovar stood upon a table.

I was examining one of the icons which I judged to be of considerable value, and turned to see Poirot prone upon the floor. Beautiful as the rug was, it hardly seemed to me to necessitate such close attention.

"Is it such a very wonderful specimen?" I asked.

"Eh? Oh! the rug? But no, it was not the rug I was remarking. But it *is* a beautiful specimen, far too beautiful to have a large nail wantonly driven through the middle of it. No, Hastings," as I came forward, "the nail is not there now. But the hole remains."

A sudden sound behind us made me spin round, and Poirot spring nimbly to his feet. A girl was standing in the doorway. Her eyes, full upon us, were dark with suspicion. She was of medium height, with a beautiful, rather sullen face, dark blue eyes, and very black hair which was cut short. Her voice, when she spoke, was rich and sonorous, and completely un-English.

"I fear my uncle will be unable to see you. He is a great invalid."

"That is a pity, but perhaps you will kindly help me instead.

You are Mademoiselle Daviloff, are you not?"

"Yes, I am Sonia Daviloff. What is it you want to know?"

"I am making some inquiries about that sad affair the night before last—the death of M. Gilmour Wilson. What can you tell me about it?"

The girl's eyes opened wide.

"He died of heart failure—as he was playing chess."

"The police are not so sure that it was—heart failure, mademoiselle."

The girl gave a terrified gesture.

"It was true then," she cried. "Ivan was right."

"Who is Ivan, and why do you say he was right?"

"It was Ivan who opened the door to you—and he has already said to me that in his opinion Gilmour Wilson did not die a natural death—that he was poisoned by mistake."

"By mistake."

"Yes, the poison was meant for my uncle."

She had quite forgotten her first distrust now, and was speaking eagerly.

"Why do you say that, mademoiselle. Who should wish to poison Dr. Savaronoff?"

She shook her head.

"I do not know. I am all in the dark. And my uncle, he will not trust me. It is natural, perhaps. You see, he hardly knows me. He saw me as a child, and not since till I came to live with him here in London. But this much I do know, he is in fear of something. We have many secret societies in Russia, and one day I overheard something which made me think it was of just such a society he went in fear. Tell me, monsieur"—she came a step nearer, and dropped her voice—"have you ever heard of a society called the 'Big Four'?"

Poirot jumped nearly out of his skin. His eyes positively bulged with astonishment.

"Why do you—what do you know of the Big Four, mademoiselle?"

"There is such an association, then! I overheard a reference to them, and asked my uncle about it afterwards. Never have I seen a man so afraid. He turned all white and shaking. He was in fear of them, monsieur, in great fear, I am sure of it. And, by mistake, they killed the American, Wilson."

"The Big Four," murmured Poirot. "Always the Big Four! An astonishing coincidence, mademoiselle, your uncle is still in danger. I must save him. Now recount to me exactly the events of that fatal evening. Show me the chess-board, the table, how the two men sat—everything."

She went to the side of the room and brought out a small table. The top of it was exquisite, inlaid with squares of silver and black to represent a chess-board.

"This was sent to my uncle a few weeks ago as a present, with the request that he would use it in the next match he played. It was in the middle of the room—so."

Poirot examined the table with what seemed to me quite unnecessary attention. He was not conducting the inquiry at all as I would have done. Many of his questions seemed to me pointless, and upon really vital matters he seemed to have no questions to ask. I concluded that the unexpected mention of the Big Four had thrown him completely off his balance.

After a minute examination of the table and the exact position it had occupied, he asked to see the chessmen. Sonia Daviloff brought them to him in a box. He examined one or two of them in a perfunctory manner.

"An exquisite set," he murmured absent-mindedly.

Still not a question as to what refreshments there had been, or what people had been present.

I cleared my throat significantly.

"Don't you think, Poirot, that—"

He interrupted me peremptorily.

"Do not think, my friend. Leave all to me. Mademoiselle, is it quite impossible that I should see your uncle?"

A faint smile showed itself on her face.

"He will see you, yes. You understand, it is my part to interview all strangers first."

She disappeared. I heard a murmur of voices in the next room, and a minute later she came back and motioned us to pass into the adjoining room.

The man who lay there on a couch was an imposing figure. Tall, gaunt, with huge bushy eyebrows and white beard, and a face haggard as the result of starvation and hardships. Dr. Savaronoff was a distinct personality. I noted the peculiar formation of his head, its unusual height. A great chess player must have a great brain, I knew. I could easily understand Dr. Savaronoff being the second greatest player in the world.

Poirot bowed.

"M. le Docteur, may I speak to you alone?"

Savaronoff turned to his niece.

"Leave us, Sonia."

She disappeared obediently.

"Now, sir, what is it?"

"Dr. Savaronoff, you have recently come into an enormous fortune. If you should—die unexpectedly, who inherits it?"

"I have made a will leaving everything to my niece, Sonia Daviloff. You do not suggest—"

"I suggest nothing, but you have not seen your niece since she was a child. It would have been easy for any one to impersonate her."

Savaronoff seemed thunderstruck by the suggestion. Poirot went on easily.

"Enough as to that. I give you the word of warning, that is all. What I want you to do now is to describe to me the game of chess the other evening."

"How do you mean—describe it?"

"Well, I do not play the chess myself, but I understand that there are various regular ways of beginning—the gambit, do they not call it?"

97

Dr. Savaronoff smiled a little.

"Ah! I comprehend you now. Wilson opened Ruy Lopez—one of the soundest openings there is, and one frequently adopted in tournaments and matches."

"And how long had you been playing when the tragedy happened?"

"It must have been about the third or fourth move when Wilson suddenly fell forward over the table, stone dead."

Poirot rose to depart. He flung out his last question as though it was of absolutely no importance, but I knew better.

"Had he had anything to eat or drink?"

"A whisky and soda, I think."

"Thank you, Dr. Savaronoff. I will disturb you no longer."

Ivan was in the hall to show us out. Poirot lingered on the threshold.

"The flat below this, do you know who lives there?"

"Sir Charles Kingwell, a member of Parliament, sir. It has been let furnished lately, though."

"Thank you."

We went out into the bright winter sunlight.

"Well, really, Poirot," I burst out. "I don't think you've distinguished yourself this time. Surely your questions were very inadequate."

"You think so, Hastings?" Poirot looked at me appealingly. "I was bouleversé, yes. What would you have asked?"

I considered the question carefully, and then outlined my scheme to Poirot. He listened with what seemed to be close interest. My monologue lasted until we had nearly reached home.

"Very excellent, very searching, Hastings," said Poirot, as he inserted his key in the door and preceded me up the stairs. "But quite unnecessary."

"Unnecessary!" I cried, amazed. "If the man was poisoned—"

"Aha," cried Poirot, pouncing upon a note which lay on the table. "From Japp. Just as I thought." He flung it over to me. It was brief and to the point. No traces of poison had been found, and there was nothing to show how the man came by his death.

"You see," said Poirot, "our questions would have been quite unnecessary."

"You guessed this beforehand?"

"'Forecast the probable result of the deal,'" quoted Poirot from a recent Bridge problem on which I had spent much time. "*Mon ami*, when you do that successfully, you do not call it guessing."

"Don't let's split hairs," I said impatiently. "You foresaw this?"

"I did."

"Why?"

Poirot put his hand into his pocket and pulled out—a white bishop.

"Why," I cried, "you forgot to give it back to Dr. Savaronoff."

"You are in error, my friend. That bishop still reposes in my left-hand pocket. I took its fellow from the box of chessmen Mademoiselle Daviloff kindly permitted me to examine. The plural of one bishop is two bishops."

He sounded the final "s" with a great hiss. I was completely mystified.

"But why did you take it?"

"*Parbleu*, I wanted to see if they were exactly alike."

He stood them on the table side by side.

"Well, they are, of course," I said, "exactly alike."

Poirot looked at them with his head on one side.

"They seem so, I admit. But one should take no fact for granted until it is proved. Bring me, I pray you, my little scales."

With infinite care he weighed the two chessmen, then turned to me with a face alight with triumph.

"I was right. See you, I was right. Impossible to deceive Hercule Poirot!"

He rushed to the telephone—waited impatiently.

"Is that Japp? Ah! Japp, it is you. Hercule Poirot speaks. Watch the man-servant, Ivan. On no account let him slip through your fingers. Yes, yes, it is as I say."

He dashed down the receiver and turned to me.

"You see it not, Hastings? I will explain. Wilson was not poisoned, he was electrocuted. A thin metal rod passes up the middle of one of those chessmen. The table was prepared beforehand and set upon a certain spot on the floor. When the bishop was placed upon one of the silver squares, the current passed through Wilson's body, killing him instantly. The only mark was the electric burn upon his hand—his left hand, because he was left-handed. The 'special table' was an extremely cunning piece of mechanism. The table I examined was a duplicate, perfectly innocent. It was substituted for the other immediately after the murder. The thing was worked from the flat below, which, if you remember, was let furnished. But one accomplice at least was in Savaronoff's flat. The girl is an agent of the Big Four, working to inherit Savaronoff's money."

"And Ivan?"

"I strongly suspect that Ivan is none other than the famous Number Four."

"*What*?"

"Yes. The man is a marvellous character actor. He can assume any part he pleases."

I thought back over past adventures, the lunatic asylum keeper, the butcher's young man, the suave doctor, all the same man, and all totally unlike each other.

"It's amazing," I said at last. "Everything fits in. Savaronoff had an inkling of the plot, and that's why he was so averse to playing the match."

Poirot looked at me without speaking. Then he turned abruptly away, and began pacing up and down.

"Have you a book on chess by any chance, *mon ami*?" he asked suddenly.

"I believe I have somewhere."

It took me some time to ferret it out, but I found it at last, and brought it to Poirot, who sank down in a chair and started reading it with the greatest attention.

In about a quarter of an hour the telephone rang. I answered it. It was Japp. Ivan had left the flat, carrying a large bundle. He had sprung into a waiting taxi, and the chase had begun. He was evidently trying to lose his pursuers. In the end he seemed to fancy that he had done so, and had then driven to a big empty house at Hampstead. The house was surrounded.

I recounted all this to Poirot. He merely stared at me as though he scarcely took in what I was saying. He held out the chess book.

"Listen to this, my friend. This is the Ruy Lopez Opening. 1 P-K4, P-K4; 2 Kt-KB3, Kt-QB3; 3B-Kt5;? Then there comes a question as to Black's best third move. He has the choice of various defences. It was White's third move that killed Gilmour Wilson, 3B-Kt5. Only the third move—does that say nothing to you?"

I hadn't the least idea what he meant, and told him so.

"I suppose, Hastings, that while you were sitting in this chair, you heard the front door being opened and shut, what would you think?"

"I should think some one had gone out, I suppose."

"Yes—but there are always two ways of looking at things. Some one gone out—some one come *in*—two totally different things, Hastings. But if you assumed the wrong one, presently some little discrepancy would creep in and show you that you were on the wrong track."

"What does all this mean, Poirot?"

Poirot sprang to his feet with sudden energy.

"It means that I have been a triple imbecile. Quick, quick, to the flat in Westminster. We may yet be in time."

We tore off in a taxi. Poirot returned no answer to my excited questions. We raced up the stairs. Repeated rings and knocks brought no reply, but listening closely I could distinguish a hollow groan coming from within.

The hall porter proved to have a master key, and after a few difficulties he consented to use it.

Poirot went straight to the inner room. A whiff of chloroform met us. On the floor was Sonia Daviloff, gagged and bound, with a great wad of saturated cotton wool over her nose and mouth. Poirot tore it off and began to take measures to restore her. Presently a doctor arrived, and Poirot handed her over to his charge and drew aside with me. There was no sign of Dr. Savaronoff.

"What does it all mean?" I asked, bewildered.

"It means that before two equal deductions I chose the wrong one. You heard me say that it would be easy for any one to impersonate Sonia Daviloff because her uncle had not seen her for so many years?"

"Yes?"

"Well, precisely the opposite held good also. It was equally easy for any one to impersonate the uncle."

"What?"

"Savaronoff *did* die at the outbreak of the Revolution. The man who pretended to have escaped with such terrible hardships, the man so changed 'that his own friends could hardly recognise him,' the man who successfully laid claim to an enormous fortune—"

"Yes. Who was he?"

"*Number Four.* No wonder he was frightened when Sonia let him know she had overheard one of his private conversations about the 'Big Four.' Again he has slipped through my fingers. He guessed I should get on the right track in the end, so he sent off the honest Ivan on a tortuous wild goose chase, chloroformed the girl, and got out, having by now doubtless realised most of the securities left by Madame Gospoja."

"But—but who tried to kill him then?"

"Nobody tried to kill *him*. Wilson was the intended victim all along."

"But why?"

"My friend, Savaronoff was the second greatest chess player in the world. In all probability Number Four did not even know the rudiments of the game. Certainly he could not sustain the fiction of a match. He tried all he knew to avoid the contest. When that failed, Wilson's doom was sealed. At all costs he must be prevented from discovering that the great Savaronoff did not even know how to play chess. Wilson was fond of the Ruy Lopez opening, and was certain to use it. Number Four arranged for death to come with the third move, before any complications of defence set in."

"But, my dear Poirot," I persisted, "are we dealing with a lunatic? I quite follow your reasoning, and admit that you must be right, but to kill a man just to sustain his role! Surely there were simpler ways out of the difficulty than that? He could have said that his doctor forbade the strain of a match."

Poirot wrinkled his forehead.

"*Certainement*, Hastings," he said, "there were other ways, but none so convincing. Besides, you are assuming that to kill a man is a thing to avoid, are you not? Number Four's mind, it does not act that way. I put myself in his place, a thing impossible for you. I picture his thoughts. He enjoys himself as the professor at that match. I doubt not he has visited the chess tourneys to study his part. He sits and frowns in thought; he gives the impression that he is thinking great plans, and all the time he laughs in himself. He is aware that two moves are all that he knows—and all that he *need know*. Again, it would appeal to his mind to foresee the events and to make the man his own executioner at the exact time that suits Number Four.... Oh, yes, Hastings, I begin to understand our friend and his psychology."

I shrugged.

"Well, I suppose you're right, but I can't understand any one running a risk he could so easily avoid."

"Risk!" Poirot snorted. "Where then lay the risk? Would Japp have solved the problem? No; if Number Four had not made one small mistake he would have run no risk."

"And his mistake?" I asked, although I suspected the answer.

"*Mon ami*, he overlooked the little gray cells of Hercule Poirot."

Poirot has his virtues, but modesty is not one of them.

TWELVE
The Baited Trap

It was mid-January—a typical English winter day in London, damp and dirty. Poirot and I were sitting in two chairs well drawn up to the fire. I was aware of my friend looking at me with a quizzical smile, the meaning of which I could not fathom.

"A penny for your thoughts," I said lightly.

"I was thinking, my friend, that at midsummer, when you first arrived, you told me that you proposed to be in this country for a couple of months only."

"Did I say that?" I asked, rather awkwardly. "I don't remember."

Poirot's smile broadened.

"You did, *mon ami*. Since then, you have changed your plan, is it not so?"

"Er—yes, I have."

"And why is that?"

"Dash it all, Poirot, you don't think I'm going to leave you all alone when you're up against a thing like the 'Big Four,' do you?"

Poirot nodded gently.

"Just as I thought. You are a staunch friend, Hastings. It is to serve me that you remain on here. And your wife—little Cinderella as you call her, what does she say?"

"I haven't gone into details, of course, but she understands. She'd be the last one to wish me to turn my back on a pal."

"Yes, yes, she, too, is a loyal friend. But it is going to be a long business, perhaps."

I nodded, rather discouraged.

"Six months already," I mused, "and where are we? You know, Poirot, I can't help thinking that we ought to—well, to do something."

"Always so energetic, Hastings! And what precisely would you have me do?"

This was somewhat of a poser, but I was not going to withdraw from my position.

"We ought to take the offensive," I urged. "What have we done all this time?"

"More than you think, my friend. After all, we have established the identity of Number Two and Number Three, and we have learnt more than a little about the ways and methods of Number Four."

I brightened up a little. As Poirot put it, things didn't sound so bad.

"Oh! Yes, Hastings, we have done a great deal. It is true that I am not in a position to accuse either Ryland or Madame Olivier—who would believe me? You remember I thought once I had Ryland successfully cornered? Nevertheless I have made my suspicions known in certain quarters—the highest—Lord Aldington, who enlisted my help in the matter of the stolen submarine plans, is fully cognisant of all my information respecting the Big Four—and while others may doubt, he believes. Ryland and Madame Olivier, and Li Chang Yen himself may go their ways, but there is a searchlight turned on all their movements."

"And Number Four?" I asked.

"As I said just now—I am beginning to know and understand his methods. You may smile, Hastings—but to penetrate a man's personality, to know exactly what he will do under any given circumstances—that is the beginning of success. It is a duel between us, and whilst he is constantly giving away his mentality to me, I endeavour to let him know little or nothing of mine. He is in the light, I in the shade. I tell you, Hastings, that every day they fear me the more for my chosen inactivity."

"They've let us alone, anyway," I observed. "There have been no more attempts on your life, and no ambushes of any kind."

"No," said Poirot thoughtfully. "On the whole, that rather surprises me. Especially as there are one or two fairly obvious ways of getting at us which I should have thought certain to have occurred to them. You catch my meaning, perhaps?"

"An infernal machine of some kind?" I hazarded.

Poirot made a sharp click with his tongue expressive of impatience.

"But no! I appeal to your imagination, and you can suggest nothing more subtle than bombs in the fireplace. Well, well, I have need of some matches, I will promenade myself despite the weather. Pardon, my friend, but is it possible that you read *The Future of the Argentine, Mirror of Society, Cattle Breeding, The Clue of Crimson* and *Sport in the Rockies* at one and the same time?"

I laughed, and admitted that *The Clue of Crimson* was at present engaging my sole attention. Poirot shook his head sadly.

"But replace then the others on the bookshelf! Never, never shall I see you embrace the order and the method. Mon Dieu, what then is a bookshelf for?"

I apologised humbly, and Poirot, after replacing the offending volumes, each in its appointed place, went out and left me to uninterrupted enjoyment of my selected book.

I must admit, however, that I was half asleep when Mrs. Pearson's knock at the door aroused me.

"A telegram for you, captain."

I tore the orange envelope open without much interest.

Then I sat as though turned to stone.

It was a cable from Bronsen, my manager out at the South American ranch, and it ran as follows:—

"Mrs. Hastings disappeared yesterday, feared been kidnapped by some gang calling itself big four cable instructions have notified police but no clue as yet."

Bronsen.

I waved Mrs. Pearson out of the room, and sat as though stunned, reading the words over and over again. Cinderella—kidnapped! In the hands of the infamous Big Four! God, what could I do?

Poirot! I must have Poirot. He would advise me. He would checkmate them somehow. In a few minutes now, he would be back. I must wait patiently until then. But Cinderella—in the hands of the Big Four!

Another knock. Mrs. Pearson put her head in once more.

"A note for you, captain—brought by a heathen Chinaman. He's a-waiting downstairs."

I seized it from her. It was brief and to the point.

"If you ever wish to see your wife again, go with the bearer of this note immediately. Leave no message for your friend or she will suffer."

It was signed with a big 4.

What ought I to have done? What would you who read have done in my place?

I had no time to think. I saw only one thing—Cinderella in the power of those devils. I must obey—I dare not risk a hair of her head. I must go with this Chinaman and follow whither he led. It was a trap, yes, and it meant certain capture and possible death, but it was baited with the person dearest to me in the whole world, and I dared not hesitate.

What irked me most was to leave no word for Poirot. Once set him on my track, and all might yet be well? Dare I risk it? Apparently I was under no supervision, but yet I hesitated. It would have been so easy for the Chinaman to come up and assure himself that I was keeping to the letter of the command. Why didn't he? His very abstention made me more suspicious. I had seen so much of the omnipotence of the Big Four that I credited them with almost super-human powers. For all I know, even the little bedraggled servant girl might be one of their agents.

No, I dared not risk it. But one thing I could do, leave the telegram. He would know then that Cinderella had disappeared, and who was responsible for her disappearance.

All this passed through my head in less time than it takes to tell, and I had clapped my hat on my head and was descending the stairs to where my guide waited, in a little over a minute.

The bearer of the message was a tall impassive Chinaman, neatly but rather shabbily dressed. He bowed and spoke to me. His English was perfect, but he spoke with a slight sing-song intonation.

"You Captain Hastings?"

"Yes," I said.

"You give me note, please."

I had foreseen the request, and handed him over the scrap of paper without a word. But that was not all.

"You have telegram to-day, yes? Come along just now? From South America, yes?"

I realised anew the excellence of their espionage system—or it might have been a shrewd guess. Bronsen was bound to cable me. They would wait until the cable was delivered and would strike hard upon it.

No good could come of denying what was palpably true.

"Yes," I said. "I did get a telegram."

"You fetch him, yes? Fetch him now."

I ground my teeth, but what could I do. I ran upstairs again. As I did so, I thought of confiding in Mrs. Pearson, at any rate as far as Cinderella's disappearance went. She was on the landing, but close behind her was the little maid-servant, and I hesitated. If she *was* a spy—the words of the note danced before my eyes. "... she will suffer...." I passed into the sitting-room without speaking.

I took up the telegram and was about to pass out again when an idea struck me. Could I not leave some sign which would mean nothing to my enemies but which Poirot himself would find significant. I hurried across to the bookcase and tumbled out four books on to the floor. No fear of Poirot's not seeing them. They would outrage his eyes immediately—and coming on top of his little lecture, surely he would find them unusual. Next I put a shovelful of coal on the fire and managed to spill four knobs into the grate. I had done all I could—pray Heaven Poirot would read the sign aright.

I hurried down again. The Chinaman took the telegram from me, read it, then placed it in his pocket and with a nod beckoned me to follow him.

It was a long weary march that he led me. Once we took a bus and once we went for some considerable way in a train, and always our route led us steadily eastward. We went through strange districts, the existence of which I had never dreamed of. We were down by the docks now, I knew, and I realised that I was being taken into the heart of Chinatown.

In spite of myself I shivered. Still my guide plodded on, turning and twisting through mean streets and byways, until at last he stopped at a dilapidated house and rapped four times upon the door.

It was opened immediately by another Chinaman who stood aside to let us pass in. The clanging to of the door behind me was the knell of my last hopes. I was indeed in the hands of the enemy.

I was now handed over to the second Chinaman. He led me down some rickety stairs and into a cellar which was filled with bales and casks and which exhaled a pungent odour, as of Eastern spices. I felt wrapped all round with the atmosphere of the East, tortuous, cunning, sinister—

Suddenly my guide rolled aside two of the casks, and I saw a low tunnel-like opening in the wall. He motioned me to go ahead. The tunnel was of some length, and it was just too low for me to stand upright. At last, however, it broadened out into a passage, and a few minutes later we stood in another cellar.

My Chinaman went forward, and rapped four times on one of the walls. A whole section of the wall swung out, leaving a narrow doorway. I passed through, and to my utter astonishment found myself in a kind of Arabian Nights' palace. A low long subterranean chamber hung with rich oriental silks, brilliantly lighted and fragrant with perfumes and spices. There five or six silk covered divans, and exquisite carpets of Chinese workmanship covered the ground. At the end of the room was a curtained recess. From behind these curtains came a voice.

"You have brought our honoured guest?"

"Excellency, he is here," replied my guide.

"Let our guest enter," was the answer.

At the same moment, the curtains were drawn aside by an unseen hand, and I was facing an immense cushioned divan on which sat a tall thin Oriental dressed in wonderfully embroidered robes, and clearly, by the length of his finger nails, a great man.

"Be seated, I pray you, Captain Hastings," he said, with a wave of his hand. "You acceded to my request to come immediately, I am glad to see."

"Who are you?" I asked. "Li Chang Yen?"

"Indeed no, I am but the humblest of the master's servants. I carry out his behests, that is all—as do other of his servants in other countries—in South America, for instance."

I advanced a step.

"Where is she? What have you done with her out there?"

"She is in a place of safety—where none will find her. As yet, she is unharmed. You observe that I say—*as yet*!"

Cold shivers ran down my spine as I confronted this smiling devil.

"What do you want?" I cried. "Money?"

"My dear Captain Hastings. We have no designs on your small savings, I can assure you. Not—pardon me—a very intelligent suggestion on your part. Your colleague would not have made it, I fancy."

"I suppose," I said heavily, "you wanted to get me into your toils. Well, you have succeeded. I have come here with my eyes open. Do what you like with me, and let her go. She knows nothing, and she can be no possible use to you. You've used her to get hold of me—you've got me all right, and that settles it."

The smiling Oriental caressed his smooth cheek, watching me obliquely out of his narrow eyes.

"You go too fast," he said purringly. "That does not quite—settle it. In fact, to 'get hold of you' as you express it, is not really our objective. But through you, we hope to get hold of your friend, M. Hercule Poirot."

"I'm afraid you won't do that," I said, with a short laugh.

"What I suggest is this," continued the other, his words running on as though he had not heard me.

"You will write M. Hercule Poirot a letter, such a letter as will induce him to hasten hither and join you."

"I shall do no such thing," I said angrily.

"The consequences of refusal will be disagreeable."

"Damn your consequences."

"The alternative might be death!"

A nasty shiver ran down my spine, but I endeavoured to put a bold face upon it.

"It's no good threatening me, and bullying me. Keep your threats for Chinese cowards."

"My threats are very real ones, Captain Hastings. I ask you again, will you write this letter?"

"I will not, and what's more, you daren't kill me. You'd have the police on your tracks in no time."

My interlocutor clapped his hands swiftly. Two Chinese attendants appeared as it were out of the blue, and pinioned me by both arms. Their master said something rapidly to them in Chinese, and they dragged me across the floor to a spot in one corner of the big chamber. One of them stooped, and suddenly, without the least warning, the flooring gave beneath my feet. But for the restraining hand of the other man I should have gone down the yawning gap beneath me. It was inky black, and I could hear the rushing of water.

"The river," said my questioner from his place on the divan. "Think well, Captain Hastings. If you refuse again, you go headlong to eternity, to meet your death in the dark waters below. For the last time, will you write that letter?"

I'm not braver than most men. I admit frankly that I was scared to death, and in a blue funk. That Chinese devil meant business, I was sure of that. It was good-bye to the good old world. In spite of myself, my voice wobbled a little as I answered.

"For the last time, no! To hell with your letter!"

Then involuntarily I closed my eyes and breathed a short prayer.

THIRTEEN
The Mouse Walks In

Not often in a life-time does a man stand on the edge of eternity, but when I spoke those words in that East End cellar I was perfectly certain that they were my last words on earth. I braced myself for the shock of those black, rushing waters beneath, and experienced in advance the horror of that breath-choking fall.

But to my surprise a low laugh fell on my ears. I opened my eyes. Obeying a sign from the man on the divan, my two jailers brought me back to my old seat facing him.

"You are a brave man, Captain Hastings," he said. "We of the East appreciate bravery. I may say that I expected you to act as you have done. That brings us to the appointed second act of our little drama. Death for yourself you have faced—will you face death for another?"

"What do you mean?" I asked hoarsely, a horrible fear creeping over me.

"Surely you have not forgotten the lady who is in our power—the Rose of the Garden."

I stared at him in dumb agony.

"I think, Captain Hastings, that you will write that letter. See, I have a cable form here. The message I shall write on it depends on you, and means life or death for your wife."

The sweat broke out on my brow. My tormentor continued, smiling amiably, and speaking with perfect sangfroid:—

"There, captain, the pen is ready to your hand. You have only to write. If not—"

"If not?" I echoed.

"If not, that lady that you love dies—and dies slowly. My master, Li Chang Yen, amuses himself in his spare hours by devising new and ingenious methods of tortures—"

"My God!" I cried. "You fiend! Not that—you wouldn't do that—"

"Shall I recount to you some of his devices?"

Without heeding my cry of protest, his speech flowed on—evenly, serenely—till with a cry of horror I clapped my hands to my ears.

"It is enough, I see. Take up the pen and write."

"You would not dare—"

"Your speech is foolishness, and you know it. Take up the pen and write."

"If I do?"

"Your wife goes free. The cable shall be despatched immediately."

"How do I know that you will keep faith with me?"

"I swear it to you on the sacred tombs of my ancestors. Moreover, judge for yourself—why should I wish to do her harm? Her detention will have answered its purpose."

"And—and Poirot?"

"We will keep him in safe custody until we have concluded our operations. Then we will let him go."

"Will you swear that also on the tombs of your ancestors?"

"I have sworn one oath to you. That should be sufficient."

My heart sank. I was betraying my friend—to what? For a moment I hesitated—then the terrible alternative rose like a nightmare before my eyes. Cinderella—in the hands of these Chinese devils, dying by slow torture—

A groan rose to my lips. I seized the pen. Perhaps by careful wording of the letter, I could convey a warning, and Poirot would be enabled to avoid the trap. It was the only hope.

But even that hope was not to remain. The Chinaman's voice rose, suave and courteous.

"Permit me to dictate to you."

He paused, consulted a sheaf of notes that lay by his side, and then dictated as follows:—

"Dear Poirot, I think I'm on the track of Number Four. A Chinaman came this afternoon and lured me down here with a bogus message. Luckily I saw through his little game in time, and gave him the slip. Then I turned the tables on him, and managed to do a bit of shadowing on my own account—rather neatly too, I flatter myself. I'm getting a bright young lad to carry this to you. Give him a half a crown, will you? That's what I promised him if it was delivered safely. I'm watching the house, and daren't leave. I shall wait for you until six o'clock, and if you haven't come then, I'll have a try at getting into the house on my own. It's too good a chance to miss, and, of course, the boy mightn't find you. But if he does, get him to bring you down here right away. And cover up those precious moustaches of yours in case any one's watching out from the house and might recognise you.

"Yours in haste,

"A. H."

Every word that I wrote plunged me deeper in despair. The thing was diabolically clever. I realised how closely every detail of our life must be known. It was just such an epistle as I might have penned myself. The acknowledgment that the Chinaman who had called that afternoon had endeavoured to "lure me away" discounted any good I might have done by leaving my "sign" of four books. It *had* been a trap, and I had seen through it, that was what Poirot would think. The time, too, was cleverly planned. Poirot, on receiving the note, would have just time to rush off with his innocent-looking guide, and that he would do so, I knew.

My determination to make my way into the house would bring him post haste. He always displayed a ridiculous distrust of my capacities. He would be convinced that I was running into danger without being equal to the situation, and would rush down to take command of the situation.

But there was nothing to be done. I wrote as bidden. My captor took the note from me, read it, then nodded his head approvingly and handed it to one of the silent attendants who disappeared with it behind one of the silken hangings on the wall which masked a doorway.

With a smile the man opposite to me picked up a cable form and wrote. He handed it to me.

It read: "Release the white bird with all despatch."

I gave a sigh of relief.

"You will send it at once?" I urged.

He smiled, and shook his head.

"When M. Hercule Poirot is in my hands it shall be sent. Not until then."

"But you promised—"

"If this device fails, I may have need of our white bird—to persuade you to further efforts."

I grew white with anger.

"My God! If you—"

He waved a long slim yellow hand.

"Be reassured, I do not think it will fail. And the moment M. Poirot is in our hands, I will keep my oath."

"If you play me false."

"I have sworn it by my honoured ancestors. Have no fear. Rest here awhile. My servants will see to your needs whilst I am absent."

I was left alone in this strange underground nest of luxury. The second Chinese attendant had reappeared. One of them brought food and drink and offered it to me, but I waved them aside. I was sick—sick—at heart—

And then suddenly the master reappeared tall and stately in his silken robes. He directed operations. By his orders I was hustled back through the cellar and tunnel into the original house I had entered. There they took me into a ground floor room. The windows were shuttered, but one could see through the cracks into the street. An old ragged man was shuffling along the opposite side of the road, and when I saw him make a sign to the window, I understood that he was one of the gang on watch.

"It is well," said my Chinese friend. "Hercule Poirot has fallen into the trap. He approaches now—and alone except for the boy who guides him. Now, Captain Hastings, you have still one more part to play. Unless you show yourself he will not enter the house. When he arrives opposite, you must go out on the step and beckon him in."

"What?" I cried, revolted.

"You play that part alone. Remember the price of failure. If Hercule Poirot suspects anything is amiss and does not enter the house, your wife dies by the Seventy lingering Deaths! Ah! Here he is."

With a beating heart, and a feeling of deathly sickness, I looked through the crack in the shutters. In the figure walking along the opposite side of the street I recognised my friend at once, though his coat collar was turned up and an immense yellow muffler hid the bottom part of his face. But there was no mistaking that walk, and the poise of that egg-shaped head.

It was Poirot, coming to my aid in all good faith, suspecting nothing amiss. By his side ran a typical London urchin, grimy of face and ragged of apparel.

Poirot paused, looking across at the house, whilst the boy spoke to him eagerly and pointed. It was the time for me to act. I went out in the hall. At a sign from the tall Chinaman, one of the servants unlatched the door.

"Remember the price of failure," said my enemy in a low voice.

I was outside on the steps. I beckoned to Poirot. He hastened across.

"Aha! So all is well with you, my friend. I was beginning to be anxious. You managed to get inside? Is the house empty, then?"

"Yes," I said, in a voice I strove to make natural. "There must be a secret way out of it somewhere. Come in and let us look for it."

I stepped back across the threshold. In all innocence Poirot prepared to follow me.

And then something seemed to snap in my head. I saw only too clearly the part I was playing—the part of Judas.

"Back, Poirot!" I cried. "Back for your life. It's a trap. Never mind me. Get away at once."

Even as I spoke—or rather shouted my warning hands gripped me like a vice. One of the Chinese servants sprang past me to grab Poirot.

I saw the latter spring back, his arm raised, then suddenly a dense volume of smoke was rising round me, choking me—killing me—

I felt myself falling—suffocating—this was death—

I came to myself slowly and painfully—all my senses dazed. The first thing I saw was Poirot's face. He was sitting opposite me watching me with an anxious face. He gave a cry of joy when he saw me looking at him.

"Ah, you revive—you return to yourself. All is well! My friend—my poor friend!"

"Where am I?" I said painfully.

"Where? But *chez vous*!"

I looked round me. True enough, I was in the old familiar surroundings. And in the grate were the identical four knobs of coal I had carefully spilt there.

Poirot had followed my glance.

"But yes, that was a famous idea of yours—that and the books. See you, if they should say to me any time. 'That friend of yours, that Hastings, he has not the great brain, is it not so?' I shall reply to them: 'You are in error.' It was an idea magnificent and superb that occurred to you there."

"You understood their meaning then?"

"Am I an imbecile? Of course I understood. It gave me just the warning I needed, and the time to mature my plans. Somehow or other the Big Four had carried you off. With what object? Clearly not for your *beaux yeux*—equally clearly not because they feared you and wanted to get you out of the way. No, their object was plain. You would be used as a decoy to get the great Hercule Poirot into their clutches. I have long been prepared for something of the kind. I make my little preparations, and presently, sure enough, the messenger arrives—such an innocent little street urchin. Me, I swallow everything, and hasten away with him, and, very fortunately, they permit you to come out on the doorstep. That was my one fear, that I should have to dispose of them before I had reached the place where you were concealed, and that I should have to search for you—perhaps in vain—afterwards."

"Dispose of them, did you say?" I asked feebly. "Single-handed."

"Oh, there is nothing very clever about that. If one is prepared in advance all is simple—the motto of the Boy Scout, is it not? And a very fine one. Me, I was prepared. Not so long ago, I rendered a service to a very famous chemist, who did a lot of work in connection with poison gas during the war. He devised for me a little bomb—simple and easy to carry about—one has but to throw it and poof, the smoke—and then the unconsciousness. Immediately I blow a little whistle and straightway some of Japp's clever fellows who were watching the house here long before the boy arrived, and who managed to follow us all the way to Limehouse, came flying up and took charge of the situation."

"But how was it you weren't unconscious too?"

"Another piece of luck. Our friend Number Four (who certainly composed that ingenious letter) permitted himself a little jest at my moustaches, which rendered it extremely easy for me to adjust my respirator under the guise of a yellow muffler."

"I remember," I cried eagerly, and then with the word "Remember" all the ghastly horror that I had temporarily forgotten came back to me. *Cinderella*—

I fell back with a groan.

I must have lost consciousness again for a minute or two. I awoke to find Poirot forcing some brandy between my lips.

"What is it, *mon ami*? But what is it—then? Tell me." Word by word, I got the thing told, shuddering as I did so. Poirot uttered a cry.

"My friend! My friend! But what you must have suffered! And I who knew nothing of all this! But reassure yourself! All is well!"

"You will find her, you mean? But she is in South America. And by the time we get there—long before, she will be dead—and God knows how and in what horrible way she will have died."

"No, no, you do not understand. She is safe and well. She has never been in their hands for one instant."

"But I got a cable from Bronsen?"

"No, no, you did not. You may have got a cable from South America signed Bronsen—that is a very different matter. Tell me, has it never occurred to you that an organisation of this kind, with ramifications all over the world, might easily strike at us through that little girl, Cinderella, whom you love so well?"

"No, never," I replied.

"Well, it did to me. I said nothing to you because I did not want to upset you unnecessarily—but I took measures of my own. Your wife's letters all seem to have been written from the ranch, but in reality she has been in a place of safety devised by me for over three months."

I looked at him for a long time.

"You are sure of that?"

"*Parbleu!* I know it. They tortured you with a lie!"

I turned my head aside. Poirot put his hand on my shoulder. There was something in his voice that I had never heard there before.

"You like not that I should embrace you or display the emotion, I know well. I will be very British. I will say nothing—but nothing at all. Only this—that in this last adventure of ours, the honours are all with you, and happy is the man who has such a friend as I have!"

FOURTEEN
The Peroxide Blonde

I was very disappointed with the results of Poirot's bomb attack on the premises in Chinatown. To begin with, the leader of the gang had escaped. When Japp's men rushed up in response to Poirot's whistle they found four Chinamen unconscious in the hall, but the man who had threatened me with death was not among them. I remembered afterwards that when I was forced out on to the doorstep, to decoy Poirot into the house, this man had kept well in the background. Presumably he was out of the danger zone of the gas bomb, and made good his escape by one of the many exits which we afterwards discovered.

From the four who remained in our hands we learnt nothing. The fullest investigation by the police failed to bring to light anything to connect them with the Big Four. They were ordinary low-class residents of the district, and they professed bland ignorance of the name Li Chang Yen. A Chinese gentleman had hired them for service in the house by the waterside, and they knew nothing whatever of his private affairs.

By the next day I had, except for a slight headache, completely recovered from the effects of Poirot's gas bomb. We went down together to Chinatown and searched the house from which I had been rescued. The premises consisted of two ramshackle houses joined together by an underground passage. The ground floors and the upper stories of each were unfurnished and deserted, the broken windows covered by decaying shutters. Japp had already been prying about in the cellars, and had discovered the secret of the entrance to the subterranean chamber where I had spent such an unpleasant half-hour. Closer investigation confirmed the impression that it had made on me the night before. The silks on the walls and divan and the carpets on the floors were of exquisite workmanship. Although I know very little about Chinese art, I could appreciate that every article in the room was perfect of its kind.

With the aid of Japp and some of his men we conducted a most thorough search of the apartment. I had cherished high hopes that we would find documents of importance. A list, perhaps, of some of the more important agents of the Big Four, or cipher notes of some of their plans, but we discovered nothing of the kind. The only papers we found in the whole place were the notes which the Chinaman had consulted whilst he was dictating the letter to Poirot. These consisted of a very complete record of each of our careers, and estimate of our characters, and suggestions about the weaknesses through which we might best be attacked.

Poirot was most childishly delighted with this discovery. Personally I could not see that it was of any value whatever, especially as whoever compiled the notes was ludicrously mistaken in some of his opinions. I pointed this out to my friend when we were back in our rooms.

"My dear Poirot," I said, "you know now what the enemy thinks of us. He appears to have a grossly exaggerated idea of your brain power, and to have absurdly underrated mine, but I do not see how we are better off for knowing this."

Poirot chuckled in rather an offensive way.

"You do not see, Hastings, no? But surely now we can prepare ourselves for some of their methods of attack now that we are warned of some of our faults. For instance my friend, we know that you should think before you act. Again, if you meet a red-haired young woman in trouble you should eye her—what you say—askance, is it not?"

Their notes had contained some absurd references to my supposed impulsiveness, and had suggested that I was susceptible to the charms of young women with hair of a certain shade. I thought Poirot's reference to be in the worst of taste, but fortunately I was able to counter him.

"And what about you?" I demanded. "Are you going to try to cure your 'overweening vanity?' Your 'finicky tidiness?'"

I was quoting, and I could see that he was not pleased with my retort.

"Oh, without doubt, Hastings, in some things they deceive themselves—*tant mieux*! They will learn in due time. Meanwhile we have learnt something, and to know is to be prepared."

This last was a favourite axiom of his lately; so much so that I had begun to hate the sound of it.

"We know something, Hastings," he continued. "Yes, we know something—and that is to the good—but we do not know nearly enough. We must know more."

"In what way?"

Poirot settled himself back in his chair, straightened a box of matches which I had thrown carelessly down on the table, and assumed an attitude that I knew only too well. I saw that he was prepared to hold forth at some length.

"See you, Hastings, we have to contend against four adversaries; that is, against four different personalities. With Number One we have never come into personal contact—we know him, as it were, only by the impress of his mind—and in passing, Hastings, I will tell you that I begin to understand that mind very well—a mind most subtle and Oriental—every scheme and plot that we have encountered have emanated from the brain of Li Chang Yen. Number Two and Number Three are so powerful, so high up, that they are for the present immune from our attacks. Nevertheless what is their safeguard is, by a perverse chance, our safeguard also. They are so much in the limelight that their movements must be carefully ordered. And so we come to the last member of the gang—we come to the man known as Number Four."

Poirot's voice altered a little, as it always did when speaking of this particular individual.

"Number Two and Number Three are able to succeed, to go on their way unscathed, owing to their notoriety and their assured position. Number Four succeeds for the opposite reason—he succeeds by the way of obscurity. Who is he? Nobody knows. What does he look like? Again nobody knows. How many times have we seen him, you and I? Five times, is it not? And could either of us say truthfully that we could be sure of recognising him again?"

I was forced to shake my head, as I ran back in my mind over those five different people who, incredible as it seemed, were one and the same man. The burly lunatic asylum keeper, the man in the buttoned up overcoat in Paris, James, the footman, the quiet young medical man in the Yellow Jasmine case, and the Russian Professor. In no way did any two of these people resemble each other.

"No," I said hopelessly. "We've nothing to go by whatsoever."

Poirot smiled.

"Do not, I pray of you, give way to such enthusiastic despair. We know one or two things."

"What kind of things?" I asked sceptically.

"We know that he is a man of medium height, and of medium or fair colouring. If he were a tall man of swarthy complexion he could never have passed himself off as the fair stocky doctor. It is child's play, of course, to put on an additional inch or so for the part of James, or the Professor. In the same way he must have a short straight nose. Additions can be built on to a nose by skilful make up, but a large nose cannot be successfully reduced at a moment's notice. Then again, he must be a fairly young man, certainly not over thirty-five. You see, we are getting somewhere. A man between thirty and thirty-five, of medium height and colouring, an adept in the art of make up, and with very few or any teeth of his own."

"What?"

"Surely, Hastings. As the keeper, his teeth were broken and discoloured, in Paris they were even and white, as the doctor they protruded slightly, and as Savaronoff they had unusually long canines. Nothing alters the face so completely as a different set of teeth. You see where all this is leading us?"

"Not exactly," I said cautiously.

"A man carries his profession written in his face, they say."

"He's a criminal," I cried.

"He is an adept in the art of making up."

"It's the same thing."

"Rather a sweeping statement, Hastings, and one which would hardly be appreciated by the theatrical world. Do you not see that the man is, or has been, at one time or another, an actor?"

"An actor?"

"But certainly. He has the whole technique at his fingertips. Now there are two classes of actors, the one who sinks himself in his part, and the one who manages to impress his personality upon it. It is from the latter class that actor managers usually spring. They seize a part and mould it to their own personality. The former class is quite likely to spend its days doing Mr. Lloyd George at different music halls, or impersonating old men with beards in repertory plays. It is among that former class that we must look for our Number Four. He is a supreme artist in the way he sinks himself in each part he plays."

I was growing interested.

"So you fancy you may be able to trace his identity through his connection with the stage?"

"Your reasoning is always brilliant, Hastings."

"It might have been better," I said coldly, "if the idea had come to you sooner. We have wasted a lot of time."

"You are in error, *mon ami*. No more time has been wasted than was unavoidable. For some months now my agents have been engaged on the task. Joseph Aarons is one of them. You remember him? They have compiled a list for me of men fulfilling the necessary qualifications—young men round about the age of thirty, of more or less nondescript appearance, and with a gift for playing character parts—men, moreover, who have definitely left the stage within the last three years."

"Well?" I said, deeply interested.

"The list was, necessarily, rather a long one. For some time now, we have been engaged on the task of elimination. And finally we have boiled the whole thing down to four names. Here they are, my friend."

He tossed me over a sheet of paper. I read its contents aloud.

"*Ernest Luttrell. Son of a North Country parson. Always had a kink of some kind in his moral make-up. Was expelled from his public school. Went on the stage at the age of twenty-three.* (There followed a list of parts he had played, with dates and places.) *Addicted to drugs. Supposed to have gone to Australia four years ago. Cannot be traced after leaving England. Age 32, height 5 ft. 10-1/2 in., clean-shaven, hair brown, nose straight, complexion fair, eyes gray.*

"*John St. Maur. Assumed name. Real name not known. Believed to be of cockney extraction. On stage since quite a child. Did music hall impersonations. Not been heard of for three years. Age, about 33, height 5 ft. 10 in., slim build, blue eyes, fair colouring.*

"*Austen Lee. Assumed name. Real name Austen Foly. Good family. Always had taste for acting and distinguished himself in that way at Oxford. Brilliant war record. Acted in—*(The usual list followed. It included many Repertory plays.) *An enthusiast on criminology. Had bad nervous breakdown as the result of a motor accident three and a half years ago, and has not appeared on the stage since. No clue to his present whereabouts. Age 35, height 5 ft. 9-1/2 in., complexion fair, eyes blue, hair brown.*

"Claud Darrell. Supposed to be real name. Some mystery about his origin. Played at music halls, and also in Repertory plays. Seems to have had no intimate friends. Was in China in 1919. Returned by way of America. Played a few parts in New York. Did not appear on the stage one night, and has never been heard of since. New York police say most mysterious disappearance. Age about 33, hair brown, fair complexion, gray eyes. Height 5 ft. 10-1/2 in.

"Most interesting," I said, as I laid down the paper. "And so this is the result of the investigation of months? These four names. Which of them are you inclined to suspect?"

Poirot made an eloquent gesture.

"*Mon ami*, for the moment it is an open question. I would just point out to you that Claud Darrell has been in China and America—a fact not without significance, perhaps, but we must not allow ourselves to be unduly biased by that point. It may be a mere coincidence."

"And the next step?" I asked eagerly.

"Affairs are already in train. Every day cautiously worded advertisements will appear. Friends and relatives of one or the other will be asked to communicate with my solicitor at his office. Even to-day we might—Aha, the telephone! Probably it is, as usual, the wrong number, and they will regret to have troubled us, but it may be—yes, it may be—that something has arisen."

I crossed the room and picked up the receiver.

"Yes, yes. M. Poirot's rooms. Yes, Captain Hastings speaking. Oh, it's you, Mr. McNeil! (McNeil and Hodgson were Poirot's solicitors.) I'll tell him. Yes, we'll come round at once."

I replaced the receiver and turned to Poirot, my eyes dancing with excitement.

"I say, Poirot, there's a woman there. Friend of Claud Darrell's. Miss Flossie Monro. McNeil wants you to come round."

"At the instant!" cried Poirot, disappearing into his bedroom, and reappearing with a hat.

A taxi soon took us to our destination, and we were ushered into Mr. McNeil's private office. Sitting in the arm-chair facing the solicitor was a somewhat lurid looking lady no longer in her first youth. Her hair was of an impossible yellow, and was prolific in curls over each ear, her eyelids were heavily blackened, and she had by no means forgotten the rouge and the lip salve.

"Ah, here is M. Poirot!" said Mr. McNeil. "M. Poirot, this is Miss—er—Monro, who has very kindly called to give us some information."

"Ah, but that is most kind!" cried Poirot.

He came forward with great empressement, and shook the lady warmly by the hand.

"Mademoiselle blooms like a flower in this dry-as-dust old office," he added, careless of the feelings of Mr. McNeil.

This outrageous flattery was not without effect. Miss Monro blushed and simpered.

"Oh, go on now, Mr. Poirot!" she exclaimed. "I know what you Frenchmen are like."

"Mademoiselle, we are not mute like Englishmen before beauty. Not that I am a Frenchman—I am a Belgian, you see."

"I've been to Ostend myself," said Miss Monro.

The whole affair, as Poirot would have said, was marching splendidly.

"And so you can tell us something about Mr. Claud Darrell?" continued Poirot.

"I knew Mr. Darrell very well at one time," explained the lady. "And I saw your advertisement, being out of a shop for the moment, and my time being my own, I said to myself: There, they want to know about poor old Claudie—lawyers, too—maybe it's a fortune looking for the rightful heir, I'd better go round at once."

Mr. McNeil rose.

"Well, Monsieur Poirot, shall I leave you for a little conversation with Miss Monro?"

"You are too amiable. But stay—a little idea presents itself to me. The hour of the *déjeuner* approaches. Mademoiselle will perhaps honour me by coming out to luncheon with me?"

Miss Monro's eyes glistened. It struck me that she was in exceedingly low water, and that the chance of a square meal was not to be despised.

A few minutes later saw us all in a taxi, bound for one of London's most expensive restaurants. Once arrived there, Poirot ordered a most delectable lunch, and then turned to his guest.

"And for wine, mademoiselle? What do you say to champagne?"

Miss Monro said nothing—or everything.

The meal started pleasantly. Poirot replenished the lady's glass with thoughtful assiduity, and gradually slid on to the topic nearest his heart.

"The poor Mr. Darrell. What a pity he is not with us."

"Yes, indeed," sighed Miss Monro. "Poor boy, I do wonder what's become of him."

"It is a long time since you have seen him, yes?"

"Oh, simply ages—not since the war. He was a funny boy, Claudie, very close about things, never told you a word about himself. But, of course, that all fits in if he's a missing heir. Is it a title, Mr. Poirot?"

"Alas, a mere heritage," said Poirot unblushingly. "But you see, it may be a question of identification. That is why it is necessary for us to find some one who knew him very well indeed. You knew him very well, did you not, mademoiselle."

"I don't mind telling you, Mr. Poirot. You're a gentleman. You know how to order a lunch for a lady—which is more than some of these young whippersnappers do nowadays. Downright mean, I call it. As I was saying, you being a Frenchman won't be shocked. Ah, you Frenchmen! Naughty, naughty!" She wagged her finger at him in an excess of archness. "Well, there it was, me and Claudie, two young things—what else could you expect? And I've still a kindly feeling for him. Though, mind you, he didn't treat me well—no, he didn't—he didn't treat me well at all. Not as a lady should be treated. They're all the same when it comes to a question of money."

"No, no, mademoiselle, do not say that," protested Poirot, filling up her glass once more. "Could you now describe this Mr. Darrell to me?"

"He wasn't anything so very much to look at," said Flossie Monro dreamily. "Neither tall nor short, you know, but quite well set up. Spruce looking. Eyes a sort of blue-gray. And more or less fair-haired, I suppose. But oh, what an artist! *I* never saw any one to touch him in the profession! He'd have made his name before now if it hadn't been for jealousy. Ah, Mr. Poirot, jealousy—you wouldn't believe it, you really wouldn't, what we artists have to suffer through jealousy. Why, I remember once at Manchester—"

We displayed what patience we could in listening to a long complicated story about a pantomime, and the infamous conduct of the principal boy. Then Poirot led her gently back to the subject of Claud Darrell.

"It is very interesting, all this that you are able to tell us, mademoiselle, about Mr. Darrell. Women are such wonderful observers—they see everything, they notice the little detail that escapes the mere man. I have seen a woman identify one man out of a dozen others—and why, do you think? She had observed that he had a trick of stroking his nose when he was agitated. Now would a man ever have thought of noticing a thing like that?"

"Did you ever!" cried Miss Monro. "I suppose we do notice things. I remember Claudie, now I come to think of it, always fiddling with his bread at table. He'd get a little piece between his fingers and then dab it round to pick up crumbs. I've seen him do it a hundred times. Why, I'd know him anywhere by that one trick of his."

"Is not that just what I say? The marvellous observation of a woman. And did you ever speak to him about this little habit of his, mademoiselle?"

"No, I didn't, Mr. Poirot. You know what men are! They don't like you to notice things especially if it should seem you were telling them off about it. I never said a word—but many's the time I smiled to myself. Bless you, he never knew he was doing it even."

Poirot nodded gently. I noticed that his own hand was shaking a little as he stretched it out to his glass.

"Then there is always handwriting as a means of establishing identity," he remarked. "Without doubt you have preserved a letter written by Mr. Darrell?"

Flossie Monro shook her head regretfully.

"He was never one for writing. Never wrote me a line in his life."

"That is a pity," said Poirot.

"I tell you what, though," said Miss Monro suddenly. "I've got a photograph if that would be any good?"

"You have a photograph?"

Poirot almost sprang from his seat with excitement.

"It's quite an old one—eight years old at least."

"*Ça ne fait rien!* No matter how old and faded! Ah, *ma foi*, but what stupendous luck! You will permit me to inspect that photograph, mademoiselle?"

"Why, of course."

"Perhaps you will even permit me to have a copy made? It would not take long."

"Certainly if you like."

Miss Monro rose.

"Well, I must run away," she declared archly. "Very glad to have met you and your friend, Mr. Poirot."

"And the photograph? When may I have it?"

"I'll look it out to-night. I think I know where to lay my hand upon it. And I'll send it to you right away."

"A thousand thanks, mademoiselle. You are all that is of the most amiable. I hope that we shall soon be able to arrange another little lunch together."

"As soon as you like," said Miss Monro. "I'm willing."

"Let me see, I do not think that I have your address?"

With a grand air, Miss Monro drew a card from her handbag, and handed it to him. It was a somewhat dirty card, and the original address had been scratched out and another substituted in pencil.

Then, with a good many bows and gesticulations on Poirot's part, we bade farewell to the lady and got away.

"Do you really think this photograph so important?" I asked Poirot.

"Yes, *mon ami*. The camera does not lie. One can magnify a photograph, seize salient points that otherwise would remain unnoticed. And then there are a thousand details—such as the structure of the ears, which no one could ever describe to you in words. Oh, yes, it is a great chance, this which has come our way! That is why I propose to take precautions."

He went across to the telephone as he finished speaking, and gave a number which I knew to be that of a private detective agency which he sometimes employed. His instructions were clear and definite. Two men were to go to the address he gave, and, in general terms, were to watch over the safety of Miss Monro. They were to follow her wherever she went.

Poirot hung up the receiver and came back to me.

"Do you really think that necessary, Poirot?" I asked.

"It may be. There is no doubt that we are watched, you and I, and since that is so, they will soon know with whom we were lunching to-day. And it is possible that Number Four will scent danger."

About twenty minutes later the telephone bell rang. I answered it. A curt voice spoke into the phone.

"Is that Mr. Poirot? St. James Hospital speaking. A young woman was brought in ten minutes ago. Street accident. Miss Flossie Monro. She is asking very urgently for Mr. Poirot. But he must come at once. She can't possibly last long."

I repeated the words to Poirot. His face went white.

"Quick, Hastings. We must go like the wind."

A taxi took us to the hospital in less than ten minutes. We asked for Miss Monro, and were taken immediately to the accident ward. But a white-capped sister met us in the doorway.

Poirot read the news in her face.

"It is over, eh?"

"She died six minutes ago."

Poirot stood as though stunned.

The nurse, mistaking his emotion, began speaking gently.

"She did not suffer, and she was unconscious towards the last. She was run over by a motor, you know—and the driver of the car did not even stop. Wicked, isn't it? I hope some one took the number."

"The stars fight against us," said Poirot, in a low voice.

"You would like to see her?"

The nurse led the way, and we followed.

Poor Flossie Monro, with her rouge and her dyed hair. She lay there very peacefully, with a little smile on her lips.

"Yes," murmured Poirot. "The stars fight against us—but is it the stars?" He lifted his head as though struck by a sudden idea. "Is it the stars, Hastings? If it is not—if it is not.... Oh, I swear to you, my friend, standing here by this poor woman's body, that I will have no mercy when the time comes!"

"What do you mean?" I asked.

But Poirot had turned to the nurse and was eagerly demanding information. A list of the articles found in her hand-bag was finally obtained. Poirot gave a suppressed cry as he read it over.

"You see, Hastings, you see?"

"See what?"

"There is no mention of a latch-key. But she must have had a latch-key with her. No, she was run down in cold blood, and the first person who bent over her took the key from her bag. But we may yet be in time. He may not have been able to find at once what he sought."

Another taxi took us to the address Flossie Monro had given us, a squalid block of Mansions in an unsavoury neighbourhood. It was some time before we could gain admission to Miss Monro's flat, but we had at least the satisfaction of knowing that no one could leave it whilst we were on guard outside.

Eventually we got in. It was plain that some one had been before us. The contents of drawers and cupboards were strewn all over the floor. Locks had been forced, and small tables had even been overthrown, so violent had been the searcher's haste.

Poirot began to hunt through the débris. Suddenly he stood erect with a cry, holding out something. It was an old fashioned photograph frame—empty.

He turned it slowly over. Affixed to the back was a small round label—a price label.

"It cost four shillings," I commented.

"*Mon Dieu!* Hastings, use your eyes. That is a new clean label. It was stuck there by the man who took out the photograph, the man who was here before us, but knew that we should come, and so left this for us—Claud Darrell—alias Number Four!"

136

FIFTEEN
The Terrible Catastrophe

It was after the tragic death of Miss Flossie Monro that I began to be aware of a change in Poirot. Up to now, his invincible confidence in himself had stood the test. But it seemed as though, at last, the long strain was beginning to tell. His manner was grave and brooding, and his nerves were on edge. In these days he was as jumpy as a cat. He avoided all discussion of the Big Four as far as possible, and seemed to throw himself into his ordinary work with almost his old ardour. Nevertheless, I knew that he was secretly active in the big matter. Extraordinary-looking Slavs were constantly calling to see him, and though he vouchsafed no explanation as to these mysterious activities, I realised that he was building some new defence or weapon of opposition with the help of these somewhat repulsive-looking foreigners. Once, purely by chance, I happened to see the entries in his pass-book—he had asked me to verify some small item—and I noticed the paying out of a huge sum—a huge sum even for Poirot who was coining money nowadays—to some Russian with apparently every letter of the alphabet in his name.

But he gave no clue as to the line on which he proposed to operate. Only over and over again he gave utterance to one phrase. "It is the greatest mistake to underestimate your adversary. Remember that, *mon ami*." And I realised that that was the pitfall he was striving at all costs to avoid.

So matters went on until the end of March, and then one morning Poirot made a remark which startled me considerably.

"This morning, my friend, I should recommend the best suit. We go to call upon the Home Secretary."

"Indeed? That is very exciting. He has called you in to take up a case?"

"Not exactly. The interview is of my seeking. You may remember my saying that I once did him some small service? He is inclined to be foolishly enthusiastic over my capabilities in consequence, and I am about to trade on this attitude of his. As you know, the French Premier, M. Desjardeaux is over in London, and at my request the Home Secretary had arranged for him to be present at our little conference this morning."

The Right Honourable Sydney Crowther, His Majesty's Secretary of State for Home Affairs, was a well-known and popular figure. A man of some fifty years of age, with a quizzical expression and shrewd gray eyes, he received us with that delightful bonhomie of manner which was well known to be one of his principal assets.

Standing with his back to the fireplace was a tall thin man with a pointed black beard and a sensitive face.

"M. Desjardeaux," said Crowther. "Allow me to introduce to you M. Hercule Poirot of whom you may, perhaps, already have heard."

The Frenchman bowed and shook hands.

"I have indeed heard of M. Hercule Poirot," he said pleasantly. "Who has not?"

"You are too amiable, monsieur," said Poirot, bowing, but his face flushed with pleasure.

"Any word for an old friend?" asked a quiet voice, and a man came forward from a corner by a tall bookcase.

It was our old acquaintance, Mr. Ingles.

Poirot shook him warmly by the hand.

"And now, M. Poirot," said Crowther. "We are at your service. I understood you to say that you had a communication of the utmost importance to make to us."

"That is so, monsieur. There is in the world to-day a vast organisation—an organisation of crime. It is controlled by four individuals, who are known and spoken of as the Big Four. Number One is a Chinaman, Li Chang Yen; Number Two is the American multi-millionaire, Abe Ryland; Number Three is a Frenchwoman; Number Four I have every reason to believe is an obscure English actor called Claud Darrell. These four are banded together to destroy the existing social order, and to replace it with an anarchy in which they would reign as dictators."

"Incredible," muttered the Frenchman. "Ryland, mixed up with a thing of that kind? Surely the idea is too fantastic."

"Listen, monsieur, whilst I recount to you some of the doings of this Big Four."

It was an enthralling narrative which Poirot unfolded. Familiar as I was with all the details, they thrilled me anew as I heard the bald recital of our adventures and escapes.

M. Desjardeaux looked mutely at Mr. Crowther as Poirot finished. The other answered the look.

"Yes, M. Desjardeaux, I think we must admit the existence of a 'Big Four.' Scotland Yard was inclined to jeer at first, but they have been forced to admit that M. Poirot was right in many of his claims. The only question is the extent of its aims. I cannot but feel that M. Poirot—er—exaggerates a little."

For answer Poirot set forth ten salient points. I have been asked not to give them to the public even now, and so I refrain from doing so, but they included the extraordinary disasters to submarines which occurred in a certain month, and also a series of aeroplane accidents and forced landings. According to Poirot, these were all the work of the Big Four, and bore witness to the fact that they were in possession of various scientific secrets unknown to the world at large.

This brought us straight to the question which I had been waiting for the French Premier to ask.

"You say that the third member of this organisation is a Frenchwoman. Have you any idea of her name?"

"It is a well-known name, monsieur. An honoured name. Number Three is no less than the famous Madame Olivier."

At the mention of the world-famous scientist, successor to the Curies, M. Desjardeaux positively bounded from his chair, his face purple with emotion.

"Madame Olivier! Impossible! Absurd! It is an insult what you say there!"

Poirot shook his head gently, but made no answer.

Desjardeaux looked at him in stupefaction for some moments. Then his face cleared, and he glanced at the Home Secretary and tapped his forehead significantly.

"M. Poirot is a great man," he observed. "But even the great man—sometimes he has his little mania, does he not? And seeks in high places for fancied conspiracies. It is well known. You agree with me, do you not, Mr. Crowther?"

The Home Secretary did not answer for some minutes. Then he spoke slowly and heavily.

"Upon my soul, I don't know," he said at last. "I have always had and still have the utmost belief in M. Poirot, but—well, this takes a bit of believing."

"This Li Chang Yen, too," continued M. Desjardeaux. "Who has ever heard of him?"

"I have," said the unexpected voice of Mr. Ingles.

The Frenchman stared at him, and he stared placidly back again, looking more like a Chinese idol than ever. "Mr. Ingles," explained the Home Secretary, "is the greatest authority we have on the interior of China."

"And you have heard of this Li Chang Yen?"

"Until M. Poirot here came to me, I imagined that I was the only man in England who had. Make no mistake, M. Desjardeaux, there is only one man in China who counts to-day—Li Chang Yen. He has, perhaps, I only say perhaps, the finest brain in the world at the present time."

M. Desjardeaux sat as though stunned. Presently, however, he rallied.

"There may be something in what you say, M. Poirot," he said coldly. "But as regards Madame Olivier, you are most certainly mistaken. She is a true daughter of France, and devoted solely to the cause of science."

Poirot shrugged his shoulders and did not answer.

There was a minute or two's pause, and then my little friend rose to his feet, with an air of dignity that sat rather oddly upon his quaint personality.

"That is all I have to say, messieurs—to warn you. I thought it likely that I should not be believed. But at least you will be on your guard. My words will sink in, and each fresh event that comes along will confirm your wavering faith. It was necessary for me to speak now—later I might not have been able to do so."

"You mean—?" asked Crowther, impressed in spite of himself by the gravity of Poirot's tone.

"I mean, monsieur, that since I have penetrated the identity of Number Four, my life is not worth an hour's purchase. He will seek to destroy me at all costs—and not for nothing is he named 'The Destroyer.' Messieurs, I salute you. To you, M. Crowther, I deliver this key, and this sealed envelope. I have got together all my notes on the case, and my ideas as to how best to meet the menace that any day may break upon the world, and have placed them in a certain safe deposit. In the event of my death, M. Crowther, I authorise you to take charge of those papers and make what use you can of them. And now, messieurs, I wish you good day."

Desjardeaux merely bowed coldly, but Crowther sprang up and held out his hand.

"You have converted me, M. Poirot. Fantastic as the whole thing seems, I believe utterly in the truth of what you have told us."

Ingles left at the same time as we did.

"I am not disappointed with the interview," said Poirot, as we walked along. "I did not expect to convince Desjardeaux, but I have at least ensured that, if I die, my knowledge does not die with me. And I have made one or two converts. *Pas si mal!*"

"I'm with you, as you know," said Ingles. "By the way, I'm going out to China as soon as I can get off."

"Is that wise?"

"No," said Ingles dryly. "But it's necessary. One must do what one can."

"Ah, you are a brave man!" cried Poirot with emotion. "If we were not in the street, I would embrace you."

I fancied that Ingles looked rather relieved.

"I don't suppose that I shall be in any more danger in China than you are in London," he growled.

"That is possibly true enough," admitted Poirot. "I hope that they will not succeed in massacring Hastings also, that is all. That would annoy me greatly."

I interrupted this cheerful conversation to remark that I had no intention of letting myself be massacred, and shortly afterwards Ingles parted from us.

For some time we went along in silence, which Poirot at length broke by uttering a totally unexpected remark.

"I think—I really think—that I shall have to bring my brother into this."

"Your brother," I cried, astonished. "I never knew you had a brother?"

"You surprise me, Hastings. Do you not know that all celebrated detectives have brothers who would be even more celebrated then they are were it not for constitutional indolence?"

Poirot employs a peculiar manner sometimes which makes it wellnigh impossible to know whether he is jesting or in earnest. That manner was very evident at the moment.

"What is your brother's name?" I asked, trying to adjust myself to this new idea.

"Achille Poirot," replied Poirot gravely. "He lives near Spa in Belgium."

"What does he do?" I asked with some curiosity, putting aside a half-formed wonder as to the character and disposition of the late Madame Poirot, and her classical taste in Christian names.

"He does nothing. He is, as I tell, of a singularly indolent disposition. But his abilities are hardly less than my own—which is saying a great deal."

"Is he like you to look at?"

"Not unlike. But not nearly so handsome. And he wears no moustaches."

"Is he older than you, or younger?"

"He happens to have been born on the same day."

"A twin," I cried.

"Exactly, Hastings. You jump to the right conclusion with unfailing accuracy. But here we are at home again. Let us at once get to work on that little affair of the Duchess's necklace."

But the Duchess's necklace was doomed to wait awhile. A case of quite another description was waiting for us.

Our landlady, Mrs. Pearson, at once informed us that a hospital nurse had called and was waiting to see Poirot.

We found her sitting in the big arm-chair facing the window, a pleasant-faced woman of middle age, in a dark blue uniform. She was a little reluctant to come to the point, but Poirot soon put her at her ease, and she embarked upon her story.

"You see, M. Poirot, I've never come across anything of the kind before. I was sent for, from the Lark Sisterhood, to go down to a case in Hertfordshire. An old gentleman, it is, Mr. Templeton. Quite a pleasant house, and quite pleasant people. The wife, Mrs. Templeton, is much younger than her husband, and he has a son by his first marriage who lives there. I don't know that the young man and the step-mother always get on together. He's not quite what you'd call normal—not 'wanting' exactly, but decidedly dull in the intellect. Well, this illness of Mr. Templeton's seemed to me from the first to be very mysterious. At times there seemed really nothing the matter with him, and then he suddenly has one of these gastric attacks with pain and vomiting. But the doctor seemed quite satisfied, and it wasn't for me to say anything. But I couldn't help thinking about it. And then—"

She paused, and became rather red.

"Something happened which aroused your suspicions?" suggested Poirot.

"Yes."

But she still seemed to find it difficult to go on.

"I found the servants were passing remarks too."

"About Mr. Templeton's illness?"

"Oh, no! About—about this other thing—"

"Mrs. Templeton?"

"Yes."

"Mrs. Templeton and the doctor, perhaps?"

Poirot had an uncanny flair in these things. The nurse threw him a grateful glance and went on.

"They *were* passing remarks. And then one day I happened to see them together myself—in the garden—"

It was left at that. Our client was in such an agony of outraged propriety that no one could feel it necessary to ask exactly what she had seen in the garden. She had evidently seen quite enough to make up her own mind on the situation.

"The attacks got worse and worse. Dr. Treves said it was all perfectly natural and to be expected, and that Mr. Templeton could not possibly live long, but I've never seen anything like it before myself—not in all my long experience of nursing. It seemed to me much more like some form of—"

She paused, hesitating.

"Arsenical poisoning?" said Poirot helpfully.

She nodded.

"And then, too, he, the patient, I mean, said something queer.

'They'll do for me, the four of them. They'll do for me yet.'"

"Eh?" said Poirot quickly.

"Those were his very words, M. Poirot. He was in great pain at the time, of course, and hardly knew what he was saying."

"'They'll do for me, the four of them,'" repeated Poirot thoughtfully. "What did he mean by 'the four of them,' do you think?"

"That I can't say, M. Poirot. I thought perhaps he meant his wife and son, and the doctor, and perhaps Miss Clark, Mrs. Templeton's companion. That would make four, wouldn't it? He might think they were all in league against him."

"Quite so, quite so," said Poirot, in a preoccupied voice. "What about food? Could you take no precautions about that?"

"I'm always doing what I can. But, of course, sometimes Mrs. Templeton insists on bringing him his food herself, and then there are the times when I am off duty."

"Exactly. And you are not sure enough of your ground to go to the police?"

The nurse's face showed her horror at the mere idea.

"What I have done, M. Poirot, is this. Mr. Templeton had a very bad attack after partaking of a bowl of soup. I took a little from the bottom of the bowl afterwards, and have brought it up with me. I have been spared for the day to visit a sick mother, as Mr. Templeton was well enough to be left."

She drew out a little bottle of dark fluid and handed it to Poirot.

"Excellent, mademoiselle. We will have this analysed immediately. If you will return here in, say, an hour's time I think that we shall be able to dispose of your suspicions one way or another."

First extracting from our visitor her name and qualifications, he ushered her out. Then he wrote a note and sent it off together with the bottle of soup. Whilst we waited to hear the result, Poirot amused himself by verifying the nurse's credentials, somewhat to my surprise.

"No, no, my friend," he declared. "I do well to be careful. Do not forget the Big Four are on our track."

However, he soon elicited the information that a nurse of the name of Mabel Palmer was a member of the Lark Institute and had been sent to the case in question.

"So far, so good," he said, with a twinkle. "And now here comes Nurse Palmer back again, and here also is our analyst's report."

Both the nurse and I waited anxiously whilst Poirot read the analyst's report.

"Is there arsenic in it?" she asked breathlessly.

Poirot shook his head, refolding the paper.

"No."

We were both immeasurably surprised.

"There is no arsenic in it," continued Poirot. "But there is antimony. And that being the case, we will start immediately for Hertfordshire. Pray Heaven that we are not too late."

It was decided that the simplest plan was for Poirot to represent himself truly as a detective, but that the ostensible reason of his visit should be to question Mrs. Templeton about a servant formerly in her employment whose name he obtained from Nurse Palmer, and who he could represent as being concerned in a jewel robbery.

It was late when we arrived at Elmstead, as the house was called. We had allowed Nurse Palmer to precede us by about twenty minutes, so that there should be no question of our all arriving together.

Mrs. Templeton, a tall dark woman, with sinuous movements and uneasy eyes, received us. I noticed that as Poirot announced his profession, she drew in her breath with a sudden hiss, as though badly startled, but she answered his question about the maid-servant readily enough. And then, to test her, Poirot embarked upon a long history of a poisoning case in which a guilty wife had figured. His eyes never left her face as he talked, and try as she would, she could hardly conceal her rising agitation. Suddenly, with an incoherent word of excuse, she hurried from the room.

We were not long left alone. A squarely-built man with a small red moustache and pince-nez came in.

"Dr. Treves," he introduced himself. "Mrs. Templeton asked me to make her excuses to you. She's in a very bad state, you know. Nervous strain. Worry over her husband and all that. I've prescribed bed and bromide. But she hopes you'll stay and take pot luck, and I'm to do host. We've heard of you down here, M. Poirot, and we mean to make the most of you. Ah, here's Micky!"

A shambling young man entered the room. He had a very round face, and foolish-looking eyebrows raised as though in perpetual surprise. He grinned awkwardly as he shook hands. This was clearly the "wanting" son.

Presently we all went in to dinner. Dr. Treves left the room—to open some wine, I think—-and suddenly the boy's physiognomy underwent a startling change. He leant forward, staring at Poirot.

"You've come about father," he said, nodding his head. "I know. I know lots of things—but nobody thinks I do. Mother will be glad when father's dead and she can marry Dr. Treves. She isn't my own mother, you know. I don't like her. She wants father to die."

It was all rather horrible. Luckily, before Poirot had time to reply, the doctor came back, and we had to carry on a forced conversation.

And then suddenly Poirot lay back in his chair with a hollow groan. His face was contorted with pain.

"My dear sir, what's the matter?" cried the doctor.

"A sudden spasm. I am used to them. No, no, I require no assistance from you, doctor. If I might lie down upstairs."

His request was instantly acceded to, and I accompanied him upstairs, where he collapsed on the bed, groaning heavily.

For the first minute or two I had been taken in, but I had quickly realised that Poirot was—as he would have put it—playing the comedy, and that his object was to be left alone upstairs near the patient's room.

Hence I was quite prepared when, the instant we were alone, he sprang up.

"Quick, Hastings, the window. There is ivy outside. We can climb down before they begin to suspect."

"Climb down?"

"Yes, we must get out of this house at once. You saw him at dinner?"

"The doctor?"

"No, young Templeton. His trick with his bread. Do you remember what Flossie Monro told us before she died? That Claud Darrell had a habit of dabbing his bread on the table to pick up crumbs. Hastings, this is a vast plot, and that vacant-looking young man is our arch enemy—Number Four! Hurry."

I did not wait to argue. Incredible as the whole thing seemed, it was wiser not to delay. We scrambled down the ivy as quietly as we could and made a bee-line for the small town and the railway station. We were just able to catch the last train, the 8.34 which would land us in town about eleven o'clock.

"A plot," said Poirot thoughtfully. "How many of them were in it, I wonder? I suspect that the whole Templeton family are just so many agents of the Big Four. Did they simply want to decoy us down there? Or was it more subtle than that. Did they intend to play the comedy down there and keep me interested until they had had time to do—what? I wonder now."

He remained very thoughtful.

Arrived at our lodgings, he restrained me at the door of the sitting-room.

"Attention, Hastings. I have my suspicions. Let me enter first."

He did so, and, to my slight amusement, took the precaution to press on the electric switch with an old galosh. Then he went round the room like a strange cat, cautiously, delicately, on the alert for danger. I watched him for some time, remaining obediently where I had been put by the wall.

"It's all right, Poirot," I said impatiently.

"It seems so, *mon ami*, it seems so. But let us make sure."

"Rot," I said. "I shall light the fire, anyway, and have a pipe. I've caught you out for once. You had the matches last and you didn't put them back in the holder as usual—the very thing you're always cursing me for doing."

I stretched out my hand. I heard Poirot's warning cry—saw him leaping towards me—my hand touched the match-box.

Then—a flash of blue flame—an ear-rending crash—and darkness—

I came to myself to find the familiar face of our old friend Dr. Ridgeway bending over me. An expression of relief passed over his features.

"Keep still," he said soothingly. "You're all right. There's been an accident, you know."

"Poirot?" I murmured.

"You're in my digs. Everything's quite all right."

A cold fear clutched at my heart. His evasion woke a horrible fear.

"Poirot?" I reiterated. "What of Poirot."

He saw that I had to know and that further evasions were useless.

"By a miracle you escaped—Poirot—did not!"

A cry burst from my lips.

"Not dead? Not dead?"

Ridgeway bowed his head, his features working with emotion.

With desperate energy I pulled myself to a sitting position.

"Poirot may be dead," I said weakly. "But his spirit lives on. I will carry on his work! Death to the Big Four!"

Then I fell back, fainting.

SIXTEEN
The Dying Chinaman

E ven now I can hardly bear to write of those days in March. Poirot—the unique, the inimitable Hercule Poirot— dead! There was a particularly diabolical touch in the disarranged match-box, which was certain to catch his eye, and which he would hasten to rearrange—and thereby touch off the explosion. That, as a matter of fact, it was I who actually pre-cipitated the catastrophe never ceased to fill me with unavailing remorse. It was, as Doctor Ridgeway said, a perfect miracle that I had not been killed, but had escaped with a slight concussion.

Although it had seemed to me as though I regained conscious-ness almost immediately, it was in reality over twenty-four hours before I came back to life. It was not until the evening of the day following that I was able to stagger feebly into an adjoining room, and view with deep emotion the plain elm coffin which held the remains of one of the most marvellous men this world has ever known.

From the very first moment of regaining consciousness I had only one purpose in mind—to avenge Poirot's death, and to hunt down the Big Four remorselessly.

I had thought that Ridgeway would have been of one mind with me about this, but to my surprise the good doctor seemed unaccountably lukewarm.

"Get back to South America" was his advice, tendered on every occasion. Why attempt the impossible? Put as delicately as possible, his opinion amounted to this:—If Poirot, the unique Poirot, had failed, was it likely that I should succeed?

But I was obstinate. Putting aside any question as to whether I had the necessary qualifications for the task (and I may say in passing that I did not entirely agree with his views on this point), I had worked so long with Poirot that I knew his methods by heart, and felt fully capable of taking up the work where he had laid it down; it was, with me, a question of feeling. My friend had been foully murdered. Was I to go tamely back to South America without an effort to bring his murderers to justice?

I said all this and more to Ridgeway, who listened attentively enough.

"All the same," he said when I had finished, "my advice does not vary. I am earnestly convinced that Poirot himself, if he were here, would urge you to return. In his name, I beg of you, Hastings, abandon these wild ideas and go back to your ranch."

To that only one answer was possible, and, shaking his head sadly, he said no more.

It was a month before I was fully restored to health. Towards the end of April, I sought, and obtained, an interview with the Home Secretary.

Mr. Crowther's manner was reminiscent of that of Dr. Ridgeway. It was soothing and negative. Whilst appreciating the offer of my services, he gently and considerately declined them. The papers referred to by Poirot had passed into his keeping, and he assured me that all possible steps were being taken to deal with the approaching menace.

With that cold comfort I was forced to be satisfied. Mr. Crowther ended the interview by urging me to return to South America. I found the whole thing profoundly unsatisfactory.

I should, I suppose, in its proper place, have described Poirot's funeral. It was a solemn and moving ceremony, and the extraordinary number of floral tributes passed belief. They came from high and low alike, and bore striking testimony to the place my friend had made for himself in the country of his adoption. For myself, I was frankly overcome by emotion as I stood by the grave side and thought of all our varied experiences and the happy days we had passed together.

By the beginning of May I had mapped out a plan of campaign. I felt that I could not do better than keep Poirot's scheme of advertising for any information respecting Claud Darrell. I had an advertisement to this effect inserted in a number of morning newspapers, and I was sitting in a small restaurant in Soho, and judging of the effect of the advertisement, when a small paragraph in another part of the paper gave me a nasty shock.

Very briefly, it reported the mysterious disappearance of Mr. John Ingles from the *S.S. Shanghai* shortly after the latter had left Marseilles. Although the weather was perfectly smooth, it was feared that the unfortunate gentleman must have fallen overboard. The paragraph ended with a brief reference to Mr. Ingles's long and distinguished service in China.

The news was unpleasant. I read into Ingles's death a sinister motive. Not for one moment did I believe the theory of an accident. Ingles had been murdered, and his death was only too clearly the handiwork of that accursed Big Four.

As I sat there, stunned by the blow, and turning the whole matter over in my mind, I was startled by the remarkable behaviour of the man sitting opposite me. So far I had not paid much attention to him. He was a thin, dark man of middle age, sallow of complexion, with a small pointed beard. He had sat down opposite me so quietly that I had hardly noticed his arrival.

But his actions now were decidedly peculiar, to say the least of them. Leaning forward, he deliberately helped me to salt, putting it in four little heaps round the edge of my plate.

"You will excuse me," he said, in a melancholy voice. "To help a stranger to salt is to help them to sorrow, they say. That may be an unavoidable necessity. I hope not, though. I hope that you will be reasonable."

Then, with a certain significance, he repeated his operations with the salt on his own plate. The symbol 4 was too plain to be missed. I looked at him searchingly. In no way that I could see did he resemble young Templeton, or James the footman, or any other of the various personalities we had come across. Nevertheless, I was convinced that I had to do with no less than the redoubtable Number Four himself. In his voice there was certainly a faint resemblance to the buttoned-up-stranger who had called upon us in Paris.

I looked round, undecided as to my course of action. Reading my thoughts, he smiled and gently shook his head.

"I should not advise it," he remarked. "Remember what came of your hasty action in Paris. Let me assure you that my way of retreat is well assured. Your ideas are inclined to be a little crude, Captain Hastings, if I may say so."

"You devil," I said, choking with rage, "you incarnate devil!"

"Heated—just a trifle heated. Your late lamented friend would have told you that a man who keeps calm has always a great advantage."

"You dare to speak of him," I cried. "The man you murdered so foully. And you come here—"

He interrupted me.

"I came here for an excellent and peaceful purpose. To advise you to return at once to South America. If you do so, that is the end of the matter as far as the Big Four are concerned. You and yours will not be molested in any way. I give you my word as to that."

I laughed scornfully.

"And if I refuse to obey your autocratic command?"

"It is hardly a command. Shall we say that it is—a warning?"

There was a cold menace in his tone.

"The first warning," he said softly. "You will be well advised not to disregard it."

Then, before I had any hint of his intention, he rose and slipped quickly away towards the door. I sprang to my feet and was after him in a second, but by bad luck I cannoned straight into an enormously fat man who blocked the way between me and the next table. By the time I had disentangled myself, my quarry was just passing through the doorway, and the next delay was from a waiter carrying a huge pile of plates who crashed into me without the least warning. By the time I got to the door there was no sign of the thin man with the dark beard.

The waiter was fulsome in apologies, the fat man was sitting placidly at a table ordering his lunch. There was nothing to show that both occurrences had not been a pure accident. Nevertheless, I had my own opinion as to that. I knew well enough that the agents of the Big Four were everywhere.

Needless to say, I paid no heed to the warning given me. I would do or die in the good cause. I received in all only two answers to the advertisements. Neither of them gave me any information of value. They were both from actors who had played with Claud Darrell at one time or another. Neither of them knew him at all intimately, and no new light was thrown upon the problem of his identity and present whereabouts.

No further sign came from the Big Four until about ten days later. I was crossing Hyde Park, lost in thought, when a voice, rich with a persuasive foreign inflection, hailed me.

"Captain Hastings, is it not?"

A big limousine had just drawn up by the pavement. A woman was leaning out. Exquisitely dressed in black, with wonderful pearls, I recognised the lady first known to us as Countess Vera Rossakoff, and afterwards under a different alias as an agent of the Big Four. Poirot, for some reason or other, had always had a sneaking fondness for the countess. Something in her very flamboyance attracted the little man. She was, he was wont to declare in moments of enthusiasm, a woman in a thousand. That she was arrayed against us, on the side of our bitterest enemies, never seemed to weigh in his judgment. "Ah, do not pass on!" said the countess. "I have something most important to say to you. And do not try to have me arrested either, for that would be stupid. You were always a little stupid—yes, yes, it is so. You are stupid now, when you persist in disregarding the warning we sent you. It is the second warning I bring you. Leave England at once. You can do no good here—I tell you that frankly. You will never accomplish anything."

"In that case," I said stiffly, "it seems rather extraordinary that you are all so anxious to get me out of the country."

The countess shrugged her shoulders—magnificent shoulders, and a magnificent gesture.

"For my part, I think that, too, stupid. I would leave you here to play about happily. But the chiefs, you see, are fearful that some word of yours may give great help to those more intelligent than yourself. Hence—you are to be banished."

The countess appeared to have a flattering idea of my abilities. I concealed my annoyance. Doubtless this attitude of hers was assumed expressly to annoy me and to give me the idea that I was unimportant.

"It would, of course, be quite easy to—remove you," she continued, "but I am quite sentimental sometimes. I pleaded for you. You have a nice little wife somewhere, have you not? And it would please the poor little man who is dead to know that you were not to be killed. I always liked him, you know. He was clever—but clever! Had it not been a case of four against one I honestly believe he might have been too much for us. I confess it frankly—he was my master! I sent a wreath to the funeral as a token of my admiration—an enormous one of crimson roses. Crimson roses express my temperament."

I listened in silence and a growing distaste.

"You have the look of a mule when it puts its ears back and kicks. Well, I have delivered my warning. Remember this, the third warning will come by the hand of the Destroyer—"

She made a sign, and the car whirled away rapidly. I noted the number mechanically, but without the hope that it would lead to anything. The Big Four were not apt to be careless in details.

I went home a little sobered. One fact had emerged from the countess's flood of volubility. I was in real danger of my life. Though I had no intention of abandoning the struggle, I saw that it behoved me to walk warily and adopt every possible precaution.

Whilst I was reviewing all these facts and seeking for the best line of action, the telephone bell rang. I crossed the room and picked up the receiver.

"Yes. Hallo. Who's speaking?"

A crisp voice answered me.

"This is St. Giles' Hospital. We have a Chinaman here, knifed in the street and brought in. He can't last long. We rang you up because we found in his pocket a piece of paper with your name and address on it."

I was very much astonished. Nevertheless, after a moment's reflection I said that I would come down at once. St. Giles' Hospital was, I knew, down by the docks, and it occurred to me that the Chinaman might have just come off some ship.

It was on my way down there that a sudden suspicion shot into my mind. Was the whole thing a trap? Wherever a Chinaman was, there might be the hand of Li Chang Yen. I remembered the adventure of the Baited Trap. Was the whole thing a ruse on the part of my enemies?

A little reflection convinced me that at any rate a visit to the hospital would do no harm. It was probable that the thing was not so much a plot as what is vulgarly known as a "plant." The dying Chinaman would make some revelation to me upon which I should act, and which would have the result of leading me into the hands of the Big Four. The thing to do was to preserve an open mind, and whilst feigning credulity be secretly on my guard.

On arriving at St. Giles' Hospital, and making my business known, I was taken at once to the accident ward, to the bedside of the man in question. He lay absolutely still, his eyelids closed, and only a very faint movement of the chest showed that he still breathed. A doctor stood by the bed, his fingers on the Chinaman's pulse.

"He's almost gone," he whispered to me. "You know him, eh?"

I shook my head.

"I've never seen him before."

"Then what was he doing with your name and address in his pocket? You are Captain Hastings, aren't you?"

"Yes, but I can't explain it any more than you can."

"Curious thing. From his papers he seems to have been the servant of a man called Ingles—a retired Civil Servant. Ah, you know him, do you?" he added quickly, as I started at the name.

Ingles's servant! Then I *had* seen him before. Not that I had ever succeeded in being able to distinguish one Chinaman from another. He must have been with Ingles on his way to China, and after the catastrophe he had returned to England with a message, possibly, for me. It was vital, imperative that I should hear that message.

"Is he conscious?" I asked. "Can he speak? Mr. Ingles was an old friend of mine, and I think it possible that this poor fellow has brought me a message from him. Mr. Ingles is believed to have gone overboard about ten days ago."

"He's just conscious, but I doubt if he has the force to speak. He lost a terrible lot of blood, you know. I can administer a stimulant, of course, but we've already done all that is possible in that direction."

Nevertheless, he administered a hypodermic injection, and I stayed by the bed, hoping against hope for a word—a sign—that might be of the utmost value to me in my work. But the minutes sped on and no sign came.

And suddenly a baleful idea shot across my mind? Was I not already falling into the trap? Suppose that this Chinaman had merely assumed the part of Ingles's servant, that he was in reality

AGATHA CHRISTIE

an agent of the Big Four? Had I not once read that certain Chinese priests were capable of simulating death? Or, to go further still, Li Chang Yen might command a little band of fanatics who would welcome death itself if it came at the command of their master. I must be on my guard.

Even as these thoughts flashed across my mind, the man in the bed stirred. His eyes opened. He murmured something incoherently. Then I saw his glance fasten upon me. He made no sign of recognition, but I was at once aware that he was trying to speak to me. Be he friend or foe, I must hear what he had to say.

I leaned over the bed, but the broken sounds conveyed no sort of meaning to me. I thought I caught the word "hand," but in what connection it was used I could not tell. Then it came again, and this time I heard another word, the word "Largo." I stared in amazement, as the possible juxtaposition of the two suggested itself to me.

"Handel's Largo?" I queried.

The Chinaman's eyelids flickered rapidly, as though in assent, and he added another Italian word, the word "*carrozza*." Two or three more words of murmured Italian came to my ears, and then he fell back abruptly.

The doctor pushed me aside. It was all over. The man was dead.

I went out into the air again thoroughly bewildered.

"Handel's Largo," and a "*carrozza*." If I remembered rightly, a *carrozza* was a carriage. What possible meaning could lie behind those simple words. The man was a Chinaman, not an Italian, why should he speak in Italian? Surely, if he were indeed Ingles's servant, he must know English? The whole thing was profoundly mystifying. I puzzled over it all the way home. Oh, if only Poirot had been there to solve the problem with his lightning ingenuity!

I let myself in with my latch-key and went slowly up to my room. A letter was lying on the table, and I tore it open carelessly enough. But in a minute I stood rooted to the ground whilst I read.

It was a communication from a firm of solicitors.

"*Dear Sir* (it ran),—*As instructed by our late client, M. Hercule Poirot, we forward you the enclosed letter. This letter was placed in our hands a week before his death, with instructions that in the event of his demise, it should be sent to you at a certain date after his death.*
"*Yours faithfully, etc.*"

I turned the enclosed missive over and over. It was undoubtedly from Poirot. I knew that familiar writing only too well. With a heavy heart, yet a certain eagerness, I tore it open.

"*Mon Cher Ami* (it began),—*When you receive this I shall be no more. Do not shed tears about me, but follow my orders. Immediately upon receipt of this, return to South America. Do not be pig-headed about this. It is not for sentimental reasons that I bid you undertake the journey. It is necessary. It is part of the plan of Hercule Poirot! To say more is unnecessary, to any one who has the acute intelligence of my friend Hastings.*
"*A bas the Big Four! I salute you, my friend, from beyond the grave.*
"*Ever thine,*
"*Hercule Poirot.*"

I read and re-read this astonishing communication. One thing was evident. This amazing man had so provided for every eventuality that even his own death did not upset the sequence of his plans! Mine was to be the active part—his the directing genius. Doubtless I should find full instructions awaiting me beyond the seas. In the meantime my enemies, convinced that I was obeying their warning, would cease to trouble their heads about me. I could return, unsuspected, and work havoc in their midst.

There was now nothing to hinder my immediate departure. I

sent off cables, booked my passage, and one week later found me embarking in the *Ansonia* en route for Buenos Ayres.

Just as the boat left the quay, a steward brought me a note. It had been given him, so he explained, by a big gentleman in a fur coat who had left the boat last thing before the gangway planks were lifted.

I opened it. It was terse and to the point.

"You are wise," it ran. It was signed with a big figure 4.

I could afford to smile to myself!

The sea was not too choppy. I enjoyed a passable dinner, made up my mind as to the majority of my fellow passengers, and had a rubber or two of Bridge. Then I turned in and slept like a log as I always do on board ship.

I was awakened by feeling myself persistently shaken. Dazed and bewildered, I saw that one of the ship's officers was standing over me. He gave a sigh of relief as I sat up.

"Thank the Lord I've got you awake at last. I've had no end of a job. Do you always sleep like that?"

"What's the matter?" I asked, still bewildered and not fully awake. "Is there anything wrong with the ship?"

"I expect you know what's the matter better than I do," he replied dryly. "Special instructions from the Admiralty. There's a destroyer waiting to take you off."

"What?" I cried. "In mid-ocean?"

"It seems a most mysterious affair, but that's not my business. They've sent a young fellow aboard who is to take your place, and we are all sworn to secrecy. Will you get up and dress?"

Utterly unable to conceal my amazement I did as I was told. A boat was lowered, and I was conveyed aboard the destroyer. There I was received courteously, but got no further information. The commander's instructions were to land me at a certain spot on the Belgian coast. There his knowledge and responsibility ended.

The whole thing was like a dream. The one idea I held to firmly was that all this must be part of Poirot's plan. I must simply go forward blindly, trusting in my dead friend.

I was duly landed at the spot indicated. There a motor was waiting, and soon I was rapidly whirling along across the flat Flemish plains. I slept that night at a small hotel in Brussels. The next day we went on again. The country became wooded and hilly. I realised that we were penetrating into the Ardennes, and I suddenly remembered Poirot's saying that he had a brother who lived at Spa.

But we did not go to Spa itself. We left the main road and wound into the leafy fastnesses of the hills, till we reached a little hamlet, and an isolated white villa high on the hill-side. Here the car stopped in front of the green door of the villa.

The door opened as I alighted. An elderly man-servant stood in the doorway bowing.

"M. le Capitaine Hastings?" he said in French. "Monsieur le Capitaine is expected. If he will follow me."

He led the way across the hall, and flung open a door at the back, standing aside to let me pass in.

I blinked a little, for the room faced west and the afternoon sun was pouring in. Then my vision cleared and I saw a figure waiting to welcome me with outstretched hands.

It was—oh, impossible, it couldn't be—but yes!

"Poirot!" I cried, and for once did not attempt to evade the embrace with which he overwhelmed me.

"But yes, but yes, it is indeed I! Not so easy to kill Hercule Poirot!"

"But Poirot—*why*?"

"A *ruse de guerre*, my friend, a *ruse de guerre*. All is now ready for our grand coup."

"But you might have told *me*!"

"No, Hastings, I could not. Never, never, in a thousand years, could you have acted the part at the funeral. As it was, it was perfect. It could not fail to carry conviction to the Big Four."

"But what I've been through—"

"Do not think me too unfeeling. I carried out the deception partly for your sake. I was willing to risk my own life, but I had qualms about continually risking yours. So, after the explosion, I have an idea of great brilliancy. The good Ridgeway, he enables me to carry it out. I am dead, you will return to South America. But, *mon ami*, that is just what you would not do. In the end I have to arrange a solicitor's letter, and a long rigmarole. But, at all events, here you are—that is the great thing. And now we lie here—*perdu*—till the moment comes for the last grand coup—the final overthrowing of the Big Four."

SEVENTEEN
Number Four Wins A Trick

From our quiet retreat in the Ardennes we watched the progress of affairs in the great world. We were plentifully supplied with newspapers, and every day Poirot received a bulky envelope, evidently containing some kind of report. He never showed these reports to me, but I could usually tell from his manner whether its contents had been satisfactory or otherwise. He never wavered in his belief that our present plan was the only one likely to be crowned by success.

"As a minor point, Hastings," he remarked one day, "I was in continual fear of your death lying at my door. And that rendered me nervous—like a cat upon the jumps, as you say. But now I am well satisfied. Even if they discover that the Captain Hastings who landed in South America is an imposter (and I do not think they will discover it, they are not likely to send an agent out there who knows you personally), they will only believe that you are trying to circumvent them in some clever manner of your own, and will pay no serious attention to discovering your whereabouts. Of the one vital fact, my supposed death, they are thoroughly convinced. They will go ahead and mature their plans."

"And then?" I asked eagerly.

"And then, *mon ami*, grand resurrection of Hercule Poirot! At the eleventh hour I reappear, throw all into confusion, and achieve

163

the supreme victory in my own unique manner!"

I realised that Poirot's vanity was of the case-hardened variety which could withstand all attacks. I reminded him that once or twice the honours of the game had lain with our adversaries. But I might have known that it was impossible to diminish Hercule Poirot's enthusiasm for his own methods.

"See you, Hastings, it is like the little trick that you play with the cards. You have seen it without doubt? You take the four knaves, you divide them, one on top of the pack, one underneath, and so on—you cut and you shuffle, and there they are all together again. That is my object. So far I have been contending, now against one of the Big Four, now against another. But let me get them all together, like the four knaves in the pack of cards, and then, with one coup, I destroy them all!"

"And how do you propose to get them all together?" I asked.

"By awaiting the supreme moment. By lying *perdu* until they are ready to strike."

"That may mean a long wait," I grumbled.

"Always impatient, the good Hastings! But no, it will not be so long. The one man they were afraid of—myself—is out of the way. I give them two or three months at most."

His speaking of some one being got out of the way reminded me of Ingles and his tragic death, and I remembered that I had never told Poirot about the dying Chinaman in St. Giles' Hospital.

He listened with keen attention to my story.

"Ingles's servant, eh? And the few words he uttered were in Italian? Curious."

"That's why I suspected it might have been a plant on the part of the Big Four."

"Your reasoning is at fault, Hastings. Employ the little gray cells. If your enemies wished to deceive you they would assuredly have seen to it that the Chinaman spoke in intelligible pigeon English. No, the message was genuine. Tell me again all that you heard?"

"First of all he made a reference to Handel's Largo, and then he said something that sounded like '*carrozzo*'—that's a carriage, isn't it?"

"Nothing else?"

"Well, just at the end he murmured something like 'Cara' somebody or other—some woman's name. Zia, I think. But I don't suppose that that had any bearing on the rest of it."

"You would not suppose so, Hastings. Cara Zia is very important, very important indeed."

"I don't see—"

"My dear friend, you *never* see—and anyway the English know no geography."

"Geography?" I cried. "What has geography got to do with it?"

"I dare say M. Thomas Cook would be more to the point."

As usual, Poirot refused to say anything more—a most irritating trick of his. But I noticed that his manner became extremely cheerful, as though he had scored some point or other.

The days went on, pleasant if a trifle monotonous. There were plenty of books in the villa, and delightful rambles all around, but I chafed sometimes at the forced inactivity of our life, and marvelled at Poirot's state of placid content. Nothing occurred to ruffle our quiet existence, and it was not until the end of June, well within the limit that Poirot had given them, that we had our news of the Big Four.

A car drove up to the villa early one morning, such an unusual event in our peaceful life that I hurried down to satisfy my curiosity. I found Poirot talking to a pleasant-faced young fellow of about my own age.

He introduced me.

"This is Captain Harvey, Hastings, one of the most famous members of your Intelligence Service."

"Not famous at all, I'm afraid," said the young man, laughing pleasantly.

"Not famous except to those in the know, I should have said.

Most of Captain Harvey's friends and acquaintances consider him an amiable but brainless young man—devoted only to the trot of the fox or whatever the dance is called."

We both laughed.

"Well, well, to business," said Poirot. "You are of opinion the time has come, then?"

"We are sure of it, sir. China was isolated politically yesterday. What is going on out there, nobody knows. No news of any kind, wireless or otherwise, has come through—just a complete break—and silence!"

"Li Chang Yen has shown his hand. And the others?"

"Abe Ryland arrived in England a week ago, and left for the Continent yesterday."

"And Madame Olivier?"

"Madame Olivier left Paris last night."

"For Italy?"

"For Italy, sir. As far as we can judge, they are both making for the resort you indicated—though how you knew that—"

"Ah, that is not the cap with the feather for me! That was the work of Hastings here. He conceals his intelligence, you comprehend, but it is profound for all that."

Harvey looked at me with due appreciation, and I felt rather uncomfortable.

"All is in train, then," said Poirot. He was pale now, and completely serious. "The time has come. The arrangements are all made?"

"Everything you ordered has been carried out. The governments of Italy, France and England are behind you, and are all working harmoniously together."

"It is, in fact, a new Entente," observed Poirot dryly. "I am glad that Desjardeaux is convinced at last. *Eh bien*, then, we will start—or rather, I will start. You, Hastings, will remain here—yes, I pray of you. In verity, my friend, I am serious."

I believed him, but it was not likely that I should consent to being left behind in that fashion. Our argument was short but decisive.

It was not until we were in the train, speeding towards Paris that he admitted that he was secretly glad of my decision.

"For you have a part to play, Hastings. An important part! Without you, I might well fail. Nevertheless, I felt that it was my duty to urge you to remain behind."

"There is danger, then?"

"*Mon ami*, where there is the Big Four there is always danger."

On arrival in Paris, we drove across to the Gare de l'Est, and Poirot at last announced our destination. We were bound for Bolzano and Italian Tyrol.

During Harvey's absence from our carriage I took the opportunity of asking Poirot why he had said that the discovery of the rendezvous was my work.

"Because it was, my friend. How Ingles managed to get hold of the information I do not know, but he did, and he sent it to us by his servant. We are bound, *mon ami* for Karersee, the new Italian name for which is Lago di Carezza. You see now where your 'Cara Zia' comes in and also your 'Carrozza' and 'Largo'—the Handel was supplied by your own imagination. Possibly some reference to the information coming from the 'hand' of M. Ingles started the train of association."

"Karersee?" I queried. "I never heard of it."

"I always tell you that the English know no geography. But as a matter of fact it is a well-known and very beautiful summer resort, four thousand feet up, in the heart of the Dolomites."

"And it is in this out of the way spot that the Big Four have their rendezvous?"

"Say rather their headquarters. The signal has been given and it is their intention to disappear from the world and issue orders from their mountain fastness. I have made the inquiries—a lot of quarrying of stone and mineral deposits is done there, and the company, apparently a small Italian firm, is in reality controlled by Abe Ryland. I am prepared to swear that a vast subterranean dwelling has been hollowed out in the very heart of the mountain, secret and inaccessible. From there the leaders of the organisation will issue by wireless their orders to their followers who are numbered by thousands in every country. And from that crag in the Dolomites the dictators of the world will emerge. That is to say—they would emerge were it not for Hercule Poirot."

"Do you seriously believe all this, Poirot? What about the armies and general machinery of civilisation?"

"What about it in Russia, Hastings? This will be Russia on an infinitely larger scale—and with this additional menace—that Madame Olivier's experiments have proceeded further than she has ever given out. I believe that she has, to a certain extent, succeeded in liberating atomic energy and harnessing it to her purpose. Her experiments with the nitrogen of the air have been very remarkable, and she has also experimented in the concentration of wireless energy, so that a beam of great intensity can be focused upon some given spot. Exactly how far she has progressed, nobody knows, but it is certain that it is much farther than has ever been given out. She is a genius, that woman—the Curies were as nothing to her. Add to her genius the powers of Ryland's almost unlimited wealth, and, with the brain of Li Chang Yen, the finest criminal brain ever known, to direct and plan—*eh bien*, it will not be, as you say, all jam for civilisation."

His words made me very thoughtful. Although Poirot was given at times to exaggeration of language, he was not really an alarmist. For the first time I realised what a desperate struggle it was upon which we were engaged.

Harvey soon rejoined us and the journey went on.

We arrived at Bolzano about midday. From there the journey on was by motor. Several big blue motor-cars were waiting in the central square of the town, and we three got into one of them. Poirot, notwithstanding the heat of the day, was muffled to the eyes in greatcoat and scarf. His eyes and the tips of his ears were all that could be seen of him.

I did not know whether this was due to precaution or merely his exaggerated fear of catching a chill. The motor journey took a couple of hours. It was a really wonderful drive. For the first part of the way we wound in and out of huge cliffs, with a trickling waterfall on one hand. Then we emerged into a fertile valley, which continued for some miles, and then, still winding steadily upwards, the bare rocky peaks began to show with dense clustering pine woods at their base. The whole place was wild and lovely. Finally a series of abrupt curves, with the road running through the pine woods on either side, and we came suddenly upon a big hotel and found that we had arrived.

Our rooms had been reserved for us, and under Harvey's guidance we went straight up to them. They looked straight out over the rocky peaks and the long slopes of pine woods leading up to them. Poirot made a gesture towards them.

"It is there?" he asked in a low voice.

"Yes," replied Harvey. "There is a place called the Felsenlabyrynth—all big boulders piled about in a most fantastic way—a path winds through them. The quarrying is to the right of that, but we think that the entrance is probably in the Felsenlabyrynth."

Poirot nodded.

"Come, *mon ami*," he said to me. "Let us go down and sit upon the terrace and enjoy the sunlight."

"You think that wise?" I asked.

He shrugged his shoulders.

The sunlight was marvellous—in fact the glare was almost too great for me. We had some creamy coffee instead of tea, then went upstairs and unpacked our few belongings. Poirot was in his most unapproachable mood, lost in a kind of reverie. Once or twice he shook his head and sighed.

I had been rather intrigued by a man who had got out of our train at Bolzano, and had been met by a private car. He was a small man, and the thing about him that had attracted my attention was that he was almost as much muffled up as Poirot had been. More so, indeed, for in addition to greatcoat and muffler, he was wearing huge blue spectacles. I was convinced that here we had an emissary of the Big Four. Poirot did not seem very impressed by my idea, but when, leaning out of my bedroom window, I reported that the man in question was strolling about in the vicinity of the hotel, he admitted that there might be something in it.

I urged my friend not to go down to dinner, but he insisted on doing so. We entered the dining-room rather late, and were shown to a table by the window. As we sat down, our attention was attracted by an exclamation and a crash of falling china. A dish of *haricots verts* had been upset over a man who was sitting at the table next to ours.

The head waiter came up and was vociferous in apologies.

Presently, when the offending waiter was serving us with soup, Poirot spoke to him.

"An unfortunate accident, that. But it was not your fault."

"Monsieur saw that? No, indeed it was not my fault. The gentleman half sprung up from his chair—I thought he was going to have an attack of some kind. I could not save the catastrophe."

I saw Poirot's eyes shining with the green light I knew so well, and as the waiter departed he said to me in a low voice:—

"You see, Hastings, the effect of Hercule Poirot—alive and in the flesh?"

"You think—"

I had not time to continue. I felt Poirot's hand on my knee, as he whispered excitedly:

"Look, Hastings, look. *His trick with the bread!* Number Four!"

Sure enough, the man at the next table to ours, his face unusually pale, was dabbing a small piece of bread mechanically about the table.

I studied him carefully. His face, clean-shaven and puffily fat, was of a pasty, unhealthy sallowness, with heavy pouches under the eyes and deep lines running from his nose to the corners of his mouth. His age might have been anything from thirty-five to forty-five. In no particular did he resemble any one of the characters which Number Four had previously assumed. Indeed, had it not been for his little trick with the bread, of which he was evidently quite unaware, I would have sworn readily enough that the man sitting there was some one whom I had never seen before.

"He has recognised you," I murmured. "You should not have come down."

"My excellent Hastings, I have feigned death for three months for this one purpose."

"To startle Number Four?"

"To startle him at a moment when he must act quickly or not at all. And we have this great advantage—he does not know that we recognise him. He thinks that he is safe in his new disguise. How I bless Flossie Monro for telling us of that little habit of his."

"What will happen now?" I asked.

"What can happen? He recognises the only man he fears, miraculously resurrected from the dead, at the very minute when the plans of the Big Four are in the balance. Madame Olivier and Abe Ryland lunched here to-day, and it is thought that they went to Cortina. Only we know that they have retired to their hiding place. How much do we know? That is what Number Four is asking himself at this minute. He dare take no risks. I must be suppressed at all costs. *Eh bien*, let him try to suppress Hercule Poirot! I shall be ready for him."

As he finished speaking, the man at the next table got up and went out.

"He has gone to make his little arrangements," said Poirot placidly. "Shall we have our coffee on the terrace, my friend? It would be pleasanter, I think. I will just go up and get a coat."

I went out on to the terrace, a little disturbed in mind. Poirot's assurance did not quite content me. However, so long as we were on our guard, nothing could happen to us. I resolved to keep thoroughly on the alert.

It was quite five minutes before Poirot joined me. With his usual precautions against cold, he was muffled up to the ears. He sat down beside me and sipped his coffee appreciatively.

"Only in England is the coffee so atrocious," he remarked. "On the continent they understand how important it is for the digestion that it should be properly made."

As he finished speaking, the man from the next table suddenly appeared on the terrace. Without any hesitation, he came over and drew up a third chair to our table.

"You do not mind my joining you, I hope," he said in English.

"Not at all, monsieur," said Poirot.

I felt very uneasy. It is true that we were on the terrace of the hotel, with people all round us, but nevertheless I was not satisfied. I sensed the presence of danger.

Meanwhile Number Four chatted away in a perfectly natural manner. It seemed impossible to believe that he was anything but a *bona fide* tourist. He described excursions and motor trips, and posed as quite an authority on the neighbourhood.

He took a pipe from his pocket and began to light it. Poirot drew out his case of tiny cigarettes. As he placed one between his lips, the stranger leant forward with a match.

"Let me give you a light."

As he spoke, without the least warning, all the lights went out. There was a chink of glass, and something pungent under my nose, suffocating me—

EIGHTEEN
In The Felsenlabyrynth

I could not have been unconscious more than a minute. I came to myself being hustled along between two men. They had me under each arm, supporting my weight, and there was a gag in my mouth. It was pitch dark, but I gathered that we were not outside, but passing through the hotel. All round I could hear people shouting and demanding in every known language what had happened to the lights. My captors swung me down some stairs. We passed along a basement passage, then through a door and out into the open again through a glass door at the back of the hotel. In another moment we had gained the shelter of the pine trees.

I had caught a glimpse of another figure in a similar plight to myself, and realised that Poirot, too, was a victim of this bold coup.

By sheer audacity, Number Four had won the day. He had employed, I gathered, an instant æsthetic, probably ethyl chloride—breaking a small bulb of it under our noses. Then, in the confusion of the darkness, his accomplices, who had probably been guests sitting at the next table, had thrust gags in our mouths and hurried us away, taking us through the hotel to baffle pursuit.

I cannot describe the hour that followed. We were hurried through the woods at a break-neck pace, going uphill the whole time. At last we emerged in the open, on the mountain-side, and I saw just in front of us an extraordinary conglomeration of fantastic rocks and boulders.

This must be the Felsenlabyrynth of which Harvey had spoken. Soon we were winding in and out of its recesses. The place was like a maze devised by some evil genie.

Suddenly we stopped. An enormous rock barred our path. One of the men stooped and seemed to push on something when, without a sound, the huge mass of rock turned on itself and disclosed a small tunnel-like opening leading into the mountain-side.

Into this we were hurried. For some time the tunnel was narrow, but presently it widened, and before very long we came out into a wide rocky chamber lighted by electricity. There the gags were removed. At a sign from Number Four, who stood facing us with mocking triumph in his face, we were searched and every article was removed from our pockets, including Poirot's little automatic pistol.

A pang smote me as it was tossed down on the table. We were defeated—hopelessly defeated and outnumbered. It was the end.

"Welcome to the headquarters of the Big Four, M. Hercule Poirot," said Number Four in a mocking tone. "To meet you again is an unexpected pleasure. But was it worth while returning from the grave only for this?"

Poirot did not reply. I dared not look at him.

"Come this way," continued Number Four. "Your arrival will be somewhat of a surprise to my colleagues."

He indicated a narrow doorway in the wall. We passed through and found ourselves in another chamber. At the very end of it was a table behind which four chairs were placed. The end chair was empty, but was draped with a mandarin's cape. On the second, smoking a cigar, sat Mr. Abe Ryland. Leaning back in the third chair, with her burning eyes and her nun's face, was Madame Olivier. Number Four took his seat on the fourth chair.

We were in the presence of the Big Four.

Never before had I felt so fully the reality and the presence of Li Chang Yen as I did now when confronting his empty seat.

Far away in China, he yet controlled and directed this malign organisation.

Madame Olivier gave a faint cry on seeing us. Ryland, more self-controlled, only shifted his cigar, and raised his grizzled eyebrows.

"M. Hercule Poirot," said Ryland slowly. "This is a pleasant surprise. You put it over on us all right. We thought you were good and buried. No matter, the game is up now."

There was a ring as of steel in his voice. Madame Olivier said nothing, but her eyes burned, and I disliked the slow way she smiled.

"Madame and messieurs, I wish you good-evening," said Poirot quietly.

Something unexpected, something I had not been prepared to hear in his voice made me look at him. He seemed quite composed. Yet there was something about his whole appearance that was different.

Then there was a stir of draperies behind us, and the Countess Vera Rossakoff came in.

"Ah!" said Number Four. "Our valued and trusted lieutenant. An old friend of yours is here, my dear lady."

The countess whirled round with her usual vehemence of movement.

"God in Heaven!" she cried. "It is the little man! Ah! but he has the nine lives of a cat! Oh, little man, little man! Why did you mix yourself up in this?"

"Madame," said Poirot, with a bow. "Me, like the great Napoleon, I am on the side of the big battalions."

As he spoke I saw a sudden suspicion flash into her eyes, and at the same moment I knew the truth which subconsciously I already sensed.

The man beside me was not Hercule Poirot.

He was very like him, extraordinarily like him. There was the same egg-shaped head, the same strutting figure, delicately plump. But the voice was different, and the eyes instead of being green were dark, and surely the moustaches—those famous moustaches—?

My reflections were cut short by the countess's voice. She stepped forward, her voice ringing with excitement.

"You have been deceived. That man is not Hercule Poirot!"

Number Four uttered an incredulous exclamation, but the countess leant forward and snatched at Poirot's moustaches. They came off in her hand, and then, indeed, the truth was plain. For this man's upper lip was disfigured by a small scar which completely altered the expression of the face.

"Not Hercule Poirot," muttered Number Four. "But who can he be then?"

"I know," I cried suddenly, and then stopped dead, afraid I had ruined everything.

But the man I will still refer to as Poirot had turned to me encouragingly.

"Say it if you will. It makes no matter now. The trick has succeeded."

"This is Achille Poirot," I said slowly. "Hercule Poirot's twin brother."

"Impossible," said Ryland sharply, but he was shaken.

"Hercule's plan has succeeded to a marvel," said Achille placidly.

Number Four leapt forward, his voice harsh and menacing.

"Succeeded, has it?" he snarled. "Do you realise that before many minutes have passed you will be dead—dead?"

"Yes," said Achille Poirot gravely. "I realise that. It is you who do not realise that a man may be willing to purchase success by his life. There were men who laid down their lives for their country in the war. I am prepared to lay down mine in the same way for the world."

It struck me just then that although perfectly willing to lay down my life I might have been consulted in the matter. Then I remembered how Poirot had urged me to stay behind, and I felt appeased.

"And in what way will your laying down your life benefit the world?" asked Ryland sardonically.

"I see that you do not perceive the true inwardness of Hercule's plan. To begin with, your place of retreat was known some months ago, and practically all the visitors, hotel assistants and others are detectives or Secret Service men. A cordon has been drawn round the mountain. You may have more than one means of egress, but even so you cannot escape. Poirot himself is directing the operations outside. My boots were smeared with a preparation of aniseed to-night, before I came down to the terrace in my brother's place. Hounds are following the trail. It will lead them infallibly to the rock in the Felsenlabyrynth where the entrance is situated. You see, do what you will to us, the net is drawn tightly round you. You cannot escape."

Madame Olivier laughed suddenly.

"You are wrong. There is one way we can escape, and, like Samson of old, destroy our enemies at the same time. What do you say, my friends?"

Ryland was staring at Achille Poirot.

"Suppose he's lying," he said hoarsely.

The other shrugged his shoulders.

"In an hour it will be dawn. Then you can see for yourself the truth of my words. Already they should have traced me to the entrance in the Felsenlabyrynth."

Even as he spoke, there was a far off reverberation, and a man ran in shouting incoherently. Ryland sprang up and went out. Madame Olivier moved to the end of the room and opened a door that I had not noticed. Inside I caught a glimpse of a perfectly equipped laboratory which reminded me of the one in Paris. Number Four also sprang up and went out. He returned with Poirot's revolver which he gave to the countess.

"There is no danger of their escaping," he said grimly. "But still you had better have this."

Then he went out again.

The countess came over to us and surveyed my companion attentively for some time. Suddenly she laughed.

"You are very clever, M. Achille Poirot," she said mockingly.

"Madame, let us talk business. It is fortunate that they have left us alone together. What is your price?"

"I do not understand. What price?"

"Madame, you can aid us to escape. You know the secret ways out of this retreat. I ask you, what is your price?"

She laughed again.

"More than you could pay, little man! Why, all the money in the world would not buy me!"

"Madame, I did not speak of money. I am a man of intelligence. Nevertheless, this is a true fact—*everyone has his price*. In exchange for life and liberty, I offer you your heart's desire."

"So you are a magician!"

"You can call me so if you like."

The countess suddenly dropped her jesting manner. She spoke with passionate bitterness.

"Fool! My heart's desire! Can you give me revenge upon my enemies? Can you give me back youth and beauty and a gay heart? Can you bring the dead to life again?"

Achille Poirot was watching her very curiously.

"Which of the three, Madame? Make your choice."

She laughed sardonically.

"You will sell me the Elixir of Life, perhaps? Come, I will make a bargain with you. Once, I had a child. Find my child for me—and you shall go free."

"Madame, I agree. It is a bargain. Your child shall be restored to you. On the faith of—on the faith of Hercule Poirot himself."

Again that strange woman laughed—this time long and unrestrainedly.

"My dear M. Poirot, I am afraid I laid a little trap for you. It is very kind of you to promise to find my child for me, but, you see, I happen to know that you would not succeed, and so that would be a very one-sided bargain, would it not?"

"Madame, I swear to you by the Holy Angels that I will restore your child to you."

"I asked you before, M. Poirot, could you restore the dead to life?"

"Then the child is—"

"Dead? Yes."

He stepped forward and took her wrist.

"Madame, I—I who speak to you, swear once more. *I will bring the dead to life.*"

She stared at him as though fascinated.

"You do not believe me. I will prove my words. Get my pocket-book which they took from me."

She went out of the room, and returned with it in her hand. Throughout all she retained her grip on the revolver. I felt that Achille Poirot's chances of bluffing her were very slight. The Countess Vera Rossakoff was no fool.

"Open it, madame. The flap on the left-hand side. That is right. Now take out that photograph and look at it."

Wonderingly, she took out what seemed to be a small snapshot. No sooner had she looked at it than she uttered a cry and swayed as though about to fall. Then she almost flew at my companion.

"Where? Where? You shall tell me. Where?"

"Remember your bargain, madame."

"Yes, yes, I will trust you. Quick, before they come back."

Catching him by the hand, she drew him quickly and silently out of the room. I followed. From the outer room she led us into the tunnel by which we had first entered, but a short way along this forked, and she turned off to the right. Again and again the passage divided, but she led us on, never faltering or seeming to doubt her way, and with increasing speed.

"If only we are in time," she panted. "We must be out in the open before the explosion occurs."

Still we went on. I understood that this tunnel led right through the mountain and that we should finally emerge on the other side, facing a different valley. The sweat streamed down my face, but I raced on.

And then, far away, I saw a gleam of daylight. Nearer and nearer. I saw green bushes growing. We forced them aside, pushed our way through. We were in the open again, with the faint light of dawn making everything rosy.

Poirot's cordon was a reality. Even as we emerged, three men fell upon us, but released us again with a cry of astonishment.

"Quick," cried my companion. "Quick—there is no time to lose—"

But he was not destined to finish. The earth shook and trembled under our feet, there was a terrific roar and the whole mountain seemed to dissolve. We were flung headlong through the air.

• • • •

I came to myself at last. I was in a strange bed and a strange room. Some one was sitting by the window. He turned and came and stood by me.

It was Achille Poirot—or, stay, was it—

The well-known ironical voice dispelled any doubts I might have had.

"But yes, my friend, it is I. Brother Achille has gone home again—to the land of myths. It was I all the time. It is not only Number Four who can act a part. Belladona in the eyes, the sacrifice of the moustaches, and a real scar the inflicting of which caused me much pain two months ago—but I could not risk a fake beneath the eagle eyes of Number Four. And the final touch, your own knowledge and belief that there was such a person as Achille Poirot! It was invaluable, the assistance you rendered me, half the success of the coup is due to you! The whole crux of the affair was to make them believe that Hercule Poirot was still at large directing operations. Otherwise, everything was true, the aniseed, the cordon, etc."

"But why not really send a substitute?"

"And let you go into danger without me by your side? You have a pretty idea of me there! Besides, I always had a hope of finding a way out through the countess."

"How on earth did you manage to convince her? It was a pretty thin story to make her swallow—all that about a dead child."

"The countess has a great deal more perspicacity than you have, my dear Hastings. She was taken in at first by my disguise; but she soon saw through it. When she said, 'You are very clever, M. Achille Poirot,' I knew that she had guessed the truth. It was then or never to play my trump card."

"All that rigmarole about bringing the dead to life?"

"Exactly—but then, you see, I had the child all along."

"*What*?"

"But yes! You know my motto—Be prepared. As soon as I found that the Countess Rossakoff was mixed up with the Big Four, I had every possible inquiry made as to her antecedents. I learnt that she had had a child who was reported to have been killed, and I also found that there were discrepancies in the story which led me to wonder whether it might not, after all, be alive. In the end, I succeeded in tracing the boy, and by paying out a big sum I obtained possession of the child's person. The poor little fellow was nearly dead of starvation. I placed him in a safe place, with kindly people, and took a snapshot of him in his new surroundings. And so, when the time came, I had my little *coup de théâtre* all ready!"

"You are wonderful, Poirot; absolutely wonderful!"

"I was glad to do it, too. For I had admired the countess. I should have been sorry if she had perished in the explosion."

"I've been half afraid to ask you—what of the Big Four?"

"All the bodies have now been recovered. That of Number Four was quite unrecognisable, the head blown to pieces. I wish—I rather wish it had not been so. I should have liked to be *sure*—but no more of that. Look at this."

He handed me a newspaper in which a paragraph was marked. It reported the death, by suicide, of Li Chang Yen, who had engineered the recent revolution which had failed so disastrously.

"My great opponent," said Poirot gravely. "It was fated that he and I should never meet in the flesh. When he received the news of the disaster here, he took the simplest way out. A great brain, my friend, a great brain. But I wish I had seen the face of the man who was Number Four.... Supposing that, after all—but I romance. He is dead. Yes, *mon ami,* together we have faced and routed the Big Four; and now you will return to your charming wife, and I—I shall retire. The great case of my life is over. Anything else will seem tame after this. No, I shall retire. Possibly I shall grow vegetable marrows! I might even marry and range myself!"

He laughed heartily at the idea, but with a touch of embarrassment. I hope ... small men always admire big, flamboyant women—

"Marry and range myself," he said again. "Who knows?"

THE
MURDER
OF
ROGER ACKROYD

Agatha Christie

THE MURDER
OF
ROGER ACKROYD

PAGE CLASSICS

ISBN: 978-1-64833-754-3

First published 1926
Published by Page Publications 2024

Printed in China

Contents

1.	Dr. Sheppard at the Breakfast Table	1
2.	Who's Who in King's Abbot	6
3.	The Man Who Grew Vegetable Marrows	14
4.	Dinner at Fernly	25
5.	Murder	40
6.	The Tunisian Dagger	54
7.	I Learn My Neighbor's Profession	62
8.	Inspector Raglan Is Confident	76
9.	The Goldfish Pond	87
10.	The Parlormaid	97
11.	Poirot Pays a Call	111
12.	Round the Table	118
13.	The Goose Quill	127
14.	Mrs. Ackroyd	134
15.	Geoffrey Raymond	144
16.	An Evening at Mah Jong	153
17.	Parker	162
18.	Charles Kent	174
19.	Flora Ackroyd	180
20.	Miss Russell	189
21.	The Paragraph in the Paper	199
22.	Ursula's Story	206
23.	Poirot's Little Reunion	214
24.	Ralph Paton's Story	226
25.	The Whole Truth	230
26.	And Nothing but the Truth	237
27.	Apologia	241

ONE

Dr. Sheppard at the Breakfast Table

Mrs. Ferrars died on the night of the 16th–17th September—a Thursday. I was sent for at eight o'clock on the morning of Friday the 17th. There was nothing to be done. She had been dead some hours.

It was just a few minutes after nine when I reached home once more. I opened the front door with my latch-key, and purposely delayed a few moments in the hall, hanging up my hat and the light overcoat that I had deemed a wise precaution against the chill of an early autumn morning. To tell the truth, I was considerably upset and worried. I am not going to pretend that at that moment I foresaw the events of the next few weeks. I emphatically did not do so. But my instinct told me that there were stirring times ahead.

From the dining-room on my left there came the rattle of tea-cups and the short, dry cough of my sister Caroline.

"Is that you, James?" she called.

An unnecessary question, since who else could it be? To tell the truth, it was precisely my sister Caroline who was the cause of my few minutes' delay. The motto of the mongoose family, so Mr. Kipling tells us, is: "Go and find out." If Caroline ever adopts a crest, I should certainly suggest a mongoose rampant. One might omit the first part of the motto. Caroline can do any amount of finding out by sitting placidly at home. I don't know how she manages it, but there it is. I suspect that the servants and the tradesmen constitute her Intelligence Corps. When she goes out, it is not to gather in information, but to spread it. At that, too, she is amazingly expert.

It was really this last named trait of hers which was causing me these pangs of indecision. Whatever I told Caroline now concerning the demise of Mrs. Ferrars would be common knowledge all over the village within the space of an hour and a half. As a professional man, I naturally aim at discretion. Therefore I have got into the habit of continually withholding all information possible from my sister. She usually finds out just the same, but I have the moral satisfaction of knowing that I am in no way to blame.

Mrs. Ferrars' husband died just over a year ago, and Caroline has constantly asserted, without the least foundation for the assertion, that his wife poisoned him.

She scorns my invariable rejoinder that Mr. Ferrars died of acute gastritis, helped on by habitual over-indulgence in alcoholic beverages. The symptoms of gastritis and arsenical poisoning are not, I agree, unlike, but Caroline bases her accusation on quite different lines.

"You've only got to look at her," I have heard her say.

Mrs. Ferrars, though not in her first youth, was a very attractive woman, and her clothes, though simple, always seemed to fit her very well, but all the same, lots of women buy their clothes in Paris and have not, on that account, necessarily poisoned their husbands.

As I stood hesitating in the hall, with all this passing through my mind, Caroline's voice came again, with a sharper note in it.

"What on earth are you doing out there, James? Why don't you come and get your breakfast?"

"Just coming, my dear," I said hastily. "I've been hanging up my overcoat."

"You could have hung up half a dozen overcoats in this time."

She was quite right. I could have.

I walked into the dining-room, gave Caroline the accustomed peck on the cheek, and sat down to eggs and bacon. The bacon was rather cold.

"You've had an early call," remarked Caroline.

"Yes," I said. "King's Paddock. Mrs. Ferrars."

"I know," said my sister.

"How did you know?"

"Annie told me."

Annie is the house parlormaid. A nice girl, but an inveterate talker.

There was a pause. I continued to eat eggs and bacon. My sister's nose, which is long and thin, quivered a little at the tip, as it always does when she is interested or excited over anything.

"Well?" she demanded.

"A bad business. Nothing to be done. Must have died in her sleep."

"I know," said my sister again.

This time I was annoyed.

"You can't know," I snapped. "I didn't know myself until I got there, and I haven't mentioned it to a soul yet. If that girl Annie knows, she must be a clairvoyant."

"It wasn't Annie who told me. It was the milkman. He had it from the Ferrars' cook."

As I say, there is no need for Caroline to go out to get information. She sits at home, and it comes to her.

My sister continued:

"What did she die of? Heart failure?"

"Didn't the milkman tell you that?" I inquired sarcastically.

Sarcasm is wasted on Caroline. She takes it seriously and answers accordingly.

"He didn't know," she explained.

After all, Caroline was bound to hear sooner or later. She might as well hear from me.

3

"She died of an overdose of veronal. She's been taking it lately for sleeplessness. Must have taken too much."

"Nonsense," said Caroline immediately. "She took it on purpose. Don't tell me!"

It is odd how, when you have a secret belief of your own which you do not wish to acknowledge, the voicing of it by some one else will rouse you to a fury of denial. I burst immediately into indignant speech.

"There you go again," I said. "Rushing along without rhyme or reason. Why on earth should Mrs. Ferrars wish to commit suicide? A widow, fairly young still, very well off, good health, and nothing to do but enjoy life. It's absurd."

"Not at all. Even you must have noticed how different she has been looking lately. It's been coming on for the last six months. She's looked positively hag-ridden. And you have just admitted that she hasn't been able to sleep."

"What is your diagnosis?" I demanded coldly. "An unfortunate love affair, I suppose?"

My sister shook her head.

"*Remorse*," she said, with great gusto.

"Remorse?"

"Yes. You never would believe me when I told you she poisoned her husband. I'm more than ever convinced of it now."

"I don't think you're very logical," I objected. "Surely if a woman committed a crime like murder, she'd be sufficiently cold-blooded to enjoy the fruits of it without any weak-minded sentimentality such as repentance."

Caroline shook her head.

"There probably are women like that—but Mrs. Ferrars wasn't one of them. She was a mass of nerves. An overmastering impulse drove her on to get rid of her husband because she was the sort of person who simply can't endure suffering of any kind, and there's no doubt that the wife of a man like Ashley Ferrars must have had to suffer a good deal——"

4

I nodded.

"And ever since she's been haunted by what she did. I can't help feeling sorry for her."

I don't think Caroline ever felt sorry for Mrs. Ferrars whilst she was alive. Now that she has gone where (presumably) Paris frocks can no longer be worn, Caroline is prepared to indulge in the softer emotions of pity and comprehension.

I told her firmly that her whole idea was nonsense. I was all the more firm because I secretly agreed with some part, at least, of what she had said. But it is all wrong that Caroline should arrive at the truth simply by a kind of inspired guesswork. I wasn't going to encourage that sort of thing. She will go round the village airing her views, and every one will think that she is doing so on medical data supplied by me. Life is very trying.

"Nonsense," said Caroline, in reply to my strictures. "You'll see. Ten to one she's left a letter confessing everything."

"She didn't leave a letter of any kind," I said sharply, and not seeing where the admission was going to land me.

"Oh!" said Caroline. "So you *did* inquire about that, did you? I believe, James, that in your heart of hearts, you think very much as I do. You're a precious old humbug."

"One always has to take the possibility of suicide into consideration," I said repressively.

"Will there be an inquest?"

"There may be. It all depends. If I am able to declare myself absolutely satisfied that the overdose was taken accidentally, an inquest might be dispensed with."

"And are you absolutely satisfied?" asked my sister shrewdly.

I did not answer, but got up from table.

TWO
Who's Who in King's Abbot

Before I proceed further with what I said to Caroline and what Caroline said to me, it might be as well to give some idea of what I should describe as our local geography. Our village, King's Abbot, is, I imagine, very much like any other village. Our big town is Cranchester, nine miles away. We have a large railway station, a small post office, and two rival "General Stores." Able-bodied men are apt to leave the place early in life, but we are rich in unmarried ladies and retired military officers. Our hobbies and recreations can be summed up in the one word, "gossip."

There are only two houses of any importance in King's Abbot. One is King's Paddock, left to Mrs. Ferrars by her late husband. The other, Fernly Park, is owned by Roger Ackroyd. Ackroyd has always interested me by being a man more impossibly like a country squire than any country squire could really be. He reminds one of the red-faced sportsmen who always appeared early in the first act of an old-fashioned musical comedy, the setting being the village green. They usually sang a song about going up to London. Nowadays we have revues, and the country squire has died out of musical fashion.

Of course, Ackroyd is not really a country squire. He is an immensely successful manufacturer of (I think) wagon wheels. He is a man of nearly fifty years of age, rubicund of face and genial of manner. He is hand and glove with the vicar, subscribes liberally to parish funds (though rumor has it that he is extremely mean in personal expenditure), encourages cricket matches, Lads' Clubs, and Disabled Soldiers' Institutes. He is, in fact, the life and soul of our peaceful village of King's Abbot.

Now when Roger Ackroyd was a lad of twenty-one, he fell in love with, and married, a beautiful woman some five or six years his senior. Her name was Paton, and she was a widow with one child. The history of the marriage was short and painful. To put it bluntly, Mrs. Ackroyd was a dipsomaniac. She succeeded in drinking herself into her grave four years after her marriage.

In the years that followed, Ackroyd showed no disposition to make a second matrimonial adventure. His wife's child by her first marriage was only seven years old when his mother died. He is now twenty-five. Ackroyd has always regarded him as his own son, and has brought him up accordingly, but he has been a wild lad and a continual source of worry and trouble to his stepfather. Nevertheless we are all very fond of Ralph Paton in King's Abbot. He is such a good-looking youngster for one thing.

As I said before, we are ready enough to gossip in our village. Everybody noticed from the first that Ackroyd and Mrs. Ferrars got on very well together. After her husband's death, the intimacy became more marked. They were always seen about together, and it was freely conjectured that at the end of her period of mourning, Mrs. Ferrars would become Mrs. Roger Ackroyd. It was felt, indeed, that there was a certain fitness in the thing. Roger Ackroyd's wife had admittedly died of drink. Ashley Ferrars had been a drunkard for many years before his death. It was only fitting that these two victims of alcoholic excess should make up to each other for all that they had previously endured at the hands of their former spouses.

The Ferrars only came to live here just over a year ago, but a halo of gossip has surrounded Ackroyd for many years past. All the time that Ralph Paton was growing up to manhood, a series of lady housekeepers presided over Ackroyd's establishment, and each in turn was regarded with lively suspicion by Caroline and her cronies. It is not too much to say that for at least fifteen years the whole village has confidently expected Ackroyd to marry one of his housekeepers. The last of them, a redoubtable lady called Miss Russell, has reigned undisputed for five years, twice as long as any of her predecessors. It is felt that but for the advent of Mrs. Ferrars, Ackroyd could hardly have escaped. That—and one other factor—the unexpected arrival of a widowed sister-in-law with her daughter from Canada. Mrs. Cecil Ackroyd, widow of Ackroyd's ne'er-do-well younger brother, has taken up her residence at Fernly Park, and has succeeded, according to Caroline, in putting Miss Russell in her proper place.

I don't know exactly what a "proper place" constitutes—it sounds chilly and unpleasant—but I know that Miss Russell goes about with pinched lips, and what I can only describe as an acid smile, and that she professes the utmost sympathy for "poor Mrs. Ackroyd—dependent on the charity of her husband's brother. The bread of charity is so bitter, is it not? *I* should be quite miserable if I did not work for my living."

I don't know what Mrs. Cecil Ackroyd thought of the Ferrars affair when it came on the tapis. It was clearly to her advantage that Ackroyd should remain unmarried. She was always very charming—not to say gushing—to Mrs. Ferrars when they met. Caroline says that proves less than nothing.

Such have been our preoccupations in King's Abbot for the last few years. We have discussed Ackroyd and his affairs from every standpoint. Mrs. Ferrars has fitted into her place in the scheme.

Now there has been a rearrangement of the kaleidoscope. From a mild discussion of probable wedding presents, we have been jerked into the midst of tragedy.

Revolving these and sundry other matters in my mind, I went mechanically on my round. I had no cases of special interest to attend, which was, perhaps, as well, for my thoughts returned again and again to the mystery of Mrs. Ferrars's death. Had she taken her own life? Surely, if she had done so, she would have left some word behind to say what she contemplated doing? Women, in my experience, if they once reach the determination to commit suicide, usually wish to reveal the state of mind that led to the fatal action. They covet the limelight.

When had I last seen her? Not for over a week. Her manner then had been normal enough considering—well—considering everything.

Then I suddenly remembered that I had seen her, though not to speak to, only yesterday. She had been walking with Ralph Paton, and I had been surprised because I had had no idea that he was likely to be in King's Abbot. I thought, indeed, that he had quarreled finally with his stepfather. Nothing had been seen of him down here for nearly six months. They had been walking along, side by side, their heads close together, and she had been talking very earnestly.

I think I can safely say that it was at this moment that a foreboding of the future first swept over me. Nothing tangible as yet—but a vague premonition of the way things were setting. That earnest *tête-à-tête* between Ralph Paton and Mrs. Ferrars the day before struck me disagreeably.

I was still thinking of it when I came face to face with Roger Ackroyd.

"Sheppard!" he exclaimed. "Just the man I wanted to get hold of. This is a terrible business."

"You've heard then?"

He nodded. He had felt the blow keenly, I could see. His big red cheeks seemed to have fallen in, and he looked a positive wreck of his usual jolly, healthy self.

"It's worse than you know," he said quietly. "Look here, Sheppard, I've got to talk to you. Can you come back with me now?"

"Hardly. I've got three patients to see still, and I must be back by twelve to see my surgery patients."

"Then this afternoon—no, better still, dine to-night. At 7.30? Will that suit you?"

"Yes—I can manage that all right. What's wrong? Is it Ralph?"

I hardly knew why I said that—except, perhaps, that it had so often been Ralph.

Ackroyd stared blankly at me as though he hardly understood. I began to realize that there must be something very wrong indeed somewhere. I had never seen Ackroyd so upset before.

"Ralph?" he said vaguely. "Oh! no, it's not Ralph. Ralph's in London——Damn! Here's old Miss Ganett coming. I don't want to have to talk to her about this ghastly business. See you to-night, Sheppard. Seven-thirty."

I nodded, and he hurried away, leaving me wondering. Ralph in London? But he had certainly been in King's Abbot the preceding afternoon. He must have gone back to town last night or early this morning, and yet Ackroyd's manner had conveyed quite a different impression. He had spoken as though Ralph had not been near the place for months.

I had no time to puzzle the matter out further. Miss Ganett was upon me, thirsting for information. Miss Ganett has all the characteristics of my sister Caroline, but she lacks that unerring aim in jumping to conclusions which lends a touch of greatness to Caroline's maneuvers. Miss Ganett was breathless and interrogatory.

Wasn't it sad about poor dear Mrs. Ferrars? A lot of people were saying she had been a confirmed drug-taker for years. So wicked the way people went about saying things. And yet, the worst of it was, there was usually a grain of truth somewhere in these wild statements. No smoke without fire! They were saying too that Mr. Ackroyd had found out about it, and had broken off the engagement—because there *was* an engagement. She, Miss Ganett, had proof positive of that. Of course I must know all about it—doctors always did—but they never tell?

And all this with a sharp beady eye on me to see how I reacted to these suggestions. Fortunately long association with Caroline has led me to preserve an impassive countenance, and to be ready with small non-committal remarks.

On this occasion I congratulated Miss Ganett on not joining in ill-natured gossip. Rather a neat counterattack, I thought. It left her in difficulties, and before she could pull herself together, I had passed on.

I went home thoughtful, to find several patients waiting for me in the surgery.

I had dismissed the last of them, as I thought, and was just contemplating a few minutes in the garden before lunch when I perceived one more patient waiting for me. She rose and came towards me as I stood somewhat surprised.

I don't know why I should have been, except that there is a suggestion of cast iron about Miss Russell, a something that is above the ills of the flesh.

Ackroyd's housekeeper is a tall woman, handsome but forbidding in appearance. She has a stern eye, and lips that shut tightly, and I feel that if I were an under housemaid or a kitchenmaid I should run for my life whenever I heard her coming.

"Good morning, Dr. Sheppard," said Miss Russell. "I should be much obliged if you would take a look at my knee."

I took a look, but, truth to tell, I was very little wiser when I had done so. Miss Russell's account of vague pains was so unconvincing that with a woman of less integrity of character I should have suspected a trumped-up tale. It did cross my mind for one moment that Miss Russell might have deliberately invented this affection of the knee in order to pump me on the subject of Mrs. Ferrars's death, but I soon saw that there, at least, I had misjudged her. She made a brief reference to the tragedy, nothing more. Yet she certainly seemed disposed to linger and chat.

"Well, thank you very much for this bottle of liniment, doctor," she said at last. "Not that I believe it will do the least good."

I didn't think it would either, but I protested in duty bound. After all, it couldn't do any harm, and one must stick up for the tools of one's trade.

"I don't believe in all these drugs," said Miss Russell, her eyes sweeping over my array of bottles disparagingly. "Drugs do a lot of harm. Look at the cocaine habit."

"Well, as far as that goes——"

"It's very prevalent in high society."

I'm sure Miss Russell knows far more about high society than I do. I didn't attempt to argue with her.

"Just tell me this, doctor," said Miss Russell. "Suppose you are really a slave of the drug habit. Is there any cure?"

One cannot answer a question like that offhand. I gave her a short lecture on the subject, and she listened with close attention. I still suspected her of seeking information about Mrs. Ferrars.

"Now, veronal, for instance——" I proceeded.

But, strangely enough, she didn't seem interested in veronal. Instead she changed the subject, and asked me if it was true that there were certain poisons so rare as to baffle detection.

"Ah!" I said. "You've been reading detective stories."

She admitted that she had.

"The essence of a detective story," I said, "is to have a rare poison—if possible something from South America, that nobody has ever heard of—something that one obscure tribe of savages use to poison their arrows with. Death is instantaneous, and Western science is powerless to detect it. That is the kind of thing you mean?"

"Yes. Is there really such a thing?"

I shook my head regretfully.

"I'm afraid there isn't. There's *curare*, of course."

I told her a good deal about curare, but she seemed to have lost interest once more. She asked me if I had any in my poison cupboard, and when I replied in the negative I fancy I fell in her estimation.

She said she must be getting back, and I saw her out at the surgery door just as the luncheon gong went.

I should never have suspected Miss Russell of a fondness for detective stories. It pleases me very much to think of her stepping out of the housekeeper's room to rebuke a delinquent housemaid, and then returning to a comfortable perusal of *The Mystery of the Seventh Death*, or something of the kind.

THREE

The Man Who Grew
Vegetable Marrows

I told Caroline at lunch time that I should be dining at Fernly. She expressed no objection—on the contrary——

"Excellent," she said. "You'll hear all about it. By the way, what is the trouble with Ralph?"

"With Ralph?" I said, surprised; "there's isn't any."

"Then why is he staying at the Three Boars instead of at Fernly Park?"

I did not for a minute question Caroline's statement that Ralph Paton was staying at the local inn. That Caroline said so was enough for me.

"Ackroyd told me he was in London," I said. In the surprise of the moment I departed from my valuable rule of never parting with information.

"Oh!" said Caroline. I could see her nose twitching as she worked on this.

"He arrived at the Three Boars yesterday morning," she said. "And he's still there. Last night he was out with a girl."

That did not surprise me in the least. Ralph, I should say, is out with a girl most nights of his life. But I did rather wonder that he chose to indulge in the pastime in King's Abbot instead of in the gay metropolis.

"One of the barmaids?" I asked.

"No. That's just it. He went out to meet her. I don't know who she is."

(Bitter for Caroline to have to admit such a thing.)

"But I can guess," continued my indefatigable sister.

I waited patiently.

"His cousin."

"Flora Ackroyd?" I exclaimed in surprise.

Flora Ackroyd is, of course, no relation whatever really to Ralph Paton, but Ralph has been looked upon for so long as practically Ackroyd's own son, that cousinship is taken for granted.

"Flora Ackroyd," said my sister.

"But why not go to Fernly if he wanted to see her?"

"Secretly engaged," said Caroline, with immense enjoyment. "Old Ackroyd won't hear of it, and they have to meet this way."

I saw a good many flaws in Caroline's theory, but I forbore to point them out to her. An innocent remark about our new neighbor created a diversion.

The house next door, The Larches, has recently been taken by a stranger. To Caroline's extreme annoyance, she has not been able to find out anything about him, except that he is a foreigner. The Intelligence Corps has proved a broken reed. Presumably the man has milk and vegetables and joints of meat and occasional whitings just like everybody else, but none of the people who make it their business to supply these things seem to have acquired any information. His name, apparently, is Mr. Porrott—a name which conveys an odd feeling of unreality. The one thing we do know about him is that he is interested in the growing of vegetable marrows.

But that is certainly not the sort of information that Caroline is after. She wants to know where he comes from, what he does, whether he is married, what his wife was, or is, like, whether he has children, what his mother's maiden name was—and so on. Somebody very like Caroline must have invented the questions on passports, I think.

"My dear Caroline," I said. "There's no doubt at all about what the man's profession has been. He's a retired hairdresser. Look at that mustache of his."

Caroline dissented. She said that if the man was a hairdresser, he would have wavy hair—not straight. All hairdressers did.

I cited several hairdressers personally known to me who had straight hair, but Caroline refused to be convinced.

"I can't make him out at all," she said in an aggrieved voice. "I borrowed some garden tools the other day, and he was most polite, but I couldn't get anything out of him. I asked him point blank at last whether he was a Frenchman, and he said he wasn't—and somehow I didn't like to ask him any more."

I began to be more interested in our mysterious neighbor. A man who is capable of shutting up Caroline and sending her, like the Queen of Sheba, empty away must be something of a personality.

"I believe," said Caroline, "that he's got one of those new vacuum cleaners——"

I saw a meditated loan and the opportunity of further questioning gleaming from her eye. I seized the chance to escape into the garden. I am rather fond of gardening. I was busily exterminating dandelion roots when a shout of warning sounded from close by and a heavy body whizzed by my ear and fell at my feet with a repellant squelch. It was a vegetable marrow!

I looked up angrily. Over the wall, to my left, there appeared a face. An egg-shaped head, partially covered with suspiciously black hair, two immense mustaches, and a pair of watchful eyes. It was our mysterious neighbor, Mr. Porrott.

He broke at once into fluent apologies.

"I demand of you a thousand pardons, monsieur. I am without defense. For some months now I cultivate the marrows. This morning suddenly I enrage myself with these marrows. I send them to promenade themselves—alas! not only mentally but physically. I seize the biggest. I hurl him over the wall. Monsieur, I am

16

ashamed. I prostrate myself."

Before such profuse apologies, my anger was forced to melt. After all, the wretched vegetable hadn't hit me. But I sincerely hoped that throwing large vegetables over walls was not our new friend's hobby. Such a habit could hardly endear him to us as a neighbor.

The strange little man seemed to read my thoughts.

"Ah! no," he exclaimed. "Do not disquiet yourself. It is not with me a habit. But can you figure to yourself, monsieur, that a man may work towards a certain object, may labor and toil to attain a certain kind of leisure and occupation, and then find that, after all, he yearns for the old busy days, and the old occupations that he thought himself so glad to leave?"

"Yes," I said slowly. "I fancy that that is a common enough occurrence. I myself am perhaps an instance. A year ago I came into a legacy—enough to enable me to realize a dream. I have always wanted to travel, to see the world. Well, that was a year ago, as I said, and—I am still here."

My little neighbor nodded.

"The chains of habit. We work to attain an object, and the object gained, we find that what we miss is the daily toil. And mark you, monsieur, my work was interesting work. The most interesting work there is in the world."

"Yes?" I said encouragingly. For the moment the spirit of Caroline was strong within me.

"The study of human nature, monsieur!"

"Just so," I said kindly.

Clearly a retired hairdresser. Who knows the secrets of human nature better than a hairdresser?

"Also, I had a friend—a friend who for many years never left my side. Occasionally of an imbecility to make one afraid, nevertheless he was very dear to me. Figure to yourself that I miss even his stupidity. His *naïveté*, his honest outlook, the pleasure of delighting and surprising him by my superior gifts—all these I miss more than I can tell you."

"He died?" I asked sympathetically.

"Not so. He lives and flourishes—but on the other side of the world. He is now in the Argentine."

"In the Argentine," I said enviously.

I have always wanted to go to South America. I sighed, and then looked up to find Mr. Porrott eyeing me sympathetically. He seemed an understanding little man.

"You will go there, yes?" he asked.

I shook my head with a sigh.

"I could have gone," I said, "a year ago. But I was foolish—and worse than foolish—greedy. I risked the substance for the shadow."

"I comprehend," said Mr. Porrott. "You speculated?"

I nodded mournfully, but in spite of myself I felt secretly entertained. This ridiculous little man was so portentously solemn.

"Not the Porcupine Oilfields?" he asked suddenly.

I stared.

"I thought of them, as a matter of fact, but in the end I plumped for a gold mine in Western Australia."

My neighbor was regarding me with a strange expression which I could not fathom.

"It is Fate," he said at last.

"What is Fate?" I asked irritably.

"That I should live next to a man who seriously considers Porcupine Oilfields, and also West Australian Gold Mines. Tell me, have you also a penchant for auburn hair?"

I stared at him open-mouthed, and he burst out laughing.

"No, no, it is not the insanity that I suffer from. Make your mind easy. It was a foolish question that I put to you there, for, see you, my friend of whom I spoke was a young man, a man who thought all women good, and most of them beautiful. But you are a man of middle age, a doctor, a man who knows the folly and the vanity of most things in this life of ours. Well, well, we are neighbors. I beg of you to accept and present to your excellent sister my best marrow."

He stooped, and with a flourish produced an immense specimen of the tribe, which I duly accepted in the spirit in which it was offered.

"Indeed," said the little man cheerfully, "this has not been a wasted morning. I have made the acquaintance of a man who in some ways resembles my far-off friend. By the way, I should like to ask you a question. You doubtless know every one in this tiny village. Who is the young man with the very dark hair and eyes, and the handsome face. He walks with his head flung back, and an easy smile on his lips?"

The description left me in no doubt.

"That must be Captain Ralph Paton," I said slowly.

"I have not seen him about here before?"

"No, he has not been here for some time. But he is the son—adopted son, rather—of Mr. Ackroyd of Fernly Park."

My neighbor made a slight gesture of impatience.

"Of course, I should have guessed. Mr. Ackroyd spoke of him many times."

"You know Mr. Ackroyd?" I said, slightly surprised.

"Mr. Ackroyd knew me in London—when I was at work there. I have asked him to say nothing of my profession down here."

"I see," I said, rather amused by this patent snobbery, as I thought it.

But the little man went on with an almost grandiloquent smirk.

"One prefers to remain incognito. I am not anxious for notoriety. I have not even troubled to correct the local version of my name."

"Indeed," I said, not knowing quite what to say.

"Captain Ralph Paton," mused Mr. Porrott. "And so he is engaged to Mr. Ackroyd's niece, the charming Miss Flora."

"Who told you so?" I asked, very much surprised.

"Mr. Ackroyd. About a week ago. He is very pleased about it—has long desired that such a thing should come to pass, or so I understood from him. I even believe that he brought some pressure to bear upon the young man. That is never wise. A young man should marry to please himself—not to please a stepfather from whom he has expectations."

My ideas were completely upset. I could not see Ackroyd taking a hairdresser into his confidence, and discussing the marriage of his niece and stepson with him. Ackroyd extends a genial patronage to the lower orders, but he has a very great sense of his own dignity. I began to think that Porrott couldn't be a hairdresser after all.

To hide my confusion, I said the first thing that came into my head.

"What made you notice Ralph Paton? His good looks?"

"No, not that alone—though he is unusually good-looking for an Englishman—what your lady novelists would call a Greek God. No, there was something about that young man that I did not understand."

He said the last sentence in a musing tone of voice which made an indefinable impression upon me. It was as though he was summing up the boy by the light of some inner knowledge that I did not share. It was that impression that was left with me, for at that moment my sister's voice called me from the house.

I went in. Caroline had her hat on, and had evidently just come in from the village. She began without preamble.

"I met Mr. Ackroyd."

"Yes?" I said.

"I stopped him, of course, but he seemed in a great hurry, and anxious to get away."

I have no doubt but that that was the case. He would feel towards Caroline much as he had felt towards Miss Ganett earlier in the day—perhaps more so. Caroline is less easy to shake off.

"I asked him at once about Ralph. He was absolutely astonished. Had no idea the boy was down here. He actually said he thought I must have made a mistake. I! A mistake!"

"Ridiculous," I said. "He ought to have known you better."

"Then he went on to tell me that Ralph and Flora are engaged."

"I know that too," I interrupted, with modest pride.

"Who told you?"

"Our new neighbor."

Caroline visibly wavered for a second or two, much as a roulette ball might coyly hover between two numbers. Then she declined the tempting red herring.

"I told Mr. Ackroyd that Ralph was staying at the Three Boars."

"Caroline," I said, "do you never reflect that you might do a lot of harm with this habit of yours of repeating everything indiscriminately?"

"Nonsense," said my sister. "People ought to know things. I consider it my duty to tell them. Mr. Ackroyd was very grateful to me."

"Well?" I said, for there was clearly more to come.

"I think he went straight off to the Three Boars, but if so he didn't find Ralph there."

"No?"

"No. Because as I was coming back through the wood——"

"Coming back through the wood?" I interrupted.

Caroline had the grace to blush.

"It was such a lovely day," she exclaimed. "I thought I would make a little round. The woods with their autumnal tints are so perfect at this time of year."

Caroline does not care a hang for woods at any time of year. Normally she regards them as places where you get your feet damp, and where all kinds of unpleasant things may drop on your head. No, it was good sound mongoose instinct which took her to our local wood. It is the only place adjacent to the village of King's Abbot where you can talk with a young woman unseen by the whole of the village. It adjoins the Park of Fernly.

"Well," I said, "go on."

"As I say, I was just coming back through the wood when I heard voices."

Caroline paused.

"Yes?"

"One was Ralph Paton's—I knew it at once. The other was a girl's. Of course I didn't mean to listen——"

"Of course not," I interjected, with patent sarcasm—which was, however, wasted on Caroline.

"But I simply couldn't help overhearing. The girl said something—I didn't quite catch what it was, and Ralph answered. He sounded very angry. 'My dear girl,' he said. 'Don't you realize that it is quite on the cards the old man will cut me off with a shilling? He's been pretty fed up with me for the last few years. A little more would do it. And we need the dibs, my dear. I shall be a very rich man when the old fellow pops off. He's mean as they make 'em, but he's rolling in money really. I don't want him to go altering his will. You leave it to me, and don't worry.' Those were his exact words. I remember them perfectly. Unfortunately, just then I stepped on a dry twig or something, and they lowered their voices and moved away. I couldn't, of course, go rushing after them, so wasn't able to see who the girl was."

"That must have been most vexing," I said. "I suppose, though, you hurried on to the Three Boars, felt faint, and went into the bar for a glass of brandy, and so were able to see if both the barmaids were on duty?"

"It wasn't a barmaid," said Caroline unhesitatingly. "In fact, I'm almost sure that it was Flora Ackroyd, only——"

"Only it doesn't seem to make sense," I agreed.

"But if it wasn't Flora, who could it have been?"

Rapidly my sister ran over a list of maidens living in the neighborhood, with profuse reasons for and against.

When she paused for breath, I murmured something about a patient, and slipped out.

22

I proposed to make my way to the Three Boars. It seemed likely that Ralph Paton would have returned there by now.

I knew Ralph very well—better, perhaps, than any one else in King's Abbot, for I had known his mother before him, and therefore I understood much in him that puzzled others. He was, to a certain extent, the victim of heredity. He had not inherited his mother's fatal propensity for drink, but nevertheless he had in him a strain of weakness. As my new friend of this morning had declared, he was extraordinarily handsome. Just on six feet, perfectly proportioned, with the easy grace of an athlete, he was dark, like his mother, with a handsome, sunburnt face always ready to break into a smile. Ralph Paton was of those born to charm easily and without effort. He was self-indulgent and extravagant, with no veneration for anything on earth, but he was lovable nevertheless, and his friends were all devoted to him.

Could I do anything with the boy? I thought I could.

On inquiry at the Three Boars I found that Captain Paton had just come in. I went up to his room and entered unannounced.

For a moment, remembering what I had heard and seen, I was doubtful of my reception, but I need have had no misgivings.

"Why, it's Sheppard! Glad to see you."

He came forward to meet me, hand outstretched, a sunny smile lighting up his face.

"The one person I am glad to see in this infernal place."

I raised my eyebrows.

"What's the place been doing?"

He gave a vexed laugh.

"It's a long story. Things haven't been going well with me, doctor. But have a drink, won't you?"

"Thanks," I said, "I will."

He pressed the bell, then, coming back, threw himself into a chair.

"Not to mince matters," he said gloomily, "I'm in the devil of a mess. In fact, I haven't the least idea what to do next."

"What's the matter?" I asked sympathetically.

"It's my confounded stepfather."

"What has he done?"

"It isn't what he's done yet, but what he's likely to do."

The bell was answered, and Ralph ordered the drinks. When the man had gone again, he sat hunched in the arm-chair, frowning to himself.

"Is it really—serious?" I asked.

He nodded.

"I'm fairly up against it this time," he said soberly.

The unusual ring of gravity in his voice told me that he spoke the truth. It took a good deal to make Ralph grave.

"In fact," he continued, "I can't see my way ahead.... I'm damned if I can."

"If I could help——" I suggested diffidently.

But he shook his head very decidedly.

"Good of you, doctor. But I can't let you in on this. I've got to play a lone hand."

He was silent a minute and then repeated in a slightly different tone of voice:—

"Yes—I've got to play a lone hand...."

FOUR
Dinner at Fernly

It was just a few minutes before half-past seven when I rang the front door bell of Fernly Park. The door was opened with admirable promptitude by Parker, the butler.

The night was such a fine one that I had preferred to come on foot. I stepped into the big square hall and Parker relieved me of my overcoat. Just then Ackroyd's secretary, a pleasant young fellow by the name of Raymond, passed through the hall on his way to Ackroyd's study, his hands full of papers.

"Good-evening, doctor. Coming to dine? Or is this a professional call?"

The last was in allusion to my black bag, which I had laid down on the oak chest.

I explained that I expected a summons to a confinement case at any moment, and so had come out prepared for an emergency call. Raymond nodded, and went on his way, calling over his shoulder:—

"Go into the drawing-room. You know the way. The ladies will be down in a minute. I must just take these papers to Mr. Ackroyd, and I'll tell him you're here."

On Raymond's appearance Parker had withdrawn, so I was alone in the hall. I settled my tie, glanced in a large mirror which hung there, and crossed to the door directly facing me, which was, as I knew, the door of the drawing-room.

I noticed, just as I was turning the handle, a sound from within—the shutting down of a window, I took it to be. I noted it, I may say, quite mechanically, without attaching any importance to it at the time.

I opened the door and walked in. As I did so, I almost collided with Miss Russell, who was just coming out. We both apologized.

For the first time I found myself appraising the housekeeper and thinking what a handsome woman she must once have been—indeed, as far as that goes, still was. Her dark hair was unstreaked with gray, and when she had a color, as she had at this minute, the stern quality of her looks was not so apparent.

Quite subconsciously I wondered whether she had been out, for she was breathing hard, as though she had been running.

"I'm afraid I'm a few minutes early," I said.

"Oh! I don't think so. It's gone half-past seven, Dr. Sheppard." She paused a minute before saying, "I—didn't know you were expected to dinner to-night. Mr. Ackroyd didn't mention it."

I received a vague impression that my dining there displeased her in some way, but I couldn't imagine why.

"How's the knee?" I inquired.

"Much the same, thank you, doctor. I must be going now. Mrs. Ackroyd will be down in a moment. I—I only came in here to see if the flowers were all right."

She passed quickly out of the room. I strolled to the window, wondering at her evident desire to justify her presence in the room. As I did so, I saw what, of course, I might have known all the time had I troubled to give my mind to it, namely, that the windows were long French ones opening on the terrace. The sound I had heard, therefore, could not have been that of a window being shut down.

Quite idly, and more to distract my mind from painful thoughts than for any other reason, I amused myself by trying to guess what could have caused the sound in question.

Coals on the fire? No, that was not the kind of noise at all. A drawer of the bureau pushed in? No, not that.

Then my eye was caught by what, I believe, is called a silver table, the lid of which lifts, and through the glass of which you can see the contents. I crossed over to it, studying the things. There were one or two pieces of old silver, a baby shoe belonging to King Charles the First, some Chinese jade figures, and quite a number of African implements and curios. Wanting to examine one of the jade figures more closely, I lifted the lid. It slipped through my fingers and fell.

At once I recognized the sound I had heard. It was this same table lid being shut down gently and carefully. I repeated the action once or twice for my own satisfaction. Then I lifted the lid to scrutinize the contents more closely.

I was still bending over the open silver table when Flora Ackroyd came into the room.

Quite a lot of people do not like Flora Ackroyd, but nobody can help admiring her. And to her friends she can be very charming. The first thing that strikes you about her is her extraordinary fairness. She has the real Scandinavian pale gold hair. Her eyes are blue—blue as the waters of a Norwegian fiord, and her skin is cream and roses. She has square, boyish shoulders and slight hips. And to a jaded medical man it is very refreshing to come across such perfect health.

A simple straight-forward English girl—I may be old-fashioned, but I think the genuine article takes a lot of beating.

Flora joined me by the silver table, and expressed heretical doubts as to King Charles I ever having worn the baby shoe.

"And anyway," continued Miss Flora, "all this making a fuss about things because some one wore or used them seems to me all nonsense. They're not wearing or using them now. The pen that George Eliot wrote *The Mill on the Floss* with—that sort of thing—well, it's only just a pen after all. If you're really keen on George Eliot, why not get *The Mill on the Floss* in a cheap edition and read it."

"I suppose you never read such old out-of-date stuff, Miss Flora?"

"You're wrong, Dr. Sheppard. I love *The Mill on the Floss*."

I was rather pleased to hear it. The things young women read nowadays and profess to enjoy positively frighten me.

"You haven't congratulated me yet, Dr. Sheppard," said Flora. "Haven't you heard?"

She held out her left hand. On the third finger of it was an exquisitely set single pearl.

"I'm going to marry Ralph, you know," she went on. "Uncle is very pleased. It keeps me in the family, you see."

I took both her hands in mine.

"My dear," I said, "I hope you'll be very happy."

"We've been engaged for about a month," continued Flora in her cool voice, "but it was only announced yesterday. Uncle is going to do up Cross-stones, and give it to us to live in, and we're going to pretend to farm. Really, we shall hunt all the winter, town for the season, and then go yachting. I love the sea. And, of course, I shall take a great interest in the parish affairs, and attend all the Mothers' Meetings."

Just then Mrs. Ackroyd rustled in, full of apologies for being late.

I am sorry to say I detest Mrs. Ackroyd. She is all chains and teeth and bones. A most unpleasant woman. She has small pale flinty blue eyes, and however gushing her words may be, those eyes of hers always remain coldly speculative.

I went across to her, leaving Flora by the window. She gave me a handful of assorted knuckles and rings to squeeze, and began talking volubly.

Had I heard about Flora's engagement? So suitable in every way. The dear young things had fallen in love at first sight. Such a perfect pair, he so dark and she so fair.

"I can't tell you, my dear Dr. Sheppard, the relief to a mother's heart."

Mrs. Ackroyd sighed—a tribute to her mother's heart, whilst her eyes remained shrewdly observant of me.

"I was wondering. You are such an old friend of dear Roger's. We know how much he trusts to your judgment. So difficult for me—in my position, as poor Cecil's widow. But there are so many tiresome things—settlements, you know—all that. I fully believe that Roger intends to make settlements upon dear Flora, but, as you know, he is just a *leetle* peculiar about money. Very usual, I've heard, amongst men who are captains of industry. I wondered, you know, if you could just *sound* him on the subject? Flora is so fond of you. We feel you are quite an old friend, although we have only really known you just over two years."

Mrs. Ackroyd's eloquence was cut short as the drawing-room door opened once more. I was pleased at the interruption. I hate interfering in other people's affairs, and I had not the least intention of tackling Ackroyd on the subject of Flora's settlements. In another moment I should have been forced to tell Mrs. Ackroyd as much.

"You know Major Blunt, don't you, doctor?"

"Yes, indeed," I said.

A lot of people know Hector Blunt—at least by repute. He has shot more wild animals in unlikely places than any man living, I suppose. When you mention him, people say: "Blunt—you don't mean the big game man, do you?"

His friendship with Ackroyd has always puzzled me a little. The two men are so totally dissimilar. Hector Blunt is perhaps five years Ackroyd's junior. They made friends early in life, and though their ways have diverged, the friendship still holds. About once in two years Blunt spends a fortnight at Fernly, and an immense animal's head, with an amazing number of horns which fixes you with a glazed stare as soon as you come inside the front door, is a permanent reminder of the friendship.

Blunt had entered the room now with his own peculiar, deliberate, yet soft-footed tread. He is a man of medium height, sturdily and rather stockily built. His face is almost mahogany-colored, and is peculiarly expressionless. He has gray eyes that give the impression of always watching something that is happening very far away. He talks little, and what he does say is said jerkily, as though the words were forced out of him unwillingly.

He said now: "How are you, Sheppard?" in his usual abrupt fashion, and then stood squarely in front of the fireplace looking over our heads as though he saw something very interesting happening in Timbuctoo.

"Major Blunt," said Flora, "I wish you'd tell me about these African things. I'm sure you know what they all are."

I have heard Hector Blunt described as a woman hater, but I noticed that he joined Flora at the silver table with what might be described as alacrity. They bent over it together.

I was afraid Mrs. Ackroyd would begin talking about settlements again, so I made a few hurried remarks about the new sweet pea. I knew there was a new sweet pea because the *Daily Mail* had told me so that morning. Mrs. Ackroyd knows nothing about horticulture, but she is the kind of woman who likes to appear well-informed about the topics of the day, and she, too, reads the *Daily Mail*. We were able to converse quite intelligently until Ackroyd and his secretary joined us, and immediately afterwards Parker announced dinner.

My place at table was between Mrs. Ackroyd and Flora. Blunt was on Mrs. Ackroyd's other side, and Geoffrey Raymond next to him.

Dinner was not a cheerful affair. Ackroyd was visibly preoccupied. He looked wretched, and ate next to nothing. Mrs. Ackroyd, Raymond, and I kept the conversation going. Flora seemed affected by her uncle's depression, and Blunt relapsed into his usual taciturnity.

Immediately after dinner Ackroyd slipped his arm through mine and led me off to his study.

"Once we've had coffee, we shan't be disturbed again," he

explained. "I told Raymond to see to it that we shouldn't be interrupted."

I studied him quietly without appearing to do so. He was clearly under the influence of some strong excitement. For a minute or two he paced up and down the room, then, as Parker entered with the coffee tray, he sank into an arm-chair in front of the fire.

The study was a comfortable apartment. Book-shelves lined one wall of it. The chairs were big and covered in dark blue leather. A large desk stood by the window and was covered with papers neatly docketed and filed. On a round table were various magazines and sporting papers.

"I've had a return of that pain after food lately," remarked Ackroyd casually, as he helped himself to coffee. "You must give me some more of those tablets of yours."

It struck me that he was anxious to convey the impression that our conference was a medical one. I played up accordingly.

"I thought as much. I brought some up with me."

"Good man. Hand them over now."

"They're in my bag in the hall. I'll get them."

Ackroyd arrested me.

"Don't you trouble. Parker will get them. Bring in the doctor's bag, will you, Parker?"

"Very good, sir."

Parker withdrew. As I was about to speak, Ackroyd threw up his hand.

"Not yet. Wait. Don't you see I'm in such a state of nerves that I can hardly contain myself?"

I saw that plainly enough. And I was very uneasy. All sorts of forebodings assailed me.

Ackroyd spoke again almost immediately.

"Make certain that window's closed, will you?" he asked.

Somewhat surprised, I got up and went to it. It was not a French window, but one of the ordinary sash type. The heavy blue velvet curtains were drawn in front of it, but the window itself was open at the top.

Parker reëntered the room with my bag while I was still at the window.

"That's all right," I said, emerging again into the room.

"You've put the latch across?"

"Yes, yes. What's the matter with you, Ackroyd?"

The door had just closed behind Parker, or I would not have put the question.

Ackroyd waited just a minute before replying.

"I'm in hell," he said slowly, after a minute. "No, don't bother with those damned tablets. I only said that for Parker. Servants are so curious. Come here and sit down. The door's closed too, isn't it?"

"Yes. Nobody can overhear; don't be uneasy."

"Sheppard, nobody knows what I've gone through in the last twenty-four hours. If a man's house ever fell in ruins about him, mine has about me. This business of Ralph's is the last straw. But we won't talk about that now. It's the other—the other——! I don't know what to do about it. And I've got to make up my mind soon."

"What's the trouble?"

Ackroyd remained silent for a minute or two. He seemed curiously averse to begin. When he did speak, the question he asked came as a complete surprise. It was the last thing I expected.

"Sheppard, you attended Ashley Ferrars in his last illness, didn't you?"

"Yes, I did."

He seemed to find even greater difficulty in framing his next question.

"Did you never suspect—did it ever enter your head—that—well, that he might have been poisoned?"

I was silent for a minute or two. Then I made up my mind what to say. Roger Ackroyd was not Caroline.

"I'll tell you the truth," I said. "At the time I had no suspicion whatever, but since—well, it was mere idle talk on my sister's part that first put the idea into my head. Since then I haven't been able to get it out again. But, mind you, I've no foundation whatever for that suspicion."

"He *was* poisoned," said Ackroyd.

He spoke in a dull heavy voice.

"Who by?" I asked sharply.

"His wife."

"How do you know that?"

"She told me so herself."

"When?"

"Yesterday! My God! yesterday! It seems ten years ago."

I waited a minute, and then he went on.

"You understand, Sheppard, I'm telling you this in confidence. It's to go no further. I want your advice—I can't carry the whole weight by myself. As I said just now, I don't know what to do."

"Can you tell me the whole story?" I said. "I'm still in the dark. How did Mrs. Ferrars come to make this confession to you?"

"It's like this. Three months ago I asked Mrs. Ferrars to marry me. She refused. I asked her again and she consented, but she refused to allow me to make the engagement public until her year of mourning was up. Yesterday I called upon her, pointed out that a year and three weeks had now elapsed since her husband's death, and that there could be no further objection to making the engagement public property. I had noticed that she had been very strange in her manner for some days. Now, suddenly, without the least warning, she broke down completely. She—she told me everything. Her hatred of her brute of a husband, her growing love for me, and the—the dreadful means she had taken. Poison! My God! It was murder in cold blood."

I saw the repulsion, the horror, in Ackroyd's face. So Mrs. Ferrars must have seen it. Ackroyd is not the type of the great lover who can forgive all for love's sake. He is fundamentally a good citizen. All that was sound and wholesome and law-abiding

33

in him must have turned from her utterly in that moment of revelation.

"Yes," he went on, in a low, monotonous voice, "she confessed everything. It seems that there is one person who has known all along—who has been blackmailing her for huge sums. It was the strain of that that drove her nearly mad."

"Who was the man?"

Suddenly before my eyes there arose the picture of Ralph Paton and Mrs. Ferrars side by side. Their heads so close together. I felt a momentary throb of anxiety. Supposing—oh! but surely that was impossible. I remembered the frankness of Ralph's greeting that very afternoon. Absurd!

"She wouldn't tell me his name," said Ackroyd slowly. "As a matter of fact, she didn't actually say that it was a man. But of course——"

"Of course," I agreed. "It must have been a man. And you've no suspicion at all?"

For answer Ackroyd groaned and dropped his head into his hands.

"It can't be," he said. "I'm mad even to think of such a thing. No, I won't even admit to you the wild suspicion that crossed my mind. I'll tell you this much, though. Something she said made me think that the person in question might be actually among my household—but that can't be so. I must have misunderstood her."

"What did you say to her?" I asked.

"What could I say? She saw, of course, the awful shock it had been to me. And then there was the question, what was my duty in the matter? She had made me, you see, an accessory after the fact. She saw all that, I think, quicker than I did. I was stunned, you know. She asked me for twenty-four hours—made me promise to do nothing till the end of that time. And she steadfastly refused to give me the name of the scoundrel who had been blackmailing her. I suppose she was afraid that I might go straight off and hammer him, and then the fat would have been in the fire as far as she was concerned. She told me that I should hear from her before twenty-four hours had passed. My God! I swear to you, Sheppard, that it never entered my head what she meant to do. Suicide! And I drove her to it."

"No, no," I said. "Don't take an exaggerated view of things. The responsibility for her death doesn't lie at your door."

"The question is, what am I to do now? The poor lady is dead. Why rake up past trouble?"

"I rather agree with you," I said.

"But there's another point. How am I to get hold of that scoundrel who drove her to death as surely as if he'd killed her. He knew of the first crime, and he fastened on to it like some obscene vulture. She's paid the penalty. Is he to go scot-free?"

"I see," I said slowly. "You want to hunt him down? It will mean a lot of publicity, you know."

"Yes, I've thought of that. I've zigzagged to and fro in my mind."

"I agree with you that the villain ought to be punished, but the cost has got to be reckoned."

Ackroyd rose and walked up and down. Presently he sank into the chair again.

"Look here, Sheppard, suppose we leave it like this. If no word comes from her, we'll let the dead things lie."

"What do you mean by word coming from her?" I asked curiously.

"I have the strongest impression that somewhere or somehow she must have left a message for me—before she went. I can't argue about it, but there it is."

I shook my head.

"She left no letter or word of any kind. I asked."

"Sheppard, I'm convinced that she did. And more, I've a feeling that by deliberately choosing death, she wanted the whole thing to come out, if only to be revenged on the man who drove her to desperation. I believe that if I could have seen her then, she would have told me his name and bid me go for him for all I was worth."

He looked at me.

"You don't believe in impressions?"

"Oh, yes, I do, in a sense. If, as you put it, word should come from her——"

I broke off. The door opened noiselessly and Parker entered with a salver on which were some letters.

"The evening post, sir," he said, handing the salver to Ackroyd.

Then he collected the coffee cups and withdrew.

My attention, diverted for a moment, came back to Ackroyd. He was staring like a man turned to stone at a long blue envelope. The other letters he had let drop to the ground.

"*Her writing*," he said in a whisper. "She must have gone out and posted it last night, just before—before——"

He ripped open the envelope and drew out a thick enclosure. Then he looked up sharply.

"You're sure you shut the window?" he said.

"Quite sure," I said, surprised. "Why?"

"All this evening I've had a queer feeling of being watched, spied upon. What's that——?"

He turned sharply. So did I. We both had the impression of hearing the latch of the door give ever so slightly. I went across to it and opened it. There was no one there.

"Nerves," murmured Ackroyd to himself.

He unfolded the thick sheets of paper, and read aloud in a low voice.

"*My dear, my very dear Roger,—A life calls for a life. I see that—I saw it in your face this afternoon. So I am taking the only road open to me. I leave to you the punishment of the person who has made my life a hell upon earth for the last year. I would not tell you the name this afternoon, but I propose to write it to you now. I have no children or near relations to be spared, so do not fear publicity. If you can, Roger, my very dear Roger, forgive me*

36

the wrong I meant to do you, since when the time came, I could not do it after all...."

Ackroyd, his finger on the sheet to turn it over, paused.

"Sheppard, forgive me, but I must read this alone," he said unsteadily. "It was meant for my eyes, and my eyes only."

He put the letter in the envelope and laid it on the table.

"Later, when I am alone."

"No," I cried impulsively, "read it now."

Ackroyd stared at me in some surprise.

"I beg your pardon," I said, reddening. "I do not mean read it aloud to me. But read it through whilst I am still here."

Ackroyd shook his head.

"No, I'd rather wait."

But for some reason, obscure to myself, I continued to urge him.

"At least, read the name of the man," I said.

Now Ackroyd is essentially pig-headed. The more you urge him to do a thing, the more determined he is not to do it. All my arguments were in vain.

The letter had been brought in at twenty minutes to nine. It was just on ten minutes to nine when I left him, the letter still unread. I hesitated with my hand on the door handle, looking back and wondering if there was anything I had left undone. I could think of nothing. With a shake of the head I passed out and closed the door behind me.

I was startled by seeing the figure of Parker close at hand. He looked embarrassed, and it occurred to me that he might have been listening at the door.

What a fat, smug, oily face the man had, and surely there was something decidedly shifty in his eye.

"Mr. Ackroyd particularly does not want to be disturbed," I said coldly. "He told me to tell you so."

"Quite so, sir. I—I fancied I heard the bell ring."

This was such a palpable untruth that I did not trouble to

reply. Preceding me to the hall, Parker helped me on with my overcoat, and I stepped out into the night. The moon was overcast and everything seemed very dark and still. The village church clock chimed nine o'clock as I passed through the lodge gates. I turned to the left towards the village, and almost cannoned into a man coming in the opposite direction.

"This the way to Fernly Park, mister?" asked the stranger in a hoarse voice.

I looked at him. He was wearing a hat pulled down over his eyes, and his coat collar turned up. I could see little or nothing of his face, but he seemed a young fellow. The voice was rough and uneducated.

"These are the lodge gates here," I said.

"Thank you, mister." He paused, and then added, quite unnecessarily, "I'm a stranger in these parts, you see."

He went on, passing through the gates as I turned to look after him.

The odd thing was that his voice reminded me of some one's voice that I knew, but whose it was I could not think.

Ten minutes later I was at home once more. Caroline was full of curiosity to know why I had returned so early. I had to make up a slightly fictitious account of the evening in order to satisfy her, and I had an uneasy feeling that she saw through the transparent device.

At ten o'clock I rose, yawned, and suggested bed. Caroline acquiesced.

It was Friday night, and on Friday night I wind the clocks. I did it as usual, whilst Caroline satisfied herself that the servants had locked up the kitchen properly.

It was a quarter past ten as we went up the stairs. I had just reached the top when the telephone rang in the hall below.

"Mrs. Bates," said Caroline immediately.

"I'm afraid so," I said ruefully.

I ran down the stairs and took up the receiver.

"What?" I said. "*What?* Certainly, I'll come at once."

I ran upstairs, caught up my bag, and stuffed a few extra dressings into it.

"Parker telephoning," I shouted to Caroline, "from Fernly. They've just found Roger Ackroyd murdered."

FIVE
Murder

I got out the car in next to no time, and drove rapidly to Fernly. Jumping out, I pulled the bell impatiently. There was some delay in answering, and I rang again.

Then I heard the rattle of the chain and Parker, his impassivity of countenance quite unmoved, stood in the open doorway.

I pushed past him into the hall.

"Where is he?" I demanded sharply.

"I beg your pardon, sir?"

"Your master. Mr. Ackroyd. Don't stand there staring at me, man. Have you notified the police?"

"The police, sir? Did you say the police?" Parker stared at me as though I were a ghost.

"What's the matter with you, Parker? If, as you say, your master has been murdered——"

A gasp broke from Parker.

"The master? Murdered? Impossible, sir!"

It was my turn to stare.

"Didn't you telephone to me, not five minutes ago, and tell me that Mr. Ackroyd had been found murdered?"

"Me, sir? Oh! no indeed, sir. I wouldn't dream of doing such a thing."

"Do you mean to say it's all a hoax? That there's nothing the matter with Mr. Ackroyd?"

"Excuse me, sir, did the person telephoning use my name?"

"I'll give you the exact words I heard. *'Is that Dr. Sheppard? Parker, the butler at Fernly, speaking. Will you please come at once, sir. Mr. Ackroyd has been murdered.'*"

Parker and I stared at each other blankly.

"A very wicked joke to play, sir," he said at last, in a shocked tone. "Fancy saying a thing like that."

"Where is Mr. Ackroyd?" I asked suddenly.

"Still in the study, I fancy, sir. The ladies have gone to bed, and Major Blunt and Mr. Raymond are in the billiard room."

"I think I'll just look in and see him for a minute," I said. "I know he didn't want to be disturbed again, but this odd practical joke has made me uneasy. I'd just like to satisfy myself that he's all right."

"Quite so, sir. It makes me feel quite uneasy myself. If you don't object to my accompanying you as far as the door, sir——?"

"Not at all," I said. "Come along."

I passed through the door on the right, Parker on my heels, traversed the little lobby where a small flight of stairs led upstairs to Ackroyd's bedroom, and tapped on the study door.

There was no answer. I turned the handle, but the door was locked.

"Allow me, sir," said Parker.

Very nimbly, for a man of his build, he dropped on one knee and applied his eye to the keyhole.

"Key is in the lock all right, sir," he said, rising. "On the inside. Mr. Ackroyd must have locked himself in and possibly just dropped off to sleep."

I bent down and verified Parker's statement.

"It seems all right," I said, "but, all the same, Parker, I'm going to wake your master up. I shouldn't be satisfied to go home without hearing from his own lips that he's quite all right."

So saying, I rattled the handle and called out, "Ackroyd, Ackroyd, just a minute."

But still there was no answer. I glanced over my shoulder.

"I don't want to alarm the household," I said hesitatingly.

Parker went across and shut the door from the big hall through which we had come.

"I think that will be all right now, sir. The billiard room is at the other side of the house, and so are the kitchen quarters and the ladies' bedrooms."

I nodded comprehendingly. Then I banged once more frantically on the door, and stooping down, fairly bawled through the keyhole:—

"Ackroyd, Ackroyd! It's Sheppard. Let me in."

And still—silence. Not a sign of life from within the locked room. Parker and I glanced at each other.

"Look here, Parker," I said, "I'm going to break this door in—or rather, we are. I'll take the responsibility."

"If you say so, sir," said Parker, rather doubtfully.

"I do say so. I'm seriously alarmed about Mr. Ackroyd."

I looked round the small lobby and picked up a heavy oak chair. Parker and I held it between us and advanced to the assault. Once, twice, and three times we hurled it against the lock. At the third blow it gave, and we staggered into the room.

Ackroyd was sitting as I had left him in the arm-chair before the fire. His head had fallen sideways, and clearly visible, just below the collar of his coat, was a shining piece of twisted metalwork.

Parker and I advanced till we stood over the recumbent figure. I heard the butler draw in his breath with a sharp hiss.

"Stabbed from be'ind," he murmured. "'Orrible!"

He wiped his moist brow with his handkerchief, then stretched out a hand gingerly towards the hilt of the dagger.

"You mustn't touch that," I said sharply. "Go at once to the telephone and ring up the police station. Inform them of what has happened. Then tell Mr. Raymond and Major Blunt."

"Very good, sir."

Parker hurried away, still wiping his perspiring brow.

I did what little had to be done. I was careful not to disturb the position of the body, and not to handle the dagger at all. No object was to be attained by moving it. Ackroyd had clearly been dead some little time.

Then I heard young Raymond's voice, horror-stricken and incredulous, outside.

"What do you say? Oh! impossible! Where's the doctor?"

He appeared impetuously in the doorway, then stopped dead, his face very white. A hand put him aside, and Hector Blunt came past him into the room.

"My God!" said Raymond from behind him; "it's true, then."

Blunt came straight on till he reached the chair. He bent over the body, and I thought that, like Parker, he was going to lay hold of the dagger hilt. I drew him back with one hand.

"Nothing must be moved," I explained. "The police must see him exactly as he is now."

Blunt nodded in instant comprehension. His face was expressionless as ever, but I thought I detected signs of emotion beneath the stolid mask. Geoffrey Raymond had joined us now, and stood peering over Blunt's shoulder at the body.

"This is terrible," he said in a low voice.

He had regained his composure, but as he took off the pince-nez he habitually wore and polished them I observed that his hand was shaking.

"Robbery, I suppose," he said. "How did the fellow get in? Through the window? Has anything been taken?"

He went towards the desk.

"You think it's burglary?" I said slowly.

"What else could it be? There's no question of suicide, I suppose?"

"No man could stab himself in such a way," I said confidently.

"It's murder right enough. But with what motive?"

"Roger hadn't an enemy in the world," said Blunt quietly. "Must have been burglars. But what was the thief after? Nothing seems to be disarranged?"

He looked round the room. Raymond was still sorting the papers on the desk.

"There seems nothing missing, and none of the drawers show signs of having been tampered with," the secretary observed at last. "It's very mysterious."

Blunt made a slight motion with his head.

"There are some letters on the floor here," he said.

I looked down. Three or four letters still lay where Ackroyd had dropped them earlier in the evening.

But the blue envelope containing Mrs. Ferrars's letter had disappeared. I half opened my mouth to speak, but at that moment the sound of a bell pealed through the house. There was a confused murmur of voices in the hall, and then Parker appeared with our local inspector and a police constable.

"Good evening, gentlemen," said the inspector. "I'm terribly sorry for this! A good kind gentleman like Mr. Ackroyd. The butler says it is murder. No possibility of accident or suicide, doctor?"

"None whatever," I said.

"Ah! A bad business."

He came and stood over the body.

"Been moved at all?" he asked sharply.

"Beyond making certain that life was extinct—an easy matter—I have not disturbed the body in any way."

"Ah! And everything points to the murderer having got clear away—for the moment, that is. Now then, let me hear all about it. Who found the body?"

I explained the circumstances carefully.

"A telephone message, you say? From the butler?"

"A message that I never sent," declared Parker earnestly. "I've not been near the telephone the whole evening. The others can bear me out that I haven't."

"Very odd, that. Did it sound like Parker's voice, doctor?"

"Well—I can't say I noticed. I took it for granted, you see."

"Naturally. Well, you got up here, broke in the door, and found poor Mr. Ackroyd like this. How long should you say he had been dead, doctor?"

"Half an hour at least—perhaps longer," I said.

"The door was locked on the inside, you say? What about the window?"

"I myself closed and bolted it earlier in the evening at Mr. Ackroyd's request."

The inspector strode across to it and threw back the curtains.

"Well, it's open now anyway," he remarked.

True enough, the window was open, the lower sash being raised to its fullest extent.

The inspector produced a pocket torch and flashed it along the sill outside.

"This is the way he went all right," he remarked, "*and* got in. See here."

In the light of the powerful torch, several clearly defined footmarks could be seen. They seemed to be those of shoes with rubber studs in the soles. One particularly clear one pointed inwards, another, slightly overlapping it, pointed outwards.

"Plain as a pikestaff," said the inspector. "Any valuables missing?"

Geoffrey Raymond shook his head.

"Not so that we can discover. Mr. Ackroyd never kept anything of particular value in this room."

"H'm," said the inspector. "Man found an open window. Climbed in, saw Mr. Ackroyd sitting there—maybe he'd fallen asleep. Man stabbed him from behind, then lost his nerve and made off. But he's left his tracks pretty clearly. We ought to get hold of *him* without much difficulty. No suspicious strangers been hanging about anywhere?"

"Oh!" I said suddenly.

"What is it, doctor?"

"I met a man this evening—just as I was turning out of the gate. He asked me the way to Fernly Park."

"What time would that be?"

"Just nine o'clock. I heard it chime the hour as I was turning out of the gate."

"Can you describe him?"

I did so to the best of my ability.

The inspector turned to the butler.

"Any one answering that description come to the front door?"

"No, sir. No one has been to the house at all this evening."

"What about the back?"

"I don't think so, sir, but I'll make inquiries."

He moved towards the door, but the inspector held up a large hand.

"No, thanks. I'll do my own inquiring. But first of all I want to fix the time a little more clearly. When was Mr. Ackroyd last seen alive?"

"Probably by me," I said, "when I left at—let me see—about ten minutes to nine. He told me that he didn't wish to be disturbed, and I repeated the order to Parker."

"Just so, sir," said Parker respectfully.

"Mr. Ackroyd was certainly alive at half-past nine," put in Raymond, "for I heard his voice in here talking."

"Who was he talking to?"

"That I don't know. Of course, at the time I took it for granted that it was Dr. Sheppard who was with him. I wanted to ask him a question about some papers I was engaged upon, but when I heard the voices I remembered that he had said he wanted to talk to Dr. Sheppard without being disturbed, and I went away again. But now it seems that the doctor had already left?"

I nodded.

"I was at home by a quarter-past nine," I said. "I didn't go out again until I received the telephone call."

"Who could have been with him at half-past nine?" queried the inspector. "It wasn't you, Mr.—er——"

"Major Blunt," I said.

"Major Hector Blunt?" asked the inspector, a respectful tone creeping into his voice.

Blunt merely jerked his head affirmatively.

"I think we've seen you down here before, sir," said the inspector. "I didn't recognize you for the moment, but you were staying with Mr. Ackroyd a year ago last May."

"June," corrected Blunt.

"Just so, June it was. Now, as I was saying, it wasn't you with Mr. Ackroyd at nine-thirty this evening?"

Blunt shook his head.

"Never saw him after dinner," he volunteered.

The inspector turned once more to Raymond.

"You didn't overhear any of the conversation going on, did you, sir?"

"I did catch just a fragment of it," said the secretary, "and, supposing as I did that it was Dr. Sheppard who was with Mr. Ackroyd, that fragment struck me as distinctly odd. As far as I can remember, the exact words were these. Mr. Ackroyd was speaking. 'The calls on my purse have been so frequent of late'— that is what he was saying—'of late, that I fear it is impossible for me to accede to your request....' I went away again at once, of course, so did not hear any more. But I rather wondered because Dr. Sheppard——"

"——Does not ask for loans for himself or subscriptions for others," I finished.

"A demand for money," said the inspector musingly. "It may be that here we have a very important clew." He turned to the butler. "You say, Parker, that nobody was admitted by the front door this evening?"

"That's what I say, sir."

"Then it seems almost certain that Mr. Ackroyd himself must have admitted this stranger. But I don't quite see——"

The inspector went into a kind of day-dream for some minutes.

"One thing's clear," he said at length, rousing himself from his absorption. "Mr. Ackroyd was alive and well at nine-thirty. That is the last moment at which he is known to have been alive."

Parker gave vent to an apologetic cough which brought the inspector's eyes on him at once.

"Well?" he said sharply.

"If you'll excuse me, sir, Miss Flora saw him after that."

"Miss Flora?"

"Yes, sir. About a quarter to ten that would be. It was after that that she told me Mr. Ackroyd wasn't to be disturbed again to-night."

"Did he send her to you with that message?"

"Not exactly, sir. I was bringing a tray with soda and whisky when Miss Flora, who was just coming out of this room, stopped me and said her uncle didn't want to be disturbed."

The inspector looked at the butler with rather closer attention than he had bestowed on him up to now.

"You'd already been told that Mr. Ackroyd didn't want to be disturbed, hadn't you?"

Parker began to stammer. His hands shook.

"Yes, sir. Yes, sir. Quite so, sir."

"And yet you were proposing to do so?"

"I'd forgotten, sir. At least I mean, I always bring the whisky and soda about that time, sir, and ask if there's anything more, and I thought—well, I was doing as usual without thinking."

It was at this moment that it began to dawn upon me that Parker was most suspiciously flustered. The man was shaking and twitching all over.

"H'm," said the inspector. "I must see Miss Ackroyd at once.

For the moment we'll leave this room exactly as it is. I can return here after I've heard what Miss Ackroyd has to tell me. I shall just take the precaution of shutting and bolting the window."

This precaution accomplished, he led the way into the hall and we followed him. He paused a moment, as he glanced up at the little staircase, then spoke over his shoulder to the constable.

"Jones, you'd better stay here. Don't let any one go into that room."

Parker interposed deferentially.

"If you'll excuse me, sir. If you were to lock the door into the main hall, nobody could gain access to this part. That staircase leads only to Mr. Ackroyd's bedroom and bathroom. There is no communication with the other part of the house. There once was a door through, but Mr. Ackroyd had it blocked up. He liked to feel that his suite was entirely private."

To make things clear and explain the position, I have appended a rough sketch of the right-hand wing of the house. The small staircase leads, as Parker explained, to a big bedroom (made by two being knocked into one) and an adjoining bathroom and lavatory.

The inspector took in the position at a glance. We went through into the large hall and he locked the door behind him, slipping the key into his pocket. Then he gave the constable some low-voiced instructions, and the latter prepared to depart.

"We must get busy on those shoe tracks," explained the inspector. "But first of all, I must have a word with Miss Ackroyd. She was the last person to see her uncle alive. Does she know yet?"

Raymond shook his head.

"Well, no need to tell her for another five minutes. She can answer my questions better without being upset by knowing the truth about her uncle. Tell her there's been a burglary, and ask her if she would mind dressing and coming down to answer a few questions."

It was Raymond who went upstairs on this errand.

"Miss Ackroyd will be down in a minute," he said, when he returned. "I told her just what you suggested."

In less than five minutes Flora descended the staircase. She was wrapped in a pale pink silk kimono. She looked anxious and excited.

The inspector stepped forward.

"Good-evening, Miss Ackroyd," he said civilly. "We're afraid there's been an attempt at robbery, and we want you to help us. What's this room—the billiard room? Come in here and sit down."

Flora sat down composedly on the wide divan which ran the length of the wall, and looked up at the inspector.

"I don't quite understand. What has been stolen? What do you want me to tell you?"

"It's just this, Miss Ackroyd. Parker here says you came out of your uncle's study at about a quarter to ten. Is that right?"

"Quite right. I had been to say good-night to him."

"And the time is correct?"

"Well, it must have been about then. I can't say exactly. It might have been later."

"Was your uncle alone, or was there any one with him?"

"He was alone. Dr. Sheppard had gone."

"Did you happen to notice whether the window was open or shut?"

Flora shook her head.

"I can't say. The curtains were drawn."

"Exactly. And your uncle seemed quite as usual?"

"I think so."

"Do you mind telling us exactly what passed between you?"

Flora paused a minute, as though to collect her recollections.

"I went in and said, 'Good-night, uncle, I'm going to bed now. I'm tired to-night.' He gave a sort of grunt, and—I went over and kissed him, and he said something about my looking nice in the frock I had on, and then he told me to run away as he was busy. So I went."

"Did he ask specially not to be disturbed?"

"Oh! yes, I forgot. He said: 'Tell Parker I don't want anything more to-night, and that he's not to disturb me.' I met Parker just outside the door and gave him uncle's message."

"Just so," said the inspector.

"Won't you tell me what it is that has been stolen?"

"We're not quite—certain," said the inspector hesitatingly.

A wide look of alarm came into the girl's eyes. She started up.

"What is it? You're hiding something from me?"

Moving in his usual unobtrusive manner, Hector Blunt came between her and the inspector. She half stretched out her hand, and he took it in both of his, patting it as though she were a very small child, and she turned to him as though something in his stolid, rocklike demeanor promised comfort and safety.

"It's bad news, Flora," he said quietly. "Bad news for all of us. Your Uncle Roger——"

"Yes?"

"It will be a shock to you. Bound to be. Poor Roger's dead."

Flora drew away from him, her eyes dilating with horror.

"When?" she whispered. "When?"

"Very soon after you left him, I'm afraid," said Blunt gravely.

Flora raised her hand to her throat, gave a little cry, and I hurried to catch her as she fell. She had fainted, and Blunt and I carried her upstairs and laid her on her bed. Then I got him to wake Mrs. Ackroyd and tell her the news. Flora soon revived, and I brought her mother to her, telling her what to do for the girl. Then I hurried downstairs again.

SIX
The Tunisian Dagger

I met the inspector just coming from the door which led into the kitchen quarters.

"How's the young lady, doctor?"

"Coming round nicely. Her mother's with her."

"That's good. I've been questioning the servants. They all declare that no one has been to the back door tonight. Your description of that stranger was rather vague. Can't you give us something more definite to go upon?"

"I'm afraid not," I said regretfully. "It was a dark night, you see, and the fellow had his coat collar well pulled up and his hat squashed down over his eyes."

"H'm," said the inspector. "Looked as though he wanted to conceal his face. Sure it was no one you know?"

I replied in the negative, but not as decidedly as I might have done. I remembered my impression that the stranger's voice was not unfamiliar to me. I explained this rather haltingly to the inspector.

"It was a rough, uneducated voice, you say?"

I agreed, but it occurred to me that the roughness had been of an almost exaggerated quality. If, as the inspector thought, the man had wished to hide his face, he might equally well have tried to disguise his voice.

"Do you mind coming into the study with me again, doctor? There are one or two things I want to ask you."

I acquiesced. Inspector Davis unlocked the door of the lobby, we passed through, and he locked the door again behind him.

"We don't want to be disturbed," he said grimly. "And we don't want any eavesdropping either. What's all this about blackmail?"

"Blackmail!" I exclaimed, very much startled.

"Is it an effort of Parker's imagination? Or is there something in it?"

"If Parker heard anything about blackmail," I said slowly, "he must have been listening outside this door with his ear glued against the keyhole."

Davis nodded.

"Nothing more likely. You see, I've been instituting a few inquiries as to what Parker has been doing with himself this evening. To tell the truth, I didn't like his manner. The man knows something. When I began to question him, he got the wind up, and plumped out some garbled story of blackmail."

I took an instant decision.

"I'm rather glad you've brought the matter up," I said. "I've been trying to decide whether to make a clean breast of things or not. I'd already practically decided to tell you everything, but I was going to wait for a favorable opportunity. You might as well have it now."

And then and there I narrated the whole events of the evening as I have set them down here. The inspector listened keenly, occasionally interjecting a question.

"Most extraordinary story I ever heard," he said, when I had finished. "And you say that letter has completely disappeared? It looks bad—it looks very bad indeed. It gives us what we've been looking for—a motive for the murder."

I nodded.

"I realize that."

"You say that Mr. Ackroyd hinted at a suspicion he had that some member of his household was involved? Household's rather an elastic term."

"You don't think that Parker himself might be the man we're after?" I suggested.

"It looks very like it. He was obviously listening at the door when you came out. Then Miss Ackroyd came across him later bent on entering the study. Say he tried again when she was safely out of the way. He stabbed Ackroyd, locked the door on the inside, opened the window, and got out that way, and went round to a side door which he had previously left open. How's that?"

"There's only one thing against it," I said slowly. "If Ackroyd went on reading that letter as soon as I left, as he intended to do, I don't see him continuing to sit on here and turn things over in his mind for another hour. He'd have had Parker in at once, accused him then and there, and there would have been a fine old uproar. Remember, Ackroyd was a man of choleric temper."

"Mightn't have had time to go on with the letter just then," suggested the inspector. "We know some one was with him at half-past nine. If that visitor turned up as soon as you left, and after he went, Miss Ackroyd came in to say good-night—well, he wouldn't be able to go on with the letter until close upon ten o'clock."

"And the telephone call?"

"Parker sent that all right—perhaps before he thought of the locked door and open window. Then he changed his mind—or got in a panic—and decided to deny all knowledge of it. That was it, depend upon it."

"Ye-es," I said rather doubtfully.

"Anyway, we can find out the truth about the telephone call from the exchange. If it was put through from here, I don't see how any one else but Parker could have sent it. Depend upon it, he's our man. But keep it dark—we don't want to alarm him just yet, till we've got all the evidence. I'll see to it he doesn't give us the slip. To all appearances we'll be concentrating on your mysterious stranger."

He rose from where he had been sitting astride the chair belonging to the desk, and crossed over to the still form in the arm-chair.

"The weapon ought to give us a clew," he remarked, looking up. "It's something quite unique—a curio, I should think, by the look of it."

He bent down, surveying the handle attentively, and I heard him give a grunt of satisfaction. Then, very gingerly, he pressed his hands down below the hilt and drew the blade out from the wound. Still carrying it so as not to touch the handle, he placed it in a wide china mug which adorned the mantelpiece.

"Yes," he said, nodding at it. "Quite a work of art. There can't be many of them about."

It was indeed a beautiful object. A narrow, tapering blade, and a hilt of elaborately intertwined metals of curious and careful workmanship. He touched the blade gingerly with his finger, testing its sharpness, and made an appreciative grimace.

"Lord, what an edge," he exclaimed. "A child could drive that into a man—as easy as cutting butter. A dangerous sort of toy to have about."

"May I examine the body properly now?" I asked.

He nodded.

"Go ahead."

I made a thorough examination.

"Well?" said the inspector, when I had finished.

"I'll spare you the technical language," I said. "We'll keep that for the inquest. The blow was delivered by a right-handed man standing behind him, and death must have been instantaneous. By the expression on the dead man's face, I should say that the blow was quite unexpected. He probably died without knowing who his assailant was."

"Butlers can creep about as soft-footed as cats," said Inspector Davis. "There's not going to be much mystery about this crime. Take a look at the hilt of that dagger."

I took the look.

"I dare say they're not apparent to you, but I can see them clearly enough." He lowered his voice. *"Fingerprints!"*

He stood off a few steps to judge of his effect.

"Yes," I said mildly. "I guessed that."

I do not see why I should be supposed to be totally devoid of intelligence. After all, I read detective stories, and the newspapers, and am a man of quite average ability. If there had been toe marks on the dagger handle, now, that would have been quite a different thing. I would then have registered any amount of surprise and awe.

I think the inspector was annoyed with me for declining to get thrilled. He picked up the china mug and invited me to accompany him to the billiard room.

"I want to see if Mr. Raymond can tell us anything about this dagger," he explained.

Locking the outer door behind us again, we made our way to the billiard room, where we found Geoffrey Raymond. The inspector held up his exhibit.

"Ever seen this before, Mr. Raymond?"

"Why—I believe—I'm almost sure that is a curio given to Mr. Ackroyd by Major Blunt. It comes from Morocco—no, Tunis. So the crime was committed with that? What an extraordinary thing. It seems almost impossible, and yet there could hardly be two daggers the same. May I fetch Major Blunt?"

Without waiting for an answer, he hurried off.

"Nice young fellow that," said the inspector. "Something honest and ingenuous about him."

I agreed. In the two years that Geoffrey Raymond has been secretary to Ackroyd, I have never seen him ruffled or out of temper. And he has been, I know, a most efficient secretary.

In a minute or two Raymond returned, accompanied by Blunt.

"I was right," said Raymond excitedly. "It *is* the Tunisian dagger."

"Major Blunt hasn't looked at it yet," objected the inspector.

"Saw it the moment I came into the study," said the quiet man.

"You recognized it then?"

Blunt nodded.

"You said nothing about it," said the inspector suspiciously.

"Wrong moment," said Blunt. "Lot of harm done by blurting out things at the wrong time."

He returned the inspector's stare placidly enough.

The latter grunted at last and turned away. He brought the dagger over to Blunt.

"You're quite sure about it, sir. You identify it positively?"

"Absolutely. No doubt whatever."

"Where was this—er—curio usually kept? Can you tell me that, sir?"

It was the secretary who answered.

"In the silver table in the drawing-room."

"What?" I exclaimed.

The others looked at me.

"Yes, doctor?" said the inspector encouragingly.

"It's nothing."

"Yes, doctor?" said the inspector again, still more encouragingly.

"It's so trivial," I explained apologetically. "Only that when I arrived last night for dinner I heard the lid of the silver table being shut down in the drawing-room."

I saw profound skepticism and a trace of suspicion on the inspector's countenance.

"How did you know it was the silver table lid?"

I was forced to explain in detail—a long, tedious explanation which I would infinitely rather not have had to make.

The inspector heard me to the end.

"Was the dagger in its place when you were looking over the contents?" he asked.

"I don't know," I said. "I can't say I remember noticing it—but, of course, it may have been there all the time."

"We'd better get hold of the housekeeper," remarked the inspector, and pulled the bell.

A few minutes later Miss Russell, summoned by Parker, entered the room.

"I don't think I went near the silver table," she said, when the inspector had posed his question. "I was looking to see that all the flowers were fresh. Oh! yes, I remember now. The silver table was open—which it had no business to be, and I shut the lid down as I passed."

She looked at him aggressively.

"I see," said the inspector. "Can you tell me if this dagger was in its place then?"

Miss Russell looked at the weapon composedly.

"I can't say, I'm sure," she replied. "I didn't stop to look. I knew the family would be down any minute, and I wanted to get away."

"Thank you," said the inspector.

There was just a trace of hesitation in his manner, as though he would have liked to question her further, but Miss Russell clearly accepted the words as a dismissal, and glided from the room.

"Rather a Tartar, I should fancy, eh?" said the inspector, looking after her. "Let me see. This silver table is in front of one of the windows, I think you said, doctor?"

Raymond answered for me.

"Yes, the left-hand window."

"And the window was open?"

"They were both ajar."

"Well, I don't think we need go into the question much further. Somebody—I'll just say somebody—could get that dagger any time he liked, and exactly when he got it doesn't matter in the least. I'll be coming up in the morning with the chief constable, Mr. Raymond. Until then, I'll keep the key of that door. I want Colonel Melrose to see everything exactly as it is. I happen to know that he's dining out the other side of the county, and, I believe, staying the night...."

We watched the inspector take up the jar.

"I shall have to pack this carefully," he observed. "It's going to be an important piece of evidence in more ways than one."

A few minutes later as I came out of the billiard room with Raymond, the latter gave a low chuckle of amusement.

I felt the pressure of his hand on my arm, and followed the direction of his eyes. Inspector Davis seemed to be inviting Parker's opinion of a small pocket diary.

"A little obvious," murmured my companion. "So Parker is the suspect, is he? Shall we oblige Inspector Davis with a set of our fingerprints also?"

He took two cards from the card tray, wiped them with his silk handkerchief, then handed one to me and took the other himself. Then, with a grin, he handed them to the police inspector.

"Souvenirs," he said. "No. 1, Dr. Sheppard; No. 2, my humble self. One from Major Blunt will be forthcoming in the morning."

Youth is very buoyant. Even the brutal murder of his friend and employer could not dim Geoffrey Raymond's spirits for long. Perhaps that is as it should be. I do not know. I have lost the quality of resilience long since myself.

It was very late when I got back, and I hoped that Caroline would have gone to bed. I might have known better.

She had hot cocoa waiting for me, and whilst I drank it, she extracted the whole history of the evening from me. I said nothing of the blackmailing business, but contented myself with giving her the facts of the murder.

"The police suspect Parker," I said, as I rose to my feet and prepared to ascend to bed. "There seems a fairly clear case against him."

"Parker!" said my sister. "Fiddlesticks! That inspector must be a perfect fool. Parker indeed! Don't tell me."

With which obscure pronouncement we went up to bed.

SEVEN
I Learn My Neighbor's Profession

On the following morning I hurried unforgivably over my round. My excuse can be that I had no very serious cases to attend. On my return Caroline came into the hall to greet me.

"Flora Ackroyd is here," she announced in an excited whisper.

"What?"

I concealed my surprise as best I could.

"She's very anxious to see you. She's been here half an hour."

Caroline led the way into our small sitting-room, and I followed.

Flora was sitting on the sofa by the window. She was in black and she sat nervously twisting her hands together. I was shocked by the sight of her face. All the color had faded away from it. But when she spoke her manner was as composed and resolute as possible.

"Dr. Sheppard, I have come to ask you to help me."

"Of course he'll help you, my dear," said Caroline.

I don't think Flora really wished Caroline to be present at the interview. She would, I am sure, have infinitely preferred to speak to me privately. But she also wanted to waste no time, so she made the best of it.

"I want you to come to The Larches with me."

"The Larches?" I queried, surprised.

"To see that funny little man?" exclaimed Caroline.

"Yes. You know who he is, don't you?"

"We fancied," I said, "that he might be a retired hairdresser."
Flora's blue eyes opened very wide.

"Why, he's Hercule Poirot! You know who I mean—the private detective. They say he's done the most wonderful things—just like detectives do in books. A year ago he retired and came to live down here. Uncle knew who he was, but he promised not to tell any one, because M. Poirot wanted to live quietly without being bothered by people."

"So that's who he is," I said slowly.

"You've heard of him, of course?"

"I'm rather an old fogey, as Caroline tells me," I said, "but I *have* just heard of him."

"Extraordinary!" commented Caroline.

I don't know what she was referring to—possibly her own failure to discover the truth.

"You want to go and see him?" I asked slowly. "Now why?"

"To get him to investigate this murder, of course," said Caroline sharply. "Don't be so stupid, James."

I was not really being stupid. Caroline does not always understand what I am driving at.

"You haven't got confidence in Inspector Davis?" I went on.

"Of course she hasn't," said Caroline. "I haven't either."

Any one would have thought it was Caroline's uncle who had been murdered.

"And how do you know he would take up the case?" I asked. "Remember he has retired from active work."

"That's just it," said Flora simply. "I've got to persuade him."

"You are sure you are doing wisely?" I asked gravely.

"Of course she is," said Caroline. "I'll go with her myself if she likes."

"I'd rather the doctor came with me if you don't mind, Miss

Sheppard," said Flora.

She knows the value of being direct on certain occasions. Any hints would certainly have been wasted on Caroline.

"You see," she explained, following directness with tact, "Dr. Sheppard being the doctor, and having found the body, he would be able to give all the details to M. Poirot."

"Yes," said Caroline grudgingly, "I see that."

I took a turn or two up and down the room.

"Flora," I said gravely, "be guided by me. I advise you not to drag this detective into the case."

Flora sprang to her feet. The color rushed into her cheeks.

"I know why you say that," she cried. "But it's exactly for that reason I'm so anxious to go. You're afraid! But I'm not. I know Ralph better than you do."

"Ralph," said Caroline. "What has Ralph got to do with it?"

Neither of us heeded her.

"Ralph may be weak," continued Flora. "He may have done foolish things in the past—wicked things even—but he wouldn't murder any one."

"No, no," I exclaimed. "I never thought it of him."

"Then why did you go to the Three Boars last night?" demanded Flora, "on your way home—after uncle's body was found?"

I was momentarily silenced. I had hoped that that visit of mine would remain unnoticed.

"How did you know about that?" I countered.

"I went there this morning," said Flora. "I heard from the servants that Ralph was staying there——"

I interrupted her.

"You had no idea that he was in King's Abbot?"

"No. I was astounded. I couldn't understand it. I went there and asked for him. They told me, what I suppose they told you last night, that he went out at about nine o'clock yesterday evening—and—and never came back."

Her eyes met mine defiantly, and as though answering

something in my look, she burst out:—

"Well, why shouldn't he? He might have gone—anywhere. He may even have gone back to London."

"Leaving his luggage behind?" I asked gently.

Flora stamped her foot.

"I don't care. There must be a simple explanation."

"And that's why you want to go to Hercule Poirot? Isn't it better to leave things as they are? The police don't suspect Ralph in the least, remember. They're working on quite another tack."

"But that's just *it*," cried the girl. "They *do* suspect him. A man from Cranchester turned up this morning—Inspector Raglan, a horrid, weaselly little man. I found he had been to the Three Boars this morning before me. They told me all about his having been there, and the questions he had asked. He must think Ralph did it."

"That's a change of mind from last night, if so," I said slowly. "He doesn't believe in Davis's theory that it was Parker then?"

"Parker indeed," said my sister, and snorted.

Flora came forward and laid her hand on my arm.

"Oh! Dr. Sheppard, let us go at once to this M. Poirot. He will find out the truth."

"My dear Flora," I said gently, laying my hand on hers. "Are you quite sure it is the truth we want?"

She looked at me, nodding her head gravely.

"You're not sure," she said. "I am. I know Ralph better than you do."

"Of course he didn't do it," said Caroline, who had been keeping silent with great difficulty. "Ralph may be extravagant, but he's a dear boy, and has the nicest manners."

I wanted to tell Caroline that large numbers of murderers have had nice manners, but the presence of Flora restrained me. Since the girl was determined, I was forced to give in to her and we started at once, getting away before my sister was able to fire off any more pronouncements beginning with her favorite words, "Of course."

An old woman with an immense Breton cap opened the door of The Larches to us. M. Poirot was at home, it seemed.

We were ushered into a little sitting-room arranged with formal precision, and there, after the lapse of a minute or so, my friend of yesterday came to us.

"Monsieur le docteur," he said, smiling. "Mademoiselle."

He bowed to Flora.

"Perhaps," I began, "you have heard of the tragedy which occurred last night."

His face grew grave.

"But certainly I have heard. It is horrible. I offer mademoiselle all my sympathy. In what way can I serve you?"

"Miss Ackroyd," I said, "wants you to—to———"

"To find the murderer," said Flora in a clear voice.

"I see," said the little man. "But the police will do that, will they not?"

"They might make a mistake," said Flora. "They are on their way to make a mistake now, I think. Please, M. Poirot, won't you help us? If—if it is a question of money———"

Poirot held up his hand.

"Not that, I beg of you, mademoiselle. Not that I do not care for money." His eyes showed a momentary twinkle. "Money, it means much to me and always has done. No, if I go into this, you must understand one thing clearly. *I shall go through with it to the end.* The good dog, he does not leave the scent, remember! You may wish that, after all, you had left it to the local police."

"I want the truth," said Flora, looking him straight in the eyes.

"All the truth?"

"All the truth."

"Then I accept," said the little man quietly. "And I hope you will not regret those words. Now, tell me all the circumstances."

"Dr. Sheppard had better tell you," said Flora. "He knows more than I do."

Thus enjoined, I plunged into a careful narrative, embodying all the facts I have previously set down. Poirot listened carefully, inserting a question here and there, but for the most part sitting in silence, his eyes on the ceiling.

I brought my story to a close with the departure of the inspector and myself from Fernly Park the previous night.

"And now," said Flora, as I finished, "tell him all about Ralph."

I hesitated, but her imperious glance drove me on.

"You went to this inn—this Three Boars—last night on your way home?" asked Poirot, as I brought my tale to a close. "Now exactly why was that?"

I paused a moment to choose my words carefully.

"I thought some one ought to inform the young man of his uncle's death. It occurred to me after I had left Fernly that possibly no one but myself and Mr. Ackroyd were aware that he was staying in the village."

Poirot nodded.

"Quite so. That was your only motive in going there, eh?"

"That was my only motive," I said stiffly.

"It was not to—shall we say—reassure yourself about *ce jeune homme*?"

"Reassure myself?"

"I think, M. le docteur, that you know very well what I mean, though you pretend not to do so. I suggest that it would have been a relief to you if you had found that Captain Paton had been at home all the evening."

"Not at all," I said sharply.

The little detective shook his head at me gravely.

"You have not the trust in me of Miss Flora," he said. "But no matter. What we have to look at is this—Captain Paton is missing, under circumstances which call for an explanation. I will not hide from you that the matter looks grave. Still, it may admit of a perfectly simple explanation."

"That's just what I keep saying," cried Flora eagerly.

Poirot touched no more upon that theme. Instead he suggested an immediate visit to the local police. He thought it better for Flora to return home, and for me to be the one to accompany him there and introduce him to the officer in charge of the case.

We carried out this plan forthwith. We found Inspector Davis outside the police station looking very glum indeed. With him was Colonel Melrose, the Chief Constable, and another man whom, from Flora's description of "weaselly," I had no difficulty in recognizing as Inspector Raglan from Cranchester.

I know Melrose fairly well, and I introduced Poirot to him and explained the situation. The chief constable was clearly vexed, and Inspector Raglan looked as black as thunder. Davis, however, seemed slightly exhilarated by the sight of his superior officer's annoyance.

"The case is going to be plain as a pikestaff," said Raglan. "Not the least need for amateurs to come butting in. You'd think any fool would have seen the way things were last night, and then we shouldn't have lost twelve hours."

He directed a vengeful glance at poor Davis, who received it with perfect stolidity.

"Mr. Ackroyd's family must, of course, do what they see fit," said Colonel Melrose. "But we cannot have the official investigation hampered in any way. I know M. Poirot's great reputation, of course," he added courteously.

"The police can't advertise themselves, worse luck," said Raglan.

It was Poirot who saved the situation.

"It is true that I have retired from the world," he said. "I never intended to take up a case again. Above all things, I have a horror of publicity. I must beg, that in the case of my being able to contribute something to the solution of the mystery, my name may not be mentioned."

Inspector Raglan's face lightened a little.

"I've heard of some very remarkable successes of yours," observed the colonel, thawing.

"I have had much experience," said Poirot quietly. "But most of my successes have been obtained by the aid of the police. I admire enormously your English police. If Inspector Raglan permits me to assist him, I shall be both honored and flattered."

The inspector's countenance became still more gracious.

Colonel Melrose drew me aside.

"From all I hear, this little fellow's done some really remarkable things," he murmured. "We're naturally anxious not to have to call in Scotland Yard. Raglan seems very sure of himself, but I'm not quite certain that I agree with him. You see, I—er—know the parties concerned better than he does. This fellow doesn't seem out after kudos, does he? Would work in with us unobtrusively, eh?"

"To the greater glory of Inspector Raglan," I said solemnly.

"Well, well," said Colonel Melrose breezily in a louder voice, "we must put you wise to the latest developments, M. Poirot."

"I thank you," said Poirot. "My friend, Dr. Sheppard, said something of the butler being suspected?"

"That's all bunkum," said Raglan instantly. "These high-class servants get in such a funk that they act suspiciously for nothing at all."

"The fingerprints?" I hinted.

"Nothing like Parker's." He gave a faint smile, and added: "And yours and Mr. Raymond's don't fit either, doctor."

"What about those of Captain Ralph Paton?" asked Poirot quietly.

I felt a secret admiration for the way he took the bull by the horns. I saw a look of respect creep into the inspector's eye.

"I see you don't let the grass grow under your feet, Mr. Poirot.

It will be a pleasure to work with you, I'm sure. We're going to take that young gentleman's fingerprints as soon as we can lay hands upon him."

"I can't help thinking you're mistaken, inspector," said Colonel Melrose warmly. "I've known Ralph Paton from a boy upward. He'd never stoop to murder."

"Maybe not," said the inspector tonelessly.

"What have you got against him?" I asked.

"Went out just on nine o'clock last night. Was seen in neighborhood of Fernly Park somewhere about nine-thirty. Not been seen since. Believed to be in serious money difficulties. I've got a pair of his shoes here—shoes with rubber studs in them. He had two pairs, almost exactly alike. I'm going up now to compare them with those footmarks. The constable is up there seeing that no one tampers with them."

"We'll go at once," said Colonel Melrose. "You and M. Poirot will accompany us, will you not?"

We assented, and all drove up in the colonel's car. The inspector was anxious to get at once to the footmarks, and asked to be put down at the lodge. About half-way up the drive, on the right, a path branched off which led round to the terrace and the window of Ackroyd's study.

"Would you like to go with the inspector, M. Poirot?" asked the chief constable, "or would you prefer to examine the study?"

Poirot chose the latter alternative. Parker opened the door to us. His manner was smug and deferential, and he seemed to have recovered from his panic of the night before.

Colonel Melrose took a key from his pocket, and unlocking the door which led into the lobby, he ushered us through into the study.

"Except for the removal of the body, M. Poirot, this room is exactly as it was last night."

"And the body was found—where?"

As precisely as possible, I described Ackroyd's position. The arm-chair still stood in front of the fire.

Poirot went and sat down in it.

"The blue letter you speak of, where was it when you left the room?"

"Mr. Ackroyd had laid it down on this little table at his right hand."

Poirot nodded.

"Except for that, everything was in its place?"

"Yes, I think so."

"Colonel Melrose, would you be so extremely obliging as to sit down in this chair a minute. I thank you. Now, M. le docteur, will you kindly indicate to me the exact position of the dagger?"

I did so, whilst the little man stood in the doorway.

"The hilt of the dagger was plainly visible from the door then. Both you and Parker could see it at once?"

"Yes."

Poirot went next to the window.

"The electric light was on, of course, when you discovered the body?" he asked over his shoulder.

I assented, and joined him where he was studying the marks on the window-sill.

"The rubber studs are the same pattern as those in Captain Paton's shoes," he said quietly.

Then he came back once more to the middle of the room. His eye traveled round, searching everything in the room with a quick, trained glance.

"Are you a man of good observation, Dr. Sheppard?" he asked at last.

"I think so," I said, surprised.

"There was a fire in the grate, I see. When you broke the door down and found Mr. Ackroyd dead, how was the fire? Was it low?"

I gave a vexed laugh.

"I—I really can't say. I didn't notice. Perhaps Mr. Raymond

or Major Blunt——"

The little man opposite me shook his head with a faint smile.

"One must always proceed with method. I made an error of judgment in asking you that question. To each man his own knowledge. You could tell me the details of the patient's appearance—nothing there would escape you. If I wanted information about the papers on that desk, Mr. Raymond would have noticed anything there was to see. To find out about the fire, I must ask the man whose business it is to observe such things. You permit——"

He moved swiftly to the fireplace and rang the bell.

After a lapse of a minute or two Parker appeared.

"The bell rang, sir," he said hesitatingly.

"Come in, Parker," said Colonel Melrose. "This gentleman wants to ask you something."

Parker transferred a respectful attention to Poirot.

"Parker," said the little man, "when you broke down the door with Dr. Sheppard last night, and found your master dead, what was the state of the fire?"

Parker replied without a pause.

"It had burned very low, sir. It was almost out."

"Ah!" said Poirot. The exclamation sounded almost triumphant. He went on:—

"Look round you, my good Parker. Is this room exactly as it was then?"

The butler's eye swept round. It came to rest on the windows.

"The curtains were drawn, sir, and the electric light was on."

Poirot nodded approval.

"Anything else?"

"Yes, sir, this chair was drawn out a little more."

He indicated a big grandfather chair to the left of the door between it and the window. I append a plan of the room with the chair in question marked with an X.

"Just show me," said Poirot.

The butler drew the chair in question out a good two feet from the wall, turning it so that the seat faced the door.

"*Voilà ce qui est curieux*," murmured Poirot. "No one would want to sit in a chair in such a position, I fancy. Now who pushed it back into place again, I wonder? Did you, my friend?"

"No, sir," said Parker. "I was too upset with seeing the master and all."

Poirot looked across at me.

"Did you, doctor?"

I shook my head.

"It was back in position when I arrived with the police, sir," put in Parker. "I'm sure of that."

"Curious," said Poirot again.

"Raymond or Blunt must have pushed it back," I suggested. "Surely it isn't important?"

"It is completely unimportant," said Poirot. "That is why it is so interesting," he added softly.

"Excuse me a minute," said Colonel Melrose. He left the room with Parker.

"Do you think Parker is speaking the truth?" I asked.

"About the chair, yes. Otherwise I do not know. You will find, M. le docteur, if you have much to do with cases of this kind, that they all resemble each other in one thing."

"What is that?" I asked curiously.

"Every one concerned in them has something to hide."

"Have I?" I asked, smiling.

Poirot looked at me attentively.

"I think you have," he said quietly.

"But——"

"Have you told me everything known to you about this young man Paton?" He smiled as I grew red. "Oh! do not fear. I will not press you. I shall learn it in good time."

"I wish you'd tell me something of your methods," I said hastily, to cover my confusion. "The point about the fire, for instance?"

"Oh! that was very simple. You leave Mr. Ackroyd at—ten minutes to nine, was it not?"

"Yes, exactly, I should say."

"The window is then closed and bolted and the door unlocked. At a quarter past ten when the body is discovered, the door is locked and the window is open. Who opened it? Clearly only Mr. Ackroyd himself could have done so, and for one of two reasons. Either because the room became unbearably hot (but since the fire was nearly out and there was a sharp drop in temperature last night, that cannot be the reason), or because he admitted some one that way. And if he admitted some one that way, it must have been some one well known to him, since he had previously shown himself uneasy on the subject of that same window."

"It sounds very simple," I said.

"Everything is simple, if you arrange the facts methodically. We are concerned now with the personality of the person who was with him at nine-thirty last night. Everything goes to show that

that was the individual admitted by the window, and though Mr. Ackroyd was seen alive later by Miss Flora, we cannot approach a solution of the mystery until we know who that visitor was. The window may have been left open after his departure and so afforded entrance to the murderer, or the same person may have returned a second time. Ah! here is the colonel who returns."

Colonel Melrose entered with an animated manner.

"That telephone call has been traced at last," he said. "It did not come from here. It was put through to Dr. Sheppard at 10.15 last night from a public call office at King's Abbot station. And at 10.23 the night mail leaves for Liverpool."

EIGHT
Inspector Raglan Is Confident

We looked at each other.

"You'll have inquiries made at the station, of course?" I said.

"Naturally, but I'm not over sanguine as to the result. You know what that station is like."

I did. King's Abbot is a mere village, but its station happens to be an important junction. Most of the big expresses stop there, and trains are shunted, re-sorted, and made up. It has two or three public telephone boxes. At that time of night three local trains come in close upon each other, to catch the connection with the express for the north which comes in at 10.19 and leaves at 10.23. The whole place is in a bustle, and the chances of one particular person being noticed telephoning or getting into the express are very small indeed.

"But why telephone at all?" demanded Melrose. "That is what I find so extraordinary. There seems no rhyme or reason in the thing."

Poirot carefully straightened a china ornament on one of the bookcases.

"Be sure there was a reason," he said over his shoulder.

"But what reason could it be?"

"When we know that, we shall know everything. This case is very curious and very interesting."

76

There was something almost indescribable in the way he said those last words. I felt that he was looking at the case from some peculiar angle of his own, and what he saw I could not tell.

He went to the window and stood there, looking out.

"You say it was nine o'clock, Dr. Sheppard, when you met this stranger outside the gate?"

He asked the question without turning round.

"Yes," I replied. "I heard the church clock chime the hour."

"How long would it take him to reach the house—to reach this window, for instance?"

"Five minutes at the outside. Two or three minutes only if he took the path at the right of the drive and came straight here."

"But to do that he would have to know the way. How can I explain myself?—it would mean that he had been here before— that he knew his surroundings."

"That is true," replied Colonel Melrose.

"We could find out, doubtless, if Mr. Ackroyd had received any strangers during the past week?"

"Young Raymond could tell us that," I said.

"Or Parker," suggested Colonel Melrose.

"*Ou tous les deux*," suggested Poirot, smiling.

Colonel Melrose went in search of Raymond, and I rang the bell once more for Parker.

Colonel Melrose returned almost immediately, accompanied by the young secretary, whom he introduced to Poirot. Geoffrey Raymond was fresh and debonair as ever. He seemed surprised and delighted to make Poirot's acquaintance.

"No idea you'd been living among us incognito, M. Poirot," he said. "It will be a great privilege to watch you at work——Hallo, what's this?"

Poirot had been standing just to the left of the door. Now he moved aside suddenly, and I saw that while my back was turned he must have swiftly drawn out the arm-chair till it stood in the position Parker had indicated.

"Want me to sit in the chair whilst you take a blood test?" asked Raymond good-humoredly. "What's the idea?"

"M. Raymond, this chair was pulled out—so—last night when Mr. Ackroyd was found killed. Some one moved it back again into place. Did you do so?"

The secretary's reply came without a second's hesitation.

"No, indeed I didn't. I don't even remember that it was in that position, but it must have been if you say so. Anyway, somebody else must have moved it back to its proper place. Have they destroyed a clew in doing so? Too bad!"

"It is of no consequence," said the detective. "Of no consequence whatever. What I really want to ask you is this, M. Raymond: Did any stranger come to see Mr. Ackroyd during this past week?"

The secretary reflected for a minute or two, knitting his brows, and during the pause Parker appeared in answer to the bell.

"No," said Raymond at last. "I can't remember any one. Can you, Parker?"

"I beg your pardon, sir?"

"Any stranger coming to see Mr. Ackroyd this week?"

The butler reflected for a minute or two.

"There was the young man who came on Wednesday, sir," he said at last. "From Curtis and Troute, I understood he was."

Raymond moved this aside with an impatient hand.

"Oh! yes, I remember, but that is not the kind of stranger this gentleman means." He turned to Poirot. "Mr. Ackroyd had some idea of purchasing a dictaphone," he explained. "It would have enabled us to get through a lot more work in a limited time. The firm in question sent down their representative, but nothing came of it. Mr. Ackroyd did not make up his mind to purchase."

Poirot turned to the butler.

"Can you describe this young man to me, my good Parker?"

"He was fair-haired, sir, and short. Very neatly dressed in a blue serge suit. A very presentable young man, sir, for his station in life."

Poirot turned to me.

"The man you met outside the gate, doctor, was tall, was he not?"

"Yes," I said. "Somewhere about six feet, I should say."

"There is nothing in that, then," declared the Belgian. "I thank you, Parker."

The butler spoke to Raymond.

"Mr. Hammond has just arrived, sir," he said. "He is anxious to know if he can be of any service, and he would be glad to have a word with you."

"I'll come at once," said the young man. He hurried out. Poirot looked inquiringly at the chief constable.

"The family solicitor, M. Poirot," said the latter.

"It is a busy time for this young M. Raymond," murmured M. Poirot. "He has the air efficient, that one."

"I believe Mr. Ackroyd considered him a most able secretary."

"He has been here—how long?"

"Just on two years, I fancy."

"His duties he fulfills punctiliously. Of that I am sure. In what manner does he amuse himself? Does he go in for *le sport*?"

"Private secretaries haven't much time for that sort of thing," said Colonel Melrose, smiling. "Raymond plays golf, I believe. And tennis in the summer time."

"He does not attend the courses—I should say the running of the horses?"

"Race meetings? No, I don't think he's interested in racing."

Poirot nodded and seemed to lose interest. He glanced slowly round the study.

"I have seen, I think, all that there is to be seen here."

I, too, looked round.

"If those walls could speak," I murmured.

Poirot shook his head.

"A tongue is not enough," he said. "They would have to have also eyes and ears. But do not be too sure that these dead things"—he touched the top of the bookcase as he spoke—"are always dumb. To me they speak sometimes—chairs, tables—they have their message!"

He turned away towards the door.

"What message?" I cried. "What have they said to you to-day?"

He looked over his shoulder and raised one eyebrow quizzically.

"An opened window," he said. "A locked door. A chair that apparently moved itself. To all three I say, 'Why?' and I find no answer."

He shook his head, puffed out his chest, and stood blinking at us. He looked ridiculously full of his own importance. It crossed my mind to wonder whether he was really any good as a detective. Had his big reputation been built up on a series of lucky chances?

I think the same thought must have occurred to Colonel Melrose, for he frowned.

"Anything more you want to see, M. Poirot?" he inquired brusquely.

"You would perhaps be so kind as to show me the silver table from which the weapon was taken? After that, I will trespass on your kindness no longer."

We went to the drawing-room, but on the way the constable waylaid the colonel, and after a muttered conversation the latter excused himself and left us together. I showed Poirot the silver table, and after raising the lid once or twice and letting it fall, he pushed open the window and stepped out on the terrace. I followed him.

Inspector Raglan had just turned the corner of the house, and was coming towards us. His face looked grim and satisfied.

"So there you are, M. Poirot," he said. "Well, this isn't going to be much of a case. I'm sorry, too. A nice enough young fellow gone wrong."

Poirot's face fell, and he spoke very mildly.

"I'm afraid I shall not be able to be of much aid to you, then?"

"Next time, perhaps," said the inspector soothingly. "Though we don't have murders every day in this quiet little corner of the world."

Poirot's gaze took on an admiring quality.

"You have been of a marvelous promptness," he observed. "How exactly did you go to work, if I may ask?"

"Certainly," said the inspector. "To begin with—method. That's what I always say—method!"

"Ah!" cried the other. "That, too, is my watchword. Method, order, and the little gray cells."

"The cells?" said the inspector, staring.

"The little gray cells of the brain," explained the Belgian.

"Oh, of course; well, we all use them, I suppose."

"In a greater or lesser degree," murmured Poirot. "And there are, too, differences in quality. Then there is the psychology of a crime. One must study that."

"Ah!" said the inspector, "you've been bitten with all this psychoanalysis stuff? Now, I'm a plain man——"

"Mrs. Raglan would not agree, I am sure, to that," said Poirot, making him a little bow.

Inspector Raglan, a little taken aback, bowed.

"You don't understand," he said, grinning broadly. "Lord, what a lot of difference language makes. I'm telling you how I set to work. First of all, method. Mr. Ackroyd was last seen alive at a quarter to ten by his niece, Miss Flora Ackroyd. That's fact number one, isn't it?"

"If you say so."

"Well, it is. At half-past ten, the doctor here says that Mr. Ackroyd has been dead at least half an hour. You stick to that, doctor?"

"Certainly," I said. "Half an hour or longer."

"Very good. That gives us exactly a quarter of an hour in which

81

the crime must have been committed. I make a list of every one in the house, and work through it, setting down opposite their names where they were and what they were doing between the hour of 9.45 and 10 p.m."

He handed a sheet of paper to Poirot. I read it over his shoulder. It ran as follows, written in a neat script:—

Major Blunt.—In billiard room with Mr. Raymond. (Latter confirms.)

Mr. Raymond.—Billiard room. (See above.)

Mrs. Ackroyd.—9.45 watching billiard match. Went up to bed 9.55. (Raymond and Blunt watched her up staircase.)

Miss Ackroyd.—Went straight from her uncle's room upstairs. (Confirmed by Parker, also housemaid, Elsie Dale.)

Servants:—

Parker.—Went straight to butler's pantry. (Confirmed by housekeeper, Miss Russell, who came down to speak to him about something at 9.47, and remained at least ten minutes.)

Miss Russell.—As above. Spoke to housemaid, Elsie Dale, upstairs at 9.45.

Ursula Bourne (parlormaid).—In her own room until 9.55. Then in Servants' Hall.

Mrs. Cooper (cook).—In Servants' Hall.

Gladys Jones (second housemaid).—In Servants' Hall.

Elsie Dale.—Upstairs in bedroom. Seen there by Miss Russell and Miss Flora Ackroyd.

Mary Thripp (kitchenmaid).—Servants' Hall.

"The cook has been here seven years, the parlormaid eighteen months, and Parker just over a year. The others are new. Except for something fishy about Parker, they all seem quite all right."

"A very complete list," said Poirot, handing it back to him. "I am quite sure that Parker did not do the murder," he added gravely.

"So is my sister," I struck in. "And she's usually right." Nobody paid any attention to my interpolation.

"That disposes pretty effectually of the household," continued the inspector. "Now we come to a very grave point. The woman at the lodge—Mary Black—was pulling the curtains last night when she saw Ralph Paton turn in at the gate and go up towards the house."

"She is sure of that?" I asked sharply.

"Quite sure. She knows him well by sight. He went past very quickly and turned off by the path to the right, which is a short cut to the terrace."

"And what time was that?" asked Poirot, who had sat with an immovable face.

"Exactly twenty-five minutes past nine," said the inspector gravely.

There was a silence. Then the inspector spoke again.

"It's all clear enough. It fits in without a flaw. At twenty-five minutes past nine, Captain Paton is seen passing the lodge; at nine-thirty or thereabouts, Mr. Geoffrey Raymond hears some one in here asking for money and Mr. Ackroyd refusing. What happens next? Captain Paton leaves the same way—through the window. He walks along the terrace, angry and baffled. He comes to the open drawing-room window. Say it's now a quarter to ten. Miss Flora Ackroyd is saying good-night to her uncle. Major Blunt, Mr. Raymond, and Mrs. Ackroyd are in the billiard room. The drawing-room is empty. He steals in, takes the dagger from the silver table, and returns to the study window. He slips off his shoes, climbs in, and—well, I don't need to go into details. Then he slips out again and goes off. Hadn't the nerve to go back to the inn. He makes for the station, rings up from there——"

"Why?" said Poirot softly.

I jumped at the interruption. The little man was leaning forward. His eyes shone with a queer green light.

For a moment Inspector Raglan was taken aback by the question.

"It's difficult to say exactly why he did that," he said at last.

"But murderers do funny things. You'd know that if you were in the police force. The cleverest of them make stupid mistakes sometimes. But come along and I'll show you those footprints."

We followed him round the corner of the terrace to the study window. At a word from Raglan a police constable produced the shoes which had been obtained from the local inn.

The inspector laid them over the marks.

"They're the same," he said confidently. "That is to say, they're not the same pair that actually made these prints. He went away in those. This is a pair just like them, but older—see how the studs are worn down."

"Surely a great many people wear shoes with rubber studs in them?" asked Poirot.

"That's so, of course," said the inspector. "I shouldn't put so much stress on the footmarks if it wasn't for everything else."

"A very foolish young man, Captain Ralph Paton," said Poirot thoughtfully. "To leave so much evidence of his presence."

"Ah! well," said the inspector, "it was a dry, fine night, you know. He left no prints on the terrace or on the graveled path. But, unluckily for him, a spring must have welled up just lately at the end of the path from the drive. See here."

A small graveled path joined the terrace a few feet away. In one spot, a few yards from its termination, the ground was wet and boggy. Crossing this wet place there were again the marks of footsteps, and amongst them the shoes with rubber studs.

Poirot followed the path on a little way, the inspector by his side.

"You noticed the women's footprints?" he said suddenly.

The inspector laughed.

"Naturally. But several different women have walked this way—and men as well. It's a regular short cut to the house, you see. It would be impossible to sort out all the footsteps. After all, it's the ones on the window-sill that are really important."

Poirot nodded.

"It's no good going farther," said the inspector, as we came in view of the drive. "It's all graveled again here, and hard as it can be."

Again Poirot nodded, but his eyes were fixed on a small garden house—a kind of superior summer-house. It was a little to the left of the path ahead of us, and a graveled walk ran up to it.

Poirot lingered about until the inspector had gone back towards the house. Then he looked at me.

"You must have indeed been sent from the good God to replace my friend Hastings," he said, with a twinkle. "I observe that you do not quit my side. How say you, Dr. Sheppard, shall we investigate that summer-house? It interests me."

He went up to the door and opened it. Inside, the place was almost dark. There were one or two rustic seats, a croquet set, and some folded deck-chairs.

I was startled to observe my new friend. He had dropped to his hands and knees and was crawling about the floor. Every now and then he shook his head as though not satisfied. Finally, he sat back on his heels.

"Nothing," he murmured. "Well, perhaps it was not to be expected. But it would have meant so much——"

He broke off, stiffening all over. Then he stretched out his hand to one of the rustic chairs. He detached something from one side of it.

"What is it?" I cried. "What have you found?"

He smiled, unclosing his hand so that I should see what lay in the palm of it. A scrap of stiff white cambric.

I took it from him, looked at it curiously, and then handed it back.

"What do you make of it, eh, my friend?" he asked, eyeing me keenly.

"A scrap torn from a handkerchief," I suggested, shrugging my shoulders.

He made another dart and picked up a small quill—a goose

quill by the look of it.

"And that?" he cried triumphantly. "What do you make of that?"

I only stared.

He slipped the quill into his pocket, and looked again at the scrap of white stuff.

"A fragment of a handkerchief?" he mused. "Perhaps you are right. But remember this—*a good laundry does not starch a handkerchief.*"

He nodded at me triumphantly, then he put away the scrap carefully in his pocket-book.

NINE
The Goldfish Pond

We walked back to the house together. There was no sign of the inspector. Poirot paused on the terrace and stood with his back to the house, slowly turning his head from side to side.

"*Une belle propriété*," he said at last appreciatively. "Who inherits it?"

His words gave me almost a shock. It is an odd thing, but until that moment the question of inheritance had never come into my head. Poirot watched me keenly.

"It is a new idea to you, that," he said at last. "You had not thought of it before—eh?"

"No," I said truthfully. "I wish I had."

He looked at me again curiously.

"I wonder just what you mean by that," he said thoughtfully. "Ah! no," as I was about to speak. "*Inutile!* You would not tell me your real thought."

"Every one has something to hide," I quoted, smiling.

"Exactly."

"You still believe that?"

"More than ever, my friend. But it is not easy to hide things from Hercule Poirot. He has a knack of finding out."

He descended the steps of the Dutch garden as he spoke.

"Let us walk a little," he said over his shoulder. "The air is pleasant to-day."

I followed him. He led me down a path to the left enclosed in yew hedges. A walk led down the middle, bordered each side with formal flower beds, and at the end was a round paved recess with a seat and a pond of goldfish. Instead of pursuing the path to the end, Poirot took another which wound up the side of a wooded slope. In one spot the trees had been cleared away, and a seat had been put. Sitting there one had a splendid view over the countryside, and one looked right down on the paved recess and the goldfish pond.

"England is very beautiful," said Poirot, his eyes straying over the prospect. Then he smiled. "And so are English girls," he said in a lower tone. "Hush, my friend, and look at the pretty picture below us."

It was then that I saw Flora. She was moving along the path we had just left and she was humming a little snatch of song. Her step was more dancing than walking, and in spite of her black dress, there was nothing but joy in her whole attitude. She gave a sudden pirouette on her toes, and her black draperies swung out. At the same time she flung her head back and laughed outright.

As she did so a man stepped out from the trees. It was Hector Blunt.

The girl started. Her expression changed a little.

"How you startled me—I didn't see you."

Blunt said nothing, but stood looking at her for a minute or two in silence.

"What I like about you," said Flora, with a touch of malice, "is your cheery conversation."

I fancy that at that Blunt reddened under his tan. His voice, when he spoke, sounded different—it had a curious sort of humility in it.

"Never was much of a fellow for talking. Not even when I was young."

"That was a very long time ago, I suppose," said Flora gravely.

I caught the undercurrent of laughter in her voice, but I don't think Blunt did.

"Yes," he said simply, "it was."

"How does it feel to be Methuselah?" asked Flora.

This time the laughter was more apparent, but Blunt was following out an idea of his own.

"Remember the Johnny who sold his soul to the devil? In return for being made young again? There's an opera about it."

"Faust, you mean?"

"That's the beggar. Rum story. Some of us would do it if we could."

"Any one would think you were creaking at the joints to hear you talk," cried Flora, half vexed, half amused.

Blunt said nothing for a minute or two. Then he looked away from Flora into the middle distance and observed to an adjacent tree trunk that it was about time he got back to Africa.

"Are you going on another expedition—shooting things?"

"Expect so. Usually do, you know—shoot things, I mean."

"You shot that head in the hall, didn't you?"

Blunt nodded. Then he jerked out, going rather red, as he did so:—

"Care for some decent skins any time? If so, I could get 'em for you."

"Oh! please do," cried Flora. "Will you really? You won't forget?"

"I shan't forget," said Hector Blunt.

He added, in a sudden burst of communicativeness:—

"Time I went. I'm no good in this sort of life. Haven't got the manners for it. I'm a rough fellow, no use in society. Never remember the things one's expected to say. Yes, time I went."

"But you're not going at once," cried Flora. "Not—not while we're in all this trouble. Oh! please. If you go——"

She turned away a little.

89

"You want me to stay?" asked Blunt.

He spoke deliberately but quite simply.

"We all——"

"I meant you personally," said Blunt, with directness.

Flora turned slowly back again and met his eyes.

"I want you to stay," she said, "if—if that makes any difference."

"It makes all the difference," said Blunt.

There was a moment's silence. They sat down on the stone seat by the goldfish pond. It seemed as though neither of them knew quite what to say next.

"It—it's such a lovely morning," said Flora at last. "You know, I can't help feeling happy, in spite—in spite of everything. That's awful, I suppose?"

"Quite natural," said Blunt. "Never saw your uncle until two years ago, did you? Can't be expected to grieve very much. Much better to have no humbug about it."

"There's something awfully consoling about you," said Flora. "You make things so simple."

"Things are simple as a rule," said the big game hunter.

"Not always," said Flora.

Her voice had lowered itself, and I saw Blunt turn and look at her, bringing his eyes back from (apparently) the coast of Africa to do so. He evidently put his own construction on her change of tone, for he said, after a minute or two, in rather an abrupt manner:—

"I say, you know, you mustn't worry. About that young chap, I mean. Inspector's an ass. Everybody knows—utterly absurd to think he could have done it. Man from outside. Burglar chap. That's the only possible solution."

Flora turned to look at him.

"You really think so?"

"Don't you?" said Blunt quickly.

"I—oh, yes, of course."

Another silence, and then Flora burst out:—

"I'm—I'll tell you why I felt so happy this morning. However heartless you think me, I'd rather tell you. It's because the lawyer has been—Mr. Hammond. He told us about the will. Uncle Roger has left me twenty thousand pounds. Think of it—twenty thousand beautiful pounds."

Blunt looked surprised.

"Does it mean so much to you?"

"Mean much to me? Why, it's everything. Freedom—life—no more scheming and scraping and lying——"

"Lying?" said Blunt, sharply interrupting.

Flora seemed taken aback for a minute.

"You know what I mean," she said uncertainly. "Pretending to be thankful for all the nasty castoff things rich relations give you. Last year's coats and skirts and hats."

"Don't know much about ladies' clothes; should have said you were always very well turned out."

"It's cost me something, though," said Flora in a low voice. "Don't let's talk of horrid things. I'm so happy. I'm free. Free to do what I like. Free not to——"

She stopped suddenly.

"Not to what?" asked Blunt quickly.

"I forget now. Nothing important."

Blunt had a stick in his hand, and he thrust it into the pond, poking at something.

"What are you doing, Major Blunt?"

"There's something bright down there. Wondered what it was—looks like a gold brooch. Now I've stirred up the mud and it's gone."

"Perhaps it's a crown," suggested Flora. "Like the one Mélisande saw in the water."

"Mélisande," said Blunt reflectively—"she's in an opera, isn't she?"

"Yes, you seem to know a lot about operas."

"People take me sometimes," said Blunt sadly. "Funny idea

of pleasure—worse racket than the natives make with their tom-toms."

Flora laughed.

"I remember Mélisande," continued Blunt, "married an old chap old enough to be her father."

He threw a small piece of flint into the goldfish pond. Then, with a change of manner, he turned to Flora.

"Miss Ackroyd, can I do anything? About Paton, I mean. I know how dreadfully anxious you must be."

"Thank you," said Flora in a cold voice. "There is really nothing to be done. Ralph will be all right. I've got hold of the most wonderful detective in the world, and he's going to find out all about it."

For some time I had felt uneasy as to our position. We were not exactly eavesdropping, since the two in the garden below had only to lift their heads to see us. Nevertheless, I should have drawn attention to our presence before now, had not my companion put a warning pressure on my arm. Clearly he wished me to remain silent.

But now he rose briskly to his feet, clearing his throat.

"I demand pardon," he cried. "I cannot allow mademoiselle thus extravagantly to compliment me, and not draw attention to my presence. They say the listener hears no good of himself, but that is not the case this time. To spare my blushes, I must join you and apologize."

He hurried down the path with me close behind him, and joined the others by the pond.

"This is M. Hercule Poirot," said Flora. "I expect you've heard of him."

Poirot bowed.

"I know Major Blunt by reputation," he said politely. "I am glad to have encountered you, monsieur. I am in need of some information that you can give me."

Blunt looked at him inquiringly.

"When did you last see M. Ackroyd alive?"

"At dinner."

"And you neither saw nor heard anything of him after that?"

"Didn't see him. Heard his voice."

"How was that?"

"I strolled out on the terrace——"

"Pardon me, what time was this?"

"About half-past nine. I was walking up and down smoking in front of the drawing-room window. I heard Ackroyd talking in his study——"

Poirot stooped and removed a microscopic weed.

"Surely you couldn't hear voices in the study from that part of the terrace," he murmured.

He was not looking at Blunt, but I was, and to my intense surprise, I saw the latter flush.

"Went as far as the corner," he explained unwillingly.

"Ah! indeed?" said Poirot.

In the mildest manner he conveyed an impression that more was wanted.

"Thought I saw—a woman disappearing into the bushes. Just a gleam of white, you know. Must have been mistaken. It was while I was standing at the corner of the terrace that I heard Ackroyd's voice speaking to that secretary of his."

"Speaking to Mr. Geoffrey Raymond?"

"Yes—that's what I supposed at the time. Seems I was wrong."

"Mr. Ackroyd didn't address him by name?"

"Oh, no."

"Then, if I may ask, why did you think——?"

Blunt explained laboriously.

"Took it for granted that it *would* be Raymond, because he had said just before I came out that he was taking some papers to Ackroyd. Never thought of it being anybody else."

"Can you remember what the words you heard were?"

"Afraid I can't. Something quite ordinary and unimportant.

Only caught a scrap of it. I was thinking of something else at the time."

"It is of no importance," murmured Poirot. "Did you move a chair back against the wall when you went into the study after the body was discovered?"

"Chair? No—why should I?"

Poirot shrugged his shoulders but did not answer. He turned to Flora.

"There is one thing I should like to know from you, mademoiselle. When you were examining the things in the silver table with Dr. Sheppard, was the dagger in its place, or was it not?"

Flora's chin shot up.

"Inspector Raglan has been asking me that," she said resentfully. "I've told him, and I'll tell you. I'm perfectly certain the dagger was *not* there. He thinks it was and that Ralph sneaked it later in the evening. And—and he doesn't believe me. He thinks I'm saying it to—to shield Ralph."

"And aren't you?" I asked gravely.

Flora stamped her foot.

"You, too, Dr. Sheppard! Oh! it's too bad."

Poirot tactfully made a diversion.

"It is true what I heard you say, Major Blunt. There is something that glitters in this pond. Let us see if I can reach it."

He knelt down by the pond, baring his arm to the elbow, and lowered it in very slowly, so as not to disturb the bottom of the pond. But in spite of all his precautions the mud eddied and swirled, and he was forced to draw his arm out again empty-handed.

He gazed ruefully at the mud upon his arm. I offered him my handkerchief, which he accepted with fervent protestations of thanks. Blunt looked at his watch.

"Nearly lunch time," he said. "We'd better be getting back to the house."

"You will lunch with us, M. Poirot?" asked Flora. "I should like you to meet my mother. She is—very fond of Ralph."

The little man bowed.

"I shall be delighted, mademoiselle."

"And you will stay, too, won't you, Dr. Sheppard?"

I hesitated.

"Oh, do!"

I wanted to, so I accepted the invitation without further ceremony.

We set out towards the house, Flora and Blunt walking ahead.

"What hair," said Poirot to me in a low tone, nodding towards Flora. "The real gold! They will make a pretty couple. She and the dark, handsome Captain Paton. Will they not?"

I looked at him inquiringly, but he began to fuss about a few microscopic drops of water on his coat sleeve. The man reminded me in some ways of a cat. His green eyes and his finicking habits.

"And all for nothing, too," I said sympathetically. "I wonder what it was in the pond?"

"Would you like to see?" asked Poirot.

I stared at him. He nodded.

"My good friend," he said gently and reproachfully, "Hercule Poirot does not run the risk of disarranging his costume without being sure of attaining his object. To do so would be ridiculous and absurd. I am never ridiculous."

"But you brought your hand out empty," I objected.

"There are times when it is necessary to have discretion. Do you tell your patients everything—everything, doctor? I think not. Nor do you tell your excellent sister everything either, is it not so? Before showing my empty hand, I dropped what it contained into my other hand. You shall see what that was."

He held out his left hand, palm open. On it lay a little circlet of gold. A woman's wedding ring.

I took it from him.

"Look inside," commanded Poirot.

I did so. Inside was an inscription in fine writing:—

From R., March 13th.

I looked at Poirot, but he was busy inspecting his appearance in a tiny pocket glass. He paid particular attention to his mustaches, and none at all to me. I saw that he did not intend to be communicative.

TEN
The Parlormaid

We found Mrs. Ackroyd in the hall. With her was a small dried-up little man, with an aggressive chin and sharp gray eyes, and "lawyer" written all over him.

"Mr. Hammond is staying to lunch with us," said Mrs. Ackroyd. "You know Major Blunt, Mr. Hammond? And dear Dr. Sheppard—also a close friend of poor Roger's. And, let me see——"

She paused, surveying Hercule Poirot in some perplexity.

"This is M. Poirot, mother," said Flora. "I told you about him this morning."

"Oh! yes," said Mrs. Ackroyd vaguely. "Of course, my dear, of course. He is to find Ralph, is he not?"

"He is to find out who killed uncle," said Flora.

"Oh! my dear," cried her mother. "Please! My poor nerves. I am a wreck this morning, a positive wreck. Such a dreadful thing to happen. I can't help feeling that it must have been an accident of some kind. Roger was so fond of handling queer curios. His hand must have slipped, or something."

This theory was received in polite silence. I saw Poirot edge up to the lawyer, and speak to him in a confidential undertone. They moved aside into the embrasure of the window. I joined them—then hesitated.

"Perhaps I'm intruding," I said.

"Not at all," cried Poirot heartily. "You and I, M. le docteur, we investigate this affair side by side. Without you I should be lost. I desire a little information from the good Mr. Hammond."

"You are acting on behalf of Captain Ralph Paton, I understand," said the lawyer cautiously.

Poirot shook his head.

"Not so. I am acting in the interests of justice. Miss Ackroyd has asked me to investigate the death of her uncle."

Mr. Hammond seemed slightly taken aback.

"I cannot seriously believe that Captain Paton can be concerned in this crime," he said, "however strong the circumstantial evidence against him may be. The mere fact that he was hard pressed for money——"

"Was he hard pressed for money?" interpolated Poirot quickly.

The lawyer shrugged his shoulders.

"It was a chronic condition with Ralph Paton," he said dryly. "Money went through his hands like water. He was always applying to his stepfather."

"Had he done so of late? During the last year, for instance?"

"I cannot say. Mr. Ackroyd did not mention the fact to me."

"I comprehend. Mr. Hammond, I take it that you are acquainted with the provisions of Mr. Ackroyd's will?"

"Certainly. That is my principal business here to-day."

"Then, seeing that I am acting for Miss Ackroyd, you will not object to telling me the terms of that will?"

"They are quite simple. Shorn of legal phraseology, and after paying certain legacies and bequests——"

"Such as——?" interrupted Poirot.

Mr. Hammond seemed a little surprised.

"A thousand pounds to his housekeeper, Miss Russell; fifty pounds to the cook, Emma Cooper; five hundred pounds to his secretary, Mr. Geoffrey Raymond. Then to various hospitals——"

Poirot held up his hand.

"Ah! the charitable bequests, they interest me not."

"Quite so. The income on ten thousand pounds' worth of shares to be paid to Mrs. Cecil Ackroyd during her lifetime. Miss Flora Ackroyd inherits twenty thousand pounds outright. The residue—including this property, and the shares in Ackroyd and Son—to his adopted son, Ralph Paton."

"Mr. Ackroyd possessed a large fortune?"

"A very large fortune. Captain Paton will be an exceedingly wealthy young man."

There was a silence. Poirot and the lawyer looked at each other.

"Mr. Hammond," came Mrs. Ackroyd's voice plaintively from the fireplace.

The lawyer answered the summons. Poirot took my arm and drew me right into the window.

"Regard the irises," he remarked in rather a loud voice. "Magnificent, are they not? A straight and pleasing effect."

At the same time I felt the pressure of his hand on my arm, and he added in a low tone:—

"Do you really wish to aid me? To take part in this investigation?"

"Yes, indeed," I said eagerly. "There's nothing I should like better. You don't know what a dull old fogey's life I lead. Never anything out of the ordinary."

"Good, we will be colleagues then. In a minute or two I fancy Major Blunt will join us. He is not happy with the good mamma. Now there are some things I want to know—but I do not wish to seem to want to know them. You comprehend? So it will be your part to ask the questions."

"What questions do you want me to ask?" I asked apprehensively.

"I want you to introduce the name of Mrs. Ferrars."

"Yes?"

"Speak of her in a natural fashion. Ask him if he was down here when her husband died. You understand the kind of thing

I mean. And while he replies, watch his face without seeming to watch it. *C'est compris?*"

There was no time for more, for at that minute, as Poirot had prophesied, Blunt left the others in his abrupt fashion and came over to us.

I suggested strolling on the terrace, and he acquiesced. Poirot stayed behind.

I stopped to examine a late rose.

"How things change in the course of a day or so," I observed. "I was up here last Wednesday, I remember, walking up and down this same terrace. Ackroyd was with me—full of spirits. And now—three days later—Ackroyd's dead, poor fellow, Mrs. Ferrars's dead—you knew her, didn't you? But of course you did."

Blunt nodded his head.

"Had you seen her since you'd been down this time?"

"Went with Ackroyd to call. Last Tuesday, think it was. Fascinating woman—but something queer about her. Deep—one would never know what she was up to."

I looked into his steady gray eyes. Nothing there surely. I went on:—

"I suppose you'd met her before."

"Last time I was here—she and her husband had just come here to live." He paused a minute and then added: "Rum thing, she had changed a lot between then and now."

"How—changed?" I asked.

"Looked ten years older."

"Were you down here when her husband died?" I asked, trying to make the question sound as casual as possible.

"No. From all I heard it would be a good riddance. Uncharitable, perhaps, but the truth."

I agreed.

"Ashley Ferrars was by no means a pattern husband," I said cautiously.

"Blackguard, I thought," said Blunt.

100

"No," I said, "only a man with more money than was good for him."

"Oh! money! All the troubles in the world can be put down to money—or the lack of it."

"Which has been your particular trouble?" I asked.

"I've enough for what I want. I'm one of the lucky ones."

"Indeed."

"I'm not too flush just now, as a matter of fact. Came into a legacy a year ago, and like a fool let myself be persuaded into putting it into some wild-cat scheme."

I sympathized, and narrated my own similar trouble.

Then the gong pealed out, and we all went in to lunch. Poirot drew me back a little.

"*Eh! bien?*"

"He's all right," I said. "I'm sure of it."

"Nothing—disturbing?"

"He had a legacy just a year ago," I said. "But why not? Why shouldn't he? I'll swear the man is perfectly square and aboveboard."

"Without doubt, without doubt," said Poirot soothingly. "Do not upset yourself."

He spoke as though to a fractious child.

We all trooped into the dining-room. It seemed incredible that less than twenty-four hours had passed since I last sat at that table.

Afterwards, Mrs. Ackroyd took me aside and sat down with me on a sofa.

"I can't help feeling a little hurt," she murmured, producing a handkerchief of the kind obviously not meant to be cried into. "Hurt, I mean, by Roger's lack of confidence in me. That twenty thousand pounds ought to have been left to *me*—not to Flora. A mother could be trusted to safeguard the interests of her child. A lack of trust, I call it."

"You forget, Mrs. Ackroyd," I said, "Flora was Ackroyd's own niece, a blood relation. It would have been different had you been his sister instead of his sister-in-law."

"As poor Cecil's widow, I think my feelings ought to have been considered," said the lady, touching her eye-lashes gingerly with the handkerchief. "But Roger was always most peculiar—not to say *mean*—about money matters. It has been a most difficult position for both Flora and myself. He did not even give the poor child an allowance. He would pay her bills, you know, and even that with a good deal of reluctance and asking what she wanted all those fal-lals for—so like a man—but—now I've forgotten what it was I was going to say! Oh, yes, not a penny we could call our own, you know. Flora resented it—yes, I must say she resented it—very strongly. Though devoted to her uncle, of course. But any girl would have resented it. Yes, I must say Roger had very strange ideas about money. He wouldn't even buy new face towels, though I told him the old ones were in holes. And then," proceeded Mrs. Ackroyd, with a sudden leap highly characteristic of her conversation, "to leave all that money—a thousand pounds—fancy, a thousand pounds!—to that woman."

"What woman?"

"That Russell woman. Something very queer about her, and so I've always said. But Roger wouldn't hear a word against her. Said she was a woman of great force of character, and that he admired and respected her. He was always going on about her rectitude and independence and moral worth. *I* think there's something fishy about her. She was certainly doing her best to marry Roger. But I soon put a stop to that. She's always hated me. Naturally. *I* saw through her."

I began to wonder if there was any chance of stemming Mrs. Ackroyd's eloquence, and getting away.

Mr. Hammond provided the necessary diversion by coming up to say good-by. I seized my chance and rose also.

"About the inquest," I said. "Where would you prefer it to be held. Here, or at the Three Boars?"

Mrs. Ackroyd stared at me with a dropped jaw.

"The inquest?" she asked, the picture of consternation. "But surely there won't have to be an inquest?"

Mr. Hammond gave a dry little cough and murmured, "Inevitable. Under the circumstances," in two short little barks.

"But surely Dr. Sheppard can arrange——"

"There are limits to my powers of arrangement," I said dryly.

"If his death was an accident——"

"He was murdered, Mrs. Ackroyd," I said brutally.

She gave a little cry.

"No theory of accident will hold water for a minute."

Mrs. Ackroyd looked at me in distress. I had no patience with what I thought was her silly fear of unpleasantness.

"If there's an inquest, I—I shan't have to answer questions and all that, shall I?" she asked.

"I don't know what will be necessary," I answered. "I imagine Mr. Raymond will take the brunt of it off you. He knows all the circumstances, and can give formal evidence of identification."

The lawyer assented with a little bow.

"I really don't think there is anything to dread, Mrs. Ackroyd," he said. "You will be spared all unpleasantness. Now, as to the question of money, have you all you need for the present? I mean," he added, as she looked at him inquiringly, "ready money. Cash, you know. If not, I can arrange to let you have whatever you require."

"That ought to be all right," said Raymond, who was standing by. "Mr. Ackroyd cashed a cheque for a hundred pounds yesterday."

"A hundred pounds?"

"Yes. For wages and other expenses due to-day. At the moment it is still intact."

"Where is this money? In his desk?"

"No, he always kept his cash in his bedroom. In an old collar-box, to be accurate. Funny idea, wasn't it?"

"I think," said the lawyer, "we ought to make sure the money is there before I leave."

"Certainly," agreed the secretary. "I'll take you up now.... Oh! I forgot. The door's locked."

Inquiry from Parker elicited the information that Inspector Raglan was in the housekeeper's room asking a few supplementary questions. A few minutes later the inspector joined the party in the hall, bringing the key with him. He unlocked the door and we passed into the lobby and up the small staircase. At the top of the stairs the door into Ackroyd's bedroom stood open. Inside the room it was dark, the curtains were drawn, and the bed was turned down just as it had been last night. The inspector drew the curtains, letting in the sunlight, and Geoffrey Raymond went to the top drawer of a rosewood bureau.

"He kept his money like that, in an unlocked drawer. Just fancy," commented the inspector.

The secretary flushed a little.

"Mr. Ackroyd had perfect faith in the honesty of all the servants," he said hotly.

"Oh! quite so," said the inspector hastily.

Raymond opened the drawer, took out a round leather collar-box from the back of it, and opening it, drew out a thick wallet.

"Here is the money," he said, taking out a fat roll of notes. "You will find the hundred intact, I know, for Mr. Ackroyd put it in the collar-box in my presence last night when he was dressing for dinner, and of course it has not been touched since."

Mr. Hammond took the roll from him and counted it. He looked up sharply.

"A hundred pounds, you said. But there is only sixty here."

Raymond stared at him.

"Impossible," he cried, springing forward. Taking the notes from the other's hand, he counted them aloud.

Mr. Hammond had been right. The total amounted to sixty pounds.

"But—I can't understand it," cried the secretary, bewildered.

Poirot asked a question.

"You saw Mr. Ackroyd put this money away last night when he was dressing for dinner? You are sure he had not paid away any of it already?"

"I'm sure he hadn't. He even said, 'I don't want to take a hundred pounds down to dinner with me. Too bulgy.'"

"Then the affair is very simple," remarked Poirot. "Either he paid out that forty pounds sometime last evening, or else it has been stolen."

"That's the matter in a nutshell," agreed the inspector. He turned to Mrs. Ackroyd. "Which of the servants would come in here yesterday evening?"

"I suppose the housemaid would turn down the bed."

"Who is she? What do you know about her?"

"She's not been here very long," said Mrs. Ackroyd. "But she's a nice ordinary country girl."

"I think we ought to clear this matter up," said the inspector. "If Mr. Ackroyd paid that money away himself, it may have a bearing on the mystery of the crime. The other servants all right, as far as you know?"

"Oh, I think so."

"Not missed anything before?"

"No."

"None of them leaving, or anything like that?"

"The parlormaid is leaving."

"When?"

"She gave notice yesterday, I believe."

"To you?"

"Oh, no. I have nothing to do with the servants. Miss Russell attends to the household matters."

The inspector remained lost in thought for a minute or two. Then he nodded his head and remarked, "I think I'd better have a word with Miss Russell, and I'll see the girl Dale as well."

Poirot and I accompanied him to the housekeeper's room. Miss Russell received us with her usual sang-froid.

Elsie Dale had been at Fernly five months. A nice girl, quick at her duties, and most respectable. Good references. The last girl in the world to take anything not belonging to her.

What about the parlormaid?

"She, too, was a most superior girl. Very quiet and ladylike. An excellent worker."

"Then why is she leaving?" asked the inspector.

Miss Russell pursed up her lips.

"It was none of my doing. I understand Mr. Ackroyd found fault with her yesterday afternoon. It was her duty to do the study, and she disarranged some of the papers on his desk, I believe. He was very annoyed about it, and she gave notice. At least, that is what I understood from her, but perhaps you'd like to see her yourselves?"

The inspector assented. I had already noticed the girl when she was waiting on us at lunch. A tall girl, with a lot of brown hair rolled tightly away at the back of her neck, and very steady gray eyes. She came in answer to the housekeeper's summons, and stood very straight with those same gray eyes fixed on us.

"You are Ursula Bourne?" asked the inspector.

"Yes, sir."

"I understand you are leaving?"

"Yes, sir."

"Why is that?"

"I disarranged some papers on Mr. Ackroyd's desk. He was very angry about it, and I said I had better leave. He told me to go as soon as possible."

"Were you in Mr. Ackroyd's bedroom at all last night? Tidying up or anything?"

"No, sir. That is Elsie's work. I never went near that part of the house."

"I must tell you, my girl, that a large sum of money is missing from Mr. Ackroyd's room."

At last I saw her roused. A wave of color swept over her face.

"I know nothing about any money. If you think I took it, and

106

that that is why Mr. Ackroyd dismissed me, you are wrong."

"I'm not accusing you of taking it, my girl," said the inspector. "Don't flare up so."

The girl looked at him coldly.

"You can search my things if you like," she said disdainfully. "But you won't find anything."

Poirot suddenly interposed.

"It was yesterday afternoon that Mr. Ackroyd dismissed you— or you dismissed yourself, was it not?" he asked.

The girl nodded.

"How long did the interview last?"

"The interview?"

"Yes, the interview between you and Mr. Ackroyd in the study?"

"I—I don't know."

"Twenty minutes? Half an hour?"

"Something like that."

"Not longer?"

"Not longer than half an hour, certainly."

"Thank you, mademoiselle."

I looked curiously at him. He was rearranging a few objects on the table, setting them straight with precise fingers. His eyes were shining.

"That'll do," said the inspector.

Ursula Bourne disappeared. The inspector turned to Miss Russell.

"How long has she been here? Have you got a copy of the reference you had with her?"

Without answering the first question, Miss Russell moved to an adjacent bureau, opened one of the drawers, and took out a handful of letters clipped together with a patent fastener. She selected one and handed it to the inspector.

"H'm," said he. "Reads all right. Mrs. Richard Folliott, Marby Grange, Marby. Who's this woman?"

"Quite good county people," said Miss Russell.

"Well," said the inspector, handing it back, "let's have a look at the other one, Elsie Dale."

Elsie Dale was a big fair girl, with a pleasant but slightly stupid face. She answered our questions readily enough, and showed much distress and concern at the loss of the money.

"I don't think there's anything wrong with her," observed the inspector, after he had dismissed her.

"What about Parker?"

Miss Russell pursed her lips together and made no reply.

"I've a feeling there's something wrong about that man," the inspector continued thoughtfully. "The trouble is that I don't quite see when he got his opportunity. He'd be busy with his duties immediately after dinner, and he's got a pretty good alibi all through the evening. I know, for I've been devoting particular attention to it. Well, thank you very much, Miss Russell. We'll leave things as they are for the present. It's highly probable Mr. Ackroyd paid that money away himself."

The housekeeper bade us a dry good-afternoon, and we took our leave.

I left the house with Poirot.

"I wonder," I said, breaking the silence, "what the papers the girl disarranged could have been for Ackroyd to have got into such a state about them? I wonder if there is any clew there to the mystery."

"The secretary said there were no papers of particular importance on the desk," said Poirot quietly.

"Yes, but——" I paused.

"It strikes you as odd that Ackroyd should have flown into a rage about so trivial a matter?"

"Yes, it does rather."

"But was it a trivial matter?"

"Of course," I admitted, "we don't know what those papers may have been. But Raymond certainly said——"

"Leave M. Raymond out of it for a minute. What did you think of that girl?"

"Which girl? The parlormaid?"

"Yes, the parlormaid. Ursula Bourne."

"She seemed a nice girl," I said hesitatingly.

Poirot repeated my words, but whereas I had laid a slight stress on the fourth word, he put it on the second.

"She *seemed* a nice girl—yes."

Then, after a minute's silence, he took something from his pocket and handed it to me.

"See, my friend, I will show you something. Look there."

The paper he had handed me was that compiled by the inspector and given by him to Poirot that morning. Following the pointing finger, I saw a small cross marked in pencil opposite the name Ursula Bourne.

"You may not have noticed it at the time, my good friend, but there was one person on this list whose alibi had no kind of confirmation. Ursula Bourne."

"You don't think——"

"Dr. Sheppard, I dare to think anything. Ursula Bourne may have killed Mr. Ackroyd, but I confess I can see no motive for her doing so. Can you?"

He looked at me very hard—so hard that I felt uncomfortable.

"Can you?" he repeated.

"No motive whatsoever," I said firmly.

His gaze relaxed. He frowned and murmured to himself:—

"Since the blackmailer was a man, it follows that she cannot be the blackmailer, then——"

I coughed.

"As far as that goes——" I began doubtfully.

He spun round on me.

"What? What are you going to say?"

"Nothing. Nothing. Only that, strictly speaking, Mrs. Ferrars in her letter mentioned a *person*—she didn't actually specify a man. But we took it for granted, Ackroyd and I, that it *was* a man."

Poirot did not seem to be listening to me. He was muttering to himself again.

"But then it is possible after all—yes, certainly it is possible—but then—ah! I must rearrange my ideas. Method, order; never have I needed them more. Everything must fit in—in its appointed place—otherwise I am on the wrong tack."

He broke off, and whirled round upon me again.

"Where is Marby?"

"It's on the other side of Cranchester."

"How far away?"

"Oh!—fourteen miles, perhaps."

"Would it be possible for you to go there? To-morrow, say?"

"To-morrow? Let me see, that's Sunday. Yes, I could arrange it. What do you want me to do there?"

"See this Mrs. Folliott. Find out all you can about Ursula Bourne."

"Very well. But—I don't much care for the job."

"It is not the time to make difficulties. A man's life may hang on this."

"Poor Ralph," I said with a sigh. "You believe him to be innocent, though?"

Poirot looked at me very gravely.

"Do you want to know the truth?"

"Of course."

"Then you shall have it. My friend, everything points to the assumption that he is guilty."

"What!" I exclaimed.

Poirot nodded.

"Yes, that stupid inspector—for he is stupid—has everything pointing his way. I seek for the truth—and the truth leads me every time to Ralph Paton. Motive, opportunity, means. But I will leave no stone unturned. I promised Mademoiselle Flora. And she was very sure, that little one. But very sure indeed."

ELEVEN
Poirot Pays a Call

I was slightly nervous when I rang the bell at Marby Grange the following afternoon. I wondered very much what Poirot expected to find out. He had entrusted the job to me. Why? Was it because, as in the case of questioning Major Blunt, he wished to remain in the background? The wish, intelligible in the first case, seemed to me quite meaningless here.

My meditations were interrupted by the advent of a smart parlormaid.

Yes, Mrs. Folliott was at home. I was ushered into a big drawing-room, and looked round me curiously as I waited for the mistress of the house. A large bare room, some good bits of old china, and some beautiful etchings, shabby covers and curtains. A lady's room in every sense of the term.

I turned from the inspection of a Bartolozzi on the wall as Mrs. Folliott came into the room. She was a tall woman, with untidy brown hair, and a very winning smile.

"Dr. Sheppard," she said hesitatingly.

"That is my name," I replied. "I must apologize for calling upon you like this, but I wanted some information about a parlormaid previously employed by you, Ursula Bourne."

With the utterance of the name the smile vanished from her face, and all the cordiality froze out of her manner. She looked uncomfortable and ill at ease.

"Ursula Bourne?" she said hesitatingly.

"Yes," I said. "Perhaps you don't remember the name?"

"Oh, yes, of course. I—I remember perfectly."

"She left you just over a year ago, I understand?"

"Yes. Yes, she did. That is quite right."

"And you were satisfied with her whilst she was with you? How long was she with you, by the way?"

"Oh! a year or two—I can't remember exactly how long. She—she is very capable. I'm sure you will find her quite satisfactory. I didn't know she was leaving Fernly. I hadn't the least idea of it."

"Can you tell me anything about her?" I asked.

"Anything about her?"

"Yes, where she comes from, who her people are—that sort of thing?"

Mrs. Folliott's face wore more than ever its frozen look.

"I don't know at all."

"Who was she with before she came to you?"

"I'm afraid I don't remember."

There was a spark of anger now underlying her nervousness. She flung up her head in a gesture that was vaguely familiar.

"Is it really necessary to ask all these questions?"

"Not at all," I said, with an air of surprise and a tinge of apology in my manner. "I had no idea you would mind answering them. I am very sorry."

Her anger left her and she became confused again.

"Oh! I don't mind answering them. I assure you I don't. Why should I? It—it just seemed a little odd, you know. That's all. A little odd."

One advantage of being a medical practitioner is that you can usually tell when people are lying to you. I should have known from Mrs. Folliott's manner, if from nothing else, that she did mind answering my questions—minded intensely. She was thoroughly uncomfortable and upset, and there was plainly some mystery in the background. I judged her to be a woman quite unused to deception of any kind, and consequently rendered acutely uneasy when forced to practice it. A child could have seen through her.

But it was also clear that she had no intention of telling me anything further. Whatever the mystery centering around Ursula Bourne might be, I was not going to learn it through Mrs. Folliott.

Defeated, I apologized once more for disturbing her, took my hat and departed.

I went to see a couple of patients and arrived home about six o'clock. Caroline was sitting beside the wreck of tea things. She had that look of suppressed exultation on her face which I know only too well. It is a sure sign with her, of either the getting or the giving of information. I wondered which it had been.

"I've had a very interesting afternoon," began Caroline as I dropped into my own particular easy chair, and stretched out my feet to the inviting blaze in the fireplace.

"Have you?" I asked. "Miss Ganett drop in to tea?"

Miss Ganett is one of the chief of our newsmongers.

"Guess again," said Caroline with intense complacency.

I guessed several times, working slowly through all the members of Caroline's Intelligence Corps. My sister received each guess with a triumphant shake of the head. In the end she volunteered the information herself.

"M. Poirot!" she said. "Now what do you think of that?"

I thought a good many things of it, but I was careful not to say them to Caroline.

"Why did he come?" I asked.

"To see me, of course. He said that knowing my brother so well, he hoped he might be permitted to make the acquaintance of his charming sister—your charming sister, I've got mixed up, but you know what I mean."

"What did he talk about?" I asked.

"He told me a lot about himself and his cases. You know that Prince Paul of Mauretania—the one who's just married a dancer?"

"Yes?"

"I saw a most intriguing paragraph about her in Society

AGATHA CHRISTIE

Snippets the other day, hinting that she was really a Russian Grand Duchess—one of the Czar's daughters who managed to escape from the Bolsheviks. Well, it seems that M. Poirot solved a baffling murder mystery that threatened to involve them both. Prince Paul was beside himself with gratitude."

"Did he give him an emerald tie pin the size of a plover's egg?" I inquired sarcastically.

"He didn't mention it. Why?"

"Nothing," I said. "I thought it was always done. It is in detective fiction anyway. The super detective always has his rooms littered with rubies and pearls and emeralds from grateful Royal clients."

"It's very interesting to hear about these things from the inside," said my sister complacently.

It would be—to Caroline. I could not but admire the ingenuity of M. Hercule Poirot, who had selected unerringly the case of all others that would most appeal to an elderly maiden lady living in a small village.

"Did he tell you if the dancer was really a Grand Duchess?" I inquired.

"He was not at liberty to speak," said Caroline importantly.

I wondered how far Poirot had strained the truth in talking to Caroline—probably not at all. He had conveyed his innuendoes by means of his eyebrows and his shoulders.

"And after all this," I remarked, "I suppose you were ready to eat out of his hand."

"Don't be coarse, James. I don't know where you get these vulgar expressions from."

"Probably from my only link with the outside world—my patients. Unfortunately my practice does not lie amongst Royal princes and interesting Russian émigrés."

Caroline pushed her spectacles up and looked at me.

"You seem very grumpy, James. It must be your liver. A blue pill, I think, to-night."

To see me in my own home, you would never imagine that

I was a doctor of medicine. Caroline does the home prescribing both for herself and me.

"Damn my liver," I said irritably. "Did you talk about the murder at all?"

"Well, naturally, James. What else is there to talk about locally? I was able to set M. Poirot right upon several points. He was very grateful to me. He said I had the makings of a born detective in me—and a wonderful psychological insight into human nature."

Caroline was exactly like a cat that is full to overflowing with rich cream. She was positively purring.

"He talked a lot about the little gray cells of the brain, and of their functions. His own, he says, are of the first quality."

"He would say so," I remarked bitterly. "Modesty is certainly not his middle name."

"I wish you would not be so horribly American, James. He thought it very important that Ralph should be found as soon as possible, and induced to come forward and give an account of himself. He says that his disappearance will produce a very unfortunate impression at the inquest."

"And what did you say to that?"

"I agreed with him," said Caroline importantly. "And I was able to tell him the way people were already talking about it."

"Caroline," I said sharply, "did you tell M. Poirot what you overheard in the wood that day?"

"I did," said Caroline complacently.

I got up and began to walk about.

"You realize what you're doing, I hope," I jerked out. "You're putting a halter round Ralph Paton's neck as surely as you're sitting in that chair."

"Not at all," said Caroline, quite unruffled. "I was surprised *you* hadn't told him."

"I took very good care not to," I said. "I'm fond of that boy."

"So am I. That's why I say you're talking nonsense. I don't believe Ralph did it, and so the truth can't hurt him, and we ought to give M. Poirot all the help we can. Why, think, very likely Ralph was out with that identical girl on the night of the murder, and if so, he's got a perfect alibi."

"If he's got a perfect alibi," I retorted, "why doesn't he come forward and say so?"

"Might get the girl into trouble," said Caroline sapiently. "But if M. Poirot gets hold of her, and puts it to her as her duty, she'll come forward of her own accord and clear Ralph."

"You seem to have invented a romantic fairy story of your own," I said. "You read too many trashy novels, Caroline. I've always told you so."

I dropped into my chair again.

"Did Poirot ask you any more questions?" I inquired.

"Only about the patients you had that morning."

"The patients?" I demanded, unbelievingly.

"Yes, your surgery patients. How many and who they were?"

"Do you mean to say you were able to tell him that?" I demanded.

Caroline is really amazing.

"Why not?" asked my sister triumphantly. "I can see the path up to the surgery door perfectly from this window. And I've got an excellent memory, James. Much better than yours, let me tell you."

"I'm sure you have," I murmured mechanically.

My sister went on, checking the names on her fingers.

"There was old Mrs. Bennett, and that boy from the farm with the bad finger, Dolly Grice to have a needle out of her finger; that American steward off the liner. Let me see—that's four. Yes, and old George Evans with his ulcer. And lastly——"

She paused significantly.

"Well?"

Caroline brought out her climax triumphantly. She hissed in the most approved style—aided by the fortunate number of s's at her disposal.

"*Miss Russell!*"

She sat back in her chair and looked at me meaningly, and when Caroline looks at you meaningly, it is impossible to miss it.

"I don't know what you mean," I said, quite untruthfully. "Why shouldn't Miss Russell consult me about her bad knee?"

"Bad knee," said Caroline. "Fiddlesticks! No more bad knee than you and I. She was after something else."

"What?" I asked.

Caroline had to admit that she didn't know.

"But depend upon it, that was what he was trying to get at, M. Poirot, I mean. There's something fishy about that woman, and he knows it."

"Precisely the remark Mrs. Ackroyd made to me yesterday," I said. "That there was something fishy about Miss Russell."

"Ah!" said Caroline darkly, "Mrs. Ackroyd! There's another!"

"Another what?"

Caroline refused to explain her remarks. She merely nodded her head several times, rolled up her knitting, and went upstairs to don the high mauve silk blouse and the gold locket which she calls dressing for dinner.

I stayed there staring into the fire and thinking over Caroline's words. Had Poirot really come to gain information about Miss Russell, or was it only Caroline's tortuous mind that interpreted everything according to her own ideas?

There had certainly been nothing in Miss Russell's manner that morning to arouse suspicion. At least——

I remembered her persistent conversation on the subject of drug-taking and from that she had led the conversation to poisons and poisoning. But there was nothing in that. Ackroyd had not been poisoned. Still, it was odd....

I heard Caroline's voice, rather acid in note, calling from the top of the stairs.

"James, you will be late for dinner."

I put some coal on the fire and went upstairs obediently.

It is well at any price to have peace in the home.

117

TWELVE
Round the Table

A joint inquest was held on Monday.

I do not propose to give the proceedings in detail. To do so would only be to go over the same ground again and again. By arrangement with the police, very little was allowed to come out. I gave evidence as to the cause of Ackroyd's death and the probable time. The absence of Ralph Paton was commented on by the coroner, but not unduly stressed.

Afterwards, Poirot and I had a few words with Inspector Raglan. The inspector was very grave.

"It looks bad, Mr. Poirot," he said. "I'm trying to judge the thing fair and square. I'm a local man, and I've seen Captain Paton many times in Cranchester. I'm not wanting him to be the guilty one—but it's bad whichever way you look at it. If he's innocent, why doesn't he come forward? We've got evidence against him, but it's just possible that that evidence could be explained away. Then why doesn't he give an explanation?"

A lot more lay behind the inspector's words than I knew at the time. Ralph's description had been wired to every port and railway station in England. The police everywhere were on the alert. His rooms in town were watched, and any houses he had been known to be in the habit of frequenting. With such a *cordon* it seemed impossible that Ralph should be able to evade detection. He had no luggage, and, as far as any one knew, no money.

"I can't find any one who saw him at the station that night," continued the inspector. "And yet he's well known down here, and you'd think somebody would have noticed him. There's no news from Liverpool either."

"You think he went to Liverpool?" queried Poirot.

"Well, it's on the cards. That telephone message from the station, just three minutes before the Liverpool express left—there ought to be something in that."

"Unless it was deliberately intended to throw you off the scent. That might just possibly be the point of the telephone message."

"That's an idea," said the inspector eagerly. "Do you really think that's the explanation of the telephone call?"

"My friend," said Poirot gravely, "I do not know. But I will tell you this: I believe that when we find the explanation of that telephone call we shall find the explanation of the murder."

"You said something like that before, I remember," I observed, looking at him curiously.

Poirot nodded.

"I always come back to it," he said seriously.

"It seems to me utterly irrelevant," I declared.

"I wouldn't say that," demurred the inspector. "But I must confess I think Mr. Poirot here harps on it a little too much. We've better clews than that. The fingerprints on the dagger, for instance."

Poirot became suddenly very foreign in manner, as he often did when excited over anything.

"M. l'Inspecteur," he said, "beware of the blind—the blind—*comment dire?*—the little street that has no end to it."

Inspector Raglan stared, but I was quicker.

"You mean a blind alley?" I said.

"That is it—the blind street that leads nowhere. So it may be with those fingerprints—they may lead you nowhere."

"I don't see how that can well be," said the police officer. "I suppose you're hinting that they're faked? I've read of such things

119

being done, though I can't say I've ever come across it in my experience. But fake or true—they're bound to lead *somewhere*."

Poirot merely shrugged his shoulders, flinging out his arms wide.

The inspector then showed us various enlarged photographs of the fingerprints, and proceeded to become technical on the subject of loops and whorls.

"Come now," he said at last, annoyed by Poirot's detached manner, "you've got to admit that those prints were made by some one who was in the house that night?"

"*Bien entendu*," said Poirot, nodding his head.

"Well, I've taken the prints of every member of the household, every one, mind you, from the old lady down to the kitchenmaid."

I don't think Mrs. Ackroyd would enjoy being referred to as the old lady. She must spend a considerable amount on cosmetics.

"Every one's," repeated the inspector fussily.

"Including mine," I said dryly.

"Very well. None of them correspond. That leaves us two alternatives. Ralph Paton, or the mysterious stranger the doctor here tells us about. When we get hold of those two——"

"Much valuable time may have been lost," broke in Poirot.

"I don't quite get you, Mr. Poirot?"

"You have taken the prints of every one in the house, you say," murmured Poirot. "Is that the exact truth you are telling me there, M. l'Inspecteur?"

"Certainly."

"Without overlooking any one?"

"Without overlooking any one."

"The quick or the dead?"

For a moment the inspector looked bewildered at what he took to be a religious observation. Then he reacted slowly.

"You mean——"

"The dead, M. l'Inspecteur."

The inspector still took a minute or two to understand.

"I am suggesting," said Poirot placidly, "that the fingerprints on the dagger handle are those of Mr. Ackroyd himself. It is an easy matter to verify. His body is still available."

"But why? What would be the point of it? You're surely not suggesting suicide, Mr. Poirot?"

"Ah! no. My theory is that the murderer wore gloves or wrapped something round his hand. After the blow was struck, he picked up the victim's hand and closed it round the dagger handle."

"But why?"

Poirot shrugged his shoulders again.

"To make a confusing case even more confusing."

"Well," said the inspector, "I'll look into it. What gave you the idea in the first place?"

"When you were so kind as to show me the dagger and draw attention to the fingerprints. I know very little of loops and whorls—see, I confess my ignorance frankly. But it did occur to me that the position of the prints was somewhat awkward. Not so would I have held a dagger in order to strike. Naturally, with the right hand brought up over the shoulder backwards, it would have been difficult to put it in exactly the right position."

Inspector Raglan stared at the little man. Poirot, with an air of great unconcern, flecked a speck of dust from his coat sleeve.

"Well," said the inspector, "it's an idea. I'll look into it all right, but don't you be disappointed if nothing comes of it."

He endeavored to make his tone kindly and patronizing. Poirot watched him go off. Then he turned to me with twinkling eyes.

"Another time," he observed, "I must be more careful of his *amour propre*. And now that we are left to our own devices, what do you think, my good friend, of a little reunion of the family?"

The "little reunion," as Poirot called it, took place about half an hour later. We sat round the table in the dining-room at Fernly—Poirot at the head of the table, like the chairman of some ghastly board meeting. The servants were not present, so we were six in all. Mrs. Ackroyd, Flora, Major Blunt, young Raymond, Poirot, and myself.

When every one was assembled, Poirot rose and bowed.

"Messieurs, mesdames, I have called you together for a certain purpose." He paused. "To begin with, I want to make a very special plea to mademoiselle."

"To me?" said Flora.

"Mademoiselle, you are engaged to Captain Ralph Paton. If any one is in his confidence, you are. I beg you, most earnestly, if you know of his whereabouts, to persuade him to come forward. One little minute"—as Flora raised her head to speak—"say nothing till you have well reflected. Mademoiselle, his position grows daily more dangerous. If he had come forward at once, no matter how damning the facts, he might have had a chance of explaining them away. But this silence—this flight—what can it mean? Surely only one thing, knowledge of guilt. Mademoiselle, if you really believe in his innocence, persuade him to come forward before it is too late."

Flora's face had gone very white.

"Too late!" she repeated, very low.

Poirot leant forward, looking at her.

"See now, mademoiselle," he said very gently, "it is Papa Poirot who asks you this. The old Papa Poirot who has much knowledge and much experience. I would not seek to entrap you, mademoiselle. Will you not trust me—and tell me where Ralph Paton is hiding?"

The girl rose, and stood facing him.

"M. Poirot," she said in a clear voice, "I swear to you—swear solemnly—that I have no idea where Ralph is, and that I have neither seen him nor heard from him either on the day of—of the murder, or since."

She sat down again. Poirot gazed at her in silence for a minute or two, then he brought his hand down on the table with a sharp rap.

"Bien! That is that," he said. His face hardened. "Now I appeal to these others who sit round this table, Mrs. Ackroyd, Major Blunt, Dr. Sheppard, Mr. Raymond. You are all friends and intimates of the missing man. If you know where Ralph Paton is hiding, speak out."

There was a long silence. Poirot looked to each in turn.

"I beg of you," he said in a low voice, "speak out."

But still there was silence, broken at last by Mrs. Ackroyd.

"I must say," she observed in a plaintive voice, "that Ralph's absence is most peculiar—most peculiar indeed. Not to come forward at such a time. It looks, you know, as though there were something *behind* it. I can't help thinking, Flora dear, that it was a very fortunate thing your engagement was never formally announced."

"Mother!" cried Flora angrily.

"Providence," declared Mrs. Ackroyd. "I have a devout belief in Providence—a divinity that shapes our ends, as Shakespeare's beautiful line runs."

"Surely you don't make the Almighty directly responsible for thick ankles, Mrs. Ackroyd, do you?" asked Geoffrey Raymond, his irresponsible laugh ringing out.

His idea was, I think, to loosen the tension, but Mrs. Ackroyd threw him a glance of reproach and took out her handkerchief.

"Flora has been saved a terrible amount of notoriety and unpleasantness. Not for a moment that I think dear Ralph had anything to do with poor Roger's death. I *don't* think so. But then I have a trusting heart—I always have had, ever since a child. I am loath to believe the worst of any one. But, of course, one must remember that Ralph was in several air raids as a young boy. The results are apparent long after, sometimes, they say. People are not responsible for their actions in the least. They lose control, you know, without being able to help it."

"Mother," cried Flora, "you don't think Ralph did it?"

"Come, Mrs. Ackroyd," said Blunt.

"I don't know what to think," said Mrs. Ackroyd tearfully. "It's all very upsetting. What would happen to the estate, I wonder, if Ralph were found guilty?"

Raymond pushed his chair away from the table violently. Major Blunt remained very quiet, looking thoughtfully at her. "Like shell-shock, you know," said Mrs. Ackroyd obstinately, "and I dare say Roger kept him very short of money—with the best intentions, of course. I can see you are all against me, but I do think it is very odd that Ralph has not come forward, and I must say I am thankful Flora's engagement was never announced formally."

"It will be to-morrow," said Flora in a clear voice.

"Flora!" cried her mother, aghast.

Flora had turned to the secretary.

"Will you send the announcement to the *Morning Post* and the *Times*, please, Mr. Raymond."

"If you are sure that it is wise, Miss Ackroyd," he replied gravely.

She turned impulsively to Blunt.

"You understand," she said. "What else can I do? As things are, I must stand by Ralph. Don't you see that I must?"

She looked very searchingly at him, and after a long pause he nodded abruptly.

Mrs. Ackroyd burst out into shrill protests. Flora remained unmoved. Then Raymond spoke.

"I appreciate your motives, Miss Ackroyd. But don't you think you're being rather precipitate? Wait a day or two."

"To-morrow," said Flora, in a clear voice. "It's no good, mother, going on like this. Whatever else I am, I'm not disloyal to my friends."

"M. Poirot," Mrs. Ackroyd appealed tearfully, "can't you say anything at all?"

"Nothing to be said," interpolated Blunt. "She's doing the right thing. I'll stand by her through thick and thin."

Flora held out her hand to him.

"Thank you, Major Blunt," she said.

"Mademoiselle," said Poirot, "will you let an old man congratulate you on your courage and your loyalty? And will you not misunderstand me if I ask you—ask you most solemnly—to postpone the announcement you speak of for at least two days more?"

Flora hesitated.

"I ask it in Ralph Paton's interests as much as in yours, mademoiselle. You frown. You do not see how that can be. But I assure you that it is so. *Pas de blagues*. You put the case into my hands—you must not hamper me now."

Flora paused a few minutes before replying.

"I do not like it," she said at last, "but I will do what you say."

She sat down again at the table.

"And now, messieurs et mesdames," said Poirot rapidly, "I will continue with what I was about to say. Understand this, I mean to arrive at the truth. The truth, however ugly in itself, is always curious and beautiful to the seeker after it. I am much aged, my powers may not be what they were." Here he clearly expected a contradiction. "In all probability this is the last case I shall ever investigate. But Hercule Poirot does not end with a failure. Messieurs et mesdames, I tell you, I mean to *know*. And I shall know—in spite of you all."

He brought out the last words provocatively, hurling them in our face as it were. I think we all flinched back a little, excepting Geoffrey Raymond, who remained good humored and imperturbable as usual.

"How do you mean—in spite of us all?" he asked, with slightly raised eyebrows.

"But—just that, monsieur. Every one of you in this room is concealing something from me." He raised his hand as a faint murmur of protest arose. "Yes, yes, I know what I am saying. It may be something unimportant—trivial—which is supposed to have no bearing on the case, but there it is. *Each one of you has something to hide.* Come, now, am I right?"

His glance, challenging and accusing, swept round the table. And every pair of eyes dropped before his. Yes, mine as well.

"I am answered," said Poirot, with a curious laugh. He got up from his seat. "I appeal to you all. Tell me the truth—the whole truth." There was a silence. "Will no one speak?"

He gave the same short laugh again.

"*C'est dommage,*" he said, and went out.

THIRTEEN
The Goose Quill

That evening, at Poirot's request, I went over to his house after dinner. Caroline saw me depart with visible reluctance. I think she would have liked to have accompanied me.

Poirot greeted me hospitably. He had placed a bottle of Irish whisky (which I detest) on a small table, with a soda water siphon and a glass. He himself was engaged in brewing hot chocolate. It was a favorite beverage of his, I discovered later.

He inquired politely after my sister, whom he declared to be a most interesting woman.

"I'm afraid you've been giving her a swelled head," I said dryly. "What about Sunday afternoon?"

He laughed and twinkled.

"I always like to employ the expert," he remarked obscurely, but he refused to explain the remark.

"You got all the local gossip anyway," I remarked. "True, and untrue."

"And a great deal of valuable information," he added quietly.

"Such as——?"

He shook his head.

"Why not have told me the truth?" he countered. "In a place like this, all Ralph Paton's doings were bound to be known. If your sister had not happened to pass through the wood that day

127

somebody else would have done so."

"I suppose they would," I said grumpily. "What about this interest of yours in my patients?"

Again he twinkled.

"Only one of them, doctor. Only one of them."

"The last?" I hazarded.

"I find Miss Russell a study of the most interesting," he said evasively.

"Do you agree with my sister and Mrs. Ackroyd that there is something fishy about her?" I asked.

"Eh? What do you say—fishy?"

I explained to the best of my ability.

"And they say that, do they?"

"Didn't my sister convey as much to you yesterday afternoon?"

"*C'est possible*."

"For no reason whatever," I declared.

"*Les femmes*," generalized Poirot. "They are marvelous! They invent haphazard—and by miracle they are right. Not that it is that, really. Women observe subconsciously a thousand little details, without knowing that they are doing so. Their subconscious mind adds these little things together—and they call the result intuition. Me, I am very skilled in psychology. I know these things."

He swelled his chest out importantly, looking so ridiculous, that I found it difficult not to burst out laughing. Then he took a small sip of his chocolate, and carefully wiped his mustache.

"I wish you'd tell me," I burst out, "what you really think of it all?"

He put down his cup.

"You wish that?"

"I do."

"You have seen what I have seen. Should not our ideas be the same?"

"I'm afraid you're laughing at me," I said stiffly. "Of course, I've no experience of matters of this kind."

Poirot smiled at me indulgently.

"You are like the little child who wants to know the way the engine works. You wish to see the affair, not as the family doctor sees it, but with the eye of a detective who knows and cares for no one—to whom they are all strangers and all equally liable to suspicion."

"You put it very well," I said.

"So I give you then, a little lecture. The first thing is to get a clear history of what happened that evening—always bearing in mind that the person who speaks may be lying."

I raised my eyebrows.

"Rather a suspicious attitude."

"But necessary—I assure you, necessary. Now first—Dr. Sheppard leaves the house at ten minutes to nine. How do I know that?"

"Because I told you so."

"But you might not be speaking the truth—or the watch you went by might be wrong. But Parker also says that you left the house at ten minutes to nine. So we accept that statement and pass on. At nine o'clock you run into a man—and here we come to what we will call the Romance of the Mysterious Stranger—just outside the Park gates. How do I know that that is so?"

"I told you so," I began again, but Poirot interrupted me with a gesture of impatience.

"Ah! but it is that you are a little stupid to-night, my friend. *You* know that it is so—but how am *I* to know? *Eh bien*, I am able to tell you that the Mysterious Stranger was not a hallucination on your part, because the maid of a Miss Ganett met him a few minutes before you did, and of her too he inquired the way to Fernly Park. We accept his presence, therefore, and we can be fairly sure of two things about him—that he was a stranger to the neighborhood, and that whatever his object in going to Fernly, there was no great secrecy about it, since he twice asked the way there."

"Yes," I said, "I see that."

"Now I have made it my business to find out more about this man. He had a drink at the Three Boars, I learn, and the barmaid there says that he spoke with an American accent and mentioned having just come over from the States. Did it strike you that he had an American accent?"

"Yes, I think he had," I said, after a minute or two, during which I cast my mind back; "but a very slight one."

"*Précisément.* There is also this which, you will remember, I picked up in the summer-house?"

He held out to me the little quill. I looked at it curiously. Then a memory of something I had read stirred in me.

Poirot, who had been watching my face, nodded.

"Yes, heroin 'snow.' Drug-takers carry it like this, and sniff it up the nose."

"Diamorphine hydrochloride," I murmured mechanically.

"This method of taking the drug is very common on the other side. Another proof, if we wanted one, that the man came from Canada or the States."

"What first attracted your attention to that summer-house?" I asked curiously.

"My friend the inspector took it for granted that any one using that path did so as a short cut to the house, but as soon as I saw the summer-house, I realized that the same path would be taken by any one using the summer-house as a rendezvous. Now it seems fairly certain that the stranger came neither to the front nor to the back door. Then did some one from the house go out and meet him? If so, what could be a more convenient place than that little summer-house? I searched it with the hope that I might find some clew inside. I found two, the scrap of cambric and the quill."

"And the scrap of cambric?" I asked curiously. "What about that?"

Poirot raised his eyebrows.

"You do not use your little gray cells," he remarked dryly. "The scrap of starched cambric should be obvious."

"Not very obvious to me." I changed the subject. "Anyway," I said, "this man went to the summer-house to meet somebody. Who was that somebody?"

"Exactly the question," said Poirot. "You will remember that Mrs. Ackroyd and her daughter came over from Canada to live here?"

"Is that what you meant to-day when you accused them of hiding the truth?"

"Perhaps. Now another point. What did you think of the parlormaid's story?"

"What story?"

"The story of her dismissal. Does it take half an hour to dismiss a servant? Was the story of those important papers a likely one? And remember, though she says she was in her bedroom from nine-thirty until ten o'clock, there is no one to confirm her statement."

"You bewilder me," I said.

"To me it grows clearer. But tell me now your own ideas and theories."

I drew a piece of paper from my pocket.

"I just scribbled down a few suggestions," I said apologetically.

"But excellent—you have method. Let us hear them."

I read out in a somewhat embarrassed voice.

"To begin with, one must look at the thing logically——"

"Just what my poor Hastings used to say," interrupted Poirot, "but alas! he never did so."

"*Point No. 1.*—Mr. Ackroyd was heard talking to some one at half-past nine.

"*Point No. 2.*—At some time during the evening Ralph Paton must have come in through the window, as evidenced by the prints of his shoes.

"*Point No. 3.*—Mr. Ackroyd was nervous that evening, and would only have admitted some one he knew.

"*Point No. 4.*—The person with Mr. Ackroyd at nine-thirty was asking for money. We know Ralph Paton was in a scrape.

"*These four points go to show that the person with Mr. Ackroyd at nine-thirty was Ralph Paton. But we know that Mr. Ackroyd was alive at a quarter to ten, therefore it was not Ralph who killed him. Ralph left the window open. Afterwards the murderer came in that way.*"

"And who was the murderer?" inquired Poirot.

"The American stranger. He may have been in league with Parker, and possibly in Parker we have the man who blackmailed Mrs. Ferrars. If so, Parker may have heard enough to realize the game was up, have told his accomplice so, and the latter did the crime with the dagger which Parker gave him."

"It is a theory that," admitted Poirot. "Decidedly you have cells of a kind. But it leaves a good deal unaccounted for."

"Such as——?"

"The telephone call, the pushed-out chair——"

"Do you really think the latter important?" I interrupted.

"Perhaps not," admitted my friend. "It may have been pulled out by accident, and Raymond or Blunt may have shoved it into place unconsciously under the stress of emotion. Then there is the missing forty pounds."

"Given by Ackroyd to Ralph," I suggested. "He may have reconsidered his first refusal."

"That still leaves one thing unexplained?"

"What?"

"Why was Blunt so certain in his own mind that it was Raymond with Mr. Ackroyd at nine-thirty?"

"He explained that," I said.

"You think so? I will not press the point. Tell me instead, what were Ralph Paton's reasons for disappearing?"

"That's rather more difficult," I said slowly. "I shall have to speak as a medical man. Ralph's nerves must have gone phut! If he suddenly found out that his uncle had been murdered within a few minutes of his leaving him—after, perhaps, a rather stormy interview—well, he might get the wind up and clear right out. Men have been known to do that—act guiltily when they're perfectly innocent."

"Yes, that is true," said Poirot. "But we must not lose sight of one thing."

"I know what you're going to say," I remarked: "motive. Ralph Paton inherits a great fortune by his uncle's death."

"That is one motive," agreed Poirot.

"One?"

"*Mais oui.* Do you realize that there are three separate motives staring us in the face. Somebody certainly stole the blue envelope and its contents. That is one motive. Blackmail! Ralph Paton may have been the man who blackmailed Mrs. Ferrars. Remember, as far as Hammond knew, Ralph Paton had not applied to his uncle for help of late. That looks as though he were being supplied with money elsewhere. Then there is the fact that he was in some—how do you say—scrape?—which he feared might get to his uncle's ears. And finally there is the one you have just mentioned."

"Dear me," I said, rather taken aback. "The case does seem black against him."

"Does it?" said Poirot. "That is where we disagree, you and I. Three motives—it is almost too much. I am inclined to believe that, after all, Ralph Paton is innocent."

FOURTEEN
Mrs. Ackroyd

After the evening talk I have just chronicled, the affair seemed to me to enter on a different phase. The whole thing can be divided into two parts, each clear and distinct from the other. Part I. ranges from Ackroyd's death on the Friday evening to the following Monday night. It is the straight-forward narrative of what occurred, as presented to Hercule Poirot. I was at Poirot's elbow the whole time. I saw what he saw. I tried my best to read his mind. As I know now, I failed in this latter task. Though Poirot showed me all his discoveries—as, for instance, the gold wedding-ring—he held back the vital and yet logical impressions that he formed. As I came to know later, this secrecy was characteristic of him. He would throw out hints and suggestions, but beyond that he would not go.

As I say, up till the Monday evening, my narrative might have been that of Poirot himself. I played Watson to his Sherlock. But after Monday our ways diverged. Poirot was busy on his own account. I got to hear of what he was doing, because, in King's Abbot, you get to hear of everything, but he did not take me into his confidence beforehand. And I, too, had my own preoccupations.

On looking back, the thing that strikes me most is the piecemeal character of this period. Every one had a hand in the elucidation of the mystery. It was rather like a jig-saw puzzle to which every one contributed their own little piece of knowledge or discovery. But their task ended there. To Poirot alone belongs the renown of fitting those pieces into their correct place.

Some of the incidents seemed at the time irrelevant and unmeaning. There was, for instance, the question of the black boots. But that comes later.... To take things strictly in chronological order, I must begin with the summons from Mrs. Ackroyd.

She sent for me early on Tuesday morning, and since the summons sounded an urgent one, I hastened there, expecting to find her *in extremis*.

The lady was in bed. So much did she concede to the etiquette of the situation. She gave me her bony hand, and indicated a chair drawn up to the bedside.

"Well, Mrs. Ackroyd," I said, "and what's the matter with you?"

I spoke with that kind of spurious geniality which seems to be expected of general practitioners.

"I'm prostrated," said Mrs. Ackroyd in a faint voice. "Absolutely prostrated. It's the shock of poor Roger's death. They say these things often aren't felt at the *time*, you know. It's the reaction afterwards."

It is a pity that a doctor is precluded by his profession from being able sometimes to say what he really thinks.

I would have given anything to be able to answer "Bunkum!"

Instead, I suggested a tonic. Mrs. Ackroyd accepted the tonic. One move in the game seemed now to be concluded. Not for a moment did I imagine that I had been sent for because of the shock occasioned by Ackroyd's death. But Mrs. Ackroyd is totally incapable of pursuing a straight-forward course on any subject. She always approaches her object by tortuous means. I wondered very much why it was she had sent for me.

"And then that scene—yesterday," continued my patient.

She paused as though expecting me to take up a cue.

"What scene?"

135

"Doctor, how can you? Have you forgotten? That dreadful little Frenchman—or Belgian—or whatever he is. Bullying us all like he did. It has quite upset me. Coming on top of Roger's death."

"I'm very sorry, Mrs. Ackroyd," I said.

"I don't know what he meant—shouting at us like he did. I should hope I know my duty too well to *dream* of concealing anything. I have given the police *every* assistance in my power."

Mrs. Ackroyd paused, and I said, "Quite so." I was beginning to have a glimmering of what all the trouble was about.

"No one can say that I have failed in my duty," continued Mrs. Ackroyd. "I am sure Inspector Raglan is perfectly satisfied. Why should this little upstart of a foreigner make a fuss? A most ridic-ulous-looking creature he is too—just like a comic Frenchman in a revue. I can't think why Flora insisted on bringing him into the case. She never said a word to me about it. Just went off and did it on her own. Flora is too independent. I am a woman of the world and her mother. She should have come to me for advice first."

I listened to all this in silence.

"What does he think? That's what I want to know. Does he actually imagine I'm hiding something? He—he—positively *accused* me yesterday."

I shrugged my shoulders.

"It is surely of no consequence, Mrs. Ackroyd," I said. "Since you are not concealing anything, any remarks he may have made do not apply to you."

Mrs. Ackroyd went off at a tangent, after her usual fashion.

"Servants are so tiresome," she said. "They gossip, and talk amongst themselves. And then it gets round—and all the time there's probably nothing in it at all."

"Have the servants been talking?" I asked. "What about?"

Mrs. Ackroyd cast a very shrewd glance at me. It quite threw me off my balance.

"I was sure *you'd* know, doctor, if any one did. You were with M. Poirot all the time, weren't you?"

"I was."

"Then of course you know. It was that girl, Ursula Bourne, wasn't it? Naturally—she's leaving. She *would* want to make all the trouble she could. Spiteful, that's what they are. They're all alike. Now, you being there, doctor, you must know exactly what she did say? I'm most anxious that no wrong impression should get about. After all, you don't repeat every little detail to the police, do you? There are family matters sometimes—nothing to do with the question of the murder. But if the girl was spiteful, she may have made out all sorts of things."

I was shrewd enough to see that a very real anxiety lay behind these outpourings. Poirot had been justified in his premises. Of the six people round the table yesterday, Mrs. Ackroyd at least had had something to hide. It was for me to discover what that something might be.

"If I were you, Mrs. Ackroyd," I said brusquely, "I should make a clean breast of things."

She gave a little scream.

"Oh! doctor, how can you be so abrupt. It sounds as though—as though——And I can explain everything so simply."

"Then why not do so," I suggested.

Mrs. Ackroyd took out a frilled handkerchief, and became tearful.

"I thought, doctor, that you might put it to M. Poirot—explain it, you know—because it's so difficult for a foreigner to see our point of view. And you don't know—nobody could know—what I've had to contend with. A martyrdom—a long martyrdom. That's what my life has been. I don't like to speak ill of the dead—but there it is. Not the smallest bill, but it had all to be gone over—just as though Roger had had a few miserly hundreds a year instead of being (as Mr. Hammond told me yesterday) one of the wealthiest men in these parts."

Mrs. Ackroyd paused to dab her eyes with the frilled handkerchief.

"Yes," I said encouragingly. "You were talking about bills?"

"Those dreadful bills. And some I didn't like to show Roger at all. They were things a man wouldn't understand. He would have said the things weren't necessary. And of course they mounted up, you know, and they kept coming in——"

She looked at me appealingly, as though asking me to condole with her on this striking peculiarity.

"It's a habit they have," I agreed.

"And the tone altered—became quite abusive. I assure you, doctor, I was becoming a nervous wreck. I couldn't sleep at nights. And a dreadful fluttering round the heart. And then I got a letter from a Scotch gentleman—as a matter of fact there were two letters—both Scotch gentlemen. Mr. Bruce MacPherson was one, and the other were Colin MacDonald. Quite a coincidence."

"Hardly that," I said dryly. "They are usually Scotch gentlemen, but I suspect a Semitic strain in their ancestry."

"Ten pounds to ten thousand on note of hand alone," murmured Mrs. Ackroyd reminiscently. "I wrote to one of them, but it seemed there were difficulties."

She paused.

I gathered that we were just coming to delicate ground. I have never known any one more difficult to bring to the point.

"You see," murmured Mrs. Ackroyd, "it's all a question of expectations, isn't it? Testamentary expectations. And though, of course, I expected that Roger would provide for me, I didn't *know*. I thought that if only I could glance over a copy of his will—not in any sense of vulgar prying—but just so that I could make my own arrangements."

She glanced sideways at me. The position was now very delicate indeed. Fortunately words, ingeniously used, will serve to mask the ugliness of naked facts.

"I could only tell this to you, dear Dr. Sheppard," said Mrs. Ackroyd rapidly. "I can trust you not to misjudge me, and to represent the matter in the right light to M. Poirot. It was on Friday afternoon———"

She came to a stop and swallowed uncertainly.

"Yes," I repeated encouragingly. "On Friday afternoon. Well?"

"Every one was out, or so I thought. And I went into Roger's study—I had some real reason for going there—I mean, there was nothing underhand about it. And as I saw all the papers heaped on the desk, it just came to me, like a flash: 'I wonder if Roger keeps his will in one of the drawers of the desk.' I'm so impulsive, always was, from a child. I do things on the spur of the moment. He'd left his keys—very careless of him—in the lock of the top drawer."

"I see," I said helpfully. "So you searched the desk. Did you find the will?"

Mrs. Ackroyd gave a little scream, and I realized that I had not been sufficiently diplomatic.

"How dreadful it sounds. But it wasn't at all like that really."

"Of course it wasn't," I said hastily. "You must forgive my unfortunate way of putting things."

"You see, men are so peculiar. In dear Roger's place, I should not have objected to revealing the provisions of my will. But men are so secretive. One is forced to adopt little subterfuges in self-defence."

"And the result of the little subterfuge?" I asked.

"That's just what I'm telling you. As I got to the bottom drawer, Bourne came in. Most awkward. Of course I shut the drawer and stood up, and I called her attention to a few specks of dust on the surface. But I didn't like the way she looked—quite respectful in manner, but a very nasty light in her eyes. Almost contemptuous, if you know what I mean. I never have liked that girl very much. She's a good servant, and she says Ma'am, and doesn't object to wearing caps and aprons (which I declare to you a lot of them do nowadays), and she can say 'Not at home' without scruples if she has to answer the door instead of Parker, and she doesn't have those peculiar gurgling noises inside which so many parlormaids seem to have when they wait at table———Let me see, where was I?"

"You were saying, that in spite of several valuable qualities, you never liked Bourne."

"No more I do. She's—odd. There's something different about her from the others. Too well educated, that's my opinion. You can't tell who are ladies and who aren't nowadays."

"And what happened next?" I asked.

"Nothing. At least, Roger came in. And I thought he was out for a walk. And he said: 'What's all this?' and I said, 'Nothing. I just came in to fetch *Punch*.' And I took *Punch* and went out with it. Bourne stayed behind. I heard her asking Roger if she could speak to him for a minute. I went straight up to my room, to lie down. I was very upset."

There was a pause.

"You will explain to M. Poirot, won't you? You can see for yourself what a trivial matter the whole thing was. But, of course, when he was so stern about concealing things, I thought of this at once. Bourne may have made some extraordinary story out of it, but you can explain, can't you?"

"That is all?" I said. "You have told me everything?"

"Ye-es," said Mrs. Ackroyd. "Oh! yes," she added firmly.

But I had noted the momentary hesitation, and I knew that there was still something she was keeping back. It was nothing less than a flash of sheer genius that prompted me to ask the question I did.

"Mrs. Ackroyd," I said, "was it you who left the silver table open?"

I had my answer in the blush of guilt that even rouge and powder could not conceal.

"How did you know?" she whispered.

"It was you, then?"

"Yes—I—you see—there were one or two pieces of old silver—very interesting. I had been reading up the subject and there was an illustration of quite a small piece which had fetched an immense sum at Christy's. It looked to me just the same as the one in the silver table. I thought I would take it up to London with me when I went—and—and have it valued. Then if it really was a valuable piece, just think what a charming surprise it would have been for Roger?"

I refrained from comments, accepting Mrs. Ackroyd's story on its merits. I even forbore to ask her why it was necessary to abstract what she wanted in such a surreptitious manner.

"Why did you leave the lid open?" I asked. "Did you forget?"

"I was startled," said Mrs. Ackroyd. "I heard footsteps coming along the terrace outside. I hastened out of the room and just got up the stairs before Parker opened the front door to you."

"That must have been Miss Russell," I said thoughtfully. Mrs. Ackroyd had revealed to me one fact that was extremely interesting. Whether her designs upon Ackroyd's silver had been strictly honorable I neither knew nor cared. What did interest me was the fact that Miss Russell must have entered the drawing-room by the window, and that I had not been wrong when I judged her to be out of breath with running. Where had she been? I thought of the summer-house and the scrap of cambric.

"I wonder if Miss Russell has her handkerchiefs starched!" I exclaimed on the spur of the moment.

Mrs. Ackroyd's start recalled me to myself, and I rose.

"You think you can explain to M. Poirot?" she asked anxiously.

"Oh, certainly. Absolutely."

I got away at last, after being forced to listen to more justifications of her conduct.

The parlormaid was in the hall, and it was she who helped me on with my overcoat. I observed her more closely than I had done heretofore. It was clear that she had been crying.

"How is it," I asked, "that you told us that Mr. Ackroyd sent for you on Friday to his study? I hear now that it was *you* who asked to speak to *him*?"

For a minute the girl's eyes dropped before mine.

Then she spoke.

141

"I meant to leave in any case," she said uncertainly.

I said no more. She opened the front door for me. Just as I was passing out, she said suddenly in a low voice:—

"Excuse me, sir, is there any news of Captain Paton?"

I shook my head, looking at her inquiringly.

"He ought to come back," she said. "Indeed—indeed he ought to come back."

She was looking at me with appealing eyes.

"Does no one know where he is?" she asked.

"Do you?" I said sharply.

She shook her head.

"No, indeed. I know nothing. But any one who was a friend to him would tell him this: he ought to come back."

I lingered, thinking that perhaps the girl would say more. Her next question surprised me.

"When do they think the murder was done? Just before ten o'clock?"

"That is the idea," I said. "Between a quarter to ten and the hour."

"Not earlier? Not before a quarter to ten?"

I looked at her attentively. She was so clearly eager for a reply in the affirmative.

"That's out of the question," I said. "Miss Ackroyd saw her uncle alive at a quarter to ten."

She turned away, and her whole figure seemed to droop.

"A handsome girl," I said to myself as I drove off. "An exceedingly handsome girl."

Caroline was at home. She had had a visit from Poirot and was very pleased and important about it.

"I am helping him with the case," she explained.

I felt rather uneasy. Caroline is bad enough as it is. What will she be like with her detective instincts encouraged?

"Are you going round the neighborhood looking for Ralph Paton's mysterious girl?" I inquired.

"I might do that on my own account," said Caroline. "No, this is a special thing M. Poirot wants me to find out for him."

"What is it?" I asked.

"He wants to know whether Ralph Paton's boots were black or brown," said Caroline with tremendous solemnity.

I stared at her. I see now that I was unbelievably stupid about these boots. I failed altogether to grasp the point.

"They were brown shoes," I said. "I saw them."

"Not shoes, James, boots. M. Poirot wants to know whether a pair of boots Ralph had with him at the hotel were brown or black. A lot hangs on it."

Call me dense if you like. I didn't see.

"And how are you going to find out?" I asked.

Caroline said there would be no difficulty about that. Our Annie's dearest friend was Miss Ganett's maid, Clara. And Clara was walking out with the boots at the Three Boars. The whole thing was simplicity itself, and by the aid of Miss Ganett, who coöperated loyally, at once giving Clara leave of absence, the matter was rushed through at express speed.

It was when we were sitting down to lunch that Caroline remarked, with would-be unconcern:—

"About those boots of Ralph Paton's."

"Well," I said, "what about them?"

"M. Poirot thought they were probably brown. He was wrong. They're black."

And Caroline nodded her head several times. She evidently felt that she had scored a point over Poirot.

I did not answer. I was puzzling over what the color of a pair of Ralph Paton's boots had to do with the case.

FIFTEEN
Geoffrey Raymond

I was to have a further proof that day of the success of Poirot's tactics. That challenge of his had been a subtle touch born of his knowledge of human nature. A mixture of fear and guilt had wrung the truth from Mrs. Ackroyd. She was the first to react.

That afternoon when I returned from seeing my patients, Caroline told me that Geoffrey Raymond had just left.

"Did he want to see me?" I asked, as I hung up my coat in the hall.

Caroline was hovering by my elbow.

"It was M. Poirot he wanted to see," she said. "He'd just come from The Larches. M. Poirot was out. Mr. Raymond thought that he might be here, or that you might know where he was."

"I haven't the least idea."

"I tried to make him wait," said Caroline, "but he said he would call back at The Larches in half an hour, and went away down the village. A great pity, because M. Poirot came in practically the minute after he left."

"Came in here?"

"No, to his own house."

"How do you know?"

"The side window," said Caroline briefly.

It seemed to me that we had now exhausted the topic. Caroline thought otherwise.

"Aren't you going across?"

"Across where?"

"To The Larches, of course."

"My dear Caroline," I said, "what for?"

"Mr. Raymond wanted to see him very particularly," said Caroline. "You might hear what it's all about."

I raised my eyebrows.

"Curiosity is not my besetting sin," I remarked coldly. "I can exist comfortably without knowing exactly what my neighbors are doing and thinking."

"Stuff and nonsense, James," said my sister. "You want to know just as much as I do. You're not so honest, that's all. You always have to pretend."

"Really, Caroline," I said, and retired into my surgery.

Ten minutes later Caroline tapped at the door and entered. In her hand she held what seemed to be a pot of jam.

"I wonder, James," she said, "if you would mind taking this pot of medlar jelly across to M. Poirot? I promised it to him. He has never tasted any home-made medlar jelly."

"Why can't Annie go?" I asked coldly.

"She's doing some mending. I can't spare her."

Caroline and I looked at each other.

"Very well," I said, rising. "But if I take the beastly thing, I shall just leave it at the door. You understand that?"

My sister raised her eyebrows.

"Naturally," she said. "Who suggested you should do anything else?"

The honors were with Caroline.

"If you *do* happen to see M. Poirot," she said, as I opened the front door, "you might tell him about the boots."

It was a most subtle parting shot. I wanted dreadfully to understand the enigma of the boots. When the old lady with the Breton cap opened the door to me, I found myself asking if M. Poirot was in, quite automatically.

Poirot sprang up to meet me, with every appearance of pleasure.

"Sit down, my good friend," he said. "The big chair? This small one? The room is not too hot, no?"

I thought it was stifling, but refrained from saying so. The windows were closed, and a large fire burned in the grate.

"The English people, they have a mania for the fresh air," declared Poirot. "The big air, it is all very well outside, where it belongs. Why admit it to the house? But let us not discuss such banalities. You have something for me, yes?"

"Two things," I said. "First—this—from my sister."

I handed over the pot of medlar jelly.

"How kind of Mademoiselle Caroline. She has remembered her promise. And the second thing?"

"Information—of a kind."

And I told him of my interview with Mrs. Ackroyd. He listened with interest, but not much excitement.

"It clears the ground," he said thoughtfully. "And it has a certain value as confirming the evidence of the housekeeper. She said, you remember, that she found the silver table lid open and closed it down in passing."

"What about her statement that she went into the drawing-room to see if the flowers were fresh?"

"Ah! we never took that very seriously, did we, my friend? It was patently an excuse, trumped up in a hurry, by a woman who felt it urgent to explain her presence—which, by the way, you would probably never have thought of questioning. I considered it possible that her agitation might arise from the fact that she had been tampering with the silver table, but I think now that we must look for another cause."

"Yes," I said. "Whom did she go out to meet? And why?"

"You think she went to meet some one?"

"I do."

Poirot nodded.

"So do I," he said thoughtfully.

There was a pause.

"By the way," I said, "I've got a message for you from my sister. Ralph Paton's boots were black, not brown."

I was watching him closely as I gave the message, and I fancied that I saw a momentary flicker of discomposure. If so, it passed almost immediately.

"She is absolutely positive they are not brown?"

"Absolutely."

"Ah!" said Poirot regretfully. "That is a pity."

And he seemed quite crestfallen.

He entered into no explanations, but at once started a new subject of conversation.

"The housekeeper, Miss Russell, who came to consult you on that Friday morning—is it indiscreet to ask what passed at the interview—apart from the medical details, I mean?"

"Not at all," I said. "When the professional part of the conversation was over, we talked for a few minutes about poisons, and the ease or difficulty of detecting them, and about drug-taking and drug-takers."

"With special reference to cocaine?" asked Poirot.

"How did you know?" I asked, somewhat surprised.

For answer, the little man rose and crossed the room to where newspapers were filed. He brought me a copy of the *Daily Budget*, dated Friday, 16th September, and showed me an article dealing with the smuggling of cocaine. It was a somewhat lurid article, written with an eye to picturesque effect.

"That is what put cocaine into her head, my friend," he said.

I would have catechized him further, for I did not quite understand his meaning, but at that moment the door opened and Geoffrey Raymond was announced.

He came in fresh and debonair as ever, and greeted us both.

"How are you, doctor? M. Poirot, this is the second time I've been here this morning. I was anxious to catch you."

"Perhaps I'd better be off," I suggested rather awkwardly.

"Not on my account, doctor. No, it's just this," he went on, seating himself at a wave of invitation from Poirot, "I've got a confession to make."

"*En verité?*" said Poirot, with an air of polite interest.

"Oh, it's of no consequence, really. But, as a matter of fact, my conscience has been pricking me ever since yesterday afternoon. You accused us all of keeping back something, M. Poirot. I plead guilty. I've had something up my sleeve."

"And what is that, M. Raymond?"

"As I say, it's nothing of consequence—just this. I was in debt—badly, and that legacy came in the nick of time. Five hundred pounds puts me on my feet again with a little to spare."

He smiled at us both with that engaging frankness that made him such a likable youngster.

"You know how it is. Suspicious looking policeman—don't like to admit you were hard up for money—think it will look bad to them. But I was a fool, really, because Blunt and I were in the billiard room from a quarter to ten onwards, so I've got a watertight alibi and nothing to fear. Still, when you thundered out that stuff about concealing things, I felt a nasty prick of conscience, and I thought I'd like to get it off my mind."

He got up again and stood smiling at us.

"You are a very wise young man," said Poirot, nodding at him with approval. "See you, when I know that any one is hiding things from me, I suspect that the thing hidden may be something very bad indeed. You have done well."

"I'm glad I'm cleared from suspicion," laughed Raymond. "I'll be off now."

"So that is that," I remarked, as the door closed behind the young secretary.

"Yes," agreed Poirot. "A mere bagatelle—but if he had not been in the billiard room—who knows? After all, many crimes have been committed for the sake of less than five hundred pounds. It all depends on what sum is sufficient to break a man. A question of the relativity, is it not so? Have you reflected, my friend, that many people in that house stood to benefit by Mr. Ackroyd's death? Mrs. Ackroyd, Miss Flora, young Mr. Raymond, the housekeeper, Miss Russell. Only one, in fact, does not, Major Blunt."

His tone in uttering that name was so peculiar that I looked up, puzzled.

"I don't quite understand you?" I said.

"Two of the people I accused have given me the truth."

"You think Major Blunt has something to conceal also?"

"As for that," remarked Poirot nonchalantly, "there is a saying, is there not, that Englishmen conceal only one thing—their love? And Major Blunt, I should say, is not good at concealments."

"Sometimes," I said, "I wonder if we haven't rather jumped to conclusions on one point."

"What is that?"

"We've assumed that the blackmailer of Mrs. Ferrars is necessarily the murderer of Mr. Ackroyd. Mightn't we be mistaken?"

Poirot nodded energetically.

"Very good. Very good indeed. I wondered if that idea would come to you. Of course it is possible. But we must remember one point. The letter disappeared. Still, that, as you say, may not necessarily mean that the murderer took it. When you first found the body, Parker may have abstracted the letter unnoticed by you."

"Parker?"

"Yes, Parker. I always come back to Parker—not as the murderer—no, he did not commit the murder; but who is more suitable than he as the mysterious scoundrel who terrorized Mrs. Ferrars? He may have got his information about Mr. Ferrars's death from one of the King's Paddock servants. At any rate, he is more likely to have come upon it than a casual guest such as Blunt, for instance."

"Parker might have taken the letter," I admitted. "It wasn't till later that I noticed it was gone."

"How much later? After Blunt and Raymond were in the room, or before?"

"I can't remember," I said slowly. "I think it was before—no, afterwards. Yes, I'm almost sure it was afterwards."

"That widens the field to three," said Poirot thoughtfully. "But Parker is the most likely. It is in my mind to try a little experiment with Parker. How say you, my friend, will you accompany me to Fernly?"

I acquiesced, and we set out at once. Poirot asked to see Miss Ackroyd, and presently Flora came to us.

"Mademoiselle Flora," said Poirot, "I have to confide in you a little secret. I am not yet satisfied of the innocence of Parker. I propose to make a little experiment with your assistance. I want to reconstruct some of his actions on that night. But we must think of something to tell him—ah! I have it. I wish to satisfy myself as to whether voices in the little lobby could have been heard outside on the terrace. Now, ring for Parker, if you will be so good."

I did so, and presently the butler appeared, suave as ever.

"You rang, sir?"

"Yes, my good Parker. I have in mind a little experiment. I have placed Major Blunt on the terrace outside the study window. I want to see if any one there could have heard the voices of Miss Ackroyd and yourself in the lobby that night. I want to enact that little scene over again. Perhaps you would fetch the tray or whatever it was you were carrying?"

Parker vanished, and we repaired to the lobby outside the study door. Presently we heard a chink in the outer hall, and Parker appeared in the doorway carrying a tray with a siphon, a decanter of whisky, and two glasses on it.

"One moment," cried Poirot, raising his hand and seemingly very excited. "We must have everything in order. Just as it occurred. It is a little method of mine."

"A foreign custom, sir," said Parker. "Reconstruction of the crime they call it, do they not?"

He was quite imperturbable as he stood there politely waiting on Poirot's orders.

"Ah! he knows something, the good Parker," cried Poirot. "He has read of these things. Now, I beg you, let us have everything of the most exact. You came from the outer hall—so. Mademoiselle was—where?"

"Here," said Flora, taking up her stand just outside the study door.

"Quite right, sir," said Parker.

"I had just closed the door," continued Flora.

"Yes, miss," agreed Parker. "Your hand was still on the handle as it is now."

"Then *allez*," said Poirot. "Play me the little comedy."

Flora stood with her hand on the door handle, and Parker came stepping through the door from the hall, bearing the tray.

He stopped just inside the door. Flora spoke.

"Oh! Parker. Mr. Ackroyd doesn't want to be disturbed again to-night."

"Is that right?" she added in an undertone.

"To the best of my recollection, Miss Flora," said Parker, "but I fancy you used the word evening instead of night." Then, raising his voice in a somewhat theatrical fashion: "Very good, miss. Shall I lock up as usual?"

"Yes, please."

Parker retired through the door, Flora followed him, and started to ascend the main staircase.

"Is that enough?" she asked over her shoulder.

"Admirable," declared the little man, rubbing his hands. "By the way, Parker, are you sure there were two glasses on the tray that evening? Who was the second one for?"

"I always bring two glasses, sir," said Parker. "Is there anything further?"

"Nothing. I thank you."

Parker withdrew, dignified to the last.

Poirot stood in the middle of the hall frowning. Flora came down and joined us.

"Has your experiment been successful?" she asked. "I don't quite understand, you know——"

Poirot smiled admiringly at her.

"It is not necessary that you should," he said. "But tell me, were there indeed two glasses on Parker's tray that night?"

Flora wrinkled her brows a minute.

"I really can't remember," she said. "I think there were. Is—is that the object of your experiment?"

Poirot took her hand and patted it.

"Put it this way," he said. "I am always interested to see if people will speak the truth."

"And did Parker speak the truth?"

"I rather think he did," said Poirot thoughtfully.

A few minutes later saw us retracing our steps to the village.

"What was the point of that question about the glasses?" I asked curiously.

Poirot shrugged his shoulders.

"One must say something," he remarked. "That particular question did as well as any other."

I stared at him.

"At any rate, my friend," he said more seriously, "I know now something I wanted to know. Let us leave it at that."

SIXTEEN
An Evening at Mah Jong

That night we had a little Mah Jong party. This kind of simple entertainment is very popular in King's Abbot. The guests arrive in goloshes and waterproofs after dinner. They partake of coffee and later of cake, sandwiches, and tea.

On this particular night our guests were Miss Ganett and Colonel Carter, who lives near the church. A good deal of gossip is handed round at these evenings, sometimes seriously interfering with the game in progress. We used to play bridge—chatty bridge of the worst description. We find Mah Jong much more peaceful. The irritated demand as to why on earth your partner did not lead a certain card is entirely done away with, and though we still express criticisms frankly, there is not the same acrimonious spirit.

"Very cold evening, eh, Sheppard?" said Colonel Carter, standing with his back to the fire. Caroline had taken Miss Ganett to her own room, and was there assisting her to disentangle herself from her many wraps. "Reminds me of the Afghan passes."

"Indeed?" I said politely.

"Very mysterious business this about poor Ackroyd," continued the colonel, accepting a cup of coffee. "A deuce of a lot behind it—that's what I say. Between you and me, Sheppard, I've heard the word blackmail mentioned!"

The colonel gave me the look which might be tabulated "one man of the world to another."

"A woman in it, no doubt," he said. "Depend upon it, a woman in it."

Caroline and Miss Ganett joined us at this minute. Miss Ganett drank coffee whilst Caroline got out the Mah Jong box and poured out the tiles upon the table.

"Washing the tiles," said the colonel facetiously. "That's right—washing the tiles, as we used to say in the Shanghai Club."

It is the private opinion of both Caroline and myself that Colonel Carter has never been in the Shanghai Club in his life. More, that he has never been farther east than India, where he juggled with tins of bully beef and plum and apple jam during the Great War. But the colonel is determinedly military, and in King's Abbot we permit people to indulge their little idiosyncrasies freely.

"Shall we begin?" said Caroline.

We sat round the table. For some five minutes there was complete silence, owing to the fact that there is tremendous secret competition amongst us as to who can build their wall quickest.

"Go on, James," said Caroline at last. "You're East Wind."

I discarded a tile. A round or two proceeded, broken by the monotonous remarks of "Three Bamboos," "Two Circles," "Pung," and frequently from Miss Ganett "Unpung," owing to that lady's habit of too hastily claiming tiles to which she had no right.

"I saw Flora Ackroyd this morning," said Miss Ganett. "Pung—no—Unpung. I made a mistake."

"Four Circles," said Caroline. "Where did you see her?"

"She didn't see *me*," said Miss Ganett, with that tremendous significance only to be met with in small villages.

"Ah!" said Caroline interestedly. "Chow."

"I believe," said Miss Ganett, temporarily diverted, "that it's the right thing nowadays to say 'Chee' not 'Chow.'"

"Nonsense," said Caroline. "I have always said '*Chow*.'"

"In the Shanghai Club," said Colonel Carter, "they say '*Chow*.'"

Miss Ganett retired, crushed.

"What were you saying about Flora Ackroyd?" asked Caroline,

after a moment or two devoted to the game. "Was she with any one?"

"Very much so," said Miss Ganett.

The eyes of the two ladies met, and seemed to exchange information.

"Really," said Caroline interestedly. "Is that it? Well, it doesn't surprise me in the least."

"We're waiting for you to discard, Miss Caroline," said the colonel. He sometimes affects the pose of the bluff male, intent on the game and indifferent to gossip. But nobody is deceived.

"If you ask me," said Miss Ganett. ("Was that a Bamboo you discarded, dear? Oh! no, I see now—it was a Circle.) As I was saying, if you ask me, Flora's been exceedingly lucky. Exceedingly lucky she's been."

"How's that, Miss Ganett?" asked the colonel. "I'll Pung that Green Dragon. How do you make out that Miss Flora's been lucky? Very charming girl and all that, I know."

"I mayn't know very much about crime," said Miss Ganett, with the air of one who knows everything there is to know, "but I can tell you one thing. The first question that's always asked is 'Who last saw the deceased alive?' And the person who did is regarded with suspicion. Now, Flora Ackroyd last saw her uncle alive. It might have looked very nasty for her—very nasty indeed. It's my opinion—and I give it for what it's worth, that Ralph Paton is staying away on her account, to draw suspicion away from her."

"Come, now," I protested mildly, "you surely can't suggest that a young girl like Flora Ackroyd is capable of stabbing her uncle in cold blood?"

"Well, I don't know," said Miss Ganett. "I've just been reading a book from the library about the underworld of Paris, and it says that some of the worst women criminals are young girls with the faces of angels."

"That's in France," said Caroline instantly.

"Just so," said the colonel. "Now, I'll tell you a very curious thing—a story that was going round the Bazaars in India...."

The colonel's story was one of interminable length, and of curiously little interest. A thing that happened in India many years ago cannot compare for a moment with an event that took place in King's Abbot the day before yesterday.

It was Caroline who brought the colonel's story to a close by fortunately going Mah Jong. After the slight unpleasantness always occasioned by my corrections of Caroline's somewhat faulty arithmetic, we started a new hand.

"East Wind passes," said Caroline. "I've got an idea of my own about Ralph Paton. Three Characters. But I'm keeping it to myself for the present."

"Are you, dear?" said Miss Ganett. "Chow—I mean Pung."

"Yes," said Caroline firmly.

"Was it all right about the boots?" asked Miss Ganett. "Their being black, I mean?"

"Quite all right," said Caroline.

"What was the point, do you think?" asked Miss Ganett.

Caroline pursed up her lips, and shook her head with an air of knowing all about it.

"Pung," said Miss Ganett. "No—Unpung. I suppose that now the doctor's in with M. Poirot he knows all the secrets?"

"Far from it," I said.

"James is so modest," said Caroline. "Ah! a concealed Kong."

The colonel gave vent to a whistle. For the moment gossip was forgotten.

"Your own wind, too," he said. "*And* you've got two Pungs of Dragons. We must be careful. Miss Caroline's out for a big hand."

We played for some minutes with no irrelevant conversation.

"This M. Poirot now," said Colonel Carter, "is he really such a great detective?"

"The greatest the world has ever known," said Caroline solemnly. "He had to come here incognito to avoid publicity."

"Chow," said Miss Ganett. "Quite wonderful for our little

village, I'm sure. By the way, Clara—my maid, you know—is great friends with Elsie, the housemaid at Fernly, and what do you think Elsie told her? That there's been a lot of money stolen, and it's her opinion—Elsie's—I mean, that the parlormaid had something to do with it. She's leaving at the month, and she's crying a good deal at night. If you ask me, the girl is very likely in league with a *gang*. She's always been a queer girl—she's not friends with any of the girls round here. She goes off by herself on her days out— very unnatural, I call it, and most suspicious. I asked her once to come to our Girls' Friendly Evenings, but she refused, and then I asked her a few questions about her home and her family—all that sort of thing, and I'm bound to say I considered her manner most impertinent. Outwardly very respectful—but she shut me up in the most barefaced way."

Miss Ganett stopped for breath, and the colonel, who was totally uninterested in the servant question, remarked that in the Shanghai Club brisk play was the invariable rule.

We had a round of brisk play.

"That Miss Russell," said Caroline. "She came here pretending to consult James on Friday morning. It's my opinion she wanted to see where the poisons were kept. Five Characters."

"Chow," said Miss Ganett. "What an extraordinary idea? I wonder if you can be right."

"Talking of poisons," said the colonel. "Eh—what? Haven't I discarded? Oh! Eight Bamboos."

"Mah Jong!" said Miss Ganett.

Caroline was very much annoyed.

"One Red Dragon," she said regretfully, "and I should have had a hand of three doubles."

"I've had two Red Dragons all the time," I mentioned.

"So exactly like you, James," said Caroline reproachfully. "You've no conception of the spirit of the game."

I myself thought I had played rather cleverly. I should have had to pay Caroline an enormous amount if she had gone Mah

Jong. Miss Ganett's Mah Jong was of the poorest variety possible, as Caroline did not fail to point out to her.

East Wind passed, and we started a new hand in silence.

"What I was going to tell you just now was this," said Caroline.

"Yes?" said Miss Ganett encouragingly.

"My idea about Ralph Paton, I mean."

"Yes, dear," said Miss Ganett, still more encouragingly. "Chow!"

"It's a sign of weakness to Chow so early," said Caroline severely. "You should go for a big hand."

"I know," said Miss Ganett. "You were saying—about Ralph Paton, you know?"

"Yes. Well, I've a pretty shrewd idea where he is."

We all stopped to stare at her.

"This is very interesting, Miss Caroline," said Colonel Carter. "All your own idea, eh?"

"Well, not exactly. I'll tell you about it. You know that big map of the county we have in the hall?"

We all said Yes.

"As M. Poirot was going out the other day, he stopped and looked at it, and he made some remark—I can't remember exactly what it was. Something about Cranchester being the only big town anywhere near us—which is true, of course. But after he had gone—it came to me suddenly."

"What came to you?"

"His meaning. Of course Ralph is in Cranchester."

It was at that moment that I knocked down the rack that held my pieces. My sister immediately reproved me for clumsiness, but half-heartedly. She was intent on her theory.

"Cranchester, Miss Caroline?" said Colonel Carter. "Surely not Cranchester! It's so near."

"That's exactly it," cried Caroline triumphantly. "It seems quite clear by now that he didn't get away from here by train. He must simply have walked into Cranchester. And I believe he's there still. No one would dream of his being so near at hand."

I pointed out several objections to the theory, but when once Caroline has got something firmly into her head, nothing dislodges it.

"And you think M. Poirot has the same idea," said Miss Ganett thoughtfully. "It's a curious coincidence, but I was out for a walk this afternoon on the Cranchester road, and he passed me in a car coming from that direction."

We all looked at each other.

"Why, dear me," said Miss Ganett suddenly, "I'm Mah Jong all the time, and I never noticed it."

Caroline's attention was distracted from her own inventive exercises. She pointed out to Miss Ganett that a hand consisting of mixed suits and too many Chows was hardly worth going Mah Jong on. Miss Ganett listened imperturbably and collected her counters.

"Yes, dear, I know what you mean," she said. "But it rather depends on what kind of a hand you have to start with, doesn't it?"

"You'll never get the big hands if you don't go for them," urged Caroline.

"Well, we must all play our own way, mustn't we?" said Miss Ganett. She looked down at her counters. "After all, I'm up, so far."

Caroline, who was considerably down, said nothing.

East Wind passed, and we set to once more. Annie brought in the tea things. Caroline and Miss Ganett were both slightly ruffled as is often the case during one of these festive evenings.

"If you would only play a leetle quicker, dear," said Caroline, as Miss Ganett hesitated over her discard. "The Chinese put down the tiles so quickly it sounds like little birds pattering."

For some few minutes we played like the Chinese.

"You haven't contributed much to the sum of information, Sheppard," said Colonel Carter genially. "You're a sly dog. Hand in glove with the great detective, and not a hint as to the way things are going."

"James is an extraordinary creature," said Caroline. "He can *not* bring himself to part with information."

She looked at me with some disfavor.

"I assure you," I said, "that I don't know anything. Poirot keeps his own counsel."

"Wise man," said the colonel with a chuckle. "He doesn't give himself away. But they're wonderful fellows, these foreign detectives. Up to all sorts of dodges, I believe."

"Pung," said Miss Ganett, in a tone of quiet triumph. "And Mah Jong."

The situation became more strained. It was annoyance at Miss Ganett's going Mah Jong for the third time running which prompted Caroline to say to me as we built a fresh wall:—

"You are too tiresome, James. You sit there like a dead head, and say nothing at all!"

"But, my dear," I protested, "I have really nothing to say—that is, of the kind you mean."

"Nonsense," said Caroline, as she sorted her hand. "You *must* know something interesting."

I did not answer for a moment. I was overwhelmed and intoxicated. I had read of there being such a thing as the Perfect Winning—going Mah Jong on one's original hand. I had never hoped to hold the hand myself.

With suppressed triumph I laid my hand face upwards on the table.

"As they say in the Shanghai Club," I remarked, "Tin-ho—the Perfect Winning!"

The colonel's eyes nearly bulged out of his head.

"Upon my soul," he said. "What an extraordinary thing. I never saw that happen before!"

It was then that I went on, goaded by Caroline's gibes, and rendered reckless by my triumph.

"And as to anything interesting," I said. "What about a gold wedding ring with a date and 'From R.' inside."

I pass over the scene that followed. I was made to say exactly where this treasure was found. I was made to reveal the date.

"March 13th," said Caroline. "Just six months ago. Ah!"

Out of the babel of excited suggestions and suppositions three theories were evolved:—

1 That of Colonel Carter: that Ralph was secretly married to Flora. The first or most simple solution.

2 That of Miss Ganett: that Roger Ackroyd had been secretly married to Mrs. Ferrars.

3 That of my sister: that Roger Ackroyd had married his housekeeper, Miss Russell.

A fourth or super-theory was propounded by Caroline later as we went up to bed.

"Mark my words," she said suddenly, "I shouldn't be at all surprised if Geoffrey Raymond and Flora weren't married."

"Surely it would be 'From G,' not 'From R' then," I suggested.

"You never know. Some girls call men by their surnames. And you heard what Miss Ganett said this evening—about Flora's carryings on."

Strictly speaking, I had not heard Miss Ganett say anything of the kind, but I respected Caroline's knowledge of innuendoes.

"How about Hector Blunt," I hinted. "If it's anybody——"

"Nonsense," said Caroline. "I dare say he admires her—may even be in love with her. But depend upon it a girl isn't going to fall in love with a man old enough to be her father when there's a good-looking young secretary about. She may encourage Major Blunt just as a blind. Girls are very artful. But there's one thing I *do* tell you, James Sheppard. Flora Ackroyd does not care a penny piece for Ralph Paton, and never has. You can take it from me."

I took it from her meekly.

SEVENTEEN
Parker

I t occurred to me the next morning that under the exhilaration produced by Tin-ho, or the Perfect Winning, I might have been slightly indiscreet. True, Poirot had not asked me to keep the discovery of the ring to myself. On the other hand, he had said nothing about it whilst at Fernly, and as far as I knew, I was the only person aware that it had been found. I felt distinctly guilty. The fact was by now spreading through King's Abbot like wildfire. I was expecting wholesale reproaches from Poirot any minute.

The joint funeral of Mrs. Ferrars and Roger Ackroyd was fixed for eleven o'clock. It was a melancholy and impressive ceremony. All the party from Fernly were there.

After it was over, Poirot, who had also been present, took me by the arm, and invited me to accompany him back to The Larches. He was looking very grave, and I feared that my indiscretion of the night before had got round to his ears. But it soon transpired that his thoughts were occupied by something of a totally different nature.

"See you," he said. "We must act. With your help I propose to examine a witness. We will question him, we will put such fear into him that the truth is bound to come out."

"What witness are you talking of?" I asked, very much surprised.

"Parker!" said Poirot. "I asked him to be at my house this

morning at twelve o'clock. He should await us there at this very minute."

"What do you think," I ventured, glancing sideways at his face.

"I know this—that I am not satisfied."

"You think that it was he who blackmailed Mrs. Ferrars?"

"Either that, or——"

"Well?" I said, after waiting a minute or two.

"My friend, I will say this to you—I hope it was he."

The gravity of his manner, and something indefinable that tinged it, reduced me to silence.

On arrival at The Larches, we were informed that Parker was already there awaiting our return. As we entered the room, the butler rose respectfully.

"Good morning, Parker," said Poirot pleasantly. "One instant, I pray of you."

He removed his overcoat and gloves.

"Allow me, sir," said Parker, and sprang forward to assist him. He deposited the articles neatly on a chair by the door. Poirot watched him with approval.

"Thank you, my good Parker," he said. "Take a seat, will you not? What I have to say may take some time."

Parker seated himself with an apologetic bend of the head.

"Now what do you think I asked you to come here for this morning—eh?"

Parker coughed.

"I understood, sir, that you wished to ask me a few questions about my late master—private like."

"*Précisément*," said Poirot, beaming. "Have you made many experiments in blackmail?"

"Sir!"

The butler sprang to his feet.

"Do not excite yourself," said Poirot placidly. "Do not play the farce of the honest, injured man. You know all there is to know about the blackmail, is it not so?"

"Sir, I—I've never—never been———"

"Insulted," suggested Poirot, "in such a way before. Then why, my excellent Parker, were you so anxious to overhear the conversation in Mr. Ackroyd's study the other evening, after you had caught the word blackmail?"

"I wasn't—I———"

"Who was your last master?" rapped out Poirot suddenly.

"My last master?"

"Yes, the master you were with before you came to Mr. Ackroyd."

"A Major Ellerby, sir———"

Poirot took the words out of his mouth.

"Just so, Major Ellerby. Major Ellerby was addicted to drugs, was he not? You traveled about with him. When he was in Bermuda there was some trouble—a man was killed. Major Ellerby was partly responsible. It was hushed up. But you knew about it. How much did Major Ellerby pay you to keep your mouth shut?"

Parker was staring at him open-mouthed. The man had gone to pieces, his cheeks shook flabbily.

"You see, me, I have made inquiries," said Poirot pleasantly. "It is as I say. You got a good sum then as blackmail, and Major Ellerby went on paying you until he died. Now I want to hear about your latest experiment."

Parker still stared.

"It is useless to deny. Hercule Poirot *knows*. It is so, what I have said about Major Ellerby, is it not?"

As though against his will, Parker nodded reluctantly once. His face was ashen pale.

"But I never hurt a hair of Mr. Ackroyd's head," he moaned. "Honest to God, sir, I didn't. I've been afraid of this coming all the time. And I tell you I didn't—I didn't kill him."

His voice rose almost to a scream.

"I am inclined to believe you, my friend," said Poirot. "You have not the nerve—the courage. But I must have the truth."

"I'll tell you anything, sir, anything you want to know. It's true that I tried to listen that night. A word or two I heard made me curious. And Mr. Ackroyd's wanting not to be disturbed, and shutting himself up with the doctor the way he did. It's God's own truth what I told the police. I heard the word blackmail, sir, and well——"

He paused.

"You thought there might be something in it for you?" suggested Poirot smoothly.

"Well—well, yes, I did, sir. I thought that if Mr. Ackroyd was being blackmailed, why shouldn't I have a share of the pickings?"

A very curious expression passed over Poirot's face. He leaned forward.

"Had you any reason to suppose before that night that Mr. Ackroyd was being blackmailed?"

"No, indeed, sir. It was a great surprise to me. Such a regular gentleman in all his habits."

"How much did you overhear?"

"Not very much, sir. There seemed what I might call a spite against me. Of course I had to attend to my duties in the pantry. And when I did creep along once or twice to the study it was no use. The first time Dr. Sheppard came out and almost caught me in the act, and another time Mr. Raymond passed me in the big hall and went that way, so I knew it was no use; and when I went with the tray, Miss Flora headed me off."

Poirot stared for a long time at the man, as if to test his sincerity. Parker returned his gaze earnestly.

"I hope you believe me, sir. I've been afraid all along the police would rake up that old business with Major Ellerby and be suspicious of me in consequence."

"*Eh bien*," said Poirot at last. "I am disposed to believe you. But there is one thing I must request of you—to show me your bank-book. You have a bank-book, I presume?"

"Yes, sir, as a matter of fact, I have it with me now."

With no sign of confusion, he produced it from his pocket. Poirot took the slim, green-covered book and perused the entries.

"Ah! I perceive you have purchased £500 of National Savings Certificates this year?"

"Yes, sir. I have already over a thousand pounds saved—the result of my connection with—er—my late master, Major Ellerby. And I have had quite a little flutter on some horses this year—very successful. If you remember, sir, a rank outsider won the Jubilee. I was fortunate enough to back it—£20."

Poirot handed him back the book.

"I will wish you good-morning. I believe that you have told me the truth. If you have not—so much the worse for you, my friend."

When Parker had departed, Poirot picked up his overcoat once more.

"Going out again?" I asked.

"Yes, we will pay a little visit to the good M. Hammond."

"You believe Parker's story?"

"It is credible enough on the face of it. It seems clear that—unless he is a very good actor indeed—he genuinely believes it was Ackroyd himself who was the victim of blackmail. If so, he knows nothing at all about the Mrs. Ferrars business."

"Then in that case—who——"

"*Précisément!* Who? But our visit to M. Hammond will accomplish one purpose. It will either clear Parker completely or else——"

"Well?"

"I fall into the bad habit of leaving my sentences unfinished this morning," said Poirot apologetically. "You must bear with me."

"By the way," I said, rather sheepishly, "I've got a confession to make. I'm afraid I have inadvertently let out something about that ring."

"What ring?"

"The ring you found in the goldfish pond."

"Ah! yes," said Poirot, smiling broadly.

"I hope you're not annoyed? It was very careless of me."

"But not at all, my good friend, not at all. I laid no commands upon you. You were at liberty to speak of it if you so wished. She was interested, your sister?"

"She was indeed. It created a sensation. All sorts of theories are flying about."

"Ah! And yet it is so simple. The true explanation leapt to the eye, did it not?"

"Did it?" I said dryly.

Poirot laughed.

"The wise man does not commit himself," he observed. "Is not that so? But here we are at Mr. Hammond's."

The lawyer was in his office, and we were ushered in without any delay. He rose and greeted us in his dry, precise manner.

Poirot came at once to the point.

"Monsieur, I desire from you certain information, that is, if you will be so good as to give it to me. You acted, I understand, for the late Mrs. Ferrars of King's Paddock?"

I noticed the swift gleam of surprise which showed in the lawyer's eyes, before his professional reserve came down once more like a mask over his face.

"Certainly. All her affairs passed through our hands."

"Very good. Now, before I ask you to tell me anything, I should like you to listen to the story Dr. Sheppard will relate to you. You have no objection, have you, my friend, to repeating the conversation you had with Mr. Ackroyd last Friday night?"

"Not in the least," I said, and straightway began the recital of that strange evening.

Hammond listened with close attention.

"That is all," I said, when I had finished.

"Blackmail," said the lawyer thoughtfully.

"You are surprised?" asked Poirot.

The lawyer took off his pince-nez and polished them with his handkerchief.

"No," he replied, "I can hardly say that I am surprised. I have suspected something of the kind for some time."

"That brings us," said Poirot, "to the information for which I am asking. If any one can give us an idea of the actual sums paid, you are the man, monsieur."

"I see no object in withholding the information," said Hammond, after a moment or two. "During the past year, Mrs. Ferrars has sold out certain securities, and the money for them was paid into her account and not reinvested. As her income was a large one, and she lived very quietly after her husband's death, it seems certain that these sums of money were paid away for some special purpose. I once sounded her on the subject, and she said that she was obliged to support several of her husband's poor relations. I let the matter drop, of course. Until now, I have always imagined that the money was paid to some woman who had had a claim on Ashley Ferrars. I never dreamed that Mrs. Ferrars herself was involved."

"And the amount?" asked Poirot.

"In all, I should say the various sums totaled at least twenty thousand pounds."

"Twenty thousand pounds!" I exclaimed. "In one year!"

"Mrs. Ferrars was a very wealthy woman," said Poirot dryly. "And the penalty for murder is not a pleasant one."

"Is there anything else that I can tell you?" inquired Mr. Hammond.

"I thank you, no," said Poirot, rising. "All my excuses for having deranged you."

"Not at all, not at all."

"The word derange," I remarked, when we were outside again, "is applicable to mental disorder only."

"Ah!" cried Poirot, "never will my English be quite perfect. A curious language. I should then have said disarranged, *n'est-ce pas*?"

"Disturbed is the word you had in mind."

"I thank you, my friend. The word exact, you are zealous for it. *Eh bien*, what about our friend Parker now? With twenty thousand pounds in hand, would he have continued being a butler? *Je ne pense pas*. It is, of course, possible that he banked the money under another name, but I am disposed to believe he spoke the truth to us. If he is a scoundrel, he is a scoundrel on a mean scale. He has not the big ideas. That leaves us as a possibility, Raymond, or—well—Major Blunt."

"Surely not Raymond," I objected. "Since we know that he was desperately hard up for a matter of five hundred pounds."

"That is what he says, yes."

"And as to Hector Blunt——"

"I will tell you something as to the good Major Blunt," interrupted Poirot. "It is my business to make inquiries. I make them. *Eh bien*—that legacy of which he speaks, I have discovered that the amount of it was close upon twenty thousand pounds. What do you think of that?"

I was so taken aback that I could hardly speak.

"It's impossible," I said at last. "A well-known man like Hector Blunt."

Poirot shrugged his shoulders.

"Who knows? At least he is a man with big ideas. I confess that I hardly see him as a blackmailer, but there is another possibility that you have not even considered."

"What is that?"

"The fire, my friend. Ackroyd himself may have destroyed that letter, blue envelope and all, after you left him."

"I hardly think that likely," I said slowly. "And yet—of course, it may be so. He might have changed his mind."

We had just arrived at my house, and on the spur of the moment I invited Poirot to come in and take pot luck.

I thought Caroline would be pleased with me, but it is hard to satisfy one's women folk. It appears that we were eating chops for lunch—the kitchen staff being regaled on tripe and onions. And two chops set before three people are productive of embarrassment.

But Caroline is seldom daunted for long. With magnificent mendacity, she explained to Poirot that although James laughed at her for doing so, she adhered strictly to a vegetarian diet. She descanted ecstatically on the delights of nut cutlets (which I am quite sure she has never tasted) and ate a Welsh rarebit with gusto and frequent cutting remarks as to the dangers of "flesh" foods.

Afterwards, when we were sitting in front of the fire and smoking, Caroline attacked Poirot directly.

"Not found Ralph Paton yet?" she asked.

"Where should I find him, mademoiselle?"

"I thought, perhaps, you'd found him in Cranchester," said Caroline, with intense meaning in her tone.

Poirot looked merely bewildered.

"In Cranchester? But why in Cranchester?"

I enlightened him with a touch of malice.

"One of our ample staff of private detectives happened to see you in a car on the Cranchester road yesterday," I explained.

Poirot's bewilderment vanished. He laughed heartily.

"Ah, that! A simple visit to the dentist, *c'est tout*. My tooth, it aches. I go there. My tooth, it is at once better. I think to return quickly. The dentist, he says No. Better to have it out. I argue. He insists. He has his way! That particular tooth, it will never ache again."

Caroline collapsed rather like a pricked balloon.

We fell to discussing Ralph Paton.

"A weak nature," I insisted. "But not a vicious one."

"Ah!" said Poirot. "But weakness, where does it end?"

"Exactly," said Caroline. "Take James here—weak as water, if I weren't about to look after him."

"My dear Caroline," I said irritably, "can't you talk without dragging in personalities?"

"You *are* weak, James," said Caroline, quite unmoved. "I'm

eight years older than you are—oh! I don't mind M. Poirot knowing that——"

"I should never have guessed it, mademoiselle," said Poirot,
with a gallant little bow.

"Eight years older. But I've always considered it my duty to
look after you. With a bad bringing up, Heaven knows what mischief you might have got into by now."

"I might have married a beautiful adventuress," I murmured,
gazing at the ceiling, and blowing smoke rings.

"Adventuress!" said Caroline, with a snort. "If we're talking
of adventuresses——"

She left the sentence unfinished.

"Well?" I said, with some curiosity.

"Nothing. But I can think of some one not a hundred miles
away."

Then she turned to Poirot suddenly.

"James sticks to it that you believe some one in the house
committed the murder. All I can say is, you're wrong."

"I should not like to be wrong," said Poirot. "It is not—how
do you say—my *métier*?"

"I've got the facts pretty clearly," continued Caroline, taking
no notice of Poirot's remark, "from James and others. As far as I
can see, of the people in the house, only two *could* have had the
chance of doing it. Ralph Paton and Flora Ackroyd."

"My dear Caroline——"

"Now, James, don't interrupt me. I know what I'm talking
about. Parker met her *outside* the door, didn't he? He didn't hear
her uncle saying good-night to her. She could have killed him
then and there."

"Caroline."

"I'm not saying she *did*, James. I'm saying she *could* have
done. As a matter of fact, though Flora is like all these young girls
nowadays, with no veneration for their betters and thinking they
know best on every subject under the sun, I don't for a minute

believe she'd kill even a chicken. But there it is. Mr. Raymond and Major Blunt have alibis. Mrs. Ackroyd's got an alibi. Even that Russell woman seems to have one—and a good job for her it is she has. Who is left? Only Ralph and Flora! And say what you will, I don't believe Ralph Paton is a murderer. A boy we've known all our lives."

Poirot was silent for a minute, watching the curling smoke rise from his cigarette. When at last he spoke, it was in a gentle far-away voice that produced a curious impression. It was totally unlike his usual manner.

"Let us take a man—a very ordinary man. A man with no idea of murder in his heart. There is in him somewhere a strain of weakness—deep down. It has so far never been called into play. Perhaps it never will be—and if so he will go to his grave honored and respected by every one. But let us suppose that something occurs. He is in difficulties—or perhaps not that even. He may stumble by accident on a secret—a secret involving life or death to some one. And his first impulse will be to speak out—to do his duty as an honest citizen. And then the strain of weakness tells. Here is a chance of money—a great amount of money. He wants money—he desires it—and it is so easy. He has to do nothing for it—just keep silence. That is the beginning. The desire for money grows. He must have more—and more! He is intoxicated by the gold mine which has opened at his feet. He becomes greedy. And in his greed he overreaches himself. One can press a man as far as one likes—but with a woman one must not press too far. For a woman has at heart a great desire to speak the truth. How many husbands who have deceived their wives go comfortably to their graves, carrying their secret with them! How many wives who have deceived their husbands wreck their lives by throwing the fact in those same husbands' teeth! They have been pressed too far. In a reckless moment (which they will afterwards regret, *bien entendu*) they fling safety to the winds and turn at bay, proclaiming the truth with great momentary satisfaction to themselves. So it was, I think, in this case. The strain was too great. And so there came your proverb, the death of the goose that laid the golden eggs. But that is not the end. Exposure faced the man of whom we are speaking. And he is not the same man he was—say, a year ago. His moral fiber is blunted. He is desperate. He is fighting a losing battle, and he is prepared to take any means that come to his hand, for exposure means ruin to him. And so—the dagger strikes!"

He was silent for a moment. It was as though he had laid a spell upon the room. I cannot try to describe the impression his words produced. There was something in the merciless analysis, and the ruthless power of vision which struck fear into both of us.

"Afterwards," he went on softly, "the danger removed, he will be himself again, normal, kindly. But if the need again arises, then once more he will strike."

Caroline roused herself at last.

"You are speaking of Ralph Paton," she said. "You may be right, you may not, but you have no business to condemn a man unheard."

The telephone bell rang sharply. I went out into the hall, and took off the receiver.

"What?" I said. "Yes. Dr. Sheppard speaking."

I listened for a minute or two, then replied briefly. Replacing the receiver, I went back into the drawing-room.

"Poirot," I said, "they have detained a man at Liverpool. His name is Charles Kent, and he is believed to be the stranger who visited Fernly that night. They want me to go to Liverpool at once and identify him."

EIGHTEEN
Charles Kent

Half an hour later saw Poirot, myself, and Inspector Raglan in the train on the way to Liverpool. The inspector was clearly very excited.

"We may get a line on the blackmailing part of the business, if on nothing else," he declared jubilantly. "He's a rough customer, this fellow, by what I heard over the phone. Takes dope, too. We ought to find it easy to get what we want out of him. If there was the shadow of a motive, nothing's more likely than that he killed Mr. Ackroyd. But in that case, why is young Paton keeping out of the way? The whole thing's a muddle—that's what it is. By the way, M. Poirot, you were quite right about those fingerprints. They were Mr. Ackroyd's own. I had rather the same idea myself, but I dismissed it as hardly feasible."

I smiled to myself. Inspector Raglan was so very plainly saving his face.

"As regards this man," said Poirot, "he is not yet arrested, eh?"

"No, detained under suspicion."

"And what account does he give of himself?"

"Precious little," said the inspector, with a grin. "He's a wary bird, I gather. A lot of abuse, but very little more."

On arrival at Liverpool I was surprised to find that Poirot was welcomed with acclamation. Superintendent Hayes, who met us, had worked with Poirot over some case long ago, and had evidently an exaggerated opinion of his powers.

"Now we've got M. Poirot here we shan't be long," he said cheerfully. "I thought you'd retired, moosior?"

"So I had, my good Hayes, so I had. But how tedious is retirement! You cannot imagine to yourself the monotony with which day comes after day."

"Very likely. So you've come to have a look at our own particular find? Is this Dr. Sheppard? Think you'll be able to identify him, sir?"

"I'm not very sure," I said doubtfully.

"How did you get hold of him?" inquired Poirot.

"Description was circulated, as you know. In the press and privately. Not much to go on, I admit. This fellow has an American accent all right, and he doesn't deny that he was near King's Abbot that night. Just asks what the hell it is to do with us, and that he'll see us in —— before he answers any questions."

"Is it permitted that I, too, see him?" asked Poirot.

The superintendent closed one eye knowingly.

"Very glad to have you, sir. You've got permission to do anything you please. Inspector Japp of Scotland Yard was asking after you the other day. Said he'd heard you were connected unofficially with this case. Where's Captain Paton hiding, sir, can you tell me that?"

"I doubt if it would be wise at the present juncture," said Poirot primly, and I bit my lips to prevent a smile.

The little man really did it very well.

After some further parley, we were taken to interview the prisoner.

He was a young fellow, I should say not more than twenty-two or three. Tall, thin, with slightly shaking hands, and the evidences of considerable physical strength somewhat run to seed. His hair was dark, but his eyes were blue and shifty, seldom meeting a glance squarely. I had all along cherished the illusion that there was something familiar about the figure I had met that night, but if this were indeed he, I was completely mistaken. He did not remind me in the least of any one I knew.

"Now then, Kent," said the superintendent, "stand up. Here are some visitors come to see you. Recognize any of them."

Kent glared at us sullenly, but did not reply. I saw his glance waver over the three of us, and come back to rest on me.

"Well, sir," said the superintendent to me, "what do you say?"

"The height's the same," I said, "and as far as general appearance goes it might well be the man in question. Beyond that, I couldn't go."

"What the hell's the meaning of all this?" asked Kent. "What have you got against me? Come on, out with it! What am I supposed to have done?"

I nodded my head.

"It's the man," I said. "I recognize the voice."

"Recognize my voice, do you? Where do you think you heard it before?"

"On Friday evening last, outside the gates of Fernly Park. You asked me the way there."

"I did, did I?"

"Do you admit it?" asked the inspector.

"I don't admit anything. Not till I know what you've got on me."

"Have you not read the papers in the last few days?" asked Poirot, speaking for the first time.

The man's eyes narrowed.

"So that's it, is it? I saw an old gent had been croaked at Fernly. Trying to make out I did the job, are you?"

"You were there that night," said Poirot quietly.

"How do you know, mister?"

"By this." Poirot took something from his pocket and held it out.

It was the goose quill we had found in the summer-house.

At the sight of it the man's face changed. He half held out his hand.

"Snow," said Poirot thoughtfully. "No, my friend, it is empty.

It lay where you dropped it in the summer-house that night."

Charles Kent looked at him uncertainly.

"You seem to know a hell of a lot about everything, you little foreign cock duck. Perhaps you remember this: the papers say that the old gent was croaked between a quarter to ten and ten o'clock?"

"That is so," agreed Poirot.

"Yes, but is it really so? That's what I'm getting at."

"This gentleman will tell you," said Poirot.

He indicated Inspector Raglan. The latter hesitated, glanced at Superintendent Hayes, then at Poirot, and finally, as though receiving sanction, he said:—

"That's right. Between a quarter to ten and ten o'clock."

"Then you've nothing to keep me here for," said Kent. "I was away from Fernly Park by twenty-five minutes past nine. You can ask at the Dog and Whistle. That's a saloon about a mile out of Fernly on the road to Cranchester. I kicked up a bit of a row there, I remember. As near as nothing to quarter to ten, it was. How about that?"

Inspector Raglan wrote down something in his notebook.

"Well?" demanded Kent.

"Inquiries will be made," said the inspector. "If you've spoken the truth, you won't have anything to complain about. What were you doing at Fernly Park anyway?"

"Went there to meet some one."

"Who?"

"That's none of your business."

"You'd better keep a civil tongue in your head, my man," the superintendent warned him.

"To hell with a civil tongue. I went there on my own business, and that's all there is to it. If I was clear away before the murder was done, that's all that concerns the cops."

"Your name, it is Charles Kent," said Poirot. "Where were you born?"

The man stared at him, then he grinned.

"I'm a full-blown Britisher all right," he said.

"Yes," said Poirot meditatively, "I think you are. I fancy you were born in Kent."

The man stared.

"Why's that? Because of my name? What's that to do with it? Is a man whose name is Kent bound to be born in that particular county?"

"Under certain circumstances, I can imagine he might be," said Poirot very deliberately. "Under certain circumstances, you comprehend."

There was so much meaning in his voice as to surprise the two police officers. As for Charles Kent, he flushed a brick red, and for a moment I thought he was going to spring at Poirot. He thought better of it, however, and turned away with a kind of laugh.

Poirot nodded as though satisfied, and made his way out through the door. He was joined presently by the two officers.

"We'll verify that statement," remarked Raglan. "I don't think he's lying, though. But he's got to come clear with a statement as to what he was doing at Fernly. It looks to me as though we'd got our blackmailer all right. On the other hand, granted his story's correct, he couldn't have had anything to do with the actual murder. He'd got ten pounds on him when he was arrested—rather a large sum. I fancy that forty pounds went to him—the numbers of the notes didn't correspond, but of course he'd have changed them first thing. Mr. Ackroyd must have given him the money, and he made off with it as fast as possible. What was that about Kent being his birthplace? What's that got to do with it?"

"Nothing whatever," said Poirot mildly. "A little idea of mine, that was all. Me, I am famous for my little ideas."

"Are you really?" said Raglan, studying him with a puzzled expression.

The superintendent went into a roar of laughter.

"Many's the time I've heard Inspector Japp say that. M. Poirot

178

and his little ideas! Too fanciful for me, he'd say, but always something in them."

"You mock yourself at me," said Poirot, smiling; "but never mind. The old ones they laugh last sometimes, when the young, clever ones do not laugh at all."

And nodding his head at them in a sage manner, he walked out into the street.

He and I lunched together at an hotel. I know now that the whole thing lay clearly unravelled before him. He had got the last thread he needed to lead him to the truth.

But at the time I had no suspicion of the fact. I overestimated his general self-confidence, and I took it for granted that the things which puzzled me must be equally puzzling to him.

My chief puzzle was what the man Charles Kent could have been doing at Fernly. Again and again I put the question to myself and could get no satisfactory reply.

At last I ventured a tentative query to Poirot. His reply was immediate.

"*Mon ami*, I do not think; I know."

"Really?" I said incredulously.

"Yes, indeed. I suppose now that to you it would not make sense if I said that he went to Fernly that night because he was born in Kent?"

I stared at him.

"It certainly doesn't seem to make sense to me," I said dryly.

"Ah!" said Poirot pityingly. "Well, no matter. I have still my little idea."

NINETEEN
Flora Ackroyd

As I was returning from my round the following morning, I was hailed by Inspector Raglan. I pulled up, and the inspector mounted on the step.

"Good-morning, Dr. Sheppard," he said. "Well, that alibi is all right enough."

"Charles Kent's?"

"Charles Kent's. The barmaid at the Dog and Whistle, Sally Jones, she remembers him perfectly. Picked out his photograph from among five others. It was just a quarter to ten when he came into the bar, and the Dog and Whistle is well over a mile from Fernly Park. The girl mentions that he had a lot of money on him—she saw him take a handful of notes out of his pocket. Rather surprised her, it did, seeing the class of fellow he was, with a pair of boots clean dropping off him. That's where that forty pounds went right enough."

"The man still refuses to give an account of his visit to Fernly?"

"Obstinate as a mule he is. I had a chat with Hayes at Liverpool over the wire this morning."

"Hercule Poirot says he knows the reason the man went there that night," I observed.

"Does he?" cried the inspector eagerly.

"Yes," I said maliciously. "He says he went there because he was born in Kent."

I felt a distinct pleasure in passing on my own discomfiture.

Raglan stared at me for a moment or two uncomprehendingly. Then a grin overspread his weaselly countenance and he tapped his forehead significantly.

"Bit gone here," he said. "I've thought so for some time. Poor old chap, so that's why he had to give up and come down here. In the family, very likely. He's got a nephew who's quite off his crumpet."

"Poirot has?" I said, very surprised.

"Yes. Hasn't he ever mentioned him to you? Quite docile, I believe, and all that, but mad as a hatter, poor lad."

"Who told you that?"

Again a grin showed itself on Inspector Raglan's face.

"Your sister, Miss Sheppard, she told me all about it."

Really, Caroline is amazing. She never rests until she knows the last details of everybody's family secrets. Unfortunately, I have never been able to instill into her the decency of keeping them to herself.

"Jump in, inspector," I said, opening the door of the car. "We'll go up to The Larches together, and acquaint our Belgian friend with the latest news."

"Might as well, I suppose. After all, even if he is a bit balmy, it was a useful tip he gave me about those fingerprints. He's got a bee in his bonnet about the man Kent, but who knows—there may be something useful behind it."

Poirot received us with his usual smiling courtesy.

He listened to the information we had brought him, nodding his head now and then.

"Seems quite O.K., doesn't it?" said the inspector rather gloomily. "A chap can't be murdering some one in one place when he's drinking in the bar in another place a mile away."

"Are you going to release him?"

"Don't see what else we can do. We can't very well hold him for obtaining money on false pretences. Can't prove a ruddy thing."

The inspector tossed a match into the grate in a disgruntled fashion. Poirot retrieved it and put it neatly in a little receptacle designed for the purpose. His action was purely mechanical. I could see that his thoughts were on something very different.

"If I were you," he said at last, "I should not release the man Charles Kent yet."

"What do you mean?"

Raglan stared at him.

"What I say. I should not release him yet."

"You don't think he can have had anything to do with the murder, do you?"

"I think probably not—but one cannot be certain yet."

"But haven't I just told you——"

Poirot raised a hand protestingly.

"*Mais oui, mais oui.* I heard. I am not deaf—nor stupid, thank the good God! But see you, you approach the matter from the wrong—the wrong—premises, is not that the word?"

The inspector stared at him heavily.

"I don't see how you make that out. Look here, we know Mr. Ackroyd was alive at a quarter to ten. You admit that, don't you?"

Poirot looked at him for a moment, then shook his head with a quick smile.

"I admit nothing that is not—*proved*!"

"Well, we've got proof enough of that. We've got Miss Flora Ackroyd's evidence."

"That she said good-night to her uncle? But me—I do not always believe what a young lady tells me—no, not even when she is charming and beautiful."

"But hang it all, man, Parker saw her coming out of the door."

"No." Poirot's voice rang out with sudden sharpness. "That is just what he did not see. I satisfied myself of that by a little experiment the other day—you remember, doctor? Parker saw her *outside* the door, with her hand on the handle. He did not see her come out of the room."

"But—where else could she have been?"

"Perhaps on the stairs."

"The stairs?"

"That is my little idea—yes."

"But those stairs only lead to Mr. Ackroyd's bedroom."

"Precisely."

And still the inspector stared.

"You think she'd been up to her uncle's bedroom? Well, why not? Why should she lie about it?"

"Ah! that is just the question. It depends on what she was doing there, does it not?"

"You mean—the money? Hang it all, you don't suggest that it was Miss Ackroyd who took that forty pounds?"

"I suggest nothing," said Poirot. "But I will remind you of this. Life was not very easy for that mother and daughter. There were bills—there was constant trouble over small sums of money. Roger Ackroyd was a peculiar man over money matters. The girl might be at her wit's end for a comparatively small sum. Figure to yourself then what happens. She has taken the money, she descends the little staircase. When she is half-way down she hears the chink of glass from the hall. She has not a doubt of what it is—Parker coming to the study. At all costs she must not be found on the stairs—Parker will not forget it, he will think it odd. If the money is missed, Parker is sure to remember having seen her come down those stairs. She has just time to rush down to the study door—with her hand on the handle to show that she has just come out, when Parker appears in the doorway. She says the first thing that comes into her head, a repetition of Roger Ackroyd's orders earlier in the evening, and then goes upstairs to her own room."

"Yes, but later," persisted the inspector, "she must have realized the vital importance of speaking the truth? Why, the whole case hinges on it!"

"Afterwards," said Poirot dryly, "it was a little difficult for Mademoiselle Flora. She is told simply that the police are here and that there has been a robbery. Naturally she jumps to the conclusion that the theft of the money has been discovered. Her one idea is to stick to her story. When she learns that her uncle is dead she is panic-stricken. Young women do not faint nowadays, monsieur, without considerable provocation. *Eh bien!* there it is. She is bound to stick to her story, or else confess everything. And a young and pretty girl does not like to admit that she is a thief—especially before those whose esteem she is anxious to retain."

Raglan brought his fist down with a thump on the table.

"I'll not believe it," he said. "It's—it's not credible. And you—you've known this all along?"

"The possibility has been in my mind from the first," admitted Poirot. "I was always convinced that Mademoiselle Flora was hiding something from us. To satisfy myself, I made the little experiment I told you of. Dr. Sheppard accompanied me."

"A test for Parker, you said it was," I remarked bitterly.

"*Mon ami*," said Poirot apologetically, "as I told you at the time, one must say something."

The inspector rose.

"There's only one thing for it," he declared. "We must tackle the young lady right away. You'll come up to Fernly with me, M. Poirot?"

"Certainly. Dr. Sheppard will drive us up in his car."

I acquiesced willingly.

On inquiry for Miss Ackroyd, we were shown into the billiard room. Flora and Major Hector Blunt were sitting on the long window seat.

"Good-morning, Miss Ackroyd," said the inspector. "Can we have a word or two alone with you?"

Blunt got up at once and moved to the door.

"What is it?" asked Flora nervously. "Don't go, Major Blunt. He can stay, can't he?" she asked, turning to the inspector.

"That's as you like," said the inspector dryly. "There's a question or two it's my duty to put to you, miss, but I'd prefer to do so privately, and I dare say you'd prefer it also."

Flora looked keenly at him. I saw her face grow whiter. Then she turned and spoke to Blunt.

"I want you to stay—please—yes, I mean it. Whatever the inspector has to say to me, I'd rather you heard it."

Raglan shrugged his shoulders.

"Well, if you will have it so, that's all there is to it. Now, Miss Ackroyd, M. Poirot here has made a certain suggestion to me. He suggests that you weren't in the study at all last Friday night, that you never saw Mr. Ackroyd to say good-night to him, that instead of being in the study you were on the stairs leading down from your uncle's bedroom when you heard Parker coming across the hall."

Flora's gaze shifted to Poirot. He nodded back at her.

"Mademoiselle, the other day, when we sat round the table, I implored you to be frank with me. What one does not tell to Papa Poirot he finds out. It was that, was it not? See, I will make it easy for you. You took the money, did you not?"

"The money," said Blunt sharply.

There was a silence which lasted for at least a minute.

Then Flora drew herself up and spoke.

"M. Poirot is right. I took that money. I stole. I am a thief— yes, a common, vulgar little thief. Now you know! I am glad it has come out. It's been a nightmare, these last few days!" She sat down suddenly and buried her face in her hands. She spoke huskily through her fingers. "You don't know what my life has been since I came here. Wanting things, scheming for them, lying, cheating, running up bills, promising to pay—oh! I hate myself when I think of it all! That's what brought us together, Ralph and I. We were both weak! I understood him, and I was sorry—because I'm the same underneath. We're not strong enough to stand alone, either of us. We're weak, miserable, despicable things."

She looked at Blunt and suddenly stamped her foot.

"Why do you look at me like that—as though you couldn't believe? I may be a thief—but at any rate I'm real now. I'm not lying any more. I'm not pretending to be the kind of girl you like, young and innocent and simple. I don't care if you never want to see me again. I hate myself, despise myself—but you've got to believe one thing, if speaking the truth would have made things better for Ralph, I would have spoken out. But I've seen all along that it wouldn't be better for Ralph—it makes the case against him blacker than ever. I was not doing him any harm by sticking to my lie."

"Ralph," said Blunt. "I see—always Ralph."

"You don't understand," said Flora hopelessly. "You never will."

She turned to the inspector.

"I admit everything; I was at my wit's end for money. I never saw my uncle that evening after he left the dinner-table. As to the money, you can take what steps you please. Nothing could be worse than it is now!"

Suddenly she broke down again, hid her face in her hands, and rushed from the room.

"Well," said the inspector in a flat tone, "so that's that."

He seemed rather at a loss what to do next.

Blunt came forward.

"Inspector Raglan," he said quietly, "that money was given to me by Mr. Ackroyd for a special purpose. Miss Ackroyd never touched it. When she says she did, she is lying with the idea of shielding Captain Paton. The truth is as I said, and I am prepared to go into the witness box and swear to it."

He made a kind of jerky bow, then turning abruptly, he left the room.

Poirot was after him in a flash. He caught the other up in the hall.

"Monsieur—a moment, I beg of you, if you will be so good."

"Well, sir?"

Blunt was obviously impatient. He stood frowning down on Poirot.

"It is this," said Poirot rapidly: "I am not deceived by your little fantasy. No, indeed. It was truly Miss Flora who took the money. All the same it is well imagined what you say—it pleases me. It is very good what you have done there. You are a man quick to think and to act."

"I'm not in the least anxious for your opinion, thank you," said Blunt coldly.

He made once more as though to pass on, but Poirot, not at all offended, laid a detaining hand on his arm.

"Ah! but you are to listen to me. I have more to say. The other day I spoke of concealments. Very well, all along have I seen what you are concealing. Mademoiselle Flora, you love her with all your heart. From the first moment you saw her, is it not so? Oh! let us not mind saying these things—why must one in England think it necessary to mention love as though it were some disgraceful secret? You love Mademoiselle Flora. You seek to conceal that fact from all the world. That is very good—that is as it should be. But take the advice of Hercule Poirot—do not conceal it from mademoiselle herself."

Blunt had shown several signs of restlessness whilst Poirot was speaking, but the closing words seemed to rivet his attention.

"What d'you mean by that?" he said sharply.

"You think that she loves the Capitaine Ralph Paton—but I, Hercule Poirot, tell you that that is not so. Mademoiselle Flora accepted Captain Paton to please her uncle, and because she saw in the marriage a way of escape from her life here which was becoming frankly insupportable to her. She liked him, and there was much sympathy and understanding between them. But love— no! It is not Captain Paton Mademoiselle Flora loves."

"What the devil do you mean?" asked Blunt.

I saw the dark flush under his tan.

"You have been blind, monsieur. Blind! She is loyal, the little one. Ralph Paton is under a cloud, she is bound in honor to stick by him."

I felt it was time I put in a word to help on the good work.

"My sister told me the other night," I said encouragingly, "that Flora had never cared a penny piece for Ralph Paton, and never would. My sister is always right about these things."

Blunt ignored my well-meant efforts. He spoke to Poirot.

"D'you really think——" he began, and stopped.

He is one of those inarticulate men who find it hard to put things into words.

Poirot knows no such disability.

"If you doubt me, ask her yourself, monsieur. But perhaps you no longer care to—the affair of the money——"

Blunt gave a sound like an angry laugh.

"Think I'd hold that against her? Roger was always a queer chap about money. She got in a mess and didn't dare tell him. Poor kid. Poor lonely kid."

Poirot looked thoughtfully at the side door.

"Mademoiselle Flora went into the garden, I think," he murmured.

"I've been every kind of a fool," said Blunt abruptly. "Rum conversation we've been having. Like one of those Danish plays. But you're a sound fellow, M. Poirot. Thank you."

He took Poirot's hand and gave it a grip which caused the other to wince in anguish. Then he strode to the side door and passed out into the garden.

"Not every kind of a fool," murmured Poirot, tenderly nursing the injured member. "Only one kind—the fool in love."

TWENTY

Miss Russell

Inspector Raglan had received a bad jolt. He was not deceived by Blunt's valiant lie any more than we had been. Our way back to the village was punctuated by his complaints.

"This alters everything, this does. I don't know whether you've realized it, Monsieur Poirot?"

"I think so, yes, I think so," said Poirot. "You see, me, I have been familiar with the idea for some time."

Inspector Raglan, who had only had the idea presented to him a short half-hour ago, looked at Poirot unhappily, and went on with his discoveries.

"Those alibis now. Worthless! Absolutely worthless. Got to start again. Find out what every one was doing from nine-thirty onwards. Nine-thirty—that's the time we've got to hang on to. You were quite right about the man Kent—we don't release *him* yet awhile. Let me see now—nine-forty-five at the Dog and Whistle. He might have got there in a quarter of an hour if he ran. It's just possible that it was *his* voice Mr. Raymond heard talking to Mr. Ackroyd—asking for money which Mr. Ackroyd refused. But one thing's clear—it wasn't he who sent the telephone message. The station is half a mile in the other direction—over a mile and a half from the Dog and Whistle, and he was at the Dog and Whistle until about ten minutes past ten. Dang that telephone call! We always come up against it."

"We do indeed," agreed Poirot. "It is curious."

"It's just possible that if Captain Paton climbed into his uncle's room and found him there murdered, *he* may have sent it. Got the wind up, thought he'd be accused, and cleared out. That's possible, isn't it?"

"Why should he have telephoned?"

"May have had doubts if the old man was really dead. Thought he'd get the doctor up there as soon as possible, but didn't want to give himself away. Yes, I say now, how's that for a theory? Something in that, I should say."

The inspector swelled his chest out importantly. He was so plainly delighted with himself that any words of ours would have been quite superfluous.

We arrived back at my house at this minute, and I hurried in to my surgery patients, who had all been waiting a considerable time, leaving Poirot to walk to the police station with the inspector.

Having dismissed the last patient, I strolled into the little room at the back of the house which I call my workshop—I am rather proud of the home-made wireless set I turned out. Caroline hates my workroom. I keep my tools there, and Annie is not allowed to wreak havoc with a dustpan and brush. I was just adjusting the interior of an alarm clock which had been denounced as wholly unreliable by the household, when the door opened and Caroline put her head in.

"Oh! there you are, James," she said, with deep disapproval. "M. Poirot wants to see you."

"Well," I said, rather irritably, for her sudden entrance had startled me and I had let go of a piece of delicate mechanism, "if he wants to see me, he can come in here."

"In here?" said Caroline.

"That's what I said—in here."

Caroline gave a sniff of disapproval and retired. She returned in a moment or two, ushering in Poirot, and then retired again, shutting the door with a bang.

"Aha! my friend," said Poirot, coming forward and rubbing his hands. "You have not got rid of me so easily, you see!"

"Finished with the inspector?" I asked.

"For the moment, yes. And you, you have seen all the patients?"

"Yes."

Poirot sat down and looked at me, tilting his egg-shaped head on one side, with the air of one who savors a very delicious joke.

"You are in error," he said at last. "You have still one patient to see."

"Not you?" I exclaimed in surprise.

"Ah, not me, *bien entendu*. Me, I have the health magnificent. No, to tell you the truth, it is a little *complot* of mine. There is some one I wish to see, you understand—and at the same time it is not necessary that the whole village should intrigue itself about the matter—which is what would happen if the lady were seen to come to my house—for it is a lady. But to you she has already come as a patient before."

"Miss Russell!" I exclaimed.

"*Précisément*. I wish much to speak with her, so I send her the little note and make the appointment in your surgery. You are not annoyed with me?"

"On the contrary," I said. "That is, presuming I am allowed to be present at the interview?"

"But naturally! In your own surgery!"

"You know," I said, throwing down the pincers I was holding, "it's extraordinarily intriguing, the whole thing. Every new development that arises is like the shake you give to a kaleidoscope—the thing changes entirely in aspect. Now, why are you so anxious to see Miss Russell?"

Poirot raised his eyebrows.

"Surely it is obvious?" he murmured.

"There you go again," I grumbled. "According to you everything is obvious. But you leave me walking about in a fog."

Poirot shook his head genially at me.

"You mock yourself at me. Take the matter of Mademoiselle Flora. The inspector was surprised—but you—you were not."

"I never dreamed of her being the thief," I expostulated.

"That—perhaps no. But I was watching your face and you were not—like Inspector Raglan—startled and incredulous."

I thought for a minute or two.

"Perhaps you are right," I said at last. "All along I've felt that Flora was keeping back something—so the truth, when it came, was subconsciously expected. It upset Inspector Raglan very much indeed, poor man."

"Ah! *pour ça, oui!* The poor man must rearrange all his ideas. I profited by his state of mental chaos to induce him to grant me a little favor."

"What was that?"

Poirot took a sheet of notepaper from his pocket. Some words were written on it, and he read them aloud.

"The police have, for some days, been seeking for Captain Ralph Paton, the nephew of Mr. Ackroyd of Fernly Park, whose death occurred under such tragic circumstances last Friday. Captain Paton has been found at Liverpool, where he was on the point of embarking for America."

He folded up the piece of paper again.

"That, my friend, will be in the newspapers to-morrow morning."

I stared at him, dumbfounded.

"But—but it isn't true! He's not at Liverpool!"

Poirot beamed on me.

"You have the intelligence so quick! No, he has not been found at Liverpool. Inspector Raglan was very loath to let me send this paragraph to the press, especially as I could not take him into my confidence. But I assured him most solemnly that very interesting results would follow its appearance in print, so he gave in, after stipulating that he was, on no account, to bear the responsibility."

I stared at Poirot. He smiled back at me.

"It beats me," I said at last, "what you expect to get out of that."

"You should employ your little gray cells," said Poirot gravely. He rose and came across to the bench.

"It is that you have really the love of the machinery," he said, after inspecting the débris of my labors.

Every man has his hobby. I immediately drew Poirot's attention to my home-made wireless. Finding him sympathetic, I showed him one or two little inventions of my own—trifling things, but useful in the house.

"Decidedly," said Poirot, "you should be an inventor by trade, not a doctor. But I hear the bell—that is your patient. Let us go into the surgery."

Once before I had been struck by the remnants of beauty in the housekeeper's face. This morning I was struck anew. Very simply dressed in black, tall, upright and independent as ever, with her big dark eyes and an unwonted flush of color in her usually pale cheeks, I realized that as a girl she must have been startlingly handsome.

"Good-morning, mademoiselle," said Poirot. "Will you be seated? Dr. Sheppard is so kind as to permit me the use of his surgery for a little conversation I am anxious to have with you."

Miss Russell sat down with her usual composure. If she felt any inward agitation, it did not display itself in any outward manifestation.

"It seems a queer way of doing things, if you'll allow me to say so," she remarked.

"Miss Russell—I have news to give you."

"Indeed!"

"Charles Kent has been arrested at Liverpool."

Not a muscle of her face moved. She merely opened her eyes a trifle wider, and asked, with a tinge of defiance:

"Well, what of it?"

But at that moment it came to me—the resemblance that had haunted me all along, something familiar in the defiance of Charles Kent's manner. The two voices, one rough and coarse, the other painfully ladylike—were strangely the same in timbre. It was of Miss Russell that I had been reminded that night outside the gates of Fernly Park.

I looked at Poirot, full of my discovery, and he gave me an imperceptible nod.

In answer to Miss Russell's question, he threw out his hands in a thoroughly French gesture.

"I thought you might be interested, that is all," he said mildly.

"Well, I'm not particularly," said Miss Russell. "Who is this Charles Kent anyway?"

"He is a man, mademoiselle, who was at Fernly on the night of the murder."

"Really?"

"Fortunately for him, he has an alibi. At a quarter to ten he was at a public-house a mile from here."

"Lucky for him," commented Miss Russell.

"But we still do not know what he was doing at Fernly—who it was he went to meet, for instance."

"I'm afraid I can't help you at all," said the housekeeper politely. "Nothing came to *my* ears. If that is all——"

She made a tentative movement as though to rise. Poirot stopped her.

"It is not quite all," he said smoothly. "This morning fresh developments have arisen. It seems now that Mr. Ackroyd was murdered, not at a quarter to ten, but *before*. Between ten minutes to nine, when Dr. Sheppard left, and a quarter to ten."

I saw the color drain from the housekeeper's face, leaving it dead white. She leaned forward, her figure swaying.

"But Miss Ackroyd said—Miss Ackroyd said——"

"Miss Ackroyd has admitted that she was lying. She was never in the study at all that evening."

"Then——?"

"Then it would seem that in this Charles Kent we have the man we are looking for. He came to Fernly, can give no account of what he was doing there——"

"I can tell you what he was doing there. He never touched a hair of old Ackroyd's head—he never went near the study. He didn't do it, I tell you."

She was leaning forward. That iron self-control was broken through at last. Terror and desperation were in her face.

"M. Poirot! M. Poirot! Oh, do believe me."

Poirot got up and came to her. He patted her reassuringly on the shoulder.

"But yes—but yes, I will believe. I had to make you speak, you know."

For an instant suspicion flared up in her.

"Is what you said true?"

"That Charles Kent is suspected of the crime? Yes, that is true. You alone can save him, by telling the reason for his being at Fernly."

"He came to see me." She spoke in a low, hurried voice. "I went out to meet him——"

"In the summer-house, yes, I know."

"How do you know?"

"Mademoiselle, it is the business of Hercule Poirot to know things. I know that you went out earlier in the evening, that you left a message in the summer-house to say what time you would be there."

"Yes, I did. I had heard from him—saying he was coming. I dared not let him come to the house. I wrote to the address he gave me and said I would meet him in the summer-house, and described it to him so that he would be able to find it. Then I was afraid he might not wait there patiently, and I ran out and left a piece of paper to say I would be there about ten minutes past nine. I didn't want the servants to see me, so I slipped out through the drawing-room window. As I came back, I met Dr. Sheppard, and I fancied that he would think it queer. I was out of breath, for I had been running. I had no idea that he was expected to dinner that night."

She paused.

"Go on," said Poirot. "You went out to meet him at ten minutes past nine. What did you say to each other?"

"It's difficult. You see——"

"Mademoiselle," said Poirot, interrupting her, "in this matter I must have the whole truth. What you tell us need never go beyond these four walls. Dr. Sheppard will be discreet, and so shall I. See, I will help you. This Charles Kent, he is your son, is he not?"

She nodded. The color had flamed into her cheeks.

"No one has ever known. It was long ago—long ago—down in Kent. I was not married...."

"So you took the name of the county as a surname for him. I understand."

"I got work. I managed to pay for his board and lodging. I never told him that I was his mother. But he turned out badly, he drank, then took to drugs. I managed to pay his passage out to Canada. I didn't hear of him for a year or two. Then, somehow or other, he found out that I was his mother. He wrote asking me for money. Finally, I heard from him back in this country again. He was coming to see me at Fernly, he said. I dared not let him come to the house. I have always been considered so—so very respectable. If any one got an inkling—it would have been all up with my post as housekeeper. So I wrote to him in the way I have just told you."

"And in the morning you came to see Dr. Sheppard?"

"Yes. I wondered if something could be done. He was not a bad boy—before he took to drugs."

"I see," said Poirot. "Now let us go on with the story. He came that night to the summer-house?"

"Yes, he was waiting for me when I got there. He was very

rough and abusive. I had brought with me all the money I had, and I gave it to him. We talked a little, and then he went away."

"What time was that?"

"It must have been between twenty and twenty-five minutes past nine. It was not yet half-past when I got back to the house."

"Which way did he go?"

"Straight out the same way he came, by the path that joined the drive just inside the lodge gates."

Poirot nodded.

"And you, what did you do?"

"I went back to the house. Major Blunt was walking up and down the terrace smoking, so I made a detour to get round to the side door. It was then just on half-past nine, as I tell you."

Poirot nodded again. He made a note or two in a microscopic pocket-book.

"I think that is all," he said thoughtfully.

"Ought I——" she hesitated. "Ought I to tell all this to Inspector Raglan?"

"It may come to that. But let us not be in a hurry. Let us proceed slowly, with due order and method. Charles Kent is not yet formally charged with murder. Circumstances may arise which will render your story unnecessary."

Miss Russell rose.

"Thank you very much, M. Poirot," she said. "You have been very kind—very kind indeed. You—you do believe me, don't you? That Charles had nothing to do with this wicked murder!"

"There seems no doubt that the man who was talking to Mr. Ackroyd in the library at nine-thirty could not possibly have been your son. Be of good courage, mademoiselle. All will yet be well."

Miss Russell departed. Poirot and I were left together.

"So that's that," I said. "Every time we come back to Ralph Paton. How did you manage to spot Miss Russell as the person Charles Kent came to meet? Did you notice the resemblance?"

"I had connected her with the unknown man long before we

actually came face to face with him. As soon as we found that quill. The quill suggested dope, and I remembered your account of Miss Russell's visit to you. Then I found the article on cocaine in that morning's paper. It all seemed very clear. She had heard from some one that morning—some one addicted to drugs, she read the article in the paper, and she came to you to ask a few tentative questions. She mentioned cocaine, since the article in question was on cocaine. Then, when you seemed too interested, she switched hurriedly to the subject of detective stories and untraceable poisons. I suspected a son or a brother, or some other undesirable male relation. Ah! but I must go. It is the time of the lunch."

"Stay and lunch with us," I suggested.

Poirot shook his head. A faint twinkle came into his eye.

"Not again to-day. I should not like to force Mademoiselle Caroline to adopt a vegetarian diet two days in succession."

It occurred to me that there was not much which escaped Hercule Poirot.

TWENTY ONE
The Paragraph in the Paper

Caroline, of course, had not failed to see Miss Russell come to the surgery door. I had anticipated this, and had ready an elaborate account of the lady's bad knee. But Caroline was not in a cross-questioning mood. Her point of view was that she knew what Miss Russell had really come for and that *I* didn't.

"Pumping you, James," said Caroline. "Pumping you in the most shameless manner, I've not a doubt. It's no good interrupting. I dare say you hadn't the least idea she was doing it even. Men *are* so simple. She knows that you are in M. Poirot's confidence, and she wants to find out things. Do you know what I think, James?"

"I couldn't begin to imagine. You think so many extraordinary things."

"It's no good being sarcastic. I think Miss Russell knows more about Mr. Ackroyd's death than she is prepared to admit."

Caroline leaned back triumphantly in her chair.

"Do you really think so?" I said absently.

"You are very dull to-day, James. No animation about you. It's that liver of yours."

Our conversation then dealt with purely personal matters.

The paragraph inspired by Poirot duly appeared in our daily paper the next morning. I was in the dark as to its purpose, but its effect on Caroline was immense.

She began by stating, most untruly, that she had said as

much all along. I raised my eyebrows, but did not argue. Caroline, however, must have felt a prick of conscience, for she went on:—

"I mayn't have actually mentioned Liverpool, but I knew he'd try to get away to America. That's what Crippen did."

"Without much success," I reminded her.

"Poor boy, and so they've caught him. I consider, James, that it's your duty to see that he isn't hung."

"What do you expect me to do?"

"Why, you're a medical man, aren't you? You've known him from a boy upwards. Not mentally responsible. That's the line to take, clearly. I read only the other day that they're very happy in Broadmoor—it's quite like a high-class club."

But Caroline's words had reminded me of something.

"I never knew that Poirot had an imbecile nephew?" I said curiously.

"Didn't you? Oh, he told me all about it. Poor lad. It's a great grief to all the family. They've kept him at home so far, but it's getting to such a pitch that they're afraid he'll have to go into some kind of institution."

"I suppose you know pretty well everything there is to know about Poirot's family by this time," I said, exasperated.

"Pretty well," said Caroline complacently. "It's a great relief to people to be able to tell all their troubles to some one."

"It might be," I said, "if they were ever allowed to do so spontaneously. Whether they enjoy having confidences screwed out of them by force is another matter."

Caroline merely looked at me with the air of a Christian martyr enjoying martyrdom.

"You are so self-contained, James," she said. "You hate speaking out, or parting with any information yourself, and you think everybody else must be just like you. I should hope that I never screw confidences out of anybody. For instance, if M. Poirot comes in this afternoon, as he said he might do, I shall not dream of asking him who it was arrived at his house early this morning."

"Early this morning?" I queried.

"Very early," said Caroline. "Before the milk came. I just happened to be looking out of the window—the blind was flapping. It was a man. He came in a closed car, and he was all muffled up. I couldn't get a glimpse of his face. But I will tell you *my* idea, and you'll see that I'm right."

"What's your idea?"

Caroline dropped her voice mysteriously.

"A Home Office expert," she breathed.

"A Home Office expert," I said, amazed. "My dear Caroline!"

"Mark my words, James, you'll see that I'm right. That Russell woman was here that morning after your poisons. Roger Ackroyd might easily have been poisoned in his food that night."

I laughed out loud.

"Nonsense," I cried. "He was stabbed in the neck. You know that as well as I do."

"After death, James," said Caroline; "to make a false clew."

"My good woman," I said, "I examined the body, and I know what I'm talking about. That wound wasn't inflicted after death— it was the cause of death, and you need make no mistake about it."

Caroline merely continued to look omniscient, which so annoyed me that I went on:—

"Perhaps you will tell me, Caroline, if I have a medical degree or if I have not?"

"You have the medical degree, I dare say, James—at least, I mean I know you have. But you've no imagination whatever."

"Having endowed you with a treble portion, there was none left over for me," I said dryly.

I was amused to notice Caroline's maneuvers that afternoon when Poirot duly arrived. My sister, without asking a direct question, skirted the subject of the mysterious guest in every way imaginable. By the twinkle in Poirot's eyes, I saw that he realized her object. He remained blandly impervious, and blocked her bowling so successfully that she herself was at a loss how to proceed.

Having, I suspect, quietly enjoyed the little game, he rose to his feet and suggested a walk.

"It is that I need to reduce the figure a little," he explained. "You will come with me, doctor? And perhaps later Miss Caroline will give us some tea."

"Delighted," said Caroline. "Won't your—er—guest come in also?"

"You are too kind," said Poirot. "But no, my friend reposes himself. Soon you must make his acquaintance."

"Quite an old friend of yours, so somebody told me," said Caroline, making one last valiant effort.

"Did they?" murmured Poirot. "Well, we must start."

Our tramp took us in the direction of Fernly. I had guessed beforehand that it might do so. I was beginning to understand Poirot's methods. Every little irrelevancy had a bearing upon the whole.

"I have a commission for you, my friend," he said at last. "To-night, at my house, I desire to have a little conference. You will attend, will you not?"

"Certainly," I said.

"Good. I need also all those in the house—that is to say: Mrs. Ackroyd, Mademoiselle Flora, Major Blunt, M. Raymond. I want you to be my ambassador. This little reunion is fixed for nine o'clock. You will ask them—yes?"

"With pleasure; but why not ask them yourself?"

"Because they will then put the questions: Why? What for? They will demand what my idea is. And, as you know, my friend, I much dislike to have to explain my little ideas until the time comes."

I smiled a little.

"My friend Hastings, he of whom I told you, used to say of me that I was the human oyster. But he was unjust. Of facts, I keep nothing to myself. But to every one his own interpretation of them."

"When do you want me to do this?"

"Now, if you will. We are close to the house."

"Aren't you coming in?"

"No, me, I will promenade myself in the grounds. I will rejoin you by the lodge gates in a quarter of an hour's time."

I nodded, and set off on my task. The only member of the family at home proved to be Mrs. Ackroyd, who was sipping an early cup of tea. She received me very graciously.

"So grateful to you, doctor," she murmured, "for clearing up that little matter with M. Poirot. But life is one trouble after another. You have heard about Flora, of course?"

"What exactly?" I asked cautiously.

"This new engagement. Flora and Hector Blunt. Of course not such a good match as Ralph would have been. But after all, happiness comes first. What dear Flora needs is an older man—some one steady and reliable, and then Hector is really a very distinguished man in his way. You saw the news of Ralph's arrest in the paper this morning?"

"Yes," I said, "I did."

"Horrible." Mrs. Ackroyd closed her eyes and shuddered. "Geoffrey Raymond was in a terrible way. Rang up Liverpool. But they wouldn't tell him anything at the police station there. In fact, they said they hadn't arrested Ralph at all. Mr. Raymond insists that it's all a mistake—a—what do they call it?—*canard* of the newspaper's. I've forbidden it to be mentioned before the servants. Such a terrible disgrace. Fancy if Flora had actually been married to him."

Mrs. Ackroyd shut her eyes in anguish. I began to wonder how soon I should be able to deliver Poirot's invitation.

Before I had time to speak, Mrs. Ackroyd was off again.

"You were here yesterday, weren't you, with that dreadful Inspector Raglan? Brute of a man—he terrified Flora into saying she took that money from poor Roger's room. And the matter was so simple, really. The dear child wanted to borrow a few pounds, didn't like to disturb her uncle since he'd given strict orders against it, but knowing where he kept his notes she went there and took what she needed."

"Is that Flora's account of the matter?" I asked.

"My dear doctor, you know what girls are nowadays. So easily acted on by suggestion. You, of course, know all about hypnosis and that sort of thing. The inspector shouts at her, says the word 'steal' over and over again, until the poor child gets an inhibition—or is it a complex?—I always mix up those two words—and actually thinks herself that she has stolen the money. I saw at once how it was. But I can't be too thankful for the whole misunderstanding in one way—it seems to have brought those two together—Hector and Flora, I mean. And I assure you that I have been very much worried about Flora in the past: why, at one time I actually thought there was going to be some kind of understanding between her and young Raymond. Just think of it!" Mrs. Ackroyd's voice rose in shrill horror. "A private secretary—with practically no means of his own."

"It would have been a severe blow to you," I said. "Now, Mrs. Ackroyd, I've got a message for you from M. Hercule Poirot."

"For me?"

Mrs. Ackroyd looked quite alarmed.

I hastened to reassure her, and I explained what Poirot wanted.

"Certainly," said Mrs. Ackroyd rather doubtfully, "I suppose we must come if M. Poirot says so. But what is it all about? I like to know beforehand."

I assured the lady truthfully that I myself did not know any more than she did.

"Very well," said Mrs. Ackroyd at last, rather grudgingly, "I will tell the others, and we will be there at nine o'clock."

Thereupon I took my leave, and joined Poirot at the agreed meeting-place.

"I've been longer than a quarter of an hour, I'm afraid," I

remarked. "But once that good lady starts talking it's a matter of the utmost difficulty to get a word in edgeways."

"It is of no matter," said Poirot. "Me, I have been well amused. This park is magnificent."

We set off homewards. When we arrived, to our great surprise Caroline, who had evidently been watching for us, herself opened the door.

She put her fingers to her lips. Her face was full of importance and excitement.

"Ursula Bourne," she said, "the parlormaid from Fernly. She's here! I've put her in the dining-room. She's in a terrible way, poor thing. Says she must see M. Poirot at once. I've done all I could. Taken her a cup of hot tea. It really goes to one's heart to see any one in such a state."

"In the dining-room?" asked Poirot.

"This way," I said, and flung open the door.

Ursula Bourne was sitting by the table. Her arms were spread out in front of her, and she had evidently just lifted her head from where it had been buried. Her eyes were red with weeping.

"Ursula Bourne," I murmured.

But Poirot went past me with outstretched hands.

"No," he said, "that is not quite right, I think. It is not Ursula Bourne, is it, my child—but Ursula Paton? Mrs. Ralph Paton."

TWENTY TWO
Ursula's Story

For a moment or two the girl looked mutely at Poirot. Then, her reserve breaking down completely, she nodded her head once, and burst into an outburst of sobs.

Caroline pushed past me, and putting her arm round the girl, patted her on the shoulder.

"There, there, my dear," she said soothingly, "it will be all right. You'll see—everything will be all right."

Buried under curiosity and scandal-mongering there is a lot of kindness in Caroline. For the moment, even the interest of Poirot's revelation was lost in the sight of the girl's distress.

Presently Ursula sat up and wiped her eyes.

"This is very weak and silly of me," she said.

"No, no, my child," said Poirot kindly. "We can all realize the strain of this last week."

"It must have been a terrible ordeal," I said.

"And then to find that you knew," continued Ursula. "How did you know? Was it Ralph who told you?"

Poirot shook his head.

"You know what brought me to you to-night," went on the girl. "*This——*"

She held out a crumpled piece of newspaper, and I recognized the paragraph that Poirot had had inserted.

"It says that Ralph has been arrested. So everything is useless.

I need not pretend any longer."

"Newspaper paragraphs are not always true, mademoiselle," murmured Poirot, having the grace to look ashamed of himself. "All the same, I think you will do well to make a clean breast of things. The truth is what we need now."

The girl hesitated, looking at him doubtfully.

"You do not trust me," said Poirot gently. "Yet all the same you came here to find me, did you not? Why was that?"

"Because I don't believe that Ralph did it," said the girl in a very low voice. "And I think that you are clever, and will find out the truth. And also——"

"Yes?"

"I think you are kind."

Poirot nodded his head several times.

"It is very good that—yes, it is very good. Listen, I do in verity believe that this husband of yours is innocent—but the affair marches badly. If I am to save him, I must know all there is to know—even if it should seem to make the case against him blacker than before."

"How well you understand," said Ursula.

"So you will tell me the whole story, will you not? From the beginning."

"You're not going to send *me* away, I hope," said Caroline, settling herself comfortably in an arm-chair. "What I want to know," she continued, "is why this child was masquerading as a parlormaid?"

"Masquerading?" I queried.

"That's what I said. Why did you do it, child? For a wager?"

"For a living," said Ursula dryly.

And encouraged, she began the story which I reproduce here in my own words.

Ursula Bourne, it seemed, was one of a family of seven—impoverished Irish gentlefolk. On the death of her father, most of the girls were cast out into the world to earn their own living.

Ursula's eldest sister was married to Captain Folliott. It was she whom I had seen that Sunday, and the cause of her embarrassment was clear enough now. Determined to earn her living and not attracted to the idea of being a nursery governess—the one profession open to an untrained girl, Ursula preferred the job of parlormaid. She scorned to label herself a "lady parlormaid." She would be the real thing, her reference being supplied by her sister. At Fernly, despite an aloofness which, as has been seen, caused some comment, she was a success at her job—quick, competent, and thorough.

"I enjoyed the work," she explained. "And I had plenty of time to myself."

And then came her meeting with Ralph Paton, and the love affair which culminated in a secret marriage. Ralph had persuaded her into that, somewhat against her will. He had declared that his stepfather would not hear of his marrying a penniless girl. Better to be married secretly, and break the news to him at some later and more favorable minute.

And so the deed was done, and Ursula Bourne became Ursula Paton. Ralph had declared that he meant to pay off his debts, find a job, and then, when he was in a position to support her, and independent of his adopted father, they would break the news to him.

But to people like Ralph Paton, turning over a new leaf is easier in theory than in practice. He hoped that his stepfather, whilst still in ignorance of the marriage, might be persuaded to pay his debts and put him on his feet again. But the revelation of the amount of Ralph's liabilities merely enraged Roger Ackroyd, and he refused to do anything at all. Some months passed, and then Ralph was bidden once more to Fernly. Roger Ackroyd did not beat about the bush. It was the desire of his heart that Ralph should marry Flora, and he put the matter plainly before the young man.

And here it was that the innate weakness of Ralph Paton showed itself. As always, he grasped at the easy, the immediate solution. As far as I could make out, neither Flora nor Ralph made any pretence of love. It was, on both sides, a business arrangement. Roger Ackroyd dictated his wishes—they agreed to them. Flora accepted a chance of liberty, money, and an enlarged horizon, Ralph, of course, was playing a different game. But he was in a very awkward hole financially. He seized at the chance. His debts would be paid. He could start again with a clean sheet. His was not a nature to envisage the future, but I gather that he saw vaguely the engagement with Flora being broken off after a decent interval had elapsed. Both Flora and he stipulated that it should be kept a secret for the present. He was anxious to conceal it from Ursula. He felt instinctively that her nature, strong and resolute, with an inherent distaste for duplicity, was not one to welcome such a course.

Then came the crucial moment when Roger Ackroyd, always high-handed, decided to announce the engagement. He said no word of his intention to Ralph—only to Flora, and Flora, apathetic, raised no objection. On Ursula, the news fell like a bombshell. Summoned by her, Ralph came hurriedly down from town. They met in the wood, where part of their conversation was overheard by my sister. Ralph implored her to keep silent for a little while longer, Ursula was equally determined to have done with concealments. She would tell Mr. Ackroyd the truth without any further delay. Husband and wife parted acrimoniously.

Ursula, steadfast in her purpose, sought an interview with Roger Ackroyd that very afternoon, and revealed the truth to him. Their interview was a stormy one—it might have been even more stormy had not Roger Ackroyd been already obsessed with his own troubles. It was bad enough, however. Ackroyd was not the kind of man to forgive the deceit that had been practiced upon him. His rancor was mainly directed to Ralph, but Ursula came in for her share, since he regarded her as a girl who had deliberately tried to "entrap" the adopted son of a very wealthy man. Unforgivable things were said on both sides.

That same evening Ursula met Ralph by appointment in the small summer-house, stealing out from the house by the side door in order to do so. Their interview was made up of reproaches on both sides. Ralph charged Ursula with having irretrievably ruined his prospects by her ill-timed revelation. Ursula reproached Ralph with his duplicity.

They parted at last. A little over half an hour later came the discovery of Roger Ackroyd's body. Since that night Ursula had neither seen nor heard from Ralph.

As the story unfolded itself, I realized more and more what a damning series of facts it was. Alive, Ackroyd could hardly have failed to alter his will—I knew him well enough to realize that to do so would be his first thought. His death came in the nick of time for Ralph and Ursula Paton. Small wonder the girl had held her tongue, and played her part so consistently.

My meditations were interrupted. It was Poirot's voice speaking, and I knew from the gravity of his tone that he, too, was fully alive to the implications of the position.

"Mademoiselle, I must ask you one question, and you must answer it truthfully, for on it everything may hang: What time was it when you parted from Captain Ralph Paton in the summer-house? Now, take a little minute so that your answer may be very exact."

The girl gave a half laugh, bitter enough in all conscience.

"Do you think I haven't gone over that again and again in my own mind? It was just half-past nine when I went out to meet him. Major Blunt was walking up and down the terrace, so I had to go round through the bushes to avoid him. It must have been about twenty-seven minutes to ten when I reached the summer-house. Ralph was waiting for me. I was with him ten minutes—not longer, for it was just a quarter to ten when I got back to the house."

I saw now the insistence of her question the other day. If only Ackroyd could have been proved to have been killed before a quarter to ten, and not after.

I saw the reflection of that thought in Poirot's next question.

"Who left the summer-house first?"

"I did."

"Leaving Ralph Paton in the summer-house?"

"Yes—but you don't think——"

"Mademoiselle, it is of no importance what I think. What did you do when you got back to the house?"

"I went up to my room."

"And stayed there until when?"

"Until about ten o'clock."

"Is there any one who can prove that?"

"Prove? That I was in my room, you mean? Oh! no. But surely—oh! I see, they might think—they might think——"

I saw the dawning horror in her eyes.

Poirot finished the sentence for her.

"That it was *you* who entered by the window and stabbed Mr. Ackroyd as he sat in his chair? Yes, they might think just that."

"Nobody but a fool would think any such thing," said Caroline indignantly.

She patted Ursula on the shoulder.

The girl had her face hidden in her hands.

"Horrible," she was murmuring. "Horrible."

Caroline gave her a friendly shake.

"Don't worry, my dear," she said. "M. Poirot doesn't think that really. As for that husband of yours, I don't think much of him, and I tell you so candidly. Running away and leaving you to face the music."

But Ursula shook her head energetically.

"Oh, no," she cried. "It wasn't like that at all. Ralph would not run away on his own account. I see now. If he heard of his stepfather's murder, he might think himself that I had done it."

"He wouldn't think any such thing," said Caroline.

"I was so cruel to him that night—so hard and bitter. I wouldn't listen to what he was trying to say—wouldn't believe that he really cared. I just stood there telling him what I thought of him, and saying the coldest, cruelest things that came into my mind—trying my best to hurt him."

"Do him no harm," said Caroline. "Never worry about what you say to a man. They're so conceited that they never believe you mean it if it's unflattering."

Ursula went on, nervously twisting and untwisting her hands.

"When the murder was discovered and he didn't come forward, I was terribly upset. Just for a moment I wondered—but then I knew he couldn't—he couldn't.... But I wished he would come forward and say openly that he'd had nothing to do with it. I knew that he was very fond of Dr. Sheppard, and I fancied that perhaps Dr. Sheppard might know where he was hiding."

She turned to me.

"That's why I said what I did to you that day. I thought, if you knew where he was, you might pass on the message to him."

"I?" I exclaimed.

"Why should James know where he was?" demanded Caroline sharply.

"It was very unlikely, I know," admitted Ursula, "but Ralph had often spoken of Dr. Sheppard, and I knew that he would be likely to consider him as his best friend in King's Abbot."

"My dear child," I said, "I have not the least idea where Ralph Paton is at the present moment."

"That is true enough," said Poirot.

"But——" Ursula held out the newspaper cutting in a puzzled fashion.

"Ah! that," said Poirot, slightly embarrassed; "a *bagatelle*, mademoiselle. A *rien du tout*. Not for a moment do I believe that Ralph Paton has been arrested."

"But then——" began the girl slowly.

Poirot went on quickly:—

"There is one thing I should like to know—did Captain Paton wear shoes or boots that night?"

Ursula shook her head.

"I can't remember."

"A pity! But how should you? Now, madame," he smiled at her, his head on one side, his forefinger wagging eloquently, "no questions. And do not torment yourself. Be of good courage, and place your faith in Hercule Poirot."

TWENTY THREE
Poirot's Little Reunion

And now," said Caroline, rising, "that child is coming upstairs to lie down. Don't you worry, my dear. M. Poirot will do everything he can for you—be sure of that."

"I ought to go back to Fernly," said Ursula uncertainly.

But Caroline silenced her protests with a firm hand.

"Nonsense. You're in my hands for the time being. You'll stay here for the present, anyway—eh, M. Poirot?"

"It will be the best plan," agreed the little Belgian. "This evening I shall want mademoiselle—I beg her pardon, madame—to attend my little reunion. Nine o'clock at my house. It is most necessary that she should be there."

Caroline nodded, and went with Ursula out of the room. The door shut behind them. Poirot dropped down into a chair again.

"So far, so good," he said. "Things are straightening themselves out."

"They're getting to look blacker and blacker against Ralph Paton," I observed gloomily.

Poirot nodded.

"Yes, that is so. But it was to be expected, was it not?"

I looked at him, slightly puzzled by the remark. He was leaning back in the chair, his eyes half closed, the tips of his fingers just touching each other. Suddenly he sighed and shook his head.

"What is it?" I asked.

"It is that there are moments when a great longing for my friend Hastings comes over me. That is the friend of whom I spoke to you—the one who resides now in the Argentine. Always, when I have had a big case, he has been by my side. And he has helped me—yes, often he has helped me. For he had a knack, that one, of stumbling over the truth unawares—without noticing it himself, *bien entendu*. At times he has said something particularly foolish, and behold that foolish remark has revealed the truth to me! And then, too, it was his practice to keep a written record of the cases that proved interesting."

I gave a slight embarrassed cough.

"As far as that goes," I began, and then stopped.

Poirot sat upright in his chair. His eyes sparkled.

"But yes? What is it that you would say?"

"Well, as a matter of fact, I've read some of Captain Hastings's narratives, and I thought, why not try my hand at something of the same kind? Seemed a pity not to—unique opportunity—probably the only time I'll be mixed up with anything of this kind."

I felt myself getting hotter and hotter, and more and more incoherent, as I floundered through the above speech.

Poirot sprang from his chair. I had a moment's terror that he was going to embrace me French fashion, but mercifully he refrained.

"But this is magnificent—you have then written down your impressions of the case as you went along?"

I nodded.

"*Epatant!*" cried Poirot. "Let me see them—this instant."

I was not quite prepared for such a sudden demand. I racked my brains to remember certain details.

"I hope you won't mind," I stammered. "I may have been a little—er—*personal* now and then."

"Oh! I comprehend perfectly; you have referred to me as comic—as, perhaps, ridiculous now and then? It matters not at all. Hastings, he also was not always polite. Me, I have the mind above such trivialities."

Still somewhat doubtful, I rummaged in the drawers of my desk and produced an untidy pile of manuscript which I handed over to him. With an eye on possible publication in the future, I had divided the work into chapters, and the night before I had brought it up to date with an account of Miss Russell's visit. Poirot had therefore twenty chapters.

I left him with them.

I was obliged to go out to a case at some distance away, and it was past eight o'clock when I got back, to be greeted with a plate of hot dinner on a tray, and the announcement that Poirot and my sister had supped together at half-past seven, and that the former had then gone to my workshop to finish his reading of the manuscript.

"I hope, James," said my sister, "that you've been careful in what you say about me in it?"

My jaw dropped. I had not been careful at all.

"Not that it matters very much," said Caroline, reading my expression correctly. "M. Poirot will know what to think. He understands me much better than you do."

I went into the workshop. Poirot was sitting by the window. The manuscript lay neatly piled on a chair beside him. He laid his hand on it and spoke.

"*Eh bien*," he said, "I congratulate you—on your modesty!"

"Oh!" I said, rather taken aback.

"And on your reticence," he added.

I said "Oh!" again.

"Not so did Hastings write," continued my friend. "On every page, many, many times was the word 'I.' What *he* thought—what *he* did. But you—you have kept your personality in the back-ground; only once or twice does it obtrude—in scenes of home life, shall we say?"

I blushed a little before the twinkle in his eye.

"What do you really think of the stuff?" I asked nervously.

"You want my candid opinion?"

"Yes."

Poirot laid his jesting manner aside.

"A very meticulous and accurate account," he said kindly. "You have recorded all the facts faithfully and exactly—though you have shown yourself becomingly reticent as to your own share in them."

"And it has helped you?"

"Yes. I may say that it has helped me considerably. Come, we must go over to my house and set the stage for my little performance."

Caroline was in the hall. I think she hoped that she might be invited to accompany us. Poirot dealt with the situation tactfully.

"I should much like to have had you present, mademoiselle," he said regretfully, "but at this juncture it would not be wise. See you, all these people to-night are suspects. Amongst them, I shall find the person who killed Mr. Ackroyd."

"You really believe that?" I said incredulously.

"I see that you do not," said Poirot dryly. "Not yet do you appreciate Hercule Poirot at his true worth."

At that minute Ursula came down the staircase.

"You are ready, my child?" said Poirot. "That is good. We will go to my house together. Mademoiselle Caroline, believe me, I do everything possible to render you service. Good-evening."

We went out, leaving Caroline, rather like a dog who has been refused a walk, standing on the front door step gazing after us.

The sitting-room at The Larches had been got ready. On the table were various *sirops* and glasses. Also a plate of biscuits. Several chairs had been brought in from the other room.

Poirot ran to and fro rearranging things. Pulling out a chair here, altering the position of a lamp there, occasionally stooping to straighten one of the mats that covered the floor. He was specially fussy over the lighting. The lamps were arranged in such a way as to throw a clear light on the side of the room where the chairs were grouped, at the same time leaving the other end of the room, where I presumed Poirot himself would sit, in a dim twilight.

Ursula and I watched him. Presently a bell was heard.

"They arrive," said Poirot. "Good, all is in readiness."

The door opened and the party from Fernly filed in. Poirot went forward and greeted Mrs. Ackroyd and Flora.

"It is most good of you to come," he said. "And Major Blunt and Mr. Raymond."

The secretary was debonair as ever.

"What's the great idea?" he said, laughing. "Some scientific machine? Do we have bands round our wrists which register guilty heart-beats? There is such an invention, isn't there?"

"I have read of it, yes," admitted Poirot. "But me, I am old-fashioned. I use the old methods. I work only with the little gray cells. Now let us begin—but first I have an announcement to make to you all."

He took Ursula's hand and drew her forward.

"This lady is Mrs. Ralph Paton. She was married to Captain Paton last March."

A little shriek burst from Mrs. Ackroyd.

"Ralph! Married! Last March! Oh! but it's absurd. How could he be?"

She stared at Ursula as though she had never seen her before.

"Married to Bourne?" she said. "Really, M. Poirot, I don't believe you."

Ursula flushed and began to speak, but Flora forestalled her.

Going quickly to the other girl's side, she passed her hand through her arm.

"You must not mind our being surprised," she said. "You see, we had no idea of such a thing. You and Ralph have kept your secret very well. I am—very glad about it."

"You are very kind, Miss Ackroyd," said Ursula in a low voice, "and you have every right to be exceedingly angry. Ralph behaved very badly—especially to you."

"You needn't worry about that," said Flora, giving her arm a consoling little pat. "Ralph was in a corner and took the only way out. I should probably have done the same in his place. I do think he might have trusted me with the secret, though. I wouldn't have let him down."

Poirot rapped gently on a table and cleared his throat significantly.

"The board meeting's going to begin," said Flora. "M. Poirot hints that we mustn't talk. But just tell me one thing. Where is Ralph? You must know if any one does."

"But I don't," cried Ursula, almost in a wail. "That's just it, I don't."

"Isn't he detained at Liverpool?" asked Raymond. "It said so in the paper."

"He is not at Liverpool," said Poirot shortly.

"In fact," I remarked, "no one knows where he is."

"Excepting Hercule Poirot, eh?" said Raymond.

Poirot replied seriously to the other's banter.

"Me, I know everything. Remember that."

Geoffrey Raymond lifted his eyebrows.

"Everything?" He whistled. "Whew! that's a tall order."

"Do you mean to say you can really guess where Ralph Paton is hiding?" I asked incredulously.

"You call it guessing. I call it knowing, my friend."

"In Cranchester?" I hazarded.

"No," replied Poirot gravely, "not in Cranchester."

He said no more, but at a gesture from him the assembled party took their seats. As they did so, the door opened once more and two other people came in and sat down near the door. They were Parker and the housekeeper.

"The number is complete," said Poirot. "Every one is here."

There was a ring of satisfaction in his tone. And with the sound of it I saw a ripple of something like uneasiness pass over all those faces grouped at the other end of the room. There was a suggestion in all this as of a trap—a trap that had closed.

Poirot read from a list in an important manner.

"Mrs. Ackroyd, Miss Flora Ackroyd, Major Blunt, Mr. Geoffrey Raymond, Mrs. Ralph Paton, John Parker, Elizabeth Russell."

He laid the paper down on the table.

"What's the meaning of all this?" began Raymond.

"The list I have just read," said Poirot, "is a list of suspected persons. Every one of you present had the opportunity to kill Mr. Ackroyd——"

With a cry Mrs. Ackroyd sprang up, her throat working.

"I don't like it," she wailed. "I don't like it. I would much prefer to go home."

"You cannot go home, madame," said Poirot sternly, "until you have heard what I have to say."

He paused a moment, then cleared his throat.

"I will start at the beginning. When Miss Ackroyd asked me to investigate the case, I went up to Fernly Park with the good Dr. Sheppard. I walked with him along the terrace, where I was shown the footprints on the window-sill. From there Inspector Raglan took me along the path which leads to the drive. My eye was caught by a little summer-house, and I searched it thoroughly. I found two things—a scrap of starched cambric and an empty goose quill. The scrap of cambric immediately suggested to me a maid's apron. When Inspector Raglan showed me his list of the people in the house, I noticed at once that one of the maids—Ursula Bourne, the parlormaid—had no real alibi. According to her own story, she was in her bedroom from nine-thirty until ten. But supposing that instead she was in the summer-house? If so, she must have gone there to meet some one. Now we know from Dr. Sheppard that some one from outside *did* come to the house that night—the stranger whom he met just by the gate. At a first glance it would seem that our problem was solved, and that the stranger went to the summer-house to meet Ursula Bourne. It was fairly certain that he *did* go to the summer-house because of the goose quill. That suggested at once to my mind a taker of drugs—and one who had acquired the habit on the other side of the Atlantic where sniffing 'snow' is more common than in this country. The man whom Dr. Sheppard met had an American accent, which fitted in with that supposition.

"But I was held up by one point. *The times did not fit.* Ursula Bourne could certainly not have gone to the summer-house before nine-thirty, whereas the man must have got there by a few minutes past nine. I could, of course, assume that he waited there for half an hour. The only alternative supposition was that there had been two separate meetings in the summer-house that night. *Eh bien*, as soon as I went into that alternative I found several significant facts. I discovered that Miss Russell, the housekeeper, had visited Dr. Sheppard that morning, and had displayed a good deal of interest in cures for victims of the drug habit. Taking that in conjunction with the goose quill, I assumed that the man in question came to Fernly to meet the housekeeper, and not Ursula Bourne. Who, then, did Ursula Bourne come to the rendezvous to meet? I was not long in doubt. First I found a ring—a wedding ring—with 'From R.' and a date inside it. Then I learnt that Ralph Paton had been seen coming up the path which led to the summer-house at twenty-five minutes past nine, and I also heard of a certain conversation which had taken place in the wood near the village that very afternoon—a conversation between Ralph Paton and some unknown girl. So I had my facts succeeding each other in a neat and orderly manner. A secret marriage, an engagement announced on the day of the tragedy, the stormy interview in the wood, and the meeting arranged for the summer-house that night.

"Incidentally this proved to me one thing, that both Ralph Paton and Ursula Bourne (or Paton) had the strongest motives for wishing Mr. Ackroyd out of the way. And it also made one other point unexpectedly clear. It could not have been Ralph Paton who was with Mr. Ackroyd in the study at nine-thirty.

"So we come to another and most interesting aspect of the

crime. Who was it in the room with Mr. Ackroyd at nine-thirty? Not Ralph Paton, who was in the summer-house with his wife. Not Charles Kent, who had already left. Who, then? I posed my cleverest—my most audacious question: *Was any one with him?*"

Poirot leaned forward and shot the last words triumphantly at us, drawing back afterwards with the air of one who has made a decided hit.

Raymond, however, did not seem impressed, and lodged a mild protest.

"I don't know if you're trying to make me out a liar, M. Poirot, but the matter does not rest on my evidence alone—except perhaps as to the exact words used. Remember, Major Blunt also heard Mr. Ackroyd talking to some one. He was on the terrace outside, and couldn't catch the words clearly, but he distinctly heard the voices."

Poirot nodded.

"I have not forgotten," he said quietly. "But Major Blunt was under the impression that it was *you* to whom Mr. Ackroyd was speaking."

For a moment Raymond seemed taken aback. Then he recovered himself.

"Blunt knows now that he was mistaken," he said.

"Exactly," agreed the other man.

"Yet there must have been some reason for his thinking so," mused Poirot. "Oh! no," he held up his hand in protest, "I know the reason you will give—but it is not enough. We must seek elsewhere. I will put it this way. From the beginning of the case I have been struck by one thing—the nature of those words which Mr. Raymond overheard. It has been amazing to me that no one has commented on them—has seen anything odd about them."

He paused a minute, and then quoted softly:—

"... *The calls on my purse have been so frequent of late that I fear it is impossible for me to accede to your request.* Does nothing strike you as odd about that?"

"I don't think so," said Raymond. "He has frequently dictated letters to me, using almost exactly those same words."

"Exactly," cried Poirot. "That is what I seek to arrive at. Would any man use such a phrase in *talking* to another? Impossible that that should be part of a real conversation. Now, if he had been dictating a letter——"

"You mean he was reading a letter aloud," said Raymond slowly. "Even so, he must have been reading to some one."

"But why? We have no evidence that there was any one else in the room. No other voice but Mr. Ackroyd's was heard, remember."

"Surely a man wouldn't read letters of that type aloud to himself—not unless he was—well—going balmy."

"You have all forgotten one thing," said Poirot softly: "the stranger who called at the house the preceding Wednesday."

They all stared at him.

"But yes," said Poirot, nodding encouragingly, "on Wednesday. The young man was not of himself important. But the firm he represented interested me very much."

"The Dictaphone Company," gasped Raymond. "I see it now. A dictaphone. That's what you think?"

Poirot nodded.

"Mr. Ackroyd had promised to invest in a dictaphone, you remember. Me, I had the curiosity to inquire of the company in question. Their reply is that Mr. Ackroyd *did* purchase a dictaphone from their representative. Why he concealed the matter from you, I do not know."

"He must have meant to surprise me with it," murmured Raymond. "He had quite a childish love of surprising people. Meant to keep it up his sleeve for a day or so. Probably was playing with it like a new toy. Yes, it fits in. You're quite right—no one would use quite those words in casual conversation."

"It explains, too," said Poirot, "why Major Blunt thought it was you who were in the study. Such scraps as came to him were

223

fragments of dictation, and so his subconscious mind deduced that you were with him. His conscious mind was occupied with something quite different—the white figure he had caught a glimpse of. He fancied it was Miss Ackroyd. Really, of course, it was Ursula Bourne's white apron he saw as she was stealing down to the summer-house."

Raymond had recovered from his first surprise.

"All the same," he remarked, "this discovery of yours, brilliant though it is (I'm quite sure I should never have thought of it), leaves the essential position unchanged. Mr. Ackroyd was alive at nine-thirty, since he was speaking into the dictaphone. It seems clear that the man Charles Kent was really off the premises by then. As to Ralph Paton——?"

He hesitated, glancing at Ursula.

Her color flared up, but she answered steadily enough.

"Ralph and I parted just before a quarter to ten. He never went near the house, I am sure of that. He had no intention of doing so. The last thing on earth he wanted was to face his stepfather. He would have funked it badly."

"It isn't that I doubt your story for a moment," explained Raymond. "I've always been quite sure Captain Paton was innocent. But one has to think of a court of law—and the questions that would be asked. He is in a most unfortunate position, but if he were to come forward——"

Poirot interrupted.

"That is your advice, yes? That he should come forward?"

"Certainly. If you know where he is——"

"I perceive that you do not believe that I do know. And yet I have told you just now that I know everything. The truth of the telephone call, of the footprints on the window-sill, of the hiding-place of Ralph Paton——"

"Where is he?" said Blunt sharply.

"Not very far away," said Poirot, smiling.

"In Cranchester?" I asked.

Poirot turned towards me.

"Always you ask me that. The idea of Cranchester it is with you an *idée fixe*. No, he is not in Cranchester. He is—*there!*"

He pointed a dramatic forefinger. Every one's head turned.

Ralph Paton was standing in the doorway.

TWENTY FOUR
Ralph Paton's Story

It was a very uncomfortable minute for *me*. I hardly took in what happened next, but there were exclamations and cries of surprise! When I was sufficiently master of myself to be able to realize what was going on, Ralph Paton was standing by his wife, her hand in his, and he was smiling across the room at me.

Poirot, too, was smiling, and at the same time shaking an eloquent finger at me.

"Have I not told you at least thirty-six times that it is useless to conceal things from Hercule Poirot?" he demanded. "That in such a case he finds out?"

He turned to the others.

"One day, you remember, we held a little séance about a table—just the six of us. I accused the other five persons present of concealing something from me. Four of them gave up their secret. Dr. Sheppard did not give up his. But all along I have had my suspicions. Dr. Sheppard went to the Three Boars that night hoping to find Ralph. He did not find him there; but supposing, I said to myself, that he met him in the street on his way home? Dr. Sheppard was a friend of Captain Paton's, and he had come straight from the scene of the crime. He must know that things looked very black against him. Perhaps he knew more than the general public did——"

"I did," I said ruefully. "I suppose I might as well make a clean breast of things now. I went to see Ralph that afternoon. At first he refused to take me into his confidence, but later he told me about his marriage, and the hole he was in. As soon as the murder was discovered, I realized that once the facts were known, suspicion could not fail to attach to Ralph—or, if not to him, to the girl he loved. That night I put the facts plainly before him. The thought of having possibly to give evidence which might incriminate his wife made him resolve at all costs to—to——"

I hesitated, and Ralph filled up the gap.

"To do a bunk," he said graphically. "You see, Ursula left me to go back to the house. I thought it possible that she might have attempted to have another interview with my stepfather. He had already been very rude to her that afternoon. It occurred to me that he might have so insulted her—in such an unforgivable manner—that without knowing what she was doing——"

He stopped. Ursula released her hand from his, and stepped back.

"You thought that, Ralph! You actually thought that I might have done it?"

"Let us get back to the culpable conduct of Dr. Sheppard," said Poirot dryly. "Dr. Sheppard consented to do what he could to help him. He was successful in hiding Captain Paton from the police."

"Where?" asked Raymond. "In his own house?"

"Ah, no, indeed," said Poirot. "You should ask yourself the question that I did. If the good doctor is concealing the young man, what place would he choose? It must necessarily be somewhere near at hand. I think of Cranchester. A hotel? No. Lodgings? Even more emphatically, no. Where, then? Ah! I have it. A nursing home. A home for the mentally unfit. I test my theory. I invent a nephew with mental trouble. I consult Mademoiselle Sheppard as to suitable homes. She gives me the names of two near Cranchester to which her brother has sent patients. I make inquiries. Yes, at one of them a patient was brought there by the doctor himself early on Saturday morning. That patient, though known by another name, I had no difficulty in identifying as Captain Paton. After certain necessary formalities, I was allowed to bring him away. He arrived at my house in the early hours of yesterday morning."

I looked at him ruefully.

"Caroline's Home Office expert," I murmured. "And to think I never guessed!"

"You see now why I drew attention to the reticence of your manuscript," murmured Poirot. "It was strictly truthful as far as it went—but it did not go very far, eh, my friend?"

I was too abashed to argue.

"Dr. Sheppard has been very loyal," said Ralph. "He has stood by me through thick and thin. He did what he thought was the best. I see now, from what M. Poirot has told me, that it was not really the best. I should have come forward and faced the music. You see, in the home, we never saw a newspaper. I knew nothing of what was going on."

"Dr. Sheppard has been a model of discretion," said Poirot dryly. "But me, I discover all the little secrets. It is my business."

"Now we can have your story of what happened that night," said Raymond impatiently.

"You know it already," said Ralph. "There's very little for me to add. I left the summer-house about nine-forty-five, and tramped about the lanes, trying to make up my mind as to what to do next—what line to take. I'm bound to admit that I've not the shadow of an alibi, but I give you my solemn word that I never went to the study, that I never saw my stepfather alive—or dead. Whatever the world thinks, I'd like all of you to believe me."

"No alibi," murmured Raymond. "That's bad. I believe you, of course, but—it's a bad business."

"It makes things very simple, though," said Poirot, in a cheerful voice. "Very simple indeed."

We all stared at him.

"You see what I mean? No? Just this—to save Captain Paton the real criminal must confess."

He beamed round at us all.

"But yes—I mean what I say. See now, I did not invite Inspector Raglan to be present. That was for a reason. I did not want to tell him all that I knew—at least I did not want to tell him to-night."

He leaned forward, and suddenly his voice and his whole personality changed. He suddenly became dangerous.

"I who speak to you—I know the murderer of Mr. Ackroyd is in this room now. It is to the murderer I speak. *To-morrow the truth goes to Inspector Raglan.* You understand?"

There was a tense silence. Into the midst of it came the old Breton woman with a telegram on a salver. Poirot tore it open.

Blunt's voice rose abrupt and resonant.

"The murderer is amongst us, you say? You know—which?"

Poirot had read the message. He crumpled it up in his hand.

"I know—now."

He tapped the crumpled ball of paper.

"What is that?" said Raymond sharply.

"A wireless message—from a steamer now on her way to the United States."

There was a dead silence. Poirot rose to his feet bowing.

"Messieurs et Mesdames, this reunion of mine is at an end. Remember—*the truth goes to Inspector Raglan in the morning.*"

TWENTY FIVE
The Whole Truth

Aslight gesture from Poirot enjoined me to stay behind the rest. I obeyed, going over to the fire and thoughtfully stirring the big logs on it with the toe of my boot.

I was puzzled. For the first time I was absolutely at sea as to Poirot's meaning. For a moment I was inclined to think that the scene I had just witnessed was a gigantic piece of bombast—that he had been what he called "playing the comedy" with a view to making himself interesting and important. But, in spite of myself, I was forced to believe in an underlying reality. There had been real menace in his words—a certain indisputable sincerity. But I still believed him to be on entirely the wrong tack.

When the door shut behind the last of the party he came over to the fire.

"Well, my friend," he said quietly, "and what do you think of it all?"

"I don't know what to think," I said frankly. "What was the point? Why not go straight to Inspector Raglan with the truth instead of giving the guilty person this elaborate warning?"

Poirot sat down and drew out his case of tiny Russian cigarettes. He smoked for a minute or two in silence. Then:—

"Use your little gray cells," he said. "There is always a reason behind my actions."

I hesitated for a moment, and then I said slowly:

230

"The first one that occurs to me is that you yourself do not know who the guilty person is, but that you are sure that he is to be found amongst the people here to-night. Therefore your words were intended to force a confession from the unknown murderer?"

Poirot nodded approvingly.

"A clever idea, but not the truth."

"I thought, perhaps, that by making him believe you knew, you might force him out into the open—not necessarily by confession. He might try to silence you as he formerly silenced Mr. Ackroyd—before you could act to-morrow morning."

"A trap with myself as the bait! *Merci, mon ami*, but I am not sufficiently heroic for that."

"Then I fail to understand you. Surely you are running the risk of letting the murderer escape by thus putting him on his guard?"

Poirot shook his head.

"He cannot escape," he said gravely. "There is only one way out—and that way does not lead to freedom."

"You really believe that one of those people here to-night committed the murder?" I asked incredulously.

"Yes, my friend."

"Which one?"

There was a silence for some minutes. Then Poirot tossed the stump of his cigarette into the grate and began to speak in a quiet, reflective tone.

"I will take you the way that I have traveled myself. Step by step you shall accompany me, and see for yourself that all the facts point indisputably to one person. Now, to begin with, there were two facts and one little discrepancy in time which especially attracted my attention. The first fact was the telephone call. If Ralph Paton were indeed the murderer, the telephone call became meaningless and absurd. Therefore, I said to myself, Ralph Paton is not the murderer.

"I satisfied myself that the call could not have been sent by any one in the house, yet I was convinced that it was amongst

231

those present on the fatal evening that I had to look for my criminal. Therefore I concluded that the telephone call must have been sent by an accomplice. I was not quite pleased with that deduction, but I let it stand for the minute.

"I next examined the *motive* for the call. That was difficult. I could only get at it by judging its *result*. Which was—that the murder was discovered that night instead of—in all probability— the following morning. You agree with that?"

"Ye-es," I admitted. "Yes. As you say, Mr. Ackroyd, having given orders that he was not to be disturbed, nobody would have been likely to go to the study that night."

"*Très bien.* The affair marches, does it not? But matters were still obscure. What was the advantage of having the crime discovered that night in preference to the following morning? The only idea I could get hold of was that the murderer, knowing the crime was to be discovered at a certain time, could make sure of being present when the door was broken in—or at any rate immediately afterwards. And now we come to the second fact—the chair pulled out from the wall. Inspector Raglan dismissed that as of no importance. I, on the contrary, have always regarded it as of supreme importance.

"In your manuscript you have drawn a neat little plan of the study. If you had it with you this minute you would see that— the chair being drawn out in the position indicated by Parker—it would stand in a direct line between the door and the window."

"The window!" I said quickly.

"You, too, have my first idea. I imagined that the chair was drawn out so that something connected with the window should not be seen by any one entering through the door. But I soon abandoned that supposition, for though the chair was a grandfather with a high back, it obscured very little of the window—only the part between the sash and the ground. No, *mon ami*—but remember that just in front of the window there stood a table with books and magazines upon it. Now that table *was* completely hidden by the drawn-out chair—and immediately I had my first shadowy suspicion of the truth.

"Supposing that there had been something on that table not intended to be seen? Something placed there by the murderer? As yet I had no inkling of what that something might be. But I knew certain very interesting facts about it. For instance, it was something that the murderer had not been able to take away with him at the time that he committed the crime. At the same time it was vital that it should be removed as soon as possible after the crime had been discovered. And so—the telephone message, and the opportunity for the murderer to be on the spot when the body was discovered.

"Now four people were on the scene before the police arrived. Yourself, Parker, Major Blunt, and Mr. Raymond. Parker I eliminated at once, since at whatever time the crime was discovered, he was the one person certain to be on the spot. Also it was he who told me of the pulled-out chair. Parker, then, was cleared (of the murder, that is. I still thought it possible that he had been blackmailing Mrs. Ferrars). Raymond and Blunt, however, remained under suspicion since, if the crime had been discovered in the early hours of the morning, it was quite possible that they might have arrived on the scene too late to prevent the object on the round table being discovered.

"Now what was that object? You heard my arguments to-night in reference to the scrap of conversation overheard? As soon as I learned that a representative of a dictaphone company had called, the idea of a dictaphone took root in my mind. You heard what I said in this room not half an hour ago? They all agreed with my theory—but one vital fact seems to have escaped them. Granted that a dictaphone was being used by Mr. Ackroyd that night—why was no dictaphone found?"

"I never thought of that," I said.

"We know that a dictaphone was supplied to Mr. Ackroyd. But no dictaphone has been found amongst his effects. So, if something was taken from that table—why should not that something be the dictaphone? But there were certain difficulties in the way. The attention of every one was, of course, focused on the murdered man. I think any one could have gone to the table unnoticed by the other people in the room. But a dictaphone has a certain bulk—it cannot be slipped casually into a pocket. There must have been a receptacle of some kind capable of holding it.

"You see where I am arriving? The figure of the murderer is taking shape. A person who was on the scene straightway, but who might not have been if the crime had been discovered the following morning. A person carrying a receptacle into which the dictaphone might be fitted——"

I interrupted.

"But why remove the dictaphone? What was the point?"

"You are like Mr. Raymond. You take it for granted that what was heard at nine-thirty was Mr. Ackroyd's voice speaking into a dictaphone. But consider this useful invention for a little minute. You dictate into it, do you not? And at some later time a secretary or a typist turns it on, and the voice speaks again."

"You mean——" I gasped.

Poirot nodded.

"Yes, I mean that. *At nine-thirty Mr. Ackroyd was already dead.* It was the dictaphone speaking—not the man."

"And the murderer switched it on. Then he must have been in the room at that minute?"

"Possibly. But we must not exclude the likelihood of some mechanical device having been applied—something after the nature of a time lock, or even of a simple alarm clock. But in that case we must add two qualifications to our imaginary portrait of the murderer. It must be some one who knew of Mr. Ackroyd's purchase of the dictaphone and also some one with the necessary mechanical knowledge.

"I had got thus far in my own mind when we came to the footprints on the window ledge. Here there were three conclusions open to me. (1) They might really have been made by Ralph Paton. He had been at Fernly that night, and might have climbed into the study and found his uncle dead there. That was one hypothesis. (2) There was the possibility that the footmarks might have been made by somebody else who happened to have the same kind of studs in his shoes. But the inmates of the house had shoes soled with crepe rubber, and I declined to believe in the coincidence of some one from outside having the same kind of shoes as Ralph Paton wore. Charles Kent, as we know from the barmaid of the Dog and Whistle, had on a pair of boots 'clean dropping off him.' (3) Those prints were made by some one deliberately trying to throw suspicion on Ralph Paton. To test this last conclusion, it was necessary to ascertain certain facts. One pair of Ralph's shoes had been obtained from the Three Boars by the police. Neither Ralph nor any one else could have worn them that evening, since they were downstairs being cleaned. According to the police theory, Ralph was wearing another pair of the same kind, and I found out that it was true that he had two pairs. Now for my theory to be proved correct it was necessary for the murderer to have worn Ralph's shoes that evening—in which case Ralph must have been wearing yet a *third* pair of footwear of some kind. I could hardly suppose that he would bring three pairs of shoes all alike—the third pair of footwear were more likely to be boots. I got your sister to make inquiries on this point—laying some stress on the color, in order—I admit it frankly—to obscure the real reason for my asking.

"You know the result of her investigations. Ralph Paton *had* had a pair of boots with him. The first question I asked him when he came to my house yesterday morning was what he was wearing on his feet on the fatal night. He replied at once that he had worn *boots*—he was still wearing them, in fact—having nothing else to put on.

"So we get a step further in our description of the murderer—a person who had the opportunity to take these shoes of Ralph

Paton's from the Three Boars that day."

He paused, and then said, with a slightly raised voice:—

"There is one further point. The murderer must have been a person who had the opportunity to purloin that dagger from the silver table. You might argue that any one in the house might have done so, but I will recall to you that Miss Ackroyd was very positive that the dagger was not there when she examined the silver table."

He paused again.

"Let us recapitulate—now that all is clear. A person who was at the Three Boars earlier that day, a person who knew Ackroyd well enough to know that he had purchased a dictaphone, a person who was of a mechanical turn of mind, who had the opportunity to take the dagger from the silver table before Miss Flora arrived, who had with him a receptacle suitable for hiding the dictaphone— such as a black bag, and who had the study to himself for a few minutes after the crime was discovered while Parker was tele- phoning for the police. In fact—*Dr. Sheppard!*"

TWENTY SIX
And Nothing but the Truth

There was a dead silence for a minute and a half.

Then I laughed.

"You're mad," I said.

"No," said Poirot placidly. "I am not mad. It was the little discrepancy in time that first drew my attention to you—right at the beginning."

"Discrepancy in time?" I queried, puzzled.

"But yes. You will remember that every one agreed—you yourself included—that it took five minutes to walk from the lodge to the house—less if you took the short cut to the terrace. But you left the house at ten minutes to nine—both by your own statement and that of Parker, and yet it was nine o'clock as you passed through the lodge gates. It was a chilly night—not an evening a man would be inclined to dawdle; why had you taken ten minutes to do a five-minutes' walk? All along I realized that we had only your statement for it that the study window was ever fastened. Ackroyd asked you if you had done so—he never looked to see. Supposing, then, that the study window was unfastened? Would there be time in that ten minutes for you to run round the outside of the house, change your shoes, climb in through the window, kill Ackroyd, and get to the gate by nine o'clock? I decided against that theory since in all probability a man as nervous as Ackroyd was that night would hear you climbing in, and then there would have

237

been a struggle. But supposing that you killed Ackroyd *before* you left—as you were standing beside his chair? Then you go out of the front door, run round to the summer-house, take Ralph Paton's shoes out of the bag you brought up with you that night, slip them on, walk through the mud in them, and leave prints on the window ledge, you climb in, lock the study door on the inside, run back to the summer-house, change back into your own shoes, and race down to the gate. (I went through similar actions the other day, when you were with Mrs. Ackroyd—it took ten minutes exactly.) Then home—and an alibi—since you had timed the dictaphone for half-past nine."

"My dear Poirot," I said in a voice that sounded strange and forced to my own ears, "you've been brooding over this case too long. What on earth had I to gain by murdering Ackroyd?"

"Safety. It was you who blackmailed Mrs. Ferrars. Who could have had a better knowledge of what killed Mr. Ferrars than the doctor who was attending him? When you spoke to me that first day in the garden, you mentioned a legacy received about a year ago. I have been unable to discover any trace of a legacy. You had to invent some way of accounting for Mrs. Ferrars's twenty thousand pounds. It has not done you much good. You lost most of it in speculation—then you put the screw on too hard, and Mrs. Ferrars took a way out that you had not expected. If Ackroyd had learnt the truth he would have had no mercy on you—you were ruined for ever."

"And the telephone call?" I asked, trying to rally. "You have a plausible explanation of that also, I suppose?"

"I will confess to you that it was my greatest stumbling block when I found that a call had actually been put through to you from King's Abbot station. I at first believed that you had simply invented the story. It was a very clever touch, that. You must have some excuse for arriving at Fernly, finding the body, and so getting the chance to remove the dictaphone on which your alibi depended. I had a very vague notion of how it was worked when

I came to see your sister that first day and inquired as to what patients you had seen on Friday morning. I had no thought of Miss Russell in my mind at that time. Her visit was a lucky coincidence, since it distracted your mind from the real object of my questions. I found what I was looking for. Among your patients that morning was the steward of an American liner. Who more suitable than he to be leaving for Liverpool by the train that evening? And afterwards he would be on the high seas, well out of the way. I noted that the *Orion* sailed on Saturday, and having obtained the name of the steward I sent him a wireless message asking a certain question. This is his reply you saw me receive just now."

He held out the message to me. It ran as follows—

"Quite correct. Dr. Sheppard asked me to leave a note at a patient's house. I was to ring him up from the station with the reply. Reply was 'No answer.'"

* * *

"It was a clever idea," said Poirot. "The call was genuine. Your sister saw you take it. But there was only one man's word as to what was actually said—your own!"

I yawned.

"All this," I said, "is very interesting—but hardly in the sphere of practical politics."

"You think not? Remember what I said—the truth goes to Inspector Raglan in the morning. But, for the sake of your good sister, I am willing to give you the chance of another way out. There might be, for instance, an overdose of a sleeping draught. You comprehend me? But Captain Ralph Paton must be cleared—*ça va sans dire*. I should suggest that you finish that very interesting manuscript of yours—but abandoning your former reticence."

"You seem to be very prolific of suggestions," I remarked. "Are you sure you've quite finished."

"Now that you remind me of the fact, it is true that there is one thing more. It would be most unwise on your part to attempt to silence me as you silenced M. Ackroyd. That kind of business does not succeed against Hercule Poirot, you understand."

"My dear Poirot," I said, smiling a little, "whatever else I may be, I am not a fool."

I rose to my feet.

"Well, well," I said, with a slight yawn, "I must be off home. Thank you for a most interesting and instructive evening."

Poirot also rose and bowed with his accustomed politeness as I passed out of the room.

TWENTY-SEVEN
Apologia

Five a.m. I am very tired—but I have finished my task. My arm aches from writing.

A strange end to my manuscript. I meant it to be published some day as the history of one of Poirot's failures! Odd, how things pan out.

All along I've had a premonition of disaster, from the moment I saw Ralph Paton and Mrs. Ferrars with their heads together. I thought then that she was confiding in him; as it happened I was quite wrong there, but the idea persisted even after I went into the study with Ackroyd that night, until he told me the truth.

Poor old Ackroyd. I'm always glad that I gave him a chance. I urged him to read that letter before it was too late. Or let me be honest—didn't I subconsciously realize that with a pig-headed chap like him, it was my best chance of getting him *not* to read it? His nervousness that night was interesting psychologically. He knew danger was close at hand. And yet he never suspected *me*.

The dagger was an afterthought. I'd brought up a very handy little weapon of my own, but when I saw the dagger lying in the silver table, it occurred to me at once how much better it would be to use a weapon that couldn't be traced to me.

I suppose I must have meant to murder him all along. As soon as I heard of Mrs. Ferrars's death, I felt convinced that she would have told him everything before she died. When I met him and he seemed so agitated, I thought that perhaps he knew the truth, but that he couldn't bring himself to believe it, and was going to give me the chance of refuting it.

So I went home and took my precautions. If the trouble were after all only something to do with Ralph—well, no harm would have been done. The dictaphone he had given me two days before to adjust. Something had gone a little wrong with it, and I persuaded him to let me have a go at it, instead of sending it back. I did what I wanted to it, and took it up with me in my bag that evening.

I am rather pleased with myself as a writer. What could be neater, for instance, than the following:—

"The letters were brought in at twenty minutes to nine. It was just on ten minutes to nine when I left him, the letter still unread. I hesitated with my hand on the door handle, looking back and wondering if there was anything I had left undone."

All true, you see. But suppose I had put a row of stars after the first sentence! Would somebody then have wondered what exactly happened in that blank ten minutes?

When I looked round the room from the door, I was quite satisfied. Nothing had been left undone. The dictaphone was on the table by the window, timed to go off at nine-thirty (the mechanism of that little device was rather clever—based on the principle of an alarm clock), and the arm-chair was pulled out so as to hide it from the door.

I must admit that it gave me rather a shock to run into Parker just outside the door. I have faithfully recorded that fact.

Then later, when the body was discovered, and I had sent Parker to telephone for the police, what a judicious use of words: *"I did what little had to be done!"* It was quite little—just to shove the dictaphone into my bag and push back the chair against the wall in its proper place. I never dreamed that Parker would have noticed that chair. Logically, he ought to have been so agog over the body as to be blind to everything else. But I hadn't reckoned with the trained-servant complex.

I wish I could have known beforehand that Flora was going to say she'd seen her uncle alive at a quarter to ten. That puzzled me more than I can say. In fact, all through the case there have been things that puzzled me hopelessly. Every one seems to have taken a hand.

My greatest fear all through has been Caroline. I have fancied she might guess. Curious the way she spoke that day of my "strain of weakness."

Well, she will never know the truth. There is, as Poirot said, one way out....

I can trust him. He and Inspector Raglan will manage it between them. I should not like Caroline to know. She is fond of me, and then, too, she is proud.... My death will be a grief to her, but grief passes....

When I have finished writing, I shall enclose this whole man-uscript in an envelope and address it to Poirot.

And then—what shall it be? Veronal? There would be a kind of poetic justice. Not that I take any responsibility for Mrs. Ferrars's death. It was the direct consequence of her own actions. I feel no pity for her.

I have no pity for myself either.

So let it be veronal.

But I wish Hercule Poirot had never retired from work and come here to grow vegetable marrows.

THE END

POIROT
INVESTIGATES

AGATHA CHRISTIE

POIROT INVESTIGATES

PAGE CLASSICS

ISBN: 978-1-64833-756-7

First published 1924
Published by Page Publications 2024

Printed in China

Contents

1. The Adventure of "The Western Star"   1

2. The Tragedy at Marsdon Manor   25

3. The Adventure of the Cheap Flat   40

4. The Mystery of Hunter's Lodge   56

5. The Million Dollar Bond Robbery   70

6. The Adventure of the Egyptian Tomb   81

7. The Jewel Robbery at the *Grand Metropolitan*   97

8. The Kidnapped Prime Minister   115

9. The Disappearance of Mr. Davenheim   136

10. The Adventure of the Italian Nobleman   152

11. The Case of the Missing Will   164

ONE
The Adventure of "The Western Star"

I was standing at the window of Poirot's rooms looking out idly on the street below.

"That's queer," I ejaculated suddenly beneath my breath.

"What is, *mon ami*?" asked Poirot placidly, from the depths of his comfortable chair.

"Deduce, Poirot, from the following facts! Here is a young lady, richly dressed—fashionable hat, magnificent furs. She is coming along slowly, looking up at the houses as she goes. Unknown to her, she is being shadowed by three men and a middle-aged woman. They have just been joined by an errand boy who points after the girl, gesticulating as he does so. What drama is this being played? Is the girl a crook, and are the shadowers detectives preparing to arrest her? Or are *they* the scoundrels, and are they plotting to attack an innocent victim? What does the great detective say?"

"The great detective, *mon ami*, chooses, as ever, the simplest course. He rises to see for himself." And my friend joined me at the window.

In a minute he gave vent to an amused chuckle.

"As usual, your facts are tinged with your incurable romanticism. That is Miss Mary Marvell, the film star. She is being followed by a bevy of admirers who have recognized her. And, *en passant*, my dear Hastings, she is quite aware of the fact!"

I laughed.

"So all is explained! But you get no marks for that, Poirot. It was a mere matter of recognition."

"*En vérité!* And how many times have you seen Mary Marvell on the screen, *mon cher*?"

I thought.

"About a dozen times perhaps."

"And I—once! Yet *I* recognize her, and *you* do not."

"She looks so different," I replied rather feebly.

"Ah! *Sacré!*" cried Poirot. "Is it that you expect her to promenade herself in the streets of London in a cowboy hat, or with bare feet, and a bunch of curls, as an Irish colleen? Always with you it is the non-essentials! Remember the case of the dancer, Valerie Saintclair."

I shrugged my shoulders, slightly annoyed.

"But console yourself, *mon ami*," said Poirot, calming down. "All cannot be as Hercule Poirot! I know it well."

"You really have the best opinion of yourself of anyone I ever knew!" I cried, divided between amusement and annoyance.

"What will you? When one is unique, one knows it! And others share that opinion—even, if I mistake not, Miss Mary Marvell."

"What?"

"Without doubt. She is coming here."

"How do you make that out?"

"Very simply. This street, it is not aristocratic, *mon ami*! In it there is no fashionable doctor, no fashionable dentist—still less is there a fashionable milliner! But there *is* a fashionable detective. *Oui*, my friend, it is true—I am become the mode, the *dernier cri*! One says to another: '*Comment?* You have lost your gold pencil-case? You must go to the little Belgian. He is too marvellous! Every one goes! *Courez!*' And they arrive! In flocks, *mon ami*! With problems of the most foolish!" A bell rang below. "What did I tell you? That is Miss Marvell."

As usual, Poirot was right. After a short interval, the American film star was ushered in, and we rose to our feet.

Mary Marvell was undoubtedly one of the most popular actresses on the screen. She had only lately arrived in England in company with her husband, Gregory B. Rolf, also a film actor. Their marriage had taken place about a year ago in the States and this was their first visit to England. They had been given a great reception. Every one was prepared to go mad over Mary Marvell, her wonderful clothes, her furs, her jewels, above all one jewel, the great diamond which had been nicknamed, to match its owner, "The Western Star." Much, true and untrue, had been written about this famous stone which was reported to be insured for the enormous sum of fifty thousand pounds.

All these details passed rapidly through my mind as I joined with Poirot in greeting our fair client.

Miss Marvell was small and slender, very fair and girlish-looking, with the wide innocent blue eyes of a child.

Poirot drew forward a chair for her, and she commenced talking at once.

"You will probably think me very foolish, Monsieur Poirot, but Lord Cronshaw was telling me last night how wonderfully you cleared up the mystery of his nephew's death, and I felt that I just must have your advice. I dare say it's only a silly hoax—Gregory says so—but it's just worrying me to death."

She paused for breath. Poirot beamed encouragement.

"Proceed, Madame. You comprehend, I am still in the dark."

"It's these letters." Miss Marvell unclasped her handbag, and drew out three envelopes which she handed to Poirot.

The latter scrutinized them closely.

"Cheap paper—the name and address carefully printed. Let us see the inside." He drew out the enclosure.

I had joined him, and was leaning over his shoulder. The writing consisted of a single sentence, carefully printed like the envelope. It ran as follows:

"The great diamond which is the left eye of the god must return whence it came."

The second letter was couched in precisely the same terms, but the third was more explicit:

"You have been warned. You have not obeyed. Now the diamond will be taken from you. At the full of the moon, the two diamonds which are the left and right eye of the god shall return. So it is written."

"The first letter I treated as a joke," explained Miss Marvell. "When I got the second, I began to wonder. The third one came yesterday, and it seemed to me that, after all, the matter might be more serious than I had imagined."

"I see they did not come by post, these letters."

"No; they were left by hand—by a *Chinaman*. That is what frightens me."

"Why?"

"Because it was from a Chink in San Francisco that Gregory bought the stone three years ago."

"I see, madame, that you believe the diamond referred to to be——"

"'The Western Star,'" finished Miss Marvell. "That's so. At the time, Gregory remembers that there was some story attached to the stone, but the Chink wasn't handing out any information. Gregory says he seemed just scared to death, and in a mortal hurry to get rid of the thing. He only asked about a tenth of its value. It was Greg's wedding present to me."

Poirot nodded thoughtfully.

"The story seems of an almost unbelievable romanticism. And yet—who knows? I pray of you, Hastings, hand me my little almanac."

I complied.

"*Voyons!*" said Poirot, turning the leaves.

"When is the date of the full moon? Ah, Friday next. That is in three days' time. *Eh bien*, madame, you seek my advice—I

4

give it to you. This *belle histoire* may be a hoax—but it may not! Therefore I counsel you to place the diamond in my keeping until after Friday next. Then we can take what steps we please."

A slight cloud passed over the actress's face, and she replied constrainedly:

"I'm afraid that's impossible."

"You have it with you—*hein*?" Poirot was watching her narrowly.

The girl hesitated a moment, then slipped her hand into the bosom of her gown, drawing out a long thin chain. She leaned forward, unclosing her hand. In the palm, a stone of white fire, exquisitely set in platinum, lay and winked at us solemnly.

Poirot drew in his breath with a long hiss.

"*Épatant!*" he murmured. "You permit, madame?" He took the jewel in his own hand and scrutinized it keenly, then restored it to her with a little bow. "A magnificent stone—without a flaw. Ah, *cent tonnerres!* and you carry it about with you, *comme ça!*"

"No, no, I'm very careful really, Monsieur Poirot. As a rule it's locked up in my jewel-case, and left in the hotel safe deposit. We're staying at the *Magnificent*, you know. I just brought it along to-day for you to see."

"And you will leave it with me, *n'est-ce pas?* You will be advised by Papa Poirot?"

"Well, you see, it's this way, Monsieur Poirot. On Friday we're going down to Yardly Chase to spend a few days with Lord and Lady Yardly."

Her words awoke a vague echo of remembrance in my mind. Some gossip—what was it now? A few years ago Lord and Lady Yardly had paid a visit to the States, rumour had it that his lordship had rather gone the pace out there with the assistance of some lady friends—but surely there was something more, some gossip which coupled Lady Yardly's name with that of a "movie" star in California—why! it came to me in a flash—of course it was none other than Gregory B. Rolf.

"I'll let you into a little secret, Monsieur Poirot," Miss Marvell was continuing. "We've got a deal on with Lord Yardly. There's some chance of our arranging to film a play down there in his ancestral pile."

"At Yardly Chase?" I cried, interested. "Why, it's one of the show places of England."

Miss Marvell nodded.

"I guess it's the real old feudal stuff all right. But he wants a pretty stiff price, and of course I don't know yet whether the deal will go through, but Greg and I always like to combine business with pleasure."

"But—I demand pardon if I am dense, madame—surely it is possible to visit Yardly Chase without taking the diamond with you?"

A shrewd, hard look came into Miss Marvell's eyes which belied their childlike appearance. She looked suddenly a good deal older.

"I want to wear it down there."

"Surely" I said suddenly, "there are some very famous jewels in the Yardly collection, a large diamond amongst them?"

"That's so," said Miss Marvell briefly.

I heard Poirot murmur beneath his breath: "Ah, *c'est comme ça!*" Then he said aloud, with his usual uncanny luck in hitting the bull's-eye (he dignifies it by the name of psychology): "Then you are without doubt already acquainted with Lady Yardly, or perhaps your husband is?"

"Gregory knew her when she was out West three years ago," said Miss Marvell. She hesitated a moment, and then added abruptly: "Do either of you ever see *Society Gossip*?"

We both pleaded guilty rather shamefacedly.

"I ask because in this week's number there is an article on famous jewels, and it's really very curious——" She broke off.

I rose, went to the table at the other side of the room and returned with the paper in question in my hand. She took it from

6

me, found the article, and began to read aloud:

". . . Amongst other famous stones may be included the Star of the East, a diamond in the possession of the Yardly family. An ancestor of the present Lord Yardly brought it back with him from China, and a romantic story is said to attach to it. According to this, the stone was once the right eye of a temple god. Another diamond, exactly similar in form and size, formed the left eye, and the story goes that this jewel, too, would in course of time be stolen. 'One eye shall go West, the other East, till they shall meet once more. Then, in triumph shall they return to the god.' It is a curious coincidence that there is at the present time a stone corresponding closely in description with this one, and known as 'The Star of the West,' or 'The Western Star.' It is the property of the celebrated film actress, Miss Mary Marvell. A comparison of the two stones would be interesting."

She stopped.

"*Épatant!*" murmured Poirot. "Without doubt a romance of the first water." He turned to Mary Marvell. "And you are not afraid, madame? You have no superstitious terrors? You do not fear to introduce these two Siamese twins to each other lest a Chinaman should appear and, hey presto! whisk them both back to China?"

His tone was mocking, but I fancied that an undercurrent of seriousness lay beneath it.

"I don't believe that Lady Yardly's diamond is anything like as good a stone as mine," said Miss Marvell. "Anyway, I'm going to see."

What more Poirot would have said I do not know, for at that moment the door flew open, and a splendid-looking man strode into the room. From his crisply curling black head, to the tips of his patent-leather boots, he was a hero fit for romance.

"I said I'd call round for you, Mary," said Gregory Rolf, "and here I am. Well, what does Monsieur Poirot say to our little problem? Just one big hoax, same as I do?"

Poirot smiled up at the big actor. They made a ridiculous contrast.

"Hoax or no hoax, Mr. Rolf," he said dryly, "I have advised Madame your wife not to take the jewel with her to Yardly Chase on Friday."

"I'm with you there, sir. I've already said so to Mary. But there! She's a woman through and through, and I guess she can't bear to think of another woman outshining her in the jewel line."

"What nonsense, Gregory!" said Mary Marvell sharply. But she flushed angrily.

Poirot shrugged his shoulders.

"Madame, I have advised. I can do no more. *C'est fini.*"

He bowed them both to the door.

"Ah! *la la,*" he observed, returning. "*Histoire de femmes!* The good husband, he hit the nail on the head—*tout de même*, he was not tactful! Assuredly not."

I imparted to him my vague remembrances, and he nodded vigorously.

"So I thought. All the same, there is something curious underneath all this. With your permission, *mon ami*, I will take the air. Await my return, I beg of you. I shall not be long."

I was half asleep in my chair when the landlady tapped on the door, and put her head in.

"It's another lady to see Mr. Poirot, sir. I've told her he was out, but she says as how she'll wait, seeing as she's come up from the country."

"Oh, show her in here, Mrs. Murchison. Perhaps I can do something for her."

In another moment the lady had been ushered in. My heart gave a leap as I recognized her. Lady Yardly's portrait had figured too often in the Society papers to allow her to remain unknown.

"Do sit down, Lady Yardly," I said, drawing forward a chair. "My friend Poirot is out, but I know for a fact that he'll be back very shortly."

She thanked me and sat down. A very different type, this, from Miss Mary Marvell. Tall, dark, with flashing eyes, and a pale proud face—yet something wistful in the curves of the mouth.

I felt a desire to rise to the occasion. Why not? In Poirot's presence I have frequently felt a difficulty—I do not appear at my best. And yet there is no doubt that I, too, possess the deductive sense in a marked degree. I leant forward on a sudden impulse.

"Lady Yardly," I said, "I know why you have come here. You have received blackmailing letters about the diamond."

There was no doubt as to my bolt having shot home. She stared at me open-mouthed, all colour banished from her cheeks.

"You know?" she gasped. "How?"

I smiled.

"By a perfectly logical process. If Miss Marvell has had warning letters——"

"Miss Marvell? She has been here?"

"She has just left. As I was saying, if she, as the holder of one of the twin diamonds, has received a mysterious series of warnings, you, as the holder of the other stone, must necessarily have done the same. You see how simple it is? I am right, then, you have received these strange communications also?"

For a moment she hesitated, as though in doubt whether to trust me or not, then she bowed her head in assent with a little smile.

"That is so," she acknowledged.

"Were yours, too, left by hand—by a Chinaman?"

"No, they came by post; but, tell me, has Miss Marvell undergone the same experience, then?"

I recounted to her the events of the morning. She listened attentively.

"It all fits in. My letters are the duplicates of hers. It is true that they came by post, but there is a curious perfume impregnating them—something in the nature of joss-stick—that at once suggested the East to me. What does it all mean?"

I shook my head.

"That is what we must find out. You have the letters with you? We might learn something from the postmarks."

"Unfortunately I destroyed them. You understand, at the time I regarded it as some foolish joke. Can it be true that some Chinese gang are really trying to recover the diamonds? It seems too incredible."

We went over the facts again and again, but could get no further towards the elucidation of the mystery. At last Lady Yardly rose.

"I really don't think I need wait for Monsieur Poirot. You can tell him all this, can't you? Thank you so much, Mr.——"

She hesitated, her hand outstretched.

"Captain Hastings."

"Of course! How stupid of me. You're a friend of the Cavendishes, aren't you? It was Mary Cavendish who sent me to Monsieur Poirot."

When my friend returned, I enjoyed telling him the tale of what had occurred during his absence. He cross-questioned me rather sharply over the details of our conversation and I could read between the lines that he was not best pleased to have been absent. I also fancied that the dear old fellow was just the least inclined to be jealous. It had become rather a pose with him to consistently belittle my abilities, and I think he was chagrined at finding no loophole for criticism. I was secretly rather pleased with myself, though I tried to conceal the fact for fear of irritating him. In spite of his idiosyncrasies, I was deeply attached to my quaint little friend.

"*Bien!*" he said at length, with a curious look on his face. "The plot develops. Pass me, I pray you, that 'Peerage' on the top shelf there." He turned the leaves. "Ah, here we are! 'Yardly . . . 10th viscount, served South African War' . . . *tout ça n'a pas d'importance* . . . 'mar. 1907 Hon. Maude Stopperton, fourth daughter of 3rd Baron Cotteril' . . . um, um, um, . . . 'has iss. two daughters, born 1908, 1910. . . . Clubs . . . residences.' . . . *Voilà*, that does not tell us much. But to-morrow morning we see this *milord*!"

"What?"

"Yes. I telegraphed to him."

"I thought you had washed your hands of the case?"

"I am not acting for Miss Marvell since she refuses to be guided by my advice. What I do now is for my own satisfaction—the satisfaction of Hercule Poirot! Decidedly, I must have a finger in this pie."

"And you calmly wire Lord Yardly to dash up to town just to suit your convenience. He won't be pleased."

"*Au contraire*, if I preserve for him his family diamond, he ought to be very grateful."

"Then you really think there is a chance of it being stolen?" I asked eagerly.

"Almost a certainty," replied Poirot placidly. "Everything points that way."

"But how——"

Poirot stopped my eager questions with an airy gesture of the hand.

"Not now, I pray you. Let us not confuse the mind. And observe that 'Peerage'—how you have replaced him! See you not that the tallest books go in the top shelf, the next tallest in the row beneath, and so on. Thus we have order, *method*, which, as I have often told you, Hastings——"

"Exactly," I said hastily, and put the offending volume in its proper place.

* * *

Lord Yardly turned out to be a cheery, loud-voiced sportsman with a rather red face, but with a good-humoured bonhomie about him that was distinctly attractive and made up for any lack of mentality.

"Extraordinary business this, Monsieur Poirot. Can't make

head or tail of it. Seems my wife's been getting odd kind of letters, and that this Miss Marvell's had 'em too. What does it all mean?"

Poirot handed him the copy of *Society Gossip*.

"First, *milord*, I would ask you if these facts are substantially correct?"

The peer took it. His face darkened with anger as he read.

"Damned nonsense!" he spluttered. "There's never been any romantic story attaching to the diamond. It came from India originally, I believe. I never heard of all this Chinese god stuff."

"Still, the stone *is* known as 'The Star of the East.'"

"Well, what if it is?" he demanded wrathfully.

Poirot smiled a little, but made no direct reply. "What I would ask you to do, *milord*, is to place yourself in my hands. If you do so unreservedly, I have great hopes of averting the catastrophe."

"Then you think there's actually something in these wild-cat tales?"

"Will you do as I ask you?"

"Of course I will, but——"

"*Bien!* Then permit that I ask you a few questions. This affair of Yardly Chase, is it, as you say, all fixed up between you and Mr. Rolf?"

"Oh, he told you about it, did he? No, there's nothing settled." He hesitated, the brick-red colour of his face deepening. "Might as well get the thing straight. I've made rather an ass of myself in many ways, Monsieur Poirot—and I'm head over ears in debt—but I want to pull up. I'm fond of the kids, and I want to straighten things up, and be able to live on at the old place. Gregory Rolf is offering me big money—enough to set me on my feet again. I don't want to do it—I hate the thought of all that crowd play-acting round the Chase—but I may have to, unless——" He broke off.

Poirot eyed him keenly. "You have, then, another string to your bow? Permit that I make a guess? It is to sell the Star of the East?"

Lord Yardly nodded. "That's it. It's been in the family for some generations, but it's not entailed. Still, it's not the easiest thing in the world to find a purchaser. Hoffberg, the Hatton Garden man, is on the look-out for a likely customer, but he'll have to find one soon, or it's a washout."

"One more question, *permettez*—Lady Yardly, which plan does she approve?"

"Oh, she's bitterly opposed to my selling the jewel. You know what women are. She's all for this film stunt."

"I comprehend," said Poirot. He remained a moment or so in thought, then rose briskly to his feet. "You return to Yardly Chase at once? *Bien!* Say no word to anyone—to *anyone* mind— but expect us there this evening. We will arrive shortly after five."

"All right, but I don't see——"

"*Ça n'a pas d'importance*," said Poirot kindly. "You will that I preserve for you your diamond, *n'est-ce pas?*"

"Yes, but——"

"Then do as I say."

A sadly bewildered nobleman left the room.

* * *

It was half-past five when we arrived at Yardly Chase, and followed the dignified butler to the old panelled hall with its fire of blazing logs. A pretty picture met our eyes: Lady Yardly and her two children, the mother's proud dark head bent down over the two fair ones. Lord Yardly stood near, smiling down on them.

"Monsieur Poirot and Captain Hastings," announced the butler.

Lady Yardly looked up with a start, her husband came forward uncertainly, his eyes seeking instruction from Poirot. The little man was equal to the occasion.

"All my excuses! It is that I investigate still this affair of Miss Marvell's. She comes to you on Friday, does she not? I make a little tour first to make sure that all is secure. Also I wanted to ask of Lady Yardly if she recollected at all the postmarks on the letters she received?"

Lady Yardly shook her head regretfully. "I'm afraid I don't. It is stupid of me. But, you see, I never dreamt of taking them seriously."

"You'll stay the night?" said Lord Yardly.

"Oh, *milord*, I fear to incommode you. We have left our bags at the inn."

"That's all right." Lord Yardly had his cue. "We'll send down for them. No, no—no trouble, I assure you."

Poirot permitted himself to be persuaded, and sitting down by Lady Yardly, began to make friends with the children. In a short time they were all romping together, and had dragged me into the game.

"*Vous êtes bonne mère*," said Poirot, with a gallant little bow, as the children were removed reluctantly by a stern nurse.

Lady Yardly smoothed her ruffled hair.

"I adore them," she said with a little catch in her voice.

"And they you—with reason!" Poirot bowed again.

A dressing-gong sounded, and we rose to go up to our rooms. At that moment the butler entered with a telegram on a salver which he handed to Lord Yardly. The latter tore it open with a brief word of apology. As he read it he stiffened visibly.

With an ejaculation, he handed it to his wife. Then he glanced at my friend.

"Just a minute, Monsieur Poirot. I feel you ought to know about this. It's from Hoffberg. He thinks he's found a customer for the diamond—an American, sailing for the States to-morrow. They're sending down a chap to-night to vet the stone. By Jove, though, if this goes through——" Words failed him.

Lady Yardly had turned away. She still held the telegram in her hand.

"I wish you wouldn't sell it, George," she said, in a low voice.

"It's been in the family so long." She waited, as though for a reply, but when none came her face hardened. She shrugged her shoulders. "I must go and dress. I suppose I had better display 'the goods.'" She turned to Poirot with a slight grimace. "It's one of the most hideous necklaces that was ever designed! George has always promised to have the stones reset for me, but it's never been done." She left the room.

Half an hour later, we three were assembled in the great drawing-room awaiting the lady. It was already a few minutes past the dinner hour.

Suddenly there was a low rustle, and Lady Yardly appeared framed in the doorway, a radiant figure in a long white shimmering dress. Round the column of her neck was a rivulet of fire. She stood there with one hand just touching the necklace.

"Behold the sacrifice," she said gaily. Her ill-humour seemed to have vanished. "Wait while I turn the big light on and you shall feast your eyes on the ugliest necklace in England."

The switches were just outside the door. As she stretched out her hand to them, the incredible thing happened. Suddenly without any warning, every light was extinguished, the door banged, and from the other side of it came a long-drawn piercing woman's scream.

"My God!" cried Lord Yardly. "That was Maude's voice! What has happened?"

We rushed blindly for the door, cannoning into each other in the darkness. It was some minutes before we could find it. What a sight met our eyes! Lady Yardly lay senseless on the marble floor, a crimson mark on her white throat where the necklace had been wrenched from her neck.

As we bent over her, uncertain for the moment whether she were dead or alive, her eyelids opened.

"The Chinaman," she whispered painfully. "The Chinaman—the side door."

Lord Yardly sprang up with an oath. I accompanied him, my

15

heart beating wildly. The Chinaman again! The side door in question was a small one in the angle of the wall, not more than a dozen
yards from the scene of the tragedy. As we reached it, I gave a
cry. There, just short of the threshold, lay the glittering necklace,
evidently dropped by the thief in the panic of his flight. I swooped
joyously down on it. Then I uttered another cry which Lord Yardly
echoed. For in the middle of the necklace was a great gap. The
Star of the East was missing!

"That settles it," I breathed. "These were no ordinary thieves.
This one stone was all they wanted."

"But how did the fellow get in?"

"Through this door."

"But it's always locked."

I shook my head. "It's not locked now. See." I pulled it open
as I spoke.

As I did so something fluttered to the ground. I picked it up.
It was a piece of silk, and the embroidery was unmistakable. It
had been torn from a Chinaman's robe.

"In his haste it caught in the door," I explained. "Come, hurry.
He cannot have gone far as yet."

But in vain we hunted and searched. In the pitch darkness
of the night, the thief had found it easy to make his getaway. We
returned reluctantly, and Lord Yardly sent off one of the footmen
post-haste to fetch the police.

Lady Yardly, aptly ministered to by Poirot, who is as good as
a woman in these matters, was sufficiently recovered to be able
to tell her story.

"I was just going to turn on the other light," she said, "when
a man sprang on me from behind. He tore my necklace from my
neck with such force that I fell headlong to the floor. As I fell I
saw him disappearing through the side door. Then I realized by
the pig-tail and the embroidered robe that he was a Chinaman."
She stopped with a shudder.

The butler reappeared. He spoke in a low voice to Lord Yardly.

16

"A gentleman from Mr. Hoffberg's, m'lord. He says you expect him."

"Good heavens!" cried the distracted nobleman. "I must see him, I suppose. No, not here, Mullings, in the library."

I drew Poirot aside.

"Look here, my dear fellow, hadn't we better get back to London?"

"You think so, Hastings? Why?"

"Well"—I coughed delicately—"things haven't gone very well, have they? I mean, you tell Lord Yardly to place himself in your hands and all will be well—and then the diamond vanishes from under your very nose!"

"True," said Poirot, rather crestfallen. "It was not one of my most striking triumphs."

This way of describing events almost caused me to smile, but I stuck to my guns.

"So, having—pardon the expression—rather made a mess of things, don't you think it would be more graceful to leave immediately?"

"And the dinner, the without doubt excellent dinner, that the *chef* of Lord Yardly has prepared?"

"Oh, what's dinner!" I said impatiently.

Poirot held up his hands in horror.

"*Mon Dieu!* It is that in this country you treat the affairs gastronomic with a criminal indifference."

"There's another reason why we should get back to London as soon as possible," I continued.

"What is that, my friend?"

"The other diamond," I said, lowering my voice. "Miss Marvell's."

"*Eh bien*, what of it?"

"Don't you see?" His unusual obtuseness annoyed me. What had happened to his usually keen wits? "They've got one, now they'll go for the other."

"*Tiens!*" cried Poirot, stepping back a pace and regarding me with admiration. "But your brain marches to a marvel, my friend! Figure to yourself that for the moment I had not thought of that! But there is plenty of time. The full of the moon, it is not until Friday."

I shook my head dubiously. The full of the moon theory left me entirely cold. I had my way with Poirot, however, and we departed immediately, leaving behind us a note of explanation and apology for Lord Yardly.

My idea was to go at once to the *Magnificent*, and relate to Miss Marvell what had occurred, but Poirot vetoed the plan, and insisted that the morning would be time enough. I gave in rather grudgingly.

In the morning Poirot seemed strangely disinclined to stir out. I began to suspect that, having made a mistake to start with, he was singularly loath to proceed with the case. In answer to my persuasions, he pointed out, with admirable common sense, that as the details of the affair at Yardly Chase were already in the morning papers the Rolfs would know quite as much as we could tell them. I gave way unwillingly.

Events proved my forebodings to be justified. About two o'clock, the telephone rang. Poirot answered it. He listened for some moments, then with a brief "*Bien, j'y serai*" he rang off, and turned to me.

"What do you think, *mon ami*?" He looked half ashamed, half excited. "The diamond of Miss Marvell, it has been stolen."

"What?" I cried, springing up. "And what about the 'full of the moon' now?" Poirot hung his head. "When did this happen?"

"This morning, I understand."

I shook my head sadly. "If only you had listened to me. You see I was right."

"It appears so, *mon ami*," said Poirot cautiously. "Appearances are deceptive, they say, but it certainly appears so."

As we hurried in a taxi to the *Magnificent*, I puzzled out the true inwardness of the scheme.

"That 'full of the moon' idea was clever. The whole point of it was to get us to concentrate on the Friday, and so be off our guard beforehand. It is a pity you did not realize that."

"*Ma foi!*" said Poirot airily, his nonchalance quite restored after its brief eclipse. "One cannot think of everything!"

I felt sorry for him. He did so hate failure of any kind.

"Cheer up," I said consolingly. "Better luck next time."

At the *Magnificent*, we were ushered at once into the manager's office. Gregory Rolf was there with two men from Scotland Yard. A pale-faced clerk sat opposite them.

Rolf nodded to us as we entered.

"We're getting to the bottom of it," he said. "But it's almost unbelievable. How the guy had the nerve I can't think."

A very few minutes sufficed to give us the facts. Mr. Rolf had gone out of the hotel at 11.15. At 11.30, a gentleman, so like him in appearance as to pass muster, entered the hotel and demanded the jewel-case from the safe deposit. He duly signed the receipt, remarking carelessly as he did so: "Looks a bit different from my ordinary one, but I hurt my hand getting out of the taxi." The clerk merely smiled and remarked that he saw very little difference. Rolf laughed and said: "Well, don't run me in as a crook this time, anyway. I've been getting threatening letters from a Chinaman, and the worst of it is I look rather like a Chink myself—it's something about the eyes."

"I looked at him," said the clerk who was telling us this, "and I saw at once what he meant. The eyes slanted up at the corners like an Oriental's. I'd never noticed it before."

"Darn it all, man," roared Gregory Rolf, leaning forward, "do you notice it now?"

The man looked up at him and started.

"No, sir," he said. "I can't say I do." And indeed there was nothing even remotely Oriental about the frank brown eyes that looked into ours.

The Scotland Yard man grunted. "Bold customer. Thought the eyes might be noticed, and took the bull by the horns to disarm suspicion. He must have watched you out of the hotel, sir, and nipped in as soon as you were well away."

"What about the jewel-case?" I asked.

"It was found in a corridor of the hotel. Only one thing had been taken—'the Western Star.'"

We stared at each other—the whole thing was so bizarre, so unreal.

Poirot hopped briskly to his feet. "I have not been of much use, I fear," he said regretfully. "Is it permitted to see Madame?"

"I guess she's prostrated with the shock," explained Rolf.

"Then perhaps I might have a few words alone with you, monsieur?"

"Certainly."

In about five minutes Poirot reappeared.

"Now, my friend," he said gaily. "To a post office. I have to send a telegram."

"Who to?"

"Lord Yardly." He discounted further inquiries by slipping his arm through mine. "Come, come, *mon ami*. I know all that you feel about this miserable business. I have not distinguished myself! You, in my place, might have distinguished yourself! *Bien!* All is admitted. Let us forget it and have lunch."

It was about four o'clock when we entered Poirot's rooms. A figure rose from a chair by the window. It was Lord Yardly. He looked haggard and distraught.

"I got your wire and came up at once. Look here, I've been round to Hoffberg, and they know nothing about that man of theirs last night, or the wire either. Do you think that——"

Poirot held up his hand.

"My excuses! I sent that wire, and hired the gentleman in question."

"*You*—but why? What?" The nobleman spluttered impotently.

20

"My little idea was to bring things to a head," explained Poirot placidly.

"Bring things to a head! Oh, my God!" cried Lord Yardly.

"And the ruse succeeded," said Poirot cheerfully. "Therefore, *milord*, I have much pleasure in returning you—this!" With a dramatic gesture he produced a glittering object. It was a great diamond.

"The Star of the East," gasped Lord Yardly. "But I don't understand——"

"No?" said Poirot. "It makes no matter. Believe me, it was necessary for the diamond to be stolen. I promised you that it should be preserved to you, and I have kept my word. You must permit me to keep my little secret. Convey, I beg of you, the assurances of my deepest respect to Lady Yardly, and tell her how pleased I am to be able to restore her jewel to her. What *beau temps*, is it not? Good day, *milord*."

And smiling and talking, the amazing little man conducted the bewildered nobleman to the door. He returned gently rubbing his hands.

"Poirot," I said. "Am I quite demented?"

"No, *mon ami*, but you are, as always, in a mental fog."

"How did you get the diamond."

"From Mr. Rolf."

"Rolf?"

"*Mais oui!* The warning letters, the Chinaman, the article in *Society Gossip*, all sprang from the ingenious brain of Mr. Rolf! The two diamonds, supposed to be so miraculously alike—bah! they did not exist. There was only *one* diamond, my friend! Originally in the Yardly collection, for three years it has been in the possession of Mr. Rolf. He stole it this morning with the assistance of a touch of grease paint at the corner of each eye! Ah, I must see him on the film, he is indeed an artist, *celui-là!*"

"But why should he steal his own diamond?" I asked, puzzled.

"For many reasons. To begin with, Lady Yardly was getting restive."

"Lady Yardly?"

"You comprehend she was left much alone in California. Her husband was amusing himself elsewhere. Mr. Rolf was handsome, he had an air about him of romance. But *au fond*, he is very business-like, *ce monsieur*! He made love to Lady Yardly, and then he blackmailed her. I taxed the lady with the truth the other night, and she admitted it. She swore that she had only been indiscreet, and I believe her. But, undoubtedly, Rolf had letters of hers that could be twisted to bear a different interpretation. Terrified by the threat of a divorce, and the prospect of being separated from her children, she agreed to all he wished. She had no money of her own, and she was forced to permit him to substitute a paste replica for the real stone. The coincidence of the date of the appearance of 'The Western Star' struck me at once. All goes well. Lord Yardly prepares to range himself—to settle down. And then comes the menace of the possible sale of the diamond. The substitution will be discovered. Without doubt she writes off frantically to Gregory Rolf who has just arrived in England. He soothes her by promising to arrange all—and prepares for a double robbery. In this way he will quiet the lady, who might conceivably tell all to her husband, an affair which would not suit our blackmailer at all, he will have £50,000 insurance money (aha, you had forgotten that!), and he will still have the diamond! At this point I put my finger in the pie. The arrival of a diamond expert is announced. Lady Yardly, as I felt sure she would, immediately arranges a robbery—and does it very well too! But Hercule Poirot, he sees nothing but facts. What happens in actuality? The lady switches off the light, bangs the door, throws the necklace down the passage, and screams. She has already wrenched out the diamond with pliers upstairs——"

"But we saw the necklace round her neck!" I objected.

"I demand pardon, my friend. Her hand concealed the part of it where the gap would have shown. To place a piece of silk in the door beforehand is child's play! Of course, as soon as Rolf read of the robbery, he arranged his own little comedy. And very well he played it!"

"What did you say to him?" I asked with lively curiosity.

"I said to him that Lady Yardly had told her husband all, that I was empowered to recover the jewel, and that if it were not immediately handed over proceedings would be taken. Also a few more little lies which occurred to me. He was as wax in my hands!"

I pondered the matter.

"It seems a little unfair on Mary Marvell. She has lost her diamond through no fault of her own."

"Bah!" said Poirot brutally. "She has a magnificent advertisement. That is all she cares for, that one! Now the other, she is different. *Bonne mère, très femme!*"

"Yes," I said doubtfully, hardly sharing Poirot's views on femininity. "I suppose it was Rolf who sent her the duplicate letters."

"*Pas du tout,*" said Poirot briskly. "She came by the advice of Mary Cavendish to seek my aid in her dilemma. Then she heard that Mary Marvell, whom she knew to be her enemy, had been here, and she changed her mind, jumping at a pretext that *you,* my friend, offered her. A very few questions sufficed to show me that *you* told her of the letters, not she you! She jumped at the chance your words offered."

"I don't believe it," I cried, stung.

"*Si, si, mon ami,* it is a pity that you study not the psychology. She told you that the letters were destroyed? Oh, la la, *never* does a woman destroy a letter if she can avoid it! Not even if it would be more prudent to do so!"

"It's all very well," I said, my anger rising, "but you've made a perfect fool of me! From beginning to end! No, it's all very well to try and explain it away afterwards. There really is a limit!"

"But you were so enjoying yourself, my friend. I had not the heart to shatter your illusions."

"It's no good. You've gone a bit too far this time."

"*Mon Dieu!* but how you enrage yourself for nothing, *mon ami!*"

"I'm fed up!" I went out, banging the door. Poirot had made an absolute laughing-stock of me. I decided that he needed a sharp lesson. I would let some time elapse before I forgave him. He had encouraged me to make a perfect fool of myself!

TWO

The Tragedy at Marsdon Manor

I had been called away from town for a few days, and on my return found Poirot in the act of strapping up his small valise.

"*A la bonne heure*, Hastings. I feared you would not have returned in time to accompany me."

"You are called away on a case, then?"

"Yes, though I am bound to admit that, on the face of it, the affair does not seem promising. The Northern Union Insurance Company have asked me to investigate the death of a Mr. Maltravers who a few weeks ago insured his life with them for the large sum of fifty thousand pounds."

"Yes?" I said, much interested.

"There was, of course, the usual suicide clause in the policy. In the event of his committing suicide within a year the premiums would be forfeited. Mr. Maltravers was duly examined by the Company's own doctor, and although he was a man slightly past the prime of life was passed as being in quite sound health. However, on Wednesday last—the day before yesterday—the body of Mr. Maltravers was found in the grounds of his house in Essex, Marsdon Manor, and the cause of his death is described as some kind of internal hæmorrhage. That in itself would be nothing remarkable, but sinister rumours as to Mr. Maltravers' financial position have been in the air of late, and the Northern Union have ascertained beyond any possible doubt that the

25

deceased gentleman stood upon the verge of bankruptcy. Now that alters matters considerably. Maltravers had a beautiful young wife, and it is suggested that he got together all the ready money he could for the purpose of paying the premiums on a life insurance for his wife's benefit, and then committed suicide. Such a thing is not uncommon. In any case, my friend Alfred Wright, who is a director of the Northern Union, has asked me to investigate the facts of the case, but, as I told him, I am not very hopeful of success. If the cause of the death had been heart failure, I should have been more sanguine. Heart failure may always be translated as the inability of the local G.P. to discover what his patient really did die of, but a hæmorrhage seems fairly definite. Still, we can but make some necessary inquiries. Five minutes to pack your bag, Hastings, and we will take a taxi to Liverpool Street."

About an hour later, we alighted from a Great Eastern train at the little station of Marsdon Leigh. Inquiries at the station yielded the information that Marsdon Manor was about a mile distant. Poirot decided to walk, and we betook ourselves along the main street.

"What is our plan of campaign?" I asked.

"First I will call upon the doctor. I have ascertained that there is only one doctor in Marsdon Leigh, Dr. Ralph Bernard. Ah, here we are at his house."

The house in question was a kind of superior cottage, standing back a little from the road. A brass plate on the gate bore the doctor's name. We passed up the path and rang the bell.

We proved to be fortunate in our call. It was the doctor's consulting hour, and for the moment there were no patients waiting for him. Dr. Bernard was an elderly man, high-shouldered and stooping, with a pleasant vagueness of manner.

Poirot introduced himself and explained the purpose of our visit, adding that Insurance Companies were bound to investigate fully in a case of this kind.

"Of course, of course," said Dr. Bernard vaguely. "I suppose, as he was such a rich man, his life was insured for a big sum?"

"You consider him a rich man, doctor?"

The doctor looked rather surprised.

"Was he not? He kept two cars, you know, and Marsdon Manor is a pretty big place to keep up, although I believe he bought it very cheap."

"I understand that he had had considerable losses of late," said Poirot, watching the doctor narrowly.

The latter, however, merely shook his head sadly.

"Is that so? Indeed. It is fortunate for his wife, then, that there is this life insurance. A very beautiful and charming young creature, but terribly unstrung by this sad catastrophe. A mass of nerves, poor thing. I have tried to spare her all I can, but of course the shock was bound to be considerable."

"You had been attending Mr. Maltravers recently?"

"My dear sir, I never attended him."

"What?"

"I understand Mr. Maltravers was a Christian Scientist—or something of that kind."

"But you examined the body?"

"Certainly. I was fetched by one of the under-gardeners."

"And the cause of death was clear?"

"Absolutely. There was blood on the lips, but most of the bleeding must have been internal."

"Was he still lying where he had been found?"

"Yes, the body had not been touched. He was lying at the edge of a small plantation. He had evidently been out shooting rooks, a small rook rifle lay beside him. The hæmorrhage must have occurred quite suddenly. Gastric ulcer, without a doubt."

"No question of his having been shot, eh?"

"My dear sir!"

"I demand pardon," said Poirot humbly. "But, if my memory is not at fault, in the case of a recent murder, the doctor first gave a verdict of heart failure—altering it when the local constable pointed out that there was a bullet wound through the head!"

"You will not find any bullet wounds on the body of Mr. Maltravers," said Dr. Bernard dryly. "Now, gentlemen, if there is nothing further——"

We took the hint.

"Good morning, and many thanks to you, doctor, for so kindly answering our questions. By the way, you saw no need for an autopsy?"

"Certainly not." The doctor became quite apoplectic. "The cause of death was clear, and in my profession we see no need to distress unduly the relatives of a dead patient."

And, turning, the doctor slammed the door sharply in our faces.

"And what do you think of Dr. Bernard, Hastings?" inquired Poirot, as we proceeded on our way to the Manor.

"Rather an old ass."

"Exactly. Your judgments of character are always profound, my friend."

I glanced at him uneasily, but he seemed perfectly serious. A twinkle, however, came into his eye, and he added slyly:

"That is to say, when there is no question of a beautiful woman!"

I looked at him coldly.

On our arrival at the manor-house, the door was opened to us by a middle-aged parlourmaid. Poirot handed her his card, and a letter from the Insurance Company for Mrs. Maltravers. She showed us into a small morning-room, and retired to tell her mistress. About ten minutes elapsed, and then the door opened, and a slender figure in widow's weeds stood upon the threshold.

"Monsieur Poirot?" she faltered.

"Madame!" Poirot sprang gallantly to his feet and hastened towards her. "I cannot tell you how I regret to derange you in this way. But what will you? *Les affaires*—they know no mercy."

Mrs. Maltravers permitted him to lead her to a chair. Her eyes were red with weeping, but the temporary disfigurement could not conceal her extraordinary beauty. She was about twenty-seven or eight, and very fair, with large blue eyes and a pretty pouting mouth.

"It is something about my husband's insurance, is it? But must I be bothered *now*—so soon?"

"Courage, my dear Madame. Courage! You see, your late husband insured his life for rather a large sum, and in such a case the Company always has to satisfy itself as to a few details. They have empowered me to act for them. You can rest assured that I will do all in my power to render the matter not too unpleasant for you. Will you recount to me briefly the sad events of Wednesday?"

"I was changing for tea when my maid came up—one of the gardeners had just run to the house. He had found——"

Her voice trailed away. Poirot pressed her hand sympathetically.

"I comprehend. Enough! You had seen your husband earlier in the afternoon?"

"Not since lunch. I had walked down to the village for some stamps, and I believe he was out pottering round the grounds."

"Shooting rooks, eh?"

"Yes, he usually took his little rook rifle with him, and I heard one or two shots in the distance."

"Where is this little rook rifle now?"

"In the hall, I think."

She led the way out of the room and found and handed the little weapon to Poirot, who examined it cursorily.

"Two shots fired, I see," he observed, as he handed it back. "And now, madame, if I might see——"

He paused delicately.

"The servant shall take you," she murmured, averting her head.

The parlourmaid, summoned, led Poirot upstairs. I remained

with the lovely and unfortunate woman. It was hard to know whether to speak or remain silent. I essayed one or two general reflections to which she responded absently, and in a very few minutes Poirot rejoined us.

"I thank you for all your courtesy, madame. I do not think you need be troubled any further with this matter. By the way, do you know anything of your husband's financial position?"

She shook her head.

"Nothing whatever. I am very stupid over business things."

"I see. Then you can give us no clue as to why he suddenly decided to insure his life? He had not done so previously, I understand."

"Well, we had only been married a little over a year. But, as to why he insured his life, it was because he had absolutely made up his mind that he would not live long. He had a strong premonition of his own death. I gather that he had had one hæmorrhage already, and that he knew that another one would prove fatal. I tried to dispel these gloomy fears of his, but without avail. Alas, he was only too right!"

Tears in her eyes, she bade us a dignified farewell. Poirot made a characteristic gesture as we walked down the drive together.

"*Eh bien*, that is that! Back to London, my friend, there appears to be no mouse in this mouse-hole. And yet——"

"Yet what?"

"A slight discrepancy, that is all! You noticed it? You did not? Still, life is full of discrepancies, and assuredly the man cannot have taken his own life—there is no poison that would fill his mouth with blood. No, no, I must resign myself to the fact that all here is clear and above-board—but who is this?"

A tall young man was striding up the drive towards us. He passed us without making any sign, but I noted that he was not ill-looking, with a lean, deeply bronzed face that spoke of life in a tropic clime. A gardener who was sweeping up leaves had paused for a minute in his task, and Poirot ran quickly up to him.

"Tell me, I pray you, who is that gentleman? Do you know him?"

"I don't remember his name, sir, though I did hear it. He was staying down here last week for a night. Tuesday, it was."

"Quick, *mon ami*, let us follow him."

We hastened up the drive after the retreating figure. A glimpse of a black-robed figure on the terrace at the side of the house, and our quarry swerved and we after him, so that we were witnesses of the meeting.

Mrs. Maltravers almost staggered where she stood, and her face blanched noticeably.

"You," she gasped. "I thought you were on the sea—on your way to East Africa?"

"I got some news from my lawyers that detained me," explained the young man. "My old uncle in Scotland died unexpectedly and left me some money. Under the circumstances I thought it better to cancel my passage. Then I saw this bad news in the paper and I came down to see if there was anything I could do. You'll want some one to look after things for you a bit perhaps."

At that moment they became aware of our presence. Poirot stepped forward, and with many apologies explained that he had left his stick in the hall. Rather reluctantly, it seemed to me, Mrs. Maltravers made the necessary introduction.

"Monsieur Poirot, Captain Black."

A few minutes' chat ensued, in the course of which Poirot elicited the fact that Captain Black was putting up at the Anchor Inn. The missing stick not having been discovered (which was not surprising), Poirot uttered more apologies and we withdrew.

We returned to the village at a great pace, and Poirot made a bee line for the Anchor Inn.

"Here we establish ourselves until our friend the Captain returns," he explained. "You notice that I emphasized the point that we were returning to London by the first train? Possibly you thought I meant it. But no—you observed Mrs. Maltravers' face when she caught sight of this young Black? She was clearly taken aback, and he—*eh bien*, he was very devoted, did you not think so? And he was here on Tuesday night—the day before Mr. Maltravers died. We must investigate the doings of Captain Black, Hastings."

In about half an hour we espied our quarry approaching the inn. Poirot went out and accosted him and presently brought him up to the room we had engaged.

"I have been telling Captain Black of the mission which brings us here," he explained. "You can understand, *monsieur le capitaine*, that I am anxious to arrive at Mr. Maltravers' state of mind immediately before his death, and that at the same time I do not wish to distress Mrs. Maltravers unduly by asking her painful questions. Now, you were here just before the occurrence, and can give us equally valuable information."

"I'll do anything I can to help you, I'm sure," replied the young soldier; "but I'm afraid I didn't notice anything out of the ordinary. You see, although Maltravers was an old friend of my people's, I didn't know him very well myself."

"You came down—when?"

"Tuesday afternoon. I went up to town early Wednesday morning, as my boat sailed from Tilbury about twelve o'clock. But some news I got made me alter my plans, as I dare say you heard me explain to Mrs. Maltravers."

"You were returning to East Africa, I understand?"

"Yes. I've been out there ever since the War—a great country."

"Exactly. Now what was the talk about at dinner on Tuesday night?"

"Oh, I don't know. The usual odd topics. Maltravers asked after my people, and then we discussed the question of German reparations, and then Mrs. Maltravers asked a lot of questions about East Africa, and I told them one or two yarns, that's about all, I think."

"Thank you."

Poirot was silent for a moment, then he said gently: "With

your permission, I should like to try a little experiment. You have told us all that your conscious self knows, I want now to question your subconscious self."

"Psychoanalysis, what?" said Black, with visible alarm.

"Oh, no," said Poirot reassuringly. "You see, it is like this, I give you a word, you answer with another, and so on. Any word, the first one you think of. Shall we begin?"

"All right," said Black slowly, but he looked uneasy.

"Note down the words, please, Hastings," said Poirot. Then he took from his pocket his big turnip-faced watch and laid it on the table beside him. "We will commence. Day."

There was a moment's pause, and then Black replied:

"*Night.*"

As Poirot proceeded, his answers came quicker.

"Name," said Poirot.

"*Place.*"

"Bernard."

"*Shaw.*"

"Tuesday."

"*Dinner.*"

"Journey."

"*Ship.*"

"Country."

"*Uganda.*"

"Story."

"*Lions.*"

"Rook Rifle."

"*Farm.*"

"Shot."

"*Suicide.*"

"Elephant."

"*Tusks.*"

"Money."

"*Lawyers.*"

"Thank you, Captain Black. Perhaps you could spare me a few minutes in about half an hour's time?"

"Certainly." The young soldier looked at him curiously and wiped his brow as he got up.

"And now, Hastings," said Poirot, smiling at me as the door closed behind him. "You see it all, do you not?"

"I don't know what you mean."

"Does that list of words tell you nothing?"

I scrutinized it, but was forced to shake my head.

"I will assist you. To begin with, Black answered well within the normal time limit, with no pauses, so we can take it that he himself has no guilty knowledge to conceal. 'Day' to 'Night' and 'Place' to 'Name' are normal associations. I began work with 'Bernard' which might have suggested the local doctor had he come across him at all. Evidently he had not. After our recent conversation, he gave 'Dinner' to my 'Tuesday,' but 'Journey' and 'Country' were answered by 'Ship' and 'Uganda,' showing clearly that it was his journey abroad that was important to him and not the one which brought him down here. 'Story' recalls to him one of the 'Lion' stories he told at dinner. I proceed to 'Rook Rifle' and he answered with the totally unexpected word 'Farm.' When I say 'Shot,' he answers at once 'Suicide.' The association seems clear. A man he knows committed suicide with a rook rifle on a farm somewhere. Remember, too, that his mind is still on the stories he told at dinner, and I think you will agree that I shall not be far from the truth if I recall Captain Black and ask him to repeat the particular suicide story which he told at the dinner-table on Tuesday evening."

Black was straightforward enough over the matter.

"Yes, I did tell them that story now that I come to think of it. Chap shot himself on a farm out there. Did it with a rook rifle through the roof of the mouth, bullet lodged in the brain. Doctors were no end puzzled over it—there was nothing to show except a little blood on the lips. But what——"

"What has it got to do with Mr. Maltravers? You did not know, I see, that he was found with a rook rifle by his side."

"You mean my story suggested to him—oh, but that is awful!"

"Do not distress yourself—it would have been one way or another. Well, I must get on the telephone to London."

Poirot had a lengthy conversation over the wire, and came back thoughtful. He went off by himself in the afternoon, and it was not till seven o'clock that he announced that he could put it off no longer, but must break the news to the young widow. My sympathy had already gone out to her unreservedly. To be left penniless, and with the knowledge that her husband had killed himself to assure her future was a hard burden for any woman to bear. I cherished a secret hope, however, that young Black might prove capable of consoling her after her first grief had passed. He evidently admired her enormously.

Our interview with the lady was painful. She refused vehemently to believe the facts that Poirot advanced, and when she was at last convinced broke down into bitter weeping. An examination of the body turned our suspicions into certainty. Poirot was very sorry for the poor lady, but, after all, he was employed by the Insurance Company, and what could he do? As he was preparing to leave he said gently to Mrs. Maltravers:

"Madame, you of all people should know that there are no dead!"

"What do you mean?" she faltered, her eyes growing wide.

"Have you never taken part in any spiritualistic séances? You are mediumistic, you know."

"I have been told so. But you do not believe in Spiritualism, surely?"

"Madame, I have seen some strange things. You know that they say in the village that this house is haunted?"

She nodded, and at that moment the parlourmaid announced that dinner was ready.

"Won't you just stay and have something to eat?"

35

We accepted gratefully, and I felt that our presence could not but help distract her a little from her own griefs.

We had just finished our soup, when there was a scream outside the door, and the sound of breaking crockery. We jumped up. The parlourmaid appeared, her hand to her heart.

"It was a man—standing in the passage."

Poirot rushed out, returning quickly.

"There is no one there."

"Isn't there, sir?" said the parlourmaid weakly. "Oh, it did give me a start!"

"But why?"

She dropped her voice to a whisper.

"I thought—I thought it was the master—it looked like 'im."

I saw Mrs. Maltravers give a terrified start, and my mind flew to the old superstition that a suicide cannot rest. She thought of it too, I am sure, for a minute later, she caught Poirot's arm with a scream.

"Didn't you hear that? Those three taps on the window? That's how *he* always used to tap when he passed round the house."

"The ivy," I cried. "It was the ivy against the pane."

But a sort of terror was gaining on us all. The parlourmaid was obviously unstrung, and when the meal was over Mrs. Maltravers besought Poirot not to go at once. She was clearly terrified to be left alone. We sat in the little morning-room. The wind was getting up, and moaning round the house in an eerie fashion. Twice the door of the room came unlatched and the door slowly opened, and each time she clung to me with a terrified gasp.

"Ah, but this door, it is bewitched!" cried Poirot angrily at last. He got up and shut it once more, then turned the key in the lock. "I shall lock it, so!"

"Don't do that," she gasped, "if it should come open now——"

And even as she spoke the impossible happened. The locked door slowly swung open. I could not see into the passage from where I sat, but she and Poirot were facing it. She gave one long shriek as she turned to him.

"You saw him—there in the passage?" she cried.

He was staring down at her with a puzzled face, then shook his head.

"I saw him—my husband—you must have seen him too?"

"Madame, I saw nothing. You are not well—unstrung——"

"I am perfectly well, I——Oh, God!"

Suddenly, without any warning, the lights quivered and went out. Out of the darkness came three loud raps. I could hear Mrs. Maltravers moaning.

And then—I saw!

The man I had seen on the bed upstairs stood there facing us, gleaming with a faint ghostly light. There was blood on his lips, and he held his right hand out, pointing. Suddenly a brilliant light seemed to proceed from it. It passed over Poirot and me, and fell on Mrs. Maltravers. I saw her white terrified face, and something else!

"My God, Poirot!" I cried. "Look at her hand, her right hand. It's all red!"

Her own eyes fell on it, and she collapsed in a heap on the floor.

"Blood," she cried hysterically. "Yes, it's blood. I killed him. I did it. He was showing me, and then I put my hand on the trigger and pressed. Save me from him—save me! he's come back!"

Her voice died away in a gurgle.

"Lights," said Poirot briskly.

The lights went on as if by magic.

"That's it," he continued. "You heard, Hastings? And you, Everett? Oh, by the way, this is Mr. Everett, rather a fine member of the theatrical profession. I 'phoned to him this afternoon. His make-up is good, isn't it? Quite like the dead man, and with a pocket torch and the necessary phosphorescence he made the proper impression. I shouldn't touch her right hand if I were you,

Hastings. Red paint marks so. When the lights went out I clasped her hand, you see. By the way, we mustn't miss our train. Inspector Japp is outside the window. A bad night—but he has been able to while away the time by tapping on the window every now and then."

"You see," continued Poirot, as we walked briskly through the wind and rain, "there was a little discrepancy. The doctor seemed to think the deceased was a Christian Scientist, and who could have given him that impression but Mrs. Maltravers? But to us she represented him as being in a grave state of apprehension about his own health. Again, why was she so taken aback by the reappearance of young Black? And lastly, although I know that convention decrees that a woman must make a decent pretence of mourning for her husband, I do not care for such heavily-rouged eyelids! You did not observe them, Hastings? No? As I always tell you, you see nothing!"

"Well, there it was. There were the two possibilities. Did Black's story suggest an ingenious method of committing suicide to Mr. Maltravers, or did his other listener, the wife, see an equally ingenious method of committing murder? I inclined to the latter view. To shoot himself in the way indicated, he would probably have had to pull the trigger with his toe—or at least so I imagine. Now if Maltravers had been found with one boot off, we should almost certainly have heard of it from some one. An odd detail like that would have been remembered.

"No, as I say, I inclined to the view that it was a case of murder, not suicide, but I realized that I had not a shadow of proof in support of my theory. Hence the elaborate little comedy you saw played to-night."

"Even now I don't quite see all the details of the crime?" I said.

"Let us start from the beginning. Here is a shrewd and scheming woman who, knowing of her husband's financial *débâcle* and tired of the elderly mate she has only married for his money, induces him to insure his life for a large sum, and then seeks for the means to accomplish her purpose. An accident gives her that—the young soldier's strange story. The next afternoon when *monsieur le capitaine*, as she thinks, is on the high seas, she and her husband are strolling round the grounds. 'What a curious story that was last night!' she observes. 'Could a man shoot himself in such a way? Do show me if it is possible!' The poor fool—he shows her. He places the end of the rifle in his mouth. She stoops down, and puts her finger on the trigger, laughing up at him. 'And now, sir,' she says saucily, 'supposing I pull the trigger?'

"And then—and then, Hastings—she pulls it!"

THREE
The Adventure of the Cheap Flat

So far, in the cases which I have recorded, Poirot's investigations have started from the central fact, whether murder or robbery, and have proceeded from thence by a process of logical deduction to the final triumphant unravelling. In the events I am now about to chronicle, a remarkable chain of circumstances led from the apparently trivial incidents which first attracted Poirot's attention to the sinister happenings which completed a most unusual case.

I had been spending the evening with an old friend of mine, Gerald Parker. There had been, perhaps, about half a dozen people there besides my host and myself, and the talk fell, as it was bound to do sooner or later wherever Parker found himself, on the subject of house-hunting in London. Houses and flats were Parker's special hobby. Since the end of the War, he had occupied at least half a dozen different flats and maisonnettes. No sooner was he settled anywhere than he would light unexpectedly upon a new find, and would forthwith depart bag and baggage. His moves were nearly always accomplished at a slight pecuniary gain, for he had a shrewd business head, but it was sheer love of the sport that actuated him, and not a desire to make money at it. We listened to Parker for some time with the respect of the novice for the expert. Then it was our turn, and a perfect babel of tongues was let loose. Finally the floor was left to Mrs. Robinson, a charming little bride who was there with her husband. I had never met them before, as Robinson was only a recent acquaintance of Parker's.

"Talking of flats," she said, "have you heard of our piece of luck, Mr. Parker? We've got a flat—at last! In Montagu Mansions."

"Well," said Parker, "I've always said there are plenty of flats—at a price!"

"Yes, but this isn't at a price. It's dirt cheap. Eighty pounds a year!"

"But—but Montagu Mansions is just off Knightsbridge, isn't it? Big handsome building. Or are you talking of a poor relation of the same name stuck in the slums somewhere?"

"No, it's the Knightsbridge one. That's what makes it so wonderful."

"Wonderful is the word! It's a blinking miracle. But there must be a catch somewhere. Big premium, I suppose?"

"No premium!"

"No prem—oh, hold my head, somebody!" groaned Parker.

"But we've got to buy the furniture," continued Mrs. Robinson.

"Ah!" Parker brisked up. "I knew there was a catch!"

"For fifty pounds. And it's beautifully furnished!"

"I give it up," said Parker. "The present occupants must be lunatics with a taste for philanthropy."

Mrs. Robinson was looking a little troubled. A little pucker appeared between her dainty brows.

"It *is* queer, isn't it? You don't think that—that—the place is *haunted*?"

"Never heard of a haunted flat," declared Parker decisively.

"N-o." Mrs. Robinson appeared far from convinced. "But there were several things about it all that struck me as—well, queer."

"For instance——" I suggested.

"Ah," said Parker, "our criminal expert's attention is aroused! Unburden yourself to him, Mrs. Robinson. Hastings is a great unraveller of mysteries."

I laughed, embarrassed but not wholly displeased with the rôle thrust upon me.

"Oh, not really queer, Captain Hastings, but when we went to the agents, Stosser and Paul—we hadn't tried them before because they only have the expensive Mayfair flats, but we thought at any rate it would do no harm—everything they offered us was four and five hundred a year, or else huge premiums, and then, just as we were going, they mentioned that they had a flat at eighty, but that they doubted if it would be any good our going there, because it had been on their books some time and they had sent so many people to see it that it was almost sure to be taken—'snapped up' as the clerk put it—only people were so tiresome in not letting them know, and then they went on sending, and people get annoyed at being sent to a place that had, perhaps, been let some time."

Mrs. Robinson paused for some much needed breath, and then continued: "We thanked him, and said that we quite understood it would probably be no good, but that we should like an order all the same—just in case. And we went there straight away in a taxi, for, after all, you never know. No. 4 was on the second floor, and just as we were waiting for the lift, Elsie Ferguson—she's a friend of mine, Captain Hastings, and they are looking for a flat too—came hurrying down the stairs. 'Ahead of you for once, my dear,' she said. 'But it's no good. It's already let.' That seemed to finish it, but—well, as John said, the place was very cheap, we could afford to give more, and perhaps if we offered a premium.——A horrid thing to do, of course, and I feel quite ashamed of telling you, but you know what flat-hunting is."

I assured her that I was well aware that in the struggle for house-room the baser side of human nature frequently triumphed over the higher, and that the well-known rule of dog eat dog always applied.

"So we went up and, would you believe it, the flat wasn't let at all. We were shown over it by the maid, and then we saw the mistress, and the thing was settled then and there. Immediate possession and fifty pounds for the furniture. We signed the agreement next day, and we are to move in to-morrow!" Mrs. Robinson paused triumphantly.

"And what about Mrs. Ferguson?" asked Parker. "Let's have your deductions, Hastings."

"'Obvious, my dear Watson,'" I quoted lightly. "She went to the wrong flat."

"Oh, Captain Hastings, how clever of you!" cried Mrs. Robinson admiringly.

I rather wished Poirot had been there. Sometimes I have the feeling that he rather underestimates my capabilities.

* * *

The whole thing was rather amusing, and I propounded the thing as a mock problem to Poirot on the following morning. He seemed interested, and questioned me rather narrowly as to the rents of flats in various localities.

"A curious story," he said thoughtfully. "Excuse me, Hastings, I must take a short stroll."

When he returned, about an hour later, his eyes were gleaming with a peculiar excitement. He laid his stick on the table, and brushed the nap of his hat with his usual tender care before he spoke.

"It is as well, *mon ami*, that we have no affairs of moment on hand. We can devote ourselves wholly to the present investigation."

"What investigation are you talking about?"

"The remarkable cheapness of your friend's, Mrs. Robinson's, new flat."

"Poirot, you are not serious!"

"I am most serious. Figure to yourself, my friend, that the real rent of those flats is £350. I have just ascertained that from

43

the landlord's agents. And yet this particular flat is being sublet at eighty pounds! Why?"

"There must be something wrong with it. Perhaps it is haunted, as Mrs. Robinson suggested."

Poirot shook his head in a dissatisfied manner.

"Then again how curious it is that her friend tells her the flat is let, and, when she goes up, behold, it is not so at all!"

"But surely you agree with me that the other woman must have gone to the wrong flat. That is the only possible solution."

"You may or may not be right on that point, Hastings. The fact still remains that numerous other applicants were sent to see it, and yet, in spite of its remarkable cheapness, it was still in the market when Mrs. Robinson arrived."

"That shows that there must be something wrong about it."

"Mrs. Robinson did not seem to notice anything amiss. Very curious, is it not? Did she impress you as being a truthful woman, Hastings?"

"She was a delightful creature!"

"*Évidemment!* since she renders you incapable of replying to my question. Describe her to me, then."

"Well, she's tall and fair; her hair's really a beautiful shade of auburn——"

"Always you have had a penchant for auburn hair!" murmured Poirot. "But continue."

"Blue eyes and a very nice complexion and—well, that's all, I think," I concluded lamely.

"And her husband?"

"Oh, he's quite a nice fellow—nothing startling."

"Dark or fair?"

"I don't know—betwixt and between, and just an ordinary sort of face."

Poirot nodded.

"Yes, there are hundreds of these average men—and, anyway, you bring more sympathy and appreciation to your description of women. Do you know anything about these people? Does Parker know them well."

"They are just recent acquaintances, I believe. But surely, Poirot, you don't think for an instant——"

Poirot raised his hand.

"*Tout doucement, mon ami.* Have I said that I think anything? All I say is—it is a curious story. And there is nothing to throw light upon it; except perhaps the lady's name, eh, Hastings?"

"Her name is Stella," I said stiffly, "but I don't see——"

Poirot interrupted me with a tremendous chuckle. Something seemed to be amusing him vastly.

"And Stella means a star, does it not? Famous!"

"What on earth——"

"And stars give light! *Voilà!* Calm yourself, Hastings. Do not put on that air of injured dignity. Come, we will go to Montagu Mansions and make a few inquiries."

I accompanied him, nothing loath. The Mansions were a handsome block of buildings in excellent repair. A uniformed porter was sunning himself on the threshold, and it was to him that Poirot addressed himself:

"Pardon, but could you tell me if a Mr. and Mrs. Robinson reside here?"

The porter was a man of few words and apparently of a sour or suspicious disposition. He hardly looked at us and grunted out:

"No. 4. Second floor."

"I thank you. Can you tell me how long they have been here?"

"Six months."

I started forward in amazement, conscious as I did so of Poirot's malicious grin.

"Impossible," I cried. "You must be making a mistake."

"Six months."

"Are you sure? The lady I mean is tall and fair with reddish gold hair and——"

"That's 'er," said the porter. "Come in the Michaelmas quarter, they did. Just six months ago."

He appeared to lose interest in us and retreated slowly up the hall. I followed Poirot outside.

"*Eh bien*, Hastings?" my friend demanded slyly. "Are you so sure now that delightful women always speak the truth?"

I did not reply.

Poirot had steered his way into Brompton Road before I asked him what he was going to do and where we were going.

"To the house agents, Hastings. I have a great desire to have a flat in Montagu Mansions. If I am not mistaken, several interesting things will take place there before long."

We were fortunate in our quest. No. 8, on the fourth floor, was to be let furnished at ten guineas a week. Poirot promptly took it for a month. Outside in the street again, he silenced my protests:

"But I make money nowadays! Why should I not indulge a whim? By the way, Hastings, have you a revolver?"

"Yes—somewhere," I answered, slightly thrilled. "Do you think——"

"That you will need it? It is quite possible. The idea pleases you, I see. Always the spectacular and romantic appeals to you."

The following day saw us installed in our temporary home. The flat was pleasantly furnished. It occupied the same position in the building as that of the Robinsons, but was two floors higher.

The day after our installation was a Sunday. In the afternoon, Poirot left the front door ajar, and summoned me hastily as a bang reverberated from somewhere below.

"Look over the banisters. Are those your friends. Do not let them see you."

I craned my neck over the staircase.

"That's them," I declared in an ungrammatical whisper.

"Good. Wait awhile."

About half an hour later, a young woman emerged in brilliant and varied clothing. With a sigh of satisfaction, Poirot tiptoed back into the flat.

"*C'est ça*. After the master and mistress, the maid. The flat should now be empty."

"What are we going to do?" I asked uneasily.

Poirot had trotted briskly into the scullery and was hauling at the rope of the coal-lift.

"We are about to descend after the method of the dustbins," he explained cheerfully. "No one will observe us. The Sunday concert, the Sunday 'afternoon out,' and finally the Sunday nap after the Sunday dinner of England—*le rosbif*—all these will distract attention from the doings of Hercule Poirot. Come, my friend."

He stepped into the rough wooden contrivance and I followed him gingerly.

"Are we going to break into the flat?" I asked dubiously.

Poirot's answer was not too reassuring:

"Not precisely to-day," he replied.

Pulling on the rope, we descended slowly till we reached the second floor. Poirot uttered an exclamation of satisfaction as he perceived that the wooden door into the scullery was open.

"You observe? Never do they bolt these doors in the daytime. And yet anyone could mount or descend as we have done. At night yes—though not always then—and it is against that that we are going to make provision."

He had drawn some tools from his pocket as he spoke, and at once set deftly to work, his object being to arrange the bolt so that it could be pulled back from the lift. The operation only occupied about three minutes. Then Poirot returned the tools to his pocket, and we reascended once more to our own domain.

* * *

On Monday Poirot was out all day, but when he returned in the evening he flung himself into his chair with a sigh of satisfaction.

"Hastings, shall I recount to you a little history? A story

47

after your own heart and which will remind you of your favourite cinema?"

"Go ahead," I laughed. "I presume that it is a true story, not one of your efforts of fancy."

"It is true enough. Inspector Japp of Scotland Yard will vouch for its accuracy, since it was through his kind offices that it came to my ears. Listen, Hastings. A little over six months ago some important Naval plans were stolen from an American Government department. They showed the position of some of the most important Harbour defences, and would be worth a considerable sum to any foreign Government—that of Japan, for example. Suspicion fell upon a young man named Luigi Valdarno, an Italian by birth, who was employed in a minor capacity in the Department and who was missing at the same time as the papers. Whether Luigi Valdarno was the thief or not, he was found two days later on the East Side in New York, shot dead. The papers were not on him. Now for some time past Luigi Valdarno had been going about with a Miss Elsa Hardt, a young concert singer who had recently appeared and who lived with a brother in an apartment in Washington. Nothing was known of the antecedents of Miss Elsa Hardt, and she disappeared suddenly about the time of Valdarno's death. There are reasons for believing that she was in reality an accomplished international spy who has done much nefarious work under various *aliases*. The American Secret Service, whilst doing their best to trace her, also kept an eye upon certain insignificant Japanese gentlemen living in Washington. They felt pretty certain that, when Elsa Hardt had covered her tracks sufficiently, she would approach the gentlemen in question. One of them left suddenly for England a fortnight ago. On the face of it, therefore, it would seem that Elsa Hardt is in England." Poirot paused, and then added softly: "The official description of Elsa Hardt is: Height 5 ft. 7, eyes blue, hair auburn, fair complexion, nose straight, no special distinguishing marks."

"Mrs. Robinson!" I gasped.

"Well, there is a chance of it, anyhow," amended Poirot. "Also, I learn that a swarthy man, a foreigner of some kind, was inquiring about the occupants of No. 4 only this morning. Therefore, *mon ami*, I fear that you must forswear your beauty sleep to-night, and join me in my all-night vigil in the flat below—armed with that excellent revolver of yours, *bien entendu!*"

"Rather," I cried with enthusiasm. "When shall we start?"

"The hour of midnight is both solemn and suitable, I fancy. Nothing is likely to occur before then."

At twelve o'clock precisely, we crept cautiously into the coal-lift and lowered ourselves to the second floor. Under Poirot's manipulation, the wooden door quickly swung inwards, and we climbed into the flat. From the scullery we passed into the kitchen where we established ourselves comfortably in two chairs with the door into the hall ajar.

"Now we have but to wait," said Poirot contentedly, closing his eyes.

To me, the waiting appeared endless. I was terrified of going to sleep. Just when it seemed to me that I had been there about eight hours—and had, as I found out afterwards, in reality been exactly one hour and twenty minutes—a faint scratching sound came to my ears. Poirot's hand touched mine. I rose, and together we moved carefully in the direction of the hall. The noise came from there. Poirot placed his lips to my ear.

"Outside the front door. They are cutting out the lock. When I give the word, not before, fall upon him from behind and hold him fast. Be careful, he will have a knife."

Presently there was a rending sound, and a little circle of light appeared through the door. It was extinguished immediately and then the door was slowly opened. Poirot and I flattened ourselves against the wall. I heard a man's breathing as he passed us. Then he flashed on his torch, and as he did so, Poirot hissed in my ear:

"*Allez.*"

We sprang together, Poirot with a quick movement enveloped the intruder's head with a light woollen scarf whilst I pinioned his arms. The whole affair was quick and noiseless. I twisted a dagger from his hand, and as Poirot brought down the scarf from his eyes, whilst keeping it wound tightly round his mouth, I jerked up my revolver where he could see it and understand that resistance was useless. As he ceased to struggle Poirot put his mouth close to his ear and began to whisper rapidly. After a minute the man nodded. Then enjoining silence with a movement of the hand, Poirot led the way out of the flat and down the stairs. Our captive followed, and I brought up the rear with the revolver. When we were out in the street, Poirot turned to me.

"There is a taxi waiting just round the corner. Give me the revolver. We shall not need it now."

"But if this fellow tries to escape?"

Poirot smiled.

"He will not."

I returned in a minute with the waiting taxi. The scarf had been unwound from the stranger's face, and I gave a start of surprise.

"He's not a Jap," I ejaculated in a whisper to Poirot.

"Observation was always your strong point, Hastings! Nothing escapes you. No, the man is not a Jap. He is an Italian."

We got into the taxi, and Poirot gave the driver an address in St. John's Wood. I was by now completely fogged. I did not like to ask Poirot where we were going in front of our captive, and strove in vain to obtain some light upon the proceedings.

We alighted at the door of a small house standing back from the road. A returning wayfarer, slightly drunk, was lurching along the pavement and almost collided with Poirot, who said something sharply to him which I did not catch. All three of us went up the steps of the house. Poirot rang the bell and motioned us to stand a little aside. There was no answer and he rang again and then seized the knocker which he plied for some minutes vigorously.

A light appeared suddenly above the fanlight, and the door was opened cautiously a little way.

"What the devil do you want?" a man's voice demanded harshly.

"I want the doctor. My wife is taken ill."

"There's no doctor here."

The man prepared to shut the door, but Poirot thrust his foot in adroitly. He became suddenly a perfect caricature of an infuriated Frenchman.

"What you say, there is no doctor? I will have the law of you. You must come! I will stay here and ring and knock all night."

"My dear sir——" The door was opened again, the man, clad in a dressing-gown and slippers, stepped forward to pacify Poirot with an uneasy glance round.

"I will call the police."

Poirot prepared to descend the steps.

"No, don't do that for Heaven's sake!" The man dashed after him.

With a neat push Poirot sent him staggering down the steps. In another minute all three of us were inside the door and it was pushed to and bolted.

"Quick—in here." Poirot led the way into the nearest room switching on the light as he did so. "And you—behind the curtain."

"Si, signor," said the Italian and slid rapidly behind the full folds of rose-coloured velvet which draped the embrasure of the window.

Not a minute too soon. Just as he disappeared from view a woman rushed into the room. She was tall with reddish hair and held a scarlet kimono round her slender form.

"Where is my husband?" she cried, with a quick frightened glance. "Who are you?"

Poirot stepped forward with a bow.

"It is to be hoped your husband will not suffer from a chill. I observed that he had slippers on his feet, and that his dressing-gown was a warm one."

"Who are you? What are you doing in my house?"

"It is true that none of us have the pleasure of your acquaintance, madame. It is especially to be regretted as one of our number has come specially from New York in order to meet you."

The curtains parted and the Italian stepped out. To my horror I observed that he was brandishing my revolver, which Poirot must doubtless have put down through inadvertence in the cab.

The woman gave a piercing scream and turned to fly, but Poirot was standing in front of the closed door.

"Let me by," she shrieked. "He will murder me."

"Who was it dat croaked Luigi Valdarno?" asked the Italian hoarsely, brandishing the weapon, and sweeping each one of us with it. We dared not move.

"My God, Poirot, this is awful. What shall we do?" I cried.

"You will oblige me by refraining from talking so much, Hastings. I can assure you that our friend will not shoot until I give the word."

"Youse sure o' dat, eh?" said the Italian, leering unpleasantly.

It was more than I was, but the woman turned to Poirot like a flash.

"What is it you want?"

Poirot bowed.

"I do not think it is necessary to insult Miss Elsa Hardt's intelligence by telling her."

With a swift movement, the woman snatched up a big black velvet cat which served as a cover for the telephone.

"They are stitched in the lining of that."

"Clever," murmured Poirot appreciatively. He stood aside from the door. "Good evening, madame. I will detain your friend from New York whilst you make your getaway."

"Whatta fool!" roared the big Italian, and raising the revolver he fired point-blank at the woman's retreating figure just as I flung myself upon him.

But the weapon merely clicked harmlessly and Poirot's voice rose in mild reproof.

"Never will you trust your old friend, Hastings. I do not care for my friends to carry loaded pistols about with them and never would I permit a mere acquaintance to do so. No, no, *mon ami.*" This to the Italian who swearing hoarsely. Poirot continued to address him in a tone of mild reproof: "See now, what I have done for you. I have saved you from being hanged. And do not think that our beautiful lady will escape. No, no, the house is watched, back and front. Straight into the arms of the police they will go. Is not that a beautiful and consoling thought? Yes, you may leave the room now. But be careful—be very careful. I——Ah, he is gone! And my friend Hastings looks at me with eyes of reproach. But it was all so simple! It was clear, from the first, that out of several hundred, probably, applicants for No. 4, Montagu Mansions only the Robinsons were considered suitable. Why? What was there that singled them out from the rest—at practically a glance. Their appearance? Possibly, but it was not so unusual. Their name, then!"

"But there's nothing unusual about the name of Robinson," I cried. "It's quite a common name."

"Ah! *Sapristi*, but exactly! That was the point. Elsa Hardt and her husband, or brother or whatever he really is, come from New York, and take a flat in the name of Mr. and Mrs. Robinson. Suddenly they learn that one of these secret societies, the Mafia, or the Camorra, to which doubtless Luigi Valdarno belonged, is on their track. What do they do? They hit on a scheme of transparent simplicity. Evidently they knew that their pursuers were not personally acquainted with either of them. What then can be simpler? They offer the flat at an absurdly low rental. Of the thousands of young couples in London looking for flats, there cannot fail to be several Robinsons. It is only a matter of waiting. If you will look at the name of Robinson in the telephone directory, you will realize that a fair-haired Mrs. Robinson was pretty sure to come along sooner or later. Then what will happen? The avenger arrives. He knows the name, he knows the address. He strikes! All is over, vengeance is satisfied, and Miss Elsa Hardt has escaped by the skin of her teeth once more. By the way, Hastings, you must present me to the real Mrs. Robinson—that delightful and truthful creature! What will they think when they find their flat has been broken into! We must hurry back. Ah, that sounds like Japp and his friends arriving."

A mighty tattoo sounded on the knocker.

"How did you know this address?" I asked as I followed Poirot out into the hall. "Oh, of course, you had the first Mrs. Robinson followed when she left the other flat."

"*A la bonne heure*, Hastings. You use your grey cells at last. Now for a little surprise for Japp."

Softly unbolting the door, he stuck the cat's head round the edge and ejaculated a piercing "Miaow."

The Scotland Yard inspector, who was standing outside with another man, jumped in spite of himself.

"Oh, it's only Monsieur Poirot at one of his little jokes!" he exclaimed, as Poirot's head followed that of the cat. "Let us in, moosior."

"You have our friends safe and sound?"

"Yes, we've got the birds all right. But they hadn't got the goods with them."

"I see. So you come to search. Well, I am about to depart with Hastings, but I should like to give you a little lecture upon the history and habits of the domestic cat."

"For the Lord's sake, have you gone completely balmy?"

"The cat," declaimed Poirot, "was worshipped by the ancient Egyptians. It is still regarded as a symbol of good luck if a black cat crosses your path. This cat crossed your path to-night, Japp. To speak of the interior of any animal or any person is not, I know, considered polite in England. But the interior of this cat is perfectly delicate. I refer to the lining."

With a sudden grunt, the second man seized the cat from Poirot's hand.

"Oh, I forgot to introduce you," said Japp. "Mr. Poirot, this is Mr. Burt of the United States Secret Service."

The American's trained fingers had felt what he was looking for. He held out his hand, and for a moment speech failed him. Then he rose to the occasion.

"Pleased to meet you," said Mr. Burt.

FOUR
The Mystery of Hunter's Lodge

A fter all," murmured Poirot, "it is possible that I shall not die this time."

Coming from a convalescent influenza patient, I hailed the remark as showing a beneficial optimism. I myself had been the first sufferer from the disease. Poirot in his turn had gone down. He was now sitting up in bed, propped up with pillows, his head muffled in a woollen shawl, and was slowly sipping a particularly noxious tisane which I had prepared according to his directions. His eye rested with pleasure upon a neatly graduated row of medicine bottles which adorned the mantelpiece.

"Yes, yes," my little friend continued. "Once more shall I be myself again, the great Hercule Poirot, the terror of evil-doers! Figure to yourself, *mon ami*, that I have a little paragraph to myself in *Society Gossip*. But yes! Here it is! 'Go it—criminals—all out! Hercule Poirot—and believe me, girls, he's some Hercules!—our own pet society detective can't get a grip on you. 'Cause why? 'Cause he's got *la grippe* himself!'"

I laughed.

"Good for you, Poirot. You are becoming quite a public character. And fortunately you haven't missed anything of particular interest during this time."

"That is true. The few cases I have had to decline did not fill me with any regret."

Our landlady stuck her head in at the door.

"There's a gentleman downstairs. Says he must see Monsieur Poirot or you, Captain. Seeing as he was in a great to-do—and with all that quite the gentleman—I brought up 'is card."

She handed me the bit of pasteboard. "Mr. Roger Havering," I read.

Poirot motioned with his head towards the bookcase, and I obediently pulled forth "Who's Who." Poirot took it from me and scanned the pages rapidly.

"Second son of fifth Baron Windsor. Married 1913 Zoe, fourth daughter of William Crabb."

"H'm!" I said. "I rather fancy that's the girl who used to act at the Frivolity—only she called herself Zoe Carrisbrook. I remember she married some young man about town just before the War."

"Would it interest you, Hastings, to go down and hear what our visitor's particular little trouble is? Make him all my excuses."

Roger Havering was a man of about forty, well set up and of smart appearance. His face, however, was haggard, and he was evidently labouring under great agitation.

"Captain Hastings? You are Monsieur Poirot's partner, I understand. It is imperative that he should come with me to Derbyshire to-day."

"I'm afraid that's impossible," I replied. "Poirot is ill in bed—influenza."

His face fell.

"Dear me, that is a great blow to me."

"The matter on which you want to consult him is serious?"

"My God, yes! My uncle, the best friend I have in the world, was foully murdered last night."

"Here in London?"

"No, in Derbyshire. I was in town and received a telegram from my wife this morning. Immediately upon its receipt I determined to come round and beg Monsieur Poirot to undertake the case."

"If you will excuse me a minute," I said, struck by a sudden idea.

I rushed upstairs, and in a few brief words acquainted Poirot with the situation. He took any further words out of my mouth.

"I see. I see. You want to go yourself, is it not so? Well, why not? You should know my methods by now. All I ask is that you should report to me fully every day, and follow implicitly any instructions I may wire you."

To this I willingly agreed.

* * *

An hour later I was sitting opposite Mr. Havering in a first-class carriage on the Midland Railway, speeding rapidly away from London.

"To begin with, Captain Hastings, you must understand that Hunter's Lodge, where we are going, and where the tragedy took place, is only a small shooting-box in the heart of the Derbyshire moors. Our real home is near Newmarket, and we usually rent a flat in town for the season. Hunter's Lodge is looked after by a housekeeper who is quite capable of doing all we need when we run down for an occasional week-end. Of course, during the shooting season, we take down some of our own servants from Newmarket. My uncle, Mr. Harrington Pace (as you may know, my mother was a Miss Pace of New York), has, for the last three years, made his home with us. He never got on well with my father, or my elder brother, and I suspect that my being somewhat of a prodigal son myself rather increased than diminished his affection towards me. Of course I am a poor man, and my uncle was a rich one—in other words, he paid the piper! But, though exacting in many ways, he was not really hard to get on with, and we all three lived very harmoniously together. Two days ago my uncle, rather wearied with some recent gaieties of ours in town, suggested that we should run down to Derbyshire for a day or two. My wife telegraphed to Mrs. Middleton, the housekeeper, and we went down that same afternoon. Yesterday evening I was forced to return to town, but my wife and my uncle remained on. This morning I received this telegram." He handed it over to me:

"Come at once uncle Harrington murdered last night bring good detective if you can but do come—Zoe."

"Then, as yet you know no details?"

"No, I suppose it will be in the evening papers. Without doubt the police are in charge."

It was about three o'clock when we arrived at the little station of Elmer's Dale. From there a five-mile drive brought us to a small grey stone building in the midst of the rugged moors.

"A lonely place," I observed with a shiver.

Havering nodded.

"I shall try and get rid of it. I could never live here again."

We unlatched the gate and were walking up the narrow path to the oak door when a familiar figure emerged and came to meet us.

"Japp!" I ejaculated.

The Scotland Yard inspector grinned at me in a friendly fashion before addressing my companion.

"Mr. Havering, I think? I've been sent down from London to take charge of this case, and I'd like a word with you, if I may, sir."

"My wife——"

"I've seen your good lady, sir—and the housekeeper. I won't keep you a moment, but I'm anxious to get back to the village now that I've seen all there is to see here."

"I know nothing as yet as to what——"

"Ex-actly," said Japp soothingly. "But there are just one or two little points I'd like your opinion about all the same. Captain Hastings here, he knows me, and he'll go on up to the house and tell them you're coming. What have you done with the little man, by the way, Captain Hastings?"

"He's ill in bed with influenza."

"Is he now? I'm sorry to hear that. Rather the case of the cart without the horse, your being here without him, isn't it?"

And on his rather ill-timed jest I went on to the house. I rang the bell, as Japp had closed the door behind him. After some moments it was opened to me by a middle-aged woman in black.

"Mr. Havering will be here in a moment," I explained. "He has been detained by the inspector. I have come down with him from London to look into the case. Perhaps you can tell me briefly what occurred last night."

"Come inside, sir." She closed the door behind me, and we stood in the dimly-lighted hall. "It was after dinner last night, sir, that the man came. He asked to see Mr. Pace, sir, and, seeing that he spoke the same way, I thought it was an American gentleman friend of Mr. Pace's and I showed him into the gun-room, and then went to tell Mr. Pace. He wouldn't give any name, which, of course, was a bit odd, now I come to think of it. I told Mr. Pace, and he seemed puzzled like, but he said to the mistress: 'Excuse me, Zoe, while I just see what this fellow wants.' He went off to the gun-room, and I went back to the kitchen, but after a while I heard loud voices, as if they were quarrelling, and I came out into the hall. At the same time, the mistress she comes out too, and just then there was a shot and then a dreadful silence. We both ran to the gun-room door, but it was locked and we had to go round to the window. It was open, and there inside was Mr. Pace, all shot and bleeding."

"What became of the man?"

"He must have got away through the window, sir, before we got to it."

"And then?"

"Mrs. Havering sent me to fetch the police. Five miles to walk it was. They came back with me, and the constable he stayed all night, and this morning the police gentleman from London arrived."

"What was this man like who called to see Mr. Pace?"

The housekeeper reflected.

"He had a black beard, sir, and was about middle-aged, and had on a light overcoat. Beyond the fact that he spoke like an American I didn't notice much about him."

"I see. Now I wonder if I can see Mrs. Havering?"

"She's upstairs, sir. Shall I tell her?"

"If you please. Tell her that Mr. Havering is outside with Inspector Japp, and that the gentleman he has brought back with him from London is anxious to speak to her as soon as possible."

"Very good, sir."

I was in a fever of impatience to get at all the facts. Japp had two or three hours' start of me, and his anxiety to be gone made me keen to be close at his heels.

Mrs. Havering did not keep me waiting long. In a few minutes I heard a light step descending the stairs, and looked up to see a very handsome young woman coming towards me. She wore a flame-coloured jumper, that set off the slender boyishness of her figure. On her dark head was a little hat of flame-coloured leather. Even the present tragedy could not dim the vitality of her personality.

I introduced myself, and she nodded in quick comprehension.

"Of course I have often heard of you and your colleague, Monsieur Poirot. You have done some wonderful things together, haven't you? It was very clever of my husband to get you so promptly. Now will you ask me questions? That is the easiest way, isn't it, of getting to know all you want to about this dreadful affair?"

"Thank you, Mrs. Havering. Now what time was it that this man arrived?"

"It must have been just before nine o'clock. We had finished dinner, and were sitting over our coffee and cigarettes."

"Your husband had already left for London?"

"Yes, he went up by the 6.15."

"Did he go by car to the station, or did he walk?"

"Our own car isn't down here. One came out from the garage in Elmer's Dale to fetch him in time for the train."

"Was Mr. Pace quite his usual self?"

"Absolutely. Most normal in every way."

"Now, can you describe this visitor at all?"

"I'm afraid not. I didn't see him. Mrs. Middleton showed him straight into the gun-room and then came to tell my uncle."

"What did your uncle say?"

"He seemed rather annoyed, but went off at once. It was about five minutes later that I heard the sound of raised voices. I ran out into the hall and almost collided with Mrs. Middleton. Then we heard the shot. The gun-room door was locked on the inside, and we had to go right round the house to the window. Of course that took some time, and the murderer had been able to get well away. My poor uncle"—her voice faltered—"had been shot through the head. I saw at once that he was dead. I sent Mrs. Middleton for the police. I was careful to touch nothing in the room but to leave it exactly as I found it."

I nodded approval.

"Now, as to the weapon?"

"Well, I can make a guess at it, Captain Hastings. A pair of revolvers of my husband's were mounted upon the wall. One of them is missing. I pointed this out to the police, and they took the other one away with them. When they have extracted the bullet, I suppose they will know for certain."

"May I go to the gun-room?"

"Certainly. The police have finished with it. But the body has been removed."

She accompanied me to the scene of the crime. At that moment Havering entered the hall, and with a quick apology his wife ran to him. I was left to undertake my investigations alone.

I may as well confess at once that they were rather disappointing. In detective novels clues abound, but here I could find nothing that struck me as out of the ordinary except a large blood-stain on the carpet where I judged the dead man had fallen. I examined everything with painstaking care and took a couple of pictures of the room with my little camera which I had brought with me. I also examined the ground outside the window, but it appeared to have been so heavily trampled underfoot that I judged it was useless to waste time over it. No, I had seen all that Hunter's Lodge had to show me. I must go back to Elmer's Dale and get into touch with Japp. Accordingly I took leave of the Haverings, and was driven off in the car that had brought us up from the station.

I found Japp at the Matlock Arms and he took me forthwith to see the body. Harrington Pace was a small, spare clean-shaven man, typically American in appearance. He had been shot through the back of the head, and the revolver had been discharged at close quarters.

"Turned away for a moment," remarked Japp, "and the other fellow snatched up a revolver and shot him. The one Mrs. Havering handed over to us was fully loaded and I suppose the other one was also. Curious what darn fool things people do. Fancy keeping two loaded revolvers hanging up on your wall."

"What do you think of the case?" I asked, as we left the grue-some chamber behind us.

"Well, I'd got my eye on Havering to begin with. Oh, yes!" noting my exclamation of astonishment. "Havering has one or two shady incidents in his past. When he was a boy at Oxford there was some funny business about the signature on one of his father's cheques. All hushed up of course. Then, he's pretty heavily in debt now, and they're the kind of debts he wouldn't like to go to his uncle about, whereas you may be sure the uncle's will would be in his favour. Yes, I'd got my eye on him, and that's why I wanted to speak to him before he saw his wife, but their statements dovetail all right, and I've been to the station and there's no doubt whatever that he left by the 6.15. That gets up to London about 10.30. He went straight to his club, he says, and if that's confirmed all right—why, he couldn't have been shooting his uncle here at nine o'clock in a black beard!"

"Ah, yes, I was going to ask you what you thought about that beard?"

Japp winked.

"I think it grew pretty fast—grew in the five miles from Elmer's Dale to Hunter's Lodge. Americans that I've met are mostly clean-shaven. Yes, it's amongst Mr. Pace's American associates that we'll have to look for the murderer. I questioned the housekeeper first, and then her mistress, and their stories agree all right, but I'm sorry Mrs. Havering didn't get a look at the fellow. She's a smart woman, and she might have noticed something that would set us on the track."

I sat down and wrote a minute and lengthy account to Poirot. I was able to add various further items of information before I posted the letter.

The bullet had been extracted and was proved to have been fired from a revolver identical with the one held by the police. Furthermore, Mr. Havering's movements on the night in question had been checked and verified, and it was proved beyond doubt that he had actually arrived in London by the train in question. And, thirdly, a sensational development had occurred. A city gentleman, living at Ealing, on crossing Haven Green to get to the District Railway Station that morning, had observed a brown-paper parcel stuck between the railings. Opening it, he found that it contained a revolver. He handed the parcel over to the local police station, and before night it was proved to be the one we were in search of, the fellow to that given us by Mrs. Havering. One bullet had been fired from it.

All this I added to my report. A wire from Poirot arrived whilst I was at breakfast the following morning:

"Of course black bearded man was not Havering only you or Japp would have such an idea wire me description of housekeeper and what clothes she wore this morning same of Mrs. Havering do *not waste time taking photographs of interiors they are underexposed and not in the least artistic."*

It seemed to me that Poirot's style was unnecessarily facetious. I also fancied he was a shade jealous of my position on the spot with full facilities for handling the case. His request for a description of the clothes worn by the two women appeared to me to be simply ridiculous, but I complied as well as I, a mere man, was able to.

At eleven a reply wire came from Poirot:

"Advise Japp arrest housekeeper before it is too late."

Dumbfounded, I took the wire to Japp. He swore softly under his breath.

"He's the goods, Monsieur Poirot! If he says so, there's something in it. And I hardly noticed the woman. I don't know that I can go so far as arresting her, but I'll have her watched. We'll go up right away, and take another look at her."

But it was too late. Mrs. Middleton, that quiet middle-aged woman, who had appeared so normal and respectable, had vanished into thin air. Her box had been left behind. It contained only ordinary wearing apparel. There was no clue in it to her identity, or as to her whereabouts.

From Mrs. Havering we elicited all the facts we could:

"I engaged her about three weeks ago when Mrs. Emery, our former housekeeper, left. She came to me from Mrs. Selbourne's Agency in Mount Street—a very well-known place. I get all my servants from there. They sent several women to see me, but this Mrs. Middleton seemed much the nicest, and had splendid references. I engaged her on the spot, and notified the Agency of the fact. I can't believe that there was anything wrong with her. She was such a nice quiet woman."

The thing was certainly a mystery. Whilst it was clear that the woman herself could not have committed the crime, since at the moment the shot was fired Mrs. Havering was with her in the hall, nevertheless she must have some connection with the murder, or why should she suddenly take to her heels and bolt? I wired the latest development to Poirot and suggested returning to London and making inquiries at Selbourne's Agency.

Poirot's reply was prompt:

"Useless to inquire at agency they will never have heard of her find out what vehicle took her up to hunters lodge when she first arrived there."

Though mystified, I was obedient. The means of transport in Elmer's Dale were limited. The local garage had two battered Ford cars, and there were two station flies. None of these had been requisitioned on the date in question. Questioned, Mrs. Havering explained that she had given the woman the money for her fare down to Derbyshire and sufficient to hire a car or fly to take her up to Hunter's Lodge. There was usually one of the Fords at the station on the chance of its being required. Taking into consideration the further fact that nobody at the station had noticed the arrival of a stranger, black-bearded or otherwise, on the fatal evening, everything seemed to point to the conclusion that the murderer had come to the spot in a car, which had been waiting near at hand to aid his escape, and that the same car had brought the mysterious housekeeper to her new post. I may mention that inquiries at the Agency in London bore out Poirot's prognostication. No such woman as "Mrs. Middleton" had ever been on their books. They had received the Hon. Mrs. Havering's application for a housekeeper, and had sent her various applicants for the post. When she sent them the engagement fee, she omitted to mention which woman she had selected.

Somewhat crestfallen, I returned to London. I found Poirot established in an arm-chair by the fire in a garish, silk dressing-gown. He greeted me with much affection.

"*Mon ami* Hastings! But how glad I am to see you. Veritably I have for you a great affection. And you have enjoyed yourself? You have run to and fro with the good Japp? You have interrogated and investigated to your heart's content?"

"Poirot," I cried, "the thing's a dark mystery! It will never be solved."

"It is true that we are not likely to cover ourselves with glory over it."

"No, indeed. It's a hard nut to crack."

"Oh, as far as that goes, I am very good at cracking the nuts! A veritable squirrel! It is not that which embarrasses me. I know well enough who killed Mr. Harrington Pace."

"You know? How did you find out?"

"Your illuminating answers to my wires supplied me with the truth. See here, Hastings, let us examine the facts methodically and in order. Mr. Harrington Pace is a man with a considerable fortune which at his death will doubtless pass to his nephew. Point No. 1. His nephew is known to be desperately hard up. Point No. 2. His nephew is also known to be—shall we say a man of rather loose moral fibre? Point No. 3."

"But Roger Havering is proved to have journeyed straight up to London."

"*Précisément*—and therefore, as Mr. Havering left Elmer's Dale at 6.15, and since Mr. Pace cannot have been killed before he left, or the doctor would have spotted the time of the crime as being given wrongly when he examined the body, we conclude quite rightly, that Mr. Havering did not shoot his uncle. But there is a Mrs. Havering, Hastings."

"Impossible! The housekeeper was with her when the shot was fired."

"Ah, yes, the housekeeper. But she has disappeared."

"She will be found."

"I think not. There is something peculiarly elusive about that housekeeper, don't you think so, Hastings? It struck me at once."

"She played her part, I suppose, and then got out in the nick of time."

"And what was her part?"

"Well, presumably to admit her confederate, the black-bearded man."

"Oh, no, that was not her part! Her part was what you have just mentioned, to provide an alibi for Mrs. Havering at the moment the shot was fired. And no one will ever find her, *mon ami*, because she does not exist! 'There's no sech person,' as your so great Shakespeare says."

"It was Dickens," I murmured, unable to suppress a smile. "But what do you mean, Poirot?"

"I mean that Zoe Havering was an actress before her marriage, that you and Japp only saw the housekeeper in a dark hall, a dim middle-aged figure in black with a faint subdued voice, and finally that neither you nor Japp, nor the local police whom the housekeeper fetched, ever saw Mrs. Middleton and her mistress at one and the same time. It was child's play for that clever and daring woman. On the pretext of summoning her mistress, she runs upstairs, slips on a bright jumper and a hat with black curls attached which she jams down over the grey transformation. A few deft touches, and the make-up is removed, a slight dusting of rouge, and the brilliant Zoe Havering comes down with her clear ringing voice. Nobody looks particularly at the housekeeper. Why should they? There is nothing to connect her with the crime. She, too, has an alibi."

"But the revolver that was found at Ealing? Mrs. Havering could not have placed it there?"

"No, that was Roger Havering's job—but it was a mistake on their part. It put me on the right track. A man who has committed a murder with a revolver which he found on the spot would fling it away at once, he would not carry it up to London with him. No, the motive was clear, the criminals wished to focus the interest of the police on a spot far removed from Derbyshire they were anxious to get the police away as soon as possible from the vicinity of Hunter's Lodge. Of course the revolver found at Ealing was not the one with which Mr. Pace was shot. Roger Havering discharged one shot from it, brought it up to London, went straight to his club to establish his alibi, then went quickly out to Ealing by the district, a matter of about twenty minutes only, placed the parcel where it was found and so back to town. That charming creature, his wife, quietly shoots Mr. Pace after dinner—you remember he was shot from behind? Another significant point, that!—reloads the revolver and puts it back in its place, and then starts off with her desperate little comedy."

"It's incredible," I murmured, fascinated, "and yet——"

"And yet it is true. *Bien sur*, my friend, it is true. But to bring that precious pair to justice, that is another matter. Well, Japp must do what he can—I have written him fully—but I very much fear, Hastings, that we shall be obliged to leave them to Fate, or *le bon Dieu*, whichever you prefer."

"The wicked flourish like a green bay tree," I reminded him.

"But at a price, Hastings, always at a price, *croyez-moi!*"

Poirot's forebodings were confirmed. Japp, though convinced of the truth of his theory, was unable to get together the necessary evidence to ensure a conviction.

Mr. Pace's huge fortune passed into the hands of his murderers. Nevertheless, Nemesis did overtake them, and when I read in the paper that the Hon. Roger and Mrs. Havering were amongst those killed in the crashing of the Air Mail to Paris I knew that Justice was satisfied.

FIVE
The Million Dollar Bond Robbery

W hat a number of bond robberies there have been lately!" I observed one morning, laying aside the newspaper. "Poirot, let us forsake the science of detection, and take to crime instead!"

"You are on the—how do you say it?—get-rich-quick tack, eh, *mon ami?*"

"Well, look at this last *coup*, the million dollars' worth of Liberty Bonds which the London and Scottish Bank were sending to New York, and which disappeared in such a remarkable manner on board the *Olympia*."

"If it were not for the *mal de mer*, and the difficulty of practising the so excellent method of Laverguier for a longer time than the few hours of crossing the channel, I should delight to voyage myself on one of these big liners," murmured Poirot dreamily.

"Yes, indeed," I said enthusiastically. "Some of them must be perfect palaces; the swimming-baths, the lounges, the restaurant, the palm courts—really, it must be hard to believe that one is on the sea."

"Me, I always know when I am on the sea," said Poirot sadly. "And all those bagatelles that you enumerate, they say nothing to me; but, my friend, consider for a moment the geniuses that travel as it were incognito! On board these floating palaces, as you so justly call them, one would meet the élite, the *haute noblesse* of the criminal world!"

I laughed.

"So that's the way your enthusiasm runs! You would have liked to cross swords with the man who sneaked the Liberty Bonds?"

The landlady interrupted us.

"A young lady as wants to see you, Mr. Poirot. Here's her card."

The card bore the inscription: Miss Esmée Farquhar, and Poirot, after diving under the table to retrieve a stray crumb, and putting it carefully in the waste-paper-basket, nodded to the landlady to admit her.

In another minute one of the most charming girls I have ever seen was ushered into the room. She was perhaps about five-and-twenty, with big brown eyes and a perfect figure. She was well-dressed and perfectly composed in manner.

"Sit down, I beg of you, mademoiselle. This is my friend, Captain Hastings, who aids me in my little problems."

"I am afraid it is a big problem I have brought you to-day, Monsieur Poirot," said the girl, giving me a pleasant bow as she seated herself. "I dare say you have read about it in the papers. I am referring to the theft of Liberty Bonds on the *Olympia*." Some astonishment must have shown itself in Poirot's face, for she continued quickly: "You are doubtless asking yourself what I have to do with a grave institution like the London and Scottish Bank. In one sense nothing, in another sense everything. You see, Monsieur Poirot, I am engaged to Mr. Philip Ridgeway."

"Aha! and Mr. Philip Ridgeway——"

"Was in charge of the bonds when they were stolen. Of course no actual blame can attach to him, it was not his fault in any way. Nevertheless, he is half distraught over the matter, and his uncle, I know, insists that he must carelessly have mentioned having them in his possession. It is a terrible set-back in his career."

"Who is his uncle?"

"Mr. Vavasour, joint general manager of the London and Scottish Bank."

"Suppose, Miss Farquhar, that you recount to me the whole story?"

"Very well. As you know, the Bank wished to extend their credits in America, and for this purpose decided to send over a million dollars in Liberty Bonds. Mr. Vavasour selected his nephew, who had occupied a position of trust in the Bank for many years and who was conversant with all the details of the Bank's dealings in New York, to make the trip. The Olympia sailed from Liverpool on the 23rd, and the bonds were handed over to Philip on the morning of that day by Mr. Vavasour and Mr. Shaw, the two joint general managers of the London and Scottish Bank. They were counted, enclosed in a package, and sealed in his presence, and he then locked the package at once in his portmanteau."

"A portmanteau with an ordinary lock?"

"No, Mr. Shaw insisted on a special lock being fitted to it by Hubbs's. Philip, as I say, placed the package at the bottom of the trunk. It was stolen just a few hours before reaching New York. A rigorous search of the whole ship was made, but without result. The bonds seemed literally to have vanished into thin air."

Poirot made a grimace.

"But they did not vanish absolutely, since I gather that they were sold in small parcels within half an hour of the docking of the Olympia! Well, undoubtedly the next thing is for me to see Mr. Ridgeway."

"I was about to suggest that you should lunch with me at the 'Cheshire Cheese.' Philip will be there. He is meeting me, but does not yet know that I have been consulting you on his behalf."

We agreed to this suggestion readily enough, and drove there in a taxi.

Mr. Philip Ridgeway was there before us, and looked somewhat surprised to see his fiancée arriving with two complete strangers. He was a nice-looking young fellow, tall and spruce, with a touch of greying hair at the temples, though he could not have been much over thirty.

Miss Farquhar went up to him and laid her hand on his arm.

"You must forgive my acting without consulting you, Philip," she said. "Let me introduce you to Monsieur Hercule Poirot, of whom you must often have heard, and his friend, Captain Hastings."

Ridgeway looked very astonished.

"Of course I have heard of you, Monsieur Poirot," he said, as he shook hands. "But I had no idea that Esmée was thinking of consulting you about my—our trouble."

"I was afraid you would not let me do it, Philip," said Miss Farquhar meekly.

"So you took care to be on the safe side," he observed, with a smile. "I hope Monsieur Poirot will be able to throw some light on this extraordinary puzzle, for I confess frankly that I am nearly out of my mind with worry and anxiety about it."

Indeed, his face looked drawn and haggard and showed only too clearly the strain under which he was labouring.

"Well, well," said Poirot. "Let us lunch, and over lunch we will put our heads together and see what can be done. I want to hear Mr. Ridgeway's story from his own lips."

Whilst we discussed the excellent steak and kidney pudding of the establishment, Philip Ridgeway narrated the circumstances leading to the disappearance of the bonds. His story agreed with that of Miss Farquhar in every particular. When he had finished, Poirot took up the thread with a question.

"What exactly led you to discover that the bonds had been stolen, Mr. Ridgeway?"

He laughed rather bitterly.

"The thing stared me in the face, Monsieur Poirot. I couldn't have missed it. My cabin trunk was half out from under the bunk and all scratched and cut about where they'd tried to force the lock."

"But I understood that it had been opened with a key?"

"That's so. They tried to force it, but couldn't. And, in the end, they must have got it unlocked somehow or other."

"Curious," said Poirot, his eyes beginning to flicker with the green light I knew so well. "Very curious! They waste much, much time trying to prise it open, and then—*sapristi!* they find that they have the key all the time—for each of Hubbs's locks are unique."

"That's just why they couldn't have had the key. It never left me day or night."

"You are sure of that?"

"I can swear to it, and besides, if they had had the key or a duplicate, why should they waste time trying to force an obviously unforceable lock?"

"Ah! there is exactly the question we are asking ourselves! I venture to prophesy that the solution, if we ever find it, will hinge on that curious fact. I beg of you not to assault me if I ask you one more question: *Are you perfectly certain you did not leave the trunk unlocked?*"

Philip Ridgeway merely looked at him, and Poirot gesticulated apologetically.

"Ah, but these things can happen, I assure you! Very well, the bonds were stolen from the trunk. What did the thief do with them? How did he manage to get ashore with them?"

"Ah!" cried Ridgeway. "That's just it. How? Word was passed to the Customs authorities, and every soul that left the ship was gone over with a toothcomb!"

"And the bonds, I gather, made a bulky package?"

"Certainly they did. They could hardly have been hidden on board—and anyway we know they weren't because they were offered for sale within half an hour of the *Olympia's* arrival, long before I got the cables going and the numbers sent out. One broker swears he bought some of them even before the *Olympia* got in. But you can't send bonds by wireless."

"Not by wireless, but did any tug come alongside?"

"Only the official ones, and that was after the alarm was given when every one was on the look-out. I was watching out myself for their being passed over to some one that way. My God, Monsieur Poirot, this thing will drive me mad! People are beginning to say I stole them myself."

"But you also were searched on landing, weren't you?" asked Poirot gently.

"Yes."

The young man stared at him in a puzzled manner.

"You do not catch my meaning, I see," said Poirot, smiling enigmatically. "Now I should like to make a few inquiries at the Bank."

Ridgeway produced a card and scribbled a few words on it.

"Send this in and my uncle will see you at once."

Poirot thanked him, bade farewell to Miss Farquhar, and together we started out for Threadneedle Street and the head office of the London and Scottish Bank. On production of Ridgeway's card, we were led through the labyrinth of counters and desks, skirting paying-in clerks and paying-out clerks and up to a small office on the first floor where the joint general managers received us. They were two grave gentlemen, who had grown grey in the service of the Bank. Mr. Vavasour had a short white beard, Mr. Shaw was clean shaven.

"I understand you are strictly a private inquiry agent?" said Mr. Vavasour. "Quite so, quite so. We have, of course, placed ourselves in the hands of Scotland Yard. Inspector McNeil has charge of the case. A very able officer, I believe."

"I am sure of it," said Poirot politely. "You will permit a few questions, on your nephew's behalf? About this lock, who ordered it from Hubbs's?"

"I ordered it myself," said Mr. Shaw. "I would not trust to any clerk in the matter. As to the keys, Mr. Ridgeway had one, and the other two are held by my colleague and myself."

"And no clerk has had access to them?"

Mr. Shaw turned inquiringly to Mr. Vavasour. "I think I am correct in saying that they have remained in the safe where we placed them on the 23rd," said Mr. Vavasour. "My colleague was unfortunately taken ill a fortnight ago—in fact on the very day that Philip left us. He has only just recovered."

"Severe bronchitis is no joke to a man of my age," said Mr. Shaw ruefully. "But I am afraid Mr. Vavasour has suffered from the hard work entailed by my absence, especially with this unexpected worry coming on top of everything."

Poirot asked a few more questions. I judged that he was endeavouring to gauge the exact amount of intimacy between uncle and nephew. Mr. Vavasour's answers were brief and punctilious. His nephew was a trusted official of the Bank, and had no debts or money difficulties that he knew of. He had been entrusted with similar missions in the past. Finally we were politely bowed out.

"I am disappointed," said Poirot, as we emerged into the street.

"You hoped to discover more? They are such stodgy old men."

"It is not their stodginess which disappoints me, *mon ami*. I do not expect to find in a Bank manager a 'keen financier with an eagle glance' as your favourite works of fiction put it. No, I am disappointed in the case—it is too easy!"

"*Easy?*"

"Yes, do you not find it almost childishly simple?"

"You know who stole the bonds?"

"I do."

"But then—we must—why——"

"Do not confuse and fluster yourself, Hastings. We are not going to do anything at present."

"But why? What are you waiting for?"

"For the *Olympia*. She is due on her return trip from New York on Tuesday."

"But if you know who stole the bonds, why wait? He may escape."

"To a South Sea island where there is no extradition? No, *mon ami*, he would find life very uncongenial there. As to why I wait—*eh bien* to the intelligence of Hercule Poirot the case is perfectly clear, but for the benefit of others, not so greatly gifted by the good God—the Inspector McNeil, for instance—it would be as well to make a few inquiries to establish the facts. One must have consideration for those less gifted than oneself."

"Good Lord, Poirot! Do you know, I'd give a considerable sum of money to see you make a thorough ass of yourself—just for once. You're so confoundedly conceited!"

"Do not enrage yourself, Hastings. In verity, I observe that there are times when you almost detest me! Alas, I suffer the penalties of greatness!"

The little man puffed out his chest, and sighed so comically that I was forced to laugh.

* * *

Tuesday saw us speeding to Liverpool in a first-class carriage of the L. & N.W.R. Poirot had obstinately refused to enlighten me as to his suspicions—or certainties. He contented himself with expressing surprise that I, too, was not equally *au fait* with the situation. I disdained to argue, and entrenched my curiosity behind a rampart of pretended indifference.

Once arrived at the quay alongside which lay the big trans-atlantic liner, Poirot became brisk and alert. Our proceedings consisted in interviewing four successive stewards and inquiring after a friend of Poirot's who had crossed to New York on the 23rd.

"An elderly gentleman, wearing glasses. A great invalid, hardly moved out of his cabin."

The description appeared to tally with one Mr. Ventnor who had occupied the cabin C 24 which was next to that of Philip Ridgeway. Although unable to see how Poirot had deduced Mr. Ventnor's existence and personal appearance, I was keenly excited.

"Tell me," I cried, "was this gentleman one of the first to land when you got to New York?" The steward shook his head.

"No, indeed, sir, he was one of the last off the boat."

I retired crestfallen, and observed Poirot grinning at me. He thanked the steward, a note changed hands, and we took our departure.

"It's all very well," I remarked heatedly, "but that last answer must have damped your precious theory, grin as you please!"

"As usual, you see nothing, Hastings. That last answer is, on the contrary, the coping-stone of my theory."

I flung up my hands in despair.

"I give it up."

* * *

When we were in the train, speeding towards London, Poirot wrote busily for a few minutes, sealing up the result in an envelope.

"This is for the good Inspector McNeil. We will leave it at Scotland Yard in passing, and then to the Rendezvous Restaurant, where I have asked Miss Esmée Farquhar to do us the honour of dining with us."

"What about Ridgeway?"

"What about him?" asked Poirot with a twinkle.

"Why, you surely don't think—you can't——"

"The habit of incoherence is growing upon you, Hastings. As a matter of fact I *did* think. If Ridgeway had been the thief—which was perfectly possible—the case would have been charming; a piece of neat methodical work."

"But not so charming for Miss Farquhar."

"Possibly you are right. Therefore all is for the best. Now, Hastings, let us review the case. I can see that you are dying to do so. The sealed package is removed from the trunk and vanishes, as Miss Farquhar puts it, into thin air. We will dismiss the thin air theory, which is not practicable at the present stage of science, and consider what is likely to have become of it. Every one asserts the incredibility of its being smuggled ashore——"

"Yes, but we know——"

"*You* may know, Hastings. I do not. I take the view that, since it seemed incredible, it *was* incredible. Two possibilities remain: it was hidden on board—also rather difficult—or it was thrown overboard."

"With a cork on it, do you mean?"

"Without a cork."

I stared.

"But if the bonds were thrown overboard, they couldn't have been sold in New York."

"I admire your logical mind, Hastings. The bonds were sold in New York, therefore they were not thrown overboard. You see where that leads us?"

"Where we were when we started."

"*Jamais de la vie!* If the package was thrown overboard, and the bonds were sold in New York, the package could not have contained the bonds. Is there any evidence that the package *did* contain the bonds? Remember, Mr. Ridgeway never opened it from the time it was placed in his hands in London."

"Yes, but then——"

Poirot waved an impatient hand.

"Permit me to continue. The last moment that the bonds are seen as bonds is in the office of the London and Scottish Bank on the morning of the 23rd. They reappear in New York half an hour after the *Olympia* gets in, and according to one man, whom nobody listens to, actually *before* she gets in. Supposing then, that they have never been on the *Olympia* at all? Is there any other way they could get to New York? Yes. The *Gigantic* leaves Southampton on the same day as the *Olympia*, and she holds the record for the Atlantic. Mailed by the *Gigantic*, the bonds would be in New York the day before the *Olympia* arrived. All is clear, the case begins to explain itself. The sealed packet is only a dummy, and the moment of its substitution must be in the office in the Bank. It would be an easy matter for any of the three men present to have prepared a duplicate package which could be substituted for the genuine one. *Très bien*, the bonds are mailed to a confederate in New York, with instructions to sell as soon as the *Olympia* is in, but some one must travel on the *Olympia* to engineer the supposed moment of the robbery."

"But why?"

"Because if Ridgeway merely opens the packet and finds it a dummy, suspicion flies at once to London. No, the man on board in the cabin next door does his work, pretends to force the lock in an obvious manner so as to draw immediate attention to the theft, really unlocks the trunk with a duplicate key, throws the package overboard and waits until the last to leave the boat. Naturally he wears glasses to conceal his eyes, and is an invalid since he does not want to run the risk of meeting Ridgeway. He steps ashore in New York and returns by the first boat available."

"But who—which was he?"

"The man who had a duplicate key, the man who ordered the lock, the man who has *not* been severely ill with bronchitis at his home in the country—*enfin*, that 'stodgy' old man, Mr. Shaw! There are criminals in high places sometimes, my friend. Ah, here we are. Mademoiselle, I have succeeded! You permit?"

And, beaming, Poirot kissed the astonished girl lightly on either cheek!

SIX

The Adventure of the Egyptian Tomb

I have always considered that one of the most thrilling and dramatic of the many adventures I have shared with Poirot was that of our investigation into the strange series of deaths which followed upon the discovery and opening of the Tomb of King Men-her-Ra.

Hard upon the discovery of the Tomb of Tut-ankh-Amen by Lord Carnarvon, Sir John Willard and Mr. Bleibner of New York, pursuing their excavations not far from Cairo, in the vicinity of the Pyramids of Gizeh, came unexpectedly on a series of funeral chambers. The greatest interest was aroused by their discovery. The Tomb appeared to be that of King Men-her-Ra, one of those shadowy kings of the Eighth Dynasty, when the Old Kingdom was falling to decay. Little was known about this period, and the discoveries were fully reported in the newspapers.

An event soon occurred which took a profound hold on the public mind. Sir John Willard died quite suddenly of heart failure.

The more sensational newspapers immediately took the opportunity of reviving all the old superstitious stories connected with the ill luck of certain Egyptian treasures. The unlucky Mummy at the British Museum, that hoary old chestnut, was dragged out with fresh zest, was quietly denied by the Museum, but nevertheless enjoyed all its usual vogue.

A fortnight later Mr. Bleibner died of acute blood poisoning, and a few days afterwards a nephew of his shot himself in New York. The "Curse of Men-her-Ra" was the talk of the day, and the magic power of dead and gone Egypt was exalted to a fetish point.

It was then that Poirot received a brief note from Lady Willard, widow of the dead archaeologist, asking him to go and see her at her house in Kensington Square. I accompanied him.

Lady Willard was a tall, thin woman, dressed in deep mourning. Her haggard face bore eloquent testimony to her recent grief.

"It is kind of you to have come so promptly, Monsieur Poirot."

"I am at your service, Lady Willard. You wished to consult me?"

"You are, I am aware, a detective, but it is not only as a detective that I wish to consult you. You are a man of original views, I know, you have imagination, experience of the world, tell me, Monsieur Poirot, what are your views on the supernatural?"

Poirot hesitated for a moment before he replied. He seemed to be considering. Finally he said:

"Let us not misunderstand each other, Lady Willard. It is not a general question that you are asking me there. It has a personal application, has it not? You are referring obliquely to the death of your late husband?"

"That is so," she admitted.

"You want me to investigate the circumstances of his death?"

"I want you to ascertain for me exactly how much is newspaper chatter, and how much may be said to be founded on fact? Three deaths, Monsieur Poirot—each one explicable taken by itself, but taken together surely an almost unbelievable coincidence, and all within a month of the opening of the tomb! It may be mere superstition, it may be some potent curse from the past that operates in ways undreamed of by modern science. The fact remains—three deaths! And I am afraid, Monsieur Poirot, horribly afraid. It may not yet be the end."

"For whom do you fear?"

"For my son. When the news of my husband's death came I was ill. My son, who has just come down from Oxford, went out there. He brought the—the body home, but now he has gone out again, in spite of my prayers and entreaties. He is so fascinated by the work that he intends to take his father's place and carry on the system of excavations. You may think me a foolish, credulous woman, but, Monsieur Poirot, I am afraid. Supposing that the spirit of the dead King is not yet appeased? Perhaps to you I seem to be talking nonsense——"

"No, indeed, Lady Willard," said Poirot quickly. "I, too, believe in the force of superstition, one of the greatest forces the world has ever known."

I looked at him in surprise. I should never have credited Poirot with being superstitious. But the little man was obviously in earnest.

"What you really demand is that I shall protect your son? I will do my utmost to keep him from harm."

"Yes, in the ordinary way, but against an occult influence?"

"In volumes of the Middle Ages, Lady Willard, you will find many ways of counteracting black magic. Perhaps they knew more than we moderns with all our boasted science. Now let us come to facts, that I may have guidance. Your husband had always been a devoted Egyptologist, hadn't he?"

"Yes, from his youth upwards. He was one of the greatest living authorities upon the subject."

"But Mr. Bleibner, I understand, was more or less of an amateur?"

"Oh, quite. He was a very wealthy man who dabbled freely in any subject that happened to take his fancy. My husband managed to interest him in Egyptology, and it was his money that was so useful in financing the expedition."

"And the nephew? What do you know of his tastes? Was he with the party at all?"

"I do not think so. In fact I never knew of his existence till I read of his death in the paper, I do not think he and Mr. Bleibner can have been at all intimate. He never spoke of having any relations."

"Who are the other members of the party?"

"Well, there is Dr. Tosswill, a minor official connected with the British Museum; Mr. Schneider of the Metropolitan Museum in New York; a young American secretary; Dr. Ames, who accompanies the expedition in his professional capacity; and Hassan, my husband's devoted native servant."

"Do you remember the name of the American secretary?"

"Harper, I think, but I cannot be sure. He had not been with Mr. Bleibner very long, I know. He was a very pleasant young fellow."

"Thank you, Lady Willard."

"If there is anything else——?"

"For the moment, nothing. Leave it now in my hands, and be assured that I will do all that is humanly possible to protect your son."

They were not exactly reassuring words, and I observed Lady Willard wince as he uttered them. Yet, at the same time, the fact that he had not pooh-poohed her fears seemed in itself to be a relief to her.

For my part I had never before suspected that Poirot had so deep a vein of superstition in his nature. I tackled him on the subject as we went homewards. His manner was grave and earnest.

"But yes, Hastings. I believe in these things. You must not underrate the force of superstition."

"What are we going to do about it?"

"*Toujours pratique*, the good Hastings! *Eh bien*, to begin with we are going to cable to New York for fuller details of young Mr. Bleibner's death."

He duly sent off his cable. The reply was full and precise. Young Rupert Bleibner had been in low water for several years. He had been a beach-comber and a remittance man in several South Sea islands, but had returned to New York two years ago, where he had rapidly sunk lower and lower. The most significant thing, to my mind, was that he had recently managed to borrow enough money to take him to Egypt. "I've a good friend there I can borrow from," he had declared. Here, however, his plans had gone awry. He had returned to New York cursing his skinflint of an uncle who cared more for the bones of dead and gone kings than his own flesh and blood. It was during his sojourn in Egypt that the death of Sir John Willard occurred. Rupert had plunged once more into his life of dissipation in New York, and then, without warning, he had committed suicide, leaving behind him a letter which contained some curious phrases. It seemed written in a sudden fit of remorse. He referred to himself as a leper and an outcast, and the letter ended by declaring that such as he were better dead.

A shadowy theory leapt into my brain. I had never really believed in the vengeance of a long dead Egyptian king. I saw here a more modern crime. Supposing this young man had decided to do away with his uncle—preferably by poison. By mistake, Sir John Willard receives the fatal dose. The young man returns to New York, haunted by his crime. The news of his uncle's death reaches him. He realizes how unnecessary his crime has been, and stricken with remorse takes his own life.

I outlined my solution to Poirot. He was interested.

"It is ingenious what you have thought of there—decidedly it is ingenious. It may even be true. But you leave out of count the fatal influence of the Tomb."

I shrugged my shoulders.

"You still think that has something to do with it?"

"So much so, *mon ami*, that we start for Egypt to-morrow."

"What?" I cried, astonished.

"I have said it." An expression of conscious heroism spread over Poirot's face. Then he groaned. "But, oh," he lamented, "the sea! The hateful sea!"

* * *

It was a week later. Beneath our feet was the golden sand of the desert. The hot sun poured down overhead. Poirot, the picture of misery, wilted by my side. The little man was not a good traveller. Our four days' voyage from Marseilles had been one long agony to him. He had landed at Alexandria the wraith of his former self, even his usual neatness had deserted him. We had arrived in Cairo and had driven out at once to the Mena House Hotel, right in the shadow of the Pyramids.

The charm of Egypt had laid hold of me. Not so Poirot. Dressed precisely the same as in London, he carried a small clothes-brush in his pocket and waged an unceasing war on the dust which accumulated on his dark apparel.

"And my boots," he wailed. "Regard them, Hastings. My boots, of the neat patent leather, usually so smart and shining. See, the sand is inside them, which is painful, and outside them, which outrages the eyesight. Also the heat, it causes my moustaches to become limp—but limp!"

"Look at the Sphinx," I urged. "Even I can feel the mystery and the charm it exhales."

Poirot looked at it discontentedly.

"It has not the air happy," he declared. "How could it, half-buried in sand in that untidy fashion. Ah, this cursed sand!"

"Come, now, there's a lot of sand in Belgium," I reminded him, mindful of a holiday spent at Knocke-sur-mer in the midst of "*les dunes impeccables*" as the guide-book had phrased it.

"Not in Brussels," declared Poirot. He gazed at the Pyramids thoughtfully. "It is true that they, at least, are of a shape solid and geometrical, but their surface is of an unevenness most unpleasing. And the palm-trees I like them not. Not even do they plant them in rows!"

I cut short his lamentations, by suggesting that we should start for the camp. We were to ride there on camels, and the beasts were patiently kneeling, waiting for us to mount, in charge of several picturesque boys headed by a voluble dragoman.

I pass over the spectacle of Poirot on a camel. He started by groans and lamentations and ended by shrieks, gesticulations and invocations to the Virgin Mary and every Saint in the calendar. In the end, he descended ignominiously and finished the journey on a diminutive donkey. I must admit that a trotting camel is no joke for the amateur. I was stiff for several days.

At last we neared the scene of the excavations. A sunburnt man with a grey beard, in white clothes and wearing a helmet, came to meet us.

"Monsieur Poirot and Captain Hastings? We received your cable. I'm sorry that there was no one to meet you in Cairo. An unforeseen event occurred which completely disorganized our plans."

Poirot paled. His hand, which had stolen to his clothes-brush, stayed its course.

"Not another death?" he breathed.

"Yes."

"Sir Guy Willard?" I cried.

"No, Captain Hastings. My American colleague, Mr. Schneider."

"And the cause?" demanded Poirot.

"Tetanus."

I blanched. All around me I seemed to feel an atmosphere of evil, subtle and menacing. A horrible thought flashed across me. Supposing I were the next?

"*Mon Dieu*," said Poirot, in a very low voice, "I do not understand this. It is horrible. Tell me, monsieur, there is no doubt that it was tetanus?"

"I believe not. But Dr. Ames will tell you more than I can do."

"Ah, of course, you are not the doctor."

"My name is Tosswill."

This, then, was the British expert described by Lady Willard as being a minor official at the British Museum. There was something at once grave and steadfast about him that took my fancy.

"If you will come with me," continued Dr. Tosswill, "I will take you to Sir Guy Willard. He was most anxious to be informed as soon as you should arrive."

We were taken across the camp to a large tent. Dr. Tosswill lifted up the flap and we entered. Three men were sitting inside.

"Monsieur Poirot and Captain Hastings have arrived, Sir Guy," said Tosswill.

The youngest of the three men jumped up and came forward to greet us. There was a certain impulsiveness in his manner which reminded me of his mother. He was not nearly so sunburnt as the others, and that fact, coupled with a certain haggardness round the eyes, made him look older than his twenty-two years. He was clearly endeavouring to bear up under a severe mental strain.

He introduced his two companions, Dr. Ames, a capable looking man of thirty odd, with a touch of greying hair at the temples, and Mr. Harper, the secretary, a pleasant lean young man wearing the national insignia of horn-rimmed spectacles.

After a few minutes' desultory conversation the latter went out, and Dr. Tosswill followed him. We were left alone with Sir Guy and Dr. Ames.

"Please ask any questions you want to ask, Monsieur Poirot," said Willard. "We are utterly dumbfounded at this strange series of disasters, but it isn't—it can't be, anything but coincidence."

There was a nervousness about his manner which rather belied the words. I saw that Poirot was studying him keenly.

"Your heart is really in this work, Sir Guy?"

"Rather. No matter what happens, or what comes of it, the work is going on. Make up your mind to that."

Poirot wheeled round on the other.

"What have you to say to that, *monsieur le docteur?*"

"Well," drawled the doctor, "I'm not for quitting myself."

Poirot made one of those expressive grimaces of his.

"Then, *évidemment*, we must find out just how we stand. When did Mr. Schneider's death take place?"

"Three days ago."

"You are sure it was tetanus?"

"Dead sure."

"It couldn't have been a case of strychnine poisoning, for instance?"

"No, Monsieur Poirot. I see what you're getting at. But it was a clear case of tetanus."

"Did you not inject anti-serum?"

"Certainly we did," said the doctor dryly. "Every conceivable thing that could be done was tried."

"Had you the anti-serum with you?"

"No. We procured it from Cairo."

"Have there been any other cases of tetanus in the camp?"

"No, not one."

"Are you certain that the death of Mr. Bleibner was not due to tetanus?"

"Absolutely plumb certain. He had a scratch upon his thumb which became poisoned, and septicæmia set in. It sounds pretty much the same to a layman, I dare say, but the two things are entirely different."

"Then we have four deaths—all totally dissimilar, one heart failure, one blood poisoning, one suicide and one tetanus."

"Exactly, Monsieur Poirot."

"Are you certain that there is nothing which might link the four together?"

"I don't quite understand you?"

"I will put it plainly. Was any act committed by those four men which might seem to denote disrespect to the spirit of Men-her-Ra?"

The doctor gazed at Poirot in astonishment.

"You're talking through your hat, Monsieur Poirot. Surely

you've not been guyed into believing all that fool talk?"

"Absolute nonsense," muttered Willard angrily.

Poirot remained placidly immovable, blinking a little out of his green cat's eyes.

"So you do not believe it, *monsieur le docteur*?"

"No, sir, I do not," declared the doctor emphatically. "I am a scientific man, and I believe only what science teaches."

"Was there no science then in Ancient Egypt?" asked Poirot softly. He did not wait for a reply, and indeed Dr. Ames seemed rather at a loss for the moment. "No, no, do not answer me, but tell me this. What do the native workmen think?"

"I guess," said Dr. Ames, "that, where white folk lose their heads, natives aren't going to be far behind. I'll admit that they're getting what you might call scared—but they've no cause to be."

"I wonder," said Poirot non-committally.

Sir Guy leant forward.

"Surely," he cried incredulously, "you cannot believe in—oh, but the thing's absurd! You can know nothing of Ancient Egypt if you think that."

For answer Poirot produced a little book from his pocket—an ancient tattered volume. As he held it out I saw its title, *The Magic of the Egyptians and Chaldeans*. Then, wheeling round, he strode out of the tent. The doctor stared at me.

"What is his little idea?"

The phrase, so familiar on Poirot's lips, made me smile as it came from another.

"I don't know exactly," I confessed. "He's got some plan of exorcizing the evil spirits, I believe."

I went in search of Poirot, and found him talking to the lean-faced young man who had been the late Mr. Bleibner's secretary.

"No," Mr. Harper was saying, "I've only been six months with the expedition. Yes, I knew Mr. Bleibner's affairs pretty well."

"Can you recount to me anything concerning his nephew?"

"He turned up here one day, not a bad-looking fellow. I'd

never met him before, but some of the others had—Ames, I think, and Schneider. The old man wasn't at all pleased to see him. They were at it in no time, hammer and tongs. 'Not a cent,' the old man shouted. 'Not one cent now or when I'm dead. I intend to leave my money to the furtherance of my life's work. I've been talking it over with Mr. Schneider to-day.' And a bit more of the same. Young Bleibner lit out for Cairo right away."

"Was he in perfectly good health at the time?"

"The old man?"

"No, the young one."

"I believe he did mention there was something wrong with him. But it couldn't have been anything serious, or I should have remembered."

"One thing more, has Mr. Bleibner left a will?"

"So far as we know, he has not."

"Are you remaining with the expedition, Mr. Harper?"

"No, sir, I am not. I'm for New York as soon as I can square up things here. You may laugh if you like, but I'm not going to be this blasted old Men-her-Ra's next victim. He'll get me if I stop here."

The young man wiped the perspiration from his brow.

Poirot turned away. Over his shoulder he said with a peculiar smile:

"Remember, he got one of his victims in New York."

"Oh, hell!" said Mr. Harper forcibly.

"That young man is nervous," said Poirot thoughtfully. "He is on the edge, but absolutely on the edge."

I glanced at Poirot curiously, but his enigmatical smile told me nothing. In company with Sir Guy Willard and Dr. Tosswill we were taken round the excavations. The principal finds had been removed to Cairo, but some of the tomb furniture was extremely interesting. The enthusiasm of the young baronet was obvious, but I fancied that I detected a shade of nervousness in his manner as though he could not quite escape from the feeling of menace in the air. As we entered the tent which had been assigned to us, for a wash before joining the evening meal, a tall dark figure in white robes stood aside to let us pass with a graceful gesture and a murmured greeting in Arabic. Poirot stopped.

"You are Hassan, the late Sir John Willard's servant?"

"I served my Lord Sir John, now I serve his son." He took a step nearer to us and lowered his voice. "You are a wise one, they say, learned in dealing with evil spirits. Let the young master depart from here. There is evil in the air around us."

And with an abrupt gesture, not waiting for a reply, he strode away.

"Evil in the air," muttered Poirot. "Yes, I feel it."

Our meal was hardly a cheerful one. The floor was left to Dr. Tosswill, who discoursed at length upon Egyptian antiquities. Just as we were preparing to retire to rest, Sir Guy caught Poirot by the arm and pointed. A shadowy figure was moving amidst the tents. It was no human one: I recognized distinctly the dog-headed figure I had seen carved on the walls of the tomb.

My blood literally froze at the sight.

"*Mon Dieu!*" murmured Poirot, crossing himself vigorously. "Anubis, the jackal-headed, the god of departing souls."

"Some one is hoaxing us," cried Dr. Tosswill, rising indignantly to his feet.

"It went into your tent, Harper," muttered Sir Guy, his face dreadfully pale.

"No," said Poirot, shaking his head, "into that of the Dr. Ames."

The doctor stared at him incredulously; then, repeating Dr. Tosswill's words, he cried:

"Some one is hoaxing us. Come, we'll soon catch the fellow."

He dashed energetically in pursuit of the shadowy apparition. I followed him, but, search as we would, we could find no trace of any living soul having passed that way. We returned, somewhat disturbed in mind, to find Poirot taking energetic measures, in his own way, to ensure his personal safety. He was busily surrounding our tent with various diagrams and inscriptions which he was drawing in the sand. I recognized the five-pointed star or Pentagon many times repeated. As was his wont, Poirot was at the same time delivering an impromptu lecture on witchcraft and magic in general, White Magic as opposed to Black, with various references to the Ka and the Book of the Dead thrown in.

It appeared to excite the liveliest contempt in Dr. Tosswill, who drew me aside, literally snorting with rage.

"Balderdash, sir," he exclaimed angrily. "Pure balderdash. The man's an impostor. He doesn't know the difference between the superstitions of the Middle Ages and the beliefs of Ancient Egypt. Never have I heard such a hotch-potch of ignorance and credulity."

I calmed the excited expert, and joined Poirot in the tent. My little friend was beaming cheerfully.

"We can now sleep in peace," he declared happily. "And I can do with some sleep. My head, it aches abominably. Ah, for a good *tisane!*"

As though in answer to prayer, the flap of the tent was lifted and Hassan appeared, bearing a steaming cup which he offered to Poirot. It proved to be camomile tea, a beverage of which he is inordinately fond. Having thanked Hassan and refused his offer of another cup for myself, we were left alone once more. I stood at the door of the tent some time after undressing, looking out over the desert.

"A wonderful place," I said aloud, "and a wonderful work. I can feel the fascination. This desert life, this probing into the heart of a vanished civilization. Surely, Poirot, you, too, must feel the charm?"

I got no answer, and I turned, a little annoyed. My annoyance was quickly changed to concern. Poirot was lying back across the rude couch, his face horribly convulsed. Beside him was the empty cup. I rushed to his side, then dashed out and across the camp to Dr. Ames's tent.

"Dr. Ames!" I cried. "Come at once."

"What's the matter?" said the doctor, appearing in pyjamas.

"My friend. He's ill. Dying. The camomile tea. Don't let Hassan leave the camp."

Like a flash the doctor ran to our tent. Poirot was lying as I left him.

"Extraordinary," cried Ames. "Looks like a seizure—or—what did you say about something he drank?" He picked up the empty cup.

"Only I did not drink it!" said a placid voice.

We turned in amazement. Poirot was sitting up on the bed. He was smiling.

"No," he said gently. "I did not drink it. While my good friend Hastings was apostrophizing the night, I took the opportunity of pouring it, not down my throat, but into a little bottle. That little bottle will go to the analytical chemist. No"—as the doctor made a sudden movement—"as a sensible man, you will understand that violence will be of no avail. During Hastings' brief absence to fetch you, I have had time to put the bottle in safe keeping. Ah, quick, Hastings, hold him!"

I misunderstood Poirot's anxiety. Eager to save my friend, I flung myself in front of him. But the doctor's swift movement had another meaning. His hand went to his mouth, a smell of bitter almonds filled the air, and he swayed forward and fell.

"Another victim," said Poirot gravely, "but the last. Perhaps it is the best way. He has three deaths on his head."

"Dr. Ames?" I cried, stupefied. "But I thought you believed in some occult influence?"

"You misunderstood me, Hastings. What I meant was that I believe in the terrific force of superstition. Once get it firmly established that a series of deaths are supernatural, and you might almost stab a man in broad daylight, and it would still be put down to the curse, so strongly is the instinct of the supernatural implanted in the human race. I suspected from the first that a man was taking advantage of that instinct. The idea came to him, I imagine, with the death of Sir John Willard. A fury of superstition arose at once. As far as I could see, nobody could derive any particular profit from Sir John's death. Mr. Bleibner was a different case. He was a man of great wealth. The information I received from New York contained several suggestive points. To begin with, young Bleibner was reported to have said he had a good friend in Egypt from whom he could borrow. It was tacitly understood that he meant his uncle, but it seemed to me that in that case he would have said so outright. The words suggest some boon companion of his own. Another thing, he scraped up enough money to take him to Egypt, his uncle refused outright to advance him a penny, yet he was able to pay the return passage to New York. Some one must have lent him the money."

"All that was very thin," I objected.

"But there was more. Hastings, there occur often enough words spoken metaphorically which are taken literally. The opposite can happen too. In this case, words which were meant literally were taken metaphorically. Young Bleibner wrote plainly enough: 'I am a leper,' but nobody realized that he shot himself because he believed that he had contracted the dread disease of leprosy."

"What?" I ejaculated.

"It was the clever invention of a diabolical mind. Young Bleibner was suffering from some minor skin trouble, he had lived in the South Sea Islands, where the disease is common enough. Ames was a former friend of his, and a well-known medical man, he would never dream of doubting his word. When I arrived here, my suspicions were divided between Harper and Dr. Ames, but I soon realized that only the doctor could have perpetrated and concealed the crimes, and I learnt from Harper that he was previously acquainted with young Bleibner. Doubtless the latter at some time or another had made a will or had insured his life in favour of the doctor. The latter saw his chance of acquiring wealth. It was easy for him to inoculate Mr. Bleibner with the deadly germs.

Then the nephew, overcome with despair at the dread news his friend had conveyed to him, shot himself. Mr. Bleibner, whatever his intentions, had made no will. His fortune would pass to his nephew and from him to the doctor."

"And Mr. Schneider?"

"We cannot be sure. He knew young Bleibner too, remember, and may have suspected something, or, again, the doctor may have thought that a further death motiveless and purposeless would strengthen the coils of superstition. Furthermore, I will tell you an interesting psychological fact, Hastings. A murderer has always a strong desire to repeat his successful crime, the performance of it grows upon him. Hence my fears for young Willard. The figure of Anubis you saw to-night was Hassan, dressed up by my orders. I wanted to see if I could frighten the doctor. But it would take more than the supernatural to frighten him. I could see that he was not entirely taken in by my pretences of belief in the occult. The little comedy I played for him did not deceive him. I suspected that he would endeavour to make me the next victim. Ah, but in spite of *la mer maudite*, the heat abominable, and the annoyances of the sand, the little grey cells still functioned!"

Poirot proved to be perfectly right in his premises. Young Bleibner, some years ago, in a fit of drunken merriment, had made a jocular will, leaving "my cigarette case you admire so much and everything else of which I die possessed which will be principally debts to my good friend Robert Ames who once saved my life from drowning."

The case was hushed up as far as possible, and, to this day, people talk of the remarkable series of deaths in connection with the Tomb of Men-her-Ra as a triumphal proof of the vengeance of a bygone king upon the desecrators of his tomb—a belief which, as Poirot pointed out to me, is contrary to all Egyptian belief and thought.

SEVEN
The Jewel Robbery at the
Grand Metropolitan

P oirot," I said, "a change of air would do you good."

"You think so, *mon ami*?"

"I am sure of it."

"Eh—eh?" said my friend, smiling. "It is all arranged, then?"
"You will come?"

"Where do you propose to take me?"

"Brighton. As a matter of fact, a friend of mine in the City put me on to a very good thing, and—well, I have money to burn, as the saying goes. I think a week-end at the *Grand Metropolitan* would do us all the good in the world."

"Thank you, I accept most gratefully. You have the good heart to think of an old man. And the good heart, it is in the end worth all the little grey cells. Yes, yes, I who speak to you am in danger of forgetting that sometimes."

I did not quite relish the implication. I fancy that Poirot is sometimes a little inclined to underestimate my mental capacities. But his pleasure was so evident that I put my slight annoyance aside.

"Then, that's all right," I said hastily.

Saturday evening saw us dining at the *Grand Metropolitan* in the midst of a gay throng. All the world and his wife seemed to be at Brighton. The dresses were marvellous, and the jewels—worn sometimes with more love of display than good taste—were something magnificent.

"*Hein*, it is a sight this!" murmured Poirot. "This is the home of the Profiteer, is it not so, Hastings?"

"Supposed to be," I replied. "But we'll hope they aren't all tarred with the Profiteering brush."

Poirot gazed round him placidly.

"The sight of so many jewels makes me wish I had turned my brains to crime, instead of to its detection. What a magnificent opportunity for some thief of distinction! Regard, Hastings, that stout woman by the pillar. She is, as you would say, plastered with gems."

I followed his eyes.

"Why," I exclaimed, "it's Mrs. Opalsen."

"You know her?"

"Slightly. Her husband is a rich stockbroker who made a fortune in the recent Oil boom."

After dinner we ran across the Opalsens in the lounge, and I introduced Poirot to them. We chatted for a few minutes, and ended by having our coffee together.

Poirot said a few words in praise of some of the costlier gems displayed on the lady's ample bosom, and she brightened up at once.

"It's a perfect hobby of mine, Mr. Poirot. I just *love* jewellery. Ed knows my weakness, and every time things go well he brings me something new. You are interested in precious stones?"

"I have had a good deal to do with them one time and another, madame. My profession has brought me into contact with some of the most famous jewels in the world."

He went on to narrate, with discreet pseudonyms, the story of the historic jewels of a reigning house, and Mrs. Opalsen listened with bated breath.

"There now!" she exclaimed, as he ended. "If it isn't just like a play! You know, I've got some pearls of my own that have a history attached to them. I believe it's supposed to be one of the finest necklaces in the world—the pearls are so beautifully matched and so perfect in colour. I declare I really must run up and get it!"

"Oh, madame," protested Poirot, "you are too amiable. Pray do not derange yourself!"

"Oh, but I'd like to show it to you."

The buxom dame waddled across to the lift briskly enough. Her husband, who had been talking to me, looked at Poirot inquiringly.

"Madame your wife is so amiable as to insist on showing me her pearl necklace," explained the latter.

"Oh, the pearls!" Opalsen smiled in a satisfied fashion. "Well, they *are* worth seeing. Cost a pretty penny too! Still, the money's there all right; I could get what I paid for them any day—perhaps more. May have to, too, if things go on as they are now. Money's confoundedly tight in the City. All this infernal E.P.D." He rambled on, launching into technicalities where I could not follow him.

He was interrupted by a small page-boy who approached and murmured something in his ear.

"Eh—what? I'll come at once. Not taken ill, is she? Excuse me, gentlemen."

He left us abruptly. Poirot leaned back and lit one of his tiny Russian cigarettes. Then, carefully and meticulously, he arranged the empty coffee-cups in a neat row, and beamed happily on the result.

The minutes passed. The Opalsens did not return.

"Curious," I remarked, at length. "I wonder when they will come back."

Poirot watched the ascending spirals of smoke, and then said thoughtfully:

"They will not come back."

"Why?"

"Because, my friend, something has happened."

"What sort of thing? How do you know?" I asked curiously.
Poirot smiled.

"A few moments ago the manager came hurriedly out of his office and ran upstairs. He was much agitated. The lift-boy is deep in talk with one of the pages. The lift-bell has rung three times, but he heeds it not. Thirdly, even the waiters are *distrait*; and to make a waiter *distrait*——" Poirot shook his head with an air of finality. "The affair must indeed be of the first magnitude. Ah, it is as I thought! Here come the police."

Two men had just entered the hotel—one in uniform, the other in plain clothes. They spoke to a page, and were immediately ushered upstairs. A few minutes later, the same boy descended and came up to where we were sitting.

"Mr. Opalsen's compliments, and would you step upstairs."

Poirot sprang nimbly to his feet. One would have said that he awaited the summons. I followed with no less alacrity.

The Opalsens' apartments were situated on the first floor. After knocking on the door, the page-boy retired, and we answered the summons, "Come in!" A strange scene met our eyes. The room was Mrs. Opalsen's bedroom, and in the centre of it, lying back in an arm-chair, was the lady herself, weeping violently. She presented an extraordinary spectacle, with the tears making great furrows in the powder with which her complexion was liberally coated. Mr. Opalsen was striding up and down angrily. The two police officials stood in the middle of the room, one with a notebook in hand. An hotel chambermaid, looking frightened to death, stood by the fire-place; and on the other side of the room a Frenchwoman, obviously Mrs. Opalsen's maid, was weeping and wringing her hands, with an intensity of grief that rivalled that of her mistress.

Into this pandemonium stepped Poirot, neat and smiling. Immediately, with an energy surprising in one of her bulk, Mrs. Opalsen sprang from her chair towards him.

"There now; Ed may say what he likes, but I believe in luck, I do. It was fated I should meet you the way I did this evening, and I've a feeling that if you can't get my pearls back for me nobody can."

"Calm yourself, I pray of you, madame." Poirot patted her hand soothingly. "Reassure yourself. All will be well. Hercule Poirot will aid you!"

Mr. Opalsen turned to the police inspector.

"There will be no objection to my—er—calling in this gentleman, I suppose?"

"None at all, sir," replied the man civilly, but with complete indifference. "Perhaps now your lady's feeling better she'll just let us have the facts?"

Mrs. Opalsen looked helplessly at Poirot. He led her back to her chair.

"Seat yourself, madame, and recount to us the whole history without agitating yourself."

Thus abjured, Mrs. Opalsen dried her eyes gingerly, and began.

"I came upstairs after dinner to fetch my pearls for Mr. Poirot here to see. The chambermaid and Célestine were both in the room as usual——"

"Excuse me, madame, but what do you mean by 'as usual'?"

Mr. Opalsen explained.

"I make it a rule that no one is to come into this room unless Célestine, the maid, is there also. The chambermaid does the room in the morning while Célestine is present, and comes in after dinner to turn down the beds under the same conditions; otherwise she never enters the room."

"Well, as I was saying," continued Mrs. Opalsen, "I came up. I went to the drawer here,"—she indicated the bottom right-hand drawer of the knee-hole dressing-table—"took out my jewel-case and unlocked it. It seemed quite as usual—but the pearls were not there!"

The inspector had been busy with his notebook. "When had

you last seen them?" he asked.

"They were there when I went down to dinner."

"You are sure?"

"Quite sure. I was uncertain whether to wear them or not, but in the end I decided on the emeralds, and put them back in the jewel-case."

"Who locked up the jewel-case?"

"I did. I wear the key on a chain round my neck." She held it up as she spoke.

The inspector examined it, and shrugged his shoulders.

"The thief must have had a duplicate key. No difficult matter. The lock is quite a simple one. What did you do after you'd locked the jewel-case?"

"I put it back in the bottom drawer where I always keep it."

"You didn't lock the drawer?"

"No, I never do. My maid remains in the room till I come up, so there's no need."

The inspector's face grew graver.

"Am I to understand that the jewels were there when you went down to dinner, and that since then *the maid has not left the room?*"

Suddenly, as though the horror of her own situation for the first time burst upon her, Célestine uttered a piercing shriek, and, flinging herself upon Poirot, poured out a torrent of incoherent French.

The suggestion was infamous! That she should be suspected of robbing Madame! The police were well known to be of a stupidity incredible! But Monsieur, who was a Frenchman—

"A Belgian," interjected Poirot, but Célestine paid no attention to the correction.

Monsieur would not stand by and see her falsely accused, while that infamous chambermaid was allowed to go scot-free. She had never liked her—a bold, red-faced thing—a born thief. She had said from the first that she was not honest. And had kept a sharp watch over her too, when she was doing Madame's room!

Let those idiots of policemen search her, and if they did not find Madame's pearls on her it would be very surprising!

Although this harangue was uttered in rapid and virulent French, Célestine had interlarded it with a wealth of gesture, and the chambermaid realized at least a part of her meaning. She reddened angrily.

"If that foreign woman's saying I took the pearls, it's a lie!" she declared heatedly. "I never so much as saw them."

"Search her!" screamed the other. "You will find it is as I say."

"You're a liar—do you hear?" said the chambermaid, advancing upon her. "Stole 'em yourself, and want to put it on me. Why, I was only in the room about three minutes before the lady come up, and then you were sitting here the whole time, as you always do, like a cat watching a mouse."

The inspector looked across inquiringly at Célestine. "Is that true? Didn't you leave the room at all?"

"I did not actually leave her alone," admitted Célestine reluctantly, "but I went into my own room through the door here twice—once to fetch a reel of cotton, and once for my scissors. She must have done it then."

"You wasn't gone a minute," retorted the chambermaid angrily. "Just popped out and in again. I'd be glad if the police *would* search me. *I've nothing to be afraid of.*"

At this moment there was a tap at the door. The inspector went to it. His face brightened when he saw who it was.

"Ah!" he said. "That's rather fortunate. I sent for one of our female searchers, and she's just arrived. Perhaps if you wouldn't mind going into the room next door."

He looked at the chambermaid, who stepped across the threshold with a toss of her head, the searcher following her closely.

The French girl had sunk sobbing into a chair. Poirot was looking round the room, the main features of which I have made clear by a sketch.

"Where does that door lead?" he inquired, nodding his head towards the one by the window.

"Into the next apartment, I believe," said the inspector. "It's bolted, anyway, on this side."

Poirot walked across to it, tried it, then drew back the bolt and tried it again.

"And on the other side as well," he remarked. "Well, that seems to rule out that."

He walked over to the windows, examining each of them in turn.

"And again—nothing. Not even a balcony outside."

"Even if there were," said the inspector impatiently, "I don't see how that would help us, if the maid never left the room."

"*Évidemment*," said Poirot, not disconcerted. "As Mademoiselle is positive she did not leave the room——"

He was interrupted by the reappearance of the chambermaid and the police searcher.

"Nothing," said the latter laconically.

"I should hope not, indeed," said the chambermaid virtuously. "And that French hussy ought to be ashamed of herself taking away an honest girl's character!"

"There, there, my girl; that's all right," said the inspector, opening the door. "Nobody suspects you. You go along and get on with your work."

The chambermaid went unwillingly.

"Going to search *her?*" she demanded, pointing at Célestine.

"Yes, yes!" He shut the door on her and turned the key.

Célestine accompanied the searcher into the small room in her turn. A few minutes later she also returned. Nothing had been found on her.

The inspector's face grew graver.

"I'm afraid I'll have to ask you to come along with me all the same, miss." He turned to Mrs. Opalsen. "I'm sorry, madam, but all the evidence points that way. If she's not got them on her, they're hidden somewhere about the room."

Célestine uttered a piercing shriek, and clung to Poirot's arm. The latter bent and whispered something in the girl's ear. She looked up at him doubtfully.

"*Si, si, mon enfant*—I assure you it is better not to resist." Then he turned to the inspector. "You permit, monsieur? A little experiment—purely for my own satisfaction."

"Depends on what it is," replied the police officer non-committally.

Poirot addressed Célestine once more.

"You have told us that you went into your room to fetch a reel of cotton. Whereabouts was it?"

"On the top of the chest of drawers, monsieur."

"And the scissors?"

"They also."

"Would it be troubling you too much, mademoiselle, to ask you to repeat those two actions? You were sitting here with your work, you say?"

Célestine sat down, and then, at a sign from Poirot, rose, passed into the adjoining room, took up an object from the chest of drawers, and returned.

Poirot divided his attention between her movements and a large turnip of a watch which he held in the palm of his hand.

"Again, if you please, mademoiselle."

At the conclusion of the second performance, he made a note in his pocket-book, and returned the watch to his pocket.

"Thank you, mademoiselle. And you, monsieur,"—he bowed to the inspector—"for your courtesy."

The inspector seemed somewhat entertained by this excessive politeness. Célestine departed in a flood of tears, accompanied by the woman and the plain-clothes official.

Then, with a brief apology to Mrs. Opalsen, the inspector set to work to ransack the room. He pulled out drawers, opened cupboards, completely unmade the bed, and tapped the floor. Mr. Opalsen looked on sceptically.

"You really think you will find them?"

"Yes, sir. It stands to reason. She hadn't time to take them out of the room. The lady's discovering the robbery so soon upset her plans. No, they're here right enough. One of the two must have hidden them—and it's very unlikely for the chambermaid to have done so."

"More than unlikely—impossible!" said Poirot quietly.

"Eh?" The inspector stared.

Poirot smiled modestly.

"I will demonstrate. Hastings, my good friend, take my watch in your hand—with care. It is a family heirloom! Just now I timed Mademoiselle's movements—her first absence from the room was of twelve seconds, her second of fifteen. Now observe my actions. Madame will have the kindness to give me the key of the jewel-case. I thank you. My friend Hastings will have the kindness to say 'Go!'"

"Go!" I said.

With almost incredible swiftness, Poirot wrenched open the drawer of the dressing-table, extracted the jewel-case, fitted the key in the lock, opened the case, selected a piece of jewellery, shut and locked the case, and returned it to the drawer, which he pushed to again. His movements were like lightning.

"Well, *mon ami*?" he demanded of me breathlessly.

"Forty-six seconds," I replied.

"You see?" He looked round. "There would not have been time for the chambermaid even to take the necklace out, far less hide it."

"Then that settles it on the maid," said the inspector with satisfaction, and returned to his search. He passed into the maid's bedroom next door.

Poirot was frowning thoughtfully. Suddenly he shot a question at Mr. Opalsen.

"This necklace—it was, without doubt, insured?"

Mr. Opalsen looked a trifle surprised at the question.

"Yes," he said hesitatingly, "that is so."

"But what does that matter?" broke in Mrs. Opalsen tearfully. "It's my necklace I want. It was unique. No money could be the same."

"I comprehend, madame," said Poirot soothingly. "I comprehend perfectly. To *la femme* sentiment is everything—is it not so? But monsieur, who has not the so fine susceptibility, will doubtless find some slight consolation in the fact."

"Of course, of course," said Mr. Opalsen rather uncertainly. "Still——"

He was interrupted by a shout of triumph from the inspector. He came in dangling something from his fingers.

With a cry, Mrs. Opalsen heaved herself up from her chair. She was a changed woman.

"Oh, oh, my necklace!"

She clasped it to her breast with both hands. We crowded round.

"Where was it?" demanded Opalsen.

"Maid's bed. In among the springs of the wire mattress. She must have stolen it and hidden it there before the chambermaid arrived on the scene."

"You permit, madame?" said Poirot gently. He took the

necklace from her and examined it closely; then handed it back with a bow.

"I'm afraid, madam, you'll have to hand it over to us for the time being," said the inspector. "We shall want it for the charge. But it shall be returned to you as soon as possible."

Mr. Opalsen frowned.

"Is that necessary?"

"I'm afraid so, sir. Just a formality."

"Oh, let him take it, Ed!" cried his wife. "I'd feel safer if he did. I shouldn't sleep a wink thinking some one else might try and get hold of it. That wretched girl! And I would never have believed it of her."

"There, there, my dear, don't take on so."

I felt a gentle pressure on my arm. It was Poirot.

"Shall we slip away, my friend? I think our services are no longer needed."

Once outside, however, he hesitated, and then, much to my surprise, he remarked:

"I should rather like to see the room next door."

The door was not locked, and we entered. The room, which was a large double one, was unoccupied. Dust lay about rather noticeably, and my sensitive friend gave a characteristic grimace as he ran his finger round a rectangular mark on a table near the window.

"The *service* leaves to be desired," he observed dryly.

He was staring thoughtfully out of the window, and seemed to have fallen into a brown study.

"Well?" I demanded impatiently. "What did we come in here for?"

He started.

"*Je vous demande pardon, mon ami.* I wished to see if the door was really bolted on this side also."

"Well," I said, glancing at the door which communicated with the room we had just left, "it *is* bolted."

Poirot nodded. He still seemed to be thinking.

"And, anyway," I continued, "what does it matter? The case is over. I wish you'd had more chance of distinguishing yourself. But it was the kind of case that even a stiff-backed idiot like that inspector couldn't go wrong over."

Poirot shook his head.

"The case is not over, my friend. It will not be over until we find out who stole the pearls."

"But the maid did!"

"Why do you say that?"

"Why," I stammered, "they were found—actually in her mattress."

"Ta, ta, ta!" said Poirot impatiently. "Those were not the pearls."

"What?"

"Imitation, *mon ami*."

The statement took my breath away. Poirot was smiling placidly.

"The good inspector obviously knows nothing of jewels. But presently there will be a fine hullabaloo!"

"Come!" I cried, dragging at his arm.

"Where?"

"We must tell the Opalsens at once."

"I think not."

"But that poor woman——"

"*Eh bien*; that poor woman, as you call her, will have a much better night believing the jewels to be safe."

"But the thief may escape with them!"

"As usual, my friend, you speak without reflection. How do you know that the pearls Mrs. Opalsen locked up so carefully to-night were not the false ones, and that the real robbery did not take place at a much earlier date?"

"Oh!" I said, bewildered.

"Exactly," said Poirot, beaming. "We start again."

He led the way out of the room, paused a moment as though considering, and then walked down to the end of the corridor, stopping outside the small den where the chambermaids and valets of the respective floors congregated. Our particular chambermaid appeared to be holding a small court there, and to be retailing her late experiences to an appreciative audience. She stopped in the middle of a sentence. Poirot bowed with his usual politeness.

"Excuse that I derange you, but I shall be obliged if you will unlock for me the door of Mr. Opalsen's room."

The woman rose willingly, and we accompanied her down the passage again. Mr. Opalsen's room was on the other side of the corridor, its door facing that of his wife's room. The chambermaid unlocked it with her pass-key, and we entered.

As she was about to depart Poirot detained her.

"One moment; have you ever seen among the effects of Mr. Opalsen a card like this?"

He held out a plain white card, rather highly glazed and uncommon in appearance. The maid took it and scrutinized it carefully.

"No, sir, I can't say I have. But, anyway, the valet has most to do with the gentlemen's rooms."

"I see. Thank you."

Poirot took back the card. The woman departed. Poirot appeared to reflect a little. Then he gave a short, sharp nod of the head.

"Ring the bell, I pray of you, Hastings. Three times, for the valet."

I obeyed, devoured with curiosity. Meanwhile Poirot had emptied the waste-paper-basket on the floor, and was swiftly going through its contents.

In a few moments the valet answered the bell. To him Poirot put the same question, and handed him the card to examine. But the response was the same. The valet had never seen a card of that particular quality among Mr. Opalsen's belongings. Poirot thanked him, and he withdrew, somewhat unwillingly, with an inquisitive glance at the overturned waste-paper-basket and the litter on the floor. He could hardly have helped overhearing Poirot's thoughtful remark as he bundled the torn papers back again:

"And the necklace was heavily insured. . . ."

"Poirot," I cried, "I see——"

"You see nothing, my friend," he replied quickly. "As usual, nothing at all! It is incredible—but there it is. Let us return to our own apartments."

We did so in silence. Once there, to my intense surprise, Poirot effected a rapid change of clothing.

"I go to London to-night," he explained. "It is imperative."

"What?"

"Absolutely. The real work, that of the brain (ah, those brave little grey cells), it is done. I go to seek the confirmation. I shall find it! Impossible to deceive Hercule Poirot!"

"You'll come a cropper one of these days," I observed, rather disgusted by his vanity.

"Do not be enraged, I beg of you, *mon ami*. I count on you to do me a service—of your friendship."

"Of course," I said eagerly, rather ashamed of my moroseness. "What is it?"

"The sleeve of my coat that I have taken off—will you brush it? See you, a little white powder has clung to it. You without doubt observed me run my finger round the drawer of the dressing-table?"

"No, I didn't."

"You should observe my actions, my friend. Thus I obtained the powder on my finger, and, being a little over-excited, I rubbed it on my sleeve; an action without method which I deplore—false to all my principles."

"But what was the powder?" I asked, not particularly interested in Poirot's principles.

"Not the poison of the Borgias," replied Poirot, with a twinkle.

"I see your imagination mounting. I should say it was French chalk."

"French chalk?"

"Yes, cabinet-makers use it to make drawers run smoothly."

I laughed.

"You old sinner! I thought you were working up to something exciting."

"Au revoir, my friend. I save myself. I fly!"

The door shut behind him. With a smile, half of derision, half of affection, I picked up the coat, and stretched out my hand for the clothes-brush.

* * *

The next morning, hearing nothing from Poirot, I went out for a stroll, met some old friends, and lunched with them at their hotel. In the afternoon we went for a spin. A punctured tyre delayed us, and it was past eight when I got back to the *Grand Metropolitan*.

The first sight that met my eyes was Poirot, looking even more diminutive than usual, sandwiched between the Opalsens, beaming in a state of placid satisfaction.

"*Mon ami* Hastings!" he cried, and sprang to meet me. "Embrace me, my friend; all has marched to a marvel!"

Luckily, the embrace was merely figurative—not a thing one is always sure of with Poirot.

"Do you mean——" I began.

"Just wonderful, I call it!" said Mrs. Opalsen, smiling all over her fat face. "Didn't I tell you, Ed, that if he couldn't get back my pearls nobody would?"

"You did, my dear, you did. And you were right."

I looked helplessly at Poirot, and he answered the glance.

"My friend Hastings is, as you say in England, all at the

seaside. Seat yourself, and I will recount to you all the affair that has so happily ended."

"Ended?"

"But yes. They are arrested."

"Who are arrested?"

"The chambermaid and the valet, *parbleu*! You did not suspect? Not with my parting hint about the French chalk?"

"You said cabinet-makers used it."

"Certainly they do—to make drawers slide easily. Somebody wanted that drawer to slide in and out without any noise. Who could that be? Obviously, only the chambermaid. The plan was so ingenious that it did not at once leap to the eye—not even to the eye of Hercule Poirot.

"Listen, this was how it was done. The valet was in the empty room next door, waiting. The French maid leaves the room. Quick as a flash the chambermaid whips open the drawer, takes out the jewel-case, and, slipping back the bolt, passes it through the door. The valet opens it at his leisure with the duplicate key with which he has provided himself, extracts the necklace, and waits his time. Célestine leaves the room again, and—pst!—in a flash the case is passed back again and replaced in the drawer.

"Madame arrives, the theft is discovered. The chambermaid demands to be searched, with a good deal of righteous indignation, and leaves the room without a stain on her character. The imitation necklace with which they have provided themselves has been concealed in the French girl's bed that morning by the chambermaid—a master stroke, *ça!*"

"But what did you go to London for?"

"You remember the card?"

"Certainly. It puzzled me—and puzzles me still. I thought——"

I hesitated delicately, glancing at Mr. Opalsen.

Poirot laughed heartily.

"*Une blague!* For the benefit of the valet. The card was one with a specially prepared surface—for finger-prints. I went straight to Scotland Yard, asked for our old friend Inspector Japp, and laid the facts before him. As I had suspected, the finger-prints proved to be those of two well-known jewel thieves who have been 'wanted' for some time. Japp came down with me, the thieves were arrested, and the necklace was discovered in the valet's possession. A clever pair, but they failed in *method*. Have I not told you, Hastings, at least thirty-six times, that without method———"

"At least thirty-six thousand times!" I interrupted. "But where did their 'method' break down?"

"*Mon ami*, it is a good plan to take a place as chambermaid or valet—but you must not shirk your work. They left an empty room undusted; and therefore, when the man put down the jewel-case on the little table near the communicating door, it left a square mark———"

"I remember," I cried.

"Before, I was undecided. Then—I *knew*!" There was a moment's silence.

"And I've got my pearls," said Mrs. Opalsen as a sort of Greek chorus.

"Well," I said, "I'd better have some dinner." Poirot accompanied me.

"This ought to mean kudos for you," I observed.

"*Pas du tout*," replied Poirot tranquilly. "Japp and the local inspector will divide the credit between them. But"—he tapped his pocket—"I have a cheque here, from Mr. Opalsen, and, how say you, my friend? This week-end has not gone according to plan. Shall we return here next week-end—at my expense this time?"

114

EIGHT
The Kidnapped Prime Minister

N ow that war and the problems of war are things of the past, I think I may safely venture to reveal to the world the part which my friend Poirot played in a moment of national crisis. The secret has been well guarded. Not a whisper of it reached the Press. But, now that the need for secrecy has gone by, I feel it is only just that England should know the debt it owes to my quaint little friend, whose marvellous brain so ably averted a great catastrophe.

One evening after dinner—I will not particularize the date; it suffices to say that it was at the time when "Peace by negotiation" was the parrot-cry of England's enemies—my friend and I were sitting in his rooms. After being invalided out of the Army I had been given a recruiting job, and it had become my custom to drop in on Poirot in the evenings after dinner and talk with him of any cases of interest that he might have on hand.

I was attempting to discuss with him the sensational news of that day—no less than an attempted assassination of Mr. David MacAdam, England's Prime Minister. The account in the papers had evidently been carefully censored. No details were given, save that the Prime Minister had had a marvellous escape, the bullet just grazing his cheek.

I considered that our police must have been shamefully care- less for such an outrage to be possible. I could well understand that the German agents in England would be willing to risk much for such an achievement. "Fighting Mac," as his own party had nicknamed him, had strenuously and unequivocally combated the Pacifist influence which was becoming so prevalent.

He was more than England's Prime Minister—he *was* England; and to have removed him from his sphere of influence would have been a crushing and paralysing blow to Britain.

Poirot was busy mopping a grey suit with a minute sponge. Never was there a dandy such as Hercule Poirot. Neatness and order were his passion. Now, with the odour of benzine filling the air, he was quite unable to give me his full attention.

"In a little minute I am with you, my friend. I have all but finished. The spot of grease—he is not good—I remove him—so!" He waved his sponge.

I smiled as I lit another cigarette.

"Anything interesting on?" I inquired, after a minute or two.

"I assist a—how do you call it?—'charlady' to find her husband. A difficult affair, needing the tact. For I have a little idea that when he is found he will not be pleased. What would you? For my part, I sympathize with him. He was a man of discrimination to lose himself."

I laughed.

"At last! The spot of grease, he is gone! I am at your disposal."

"I was asking you what you thought of this attempt to assassinate MacAdam?"

"*Enfantillage!*" replied Poirot promptly. "One can hardly take it seriously. To fire with the rifle—never does it succeed. It is a device of the past."

"It was very near succeeding this time," I reminded him.

Poirot shook his head impatiently. He was about to reply when the landlady thrust her head round the door and informed him that there were two gentlemen below who wanted to see him.

"They won't give their names, sir, but they says as it's very important."

"Let them mount," said Poirot, carefully folding his grey trousers.

In a few minutes the two visitors were ushered in, and my heart gave a leap as in the foremost I recognized no less a personage than Lord Estair, Leader of the House of Commons; whilst his companion, Mr. Bernard Dodge, was also a member of the War Cabinet, and, as I knew, a close personal friend of the Prime Minister.

"Monsieur Poirot?" said Lord Estair interrogatively. My friend bowed. The great man looked at me and hesitated. "My business is private."

"You may speak freely before Captain Hastings," said my friend, nodding to me to remain. "He has not all the gifts, no! But I answer for his discretion."

Lord Estair still hesitated, but Mr. Dodge broke in abruptly:

"Oh, come on—don't let's beat about the bush! As far as I can see, the whole of England will know the hole we're in soon enough. Time's everything."

"Pray be seated, messieurs," said Poirot politely. "Will you take the big chair, *milord?*"

Lord Estair started slightly. "You know me?"

Poirot smiled. "Certainly. I read the little papers with the pictures. How should I not know you?"

"Monsieur Poirot, I have come to consult you upon a matter of the most vital urgency. I must ask for absolute secrecy."

"You have the word of Hercule Poirot—I can say no more!" said my friend grandiloquently.

"It concerns the Prime Minister. We are in grave trouble."

"We're up a tree!" interposed Mr. Dodge.

"The injury is serious, then?" I asked.

"What injury?"

"The bullet wound."

"Oh, that!" cried Mr. Dodge contemptuously. "That's old history."

"As my colleague says," continued Lord Estair, "that affair is over and done with. Luckily, it failed. I wished I could say as much for the second attempt."

"There has been a second attempt, then?"

"Yes, though not of the same nature. Monsieur Poirot, the Prime Minister has disappeared."

"What?"

"He has been kidnapped!"

"Impossible!" I cried, stupefied.

Poirot threw a withering glance at me, which I knew enjoined me to keep my mouth shut.

"Unfortunately, impossible as it seems, it is only too true," continued his lordship.

Poirot looked at Mr. Dodge. "You said just now, monsieur, that time was everything. What did you mean by that?"

The two men exchanged glances, and then Lord Estair said:

"You have heard, Monsieur Poirot, of the approaching Allied Conference?"

My friend nodded.

"For obvious reasons, no details have been given of when and where it is to take place. But, although it has been kept out of the newspapers, the date is, of course, widely known in diplomatic circles. The Conference is to be held to-morrow—Thursday— evening at Versailles. Now you perceive the terrible gravity of the situation. I will not conceal from you that the Prime Minister's presence at the Conference is a vital necessity. The Pacifist propaganda, started and maintained by the German agents in our midst, has been very active. It is the universal opinion that the turning point of the Conference will be the strong personality of the Prime Minister. His absence may have the most serious results—possibly a premature and disastrous peace. And we have no one who can be sent in his place. He alone can represent England."

Poirot's face had grown very grave. "Then you regard the kidnapping of the Prime Minister as a direct attempt to prevent his being present at the Conference?"

"Most certainly I do. He was actually on his way to France at the time."

"And the Conference is to be held?"

"At nine o'clock to-morrow night."

Poirot drew an enormous watch from his pocket.

"It is now a quarter to nine."

"Twenty-four hours," said Mr. Dodge thoughtfully.

"And a quarter," amended Poirot. "Do not forget the quarter, monsieur—it may come in useful. Now for the details—the abduction, did it take place in England or in France?"

"In France. Mr. MacAdam crossed to France this morning. He was to stay to-night as the guest of the Commander-in-Chief, proceeding to-morrow to Paris. He was conveyed across the Channel by destroyer. At Boulogne he was met by a car from General Headquarters and one of the Commander-in-Chief's A.D.C.s."

"*Eh bien?*"

"Well, they started from Boulogne—but they never arrived."

"What?"

"Monsieur Poirot, it was a bogus car and a bogus A.D.C. The real car was found in a side road, with the chauffeur and the A.D.C. neatly gagged and bound."

"And the bogus car?"

"Is still at large."

Poirot made a gesture of impatience. "Incredible! Surely it cannot escape attention for long?"

"So we thought. It seemed merely a question of searching thoroughly. That part of France is under Military Law. We were convinced that the car could not go long unnoticed. The French police and our own Scotland Yard men, and the military are straining every nerve. It is, as you say, incredible—but nothing has been discovered!"

At that moment a tap came at the door, and a young officer entered with a heavily sealed envelope which he handed to Lord Estair.

"Just through from France, sir. I brought it on here, as you directed."

The Minister tore it open eagerly, and uttered an exclamation. The officer withdrew.

"Here is news at last! This telegram has just been decoded. They have found the second car, also the secretary, Daniels, chloroformed, gagged, and bound, in an abandoned farm near C——. He remembers nothing, except something being pressed against his mouth and nose from behind, and struggling to free himself. The police are satisfied as to the genuineness of his statement."

"And they have found nothing else?"

"No."

"Not the Prime Minister's dead body? Then, there is hope. But it is strange. Why, after trying to shoot him this morning, are they now taking so much trouble to keep him alive?"

Dodge shook his head. "One thing's quite certain. They're determined at all costs to prevent his attending the Conference."

"If it is humanly possible, the Prime Minister shall be there. God grant it is not too late. Now, messieurs, recount to me everything—from the beginning. I must know about this shooting affair as well."

"Last night, the Prime Minister, accompanied by one of his secretaries, Captain Daniels——"

"The same who accompanied him to France?"

"Yes. As I was saying, they motored down to Windsor, where the Prime Minister was granted an Audience. Early this morning, he returned to town, and it was on the way that the attempted assassination took place."

"One moment, if you please. Who is this Captain Daniels? You have his dossier?"

Lord Estair smiled. "I thought you would ask me that. We do not know very much of him. He is of no particular family. He has served in the English Army, and is an extremely able secretary, being an exceptionally fine linguist. I believe he speaks seven languages. It is for that reason that the Prime Minister chose him to accompany him to France."

"Has he any relatives in England?"

"Two aunts. A Mrs. Everard, who lives at Hampstead, and a Miss Daniels, who lives near Ascot."

"Ascot? That is near to Windsor, is it not?"

"That point has not been overlooked. But it has led to nothing."

"You regard the Capitaine Daniels, then, as above suspicion?"

A shade of bitterness crept into Lord Estair's voice, as he replied:

"No, Monsieur Poirot. In these days, I should hesitate before I pronounced *anyone* above suspicion."

"*Très bien.* Now I understand, *milord,* that the Prime Minister would, as a matter of course, be under vigilant police protection, which ought to render any assault upon him an impossibility?"

Lord Estair bowed his head. "That is so. The Prime Minister's car was closely followed by another car containing detectives in plain clothes. Mr. MacAdam knew nothing of these precautions. He is personally a most fearless man, and would be inclined to sweep them away arbitrarily. But, naturally, the police make their own arrangements. In fact, the Premier's chauffeur, O'Murphy, is a C.I.D. man."

"O'Murphy? That is a name of Ireland, is it not so?"

"Yes, he is an Irishman."

"From what part of Ireland?"

"County Clare, I believe."

"*Tiens!* But proceed, *milord.*"

"The Premier started for London. The car was a closed one. He and Captain Daniels sat inside. The second car followed as usual. But, unluckily, for some unknown reason, the Prime Minister's car deviated from the main road——"

"At a point where the road curves?" interrupted Poirot.

"Yes—but how did you know?"

"Oh, *c'est évident!* Continue!"

"For some unknown reason," continued Lord Estair, "the Premier's car left the main road. The police car, unaware of the deviation, continued to keep to the high road. At a short distance down the unfrequented lane, the Prime Minister's car was suddenly held up by a band of masked men. The chauffeur——"

"That brave O'Murphy!" murmured Poirot thoughtfully.

"The chauffeur, momentarily taken aback, jammed on the brakes. The Prime Minister put his head out of the window. Instantly a shot rang out—then another. The first one grazed his cheek, the second, fortunately, went wide. The chauffeur, now realizing the danger, instantly forged straight ahead, scattering the band of men."

"A near escape," I ejaculated, with a shiver.

"Mr. MacAdam refused to make any fuss over the slight wound he had received. He declared it was only a scratch. He stopped at a local cottage hospital, where it was dressed and bound up—he did not, of course, reveal his identity. He then drove, as per schedule, straight to Charing Cross, where a special train for Dover was awaiting him, and, after a brief account of what had happened had been given to the anxious police by Captain Daniels, he duly departed for France. At Dover, he went on board the waiting destroyer. At Boulogne, as you know, the bogus car was waiting for him, carrying the Union Jack, and correct in every detail."

"That is all you have to tell me?"

"Yes."

"There is no other circumstance that you have omitted, milord?"

"Well, there is one rather peculiar thing."

"Yes?"

"The Prime Minister's car did not return home after leaving the Prime Minister at Charing Cross. The police were anxious to interview O'Murphy, so a search was instituted at once. The car was discovered standing outside a certain unsavoury little restaurant in Soho, which is well known as a meeting-place of German agents."

"And the chauffeur?"

"The chauffeur was nowhere to be found. He, too, had disappeared."

"So," said Poirot thoughtfully, "there are two disappearances: the Prime Minister in France, and O'Murphy in London."

He looked keenly at Lord Estair, who made a gesture of despair.

"I can only tell you, Monsieur Poirot, that, if anyone had suggested to me yesterday that O'Murphy was a traitor, I should have laughed in his face."

"And to-day?"

"To-day I do not know what to think."

Poirot nodded gravely. He looked at his turnip of a watch again.

"I understand that I have carte blanche, messieurs—in every way, I mean? I must be able to go where I choose, and how I choose."

"Perfectly. There is a special train leaving for Dover in an hour's time, with a further contingent from Scotland Yard. You shall be accompanied by a Military officer and a C.I.D. man, who will hold themselves at your disposal in every way. Is that satisfactory?"

"Quite. One more question before you leave, messieurs. What made you come to me? I am unknown, obscure, in this great London of yours."

"We sought you out on the express recommendation and wish of a very great man of your own country."

"*Comment?* My old friend the *Préfet*——?"

Lord Estair shook his head.

"One higher than the *Préfet*. One whose word was once law in Belgium—and shall be again! That England has sworn!"

Poirot's hand flew swiftly to a dramatic salute. "Amen to that!

Ah, but my Master does not forget. . . . Messieurs, I, Hercule Poirot, will serve you faithfully. Heaven only send that it will be in time. But this is dark—dark. . . . I cannot see."

"Well, Poirot," I cried impatiently, as the door closed behind the Ministers, "what do you think?"

My friend was busy packing a minute suitcase, with quick, deft movements. He shook his head thoughtfully.

"I do not know what to think. My brains desert me."

"Why, as you said, kidnap him, when a knock on the head would do as well?" I mused.

"Pardon me, *mon ami*, but I did not quite say that. It is undoubtedly far more their affair to kidnap him."

"But why?"

"Because uncertainty creates panic. That is one reason. Were the Prime Minister dead, it would be a terrible calamity, but the situation would have to be faced. But now you have paralysis. Will the Prime Minister reappear, or will he not? Is he dead or alive? Nobody knows, and until they know nothing definite can be done. And, as I tell you, uncertainty breeds panic, which is what *les Boches* are playing for. Then, again, if the kidnappers are holding him secretly somewhere, they have the advantage of being able to make terms with both sides. The German Government is not a liberal paymaster, as a rule, but no doubt they can be made to disgorge substantial remittances in such a case as this. Thirdly, they run no risk of the hangman's rope. Oh, decidedly, kidnapping is their affair."

"Then, if that is so, why should they first try to shoot him?"

Poirot made a gesture of anger. "Ah, that is just what I do not understand! It is inexplicable—stupid! They have all their arrangements made (and very good arrangements too!) for the abduction, and yet they imperil the whole affair by a melodramatic attack, worthy of a Cinema, and quite as unreal. It is almost impossible to believe in it, with its band of masked men, not twenty miles from London!"

"Perhaps they were two quite separate attempts which happened irrespective of each other," I suggested.

"Ah, no, that would be too much of a coincidence! Then, further—who is the traitor? There must have been a traitor—in the first affair, anyway. But who was it—Daniels or O'Murphy? It must have been one of the two, or why did the car leave the main road? We cannot suppose that the Prime Minister connived at his own assassination! Did O'Murphy take that turning of his own accord, or was it Daniels who told him to do so?"

"Surely it must have been O'Murphy's doing."

"Yes, because if it was Daniels' the Prime Minister would have heard the order, and would have asked the reason. But there are altogether too many 'whys' in this affair, and they contradict each other. If O'Murphy is an honest man, *why* did he leave the main road? But if he was a dishonest man, *why* did he start the car again when only two shots had been fired—thereby, in all probability, saving the Prime Minister's life? And, again, if he was honest, why did he, immediately on leaving Charing Cross, drive to a well-known rendezvous of German spies?"

"It looks bad," I said.

"Let us look at the case with method. What have we for and against these two men? Take O'Murphy first. Against: that his conduct in leaving the main road was suspicious; that he is an Irishman from County Clare; that he has disappeared in a highly suggestive manner. For: that his promptness in restarting the car saved the Premier's life; that he is a Scotland Yard man, and, obviously, from the post allotted to him, a trusted detective. Now for Daniels. There is not much against him, except the fact that nothing is known of his antecedents, and that he speaks too many languages for a good Englishman! (Pardon me, *mon ami*, but, as linguists, you are deplorable!) *Now for him*, we have the fact that he was found gagged, bound, and chloroformed—which does not look as though he had anything to do with the matter."

"He might have gagged and bound himself, to divert suspicion."

Poirot shook his head. "The French police would make no mistake of that kind. Besides, once he had attained his object, and the Prime Minister was safely abducted, there would not be much point in his remaining behind. His accomplices *could* have gagged and chloroformed him, of course, but I fail to see what object they hoped to accomplish by it. He can be of little use to them now, for, until the circumstances concerning the Prime Minister have been cleared up, he is bound to be closely watched."

"Perhaps he hoped to start the police on a false scent?"

"Then why did he not do so? He merely says that something was pressed over his nose and mouth, and that he remembers nothing more. There is no false scent there. It sounds remarkably like the truth."

"Well," I said, glancing at the clock, "I suppose we'd better start for the station. You may find more clues in France."

"Possibly, *mon ami*, but I doubt it. It is still incredible to me that the Prime Minister has not been discovered in that limited area, where the difficulty of concealing him must be tremendous. If the military and the police of two countries have not found him, how shall I?"

At Charing Cross we were met by Mr. Dodge.

"This is Detective Barnes, of Scotland Yard, and Major Norman. They will hold themselves entirely at your disposal. Good luck to you. It's a bad business, but I've not given up hope. Must be off now." And the Minister strode rapidly away.

We chatted in a desultory fashion with Major Norman. In the centre of the little group of men on the platform I recognized a little ferret-faced fellow talking to a tall, fair man. He was an old acquaintance of Poirot's—Detective-Inspector Japp, supposed to be one of the smartest of Scotland Yard's officers. He came over and greeted my friend cheerfully.

"I heard you were on this job too. Smart bit of work. So far they've got away with the goods all right. But I can't believe they can keep him hidden long. Our people are going through France with a toothcomb. So are the French. I can't help feeling it's only a matter of hours now."

"That is, if he's still alive," remarked the tall detective gloomily.

Japp's face fell. "Yes. . . . But somehow I've got the feeling he's alive all right."

Poirot nodded. "Yes, yes; he's alive. But can he be found in time? I, like you, did not believe he could be hidden so long."

The whistle blew, and we all trooped up into the Pullman car. Then, with a slow, unwilling jerk, the train drew out of the station.

It was a curious journey. The Scotland Yard men crowded together. Maps of Northern France were spread out, and eager forefingers traced the lines of roads and villages. Each man had his own pet theory. Poirot showed none of his usual loquacity, but sat staring in front of him, with an expression on his face that reminded me of a puzzled child. I talked to Norman, whom I found quite an amusing fellow. On arriving at Dover Poirot's behaviour moved me to intense amusement. The little man, as he went on board the boat, clutched desperately at my arm. The wind was blowing lustily.

"*Mon Dieu!*" he murmured. "This is terrible!"

"Have courage, Poirot," I cried. "You will succeed. You will find him. I am sure of it."

"Ah, *mon ami*, you mistake my emotion. It is this villainous sea that troubles me! The *mal de mer*—it is horrible suffering!"

"Oh!" I said, rather taken aback.

The first throb of the engines was felt, and Poirot groaned and closed his eyes.

"Major Norman has a map of Northern France if you would like to study it?"

Poirot shook his head impatiently.

"But no, but no! Leave me, my friend. See you, to think, the stomach and the brain must be in harmony. Laverguier has a method most excellent for averting the *mal de mer*. You breathe in—and out—slowly, so—turning the head from left to right and counting six between each breath."

I left him to his gymnastic endeavours, and went on deck.

As we came slowly into Boulogne Harbour Poirot appeared, neat and smiling, and announced to me in a whisper that Laverguier's system had succeeded "to a marvel!"

Japp's forefinger was still tracing imaginary routes on his map. "Nonsense! The car started from Boulogne—here they branched off. Now, my idea is that they transferred the Prime Minister to another car. See?"

"Well," said the tall detective, "I shall make for the seaports. Ten to one, they've smuggled him on board a ship."

Japp shook his head. "Too obvious. The order went out at once to close all the ports."

The day was just breaking as we landed. Major Norman touched Poirot on the arm. "There's a military car here waiting for you, sir."

"Thank you, monsieur. But, for the moment, I do not propose to leave Boulogne."

"What?"

"No, we will enter this hotel here, by the quay."

He suited the action to the word, demanded and was accorded a private room. We three followed him, puzzled and uncomprehending.

He shot a quick glance at us. "It is not so that the good detective should act, eh? I perceive your thought. He must be full of energy. He must rush to and fro. He should prostrate himself on the dusty road and seek the marks of tyres through a little glass. He must gather up the cigarette-end, the fallen match? That is your idea, is it not?"

His eyes challenged us. "But I—Hercule Poirot—tell you that it is not so! The true clues are within—*here!*" He tapped his forehead. "See you, I need not have left London. It would have been sufficient for me to sit quietly in my rooms there. All that matters is the little grey cells within. Secretly and silently they do their part, until suddenly I call for a map, and I lay my finger on a spot—so—and I say: the Prime Minister is *there*! And it is so! With method and logic one can accomplish anything! This frantic rushing to France was a mistake—it is playing a child's game of hide-and-seek. But now, though it may be too late, I will set to work the right way, from within. Silence, my friends, I beg of you."

And for five long hours the little man sat motionless, blinking his eyelids like a cat, his green eyes flickering and becoming steadily greener and greener. The Scotland Yard man was obviously contemptuous, Major Norman was bored and impatient, and I myself found the time pass with wearisome slowness.

Finally, I got up, and strolled as noiselessly as I could to the window. The matter was becoming a farce. I was secretly concerned for my friend. If he failed, I would have preferred him to fail in a less ridiculous manner. Out of the window I idly watched the daily leave boat, belching forth columns of smoke, as she lay alongside the quay.

Suddenly I was aroused by Poirot's voice close to my elbow.

"*Mes amis*, let us start!"

I turned. An extraordinary transformation had come over my friend. His eyes were flickering with excitement, his chest was swelled to the uttermost.

"I have been an imbecile, my friends! But I see daylight at last."

Major Norman moved hastily to the door. "I'll order the car."

"There is no need. I shall not use it. Thank Heaven the wind has fallen."

"Do you mean you are going to walk, sir?"

"No, my young friend. I am no St. Peter. I prefer to cross the sea by boat."

"To cross the *sea*?"

"Yes. To work with method, one must begin from the beginning. And the beginning of this affair was in England. Therefore, we return to England."

* * *

At three o'clock, we stood once more upon Charing Cross platform. To all our expostulations, Poirot turned a deaf ear, and reiterated again and again that to start at the beginning was not a waste of time, but the only way. On the way over, he had conferred with Norman in a low voice, and the latter had despatched a sheaf of telegrams from Dover.

Owing to the special passes held by Norman, we got through everywhere in record time. In London, a large police car was waiting for us, with some plain-clothes men, one of whom handed a typewritten sheet of paper to my friend. He answered my inquiring glance.

"A list of the cottage hospitals within a certain radius west of London. I wired for it from Dover."

We were whirled rapidly through the London streets. We were on the Bath Road. On we went, through Hammersmith, Chiswick and Brentford. I began to see our objective. Through Windsor and on to Ascot. My heart gave a leap. Ascot was where Daniels had an aunt living. We were after *him*, then, not O'Murphy.

We duly stopped at the gate of a trim villa. Poirot jumped out and rang the bell. I saw a perplexed frown dimming the radiance of his face. Plainly, he was not satisfied. The bell was answered. He was ushered inside. In a few moments he reappeared, and climbed into the car with a short, sharp shake of his head. My hopes began to die down. It was past four now. Even if he found certain evidence incriminating Daniels, what would be the good of it, unless he could wring from some one the exact spot in France where they were holding the Prime Minister?

Our return progress towards London was an interrupted one. We deviated from the main road more than once, and occasionally stopped at a small building, which I had no difficulty in recognizing as a cottage hospital. Poirot only spent a few minutes at each, but at every halt his radiant assurance was more and more restored.

He whispered something to Norman, to which the latter replied:

"Yes, if you turn off to the left, you will find them waiting by the bridge."

We turned up a side road, and in the failing light I discerned a second car, waiting by the side of the road. It contained two men in plain clothes. Poirot got down and spoke to them, and then we started off in a northerly direction, the other car following close behind.

We drove for some time, our objective being obviously one of the northern suburbs of London. Finally, we drove up to the front door of a tall house, standing a little back from the road in its own grounds.

Norman and I were left with the car. Poirot and one of the detectives went up to the door and rang. A neat parlourmaid opened it. The detective spoke.

"I am a police officer, and I have a warrant to search this house."

The girl gave a little scream, and a tall, handsome woman of middle-age appeared behind her in the hall.

"Shut the door, Edith. They are burglars, I expect."

But Poirot swiftly inserted his foot in the door, and at the same moment blew a whistle. Instantly the other detectives ran up, and poured into the house, shutting the door behind them.

Norman and I spent about five minutes cursing our forced inactivity. Finally the door reopened, and the men emerged, escorting three prisoners—a woman and two men. The woman, and one of the men, were taken to the second car. The other man was placed in our car by Poirot himself.

"I must go with the others, my friend. But have great care of this gentleman. You do not know him, no? *Eh bien*, let me present to you, Monsieur O'Murphy!"

O'Murphy! I *gaped* at him open-mouthed as we started again.
He was not handcuffed, but I did not fancy he would try to escape.
He sat there staring in front of him as though dazed. Anyway,
Norman and I would be more than a match for him.

To my surprise, we still kept a northerly route. We were not
returning to London, then! I was much puzzled. Suddenly, as
the car slowed down, I recognized that we were close to Hendon
Aerodrome. Immediately I grasped Poirot's idea. He proposed to
reach France by aeroplane.

It was a sporting idea, but, on the face of it, impracticable.
A telegram would be far quicker. Time was everything. He must
leave the personal glory of rescuing the Prime Minister to others.

As we drew up, Major Norman jumped out, and a plain-
clothes man took his place. He conferred with Poirot for a few
minutes, and then went off briskly.

I, too, jumped out, and caught Poirot by the arm.

"I congratulate you, old fellow! They have told you the hiding-place? But, look here, you must wire to France at once. You'll
be too late if you go yourself."

Poirot looked at me curiously for a minute or two.

"Unfortunately, my friend, there are some things that cannot
be sent by telegram."

* * *

At that moment Major Norman returned, accompanied by a young
officer in the uniform of the Flying Corps.

"This is Captain Lyall, who will fly you over to France. He
can start at once."

"Wrap up warmly, sir," said the young pilot. "I can lend you
a coat, if you like."

Poirot was consulting his enormous watch. He murmured to
himself: "Yes, there is time—just time." Then he looked up, and

bowed politely to the young officer. "I thank you, monsieur. But it is not I who am your passenger. It is this gentleman here."

He moved a little aside as he spoke, and a figure came forward out of the darkness. It was the second male prisoner who had gone in the other car, and as the light fell on his face, I gave a gasp of surprise.

It was the Prime Minister!

* * *

"For Heaven's sake, tell me all about it," I cried impatiently, as Poirot, Norman, and I motored back to London. "How in the world did they manage to smuggle him back to England?"

"There was no need to smuggle him back," replied Poirot dryly. "The Prime Minister has never left England. He was kidnapped on his way from Windsor to London."

"What?"

"I will make all clear. The Prime Minister was in his car, his secretary beside him. Suddenly a pad of chloroform is clapped on his face——"

"But by whom?"

"By the clever linguistic Captain Daniels. As soon as the Prime Minister is unconscious, Daniels picks up the speaking-tube, and directs O'Murphy to turn to the right, which the chauffeur, quite unsuspicious, does. A few yards down that unfrequented road, a large car is standing, apparently broken down. Its driver signals to O'Murphy to stop. O'Murphy slows up. The stranger approaches. Daniels leans out of the window, and, probably with the aid of an instantaneous anæsthetic, such as ethylchloride, the chloroform trick is repeated. In a few seconds, the two helpless men are dragged out and transferred to the other car, and a pair of substitutes take their places."

"Impossible!"

"*Pas du tout!* Have you not seen music-hall turns imitating celebrities with marvellous accuracy? Nothing is easier than to personate a public character. The Prime Minister of England is far easier to understudy than Mr. John Smith of Clapham, say. As for O'Murphy's 'double,' no one was going to take much notice of him until after the departure of the Prime Minister, and by then he would have made himself scarce. He drives straight from Charing Cross to the meeting-place of his friends. He goes in as O'Murphy, he emerges as some one quite different. O'Murphy has disappeared, leaving a conveniently suspicious trail behind him."

"But the man who personated the Prime Minister was seen by every one!"

"He was not seen by anyone who knew him privately or intimately. And Daniels shielded him from contact with anyone as much as possible. Moreover, his face was bandaged up, and anything unusual in his manner would be put down to the fact that he was suffering from shock as a result of the attempt upon his life. Mr. MacAdam has a weak throat, and always spares his voice as much as possible before any great speech. The deception was perfectly easy to keep up as far as France. There it would be impracticable and impossible—so the Prime Minister disappears. The police of this country hurry across the Channel, and no one bothers to go into the details of the first attack. To sustain the illusion that the abduction has taken place in France, Daniels is gagged and chloroformed in a convincing manner."

"And the man who has enacted the part of the Prime Minister?"

"Rids himself of his disguise. He and the bogus chauffeur may be arrested as suspicious characters, but no one will dream of suspecting their real part in the drama, and they will eventually be released for lack of evidence."

"And the real Prime Minister?"

"He and O'Murphy were driven straight to the house of 'Mrs. Everard,' at Hampstead, Daniels' so-called 'aunt.' In reality, she is

Frau Bertha Ebenthal, and the police have been looking for her for some time. It is a valuable little present that I have made to them—to say nothing of Daniels! Ah, it was a clever plan, but he did not reckon on the cleverness of Hercule Poirot!"

I think my friend might well be excused his moment of vanity.

"When did you first begin to suspect the truth of the matter?"

"When I began to work the right way—from *within*! I could not make that shooting affair fit in—but when I saw that the net result of it was that *the Prime Minister went to France with his face bound up* I began to comprehend! And when I visited all the cottage hospitals between Windsor and London, and found that no one answering to my description had had his face bound up and dressed that morning, I was sure! After that, it was child's-play for a mind like mine!"

* * *

The following morning, Poirot showed me a telegram he had just received. It had no place of origin, and was unsigned. It ran:

"In time."

Later in the day the evening papers published an account of the Allied Conference. They laid particular stress on the magnificent ovation accorded to Mr. David MacAdam, whose inspiring speech had produced a deep and lasting impression.

NINE
The Disappearance of
Mr. Davenheim

Poirot and I were expecting our old friend Inspector Japp of Scotland Yard to tea. We were sitting round the tea-table awaiting his arrival. Poirot had just finished carefully straightening the cups and saucers which our landlady was in the habit of throwing, rather than placing, on the table. He had also breathed heavily on the metal teapot, and polished it with a silk handkerchief. The kettle was on the boil, and a small enamel saucepan beside it contained some thick, sweet chocolate which was more to Poirot's palate than what he described as "your English poison." A sharp "rat-tat" sounded below, and a few minutes afterwards Japp entered briskly.

"Hope I'm not late," he said as he greeted us. "To tell the truth, I was yarning with Miller, the man who's in charge of the Davenheim case."

I pricked up my ears. For the last three days the papers had been full of the strange disappearance of Mr. Davenheim, senior partner of Davenheim and Salmon, the well-known bankers and financiers. On Saturday last he had walked out of his house, and had never been seen since. I looked forward to extracting some interesting details from Japp.

"I should have thought," I remarked, "that it would be almost impossible for anyone to 'disappear' nowadays."

Poirot moved a plate of bread and butter the eighth of an inch, and said sharply:

"Be exact, my friend. What do you mean by 'disappear'? To which class of disappearance are you referring?"

"Are disappearances classified and labelled, then?" I laughed.

Japp smiled also. Poirot frowned at us both.

"But certainly they are! They fall into three categories: First, and most common, the voluntary disappearance. Second, the much abused 'loss of memory' case—rare, but occasionally genuine. Third, murder, and a more or less successful disposal of the body. Do you refer to all three as impossible of execution?"

"Very nearly so, I should think. You might lose your own memory, but some one would be sure to recognize you—especially in the case of a well-known man like Davenheim. Then 'bodies' can't be made to vanish into thin air. Sooner or later they turn up, concealed in lonely places, or in trunks. Murder will out. In the same way, the absconding clerk, or the domestic defaulter, is bound to be run down in these days of wireless telegraphy. He can be headed off from foreign countries; ports and railway stations are watched; and, as for concealment in this country, his features and appearance will be known to every one who reads a daily newspaper. He's up against civilization."

"*Mon ami*," said Poirot, "you make one error. You do not allow for the fact that a man who had decided to make away with another man—or with himself in a figurative sense—might be that rare machine, a man of method. He might bring intelligence, talent, a careful calculation of detail to the task; and then I do not see why he should not be successful in baffling the police force."

"But not *you*, I suppose?" said Japp good-humouredly, winking at me. "He couldn't baffle *you*, eh, Monsieur Poirot?"

Poirot endeavoured, with a marked lack of success, to look modest. "Me, also! Why not? It is true that I approach such problems with an exact science, a mathematical precision, which seems, alas, only too rare in the new generation of detectives!"

137

Japp grinned more widely.

"I don't know," he said. "Miller, the man who's on this case, is a smart chap. You may be very sure he won't overlook a footprint, or a cigar-ash, or a crumb even. He's got eyes that see everything."

"So, *mon ami*," said Poirot, "has the London sparrow. But all the same, I should not ask the little brown bird to solve the problem of Mr. Davenheim."

"Come now, monsieur, you're not going to run down the value of details as clues?"

"By no means. These things are all good in their way. The danger is they may assume undue importance. Most details are insignificant; one or two are vital. It is the brain, the little grey cells"—he tapped his forehead—"on which one must rely. The senses mislead. One must seek the truth within—not without."

"You don't mean to say, Monsieur Poirot, that you would undertake to solve a case without moving from your chair, do you?"

"That is exactly what I do mean—granted the facts were placed before me. I regard myself as a consulting specialist."

Japp slapped his knee. "Hanged if I don't take you at your word. Bet you a fiver that you can't lay your hand—or rather tell me where to lay my hand—on Mr. Davenheim, dead or alive, before a week is out."

Poirot considered. "*Eh bien, mon ami,* I accept. *Le sport,* it is the passion of you English. Now—the facts."

"On Saturday last, as is his usual custom, Mr. Davenheim took the 12.40 train from Victoria to Chingside, where his palatial country place, The Cedars, is situated. After lunch, he strolled round the grounds, and gave various directions to the gardeners. Everybody agrees that his manner was absolutely normal and as usual. After tea he put his head into his wife's boudoir, saying that he was going to stroll down to the village and post some letters. He added that he was expecting a Mr. Lowen, on business. If he should come before he himself returned, he was to be shown into the study and asked to wait. Mr. Davenheim then left the house by the front door, passed leisurely down the drive, and out at the gate, and—was never seen again. From that hour, he vanished completely."

"Pretty—very pretty—altogether a charming little problem," murmured Poirot. "Proceed, my good friend."

"About a quarter of an hour later a tall, dark man with a thick black moustache rang the front-door bell, and explained that he had an appointment with Mr. Davenheim. He gave the name of Lowen, and in accordance with the banker's instructions was shown into the study. Nearly an hour passed. Mr. Davenheim did not return. Finally Mr. Lowen rang the bell, and explained that he was unable to wait any longer, as he must catch his train back to town. Mrs. Davenheim apologized for her husband's absence, which seemed unaccountable, as she knew him to have been expecting the visitor. Mr. Lowen reiterated his regrets and took his departure.

"Well, as every one knows, Mr. Davenheim did not return. Early on Sunday morning the police were communicated with, but could make neither head nor tail of the matter. Mr. Davenheim seemed literally to have vanished into thin air. He had not been to the post office; nor had he been seen passing through the village. At the station they were positive he had not departed by any train. His own motor had not left the garage. If he had hired a car to meet him in some lonely spot, it seems almost certain that by this time, in view of the large reward offered for information, the driver of it would have come forward to tell what he knew. True, there was a small race-meeting at Entfield, five miles away, and if he had walked to that station he might have passed unnoticed in the crowd. But since then his photograph and a full description of him have been circulated in every newspaper, and nobody has been able to give any news of him. We have, of course, received many letters from all over England, but each clue, so far, has ended in disappointment.

"On Monday morning a further sensational discovery came to

light. Behind a portière in Mr. Davenheim's study stands a safe, and that safe had been broken into and rifled. The windows were fastened securely on the inside, which seems to put an ordinary burglary out of court, unless, of course, an accomplice within the house fastened them again afterwards. On the other hand, Sunday having intervened, and the household being in a state of chaos, it is likely that the burglary was committed on the Saturday, and remained undetected until Monday."

"*Précisément*," said Poirot dryly. "Well, is he arrested, *ce pauvre M. Lowen*?"

Japp grinned. "Not yet. But he's under pretty close supervision."

Poirot nodded. "What was taken from the safe? Have you any idea?"

"We've been going into that with the junior partner of the firm and Mrs. Davenheim. Apparently there was a considerable amount in bearer bonds, and a very large sum in notes, owing to some large transaction having been just carried through. There was also a small fortune in jewellery. All Mrs. Davenheim's jewels were kept in the safe. The purchasing of them had become a passion with her husband of late years, and hardly a month passed that he did not make her a present of some rare and costly gem."

"Altogether a good haul," said Poirot thoughtfully. "Now, what about Lowen? Is it known what his business was with Davenheim that evening?"

"Well, the two men were apparently not on very good terms. Lowen is a speculator in quite a small way. Nevertheless, he has been able once or twice to score a *coup* off Davenheim in the market, though it seems they seldom or never actually met. It was a matter concerning some South American shares which led the banker to make his appointment."

"Had Davenheim interests in South America, then?"

"I believe so. Mrs. Davenheim happened to mention that he spent all last autumn in Buenos Ayres."

"Any trouble in his home life? Were the husband and wife

on good terms?"

"I should say his domestic life was quite peaceful and uneventful. Mrs. Davenheim is a pleasant, rather unintelligent woman. Quite a nonentity, I think."

"Then we must not look for the solution of the mystery there. Had he any enemies?"

"He had plenty of financial rivals, and no doubt there are many people whom he has got the better of who bear him no particular good-will. But there was no one likely to make away with him—and, if they had, where is the body?"

"Exactly. As Hastings says, bodies have a habit of coming to light with fatal persistency."

"By the way, one of the gardeners says he saw a figure going round to the side of the house toward the rose-garden. The long French window of the study opens on to the rose-garden, and Mr. Davenheim frequently entered and left the house that way. But the man was a good way off, at work on some cucumber frames, and cannot even say whether it was the figure of his master or not. Also, he cannot fix the time with any accuracy. It must have been before six, as the gardeners cease work at that time."

"And Mr. Davenheim left the house?"

"About half-past five or thereabouts."

"What lies beyond the rose-garden?"

"A lake."

"With a boathouse?"

"Yes, a couple of punts are kept there. I suppose you're thinking of suicide, Monsieur Poirot? Well, I don't mind telling you that Miller's going down to-morrow expressly to see that piece of water dragged. That's the kind of man he is!"

Poirot smiled faintly, and turned to me. "Hastings, I pray you, hand me that copy of the *Daily Megaphone*. If I remember rightly, there is an unusually clear photograph there of the missing man."

I rose, and found the sheet required. Poirot studied the features attentively.

"H'm!" he murmured. "Wears his hair rather long and wavy, full moustache and pointed beard, bushy eyebrows. Eyes dark?"

"Yes."

"Hair and beard turning grey?"

The detective nodded. "Well, Monsieur Poirot, what have you got to say to it all? Clear as daylight, eh?"

"On the contrary, most obscure."

The Scotland Yard man looked pleased.

"Which gives me great hopes of solving it," finished Poirot placidly.

"Eh?"

"I find it a good sign when a case is obscure. If a thing is clear as daylight—*eh bien*, mistrust it! Some one has made it so."

Japp shook his head almost pityingly. "Well, each to their fancy. But it's not a bad thing to see your way clear ahead."

"I do not see," murmured Poirot. "I shut my eyes—and think."

Japp sighed. "Well, you've got a clear week to think in."

"And you will bring me any fresh developments that arise—the result of the labours of the hard-working and lynx-eyed Inspector Miller, for instance?"

"Certainly. That's in the bargain."

"Seems a shame, doesn't it?" said Japp to me as I accompanied him to the door. "Like robbing a child!"

I could not help agreeing with a smile. I was still smiling as I re-entered the room.

"*Eh bien!*" said Poirot immediately. "You make fun of Papa Poirot, is it not so?" He shook his finger at me. "You do not trust his grey cells? Ah, do not be confused! Let us discuss this little problem—incomplete as yet, I admit, but already showing one or two points of interest."

"The lake!" I said significantly.

"And even more than the lake, the boathouse!"

I looked sidewise at Poirot. He was smiling in his most inscrutable fashion. I felt that, for the moment, it would be quite useless to question him further.

We heard nothing of Japp until the following evening, when he walked in about nine o'clock. I saw at once by his expression that he was bursting with news of some kind.

"*Eh bien*, my friend," remarked Poirot. "All goes well? But do not tell me that you have discovered the body of Mr. Davenheim in your lake, because I shall not believe you."

"We haven't found the body, but we did find his *clothes*—the identical clothes he was wearing that day. What do you say to that?"

"Any other clothes missing from the house?"

"No, his valet is quite positive on that point. The rest of his wardrobe is intact. There's more. We've arrested Lowen. One of the maids, whose business it is to fasten the bedroom windows, declares that she saw Lowen coming *towards* the study through the rose-garden about a quarter past six. That would be about ten minutes before he left the house."

"What does he himself say to that?"

"Denied first of all that he had ever left the study. But the maid was positive, and he pretended afterwards that he had forgotten just stepping out of the window to examine an unusual species of rose. Rather a weak story! And there's fresh evidence against him come to light. Mr. Davenheim always wore a thick gold ring set with a solitaire diamond on the little finger of his right hand. Well, that ring was pawned in London on Saturday night by a man called Billy Kellett! He's already known to the police—did three months last autumn for lifting an old gentleman's watch. It seems he tried to pawn the ring at no less than five different places, succeeded at the last one, got gloriously drunk on the proceeds, assaulted a policeman, and was run in in consequence. I went to Bow Street with Miller and saw him. He's sober enough now, and I don't mind admitting we pretty well frightened the life out of him, hinting he might be charged with murder. This is his yarn, and a very queer one it is.

"He was at Entfield races on Saturday, though I dare say

scarfpins was his line of business, rather than betting. Anyway, he had a bad day, and was down on his luck. He was tramping along the road to Chingside, and sat down in a ditch to rest just before he got into the village. A few minutes later he noticed a man coming along the road to the village, 'dark-complexioned gent, with a big moustache, one of them city toffs,' is his description of the man.

"Kellett was half concealed from the road by a heap of stones. Just before he got abreast of him, the man looked quickly up and down the road, and seeing it apparently deserted he took a small object from his pocket and threw it over the hedge. Then he went on towards the station. Now, the object he had thrown over the hedge had fallen with a slight 'chink' which aroused the curiosity of the human derelict in the ditch. He investigated and, after a short search, discovered the ring! That is Kellett's story. It's only fair to say that Lowen denies it utterly, and of course the word of a man like Kellett can't be relied upon in the slightest. It's within the bounds of possibility that he met Davenheim in the lane and robbed and murdered him."

Poirot shook his head.

"Very improbable, *mon ami*. He had no means of disposing of the body. It would have been found by now. Secondly, the open way in which he pawned the ring makes it unlikely that he did murder to get it. Thirdly, your sneak-thief is rarely a murderer. Fourthly, as he has been in prison since Saturday, it would be too much of a coincidence that he is able to give so accurate a description of Lowen."

Japp nodded. "I don't say you're not right. But all the same, you won't get a jury to take much note of a jailbird's evidence. What seems odd to me is that Lowen couldn't find a cleverer way of disposing of the ring."

Poirot shrugged his shoulders. "Well, after all, if it were found in the neighbourhood, it might be argued that Davenheim himself had dropped it."

"But why remove it from the body at all?" I cried.

"There might be a reason for that," said Japp. "Do you know that just beyond the lake, a little gate leads out on to the hill, and not three minutes' walk brings you to—what do you think?—a *lime kiln*."

"Good heavens!" I cried. "You mean that the lime which destroyed the body would be powerless to affect the metal of the ring?"

"Exactly."

"It seems to me," I said, "that that explains everything. What a horrible crime!"

By common consent we both turned and looked at Poirot. He seemed lost in reflection, his brow knitted, as though with some supreme mental effort. I felt that at last his keen intellect was asserting itself. What would his first words be? We were not long left in doubt. With a sigh, the tension of his attitude relaxed, and turning to Japp, he asked:

"Have you any idea, my friend, whether Mr. and Mrs. Davenheim occupied the same bedroom?"

The question seemed so ludicrously inappropriate that for a moment we both stared in silence. Then Japp burst into a laugh. "Good Lord, Monsieur Poirot, I thought you were coming out with something startling. As to your question, I'm sure I don't know."

"You could find out?" asked Poirot with curious persistence.

"Oh, certainly—if you *really* want to know."

"*Merci, mon ami.* I should be obliged if you would make a point of it."

Japp stared at him a few minutes longer, but Poirot seemed to have forgotten us both. The detective shook his head sadly at me, and murmuring, "Poor old fellow! War's been too much for him!" gently withdrew from the room.

As Poirot still seemed sunk in a daydream, I took a sheet of paper, and amused myself by scribbling notes upon it. My friend's voice aroused me. He had come out of his reverie, and was looking brisk and alert.

"*Que faites-vous là, mon ami?*"

"I was jotting down what occurred to me as the main points of interest in this affair."

"You become methodical—at last!" said Poirot approvingly.

I concealed my pleasure. "Shall I read them to you?"

"By all means."

I cleared my throat.

"'One: All the evidence points to Lowen having been the man who forced the safe.

"'Two: He had a grudge against Davenheim.

"'Three: He lied in his first statement that he had never left the study.

"'Four: If you accept Billy Kellett's story as true, Lowen is unmistakably implicated.'"

I paused. "Well?" I asked, for I felt that I had put my finger on all the vital facts.

Poirot looked at me pityingly, shaking his head very gently. "*Mon pauvre ami!* But it is that you have not the gift! The important detail, you appreciate him never! Also, your reasoning is false."

"How?"

"Let me take your four points.

"One: Mr. Lowen could not possibly know that he would have the chance to open the safe. He came for a business interview. He could not know beforehand that Mr. Davenheim would be absent posting a letter, and that he would consequently be alone in the study!"

"He might have seized his opportunity," I suggested.

"And the tools? City gentlemen do not carry round housebreaker's tools on the off chance! And one could not cut into that safe with a penknife, *bien entendu!*"

"Well, what about Number Two?"

"You say Lowen had a grudge against Mr. Davenheim. What you mean is that he had once or twice got the better of him. And presumably those transactions were entered into with the view of

146

benefiting himself. In any case you do not as a rule bear a grudge against a man you have got the better of—it is more likely to be the other way about. Whatever grudge there might have been would have been on Mr. Davenheim's side."

"Well, you can't deny that he lied about never having left the study?"

"No. But he may have been frightened. Remember, the missing man's clothes had just been discovered in the lake. Of course, as usual, he would have done better to speak the truth."

"And the fourth point?"

"I grant you that. If Kellett's story is true, Lowen is undeniably implicated. That is what makes the affair so very interesting."

"Then I did appreciate *one* vital fact?"

"Perhaps—but you have entirely overlooked the two most important points, the ones which undoubtedly hold the clue to the whole matter."

"And pray, what are they?"

"One, the passion which has grown upon Mr. Davenheim in the last few years for buying jewellery. Two, his trip to Buenos Ayres last autumn."

"Poirot, you are joking!"

"I am most serious. Ah, sacred thunder, but I hope Japp will not forget my little commission."

But the detective, entering into the spirit of the joke, had remembered it so well that a telegram was handed to Poirot about eleven o'clock the next day. At his request I opened it and read it out:

"'Husband and wife have occupied separate rooms since last winter.'"

"Aha!" cried Poirot. "And now we are in mid June! All is solved!"

I stared at him.

"You have no moneys in the bank of Davenheim and Salmon, *mon ami*?"

"No," I said, wondering. "Why?"

"Because I should advise you to withdraw it—before it is too late."

"Why, what do you expect?"

"I expect a big smash in a few days—perhaps sooner. Which reminds me, we will return the compliment of a *dépêche* to Japp. A pencil, I pray you, and a form. *Voilà!* 'Advise you to withdraw any money deposited with firm in question.' That will intrigue him, the good Japp! His eyes will open wide—wide! He will not comprehend in the slightest—until to-morrow, or the next day!"

I remained sceptical, but the morrow forced me to render tribute to my friend's remarkable powers. In every paper was a huge headline telling of the sensational failure of the Davenheim bank. The disappearance of the famous financier took on a totally different aspect in the light of the revelation of the financial affairs of the bank.

Before we were half-way through breakfast, the door flew open and Japp rushed in. In his left hand was a paper; in his right was Poirot's telegram, which he banged down on the table in front of my friend.

"How did you know, Monsieur Poirot? How the blazes could you know?"

Poirot smiled placidly at him. "Ah, *mon ami*, after your wire, it was a certainty! From the commencement, see you, it struck me that the safe burglary was somewhat remarkable. Jewels, ready money, bearer bonds—all so conveniently arranged for—whom? Well, the good Monsieur Davenheim was of those who 'look after Number One' as your saying goes! It seemed almost certain that it was arranged for—himself! Then his passion of late years for buying jewellery! How simple! The funds he embezzled, he converted into jewels, very likely replacing them in turn with paste duplicates, and so he put away in a safe place, under another name, a considerable fortune to be enjoyed all in good time when every one has been thrown off the track. His arrangements completed, he makes an appointment with Mr. Lowen (who has been imprudent enough in the past to cross the great man once or twice), drills a hole in the safe, leaves orders that the guest is to be shown into the study, and walks out of the house—where?" Poirot stopped, and stretched out his hand for another boiled egg. He frowned. "It is really insupportable," he murmured, "that every hen lays an egg of a different size! What symmetry can there be on the breakfast table? At least they should sort them in dozens at the shop!"

"Never mind the eggs," said Japp impatiently. "Let 'em lay 'em square if they like. Tell us where our customer went to when he left The Cedars—that is, if you know!"

"*Eh bien*, he went to his hiding-place. Ah, this Monsieur Davenheim, there may be some malformation in his grey cells, but they are of the first quality!"

"Do you know where he is hiding?"

"Certainly! It is most ingenious."

"For the Lord's sake, tell us, then!"

Poirot gently collected every fragment of shell from his plate, placed them in the egg-cup, and reversed the empty egg-shell on top of them. This little operation concluded, he smiled on the neat effect, and then beamed affectionately on us both.

"Come, my friends, you are men of intelligence. Ask yourselves the question which I asked myself. 'If I were this man, where should *I* hide?' Hastings, what do you say?"

"Well," I said, "I'm rather inclined to think I'd not do a bolt at all. I'd stay in London—in the heart of things, travel by tubes and buses; ten to one I'd never be recognized. There's safety in a crowd."

Poirot turned inquiringly to Japp.

"I don't agree. Get clear away at once—that's the only chance. I would have had plenty of time to prepare things beforehand. I'd have a yacht waiting, with steam up, and I'd be off to one of the most out-of-the-way corners of the world before the hue and cry began!"

We both looked at Poirot. "What do *you* say, monsieur?"

For a moment he remained silent. Then a very curious smile flitted across his face.

"My friends, if *I* were hiding from the police, do you know *where* I should hide? *In a prison!*"

"What?"

"You are seeking Monsieur Davenheim in order to put him in prison, so you never dream of looking to see if he may not be already there!"

"What do you mean?"

"You tell me Madame Davenheim is not a very intelligent woman. Nevertheless I think that if you took her to Bow Street and confronted her with the man Billy Kellett, she would recognize him! In spite of the fact that he has shaved his beard and moustache and those bushy eyebrows, and has cropped his hair close. A woman nearly always knows her husband, though the rest of the world may be deceived!"

"Billy Kellett? But he's known to the police!"

"Did I not tell you Davenheim was a clever man? He prepared his alibi long beforehand. He was not in Buenos Ayres last autumn—he was creating the character of Billy Kellett, 'doing three months,' so that the police should have no suspicions when the time came. He was playing, remember, for a large fortune, as well as liberty. It was worth while doing the thing thoroughly. Only——"

"Yes?"

"*Eh bien*, afterwards he had to wear a false beard and wig, had to *make up as himself* again, and to sleep with a false beard is not easy—it invites detection! He cannot risk continuing to share the chamber of madame his wife. You found out for me that for the last six months, or ever since his supposed return from Buenos Ayres, he and Mrs. Davenheim occupied separate rooms. Then I was sure! Everything fitted in. The gardener who fancied he saw his master going round to the side of the house was quite right.

He went to the boathouse, donned his 'tramp' clothes, which you may be sure had been safely hidden from the eyes of his valet, dropped the others in the lake, and proceeded to carry out his plan by pawning the ring in an obvious manner, and then assaulting a policeman, getting himself safely into the haven of Bow Street, where nobody would ever dream of looking for him!"

"It's impossible," murmured Japp.

"Ask Madame," said my friend, smiling.

The next day a registered letter lay beside Poirot's plate. He opened it, and a five-pound note fluttered out. My friend's brow puckered.

"*Ah, sacré!* But what shall I do with it? I have much remorse! *Ce pauvre Japp!* Ah, an idea! We will have a little dinner, we three! That consoles me. It was really too easy. I am ashamed. I, who would not rob a child—*mille tonnerres! Mon ami*, what have you, that you laugh so heartily?"

TEN

The Adventure of the Italian Nobleman

Poirot and I had many friends and acquaintances of an informal nature. Amongst these was to be numbered Dr. Hawker, a near neighbour of ours, and a member of the medical profession. It was the genial doctor's habit to drop in sometimes of an evening and have a chat with Poirot, of whose genius he was an ardent admirer. The doctor himself, frank and unsuspicious to the last degree, admired the talents so far removed from his own.

On one particular evening in early June, he arrived about half-past eight and settled down to a comfortable discussion on the cheery topic of the prevalence of arsenical poisoning in crimes. It must have been about a quarter of an hour later when the door of our sitting-room flew open, and a distracted female precipitated herself into the room.

"Oh, doctor, you're wanted! Such a terrible voice. It gave me a turn, it did indeed."

I recognized in our new visitor Dr. Hawker's housekeeper, Miss Rider. The doctor was a bachelor, and lived in a gloomy old house a few streets away. The usually placid Miss Rider was now in a state bordering on incoherence.

"What terrible voice? Who is it, and what's the trouble?"

"It was the telephone, doctor. I answered it—and a voice spoke. 'Help,' it said. 'Doctor—help. They've killed me!' Then it sort of tailed away. 'Who's speaking?' I said. 'Who's speaking?' Then I got a reply, just a whisper, it seemed, 'Foscatine'—something like that—'Regent's Court.'"

The doctor uttered an exclamation.

"Count Foscatini. He has a flat in Regent's Court. I must go at once. What can have happened?"

"A patient of yours?" asked Poirot.

"I attended him for some slight ailment a few weeks ago. An Italian, but he speaks English perfectly. Well, I must wish you good night, Monsieur Poirot, unless——" He hesitated.

"I perceive the thought in your mind," said Poirot, smiling. "I shall be delighted to accompany you. Hastings, run down and get hold of a taxi."

Taxis always make themselves sought for when one is particularly pressed for time, but I captured one at last, and we were soon bowling along in the direction of Regent's Park. Regent's Court was a new block of flats, situated just off St. John's Wood Road. They had only recently been built, and contained the latest service devices.

There was no one in the hall. The doctor pressed the lift-bell impatiently, and when the lift arrived questioned the uniformed attendant sharply.

"Flat 11. Count Foscatini. There's been an accident there, I understand."

The man stared at him.

"First I've heard of it. Mr. Graves—that's Count Foscatini's man—went out about half an hour ago, and he said nothing."

"Is the Count alone in the flat?"

"No, sir, he's got two gentlemen dining with him."

"What are they like?" I asked eagerly.

We were in the lift now, ascending rapidly to the second floor, on which Flat 11 was situated.

"I didn't see them myself, sir, but I understand that they were foreign gentlemen."

He pulled back the iron door, and we stepped out on the landing. No. 11 was opposite to us. The doctor rang the bell. There was no reply, and we could hear no sound from within. The doctor rang again and again; we could hear the bell trilling within, but no sign of life rewarded us.

"This is getting serious," muttered the doctor. He turned to the lift attendant.

"Is there any pass-key to this door?"

"There is one in the porter's office downstairs."

"Get it, then, and, look here, I think you'd better send for the police."

Poirot approved with a nod of the head.

The man returned shortly; with him came the manager.

"Will you tell me, gentlemen, what is the meaning of all this?"

"Certainly. I received a telephone message from Count Foscatini stating that he had been attacked and was dying. You can understand that we must lose no time—if we are not already too late."

The manager produced the key without more ado, and we all entered the flat.

We passed first into a small square lounge hall. A door on the right of it was half open. The manager indicated it with a nod.

"The dining-room."

Dr. Hawker led the way. We followed close on his heels. As we entered the room I gave a gasp. The round table in the centre bore the remains of a meal; three chairs were pushed back, as though their occupants had just risen. In the corner, to the right of the fire-place, was a big writing-table, and sitting at it was a man—or what had been a man. His right hand still grasped the base of the telephone, but he had fallen forward, struck down by a terrific blow on the head from behind. The weapon was not far to seek. A marble statuette stood where it had been hurriedly put down, the base of it stained with blood.

The doctor's examination did not take a minute. "Stone dead.

154

Must have been almost instantaneous. I wonder he even managed to telephone. It will be better not to move him until the police arrive."

On the manager's suggestion we searched the flat, but the result was a foregone conclusion. It was not likely that the murderers would be concealed there when all they had to do was to walk out.

We came back to the dining-room. Poirot had not accompanied us in our tour. I found him studying the centre table with close attention. I joined him. It was a well-polished round mahogany table. A bowl of roses decorated the centre, and white lace mats reposed on the gleaming surface. There was a dish of fruit, but the three dessert plates were untouched. There were three coffee-cups with remains of coffee in them—two black, one with milk. All three men had taken port, and the decanter, half-full, stood before the centre plate. One of the men had smoked a cigar, the other two cigarettes. A tortoiseshell-and-silver box, holding cigars and cigarettes, stood open upon the table.

I enumerated all these facts to myself, but I was forced to admit that they did not shed any brilliant light on the situation. I wondered what Poirot saw in them to make him so intent. I asked him.

"*Mon ami*," he replied, "you miss the point. I am looking for something that I do *not* see."

"What is that?"

"A mistake—even a little mistake—on the part of the murderer."

He stepped swiftly to the small adjoining kitchen, looked in, and shook his head.

"Monsieur," he said to the manager, "explain to me, I pray, your system of serving meals here."

The manager stepped to a small hatch in the wall.

"This is the service lift," he explained. "It runs to the kitchens at the top of the building. You order through this telephone, and

155

the dishes are sent down in the lift, one course at a time. The dirty plates and dishes are sent up in the same manner. No domestic worries, you understand, and at the same time you avoid the wearying publicity of always dining in a restaurant."

Poirot nodded.

"Then the plates and dishes that were used to-night are on high in the kitchen. You permit that I mount there?"

"Oh, certainly, if you like! Roberts, the lift man, will take you up and introduce you; but I'm afraid you won't find anything that's of any use. They're handling hundreds of plates and dishes, and they'll be all lumped together."

Poirot remained firm, however, and together we visited the kitchens and questioned the man who had taken the order from Flat 11.

"The order was given from the *à la carte menu*—for three," he explained. "Soup julienne, filet de sole normande, tournedos of beef, and a rice soufflé. What time? Just about eight o'clock, I should say. No, I'm afraid the plates and dishes have been all washed up by now. Unfortunate. You were thinking of finger-prints, I suppose?"

"Not exactly," said Poirot, with an enigmatical smile. "I am more interested in Count Foscatini's appetite. Did he partake of every dish?"

"Yes; but of course I can't say how much of each he ate. The plates were all soiled, and the dishes empty—that is to say, with the exception of the rice soufflé. There was a fair amount of that left."

"Ah!" said Poirot, and seemed satisfied with the fact.

As we descended to the flat again he remarked in a low tone:

"We have decidedly to do with a man of method."

"Do you mean the murderer, or Count Foscatini?"

"The latter was undoubtedly an orderly gentleman. After imploring help and announcing his approaching demise, he carefully hung up the telephone receiver."

I stared at Poirot. His words now and his recent inquiries gave me the glimmering of an idea.

"You suspect poison?" I breathed. "The blow on the head was a blind."

Poirot merely smiled.

We re-entered the flat to find the local inspector of police had arrived with two constables. He was inclined to resent our appearance, but Poirot calmed him with the mention of our Scotland Yard friend, Inspector Japp, and we were accorded a grudging permission to remain. It was a lucky thing we were, for we had not been back five minutes before an agitated middle-aged man came rushing into the room with every appearance of grief and agitation.

This was Graves, valet-butler to the late Count Foscatini. The story he had to tell was a sensational one.

On the previous morning, two gentlemen had called to see his master. They were Italians, and the elder of the two, a man of about forty, gave his name as Signor Ascanio. The younger was a well-dressed lad of about twenty-four.

Count Foscatini was evidently prepared for their visit and immediately sent Graves out upon some trivial errand. Here the man paused and hesitated in his story. In the end, however, he admitted that, curious as to the purport of the interview, he had not obeyed immediately, but had lingered about endeavouring to hear something of what was going on.

The conversation was carried on in so low a tone that he was not as successful as he had hoped; but he gathered enough to make it clear that some kind of monetary proposition was being discussed, and that the basis of it was a threat. The discussion was anything but amicable. In the end, Count Foscatini raised his voice slightly, and the listener heard these words clearly:

"I have no time to argue further now, gentlemen. If you will dine with me to-morrow night at eight o'clock, we will resume the discussion."

Afraid of being discovered listening, Graves had then hurried out to do his master's errand. This evening the two men had arrived punctually at eight. During dinner they had talked of indifferent matters—politics, the weather, and the theatrical world. When Graves had placed the port upon the table and brought in the coffee his master told him that he might have the evening off.

"Was that a usual proceeding of his when he had guests?" asked the inspector.

"No, sir; it wasn't. That's what made me think it must be some business of a very unusual kind that he was going to discuss with these gentlemen."

That finished Graves's story. He had gone out about 8.30, and, meeting a friend, had accompanied him to the Metropolitan Music Hall in Edgware Road.

Nobody had seen the two men leave, but the time of the murder was fixed clearly enough at 8.47. A small clock on the writing-table had been swept off by Foscatini's arm, and had stopped at that hour, which agreed with Miss Rider's telephone summons.

The police surgeon had made his examination of the body, and it was now lying on the couch. I saw the face for the first time—the olive complexion, the long nose, the luxuriant black moustache, and the full red lips drawn back from the dazzlingly white teeth. Not altogether a pleasant face.

"Well," said the inspector, refastening his notebook. "The case seems clear enough. The only difficulty will be to lay our hands on this Signor Ascanio. I suppose his address is not in the dead man's pocket-book by any chance?"

As Poirot had said, the late Foscatini was an orderly man. Neatly written in small, precise handwriting was the inscription, "Signor Paolo Ascanio, Grosvenor Hotel."

The inspector busied himself with the telephone, then turned to us with a grin.

"Just in time. Our fine gentleman was off to catch the boat

train to the Continong. Well, gentlemen, that's about all we can do here. It's a bad business, but straightforward enough. One of these Italian vendetta things, as likely as not."

Thus airily dismissed, we found our way downstairs. Dr. Hawker was full of excitement.

"Like the beginning of a novel, eh? Real exciting stuff. Wouldn't believe it if you read about it."

Poirot did not speak. He was very thoughtful. All the evening he had hardly opened his lips.

"What says the master detective, eh?" asked Hawker, clapping him on the back. "Nothing to work your grey cells over this time."

"You think not?"

"What could there be?"

"Well, for example, there is the window."

"The window? But it was fastened. Nobody could have got out or in that way. I noticed it specially."

"And why were you able to notice it?"

The doctor looked puzzled. Poirot hastened to explain.

"It is to the curtains I refer. They were not drawn. A little odd, that. And then there was the coffee. It was very black coffee."

"Well, what of it?"

"Very black," repeated Poirot. "In conjunction with that let us remember that very little of the rice soufflé was eaten, and we get—what?"

"Moonshine," laughed the doctor. "You're pulling my leg."

"Never do I pull the leg. Hastings here knows that I am perfectly serious."

"I don't know what you are getting at, all the same," I confessed. "You don't suspect the manservant, do you? He might have been in with the gang, and put some dope in the coffee. I suppose they'll test his alibi?"

"Without doubt, my friend; but it is the alibi of Signor Ascanio that interests me."

"You think he has an alibi?"

159

"That is just what worries me. I have no doubt that we shall soon be enlightened on that point."

The *Daily Newsmonger* enabled us to become conversant with succeeding events.

Signor Ascanio was arrested and charged with the murder of Count Foscatini. When arrested, he denied knowing the Count, and declared he had never been near Regent's Court either on the evening of the crime or on the previous morning. The younger man had disappeared entirely. Signor Ascanio had arrived alone at the Grosvenor Hotel from the Continent two days before the murder. All efforts to trace the second man failed.

Ascanio, however, was not sent for trial. No less a personage than the Italian Ambassador himself came forward and testified at the police-court proceedings that Ascanio had been with him at the Embassy from eight till nine that evening. The prisoner was discharged. Naturally, a lot of people thought that the crime was a political one, and was being deliberately hushed up.

Poirot had taken a keen interest in all these points. Nevertheless, I was somewhat surprised when he suddenly informed me one morning that he was expecting a visitor at eleven o'clock, and that that visitor was none other than Ascanio himself.

"He wishes to consult you?"

"*Du tout*, Hastings. I wish to consult him."

"What about?"

"The Regent's Court murder."

"You are going to prove that he did it?"

"A man cannot be tried twice for murder, Hastings. Endeavour to have the common sense. Ah, that is our friend's ring."

A few minutes later Signor Ascanio was ushered in—a small, thin man with a secretive and furtive glance in his eyes. He remained standing, darting suspicious glances from one to the other of us.

"Monsieur Poirot?"

My little friend tapped himself gently on the chest.

160

"Be seated, signor. You received my note. I am determined to get to the bottom of this mystery. In some small measure you can aid me. Let us commence. You—in company with a friend—visited the late Count Foscatini on the morning of Tuesday the 9th——"

The Italian made an angry gesture.

"I did nothing of the sort. I have sworn in court——"

"*Précisément*—and I have a little idea that you have sworn falsely."

"You threaten me? Bah! I have nothing to fear from you. I have been acquitted."

"Exactly; and as I am not an imbecile, it is not with the gallows I threaten you—but with publicity. Publicity! I see that you do not like the word. I had an idea that you would not. My little ideas, you know, they are very valuable to me. Come, signor, your only chance is to be frank with me. I do not ask to know whose indiscretions brought you to England. I know this much, you came for the especial purpose of seeing Count Foscatini."

"He was not a count," growled the Italian.

"I have already noted the fact that his name does not appear in the *Almanach de Gotha*. Never mind, the title of count is often useful in the profession of blackmailing."

"I suppose I might as well be frank. You seem to know a good deal."

"I have employed my grey cells to some advantage. Come, Signor Ascanio, you visited the dead man on the Tuesday morning—that is so, is it not?"

"Yes; but I never went there on the following evening. There was no need. I will tell you all. Certain information concerning a man of great position in Italy had come into this scoundrel's possession. He demanded a big sum of money in return for the papers. I came over to England to arrange the matter. I called upon him by appointment that morning. One of the young secretaries of the Embassy was with me. The Count was more reasonable than I had hoped, although even then the sum of money I paid him was a huge one."

"Pardon, how was it paid?"

"In Italian notes of comparatively small denomination. I paid over the money then and there. He handed me the incriminating papers. I never saw him again."

"Why did you not say all this when you were arrested?"

"In my delicate position I was forced to deny any association with the man."

"And how do you account for the events of the evening, then?"

"I can only think that some one must have deliberately impersonated me. I understand that no money was found in the flat."

Poirot looked at him and shook his head.

"Strange," he murmured. "We all have the little grey cells. And so few of us know how to use them. Good morning, Signor Ascanio. I believe your story. It is very much as I had imagined. But I had to make sure."

After bowing his guest out, Poirot returned to his arm-chair and smiled at me.

"Let us hear M. le Capitaine Hastings on the case?"

"Well, I suppose Ascanio is right—somebody impersonated him."

"Never, never will you use the brains the good God has given you. Recall to yourself some words I uttered after leaving the flat that night. I referred to the window-curtains not being drawn. We are in the month of June. It is still light at eight o'clock. The light is failing by half-past. *Ça vous dit quelque chose?* I perceive a struggling impression that you will arrive some day. Now let us continue. The coffee was, as I said, very black. Count Foscatini's teeth were magnificently white. Coffee stains the teeth. We reason from that that Count Foscatini did not drink any coffee. Yet there was coffee in all three cups. Why should anyone pretend Count Foscatini had drunk coffee when he had not done so?"

I shook my head, utterly bewildered.

"Come, I will help you. What evidence have we that Ascanio and his friend, or two men posing as them, ever came to the flat that night? Nobody saw them go in; nobody saw them go out. We have the evidence of one man and of a host of inanimate objects."

"You mean?"

"I mean knives and forks and plates and empty dishes. Ah, but it was a clever idea! Graves is a thief and a scoundrel, but what a man of method! He overhears a portion of the conversation in the morning, enough to realize that Ascanio will be in awkward position to defend himself. The following evening, about eight o'clock, he tells his master he is wanted at the telephone. Foscatini sits down, stretches out his hand to the telephone, and from behind Graves strikes him down with the marble figure. Then quickly to the service telephone—dinner for three! It comes, he lays the table, dirties the plates, knives, and forks, etc. But he has to get rid of the food too. Not only is he a man of brain; he has a resolute and capacious stomach! But after eating three tournedos, the rice soufflé is too much for him! He even smokes a cigar and two cigarettes to carry out the illusion. Ah, but it was magnificently thorough! Then, having moved on the hands of the clock to 8.47, he smashes it and stops it. The one thing he does not do is to draw the curtains. But if there had been a real dinner party the curtains would have been drawn as soon as the light began to fail. Then he hurries out, mentioning the guests to the lift man in passing. He hurries to a telephone box, and as near as possible to 8.47 rings up the doctor with his master's dying cry. So successful is his idea that no one ever inquires if a call was put through from Flat 11 at that time."

"Except Hercule Poirot, I suppose?" I said sarcastically.

"Not even Hercule Poirot," said my friend, with a smile. "I am about to inquire now. I had to prove my point to you first. But you will see, I shall be right; and then Japp, to whom I have already given a hint, will be able to arrest the respectable Graves. I wonder how much of the money he has spent."

Poirot *was* right. He always is, confound him!

ELEVEN
The Case of the Missing Will

The problem presented to us by Miss Violet Marsh made rather a pleasant change from our usual routine work. Poirot had received a brisk and business-like note from the lady asking for an appointment, and he had replied asking her to call upon him at eleven o'clock the following day.

She arrived punctually—a tall, handsome young woman, plainly but neatly dressed, with an assured and business-like manner. Clearly a young woman who meant to get on in the world. I am not a great admirer of the so-called New Woman myself, and, in spite of her good looks, I was not particularly prepossessed in her favour.

"My business is of a somewhat unusual nature, Monsieur Poirot," she began, after she had accepted a chair. "I had better begin at the beginning and tell you the whole story."

"If you please, mademoiselle."

"I am an orphan. My father was one of two brothers, sons of a small yeoman farmer in Devonshire. The farm was a poor one, and the elder brother, Andrew, emigrated to Australia, where he did very well indeed, and by means of successful speculation in land became a very rich man. The younger brother, Roger (my father), had no leanings towards the agricultural life. He managed to educate himself a little, and obtained a post as a clerk with a small firm. He married slightly above him; my mother was the daughter of a poor artist. My father died when I was six years old. When I was fourteen, my mother followed him to the grave. My only living relation then was my Uncle Andrew, who had recently returned from Australia and bought a small place, Crabtree Manor, in his native county. He was exceedingly kind to his brother's orphan child, took me to live with him, and treated me in every way as though I was his own daughter.

"Crabtree Manor, in spite of its name, is really only an old farmhouse. Farming was in my uncle's blood, and he was intensely interested in various modern farming experiments. Although kindness itself to me, he had certain peculiar and deeply-rooted ideas as to the up-bringing of women. Himself a man of little or no education, though possessing remarkable shrewdness, he placed little value on what he called 'book knowledge.' He was especially opposed to the education of women. In his opinion, girls should learn practical housework and dairy-work, be useful about the home, and have as little to do with book learning as possible. He proposed to bring me up on these lines, to my bitter disappointment and annoyance. I rebelled frankly. I knew that I possessed a good brain, and had absolutely no talent for domestic duties. My uncle and I had many bitter arguments on the subject, for, though much attached to each other, we were both self-willed. I was lucky enough to win a scholarship, and up to a certain point was successful in getting my own way. The crisis arose when I resolved to go to Girton. I had a little money of my own, left me by my mother, and I was quite determined to make the best use of the gifts God had given me. I had one long, final argument with my uncle. He put the facts plainly before me. He had no other relations, and he had intended me to be his sole heiress. As I have told you, he was a very rich man. If I persisted in these 'new-fangled notions' of mine, however, I need look for nothing from him. I remained polite, but firm. I should always be deeply attached to him, I told him, but I must lead my own life. We parted on that note. 'You fancy your brains, my girl,' were his last words. 'I've no book learning, but, for all that, I'll pit mine against yours any day. We'll see what we shall see.'

"That was nine years ago. I have stayed with him for a weekend occasionally, and our relations were perfectly amicable, though his views remained unaltered. He never referred to my having matriculated, nor to my B.Sc. For the last three years his health had been failing, and a month ago he died.

"I am now coming to the point of my visit. My uncle left a most extraordinary will. By its terms, Crabtree Manor and its contents are to be at my disposal for a year from his death—'during which time my clever niece may prove her wits,' the actual words run. At the end of that period, 'my wits having proved better than hers,' the house and all my uncle's large fortune pass to various charitable institutions."

"That is a little hard on you, mademoiselle, seeing that you were Mr. Marsh's only blood relation."

"I do not look on it in that way. Uncle Andrew warned me fairly, and I chose my own path. Since I would not fall in with his wishes, he was at perfect liberty to leave his money to whom he pleased."

"Was the will drawn up by a lawyer?"

"No; it was written on a printed will-form and witnessed by the man and his wife who live in the house and do for my uncle."

"There might be a possibility of upsetting such a will?"

"I would not even attempt to do such a thing."

"You regard it, then, as a sporting challenge on the part of your uncle?"

"That is exactly how I look upon it."

"It bears that interpretation, certainly," said Poirot thoughtfully. "Somewhere in this rambling old manor-house your uncle has concealed either a sum of money in notes or possibly a second will, and has given you a year in which to exercise your ingenuity to find it."

"Exactly, Monsieur Poirot; and I am paying you the compliment

166

of assuming that your ingenuity will be greater than mine."

"Eh, eh! but that is very charming of you. My grey cells are at your disposal. You have made no search yourself?"

"Only a cursory one; but I have too much respect for my uncle's undoubted abilities to fancy that the task will be an easy one."

"Have you the will or a copy of it with you?"

Miss Marsh handed a document across the table. Poirot ran through it, nodding to himself.

"Made three years ago. Dated March 25; and the time is given also—11 a.m.—that is very suggestive. It narrows the field of search. Assuredly it is another will we have to seek for. A will made even half-an-hour later would upset this. *Eh bien*, mademoiselle, it is a problem charming and ingenious that you have presented to me here. I shall have all the pleasure in the world in solving it for you. Granted that your uncle was a man of ability, his grey cells cannot have been of the quality of Hercule Poirot's!"

(Really, Poirot's vanity is blatant!)

"Fortunately, I have nothing of moment on hand at the minute. Hastings and I will go down to Crabtree Manor to-night. The man and wife who attended on your uncle are still there, I presume?"

"Yes, their name is Baker."

* * *

The following morning saw us started on the hunt proper. We had arrived late the night before. Mr. and Mrs. Baker, having received a telegram from Miss Marsh, were expecting us. They were a pleasant couple, the man gnarled and pink-cheeked, like a shrivelled pippin, and his wife a woman of vast proportions and true Devonshire calm.

Tired with our journey and the eight-mile drive from the station, we had retired at once to bed after a supper of roast chicken, apple pie, and Devonshire cream. We had now disposed of an excellent breakfast, and were sitting in a small panelled room which had been the late Mr. Marsh's study and living-room. A roll-top desk stuffed with papers, all neatly docketed, stood against the wall, and a big leather armchair showed plainly that it had been its owner's constant resting-place. A big chintz-covered settee ran along the opposite wall, and the deep low window seats were covered with the same faded chintz of an old-fashioned pattern.

"*Eh bien, mon ami,*" said Poirot, lighting one of his tiny cigarettes, "we must map out our plan of campaign. Already I have made a rough survey of the house, but I am of opinion that any clue will be found in this room. We shall have to go through the documents in the desk with meticulous care. Naturally, I do not expect to find the will amongst them; but it is likely that some apparently innocent paper may conceal the clue to its hiding-place. But first we must have a little information. Ring the bell, I pray of you."

I did so. While we were waiting for it to be answered, Poirot walked up and down, looking about him approvingly.

"A man of method this Mr. Marsh. See how neatly the packets of papers are docketed; then the key to each drawer has its ivory label—so has the key of the china cabinet on the wall; and see with what precision the china within is arranged. It rejoices the heart. Nothing here offends the eye——"

He came to an abrupt pause, as his eye was caught by the key of the desk itself, to which a dirty envelope was affixed. Poirot frowned at it and withdrew it from the lock. On it were scrawled the words: "Key of Roll Top Desk," in a crabbed handwriting, quite unlike the neat superscriptions on the other keys.

"An alien note," said Poirot, frowning. "I could swear that here we have no longer the personality of Mr. Marsh. But who else has been in the house? Only Miss Marsh, and she, if I mistake not, is also a young lady of method and order."

Baker came in answer to the bell.

"Will you fetch madame your wife, and answer a few questions?"

Baker departed, and in a few moments returned with Mrs. Baker, wiping her hands on her apron and beaming all over her face.

In a few clear words Poirot set forth the object of his mission. The Bakers were immediately sympathetic.

"Us don't want to see Miss Violet done out of what's hers," declared the woman. "Cruel hard 'twould be for hospitals to get it all."

Poirot proceeded with his questions. Yes, Mr. and Mrs. Baker remembered perfectly witnessing the will. Baker had previously been sent into the neighbouring town to get two printed will-forms.

"Two?" said Poirot sharply.

"Yes, sir, for safety like, I suppose, in case he should spoil one—and sure enough, so he did do. Us had signed one——"

"What time of day was that?"

Baker scratched his head, but his wife was quicker.

"Why, to be sure, I'd just put the milk on for the cocoa at eleven. Don't ee remember? It had all boiled over on the stove when us got back to kitchen."

"And afterwards?"

"'Twould be about an hour later. Us had to go in again. 'I've made a mistake,' says old master, 'had to tear the whole thing up. I'll trouble you to sign again,' and us did. And afterwards master give us a tidy sum of money each. 'I've left you nothing in my will,' says he, 'but each year I live you'll have this to be a nest-egg when I'm gone'; and sure enough, so he did."

Poirot reflected.

"After you had signed the second time, what did Mr. Marsh do? Do you know?"

"Went out to the village to pay tradesmen's books."

That did not seem very promising. Poirot tried another tack. He held out the key of the desk.

169

"Is that your master's writing?"

I may have imagined it, but I fancied that a moment or two elapsed before Baker replied: "Yes, sir, it is."

"He's lying," I thought. "But why?"

"Has your master let the house?—have there been any strangers in it during the last three years?"

"No, sir."

"No visitors?"

"Only Miss Violet."

"No strangers of any kind been inside this room?"

"No, sir."

"You forget the workmen, Jim," his wife reminded him.

"Workmen?" Poirot wheeled round on her. "What workmen?"

The woman explained that about two years and a half ago workmen had been in the house to do certain repairs. She was quite vague as to what the repairs were. Her view seemed to be that the whole thing was a fad of her master's and quite unnecessary. Part of the time the workmen had been in the study; but what they had done there she could not say, as her master had not let either of them into the room whilst the work was in progress. Unfortunately, they could not remember the name of the firm employed, beyond the fact that it was a Plymouth one.

"We progress, Hastings," said Poirot, rubbing his hands as the Bakers left the room. "Clearly he made a second will and then had workmen from Plymouth in to make a suitable hiding-place. Instead of wasting time taking up the floor and tapping the walls, we will go to Plymouth."

With a little trouble, we were able to get the information we wanted. After one or two essays, we found the firm employed by Mr. Marsh.

Their employees had all been with them many years, and it was easy to find the two men who had worked under Mr. Marsh's orders. They remembered the job perfectly. Amongst various other minor jobs, they had taken up one of the bricks of the old-fashioned fireplace, made a cavity beneath, and so cut the brick that it was impossible to see the join. By pressing on the second brick from the end, the whole thing was raised. It had been quite a complicated piece of work, and the old gentleman had been very fussy about it. Our informant was a man called Coghan, a big, gaunt man with a grizzled moustache. He seemed an intelligent fellow.

We returned to Crabtree Manor in high spirits, and, locking the study door, proceeded to put our newly acquired knowledge into effect. It was impossible to see any sign on the bricks, but when we pressed in the manner indicated, a deep cavity was at once disclosed.

Eagerly Poirot plunged in his hand. Suddenly his face fell from complacent elation to consternation. All he held was a charred fragment of stiff paper. But for it, the cavity was empty.

"*Sacré!*" cried Poirot angrily. "Some one has been before us."

We examined the scrap of paper anxiously. Clearly it was a fragment of what we sought. A portion of Baker's signature remained, but no indication of what the terms of the will had been.

Poirot sat back on his heels. His expression would have been comical if we had not been so overcome.

"I understand it not," he growled. "Who destroyed this? And what was their object?"

"The Bakers?" I suggested.

"*Pourquoi?* Neither will makes any provision for them, and they are more likely to be kept on with Miss Marsh than if the place became the property of a hospital. How could it be to anyone's advantage to destroy the will? The hospitals benefit—yes; but one cannot suspect institutions."

"Perhaps the old man changed his mind and destroyed it himself," I suggested.

Poirot rose to his feet, dusting his knees with his usual care.

"That may be," he admitted. "One of your more sensible observations, Hastings. Well, we can do no more here. We have done all that mortal man can do. We have successfully pitted our wits against the late Andrew Marsh's; but, unfortunately, his niece is no better off for our success."

By driving to the station at once, we were just able to catch a train to London, though not the principal express. Poirot was sad and dissatisfied. For my part, I was tired and dozed in a corner. Suddenly, as we were just moving out of Taunton, Poirot uttered a piercing squeal.

"*Vite*, Hastings! Awake and jump! But jump I say!"

Before I knew where I was we were standing on the platform, bareheaded and minus our valises, whilst the train disappeared into the night. I was furious. But Poirot paid no attention.

"Imbecile that I have been!" he cried. "Triple imbecile! Not again will I vaunt my little grey cells!"

"That's a good job at any rate," I said grumpily. "But what is this all about?"

As usual, when following out his own ideas, Poirot paid absolutely no attention to me.

"The tradesmen's books—I have left them entirely out of account! Yes, but where? Where? Never mind, I cannot be mistaken. We must return at once."

Easier said than done. We managed to get a slow train to Exeter, and there Poirot hired a car. We arrived back at Crabtree Manor in the small hours of the morning. I pass over the bewilderment of the Bakers when we had at last aroused them. Paying no attention to anybody, Poirot strode at once to the study.

"I have been, not a triple imbecile, but thirty-six times one, my friend," he deigned to remark. "Now, behold!"

Going straight to the desk, he drew out the key, and detached the envelope from it. I stared at him stupidly. How could he possibly hope to find a big will-form in that tiny envelope? With great care he cut open the envelope, laying it out flat. Then he lighted the fire and held the plain inside surface of the envelope to the flame. In a few minutes faint characters began to appear.

"Look, *mon ami*!" cried Poirot in triumph.

I looked. There were just a few lines of faint writing stating briefly that he left everything to his niece, Violet Marsh. It was dated March 25, 12.30 p.m., and witnessed by Albert Pike, confectioner, and Jessie Pike, married woman.

"But is it legal?" I gasped.

"As far as I know, there is no law against writing your will in a blend of disappearing and sympathetic ink. The intention of the testator is clear, and the beneficiary is his only living relation. But the cleverness of him! He foresaw every step that a searcher would take—that I, miserable imbecile, took. He gets two will-forms, makes the servants sign twice, then sallies out with his will written on the inside of a dirty envelope and a fountain-pen containing his little ink mixture. On some excuse he gets the confectioner and his wife to sign their names under his own signature, then he ties it to the key of his desk and chuckles to himself. If his niece sees through his little ruse, she will have justified her choice of life and elaborate education, and be thoroughly welcome to his money."

"She didn't see through it, did she?" I said slowly. "It seems rather unfair. The old man really won."

"But no, Hastings. It is *your* wits that go astray. Miss Marsh proved the astuteness of her wits and the value of the higher education for women by at once putting the matter in *my* hands. Always employ the expert. She has amply proved her right to the money."

I wonder—I very much wonder—what old Andrew Marsh would have thought!

THE END

THE MURDER
⊸ ON ⊷
THE LINKS

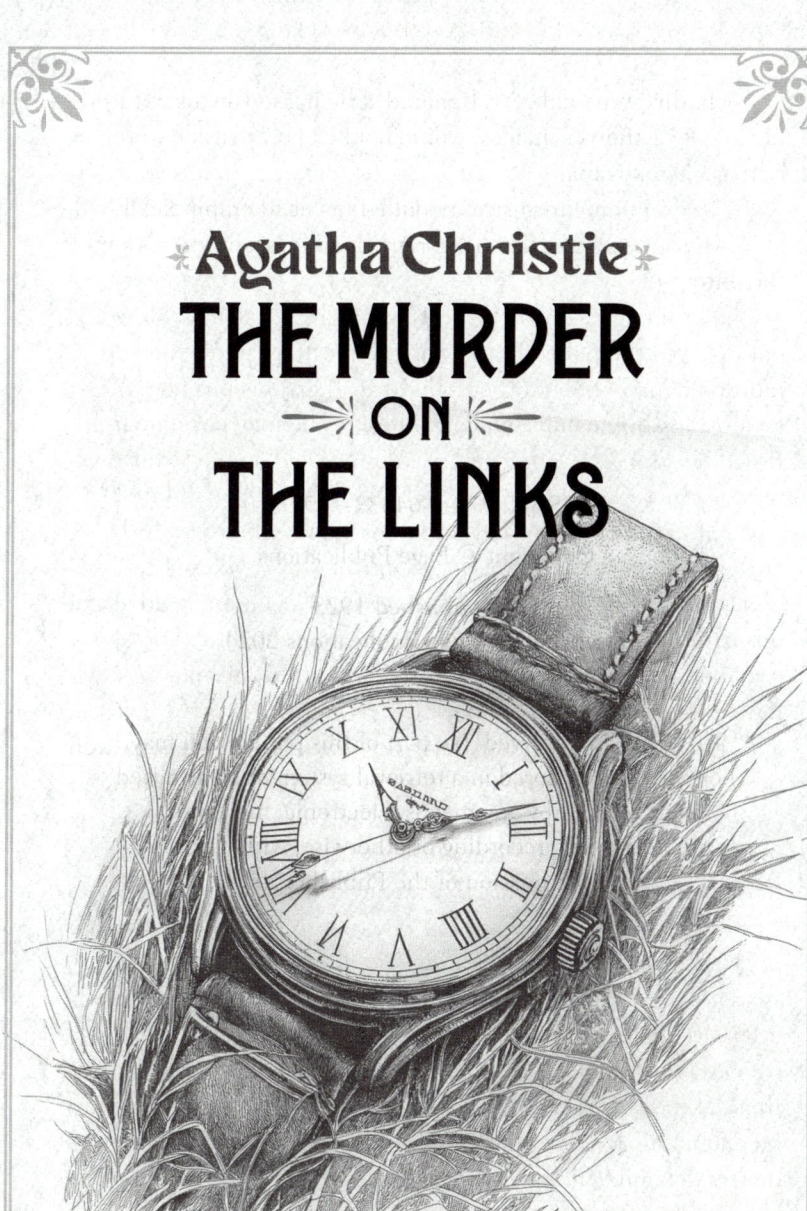

Agatha Christie
THE MURDER
ON
THE LINKS

PAGE CLASSICS

ISBN: 978-1-64833-749-9

First published 1923
Published by Page Publications 2024

Printed in China

Contents

1.	A Fellow Traveller	1
2.	An Appeal for Help	7
3.	At the Villa Geneviève	18
4.	The Letter Signed "Bella"	28
5.	Mrs. Renauld's Story	36
6.	The Scene of the Crime	45
7.	The Mysterious Madame Daubreuil	52
8.	An Unexpected Meeting	63
9.	M. Giraud Finds Some Clues	72
10.	Gabriel Stonor	79
11.	Jack Renauld	86
12.	Poirot Elucidates Certain Points	97
13.	The Girl with the Anxious Eyes	105
14.	The Second Body	114
15.	A Photograph	121
16.	The Beroldy Case	129
17.	We Make Further Investigations	135
18.	Giraud Acts	142

19.	I Use My Grey Cells	148
20.	An Amazing Statement	154
21.	Hercule Poirot on the Case!	164
22.	I Find Love	171
23.	Difficulties Ahead	180
24.	"Save Him!"	185
25.	An Unexpected Dénouement	193
26.	I Receive a Letter	198
27.	Jack Renauld's Story	203
28.	Journey's End	214

ONE
A Fellow Traveller

I believe that a well-known anecdote exists to the effect that a young writer, determined to make the commencement of his story forcible and original enough to catch and rivet the attention of the most blasé of editors, penned the following sentence: "'Hell!' said the Duchess."

Strangely enough, this tale of mine opens in much the same fashion. Only the lady who gave utterance to the exclamation was not a Duchess!

It was a day in early June. I had been transacting some business in Paris and was returning by the morning service to London where I was still sharing rooms with my old friend, the Belgian ex-detective, Hercule Poirot.

The Calais express was singularly empty—in fact, my own compartment held only one other traveller. I had made a somewhat hurried departure from the hotel and was busy assuring myself that I had duly collected all my traps when the train started. Up till then I had hardly noticed my companion, but I was now violently recalled to the fact of her existence. Jumping up from her seat, she let down the window and stuck her head out, withdrawing it a moment later with the brief and forcible ejaculation "Hell!"

Now I am old-fashioned. A woman, I consider, should be womanly. I have no patience with the modern neurotic girl who jazzes from morning to night, smokes like a chimney, and uses language which would make a Billingsgate fishwoman blush!

I looked up now, frowning slightly, into a pretty, impudent face, surmounted by a rakish little red hat. A thick cluster of black curls hid each ear. I judged that she was little more than seventeen, but her face was covered with powder, and her lips were quite impossibly scarlet.

Nothing abashed, she returned my glance, and executed an expressive grimace.

"Dear me, we've shocked the kind gentleman!" she observed to an imaginary audience. "I apologize for my language! Most unladylike, and all that, but Oh, Lord, there's reason enough for it! Do you know I've lost my only sister?"

"Really?" I said politely. "How unfortunate."

"He disapproves!" remarked the lady. "He disapproves utterly—of me, and my sister—which last is unfair, because he hasn't seen her!"

I opened my mouth, but she forestalled me.

"Say no more! Nobody loves me! I shall go into the garden and eat worms! Boohoo! I am crushed!"

She buried herself behind a large comic French paper. In a minute or two I saw her eyes stealthily peeping at me over the top. In spite of myself I could not help smiling, and in a minute she had tossed the paper aside, and had burst into a merry peal of laughter.

"I knew you weren't such a mutt as you looked," she cried.

Her laughter was so infectious that I could not help joining in, though I hardly cared for the word "mutt." The girl was certainly all that I most disliked, but that was no reason why I should make myself ridiculous by my attitude. I prepared to unbend. After all, she was decidedly pretty....

"There! Now we're friends!" declared the minx. "Say you're sorry about my sister—"

"I am desolated!"

"That's a good boy!"

"Let me finish. I was going to add that, although I am

2

desolated, I can manage to put up with her absence very well." I made a little bow.

But this most unaccountable of damsels frowned and shook her head.

"Cut it out. I prefer the 'dignified disapproval' stunt. Oh, your face! 'Not one of us,' it said. And you were right there—though, mind you, it's pretty hard to tell nowadays. It's not every one who can distinguish between a demi and a duchess. There now, I believe I've shocked you again! You've been dug out of the back-woods, you have. Not that I mind that. We could do with a few more of your sort. I just hate a fellow who gets fresh. It makes me mad."

She shook her head vigorously.

"What are you like when you're mad?" I inquired with a smile.

"A regular little devil! Don't care what I say, or what I do, either! I nearly did a chap in once. Yes, really. He'd have deserved it too. Italian blood I've got. I shall get into trouble one of these days."

"Well," I begged, "don't get mad with me."

"I shan't. I like you—did the first moment I set eyes on you. But you looked so disapproving that I never thought we should make friends."

"Well, we have. Tell me something about yourself."

"I'm an actress. No—not the kind you're thinking of, lunching at the Savoy covered with jewellery, and with their photograph in every paper saying how much they love Madame So and So's face cream. I've been on the boards since I was a kid of six—tumbling."

"I beg your pardon," I said puzzled.

"Haven't you seen child acrobats?"

"Oh, I understand."

"I'm American born, but I've spent most of my life in England. We got a new show now—"

"We?"

"My sister and I. Sort of song and dance, and a bit of patter, and a dash of the old business thrown in. It's quite a new idea, and it hits them every time. There's to be money in it—"

My new acquaintance leaned forward, and discoursed volubly, a great many of her terms being quite unintelligible to me. Yet I found myself evincing an increasing interest in her. She seemed such a curious mixture of child and woman. Though perfectly worldly-wise, and able, as she expressed it, to take care of herself, there was yet something curiously ingenuous in her single-minded attitude towards life, and her whole-hearted determination to "make good." This glimpse of a world unknown to me was not without its charm, and I enjoyed seeing her vivid little face light up as she talked.

We passed through Amiens. The name awakened many memories. My companion seemed to have an intuitive knowledge of what was in my mind.

"Thinking of the War?"

I nodded.

"You were through it, I suppose?"

"Pretty well. I was wounded once, and after the Somme they invalided me out altogether. I had a half fledged Army job for a bit. I'm a sort of private secretary now to an M. P."

"My! That's brainy!"

"No, it isn't. There's really awfully little to do. Usually a couple of hours every day sees me through. It's dull work too. In fact, I don't know what I should do if I hadn't got something to fall back upon."

"Don't say you collect bugs!"

"No. I share rooms with a very interesting man. He's a Belgian—an ex-detective. He's set up as a private detective in London, and he's doing extraordinarily well. He's really a very marvellous little man. Time and again he has proved to be right where the official police have failed."

My companion listened with widening eyes.

"Isn't that interesting, now? I just adore crime. I go to all the mysteries on the movies. And when there's a murder on I just devour the papers."

"Do you remember the Styles Case?" I asked.

"Let me see, was that the old lady who was poisoned? Somewhere down in Essex?"

I nodded.

"That was Poirot's first big case. Undoubtedly, but for him, the murderer would have escaped scot-free. It was a most wonderful bit of detective work."

Warming to my subject, I ran over the heads of the affair, working up to the triumphant and unexpected dénouement. The girl listened spellbound. In fact, we were so absorbed that the train drew into Calais station before we realized it.

"My goodness gracious me!" cried my companion. "Where's my powder-puff?"

She proceeded to bedaub her face liberally, and then applied a stick of lip salve to her lips, observing the effect in a small pocket glass, and betraying not the faintest sign of self-consciousness.

"I say," I hesitated. "I dare say it's cheek on my part, but why do all that sort of thing?"

The girl paused in her operations, and stared at me with undisguised surprise.

"It isn't as though you weren't so pretty that you can afford to do without it," I said stammeringly.

"My dear boy! I've got to do it. All the girls do. Think I want to look like a little frump up from the country?" She took one last look in the mirror, smiled approval, and put it and her vanity-box away in her bag. "That's better. Keeping up appearances is a bit of a fag, I grant, but if a girl respects herself it's up to her not to let herself get slack."

To this essentially moral sentiment, I had no reply. A point of view makes a great difference.

I secured a couple of porters, and we alighted on the platform. My companion held out her hand.

"Good-bye, and I'll mind my language better in future."

"Oh, but surely you'll let me look after you on the boat?"

"Mayn't be on the boat. I've got to see whether that sister of mine got aboard after all anywhere. But thanks all the same."

"Oh, but we're going to meet again, surely? I—" I hesitated. "I want to meet your sister."

We both laughed.

"That's real nice of you. I'll tell her what you say. But I don't fancy we'll meet again. You've been very good to me on the journey, especially after I cheeked you as I did. But what your face expressed first thing is quite true. I'm not your kind. And that brings trouble—*I* know that well enough...."

Her face changed. For the moment all the light-hearted gaiety died out of it. It looked angry—revengeful....

"So good-bye," she finished, in a lighter tone.

"Aren't you even going to tell me your name?" I cried, as she turned away.

She looked over her shoulder. A dimple appeared in each cheek. She was like a lovely picture by Greuze.

"Cinderella," she said, and laughed.

But little did I think when and how I should see Cinderella again.

TWO
An Appeal for Help

It was five minutes past nine when I entered our joint sitting-room for breakfast on the following morning.

My friend Poirot, exact to the minute as usual, was just tapping the shell of his second egg.

He beamed upon me as I entered.

"You have slept well, yes? You have recovered from the crossing so terrible? It is a marvel, almost you are exact this morning. *Pardon*, but your tie is not symmetrical. Permit that I rearrange him."

Elsewhere, I have described Hercule Poirot. An extraordinary little man! Height, five feet four inches, egg-shaped head carried a little to one side, eyes that shone green when he was excited, stiff military moustache, air of dignity immense! He was neat and dandified in appearance. For neatness of any kind, he had an absolute passion. To see an ornament set crooked, or a speck of dust, or a slight disarray in one's attire, was torture to the little man until he could ease his feelings by remedying the matter. "Order" and "Method" were his gods. He had a certain disdain for tangible evidence, such as footprints and cigarette ash, and would maintain that, taken by themselves, they would never enable a detective to solve a problem. Then he would tap his egg-shaped head with absurd complacency, and remark with great satisfaction: "The true work, it is done from *within*. The little grey cells—remember always the little grey cells, *mon ami!*"

I slipped into my seat, and remarked idly, in answer to Poirot's greeting, that an hour's sea passage from Calais to Dover could hardly be dignified by the epithet "terrible."

Poirot waved his egg-spoon in vigorous refutation of my remark.

"*Du tout!* If for an hour one experiences sensations and emotions of the most terrible, one has lived many hours! Does not one of your English poets say that time is counted, not by hours, but by heart-beats?"

"I fancy Browning was referring to something more romantic than sea sickness, though."

"Because he was an Englishman, an Islander to whom *la Manche* was nothing. Oh, you English! With *nous autres* it is different. Figure to yourself that a lady of my acquaintance at the beginning of the war fled to Ostend. There she had a terrible crisis of the nerves. Impossible to escape further except by crossing the sea! And she had a horror—*mais une horreur!*—of the sea! What was she to do? Daily *les Boches* were drawing nearer. Imagine to yourself the terrible situation!"

"What did she do?" I inquired curiously.

"Fortunately her husband was *homme pratique*. He was also very calm, the crises of the nerves, they affected him not. *Il l'a emportée simplement!* Naturally when she reached England she was prostrate, but she still breathed."

Poirot shook his head seriously. I composed my face as best I could.

Suddenly he stiffened and pointed a dramatic finger at the toast rack.

"Ah, par exemple, c'est trop fort!" he cried.

"What is it?"

"This piece of toast. You remark him not?" He whipped the offender out of the rack, and held it up for me to examine.

"Is it square? No. Is it a triangle? Again no. Is it even round?

No. Is it of any shape remotely pleasing to the eye? What symmetry have we here? None."

"It's cut from a cottage loaf," I explained soothingly.

Poirot threw me a withering glance.

"What an intelligence has my friend Hastings!" he exclaimed sarcastically. "Comprehend you not that I have forbidden such a loaf—a loaf haphazard and shapeless, that no baker should permit himself to bake!"

I endeavoured to distract his mind.

"Anything interesting come by the post?"

Poirot shook his head with a dissatisfied air.

"I have not yet examined my letters, but nothing of interest arrives nowadays. The great criminals, the criminals of method, they do not exist. The cases I have been employed upon lately were *banal* to the last degree. In verity I am reduced to recovering lost lap-dogs for fashionable ladies! The last problem that presented any interest was that intricate little affair of the Yardly diamond, and that was—how many months ago, my friend?"

He shook his head despondently, and I roared with laughter.

"Cheer up, Poirot, the luck will change. Open your letters. For all you know, there may be a great Case looming on the horizon."

Poirot smiled, and taking up the neat little letter opener with which he opened his correspondence he slit the tops of the several envelopes that lay by his plate.

"A bill. Another bill. It is that I grow extravagant in my old age. Aha! a note from Japp."

"Yes?" pricked up my ears. The Scotland Yard Inspector had more than once introduced us to an interesting case.

"He merely thanks me (in his fashion) for a little point in the Aberystwyth Case on which I was able to set him right. I am delighted to have been of service to him."

"How does he thank you?" I asked curiously, for I knew my Japp.

"He is kind enough to say that I am a wonderful sport for my age, and that he was glad to have had the chance of letting me in on the case."

This was so typical of Japp, that I could not forbear a chuckle. Poirot continued to read his correspondence placidly.

"A suggestion that I should give a lecture to our local boy scouts. The Countess of Forfanock will be obliged if I will call and see her. Another lap-dog without doubt! And now for the last. Ah—"

I looked up, quick to notice the change of tone. Poirot was reading attentively. In a minute he tossed the sheet over to me.

"This is out of the ordinary, *mon ami*. Read for yourself."

The letter was written on a foreign type of paper, in a bold characteristic hand:

"Villa Geneviève
Merlinville-sur-Mer
France

"*Dear Sir,*

"I am in need of the services of a detective and, for reasons which I will give you later, do not wish to call in the official police. I have heard of you from several quarters, and all reports go to show that you are not only a man of decided ability, but one who also knows how to be discreet. I do not wish to trust details to the post, but, on account of a secret I possess, I go in daily fear of my life. I am convinced that the danger is imminent, and therefore I beg that you will lose no time in crossing to France. I will send a car to meet you at Calais, if you will wire me when you are arriving. I shall be obliged if you will drop all cases you have on hand, and devote yourself solely to my interests. I am prepared to pay any compensation necessary. I shall probably need your services for a considerable period of time, as it may be necessary for you to go out to Santiago, where I spent

10

several years of my life. I shall be content for you to name your own fee.

Assuring you once more that the matter is *urgent*,

"Yours faithfully
"P. T. RENAULD."

Below the signature was a hastily scrawled line, almost illegible: "For God's sake, come!"

I handed the letter back with quickened pulses.

"At last!" I said. "Here is something distinctly out of the ordinary."

"Yes, indeed," said Poirot meditatively.

"You will go of course," I continued.

Poirot nodded. He was thinking deeply. Finally he seemed to make up his mind, and glanced up at the clock. His face was very grave.

"See you, my friend, there is no time to lose. The Continental express leaves Victoria at 11 o'clock. Do not agitate yourself. There is plenty of time. We can allow ten minutes for discussion. You accompany me, *n'est-ce pas?*"

"Well—"

"You told me yourself that your employer needed you not for the next few weeks."

"Oh, that's all right. But this Mr. Renauld hints strongly that his business is private."

"Ta-ta-ta. I will manage M. Renauld. By the way, I seem to know the name?"

"There's a well-known South American millionaire fellow. His name's Renauld. I don't know whether it could be the same."

"But without doubt. That explains the mention of Santiago. Santiago is in Chile, and Chile it is in South America! Ah, but we progress finely."

"Dear me, Poirot," I said, my excitement rising, "I smell some goodly shekels in this. If we succeed, we shall make our fortunes!"

11

"Do not be too sure of that, my friend. A rich man and his money are not so easily parted. Me, I have seen a well-known millionaire turn out a tramful of people to seek for a dropped halfpenny."

I acknowledged the wisdom of this.

"In any case," continued Poirot, "it is not the money which attracts me here. Certainly it will be pleasant to have *carte blanche* in our investigations; one can be sure that way of wasting no time, but it is something a little bizarre in this problem which arouses my interest. You remarked the postscript? How did it strike you?"

I considered.

"Clearly he wrote the letter keeping himself well in hand, but at the end his self-control snapped and, on the impulse of the moment, he scrawled those four desperate words."

But my friend shook his head energetically.

"You are in error. See you not that while the ink of the signature is nearly black, that of the postscript is quite pale?"

"Well?" I said puzzled.

"*Mon Dieu, mon ami*, but use your little grey cells! Is it not obvious? M. Renauld wrote his letter. Without blotting it, he reread it carefully. Then, not on impulse, but deliberately, he added those last words, and blotted the sheet."

"But why?"

"*Parbleu!* so that it should produce the effect upon me that it has upon you."

"What?"

"*Mais, oui*—to make sure of my coming! He reread the letter and was dissatisfied. It was not strong enough!"

He paused, and then added softly, his eyes shining with that green light that always betokened inward excitement: "And so, *mon ami*, since that postscript was added, not on impulse, but soberly, in cold blood, the urgency is very great, and we must reach him as soon as possible."

"Merlinville," I murmured thoughtfully. "I've heard of it, I think."

Poirot nodded.

"It is a quiet little place—but chic! It lies about midway between Bolougne and Calais. It is rapidly becoming the fashion. Rich English people who wish to be quiet are taking it up. M. Renauld has a house in England, I suppose?"

"Yes, in Rutland Gate, as far as I remember. Also a big place in the country, somewhere in Hertfordshire. But I really know very little about him, he doesn't do much in a social way. I believe he has large South American interests in the City, and has spent most of his life out in Chile and the Argentino."

"Well, we shall hear all details from the man himself. Come, let us pack. A small suit-case each, and then a taxi to Victoria."

"And the Countess?" I inquired with a smile.

"Ah! *je m'en fiche!* Her case was certainly not interesting."

"Why so sure of that?"

"Because in that case she would have come, not written. A woman cannot wait—always remember that, Hastings."

Eleven o'clock saw our departure from Victoria on our way to Dover. Before starting Poirot had despatched a telegram to Mr. Renauld giving the time of our arrival at Calais. "I'm surprised you haven't invested in a few bottles of some sea sick remedy, Poirot," I observed maliciously, as I recalled our conversation at breakfast.

My friend, who was anxiously scanning the weather, turned a reproachful face upon me.

"Is it that you have forgotten the method most excellent of Laverguier? His system, I practise it always. One balances oneself, if you remember, turning the head from left to right, breathing in and out, counting six between each breath."

"H'm," I demurred. "You'll be rather tired of balancing yourself and counting six by the time you get to Santiago, or Buenos Ayres, or wherever it is you land."

"*Quelle idée!* You do not figure to yourself that I shall go to Santiago?"

"Mr. Renauld suggests it in his letter."

"He did not know the methods of Hercule Poirot. I do not run to and fro, making journeys, and agitating myself. My work is done from within—*here*—" he tapped his forehead significantly.

As usual, this remark roused my argumentative faculty.

"It's all very well, Poirot, but I think you are falling into the habit of despising certain things too much. A finger-print has led sometimes to the arrest and conviction of a murderer."

"And has, without doubt, hanged more than one innocent man," remarked Poirot dryly.

"But surely the study of finger-prints and footprints, cigarette ash, different kinds of mud, and other clues that comprise the minute observation of details—all these are of vital importance?"

"But certainly. I have never said otherwise. The trained observer, the expert, without doubt he is useful! But the others, the Hercules Poirots, they are above the experts! To them the experts bring the facts, their business is the method of the crime, its logical deduction, the proper sequence and order of the facts; above all, the true psychology of the case. You have hunted the fox, yes?"

"I have hunted a bit, now and again," I said, rather bewildered by this abrupt change of subject. "Why?"

"*Eh bien*, this hunting of the fox, you need the dogs, no?"

"Hounds," I corrected gently. "Yes, of course."

"But yet," Poirot wagged his finger at me. "You did not descend from your horse and run along the ground smelling with your nose and uttering loud Ow Ows?"

In spite of myself I laughed immoderately. Poirot nodded in a satisfied manner.

"So. You leave the work of the d— hounds to the hounds. Yet you demand that I, Hercule Poirot, should make myself ridiculous by lying down (possibly on damp grass) to study hypothetical footprints, and should scoop up cigarette ash when I do not know one kind from the other. Remember the Plymouth Express mystery.

The good Japp departed to make a survey of the railway line. When he returned, I, without having moved from my apartments, was able to tell him exactly what he had found."

"So you are of the opinion that Japp wasted his time."

"Not at all, since his evidence confirmed my theory. But *I* should have wasted my time if *I* had gone. It is the same with so called 'experts.' Remember the handwriting testimony in the Cavendish Case. One counsel's questioning brings out testimony as to the resemblances, the defence brings evidence to show dissimilarity. All the language is very technical. And the result? What we all knew in the first place. The writing was very like that of John Cavendish. And the psychological mind is faced with the question 'Why?' Because it was actually his? Or because some one wished us to think it was his? I answered that question, *mon ami*, and answered it correctly."

And Poirot, having effectually silenced, if not convinced me, leaned back with a satisfied air.

On the boat, I knew better than to disturb my friend's solitude. The weather was gorgeous, and the sea as smooth as the proverbial mill-pond, so I was hardly surprised to hear that Laverguier's method had once more justified itself when a smiling Poirot joined me on disembarking at Calais. A disappointment was in store for us, as no car had been sent to meet us, but Poirot put this down to his telegram having been delayed in transit.

"Since it is *carte blanche*, we will hire a car," he said cheerfully. And a few minutes later saw us creaking and jolting along, in the most ramshackle of automobiles that ever plied for hire, in the direction of Merlinville.

My spirits were at their highest.

"What gorgeous air!" I exclaimed. "This promises to be a delightful trip."

"For you, yes. For me, I have work to do, remember, at our journey's end."

"Bah!" I said cheerfully. "You will discover all, ensure this Mr.

Renauld's safety, run the would-be assassins to earth, and all will finish in a blaze of glory."

"You are sanguine, my friend."

"Yes, I feel absolutely assured of success. Are you not the one and only Hercule Poirot?"

But my little friend did not rise to the bait. He was observing me gravely.

"You are what the Scotch people call 'fey,' Hastings. It presages disaster."

"Nonsense. At any rate, you do not share my feelings."

"No, but I am afraid."

"Afraid of what?"

"I do not know. But I have a premonition—a *je ne sais quoi!*" He spoke so gravely, that I was impressed in spite of myself.

"I have a feeling," he said slowly, "that this is going to be a big affair—a long, troublesome problem that will not be easy to work out."

I would have questioned him further, but we were just coming into the little town of Merlinville, and we slowed up to inquire the way to the Villa Geneviève.

"Straight on, monsieur, through the town. The Villa Geneviève is about half a mile the other side. You cannot miss it. A big Villa, overlooking the sea."

We thanked our informant, and drove on, leaving the town behind. A fork in the road brought us to a second halt. A peasant was trudging towards us, and we waited for him to come up to us in order to ask the way again. There was a tiny Villa standing right by the road, but it was too small and dilapidated to be the one we wanted. As we waited, the gate of it swung open and a girl came out.

The peasant was passing us now, and the driver leaned forward from his seat and asked for direction.

"The Villa Geneviève? Just a few steps up this road to the right, monsieur. You could see it if it were not for the curve."

The chauffeur thanked him, and started the car again. My eyes were fascinated by the girl who still stood, with one hand on the gate, watching us. I am an admirer of beauty, and here was one whom nobody could have passed without remark. Very tall, with the proportions of a young goddess, her uncovered golden head gleaming in the sunlight, I swore to myself that she was one of the most beautiful girls I had ever seen. As we swung up the rough road, I turned my head to look after her.

"By Jove, Poirot," I exclaimed, "did you see that young goddess."

Poirot raised his eyebrows.

"*Ça commence!*" he murmured. "Already you have seen a goddess!"

"But, hang it all, wasn't she?"

"Possibly. I did not remark the fact."

"Surely you noticed her?"

"*Mon ami*, two people rarely see the same thing. You, for instance, saw a goddess. I…" he hesitated.

"Yes?"

"I saw only a girl with anxious eyes," said Poirot gravely.

But at that moment we drew up at a big green gate, and, simultaneously, we both uttered an exclamation. Before it stood an imposing *sergent de ville*. He held up his hand to bar our way.

"You cannot pass, monsieurs."

"But we wish to see Mr. Renauld," I cried. "We have an appointment. This is his Villa, isn't it?"

"Yes, monsieur, but—"

Poirot leaned forward.

"But what?"

"M. Renauld was murdered this morning."

THREE
At the Villa Geneviève

In a moment Poirot had leapt from the car, his eyes blazing with excitement. He caught the man by the shoulder.

"What is that you say? Murdered? When? How?"

The *sergent de ville* drew himself up.

"I cannot answer any questions, monsieur."

"True. I comprehend." Poirot reflected for a minute. "The Commissary of Police, he is without doubt within?"

"Yes, monsieur."

Poirot took out a card, and scribbled a few words on it.

"*Voilà!* Will you have the goodness to see that this card is sent in to the commissary at once?"

The man took it and, turning his head over his shoulder, whistled. In a few seconds a comrade joined him and was handed Poirot's message. There was a wait of some minutes, and then a short stout man with a huge moustache came bustling down to the gate. The *sergent de ville* saluted and stood aside.

"My dear M. Poirot," cried the new-comer, "I am delighted to see you. Your arrival is most opportune."

Poirot's face had lighted up.

"M. Bex! This is indeed a pleasure." He turned to me. "This is an English friend of mine, Captain Hastings—M. Lucien Bex."

The commissary and I bowed to each other ceremoniously, then M. Bex turned once more to Poirot.

"*Mon vieux*, I have not seen you since 1909, that time in Ostend. I heard that you had left the Force?"

"So I have. I run a private business in London."

"And you say you have information to give which may assist us?"

"Possibly you know it already. You were aware that I had been sent for?"

"No. By whom?"

"The dead man. It seems he knew an attempt was going to be made on his life. Unfortunately he sent for me too late."

"*Sacri tonnerre!*" ejaculated the Frenchman. "So he foresaw his own murder? That upsets our theories considerably! But come inside."

He held the gate open, and we commenced walking towards the house. M. Bex continued to talk:

"The examining magistrate, M. Hautet, must hear of this at once. He has just finished examining the scene of the crime and is about to begin his interrogations. A charming man. You will like him. Most sympathetic. Original in his methods, but an excellent judge."

"When was the crime committed?" asked Poirot.

"The body was discovered this morning about nine o'clock. Madame Renauld's evidence, and that of the doctors goes to show that the death must have occurred about 2 a.m. But enter, I pray of you."

We had arrived at the steps which led up to the front door of the Villa. In the hall another *sergent de ville* was sitting. He rose at sight of the commissary.

"Where is M. Hautet now?" inquired the latter.

"In the *salon*, monsieur."

M. Bex opened a door to the left of the hall, and we passed in. M. Hautet and his clerk were sitting at a big round table. They looked up as we entered. The commissary introduced us, and explained our presence.

M. Hautet, the Juge d'Instruction, was a tall, gaunt man, with piercing dark eyes, and a neatly cut grey beard, which he had a habit of caressing as he talked. Standing by the mantelpiece was an elderly man, with slightly stooping shoulders, who was introduced to us as Dr. Durand.

"Most extraordinary," remarked M. Hautet, as the commissary finished speaking. "You have the letter here, monsieur?"

Poirot handed it to him, and the magistrate read it.

"H'm. He speaks of a secret. What a pity he was not more explicit. We are much indebted to you, M. Poirot. I hope you will do us the honour of assisting us in our investigations. Or are you obliged to return to London?"

"M. le juge, I propose to remain. I did not arrive in time to prevent my client's death, but I feel myself bound in honour to discover the assassin."

The magistrate bowed.

"These sentiments do you honour. Also, without doubt, Madame Renauld will wish to retain your services. We are expecting M. Giraud from the Sûreté in Paris any moment, and I am sure that you and he will be able to give each other mutual assistance in your investigations. In the meantime, I hope that you will do me the honour to be present at my interrogations, and I need hardly say that if there is any assistance you require it is at your disposal."

"I thank you, monsieur. You will comprehend that at present I am completely in the dark. I know nothing whatever."

M. Hautet nodded to the commissary, and the latter took up the tale:

"This morning, the old servant Françoise, on descending to start her work, found the front door ajar. Feeling a momentary alarm as to burglars, she looked into the dining-room, but seeing the silver was safe she thought no more about it, concluding that her master had, without doubt, risen early, and gone for a stroll."

"Pardon, monsieur, for interrupting, but was that a common practice of his?"

"No, it was not, but old Françoise has the common idea as regards the English—that they are mad, and liable to do the most unaccountable things at any moment! Going to call her mistress as usual, a younger maid, Léonie, was horrified to discover her gagged and bound, and almost at the same moment news was brought that M. Renauld's body had been discovered, stone dead, stabbed in the back."

"Where?"

"That is one of the most extraordinary features of the case. M. Poirot, the body was lying, face downwards, *in an open grave.*"

"What?"

"Yes. The pit was freshly dug—just a few yards outside the boundary of the Villa grounds."

"And he had been dead—how long?"

Dr. Durand answered this.

"I examined the body this morning at ten o'clock. Death must have taken place at least seven, and possibly ten hours previously."

"H'm, that fixes it at between midnight and 3 a.m."

"Exactly, and Madame Renauld's evidence places it at after 2 a.m. which narrows the field still further. Death must have been instantaneous, and naturally could not have been self-inflicted."

Poirot nodded, and the commissary resumed:

"Madame Renauld was hastily freed from the cords that bound her by the horrified servants. She was in a terrible condition of weakness, almost unconscious from the pain of her bonds. It appears that two masked men entered the bedroom, gagged and bound her, whilst forcibly abducting her husband. This we know at second hand from the servants. On hearing the tragic news, she fell at once into an alarming state of agitation. On arrival, Dr. Durand immediately prescribed a sedative, and we have not yet been able to question her. But without doubt she will awake more calm, and be equal to bearing the strain of the interrogation."

The commissary paused.

"And the inmates of the house, monsieur?"

"There is old Françoise, the housekeeper, she lived for many years with the former owners of the Villa Geneviève. Then there are two young girls, sisters, Denise and Léonie Oulard. Their home is in Merlinville, and they come of the most respectable parents. Then there is the chauffeur whom M. Renauld brought over from England with him, but he is away on a holiday. Finally there are Madame Renauld and her son, M. Jack Renauld. He, too, is away from home at present."

Poirot bowed his head. M. Hautet spoke:

"Marchaud!"

The *sergent de ville* appeared.

"Bring in the woman Françoise."

The man saluted, and disappeared. In a moment or two, he returned, escorting the frightened Françoise.

"You name is Françoise Arrichet?"

"Yes, monsieur."

"You have been a long time in service at the Villa Geneviève?"

"Eleven years with Madame la Vicomtesse. Then when she sold the Villa this spring, I consented to remain on with the English milor. Never did I imagine—"

The magistrate cut her short.

"Without doubt, without doubt. Now, Françoise, in this matter of the front door, whose business was it to fasten it at night?"

"Mine, monsieur. Always I saw to it myself."

"And last night?"

"I fastened it as usual."

"You are sure of that?"

"I swear it by the blessed saints, monsieur."

"What time would that be?"

"The same time as usual, half-past ten, monsieur."

"What about the rest of the household, had they gone up to bed?"

"Madame had retired some time before. Denise and Léonie

22

went up with me. Monsieur was still in his study."

"Then, if any one unfastened the door afterwards, it must have been M. Renauld himself?"

Françoise shrugged her broad shoulders.

"What should he do that for? With robbers and assassins passing every minute! A nice idea! Monsieur was not an imbecile. It is not as though he had had to let *cette dame* out—"

The magistrate interrupted sharply:

"*Cette dame?* What lady do you mean?"

"Why, the lady who came to see him."

"Had a lady been to see him that evening?"

"But yes, monsieur—and many other evenings as well."

"Who was she? Did you know her?"

A rather cunning look spread over the woman's face. "How should I know who it was?" she grumbled. "I did not let her in last night."

"Aha!" roared the examining magistrate, bringing his hand down with a bang on the table. "You would trifle with the police, would you? I demand that you tell me at once the name of this woman who came to visit M. Renauld in the evenings."

"The police—the police," grumbled Françoise. "Never did I think that I should be mixed up with the police. But I know well enough who she was. It was Madame Daubreuil."

The commissary uttered an exclamation, and leaned forward as though in utter astonishment.

"Madame Daubreuil—from the Villa Marguerite just down the road?"

"That is what I said, monsieur. Oh, she is a pretty one, *cellela!*" The old woman tossed her head scornfully.

"Madame Daubreuil," murmured the commissary. "Impossible."

"*Voilà,*" grumbled Françoise. "That is all you get for telling the truth."

"Not at all," said the examining magistrate soothingly. "We

were surprised, that is all. Madame Daubreuil then, and Monsieur Renauld, they were—" he paused delicately. "Eh? It was that without doubt?"

"How should I know? But what will you? Monsieur, he was *milor anglais—trés riche*—and Madame Daubreuil, she was poor, that one—and *trés chic* for all that she lives so quietly with her daughter. Not a doubt of it, she has had her history! She is no longer young, but *ma foi!* I who speak to you have seen the men's heads turn after her as she goes down the street. Besides lately, she has had more money to spend—all the town knows it. The little economies, they are at an end." And Françoise shook her head with an air of unalterable certainty.

M. Hautet stroked his beard reflectively.

"And Madame Renauld?" he asked at length. "How did she take this—friendship."

Françoise shrugged her shoulders.

"She was always most amiable—most polite. One would say that she suspected nothing. But all the same, is it not so, the heart suffers, monsieur? Day by day, I have watched Madame grow paler and thinner. She was not the same woman who arrived here a month ago. Monsieur, too, has changed. He also has had his worries. One could see that he was on the brink of a crisis of the nerves. And who could wonder, with an affair conducted such a fashion? No reticence, no discretion. *Style anglais*, without doubt!"

I bounded indignantly in my seat, but the examining magistrate was continuing his questions, undistracted by side issues.

"You say that M. Renauld had not to let Madame Daubreuil out? Had she left, then?"

"Yes, monsieur. I heard them come out of the study and go to the door. Monsieur said good night, and shut the door after her."

"What time was that?"

"About twenty-five minutes after ten, monsieur."

"Do you know when M. Renauld went to bed?"

"I heard him come up about ten minutes after we did. The

stair creaks so that one hears every one who goes up and down."

"And that is all? You heard no sound of disturbance during the night?"

"Nothing whatever, monsieur."

"Which of the servants came down the first in the morning?"

"I did, monsieur. At once I saw the door swinging open."

"What about the other downstairs windows, were they all fastened?"

"Every one of them. There was nothing suspicious or out of place anywhere."

"Good, Françoise, you can go."

The old woman shuffled towards the door. On the threshold she looked back.

"I will tell you one thing, monsieur. That Madame Daubreuil she is a bad one! Oh, yes, one woman knows about another. She is a bad one, remember that." And, shaking her head sagely, Françoise left the room.

"Léonie Oulard," called the magistrate.

Léonie appeared dissolved in tears, and inclined to be hysterical. M. Hautet dealt with her adroitly. Her evidence was mainly concerned with the discovery of her mistress gagged and bound, of which she gave rather an exaggerated account. She, like Françoise, had heard nothing during the night.

Her sister, Denise, succeeded her. She agreed that her master had changed greatly of late.

"Every day he became more and more morose. He ate less. He was always depressed." But Denise had her own theory. "Without doubt it was the Mafia he had on his track! Two masked men— who else could it be? A terrible society that!"

"It is, of course, possible," said the magistrate smoothly. "Now, my girl, was it you who admitted Madame Daubreuil to the house last night?"

"Not *last* night, monsieur, the night before."

"But Françoise has just told us that Madame Daubreuil was

here last night?"

"No, monsieur. A lady *did* come to see M. Renauld last night, but it was not Madame Daubreuil."

Surprised, the magistrate insisted, but the girl held firm. She knew Madame Daubreuil perfectly by sight. This lady was dark also, but shorter, and much younger. Nothing could shake her statement.

"Had you ever seen this lady before?"

"Never, monsieur." And then the girl added diffidently: "But I think she was English."

"English?"

"Yes, monsieur. She asked for M. Renauld in quite good French, but the accent—one can always tell it, *n'est-ce pas?* Besides when they came out of the study they were speaking in English."

"Did you hear what they said? Could you understand it, I mean?"

"Me, I speak the English very well," said Denise with pride. "The lady was speaking too fast for me to catch what she said, but I heard Monsieur's last words as he opened the door for her." She paused, and then repeated carefully and laboriously:

"'Yeas—yeas—butt for Gaud's saike go nauw!'"

"Yes, yes, but for God's sake go now!" repeated the magistrate.

He dismissed Denise and, after a moment or two for consideration, recalled Françoise. To her he propounded the question as to whether she had not made a mistake in fixing the night of Madame Daubreuil's visit. Françoise, however, proved unexpectedly obstinate. It was last night that Madame Daubreuil had come. Without a doubt it was she. Denise wished to make herself interesting, *voilà tout!* So she had cooked up this fine tale about a strange lady. Airing her knowledge of English too! Probably Monsieur had never spoken that sentence in English at all, and even if he had, it proved nothing, for Madame Daubreuil spoke English perfectly, and generally used that language when talking to M. and Madame

Renauld. "You see, M. Jack, the son of Monsieur, was usually here, and he spoke the French very badly."

The magistrate did not insist. Instead he inquired about the chauffeur, and learned that only yesterday, M. Renauld had declared that he was not likely to use the car, and that Masters might just as well take a holiday.

A perplexed frown was beginning to gather between Poirot's eyes.

"What is it?" I whispered.

He shook his head impatiently, and asked a question:

"Pardon, M. Bex, but without doubt M. Renauld could drive the car himself?"

The commissary looked over at Françoise, and the old woman replied promptly:

"No, Monsieur did not drive himself."

Poirot's frown deepened.

"I wish you would tell me what is worrying you," I said impatiently.

"See you not? In his letter M. Renauld speaks of sending the car for me to Calais."

"Perhaps he meant a hired car," I suggested.

"Doubtless that is so. But why hire a car when you have one of your own. Why choose yesterday to send away the chauffeur on a holiday—suddenly, at a moment's notice? Was it that for some reason he wanted him out of the way before we arrived?"

F O U R

The Letter Signed "Bella"

Françoise had left the room. The magistrate was drumming thoughtfully on the table.

"M. Bex," he said at length, "here we have directly conflicting testimony. Which are we to believe, Françoise or Denise?"

"Denise," said the commissary decidedly. "It was she who let the visitor in. Françoise is old and obstinate, and has evidently taken a dislike to Madame Daubreuil. Besides, our own knowledge tends to show that Renauld was entangled with another woman."

"*Tiens!*" cried M. Hautet. "We have forgotten to inform M. Poirot of that." He searched amongst the papers on the table, and finally handed the one he was in search of to my friend. "This letter, M. Poirot, we found in the pocket of the dead man's overcoat."

Poirot took it and unfolded it. It was somewhat worn and crumbled, and was written in English in a rather unformed hand:

> "*My dearest one*:"
> Why have you not written for so long? You do love me
> still, don't you? Your letters lately have been so different,
> cold and strange, and now this long silence. It makes
> me afraid. If you were to stop loving me! But that's
> impossible—what a silly kid I am—always imagining
> things! But if you *did* stop loving me, I don't know what

I should do—kill myself perhaps! I couldn't live without you. Sometimes I fancy another woman is coming between us. Let her look out, that's all—and you too! I'd as soon kill you as let her have you! I mean it.

"But there, I'm writing high-flown nonsense. You love me, and I love you—yes, love you, love you, love you!

"Your own adoring
"BELLA."

There was no address or date. Poirot handed it back with a grave face.

"And the assumption is, M. le juge—?"

The examining magistrate shrugged his shoulders.

"Obviously M. Renauld was entangled with this Englishwoman—Bella. He comes over here, meets Madame Daubreuil, and starts an intrigue with her. He cools off to the other, and she instantly suspects something. This letter contains a distinct threat. M. Poirot, at first sight the case seemed simplicity itself. Jealousy! The fact that M. Renauld was stabbed in the back seemed to point distinctly to its being a woman's crime."

Poirot nodded.

"The stab in the back, yes—but not the grave! That was laborious work, hard work—no woman dug that grave, monsieur. That was a man's doing."

The commissary exclaimed excitedly: "Yes, yes, you are right. We did not think of that."

"As I said," continued M. Hautet, "at first sight the case seemed simple, but the masked men, and the letter you received from M. Renauld complicate matters. Here we seem to have an entirely different set of circumstances, with no relationship between the two. As regards the letter written to yourself, do you think it is possible that it referred in any way to this 'Bella,' and her threats?"

Poirot shook his head.

"Hardly. A man like M. Renauld, who has led an adventurous life in out-of-the-way places, would not be likely to ask for protection against a woman."

The examining magistrate nodded his head emphatically.

"My view exactly. Then we must look for the explanation of the letter—"

"In Santiago," finished the commissary. "I shall cable without delay to the police in that city, requesting full details of the murdered man's life out there, his love affairs, his business transactions, his friendships, and any enmities he may have incurred. It will be strange if, after that, we do not hold a clue to his mysterious murder."

The commissary looked round for approval.

"Excellent," said Poirot appreciatively.

"His wife, too, may be able to give us a pointer," added the magistrate.

"You have found no other letters from this Bella amongst M. Renauld's effects?" asked Poirot.

"No. Of course one of our first proceedings was to search through his private papers in the study. We found nothing of interest, however. All seemed square and above-board. The only thing at all out of the ordinary was his will. Here it is."

Poirot ran through the document.

"So. A legacy of a thousand pounds to Mr. Stonor—who is he, by the way?"

"M. Renauld's secretary. He remained in England, but was over here once or twice for a week-end."

"And everything else left unconditionally to his beloved wife, Eloise. Simply drawn up, but perfectly legal. Witnessed by the two servants, Denise and Françoise. Nothing so very unusual about that." He handed it back.

"Perhaps," began Bex, "you did not notice—"

"The date?" twinkled Poirot. "But yes, I noticed it. A fortnight ago. Possibly it marks his first intimation of danger. Many rich men die intestate through never considering the likelihood of their demise. But it is dangerous to draw conclusions prematurely. It points, however, to his having a real liking and fondness for his wife, in spite of his amorous intrigues."

"Yes," said M. Hautet doubtfully. "But it is possibly a little unfair on his son, since it leaves him entirely dependent on his mother. If she were to marry again, and her second husband obtained an ascendancy over her, this boy might never touch a penny of his father's money."

Poirot shrugged his shoulders.

"Man is a vain animal. M. Renauld figured to himself, without doubt, that his widow would never marry again. As to the son, it may have been a wise precaution to leave the money in his mother's hands. The sons of rich men are proverbially wild."

"It may be as you say. Now, M. Poirot, you would without doubt like to visit the scene of the crime. I am sorry that the body has been removed, but of course photographs have been taken from every conceivable angle, and will be at your disposal as soon as they are available."

"I thank you, monsieur, for all your courtesy."

The commissary rose.

"Come with me, monsieurs."

He opened the door, and bowed ceremoniously to Poirot to precede him. Poirot, with equal politeness, drew back and bowed to the commissary.

"Monsieur."

"Monsieur."

At last they got out into the hall.

"That room there, it is the study, *hein?*" asked Poirot suddenly, nodding towards the door opposite.

"Yes. You would like to see it?" He threw the door open as he spoke, and we entered.

The room which M. Renauld had chosen for his own particular use was small, but furnished with great taste and comfort. A businesslike writing desk, with many pigeon holes, stood in the window. Two large leather-covered armchairs faced the fireplace, and between them was a round table covered with the latest books and magazines. Bookshelves lined two of the walls, and at the end of the room opposite the window there was a handsome oak sideboard with a tantalus on top. The curtains and *portière* were of a soft dull green, and the carpet matched them in tone.

Poirot stood a moment taking in the room, then he stepped forward, passed his hand lightly over the backs of the leather chairs, picked up a magazine from the table, and drew a finger gingerly over the surface of the oak sideboard. His face expressed complete approval.

"No dust?" I asked, with a smile.

He beamed on me, appreciative of my knowledge of his peculiarities.

"Not a particle, *mon ami!* And for once, perhaps, it is a pity."

His sharp, birdlike eyes darted here and there.

"Ah!" he remarked suddenly, with an intonation of relief. "The hearth-rug is crooked," and he bent down to straighten it.

Suddenly he uttered an exclamation and rose. In his hand he held a small fragment of paper.

"In France, as in England," he remarked, "the domestics omit to sweep under the mats!"

Bex took the fragment from him, and I came closer to examine it.

"You recognize it—eh, Hastings?"

I shook my head, puzzled—and yet that particular shade of pink paper was very familiar.

The commissary's mental processes were quicker than mine.

"A fragment of a cheque," he exclaimed.

The piece of paper was roughly about two inches square. On it was written in ink the word "Duveen."

"*Bien,*" said Bex. "This cheque was payable to, or drawn by, one named Duveen."

"The former, I fancy," said Poirot, "for, if I am not mistaken, the handwriting is that of M. Renauld."

That was soon established, by comparing it with a memorandum from the desk.

"Dear me," murmured the commissary, with a crestfallen air, "I really cannot imagine how I came to overlook this."

Poirot laughed.

"The moral of that is, always look under the mats! My friend Hastings here will tell you that anything in the least crooked is a torment to me. As soon as I saw that the hearth-rug was out of the straight, I said to myself: '*Tiens!* The leg of the chair caught it in being pushed back. Possibly there may be something beneath it which the good Françoise overlooked.'"

"Françoise?"

"Or Denise, or Léonie. Whoever did this room. Since there is no dust, the room *must* have been done this morning. I reconstruct the incident like this. Yesterday, possibly last night, M. Renauld drew a cheque to the order of some one named Duveen. Afterwards it was torn up, and scattered on the floor. This morning—" But M. Bex was already pulling impatiently at the bell.

Françoise answered it. Yes, there had been a lot of pieces of paper on the floor. What had she done with them? Put them in the kitchen stove of course! What else?

With a gesture of despair, Bex dismissed her. Then, his face lightening, he ran to the desk. In a minute he was hunting through the dead man's cheque book. Then he repeated his former gesture. The last counterfoil was blank.

"Courage!" cried Poirot, clapping him on the back. "Without doubt, Madame Renauld will be able to tell us all about this mysterious person named Duveen."

The commissary's face cleared. "That is true. Let us proceed."

As we turned to leave the room, Poirot remarked casually: "It was here that M. Renauld received his guest last night, eh?"

"It was—but how did you know?"

"By *this*. I found it on the back of the leather chair."

And he held up between his finger and thumb a long black hair—a woman's hair!

M. Bex took us out by the back of the house to where there was a small shed leaning against the house. He produced a key from his pocket and unlocked it.

"The body is here. We moved it from the scene of the crime just before you arrived, as the photographers had done with it."

He opened the door and we passed in. The murdered man lay on the ground, with a sheet over him. M. Bex dexterously whipped off the covering. Renauld was a man of medium height, slender and lithe in figure. He looked about fifty years of age, and his dark hair was plentifully streaked with grey. He was clean shaven with a long thin nose, and eyes set rather close together, and his skin was deeply bronzed, as that of a man who had spent most of his life beneath tropical skies. His lips were drawn back from his teeth and an expression of absolute amazement and terror was stamped on the livid features.

"One can see by his face that he was stabbed in the back," remarked Poirot.

Very gently, he turned the dead man over. There, between the shoulder-blades, staining the light fawn overcoat, was a round dark patch. In the middle of it there was a slit in the cloth. Poirot examined it narrowly.

"Have you any idea with what weapon the crime was committed?"

"It was left in the wound." The commissary reached down a large glass jar. In it was a small object that looked to me more like a paper-knife than anything else. It had a black handle, and a narrow shining blade. The whole thing was not more than ten inches long. Poirot tested the discoloured point gingerly with his finger tip.

"*Ma foi!* but it is sharp! A nice easy little tool for murder!"

"Unfortunately, we could find no trace of fingerprints on it," remarked Bex regretfully. "The murderer must have worn gloves."

"Of course he did," said Poirot contemptuously. "Even in Santiago they know enough for that. The veriest amateur of an English Mees knows it—thanks to the publicity the Bertillon system has been given in the Press. All the same, it interests me very much that there were no finger-prints. It is so amazingly simple to leave the finger-prints of some one else! And then the police are happy." He shook his head. "I very much fear our criminal is not a man of method—either that or he was pressed for time. But we shall see."

He let the body fall back into its original position.

"He wore only underclothes under his overcoat, I see," he remarked.

"Yes, the examining magistrate thinks that is rather a curious point."

At this minute there was a tap on the door which Bex had closed after him. He strode forward and opened it. Françoise was there. She endeavoured to peep in with ghoulish curiosity.

"Well, what is it?" demanded Bex impatiently.

"Madame. She sends a message that she is much recovered, and is quite ready to receive the examining magistrate."

"Good," said M. Bex briskly. "Tell M. Hautet and say that we will come at once."

Poirot lingered a moment, looking back towards the body. I thought for a moment that he was going to apostrophize it, to declare aloud his determination never to rest till he had discovered the murderer. But when he spoke, it was tamely and awkwardly, and his comment was ludicrously inappropriate to the solemnity of the moment.

"He wore his overcoat very long," he said constrainedly.

FIVE
Mrs. Renauld's Story

We found M. Hautet awaiting us in the hall, and we all proceeded upstairs together, Françoise marching ahead to show us the way. Poirot went up in a zigzag fashion which puzzled me, until he whispered with a grimace:

"No wonder the servants heard M. Renauld mounting the stairs; not a board of them but creaks fit to wake the dead!"

At the head of the staircase, a small passage branched off.

"The servants' quarters," explained Bex.

We continued along a corridor, and Françoise tapped on the last door to the right of it.

A faint voice bade us enter, and we passed into a large sunny apartment looking out towards the sea, which showed blue and sparkling about a quarter of a mile distant.

On a couch, propped up with cushions, and attended by Dr. Durand, lay a tall, striking-looking woman. She was middle-aged, and her once dark hair was now almost entirely silvered, but the intense vitality and strength of her personality would have made itself felt anywhere. You knew at once that you were in the presence of what the French call *une maitresse femme.*

She greeted us with a dignified inclination of the head.

"Pray be seated, monsieurs."

We took chairs, and the magistrate's clerk established himself at a round table.

36

"I hope, madame," began M. Hautet, "that it will not distress you unduly to relate to us what occurred last night?"

"Not at all, monsieur. I know the value of time, if these scoundrelly assassins are to be caught and punished."

"Very well, madame. It will fatigue you less, I think, if I ask you questions and you confine yourself to answering them. At what time did you go to bed last night?"

"At half-past nine, monsieur. I was tired."

"And your husband?"

"About an hour later, I fancy."

"Did he seem disturbed—upset in any way?"

"No, not more than usual."

"What happened then?"

"We slept. I was awakened by a hand being pressed over my mouth. I tried to scream out, but the hand prevented me. There were two men in the room. They were both masked."

"Can you describe them at all, madame?"

"One was very tall, and had a long black beard, the other was short and stout. His beard was reddish. They both wore hats pulled down over their eyes."

"H'm," said the magistrate thoughtfully, "too much beard, I fear."

"You mean they were false?"

"Yes, madame. But continue your story."

"It was the short man who was holding me. He forced a gag into my mouth, and then bound me with rope hand and foot. The other man was standing over my husband. He had caught up my little dagger paper-knife from the dressing-table and was holding it with the point just over his heart. When the short man had finished with me, he joined the other, and they forced my husband to get up and accompany them into the dressing-room next door. I was nearly fainting with terror, nevertheless I listened desperately.

"They were speaking in too low a tone for me to hear what they said. But I recognized the language, a bastard Spanish such as is spoken in some parts of South America. They seemed to be demanding something from my husband, and presently they grew angry, and their voices rose a little. I think the tall man was speaking. 'You know what we want!' he said. '*The secret!* Where is it?' I do not know what my husband answered, but the other replied fiercely: 'You lie! We know you have it. Where are your keys?'

"Then I heard sounds of drawers being pulled out. There is a safe on the wall of my husband's dressing-room in which he always keeps a fairly large amount of ready money. Léonie tells me this has been rifled and the money taken, but evidently what they were looking for was not there, for presently I heard the tall man, with an oath, command my husband to dress himself. Soon after that, I think some noise in the house must have disturbed them, for they hustled my husband out into my room only half dressed."

"*Pardon*," interrupted Poirot, "but is there then no other egress from the dressing-room?"

"No, monsieur, there is only the communicating door into my room. They hurried my husband through, the short man in front, and the tall man behind him with the dagger still in his hand. Paul tried to break away to come to me. I saw his agonized eyes. He turned to his captors. 'I must speak to her,' he said. Then, coming to the side of the bed, 'It is all right, Eloise,' he said. 'Do not be afraid. I shall return before morning.' But, although he tried to make his voice confident, I could see the terror in his eyes. Then they hustled him out of the door, the tall man saying: 'One sound—and you are a dead man, remember.'

"After that," continued Mrs. Renauld, "I must have fainted. The next thing I recollect is Léonie rubbing my wrists, and giving me brandy."

"Madame Renauld," said the magistrate, "had you any idea what it was for which the assassins were searching?"

"None whatever, monsieur."

"Had you any knowledge that your husband feared something?"

38

"Yes. I had seen the change in him."

"How long ago was that?"

Mrs. Renauld reflected.

"Ten days perhaps."

"Not longer?"

"Possibly. I only noticed it then."

"Did you question your husband at all as to the cause?"

"Once. He put me off evasively. Nevertheless, I was convinced that he was suffering some terrible anxiety. However, since he evidently wished to conceal the fact from me, I tried to pretend that I had noticed nothing."

"Were you aware that he had called in the services of a detective?"

"A detective?" exclaimed Mrs. Renauld, very much surprised.

"Yes, this gentleman—M. Hercule Poirot." Poirot bowed. "He arrived today in response to a summons from your husband." And taking the letter written by M. Renauld from his pocket he handed it to the lady.

She read it with apparently genuine astonishment.

"I had no idea of this. Evidently he was fully cognizant of the danger."

"Now, madame, I will beg of you to be frank with me. Is there any incident in your husband's past life in South America which might throw light on his murder?"

Mrs. Renauld reflected deeply, but at last shook her head.

"I can think of none. Certainly my husband had many enemies, people he had got the better of in some way or another, but I can think of no one distinctive case. I do not say there is no such incident—only that I am not aware of it."

The examining magistrate stroked his beard disconsolately.

"And you can fix the time of this outrage?"

"Yes, I distinctly remember hearing the clock on the mantelpiece strike two." She nodded towards an eight-day travelling clock in a leather case which stood in the centre of the chimney-piece.

Poirot rose from his seat, scrutinized the clock carefully, and nodded, satisfied.

"And here too," exclaimed M. Bex, "is a wrist watch, knocked off the dressing-table by the assassins, without doubt, and smashed to atoms. Little did they know it would testify against them."

Gently he picked away the fragments of broken glass. Suddenly his face changed to one of utter stupefaction.

"*Mon Dieu!*" he ejaculated.

"What is it?"

"The hands of the watch point to seven o'clock!"

"What?" cried the examining magistrate, astonished.

But Poirot, deft as ever, took the broken trinket from the startled commissary, and held it to his ear. Then he smiled.

"The glass is broken, yes, but the watch itself is still going."

The explanation of the mystery was greeted with a relieved smile. But the magistrate bethought him of another point.

"But surely it is not seven o'clock now?"

"No," said Poirot gently, "it is a few minutes after five. Possibly the watch gains, is that so, madame?"

Mrs. Renauld was frowning perplexedly.

"It does gain," she admitted, "but I've never known it to gain quite so much as that."

With a gesture of impatience, the magistrate left the matter of the watch and proceeded with his interrogatory.

"Madame, the front door was found ajar. It seems almost certain that the murderers entered that way, yet it has not been forced at all. Can you suggest any explanation?"

"Possibly my husband went out for a stroll the last thing, and forgot to latch it when he came in."

"Is that a likely thing to happen?"

"Very. My husband was the most absent-minded of men."

There was a slight frown on her brow as she spoke, as though this trait in the dead man's character had at times vexed her.

"There is one inference I think we might draw," remarked the commissary suddenly. "Since the men insisted on M. Renauld dressing himself, it looks as though the place they were taking him to, the place where 'the secret' was concealed, lay some distance away."

The magistrate nodded.

"Yes, far, and yet not too far, since he spoke of being back by morning."

"What times does the last train leave the station of Merlinville?" asked Poirot.

"Eleven-fifty one way, and 12:17 the other, but it is more probable that they had a motor waiting."

"Of course," agreed Poirot, looking somewhat crestfallen.

"Indeed, that might be one way of tracing them," continued the magistrate, brightening. "A motor containing two foreigners is quite likely to have been noticed. That is an excellent point, M. Bex."

He smiled to himself, and then, becoming grave once more, he said to Mrs. Renauld:

"There is another question. Do you know any one of the name of 'Duveen'?"

"Duveen?" Mrs. Renauld repeated, thoughtfully. "No, for the moment, I cannot say I do."

"You have never heard your husband mention any one of that name?"

"Never."

"Do you know any one whose Christian name is Bella?"

He watched Mrs. Renauld narrowly as he spoke, seeking to surprise any signs of anger or consciousness, but she merely shook her head in quite a natural manner. He continued his questions.

"Are you aware that your husband had a visitor last night?"

Now he saw the red mount slightly in her cheeks, but she replied composedly.

"No, who was that?"

"A lady."

"Indeed?"

But for the moment the magistrate was content to say no more. It seemed unlikely that Madame Daubreuil had any connection with the crime, and he was anxious not to upset Mrs. Renauld more than necessary.

He made a sign to the commissary, and the latter replied with a nod. Then rising, he went across the room, and returned with the glass jar we had seen in the outhouse in his hand. From this, he took the dagger.

"Madame," he said gently, "do you recognize this?"

She gave a little cry.

"Yes, that is my little dagger." Then—she saw the stained point, and she drew back, her eyes widening with horror. "Is that—blood?"

"Yes, madame. Your husband was killed with this weapon." He removed it hastily from sight. "You are quite sure about it's being the one that was on your dressing-table last night?"

"Oh, yes. It was a present from my son. He was in the Air Force during the War. He gave his age as older than it was." There was a touch of the proud mother in her voice. "This was made from a streamline aeroplane wire, and was given to me by my son as a souvenir of the War."

"I see, madame. That brings us to another matter. Your son, where is he now? It is necessary that he should be telegraphed to without delay."

"Jack? He is on his way to Buenos Ayres."

"What?"

"Yes. My husband telegraphed to him yesterday. He had sent him on business to Paris, but yesterday he discovered that it would be necessary for him to proceed without delay to South America. There was a boat leaving Cherbourg for Buenos Ayres last night, and he wired him to catch it."

"Have you any knowledge of what the business in Buenos Ayres was?"

"No, monsieur, I know nothing of its nature, but Buenos Ayres is not my son's final destination. He was going overland from there to Santiago."

And, in unison, the magistrate and the commissary exclaimed: "Santiago! Again Santiago!"

It was at this moment, when we were all stunned by the mention of that word, that Poirot approached Mrs. Renauld. He had been standing by the window like a man lost in a dream, and I doubt if he had fully taken in what had passed. He paused by the lady's side with a bow.

"*Pardon*, madame, but may I examine your wrists."

Though slightly surprised at the request, Mrs. Renauld held them out to him. Round each of them was a cruel red mark where the cords had bitten into the flesh. As he examined them, I fancied that a momentary flicker of excitement I had seen in his eyes disappeared.

"They must cause you great pain," he said, and once more he looked puzzled.

But the magistrate was speaking excitedly.

"Young M. Renauld must be communicated with at once by wireless. It is vital that we should know anything he can tell us about this trip to Santiago." He hesitated. "I hoped he might have been near at hand, so that we could have saved you pain, madame." He paused.

"You mean," she said in a low voice, "the identification of my husband's body?"

The magistrate bowed his head.

"I am a strong woman, monsieur. I can bear all that is required of me. I am ready—now."

"Oh, tomorrow will be quite soon enough, I assure you—"

"I prefer to get it over," she said in a low tone, a spasm of pain crossing her face. "If you will be so good as to give me your arm, Doctor?"

The doctor hastened forward, a cloak was thrown over Mrs.

Renauld's shoulders, and a slow procession went down the stairs. M. Bex hurried on ahead to open the door of the shed. In a minute or two Mrs. Renauld appeared in the doorway. She was very pale, but resolute. Behind her, M. Hautet was clacking commiserations and apologies like an animated hen.

She raised her hand to her face.

"A moment, messieurs, while I steel myself."

She took her hand away and looked down at the dead man. Then the marvellous self-control which had upheld her so far deserted her.

"Paul!" she cried. "Husband! Oh, God!" And pitching forward she fell unconscious to the ground.

Instantly Poirot was beside her, he raised the lid of her eye, felt her pulse. When he had satisfied himself that she had really fainted, he drew aside. He caught me by the arm.

"I am an imbecile, my friend! If ever there was love and grief in a woman's voice, I heard it then. My little idea was all wrong. *Eh bien!* I must start again!"

SIX

The Scene of the Crime

Between them, the doctor and M. Hautet carried the unconscious woman into the house. The commissary looked after them, shaking his head.

"*Pauvre femme*," he murmured to himself. "The shock was too much for her. Well, well, we can do nothing. Now, M. Poirot, shall we visit the place where the crime was committed?"

"If you please, M. Bex."

We passed through the house, and out by the front door. Poirot had looked up at the staircase in passing, and shook his head in a dissatisfied manner.

"It is to me incredible that the servants heard nothing. The creaking of that staircase, with *three* people descending it, would awaken the dead!"

"It was the middle of the night, remember. They were sound asleep by then."

But Poirot continued to shake his head as though not fully accepting the explanation. On the sweep of the drive, he paused, looking up at the house.

"What moved them in the first place to try if the front door were open? It was a most unlikely thing that it should be. It was far more probable that they should at once try to force a window."

"But all the windows on the ground floor are barred with iron shutters," objected the commissary.

Poirot pointed to a window on the first floor.

"That is the window of the bedroom we have just come from, is it not? And see—there is a tree by which it would be the easiest thing in the world to mount."

"Possibly," admitted the other. "But they could not have done so without leaving footprints in the flower-bed."

I saw the justice of his words. There were two large oval flower-beds planted with scarlet geraniums, one each side of the steps leading up to the front door. The tree in question had its roots actually at the back of the bed itself, and it would have been impossible to reach it without stepping on the bed.

"You see," continued the commissary, "owing to the dry weather no prints would show on the drive or paths; but, on the soft mould of the flower-bed, it would have been a very different affair."

Poirot went close to the bed and studied it attentively. As Bex had said, the mould was perfectly smooth. There was not an indentation on it anywhere.

Poirot nodded, as though convinced, and we turned away, but he suddenly darted off and began examining the other flower-bed.

"M. Bex!" he called. "See here. Here are plenty of traces for you."

The commissary joined him—and smiled.

"My dear M. Poirot, those are without doubt the footprints of the gardener's large hobnailed boots. In any case, it would have no importance, since this side we have no tree, and consequently no means of gaining access to the upper story."

"True," said Poirot, evidently crestfallen. "So you think these footprints are of no importance?"

"Not the least in the world."

Then, to my utter astonishment, Poirot pronounced these words:

"I do not agree with you. I have a little idea that these footprints are the most important things we have seen yet."

46

M. Bex said nothing, merely shrugged his shoulders. He was far too courteous to utter his real opinion.

"Shall we proceed?" he asked instead.

"Certainly. I can investigate this matter of the footprints later," said Poirot cheerfully.

Instead of following the drive down to the gate, M. Bex turned up a path that branched off at right angles. It led, up a slight incline, round to the right of the house, and was bordered on either side by a kind of shrubbery. Suddenly it emerged into a little clearing from which one obtained a view of the sea. A seat had been placed here, and not far from it was a rather ramshackle shed. A few steps further on, a neat line of small bushes marked the boundary of the Villa grounds. M. Bex pushed his way through these and we found ourselves on a wide stretch of open downs. I looked round, and saw something that filled me with astonishment.

"Why, this is a golf course," I cried.

Bex nodded.

"The limits are not completed yet," he explained. "It is hoped to be able to open them sometime next month. It was some of the men working on them who discovered the body early this morning."

I gave a gasp. A little to my left, where for the moment I had overlooked it, was a long narrow pit, and by it, face downwards, was the body of a man! For a moment, my heart gave a terrible leap, and I had a wild fancy that the tragedy had been duplicated. But the commissary dispelled my illusion by moving forward with a sharp exclamation of annoyance:

"What have my police been about? They had strict orders to allow no one near the place without proper credentials!"

The man on the ground turned his head over his shoulder.

"But I have proper credentials," he remarked, and rose slowly to his feet.

"My dear M. Giraud," cried the commissary. "I had no idea

that you had arrived, even. The examining magistrate has been awaiting you with the utmost impatience."

As he spoke, I was scanning the new-comer with the keenest curiosity. The famous detective from the Paris Sûreté was familiar to me by name, and I was extremely interested to see him in the flesh. He was very tall, perhaps about thirty years of age, with auburn hair and moustache, and a military carriage. There was a trace of arrogance in his manner which showed that he was fully alive to his own importance. Bex introduced us, presenting Poirot as a colleague. A flicker of interest came into the detective's eye.

"I know you by name, M. Poirot," he said. "You cut quite a figure in the old days, didn't you? But methods are very different now."

"Crimes, though, are very much the same," remarked Poirot gently.

I saw at once that Giraud was prepared to be hostile. He resented the other being associated with him, and I felt that if he came across any clue of importance he would be more than likely to keep it to himself.

"The examining magistrate—" began Bex again. But Giraud interrupted him rudely:

"A fig for the examining magistrate! The light is the important thing. For all practical purposes it will be gone in another half-hour or so. I know all about the case, and the people at the house will do very well until tomorrow, but, if we're going to find a clue to the murderers, here is the spot we shall find it. Is it your police who have been trampling all over the place? I thought they knew better nowadays."

"Assuredly they do. The marks you complain of were made by the workmen who discovered the body."

The other grunted disgustedly.

"I can see the tracks where the three of them came through the hedge—but they were cunning. You can just recognize the centre footmarks as those of M. Renauld, but those on either side have been carefully obliterated. Not that there would really be much to see anyway on this hard ground, but they weren't taking any chances."

"The external sign," said Poirot. "That is what you seek, eh?"

The other detective stared.

"Of course."

A very faint smile came to Poirot's lips. He seemed about to speak, but checked himself. He bent down to where a spade was lying.

"That's what the grave was dug with, right enough," said Giraud. "But you'll get nothing from it. It was Renauld's own spade, and the man who used it wore gloves. Here they are." He gesticulated with his foot to where two soiled earth-stained gloves were lying. "And they're Renauld's too—or at least his gardener's. I tell you, the men who planned out this crime were taking no chances. The man was stabbed with his own dagger, and would have been buried with his own spade. They counted on leaving no traces! But I'll beat them. There's always *something*! And I mean to find it."

But Poirot was now apparently interested in something else, a short discoloured piece of lead-piping which lay beside the spade. He touched it delicately with his finger.

"And does this, too, belong to the murdered man?" he asked, and I thought I detected a subtle flavour of irony in the question.

Giraud shrugged his shoulders to indicate that he neither knew nor cared.

"May have been lying around here for weeks. Anyway, it doesn't interest me."

"I, on the contrary, find it very interesting," said Poirot sweetly.

I guessed that he was merely bent on annoying the Paris detective and, if so, he succeeded. The other turned away rudely, remarking that he had no time to waste, and bending down he resumed his minute search of the ground.

Meanwhile Poirot, as though struck by a sudden idea, stepped back over the boundary, and tried the door of the little shed.

"That's locked," said Giraud over his shoulder. "But it's only a place where the gardener keeps his rubbish. The spade didn't come from there, but from the toolshed up by the house."

"Marvellous," murmured M. Bex, to me ecstatically. "He has been here but half an hour, and he already knows everything! What a man! Undoubtedly Giraud is the greatest detective alive today."

Although I disliked the detective heartily, I nevertheless was secretly impressed. Efficiency seemed to radiate from the man. I could not help feeling that, so far, Poirot had not greatly distinguished himself, and it vexed me. He seemed to be directing his attention to all sorts of silly, puerile points that had nothing to do with the case. Indeed, at this juncture, he suddenly asked:

"M. Bex, tell me, I pray you, the meaning of this whitewashed line that extends all round the grave. Is it a device of the police?"

"No, M. Poirot, it is an affair of the golf course. It shows that there is here to be a 'bunkair,' as you call it."

"A bunkair?" Poirot turned to me. "That is the irregular hole filled with sand and a bank at one side, is it not?"

I concurred.

"You do not play the golf, M. Poirot?" inquired Bex.

"I? Never! What a game!" He became excited. "Figure to yourself, each hole it is of a different length. The obstacles, they are not arranged mathematically. Even the greens are frequently up one side! There is only one pleasing thing—the how do you call them?—tee boxes! They, at least, are symmetrical."

I could not refrain from a laugh at the way the game appeared to Poirot, and my little friend smiled at me affectionately, bearing no malice. Then he asked:

"But M. Renauld, without doubt he played the golf?"

"Yes, he was a keen golfer. It's mainly owing to him, and to his large subscriptions, that this work is being carried forward. He even had a say in the designing of it."

Poirot nodded thoughtfully.

Then he remarked:

"It was not a very good choice they made—of a spot to bury the body? When the men began to dig up the ground, all would have been discovered."

"Exactly," cried Giraud triumphantly. "And that *proves* that they were strangers to the place. It's an excellent piece of indirect evidence."

"Yes," said Poirot doubtfully. "No one who knew would bury a body there—unless—unless—they *wanted* it to be discovered. And that is clearly absurd, is it not?"

Giraud did not even trouble to reply.

"Yes," said Poirot, in a somewhat dissatisfied voice. "Yes—undoubtedly—absurd!"

SEVEN

The Mysterious Madame Daubreuil

As we retraced our steps to the house, M. Bex excused himself for leaving us, explaining that he must immediately acquaint the examining magistrate with the fact of Giraud's arrival. Giraud himself had been obviously delighted when Poirot declared that he had seen all he wanted. The last thing we observed, as we left the spot, was Giraud, crawling about on all fours, with a thoroughness in his search that I could not but admire. Poirot guessed my thoughts, for as soon as we were alone he remarked ironically:

"At last you have seen the detective you admire—the human foxhound! Is it not so, my friend?"

"At any rate, he's *doing* something," I said, with asperity. "If there's anything to find, he'll find it. Now you—"

"*Eh bien!* I also have found something! A piece of lead-piping."

"Nonsense, Poirot. You know very well that's got nothing to do with it. I meant *little* things—traces that may lead us infallibly to the murderers."

"*Mon ami*, a clue of two feet long is every bit as valuable as one measuring two millimetres! But it is the romantic idea that all important clues must be infinitesimal! As to the piece of lead-piping having nothing to do with the crime, you say that because Giraud told you so. No"—as I was about to interpose a question—"we will say no more. Leave Giraud to his search, and me to my ideas. The case seems straightforward enough—and yet—and yet, *mon ami*, I am not satisfied! And do you know why? Because of the wrist watch that is two hours fast. And then there are several curious little points that do not seem to fit in. For instance, if the object of the murderers was revenge, why did they not stab Renauld in his sleep and have done with it?"

"They wanted the 'secret,'" I reminded him.

Poirot brushed a speck of dust from his sleeve with a dissatisfied air.

"Well, where is this 'secret'? Presumably some distance away, since they wish him to dress himself. Yet he is found murdered close at hand, almost within ear-shot of the house. Then again, it is pure chance that a weapon such as the dagger should be lying about casually, ready to hand."

He paused frowning, and then went on:

"Why did the servants hear nothing? Were they drugged? Was there an accomplice and did that accomplice see to it that the front door should remain open? I wonder if—"

He stopped abruptly. We had reached the drive in front of the house. Suddenly he turned to me.

"My friend, I am about to surprise you—to please you! I have taken your reproaches to heart! We will examine some footprints!"

"Where?"

"In that right-hand bed yonder. M. Bex says that they are the footmarks of the gardener. Let us see if that is so. See, he approaches with his wheelbarrow."

Indeed an elderly man was just crossing the drive with a barrowful of seedlings. Poirot called to him, and he set down the barrow and came hobbling towards us.

"You are going to ask him for one of his boots to compare with the footmarks?" I asked breathlessly. My faith in Poirot revived a little. Since he said the footprints in this right-hand bed were important, presumably they *were*.

"Exactly," said Poirot.

"But won't he think it very odd?"

"He will not think about it at all."

We could say no more, for the old man had joined us.

"You want me for something, monsieur?"

"Yes. You have been gardener here a long time, haven't you?"

"Twenty-four years, monsieur."

"And your name is—?"

"Auguste, monsieur."

"I was admiring these magnificent geraniums. They are truly superb. They have been planted long?"

"Some time, monsieur. But of course, to keep the beds looking smart, one must keep bedding out a few new plants, and remove those that are over, besides keeping the old blooms well picked off."

"You put in some new plants yesterday, didn't you? Those in the middle there, and in the other bed also?"

"Monsieur has a sharp eye. It takes always a day or so for them to 'pick up.' Yes, I put ten new plants in each bed last night. As Monsieur doubtless knows, one should not put in plants when the sun is hot."

Auguste was charmed with Poirot's interest, and was quite inclined to be garrulous.

"That is a splendid specimen there," said Poirot, pointing. "Might I perhaps have a cutting of it?"

"But certainly, monsieur." The old fellow stepped into the bed, and carefully took a slip from the plant Poirot had admired.

Poirot was profuse in his thanks, and Auguste departed to his barrow.

"You see?" said Poirot with a smile, as he bent over the bed to examine the indentation of the gardener's hobnailed boot. "It is quite simple."

"I did not realize—"

"That the foot would be inside the boot? You do not use your excellent mental capacities sufficiently. Well, what of the footmark?"

I examined the bed carefully.

"All the footmarks in the bed were made by the same boot," I said at length after a careful study.

"You think so? *Eh bien*, I agree with you," said Poirot.

He seemed quite uninterested, and as though he were thinking of something else.

"At any rate," I remarked, "you will have one bee less in your bonnet now."

"*Mon Dieu!* But what an idiom! What does it mean?"

"What I meant was that now you will give up your interest in these footmarks."

But to my surprise Poirot shook his head.

"No, no, *mon ami*. At last I am on the right track. I am still in the dark, but, as I hinted just now to M. Bex, these footmarks are the most important and interesting things in the case! That poor Giraud—I should not be surprised if he took no notice of them whatever."

At that moment, the front door opened, and M. Hautet and the commissary came down the steps.

"Ah, M. Poirot, we were coming to look for you," said the magistrate. "It is getting late, but I wish to pay a visit to Madame Daubreuil. Without doubt she will be very much upset by M. Renauld's death, and we may be fortunate enough to get a clue from her. The secret that he did not confide to his wife, it is possible that he may have told it to the woman whose love held him enslaved. We know where our Samsons are weak, don't we?"

I admired the picturesqueness of M. Hautet's language. I suspected that the examining magistrate was by now thoroughly enjoying his part in the mysterious drama.

"Is M. Giraud not going to accompany us?" asked Poirot.

"M. Giraud has shown clearly that he prefers to conduct the case in his own way," said M. Hautet dryly. One could see easily enough that Giraud's cavalier treatment of the examining magistrate had not prejudiced the latter in his favour. We said no more, but fell into line. Poirot walked with the examining magistrate, and the commissary and I followed a few paces behind.

"There is no doubt that Françoise's story is substantially correct," he remarked to me in a confidential tone. "I have been telephoning headquarters. It seems that three times in the last six weeks—that is to say since the arrival of M. Renauld at Merlinville—Madame Daubreuil has paid a large sum in notes into her banking account. Altogether the sum totals two hundred thousand francs!"

"Dear me," I said, considering, "that must be something like four thousand pounds!"

"Precisely. Yes, there can be no doubt that he was absolutely infatuated. But it remains to be seen whether he confided his secret to her. The examining magistrate is hopeful, but I hardly share his views."

During this conversation we were walking down the lane towards the fork in the road where our car had halted earlier in the afternoon, and in another moment I realized that the Villa Marguerite, the home of the mysterious Madame Daubreuil, was the small house from which the beautiful girl had emerged.

"She has lived here for many years," said the commissary, nodding his head towards the house. "Very quietly, very unobtrusively. She seems to have no friends or relations other than the acquaintances she has made in Merlinville. She never refers to the past, nor to her husband. One does not even know if he is alive or dead. There is a mystery about her, you comprehend." I nodded, my interest growing.

"And—the daughter?" I ventured.

"A truly beautiful young girl—modest, devout, all that she should be. One pities her, for, though she may know nothing of the past, a man who wants to ask her hand in marriage must necessarily inform himself, and then—" The commissary shrugged his shoulders cynically.

"But it would not be her fault!" I cried, with rising indignation.

"No. But what will you? A man is particular about his wife's antecedents."

I was prevented from further argument by our arrival at the door. M. Hautet rang the bell. A few minutes elapsed, and then we heard a footfall within, and the door was opened. On the threshold stood my young goddess of that afternoon. When she saw us, the colour left her cheeks, leaving her deathly white, and her eyes widened with apprehension. There was no doubt about it, she was afraid!

"Mademoiselle Daubreuil," said M. Hautet, sweeping off his hat, "we regret infinitely to disturb you, but the exigencies of the Law—you comprehend? My compliments to Madame your mother, and will she have the goodness to grant me a few moments' interview."

For a moment the girl stood motionless. Her left hand was pressed to her side, as though to still the sudden unconquerable agitation of her heart. But she mastered herself, and said in a low voice:

"I will go and see. Please come inside."

She entered a room on the left of the hall, and we heard the low murmur of her voice. And then another voice, much the same in timbre, but with a slightly harder inflection behind its mellow roundness said:

"But certainly. Ask them to enter."

In another minute we were face to face with the mysterious Madame Daubreuil.

She was not nearly so tall as her daughter, and the rounded curves of her figure had all the grace of full maturity. Her hair, again unlike her daughter's, was dark, and parted in the middle in the madonna style. Her eyes, half hidden by the drooping lids, were blue. There was a dimple in the round chin, and the half parted lips seemed always to hover on the verge of a mysterious smile. There was something almost exaggeratedly feminine about her, at once yielding and seductive. Though very well preserved, she was certainly no longer young, but her charm was of the quality which is independent of age.

Standing there, in her black dress with the fresh white collar and cuffs, her hands clasped together, she looked subtly appealing and helpless.

"You wished to see me, monsieur?" she asked.

"Yes, madame." M. Hautet cleared his throat. "I am investigating the death of M. Renauld. You have heard of it, no doubt?"

She bowed her head without speaking. Her expression did not change.

"We came to ask you whether you can—er—throw any light upon the circumstances surrounding it?"

"I?" The surprise of her tone was excellent.

"Yes, madame. It would, perhaps, be better if we could speak to you alone." He looked meaningly in the direction of the girl.

Madame Daubreuil turned to her.

"Marthe, dear—"

But the girl shook her head.

"No, *maman*, I will not go. I am not a child. I am twenty-two. I shall not go."

Madame Daubreuil turned back to the examining magistrate.

"You see, monsieur."

"I should prefer not to speak before Mademoiselle Daubreuil."

"As my daughter says, she is not a child."

For a moment the magistrate hesitated, baffled.

"Very well, madame," he said at last. "Have it your own way. We have reason to believe that you were in the habit of visiting the dead man at his Villa in the evenings. Is that so?"

The colour rose in the lady's pale cheeks, but she replied quietly:

"I deny your right to ask me such a question!"

"Madame, we are investigating a murder."

"Well, what of it? I had nothing to do with the murder."

"Madame, we do not say that for a moment. But you knew the dead man well. Did he ever confide in you as to any danger that threatened him?"

"Never."

"Did he ever mention his life in Santiago, and any enemies he may have made there?"

"No."

"Then you can give us no help at all?"

"I fear not. I really do not see why you should come to me. Cannot his wife tell you what you want to know?" Her voice held a slender inflection of irony.

"Madame Renauld has told us all she can."

"Ah!" said Madame Daubreuil. "I wonder—"

"You wonder what, madame?"

"Nothing."

The examining magistrate looked at her. He was aware that he was fighting a duel, and that he had no mean antagonist.

"You persist in your statement that M. Renauld confided nothing in you?"

"Why should you think it likely that he should confide in me?"

"Because, madame," said M. Hautet, with calculated brutality. "A man tells to his mistress what he does not always tell to his wife."

"Ah!" she sprang forward. Her eyes flashed fire. "Monsieur, you insult me! And before my daughter! I can tell you nothing. Have the goodness to leave my house!"

The honours undoubtedly rested with the lady. We left the Villa Marguerite like a shamefaced pack of schoolboys. The magistrate muttered angry ejaculations to himself. Poirot seemed lost in thought. Suddenly he came out of his reverie with a start, and inquired of M. Hautet if there was a good hotel near at hand.

"There is a small place, the Hotel des Bains, on this side of town. A few hundred yards down the road. It will be handy for your investigations. We shall see you in the morning then, I presume?"

"Yes, I thank you, M. Hautet."

With mutual civilities, we parted company, Poirot and I going towards Merlinville, and the others returning to the Villa Geneviève.

"The French police system is very marvellous," said Poirot, looking after them. "The information they possess about every one's life, down to the most commonplace detail, is extraordinary. Though he has only been here a little over six weeks, they are perfectly well acquainted with M. Renauld's tastes and pursuits, and at a moment's notice they can produce information as to Madame Daubreuil's banking account, and the sums that have lately been paid in! Undoubtedly the *dossier* is a great institution. But what is that?" He turned sharply.

A figure was running hatless, down the road after us. It was Marthe Daubreuil.

"I beg your pardon," she cried breathlessly, as she reached us. "I—I should not do this, I know. You must not tell my mother. But is it true, what the people say, that M. Renauld called in a detective before he died, and—and that you are he?"

"Yes, mademoiselle," said Poirot gently. "It is quite true. But how did you learn it?"

"Françoise told our Amélie," explained Marthe, with a blush.

Poirot made a grimace.

"The secrecy, it is impossible in an affair of this kind! Not that it matters. Well, mademoiselle, what is it you want to know?"

The girl hesitated. She seemed longing, yet fearing, to speak. At last, almost in a whisper, she asked:

"Is—any one suspected?"

Poirot eyed her keenly.

Then he replied evasively:

"Suspicion is in the air at present, mademoiselle."

"Yes, I know—but—any one in particular?"

"Why do you want to know?"

The girl seemed frightened by the question. All at once Poirot's words about her earlier in the day recurred to me. The "girl with the anxious eyes!"

"M. Renauld was always very kind to me," she replied at last. "It is natural that I should be interested."

"I see," said Poirot. "Well, mademoiselle, suspicion at present is hovering round two persons."

"Two?"

I could have sworn there was a note of surprise and relief in her voice.

"Their names are unknown, but they are presumed to be Chilians from Santiago. And now, mademoiselle, you see what comes of being young and beautiful! I have betrayed professional secrets for you!"

The girl laughed merrily, and then, rather shyly, she thanked him.

"I must run back now. *Maman* will miss me."

And she turned and ran back up the road, looking like a modern Atalanta. I stared after her.

"*Mon ami,*" said Poirot, in his gentle ironical voice, "is it that we are to remain planted here all night—just because you have seen a beautiful young woman, and your head is in a whirl?"

I laughed and apologized.

"But she *is* beautiful, Poirot. Any one might be excused for being bowled over by her."

Poirot groaned.

"*Mon Dieu!* But it is that you have the susceptible heart!"

"Poirot," I said, "do you remember after the Styles Case when—"

"When you were in love with two charming women at once, and neither of them were for you? Yes, I remember."

"You consoled me by saying that perhaps some day we should hunt together again, and that then—"

"*Eh bien?*"

"Well, we are hunting together again, and—" I paused, and laughed rather self-consciously.

But to my surprise Poirot shook his head very earnestly.

"Ah, *mon ami*, do not set your heart on Marthe Daubreuil. She is not for you, that one! Take it from Papa Poirot!"

"Why," I cried, "the commissary assured me that she was as good as she is beautiful! A perfect angel!"

"Some of the greatest criminals I have known had the faces of angels," remarked Poirot cheerfully. "A malformation of the grey cells may coincide quite easily with the face of a madonna."

"Poirot," I cried, horrified, "you cannot mean that you suspect an innocent child like this!"

"Ta-ta-ta! Do not excite yourself! I have not said that I suspected her. But you must admit that her anxiety to know about the case is somewhat unusual."

"For once, I see further than you do," I said. "Her anxiety is not for herself—but for her mother."

"My friend," said Poirot, "as usual, you see nothing at all. Madame Daubreuil is very well able to look after herself without her daughter worrying about her. I admit I was teasing you just now, but all the same I repeat what I said before. Do not set your heart on that girl. She is not for you! I, Hercule Poirot, know it. *Sacré!* if only I could remember where I had seen that face!"

"What face?" I asked, surprised. "The daughter's?"

"No. The mother's."

Noting my surprise, he nodded emphatically.

"But yes—it is as I tell you. It was a long time ago, when I was still with the Police in Belgium. I have never actually seen the woman before, but I have seen her picture—and in connection with some case. I rather fancy—"

"Yes?"

"I may be mistaken, but I rather fancy that it was a murder case!"

EIGHT
An Unexpected Meeting

We were up at the Villa betimes next morning. The man on guard at the gate did not bar our way this time. Instead, he respectfully saluted us, and we passed on to the house. The maid Léonie was just coming down the stairs, and seemed not averse to the prospect of a little conversation.

Poirot inquired after the health of Mrs. Renauld.

Léonie shook her head.

"She is terribly upset, *la pauvre dame!* She will eat nothing—but nothing! And she is as pale as a ghost. It is heartrending to see her. Ah, *par exemple*, it is not I who would grieve like that for a man who had deceived me with another woman!"

Poirot nodded sympathetically.

"What you say is very just, but what will you? The heart of a woman who loves will forgive many blows. Still, undoubtedly there must have been many scenes of recrimination between them in the last few months?"

Again Léonie shook her head.

"Never, monsieur. Never have I heard Madame utter a word of protest—of reproach, even! She had the temper and disposition of an angel—quite different to Monsieur."

"Monsieur Renauld had not the temper of an angel?"

"Far from it. When he enraged himself, the whole house knew of it. The day that he quarrelled with M. Jack—*ma foi!* they might

63

have been heard in the market place, they shouted so loud!"

"Indeed," said Poirot. "And when did this quarrel take place?"

"Oh! it was just before M. Jack went to Paris. Almost he missed his train. He came out of the library, and caught up his bag which he had left in the hall. The automobile, it was being repaired, and he had to run for the station. I was dusting the salon, and I saw him pass, and his face was white—white—with two burning spots of red. Ah, but he was angry!"

Léonie was enjoying her narrative thoroughly.

"And the dispute, what was it about?"

"Ah, that I do not know," confessed Léonie. "It is true that they shouted, but their voices were so loud and high, and they spoke so fast, that only one well acquainted with English could have comprehended. But Monsieur, he was like a thundercloud all day! Impossible to please him!"

The sound of a door shutting upstairs cut short Léonie's loquacity.

"And Françoise who awaits me!" she exclaimed, awakening to a tardy remembrance of her duties. "That old one, she always scolds."

"One moment, mademoiselle. The examining magistrate, where is he?"

"They have gone out to look at the automobile in the garage. Monsieur the commissary had some idea that it might have been used on the night of the murder."

"*Quelle idée*," murmured Poirot, as the girl disappeared.

"You will go out and join them?"

"No, I shall await their return in the *salon*. It is cool there on this hot morning."

This placid way of taking things did not quite commend itself to me.

"If you don't mind—" I said, and hesitated.

"Not in the least. You wish to investigate on your own account, eh?"

64

"Well, I'd rather like to have a look at Giraud, if he's anywhere about, and see what he's up to."

"The human foxhound," murmured Poirot, as he leaned back in a comfortable chair, and closed his eyes. "By all means, my friend. Au revoir."

I strolled out of the front door. It was certainly hot. I turned up the path we had taken the day before. I had a mind to study the scene of the crime myself. I did not go directly to the spot, however, but turned aside into the bushes, so as to come out on the links some hundred yards or so further to the right. If Giraud were still on the spot, I wanted to observe his methods before he knew of my presence. But the shrubbery here was much denser, and I had quite a struggle to force my way through. When I emerged at last on the course, it was quite unexpectedly and with such vigour that I cannoned heavily into a young lady who had been standing with her back to the plantation.

She not unnaturally gave a suppressed shriek, but I, too, uttered an exclamation of surprise. For it was my friend of the train, Cinderella!

The surprise was mutual.

"You," we both exclaimed simultaneously.

The young lady recovered herself first.

"My only Aunt!" she exclaimed. "What are you doing here?"

"For the matter of that, what are you?" I retorted.

"When last I saw you, the day before yesterday, you were trotting home to England like a good little boy. Have they given you a season ticket to and fro, on the strength of your M.P.?"

I ignored the end of the speech.

"When last I saw you," I said, "you were trotting home with your sister, like a good little girl. By the way, how is your sister?"

A flash of white teeth rewarded me.

"How kind of you to ask! My sister is well, I thank you."

"She is here with you?"

"She remained in town," said the minx with dignity.

"I don't believe you've got a sister," I laughed. "If you have, her name is Harris!"

"Do you remember mine?" she asked, with a smile.

"Cinderella. But you're going to tell me the real one now, aren't you?"

She shook her head with a wicked look.

"Not even why you're here?"

"Oh, that! I suppose you've heard of members of my profession 'resting.'"

"At expensive French watering-places?"

"Dirt cheap if you know where to go."

I eyed her keenly.

"Still, you'd no intention of coming here when I met you two days ago?"

"We all have our disappointments," said Miss Cinderella sententiously. "There now, I've told you quite as much as is good for you. Little boys should not be inquisitive. You've not yet told me what you're doing here? Got the M.P. in tow, I suppose, doing the gay boy on the beach."

I shook my head. "Guess again. You remember my telling you that my great friend was a detective?"

"Yes?"

"And perhaps you've heard about this crime—at the Villa Geneviève—?"

She stared at me. Her breast heaved, and her eyes grew wide and round.

"You don't mean—that you're in on *that*?"

I nodded. There was no doubt that I had scored heavily. Her emotion, as she regarded me, was only too evident. For some few seconds, she remained silent, staring at me. Then she nodded her head emphatically.

"Well, if that doesn't beat the band! Tote me round. I want to see all the horrors."

"What do you mean?"

66

"What I say. Bless the boy, didn't I tell you I doted on crimes? What do you think I'm imperilling my ankles for in high-heeled shoes over this stubble? I've been nosing round for hours. Tried the front way in, but that old stick-in-the-mud of a French gendarme wasn't taking any. I guess Helen of Troy, and Cleopatra, and Mary, Queen of Scots, rolled in one wouldn't cut ice with him! It's a real piece of luck happening on you this way. Come on, show me all the sights."

"But look here—wait a minute—I can't. Nobody's allowed in. They're awfully strict."

"Aren't you and your friend the big bugs?"

I was loath to relinquish my position of importance.

"Why are you so keen?" I asked weakly. "And what is it you want to see."

"Oh, everything! The place where it happened, and the weapon, and the body, and any finger-prints or interesting things like that. I've never had a chance of being right in on a murder like this before. It'll last me all my life?"

I turned away, sickened. What were women coming to nowadays? The girl's ghoulish excitement nauseated me. I had read of the mobs of women who besieged the law courts when some wretched man was being tried for his life on the capital charge. I had sometimes wondered who these women were. Now I knew. They were of the likeness of Cinderella, young, yet obsessed with a yearning for morbid excitement, for sensation at any price, without regard to any decency or good feeling. The vividness of the girl's beauty had attracted me in spite of myself, yet at heart I retained my first impression of disapproval and dislike. I thought of my mother, long since dead. What would she have said of this strange modern product of girlhood? The pretty face with the paint and powder, and the ghoulish mind behind!

"Come off your high horse," said the lady suddenly. "And don't give yourself airs. When you got called to this job, did you put your nose in the air and say it was a nasty business, and you wouldn't be mixed up in it?"

"No, but—"

"If you'd been here on a holiday, wouldn't you be nosing round just the same as I am? Of course you would."

"I'm a man. You're a woman."

"Your idea of a woman is some one who gets on a chair and shrieks if she sees a mouse. That's all prehistoric. But you *will* show me round, won't you? You see, it might make a big difference to me."

"In what way?"

"They're keeping all the reporters out. I might make a big scoop with one of the papers. You don't know how much they pay for a bit of inside stuff."

I hesitated. She slipped a small soft hand into mine.

"*Please*—there's a dear."

I capitulated. Secretly, I knew that I should rather enjoy the part of showman. After all, the moral attitude displayed by the girl was none of my business. I was a little nervous as to what the examining magistrate might say, but I reassured myself by the reflection that no harm could possibly be done.

We repaired first to the spot where the body had been discovered. A man was on guard there, who saluted respectfully, knowing me by sight, and raised no question as to my companion. Presumably he regarded her as vouched for by me. I explained to Cinderella just how the discovery had been made, and she listened attentively, sometimes putting an intelligent question. Then we turned our steps in the direction of the Villa. I proceeded rather cautiously, for, truth to tell, I was not at all anxious to meet any one. I took the girl through the shrubbery round to the back of the house where the small shed was. I recollected that yesterday evening, after relocking the door, M. Bex had left the key with the *sergent de ville* Marchaud, "in case M. Giraud should require it while we are upstairs." I thought it quite likely that the Sûreté detective, after using it, had returned it to Marchaud again.

Leaving the girl out of sight in the shrubbery, I entered the house. Marchaud was on duty outside the door of the *salon*. From within came the murmur of voices.

"Monsieur desires Hautet? He is within. He is again interrogating Françoise."

"No," I said hastily, "I don't want him. But I should very much like the key of the shed outside if it is not against regulations."

"But certainly, monsieur." He produced it. "Here it is. M. le juge gave orders that all facilities were to be placed at your disposal. You will return it to me when you have finished out there, that is all."

"Of course."

I felt a thrill of satisfaction as I realized that in Marchaud's eyes, at least, I ranked equally in importance with Poirot. The girl was waiting for me. She gave an exclamation of delight as she saw the key in my hand.

"You've got it then?"

"Of course," I said coolly. "All the same, you know, what I'm doing is highly irregular."

"You've been a perfect duck, and I shan't forget it. Come along. They can't see us from the house, can they?"

"Wait a minute." I arrested her eager advance. "I won't stop you if you really wish to go in. But do you? You've seen the grave, and the grounds, and you've heard all the details of the affair. Isn't that enough for you? This is going to be gruesome, you know, and—unpleasant."

She looked at me for a moment with an expression that I could not quite fathom. Then she laughed.

"Me for the horrors," she said. "Come along."

In silence we arrived at the door of the shed. I opened it and we passed in. I walked over to the body, and gently pulled down the sheet as M. Bex had done the preceding afternoon. A little gasping sound escaped from the girl's lips, and I turned and looked at her. There was horror on her face now, and those debonair high spirits of hers were quenched utterly. She had not chosen to listen to my advice, and she was punished now for her disregard of it. I felt singularly merciless towards her. She should go through with it now. I turned the corpse gently over.

"You see," I said, "he was stabbed in the back."

Her voice was almost soundless.

"With what?"

I nodded towards the glass jar.

"That dagger."

Suddenly the girl reeled, and then sank down in a heap. I sprang to her assistance.

"You are faint. Come out of here. It has been too much for you."

"Water," she murmured. "Quick. Water...."

I left her, and rushed into the house. Fortunately none of the servants were about, and I was able to secure a glass of water unobserved and add a few drops of brandy from a pocket flask. In a few minutes I was back again. The girl was lying as I had left her, but a few sips of the brandy and water revived her in a marvellous manner.

"Take me out of here—oh, quickly, quickly!" she cried, shuddering.

Supporting her with my arm I led her out into the air, and she pulled the door to behind her. Then she drew a deep breath.

"That's better. Oh, it was horrible! Why did you ever let me go in?"

I felt this to be so feminine that I could not forbear a smile. Secretly, I was not dissatisfied with her collapse. It proved that she was not quite so callous as I had thought her. After all she was little more than a child, and her curiosity had probably been of the unthinking order.

"I did my best to stop you, you know," I said gently.

"I suppose you did. Well, good-bye."

"Look here, you can't start off like that—all alone. You're not fit for it. I insist on accompanying you back to Merlinville."

"Nonsense. I'm quite all right now."

"Supposing you felt faint again? No, I shall come with you."

But this she combated with a good deal of energy. In the end, however, I prevailed so far as to be allowed to accompany her to the outskirts of the town. We retraced our steps over our former route, passing the grave again, and making a detour on to the road. Where the first straggling line of shops began, she stopped and held out her hand.

"Good-bye, and thank you ever so much for coming with me."

"Are you sure you're all right now?"

"Quite, thanks. I hope you won't get into any trouble over showing me things?"

I disclaimed the idea lightly.

"Well, good-bye."

"Au revoir," I corrected. "If you're staying here, we shall meet again."

She flashed a smile at me.

"That's so. Au revoir, then."

"Wait a second, you haven't told me your address?"

"Oh, I'm staying at the Hôtel du Phare. It's a little place, but quite good. Come and look me up tomorrow."

"I will," I said, with perhaps rather unnecessary *empressement*.

I watched her out of sight, then turned and retraced my steps to the Villa. I remembered that I had not relocked the door of the shed. Fortunately no one had noticed the oversight, and turning the key I removed it and returned it to the *sergent de ville*. And, as I did so, it came upon me suddenly that though Cinderella had given me her address I still did not know her name.

NINE
M. Giraud Finds Some Clues

I n the *Salon* I found the examining magistrate busily interrogating the old gardener Auguste. Poirot and the commissary, who were both present, greeted me respectively with a smile and a polite bow. I slipped quietly into a seat. M. Hautet was painstaking and meticulous in the extreme, but did not succeed in eliciting anything of importance.

The gardening gloves Auguste admitted to be his. He wore them when handling a certain species of primula plant which was poisonous to some people. He could not say when he had worn them last. Certainly he had not missed them. Where were they kept? Sometimes in one place, sometimes in another. The spade was usually to be found in the small tool shed. Was it locked? Of course it was locked. Where was the key kept? *Parbleu*, it was in the door of course! There was nothing of value to steal. Who would have expected a party of bandits, of assassins? Such things did not happen in Madame la Vicomtesse's time. M. Hautet signifying that he had finished with him, the old man withdrew, grumbling to the last. Remembering Poirot's unaccountable insistence on the footprints in the flower beds, I scrutinized him narrowly as he gave his evidence. Either he had nothing to do with the crime or he was a consummate actor. Suddenly, just as he was going out of the door, an idea struck me. "*Pardon* M. Hautet," I cried, "but will you permit me to ask him one question?"

"But certainly, monsieur."

Thus encouraged, I turned to Auguste.

"Where do you keep your boots?"

"*Sac à papier!*" growled the old man. "On my feet. Where else?"

"But when you go to bed at night?"

"Under my bed."

"But who cleans them?"

"Nobody. Why should they be cleaned? Is it that I promenade myself on the front like a young man? On Sunday I wear the Sunday boots, *bien entendu*, but otherwise—!" he shrugged his shoulders.

I shook my head, discouraged.

"Well, well," said the magistrate. "We do not advance very much. Undoubtedly we are held up until we get the return cable from Santiago. Has any one seen Giraud? In verity that one lacks politeness! I have a very good mind to send for him and—"

"You will not have to send far, M. le juge."

The quiet voice startled us. Giraud was standing outside looking in through the open window.

He leaped lightly into the room, and advanced to the table.

"Here I am, M. le juge, at your service. Accept my excuses for not presenting myself sooner."

"Not at all. Not at all," said the magistrate, rather confused.

"Of course I am only a detective," continued the other. "I know nothing of interrogatories. Were I conducting one, I should be inclined to do so without an open window. Any one standing outside can so easily hear all that passes…. But no matter."

M. Hautet flushed angrily. There was evidently going to be no love lost between the examining magistrate and the detective in charge of the case. They had fallen foul of each other at the start. Perhaps in any event it would have been much the same. To Giraud, all examining magistrates were fools, and to M. Hautet who took himself seriously, the casual manner of the Paris detective could not fail to give offence.

"*Eh bien*, M. Giraud," said the magistrate rather sharply. "Without doubt you have been employing your time to a marvel? You have the names of the assassins for us, have you not? And also the precise spot where they find themselves now?"

Unmoved by this irony, Giraud replied:

"I know at least where they have come from."

"*Comment?*"

Giraud took two small objects from his pocket and laid them down on the table. We crowded round. The objects were very simple ones: the stub of a cigarette, and an unlighted match. The detective wheeled round on Poirot.

"What do you see there?" he asked.

There was something almost brutal in his tone. It made my cheeks flush. But Poirot remained unmoved. He shrugged his shoulders.

"A cigarette end, and a match."

"And what does that tell you?"

Poirot spread out his hands.

"It tells me—nothing."

"Ah!" said Giraud, in a satisfied voice. "You haven't made a study of these things. That's not an ordinary match—not in this country at least. It's common enough in South America. Luckily it's unlighted. I mightn't have recognized it otherwise. Evidently one of the men threw away his cigarette end, and lit another, spilling one match out of the box as he did so."

"And the other match?" asked Poirot.

"Which match?"

"The one he *did* light his cigarette with. You have found that also?"

"No."

"Perhaps you didn't search very thoroughly."

"Not search thoroughly—" For a moment it seemed as though the detective were going to break out angrily, but with an effort he controlled himself. "I see you love a joke, M. Poirot. But in any case, match or no match, the cigarette end would be sufficient. It is a South American cigarette with liquorice pectoral paper."

Poirot bowed. The commissary spoke:

"The cigarette end and match might have belonged to M. Renauld. Remember, it is only two years since he returned from South America."

"No," replied the other confidently. "I have already searched among the effects of M. Renauld. The cigarettes he smoked and the matches he used are quite different."

"You do not think it odd," asked Poirot, "that these strangers should come unprovided with a weapon, with gloves, with a spade, and that they should so conveniently find all these things?"

Giraud smiled in a rather superior manner.

"Undoubtedly it is strange. Indeed, without the theory that I hold, it would be inexplicable."

"Aha!" said M. Hautet. "An accomplice. An accomplice within the house!"

"Or outside it," said Giraud with a peculiar smile.

"But some one must have admitted them? We cannot allow that, by an unparalleled piece of good fortune, they found the door ajar for them to walk in?"

"D'accord, M. le juge. The door was opened for them, but it could just as easily be opened from outside—by some one who possessed a key."

"But who did possess a key?"

Giraud shrugged his shoulders.

"As for that, no one who possesses one is going to admit the fact if they can help it. But several people *might* have had one. M. Jack Renauld, the son, for instance. It is true that he is on his way to South America, but he might have lost the key or had it stolen from him. Then there is the gardener—he has been here many years. One of the younger servants may have a lover. It is easy to take an impression of a key and have one cut. There are many possibilities. Then there is another person who, I should judge, is exceedingly likely to have such a thing in her keeping."

"Who is that?"

"Madame Daubreuil," said the detective dryly.

"Eh, eh!" said the magistrate, his face falling a little, "so you have heard about that, have you?"

"I hear everything," said Giraud imperturbably.

"There is one thing I could swear you have not heard," said M. Hautet, delighted to be able to show superior knowledge, and without more ado, he retailed the story of the mysterious visitor the night before. He also touched on the cheque made out to "Duveen," and finally handed Giraud the letter signed "Bella."

Giraud listened in silence, studied the letter attentively, and then handed it back.

"All very interesting, M. le juge. But my theory remains unaffected."

"And your theory is?"

"For the moment I prefer not to say. Remember, I am only just beginning my investigations."

"Tell me one thing, M. Giraud," said Poirot suddenly. "Your theory allows for the door being opened. It does not explain why it was *left* open. When they departed, would it not have been natural for them to close it behind them. If a *sergent de ville* had chanced to come up to the house, as is sometimes done to see that all is well, they might have been discovered and overtaken almost at once."

"Bah! They forgot it. A mistake, I grant you."

Then, to my surprise, Poirot uttered almost the same words as he had uttered to Bex the previous evening:

"*I do not agree with you.* The door being left open was the result of either design or necessity, and any theory that does not admit that fact is bound to prove vain."

We all regarded the little man with a good deal of astonishment. The confession of ignorance drawn from him over the match end had, I thought, been bound to humiliate him, but here he was self satisfied as ever, laying down the law to the great Giraud without a tremor.

The detective twisted his moustache, eyeing my friend in a somewhat bantering fashion.

"You don't agree with me, eh? Well, what strikes you particularly about the case. Let's hear your views."

"One thing presents itself to me as being significant. Tell me, M. Giraud, does nothing strike you as familiar about this case? Is there nothing it reminds you of?"

"Familiar? Reminds me of? I can't say off-hand. I don't think so, though."

"You are wrong," said Poirot quietly. "A crime almost precisely similar has been committed before."

"When? And where?"

"Ah, that, unfortunately, I cannot for the moment remember—but I shall do so. I had hoped you might be able to assist me."

Giraud snorted incredulously.

"There have been many affairs of masked men! I cannot remember the details of them all. These crimes all resemble each other more or less."

"There is such a thing as the individual touch." Poirot suddenly assumed his lecturing manner, and addressed us collectively. "I am speaking to you now of the psychology of crime. M. Giraud knows quite well that each criminal has his particular method, and that the police, when called in to investigate—say a case of burglary—can often make a shrewd guess at the offender, simply by the peculiar method he has employed. (Japp would tell you the same, Hastings.) Man is an unoriginal animal. Unoriginal within the law in his daily respectable life, equally unoriginal outside the law. If a man commits a crime, any other crime he commits will resemble it closely. The English murderer who disposed of his wives in succession by drowning them in their baths was a case in point. Had he varied his methods, he might have escaped detection to this day. But he obeyed the common dictates of human nature, arguing that what had once succeeded would succeed again, and he paid the penalty of his lack of originality."

"And the point of all this?" sneered Giraud.

"That when you have two crimes precisely similar in design and execution, you find the same brain behind them both. I am looking for that brain, M. Giraud—and I shall find it. Here we have a true clue—a psychological clue. You may know all about cigarettes and match ends, M. Giraud, but I, Hercule Poirot, know the mind of man!" And the ridiculous little fellow tapped his forehead with emphasis.

Giraud remained singularly unimpressed.

"For your guidance," continued Poirot, "I will also advise you of one fact which might fail to be brought to your notice. The wrist watch of Madame Renauld, on the day following the tragedy, had gained two hours. It might interest you to examine it."

Giraud stared.

"Perhaps it was in the habit of gaining?"

"As a matter of fact, I am told it did."

"*Eh bien*, then!"

"All the same, two hours is a good deal," said Poirot softly. "Then there is the matter of the footprints in the flower-bed."

He nodded his head towards the open window. Giraud took two eager strides, and looked out.

"This bed here?"

"Yes."

"But I see no footprints?"

"No," said Poirot, straightening a little pile of books on a table. "There are none."

For a moment an almost murderous rage obscured Giraud's face. He took two strides towards his tormentor, but at that moment the *salon* door was opened, and Marchaud announced.

"M. Stonor, the secretary, has just arrived from England. May he enter?"

TEN
Gabriel Stonor

The man who entered the room was a striking figure. Very tall, with a well knit athletic frame, and a deeply bronzed face and neck, he dominated the assembly. Even Giraud seemed anaemic beside him. When I knew him better I realized that Gabriel Stonor was quite an unusual personality. English by birth, he had knocked about all over the world. He had shot big game in Africa, travelled in Korea, ranched in California, and traded in the South Sea Islands. He had been secretary to a New York railway magnate, and had spent a year encamped in the desert with a friendly tribe of Arabs.

His unerring eye picked out M. Hautet.

"The examining magistrate in charge of the case? Pleased to meet you, M. le juge. This is a terrible business. How's Mrs. Renauld? Is she bearing up fairly well? It must have been an awful shock to her."

"Terrible, terrible," said M. Hautet. "Permit me to introduce M. Bex—our commissary of police, M. Giraud of the Sûreté. This gentleman is M. Hercule Poirot. M. Renauld sent for him, but he arrived too late to do anything to avert the tragedy. A friend of M. Poirot's, Captain Hastings."

Stonor looked at Poirot with some interest.

"Sent for you, did he?"

"You did not know, then, that M. Renauld contemplated calling in a detective?" interposed M. Bex.

"No, I didn't. But it doesn't surprise me a bit."

"Why?"

"Because the old man was rattled! I don't know what it was all about. He didn't confide in me. We weren't on those terms. But rattled he was—and badly!"

"H'm!" said M. Hautet. "But you have no notion of the cause?"

"That's what I said, sir."

"You will pardon me, M. Stonor, but we must begin with a few formalities. Your name?"

"Gabriel Stonor."

"How long ago was it that you became secretary to M. Renauld?"

"About two years ago, when he first arrived from South America. I met him through a mutual friend, and he offered me the post. A thundering good boss he was too."

"Did he talk to you much about his life in South America?"

"Yes, a good bit."

"Do you know if he was ever in Santiago?"

"Several times, I believe."

"He never mentioned any special incident that occurred there—anything that might have provoked some vendetta against him?"

"Never."

"Did he speak of any secret that he had acquired whilst sojourning there?"

"No."

"Did he ever say anything at all about a secret?"

"Not that I can remember. But, for all that, there *was* a mystery about him. I've never heard him speak of his boyhood for instance, or of any incident prior to his arrival in South America. He was a French Canadian by birth, I believe, but I've never heard him speak of his life in Canada. He could shut up like a clam if he liked."

"So, as far as you know, he had no enemies, and you can give us no clue as to any secret to obtain possession of which he might have been murdered?"

"That's so."

"M. Stonor, have you ever heard the name of Duveen in connection with M. Renauld?"

"Duveen. Duveen." He tried the name over thoughtfully. "I don't think I have. And yet it seems familiar."

"Do you know a lady, a friend of M. Renauld's whose Christian name is Bella?"

Again Mr. Stonor shook his head.

"Bella Duveen? Is that the full name? It's curious! I'm sure I know it. But for the moment I can't remember in what connection."

The magistrate coughed.

"You understand, M. Stonor—the case is like this. *There must be no reservations.* You might, perhaps, through a feeling of consideration for Madame Renauld—for whom, I gather, you have a great esteem and affection, you might—*enfin!*" said M. Hautet getting rather tied up in his sentence, "there must absolutely be no reservations."

Stonor stared at him, a dawning light of comprehension in his eyes.

"I don't quite get you," he said gently. "Where does Mrs. Renauld come in? I've an immense respect and affection for that lady; she's a very wonderful and unusual type, but I don't quite see how my reservations, or otherwise, could affect her?"

"Not if this Bella Duveen should prove to have been something more than a friend to her husband?"

"Ah!" said Stonor. "I get you now. But I'll bet my bottom dollar that you're wrong. The old man never so much as looked at a petticoat. He just adored his own wife. They were the most devoted couple I know."

M. Hautet shook his head gently.

"M. Stonor, we hold absolute proof—a love letter written

81

by this Bella to M. Renauld, accusing him of having tired of her. Moreover, we have further proof that, at the time of his death, he was carrying on an intrigue with a Frenchwoman, a Madame Daubreuil, who rents the adjoining Villa. And this is the man who, according to you, never looked at a petticoat!"

The secretary's eyes narrowed.

"Hold on, M. le juge. You're barking up the wrong tree. I knew Paul Renauld. What you've just been saying is utterly impossible. There's some other explanation."

The magistrate shrugged his shoulders.

"What other explanation could there be?"

"What leads you to think it was a love affair?"

"Madame Daubreuil was in the habit of visiting him here in the evenings. Also, since M. Renauld came to the Villa Geneviève, Madame Daubreuil has paid large sums of money into the bank in notes. In all, the amount totals four thousand pounds of your English money."

"I guess that's right," said Stonor quietly. "I transmitted him those sums at his request. But it wasn't an intrigue."

"Eh! *mon Dieu!* What else could it be?"

"*Blackmail*," said Stonor sharply, bringing down his hand with a slam on the table. "That's what it was."

"Ah! Voilà une idée!" cried the magistrate, shaken in spite of himself.

"Blackmail," repeated Stonor. "The old man was being bled— and at a good rate too. Four thousand in a couple of months. Whew! I told you just now there was a mystery about Renauld. Evidently this Madame Daubreuil knew enough of it to put the screws on."

"It is possible," the commissary cried excitedly. "Decidedly, it is possible."

"Possible?" roared Stonor. "It's certain! Tell me, have you asked Mrs. Renauld about this love affair stunt of yours?"

"No, monsieur. We did not wish to occasion her any distress

if it could reasonably be avoided."

"Distress? Why, she'd laugh in your face. I tell you, she and Renauld were a couple in a hundred."

"Ah, that reminds me of another point," said M. Hautet. "Did M. Renauld take you into his confidence at all as to the dispositions of his will?"

"I know all about it—took it to the lawyer for him after he'd drawn it out. I can give you the name of his solicitors if you want to see it. They've got it there. Quite simple. Half in trust to his wife for her lifetime, the other half to his son. A few legacies. I rather think he left me a thousand."

"When was this will drawn up?"

"Oh, about a year and a half ago."

"Would it surprise you very much, M. Stonor, to hear that M. Renauld had made another will, less than a fortnight ago?"

Stonor was obviously very much surprised.

"I'd no idea of it. What's it like?"

"The whole of his vast fortune is left unreservedly to his wife. There is no mention of his son."

Mr. Stonor gave vent to a prolonged whistle.

"I call that rather rough on the lad. His mother adores him, of course, but to the world at large it looks rather like a want of confidence on his father's part. It will be rather galling to his pride. Still, it all goes to prove what I told you, that Renauld and his wife were on first rate terms."

"Quite so, quite so," said M. Hautet. "It is possible we shall have to revise our ideas on several points. We have, of course, cabled to Santiago, and are expecting a reply from there any minute. In all possibility, everything will then be perfectly clear and straightforward. On the other hand, if your suggestion of blackmail is true, Madame Daubreuil ought to be able to give us valuable information."

Poirot interjected a remark:

"M. Stonor, the English chauffeur, Masters, had he been long with M. Renauld?"

"Over a year?"

"Have you any idea whether he has ever been in South America?"

"I'm quite sure he hasn't. Before coming to Mr. Renauld, he had been for many years with some people in Gloucestershire whom I know well."

"In fact, you can answer for him as being above suspicion?"

"Absolutely."

Poirot seemed somewhat crest-fallen.

Meanwhile the magistrate had summoned Marchaud.

"My compliments to Madame Renauld, and I should be glad to speak to her for a few minutes. Beg her not to disturb herself. I will wait upon her upstairs."

Marchaud saluted and disappeared.

We waited some minutes, and then, to our surprise, the door opened, and Mrs. Renauld, deathly pale in her heavy mourning, entered the room.

M. Hautet brought forward a chair, uttering vigorous protestations, and she thanked him with a smile. Stonor was holding one hand of hers in his with an eloquent sympathy. Words evidently failed him. Mrs. Renauld turned to M. Hautet.

"You wished to ask me something, M. le juge."

"With your permission, madame. I understand your husband was a French Canadian by birth. Can you tell me anything of his youth, or upbringing?"

She shook her head.

"My husband was always very reticent about himself, monsieur. He came from the North West, I know, but I fancy that he had an unhappy childhood, for he never cared to speak of that time. Our life was lived entirely in the present and the future."

"Was there any mystery in his past life?"

Mrs. Renauld smiled a little, and shook her head.

"Nothing so romantic, I am sure, M. le juge."

M. Hautet also smiled.

"True, we must not permit ourselves to get melodramatic. There is one thing more—" he hesitated.

Stonor broke in impetuously:

"They've got an extraordinary idea into their heads Mrs. Renauld. They actually fancy that Mr. Renauld was carrying on an intrigue with a Madame Daubreuil who, it seems, lives next door."

The scarlet colour flamed into Mrs. Renauld's cheeks. She flung her head up, then bit her lip, her face quivering. Stonor stood looking at her in astonishment, but M. Bex leaned forward and said gently: "We regret to cause you pain, madame, but have you any reason to believe that Madame Daubreuil was your husband's mistress?"

With a sob of anguish, Mrs. Renauld buried her face in her hands. Her shoulders heaved convulsively. At last she lifted her head, and said brokenly:

"She may have been."

Never, in all my life, have I seen anything to equal the blank amazement on Stonor's face. He was thoroughly taken aback.

ELEVEN
Jack Renauld

What the next development of the conversation would have been, I cannot say, for at that moment the door was thrown violently open, and a tall young man strode into the room.

Just for a moment I had the uncanny sensation that the dead man had come to life again. Then I realized that this dark head was untouched with grey, and that, in point of fact, it was a mere boy who now burst in among us with so little ceremony. He went straight to Mrs. Renauld with an impetuosity that took no heed of the presence of others.

"Mother!"

"Jack!" With a cry she folded him in her arms. "My dearest! But what brings you here? You were to sail on the *Anzora* from Cherbourg two days ago?" Then, suddenly recalling to herself the presence of others, she turned with a certain dignity, "My son, messieurs."

"Aha!" said M. Hautet, acknowledging the young man's bow. "So you did not sail on the *Anzora?*"

"No, monsieur. As I was about to explain, the *Anzora* was detained twenty-four hours through engine trouble. I should have sailed last night instead of the night before, but, happening to buy an evening paper, I saw in it an account of the—the awful tragedy that had befallen us—" His voice broke and the tears came into his eyes. "My poor father—my poor, poor, father."

Staring at him like one in a dream, Mrs. Renauld repeated: "So you did not sail?" And then, with a gesture of infinite weariness, she murmured as though to herself, "After all, it does not matter—now."

"Sit down, M. Renauld, I beg of you," said M. Hautet, indicating a chair. "My sympathy for you is profound. It must have been a terrible shock to you to learn the news as you did. However, it is most fortunate that you were prevented from sailing. I am in hopes that you may be able to give us just the information we need to clear up this mystery."

"I am at your disposal, M. le juge. Ask me any questions you please."

"To begin with, I understand that this journey was being undertaken at your father's request?"

"Quite so, M. le juge. I received a telegram bidding me to proceed without delay to Buenos Ayres, and from thence via the Andes to Valparaiso and on to Santiago."

"Ah. And the object of this journey?"

"I have no idea, M. le juge."

"What?"

"No. See, here is the telegram."

The magistrate took it and read it aloud.

"'Proceed immediately Cherbourg embark *Anzora* sailing tonight Buenos Ayres. Ultimate destination Santiago. Further instructions will await you Buenos Ayres. Do not fail. Matter is of utmost importance. Renauld.' And there had been no previous correspondence on the matter?"

Jack Renauld shook his head.

"That is the only intimation of any kind. I knew, of course, that my father, having lived so long out there, had necessarily many interests in South America. But he had never mooted any suggestion of sending me out."

"You have, of course, been a good deal in South America, M. Renauld?"

"I was there as a child. But I was educated in England, and spent most of my holidays in that country, so I really know far less of South America than might be supposed. You see, the war broke out when I was seventeen."

"You served in the English Flying Corps, did you not?"

"Yes, M. le juge."

M. Hautet nodded his head, and proceeded with his inquiries along the, by now, well-known lines. In response, Jack Renauld declared definitely that he knew nothing of any enmity his father might have incurred in the city of Santiago, or elsewhere in the South American continent, that he had noticed no change in his father's manner of late, and that he had never heard him refer to a secret. He had regarded the mission to South America as connected with business interests.

As M. Hautet paused for a minute, the quiet voice of Giraud broke in.

"I should like to put a few questions on my own account, M. le juge."

"By all means, M. Giraud, if you wish," said the magistrate coldly.

Giraud edged his chair a little nearer to the table.

"Were you on good terms with your father, M. Renauld?"

"Certainly I was," returned the lad haughtily.

"You assert that positively?"

"Yes."

"No little disputes, eh?"

Jack shrugged his shoulders. "Every one may have a difference of opinion now and then."

"Quite so, quite so. But if any one were to assert that you had a violent quarrel with your father on the eve of your departure for Paris, that person, without doubt, would be lying?"

I could not but admire the ingenuity of Giraud. His boast "I know everything" had been no idle one. Jack Renauld was clearly disconcerted by the question.

"We—we did have an argument," he admitted.

"Ah, an argument! In the course of that argument did you use this phrase: 'When you are dead, I can do as I please?'"

"I may have done," muttered the other. "I don't know."

"In response to that, did your father say: 'But I am not dead yet!' To which you responded: 'I wish you were!'"

The boy made no answer. His hands fiddled nervously with the things on the table in front of him.

"I must request an answer, please, M. Renauld," said Giraud sharply.

With an angry exclamation, the boy swept a heavy paper-knife on to the floor.

"What does it matter? You might as well know. Yes, I did quarrel with my father. I dare say I said all those things—I was so angry I cannot even remember what I said! I was furious—I could almost have killed him at that moment—there, make the most of that!" He leant back in his chair, flushed and defiant.

Giraud smiled, then, moving his chair back a little, said:

"That is all. You would, without doubt, prefer to continue the interrogatory, M. le juge."

"Ah, yes, exactly," said M. Hautet. "And what was the subject of your quarrel?"

"I decline to state."

M. Hautet sat up in his chair.

"M. Renauld, it is not permitted to trifle with the law!" he thundered. "What was the subject of the quarrel?"

Young Renauld remained silent, his boyish face sullen and overcast. But another voice spoke, imperturbable and calm, the voice of Hercule Poirot.

"I will inform you, if you like, M. le juge."

"You know?"

"Certainly I know. The subject of the quarrel was Mademoiselle Marthe Daubreuil."

Renauld sprang round, startled. The magistrate leaned forward.

"Is this so, monsieur."

Jack Renauld bowed his head.

"Yes," he admitted. "I love Mademoiselle Daubreuil, and I wish to marry her. When I informed my father of the fact, he flew at once into a violent rage. Naturally I could not stand hearing the girl I loved insulted, and I, too, lost my temper."

M. Hautet looked across at Mrs. Renauld.

"You were aware of this—attachment, madame."

"I feared it," she replied simply.

"Mother," cried the boy. "You too! Marthe is as good as she is beautiful. What can you have against her?"

"I have nothing against Mademoiselle Daubreuil in any way. But I should prefer you to marry an Englishwoman, or if a Frenchwoman not one who has a mother of doubtful antecedents!"

Her rancour against the older woman showed plainly in her voice, and I could well understand that it must have been a bitter blow to her when her only son showed signs of falling in love with the daughter of her rival.

Mrs. Renauld continued, addressing the magistrate:

"I ought, perhaps, to have spoken to my husband on the subject, but I hoped that it was only a boy and girl flirtation which would blow over all the quicker if no notice was taken of it. I blame myself now for my silence, but my husband, as I told you, had seemed so anxious and care-worn, different altogether from his normal self, that I was chiefly concerned not to give him any additional worry."

M. Hautet nodded.

"When you informed your father of your intentions towards Mademoiselle Daubreuil," he resumed, "he was surprised?"

"He seemed completely taken aback. Then he ordered me peremptorily to dismiss any such idea from my mind. He would never give his consent to such a marriage. Nettled, I demanded what he had against Mademoiselle Daubreuil. To that he could give no satisfactory reply, but spoke in slighting terms of the mystery surrounding the lives of the mother and daughter. I answered that I was marrying Marthe, and not her antecedents, but he shouted me down with a peremptory refusal to discuss the matter in any way. The whole thing must be given up. The injustice and high-handedness of it all maddened me—especially since he himself always seemed to go out of his way to be attentive to the Daubreuils and was always suggesting that they should be asked to the house. I lost my head, and we quarrelled in earnest. My father reminded me that I was entirely dependent on him, and it must have been in answer to that that I made the remark about doing as I pleased after his death—"

Poirot interrupted with a quick question.

"You were aware, then, of the terms of your father's will?"

"I knew that he had left half his fortune to me, the other half in trust for my mother to come to me at her death," replied the lad.

"Proceed with your story," said the magistrate.

"After that we shouted at each other in sheer rage, until I suddenly realized that I was in danger of missing my train to Paris. I had to run for the station, still in a white heat of fury. However, once well away, I calmed down. I wrote to Marthe, telling her what had happened, and her reply soothed me still further. She pointed out to me that we had only to be steadfast, and any opposition was bound to give way at last. Our affection for each other must be tried and proved, and when my parents realized that it was no light infatuation on my part they would doubtless relent towards us. Of course, to her, I had not dwelt on my father's principal objection to the match. I soon saw that I should do my cause no good by violence. My father wrote me several letters to Paris, affectionate in tone, and which did not refer to our disagreement or its cause, and I replied in the same strain."

"You can produce those letters, eh?" said Giraud.

"I did not keep them."

"No matter," said the detective.

Renauld looked at him for a moment, but the magistrate was

continuing his questions.

"To pass to another matter, are you acquainted with the name of Duveen, M. Renauld?"

"Duveen?" said Jack. "Duveen?" He leant forward, and slowly picked up the paper-knife he had swept from the table. As he lifted his head, his eyes met the watching ones of Giraud. "Duveen? No, I can't say I am."

"Will you read this letter, M. Renauld? And tell me if you have any idea as to who the person was who addressed it to your father?"

Jack Renauld took the letter, and read it through, the colour mounting in his face as he did so.

"Addressed to my father?" The emotion and indignation in his tones were evident.

"Yes. We found it in the pocket of his coat."

"Does—" He hesitated, throwing the merest fraction of a glance towards his mother. The magistrate understood.

"As yet—no. Can you give us any clue as to the writer?"

"I have no idea whatsoever."

M. Hautet sighed.

"A most mysterious case. Ah, well, I suppose we can now rule out the letter altogether. What do you think, M. Giraud? It does not seem to lead us anywhere."

"It certainly does not," agreed the detective with emphasis.

"And yet," sighed the magistrate, "it promised at the beginning to be such a beautiful and simple case!" He caught Mrs. Renauld's eye, and blushed in immediate confusion. "Ah, yes," he coughed, turning over the papers on the table. "Let me see, where were we? Oh, the weapon. I fear this may give you pain, M. Renauld. I understand it was a present from you to your mother. Very sad— very distressing—"

Jack Renauld leaned forward. His face, which had flushed during the perusal of the letter, was now deadly white.

"Do you mean—that it was with an aeroplane wire paper cutter that my father was—was killed? But it's impossible! A little thing like that!"

"Alas, M. Renauld, it is only too true! An ideal little tool, I fear. Sharp and easy to handle."

"Where is it? Can I see it? Is it still in the—the body?"

"Oh, no, it had been removed. You would like to see it? To make sure? It would be as well, perhaps, though madame has already identified it. Still—M. Bex, might I trouble you?"

"Certainly, M. le juge. I will fetch it immediately."

"Would it not be better to take M. Renauld to the shed?" suggested Giraud smoothly. "Without doubt he would wish to see his father's body."

The boy made a shivering gesture of negation, and the magistrate, always disposed to cross Giraud whenever possible, replied.

"But no—not at present. M. Bex will be so kind as to bring it to us here."

The commissary left the room. Stonor crossed to Jack, and wrung him by the hand. Poirot had risen and was adjusting a pair of candlesticks that struck his trained eye as being a shade askew. The magistrate was reading the mysterious love-letter through a last time, clinging desperately to his first theory of jealousy and a stab in the back.

Suddenly the door burst open and the commissary rushed in.

"M. le juge! M. le juge!"

"But yes. What is it?"

"The dagger! It is gone!"

"*Comment*—gone?"

"Vanished. Disappeared. The glass jar that contained it is empty!"

"What?" I cried. "Impossible. Why, only this morning I saw—" The words died on my tongue.

But the attention of the entire room was diverted to me.

"What is that you say?" cried the commissary. "This morning?"

"I saw it there this morning," I said slowly. "About an hour and a half ago, to be accurate."

"You went to the shed, then? How did you get the key?"

"I asked the *sergent de ville* for it."

"And you went there? Why?"

I hesitated, but in the end I decided that the only thing to do was to make a clean breast of it.

"M. le juge," I said. "I have committed a grave fault, for which I must crave your indulgence."

"*Eh bien!* Proceed, monsieur."

"The fact of the matter is," I said, wishing myself anywhere else than where I was, "that I met a young lady, an acquaintance of mine. She displayed a great desire to see everything that was to be seen, and I—well, in short, I took the key to show her the body."

"Ah, *par exemple*," cried the magistrate indignantly. "But it is a grave fault you have committed there, Captain Hastings. It is altogether most irregular. You should not have permitted yourself this folly."

"I know," I said meekly. "Nothing that you can say could be too severe, M. le juge."

"You did not invite this lady to come here?"

"Certainly not. I met her quite by accident. She is an English lady who happens to be staying in Merlinville, though I was not aware of that until my unexpected meeting with her."

"Well, well," said the magistrate, softening. "It was most irregular, but the lady is without doubt young and beautiful, *n'est-ce pas?* What it is to be young! *O jeunesse, jeunesse!*" And he sighed sentimentally.

But the commissary, less romantic, and more practical, took up the tale:

"But did not you reclose and lock the door when you departed."

"That's just it," I said slowly. "That's what I blame myself for so terribly. My friend was upset at the sight. She nearly fainted. I got her some brandy and water, and afterwards insisted on accompanying her back to town. In the excitement, I forgot to relock the door. I only did so when I got back to the Villa."

"Then for twenty minutes at least—" said the commissary slowly. He stopped.

"Exactly," I said.

"Twenty minutes," mused the commissary.

"It is deplorable," said M. Hautet, his sternness of manner returning. "Without precedent."

Suddenly another voice spoke.

"You find it deplorable, M. le juge?" asked Giraud.

"Certainly I do."

"*Eh bien!* I find it admirable," said the other imperturbably.

This unexpected ally quite bewildered me.

"Admirable, M. Giraud?" asked the magistrate, studying him cautiously out of the corner of his eye.

"Precisely."

"And why?"

"Because we know now that the assassin, or an accomplice of the assassin, has been near the Villa only an hour ago. It will be strange if, with that knowledge, we do not shortly lay hands upon him." There was a note of menace in his voice. He continued: "He risked a good deal to gain possession of that dagger. Perhaps he feared that finger-prints might be discovered on it."

Poirot turned to Bex.

"You said there were none?"

Giraud shrugged his shoulders.

"Perhaps he could not be sure."

Poirot looked at him.

"You are wrong, M. Giraud. The assassin wore gloves. So he must have been sure."

"I do not say it was the assassin himself. It may have been an accomplice who was not aware of that fact."

"*Ils sont mal renseignés, les accomplices!*" muttered Poirot, but he said no more.

The magistrate's clerk was gathering up the papers on the table. M. Hautet addressed us:

"Our work here is finished. Perhaps, M. Renauld, you will listen whilst your evidence is read over to you. I have purposely kept all the proceedings as informal as possible. I have been called original in my methods, but I maintain that there is much to be said for originality. The case is now in the clever hands of the renowned M. Giraud. He will without doubt distinguish himself. Indeed, I wonder that he has not already laid his hands upon the murderers! Madame, again let me assure you of my heart-felt sympathy. Messieurs, I wish you all good day." And, accompanied by his clerk and the commissary, he took his departure.

Poirot tugged out that large turnip of a watch of his, and observed the time.

"Let us return to the hotel for lunch, my friend," he said. "And you shall recount to me in full the indiscretions of this morning. No one is observing us. We need make no adieux."

We went quietly out of the room. The examining magistrate had just driven off in his car. I was going down the steps when Poirot's voice arrested me:

"One little moment, my friend." Dexterously, he whipped out his yard measure, and proceeded, quite solemnly, to measure an overcoat hanging in the hall from the collar to the hem. I had not seen it hanging there before, and guessed that it belonged to either Mr. Stonor, or Jack Renauld.

Then, with a little satisfied grunt, Poirot returned the measure to his pocket, and followed me out into the open air.

TWELVE
Poirot Elucidates Certain Points

"W hy did you measure that overcoat?" I asked, with some curiosity, as we walked down the hot white road at a leisurely pace.

"*Parbleu!* to see how long it was," replied my friend imperturbably.

I was vexed. Poirot's incurable habit of making a mystery out of nothing never failed to irritate me. I relapsed into silence, and followed a train of thought of my own. Although I had not noticed them specially at the time, certain words Mrs. Renauld had addressed to her son now recurred to me, fraught with a new significance. "So you did not sail?" she had said, and then had added: "*After all, it does not matter—now.*"

What had she meant by that? The words were enigmatical—significant. Was it possible that she knew more than we supposed? She had denied all knowledge of the mysterious mission with which her husband was to have entrusted his son. But was she really less ignorant than she pretended? Could she enlighten us if she chose, and was her silence part of a carefully thought out and preconceived plan?

The more I thought about it, the more I was convinced that I was right. Mrs. Renauld knew more than she chose to tell. In her surprise at seeing her son, she had momentarily betrayed herself. I felt convinced that she knew, if not the assassins, at least the motive for the assassination. But some very powerful consider-ations must keep her silent.

"You think profoundly, my friend," remarked Poirot, breaking in upon my reflections. "What is it that intrigues you so?"

I told him, sure of my ground, though feeling expectant that he would ridicule my suspicions. But to my surprise he nodded thoughtfully.

"You are quite right, Hastings. From the beginning I have been sure that she was keeping something back. At first I sus-pected her, if not of inspiring, at least of conniving at the crime."

"You suspected *her?*" I cried.

"But certainly! She benefits enormously—in fact, by this new will, she is the only person to benefit. So, from the start, she was singled out for attention. You may have noticed that I took an early opportunity of examining her wrists. I wished to see whether there was any possibility that she had gagged and bound herself. *Eh bien*, I saw at once that there was no fake, the cords had actually been drawn so tight as to cut into the flesh. That ruled out the possibility of her having committed the crime single-handed. But it was still possible for her to have connived at it, or to have been the instigator with an accomplice. Moreover, the story, as she told it, was singularly familiar to me—the masked men that she could not recognize, the mention of 'the secret'—I had heard, or read, all these things before. Another little detail confirmed my belief that she was not speaking the truth. *The wrist watch, Hastings, the wrist watch!*"

Again that wrist watch! Poirot was eyeing me curiously.

"You see, *mon ami?* You comprehend?"

"No," I replied with some ill humour. "I neither see nor comprehend. You make all these confounded mysteries, and it's useless asking you to explain. You always like keeping everything up your sleeve to the last minute."

"Do not enrage yourself, my friend," said Poirot with a smile. "I will explain if you wish. But not a word to Giraud, *c'est entendu?*

He treats me as an old one of no importance! *We shall see!* In common fairness I gave him a hint. If he does not choose to act upon it, that is his own look out."

I assured Poirot that he could rely upon my discretion.

"*C'est bien!* Let us then employ our little grey cells. Tell me, my friend, at what time, according to you, did the tragedy take place?"

"Why, at two o'clock or thereabouts," I said, astonished. "You remember, Mrs. Renauld told us that she heard the clock strike while the men were in the room."

"Exactly, and on the strength of that, you, the examining magistrate, Bex, and every one else, accept the time without further question. But I, Hercule Poirot, say that Madame Renauld lied. *The crime took place at least two hours earlier.*"

"But the doctors—"

"They declared, after examination of the body, that death had taken place between ten and seven hours previously. *Mon ami,* for some reason, it was imperative that the crime should seem to have taken place later than it actually did. You have read of a smashed watch or clock recording the exact hour of a crime? So that the time should not rest on Mrs. Renauld's testimony alone, some one moved on the hands of that wrist watch to two o'clock, and then dashed it violently to the ground. But, as is often the case, they defeated their own object. The glass was smashed, but the mechanism of the watch was uninjured. It was a most disastrous manoeuvre on their part, for it at once drew my attention to two points—first, that Madame Renauld was lying; secondly, that there must be some vital reason for the postponement of the time."

"But what reason could there be?"

"Ah, that is the question! There we have the whole mystery. As yet, I cannot explain it. There is only one idea that presents itself to me as having a possible connection."

"And that is?"

"The last train left Merlinville at seventeen minutes past twelve."

I followed it out slowly.

"So that, the crime apparently taking place some two hours later, any one leaving by that train would have an unimpeachable alibi!"

"Perfect, Hastings! You have it!"

I sprang up.

"But we must inquire at the station. Surely they cannot have failed to notice two foreigners who left by that train! We must go there at once!"

"You think so, Hastings?"

"Of course. Let us go there now."

Poirot restrained my ardour with a light touch upon the arm.

"Go by all means if you wish, *mon ami*—but if you go, I should not ask for particulars of two foreigners."

I stared, and he said rather impatiently:

"Là, là, you do not believe all that rigmarole, do you? The masked men and all the rest of *cette histoire-là!*"

His words took me so much aback that I hardly knew how to respond. He went on serenely:

"You heard me say to Giraud, did you not, that all the details of this crime were familiar to me? *Eh bien*, that presupposes one of two things, either the brain that planned the first crime also planned this one, or else an account read of a *cause célèbre* unconsciously remained in our assassin's memory and prompted the details. I shall be able to pronounce definitely on that after—" he broke off.

I was revolving sundry matters in my mind.

"But Mr. Renauld's letter? It distinctly mentions a secret and Santiago?"

"Undoubtedly there was a secret in M. Renauld's life—there can be no doubt of that. On the other hand, the word Santiago, to my mind, is a red herring, dragged continually across the track to put us off the scent. It is possible that it was used in the same way on M. Renauld, to keep him from directing his suspicions into a quarter nearer at hand. Oh, be assured, Hastings, the danger that threatened him was not in Santiago, it was near at hand, in France."

He spoke so gravely, and with such assurance, that I could not fail to be convinced. But I essayed one final objection:

"And the match and cigarette end found near the body? What of them."

A light of pure enjoyment lit up Poirot's face.

"Planted! Deliberately planted there for Giraud or one of his tribe to find! Ah, he is smart, Giraud, he can do his tricks! So can a good retriever dog. He comes in so pleased with himself. For hours he has crawled on his stomach. 'See what I have found,' he says. And then again to me: 'What do you see here?' Me, I answer, with profound and deep truth, 'Nothing.' And Giraud, the great Giraud, he laughs, he thinks to himself, 'Oh, that he is imbecile, this old one!' *But we shall see....*"

But my mind had reverted to the main facts.

"Then all this story of the masked men——?"

"Is false."

"What really happened?"

Poirot shrugged his shoulders.

"One person could tell us—Madame Renauld. But she will not speak. Threats and entreaties would not move her. A remarkable woman that, Hastings. I recognized as soon as I saw her that I had to deal with a woman of unusual character. At first, as I told you, I was inclined to suspect her of being concerned in the crime. Afterwards I altered my opinion."

"What made you do that?"

"Her spontaneous and genuine grief at the sight of her husband's body. I could swear that the agony in that cry of hers was genuine."

"Yes," I said thoughtfully, "one cannot mistake these things."

"I beg your pardon, my friend—one can always be mistaken. Regard a great actress, does not her acting of grief carry you away and impress you with its reality? No, however strong my own

101

impression and belief, I needed other evidence before I allowed myself to be satisfied. The great criminal can be a great actor. I base my certainty in this case, not upon my own impression, but upon the undeniable fact that Mrs. Renauld actually fainted. I turned up her eyelids and felt her pulse. There was no deception—the swoon was genuine. Therefore I was satisfied that her anguish was real and not assumed. Besides, a small additional point not without interest, it was unnecessary for Mrs. Renauld to exhibit unrestrained grief. She had had one paroxysm on learning of her husband's death, and there would be no need for her to simulate another such a violent one on beholding his body. No, Mrs. Renauld was not her husband's murderess. But why has she lied? She lied about the wrist watch, she lied about the masked men—she lied about a third thing. Tell me, Hastings, what is your explanation of the open door?"

"Well," I said, rather embarrassed, "I suppose it was an oversight. They forgot to shut it."

Poirot shook his head, and sighed.

"That is the explanation of Giraud. It does not satisfy me. There is a meaning behind that open door which for a moment I cannot fathom."

"I have an idea," I cried suddenly.

"*A la bonne heure!* Let us hear it."

"Listen. We are agreed that Mrs. Renauld's story is a fabrication. Is it not possible, then, that Mr. Renauld left the house to keep an appointment—possibly with the murderer—leaving the front door open for his return. But he did not return, and the next morning he is found, stabbed in the back."

"An admirable theory, Hastings, but for two facts which you have characteristically overlooked. In the first place, who gagged and bound Madame Renauld? And why on earth should they return to the house to do so? In the second place, no man on earth would go out to keep an appointment wearing his underclothes and an overcoat. There are circumstances in which a man might wear pajamas and an overcoat—but the other, never!"

"True," I said, rather crest-fallen.

"No," continued Poirot, "we must look elsewhere for a solution of the open door mystery. One thing I am fairly sure of—they did not leave through the door. They left by the window."

"What?"

"Precisely."

"But there were no footmarks in the flower bed underneath."

"No—*and there ought to have been*. Listen, Hastings. The gardener, Auguste, as you heard him say, planted both those beds the preceding afternoon. In the one there are plentiful impressions of his big hobnailed boots—in the other, *none!* You see? Some one had passed that way, some one who, to obliterate their footprints, smoothed over the surface of the bed with a rake."

"Where did they get a rake?"

"Where they got the spade and the gardening gloves," said Poirot impatiently. "There is no difficulty about that."

"What makes you think that they left that way, though? Surely it is more probable that they entered by the window, and left by the door."

"That is possible of course. Yet I have a strong idea that they left by the window."

"I think you are wrong."

"Perhaps, *mon ami*."

I mused, thinking over the new field of conjecture that Poirot's deductions had opened up to me. I recalled my wonder at his cryptic allusions to the flower bed and the wrist watch. His remarks had seemed so meaningless at the moment and now, for the first time, I realized how remarkably, from a few slight incidents, he had unravelled much of the mystery that surrounded the case. I paid a belated homage to my friend. As though he read my thoughts, he nodded sagely.

"Method, you comprehend! Method! Arrange your facts. Arrange your ideas. And if some little fact will not fit in—do not reject it but consider it closely. Though its significance escapes you, be sure that it is significant."

"In the meantime," I said, considering, "although we know a great deal more than we did, we are no nearer to solving the mystery of who killed Mr. Renauld."

"No," said Poirot cheerfully. "In fact we are a great deal further off."

The fact seemed to afford him such peculiar satisfaction that I gazed at him in wonder. He met my eye and smiled.

"But yes, it is better so. Before, there was at all events a clear theory as to how and by whose hands he met his death. Now that is all gone. We are in darkness. A hundred conflicting points confuse and worry us. That is well. That is excellent. Out of confusion comes forth order. But if you find order to start with, if a crime seems simple and above-board, *eh bien, méfiez vous!* It is, how do you say it?—*cooked!* The great criminal is simple—but very few criminals *are* great. In trying to cover up their tracks, they invariably betray themselves. Ah, *mon ami,* I would that some day I could meet a really great criminal—one who commits his crime, and then—does nothing! Even I, Hercule Poirot, might fail to catch such a one."

But I had not followed his words. A light had burst upon me.

"Poirot! Mrs. Renauld! I see it now. She must be shielding somebody."

From the quietness with which Poirot received my remark, I could see that the idea had already occurred to him.

"Yes," he said thoughtfully. "Shielding some one—or screening some one. One of the two."

I saw very little difference between the two words, but I developed my theme with a good deal of earnestness. Poirot maintained a strictly non-committal attitude, repeating:

"It may be—yes, it may be. But as yet I do not know! There is something very deep underneath all this. You will see. Something very deep."

Then, as we entered our hotel, he enjoined silence on me with a gesture.

THIRTEEN
The Girl with the Anxious Eyes

W e lunched with an excellent appetite. I understood well enough that Poirot did not wish to discuss the tragedy where we could so easily be overheard. But, as is usual when one topic fills the mind to the exclusion of everything else, no other subject of interest seemed to present itself. For a while we ate in silence, and then Poirot observed maliciously:

"*Eh bien!* And your indiscretions! You recount them not?"

I felt myself blushing.

"Oh, you mean this morning?" I endeavoured to adopt a tone of absolute nonchalance.

But I was no match for Poirot. In a very few minutes he had extracted the whole story from me, his eyes twinkling as he did so.

"*Tiens!* A story of the most romantic. What is her name, this charming young lady?"

I had to confess that I did not know.

"Still more romantic! The first *rencontre* in the train from Paris, the second here. Journeys end in lovers' meetings, is not that the saying?"

"Don't be an ass, Poirot."

"Yesterday it was Mademoiselle Daubreuil, today it is Mademoiselle—Cinderella! Decidedly you have the heart of a Turk, Hastings! You should establish a harem!"

"It's all very well to rag me. Mademoiselle Daubreuil is a

very beautiful girl, and I do admire her immensely—I don't mind admitting it. The other's nothing—don't suppose I shall ever see her again. She was quite amusing to talk to just for a railway journey, but she's not the kind of girl I should ever get keen on."

"Why?"

"Well—it sounds snobbish perhaps—but she's not a lady, not in any sense of the word."

Poirot nodded thoughtfully. There was less raillery in his voice as he asked:

"You believe, then, in birth and breeding?"

"I may be old-fashioned, but I certainly don't believe in marrying out of one's class. It never answers."

"I agree with you, *mon ami*. Ninety-nine times out of a hundred, it is as you say. But there is always the hundredth time! Still, that does not arise, as you do not propose to see the lady again."

His last words were almost a question, and I was aware of the sharpness with which he darted a glance at me. And before my eyes, writ large in letters of fire, I saw the words "Hôtel du Phare," and I heard again her voice saying "Come and look me up" and my own answering with *empressement*: "I will."

Well, what of it? I had meant to go at the time. But since then, I had had time to reflect. I did not like the girl. Thinking it over in cold blood, I came definitely to the conclusion that I disliked her intensely. I had got hauled over the coals for foolishly gratifying her morbid curiosity, and I had not the least wish to see her again.

I answered Poirot lightly enough.

"She asked me to look her up, but of course I shan't."

"Why 'of course'?"

"Well—I don't want to."

"I see." He studied me attentively for some minutes. "Yes. I see very well. And you are wise. Stick to what you have said."

"That seems to be your invariable advice," I remarked, rather piqued.

"Ah, my friend, have faith in Papa Poirot. Some day, if you

permit, I will arrange you a marriage of great suitability."

"Thank you," I said laughing, "but the prospect leaves me cold."

Poirot sighed and shook his head.

"*Les Anglais!*" he murmured. "No method—absolutely none whatever. They leave all to chance!" He frowned, and altered the position of the salt cellar.

"Mademoiselle Cinderella is staying at the Hôtel d'Angleterre you told me, did you not?"

"No. Hôtel du Phare."

"True, I forgot."

A moment's misgiving shot across my mind. Surely I had never mentioned any hotel to Poirot. I looked across at him, and felt reassured. He was cutting his bread into neat little squares, completely absorbed in his task. He must have fancied I had told him where the girl was staying.

We had coffee outside facing the sea. Poirot smoked one of his tiny cigarettes, and then drew his watch from his pocket.

"The train to Paris leaves at 2:25," he observed. "I should be starting."

"Paris?" I cried.

"That is what I said, *mon ami*."

"You are going to Paris? But why?"

He replied very seriously.

"To look for the murderer of M. Renauld."

"You think he is in Paris?"

"I am quite certain that he is not. Nevertheless, it is there that I must look for him. You do not understand, but I will explain it all to you in good time. Believe me, this journey to Paris is necessary. I shall not be away long. In all probability I shall return tomorrow. I do not propose that you should accompany me. Remain here and keep an eye on Giraud. Also cultivate the society of M. Renauld *fils*. And thirdly, if you wish, endeavour to cut him out with Mademoiselle Marthe. But I fear you will not have great success."

I did not quite relish the last remark.

"That reminds me," I said. "I meant to ask you how you knew about those two?"

"*Mon ami*—I know human nature. Throw together a boy young Renauld and a beautiful girl like Mademoiselle Marthe, and the result is almost inevitable. Then, the quarrel! It was money or a woman and, remembering Léonie's description of the lad's anger, I decided on the latter. So I made my guess—and I was right."

"And that was why you warned me against setting my heart on the lady? You already suspected that she loved young Renauld?"

Poirot smiled.

"At any rate—*I saw that she had anxious eyes.* That is how always think of Mademoiselle Daubreuil *as the girl with the anxious eyes...*"

His voice was so grave that it impressed me uncomfortably.

"What do you mean by that, Poirot?"

"I fancy, my friend, that we shall see before very long. But I must start."

"You've oceans of time."

"Perhaps—perhaps. But I like plenty of leisure at the station. I do not wish to rush, to hurry, to excite myself."

"At all events," I said, rising, "I will come and see you off."

"You will do nothing of the sort. I forbid it."

He was so peremptory that I stared at him in surprise. He nodded emphatically.

"I mean it, *mon ami*. Au revoir! You permit that I embrace you? Ah, no, I forget that it is not the English custom. Une poignee de main, alors."

I felt rather at a loose end after Poirot had left me. I strolled down the beach, and watched the bathers, without feeling energetic enough to join them. I rather fancied that Cinderella might be disporting herself amongst them in some wonderful costume, but I saw no signs of her. I strolled aimlessly along the sands towards the further end of the town. It occurred to me that, after all, it would only be decent feeling on my part to inquire after the girl. And it would save trouble in the end. The matter would then be finished with. There would be no need for me to trouble about her any further. But, if I did not go at all, she might quite possibly come and look me up at the Villa. And that would be annoying in every way. Decidedly it would be better to pay a short call, in the course of which I could make it quite clear that I could do nothing further for her in my capacity of showman.

Accordingly I left the beach, and walked inland. I soon found the Hôtel du Phare, a very unpretentious building. It was annoying in the extreme not to know the lady's name and, to save my dignity, I decided to stroll inside and look around. Probably I should find her in the lounge. Merlinville was a small place, you left your hotel to go to the beach, and you left the beach to return to the hotel. There were no other attractions. There was a Casino being built, but it was not yet completed.

I had walked the length of the beach without seeing her, therefore she must be in the hotel. I went in. Several people were sitting in the tiny lounge, but my quarry was not amongst them. I looked into some other rooms, but there was no sign of her. I waited for some time, till my impatience got the better of me. I took the concierge aside, and slipped five francs into his hand.

"I wish to see a lady who is staying here. A young English lady, small and dark. I am not sure of her name."

The man shook his head, and seemed to be suppressing a grin.

"There is no such lady as you describe staying here."

"She is American possibly," I suggested. These fellows are so stupid.

But the man continued to shake his head.

"No, monsieur. There are only six or seven English and American ladies altogether, and they are all much older than the lady you are seeking. It is not here that you will find her, monsieur."

He was so positive that I felt doubts.

"But the lady told me she was staying here."

"Monsieur must have made a mistake—or it is more likely the lady did, since there has been another gentleman here inquiring for her."

"What is that you say?" I cried, surprised.

"But yes, monsieur. A gentleman who described her just as you have done."

"What was he like?"

"He was a small gentleman, well dressed, very neat, very spotless, the moustache very stiff, the head of a peculiar shape, and the eyes green."

Poirot! So that was why he refused to let me accompany him to the station. The impertinence of it! I would thank him not to meddle in my concerns. Did he fancy I needed a nurse to look after me? Thanking the man, I departed, somewhat at a loss, and still much incensed with my meddlesome friend. I regretted that he was, for the moment, out of reach. I should have enjoyed telling him what I thought of his unwarranted interference. Had I not distinctly told him that I had no intention of seeing the girl? Decidedly, one's friends can be too zealous!

But where was the lady? I set aside my wrath, and tried to puzzle it out. Evidently, through inadvertence, she had named the wrong hotel. Then another thought struck me. Was it inadvertence? Or had she deliberately withheld her name and given me the wrong address? The more I thought about it, the more I felt convinced that this last surmise of mine was right. For some reason or other she did not wish to let the acquaintance ripen into friendship. And though half an hour earlier this had been precisely my own view, I did not enjoy having the tables turned upon me. The whole affair was profoundly unsatisfactory, and I went up to the Villa Geneviève in a condition of distinct ill humour. I did not go to the house, but went up the path to the little bench by the shed, and sat there moodily enough.

I was distracted from my thoughts by the sound of voices

close at hand. In a second or two I realized that they came, not from the garden I was in, but from the adjoining garden of the Villa Marguerite, and that they were approaching rapidly. A girl's voice was speaking, a voice that I recognized as that of the beautiful Marthe.

"*Chéri*," she was saying, "is it really true? Are all our troubles over."

"You know it, Marthe," Jack Renauld replied. "Nothing can part us now, beloved. The last obstacle to our union is removed. Nothing can take you from me."

"Nothing?" the girl murmured. "Oh, Jack, Jack—I am afraid."

I had moved to depart, realizing that I was quite unintentionally eavesdropping. As I rose to my feet, I caught sight of them through a gap in the hedge. They stood together facing me, the man's arm round the girl, his eyes looking into hers. They were a splendid looking couple, the dark, well-knit boy, and the fair young goddess. They seemed made for each other as they stood there, happy in spite of the terrible tragedy that overshadowed their young lives.

But the girl's face was troubled, and Jack Renauld seemed to recognize it, as he held her closer to him and asked:

"But what are you afraid of, darling? What is there to fear—now?"

And then I saw the look in her eyes, the look Poirot had spoken of, as she murmured, so that I almost guessed at the words. "I am afraid—for *you*...."

I did not hear young Renauld's answer, for my attention was distracted by an unusual appearance a little further down the hedge. There appeared to be a brown bush there, which seemed odd, to say the least of it, so early in the summer. I stepped along to investigate, but, at my advance, the brown bush withdrew itself precipitately, and faced me with a finger to its lips. It was Giraud.

Enjoining caution, he led the way round the shed until we were out of ear-shot.

"What were you doing there?" I asked.

"Exactly what you were doing—listening."

"But I was not there on purpose!"

"Ah!" said Giraud. "I was."

As always, I admired the man whilst disliking him. He looked me up and down with a sort of contemptuous disfavour.

"You didn't help matters by butting in. I might have heard something useful in a minute. What have you done with your old fossil?"

"M. Poirot has gone to Paris," I replied coldly.

"And I can tell you, M. Giraud, that he is anything but an old fossil. He has solved many cases that have completely baffled the English police."

"Bah! The English police!" Giraud snapped his fingers disdainfully. "They must be on a level with our examining magistrates. So he has gone to Paris, has he? Well, a good thing. The longer he stays there, the better. But what does he think he will find there?"

I thought I read in the question a tinge of uneasiness. I drew myself up.

"That I am not at liberty to say," I said quietly.

Giraud subjected me to a piercing stare.

"He has probably enough sense not to tell *you*," he remarked rudely. "Good afternoon. I'm busy."

And with that, he turned on his heel, and left me without ceremony. Matters seemed at a standstill at the Villa Geneviève. Giraud evidently did not desire my company and, from what I had seen, it seemed fairly certain that Jack Renauld did not either.

I went back to the town, had an enjoyable bath and returned to the hotel. I turned in early, wondering whether the following day would bring forth anything of interest.

I was wholly unprepared for what it did bring forth. I was eating my petit déjeuner in the dining-room, when the waiter, who had been talking to some one outside, came back in obvious excitement. He hesitated for a minute, fidgeting with his napkin, and then burst out.

"Monsieur will pardon me, but he is connected, is he not, with the affair at the Villa Geneviève?'

"Yes," I said eagerly. "Why?"

"Monsieur has not heard the news, though?"

"What news?"

"That there has been another murder there last night!"

"*What?*"

Leaving my breakfast, I caught up my hat and ran as fast as I could. Another murder—and Poirot away! What fatality. But who had been murdered?

I dashed in at the gate. A group of the servants was in the drive, talking and gesticulating. I caught hold of Françoise.

"What has happened?"

"Oh, monsieur! monsieur! Another death! It is terrible. There is a curse upon the house. But yes, I say it, a curse! They should send for M. le curé to bring some holy water. Never will I sleep another night under that roof. It might be my turn, who knows?"

She crossed herself.

"Yes," I cried, "but who has been killed?"

"Do I know—me? A man—a stranger. They found him up there—in the shed—not a hundred yards from where they found poor Monsieur. And that is not all. He is stabbed—stabbed to the heart *with the same dagger!*"

FOURTEEN
The Second Body

Waiting for no more, I turned and ran up the path to the shed. The two men on guard there stood aside to let me pass and, filled with excitement, I entered. The light was dim, the place was a mere rough wooden erection to keep old pots and tools in. I had entered impetuously, but on the threshold I checked myself, fascinated by the spectacle before me.

Giraud was on his hands and knees, a pocket torch in his hand with which he was examining every inch of the ground. He looked up with a frown at my entrance, then his face relaxed a little in a sort of good-humoured contempt.

"Ah, *c'est l'Anglais!* Enter then. Let us see what you can make of this affair."

Rather stung by his tone, I stooped my head, and passed in.

"There he is," said Giraud, flashing his torch to the far corner.

I stepped across.

The dead man lay straight upon his back. He was of medium height, swarthy of complexion, and possibly about fifty years of age. He was neatly dressed in a dark blue suit, well cut and probably made by an expensive tailor, but not new. His face was terribly convulsed, and on his left side, just over the heart, the hilt of a dagger stood up, black and shining. I recognized it. It was the same dagger I had seen reposing in the glass jar the preceding morning!

114

"I'm expecting the doctor any minute," explained Giraud. "Although we hardly need him. There's no doubt what the man died of. He was stabbed to the heart, and death must have been pretty well instantaneous."

"When was it done? Last night?"

Giraud shook his head.

"Hardly. I don't lay down the law on medical evidence, but the man's been dead well over twelve hours. When do you say you last saw that dagger?"

"About ten o'clock yesterday morning."

"Then I should be inclined to fix the crime as being done not long after that."

"But people were passing and repassing this shed continually."

Giraud laughed disagreeably.

"You progress to a marvel! Who told you he was killed in this shed?"

"Well—" I felt flustered. "I—I assumed it."

"Oh, what a fine detective! Look at him, *mon petit*—does a man stabbed to the heart fall like that—neatly with his feet together, and his arms to his side? No. Again does a man lie down on his back and permit himself to be stabbed without raising a hand to defend himself? It is absurd, is it not? But see here—and here—" He flashed the torch along the ground. I saw curious irregular marks in the soft dirt. "He was dragged here after he was dead. Half dragged, half carried by two people. Their tracks do not show on the hard ground outside, and here they have been careful to obliterate them—but one of the two was a woman, my young friend."

"A woman?"

"Yes."

"But if the tracks are obliterated, how do you know?"

"Because, blurred as they are, the prints of the woman's shoe are unmistakable. Also, by *this*—" And, leaning forward, he drew something from the handle of the dagger and held it up for me to

115

see. It was a woman's long black hair—similar to the one Poirot had taken from the arm-chair in the library.

With a slightly ironic smile he wound it round the dagger again.

"We will leave things as they are as much as possible," he explained. "It pleases the examining magistrate. *Eh bien*, do you notice anything else?"

I was forced to shake my head.

"Look at his hands."

I did. The nails were broken and discoloured, and the skin was hard. It hardly enlightened me as much as I should have liked it to have done. I looked up at Giraud.

"They are not the hands of a gentleman," he said, answering my look. "On the contrary his clothes are those of a well-to-do man. That is curious, is it not?"

"Very curious," I agreed.

"And none of his clothing is marked. What do we learn from that? This man was trying to pass himself off as other than he was. He was masquerading. Why? Did he fear something? Was he trying to escape by disguising himself? As yet we do not know, but one thing we do know—he was as anxious to conceal his identity as we are to discover it."

He looked down at the body again.

"As before there are no finger-prints on the handle of the dagger. The murderer again wore gloves."

"You think, then, that the murderer was the same in both cases?" I asked eagerly.

Giraud became inscrutable.

"Never mind what I think. We shall see. Marchaud!"

The *sergent de ville* appeared at the doorway.

"Monsieur?"

"Why is Madame Renauld not here? I sent for her a quarter of an hour ago?"

"She is coming up the path now, monsieur, and her son with her."

"Good. I only want one at a time, though."

Marchaud saluted and disappeared again. A moment later he reappeared with Mrs. Renauld.

"Here is Madame."

Giraud came forward with a curt bow.

"This way, madame." He led her across, and then, standing suddenly aside. "Here is the man. Do you know him?"

And as he spoke, his eyes, gimlet-like, bored into her face, seeking to read her mind, noting every indication of her manner.

But Mrs. Renauld remained perfectly calm—too calm, I felt. She looked down at the corpse almost without interest, certainly without any sign of agitation or recognition.

"No," she said. "I have never seen him in my life. He is quite a stranger to me."

"You are sure?"

"Quite sure."

"You do not recognize in him one of your assailants, for instance?"

"No," she seemed to hesitate, as though struck by the idea. "No, I do not think so. Of course they wore beards—false ones the examining magistrate thought, but still—no." Now she seemed to make her mind up definitely. "I am sure neither of the two was this man."

"Very well, madame. That is all, then."

She stepped out with head erect, the sun flashing on the silver threads in her hair. Jack Renauld succeeded her. He, too, failed to identify the man, in a completely natural manner.

Giraud merely grunted. Whether he was pleased or chagrined I could not tell. He merely called to Marchaud:

"You have got the other there?"

"Yes, monsieur."

"Bring her in then."

"The other" was Madame Daubreuil. She came indignantly, protesting with vehemence.

"I object, monsieur! This is an outrage! What have I to do with all this?"

"Madame," said Giraud brutally, "I am investigating not one murder, but two murders! For all I know you may have committed them both."

"How dare you?" she cried. "How dare you insult me by such a wild accusation! It is infamous."

"Infamous, is it? What about this?" Stooping, he again detached the hair, and held it up. "Do you see this, madame?" He advanced towards her. "You permit that I see whether it matches?"

With a cry she started backwards, white to the lips.

"It is false—I swear it. I know nothing of the crime—of either crime. Any one who says I do lies! Ah! *mon Dieu*, what shall I do?"

"Calm yourself, madame," said Giraud coldly. "No one has accused you as yet. But you will do well to answer my questions without more ado."

"Anything you wish, monsieur."

"Look at the dead man. Have you ever seen him before?"

Drawing nearer, a little of the colour creeping back to her face, Madame Daubreuil looked down at the victim with a certain amount of interest and curiosity. Then she shook her head.

"I do not know him."

It seemed impossible to doubt her, the words came so naturally. Giraud dismissed her with a nod of the head. "You are letting her go?" I asked in a low voice. "Is that wise? Surely that black hair is from her head."

"I do not need teaching my business," said Giraud dryly. "She is under surveillance. I have no wish to arrest her as yet."

Then, frowning, he gazed down at the body.

"Should you say that was a Spanish type at all?" he asked suddenly.

I considered the face carefully.

"No," I said at last. "I should put him down as a Frenchman most decidedly."

Giraud gave a grunt of dissatisfaction.

"Same here."

He stood there for a moment, then with an imperative gesture he waved me aside, and once more, on hands and knees, he continued his search of the floor of the shed. He was marvellous. Nothing escaped him. Inch by inch he went over the floor, turning over pots, examining old sacks. He pounced on a bundle by the door, but it proved to be only a ragged coat and trousers, and he flung it down again with a snarl. Two pairs of old gloves interested him, but in the end he shook his head and laid them aside. Then he went back to the pots, methodically turning them over one by one. In the end, he rose to his feet, and shook his head thoughtfully. He seemed baffled and perplexed. I think he had forgotten my presence.

But, at that moment, a stir and bustle was heard outside, and our old friend, the examining magistrate, accompanied by his clerk and M. Bex, with the doctor behind him, came bustling in.

"But this is extraordinary, Mr. Giraud," cried M. Hautet. "Another crime! Ah, we have not got to the bottom of this case. There is some deep mystery here. But who is the victim this time?"

"That is just what nobody can tell us, M. le juge. He has not been identified."

"Where is the body?" asked the doctor.

Giraud moved aside a little.

"There in the corner. He has been stabbed to the heart, as you see. And with the dagger that was stolen yesterday morning. I fancy that the murder followed hard upon the theft—but that is for you to say. You can handle the dagger freely—there are no finger-prints on it."

The doctor knelt down by the dead man, and Giraud turned to the examining magistrate.

"A pretty little problem, is it not? But I shall solve it."

"And so no one can identify him," mused the magistrate. "Could it possibly be one of the assassins? They may have fallen out among themselves."

Giraud shook his head.

"The man is a Frenchman—I would take my oath of that—"

But at that moment they were interrupted by the doctor who was sitting back on his heels with a perplexed expression.

"You say he was killed yesterday morning?"

"I fix it by the theft of the dagger," explained Giraud. "He may, of course, have been killed later in the day."

"Later in the day? Fiddlesticks! This man has been dead at least forty-eight hours, and probably longer."

We stared at each other in blank amazement.

FIFTEEN
A Photograph

The doctor's words were so surprising that we were all momentarily taken aback. Here was a man stabbed with a dagger which we knew to have been stolen only twenty-four hours previously, and yet Dr. Durand asserted positively that he had been dead at least forty-eight hours! The whole thing was fantastic to the last extreme.

We were still recovering from the surprise of the doctor's announcement, when a telegram was brought to me. It had been sent up from the hotel to the Villa. I tore it open. It was from Poirot, and announced his return by the train arriving at Merlinville at 12:28.

I looked at my watch and saw that I had just time to get comfortably to the station and meet him there. I felt that it was of the utmost importance that he should know at once of the new and startling developments in the case.

Evidently, I reflected, Poirot had had no difficulty in finding what he wanted in Paris. The quickness of his return proved that. Very few hours had sufficed. I wondered how he would take the exciting news I had to impart.

The train was some minutes late, and I strolled aimlessly up and down the platform, until it occurred to me that I might pass the time by asking a few questions as to who had left Merlinville by the last train on the evening of the tragedy.

I approached the chief porter, an intelligent looking man, and had little difficulty in persuading him to enter upon the subject. It was a disgrace to the Police, he hotly affirmed, that such brigands of assassins should be allowed to go about unpunished. I hinted that there was some possibility they might have left by the midnight train, but he negatived the idea decidedly. He would have noticed two foreigners—he was sure of it. Only about twenty people had left by the train, and he could not have failed to observe them.

I do not know what put the idea into my head—possibly it was the deep anxiety underlying Marthe Daubreuil's tones—but I asked suddenly:

"Young M. Renauld—he did not leave by that train, did he?"

"Ah, no, monsieur. To arrive and start off again within half an hour, it would not be amusing, that!"

I stared at the man, the significance of his words almost escaping me. Then I saw....

"You mean," I said, my heart beating a little, "that M. Jack Renauld arrived at Merlinville that evening?"

"But yes, monsieur. By the last train arriving the other way, the 11:40."

My brain whirled. That, then, was the reason of Marthe's poignant anxiety. Jack Renauld had been in Merlinville on the night of the crime! But why had he not said so? Why, on the contrary, had he led us to believe that he had remained in Cherbourg? Remembering his frank boyish countenance, I could hardly bring myself to believe that he had any connection with the crime. Yet why this silence on his part about so vital a matter? One thing was certain, Marthe had known all along. Hence her anxiety, and her eager questioning of Poirot to know whether any one were suspected.

My cogitations were interrupted by the arrival of the train, and in another moment I was greeting Poirot. The little man was radiant. He beamed and vociferated and, forgetting my English reluctance, embraced me warmly on the platform.

"*Mon cher ami*, I have succeeded—but succeeded to a marvel!"

"Indeed? I'm delighted to hear it. Have you heard the latest here?"

"How would you that I should hear anything? There have been some developments, eh? The brave Giraud, he has made an arrest? Or even arrests perhaps? Ah, but I will make him look foolish, that one! But where are you taking me, my friend? Do we not go to the hotel? It is necessary that I attend to my moustaches—they are deplorably limp from the heat of travelling. Also, without doubt, there is dust on my coat. And my tie, that I must rearrange."

I cut short his remonstrances.

"My dear Poirot—never mind all that. We must go to the Villa at once. *There has been another murder!*"

I have frequently been disappointed when fancying that I was giving news of importance to my friend. Either he has known it already or he has dismissed it as irrelevant to the main issue—and in the latter case events have usually proved him justified. But this time I could not complain of missing my effect. Never have I seen a man so flabbergasted. His jaw dropped. All the jauntiness went out of his bearing. He stared at me open-mouthed.

"What is that you say? Another murder? Ah, then, I am all wrong. I have failed. Giraud may mock himself at me—he will have reason!"

"You did not expect it, then?"

"I? Not the least in the world. It demolishes my theory—it ruins everything—it—ah, no!" He stopped dead, thumping himself on the chest. "It is impossible. I *cannot* be wrong! The facts, taken methodically and in their proper order admit of only one explanation. I must be right! I *am* right!"

"But then—"

He interrupted me.

"Wait, my friend. I must be right, therefore this new murder is impossible unless—unless—oh, wait, I implore you. Say no word—"

He was silent for a moment or two, then, resuming his normal manner, he said in a quiet assured voice: "The victim is a man of middle-age. His body was found in the locked shed near the scene of the crime and had been dead at least forty-eight hours. And it is most probable that he was stabbed in a similar manner to M. Renauld, though not necessarily in the back."

It was my turn to gape—and gape I did. In all my knowledge of Poirot he had never done anything so amazing as this. And, almost inevitably, a doubt crossed my mind.

"Poirot," I cried, "you're pulling my leg. You've heard all about it already."

He turned his earnest gaze upon me reproachfully.

"Would I do such a thing? I assure you that I have heard nothing whatsoever. Did you not observe the shock your news was to me?"

"But how on earth could you know all that?"

"I was right then? But I knew it. The little grey cells, my friend, the little grey cells! They told me. Thus, and in no other way, could there have been a second death. Now tell me all. If we go round to the left here, we can take a short cut across the golf links which will bring us to the back of the Villa Geneviève much more quickly."

As we walked, taking the way he had indicated, I recounted all I knew. Poirot listened attentively.

"The dagger was in the wound, you say? That is curious. You are sure it was the same one?"

"Absolutely certain. That's what make it so impossible."

"Nothing is impossible. There may have been two daggers."

I raised my eyebrows.

"Surely that is in the highest degree unlikely? It would be a most extraordinary coincidence."

"You speak as usual, without reflection, Hastings. In some

124

cases two identical weapons *would* be highly improbable. But not here. This particular weapon was a war souvenir which was made to Jack Renauld's orders. It is really highly unlikely, when you come to think of it, that he should have had only one made. Very probably he would have another for his own use."

"But nobody has mentioned such a thing," I objected.

A hint of the lecturer crept into Poirot's tone. "My friend, in working upon a case, one does not take into account only the things that are 'mentioned.' There is no reason to mention many things which may be important. Equally, there is often an excellent reason for *not* mentioning them. You can take your choice of the two motives."

I was silent, impressed in spite of myself. Another few minutes brought us to the famous shed. We found all our friends there and, after an interchange of polite amenities, Poirot began his task.

Having watched Giraud at work, I was keenly interested. Poirot bestowed but a cursory glance on the surroundings. The only thing he examined was the ragged coat and trousers by the door. A disdainful smile rose to Giraud's lips, and, as though noting it, Poirot flung the bundle down again.

"Old clothes of the gardener's?" he queried.

"Exactly," said Giraud.

Poirot knelt down by the body. His fingers were rapid but methodical. He examined the texture of the clothes, and satisfied himself that there were no marks on them. The boots he subjected to special care, also the dirty and broken finger-nails. Whilst examining the latter he threw a quick question at Giraud.

"You saw these?"

"Yes, I saw them," replied the other. His face remained inscrutable.

Suddenly Poirot stiffened.

"Dr. Durand!"

"Yes?" The doctor came forward.

"There is foam on the lips. You observed it?"

"I didn't notice it, I must admit."

"But you observe it now?"

"Oh, certainly."

Poirot again shot a question at Giraud.

"You noticed it without doubt?"

The other did not reply. Poirot proceeded. The dagger had been withdrawn from the wound. It reposed in a glass jar by the side of the body. Poirot examined it, then he studied the wound closely. When he looked up, his eyes were excited, and shone with the green light I knew so well.

"It is a strange wound, this! It has not bled. There is no stain on the clothes. The blade of the dagger is slightly discoloured, that is all. What do you think, M. le docteur?"

"I can only say that it is most abnormal."

"It is not abnormal at all. It is most simple. The man was stabbed *after he was dead*." And, stilling the clamour of voices that arose with a wave of his hand, Poirot turned to Giraud and added, "M. Giraud agrees with me, do you not, monsieur?"

Whatever Giraud's real belief, he accepted the position without moving a muscle. Calmly and almost scornfully he replied:

"Certainly I agree."

The murmur of surprise and interest broke out again.

"But what an idea!" cried M. Hautet. "To stab a man after he is dead! Barbaric! Unheard of! Some unappeasable hate, perhaps."

"No, M. le juge," said Poirot. "I should fancy it was done quite cold-bloodedly—to create an impression."

"What impression?"

"The impression it nearly did create," returned Poirot oracularly.

M. Bex had been thinking.

"How, then, was the man killed?"

"He was not killed. He died. He died, M. le juge, if I am not much mistaken, of an epileptic fit!"

This statement of Poirot's again aroused considerable

excitement. Dr. Durand knelt down again, and made a searching examination. At last he rose to his feet.

"Well, M. le docteur?"

"M. Poirot, I am inclined to believe that you are correct in your assertion. I was misled to begin with. The incontrovertible fact that the man had been stabbed distracted my attention from any other indications."

Poirot was the hero of the hour. The examining magistrate was profuse in compliments. Poirot responded gracefully, and then excused himself on the pretext that neither he nor I had yet lunched, and that he wished to repair the ravages of the journey. As we were about to leave the shed, Giraud approached us.

"One more thing, M. Poirot," he said, in his suave mocking voice. "We found this coiled round the handle of the dagger. A woman's hair."

"Ah!" said Poirot. "A woman's hair? What woman's, I wonder?"

"I wonder also," said Giraud. Then, with a bow, he left us.

"He was insistent, the good Giraud," said Poirot thoughtfully, as we walked towards the hotel. "I wonder in what direction he hopes to mislead me? A woman's hair—h'm!"

We lunched heartily, but I found Poirot somewhat distrait and inattentive. Afterwards we went up to our sitting-room and there I begged him to tell me something of his mysterious journey to Paris.

"Willingly, my friend. I went to Paris to find *this*."

He took from his pocket a small faded newspaper cutting. It was the reproduction of a woman's photograph. He handed it to me. I uttered an exclamation.

"You recognize it, my friend?"

I nodded. Although the photo obviously dated from very many years back, and the hair was dressed in a different style, the likeness was unmistakable.

"Madame Daubreuil!" I exclaimed.

Poirot shook his head with a smile.

"Not quite correct, my friend. She did not call herself by that name in those days. That is a picture of the notorious Madame Beroldy!"

Madame Beroldy! In a flash the whole thing came back to me. The murder trial that had evoked such world-wide interest. *The Beroldy Case.*

SIXTEEN
The Beroldy Case

S ome twenty years or so before the opening of the present story, Monsieur Arnold Beroldy, a native of Lyons, arrived in Paris accompanied by his pretty wife and their little daughter, a mere babe. Monsieur Beroldy was a junior partner in a firm of wine merchants, a stout middle-aged man, fond of the good things of life, devoted to his charming wife, and altogether unremarkable in every way. The firm in which Monsieur Beroldy was a partner was a small one, and although doing well, it did not yield a large income to the junior partner. The Beroldys had a small apartment and lived in a very modest fashion to begin with.

But unremarkable though Monsieur Beroldy might be, his wife was plentifully gilded with the brush of Romance. Young and good looking, and gifted withal with a singular charm of manner, Madame Beroldy at once created a stir in the quarter, especially when it began to be whispered that some interesting mystery surrounded her birth. It was rumoured that she was the illegitimate daughter of a Russian Grand Duke. Others asserted that it was an Austrian Archduke, and that the union was legal, though morganatic. But all stories agreed upon one point, that Jeanne Beroldy was the centre of an interesting mystery. Questioned by the curious, Madame Beroldy did not deny these rumours. On the other hand she let it be clearly understood that, though her "lips" were "sealed," all these stories had a foundation in fact. To intimate friends she unburdened herself further, spoke of political intrigues, of "papers," of obscure dangers that threatened her. There was also much talk of Crown jewels that were to be sold secretly, with herself acting as the go-between.

Amongst the friends and acquaintances of the Beroldys was a young lawyer, Georges Conneau. It was soon evident that the fascinating Jeanne had completely enslaved his heart. Madame Beroldy encouraged the young man in a discreet fashion, but being always careful to affirm her complete devotion to her middle-aged husband. Nevertheless, many spiteful persons did not hesitate to declare that young Conneau was her lover—and not the only one!

When the Beroldys had been in Paris about three months, another personage came upon the scene. This was Mr. Hiram P. Trapp, a native of the United States, and extremely wealthy. Introduced to the charming and mysterious Madame Beroldy, he fell a prompt victim to her fascinations. His admiration was obvious, though strictly respectful.

About this time, Madame Beroldy became more outspoken in her confidences. To several friends, she declared herself greatly worried on her husband's behalf. She explained that he had been drawn into several schemes of a political nature, and also referred to some important papers that had been entrusted to him for safe-keeping and which concerned a "secret" of far reaching European importance. They had been entrusted to his custody to throw pursuers off the track, but Madame Beroldy was nervous, having recognized several important members of the Revolutionary Circle in Paris.

On the 28th day of November, the blow fell. The woman who came daily to clean and cook for the Beroldys was surprised to find the door of the apartment standing wide open. Hearing faint moans issuing from the bedroom, she went in. A terrible sight met her eyes. Madame Beroldy lay on the floor, bound hand and foot, uttering feeble moans, having managed to free her mouth from a gag. On the bed was Monsieur Beroldy, lying in a pool of blood, with a knife driven through his heart.

Madame Beroldy's story was clear enough. Suddenly awakened from sleep, she had discerned two masked men bending over her. Stifling her cries, they had bound and gagged her. They had then demanded of Monsieur Beroldy the famous "secret."

But the intrepid wine merchant refused point-blank to accede to their request. Angered by his refusal, one of the men incontinently stabbed him through the heart. With the dead man's keys, they had opened the safe in the corner, and had carried away with them a mass of papers. Both men were heavily bearded, and had worn masks, but Madame Beroldy declared positively that they were Russians.

The affair created an immense sensation. It was referred to variously as "the Nihilist Atrocity," "Revolutionaries in Paris," and the "Russian Mystery." Time went on, and the mysterious bearded men were never traced. And then, just as public interest was beginning to die down, a startling development occurred. Madame Beroldy was arrested and charged with the murder of her husband.

The trial, when it came on, aroused widespread interest. The youth and beauty of the accused, and her mysterious history, were sufficient to make of it a *cause célèbre*. People ranged themselves wildly for or against the prisoner. But her partisans received several severe checks to their enthusiasm. The romantic past of Madame Beroldy, her royal blood, and the mysterious intrigues in which she had her being were shown to be mere fantasies of the imagination.

It was proved beyond doubt that Jeanne Beroldy's parents were a highly respectable and prosaic couple, fruit merchants, who lived on the outskirts of Lyons. The Russian Grand Duke, the court intrigues, and the political schemes—all the stories current were traced back to—the lady herself! From her brain had emanated these ingenious myths, and she was proved to have raised a considerable sum of money from various credulous persons by her fiction of the "Crown jewels"—the jewels in question being found to be mere paste imitations. Remorselessly the whole story of her life was laid bare. The motive for the murder was found in Mr. Hiram P. Trapp. Mr. Trapp did his best, but relentlessly and agilely cross-questioned he was forced to admit that he loved the lady, and that, had she been free, he would have asked her to be his wife. The fact that the relations between them were admittedly platonic strengthened the case against the accused. Debarred from becoming his mistress by the simple honourable nature of the man, Jeanne Beroldy had conceived the monstrous project of ridding herself of her elderly undistinguished husband, and becoming the wife of the rich American.

Throughout, Madame Beroldy confronted her accusers with complete sang froid and self possession. Her story never varied. She continued to declare strenuously that she was of royal birth, and that she had been substituted for the daughter of the fruit seller at an early age. Absurd and completely unsubstantiated as these statements were, a great number of people believed implicitly in their truth.

But the prosecution was implacable. It denounced the masked "Russians" as a myth, and asserted that the crime had been committed by Madame Beroldy and her lover, Georges Conneau. A warrant was issued for the arrest of the latter, but he had wisely disappeared. Evidence showed that the bonds which secured Madame Beroldy were so loose that she could easily have freed herself.

And then, towards the close of the trial, a letter, posted in Paris, was sent to the Public Prosecutor. It was from Georges Conneau and, without revealing his whereabouts, it contained a full confession of the crime. He declared that he had indeed struck the fatal blow at Madame Beroldy's instigation. The crime had been planned between them. Believing that her husband ill-treated her, and maddened by his own passion for her, a passion which he believed her to return, he had planned the crime and struck the fatal blow that should free the woman he loved from a hateful bondage. Now, for the first time, he learnt of Mr. Hiram P. Trapp, and realized that the woman he loved had betrayed him! Not for his sake did she wish to be free—but in order to marry the wealthy American. She had used him as a cat's-paw, and now, in his jealous rage, he turned and denounced her, declaring that throughout he had acted at her instigation.

And then Madame Beroldy proved herself the remarkable woman she undoubtedly was. Without hesitation, she dropped her previous defence, and admitted that the "Russians" were a pure invention on her part. The real murderer was Georges Conneau. Maddened by passion, he had committed the crime, vowing that if she did not keep silence he would enact a terrible vengeance from her. Terrified by his threats, she had consented—also fearing it likely that if she told the truth she might be accused of conniving at the crime. But she had steadfastly refused to have anything more to do with her husband's murderer, and it was in revenge for this attitude on her part that he had written this letter accusing her. She swore solemnly that she had had nothing to do with the planning of the crime, that she had awoke on that memorable night to find Georges Conneau standing over her, the blood-stained knife in his hand.

It was a touch and go affair. Madame Beroldy's story was hardly credible. But this woman, whose fairy tales of royal intrigues had been so easily accepted, had the supreme art of making herself believed. Her address to the jury was a masterpiece. The tears streaming down her face, she spoke of her child, of her woman's honour—of her desire to keep her reputation untarnished for the child's sake. She admitted that, Georges Conneau having been her lover, she might perhaps be held morally responsible for the crime—but, before God, nothing more! She knew that she had committed a grave fault in not denouncing Conneau to the law, but she declared in a broken voice that that was a thing no woman could have done.... She had loved him! Could she let her hand be the one to send him to the Guillotine? She had been guilty of much, but she was innocent of the terrible crime imputed to her.

However that may have been, her eloquence and personality won the day. Madame Beroldy, amidst a scene of unparalleled excitement, was acquitted. Despite the utmost endeavours of the police, Georges Conneau was never traced. As for Madame Beroldy, nothing more was heard of her. Taking the child with her, she left Paris to begin a new life.

SEVENTEEN
We Make Further Investigations

I have set down the Beroldy case in full. Of course all the details did not present themselves to my memory as I have recounted them here. Nevertheless, I recalled the case fairly accurately. It had attracted a great deal of interest at the time, and had been fully reported by the English papers, so that it did not need much effort of memory on my part to recollect the salient details.

Just for the moment, in my excitement, it seemed to clear up the whole matter. I admit that I am impulsive, and Poirot deplores my custom of jumping to conclusions, but I think I had some excuse in this instance. The remarkable way in which this discovery justified Poirot's point of view struck me at once.

"Poirot," I said, "I congratulate you. I see everything now."

"If that is indeed the truth, *I* congratulate *you, mon ami.* For as a rule you are not famous for seeing—eh, is it not so?"

I felt a little annoyed.

"Come now, don't rub it in. You've been so confoundedly mysterious all along with your hints and your insignificant details that any one might fail to see what you were driving at."

Poirot lit one of his little cigarettes with his usual precision. Then he looked up.

"And since you see everything now, *mon ami,* what exactly is it that you see?"

"Why, that it was Madame Daubreuil—Beroldy, who murdered Mr. Renauld. The similarity of the two cases proves that beyond a doubt."

"Then you consider that Madame Beroldy was wrongly acquitted? That in actual fact she was guilty of connivance in her husband's murder?"

I opened my eyes wide.

"But of course! Don't you?"

Poirot walked to the end of the room, absentmindedly straightened a chair, and then said thoughtfully.

"Yes, that is my opinion. But there is no 'of course' about it, my friend. Technically speaking, Madame Beroldy is innocent."

"Of that crime, perhaps. But not of this."

Poirot sat down again, and regarded me, his thoughtful air more marked than ever.

"So it is definitely your opinion, Hastings, that Madame Daubreuil murdered M. Renauld?"

"Yes."

"Why?"

He shot the question at me with such suddenness that I was taken aback.

"Why?" I stammered. "Why? Oh, because—" I came to a stop.

Poirot nodded his head at me.

"You see, you come to a stumbling-block at once. Why should Madame Daubreuil (I shall call her that for clearness sake) murder M. Renauld? We can find no shadow of a motive. She does not benefit by his death; considered as either mistress or blackmailer she stands to lose. You cannot have a murder without a motive. The first crime was different, there we had a rich lover waiting to step into her husband's shoes."

"Money is not the only motive for murder," I objected.

"True," agreed Poirot placidly. "There are two others, the *crime passionnel* is one. And there is the third rare motive, murder for an idea which implies some form of mental derangement on the part of the murderer. Homicidal mania, and religious fanaticism belong to that class. We can rule it out here."

"But what about the *crime passionnel*? Can you rule that out? If Madame Daubreuil was Renauld's mistress, if she found that his affection was cooling, or if her jealousy was aroused in any way, might she not have struck him down in a moment of anger?"

Poirot shook his head.

"If—I say *if*, you note—Madame Daubreuil was Renauld's mistress, he had not had time to tire of her. And in any case you mistake her character. She is a woman who can simulate great emotional stress. She is a magnificent actress. But, looked at dispassionately, her life disproves her appearance. Throughout, if we examine it, she had been cold-blooded and calculating in her motives and actions. It was not to link her life with that of her young lover that she connived at her husband's murder. The rich American, for whom she probably did not care a button, was her objective. If she committed a crime, she would always do so for gain. Here there was no gain. Besides, how do you account for the digging of the grave? That was a man's work."

"She might have had an accomplice," I suggested, unwilling to relinquish my belief.

"I pass to another objection. You have spoken of the similarity between the two crimes. Wherein does that lie, my friend?"

I stared at him in astonishment.

"Why, Poirot, it was you who remarked on that! The story of the masked men, the 'secret,' the papers!"

Poirot smiled a little.

"Do not be so indignant, I beg of you. I repudiate nothing. The similarity of the two stories links the two cases together inevitably. But reflect now on something very curious. It is not Madame Daubreuil who tells us this tale—if it were all would indeed be plain sailing—it is Madame Renauld. Is she then in league with the other?"

"I can't believe that," I said slowly. "If it is so, she must be the most consummate actress the world has ever known."

"Ta-ta-ta," said Poirot impatiently. "Again you have the sentiment, and not the logic! If it is necessary for a criminal to be a consummate actress, then by all means assume her to be one. But is it necessary? I do not believe Madame Renauld to be in league with Madame Daubreuil for several reasons, some of which I have already enumerated to you. The others are self-evident. Therefore, that possibility eliminated, we draw very near to the truth which is, as always, very curious and interesting."

"Poirot," I cried, "what more do you know?"

"*Mon ami*, you must make your own deductions. You have 'access to the facts!' Concentrate your grey cells. Reason—not like Giraud—but like Hercule Poirot."

"But are you *sure*?"

"My friend, in many ways I have been an imbecile. But at last I see clearly."

"You know everything?"

"I have discovered what M. Renauld sent for me to discover."

"And you know the murderer?"

"I know one murderer."

"What do you mean?"

"We talk a little at cross-purposes. There are here not one crime, but two. The first I have solved, the second—*eh bien*, I will confess, I am not sure!"

"But, Poirot, I thought you said the man in the shed had died a natural death?"

"Ta-ta-ta." Poirot made his favourite ejaculation of impatience. "Still you do not understand. One may have a crime without a murderer, but for two crimes it is essential to have two bodies."

His remark struck me as so peculiarly lacking in lucidity that I looked at him in some anxiety. But he appeared perfectly normal. Suddenly he rose and strolled to the window.

"Here he is," he observed.

"Who?"

"M. Jack Renauld. I sent a note up to the Villa to ask him to come here."

That changed the course of my ideas, and I asked Poirot if he knew that Jack Renauld had been in Merlinville on the night of the crime. I had hoped to catch my astute little friend napping, but as usual, he was omniscient. He, too, had inquired at the station.

"And without doubt we are not original in the idea, Hastings. The excellent Giraud, he also has probably made his inquiries."

"You don't think—" I said, and then stopped. "Ah, no, it would be too horrible!"

Poirot looked inquiringly at me, but I said no more. It had just occurred to me that though there were seven women directly or indirectly connected with the case Mrs. Renauld, Madame Daubreuil and her daughter, the mysterious visitor, and the three servants—there was, with the exception of old Auguste who could hardly count, only one man—Jack Renauld. *And a man must have dug a grave....*

I had no time to develop further the appalling idea that had occurred to me, for Jack Renauld was ushered into the room.

Poirot greeted him in a business-like manner.

"Take a seat, monsieur. I regret infinitely to derange you, but you will perhaps understand that the atmosphere of the Villa is not too congenial to me. M. Giraud and I do not see eye to eye about everything. His politeness to me has not been striking and you will comprehend that I do not intend any little discoveries I may make to benefit him in any way."

"Exactly, M. Poirot," said the lad. "That fellow Giraud is an ill-conditioned brute, and I'd be delighted to see some one score at his expense."

"Then I may ask a little favour of you?"

"Certainly."

"I will ask you to go to the railway station and take a train to the next station along the line, Abbalac. Ask there at the cloak-room whether two foreigners deposited a valise there on the night of the murder. It is a small station, and they are almost certain to remember. Will you do this?"

"Of course I will," said the boy, mystified, though ready for the task.

"I and my friend, you comprehend, have business elsewhere," explained Poirot. "There is a train in a quarter of an hour, and I will ask you not to return to the Villa, as I have no wish for Giraud to get an inkling of your errand."

"Very well, I will go straight to the station."

He rose to his feet. Poirot's voice stopped him.

"One moment, M. Renauld, there is one little matter that puzzles me. Why did you not mention to M. Hautet this morning that you were in Merlinville on the night of the crime?"

Jack Renauld's face went crimson. With an effort he controlled himself.

"You have made a mistake. I was in Cherbourg, as I told the examining magistrate this morning."

Poirot looked at him, his eyes narrowed, cat-like, until they only showed a gleam of green.

"Then it is a singular mistake that I have made there—for it is shared by the station staff. They say you arrived by the 11:40 train."

For a moment Jack Renauld hesitated, then he made up his mind.

"And if I did? I suppose you do not mean to accuse me of participating in my father's murder?" He asked the question haughtily, his head thrown back.

"I should like an explanation of the reason that brought you here."

"That is simple enough. I came to see my fiancée, Mademoiselle Daubreuil. I was on the eve of a long voyage, uncertain as to when I should return. I wished to see her before I went, to assure her of my unchanging devotion."

"And you did see her?" Poirot's eyes never left the other's face.

There was an appreciable pause before Renauld replied. Then he said:

"Yes."

"And afterwards?"

"I found I had missed the last train. I walked to St. Beauvais where I knocked up a garage and got a car to take me back to Cherbourg."

"St. Beauvais? That is fifteen kilometres. A long walk, M. Renauld."

"I—I felt like walking."

Poirot bowed his head as a sign that he accepted the explanation. Jack Renauld took up his hat and cane and departed. In a trice Poirot jumped to his feet.

"Quick, Hastings. We will go after him."

Keeping a discreet distance behind our quarry, we followed him through the streets of Merlinville. But when Poirot saw that he took the turning to the station, he checked himself.

"All is well. He has taken the bait. He will go to Abbalac, and will inquire for the mythical valise left by the mythical foreigners. Yes, *mon ami*, all that was a little invention of my own."

"You wanted him out of the way!" I exclaimed.

"Your penetration is amazing, Hastings! Now, if you please, we will go up to the Villa Geneviève."

EIGHTEEN
Giraud Acts

By the way, Poirot," I said, as we walked along the hot white road, "I've got a bone to pick with you. I dare say you meant well, but really it was no business of yours to go mouching round to the Hôtel du Phare without letting me know."

Poirot shot a quick sidelong glance at me.

"And how did you know I had been there?" he inquired.

Much to my annoyance I felt the colour rising in my cheeks.

"I happened to look in in passing," I explained with as much dignity as I could muster.

I rather feared Poirot's banter, but to my relief, and somewhat to my surprise, he only shook his head with a rather unusual gravity.

"If I have offended your susceptibilities in any way, I demand pardon of you. You will understand better soon. But, believe me, I have striven to concentrate all my energies on the case."

"Oh, it's all right," I said, mollified by the apology. "I know it's only that you have my interests at heart. But I can take care of myself all right."

Poirot seemed to be about to say something further, but checked himself.

Arrived at the Villa, Poirot led the way up to the shed where the second body had been discovered. He did not, however, go in, but paused by the bench which I have mentioned before as being set some few yards away from it. After contemplating it for a moment or two, he paced carefully from it to the hedge which marked the boundary between the Villa Geneviève and the Villa Marguerite. Then he paced back again, nodding his head as he did so. Returning again to the hedge, he parted the bushes with his hands.

"With good fortune," he remarked to me over his shoulder, "Mademoiselle Marthe may find herself in the garden. I desire to speak to her and would prefer not to call formally at the Villa Marguerite. Ah, all is well, there she is. Pst, mademoiselle! Pst! *Un moment, s'il vous plaît.*"

I joined him at the moment that Marthe Daubreuil, looking slightly startled, came running up to the hedge at his call.

"A little word with you, mademoiselle, if it is permitted?"

"Certainly, Monsieur Poirot."

Despite her acquiescence, her eyes looked troubled and afraid.

"Mademoiselle, do you remember running after me on the road the day that I came to your house with the examining magistrate? You asked me if any one were suspected of the crime."

"And you told me two Chilians." Her voice sounded rather breathless, and her left hand stole to her breast.

"Will you ask me the same question again, mademoiselle?"

"What do you mean?"

"This. If you were to ask me that question again, I should give you a different answer. Some one is suspected—but not a Chilian."

"Who?" The word came faintly between her parted lips.

"M. Jack Renauld."

"What?" It was a cry. "Jack? Impossible. Who dares to suspect him?"

"Giraud."

"Giraud!" The girl's face was ashy. "I am afraid of that man. He is cruel. He will—he will—" She broke off. There was courage

143

gathering in her face, and determination. I realized in that moment that she was a fighter. Poirot, too, watched her intently.

"You know, of course, that he was here on the night of the murder?" he asked.

"Yes," she replied mechanically. "He told me."

"It was unwise to have tried to conceal the fact," ventured Poirot.

"Yes, yes," she replied impatiently. "But we cannot waste time on regrets. We must find something to save him. He is innocent, of course, but that will not help him with a man like Giraud who has his reputation to think of. He must arrest some one, and that some one will be Jack."

"The facts will tell against him," said Poirot. "You realize that?"

She faced him squarely, and used the words I had heard her say in her mother's drawing-room.

"I am not a child, monsieur. I can be brave and look facts in the face. He is innocent, and we must save him."

She spoke with a kind of desperate energy, then was silent, frowning as she thought.

"Mademoiselle," said Poirot observing her keenly, "is there not something that you are keeping back that you could tell us?"

She nodded perplexedly.

"Yes, there is something, but I hardly know whether you will believe it—it seems so absurd."

"At any rate, tell us, mademoiselle."

"It is this. M. Giraud sent for me, as an afterthought, to see if I could identify the man in there." She signed with her head towards the shed. "I could not. At least I could not at the moment. But since I have been thinking—"

"Well?"

"It seems so queer, and yet I am almost sure. I will tell you. On the morning of the day M. Renauld was murdered, I was walking in the garden here, when I heard a sound of men's voices quarrelling. I pushed aside the bushes and looked through. One of the men was M. Renauld and the other was a tramp, a dreadful looking creature in filthy rags. He was alternately whining and threatening. I gathered he was asking for money, but at that moment *maman* called me from the house, and I had to go. That is all, only—I am almost sure that the tramp and the dead man in the shed are one and the same."

Poirot uttered an exclamation.

"But why did you not say so at the time, mademoiselle?"

"Because at first it only struck me that the face was vaguely familiar in some way. The man was differently dressed, and apparently belonged to a superior station in life. But tell me, Monsieur Poirot, is it not possible that this tramp might have attacked and killed M. Renauld, and taken his clothes and money?"

"It is an idea, mademoiselle," said Poirot slowly. "It leaves a lot unexplained, but it is certainly an idea. I will think of it."

A voice called from the house.

"*Maman,*" whispered Marthe, "I must go." And she slipped away through the trees.

"Come," said Poirot, and taking my arm, turned in the direction of the Villa.

"What do you really think?" I asked, in some curiosity. "Was that story true, or did the girl make it up in order to divert suspicion from her lover?"

"It is a curious tale," said Poirot, "but I believe it to be the absolute truth. Unwittingly, Mademoiselle Marthe told us the truth on another point—and incidentally gave Jack Renauld the lie. Did you notice his hesitation when I asked him if he saw Marthe Daubreuil on the night of the crime? He paused and then said 'Yes.' I suspected that he was lying. It was necessary for me to see Mademoiselle Marthe before he could put her on her guard. Three little words gave me the information I wanted. When I asked her if she knew that Jack Renauld was here that night, she answered 'He *told* me.' Now, Hastings, what was Jack Renauld doing here on that eventful evening, and if he did not see Mademoiselle Marthe whom did he see?"

"Surely, Poirot," I cried, aghast, "you cannot believe that a boy like that would murder his own father."

"*Mon ami*," said Poirot, "you continue to be of a sentimentality unbelievable! I have seen mothers who murdered their little children for the sake of the insurance money! After that, one can believe anything."

"And the motive?"

"Money of course. Remember that Jack Renauld thought that he would come in to half his father's fortune at the latter's death."

"But the tramp. Where does he come in?"

Poirot shrugged his shoulders.

"Giraud would say that he was an accomplice—an apache who helped young Renauld to commit the crime, and who was conveniently put out of the way afterwards."

"But the hair round the dagger? The woman's hair?"

"Ah," said Poirot, smiling broadly. "That is the cream of Giraud's little jest. According to him, it is not a woman's hair at all. Remember that the youths of today wear their hair brushed straight back from the forehead with pomade or hairwash to make it lie flat. Consequently some of the hairs are of considerable length."

"And you believe that too?"

"No," said Poirot with a curious smile. "For I know it to be the hair of a woman—and more, which woman!"

"Madame Daubreuil," I announced positively.

"Perhaps," said Poirot, regarding me quizzically.

But I refused to allow myself to get annoyed.

"What are we going to do now?" I asked, as we entered the hall of the Villa Geneviève.

"I wish to make a search amongst the effects of M. Jack Renauld. That is why I had to get him out of the way for a few hours."

"But will not Giraud have searched already?" I asked doubtfully.

"Of course. He builds a case, as a beaver builds a dam, with a fatiguing industry. But he will not have looked for the things that I am seeking—in all probability he would not have seen their importance if they stared him in the face. Let us begin."

Neatly and methodically, Poirot opened each drawer in turn, examined the contents, and returned them exactly to their places. It was a singularly dull and uninteresting proceeding. Poirot waded on through collars, pajamas and socks. A purring noise outside drew me to the window. Instantly I became galvanized into life.

"Poirot!" I cried. "A car has just driven up. Giraud is in it, and Jack Renauld, and two gendarmes."

"*Sacré tonnerre!*" growled Poirot. "That animal of a Giraud, could he not wait? I shall not be able to replace the things in this last drawer with the proper method. Let us be quick."

Unceremoniously he tumbled out the things on the floor, mostly ties and handkerchiefs. Suddenly with a cry of triumph Poirot pounced on something, a small square cardboard, evidently a photograph. Thrusting it into his pocket, he returned the things pell-mell to the drawer, and seizing me by the arm dragged me out of the room and down the stairs. In the hall stood Giraud, contemplating his prisoner.

"Good afternoon, M. Giraud," said Poirot. "What have we here?"

Giraud nodded his head towards Jack.

"He was trying to make a getaway, but I was too sharp for him. He is under arrest for the murder of his father, M. Paul Renauld."

Poirot wheeled to confront the boy who leaned limply against the door, his face ashy pale.

"What do you say to that, *jeune homme?*"

Jack Renauld stared at him stonily.

"Nothing," he said.

NINETEEN
I Use My Grey Cells

I was dumbfounded. Up to the last, I had not been able bring myself to believe Jack Renauld guilty. I had expected a ringing proclamation of his innocence when Poirot challenged him. But now, watching him as he stood, white and limp against the wall, and hearing the damning admission fall from his lips, I doubted no longer.

But Poirot had turned to Giraud.

"What are your grounds for arresting him?"

"Do you expect me to give them to you?"

"As a matter of courtesy, yes."

Giraud looked at him doubtfully. He was torn between a desire to refuse rudely and the pleasure of triumphing over his adversary.

"You think I have made a mistake, I suppose?" he sneered.

"It would not surprise me," replied Poirot, with a soupçon of malice.

Giraud's face took on a deeper tinge of red.

"*Eh bien*, come in here. You shall judge for yourself." He flung open the door of the *salon*, and we passed in, leaving Jack Renauld in the care of the two other men.

"Now, M. Poirot," said Giraud laying his hat on the table, and speaking with the utmost sarcasm, "I will treat you to a little lecture on detective work. I will show you how we moderns work."

"*Bien!*" said Poirot, composing himself to listen. "I will show you how admirably the Old Guard can listen," and he leaned back and closed his eyes, opening them for a moment to remark. "Do not fear that I shall sleep. I will attend most carefully."

"Of course," began Giraud, "I soon saw through all that Chilian tomfoolery. Two men were in it—but they were not mysterious foreigners! All that was a blind."

"Very creditable so far, my dear Giraud," murmured Poirot. "Especially after that clever trick of theirs with the match and cigarette end."

Giraud glared, but continued:

"A man must have been connected with the case, in order to dig the grave. There is no man who actually benefits by the crime, but there was a man who thought he would benefit. I heard of Jack Renauld's quarrel with his father, and of the threats that he had used. The motive was established. Now as to means. Jack Renauld was in Merlinville that night. He concealed the fact—which turned suspicion into certainty. Then we found a second victim—*stabbed with the same dagger*. We know when that dagger was stolen. Captain Hastings here can fix the time. Jack Renauld, arriving from Cherbourg, was the only person who could have taken it. I have accounted for all the other members of the household."

Poirot interrupted:

"You are wrong. There is one other person who could have taken the dagger."

"You refer to M. Stonor? He arrived at the front door, in an automobile which had brought him straight from Calais. Ah, believe me, I have looked into everything. M. Jack Renauld arrived by train. An hour elapsed between his arrival, and the moment he presented himself at the house. Without doubt, he saw Captain Hastings and his companion leave the shed, slipped in himself and took the dagger, stabbed his accomplice in the shed—"

"Who was already dead!"

Giraud shrugged his shoulders.

"Possibly he did not observe that. He may have judged him to be sleeping. Without doubt they had a rendezvous. In any case he knew this apparent second murder would greatly complicate the case. It did."

"But it could not deceive M. Giraud," murmured Poirot.

"You mock yourself at me. But I will give you one last irrefutable proof. Madame Renauld's story was false—a fabrication from beginning to end. We believe Madame Renauld to have loved her husband—*yet she lied to shield his murderer.* For whom will a woman lie? Sometimes for herself, usually for the man she loves, *always* for her children. That is the last—the irrefutable proof. You cannot get round it."

Giraud paused, flushed and triumphant. Poirot regarded him steadily.

"That is my case," said Giraud. "What have you to say to it?"

"Only that there is one thing you have failed to take into account."

"What is that?"

"Jack Renauld was presumably acquainted with the planning out of the golf course. He knew that the body would be discovered almost at once, when they started to dig the bunker."

Giraud laughed out loud.

"But it is idiotic what you say there! He wanted the body to be found! Until it was found, he could not presume death, and would have been unable to enter into his inheritance."

I saw a quick flash of green in Poirot's eyes as he rose to his feet.

"Then why bury it?" he asked softly. "Reflect, Giraud. Since it was to Jack Renauld's advantage that the body should be found without delay, *why dig a grave at all?*"

Giraud did not reply. The question found him unprepared. He shrugged his shoulders as though to intimate that it was of no importance.

Poirot moved towards the door. I followed him.

"There is one more thing that you have failed to take into account," he said over his shoulder.

"What is that?"

"The piece of lead piping," said Poirot, and left the room.

Jack Renauld still stood in the hall, with a white dumb face, but as we came out of the *salon*, he looked up sharply. At the same moment there was the sound of a footfall on the staircase. Mrs. Renauld was descending it. At the sight of her son, standing between the two myrmidons of the law, she stopped as though petrified.

"Jack," she faltered. "Jack, what is this?"

He looked up at her, his face set.

"They have arrested me, mother."

"What?"

She uttered a piercing cry, and before any one could get to her she swayed and fell heavily. We both ran to her and lifted her up. In a minute Poirot stood up again.

"She has cut her head badly, on the corner of the stairs. I fancy there is a slight concussion also. If Giraud wants a statement from her, he will have to wait. She will probably be unconscious for at least a week."

Denise and Françoise had run to their mistress, and leaving her in their charge Poirot left the house. He walked with his head bent down, frowning thoughtfully at the ground. For some time I did not speak, but at last I ventured to put a question to him.

"Do you believe then, in spite of all appearances to the contrary, that Jack Renauld may not be guilty?"

Poirot did not answer at once, but after a long wait he said gravely:

"I do not know, Hastings. There is just a chance of it. Of course Giraud is all wrong—wrong from beginning to end. If Jack Renauld is guilty, it is in spite of Giraud's arguments, not *because* of them. And the gravest indictment against him is known only to me."

"What is that?" I asked, impressed.

"If you would use your grey cells, and see the whole case clearly as I do, you too would perceive it, my friend."

This was what I called one of Poirot's irritating answers. He went on, without waiting for me to speak.

"Let us walk this way to the sea. We will sit on that little mound there, overlooking the beach, and review the case. You shall know all that I know, but I would prefer that you should come at the truth by your own efforts—not by my leading you by the hand."

We established ourselves on the grassy knoll as Poirot had suggested, looking out to sea. From farther along the sand, the cries of the bathers reached us faintly. The sea was of the palest blue, and the halcyon calm reminded me of the day we had arrived at Merlinville, my own good spirits, and Poirot's suggestion that I was "fey." What a long time seemed to have elapsed since then. And in reality it was only three days!

"Think, my friend," said Poirot's voice encouragingly. "Arrange your ideas. Be methodical. Be orderly. There is the secret of success."

I endeavoured to obey him, casting my mind back over all the details of the case. And reluctantly it seemed to me that the only clear and possible solution was that of Giraud—which Poirot despised. I reflected anew. If there was daylight anywhere it was in the direction of Madame Daubreuil. Giraud was ignorant of her connection with the Beroldy Case. Poirot had declared the Beroldy Case to be all important. It was there I must seek. I was on the right track now. And suddenly I started as an idea of bewildering luminosity shot into my brain. Trembling I built up my hypothesis.

"You have a little idea, I see, *mon ami!* Capital. We progress."

I sat up, and lit a pipe.

"Poirot," I said, "it seems to me we have been strangely remiss. I say we—although I dare say *I* would be nearer the mark. But you must pay the penalty of your determined secrecy. So I say again we have been strangely remiss. There is some one we have forgotten."

"And who is that?" inquired Poirot, with twinkling eyes.

"Georges Conneau!"

TWENTY

An Amazing Statement

The next moment Poirot embraced me warmly. "*Enfin!* You have arrived. And all by yourself. It is superb! Continue your reasoning. You are right. Decidedly we have done wrong to forget Georges Conneau."

I was so flattered by the little man's approval that I could hardly continue. But at last I collected my thoughts and went on.

"Georges Conneau disappeared twenty years ago, but we have no reason to believe that he is dead."

"*Aucunement,*" agreed Poirot. "Proceed."

"Therefore we will assume that he is alive."

"Exactly."

"Or that he was alive until recently."

"*De mieux en mieux!*"

"We will presume," I continued, my enthusiasm rising, "that he has fallen on evil days. He has become a criminal, an apache, a tramp—a what you will. He chances to come to Merlinville. There he finds the woman he has never ceased to love."

"Eh eh! The sentimentality," warned Poirot.

"Where one hates one also loves," I quoted or misquoted. "At any rate he finds her there, living under an assumed name. But she has a new lover, the Englishman, Renauld. Georges Conneau, the memory of old wrongs rising in him, quarrels with this Renauld. He lies in wait for him as he comes to visit his mistress, and stabs

154

him in the back. Then, terrified at what he has done, he starts to dig a grave. I imagine it likely that Madame Daubreuil comes out to look for her lover. She and Conneau have a terrible scene. He drags her into the shed, and there suddenly falls down in an epileptic fit. Now supposing Jack Renauld to appear. Madame Daubreuil tells him all, points out to him the dreadful consequences to her daughter if this scandal of the past is revived. His father's murderer is dead—let them do their best to hush it up. Jack Renauld consents—goes to the house and has an interview with his mother, winning her over to his point of view. Primed with the story that Madame Daubreuil has suggested to him, she permits herself to be gagged and bound. There, Poirot, what do you think of that?" I leaned back, flushed with the pride of successful reconstruction.

Poirot looked at me thoughtfully.

"I think that you should write for the Kinema, *mon ami*," he remarked at last.

"You mean—?"

"It would make a good film, the story that you have recounted to me there—but it bears no sort of resemblance to everyday life."

"I admit that I haven't gone into all the details, but—"

"You have gone further—you have ignored them magnificently. What about the way the two men were dressed? Do you suggest that after stabbing his victim, Conneau removed his suit of clothes, donned it himself, and replaced the dagger?"

"I don't see that that matters," I objected rather huffily. "He may have obtained clothes and money from Madame Daubreuil by threats earlier in the day."

"By threats—eh? You seriously advance that supposition?"

"Certainly. He could have threatened to reveal her identity to the Renaulds, which would probably have put an end to all hopes of her daughter's marriage."

"You are wrong, Hastings. He could not blackmail her, for she had the whip hand. Georges Conneau, remember, is still wanted for murder. A word from her and he is in danger of the guillotine."

I was forced, rather reluctantly, to admit the truth of this.

"*Your* theory," I remarked acidly, "is doubtless correct as to all the details?"

"My theory is the truth," said Poirot quietly. "And the truth is necessarily correct. In your theory you made a fundamental error. You permitted your imagination to lead you astray with midnight assignations and passionate love scenes. But in investigating crime we must take our stand upon the commonplace. Shall I demonstrate my methods to you?"

"Oh, by all means let us have a demonstration!"

Poirot sat very upright and began, wagging his forefinger emphatically to emphasize his points.

"I will start as you started from the basic fact of Georges Conneau. Now the story told by Madame Beroldy in court as to the 'Russians' was admittedly a fabrication. If she was innocent of connivance in the crime, it was concocted by her, and by her only as she stated. If, on the other hand, she was not innocent, it might have been invented by either her or Georges Conneau.

"Now in this case we are investigating, we meet the same tale. As I pointed out to you, the facts render it very unlikely that Madame Daubreuil inspired it. So we turn to the hypothesis that the story had its origin in the brain of Georges Conneau. Very good. Georges Conneau, therefore, planned the crime with Madame Renauld as his accomplice. She is in the limelight, and behind her is a shadowy figure whose alias is unknown to us.

"Now let us go carefully over the Renauld Case from the beginning, setting down each significant point in its chronological order. You have a notebook and pencil? Good. Now what is the earliest point to note down?"

"The letter to you?"

"That was the first we knew of it, but it is not the proper beginning of the case. The first point of any significance, I should say, is the change that came over M. Renauld shortly after arriving in Merlinville, and which is attested to by several witnesses. We have also to consider his friendship with Madame Daubreuil, and the large sums of money paid over to her. From thence we can come directly to the 23rd May."

Poirot paused, cleared his throat, and signed to me to write.

"*23rd May.* M. Renauld quarrels with his son over latter's wish to marry Marthe Daubreuil. Son leaves for Paris.

"*24th May.* M. Renauld alters his will, leaving entire control of his fortune in his wife's hands.

"*7th June.* Quarrel with tramp in garden, witnessed by Marthe Daubreuil.

"Letter written to M. Hercule Poirot, imploring assistance.

"Telegram sent to Jack Renauld, bidding him proceed by the *Anzora* to Buenos Ayres.

"Chauffeur, Masters, sent off on a holiday.

"Visit of a lady, that evening. As he is seeing her out, his words are 'Yes, yes—but for God's sake go now....'"

Poirot paused.

"There, Hastings, take each of those facts one by one, consider them carefully by themselves and in relation to the whole, and see if you do not get new light on the matter."

I endeavoured conscientiously to do as he had said. After a moment or two, I said rather doubtfully:

"As to the first points, the question seems to be whether we adopt the theory of blackmail, or of an infatuation for this woman."

"Blackmail, decidedly. You heard what Stonor said as to his character and habits."

"Mrs. Renauld did not confirm his view," I argued.

"We have already seen that Madame Renauld's testimony cannot be relied upon in any way. We must trust to Stonor on that point."

"Still, if Renauld had an affair with a woman called Bella, there seems no inherent improbability in his having another with Madame Daubreuil."

"None whatever, I grant you, Hastings. But did he?"

"The letter, Poirot. You forget the letter."

"No, I do not forget. But what makes you think that letter was written to M. Renauld?"

"Why it was found in his pocket and—and—"

"And that is all!" cut in Poirot. "There was no mention of any name to show to whom the letter was addressed. We assumed it was to the dead man because it was in the pocket of his overcoat. Now, *mon ami*, something about that overcoat struck me as unusual. I measured it, and made the remark that he wore his overcoat very long. That remark should have given you to think."

"I thought you were just saying it for the sake of saying something," I confessed.

"Ah, *quelle idée!* Later you observed me measuring the overcoat of M. Jack Renauld. *Eh bien*, M. Jack Renauld wears his overcoat very short. Put those two facts together with a third, namely that M. Jack Renauld flung out of the house in a hurry on his departure for Paris, and tell me what you make of it!"

"I see," I said slowly, as the meaning of Poirot's remarks bore in upon me. "That letter was written to Jack Renauld—not to his father. He caught up the wrong overcoat in his haste and agitation."

Poirot nodded.

"*Précisement!* We can return to this point later. For the moment let us content ourselves with accepting the letter as having nothing to do with M. Renauld *père*, and pass to the next chronological event."

"May 23rd," I read, "M. Renauld quarrels with his son over latter's wish to marry Marthe Daubreuil. Son leaves for Paris. I don't see anything much to remark upon there, and the altering of the will the following day seems straightforward enough. It was the direct result of the quarrel."

"We agree, *mon ami*—at least as to the cause. But what exact motive underlay this procedure of M. Renauld's?"

I opened my eyes in surprise.

"Anger against his son of course."

"Yet he wrote him affectionate letters to Paris?"

"So Jack Renauld says, but he cannot produce them."

"Well, let us pass from that."

"Now we come to the day of the tragedy. You have placed the events of the morning in a certain order. Have you any justification for that?"

"I have ascertained that the letter to me was posted at the same time as the telegram was despatched. Masters was informed he could take a holiday shortly afterwards. In my opinion the quarrel with the tramp took place anterior to these happenings."

"I do not see that you can fix that definitely—unless you question Mademoiselle Dabreuil again."

"There is no need. I am sure of it. And if you do not see that, you see nothing, Hastings!"

I looked at him for a moment.

"Of course! I am an idiot. If the tramp was Georges Conneau, it was after the stormy interview with him that Mr. Renauld apprehended danger. He sent away the chauffeur, Masters, whom he suspected of being in the other's pay, he wired to his son, and sent for you."

A faint smile crossed Poirot's lips.

"You do not think it strange that he should use exactly the same expressions in his letter as Madame Renauld used later in her story? If the mention of Santiago was a blind, why should Renauld speak of it, and—what is more—send his son there?"

"It is puzzling, I admit, but perhaps we shall find some explanation later. We come now to the evening, and the visit of the mysterious lady. I confess that that fairly baffles me, unless it was Madame Daubreuil, as Françoise all along maintained."

Poirot shook his head.

"My friend, my friend, where are your wits wandering? Remember the fragment of cheque, and the fact that the name Bella Duveen was faintly familiar to Stonor, and I think we may take it for granted that Bella Duveen is the full name of Jack's unknown correspondent, and that it was she who came to the Villa Geneviève that night. Whether she intended to see Jack, or whether she meant all along to appeal to his father we cannot be certain, but I think we may assume that this is what occurred. She produced her claim upon Jack, probably showed letters that he had written her, and the older man tried to buy her off by writing a cheque. This she indignantly tore up. The terms of her letter are those of a woman genuinely in love, and she would probably deeply resent being offered money. In the end he got rid of her, and here the words that he used are significant."

"Yes, yes, but for God's sake go now,'" I repeated. "They seem to me a little vehement, perhaps, that is all."

"That is enough. He was desperately anxious for the girl to go. Why? Not only because the interview was unpleasant. No, it was the time that was slipping by, and for some reason time was precious."

"Why should it be?" I asked, bewildered.

"That is what we ask ourselves. Why should it be? But later we have the incident of the wrist watch—which again shows us that time plays a very important part in the crime. We are now fast approaching the actual drama. It is half-past ten when Bella Duveen leaves, and by the evidence of the wrist watch we know that the crime was committed, or at any rate that it was staged, before twelve o'clock. We have reviewed all the events anterior to the murder, there remains only one unplaced. By the doctor's evidence, the tramp, when found, had been dead at least forty-eight hours—with a possible margin of twenty-four hours more. Now, with no other facts to help me than those we have discussed, I place the death as having occurred on the morning of June 7th."

I stared at him, stupefied.

"But how? Why? How can you possibly know?"

"Because only in that way can the sequence of events be logically explained. *Mon ami*, I have taken you step by step along the way. Do you not now see what is so glaringly plain?"

"My dear Poirot, I can't see anything glaring about it. I did think I was beginning to see my way before, but I'm now hopelessly fogged."

Poirot looked at me sadly, and shook his head. *"Mon Dieu!* But it is *triste!* A good intelligence—and so deplorably lacking in method. There is an exercise most excellent for the development of the little grey cells. I will impart it to you—"

"For Heaven's sake, not now! You really are the most irritating of fellows, Poirot. For goodness' sake, get on and tell me who killed M. Renauld."

"That is just what I am not sure of as yet."

"But you said it was glaringly clear?"

"We talk at cross-purposes, my friend. Remember, it is two crimes we are investigating—for which, as I pointed out to you, we have the necessary two bodies. There, there, *ne vous impatientez pas!* I explain all. To begin with, we apply our psychology. We find three points at which M. Renauld displays a distinct change of view and action—three psychological points therefore. The first occurs immediately after arriving in Merlinville, the second after quarrelling with his son on a certain subject, the third on the morning of June 7th. Now for the three causes. We can attribute No. 1 to meeting Madame Daubreuil. No. 2 is indirectly connected with her since it concerns a marriage between M. Renauld's son and her daughter. But the cause of No. 3 is hidden from us. We have to deduce it. Now, *mon ami*, let me ask you a question; who do we believe to have planned this crime?"

"Georges Conneau," I said doubtfully, eyeing Poirot warily.

"Exactly. Now Giraud laid it down as an axiom that a woman lies to save herself, the man she loves, and her child. Since we are satisfied that was Georges Conneau who dictated the lie to her, and as Georges Conneau is not Jack Renauld, follows that the third case is put out of court. And, still attributing the crime to Georges Conneau, the first is equally so. So we are forced to the second—that Madame Renauld lied for the sake of the man she loved—or in other words, for the sake of Georges Conneau. You agree to that."

"Yes," I admitted. "It seems logical enough."

"*Bien!* Madame Renauld loves Georges Conneau. Who, then, is Georges Conneau?"

"The tramp."

"Have we any evidence to show that Madame Renauld loved the tramp?"

"No, but—"

"Very well then. Do not cling to theories where facts no longer support them. Ask yourself instead who Madame Renauld *did* love."

I shook my head perplexed.

"*Mais, oui*, you know perfectly. Who did Madame Renauld love so dearly that when she saw his dead body, she fell down in a swoon?"

I stared dumbfounded.

"Her husband?" I gasped.

Poirot nodded.

"Her husband—or Georges Conneau, whichever you like to call him."

I rallied myself.

"But it's impossible."

"How 'impossible?' Did we not agree just now that Madame Daubreuil was in a position to blackmail Georges Conneau?"

"Yes, but—"

"And did she not very effectively blackmail M. Renauld?"

"That may be true enough, but—"

"And is it not a fact that we know nothing of M. Renauld's youth and upbringing? That he springs suddenly into existence as a French Canadian exactly twenty-two years ago?"

"All that is so," I said more firmly, "but you seem to me to be overlooking one salient point."

"What is it, my friend?"

"Why, we have admitted Georges Conneau planned the crime. That brings us to the ridiculous statement that he planned his own murder!"

"*Eh bien, mon ami,*" said Poirot placidly, "that is just what he did do!"

TWENTY-ONE
Hercule Poirot on the Case!

In a measured voice, Poirot began his exposition.

"It seems strange to you, *mon ami*, that a man should plan his own death? So strange, that you prefer to reject the truth as fantastic, and to revert to a story that is in reality ten times more impossible. Yes, M. Renauld planned his own death, but there is one detail that perhaps escapes you—he did not intend to die."

I shook my head, bewildered.

"But no, it is all most simple really," said Poirot kindly. "For the crime that M. Renauld proposed a murderer was not necessary, as I told you, but a body was. Let us reconstruct, seeing events this time from a different angle.

"Georges Conneau flies from justice—to Canada. There, under an assumed name he marries, and finally acquires a vast fortune in South America. But there is a nostalgia upon him for his own country. Twenty years have elapsed, he is considerably changed in appearance, besides being a man of such eminence that no one is likely to connect him with a fugitive from justice many years ago. He deems it quite safe to return. He takes up his headquarters in England, but intends to spend the summers in France. And ill fortune, that obscure justice which shapes men's ends, and will not allow them to evade the consequences of their acts, takes him to Merlinville. There, in the whole of France, is the one person who is capable of recognizing him. It is, of course, a gold mine to Madame Daubreuil, and a gold mine of which she is not slow to take advantage. He is helpless, absolutely in her power. And she bleeds him heavily.

"And then the inevitable happens. Jack Renauld falls in love with the beautiful girl he sees almost daily, and wishes to marry her. That rouses his father. At all costs, he will prevent his son marrying the daughter of this evil woman. Jack Renauld knows nothing of his father's past, but Madame Renauld knows everything. She is a woman of great force of character, and passionately devoted to her husband. They take counsel together. Renauld sees only one way of escape—death. He must appear to die, in reality escaping to another country where he will start again under an assumed name, and where Madame Renauld, having played the widow's part for a while, can join him. It is essential that she should have control of the money, so he alters his will. How they meant to manage the body business originally, I do not know— possibly an art student's skeleton—and a fire or something of the kind, but long before their plans have matured an event occurs which plays into their hands. A rough tramp, violent and abusive, finds his way into the garden. There is a struggle, M. Renauld seeks to eject him, and suddenly the tramp, an epileptic, falls down in a fit. He is dead. M. Renauld calls his wife. Together they drag him into the shed—as we know, the event had occurred just outside—and they realize the marvellous opportunity that has been vouchsafed them. The man bears no resemblance to M. Renauld, but he is middle-aged, of a usual French type. That is sufficient.

"I rather fancy that they sat on the bench up there, out of earshot from the house, discussing matters. Their plan was quickly made. The identification must rest solely on Madame Renauld's evidence. Jack Renauld and the chauffeur (who had been with his master two years) must be got out of the way. It was unlikely that the French women servants would go near the body, and in any case Renauld intended to take measures to deceive any one not likely to appreciate details. Masters was sent off, a telegram despatched to Jack, Buenos Ayres being selected to give credence to the story that Renauld had decided upon. Having heard of me, as a rather obscure elderly detective, he wrote his appeal for help knowing that, when I arrived, the production of the letter would have a profound effect upon the examining magistrate—which, of course, it did.

"They dressed the body of the tramp in a suit of M. Renauld's and left his ragged coat and trousers by the door of the shed, not daring to take them into the house. And then, to give credence to the tale Madame Renauld was to tell, they drove the aeroplane dagger through his heart. That night, M. Renauld will first bind and gag his wife, and then, taking a spade, will dig a grave in that particular spot of ground where he knows a—how do you call it? bunkair?—is to be made. It is essential that the body should be found—Madame Daubreuil must have no suspicions. On the other hand, if a little time elapses, any dangers as to identity will be greatly lessened. Then, M. Renauld will don the tramp's rags, and shuffle off to the station, where he will leave, unnoticed, by the 12:10 train. Since the crime will be supposed to have taken place two hours later, no suspicion can possibly attach to him.

"You see now his annoyance at the inopportune visit of the girl Bella. Every moment of delay is fatal to his plans. He gets rid of her as soon as he can, however. Then, to work! He leaves the front door slightly ajar to create the impression that the assassins left that way. He binds and gags Madame Renauld, correcting his mistake of twenty-two years ago, when the looseness of the bonds caused suspicion to fall upon his accomplice, but leaving her primed with essentially the same story as he had invented before, proving the unconscious recoil of the mind against originality. The night is chilly, and he slips on an overcoat over his underclothing, intending to cast it into the grave with the dead man. He goes out by the window, smoothing over the flower bed carefully, and thereby furnishing the most positive evidence against himself.

He goes out on to the lonely golf links, and he digs—and then—"

"Yes?"

"And then," said Poirot gravely, "the justice that he has so long eluded overtakes him. An unknown hand stabs him in the back.... Now, Hastings, you understand what I mean when I talk of *two* crimes. The first crime, the crime that M. Renauld, in his arrogance, asked us to investigate (ah, but he made a famous mistake there! He misjudged Hercule Poirot!) is solved. But behind it lies a deeper riddle. And to solve that will be difficult—since the criminal in his wisdom, has been content to avail himself of the devices prepared by M. Renauld. It has been a particularly perplexing and baffling mystery to solve. A young hand, like Giraud, who does not place any reliance on the psychology, is almost certain to fail."

"You're marvellous, Poirot," I said, with admiration. "Absolutely marvellous. No one on earth but you could have done it!"

I think my praise pleased him. For once in his life, he looked almost embarrassed.

"Ah, then you no longer despise poor old Papa Poirot? You shift your allegiance back from the human foxhound?"

His term for Giraud never failed to make me smile.

"Rather. You've scored over him handsomely."

"That poor Giraud," said Poirot, trying unsuccessfully to look modest. "Without doubt it is not all stupidity. He has had *la mauvaise chance* once or twice. That dark hair coiled round the dagger, for instance. To say the least, it was misleading."

"To tell you the truth, Poirot," I said slowly, "even now I don't quite see—whose hair was it?"

"Madame Renauld's of course. That is where *la mauvaise chance* came in. Her hair, dark originally, is almost completely silvered. It might just as easily have been a grey hair—and then, by no conceivable effort could Giraud have persuaded himself it came from the head of Jack Renauld! But it is all of a piece. Always the facts must be twisted to fit the theory! Did not Giraud find the traces of two persons, a man and a woman, in the shed? And how does that fit in with his reconstruction of the case? I will tell you—it does not fit in, and so we shall hear no more of them! I ask you, is that a methodical way of working? The great Giraud! The great Giraud is nothing but a toy balloon—swollen with its own importance. But I, Hercule Poirot, whom he despises, will be the little pin that pricks the big balloon—*comme ça!*" And he made an expressive gesture. Then, calming down, he resumed:

"Without doubt, when Madame Renauld recovers, she will speak. The possibility of her son being accused of the murder never occurred to her. How should it, when she believed him safely at sea on board the *Anzora? Ah! voilà une femme*, Hastings! What force, what self-command! She only made one slip. On his unexpected return: 'It does not matter—*now*.' And no one noticed—no one realized the significance of those words. What a terrible part she has had to play, poor woman. Imagine the shock when she goes to identify the body and, instead of what she expects, sees the actual lifeless form of the husband she has believed miles away by now. No wonder she fainted! But since then, despite her grief and her despair, how resolutely she has played her part, and how the anguish of it must wring her. She cannot say a word to set us on the track of the real murderers. For her son's sake, no one must know that Paul Renauld was Georges Conneau, the criminal. Final and most bitter blow, she has admitted publicly that Madame Daubreuil was her husband's mistress—for a hint of blackmail might be fatal to her secret. How cleverly she dealt with the examining magistrate when he asked her if there was any mystery in her husband's past life. 'Nothing so romantic, I am sure, M. le juge.' It was perfect, the indulgent tone, the *soupçon* of sad mockery. At once M. Hautet felt himself foolish and melodramatic. Yes, she is a great woman! If she loved a criminal, she loved him royally!"

Poirot lost himself in contemplation.

"One thing more, Poirot, what about the piece of lead piping?"

"You do not see? To disfigure the victim's face so that it would be unrecognizable. It was that which first set me on the right track. And that imbecile of a Giraud, swarming all over it to look for match ends! Did I not tell you that a clue of two feet long was quite as good as a clue of two inches?"

"Well, Giraud will sing small now," I observed hastily, to lead the conversation away from my own shortcomings.

"As I said before, will he? If he has arrived at the right person by the wrong method, he will not permit that to worry him."

"But surely——" I paused as I saw the new trend of things.

"You see, Hastings, we must now start again. Who killed M. Renauld? Some one who was near the Villa just before twelve o'clock that night, some one who would benefit by his death—the description fits Jack Renauld only too well. The crime need not have been premeditated. And then the dagger!"

I started, I had not realized that point.

"Of course," I said. "The second dagger we found in the tramp was Mrs. Renauld's. There *were* two, then."

"Certainly, and, since they were duplicates, it stands to reason that Jack Renauld was the owner. But that would not trouble me so much. In fact I have a little idea as to that. No, the worst indictment against him is again psychological—heredity, *mon ami*, heredity! Like father, like son—Jack Renauld, when all is said or done, is the son of Georges Conneau."

His tone was grave and earnest, and I was impressed in spite of myself.

"What is your little idea that you mentioned just now?" I asked.

For answer, Poirot consulted his turnip-faced watch, and then asked:

"What time is the afternoon boat from Calais?"

"About five, I believe."

"That will do very well. We shall just have time."

"You are going to England?"

"Yes, my friend."

"Why?"

"To find a possible—witness."

"Who?"

With a rather peculiar smile upon his face, Poirot replied: "Miss Bella Duveen."

"But how will you find her—what do you know about her?"

"I know nothing about her—but I can guess a good deal. We may take it for granted that her name *is* Bella Duveen, and since that name was faintly familiar to M. Stonor, though evidently not in connection with the Renauld family, it is probable that she is on the stage. Jack Renauld was a young man with plenty of money, and twenty years of age. The stage is sure to have been the home of his first love. It tallies, too, with M. Renauld's attempt to placate her with a cheque. I think I shall find her all right—especially with the help of *this*."

And he brought out the photograph I had seen him take from Jack Renauld's drawer. "With love from Bella," was scrawled across the corner, but it was not that which held my eyes fascinated. The likeness was not first rate—but for all that it was unmistakable to me. I felt a cold sinking, as though some unutterable calamity had befallen me.

It was the face of Cinderella.

TWENTY-TWO
I Find Love

For a moment or two I sat as though frozen, the photograph still in my hand. Then, summoning all my courage to appear unmoved, I handed it back. At the same time, I stole a quick glance at Poirot. Had he noticed anything? But to my relief he did not seem to be observing me. Anything unusual in my manner had certainly escaped him.

He rose briskly to his feet.

"We have no time to lose. We must make our departure with all despatch. All is well—the sea it will be calm!"

In the bustle of departure, I had no time for thinking, but once on board the boat, secure from Poirot's observation (he, as usual, was "practising the method most excellent of Laverguier") I pulled myself together, and attacked the facts dispassionately. How much did Poirot know? Was he aware that my acquaintance of the train and Bella Duveen were one and the same? Why had he gone to the Hôtel du Phare? On my behalf as I had believed? Or had I only fatuously thought so, and was this visit undertaken with a deeper and more sinister purpose?

But in any case, why was he bent on finding this girl? Did he suspect her of having seen Jack Renauld commit the crime? Or did he suspect—but that was impossible! The girl had no grudge against the elder Renauld, no possible motive for wishing his death. What had brought her back to the scene of the

171

murder? I went over the facts carefully. She must have left the train at Calais where I parted from her that day. No wonder I had been unable to find her on the boat. If she had dined in Calais, and then taken a train out to Merlinville, she would have arrived at the Villa Geneviève just about the time that Françoise said. What had she done when she left the house just after ten? Presumably either gone to an hotel, or returned to Calais. And then? The crime had been committed on Tuesday night. On Thursday morning, she was once more in Merlinville. Had she ever left France at all? I doubted it very much. What kept her there—the hope of seeing Jack Renauld? I had told her (as at the time we believed) that he was on the high seas *en route* to Buenos Ayres. Possibly she was aware that the *Anzora* had not sailed. But to know that she must have seen Jack. Was that what Poirot was after? Had Jack Renauld, returning to see Marthe Daubreuil, come face to face instead with Bella Duveen, the girl he had heartlessly thrown over?

I began to see daylight. If that were indeed the case, it might furnish Jack with the alibi he needed. Yet under those circumstances his silence seemed difficult to explain. Why could he not have spoken out boldly? Did he fear for this former entanglement of his to come to the ears of Marthe Daubreuil? I shook my head, dissatisfied. The thing had been harmless enough, a foolish boy and girl affair, and I reflected cynically that the son of a millionaire was not likely to be thrown over by a penniless French girl, who moreover loved him devotedly, without a much graver cause.

Altogether I found the affair puzzling and unsatisfactory. I disliked intensely being associated with Poirot in hunting this girl down, but I could not see any way of avoiding it, without revealing everything to him, and this, for some reason, I was loath to do.

Poirot reappeared brisk and smiling at Dover, and our journey to London was uneventful. It was past nine o'clock when we arrived, and I supposed that we should return straight away to our rooms and do nothing till the morning. But Poirot had other plans.

"We must lose no time, *mon ami*. The news of the arrest will not be in the English papers until the day after tomorrow, but still we must lose no time."

I did not quite follow his reasoning, but I merely asked how he proposed to find the girl.

"You remember Joseph Aarons, the theatrical agent? No? I assisted him in a little matter of a Japanese wrestler. A pretty little problem, I must recount it to you one day. He, without doubt, will be able to put us in the way of finding out what we want to know."

It took us some time to run Mr. Aarons to earth, and it was after midnight when we finally managed it. He greeted Poirot with every evidence of warmth, and professed himself ready to be of service to us in any way.

"There's not much about the profession I don't know," he said, beaming genially.

"*Eh bien*, M. Aarons, I desire to find a young girl called Bella Duveen."

"Bella Duveen. I know the name, but for the moment I can't place it. What's her line?"

"That I do not know—but here is her photograph."

Mr. Aarons studied it for a moment, then his face lighted.

"Got it!" He slapped his thigh. "The Dulcibella Kids, by the Lord!"

"The Dulcibella Kids?"

"That's it. They're sisters. Acrobats, dancers and singers. Give quite a good little turn. They're in the provinces somewhere, I believe—if they're not resting. They've been on in Paris for the last two or three weeks."

"Can you find out for me exactly where they are?"

"Easy as a bird. You go home, and I'll send you round the dope in the morning."

With this promise we took leave of him. He was as good as his word. About eleven o'clock the following day, a scribbled note reached us.

173

"The Dulcibella Sisters are on at the Palace in Coventry. Good luck to you."

Without more ado, we started for Coventry. Poirot made no inquiries at the theatre, but contented himself with booking stalls for the variety performance that evening.

The show was wearisome beyond words—or perhaps it was only my mood that made it seem so. Japanese families balanced themselves precariously, would-be fashionable men, in greenish evening dress and exquisitely slicked hair, reeled off society patter and danced marvellously, stout prima donnas sang at the top of the human register, a comic comedian endeavoured to be Mr. George Robey and failed signally.

At last the number went up which announced the Dulcibella Kids. My heart beat sickeningly. There she was—there they both were, the pair of them, one flaxen haired, one dark, matching as to size, with short fluffy skirts and immense buster brown bows. They looked a pair of extremely piquant children. They began to sing. Their voices were fresh and true, rather thin and music-hally, but attractive.

It was quite a pretty little turn. They danced neatly, and did some clever little acrobatic feats. The words of their songs were crisp and catchy. When the curtain fell, there was a full meed of applause. Evidently the Dulcibella Kids were a success.

Suddenly I felt that I could remain no longer. I must get out into the air. I suggested leaving to Poirot.

"Go by all means, *mon ami*. I amuse myself, and will stay to the end. I will rejoin you later."

It was only a few steps from the theatre to the hotel. I went up to the sitting-room, ordered a whisky and soda, and sat drinking it, staring meditatively into the empty grate. I heard the door open, and turned my head, thinking it was Poirot. Then I jumped to my feet. It was Cinderella who stood in the doorway. She spoke haltingly, her breath coming in little gasps.

"I saw you in front. You and your friend. When you got up to go, I was waiting outside and followed you. Why are you here—in Coventry? What were you doing there to-night? Is the man who was with you the—the detective?"

She stood there, the cloak she had wrapped round her stage dress slipping from her shoulders. I saw the whiteness of her cheeks under the rouge, and heard the terror in her voice. And in that moment I understood everything—understood why Poirot was seeking her, and what she feared, and understood at last my own heart....

"Yes," I said gently.

"Is he looking for—me?" she half whispered.

Then, as I did not answer for a moment, she slipped down by the big chair, and burst into violent, bitter weeping.

I knelt down by her, holding her in my arms, and smoothing the hair back from her face.

"Don't cry, child, don't cry, for God's sake. You're safe here. I'll take care of you. Don't cry, darling. Don't cry. I know—I know everything."

"Oh, but you don't!"

"I think I do." And after a moment, as her sobs grew quieter, I asked: "It was you who took the dagger, wasn't it?"

"Yes."

"That was why you wanted me to show you round? And why you pretended to faint?"

Again she nodded. It was a strange thought to come to me at the moment, but it shot into my mind that I was glad her motive was what it had been—rather than the idle and morbid curiosity I had accused her of at the time. How gallantly she had played her part that day, inwardly racked with fear and trepidation as she must have been. Poor little soul, bearing the burden of a moment's impetuous action.

"Why did you take the dagger?" I asked presently.

She replied as simply as a child:

"I was afraid there might be finger-marks on it."

"But didn't you remember that you had worn gloves?"

She shook her head as though bewildered, and then said slowly:

"Are you going to give me up to—to the Police?"

"Good God! no."

Her eyes sought mine long and earnestly, and then she asked in a little quiet voice that sounded afraid of itself:

"Why not?"

It seemed a strange place and a strange time for a declaration of love—and God knows, in all my imagining, I had never pictured love coming to me in such a guise. But I answered simply and naturally enough:

"Because I love you, Cinderella."

She bent her head down, as though ashamed, and muttered in a broken voice:

"You can't—you can't—not if you knew—" And then, as though rallying herself, she faced me squarely, and asked:

"What do you know, then?"

"I know that you came to see Mr. Renauld that night. He offered you a cheque and you tore it up indignantly. Then you left the house—" I paused.

"Go on—what next?"

"I don't know whether you knew that Jack Renauld would be coming that night, or whether you just waited about on the chance of seeing him, but you did wait about. Perhaps you were just miserable, and walked aimlessly—but at any rate just before twelve you were still near there, and you saw a man on the golf links—"

Again I paused. I had leapt to the truth in a flash as she entered the room, but now the picture rose before me even more convincingly. I saw vividly the peculiar pattern of the overcoat on the dead body of Mr. Renauld, and I remembered the amazing likeness that had startled me into believing for one instant that the dead man had risen from the dead when his son burst into our conclave in the *salon*.

"Go on," repeated the girl steadily.

"I fancy his back was to you—but you recognized him, or thought you recognized him. The gait and the carriage were familiar to you, and the pattern of his overcoat." I paused. "You told me in the train on the way from Paris that you had Italian blood in your veins, and that you had nearly got into trouble once with it. You used a threat in one of your letters to Jack Renauld. When you saw him there, your anger and jealousy drove you mad—and you struck! I don't believe for a minute that you meant to kill him. But you did kill him, Cinderella."

She had flung up her hands to cover her face, and in a choked voice she said:

"You're right... you're right... I can see it all as you tell it." Then she turned on me almost savagely. "And you love me? Knowing what you do, how can you love me?"

"I don't know," I said a little wearily. "I think love is like that—a thing one cannot help. I have tried, I know—ever since the first day I met you. And love has been too strong for me."

And then suddenly, when I least expected it, she broke down again, casting herself down on the floor and sobbing wildly.

"Oh, I can't!" she cried. "I don't know what to do. I don't know which way to turn. Oh, pity me, pity me, some one, and tell me what to do!"

Again I knelt by her, soothing her as best I could.

"Don't be afraid of me, Bella. For God's sake don't be afraid of me. I love you, that's true—but I don't want anything in return. Only let me help you. Love him still if you have to, but let me help you as he can't."

It was as though she had been turned to stone by my words. She raised her head from her hands and stared at me.

"You think that?" she whispered. "You think that I love Jack Renauld?"

Then, half laughing, half crying, she flung her arms passionately round my neck, and pressed her sweet wet face to mine.

"Not as I love you," she whispered. "Never as I love you!"

Her lips brushed my cheek, and then, seeking my mouth, kissed me again and again with a sweetness and fire beyond belief. The wildness of it—and the wonder, I shall not forget—no, not as long as I live!

It was a sound in the doorway that made us look up. Poirot was standing there looking at us.

I did not hesitate. With a bound I reached him and pinioned his arms to his sides.

"Quick," I said to the girl. "Get out of here. As fast as you can. I'll hold him."

With one look at me, she fled out of the room past us. I held Poirot in a grip of iron.

"*Mon ami*," observed the latter mildly, "you do this sort of thing very well. The strong man holds me in his grasp and I am helpless as a child. But all this is uncomfortable and slightly ridiculous. Let us sit down and be calm."

"You won't pursue her?"

"*Mon Dieu!* no. Am I Giraud? Release me, my friend."

Keeping a suspicious eye upon him, for I paid Poirot the compliment of knowing that I was no match for him in astuteness, I relaxed my grip, and he sank into an arm-chair, feeling his arms tenderly.

"It is that you have the strength of a bull when you are roused, Hastings! *Eh bien*, and do you think you have behaved well to your old friend? I show you the girl's photograph and you recognize it, but you never say a word."

"There was no need if you knew that I recognized it," I said rather bitterly. So Poirot had known all along! I had not deceived him for an instant.

"Ta-ta! You did not know that I knew that. And tonight you help the girl to escape when we have found her with so much trouble! *Eh bien!* it comes to this—are you going to work with me or against me, Hastings?"

178

For a moment or two I did not answer. To break with my old friend gave me great pain. Yet I must definitely range myself against him. Would he ever forgive me, I wondered? He had been strangely calm so far, but I knew him to possess marvellous self-command.

"Poirot," I said, "I'm sorry. I admit I've behaved badly to you over this. But sometimes one has no choice. And in future I must take my own line."

Poirot nodded his head several times.

"I understand," he said. The mocking light had quite died out of his eyes, and he spoke with a sincerity and kindness that surprised me. "It is that, my friend, is it not? It is love that has come—not as you imagined it, all cock a hoop with fine feathers, but sadly, with bleeding feet. Well, well—I warned you. When I realized that this girl must have taken the dagger, I warned you. Perhaps you remember. But already it was too late. But, tell me, how much do you know?"

I met his eyes squarely.

"Nothing that you could tell me would be any surprise to me, Poirot. Understand that. But in case you think of resuming your search for Miss Duveen, I should like you to know one thing clearly. If you have any idea that she was concerned in the crime, or was the mysterious lady who called upon Mr. Renauld that night, you are wrong. I travelled home from France with her that day, and parted from her at Victoria that evening so that it is clearly impossible for her to have been in Merlinville."

"Ah!" Poirot looked at me thoughtfully. "And you would swear to that in a court of law?"

"Most certainly I would."

Poirot rose and bowed.

"*Mon ami! Vive l'amour!* It can perform miracles. It is decidedly ingenious what you have thought of there. It defeats even Hercule Poirot!"

TWENTY-THREE
Difficulties Ahead

After a moment of stress, such as I have just described, reaction is bound to set in. I retired to rest that night on a note of triumph, but I awoke to realize that I was by no means out of the wood. True, I could see no flaw in the alibi I had so suddenly conceived. I had but to stick to my story, and I failed to see how Bella could be convicted in face of it. It was not as though there was any old friendship between us that could be raked up, and which might lead them to suspect that I was committing perjury. It could be proved that in actual fact I had only seen the girl on three occasions. No, I was still satisfied with my idea—had not even Poirot admitted that it defeated him?

But there I felt the need of treading warily. All very well for my little friend to admit himself momentarily nonplussed. I had far too much respect for his abilities to conceive of him as being content to remain in that position. I had a very humble opinion of my wits when it came to matching them against his. Poirot would not take defeat lying down. Somehow or other, he would endeavour to turn the tables on me, and that in the way, and at the moment, when I least expected it.

We met at breakfast the following morning as though nothing had happened. Poirot's good temper was imperturbable, yet I thought I detected a film of reserve in his manner which was new.

After breakfast, I announced my intention of going out for a stroll. A malicious gleam shot through Poirot's eyes.

"If it is information you seek, you need not be at the pains of deranging yourself. I can tell you all you wish to know. The Dulcibella Sisters have cancelled their contract, and have left Coventry for an unknown destination."

"Is that really so, Poirot?"

"You can take it from me, Hastings. I made inquiries the first thing this morning. After all, what else did you expect?"

True enough, nothing else could be expected under the circumstances. Cinderella had profited by the slight start I had been able to assure her, and would certainly not lose a moment in removing herself from the reach of the pursuer. It was what I had intended and planned. Nevertheless, I was aware of being plunged into a network of fresh difficulties.

I had absolutely no means of communicating with the girl, and it was vital that she should know the line of defence that had occurred to me, and which I was prepared to carry out. Of course it was possible that she might try to send word to me in some way or another, but I hardly thought it likely. She would know the risk she ran of a message being intercepted by Poirot, thus setting him on her track once more. Clearly her only course was to disappear utterly for the time being.

But, in the meantime, what was Poirot doing? I studied him attentively. He was wearing his most innocent air, and staring meditatively into the far distance. He looked altogether too placid and supine to give me reassurance. I had learned, with Poirot, that the less dangerous he looked, the more dangerous he was. His quiescence alarmed me. Observing a troubled quality in my glance, he smiled benignantly.

"You are puzzled, Hastings? You ask yourself why I do not launch myself in pursuit?"

"Well—something of the kind."

"It is what you would do, were you in my place. I understand that. But I am not of those who enjoy rushing up and down a country seeking a needle in a haystack, as you English say. No—let Mademoiselle Bella Duveen go. Without doubt, I shall be able to find her when the time comes. Until then, I am content to wait."

I stared at him doubtfully. Was he seeking to mislead me? I had an irritating feeling that, even now, he was master of the situation. My sense of superiority was gradually waning. I had contrived the girl's escape, and evolved a brilliant scheme for saving her from the consequences of her rash act—but I could not rest easy in my mind. Poirot's perfect calm awakened a thousand apprehensions.

"I suppose, Poirot," I said rather diffidently, "I mustn't ask what your plans are? I've forfeited the right."

"But not at all. There is no secret about them. We return to France without delay."

"*We?*"

"Precisely—'*we!*' You know very well that you cannot afford to let Papa Poirot out of your sight. Eh, is it not so, my friend? But remain in England by all means if you wish—"

I shook my head. He had hit the nail on the head. I could not afford to let him out of my sight. Although I could not expect his confidence after what had happened, I could still check his actions. The only danger to Bella lay with him. Giraud and the French police were indifferent to her existence. At all costs I must keep near Poirot.

Poirot observed me attentively as these reflections passed through my mind, and gave a nod of satisfaction.

"I am right, am I not? And as you are quite capable of trying to follow me, disguised with some absurdity such as a false beard—which every one would perceive, *bien entendu*—I much prefer that we should voyage together. It would annoy me greatly that any one should mock themselves at you."

"Very well, then. But it's only fair to warn you—"

"I know—I know all. You are my enemy! Be my enemy then. It does not worry me at all."

"So long as it's all fair and above-board, I don't mind."

"You have to the full the English passion for 'fair-play!' Now your scruples are satisfied, let us depart immediately. There is no time to be lost. Our stay in England has been short but sufficient. I know—what I wanted to know."

The tone was light, but I read a veiled menace into the words.

"Still—" I began, and stopped.

"Still—as you say! Without doubt you are satisfied with the part you are playing. Me, I preoccupy myself with Jack Renauld."

Jack Renauld! The words gave me a start. I had completely forgotten that aspect of the case. Jack Renauld, in prison, with the shadow of the guillotine looming over him! I saw the part I was playing in a more sinister light. I could save Bella—yes, but in doing so I ran the risk of sending an innocent man to his death.

I pushed the thought from me with horror. It could not be. He would be acquitted. Certainly he would be acquitted! But the cold fear came back. Suppose he were not? What then? Could I have it on my conscience—horrible thought! Would it come to that in the end? A decision. Bella or Jack Renauld? The promptings of my heart were to save the girl I loved at any cost to myself. But, if the cost were to another, the problem was altered.

What would the girl herself say? I remembered that no word of Jack Renauld's arrest had passed my lips. As yet she was in total ignorance of the fact that her former lover was in prison charged with a hideous crime which he had not committed. When she knew, how would she act? Would she permit her life to be saved at the expense of his? Certainly she must do nothing rash. Jack Renauld might, and probably would, be acquitted without any intervention on her part. If so, good. But if he was not…. That was the terrible, the unanswerable problem. I fancied that she ran no risk of the extreme penalty. The circumstances of the crime were quite different in her case. She could plead jealousy and extreme provocation, and her youth and beauty would go for much. The fact that by a tragic mistake it was old Mr. Renauld, and not his son, who paid the penalty would not alter the motive of the crime. But in any case, however lenient the sentence of the Court, it must mean a long term of imprisonment.

No, Bella must be protected. And, at the same time, Jack Renauld must be saved. How this was to be accomplished I did not see clearly. But I pinned my faith to Poirot. He knew. Come what might, he would manage to save an innocent man. He must find some pretext other than the real one. It might be difficult, but he would manage it somehow. And with Bella unsuspected, and Jack Renauld acquitted, all would end satisfactorily.

So I told myself repeatedly, but at the bottom of my heart there still remained a cold fear.

TWENTY-FOUR
"Save Him!"

We crossed from England by the evening boat, and the following morning saw us in Saint-Omer, whither Jack Renauld had been taken. Poirot lost no time in visiting M. Hautet. As he did not seem disposed to make any objections to my accompanying him, I bore him company.

After various formalities and preliminaries, we were conducted to the examining magistrate's room. He greeted us cordially.

"I was told that you had returned to England, M. Poirot. I am glad to find that such is not the case."

"It is true that I went there, M. le juge, but it was only for a flying visit. A side issue, but one that I fancied might repay investigation."

"And it did—eh?"

Poirot shrugged his shoulders. M. Hautet nodded, sighing.

"We must resign ourselves, I fear. That animal Giraud, his manners are abominable, but he is undoubtedly clever! Not much chance of that one making a mistake."

"You think not, M. le juge?"

It was the examining magistrate's turn to shrug his shoulders.

"*Eh bien*, speaking frankly—in confidence, *c'est entendu*—can you come to any other conclusion?"

"Frankly, M. le juge, there seem to me to be many points that are obscure."

185

"Such as—?"

But Poirot was not to be drawn.

"I have not yet tabulated them," he remarked. "It was a general reflection that I was making. I liked the young man, and should be sorry to believe him guilty of such a hideous crime. By the way, what has he to say for himself on the matter?"

The magistrate frowned.

"I cannot understand him. He seems incapable of putting up any sort of defence. It has been most difficult to get him to answer questions. He contents himself with a general denial, and beyond that takes refuge in a most obstinate silence. I am interrogating him again tomorrow; perhaps you would like to be present?"

We accepted the invitation with *empressement*.

"A distressing case," said the magistrate with a sigh. "My sympathy for Madame Renauld is profound."

"How is Madame Renauld?"

"She has not yet recovered consciousness. It is merciful in a way, poor woman, she is being spared much. The doctors say that there is no danger, but that when she comes to herself she must be kept as quiet as possible. It was, I understand, quite as much the shock as the fall which caused her present state. It would be terrible if her brain became unhinged; but I should not wonder at all—no, really, not at all."

M. Hautet leaned back, shaking his head, with a sort of mournful enjoyment, as he envisaged the gloomy prospect.

He roused himself at length, and observed with a start.

"That reminds me. I have here a letter for you, M. Poirot. Let me see, where did I put it?"

He proceeded to rummage amongst his papers. At last he found the missive, and handed it to Poirot.

"It was sent under cover to me in order that I might forward it to you," he explained. "But as you left no address I could not do so."

Poirot studied the letter curiously. It was addressed in a long, sloping, foreign hand, and the writing was decidedly a woman's. Poirot did not open it. Instead he put it in his pocket and rose to his feet.

"*A demain* then, M. le juge. Many thanks for your courtesy and amiability."

"But not at all. I am always at your service. These young detectives of the school of Giraud, they are all alike—rude, sneering fellows. They do not realize that an examining magistrate of my—er—experience is bound to have a certain discernment, a certain—*flair*. *Enfin!* the politeness of the old school is infinitely more to my taste. Therefore, my dear friend, command me in any way you will. We know a thing or two, you and I—eh?"

And laughing heartily, enchanted with himself and with us, M. Hautet bade us adieu. I am sorry to have to record that Poirot's first remark to me as we traversed the corridor was:

"A famous old imbecile, that one! Of a stupidity to make pity!"

We were just leaving the building when we came face to face with Giraud, looking more dandified than ever, and thoroughly pleased with himself.

"Aha! M. Poirot," he cried airily. "You have returned from England then?"

"As you see," said Poirot.

"The end of the case is not far off now, I fancy."

"I agree with you, M. Giraud."

Poirot spoke in a subdued tone. His crest-fallen manner seemed to delight the other.

"Of all the milk and water criminals! Not an idea of defending himself. It is extraordinary!"

"So extraordinary that it gives one to think, does it not?" suggested Poirot mildly.

But Giraud was not even listening. He twirled his cane amicably.

"Well, good day, M. Poirot. I am glad you're satisfied of young Renauld's guilt at last."

"*Pardon!* But I am not in the least satisfied. Jack Renauld is innocent."

Giraud stared for a moment—then burst out laughing, tapping his head significantly with the brief remark: "*Toqué!*"

Poirot drew himself up. A dangerous light showed in his eyes.

"M. Giraud, throughout the case your manner to me has been deliberately insulting! You need teaching a lesson. I am prepared to wager you 500 francs that I find the murderer of M. Renauld before you do. Is it agreed?"

Giraud stared helplessly at him, and murmured again: "*Toqué!*"

"Come now," urged Poirot, "is it agreed?"

"I have no wish to take your money from you."

"Make your mind easy—you will not!"

"Oh, well then, I agree! You speak of my manner to you being insulting. *Eh bien*, once or twice, *your* manner has annoyed *me*."

"I am enchanted to hear it," said Poirot. "Good morning, M. Giraud. Come, Hastings."

I said no word as we walked along the street. My heart was heavy. Poirot had displayed his intentions only too plainly. I doubted more than ever my powers of saving Bella from the consequences of her act. This unlucky encounter with Giraud had roused Poirot and put him on his mettle.

Suddenly I felt a hand laid on my shoulder, and turned to face Gabriel Stonor. We stopped and greeted him, and he proposed strolling with us back to our hotel.

"And what are you doing here, M. Stonor?" inquired Poirot.

"One must stand by one's friends," replied the other dryly. "Especially when they are unjustly accused."

"Then you do not believe that Jack Renauld committed the crime?" I asked eagerly.

"Certainly I don't. I know the lad. I admit that there have been one or two things in this business that have staggered me completely, but none the less, in spite of his fool way of taking it,

I'll never believe that Jack Renauld is a murderer."

My heart warmed to the secretary. His words seemed to lift a secret weight from my heart.

"I have no doubt that many people feel as you do," I exclaimed. "There is really absurdly little evidence against him. I should say that there was no doubt of his acquittal—no doubt whatever."

But Stonor hardly responded as I could have wished.

"I'd give a lot to think as you do," he said gravely. He turned to Poirot. "What's your opinion, monsieur?"

"I think that things look very black against him," said Poirot quietly.

"You believe him guilty?" said Stonor sharply.

"No. But I think he will find it hard to prove his innocence."

"He's behaving so damned queerly," muttered Stonor. "Of course I realize that there's a lot more in this affair than meets the eye. Giraud's not wise to that because he's an outsider, but the whole thing has been damned odd. As to that, least said soonest mended. If Mrs. Renauld wants to hush anything up, I'll take my cue from her. It's her show, and I've too much respect for her judgment to shove my oar in, but I can't get behind this attitude of Jack's. Any one would think he *wanted* to be thought guilty."

"But it's absurd," I cried, bursting in. "For one thing, the dagger—" I paused, uncertain as to how much Poirot would wish me to reveal. I continued, choosing my words carefully, "We know that the dagger could not have been in Jack Renauld's possession that evening. Mrs. Renauld knows that."

"True," said Stonor. "When she recovers, she will doubtless say all this and more. Well, I must be leaving you."

"One moment." Poirot's hand arrested his departure. "Can you arrange for word to be sent to me at once should Madame Renauld recover consciousness?"

"Certainly. That's easily done."

"That point about the dagger is good, Poirot," I urged as we went upstairs. "I couldn't speak very plainly before Stonor."

"That was quite right of you. We might as well keep the knowledge to ourselves as long as we can. As to the dagger, your point hardly helps Jack Renauld. You remember that I was absent for an hour this morning, before we started from London?"

"Yes?"

"Well, I was employed in trying to find the firm Jack Renauld employed to convert his souvenirs. It was not very difficult. *Eh bien*, Hastings, they made to his order not *two* paper-knives, but *three*."

"So that—?"

"So that, after giving one to his mother, and one to Bella Duveen, there was a third which he doubtless retained for his own use. No, Hastings, I fear the dagger question will not help us to save him from the guillotine."

"It won't come to that," I cried, stung.

Poirot shook his head uncertainly.

"You will save him," I cried positively.

Poirot glanced at me dryly.

"Have you not rendered it impossible, *mon ami?*"

"Some other way," I muttered.

"Ah! *Sapristi!* But it is miracles you ask from me. No—say no more. Let us instead see what is in this letter."

And he drew out the envelope from his breast pocket.

His face contracted as he read, then he handed the one flimsy sheet to me.

"There are other women in the world who suffer, Hastings."

The writing was blurred and the note had evidently been written in great agitation:

"Dear M. Poirot:

"If you get this, I beg of you to come to my aid. I have no one to turn to, and at all costs Jack must be saved. I implore of you on my knees to help us.

"MARTHE DAUBREUIL."

190

I handed it back, moved.

"You will go?"

"At once. We will command an auto."

Half an hour later saw us at the Villa Marguerite. Marthe was at the door to meet us, and led Poirot in, clinging with both hands to one of his.

"Ah, you have come—it is good of you. I have been in despair, not knowing what to do. They will not let me go to see him in prison even. I suffer horribly, I am nearly mad. Is it true what they say, that he does not deny the crime? But that is madness. It is impossible that he should have done it! Never for one minute will I believe it."

"Neither do I believe it, mademoiselle," said Poirot gently.

"But then why does he not speak? I do not understand."

"Perhaps because he is screening some one," suggested Poirot, watching her.

Marthe frowned.

"Screening some one? Do you mean his mother? Ah, from the beginning I have suspected her. Who inherits all that vast fortune? She does. It is easy to wear widow's weeds and play the hypocrite. And they say that when he was arrested she fell down—like *that*." She made a dramatic gesture. "And without doubt, M. Stonor, the secretary, he helped her. They are thick as thieves, those two. It is true she is older than he—but what do men care—if a woman is rich!"

There was a hint of bitterness in her tone.

"Stonor was in England," I put in.

"He says so—but who knows?"

"Mademoiselle," said Poirot quietly, "if we are to work together, you and I, we must have things clear. First, I will ask you a question."

"Yes, monsieur?"

"Are you aware of your mother's real name?"

Marthe looked at him for a minute, then, letting her head fall forward on her arms, she burst into tears.

"There, there," said Poirot, patting her on the shoulder. "Calm yourself, *petite*, I see that you know. Now a second question, did you know who M. Renauld was?"

"M. Renauld," she raised her head from her hands and gazed at him wonderingly.

"Ah, I see you do not know that. Now listen to me carefully."

Step by step, he went over the case, much as he had done to me on the day of our departure for England. Marthe listened spellbound. When he had finished, she drew a long breath.

"But you are wonderful—magnificent! You are the greatest detective in the world."

With a swift gesture she slipped off her chair and knelt before him with an abandonment that was wholly French.

"Save him, monsieur," she cried. "I love him so. Oh, save him, save him—save him!"

TWENTY-FIVE
An Unexpected Dénouement

We were present the following morning at the examination of Jack Renauld. Short as the time had been, I was shocked at the change that had taken place in the young prisoner. His cheeks had fallen in, there were deep black circles round his eyes, and he looked haggard and distraught, as one who had wooed sleep in vain for several nights. He betrayed no emotion at seeing us.

The prisoner and his counsel, Maître Grosíer, were accommodated with chairs. A formidable guard with resplendent sabre stood before the door. The patient *greffier* sat at his desk. The examination began.

"Renauld," began the magistrate, "do you deny that you were in Merlinville on the night of the crime?"

Jack did not reply at once, then he said with a hesitancy of manner which was piteous:

"I—I—told you that I was in Cherbourg."

Maître Grosíer frowned and sighed. I realized at once that Jack Renauld was obstinately bent on conducting his own case as he wished, to the despair of his legal representative.

The magistrate turned sharply.

"Send in the station witnesses."

In a moment or two the door opened to admit a man whom I recognized as being a porter at Merlinville station.

"You were on duty on the night of June 7th?"

"Yes, monsieur."

"You witnessed the arrival of the 11:40 train?"

"Yes, monsieur."

"Look at the prisoner. Do you recognize him as having been one of the passengers to alight?"

"Yes, Monsieur le juge."

"There is no possibility of your being mistaken?"

"No, monsieur. I knew M. Jack Renauld well."

"Nor of your being mistaken as to the date?"

"No, monsieur. Because it was the following morning, June 8th, that we heard of the murder."

Another railway official was brought in, and confirmed the first one's evidence. The magistrate looked at Jack Renauld.

"These men have identified you positively. What have you to say?"

Jack shrugged his shoulders.

"Nothing."

M. Hautet exchanged a glance with the *greffier*, as the scratching of the latter's pen recorded the answer.

"Renauld," continued the magistrate, "do you recognize this?"

He took something from the table by his side, and held it out to the prisoner. I shuddered as I recognized the aeroplane dagger.

"Pardon," cried Maître Grosíer. "I demand to speak to my client before he answers that question."

But Jack Renauld had no consideration for the feelings of the wretched Grosíer. He waved him aside, and replied quietly:

"Certainly I recognize it. It is a present given by me to my mother, as a souvenir of the War."

"Is there, as far as you know, any duplicate of that dagger in existence?"

Again Maître Grosíer burst out, and again Jack overrode him.

"Not that I know of. The setting was my own design."

Even the magistrate almost gasped at the boldness of the

reply. It did, in very truth, seem as though Jack was rushing on his fate. I realized, of course, the vital necessity he was under of concealing, for Bella's sake, the fact that there was a duplicate dagger in the case. So long as there was supposed to be only one weapon, no suspicion was likely to attach to the girl who had had the second paper-knife in her possession. He was valiantly shielding the woman he had once loved—but at what a cost to himself! I began to realize the magnitude of the task I had so lightly set Poirot. It would not be easy to secure the acquittal of Jack Renauld, by anything short of the truth.

M. Hautet spoke again, with a peculiarly biting inflection:

"Madame Renauld told us that this dagger was on her dressing table on the night of the crime. But Madame Renauld is a mother! It will doubtless astonish you, Renauld, but I consider it highly likely that Madame Renauld was mistaken, and that, by inadvertence perhaps, you had taken it with you to Paris. Doubtless you will contradict me—"

I saw the lad's handcuffed hands clench themselves. The perspiration stood out in beads upon his brow, as with a supreme effort he interrupted M. Hautet in a hoarse voice:

"I shall not contradict you. It is possible."

It was a stupefying moment. Maître Grosíer rose to his feet, protesting:

"My client has undergone a considerable nervous strain. I should wish it put on record that I do not consider him answerable for what he says."

The magistrate quelled him angrily. For a moment a doubt seemed to arise in his own mind. Jack Renauld had almost over-done his part. He leaned forward, and gazed at the prisoner searchingly.

"Do you fully understand, Renauld, that on the answers you have given me I shall have no alternative but to commit you for trial?"

Jack's pale face flushed. He looked steadily back.

"M. Hautet, I swear that I did not kill my father."

But the magistrate's brief moment of doubt was over. He laughed a short, unpleasant laugh.

"Without doubt, without doubt—they are always innocent, our prisoners! By your own mouth you are condemned. You can offer no defence, no alibi—only a mere assertion which would not deceive a babe!—that you are not guilty. You killed your father, Renauld—cruel and cowardly murder—for the sake of money which you believed would come to you at his death. Your mother was an accessory after the fact. Doubtless, in view of the fact that she acted as a mother, the courts will extend an indulgence to her that they will not accord to you. And rightly so! Your crime was a horrible one—to be held in abhorrence by gods and men!" M. Hautet was enjoying himself, working up his period, steeped in the solemnity of the moment, and his own role as representative of justice. "You killed—and you must pay the consequences of your action. I speak to you, not as a man, but as Justice, eternal Justice, which—"

M. Hautet was interrupted—to his intense annoyance. The door was pushed open.

"M. le juge, M. le juge," stammered the attendant, "there is a lady who says—who says—"

"Who says what?" cried the justly incensed magistrate. "This is highly irregular. I forbid it—I absolutely forbid it."

But a slender figure pushed the stammering gendarme aside. Dressed all in black, with a long veil that hid her face, she advanced into the room.

My heart gave a sickening throb. She had come then! All my efforts were in vain. Yet I could not but admire the courage that had led her to take this step so unfalteringly.

She raised her veil—and I gasped. For, though as like her as two peas, this girl was not Cinderella! On the other hand, now that I saw her without the fair wig she had worn on the stage, I recognized her as the girl of the photograph in Jack Renauld's room.

"You are the Juge d'Instruction, M. Hautet?" she queried.

"Yes, but I forbid—"

"My name is Bella Duveen. I wish to give myself up for the murder of Mr. Renauld."

197

TWENTY-SIX

I Receive a Letter

My Friend:

"You will know all when you get this. Nothing that I can say will move Bella. She has gone out to give herself up. I am tired out with struggling.

"You will know now that I deceived you, that where you gave me trust I repaid you with lies. It will seem, perhaps, indefensible to you, but I should like, before I go out of your life for ever, to show you just how it all came about. If I knew that you forgave me, it would make life easier for me. It wasn't for myself I did it—that's the only thing I can put forward to say for myself.

"I'll begin from the day I met you in the boat train from Paris. I was uneasy then about Bella. She was just desperate about Jack Renauld, she'd have lain down on the ground for him to walk on, and when he began to change, and to stop writing so often, she began getting in a state. She got it into her head that he was keen on another girl—and of course, as it turned out afterwards, she was quite right there. She'd made up her mind to go to their Villa at Merlinville, and try and see Jack. She knew I was against it, and tried to give me the slip. I found she was not on the train at Calais, and determined I would not go on to England without her. I'd an uneasy feeling that something awful was going to happen if I couldn't prevent it.

"I met the next train from Paris. She was on it, and set upon going out then and there to Merlinville. I argued with her for all I was worth, but it wasn't any good. She was all strung up and set upon having her own way. Well, I washed my hands of it. I'd done all I could! It was getting late. I went to an hotel, and Bella started for Merlinville. I still couldn't shake off my feeling of what the books call 'impending disaster.'

"The next day came—but no Bella. She'd made a date with me to meet at the hotel, but she didn't keep it. No sign of her all day. I got more and more anxious. Then came an evening paper with the news.

"It was awful! I couldn't be sure, of course—but I was terribly afraid. I figured it out that Bella had met Papa Renauld and told him about her and Jack, and that he'd insulted her or something like that. We've both got terribly quick tempers.

"Then all the masked foreigner business came out, and I began to feel more at ease. But it still worried me that Bella hadn't kept her date with me.

"By the next morning, I was so rattled that I'd just got to go and see what I could. First thing, I ran up against you. You know all that... When I saw the dead man, looking so like Jack, and wearing Jack's fancy overcoat, I knew! And there was the identical paper-knife—wicked little thing!—that Jack had given Bella! Ten to one it had her finger-marks on it. I can't hope to explain to you the sort of helpless horror of that moment. I only saw one thing clearly—I must get hold of that dagger, and get right away with it before they found out it was gone. I pretended to faint, and whilst you were away getting water I took the thing and hid it away in my dress.

"I told you that I was staying at the Hôtel du Phare, but of course really I made a bee line back to Calais, and then on to England by the first boat. When we were in mid-Channel, I dropped that little devil of a dagger into the sea. Then I felt I could breathe again.

"Bella was at our digs in London. She looked like nothing on God's earth. I told her what I'd done, and that she was pretty safe for the time being. She stared at me, and then began laughing… laughing… laughing… it was horrible to hear her! I felt that the best thing to do was to keep busy. She'd go mad if she had time to brood on what she'd done. Luckily we got an engagement at once.

"And then, I saw you and your friend, watching us that night… I was frantic. You must suspect, or you wouldn't have tracked us down. I had to know the worst, so I followed you. I was desperate. And then, before I'd had time to say anything, I tumbled to it that it was *me* you suspected, not Bella! Or at least that you thought I *was* Bella since I'd stolen the dagger.

"I wish, honey, that you could see back into my mind at that moment… you'd forgive me, perhaps… I was so frightened, and muddled, and desperate…. All I could get clearly was that you would try and save me. I didn't know whether you'd be willing to save her… I thought very likely not—it wasn't the same thing! And I couldn't risk it! Bella's my twin—I'd got to do the best for her. So I went on lying…. I felt mean—I feel mean still…. That's all—enough too, you'll say, I expect. I ought to have trusted you…. If I had—

"As soon as the news was in the paper that Jack Renauld had been arrested, it was all up. Bella wouldn't even wait to see how things went….

"I'm very tired…. I can't write any more…."

She had begun to sign herself Cinderella, but had crossed that out and written instead "Dulcie Duveen."

It was an ill-written, blurred epistle but I have kept it to this day.

Poirot was with me when I read it. The sheets fell from my hand, and I looked across at him.

"Did you know all the time that it was—the other?"

"Yes, my friend."

"Why did you not tell me?"

"To begin with, I could hardly believe it conceivable that you could make such a mistake. You had seen the photograph. The sisters are very alike, but by no means incapable of distinguishment."

"But the fair hair?"

"A wig, worn for the sake of a piquant contrast on the stage. Is it conceivable that with twins one should be fair and one dark?"

"Why didn't you tell me that night at the hotel in Coventry?"

"You were rather high-handed in your methods, *mon ami*," said Poirot dryly. "You did not give me a chance."

"But afterwards?"

"Ah, afterwards! Well, to begin with, I was hurt at your want of faith in me. And then, I wanted to see whether your—feelings would stand the test of time. In fact, whether it was love, or a flash in the pan, with you. I should not have left you long in your error."

I nodded. His tone was too affectionate for me to bear resentment. I looked down on the sheets of the letter. Suddenly I picked them up from the floor, and pushed them across to him.

"Read that," I said. "I'd like you to."

He read it through in silence, then he looked up at me.

"What is it that worries you, Hastings?"

This was quite a new mood in Poirot. His mocking manner seemed laid quite aside. I was able to say what I wanted without too much difficulty.

"She doesn't say—she doesn't say—well, not whether she cares for me or not!"

Poirot turned back the pages.

"I think you are mistaken, Hastings."

"Where?" I cried, leaning forward eagerly.

Poirot smiled.

"She tells you that in every line of the letter, *mon ami*."

"But where am I to find her? There's no address on the letter. There's a French stamp, that's all."

"Excite yourself not! Leave it to Papa Poirot. I can find her for you as soon as I have five little minutes!"

TWENTY-SEVEN
Jack Renauld's Story

C ongratulations, M. Jack," said Poirot, wringing the lad warmly by the hand.

Young Renauld had come to us as soon as he was liberated—before starting for Merlinville to rejoin Marthe and his mother. Stonor accompanied him. His heartiness was in strong contrast to the lad's wan looks. It was plain that the boy was on the verge of a nervous breakdown. Although delivered from the immediate peril that was hanging over him, the circumstances of his release were too painful to let him feel full relief. He smiled mournfully at Poirot, and said in a low voice:

"I went through it to protect her, and now it's all no use!"

"You could hardly expect the girl to accept the price of your life," remarked Stonor dryly. "She was bound to come forward when she saw you heading straight for the guillotine."

"*Eh ma foi!* and you were heading for it too!" added Poirot, with a slight twinkle. "You would have had Maître Grosíer's death from rage on your conscience if you had gone on."

"He was a well meaning ass, I suppose," said Jack. "But he worried me horribly. You see, I couldn't very well take him into my confidence. But, my God! what's going to happen about Bella?"

"If I were you," said Poirot frankly, "I should not distress myself unduly. The French Courts are very lenient to youth and beauty, and the *crime passionnel*. A clever lawyer will make out a great case of extenuating circumstances. It will not be pleasant for you—"

"I don't care about that. You see, M. Poirot, in a way I *do* feel guilty of my father's murder. But for me, and my entanglement with this girl, he would be alive and well today. And then my cursed carelessness in taking away the wrong overcoat. I can't help feeling responsible for his death. It will haunt me for ever!"

"No, no," I said soothingly.

"Of course it's horrible to me to think that Bella killed my father," resumed Jack, "but I'd treated her shamefully. After I met Marthe, and realized I'd made a mistake, I ought to have written and told her so honestly. But I was so terrified of a row, and of its coming to Marthe's ears, and her thinking there was more in it than there ever had been, that—well, I was a coward, and went on hoping the thing would die down of itself. I just drifted, in fact—not realizing that I was driving the poor kid desperate. If she'd really knifed me, as she meant to, I should have got no more than my deserts. And the way she's come forward now is downright plucky. I'd have stood the racket, you know—up to the end."

He was silent for a moment or two, and then burst out on another tack:

"What gets me is why the Governor should be wandering about in underclothes and my overcoat at that time of night. I suppose he'd just given the foreign johnnies the slip, and my mother must have made a mistake about its being 2 o'clock when they came. Or—or, it wasn't all a frame up, was it? I mean, my mother didn't think—couldn't think—that—that it was *me?*"

Poirot reassured him quickly.

"No, no, M. Jack. Have no fears on that score. As for the rest, I will explain it to you one of these days. It is rather curious. But will you recount to us exactly what did occur on that terrible evening?"

"There's very little to tell. I came from Cherbourg, as I told you, in order to see Marthe before going to the other end of the world. The train was late, and I decided to take the short cut across the golf links. I could easily get into the grounds of the Villa Marguerite from there. I had nearly reached the place when—"

He paused and swallowed.

"Yes?"

"I heard a terrible cry. It wasn't loud—a sort of choke and gasp—but it frightened me. For a moment I stood rooted to the spot. Then I came round the corner of a bush. There was moonlight. I saw the grave, and a figure lying face downwards, with a dagger sticking in the back. And then—and then—I looked up and saw *her*. She was looking at me as though she saw a ghost—it's what she must have thought me at first—all expression seemed frozen out of her face by horror. And then she gave a cry, and turned and ran."

He stopped, trying to master his emotion.

"And afterwards?" asked Poirot gently.

"I really don't know. I stayed there for a time, dazed. And then I realized I'd better get away as fast as I could. It didn't occur to me that they would suspect me, but I was afraid of being called upon to give evidence against her. I walked to St. Beauvais as I told you, and got a car from there back to Cherbourg."

A knock came at the door, and a page entered with a telegram which he delivered to Stonor. He tore it open. Then he got up from his seat.

"Mrs. Renauld has regained consciousness," he said.

"Ah!" Poirot sprang to his feet. "Let us all go to Merlinville at once!"

A hurried departure was made forthwith. Stonor, at Jack's instance, agreed to stay behind and do all that could be done for Bella Duveen. Poirot, Jack Renauld and I set off in the Renauld car.

The run took just over forty minutes. As we approached the doorway of the Villa Marguerite, Jack Renauld shot a questioning glance at Poirot.

"How would it be if you went on first—to break the news to

my mother that I am free—"

"While you break it in person to Mademoiselle Marthe, eh?" finished Poirot, with a twinkle. "But yes, by all means, I was about to propose such an arrangement myself."

Jack Renauld did not wait for more. Stopping the car, he swung himself out, and ran up the path to the front door. We went on in the car to the Villa Geneviève.

"Poirot," I said, "do you remember how we arrived here that first day? And were met by the news of M. Renauld's murder?"

"Ah! yes, truly. Not so long ago, either. But what a lot of things have happened since then—especially for you, *mon ami!*"

"Poirot, what have you done about finding Bel—I mean Dulcie?"

"Calm yourself, Hastings. I arrange everything."

"You're being a precious long time about it," I grumbled.

Poirot changed the subject.

"Then the beginning, now the end," he moralized, as we rang the bell. "And, considered as a case, the end is profoundly unsatisfactory."

"Yes, indeed," I sighed.

"You are regarding it from the sentimental standpoint, Hastings. That was not my meaning. We will hope that Mademoiselle Bella will be dealt with leniently, and after all Jack Renauld cannot marry both the girls. I spoke from a professional standpoint. This is not a crime well ordered and regular, such as a detective delights in. The *mise en scène* designed by Georges Conneau, that indeed is perfect, but the *dénouement*—ah, no! A man killed by accident in a girl's fit of anger—ah, indeed, what order or method is there in that?"

And in the midst of a fit of laughter on my part at Poirot's peculiarities, the door was opened by Françoise.

Poirot explained that he must see Mrs. Renauld at once, and the old woman conducted him upstairs. I remained in the *salon*. It was some time before Poirot reappeared. He was looking unusually grave.

"*Vous voilà*, Hastings! *Sacré tonnerre*, but there are squalls ahead!"

"What do you mean?" I cried.

"I would hardly have credited it," said Poirot thoughtfully, "but women are very unexpected."

"Here are Jack and Marthe Daubreuil," I exclaimed, looking out of the window.

Poirot bounded out of the room, and met the young couple on the steps outside.

"Do not enter. It is better not. Your mother is very upset."

"I know, I know," said Jack Renauld. "I must go up to her at once."

"But no, I tell you. It is better not."

"But Marthe and I—"

"In any case, do not take Mademoiselle with you. Mount, if you must, but you would be wise to be guided by me."

A voice on the stairs behind made us all start.

"I thank you for your good offices, M. Poirot, but I will make my own wishes clear."

We stared in astonishment. Descending the stairs, leaning upon Léonie's arm, was Mrs. Renauld, her head still bandaged. The French girl was weeping, and imploring her mistress to return to bed.

"Madame will kill herself. It is contrary to all the doctor's orders!"

But Mrs. Renauld came on.

"Mother," cried Jack, starting forward. But with a gesture she drove him back.

"I am no mother of yours! You are no son of mine! From this day and hour I renounce you."

"Mother," cried the lad, stupefied.

For a moment she seemed to waver, to falter before the anguish in his voice. Poirot made a mediating gesture, but instantly she regained command of herself.

"Your father's blood is on your head. You are morally guilty of his death. You thwarted and defied him over this girl, and by your heartless treatment of another girl, you brought about his death. Go out from my house. Tomorrow I intend to take such steps as shall make it certain that you shall never touch a penny of his money. Make your way in the world as best you can with the help of the girl who is the daughter of your father's bitterest enemy!"

And slowly, painfully, she retraced her way upstairs.

We were all dumbfounded—totally unprepared for such a demonstration. Jack Renauld, worn out with all he had already gone through, swayed and nearly fell. Poirot and I went quickly to his assistance.

"He is overdone," murmured Poirot to Marthe. "Where can we take him?"

"But home! To the Villa Marguerite. We will nurse him, my mother and I. My poor Jack!"

We got the lad to the Villa, where he dropped limply on to a chair in a semi-dazed condition. Poirot felt his head and hands.

"He has fever. The long strain begins to tell. And now this shock on top of it. Get him to bed, and Hastings and I will summon a doctor."

A doctor was soon procured. After examining the patient, he gave it as his opinion that it was simply a case of nerve strain. With perfect rest and quiet, the lad might be almost restored by the next day, but, if excited, there was a chance of brain fever. It would be advisable for some one to sit up all night with him.

Finally, having done all we could, we left him in the charge of Marthe and her mother, and set out for the town. It was past our usual hour of dining, and we were both famished. The first restaurant we came to assuaged the pangs of hunger with an excellent *omelette*, and an equally excellent *entrecôte* to follow.

"And now for quarters for the night," said Poirot, when at length *café noir* had completed the meal. "Shall we try our old friend, the Hôtel des Bains?"

We traced our steps there without more ado. Yes, Messieurs could be accommodated with two good rooms overlooking the sea. Then Poirot asked a question which surprised me.

"Has an English lady, Miss Robinson, arrived?"

"Yes, monsieur. She is in the little *salon*."

"Ah!"

"Poirot," I cried, keeping pace with him as he walked along the corridor, "who on earth is Miss Robinson?"

Poirot beamed kindly on me.

"It is that I have arranged you a marriage, Hastings."

"But, I say—"

"Bah!" said Poirot, giving me a friendly push over the threshold of the door. "Do you think I wish to trumpet aloud in Merlinville the name of Duveen?"

It was indeed Cinderella who rose to greet us. I took her hands in both of mine. My eyes said the rest.

Poirot cleared his throat.

"*Mes enfants*," he said, "for the moment we have no time for sentiment. There is work ahead of us. Mademoiselle, were you able to do what I asked you?"

In response, Cinderella took from her bag an object wrapped up in paper, and handed it silently to Poirot. The latter unwrapped it. I gave a start—for it was the aeroplane dagger which I understood she had cast into the sea. Strange, how reluctant women always are to destroy the most compromising of objects and documents!

"*Très bien, mon enfant*," said Poirot. "I am pleased with you. Go now and rest yourself. Hastings here and I have work to do. You shall see him tomorrow."

"Where are you going?" asked the girl, her eyes widening.

"You shall hear all about it tomorrow."

"Because wherever you're going, I'm coming too."

"But mademoiselle—"

"I'm coming too, I tell you."

Poirot realized that it was futile to argue further. He gave in.

"Come then, mademoiselle. But it will not be amusing. In all probability nothing will happen."

The girl made no reply.

Twenty minutes later we set forth. It was quite dark now, a close, oppressive evening. Poirot led the way out of the town in the direction of the Villa Geneviève. But when he reached the Villa Marguerite he paused.

"I should like to assure myself that all goes well with Jack Renauld. Come with me, Hastings. Mademoiselle will perhaps remain outside. Madame Daubreuil might say something which would wound her."

We unlatched the gate, and walked up the path. As we went round to the side of the house, I drew Poirot's attention to a window on the first floor. Thrown sharply on the blind was the profile of Marthe Daubreuil.

"Ah!" said Poirot. "I figure to myself that that is the room where we shall find Jack Renauld."

Madame Daubreuil opened the door to us. She explained that Jack was much the same, but perhaps we would like to see for ourselves. She led us upstairs and into the bedroom. Marthe Daubreuil was embroidering by a table with a lamp on it. She put her finger to her lips as we entered.

Jack Renauld was sleeping an uneasy fitful sleep, his head turning from side to side, and his face still unduly flushed.

"Is the doctor coming again?" asked Poirot in a whisper.

"Not unless we send. He is sleeping—that is the great thing. *Maman* made him a tisane."

She sat down again with her embroidery as we left the room. Madame Daubreuil accompanied us down the stairs. Since I had learned of her past history, I viewed this woman with increased interest. She stood there with her eyes cast down, the same very faint enigmatical smile that I remembered on her lips. And suddenly I felt afraid of her, as one might feel afraid of a beautiful poisonous snake.

"I hope we have not deranged you, madame," said Poirot politely as she opened the door for us to pass out.

"Not at all, monsieur."

"By the way," said Poirot, as though struck by an afterthought, "M. Stonor has not been in Merlinville today, has he?"

I could not at all fathom the point of this question which I well knew to be meaningless as far as Poirot was concerned.

Madame Daubreuil replied quite composedly:

"Not that I know of."

"He has not had an interview with Mrs. Renauld?"

"How should I know that, monsieur?"

"True," said Poirot. "I thought you might have seen him coming or going, that is all. Good night, madame."

"Why—" I began.

"No 'whys,' Hastings. There will be time for that later."

We rejoined Cinderella and made our way rapidly in the direction of the Villa Geneviève. Poirot looked over his shoulder once at the lighted window and the profile of Marthe as she bent over her work.

"He is being guarded at all events," he muttered.

Arrived at the Villa Geneviève, Poirot took up his stand behind some bushes to the left of the drive, where, whilst enjoying a good view ourselves, we were completely hidden from sight. The Villa itself was in total darkness, everybody was without doubt in bed and asleep. We were almost immediately under the window of Mrs. Renauld's bedroom, which window, I noticed, was open. It seemed to me that it was upon this spot that Poirot's eyes were fixed.

"What are we going to do?" I whispered.

"Watch."

"But—"

"I do not expect anything to happen for at least an hour,

probably two hours, but the—"

But his words were interrupted by a long thin drawn cry:

"Help!"

A light flashed up in the second floor room on the right hand side of the house. The cry came from there. And even as we watched there came a shadow on the blind as of two people struggling.

"*Mille tonnerres!*" cried Poirot. "She must have changed her room!"

Dashing forward, he battered wildly on the front door. Then rushing to the tree in the flower-bed, he swarmed up it with the agility of a cat. I followed him, as with a bound he sprang in through the open window. Looking over my shoulder, I saw Dulcie reaching the branch behind me.

"Take care," I exclaimed.

"Take care of your grandmother!" retorted the girl. "This is child's play to me."

Poirot had rushed through the empty room and was pounding on the door leading into the corridor.

"Locked and bolted on the outside," he growled. "And it will take time to burst it open."

The cries for help were getting noticeably fainter. I saw despair in Poirot's eyes. He and I together put our shoulders to the door.

Cinderella's voice, calm and dispassionate, came from the window:

"You'll be too late, I guess I'm the only one who can do anything."

Before I could move a hand to stop her, she appeared to leap upward into space. I rushed and looked out. To my horror, I saw her hanging by her hands from the roof, propelling herself along by jerks in the direction of the lighted window.

"Good heavens! She'll be killed," I cried.

"You forget. She's a professional acrobat, Hastings. It was the providence of the good God that made her insist on coming with us tonight. I only pray that she may be in time. Ah!"

A cry of absolute terror floated out on to the night as the girl disappeared through the right-hand window; then in Cinderella's clear tones came the words:

"No, you don't! I've got you—and my wrists are just like steel."

At the same moment the door of our prison was opened cautiously by Françoise. Poirot brushed her aside unceremoniously and rushed down the passage to where the other maids were grouped round the further door.

"It's locked on the inside, monsieur."

There was the sound of a heavy fall within. After a moment or two the key turned and the door swung slowly open. Cinderella, very pale, beckoned us in.

"She is safe?" demanded Poirot.

"Yes, I was just in time. She was exhausted."

Mrs. Renauld was half sitting, half lying on the bed. She was gasping for breath.

"Nearly strangled me," she murmured painfully. The girl picked up something from the floor and handed it to Poirot. It was a rolled up ladder of silk rope, very fine but quite strong.

"A getaway," said Poirot. "By the window, whilst we were battering at the door. Where is—the other?"

The girl stood aside a little and pointed. On the ground lay a figure wrapped in some dark material a fold of which hid the face.

"Dead?"

She nodded.

"I think so."

"Head must have struck the marble fender."

"But who is it?" I cried.

"The murderer of M. Renauld, Hastings. And the would-be murderer of Madame Renauld."

Puzzled and uncomprehending, I knelt down, and lifting the fold of cloth, looked into the dead beautiful face of Marthe Daubreuil!

TWENTY-EIGHT
Journey's End

I have confused memories of the further events of that night. Poirot seemed deaf to my repeated questions. He was engaged in overwhelming Françoise with reproaches for not having told him of Mrs. Renauld's change of sleeping quarters.

I caught him by the shoulder, determined to attract his attention, and make myself heard.

"But you *must* have known," I expostulated. "You were taken up to see her this afternoon."

Poirot deigned to attend to me for a brief moment.

"She had been wheeled on a sofa into the middle room—her boudoir," he explained.

"But, monsieur," cried Françoise, "Madame changed her room almost immediately after the crime! The associations—they were too distressing!"

"Then why was I not told," vociferated Poirot, striking the table, and working himself into a first-class passion. "I demand you—why—was—I—not—told? You are an old woman completely imbecile! And Léonie and Denise are no better. All of you are triple idiots! Your stupidity has nearly caused the death of your mistress. But for this courageous child—"

He broke off, and, darting across the room to where the girl was bending over ministering to Mrs. Renauld, he embraced her with Gallic fervour—slightly to my annoyance.

I was aroused from my condition of mental fog by a sharp command from Poirot to fetch the doctor immediately on Mrs. Renauld's behalf. After that, I might summon the police. And he added, to complete my dudgeon:

"It will hardly be worth your while to return here. I shall be too busy to attend to you, and of Mademoiselle here I make a *garde-malad.*"

I retired with what dignity I could command. Having done my errands, I returned to the hotel. I understood next to nothing of what had occurred. The events of the night seemed fantastic and impossible. Nobody would answer my questions. Nobody had seemed to hear them. Angrily, I flung myself into bed, and slept the sleep of the bewildered and utterly exhausted.

I awoke to find the sun pouring in through the open windows and Poirot, neat and smiling, sitting beside the bed.

"*Enfin* you wake! But it is that you are a famous sleeper, Hastings! Do you know that it is nearly eleven o'clock?"

I groaned and put a hand to my head.

"I must have been dreaming," I said. "Do you know, I actually dreamt that we found Marthe Daubreuil's body in Mrs. Renauld's room, and that you declared her to have murdered Mr. Renauld?"

"You were not dreaming. All that is quite true."

"But Bella Duveen killed Mr. Renauld?"

"Oh, no, Hastings, she did not! She said she did—yes—but that was to save the man she loved from the guillotine."

"What?"

"Remember Jack Renauld's story. They both arrived on the scene at the same instant, and each took the other to be the perpetrator of the crime. The girl stares at him in horror, and then with a cry rushes away. But, when she hears that the crime has been brought home to him, she cannot bear it, and comes forward to accuse herself and save him from certain death."

Poirot leaned back in his chair, and brought the tips of his fingers together in familiar style.

"The case was not quite satisfactory to me," he observed judicially. "All along I was strongly under the impression that we were dealing with a cold-blooded and premeditated crime committed by some one who had been contented (very cleverly) with using M. Renauld's own plans for throwing the police off the track. The great criminal (as you may remember my remarking to you once) is always supremely simple."

I nodded.

"Now, to support this theory, the criminal must have been fully cognizant of Mr. Renauld's plans. That leads us to Madame Renauld. But facts fail to support any theory of her guilt. Is there any one else who might have known of them? Yes. From Marthe Daubreuil's own lips we have the admission that she overheard M. Renauld's quarrel with the tramp. If she could overhear that, there is no reason why she should not have heard everything else, especially if M. and Madame Renauld were imprudent enough to discuss their plans sitting on the bench. Remember how easily you overheard Marthe's conversation with Jack Renauld from that spot."

"But what possible motive could Marthe have for murdering Mr. Renauld?" I argued.

"What motive? Money! M. Renauld was a millionaire several times over, and at his death (or so she and Jack believed) half that vast fortune would pass to his son. Let us reconstruct the scene from the standpoint of Marthe Daubreuil.

"Marthe Daubreuil overhears what passes between Renauld and his wife. So far he has been a nice little source of income to the Daubreuil mother and daughter, but now he proposes to escape from their toils. At first, possibly, her idea is to prevent that escape. But a bolder idea takes its place, and one that fails to horrify the daughter of Jeanne Beroldy! At present M. Renauld stands inexorably in the way of her marriage with Jack. If the latter defies his father, he will be a pauper—which is not at all to the mind of Mademoiselle Marthe. In fact, I doubt if she has ever cared a straw for Jack Renauld. She can simulate emotion, but in reality she is of the same cold, calculating type as her mother. I doubt, too, whether she was really very sure of her hold over the boy's affections. She had dazzled and captivated him, but separated from her, as his father could so easily manage to separate him, she might lose him. But with M. Renauld dead, and Jack the heir to half his millions, the marriage can take place at once, and at a stroke she will attain wealth—not the beggarly thousands that have been extracted from him so far. And her clever brain takes in the simplicity of the thing. It is all so easy. M. Renauld is planning all the circumstances of his death—she has only to step in at the right moment and turn the farce into a grim reality. And here comes in the second point which led me infallibly to Marthe Daubreuil—the dagger! Jack Renauld had *three* souvenirs made. One he gave to his mother, one to Bella Duveen; was it not highly probable that he had given the third one to Marthe Daubreuil?

"So then, to sum up, there were four points of note against Marthe Daubreuil:

"(1) Marthe Daubreuil could have overheard M. Renauld's plans.

"(2) Marthe Daubreuil had a direct interest in causing M. Renauld's death.

"(3) Marthe Daubreuil was the daughter of the notorious Madame Beroldy who in my opinion was morally and virtually the murderess of her husband, although it may have been Georges Conneau's hand which struck the actual blow.

"(4) Marthe Daubreuil was the only person, besides Jack Renauld, likely to have the third dagger in her possession."

Poirot paused and cleared his throat.

"Of course, when I learned of the existence of the other girl, Bella Duveen, I realized that it was quite possible that *she* might have killed M. Renauld. The solution did not commend itself to me, because, as I pointed out to you, Hastings, an expert, such as I am, likes to meet a foeman worthy of his steel. Still one must take crimes as one finds them, not as one would like them to be. It did not seem very likely that Bella Duveen would be wandering about carrying a souvenir paper-knife in her hand, but of course she might have had some idea all the time of revenging herself on Jack Renauld. When she actually came forward and confessed to the murder, it seemed that all was over. And yet—I was not satisfied, *mon ami. I was not satisfied.…*

"I went over the case again minutely, and I came to the same conclusion as before. If it was *not* Bella Duveen, the only other person who could have committed the crime was Marthe Daubreuil. But I had not one single proof against her!

"And then you showed me that letter from Mademoiselle Dulcie, and I saw a chance of settling the matter once for all. The original dagger was stolen by Dulcie Duveen and thrown into the sea—since, as she thought, it belonged to her sister. But if, by any chance, it was *not* her sister's, but the one given by Jack to Marthe Daubreuil—why then, Bella Duveen's dagger would be still intact! I said no word to you, Hastings (it was no time for romance) but I sought out Mademoiselle Dulcie, told her as much as I deemed needful, and set her to search amongst the effects of her sister. Imagine my elation, when she sought me out (according to my instructions) as Miss Robinson with the precious souvenir in her possession!

"In the meantime I had taken steps to force Mademoiselle Marthe into the open. By my orders, Mrs. Renauld repulsed her son, and declared her intention of making a will on the morrow which should cut him off from ever enjoying even a portion of his father's fortune. It was a desperate step, but a necessary one, and Madame Renauld was fully prepared to take the risk—though unfortunately she also never thought of mentioning her change of room. I suppose she took it for granted that I knew. All happened as I thought. Marthe Daubreuil made a last bold bid for the Renauld millions—and failed!"

"What absolutely bewilders me," I said, "is how she ever got into the house without our seeing her. It seems an absolute miracle. We left her behind at the Villa Marguerite, we go straight to the Villa Geneviève—and yet she is there before us!"

"Ah, but we did not leave her behind. She was out of the Villa Marguerite by the back way whilst we were talking to her mother in the hall. That is where, as the Americans say, she 'put it over' on Hercule Poirot!"

"But the shadow on the blind? We saw it from the road."

"*Eh bien*, when we looked up, Madame Daubreuil had just had time to run upstairs and take her place."

"Madame Daubreuil?"

"Yes. One is old, and one is young, one dark, and one fair, but, for the purpose of a silhouette on a blind, their profiles are singularly alike. Even I did not suspect—triple imbecile that I was! I thought I had plenty of time before me—that she would not try to gain admission to the Villa until much later. She had brains, that beautiful Mademoiselle Marthe."

"And her object was to murder Mrs. Renauld?"

"Yes. The whole fortune would then pass to her son. But it would have been suicide, *mon ami!* On the floor by Marthe Daubreuil's body, I found a pad and a little bottle of chloroform and a hypodermic syringe containing a fatal dose of morphine. You understand? The chloroform first—then when the victim is unconscious the prick of the needle. By the morning the smell of the chloroform has quite disappeared, and the syringe lies where it has fallen from Madame Renauld's hand. What would he say, the excellent M. Hautet? 'Poor woman! What did I tell you? The shock of joy, it was too much on top of the rest! Did I not say that I should not be surprised if her brain became unhinged. Altogether a most tragic case, the Renauld Case!'

"However, Hastings, things did not go quite as Mademoiselle Marthe had planned. To begin with, Madame Renauld was awake and waiting for her. There is a struggle. But Madame Renauld is terribly weak still. There is a last chance for Marthe Daubreuil.

The idea of suicide is at an end, but if she can silence Madame Renauld with her strong hands, make a getaway with her little silk ladder whilst we are still battering on the inside of the further door, and be back at the Villa Marguerite before we return there, it will be hard to prove anything against her. But she was checkmated—not by Hercule Poirot—but by *la petite acrobate* with her wrists of steel."

I mused over the whole story.

"When did you first begin to suspect Marthe Daubreuil, Poirot? When she told us she had overheard the quarrel in the garden?"

Poirot smiled.

"My friend, do you remember when we drove into Merlinville that first day? And the beautiful girl we saw standing at the gate? You asked me if I had not noticed a young goddess, and I replied to you that I had seen only a girl with anxious eyes. That is how I have thought of Marthe Daubreuil from the beginning. *The girl with the anxious eyes!* Why was she anxious? Not on Jack Renauld's behalf, for she did not know then that he had been in Merlinville the previous evening."

"By the way," I exclaimed, "how is Jack Renauld?"

"Much better. He is still at the Villa Marguerite. But Madame Daubreuil has disappeared. The police are looking for her."

"Was she in with her daughter, do you think?"

"We shall never know. Madame is a lady who can keep her secrets. And I doubt very much if the police will ever find her."

"Has Jack Renauld been—told?"

"Not yet."

"It will be a terrible shock to him."

"Naturally. And yet, do you know, Hastings, I doubt if his heart was ever seriously engaged. So far we have looked upon Bella Duveen as a siren, and Marthe Daubreuil as the girl he really loved. But I think that if we reversed the terms we should come nearer to the truth. Marthe Daubreuil was very beautiful. She set herself to fascinate Jack, and she succeeded, but remember his curious reluctance to break with the other girl. And see how he was willing to go to the guillotine rather than implicate her. I have a little idea that when he learns the truth he will be horrified—revolted, and his false love will wither away."

"What about Giraud?"

"He has a *crise* of the nerves, that one! He has been obliged to return to Paris."

We both smiled.

Poirot proved a fairly true prophet. When at length the doctor pronounced Jack Renauld strong enough to hear the truth, it was Poirot who broke it to him. The shock was indeed terrific. Yet Jack rallied better than I could have supposed possible. His mother's devotion helped him to live through those difficult days. The mother and son were inseparable now.

There was a further revelation to come. Poirot had acquainted Mrs. Renauld with the fact that he knew her secret, and had represented to her that Jack should not be left in ignorance of his father's past.

"To hide the truth, never does it avail, madame! Be brave and tell him everything."

With a heavy heart Mrs. Renauld consented, and her son learned that the father he had loved had been in actual fact a fugitive from justice. A halting question was promptly answered by Poirot.

"Reassure yourself, M. Jack. The world knows nothing. As far as I can see, there is no obligation for me to take the police into my confidence. Throughout the case I have acted, not for them, but for your father. Justice overtook him at last, but no one need ever know that he and Georges Conneau were one and the same."

There were, of course, various points in the case that remained puzzling to the police, but Poirot explained things in so plausible a fashion that all query about them was gradually stilled.

Shortly after we got back to London, I noticed a magnificent model of a foxhound adorning Poirot's mantelpiece. In answer to my inquiring glance, Poirot nodded.

"*Mais, oui!* I got my 500 francs! Is he not a splendid fellow? I call him Giraud!"

A few days later Jack Renauld came to see us with a resolute expression on his face.

"M. Poirot, I've come to say good-bye. I'm sailing for South America almost immediately. My father had large interests over the continent, and I mean to start a new life out there."

"You go alone, M. Jack?"

"My mother comes with me—and I shall keep Stonor on as my secretary. He likes out of-the-way parts of the world."

"No one else goes with you?"

Jack flushed.

"You mean—?"

"A girl who loves you very dearly—who has been willing to lay down her life for you."

"How could I ask her?" muttered the boy. "After all that has happened, could I go to her and—oh, what sort of a lame story could I tell?"

"*Les femmes*—they have a wonderful genius for manufacturing crutches for stories like that."

"Yes, but—I've been such a damned fool!"

"So have all of us, at one time and another," observed Poirot philosophically.

But Jack's face had hardened.

"There's something else. I'm my father's son. Would any one marry me, knowing that?"

"You are your father's son, you say. Hastings here will tell you that I believe in heredity—"

"Well, then—"

"Wait. I know a woman, a woman of courage and endurance, capable of great love, of supreme self-sacrifice—"

The boy looked up. His eyes softened.

222

"My mother!"

"Yes. You are your mother's son as well as your father's. Go then to Mademoiselle Bella. Tell her everything. Keep nothing back—and see what she will say!"

Jack looked irresolute.

"Go to her as a boy no longer, but a man—a man bowed by the fate of the Past, and the fate of Today, but looking forward to a new and wonderful life. Ask her to share it with you. You may not realize it, but your love for each other has been tested in the fire and not found wanting. You have both been willing to lay down your lives for each other."

And what of Captain Arthur Hastings, humble chronicler of these pages?

There is some talk of his joining the Renaulds on a ranch across the seas, but for the end of this story I prefer to go back to a morning in the garden of the Villa Geneviève.

"I can't call you Bella," I said, "since it isn't your name. And Dulcie seems so unfamiliar. So it's got to be Cinderella. Cinderella married the Prince, you remember. I'm not a Prince, but—"

She interrupted me.

"Cinderella warned him, I'm sure! You see, she couldn't promise to turn into a princess. She was only a little scullion after all—"

"It's the Prince's turn to interrupt," I interpolated. "Do you know what he said?"

"No?"

"'Hell!' said the Prince—and kissed her!"

And I suited the action to the word.

THE MYSTERIOUS AFFAIR AT STYLES

Agatha Christie
THE
MYSTERIOUS
AFFAIR
AT STYLES

PAGE CLASSICS

ISBN: 978-1-64833-747-5

First published 1920
Published by Page Publications 2024

Printed in China

Contents

1.	I Go to Styles	1
2.	The 16th and 17th of July	14
3.	The Night of the Tragedy	23
4.	Poirot Investigates	31
5.	"It Isn't Strychnine, Is It?"	52
6.	The Inquest	79
7.	Poirot Pays His Debts	93
8.	Fresh Suspicions	105
9.	Dr. Bauerstein	121
10.	The Arrest	135
11.	The Case for the Prosecution	151
12.	The Last Link	170
13.	Poirot Explains	181

ONE

I Go to Styles

The intense interest aroused in the public by what was known at the time as "The Styles Case" has now somewhat subsided. Nevertheless, in view of the world-wide notoriety which attended it, I have been asked, both by my friend Poirot and the family themselves, to write an account of the whole story. This, we trust, will effectually silence the sensational rumours which still persist.

I will therefore briefly set down the circumstances which led to my being connected with the affair.

I had been invalided home from the Front; and, after spending some months in a rather depressing Convalescent Home, was given a month's sick leave. Having no near relations or friends, I was trying to make up my mind what to do, when I ran across John Cavendish. I had seen very little of him for some years. Indeed, I had never known him particularly well. He was a good fifteen years my senior, for one thing, though he hardly looked his forty-five years. As a boy, though, I had often stayed at Styles, his mother's place in Essex.

We had a good yarn about old times, and it ended in his inviting me down to Styles to spend my leave there.

"The mater will be delighted to see you again—after all those years," he added.

"Your mother keeps well?" I asked.

"Oh, yes. I suppose you know that she has married again?"

I am afraid I showed my surprise rather plainly. Mrs. Cavendish, who had married John's father when he was a widower with two sons, had been a handsome woman of middle-age as I remembered her. She certainly could not be a day less than seventy now. I recalled her as an energetic, autocratic personality, somewhat inclined to charitable and social notoriety, with a fondness for opening bazaars and playing the Lady Bountiful. She was a most generous woman, and possessed a considerable fortune of her own.

Their country-place, Styles Court, had been purchased by Mr. Cavendish early in their married life. He had been completely under his wife's ascendancy, so much so that, on dying, he left the place to her for her lifetime, as well as the larger part of his income; an arrangement that was distinctly unfair to his two sons. Their step-mother, however, had always been most generous to them; indeed, they were so young at the time of their father's remarriage that they always thought of her as their own mother.

Lawrence, the younger, had been a delicate youth. He had qualified as a doctor but early relinquished the profession of medicine, and lived at home while pursuing literary ambitions; though his verses never had any marked success.

John practised for some time as a barrister, but had finally settled down to the more congenial life of a country squire. He had married two years ago, and had taken his wife to live at Styles, though I entertained a shrewd suspicion that he would have preferred his mother to increase his allowance, which would have enabled him to have a home of his own. Mrs. Cavendish, however, was a lady who liked to make her own plans, and expected other people to fall in with them, and in this case she certainly had the whip hand, namely: the purse strings.

John noticed my surprise at the news of his mother's remarriage and smiled rather ruefully.

"Rotten little bounder too!" he said savagely. "I can tell you,

Hastings, it's making life jolly difficult for us. As for Evie—you remember Evie?"

"No."

"Oh, I suppose she was after your time. She's the mater's factotum, companion, Jack of all trades! A great sport—old Evie! Not precisely young and beautiful, but as game as they make them."

"You were going to say——?"

"Oh, this fellow! He turned up from nowhere, on the pretext of being a second cousin or something of Evie's, though she didn't seem particularly keen to acknowledge the relationship. The fellow is an absolute outsider, anyone can see that. He's got a great black beard, and wears patent leather boots in all weathers! But the mater cottoned to him at once, took him on as secretary—you know how she's always running a hundred societies?"

I nodded.

"Well, of course the war has turned the hundreds into thousands. No doubt the fellow was very useful to her. But you could have knocked us all down with a feather when, three months ago, she suddenly announced that she and Alfred were engaged! The fellow must be at least twenty years younger than she is! It's simply bare-faced fortune hunting; but there you are—she is her own mistress, and she's married him."

"It must be a difficult situation for you all."

"Difficult! It's damnable!"

Thus it came about that, three days later, I descended from the train at Styles St. Mary, an absurd little station, with no apparent reason for existence, perched up in the midst of green fields and country lanes. John Cavendish was waiting on the platform, and piloted me out to the car.

"Got a drop or two of petrol still, you see," he remarked. "Mainly owing to the mater's activities."

The village of Styles St. Mary was situated about two miles from the little station, and Styles Court lay a mile the other side of it. It was a still, warm day in early July. As one looked out over the flat Essex country, lying so green and peaceful under the afternoon sun, it seemed almost impossible to believe that, not so very far away, a great war was running its appointed course. I felt I had suddenly strayed into another world. As we turned in at the lodge gates, John said:

"I'm afraid you'll find it very quiet down here, Hastings."

"My dear fellow, that's just what I want."

"Oh, it's pleasant enough if you want to lead the idle life. I drill with the volunteers twice a week, and lend a hand at the farms. My wife works regularly 'on the land'. She is up at five every morning to milk, and keeps at it steadily until lunchtime. It's a jolly good life taking it all round—if it weren't for that fellow Alfred Inglethorp!" He checked the car suddenly, and glanced at his watch. "I wonder if we've time to pick up Cynthia. No, she'll have started from the hospital by now."

"Cynthia! That's not your wife?"

"No, Cynthia is a protégée of my mother's, the daughter of an old schoolfellow of hers, who married a rascally solicitor. He came a cropper, and the girl was left an orphan and penniless. My mother came to the rescue, and Cynthia has been with us nearly two years now. She works in the Red Cross Hospital at Tadminster, seven miles away."

As he spoke the last words, we drew up in front of the fine old house. A lady in a stout tweed skirt, who was bending over a flower bed, straightened herself at our approach.

"Hullo, Evie, here's our wounded hero! Mr. Hastings—Miss Howard."

Miss Howard shook hands with a hearty, almost painful, grip. I had an impression of very blue eyes in a sunburnt face. She was a pleasant-looking woman of about forty, with a deep voice, almost manly in its stentorian tones, and had a large sensible square body, with feet to match—these last encased in good thick boots. Her conversation, I soon found, was couched in the telegraphic style.

"Weeds grow like house afire. Can't keep even with 'em. Shall press you in. Better be careful."

"I'm sure I shall be only too delighted to make myself useful," I responded.

"Don't say it. Never does. Wish you hadn't later."

"You're a cynic, Evie," said John, laughing. "Where's tea to-day—inside or out?"

"Out. Too fine a day to be cooped up in the house."

"Come on then, you've done enough gardening for to-day. 'The labourer is worthy of his hire', you know. Come and be refreshed."

"Well," said Miss Howard, drawing off her gardening gloves, "I'm inclined to agree with you."

She led the way round the house to where tea was spread under the shade of a large sycamore.

A figure rose from one of the basket chairs, and came a few steps to meet us.

"My wife, Hastings," said John.

I shall never forget my first sight of Mary Cavendish. Her tall, slender form, outlined against the bright light; the vivid sense of slumbering fire that seemed to find expression only in those wonderful tawny eyes of hers, remarkable eyes, different from any other woman's that I have ever known; the intense power of stillness she possessed, which nevertheless conveyed the impression of a wild untamed spirit in an exquisitely civilised body—all these things are burnt into my memory. I shall never forget them.

She greeted me with a few words of pleasant welcome in a low clear voice, and I sank into a basket chair feeling distinctly glad that I had accepted John's invitation. Mrs. Cavendish gave me some tea, and her few quiet remarks heightened my first impression of her as a thoroughly fascinating woman. An appreciative listener is always stimulating, and I described, in a humorous manner, certain incidents of my Convalescent Home, in a way which, I flatter myself, greatly amused my hostess. John, of course, good fellow though he is, could hardly be called a brilliant conversationalist.

At that moment a well remembered voice floated through the

open French window near at hand:

"Then you'll write to the Princess after tea, Alfred? I'll write to Lady Tadminster for the second day, myself. Or shall we wait until we hear from the Princess? In case of a refusal, Lady Tadminster might open it the first day, and Mrs. Crosbie the second. Then there's the Duchess—about the school fête."

There was the murmur of a man's voice, and then Mrs. Inglethorp's rose in reply:

"Yes, certainly. After tea will do quite well. You are so thoughtful, Alfred dear."

The French window swung open a little wider, and a handsome white-haired old lady, with a somewhat masterful cast of features, stepped out of it on to the lawn. A man followed her, a suggestion of deference in his manner.

Mrs. Inglethorp greeted me with effusion.

"Why, if it isn't too delightful to see you again, Mr. Hastings, after all these years. Alfred, darling, Mr. Hastings—my husband."

I looked with some curiosity at "Alfred darling". He certainly struck a rather alien note. I did not wonder at John objecting to his beard. It was one of the longest and blackest I have ever seen. He wore gold-rimmed pince-nez, and had a curious impassivity of feature. It struck me that he might look natural on a stage, but was strangely out of place in real life. His voice was rather deep and unctuous. He placed a wooden hand in mine and said:

"This is a pleasure, Mr. Hastings." Then, turning to his wife: "Emily dearest, I think that cushion is a little damp."

She beamed fondly on him, as he substituted another with every demonstration of the tenderest care. Strange infatuation of an otherwise sensible woman!

With the presence of Mr. Inglethorp, a sense of constraint and veiled hostility seemed to settle down upon the company. Miss Howard, in particular, took no pains to conceal her feelings. Mrs. Inglethorp, however, seemed to notice nothing unusual. Her volubility, which I remembered of old, had lost nothing in the intervening years, and she poured out a steady flood of conversation, mainly on the subject of the forthcoming bazaar which she was organizing and which was to take place shortly. Occasionally she referred to her husband over a question of days or dates. His watchful and attentive manner never varied. From the very first I took a firm and rooted dislike to him, and I flatter myself that my first judgments are usually fairly shrewd.

Presently Mrs. Inglethorp turned to give some instructions about letters to Evelyn Howard, and her husband addressed me in his painstaking voice:

"Is soldiering your regular profession, Mr. Hastings?"

"No, before the war I was in Lloyd's."

"And you will return there after it is over?"

"Perhaps. Either that or a fresh start altogether."

Mary Cavendish leant forward.

"What would you really choose as a profession, if you could just consult your inclination?"

"Well, that depends."

"No secret hobby?" she asked. "Tell me—you're drawn to something? Everyone is—usually something absurd."

"You'll laugh at me."

She smiled.

"Perhaps."

"Well, I've always had a secret hankering to be a detective!"

"The real thing—Scotland Yard? Or Sherlock Holmes?"

"Oh, Sherlock Holmes by all means. But really, seriously, I am awfully drawn to it. I came across a man in Belgium once, a very famous detective, and he quite inflamed me. He was a marvellous little fellow. He used to say that all good detective work was a mere matter of method. My system is based on his—though of course I have progressed rather further. He was a funny little man, a great dandy, but wonderfully clever."

"Like a good detective story myself," remarked Miss Howard. "Lots of nonsense written, though. Criminal discovered in last chapter. Everyone dumbfounded. Real crime—you'd know at once."

"There have been a great number of undiscovered crimes," I argued.

"Don't mean the police, but the people that are right in it. The family. You couldn't really hoodwink them. They'd know."

"Then," I said, much amused, "you think that if you were mixed up in a crime, say a murder, you'd be able to spot the murderer right off?"

"Of course I should. Mightn't be able to prove it to a pack of lawyers. But I'm certain I'd know. I'd feel it in my fingertips if he came near me."

"It might be a 'she'," I suggested.

"Might. But murder's a violent crime. Associate it more with a man."

"Not in a case of poisoning." Mrs. Cavendish's clear voice startled me. "Dr. Bauerstein was saying yesterday that, owing to the general ignorance of the more uncommon poisons among the medical profession, there were probably countless cases of poisoning quite unsuspected."

"Why, Mary, what a gruesome conversation!" cried Mrs. Inglethorp. "It makes me feel as if a goose were walking over my grave. Oh, there's Cynthia!"

A young girl in V.A.D. uniform ran lightly across the lawn.

"Why, Cynthia, you are late to-day. This is Mr. Hastings— Miss Murdoch."

Cynthia Murdoch was a fresh-looking young creature, full of life and vigour. She tossed off her little V.A.D. cap, and I admired the great loose waves of her auburn hair, and the smallness and whiteness of the hand she held out to claim her tea. With dark eyes and eyelashes she would have been a beauty.

She flung herself down on the ground beside John, and as I handed her a plate of sandwiches she smiled up at me.

"Sit down here on the grass, do. It's ever so much nicer."

I dropped down obediently.

"You work at Tadminster, don't you, Miss Murdoch?"

She nodded.

"For my sins."

"Do they bully you, then?" I asked, smiling.

"I should like to see them!" cried Cynthia with dignity.

"I have got a cousin who is nursing," I remarked. "And she is terrified of 'Sisters'."

"I don't wonder. Sisters *are*, you know, Mr. Hastings. They simp-ly *are*! You've no idea! But I'm not a nurse, thank heaven, I work in the dispensary."

"How many people do you poison?" I asked, smiling.

Cynthia smiled too.

"Oh, hundreds!" she said.

"Cynthia," called Mrs. Inglethorp, "do you think you could write a few notes for me?"

"Certainly, Aunt Emily."

She jumped up promptly, and something in her manner reminded me that her position was a dependent one, and that Mrs. Inglethorp, kind as she might be in the main, did not allow her to forget it.

My hostess turned to me.

"John will show you your room. Supper is at half-past seven. We have given up late dinner for some time now. Lady Tadminster, our Member's wife—she was the late Lord Abbotsbury's daughter—does the same. She agrees with me that one must set an example of economy. We are quite a war household; nothing is wasted here—every scrap of waste paper, even, is saved and sent away in sacks."

I expressed my appreciation, and John took me into the house and up the broad staircase, which forked right and left half-way to different wings of the building. My room was in the left wing, and looked out over the park.

John left me, and a few minutes later I saw him from my

window walking slowly across the grass arm in arm with Cynthia Murdoch. I heard Mrs. Inglethorp call "Cynthia" impatiently, and the girl started and ran back to the house. At the same moment, a man stepped out from the shadow of a tree and walked slowly in the same direction. He looked about forty, very dark with a melancholy clean-shaven face. Some violent emotion seemed to be mastering him. He looked up at my window as he passed, and I recognized him, though he had changed much in the fifteen years that had elapsed since we last met. It was John's younger brother, Lawrence Cavendish. I wondered what it was that had brought that singular expression to his face.

Then I dismissed him from my mind, and returned to the contemplation of my own affairs.

The evening passed pleasantly enough; and I dreamed that night of that enigmatical woman, Mary Cavendish.

The next morning dawned bright and sunny, and I was full of the anticipation of a delightful visit.

I did not see Mrs. Cavendish until lunch-time, when she volunteered to take me for a walk, and we spent a charming afternoon roaming in the woods, returning to the house about five.

As we entered the large hall, John beckoned us both into the smoking-room. I saw at once by his face that something disturbing had occurred. We followed him in, and he shut the door after us.

"Look here, Mary, there's the deuce of a mess. Evie's had a row with Alfred Inglethorp, and she's off."

"Evie? Off?"

John nodded gloomily.

"Yes; you see she went to the mater, and—Oh,—here's Evie herself."

Miss Howard entered. Her lips were set grimly together, and she carried a small suit-case. She looked excited and determined, and slightly on the defensive.

"At any rate," she burst out, "I've spoken my mind!"

"My dear Evelyn," cried Mrs. Cavendish, "this can't be true!"

Miss Howard nodded grimly.

"True enough! Afraid I said some things to Emily she won't forget or forgive in a hurry. Don't mind if they've only sunk in a bit. Probably water off a duck's back, though. I said right out: 'You're an old woman, Emily, and there's no fool like an old fool. The man's twenty years younger than you, and don't you fool yourself as to what he married you for. Money! Well, don't let him have too much of it. Farmer Raikes has got a very pretty young wife. Just ask your Alfred how much time he spends over there.' She was very angry. Natural! I went on, 'I'm going to warn you, whether you like it or not. That man would as soon murder you in your bed as look at you. He's a bad lot. You can say what you like to me, but remember what I've told you. He's a bad lot!'"

"What did she say?"

Miss Howard made an extremely expressive grimace.

"'Darling Alfred'—'dearest Alfred'—'wicked calumnies' —'wicked lies'—'wicked woman'—to accuse her 'dear husband!' The sooner I left her house the better. So I'm off."

"But not now?"

"This minute!"

For a moment we sat and stared at her. Finally John Cavendish, finding his persuasions of no avail, went off to look up the trains. His wife followed him, murmuring something about persuading Mrs. Inglethorp to think better of it.

As she left the room, Miss Howard's face changed. She leant towards me eagerly.

"Mr. Hastings, you're honest. I can trust you?"

I was a little startled. She laid her hand on my arm, and sank her voice to a whisper.

"Look after her, Mr. Hastings. My poor Emily. They're a lot of sharks—all of them. Oh, I know what I'm talking about. There isn't one of them that's not hard up and trying to get money out of her. I've protected her as much as I could. Now I'm out of the way, they'll impose upon her."

"Of course, Miss Howard," I said, "I'll do everything I can, but I'm sure you're excited and overwrought."

She interrupted me by slowly shaking her forefinger.

"Young man, trust me. I've lived in the world rather longer than you have. All I ask you is to keep your eyes open. You'll see what I mean."

The throb of the motor came through the open window, and Miss Howard rose and moved to the door. John's voice sounded outside. With her hand on the handle, she turned her head over her shoulder, and beckoned to me.

"Above all, Mr. Hastings, watch that devil—her husband!"

There was no time for more. Miss Howard was swallowed up in an eager chorus of protests and good-byes. The Inglethorps did not appear.

As the motor drove away, Mrs. Cavendish suddenly detached herself from the group, and moved across the drive to the lawn to meet a tall bearded man who had been evidently making for the house. The colour rose in her cheeks as she held out her hand to him.

"Who is that?" I asked sharply, for instinctively I distrusted the man.

"That's Dr. Bauerstein," said John shortly.

"And who is Dr. Bauerstein?"

"He's staying in the village doing a rest cure, after a bad nervous breakdown. He's a London specialist; a very clever man—one of the greatest living experts on poisons, I believe."

"And he's a great friend of Mary's," put in Cynthia, the irrepressible.

John Cavendish frowned and changed the subject.

"Come for a stroll, Hastings. This has been a most rotten business. She always had a rough tongue, but there is no stauncher friend in England than Evelyn Howard."

He took the path through the plantation, and we walked down to the village through the woods which bordered one side of the estate.

As we passed through one of the gates on our way home again, a pretty young woman of gipsy type coming in the opposite direction bowed and smiled.

"That's a pretty girl," I remarked appreciatively.

John's face hardened.

"That is Mrs. Raikes."

"The one that Miss Howard——"

"Exactly," said John, with rather unnecessary abruptness.

I thought of the white-haired old lady in the big house, and that vivid wicked little face that had just smiled into ours, and a vague chill of foreboding crept over me. I brushed it aside.

"Styles is really a glorious old place," I said to John.

He nodded rather gloomily.

"Yes, it's a fine property. It'll be mine some day—should be mine now by rights, if my father had only made a decent will. And then I shouldn't be so damned hard up as I am now."

"Hard up, are you?"

"My dear Hastings, I don't mind telling you that I'm at my wits' end for money."

"Couldn't your brother help you?"

"Lawrence? He's gone through every penny he ever had, publishing rotten verses in fancy bindings. No, we're an impecunious lot. My mother's always been awfully good to us, I must say. That is, up to now. Since her marriage, of course——" he broke off, frowning.

For the first time I felt that, with Evelyn Howard, something indefinable had gone from the atmosphere. Her presence had spelt security. Now that security was removed—and the air seemed rife with suspicion. The sinister face of Dr. Bauerstein recurred to me unpleasantly. A vague suspicion of everyone and everything filled my mind. Just for a moment I had a premonition of approaching evil.

TWO

The 16th and 17th of July

I had arrived at Styles on the 5th of July. I come now to the events of the 16th and 17th of that month. For the convenience of the reader I will recapitulate the incidents of those days in as exact a manner as possible. They were elicited subsequently at the trial by a process of long and tedious cross-examinations.

I received a letter from Evelyn Howard a couple of days after her departure, telling me she was working as a nurse at the big hospital in Middlingham, a manufacturing town some fifteen miles away, and begging me to let her know if Mrs. Inglethorp should show any wish to be reconciled.

The only fly in the ointment of my peaceful days was Mrs. Cavendish's extraordinary, and, for my part, unaccountable preference for the society of Dr. Bauerstein. What she saw in the man I cannot imagine, but she was always asking him up to the house, and often went off for long expeditions with him. I must confess that I was quite unable to see his attraction.

The 16th of July fell on a Monday. It was a day of turmoil. The famous bazaar had taken place on Saturday, and an entertainment, in connection with the same charity, at which Mrs. Inglethorp was to recite a War poem, was to be held that night. We were all busy during the morning arranging and decorating the Hall in the village where it was to take place. We had a late luncheon and spent the afternoon resting in the garden. I noticed that John's manner was somewhat unusual. He seemed very excited and restless.

After tea, Mrs. Inglethorp went to lie down to rest before her efforts in the evening and I challenged Mary Cavendish to a single at tennis.

About a quarter to seven, Mrs. Inglethorp called us that we should be late as supper was early that night. We had rather a scramble to get ready in time; and before the meal was over the motor was waiting at the door.

The entertainment was a great success, Mrs. Inglethorp's recitation receiving tremendous applause. There were also some tableaux in which Cynthia took part. She did not return with us, having been asked to a supper party, and to remain the night with some friends who had been acting with her in the tableaux.

The following morning, Mrs. Inglethorp stayed in bed to breakfast, as she was rather overtired; but she appeared in her briskest mood about 12.30, and swept Lawrence and myself off to a luncheon party.

"Such a charming invitation from Mrs. Rolleston. Lady Tadminster's sister, you know. The Rollestons came over with the Conqueror—one of our oldest families."

Mary had excused herself on the plea of an engagement with Dr. Bauerstein.

We had a pleasant luncheon, and as we drove away Lawrence suggested that we should return by Tadminster, which was barely a mile out of our way, and pay a visit to Cynthia in her dispensary. Mrs. Inglethorp replied that this was an excellent idea, but as she had several letters to write she would drop us there, and we could come back with Cynthia in the pony-trap.

We were detained under suspicion by the hospital porter, until Cynthia appeared to vouch for us, looking very cool and sweet in her long white overall. She took us up to her sanctum, and introduced us to her fellow dispenser, a rather awe-inspiring individual, whom Cynthia cheerily addressed as "Nibs."

"What a lot of bottles!" I exclaimed, as my eye travelled round the small room. "Do you really know what's in them all?"

"Say something original," groaned Cynthia. "Every single person who comes up here says that. We are really thinking of bestowing a prize on the first individual who does *not* say: 'What a lot of bottles!' And I know the next thing you're going to say is: 'How many people have you poisoned?'"

I pleaded guilty with a laugh.

"If you people only knew how fatally easy it is to poison someone by mistake, you wouldn't joke about it. Come on, let's have tea. We've got all sorts of secret stores in that cupboard. No, Lawrence—that's the poison cupboard. The big cupboard—that's right."

We had a very cheery tea, and assisted Cynthia to wash up afterwards. We had just put away the last tea-spoon when a knock came at the door. The countenances of Cynthia and Nibs were suddenly petrified into a stern and forbidding expression.

"Come in," said Cynthia, in a sharp professional tone.

A young and rather scared looking nurse appeared with a bottle which she proffered to Nibs, who waved her towards Cynthia with the somewhat enigmatical remark:

"*I'm not really here to-day.*"

Cynthia took the bottle and examined it with the severity of a judge.

"This should have been sent up this morning."

"Sister is very sorry. She forgot."

"Sister should read the rules outside the door."

I gathered from the little nurse's expression that there was not the least likelihood of her having the hardihood to retail this message to the dreaded "Sister".

"So now it can't be done until to-morrow," finished Cynthia.

"Don't you think you could possibly let us have it to-night?"

"Well," said Cynthia graciously, "we are very busy, but if we have time it shall be done."

The little nurse withdrew, and Cynthia promptly took a jar

from the shelf, refilled the bottle, and placed it on the table outside the door.

I laughed.

"Discipline must be maintained?"

"Exactly. Come out on our little balcony. You can see all the outside wards there."

I followed Cynthia and her friend and they pointed out the different wards to me. Lawrence remained behind, but after a few moments Cynthia called to him over her shoulder to come and join us. Then she looked at her watch.

"Nothing more to do, Nibs?"

"No."

"All right. Then we can lock up and go."

I had seen Lawrence in quite a different light that afternoon. Compared to John, he was an astoundingly difficult person to get to know. He was the opposite of his brother in almost every respect, being unusually shy and reserved. Yet he had a certain charm of manner, and I fancied that, if one really knew him well, one could have a deep affection for him. I had always fancied that his manner to Cynthia was rather constrained, and that she on her side was inclined to be shy of him. But they were both gay enough this afternoon, and chatted together like a couple of children.

As we drove through the village, I remembered that I wanted some stamps, so accordingly we pulled up at the post office.

As I came out again, I cannoned into a little man who was just entering. I drew aside and apologised, when suddenly, with a loud exclamation, he clasped me in his arms and kissed me warmly.

"*Mon ami* Hastings!" he cried. "It is indeed *mon ami* Hastings!"

"Poirot!" I exclaimed.

I turned to the pony-trap.

"This is a very pleasant meeting for me, Miss Cynthia. This is my old friend, Monsieur Poirot, whom I have not seen for years."

"Oh, we know Monsieur Poirot," said Cynthia gaily. "But I had no idea he was a friend of yours."

"Yes, indeed," said Poirot seriously. "I know Mademoiselle Cynthia. It is by the charity of that good Mrs. Inglethorp that I am here." Then, as I looked at him inquiringly: "Yes, my friend, she had kindly extended hospitality to seven of my countrypeople who, alas, are refugees from their native land. We Belgians will always remember her with gratitude."

Poirot was an extraordinary looking little man. He was hardly more than five feet, four inches, but carried himself with great dignity. His head was exactly the shape of an egg, and he always perched it a little on one side. His moustache was very stiff and military. The neatness of his attire was almost incredible. I believe a speck of dust would have caused him more pain than a bullet wound. Yet this quaint dandified little man who, I was sorry to see, now limped badly, had been in his time one of the most celebrated members of the Belgian police. As a detective, his *flair* had been extraordinary, and he had achieved triumphs by unravelling some of the most baffling cases of the day.

He pointed out to me the little house inhabited by him and his fellow Belgians, and I promised to go and see him at an early date. Then he raised his hat with a flourish to Cynthia, and we drove away.

"He's a dear little man," said Cynthia. "I'd no idea you knew him."

"You've been entertaining a celebrity unawares," I replied.

And, for the rest of the way home, I recited to them the various exploits and triumphs of Hercule Poirot.

We arrived back in a very cheerful mood. As we entered the hall, Mrs. Inglethorp came out of her boudoir. She looked flushed and upset.

"Oh, it's you," she said.

"Is there anything the matter, Aunt Emily?" asked Cynthia.

"Certainly not," said Mrs. Inglethorp sharply. "What should there be?" Then catching sight of Dorcas, the parlourmaid, going into the dining-room, she called to her to bring some stamps into the boudoir.

"Yes, m'm." The old servant hesitated, then added diffidently:

"Don't you think, m'm, you'd better get to bed? You're looking very tired."

"Perhaps you're right, Dorcas—yes—no—not now. I've some letters I must finish by post-time. Have you lighted the fire in my room as I told you?"

"Yes, m'm."

"Then I'll go to bed directly after supper."

She went into the boudoir again, and Cynthia stared after her.

"Goodness gracious! I wonder what's up?" she said to Lawrence.

He did not seem to have heard her, for without a word he turned on his heel and went out of the house.

I suggested a quick game of tennis before supper and, Cynthia agreeing, I ran upstairs to fetch my racquet.

Mrs. Cavendish was coming down the stairs. It may have been my fancy, but she, too, was looking odd and disturbed.

"Had a good walk with Dr. Bauerstein?" I asked, trying to appear as indifferent as I could.

"I didn't go," she replied abruptly. "Where is Mrs. Inglethorp?"

"In the boudoir."

Her hand clenched itself on the banisters, then she seemed to nerve herself for some encounter, and went rapidly past me down the stairs across the hall to the boudoir, the door of which she shut behind her.

As I ran out to the tennis court a few moments later, I had to pass the open boudoir window, and was unable to help overhearing the following scrap of dialogue. Mary Cavendish was saying in the voice of a woman desperately controlling herself:

"Then you won't show it to me?"

To which Mrs. Inglethorp replied:

"My dear Mary, it has nothing to do with that matter."

"Then show it to me."

"I tell you it is not what you imagine. It does not concern you in the least."

To which Mary Cavendish replied, with a rising bitterness:

"Of course, I might have known you would shield him."

Cynthia was waiting for me, and greeted me eagerly with:

"I say! There's been the most awful row! I've got it all out of Dorcas."

"What kind of a row?"

"Between Aunt Emily and *him*. I do hope she's found him out at last!"

"Was Dorcas there, then?"

"Of course not. She 'happened to be near the door'. It was a real old bust-up. I do wish I knew what it was all about."

I thought of Mrs. Raikes's gipsy face, and Evelyn Howard's warnings, but wisely decided to hold my peace, whilst Cynthia exhausted every possible hypothesis, and cheerfully hoped, "Aunt Emily will send him away, and will never speak to him again."

I was anxious to get hold of John, but he was nowhere to be seen. Evidently something very momentous had occurred that afternoon. I tried to forget the few words I had overheard; but, do what I would, I could not dismiss them altogether from my mind. What was Mary Cavendish's concern in the matter?

Mr. Inglethorp was in the drawing-room when I came down to supper. His face was impassive as ever, and the strange unreality of the man struck me afresh.

Mrs. Inglethorp came down last. She still looked agitated, and during the meal there was a somewhat constrained silence. Inglethorp was unusually quiet. As a rule, he surrounded his wife with little attentions, placing a cushion at her back, and altogether playing the part of the devoted husband. Immediately after supper, Mrs. Inglethorp retired to her boudoir again.

"Send my coffee in here, Mary," she called. "I've just five minutes to catch the post."

Cynthia and I went and sat by the open window in the drawing-room. Mary Cavendish brought our coffee to us. She seemed excited.

"Do you young people want lights, or do you enjoy the twilight?" she asked. "Will you take Mrs. Inglethorp her coffee, Cynthia? I will pour it out."

"Do not trouble, Mary," said Inglethorp. "I will take it to Emily." He poured it out, and went out of the room carrying it carefully.

Lawrence followed him, and Mrs. Cavendish sat down by us.

We three sat for some time in silence. It was a glorious night, hot and still. Mrs. Cavendish fanned herself gently with a palm leaf.

"It's almost too hot," she murmured. "We shall have a thunderstorm."

Alas, that these harmonious moments can never endure! My paradise was rudely shattered by the sound of a well known, and heartily disliked, voice in the hall.

"Dr. Bauerstein!" exclaimed Cynthia. "What a funny time to come."

I glanced jealously at Mary Cavendish, but she seemed quite undisturbed, the delicate pallor of her cheeks did not vary.

In a few moments, Alfred Inglethorp had ushered the doctor in, the latter laughing, and protesting that he was in no fit state for a drawing-room. In truth, he presented a sorry spectacle, being literally plastered with mud.

"What have you been doing, doctor?" cried Mrs. Cavendish.

"I must make my apologies," said the doctor. "I did not really mean to come in, but Mr. Inglethorp insisted."

"Well, Bauerstein, you are in a plight," said John, strolling in from the hall. "Have some coffee, and tell us what you have been up to."

"Thank you, I will." He laughed rather ruefully, as he described how he had discovered a very rare species of fern in an inaccessible place, and in his efforts to obtain it had lost his footing, and slipped ignominiously into a neighbouring pond.

"The sun soon dried me off," he added, "but I'm afraid my

appearance is very disreputable."

At this juncture, Mrs. Inglethorp called to Cynthia from the hall, and the girl ran out.

"Just carry up my despatch-case, will you, dear? I'm going to bed."

The door into the hall was a wide one. I had risen when Cynthia did, John was close by me. There were therefore three witnesses who could swear that Mrs. Inglethorp was carrying her coffee, as yet untasted, in her hand.

My evening was utterly and entirely spoilt by the presence of Dr. Bauerstein. It seemed to me the man would never go. He rose at last, however, and I breathed a sigh of relief.

"I'll walk down to the village with you," said Mr. Inglethorp. "I must see our agent over those estate accounts." He turned to John. "No one need sit up. I will take the latch-key."

THREE
The Night of the Tragedy

T o make this part of my story clear, I append the following plan of the first floor of Styles. The servants' rooms are reached through the door B. They have no communication with the right wing, where the Inglethorps' rooms were situated.

It seemed to be the middle of the night when I was awakened by Lawrence Cavendish. He had a candle in his hand, and the agitation of his face told me at once that something was seriously wrong.

"What's the matter?" I asked, sitting up in bed, and trying to collect my scattered thoughts.

"We are afraid my mother is very ill. She seems to be having some kind of fit. Unfortunately she has locked herself in."

"I'll come at once."

I sprang out of bed; and, pulling on a dressing-gown, followed Lawrence along the passage and the gallery to the right wing of the house.

John Cavendish joined us, and one or two of the servants were standing round in a state of awe-stricken excitement. Lawrence turned to his brother.

"What do you think we had better do?"

Never, I thought, had his indecision of character been more apparent.

John rattled the handle of Mrs. Inglethorp's door violently, but with no effect. It was obviously locked or bolted on the inside. The whole household was aroused by now. The most alarming sounds were audible from the interior of the room. Clearly something must be done.

"Try going through Mr. Inglethorp's room, sir," cried Dorcas. "Oh, the poor mistress!"

Suddenly I realized that Alfred Inglethorp was not with us— that he alone had given no sign of his presence. John opened the door of his room. It was pitch dark, but Lawrence was following with the candle, and by its feeble light we saw that the bed had not been slept in, and that there was no sign of the room having been occupied.

We went straight to the connecting door. That, too, was locked or bolted on the inside. What was to be done?

"Oh, dear, sir," cried Dorcas, wringing her hands, "what ever shall we do?"

"We must try and break the door in, I suppose. It'll be a tough job, though. Here, let one of the maids go down and wake Baily and tell him to go for Dr. Wilkins at once. Now then, we'll have a try at the door. Half a moment, though, isn't there a door into Miss Cynthia's rooms?"

"Yes, sir, but that's always bolted. It's never been undone."

"Well, we might just see."

He ran rapidly down the corridor to Cynthia's room. Mary Cavendish was there, shaking the girl—who must have been an unusually sound sleeper—and trying to wake her.

In a moment or two he was back.

"No good. That's bolted too. We must break in the door. I think this one is a shade less solid than the one in the passage."

We strained and heaved together. The framework of the door was solid, and for a long time it resisted our efforts, but at last we felt it give beneath our weight, and finally, with a resounding crash, it was burst open.

We stumbled in together, Lawrence still holding his candle. Mrs. Inglethorp was lying on the bed, her whole form agitated by violent convulsions, in one of which she must have overturned the table beside her. As we entered, however, her limbs relaxed, and she fell back upon the pillows.

John strode across the room, and lit the gas. Turning to Annie, one of the housemaids, he sent her downstairs to the dining-room for brandy. Then he went across to his mother whilst I unbolted the door that gave on the corridor.

I turned to Lawrence, to suggest that I had better leave them now that there was no further need of my services, but the words were frozen on my lips. Never have I seen such a ghastly look on any man's face. He was white as chalk, the candle he held in his shaking hand was sputtering onto the carpet, and his eyes, petrified with terror, or some such kindred emotion, stared fixedly over my head at a point on the further wall. It was as though he had seen something that turned him to stone. I instinctively followed the direction of his eyes, but I could see nothing unusual. The still feebly flickering ashes in the grate, and the row of prim ornaments on the mantelpiece, were surely harmless enough.

The violence of Mrs. Inglethorp's attack seemed to be passing. She was able to speak in short gasps.

"Better now—very sudden—stupid of me—to lock myself in."

A shadow fell on the bed and, looking up, I saw Mary Cavendish standing near the door with her arm around Cynthia. She seemed to be supporting the girl, who looked utterly dazed and unlike herself. Her face was heavily flushed, and she yawned repeatedly.

"Poor Cynthia is quite frightened," said Mrs. Cavendish in a low clear voice. She herself, I noticed, was dressed in her white land smock. Then it must be later than I thought. I saw that a faint streak of daylight was showing through the curtains of the windows, and that the clock on the mantelpiece pointed to close upon five o'clock.

A strangled cry from the bed startled me. A fresh access of pain seized the unfortunate old lady. The convulsions were of a violence terrible to behold. Everything was confusion. We thronged round her, powerless to help or alleviate. A final convulsion lifted her from the bed, until she appeared to rest upon her head and her heels, with her body arched in an extraordinary manner. In vain Mary and John tried to administer more brandy. The moments flew. Again the body arched itself in that peculiar fashion.

At that moment, Dr. Bauerstein pushed his way authoritatively into the room. For one instant he stopped dead, staring at the figure on the bed, and, at the same instant, Mrs. Inglethorp cried out in a strangled voice, her eyes fixed on the doctor:

"Alfred—Alfred——" Then she fell back motionless on the pillows.

With a stride, the doctor reached the bed, and seizing her arms worked them energetically, applying what I knew to be artificial respiration. He issued a few short sharp orders to the servants. An imperious wave of his hand drove us all to the door. We watched him, fascinated, though I think we all knew in our hearts that it was too late, and that nothing could be done now. I could see by the expression on his face that he himself had little hope.

THE MYSTERIOUS AFFAIR AT STYLES

Finally he abandoned his task, shaking his head gravely. At that moment, we heard footsteps outside, and Dr. Wilkins, Mrs. Inglethorp's own doctor, a portly, fussy little man, came bustling in.

In a few words Dr. Bauerstein explained how he had happened to be passing the lodge gates as the car came out, and had run up to the house as fast as he could, whilst the car went on to fetch Dr. Wilkins. With a faint gesture of the hand, he indicated the figure on the bed.

"Ve—ry sad. Ve—ry sad," murmured Dr. Wilkins. "Poor dear lady. Always did far too much—far too much—against my advice. I warned her. Her heart was far from strong. 'Take it easy,' I said to her, 'Take—it—easy'. But no—her zeal for good works was too great. Nature rebelled. Na—ture—re—belled."

Dr. Bauerstein, I noticed, was watching the local doctor narrowly. He still kept his eyes fixed on him as he spoke.

"The convulsions were of a peculiar violence, Dr. Wilkins. I am sorry you were not here in time to witness them. They were quite—tetanic in character."

"Ah!" said Dr. Wilkins wisely.

"I should like to speak to you in private," said Dr. Bauerstein. He turned to John. "You do not object?"

"Certainly not."

We all trooped out into the corridor, leaving the two doctors alone, and I heard the key turned in the lock behind us.

We went slowly down the stairs. I was violently excited. I have a certain talent for deduction, and Dr. Bauerstein's manner had started a flock of wild surmises in my mind. Mary Cavendish laid her hand upon my arm.

"What is it? Why did Dr. Bauerstein seem so—peculiar?"

I looked at her.

"Do you know what I think?"

"What?"

"Listen!" I looked round, the others were out of earshot. I

lowered my voice to a whisper. "I believe she has been poisoned! I'm certain Dr. Bauerstein suspects it."

"*What?*" She shrank against the wall, the pupils of her eyes dilating wildly. Then, with a sudden cry that startled me, she cried out: "No, no—not that—not that!" And breaking from me, fled up the stairs. I followed her, afraid that she was going to faint. I found her leaning against the bannisters, deadly pale. She waved me away impatiently.

"No, no—leave me. I'd rather be alone. Let me just be quiet for a minute or two. Go down to the others."

I obeyed her reluctantly. John and Lawrence were in the dining-room. I joined them. We were all silent, but I suppose I voiced the thoughts of us all when I at last broke it by saying:

"Where is Mr. Inglethorp?"

John shook his head.

"He's not in the house."

Our eyes met. Where *was* Alfred Inglethorp? His absence was strange and inexplicable. I remembered Mrs. Inglethorp's dying words. What lay beneath them? What more could she have told us, if she had had time?

At last we heard the doctors descending the stairs. Dr. Wilkins was looking important and excited, and trying to conceal an inward exultation under a manner of decorous calm. Dr. Bauerstein remained in the background, his grave bearded face unchanged. Dr. Wilkins was the spokesman for the two. He addressed himself to John:

"Mr. Cavendish, I should like your consent to a post-mortem."

"Is that necessary?" asked John gravely. A spasm of pain crossed his face.

"Absolutely," said Dr. Bauerstein.

"You mean by that——?"

"That neither Dr. Wilkins nor myself could give a death certificate under the circumstances."

John bent his head.

"In that case, I have no alternative but to agree."

"Thank you," said Dr. Wilkins briskly. "We propose that it should take place to-morrow night—or rather to-night." And he glanced at the daylight. "Under the circumstances, I am afraid an inquest can hardly be avoided—these formalities are necessary, but I beg that you won't distress yourselves."

There was a pause, and then Dr. Bauerstein drew two keys from his pocket, and handed them to John.

"These are the keys of the two rooms. I have locked them and, in my opinion, they would be better kept locked for the present."

The doctors then departed.

I had been turning over an idea in my head, and I felt that the moment had now come to broach it. Yet I was a little chary of doing so. John, I knew, had a horror of any kind of publicity, and was an easygoing optimist, who preferred never to meet trouble half-way. It might be difficult to convince him of the soundness of my plan. Lawrence, on the other hand, being less conventional, and having more imagination, I felt I might count upon as an ally. There was no doubt that the moment had come for me to take the lead.

"John," I said, "I am going to ask you something."

"Well?"

"You remember my speaking of my friend Poirot? The Belgian who is here? He has been a most famous detective."

"Yes."

"I want you to let me call him in—to investigate this matter."

"What—now? Before the post-mortem?"

"Yes, time is an advantage if—if—there has been foul play."

"Rubbish!" cried Lawrence angrily. "In my opinion the whole thing is a mare's nest of Bauerstein's! Wilkins hadn't an idea of such a thing, until Bauerstein put it into his head. But, like all specialists, Bauerstein's got a bee in his bonnet. Poisons are his hobby, so of course he sees them everywhere."

I confess that I was surprised by Lawrence's attitude. He was so seldom vehement about anything.

John hesitated.

"I can't feel as you do, Lawrence," he said at last. "I'm inclined to give Hastings a free hand, though I should prefer to wait a bit. We don't want any unnecessary scandal."

"No, no," I cried eagerly, "you need have no fear of that. Poirot is discretion itself."

"Very well, then, have it your own way. I leave it in your hands. Though, if it is as we suspect, it seems a clear enough case. God forgive me if I am wronging him!"

I looked at my watch. It was six o'clock. I determined to lose no time.

Five minutes' delay, however, I allowed myself. I spent it in ransacking the library until I discovered a medical book which gave a description of strychnine poisoning.

FOUR

Poirot Investigates

The house which the Belgians occupied in the village was quite close to the park gates. One could save time by taking a narrow path through the long grass, which cut off the detours of the winding drive. So I, accordingly, went that way. I had nearly reached the lodge, when my attention was arrested by the running figure of a man approaching me. It was Mr. Inglethorp. Where had he been? How did he intend to explain his absence?

He accosted me eagerly.

"My God! This is terrible! My poor wife! I have only just heard."

"Where have you been?" I asked.

"Denby kept me late last night. It was one o'clock before we'd finished. Then I found that I'd forgotten the latch-key after all. I didn't want to arouse the household, so Denby gave me a bed."

"How did you hear the news?" I asked.

"Wilkins knocked Denby up to tell him. My poor Emily! She was so self-sacrificing—such a noble character. She over-taxed her strength."

A wave of revulsion swept over me. What a consummate hypocrite the man was!

"I must hurry on," I said, thankful that he did not ask me whither I was bound.

In a few minutes I was knocking at the door of Leastways Cottage.

Getting no answer, I repeated my summons impatiently. A window above me was cautiously opened, and Poirot himself looked out.

He gave an exclamation of surprise at seeing me. In a few brief words, I explained the tragedy that had occurred, and that I wanted his help.

"Wait, my friend, I will let you in, and you shall recount to me the affair whilst I dress."

In a few moments he had unbarred the door, and I followed him up to his room. There he installed me in a chair, and I related the whole story, keeping back nothing, and omitting no circumstance, however insignificant, whilst he himself made a careful and deliberate toilet.

I told him of my awakening, of Mrs. Inglethorp's dying words, of her husband's absence, of the quarrel the day before, of the scrap of conversation between Mary and her mother-in-law that I had overheard, of the former quarrel between Mrs. Inglethorp and Evelyn Howard, and of the latter's innuendoes.

I was hardly as clear as I could wish. I repeated myself several times, and occasionally had to go back to some detail that I had forgotten. Poirot smiled kindly on me.

"The mind is confused? Is it not so? Take time, *mon ami*. You are agitated; you are excited—it is but natural. Presently, when we are calmer, we will arrange the facts, neatly, each in his proper place. We will examine—and reject. Those of importance we will put on one side; those of no importance, pouf!"—he screwed up his cherub-like face, and puffed comically enough—"blow them away!"

"That's all very well," I objected, "but how are you going to decide what is important, and what isn't? That always seems the difficulty to me."

Poirot shook his head energetically. He was now arranging his moustache with exquisite care.

"Not so. *Voyons!* One fact leads to another—so we continue. Does the next fit in with that? *A merveille!* Good! We can proceed. This next little fact—no! Ah, that is curious! There is something missing—a link in the chain that is not there. We examine. We search. And that little curious fact, that possibly paltry little detail that will not tally, we put it here!" He made an extravagant gesture with his hand. "It is significant! It is tremendous!"

"Y—es——"

"Ah!" Poirot shook his forefinger so fiercely at me that I quailed before it. "Beware! Peril to the detective who says: 'It is so small—it does not matter. It will not agree. I will forget it.' That way lies confusion! Everything matters."

"I know. You always told me that. That's why I have gone into all the details of this thing whether they seemed to me relevant or not."

"And I am pleased with you. You have a good memory, and you have given me the facts faithfully. Of the order in which you present them, I say nothing—truly, it is deplorable! But I make allowances—you are upset. To that I attribute the circumstance that you have omitted one fact of paramount importance."

"What is that?" I asked.

"You have not told me if Mrs. Inglethorp ate well last night."

I stared at him. Surely the war had affected the little man's brain. He was carefully engaged in brushing his coat before putting it on, and seemed wholly engrossed in the task.

"I don't remember," I said. "And, anyway, I don't see——"

"You do not see? But it is of the first importance."

"I can't see why," I said, rather nettled. "As far as I can remember, she didn't eat much. She was obviously upset, and it had taken her appetite away. That was only natural."

"Yes," said Poirot thoughtfully, "it was only natural."

He opened a drawer, and took out a small despatch-case, then turned to me.

"Now I am ready. We will proceed to the château, and study

33

matters on the spot. Excuse me, *mon ami*, you dressed in haste, and your tie is on one side. Permit me." With a deft gesture, he rearranged it.

"*Ça y est!* Now, shall we start?"

We hurried up the village, and turned in at the lodge gates. Poirot stopped for a moment, and gazed sorrowfully over the beautiful expanse of park, still glittering with morning dew.

"So beautiful, so beautiful, and yet, the poor family, plunged in sorrow, prostrated with grief."

He looked at me keenly as he spoke, and I was aware that I reddened under his prolonged gaze.

Was the family prostrated by grief? Was the sorrow at Mrs. Inglethorp's death so great? I realized that there was an emotional lack in the atmosphere. The dead woman had not the gift of commanding love. Her death was a shock and a distress, but she would not be passionately regretted.

Poirot seemed to follow my thoughts. He nodded his head gravely.

"No, you are right," he said, "it is not as though there was a blood tie. She has been kind and generous to these Cavendishes, but she was not their own mother. Blood tells—always remember that—blood tells."

"Poirot," I said, "I wish you would tell me why you wanted to know if Mrs. Inglethorp ate well last night? I have been turning it over in my mind, but I can't see how it has anything to do with the matter?"

He was silent for a minute or two as we walked along, but finally he said:

"I do not mind telling you—though, as you know, it is not my habit to explain until the end is reached. The present contention is that Mrs. Inglethorp died of strychnine poisoning, presumably administered in her coffee."

"Yes?"

"Well, what time was the coffee served?"

"About eight o'clock."

"Therefore she drank it between then and half-past eight—certainly not much later. Well, strychnine is a fairly rapid poison. Its effects would be felt very soon, probably in about an hour. Yet, in Mrs. Inglethorp's case, the symptoms do not manifest themselves until five o'clock the next morning: nine hours! But a heavy meal, taken at about the same time as the poison, might retard its effects, though hardly to that extent. Still, it is a possibility to be taken into account. But, according to you, she ate very little for supper, and yet the symptoms do not develop until early the next morning! Now that is a curious circumstance, my friend. Something may arise at the autopsy to explain it. In the meantime, remember it."

As we neared the house, John came out and met us. His face looked weary and haggard.

"This is a very dreadful business, Monsieur Poirot," he said. "Hastings has explained to you that we are anxious for no publicity?"

"I comprehend perfectly."

"You see, it is only suspicion so far. We have nothing to go upon."

"Precisely. It is a matter of precaution only."

John turned to me, taking out his cigarette-case, and lighting a cigarette as he did so.

"You know that fellow Inglethorp is back?"

"Yes. I met him."

John flung the match into an adjacent flower bed, a proceeding which was too much for Poirot's feelings. He retrieved it, and buried it neatly.

"It's jolly difficult to know how to treat him."

"That difficulty will not exist long," pronounced Poirot quietly.

John looked puzzled, not quite understanding the portent of this cryptic saying. He handed the two keys which Dr. Bauerstein had given him to me.

"Show Monsieur Poirot everything he wants to see."

"The rooms are locked?" asked Poirot.

"Dr. Bauerstein considered it advisable."

Poirot nodded thoughtfully.

"Then he is very sure. Well, that simplifies matters for us."

We went up together to the room of the tragedy. For convenience I append a plan of the room and the principal articles of furniture in it.

MRS. INGLETHORP'S BEDROOM
A.—Door into Passage
B.—Door into Mr. Inglethorp's Room.
C.—Door into Cynthia's Room

Poirot locked the door on the inside, and proceeded to a minute inspection of the room. He darted from one object to the other with the agility of a grasshopper. I remained by the door, fearing to obliterate any clues. Poirot, however, did not seem grateful to me for my forbearance.

"What have you, my friend," he cried, "that you remain there like—how do you say it?—ah, yes, the stuck pig?"

I explained that I was afraid of obliterating any foot-marks.

"Foot-marks? But what an idea! There has already been practically an army in the room! What foot-marks are we likely to find?

No, come here and aid me in my search. I will put down my little case until I need it."

He did so, on the round table by the window, but it was an ill-advised proceeding; for, the top of it being loose, it tilted up, and precipitated the despatch-case on the floor.

"*Eh voilà une table!*" cried Poirot. "Ah, my friend, one may live in a big house and yet have no comfort."

After which piece of moralizing, he resumed his search.

A small purple despatch-case, with a key in the lock, on the writing-table, engaged his attention for some time. He took out the key from the lock, and passed it to me to inspect. I saw nothing peculiar, however. It was an ordinary key of the Yale type, with a bit of twisted wire through the handle.

Next, he examined the framework of the door we had broken in, assuring himself that the bolt had really been shot. Then he went to the door opposite leading into Cynthia's room. That door was also bolted, as I had stated. However, he went to the length of unbolting it, and opening and shutting it several times; this he did with the utmost precaution against making any noise. Suddenly something in the bolt itself seemed to rivet his attention. He examined it carefully, and then, nimbly whipping out a pair of small forceps from his case, he drew out some minute particle which he carefully sealed up in a tiny envelope.

On the chest of drawers there was a tray with a spirit lamp and a small saucepan on it. A small quantity of a dark fluid remained in the saucepan, and an empty cup and saucer that had been drunk out of stood near it.

I wondered how I could have been so unobservant as to overlook this. Here was a clue worth having. Poirot delicately dipped his finger into liquid, and tasted it gingerly. He made a grimace.

"Cocoa—with—I think—rum in it."

He passed on to the debris on the floor, where the table by the bed had been overturned. A reading-lamp, some books, matches, a bunch of keys, and the crushed fragments of a coffee-cup lay scattered about.

"Ah, this is curious," said Poirot.

"I must confess that I see nothing particularly curious about it."

"You do not? Observe the lamp—the chimney is broken in two places; they lie there as they fell. But see, the coffee-cup is absolutely smashed to powder."

"Well," I said wearily, "I suppose someone must have stepped on it."

"Exactly," said Poirot, in an odd voice. "Someone stepped on it."

He rose from his knees, and walked slowly across to the mantelpiece, where he stood abstractedly fingering the ornaments, and straightening them—a trick of his when he was agitated.

"*Mon ami*," he said, turning to me, "somebody stepped on that cup, grinding it to powder, and the reason they did so was either because it contained strychnine or—which is far more serious— because it did not contain strychnine!"

I made no reply. I was bewildered, but I knew that it was no good asking him to explain. In a moment or two he roused himself, and went on with his investigations. He picked up the bunch of keys from the floor, and twirling them round in his fingers finally selected one, very bright and shining, which he tried in the lock of the purple despatch-case. It fitted, and he opened the box, but after a moment's hesitation, closed and relocked it, and slipped the bunch of keys, as well as the key that had originally stood in the lock, into his own pocket.

"I have no authority to go through these papers. But it should be done—at once!"

He then made a very careful examination of the drawers of the wash-stand. Crossing the room to the left-hand window, a round stain, hardly visible on the dark brown carpet, seemed to interest him particularly. He went down on his knees, examining it minutely—even going so far as to smell it.

38

Finally, he poured a few drops of the cocoa into a test tube, sealing it up carefully. His next proceeding was to take out a little notebook.

"We have found in this room," he said, writing busily, "six points of interest. Shall I enumerate them, or will you?"

"Oh, you," I replied hastily.

"Very well, then. One, a coffee-cup that has been ground into powder; two, a despatch-case with a key in the lock; three, a stain on the floor."

"That may have been done some time ago," I interrupted.

"No, for it is still perceptibly damp and smells of coffee. Four, a fragment of some dark green fabric—only a thread or two, but recognizable."

"Ah!" I cried. "That was what you sealed up in the envelope."

"Yes. It may turn out to be a piece of one of Mrs. Inglethorp's own dresses, and quite unimportant. We shall see. Five, *this*!" With a dramatic gesture, he pointed to a large splash of candle grease on the floor by the writing-table. "It must have been done since yesterday, otherwise a good housemaid would have at once removed it with blotting-paper and a hot iron. One of my best hats once—but that is not to the point."

"It was very likely done last night. We were very agitated. Or perhaps Mrs. Inglethorp herself dropped her candle."

"You brought only one candle into the room?"

"Yes. Lawrence Cavendish was carrying it. But he was very upset. He seemed to see something over here"—I indicated the mantelpiece—"that absolutely paralysed him."

"That is interesting," said Poirot quickly. "Yes, it is suggestive"—his eye sweeping the whole length of the wall—"but it was not his candle that made this great patch, for you perceive that this is white grease; whereas Monsieur Lawrence's candle, which is still on the dressing-table, is pink. On the other hand, Mrs. Inglethorp had no candlestick in the room, only a reading-lamp."

"Then," I said, "what do you deduce?"

To which my friend only made a rather irritating reply, urging me to use my own natural faculties.

"And the sixth point?" I asked. "I suppose it is the sample of cocoa."

"No," said Poirot thoughtfully. "I might have included that in the six, but I did not. No, the sixth point I will keep to myself for the present."

He looked quickly round the room. "There is nothing more to be done here, I think, unless"—he stared earnestly and long at the dead ashes in the grate. "The fire burns—and it destroys. But by chance—there might be—let us see!"

Deftly, on hands and knees, he began to sort the ashes from the grate into the fender, handling them with the greatest caution. Suddenly, he gave a faint exclamation.

"The forceps, Hastings!"

I quickly handed them to him, and with skill he extracted a small piece of half charred paper.

"There, *mon ami!*" he cried. "What do you think of that?"

I scrutinized the fragment. This is an exact reproduction of it:—

I was puzzled. It was unusually thick, quite unlike ordinary notepaper. Suddenly an idea struck me.

"Poirot!" I cried. "This is a fragment of a will!"

"Exactly."

I looked up at him sharply.

"You are not surprised?"

"No," he said gravely, "I expected it."

I relinquished the piece of paper, and watched him put it

away in his case, with the same methodical care that he bestowed on everything. My brain was in a whirl. What was this complication of a will? Who had destroyed it? The person who had left the candle grease on the floor? Obviously. But how had anyone gained admission? All the doors had been bolted on the inside.

"Now, my friend," said Poirot briskly, "we will go. I should like to ask a few questions of the parlourmaid—Dorcas, her name is, is it not?"

We passed through Alfred Inglethorp's room, and Poirot delayed long enough to make a brief but fairly comprehensive examination of it. We went out through that door, locking both it and that of Mrs. Inglethorp's room as before.

I took him down to the boudoir which he had expressed a wish to see, and went myself in search of Dorcas.

When I returned with her, however, the boudoir was empty.

"Poirot," I cried, "where are you?"

"I am here, my friend."

He had stepped outside the French window, and was standing, apparently lost in admiration, before the various shaped flower beds.

"Admirable!" he murmured. "Admirable! What symmetry! Observe that crescent; and those diamonds—their neatness rejoices the eye. The spacing of the plants, also, is perfect. It has been recently done; is it not so?"

"Yes, I believe they were at it yesterday afternoon. But come in—Dorcas is here."

"Eh bien, eh bien! Do not grudge me a moment's satisfaction of the eye."

"Yes, but this affair is more important."

"And how do you know that these fine begonias are not of equal importance?"

I shrugged my shoulders. There was really no arguing with him if he chose to take that line.

"You do not agree? But such things have been. Well, we will

41

come in and interview the brave Dorcas."

Dorcas was standing in the boudoir, her hands folded in front of her, and her grey hair rose in stiff waves under her white cap. She was the very model and picture of a good old-fashioned servant.

In her attitude towards Poirot, she was inclined to be suspicious, but he soon broke down her defences. He drew forward a chair.

"Pray be seated, mademoiselle."

"Thank you, sir."

"You have been with your mistress many years, is it not so?"

"Ten years, sir."

"That is a long time, and very faithful service. You were much attached to her, were you not?"

"She was a very good mistress to me, sir."

"Then you will not object to answering a few questions. I put them to you with Mr. Cavendish's full approval."

"Oh, certainly, sir."

"Then I will begin by asking you about the events of yesterday afternoon. Your mistress had a quarrel?"

"Yes, sir. But I don't know that I ought——" Dorcas hesitated.

Poirot looked at her keenly.

"My good Dorcas, it is necessary that I should know every detail of that quarrel as fully as possible. Do not think that you are betraying your mistress's secrets. Your mistress lies dead, and it is necessary that we should know all—if we are to avenge her. Nothing can bring her back to life, but we do hope, if there has been foul play, to bring the murderer to justice."

"Amen to that," said Dorcas fiercely. "And, naming no names, there's *one* in this house that none of us could ever abide! And an ill day it was when first *he* darkened the threshold."

Poirot waited for her indignation to subside, and then, resuming his business-like tone, he asked:

"Now, as to this quarrel? What is the first you heard of it?"

"Well, sir, I happened to be going along the hall outside yesterday———"

"What time was that?"

"I couldn't say exactly, sir, but it wasn't tea-time by a long way. Perhaps four o'clock—or it may have been a bit later. Well, sir, as I said, I happened to be passing along, when I heard voices very loud and angry in here. I didn't exactly mean to listen, but—well, there it is. I stopped. The door was shut, but the mistress was speaking very sharp and clear, and I heard what she said quite plainly. 'You have lied to me, and deceived me,' she said. I didn't hear what Mr. Inglethorp replied. He spoke a good bit lower than she did—but she answered: 'How dare you? I have kept you and clothed you and fed you! You owe everything to me! And this is how you repay me! By bringing disgrace upon our name!' Again I didn't hear what he said, but she went on: 'Nothing that you can say will make any difference. I see my duty clearly. My mind is made up. You need not think that any fear of publicity, or scandal between husband and wife will deter me.' Then I thought I heard them coming out, so I went off quickly."

"You are sure it was Mr. Inglethorp's voice you heard?"

"Oh, yes, sir, whose else's could it be?"

"Well, what happened next?"

"Later, I came back to the hall; but it was all quiet. At five o'clock, Mrs. Inglethorp rang the bell and told me to bring her a cup of tea—nothing to eat—to the boudoir. She was looking dreadful—so white and upset. 'Dorcas,' she says, 'I've had a great shock.' 'I'm sorry for that, m'm,' I says. 'You'll feel better after a nice hot cup of tea, m'm.' She had something in her hand. I don't know if it was a letter, or just a piece of paper, but it had writing on it, and she kept staring at it, almost as if she couldn't believe what was written there. She whispered to herself, as though she had forgotten I was there: 'These few words—and everything's changed.' And then she says to me: 'Never trust a man, Dorcas, they're not worth it!' I hurried off, and got her a good strong cup of tea, and she thanked me, and

43

said she'd feel better when she'd drunk it. 'I don't know what to do,' she says. 'Scandal between husband and wife is a dreadful thing, Dorcas. I'd rather hush it up if I could.' Mrs. Cavendish came in just then, so she didn't say any more."

"She still had the letter, or whatever it was, in her hand?"

"Yes, sir."

"What would she be likely to do with it afterwards?"

"Well, I don't know, sir, I expect she would lock it up in that purple case of hers."

"Is that where she usually kept important papers?"

"Yes, sir. She brought it down with her every morning, and took it up every night."

"When did she lose the key of it?"

"She missed it yesterday at lunch-time, sir, and told me to look carefully for it. She was very much put out about it."

"But she had a duplicate key?"

"Oh, yes, sir."

Dorcas was looking very curiously at him and, to tell the truth, so was I. What was all this about a lost key? Poirot smiled.

"Never mind, Dorcas, it is my business to know things. Is this the key that was lost?" He drew from his pocket the key that he had found in the lock of the despatch-case upstairs.

Dorcas's eyes looked as though they would pop out of her head.

"That's it, sir, right enough. But where did you find it? I looked everywhere for it."

"Ah, but you see it was not in the same place yesterday as it was to-day. Now, to pass to another subject, had your mistress a dark green dress in her wardrobe?"

Dorcas was rather startled by the unexpected question.

"No, sir."

"Are you quite sure?"

"Oh, yes, sir."

"Has anyone else in the house got a green dress?"

Dorcas reflected.

"Miss Cynthia has a green evening dress."

"Light or dark green?"

"A light green, sir; a sort of chiffon, they call it."

"Ah, that is not what I want. And nobody else has anything green?"

"No, sir—not that I know of."

Poirot's face did not betray a trace of whether he was disappointed or otherwise. He merely remarked:

"Good, we will leave that and pass on. Have you any reason to believe that your mistress was likely to take a sleeping powder last night?"

"Not *last* night, sir, I know she didn't."

"Why do you know so positively?"

"Because the box was empty. She took the last one two days ago, and she didn't have any more made up."

"You are quite sure of that?"

"Positive, sir."

"Then that is cleared up! By the way, your mistress didn't ask you to sign any paper yesterday?"

"To sign a paper? No, sir."

"When Mr. Hastings and Mr. Lawrence came in yesterday evening, they found your mistress busy writing letters. I suppose you can give me no idea to whom these letters were addressed?"

"I'm afraid I couldn't, sir. I was out in the evening. Perhaps Annie could tell you, though she's a careless girl. Never cleared the coffee-cups away last night. That's what happens when I'm not here to look after things."

Poirot lifted his hand.

"Since they have been left, Dorcas, leave them a little longer, I pray you. I should like to examine them."

"Very well, sir."

"What time did you go out last evening?"

"About six o'clock, sir."

45

"Thank you, Dorcas, that is all I have to ask you." He rose and strolled to the window. "I have been admiring these flower beds. How many gardeners are employed here, by the way?"

"Only three now, sir. Five, we had, before the war, when it was kept as a gentleman's place should be. I wish you could have seen it then, sir. A fair sight it was. But now there's only old Manning, and young William, and a new-fashioned woman gardener in breeches and such-like. Ah, these are dreadful times!"

"The good times will come again, Dorcas. At least, we hope so. Now, will you send Annie to me here?"

"Yes, sir. Thank you, sir."

"How did you know that Mrs. Inglethorp took sleeping powders?" I asked, in lively curiosity, as Dorcas left the room. "And about the lost key and the duplicate?"

"One thing at a time. As to the sleeping powders, I knew by this." He suddenly produced a small cardboard box, such as chemists use for powders.

"Where did you find it?"

"In the wash-stand drawer in Mrs. Inglethorp's bedroom. It was Number Six of my catalogue."

"But I suppose, as the last powder was taken two days ago, it is not of much importance?"

"Probably not, but do you notice anything that strikes you as peculiar about this box?"

I examined it closely.

"No, I can't say that I do."

"Look at the label."

I read the label carefully: "'One powder to be taken at bedtime, if required. Mrs. Inglethorp.' No, I see nothing unusual."

"Not the fact that there is no chemist's name?"

"Ah!" I exclaimed. "To be sure, that is odd!"

"Have you ever known a chemist to send out a box like that, without his printed name?"

"No, I can't say that I have."

I was becoming quite excited, but Poirot damped my ardour by remarking:

"Yet the explanation is quite simple. So do not intrigue yourself, my friend."

An audible creaking proclaimed the approach of Annie, so I had no time to reply.

Annie was a fine, strapping girl, and was evidently labouring under intense excitement, mingled with a certain ghoulish enjoyment of the tragedy.

Poirot came to the point at once, with a business-like briskness.

"I sent for you, Annie, because I thought you might be able to tell me something about the letters Mrs. Inglethorp wrote last night. How many were there? And can you tell me any of the names and addresses?"

Annie considered.

"There were four letters, sir. One was to Miss Howard, and one was to Mr. Wells, the lawyer, and the other two I don't think I remember, sir—oh, yes, one was to Ross's, the caterers in Tadminster. The other one, I don't remember."

"Think," urged Poirot.

Annie racked her brains in vain.

"I'm sorry, sir, but it's clean gone. I don't think I can have noticed it."

"It does not matter," said Poirot, not betraying any sign of disappointment. "Now I want to ask you about something else. There is a saucepan in Mrs. Inglethorp's room with some cocoa in it. Did she have that every night?"

"Yes, sir, it was put in her room every evening, and she warmed it up in the night—whenever she fancied it."

"What was it? Plain cocoa?"

"Yes, sir, made with milk, with a teaspoonful of sugar, and two teaspoonfuls of rum in it."

"Who took it to her room?"

47

"I did, sir."

"Always?"

"Yes, sir."

"At what time?"

"When I went to draw the curtains, as a rule, sir."

"Did you bring it straight up from the kitchen then?"

"No, sir, you see there's not much room on the gas stove, so cook used to make it early, before putting the vegetables on for supper. Then I used to bring it up, and put it on the table by the swing door, and take it into her room later."

"The swing door is in the left wing, is it not?"

"Yes, sir."

"And the table, is it on this side of the door, or on the farther—servants' side?"

"It's this side, sir."

"What time did you bring it up last night?"

"About quarter-past seven, I should say, sir."

"And when did you take it into Mrs. Inglethorp's room?"

"When I went to shut up, sir. About eight o'clock. Mrs. Inglethorp came up to bed before I'd finished."

"Then, between seven-fifteen and eight o'clock, the cocoa was standing on the table in the left wing?"

"Yes, sir." Annie had been growing redder and redder in the face, and now she blurted out unexpectedly:

"And if there *was* salt in it, sir, it wasn't me. I never took the salt near it."

"What makes you think there was salt in it?" asked Poirot.

"Seeing it on the tray, sir."

"You saw some salt on the tray?"

"Yes. Coarse kitchen salt, it looked. I never noticed it when I took the tray up, but when I came to take it into the mistress's room I saw it at once, and I suppose I ought to have taken it down again, and asked cook to make some fresh. But I was in a hurry, because Dorcas was out, and I thought maybe the cocoa itself was all right, and the salt had only gone on the tray. So I dusted it off with my apron, and took it in."

I had the utmost difficulty in controlling my excitement. Unknown to herself, Annie had provided us with an important piece of evidence. How she would have gaped if she had realized that her "coarse kitchen salt" was strychnine, one of the most deadly poisons known to mankind. I marvelled at Poirot's calm. His self-control was astonishing. I awaited his next question with impatience, but it disappointed me.

"When you went into Mrs. Inglethorp's room, was the door leading into Miss Cynthia's room bolted?"

"Oh! Yes, sir; it always was. It had never been opened."

"And the door into Mr. Inglethorp's room? Did you notice if that was bolted too?"

Annie hesitated.

"I couldn't rightly say, sir; it was shut but I couldn't say whether it was bolted or not."

"When you finally left the room, did Mrs. Inglethorp bolt the door after you?"

"No, sir, not then, but I expect she did later. She usually did lock it at night. The door into the passage, that is."

"Did you notice any candle grease on the floor when you did the room yesterday?"

"Candle grease? Oh, no, sir. Mrs. Inglethorp didn't have a candle, only a reading-lamp."

"Then, if there had been a large patch of candle grease on the floor, you think you would have been sure to have seen it?"

"Yes, sir, and I would have taken it out with a piece of blotting-paper and a hot iron."

Then Poirot repeated the question he had put to Dorcas:

"Did your mistress ever have a green dress?"

"No, sir."

"Nor a mantle, nor a cape, nor a—how do you call it?—a sports coat?"

"Not green, sir."

"Nor anyone else in the house?"

Annie reflected.

"No, sir."

"You are sure of that?"

"Quite sure."

"*Bien!* That is all I want to know. Thank you very much."

With a nervous giggle, Annie took herself creakingly out of the room. My pent-up excitement burst forth.

"Poirot," I cried, "I congratulate you! This is a great discovery."

"What is a great discovery?"

"Why, that it was the cocoa and not the coffee that was poisoned. That explains everything! Of course it did not take effect until the early morning, since the cocoa was only drunk in the middle of the night."

"So you think that the cocoa—mark well what I say, Hastings, the *cocoa*—contained strychnine?"

"Of course! That salt on the tray, what else could it have been?"

"It might have been salt," replied Poirot placidly.

I shrugged my shoulders. If he was going to take the matter that way, it was no good arguing with him. The idea crossed my mind, not for the first time, that poor old Poirot was growing old. Privately I thought it lucky that he had associated with him someone of a more receptive type of mind.

Poirot was surveying me with quietly twinkling eyes.

"You are not pleased with me, *mon ami?*"

"My dear Poirot," I said coldly, "it is not for me to dictate to you. You have a right to your own opinion, just as I have to mine."

"A most admirable sentiment," remarked Poirot, rising briskly to his feet. "Now I have finished with this room. By the way, whose is the smaller desk in the corner?"

"Mr. Inglethorp's."

"Ah!" He tried the roll top tentatively. "Locked. But perhaps one of Mrs. Inglethorp's keys would open it." He tried several, twisting and turning them with a practiced hand, and finally uttering an ejaculation of satisfaction. "*Voilà!* It is not the key, but it will open it at a pinch." He slid back the roll top, and ran a rapid eye over the neatly filed papers. To my surprise, he did not examine them, merely remarking approvingly as he relocked the desk: "Decidedly, he is a man of method, this Mr. Inglethorp!"

A "man of method" was, in Poirot's estimation, the highest praise that could be bestowed on any individual.

I felt that my friend was not what he had been as he rambled on disconnectedly:

"There were no stamps in his desk, but there might have been, eh, *mon ami?* There might have been? Yes"—his eyes wandered round the room—"this boudoir has nothing more to tell us. It did not yield much. Only this."

He pulled a crumpled envelope out of his pocket, and tossed it over to me. It was rather a curious document. A plain, dirty looking old envelope with a few words scrawled across it, apparently at random. The following is a facsimile of it.

51

FIVE

"It Isn't Strychnine, Is It?"

Where did you find this?" I asked Poirot, in lively curiosity.

"In the waste-paper basket. You recognise the handwriting?"

"Yes, it is Mrs. Inglethorp's. But what does it mean?"

Poirot shrugged his shoulders.

"I cannot say—but it is suggestive."

A wild idea flashed across me. Was it possible that Mrs. Inglethorp's mind was deranged? Had she some fantastic idea of demoniacal possession? And, if that were so, was it not also possible that she might have taken her own life?

I was about to expound these theories to Poirot, when his own words distracted me.

"Come," he said, "now to examine the coffee-cups!"

"My dear Poirot! What on earth is the good of that, now that we know about the cocoa?"

"Oh, *là là!* That miserable cocoa!" cried Poirot flippantly.

He laughed with apparent enjoyment, raising his arms to heaven in mock despair, in what I could not but consider the worst possible taste.

"And, anyway," I said, with increasing coldness, "as Mrs. Inglethorp took her coffee upstairs with her, I do not see what you expect to find, unless you consider it likely that we shall discover a packet of strychnine on the coffee tray!"

Poirot was sobered at once.

"Come, come, my friend," he said, slipping his arms through mine. "*Ne vous fâchez pas!* Allow me to interest myself in my coffee-cups, and I will respect your cocoa. There! Is it a bargain?"

He was so quaintly humorous that I was forced to laugh; and we went together to the drawing-room, where the coffee-cups and tray remained undisturbed as we had left them.

Poirot made me recapitulate the scene of the night before, listening very carefully, and verifying the position of the various cups.

"So Mrs. Cavendish stood by the tray—and poured out. Yes. Then she came across to the window where you sat with Mademoiselle Cynthia. Yes. Here are the three cups. And the cup on the mantelpiece, half drunk, that would be Mr. Lawrence Cavendish's. And the one on the tray?"

"John Cavendish's. I saw him put it down there."

"Good. One, two, three, four, five—but where, then, is the cup of Mr. Inglethorp?"

"He does not take coffee."

"Then all are accounted for. One moment, my friend."

With infinite care, he took a drop or two from the grounds in each cup, sealing them up in separate test tubes, tasting each in turn as he did so. His physiognomy underwent a curious change. An expression gathered there that I can only describe as half puzzled, and half relieved.

"*Bien!*" he said at last. "It is evident! I had an idea—but clearly I was mistaken. Yes, altogether I was mistaken. Yet it is strange. But no matter!"

And, with a characteristic shrug, he dismissed whatever it was that was worrying him from his mind. I could have told him from the beginning that this obsession of his over the coffee was bound to end in a blind alley, but I restrained my tongue. After all, though he was old, Poirot had been a great man in his day.

"Breakfast is ready," said John Cavendish, coming in from the hall. "You will breakfast with us, Monsieur Poirot?"

Poirot acquiesced. I observed John. Already he was almost restored to his normal self. The shock of the events of the last night had upset him temporarily, but his equable poise soon swung back to the normal. He was a man of very little imagination, in sharp contrast with his brother, who had, perhaps, too much.

Ever since the early hours of the morning, John had been hard at work, sending telegrams—one of the first had gone to Evelyn Howard—writing notices for the papers, and generally occupying himself with the melancholy duties that a death entails.

"May I ask how things are proceeding?" he said. "Do your investigations point to my mother having died a natural death—or—or must we prepare ourselves for the worst?"

"I think, Mr. Cavendish," said Poirot gravely, "that you would do well not to buoy yourself up with any false hopes. Can you tell me the views of the other members of the family?"

"My brother Lawrence is convinced that we are making a fuss over nothing. He says that everything points to its being a simple case of heart failure."

"He does, does he? That is very interesting—very interesting," murmured Poirot softly. "And Mrs. Cavendish?"

A faint cloud passed over John's face.

"I have not the least idea what my wife's views on the subject are."

The answer brought a momentary stiffness in its train. John broke the rather awkward silence by saying with a slight effort:

"I told you, didn't I, that Mr. Inglethorp has returned?"

Poirot bent his head.

"It's an awkward position for all of us. Of course one has to treat him as usual—but, hang it all, one's gorge does rise at sitting down to eat with a possible murderer!"

Poirot nodded sympathetically.

"I quite understand. It is a very difficult situation for you, Mr. Cavendish. I would like to ask you one question. Mr. Inglethorp's reason for not returning last night was, I believe, that he had forgotten the latch-key. Is not that so?"

"Yes."

"I suppose you are quite sure that the latch-key *was* forgotten—that he did not take it after all?"

"I have no idea. I never thought of looking. We always keep it in the hall drawer. I'll go and see if it's there now."

Poirot held up his hand with a faint smile.

"No, no, Mr. Cavendish, it is too late now. I am certain that you would find it. If Mr. Inglethorp did take it, he has had ample time to replace it by now."

"But do you think——"

"I think nothing. If anyone had chanced to look this morning before his return, and seen it there, it would have been a valuable point in his favour. That is all."

John looked perplexed.

"Do not worry," said Poirot smoothly. "I assure you that you need not let it trouble you. Since you are so kind, let us go and have some breakfast."

Everyone was assembled in the dining-room. Under the circumstances, we were naturally not a cheerful party. The reaction after a shock is always trying, and I think we were all suffering from it. Decorum and good breeding naturally enjoined that our demeanour should be much as usual, yet I could not help wondering if this self-control were really a matter of great difficulty. There were no red eyes, no signs of secretly indulged grief. I felt that I was right in my opinion that Dorcas was the person most affected by the personal side of the tragedy.

I pass over Alfred Inglethorp, who acted the bereaved widower in a manner that I felt to be disgusting in its hypocrisy. Did he know that we suspected him, I wondered. Surely he could not be unaware of the fact, conceal it as we would. Did he feel some secret stirring of fear, or was he confident that his crime would go unpunished? Surely the suspicion in the atmosphere must warn him that he was already a marked man.

But did everyone suspect him? What about Mrs. Cavendish? I watched her as she sat at the head of the table, graceful, composed, enigmatic. In her soft grey frock, with white ruffles at the wrists falling over her slender hands, she looked very beautiful. When she chose, however, her face could be sphinx-like in its inscrutability. She was very silent, hardly opening her lips, and yet in some queer way I felt that the great strength of her personality was dominating us all.

And little Cynthia? Did she suspect? She looked very tired and ill, I thought. The heaviness and languor of her manner were very marked. I asked her if she were feeling ill, and she answered frankly:

"Yes, I've got the most beastly headache."

"Have another cup of coffee, mademoiselle?" said Poirot solicitously. "It will revive you. It is unparalleled for the *mal de tête*." He jumped up and took her cup.

"No sugar," said Cynthia, watching him, as he picked up the sugar-tongs.

"No sugar? You abandon it in the war-time, eh?"

"No, I never take it in coffee."

"*Sacré!*" murmured Poirot to himself, as he brought back the replenished cup.

Only I heard him, and glancing up curiously at the little man I saw that his face was working with suppressed excitement, and his eyes were as green as a cat's. He had heard or seen something that had affected him strongly—but what was it? I do not usually label myself as dense, but I must confess that nothing out of the ordinary had attracted *my* attention.

In another moment, the door opened and Dorcas appeared.

"Mr. Wells to see you, sir," she said to John.

I remembered the name as being that of the lawyer to whom Mrs. Inglethorp had written the night before.

John rose immediately.

"Show him into my study." Then he turned to us. "My mother's lawyer," he explained. And in a lower voice: "He is also Coroner—you understand. Perhaps you would like to come with me?"

We acquiesced and followed him out of the room. John strode on ahead and I took the opportunity of whispering to Poirot:

"There will be an inquest then?"

Poirot nodded absently. He seemed absorbed in thought; so much so that my curiosity was aroused.

"What is it? You are not attending to what I say."

"It is true, my friend. I am much worried."

"Why?"

"Because Mademoiselle Cynthia does not take sugar in her coffee."

"What? You cannot be serious?"

"But I am most serious. Ah, there is something there that I do not understand. My instinct was right."

"What instinct?"

"The instinct that led me to insist on examining those coffee-cups. *Chut!* no more now!"

We followed John into his study, and he closed the door behind us.

Mr. Wells was a pleasant man of middle-age, with keen eyes, and the typical lawyer's mouth. John introduced us both, and explained the reason of our presence.

"You will understand, Wells," he added, "that this is all strictly private. We are still hoping that there will turn out to be no need for investigation of any kind."

"Quite so, quite so," said Mr. Wells soothingly. "I wish we could have spared you the pain and publicity of an inquest, but of course it's quite unavoidable in the absence of a doctor's certificate."

"Yes, I suppose so."

"Clever man, Bauerstein. Great authority on toxicology, I believe."

"Indeed," said John with a certain stiffness in his manner. Then he added rather hesitatingly: "Shall we have to appear as witnesses—all of us, I mean?"

"You, of course—and ah—er—Mr.—er—Inglethorp."

A slight pause ensued before the lawyer went on in his soothing manner:

"Any other evidence will be simply confirmatory, a mere matter of form."

"I see."

A faint expression of relief swept over John's face. It puzzled me, for I saw no occasion for it.

"If you know of nothing to the contrary," pursued Mr. Wells, "I had thought of Friday. That will give us plenty of time for the doctor's report. The post-mortem is to take place to-night, I believe?"

"Yes."

"Then that arrangement will suit you?"

"Perfectly."

"I need not tell you, my dear Cavendish, how distressed I am at this most tragic affair."

"Can you give us no help in solving it, monsieur?" interposed Poirot, speaking for the first time since we had entered the room.

"I?"

"Yes, we heard that Mrs. Inglethorp wrote to you last night. You should have received the letter this morning."

"I did, but it contains no information. It is merely a note asking me to call upon her this morning, as she wanted my advice on a matter of great importance."

"She gave you no hint as to what that matter might be?"

"Unfortunately, no."

"That is a pity," said John.

"A great pity," agreed Poirot gravely.

There was silence. Poirot remained lost in thought for a few minutes. Finally he turned to the lawyer again.

"Mr. Wells, there is one thing I should like to ask you—that is, if it is not against professional etiquette. In the event of Mrs. Inglethorp's death, who would inherit her money?"

The lawyer hesitated a moment, and then replied:

"The knowledge will be public property very soon, so if Mr. Cavendish does not object——"

"Not at all," interpolated John.

"I do not see any reason why I should not answer your question. By her last will, dated August of last year, after various unimportant legacies to servants, etc., she gave her entire fortune to her stepson, Mr. John Cavendish."

"Was not that—pardon the question, Mr. Cavendish—rather unfair to her other stepson, Mr. Lawrence Cavendish?"

"No, I do not think so. You see, under the terms of their father's will, while John inherited the property, Lawrence, at his stepmother's death, would come into a considerable sum of money. Mrs. Inglethorp left her money to her elder stepson, knowing that he would have to keep up Styles. It was, to my mind, a very fair and equitable distribution."

Poirot nodded thoughtfully.

"I see. But I am right in saying, am I not, that by your English law that will was automatically revoked when Mrs. Inglethorp remarried?"

Mr. Wells bowed his head.

"As I was about to proceed, Monsieur Poirot, that document is now null and void."

"*Hein!*" said Poirot. He reflected for a moment, and then asked: "Was Mrs. Inglethorp herself aware of that fact?"

"I do not know. She may have been."

"She was," said John unexpectedly. "We were discussing the matter of wills being revoked by marriage only yesterday."

"Ah! One more question, Mr. Wells. You say 'her last will.' Had Mrs. Inglethorp, then, made several former wills?"

"On an average, she made a new will at least once a year," said Mr. Wells imperturbably. "She was given to changing her mind as to her testamentary dispositions, now benefiting one, now another member of her family."

"Suppose," suggested Poirot, "that, unknown to you, she had made a new will in favour of someone who was not, in any sense of the word, a member of the family—we will say Miss Howard, for instance—would you be surprised?"

"Not in the least."

"Ah!" Poirot seemed to have exhausted his questions.

I drew close to him, while John and the lawyer were debating the question of going through Mrs. Inglethorp's papers.

"Do you think Mrs. Inglethorp made a will leaving all her money to Miss Howard?" I asked in a low voice, with some curiosity.

Poirot smiled.

"No."

"Then why did you ask?"

"Hush!"

John Cavendish had turned to Poirot.

"Will you come with us, Monsieur Poirot? We are going through my mother's papers. Mr. Inglethorp is quite willing to leave it entirely to Mr. Wells and myself."

"Which simplifies matters very much," murmured the lawyer. "As technically, of course, he was entitled——" He did not finish the sentence.

"We will look through the desk in the boudoir first," explained John, "and go up to her bedroom afterwards. She kept her most important papers in a purple despatch-case, which we must look through carefully."

"Yes," said the lawyer, "it is quite possible that there may be a later will than the one in my possession."

"There *is* a later will." It was Poirot who spoke.

"What?" John and the lawyer looked at him startled.

"Or, rather," pursued my friend imperturbably, "there *was* one."

"What do you mean—there was one? Where is it now?"

"Burnt!"

"Burnt?"

"Yes. See here." He took out the charred fragment we had found in the grate in Mrs. Inglethorp's room, and handed it to the lawyer with a brief explanation of when and where he had found it.

"But possibly this is an old will?"

"I do not think so. In fact I am almost certain that it was made no earlier than yesterday afternoon."

"What?" "Impossible!" broke simultaneously from both men. Poirot turned to John.

"If you will allow me to send for your gardener, I will prove it to you."

"Oh, of course—but I don't see——"

Poirot raised his hand.

"Do as I ask you. Afterwards you shall question as much as you please."

"Very well." He rang the bell.

Dorcas answered it in due course.

"Dorcas, will you tell Manning to come round and speak to me here."

"Yes, sir."

Dorcas withdrew.

We waited in a tense silence. Poirot alone seemed perfectly at his ease, and dusted a forgotten corner of the bookcase.

The clumping of hobnailed boots on the gravel outside proclaimed the approach of Manning. John looked questioningly at Poirot. The latter nodded.

"Come inside, Manning," said John, "I want to speak to you."

Manning came slowly and hesitatingly through the French window, and stood as near it as he could. He held his cap in his hands, twisting it very carefully round and round. His back was much bent, though he was probably not as old as he looked, but his eyes were sharp and intelligent, and belied his slow and rather cautious speech.

"Manning," said John, "this gentleman will put some questions to you which I want you to answer."

"Yessir," mumbled Manning.

Poirot stepped forward briskly. Manning's eye swept over him with a faint contempt.

"You were planting a bed of begonias round by the south side of the house yesterday afternoon, were you not, Manning?"

"Yes, sir, me and Willum."

"And Mrs. Inglethorp came to the window and called you, did she not?"

"Yes, sir, she did."

"Tell me in your own words exactly what happened after that."

"Well, sir, nothing much. She just told Willum to go on his bicycle down to the village, and bring back a form of will, or suchlike—I don't know what exactly—she wrote it down for him."

"Well?"

"Well, he did, sir."

"And what happened next?"

"We went on with the begonias, sir."

"Did not Mrs. Inglethorp call you again?"

"Yes, sir, both me and Willum, she called."

"And then?"

"She made us come right in, and sign our names at the bottom of a long paper—under where she'd signed."

"Did you see anything of what was written above her signature?" asked Poirot sharply.

"No, sir, there was a bit of blotting paper over that part."

"And you signed where she told you?"

"Yes, sir, first me and then Willum."

"What did she do with it afterwards?"

"Well, sir, she slipped it into a long envelope, and put it inside a sort of purple box that was standing on the desk."

"What time was it when she first called you?"

"About four, I should say, sir."

"Not earlier? Couldn't it have been about half-past three?"

"No, I shouldn't say so, sir. It would be more likely to be a bit after four—not before it."

"Thank you, Manning, that will do," said Poirot pleasantly.

The gardener glanced at his master, who nodded, whereupon Manning lifted a finger to his forehead with a low mumble, and backed cautiously out of the window.

We all looked at each other.

"Good heavens!" murmured John. "What an extraordinary coincidence."

"How—a coincidence?"

"That my mother should have made a will on the very day of her death!"

Mr. Wells cleared his throat and remarked drily:

"Are you so sure it is a coincidence, Cavendish?"

"What do you mean?"

"Your mother, you tell me, had a violent quarrel with—someone yesterday afternoon——"

"What do you mean?" cried John again. There was a tremor in his voice, and he had gone very pale.

"In consequence of that quarrel, your mother very suddenly and hurriedly makes a new will. The contents of that will we shall never know. She told no one of its provisions. This morning, no doubt, she would have consulted me on the subject—but she had no chance. The will disappears, and she takes its secret with her to her grave. Cavendish, I much fear there is no coincidence there. Monsieur Poirot, I am sure you agree with me that the facts are very suggestive."

"Suggestive, or not," interrupted John, "we are most grateful to Monsieur Poirot for elucidating the matter. But for him, we should never have known of this will. I suppose, I may not ask you, monsieur, what first led you to suspect the fact?"

Poirot smiled and answered:

"A scribbled over old envelope, and a freshly planted bed of begonias."

John, I think, would have pressed his questions further, but at that moment the loud purr of a motor was audible, and we all turned to the window as it swept past.

"Evie!" cried John. "Excuse me, Wells." He went hurriedly out into the hall.

Poirot looked inquiringly at me.

"Miss Howard," I explained.

"Ah, I am glad she has come. There is a woman with a head and a heart too, Hastings. Though the good God gave her no beauty!"

I followed John's example, and went out into the hall, where Miss Howard was endeavouring to extricate herself from the voluminous mass of veils that enveloped her head. As her eyes fell on me, a sudden pang of guilt shot through me. This was the woman who had warned me so earnestly, and to whose warning I had, alas, paid no heed! How soon, and how contemptuously, I had dismissed it from my mind. Now that she had been proved justified in so tragic a manner, I felt ashamed. She had known Alfred Inglethorp only too well. I wondered whether, if she had remained at Styles, the tragedy would have taken place, or would the man have feared her watchful eyes?

I was relieved when she shook me by the hand, with her well remembered painful grip. The eyes that met mine were sad, but not reproachful; that she had been crying bitterly, I could tell by the redness of her eyelids, but her manner was unchanged from its old gruffness.

"Started the moment I got the wire. Just come off night duty. Hired car. Quickest way to get here."

"Have you had anything to eat this morning, Evie?" asked John.

"No."

"I thought not. Come along, breakfast's not cleared away yet, and they'll make you some fresh tea." He turned to me. "Look after her, Hastings, will you? Wells is waiting for me. Oh, here's

Monsieur Poirot. He's helping us, you know, Evie."

Miss Howard shook hands with Poirot, but glanced suspiciously over her shoulder at John.

"What do you mean—helping us?"

"Helping us to investigate."

"Nothing to investigate. Have they taken him to prison yet?"

"Taken who to prison?"

"Who? Alfred Inglethorp, of course!"

"My dear Evie, do be careful. Lawrence is of the opinion that my mother died from heart seizure."

"More fool, Lawrence!" retorted Miss Howard. "Of course Alfred Inglethorp murdered poor Emily—as I always told you he would."

"My dear Evie, don't shout so. Whatever we may think or suspect, it is better to say as little as possible for the present. The inquest isn't until Friday."

"Not until fiddlesticks!" The snort Miss Howard gave was truly magnificent. "You're all off your heads. The man will be out of the country by then. If he's any sense, he won't stay here tamely and wait to be hanged."

John Cavendish looked at her helplessly.

"I know what it is," she accused him, "you've been listening to the doctors. Never should. What do they know? Nothing at all—or just enough to make them dangerous. I ought to know—my own father was a doctor. That little Wilkins is about the greatest fool that even I have ever seen. Heart seizure! Sort of thing he would say. Anyone with any sense could see at once that her husband had poisoned her. I always said he'd murder her in her bed, poor soul. Now he's done it. And all you can do is to murmur silly things about 'heart seizure' and 'inquest on Friday.' You ought to be ashamed of yourself, John Cavendish."

"What do you want me to do?" asked John, unable to help a faint smile. "Dash it all, Evie, I can't haul him down to the local police station by the scruff of his neck."

"Well, you might do something. Find out how he did it. He's a crafty beggar. Dare say he soaked fly papers. Ask cook if she's missed any."

It occurred to me very forcibly at that moment that to harbour Miss Howard and Alfred Inglethorp under the same roof, and keep the peace between them, was likely to prove a Herculean task, and I did not envy John. I could see by the expression of his face that he fully appreciated the difficulty of the position. For the moment, he sought refuge in retreat, and left the room precipitately.

Dorcas brought in fresh tea. As she left the room, Poirot came over from the window where he had been standing, and sat down facing Miss Howard.

"Mademoiselle," he said gravely, "I want to ask you something."

"Ask away," said the lady, eyeing him with some disfavour.

"I want to be able to count upon your help."

"I'll help you to hang Alfred with pleasure," she replied gruffly. "Hanging's too good for him. Ought to be drawn and quartered, like in good old times."

"We are at one then," said Poirot, "for I, too, want to hang the criminal."

"Alfred Inglethorp?"

"Him, or another."

"No question of another. Poor Emily was never murdered until *he* came along. I don't say she wasn't surrounded by sharks—she was. But it was only her purse they were after. Her life was safe enough. But along comes Mr. Alfred Inglethorp—and within two months—hey presto!"

"Believe me, Miss Howard," said Poirot very earnestly, "if Mr. Inglethorp is the man, he shall not escape me. On my honour, I will hang him as high as Haman!"

"That's better," said Miss Howard more enthusiastically.

"But I must ask you to trust me. Now your help may be very valuable to me. I will tell you why. Because, in all this house of mourning, yours are the only eyes that have wept."

Miss Howard blinked, and a new note crept into the gruffness of her voice.

"If you mean that I was fond of her—yes, I was. You know, Emily was a selfish old woman in her way. She was very generous, but she always wanted a return. She never let people forget what she had done for them—and, that way she missed love. Don't think she ever realized it, though, or felt the lack of it. Hope not, anyway. I was on a different footing. I took my stand from the first. 'So many pounds a year I'm worth to you. Well and good. But not a penny piece besides—not a pair of gloves, nor a theatre ticket.' She didn't understand—was very offended sometimes. Said I was foolishly proud. It wasn't that—but I couldn't explain. Anyway, I kept my self-respect. And so, out of the whole bunch, I was the only one who could allow myself to be fond of her. I watched over her. I guarded her from the lot of them, and then a glib-tongued scoundrel comes along, and pooh! all my years of devotion go for nothing."

Poirot nodded sympathetically.

"I understand, mademoiselle, I understand all you feel. It is most natural. You think that we are lukewarm—that we lack fire and energy—but trust me, it is not so."

John stuck his head in at this juncture, and invited us both to come up to Mrs. Inglethorp's room, as he and Mr. Wells had finished looking through the desk in the boudoir.

As we went up the stairs, John looked back to the dining-room door, and lowered his voice confidentially:

"Look here, what's going to happen when these two meet?"

I shook my head helplessly.

"I've told Mary to keep them apart if she can."

"Will she be able to do so?"

"The Lord only knows. There's one thing, Inglethorp himself won't be too keen on meeting her."

"You've got the keys still, haven't you, Poirot?" I asked, as we reached the door of the locked room.

Taking the keys from Poirot, John unlocked it, and we all passed in. The lawyer went straight to the desk, and John followed him.

"My mother kept most of her important papers in this despatch-case, I believe," he said.

Poirot drew out the small bunch of keys.

"Permit me. I locked it, out of precaution, this morning."

"But it's not locked now."

"Impossible!"

"See." And John lifted the lid as he spoke.

"*Milles tonnerres!*" cried Poirot, dumbfounded. "And I—who have both the keys in my pocket!" He flung himself upon the case. Suddenly he stiffened. "*Eh voilà une affaire!* This lock has been forced."

"What?"

Poirot laid down the case again.

"But who forced it? Why should they? When? But the door was locked?" These exclamations burst from us disjointedly.

Poirot answered them categorically—almost mechanically.

"Who? That is the question. Why? Ah, if I only knew. When? Since I was here an hour ago. As to the door being locked, it is a very ordinary lock. Probably any other of the doorkeys in this passage would fit it."

We stared at one another blankly. Poirot had walked over to the mantelpiece. He was outwardly calm, but I noticed his hands, which from long force of habit were mechanically straightening the spill vases on the mantelpiece, were shaking violently.

"See here, it was like this," he said at last. "There was something in that case—some piece of evidence, slight in itself perhaps, but still enough of a clue to connect the murderer with the crime. It was vital to him that it should be destroyed before it was discovered and its significance appreciated. Therefore, he took the risk, the great risk, of coming in here. Finding the case locked, he was obliged to force it, thus betraying his presence. For him to

68

take that risk, it must have been something of great importance."

"But what was it?"

"Ah!" cried Poirot, with a gesture of anger. "That, I do not know! A document of some kind, without doubt, possibly the scrap of paper Dorcas saw in her hand yesterday afternoon. And I—" his anger burst forth freely—"miserable animal that I am! I guessed nothing! I have behaved like an imbecile! I should never have left that case here. I should have carried it away with me. Ah, triple pig! And now it is gone. It is destroyed—but is it destroyed? Is there not yet a chance—we must leave no stone unturned—"

He rushed like a madman from the room, and I followed him as soon as I had sufficiently recovered my wits. But, by the time I had reached the top of the stairs, he was out of sight.

Mary Cavendish was standing where the staircase branched, staring down into the hall in the direction in which he had disappeared.

"What has happened to your extraordinary little friend, Mr. Hastings? He has just rushed past me like a mad bull."

"He's rather upset about something," I remarked feebly. I really did not know how much Poirot would wish me to disclose. As I saw a faint smile gather on Mrs. Cavendish's expressive mouth, I endeavoured to try and turn the conversation by saying: "They haven't met yet, have they?"

"Who?"

"Mr. Inglethorp and Miss Howard."

She looked at me in rather a disconcerting manner.

"Do you think it would be such a disaster if they did meet?"

"Well, don't you?" I said, rather taken aback.

"No." She was smiling in her quiet way. "I should like to see a good flare up. It would clear the air. At present we are all thinking so much, and saying so little."

"John doesn't think so," I remarked. "He's anxious to keep them apart."

"Oh, John!"

Something in her tone fired me, and I blurted out:

"Old John's an awfully good sort."

She studied me curiously for a minute or two, and then said, to my great surprise:

"You are loyal to your friend. I like you for that."

"Aren't you my friend too?"

"I am a very bad friend."

"Why do you say that?"

"Because it is true. I am charming to my friends one day, and forget all about them the next."

I don't know what impelled me, but I was nettled, and I said foolishly and not in the best of taste:

"Yet you seem to be invariably charming to Dr. Bauerstein!"

Instantly I regretted my words. Her face stiffened. I had the impression of a steel curtain coming down and blotting out the real woman. Without a word, she turned and went swiftly up the stairs, whilst I stood like an idiot gaping after her.

I was recalled to other matters by a frightful row going on below. I could hear Poirot shouting and expounding. I was vexed to think that my diplomacy had been in vain. The little man appeared to be taking the whole house into his confidence, a proceeding of which I, for one, doubted the wisdom. Once again I could not help regretting that my friend was so prone to lose his head in moments of excitement. I stepped briskly down the stairs. The sight of me calmed Poirot almost immediately. I drew him aside.

"My dear fellow," I said, "is this wise? Surely you don't want the whole house to know of this occurrence? You are actually playing into the criminal's hands."

"You think so, Hastings?"

"I am sure of it."

"Well, well, my friend, I will be guided by you."

"Good. Although, unfortunately, it is a little too late now."

"Sure."

He looked so crestfallen and abashed that I felt quite sorry, though I still thought my rebuke a just and wise one.

"Well," he said at last, "let us go, *mon ami*."

"You have finished here?"

"For the moment, yes. You will walk back with me to the village?"

"Willingly."

He picked up his little suit-case, and we went out through the open window in the drawing-room. Cynthia Murdoch was just coming in, and Poirot stood aside to let her pass.

"Excuse me, mademoiselle, one minute."

"Yes?" she turned inquiringly.

"Did you ever make up Mrs. Inglethorp's medicines?"

A slight flush rose in her face, as she answered rather constrainedly:

"No."

"Only her powders?"

The flush deepened as Cynthia replied:

"Oh, yes, I did make up some sleeping powders for her once."

"These?"

Poirot produced the empty box which had contained powders. She nodded.

"Can you tell me what they were? Sulphonal? Veronal?"

"No, they were bromide powders."

"Ah! Thank you, mademoiselle; good morning."

As we walked briskly away from the house, I glanced at him more than once. I had often before noticed that, if anything excited him, his eyes turned green like a cat's. They were shining like emeralds now.

"My friend," he broke out at last, "I have a little idea, a very strange, and probably utterly impossible idea. And yet—it fits in."

I shrugged my shoulders. I privately thought that Poirot was rather too much given to these fantastic ideas. In this case, surely, the truth was only too plain and apparent.

71

"So that is the explanation of the blank label on the box," I remarked. "Very simple, as you said. I really wonder that I did not think of it myself."

Poirot did not appear to be listening to me.

"They have made one more discovery, *là-bas*," he observed, jerking his thumb over his shoulder in the direction of Styles. "Mr. Wells told me as we were going upstairs."

"What was it?"

"Locked up in the desk in the boudoir, they found a will of Mrs. Inglethorp's, dated before her marriage, leaving her fortune to Alfred Inglethorp. It must have been made just at the time they were engaged. It came quite as a surprise to Wells—and to John Cavendish also. It was written on one of those printed will forms, and witnessed by two of the servants—not Dorcas."

"Did Mr. Inglethorp know of it?"

"He says not."

"One might take that with a grain of salt," I remarked sceptically. "All these wills are very confusing. Tell me, how did those scribbled words on the envelope help you to discover that a will was made yesterday afternoon?"

Poirot smiled.

"*Mon ami*, have you ever, when writing a letter, been arrested by the fact that you did not know how to spell a certain word?"

"Yes, often. I suppose everyone has."

"Exactly. And have you not, in such a case, tried the word once or twice on the edge of the blotting-paper, or a spare scrap of paper, to see if it looked right? Well, that is what Mrs. Inglethorp did. You will notice that the word 'possessed' is spelt first with one 's' and subsequently with two—correctly. To make sure, she had further tried it in a sentence, thus: 'I am possessed.' Now, what did that tell me? It told me that Mrs. Inglethorp had been writing the word 'possessed' that afternoon, and, having the fragment of paper found in the grate fresh in my mind, the possibility of a will—(a document almost certain to contain that word)—occurred to me at once. This possibility was confirmed by a further circumstance. In the general confusion, the boudoir had not been swept that morning, and near the desk were several traces of brown mould and earth. The weather had been perfectly fine for some days, and no ordinary boots would have left such a heavy deposit.

"I strolled to the window, and saw at once that the begonia beds had been newly planted. The mould in the beds was exactly similar to that on the floor of the boudoir, and also I learnt from you that they *had* been planted yesterday afternoon. I was now sure that one, or possibly both of the gardeners—for there were two sets of footprints in the bed—had entered the boudoir, for if Mrs. Inglethorp had merely wished to speak to them she would in all probability have stood at the window, and they would not have come into the room at all. I was now quite convinced that she had made a fresh will, and had called the two gardeners in to witness her signature. Events proved that I was right in my supposition."

"That was very ingenious," I could not help admitting. "I must confess that the conclusions I drew from those few scribbled words were quite erroneous."

He smiled.

"You gave too much rein to your imagination. Imagination is a good servant, and a bad master. The simplest explanation is always the most likely."

"Another point—how did you know that the key of the despatch-case had been lost?"

"I did not know it. It was a guess that turned out to be correct. You observed that it had a piece of twisted wire through the handle. That suggested to me at once that it had possibly been wrenched off a flimsy key-ring. Now, if it had been lost and recovered, Mrs. Inglethorp would at once have replaced it on her bunch; but on her bunch I found what was obviously the duplicate key, very new and bright, which led me to the hypothesis that somebody else had inserted the original key in the lock of the despatch-case."

"Yes," I said, "Alfred Inglethorp, without doubt."

Poirot looked at me curiously.

"You are very sure of his guilt?"

"Well, naturally. Every fresh circumstance seems to establish it more clearly."

"On the contrary," said Poirot quietly, "there are several points in his favour."

"Oh, come now!"

"Yes."

"I see only one."

"And that?"

"That he was not in the house last night."

"'Bad shot!' as you English say! You have chosen the one point that to my mind tells against him."

"How is that?"

"Because if Mr. Inglethorp knew that his wife would be poisoned last night, he would certainly have arranged to be away from the house. His excuse was an obviously trumped up one. That leaves us two possibilities: either he knew what was going to happen or he had a reason of his own for his absence."

"And that reason?" I asked sceptically.

Poirot shrugged his shoulders.

"How should I know? Discreditable, without doubt. This Mr. Inglethorp, I should say, is somewhat of a scoundrel—but that does not of necessity make him a murderer."

I shook my head, unconvinced.

"We do not agree, eh?" said Poirot. "Well, let us leave it. Time will show which of us is right. Now let us turn to other aspects of the case. What do you make of the fact that all the doors of the bedroom were bolted on the inside?"

"Well——" I considered. "One must look at it logically."

"True."

"I should put it this way. The doors were bolted—our own eyes have told us that—yet the presence of the candle grease on the floor, and the destruction of the will, prove that during the night someone entered the room. You agree so far?"

"Perfectly. Put with admirable clearness. Proceed."

"Well," I said, encouraged, "as the person who entered did not do so by the window, nor by miraculous means, it follows that the door must have been opened from inside by Mrs. Inglethorp herself. That strengthens the conviction that the person in question was her husband. She would naturally open the door to her own husband."

Poirot shook his head.

"Why should she? She had bolted the door leading into his room—a most unusual proceeding on her part—she had had a most violent quarrel with him that very afternoon. No, he was the last person she would admit."

"But you agree with me that the door must have been opened by Mrs. Inglethorp herself?"

"There is another possibility. She may have forgotten to bolt the door into the passage when she went to bed, and have got up later, towards morning, and bolted it then."

"Poirot, is that seriously your opinion?"

"No, I do not say it is so, but it might be. Now, to turn to another feature, what do you make of the scrap of conversation you overheard between Mrs. Cavendish and her mother-in-law?"

"I had forgotten that," I said thoughtfully. "That is as enigmatical as ever. It seems incredible that a woman like Mrs. Cavendish, proud and reticent to the last degree, should interfere so violently in what was certainly not her affair."

"Precisely. It was an astonishing thing for a woman of her breeding to do."

"It is certainly curious," I agreed. "Still, it is unimportant, and need not be taken into account."

A groan burst from Poirot.

"What have I always told you? Everything must be taken into account. If the fact will not fit the theory—let the theory go."

"Well, we shall see," I said, nettled.

"Yes, we shall see."

We had reached Leastways Cottage, and Poirot ushered me upstairs to his own room. He offered me one of the tiny Russian cigarettes he himself occasionally smoked. I was amused to notice that he stowed away the used matches most carefully in a little china pot. My momentary annoyance vanished.

Poirot had placed our two chairs in front of the open window which commanded a view of the village street. The fresh air blew in warm and pleasant. It was going to be a hot day.

Suddenly my attention was arrested by a weedy looking young man rushing down the street at a great pace. It was the expression on his face that was extraordinary—a curious mingling of terror and agitation.

"Look, Poirot!" I said.

He leant forward.

"*Tiens!*" he said. "It is Mr. Mace, from the chemist's shop. He is coming here."

The young man came to a halt before Leastways Cottage, and, after hesitating a moment, pounded vigorously at the door.

"A little minute," cried Poirot from the window. "I come."

Motioning to me to follow him, he ran swiftly down the stairs and opened the door. Mr. Mace began at once.

"Oh, Mr. Poirot, I'm sorry for the inconvenience, but I heard that you'd just come back from the Hall?"

"Yes, we have."

The young man moistened his dry lips. His face was working curiously.

"It's all over the village about old Mrs. Inglethorp dying so suddenly. They do say—" he lowered his voice cautiously—"that it's poison?"

Poirot's face remained quite impassive.

"Only the doctors can tell us that, Mr. Mace."

"Yes, exactly—of course——" The young man hesitated, and

then his agitation was too much for him. He clutched Poirot by the arm, and sank his voice to a whisper: "Just tell me this, Mr. Poirot, it isn't—it isn't strychnine, is it?"

I hardly heard what Poirot replied. Something evidently of a non-committal nature. The young man departed, and as he closed the door Poirot's eyes met mine.

"Yes," he said, nodding gravely. "He will have evidence to give at the inquest."

We went slowly upstairs again. I was opening my lips, when Poirot stopped me with a gesture of his hand.

"Not now, not now, *mon ami*. I have need of reflection. My mind is in some disorder—which is not well."

For about ten minutes he sat in dead silence, perfectly still, except for several expressive motions of his eyebrows, and all the time his eyes grew steadily greener. At last he heaved a deep sigh.

"It is well. The bad moment has passed. Now all is arranged and classified. One must never permit confusion. The case is not clear yet—no. For it is of the most complicated! It puzzles *me*. *Me*, Hercule Poirot! There are two facts of significance."

"And what are they?"

"The first is the state of the weather yesterday. That is very important."

"But it was a glorious day!" I interrupted. "Poirot, you're pulling my leg!"

"Not at all. The thermometer registered 80 degrees in the shade. Do not forget that, my friend. It is the key to the whole riddle!"

"And the second point?" I asked.

"The important fact that Monsieur Inglethorp wears very peculiar clothes, has a black beard, and uses glasses."

"Poirot, I cannot believe you are serious."

"I am absolutely serious, my friend."

"But this is childish!"

"No, it is very momentous."

"And supposing the Coroner's jury returns a verdict of Wilful Murder against Alfred Inglethorp. What becomes of your theories, then?"

"They would not be shaken because twelve stupid men had happened to make a mistake! But that will not occur. For one thing, a country jury is not anxious to take responsibility upon itself, and Mr. Inglethorp stands practically in the position of local squire. Also," he added placidly, "*I should not allow it!*"

"*You* would not allow it?"

"No."

I looked at the extraordinary little man, divided between annoyance and amusement. He was so tremendously sure of himself. As though he read my thoughts, he nodded gently.

"Oh, yes, *mon ami*, I would do what I say." He got up and laid his hand on my shoulder. His physiognomy underwent a complete change. Tears came into his eyes. "In all this, you see, I think of that poor Mrs. Inglethorp who is dead. She was not extravagantly loved—no. But she was very good to us Belgians—I owe her a debt."

I endeavoured to interrupt, but Poirot swept on.

"Let me tell you this, Hastings. She would never forgive me if I let Alfred Inglethorp, her husband, be arrested *now*—when a word from me could save him!"

SIX

The Inquest

In the interval before the inquest, Poirot was unfailing in his activity. Twice he was closeted with Mr. Wells. He also took long walks into the country. I rather resented his not taking me into his confidence, the more so as I could not in the least guess what he was driving at.

It occurred to me that he might have been making inquiries at Raikes's farm; so, finding him out when I called at Leastways Cottage on Wednesday evening, I walked over there by the fields, hoping to meet him. But there was no sign of him, and I hesitated to go right up to the farm itself. As I walked away, I met an aged rustic, who leered at me cunningly.

"You'm from the Hall, bain't you?" he asked.

"Yes. I'm looking for a friend of mine whom I thought might have walked this way."

"A little chap? As waves his hands when he talks? One of them Belgies from the village?"

"Yes," I said eagerly. "He has been here, then?"

"Oh, ay, he's been here, right enough. More'n once too. Friend of yours, is he? Ah, you gentlemen from the Hall—you'm a pretty lot!" And he leered more jocosely than ever.

"Why, do the gentlemen from the Hall come here often?" I asked, as carelessly as I could.

He winked at me knowingly.

"*One* does, mister. Naming no names, mind. And a very liberal gentleman too! Oh, thank you, sir, I'm sure."

I walked on sharply. Evelyn Howard had been right then, and I experienced a sharp twinge of disgust, as I thought of Alfred Inglethorp's liberality with another woman's money. Had that piquant gipsy face been at the bottom of the crime, or was it the baser mainspring of money? Probably a judicious mixture of both.

On one point, Poirot seemed to have a curious obsession. He once or twice observed to me that he thought Dorcas must have made an error in fixing the time of the quarrel. He suggested to her repeatedly that it was four-thirty, and not four o'clock when she had heard the voices.

But Dorcas was unshaken. Quite an hour, or even more, had elapsed between the time when she had heard the voices and five o'clock, when she had taken tea to her mistress.

The inquest was held on Friday at the Stylites Arms in the village. Poirot and I sat together, not being required to give evidence.

The preliminaries were gone through. The jury viewed the body, and John Cavendish gave evidence of identification.

Further questioned, he described his awakening in the early hours of the morning, and the circumstances of his mother's death.

The medical evidence was next taken. There was a breathless hush, and every eye was fixed on the famous London specialist, who was known to be one of the greatest authorities of the day on the subject of toxicology.

In a few brief words, he summed up the result of the post-mortem. Shorn of its medical phraseology and technicalities, it amounted to the fact that Mrs. Inglethorp had met her death as the result of strychnine poisoning. Judging from the quantity recovered, she must have taken not less than three-quarters of a grain of strychnine, but probably one grain or slightly over.

"Is it possible that she could have swallowed the poison by accident?" asked the Coroner.

"I should consider it very unlikely. Strychnine is not used for domestic purposes, as some poisons are, and there are restrictions placed on its sale."

"Does anything in your examination lead you to determine how the poison was administered?"

"No."

"You arrived at Styles before Dr. Wilkins, I believe?"

"That is so. The motor met me just outside the lodge gates, and I hurried there as fast as I could."

"Will you relate to us exactly what happened next?"

"I entered Mrs. Inglethorp's room. She was at that moment in a typical tetanic convulsion. She turned towards me, and gasped out: 'Alfred—Alfred——'"

"Could the strychnine have been administered in Mrs. Inglethorp's after-dinner coffee which was taken to her by her husband?"

"Possibly, but strychnine is a fairly rapid drug in its action. The symptoms appear from one to two hours after it has been swallowed. It is retarded under certain conditions, none of which, however, appear to have been present in this case. I presume Mrs. Inglethorp took the coffee after dinner about eight o'clock, whereas the symptoms did not manifest themselves until the early hours of the morning, which, on the face of it, points to the drug having been taken much later in the evening."

"Mrs. Inglethorp was in the habit of drinking a cup of cocoa in the middle of the night. Could the strychnine have been administered in that?"

"No, I myself took a sample of the cocoa remaining in the saucepan and had it analysed. There was no strychnine present."

I heard Poirot chuckle softly beside me.

"How did you know?" I whispered.

"Listen."

"I should say"—the doctor was continuing—"that I would have been considerably surprised at any other result."

"Why?"

"Simply because strychnine has an unusually bitter taste. It can be detected in a solution of one in seventy thousand, and can only be disguised by some strongly flavoured substance. Cocoa would be quite powerless to mask it."

One of the jury wanted to know if the same objection applied to coffee.

"No. Coffee has a bitter taste of its own which would probably cover the taste of strychnine."

"Then you consider it more likely that the drug was administered in the coffee, but that for some unknown reason its action was delayed."

"Yes, but, the cup being completely smashed, there is no possibility of analyzing its contents."

This concluded Dr. Bauerstein's evidence. Dr. Wilkins corroborated it on all points. Sounded as to the possibility of suicide, he repudiated it utterly. The deceased, he said, suffered from a weak heart, but otherwise enjoyed perfect health, and was of a cheerful and well-balanced disposition. She would be one of the last people to take her own life.

Lawrence Cavendish was next called. His evidence was quite unimportant, being a mere repetition of that of his brother. Just as he was about to step down, he paused, and said rather hesitatingly:

"I should like to make a suggestion if I may?"

He glanced deprecatingly at the Coroner, who replied briskly:

"Certainly, Mr. Cavendish, we are here to arrive at the truth of this matter, and welcome anything that may lead to further elucidation."

"It is just an idea of mine," explained Lawrence. "Of course I may be quite wrong, but it still seems to me that my mother's death might be accounted for by natural means."

"How do you make that out, Mr. Cavendish?"

"My mother, at the time of her death, and for some time before it, was taking a tonic containing strychnine."

"Ah!" said the Coroner.

The jury looked up, interested.

"I believe," continued Lawrence, "that there have been cases where the cumulative effect of a drug, administered for some time, has ended by causing death. Also, is it not possible that she may have taken an overdose of her medicine by accident?"

"This is the first we have heard of the deceased taking strychnine at the time of her death. We are much obliged to you, Mr. Cavendish."

Dr. Wilkins was recalled and ridiculed the idea.

"What Mr. Cavendish suggests is quite impossible. Any doctor would tell you the same. Strychnine is, in a certain sense, a cumulative poison, but it would be quite impossible for it to result in sudden death in this way. There would have to be a long period of chronic symptoms which would at once have attracted my attention. The whole thing is absurd."

"And the second suggestion? That Mrs. Inglethorp may have inadvertently taken an overdose?"

"Three, or even four doses, would not have resulted in death. Mrs. Inglethorp always had an extra large amount of medicine made up at a time, as she dealt with Coot's, the Cash Chemists in Tadminster. She would have had to take very nearly the whole bottle to account for the amount of strychnine found at the post-mortem."

"Then you consider that we may dismiss the tonic as not being in any way instrumental in causing her death?"

"Certainly. The supposition is ridiculous."

The same juryman who had interrupted before here suggested that the chemist who made up the medicine might have committed an error.

"That, of course, is always possible," replied the doctor.

But Dorcas, who was the next witness called, dispelled even

that possibility. The medicine had not been newly made up. On the contrary, Mrs. Inglethorp had taken the last dose on the day of her death.

So the question of the tonic was finally abandoned, and the Coroner proceeded with his task. Having elicited from Dorcas how she had been awakened by the violent ringing of her mistress's bell, and had subsequently roused the household, he passed to the subject of the quarrel on the preceding afternoon.

Dorcas's evidence on this point was substantially what Poirot and I had already heard, so I will not repeat it here.

The next witness was Mary Cavendish. She stood very upright, and spoke in a low, clear, and perfectly composed voice. In answer to the Coroner's question, she told how, her alarm clock having aroused her at four-thirty as usual, she was dressing, when she was startled by the sound of something heavy falling.

"That would have been the table by the bed?" commented the Coroner.

"I opened my door," continued Mary, "and listened. In a few minutes a bell rang violently. Dorcas came running down and woke my husband, and we all went to my mother-in-law's room, but it was locked——"

The Coroner interrupted her.

"I really do not think we need trouble you further on that point. We know all that can be known of the subsequent happenings. But I should be obliged if you would tell us all you overheard of the quarrel the day before."

"I?"

There was a faint insolence in her voice. She raised her hand and adjusted the ruffle of lace at her neck, turning her head a little as she did so. And quite spontaneously the thought flashed across my mind: "She is gaining time!"

"Yes. I understand," continued the Coroner deliberately, "that you were sitting reading on the bench just outside the long window of the boudoir. That is so, is it not?"

This was news to me and glancing sideways at Poirot, I fancied that it was news to him as well.

There was the faintest pause, the mere hesitation of a moment, before she answered:

"Yes, that is so."

"And the boudoir window was open, was it not?"

Surely her face grew a little paler as she answered:

"Yes."

"Then you cannot have failed to hear the voices inside, especially as they were raised in anger. In fact, they would be more audible where you were than in the hall."

"Possibly."

"Will you repeat to us what you overheard of the quarrel?"

"I really do not remember hearing anything."

"Do you mean to say you did not hear voices?"

"Oh, yes, I heard the voices, but I did not hear what they said." A faint spot of colour came into her cheek. "I am not in the habit of listening to private conversations."

The Coroner persisted.

"And you remember nothing at all? *Nothing*, Mrs. Cavendish? Not one stray word or phrase to make you realize that it *was* a private conversation?"

She paused, and seemed to reflect, still outwardly as calm as ever.

"Yes; I remember. Mrs. Inglethorp said something—I do not remember exactly what—about causing scandal between husband and wife."

"Ah!" the Coroner leant back satisfied. "That corresponds with what Dorcas heard. But excuse me, Mrs. Cavendish, although you realized it was a private conversation, you did not move away? You remained where you were?"

I caught the momentary gleam of her tawny eyes as she raised them. I felt certain that at that moment she would willingly have torn the little lawyer, with his insinuations, into pieces, but she replied quietly enough:

"No. I was very comfortable where I was. I fixed my mind on my book."

"And that is all you can tell us?"

"That is all."

The examination was over, though I doubted if the Coroner was entirely satisfied with it. I think he suspected that Mary Cavendish could tell more if she chose.

Amy Hill, shop assistant, was next called, and deposed to having sold a will form on the afternoon of the 17th to William Earl, under-gardener at Styles.

William Earl and Manning succeeded her, and testified to witnessing a document. Manning fixed the time at about four-thirty, William was of the opinion that it was rather earlier.

Cynthia Murdoch came next. She had, however, little to tell. She had known nothing of the tragedy, until awakened by Mrs. Cavendish.

"You did not hear the table fall?"

"No. I was fast asleep."

The Coroner smiled.

"A good conscience makes a sound sleeper," he observed. "Thank you, Miss Murdoch, that is all."

"Miss Howard."

Miss Howard produced the letter written to her by Mrs. Inglethorp on the evening of the 17th. Poirot and I had, of course already seen it. It added nothing to our knowledge of the tragedy. The following is a facsimile:

86

July 17th

Styles Court
Essex

My dear Evelyn
          Can we not bury
the hatchet? I have
found it hard to forget
the things you said
against my dear husband
but I am an old woman
     very fond of you
          yours affectionably
               Emily Inglethorp

87

It was handed to the jury who scrutinized it attentively.

"I fear it does not help us much," said the Coroner, with a sigh. "There is no mention of any of the events of that afternoon."

"Plain as a pikestaff to me," said Miss Howard shortly. "It shows clearly enough that my poor old friend had just found out she'd been made a fool of!"

"It says nothing of the kind in the letter," the Coroner pointed out.

"No, because Emily never could bear to put herself in the wrong. But *I* know her. She wanted me back. But she wasn't going to own that I'd been right. She went round about. Most people do. Don't believe in it myself."

Mr. Wells smiled faintly. So, I noticed, did several of the jury. Miss Howard was obviously quite a public character.

"Anyway, all this tomfoolery is a great waste of time," continued the lady, glancing up and down the jury disparagingly. "Talk—talk—talk! When all the time we know perfectly well——"

The Coroner interrupted her in an agony of apprehension:

"Thank you, Miss Howard, that is all."

I fancy he breathed a sigh of relief when she complied.

Then came the sensation of the day. The Coroner called Albert Mace, chemist's assistant.

It was our agitated young man of the pale face. In answer to the Coroner's questions, he explained that he was a qualified pharmacist, but had only recently come to this particular shop, as the assistant formerly there had just been called up for the army.

These preliminaries completed, the Coroner proceeded to business.

"Mr. Mace, have you lately sold strychnine to any unauthorized person?"

"Yes, sir."

"When was this?"

"Last Monday night."

"Monday? Not Tuesday?"

"No, sir, Monday, the 16th."

"Will you tell us to whom you sold it?"

You could have heard a pin drop.

"Yes, sir. It was to Mr. Inglethorp."

Every eye turned simultaneously to where Alfred Inglethorp was sitting, impassive and wooden. He started slightly, as the damning words fell from the young man's lips. I half thought he was going to rise from his chair, but he remained seated, although a remarkably well acted expression of astonishment rose on his face.

"You are sure of what you say?" asked the Coroner sternly.

"Quite sure, sir."

"Are you in the habit of selling strychnine indiscriminately over the counter?"

The wretched young man wilted visibly under the Coroner's frown.

"Oh, no, sir—of course not. But, seeing it was Mr. Inglethorp of the Hall, I thought there was no harm in it. He said it was to poison a dog."

Inwardly I sympathized. It was only human nature to endeavour to please "The Hall"—especially when it might result in custom being transferred from Coot's to the local establishment.

"Is it not customary for anyone purchasing poison to sign a book?"

"Yes, sir, Mr. Inglethorp did so."

"Have you got the book here?"

"Yes, sir."

It was produced; and, with a few words of stern censure, the Coroner dismissed the wretched Mr. Mace.

Then, amidst a breathless silence, Alfred Inglethorp was called. Did he realize, I wondered, how closely the halter was being drawn around his neck?

The Coroner went straight to the point.

"On Monday evening last, did you purchase strychnine for

the purpose of poisoning a dog?"

Inglethorp replied with perfect calmness:

"No, I did not. There is no dog at Styles, except an outdoor sheepdog, which is in perfect health."

"You deny absolutely having purchased strychnine from Albert Mace on Monday last?"

"I do."

"Do you also deny *this*?"

The Coroner handed him the register in which his signature was inscribed.

"Certainly I do. The hand-writing is quite different from mine. I will show you."

He took an old envelope out of his pocket, and wrote his name on it, handing it to the jury. It was certainly utterly dissimilar.

"Then what is your explanation of Mr. Mace's statement?"

Alfred Inglethorp replied imperturbably:

"Mr. Mace must have been mistaken."

The Coroner hesitated for a moment, and then said:

"Mr. Inglethorp, as a mere matter of form, would you mind telling us where you were on the evening of Monday, July 16th?"

"Really—I cannot remember."

"That is absurd, Mr. Inglethorp," said the Coroner sharply. "Think again."

Inglethorp shook his head.

"I cannot tell you. I have an idea that I was out walking."

"In what direction?"

"I really can't remember."

The Coroner's face grew graver.

"Were you in company with anyone?"

"No."

"Did you meet anyone on your walk?"

"No."

"That is a pity," said the Coroner dryly. "I am to take it then that you decline to say where you were at the time that Mr.

Mace positively recognized you as entering the shop to purchase strychnine?"

"If you like to take it that way, yes."

"Be careful, Mr. Inglethorp."

Poirot was fidgeting nervously.

"*Sacré!*" he murmured. "Does this imbecile of a man *want* to be arrested?"

Inglethorp was indeed creating a bad impression. His futile denials would not have convinced a child. The Coroner, however, passed briskly to the next point, and Poirot drew a deep breath of relief.

"You had a discussion with your wife on Tuesday afternoon?"

"Pardon me," interrupted Alfred Inglethorp, "you have been misinformed. I had no quarrel with my dear wife. The whole story is absolutely untrue. I was absent from the house the entire afternoon."

"Have you anyone who can testify to that?"

"You have my word," said Inglethorp haughtily.

The Coroner did not trouble to reply.

"There are two witnesses who will swear to having heard your disagreement with Mrs. Inglethorp."

"Those witnesses were mistaken."

I was puzzled. The man spoke with such quiet assurance that I was staggered. I looked at Poirot. There was an expression of exultation on his face which I could not understand. Was he at last convinced of Alfred Inglethorp's guilt?

"Mr. Inglethorp," said the Coroner, "you have heard your wife's dying words repeated here. Can you explain them in any way?"

"Certainly I can."

"You can?"

"It seems to me very simple. The room was dimly lighted. Dr. Bauerstein is much of my height and build, and, like me, wears a beard. In the dim light, and suffering as she was, my poor wife

91

mistook him for me."

"Ah!" murmured Poirot to himself. "But it is an idea, that!"

"You think it is true?" I whispered.

"I do not say that. But it is truly an ingenious supposition."

"You read my wife's last words as an accusation"—Inglethorp was continuing—"they were, on the contrary, an appeal to me."

The Coroner reflected a moment, then he said:

"I believe, Mr. Inglethorp, that you yourself poured out the coffee, and took it to your wife that evening?"

"I poured it out, yes. But I did not take it to her. I meant to do so, but I was told that a friend was at the hall door, so I laid down the coffee on the hall table. When I came through the hall again a few minutes later, it was gone."

This statement might, or might not, be true, but it did not seem to me to improve matters much for Inglethorp. In any case, he had had ample time to introduce the poison.

At that point, Poirot nudged me gently, indicating two men who were sitting together near the door. One was a little, sharp, dark, ferret-faced man, the other was tall and fair.

I questioned Poirot mutely. He put his lips to my ear.

"Do you know who that little man is?"

I shook my head.

"That is Detective Inspector James Japp of Scotland Yard—Jimmy Japp. The other man is from Scotland Yard too. Things are moving quickly, my friend."

I stared at the two men intently. There was certainly nothing of the policeman about them. I should never have suspected them of being official personages.

I was still staring, when I was startled and recalled by the verdict being given:

"Wilful Murder against some person or persons unknown."

SEVEN

Poirot Pays His Debts

As we came out of the Stylites Arms, Poirot drew me aside by a gentle pressure of the arm. I understood his object. He was waiting for the Scotland Yard men.

In a few moments, they emerged, and Poirot at once stepped forward, and accosted the shorter of the two.

"I fear you do not remember me, Inspector Japp."

"Why, if it isn't Mr. Poirot!" cried the Inspector. He turned to the other man. "You've heard me speak of Mr. Poirot? It was in 1904 he and I worked together—the Abercrombie forgery case—you remember, he was run down in Brussels. Ah, those were great days, moosier. Then, do you remember 'Baron' Altara? There was a pretty rogue for you! He eluded the clutches of half the police in Europe. But we nailed him in Antwerp—thanks to Mr. Poirot here."

As these friendly reminiscences were being indulged in, I drew nearer, and was introduced to Detective-Inspector Japp, who, in his turn, introduced us both to his companion, Superintendent Summerhaye.

"I need hardly ask what you are doing here, gentlemen," remarked Poirot.

Japp closed one eye knowingly.

"No, indeed. Pretty clear case I should say."

But Poirot answered gravely:

"There I differ from you."

"Oh, come!" said Summerhaye, opening his lips for the first time. "Surely the whole thing is clear as daylight. The man's caught red-handed. How he could be such a fool beats me!"

But Japp was looking attentively at Poirot.

"Hold your fire, Summerhaye," he remarked jocularly. "Me and Moosier here have met before—and there's no man's judgment I'd sooner take than his. If I'm not greatly mistaken, he's got something up his sleeve. Isn't that so, moosier?"

Poirot smiled.

"I have drawn certain conclusions—yes."

Summerhaye was still looking rather sceptical, but Japp continued his scrutiny of Poirot.

"It's this way," he said, "so far, we've only seen the case from the outside. That's where the Yard's at a disadvantage in a case of this kind, where the murder's only out, so to speak, after the inquest. A lot depends on being on the spot first thing, and that's where Mr. Poirot's had the start of us. We shouldn't have been here as soon as this even, if it hadn't been for the fact that there was a smart doctor on the spot, who gave us the tip through the Coroner. But you've been on the spot from the first, and you may have picked up some little hints. From the evidence at the inquest, Mr. Inglethorp murdered his wife as sure as I stand here, and if anyone but you hinted the contrary I'd laugh in his face. I must say I was surprised the jury didn't bring it in Wilful Murder against him right off. I think they would have, if it hadn't been for the Coroner—he seemed to be holding them back."

"Perhaps, though, you have a warrant for his arrest in your pocket now," suggested Poirot.

A kind of wooden shutter of officialdom came down from Japp's expressive countenance.

"Perhaps I have, and perhaps I haven't," he remarked dryly.

Poirot looked at him thoughtfully.

"I am very anxious, Messieurs, that he should not be arrested."

"I dare say," observed Summerhaye sarcastically.

Japp was regarding Poirot with comical perplexity.

"Can't you go a little further, Mr. Poirot? A wink's as good as a nod—from you. You've been on the spot—and the Yard doesn't want to make any mistakes, you know."

Poirot nodded gravely.

"That is exactly what I thought. Well, I will tell you this. Use your warrant: Arrest Mr. Inglethorp. But it will bring you no kudos—the case against him will be dismissed at once! *Comme ça!*" And he snapped his fingers expressively.

Japp's face grew grave, though Summerhaye gave an incredulous snort.

As for me, I was literally dumb with astonishment. I could only conclude that Poirot was mad.

Japp had taken out a handkerchief, and was gently dabbing his brow.

"I daren't do it, Mr. Poirot. I'd take your word, but there's others over me who'll be asking what the devil I mean by it. Can't you give me a little more to go on?"

Poirot reflected a moment.

"It can be done," he said at last. "I admit I do not wish it. It forces my hand. I would have preferred to work in the dark just for the present, but what you say is very just—the word of a Belgian policeman, whose day is past, is not enough! And Alfred Inglethorp must not be arrested. That I have sworn, as my friend Hastings here knows. See, then, my good Japp, you go at once to Styles?"

"Well, in about half an hour. We're seeing the Coroner and the doctor first."

"Good. Call for me in passing—the last house in the village. I will go with you. At Styles, Mr. Inglethorp will give you, or if he refuses—as is probable—I will give you such proofs that shall satisfy you that the case against him could not possibly be sustained. Is that a bargain?"

"That's a bargain," said Japp heartily. "And, on behalf of the Yard, I'm much obliged to you, though I'm bound to confess I can't at present see the faintest possible loop-hole in the evidence, but you always were a marvel! So long, then, moosier."

The two detectives strode away, Summerhaye with an incredulous grin on his face.

"Well, my friend," cried Poirot, before I could get in a word, "what do you think? *Mon Dieu!* I had some warm moments in that court; I did not figure to myself that the man would be so pig-headed as to refuse to say anything at all. Decidedly, it was the policy of an imbecile."

"H'm! There are other explanations besides that of imbecility," I remarked. "For, if the case against him is true, how could he defend himself except by silence?"

"Why, in a thousand ingenious ways," cried Poirot. "See; say that it is I who have committed this murder, I can think of seven most plausible stories! Far more convincing than Mr. Inglethorp's stony denials!"

I could not help laughing.

"My dear Poirot, I am sure you are capable of thinking of seventy! But, seriously, in spite of what I heard you say to the detectives, you surely cannot still believe in the possibility of Alfred Inglethorp's innocence?"

"Why not now as much as before? Nothing has changed."

"But the evidence is so conclusive."

"Yes, too conclusive."

We turned in at the gate of Leastways Cottage, and proceeded up the now familiar stairs.

"Yes, yes, too conclusive," continued Poirot, almost to himself. "Real evidence is usually vague and unsatisfactory. It has to be examined—sifted. But here the whole thing is cut and dried. No, my friend, this evidence has been very cleverly manufactured—so cleverly that it has defeated its own ends."

"How do you make that out?"

"Because, so long as the evidence against him was vague and intangible, it was very hard to disprove. But, in his anxiety, the criminal has drawn the net so closely that one cut will set Inglethorp free."

I was silent. And in a minute or two, Poirot continued:

"Let us look at the matter like this. Here is a man, let us say, who sets out to poison his wife. He has lived by his wits as the saying goes. Presumably, therefore, he has some wits. He is not altogether a fool. Well, how does he set about it? He goes boldly to the village chemist's and purchases strychnine under his own name, with a trumped up story about a dog which is bound to be proved absurd. He does not employ the poison that night. No, he waits until he has had a violent quarrel with her, of which the whole household is cognisant, and which naturally directs their suspicions upon him. He prepares no defence—no shadow of an alibi, yet he knows the chemist's assistant must necessarily come forward with the facts. Bah! Do not ask me to believe that any man could be so idiotic! Only a lunatic, who wished to commit suicide by causing himself to be hanged, would act so!"

"Still—I do not see——" I began.

"Neither do I see. I tell you, *mon ami*, it puzzles me. Me—Hercule Poirot!"

"But if you believe him innocent, how do you explain his buying the strychnine?"

"Very simply. He did *not* buy it."

"But Mace recognized him!"

"I beg your pardon, he saw a man with a black beard like Mr. Inglethorp's, and wearing glasses like Mr. Inglethorp, and dressed in Mr. Inglethorp's rather noticeable clothes. He could not recognize a man whom he had probably only seen in the distance, since, you remember, he himself had only been in the village a fortnight, and Mrs. Inglethorp dealt principally with Coot's in Tadminster."

"Then you think——"

"*Mon ami*, do you remember the two points I laid stress upon?

Leave the first one for the moment, what was the second?"

"The important fact that Alfred Inglethorp wears peculiar clothes, has a black beard, and uses glasses," I quoted.

"Exactly. Now suppose anyone wished to pass himself off as John or Lawrence Cavendish. Would it be easy?"

"No," I said thoughtfully. "Of course an actor——"

But Poirot cut me short ruthlessly.

"And why would it not be easy? I will tell you, my friend: Because they are both clean-shaven men. To make up successfully as one of these two in broad daylight, it would need an actor of genius, and a certain initial facial resemblance. But in the case of Alfred Inglethorp, all that is changed. His clothes, his beard, the glasses which hide his eyes—those are the salient points about his personal appearance. Now, what is the first instinct of the criminal? To divert suspicion from himself, is it not so? And how can he best do that? By throwing it on someone else. In this instance, there was a man ready to his hand. Everybody was predisposed to believe in Mr. Inglethorp's guilt. It was a foregone conclusion that he would be suspected; but, to make it a sure thing there must be tangible proof—such as the actual buying of the poison, and that, with a man of the peculiar appearance of Mr. Inglethorp, was not difficult. Remember, this young Mace had never actually spoken to Mr. Inglethorp. How should he doubt that the man in his clothes, with his beard and his glasses, was not Alfred Inglethorp?"

"It may be so," I said, fascinated by Poirot's eloquence. "But, if that was the case, why does he not say where he was at six o'clock on Monday evening?"

"Ah, why indeed?" said Poirot, calming down. "If he were arrested, he probably would speak, but I do not want it to come to that. I must make him see the gravity of his position. There is, of course, something discreditable behind his silence. If he did not murder his wife, he is, nevertheless, a scoundrel, and has something of his own to conceal, quite apart from the murder."

"What can it be?" I mused, won over to Poirot's views for the moment, although still retaining a faint conviction that the obvious deduction was the correct one.

"Can you not guess?" asked Poirot, smiling.

"No, can you?"

"Oh, yes, I had a little idea sometime ago—and it has turned out to be correct."

"You never told me," I said reproachfully.

Poirot spread out his hands apologetically.

"Pardon me, *mon ami*, you were not precisely *sympathique*." He turned to me earnestly. "Tell me—you see now that he must not be arrested?"

"Perhaps," I said doubtfully, for I was really quite indifferent to the fate of Alfred Inglethorp, and thought that a good fright would do him no harm.

Poirot, who was watching me intently, gave a sigh.

"Come, my friend," he said, changing the subject, "apart from Mr. Inglethorp, how did the evidence at the inquest strike you?"

"Oh, pretty much what I expected."

"Did nothing strike you as peculiar about it?"

My thoughts flew to Mary Cavendish, and I hedged:

"In what way?"

"Well, Mr. Lawrence Cavendish's evidence for instance?"

I was relieved.

"Oh, Lawrence! No, I don't think so. He's always a nervous chap."

"His suggestion that his mother might have been poisoned accidentally by means of the tonic she was taking, that did not strike you as strange— *hein?*"

"No, I can't say it did. The doctors ridiculed it of course. But it was quite a natural suggestion for a layman to make."

"But Monsieur Lawrence is not a layman. You told me your-self that he had started by studying medicine, and that he had taken his degree."

"Yes, that's true. I never thought of that." I was rather startled.

"It *is* odd."

Poirot nodded.

"From the first, his behaviour has been peculiar. Of all the household, he alone would be likely to recognize the symptoms of strychnine poisoning, and yet we find him the only member of the family to uphold strenuously the theory of death from natural causes. If it had been Monsieur John, I could have understood it. He has no technical knowledge, and is by nature unimaginative. But Monsieur Lawrence—no! And now, to-day, he puts forward a suggestion that he himself must have known was ridiculous. There is food for thought in this, *mon ami!*"

"It's very confusing," I agreed.

"Then there is Mrs. Cavendish," continued Poirot. "That's another who is not telling all she knows! What do you make of her attitude?"

"I don't know what to make of it. It seems inconceivable that she should be shielding Alfred Inglethorp. Yet that is what it looks like."

Poirot nodded reflectively.

"Yes, it is queer. One thing is certain, she overheard a good deal more of that 'private conversation' than she was willing to admit."

"And yet she is the last person one would accuse of stooping to eavesdrop!"

"Exactly. One thing her evidence *has* shown me. I made a mistake. Dorcas was quite right. The quarrel did take place earlier in the afternoon, about four o'clock, as she said."

I looked at him curiously. I had never understood his insistence on that point.

"Yes, a good deal that was peculiar came out to-day," continued Poirot. "Dr. Bauerstein, now, what was *he* doing up and dressed at that hour in the morning? It is astonishing to me that no one commented on the fact."

"He has insomnia, I believe," I said doubtfully.

"Which is a very good, or a very bad explanation," remarked

Poirot. "It covers everything, and explains nothing. I shall keep my eye on our clever Dr. Bauerstein."

"Any more faults to find with the evidence?" I inquired satirically.

"*Mon ami*," replied Poirot gravely, "when you find that people are not telling you the truth—look out! Now, unless I am much mistaken, at the inquest to-day only one—at most, two persons were speaking the truth without reservation or subterfuge."

"Oh, come now, Poirot! I won't cite Lawrence, or Mrs. Cavendish. But there's John—and Miss Howard, surely they were speaking the truth?"

"Both of them, my friend? One, I grant you, but both——!"

His words gave me an unpleasant shock. Miss Howard's evidence, unimportant as it was, had been given in such a downright straightforward manner that it had never occurred to me to doubt her sincerity. Still, I had a great respect for Poirot's sagacity— except on the occasions when he was what I described to myself as "foolishly pig-headed."

"Do you really think so?" I asked. "Miss Howard had always seemed to me so essentially honest—almost uncomfortably so."

Poirot gave me a curious look, which I could not quite fathom. He seemed to speak, and then checked himself.

"Miss Murdoch too," I continued, "there's nothing untruthful about *her*."

"No. But it was strange that she never heard a sound, sleeping next door; whereas Mrs. Cavendish, in the other wing of the building, distinctly heard the table fall."

"Well, she's young. And she sleeps soundly."

"Ah, yes, indeed! She must be a famous sleeper, that one!"

I did not quite like the tone of his voice, but at that moment a smart knock reached our ears, and looking out of the window we perceived the two detectives waiting for us below.

Poirot seized his hat, gave a ferocious twist to his moustache, and, carefully brushing an imaginary speck of dust from his sleeve, motioned me to precede him down the stairs; there we joined the detectives and set out for Styles.

I think the appearance of the two Scotland Yard men was rather a shock—especially to John, though of course after the verdict, he had realized that it was only a matter of time. Still, the presence of the detectives brought the truth home to him more than anything else could have done.

Poirot had conferred with Japp in a low tone on the way up, and it was the latter functionary who requested that the household, with the exception of the servants, should be assembled together in the drawing-room. I realized the significance of this. It was up to Poirot to make his boast good.

Personally, I was not sanguine. Poirot might have excellent reasons for his belief in Inglethorp's innocence, but a man of the type of Summerhaye would require tangible proofs, and these I doubted if Poirot could supply.

Before very long we had all trooped into the drawing-room, the door of which Japp closed. Poirot politely set chairs for everyone. The Scotland Yard men were the cynosure of all eyes. I think that for the first time we realized that the thing was not a bad dream, but a tangible reality. We had read of such things—now we ourselves were actors in the drama. To-morrow the daily papers, all over England, would blazon out the news in staring headlines:

"*MYSTERIOUS TRAGEDY IN ESSEX*"
"*WEALTHY LADY POISONED*"

There would be pictures of Styles, snap-shots of "The family leaving the Inquest"—the village photographer had not been idle! All the things that one had read a hundred times—things that happen to other people, not to oneself. And now, in this house, a murder had been committed. In front of us were "the detectives in charge of the case." The well-known glib phraseology passed rapidly through my mind in the interval before Poirot opened the proceedings.

I think everyone was a little surprised that it should be he and not one of the official detectives who took the initiative.

"*Mesdames* and *messieurs*," said Poirot, bowing as though he were a celebrity about to deliver a lecture, "I have asked you to come here all together, for a certain object. That object, it concerns Mr. Alfred Inglethorp."

Inglethorp was sitting a little by himself—I think, unconsciously, everyone had drawn his chair slightly away from him—and he gave a faint start as Poirot pronounced his name.

"Mr. Inglethorp," said Poirot, addressing him directly, "a very dark shadow is resting on this house—the shadow of murder."

Inglethorp shook his head sadly.

"My poor wife," he murmured. "Poor Emily! It is terrible."

"I do not think, monsieur," said Poirot pointedly, "that you quite realize how terrible it may be—for you." And as Inglethorp did not appear to understand, he added: "Mr. Inglethorp, you are standing in very grave danger."

The two detectives fidgeted. I saw the official caution "Anything you say will be used in evidence against you," actually hovering on Summerhaye's lips. Poirot went on.

"Do you understand now, monsieur?"

"No. What do you mean?"

"I mean," said Poirot deliberately, "that you are suspected of poisoning your wife."

A little gasp ran round the circle at this plain speaking.

"Good heavens!" cried Inglethorp, starting up. "What a monstrous idea! *I*—poison my dearest Emily!"

"I do not think"—Poirot watched him narrowly—"that you quite realize the unfavourable nature of your evidence at the inquest. Mr. Inglethorp, knowing what I have now told you, do you still refuse to say where you were at six o'clock on Monday afternoon?"

With a groan, Alfred Inglethorp sank down again and buried his face in his hands. Poirot approached and stood over him.

"Speak!" he cried menacingly.

With an effort, Inglethorp raised his face from his hands. Then, slowly and deliberately, he shook his head.

"You will not speak?"

"No. I do not believe that anyone could be so monstrous as to accuse me of what you say."

Poirot nodded thoughtfully, like a man whose mind is made up.

"*Soit!*" he said. "Then I must speak for you."

Alfred Inglethorp sprang up again.

"You? How can you speak? You do not know——" he broke off abruptly.

Poirot turned to face us. "*Mesdames* and *messieurs*! I speak! Listen! I, Hercule Poirot, affirm that the man who entered the chemist's shop, and purchased strychnine at six o'clock on Monday last was not Mr. Inglethorp, for at six o'clock on that day Mr. Inglethorp was escorting Mrs. Raikes back to her home from a neighbouring farm. I can produce no less than five witnesses to swear to having seen them together, either at six or just after and, as you may know, the Abbey Farm, Mrs. Raikes's home, is at least two and a half miles distant from the village. There is absolutely no question as to the alibi!"

EIGHT

Fresh Suspicions

There was a moment's stupefied silence. Japp, who was the least surprised of any of us, was the first to speak.

"My word," he cried, "you're the goods! And no mistake, Mr. Poirot! These witnesses of yours are all right, I suppose?"

"*Voilà!* I have prepared a list of them—names and addresses. You must see them, of course. But you will find it all right."

"I'm sure of that." Japp lowered his voice. "I'm much obliged to you. A pretty mare's nest arresting him would have been." He turned to Inglethorp. "But, if you'll excuse me, sir, why couldn't you say all this at the inquest?"

"I will tell you why," interrupted Poirot. "There was a certain rumour——"

"A most malicious and utterly untrue one," interrupted Alfred Inglethorp in an agitated voice.

"And Mr. Inglethorp was anxious to have no scandal revived just at present. Am I right?"

"Quite right." Inglethorp nodded. "With my poor Emily not yet buried, can you wonder I was anxious that no more lying rumours should be started."

"Between you and me, sir," remarked Japp, "I'd sooner have any amount of rumours than be arrested for murder. And I venture to think your poor lady would have felt the same. And, if it hadn't

105

been for Mr. Poirot here, arrested you would have been, as sure as eggs is eggs!"

"I was foolish, no doubt," murmured Inglethorp. "But you do not know, inspector, how I have been persecuted and maligned." And he shot a baleful glance at Evelyn Howard.

"Now, sir," said Japp, turning briskly to John, "I should like to see the lady's bedroom, please, and after that I'll have a little chat with the servants. Don't you bother about anything. Mr. Poirot, here, will show me the way."

As they all went out of the room, Poirot turned and made me a sign to follow him upstairs. There he caught me by the arm, and drew me aside.

"Quick, go to the other wing. Stand there—just this side of the baize door. Do not move till I come." Then, turning rapidly, he rejoined the two detectives.

I followed his instructions, taking up my position by the baize door, and wondering what on earth lay behind the request. Why was I to stand this particular spot on guard? I looked thoughtfully down the corridor in front of me. An idea struck me. With the exception of Cynthia Murdoch's, everyone's room was in this left wing. Had that anything to do with it? Was I to report who came or went? I stood faithfully at my post. The minutes passed. Nobody came. Nothing happened.

It must have been quite twenty minutes before Poirot rejoined me.

"You have not stirred?"

"No, I've stuck here like a rock. Nothing's happened."

"Ah!" Was he pleased, or disappointed? "You've seen nothing at all?"

"No."

"But you have probably heard something? A big bump—eh, *mon ami?*"

"No."

"Is it possible? Ah, but I am vexed with myself! I am not

usually clumsy. I made but a slight gesture"—I know Poirot's gestures—"with the left hand, and over went the table by the bed!"

He looked so childishly vexed and crest-fallen that I hastened to console him.

"Never mind, old chap. What does it matter? Your triumph downstairs excited you. I can tell you, that was a surprise to us all. There must be more in this affair of Inglethorp's with Mrs. Raikes than we thought, to make him hold his tongue so persistently. What are you going to do now? Where are the Scotland Yard fellows?"

"Gone down to interview the servants. I showed them all our exhibits. I am disappointed in Japp. He has no method!"

"Hullo!" I said, looking out of the window. "Here's Dr. Bauerstein. I believe you're right about that man, Poirot. I don't like him."

"He is clever," observed Poirot meditatively.

"Oh, clever as the devil! I must say I was overjoyed to see him in the plight he was in on Tuesday. You never saw such a spectacle!" And I described the doctor's adventure. "He looked a regular scarecrow! Plastered with mud from head to foot."

"You saw him, then?"

"Yes. Of course, he didn't want to come in—it was just after dinner—but Mr. Inglethorp insisted."

"What?" Poirot caught me violently by the shoulders. "Was Dr. Bauerstein here on Tuesday evening? Here? And you never told me? Why did you not tell me? Why? Why?"

He appeared to be in an absolute frenzy.

"My dear Poirot," I expostulated, "I never thought it would interest you. I didn't know it was of any importance."

"Importance? It is of the first importance! So Dr. Bauerstein was here on Tuesday night—the night of the murder. Hastings, do you not see? That alters everything—everything!"

I had never seen him so upset. Loosening his hold of me, he mechanically straightened a pair of candlesticks, still murmuring to himself: "Yes, that alters everything—everything."

Suddenly he seemed to come to a decision.

"*Allons!*" he said. "We must act at once. Where is Mr. Cavendish?"

John was in the smoking-room. Poirot went straight to him.

"Mr. Cavendish, I have some important business in Tadminster. A new clue. May I take your motor?"

"Why, of course. Do you mean at once?"

"If you please."

John rang the bell, and ordered round the car. In another ten minutes, we were racing down the park and along the high road to Tadminster.

"Now, Poirot," I remarked resignedly, "perhaps you will tell me what all this is about?"

"Well, *mon ami*, a good deal you can guess for yourself. Of course you realize that, now Mr. Inglethorp is out of it, the whole position is greatly changed. We are face to face with an entirely new problem. We know now that there is one person who did not buy the poison. We have cleared away the manufactured clues. Now for the real ones. I have ascertained that anyone in the household, with the exception of Mrs. Cavendish, who was playing tennis with you, could have personated Mr. Inglethorp on Monday evening. In the same way, we have his statement that he put the coffee down in the hall. No one took much notice of that at the inquest—but now it has a very different significance. We must find out who did take that coffee to Mrs. Inglethorp eventually, or who passed through the hall whilst it was standing there. From your account, there are only two people whom we can positively say did not go near the coffee—Mrs. Cavendish, and Mademoiselle Cynthia."

"Yes, that is so." I felt an inexpressible lightening of the heart. Mary Cavendish could certainly not rest under suspicion.

"In clearing Alfred Inglethorp," continued Poirot, "I have been obliged to show my hand sooner than I intended. As long as I might be thought to be pursuing him, the criminal would be off his guard. Now, he will be doubly careful. Yes—doubly careful." He turned to me abruptly. "Tell me, Hastings, you yourself—have you no suspicions of anybody?"

I hesitated. To tell the truth, an idea, wild and extravagant in itself, had once or twice that morning flashed through my brain. I had rejected it as absurd, nevertheless it persisted.

"You couldn't call it a suspicion," I murmured. "It's so utterly foolish."

"Come now," urged Poirot encouragingly. "Do not fear. Speak your mind. You should always pay attention to your instincts."

"Well then," I blurted out, "it's absurd—but I suspect Miss Howard of not telling all she knows!"

"Miss Howard?"

"Yes—you'll laugh at me——"

"Not at all. Why should I?"

"I can't help feeling," I continued blunderingly; "that we've rather left her out of the possible suspects, simply on the strength of her having been away from the place. But, after all, she was only fifteen miles away. A car would do it in half an hour. Can we say positively that she was away from Styles on the night of the murder?"

"Yes, my friend," said Poirot unexpectedly, "we can. One of my first actions was to ring up the hospital where she was working."

"Well?"

"Well, I learnt that Miss Howard had been on afternoon duty on Tuesday, and that—a convoy coming in unexpectedly—she had kindly offered to remain on night duty, which offer was gratefully accepted. That disposes of that."

"Oh!" I said, rather nonplussed. "Really," I continued, "it's her extraordinary vehemence against Inglethorp that started me off suspecting her. I can't help feeling she'd do anything against him. And I had an idea she might know something about the destroying of the will. She might have burnt the new one, mistaking it for the earlier one in his favour. She is so terribly bitter against him."

"You consider her vehemence unnatural?"

"Y—es. She is so very violent. I wondered really whether she is quite sane on that point."

Poirot shook his head energetically.

"No, no, you are on a wrong tack there. There is nothing weak-minded or degenerate about Miss Howard. She is an excellent specimen of well-balanced English beef and brawn. She is sanity itself."

"Yet her hatred of Inglethorp seems almost a mania. My idea was—a very ridiculous one, no doubt—that she had intended to poison him—and that, in some way, Mrs. Inglethorp got hold of it by mistake. But I don't at all see how it could have been done. The whole thing is absurd and ridiculous to the last degree."

"Still you are right in one thing. It is always wise to suspect everybody until you can prove logically, and to your own satisfaction, that they are innocent. Now, what reasons are there against Miss Howard's having deliberately poisoned Mrs. Inglethorp?"

"Why, she was devoted to her!" I exclaimed.

"Tcha! Tcha!" cried Poirot irritably. "You argue like a child. If Miss Howard were capable of poisoning the old lady, she would be quite equally capable of simulating devotion. No, we must look elsewhere. You are perfectly correct in your assumption that her vehemence against Alfred Inglethorp is too violent to be natural; but you are quite wrong in the deduction you draw from it. I have drawn my own deductions, which I believe to be correct, but I will not speak of them at present." He paused a minute, then went on. "Now, to my way of thinking, there is one insuperable objection to Miss Howard's being the murderess."

"And that is?"

"That in no possible way could Mrs. Inglethorp's death benefit Miss Howard. Now there is no murder without a motive."

I reflected.

"Could not Mrs. Inglethorp have made a will in her favour?"

Poirot shook his head.

"But you yourself suggested that possibility to Mr. Wells?"

Poirot smiled.

"That was for a reason. I did not want to mention the name of the person who was actually in my mind. Miss Howard occupied very much the same position, so I used her name instead."

"Still, Mrs. Inglethorp might have done so. Why, that will, made on the afternoon of her death may——"

But Poirot's shake of the head was so energetic that I stopped.

"No, my friend. I have certain little ideas of my own about that will. But I can tell you this much—it was not in Miss Howard's favour."

I accepted his assurance, though I did not really see how he could be so positive about the matter.

"Well," I said, with a sigh, "we will acquit Miss Howard, then. It is partly your fault that I ever came to suspect her. It was what you said about her evidence at the inquest that set me off."

Poirot looked puzzled.

"What did I say about her evidence at the inquest?"

"Don't you remember? When I cited her and John Cavendish as being above suspicion?"

"Oh—ah—yes." He seemed a little confused, but recovered himself. "By the way, Hastings, there is something I want you to do for me."

"Certainly. What is it?"

"Next time you happen to be alone with Lawrence Cavendish, I want you to say this to him. 'I have a message for you, from Poirot. He says: "Find the extra coffee-cup, and you can rest in peace!"' Nothing more. Nothing less."

"'Find the extra coffee-cup, and you can rest in peace.' Is that right?" I asked, much mystified.

"Excellent."

"But what does it mean?"

"Ah, that I will leave you to find out. You have access to the facts. Just say that to him, and see what he says."

"Very well—but it's all extremely mysterious."

We were running into Tadminster now, and Poirot directed the car to the "Analytical Chemist."

Poirot hopped down briskly, and went inside. In a few minutes he was back again.

"There," he said. "That is all my business."

"What were you doing there?" I asked, in lively curiosity.

"I left something to be analysed."

"Yes, but what?"

"The sample of cocoa I took from the saucepan in the bedroom."

"But that has already been tested!" I cried, stupefied. "Dr. Bauerstein had it tested, and you yourself laughed at the possibility of there being strychnine in it."

"I know Dr. Bauerstein had it tested," replied Poirot quietly.

"Well, then?"

"Well, I have a fancy for having it analysed again, that is all."

And not another word on the subject could I drag out of him. This proceeding of Poirot's, in respect of the cocoa, puzzled me intensely. I could see neither rhyme nor reason in it. However, my confidence in him, which at one time had rather waned, was fully restored since his belief in Alfred Inglethorp's innocence had been so triumphantly vindicated.

The funeral of Mrs. Inglethorp took place the following day, and on Monday, as I came down to a late breakfast, John drew me aside, and informed me that Mr. Inglethorp was leaving that morning, to take up his quarters at the Stylites Arms until he should have completed his plans.

"And really it's a great relief to think he's going, Hastings," continued my honest friend. "It was bad enough before, when we thought he'd done it, but I'm hanged if it isn't worse now, when we all feel guilty for having been so down on the fellow. The fact is, we've treated him abominably. Of course, things did look black against him. I don't see how anyone could blame us for jumping to the conclusions we did. Still, there it is, we were in the wrong, and now there's a beastly feeling that one ought to make amends; which is difficult, when one doesn't like the fellow a bit better than one did before. The whole thing's damned awkward! And I'm thankful he's had the tact to take himself off. It's a good thing Styles wasn't the mater's to leave to him. Couldn't bear to think of the fellow lording it here. He's welcome to her money."

"You'll be able to keep up the place all right?" I asked.

"Oh, yes. There are the death duties, of course, but half my father's money goes with the place, and Lawrence will stay with us for the present, so there is his share as well. We shall be pinched at first, of course, because, as I once told you, I am in a bit of a hole financially myself. Still, the Johnnies will wait now."

In the general relief at Inglethorp's approaching departure, we had the most genial breakfast we had experienced since the tragedy. Cynthia, whose young spirits were naturally buoyant, was looking quite her pretty self again, and we all, with the exception of Lawrence, who seemed unalterably gloomy and nervous, were quietly cheerful, at the opening of a new and hopeful future.

The papers, of course, had been full of the tragedy. Glaring headlines, sandwiched biographies of every member of the household, subtle innuendoes, the usual familiar tag about the police having a clue. Nothing was spared us. It was a slack time. The war was momentarily inactive, and the newspapers seized with avidity on this crime in fashionable life: "The Mysterious Affair at Styles" was the topic of the moment.

Naturally it was very annoying for the Cavendishes. The house was constantly besieged by reporters, who were consistently denied admission, but who continued to haunt the village and the grounds, where they lay in wait with cameras, for any unwary members of the household. We all lived in a blast of publicity. The Scotland Yard men came and went, examining, questioning, lynx-eyed and reserved of tongue. Towards what end they were working, we did not know. Had they any clue, or would the whole thing remain in the category of undiscovered crimes?

After breakfast, Dorcas came up to me rather mysteriously, and asked if she might have a few words with me.

"Certainly. What is it, Dorcas?"

"Well, it's just this, sir. You'll be seeing the Belgian gentleman to-day perhaps?" I nodded. "Well, sir, you know how he asked me so particular if the mistress, or anyone else, had a green dress?"

"Yes, yes. You have found one?" My interest was aroused.

"No, not that, sir. But since then I've remembered what the young gentlemen"—John and Lawrence were still the "young gentlemen" to Dorcas—"call the 'dressing-up box.' It's up in the front attic, sir. A great chest, full of old clothes and fancy dresses, and what not. And it came to me sudden like that there might be a green dress amongst them. So, if you'd tell the Belgian gentleman——"

"I will tell him, Dorcas," I promised.

"Thank you very much, sir. A very nice gentleman he is, sir. And quite a different class from them two detectives from London, what goes prying about, and asking questions. I don't hold with foreigners as a rule, but from what the newspapers say I make out as how these brave Belges isn't the ordinary run of foreigners, and certainly he's a most polite spoken gentleman."

Dear old Dorcas! As she stood there, with her honest face upturned to mine, I thought what a fine specimen she was of the old-fashioned servant that is so fast dying out.

I thought I might as well go down to the village at once, and look up Poirot; but I met him half-way, coming up to the house, and at once gave him Dorcas's message.

"Ah, the brave Dorcas! We will look at the chest, although— but no matter—we will examine it all the same."

We entered the house by one of the windows. There was no one in the hall, and we went straight up to the attic.

Sure enough, there was the chest, a fine old piece, all studded with brass nails, and full to overflowing with every imaginable type of garment.

Poirot bundled everything out on the floor with scant ceremony. There were one or two green fabrics of varying shades; but Poirot shook his head over them all. He seemed somewhat apathetic in the search, as though he expected no great results from it. Suddenly he gave an exclamation.

"What is it?"

"Look!"

The chest was nearly empty, and there, reposing right at the bottom, was a magnificent black beard.

"*Ohó!*" said Poirot. "*Ohó!*" He turned it over in his hands, examining it closely. "New," he remarked. "Yes, quite new."

After a moment's hesitation, he replaced it in the chest, heaped all the other things on top of it as before, and made his way briskly downstairs. He went straight to the pantry, where we found Dorcas busily polishing her silver.

Poirot wished her good morning with Gallic politeness, and went on:

"We have been looking through that chest, Dorcas. I am much obliged to you for mentioning it. There is, indeed, a fine collection there. Are they often used, may I ask?"

"Well, sir, not very often nowadays, though from time to time we do have what the young gentlemen call 'a dress-up night.' And very funny it is sometimes, sir. Mr. Lawrence, he's wonderful. Most comic! I shall never forget the night he came down as the Char of Persia, I think he called it—a sort of Eastern King it was. He had the big paper knife in his hand, and 'Mind, Dorcas,' he says, 'you'll have to be very respectful. This is my specially sharpened scimitar, and it's off with your head if I'm at all displeased with you!' Miss Cynthia, she was what they call an Apache, or some such name—a Frenchified sort of cut-throat, I take it to be. A real sight she looked. You'd never have believed a pretty young lady like that could have made herself into such a ruffian. Nobody

115

would have known her."

"These evenings must have been great fun," said Poirot genially. "I suppose Mr. Lawrence wore that fine black beard in the chest upstairs, when he was Shah of Persia?"

"He did have a beard, sir," replied Dorcas, smiling. "And well I know it, for he borrowed two skeins of my black wool to make it with! And I'm sure it looked wonderfully natural at a distance. I didn't know as there was a beard up there at all. It must have been got quite lately, I think. There was a red wig, I know, but nothing else in the way of hair. Burnt corks they use mostly—though 'tis messy getting it off again. Miss Cynthia was a nigger once, and, oh, the trouble she had."

"So Dorcas knows nothing about that black beard," said Poirot thoughtfully, as we walked out into the hall again.

"Do you think it is *the* one?" I whispered eagerly.

Poirot nodded.

"I do. You notice it had been trimmed?"

"No."

"Yes. It was cut exactly the shape of Mr. Inglethorp's, and I found one or two snipped hairs. Hastings, this affair is very deep."

"Who put it in the chest, I wonder?"

"Someone with a good deal of intelligence," remarked Poirot dryly. "You realize that he chose the one place in the house to hide it where its presence would not be remarked? Yes, he is intelligent. But we must be more intelligent. We must be so intelligent that he does not suspect us of being intelligent at all."

I acquiesced.

"There, *mon ami*, you will be of great assistance to me."

I was pleased with the compliment. There had been times when I hardly thought that Poirot appreciated me at my true worth.

"Yes," he continued, staring at me thoughtfully, "you will be invaluable."

This was naturally gratifying, but Poirot's next words were not so welcome.

"I must have an ally in the house," he observed reflectively.

"You have me," I protested.

"True, but you are not sufficient."

I was hurt, and showed it. Poirot hurried to explain himself.

"You do not quite take my meaning. You are known to be working with me. I want somebody who is not associated with us in any way."

"Oh, I see. How about John?"

"No, I think not."

"The dear fellow isn't perhaps very bright," I said thoughtfully.

"Here comes Miss Howard," said Poirot suddenly. "She is the very person. But I am in her black books, since I cleared Mr. Inglethorp. Still, we can but try."

With a nod that was barely civil, Miss Howard assented to Poirot's request for a few minutes' conversation.

We went into the little morning-room, and Poirot closed the door.

"Well, Monsieur Poirot," said Miss Howard impatiently, "what is it? Out with it. I'm busy."

"Do you remember, mademoiselle, that I once asked you to help me?"

"Yes, I do." The lady nodded. "And I told you I'd help you with pleasure—to hang Alfred Inglethorp."

"Ah!" Poirot studied her seriously. "Miss Howard, I will ask you one question. I beg of you to reply to it truthfully."

"Never tell lies," replied Miss Howard.

"It is this. Do you still believe that Mrs. Inglethorp was poisoned by her husband?"

"What do you mean?" she asked sharply. "You needn't think your pretty explanations influence me in the slightest. I'll admit that it wasn't he who bought strychnine at the chemist's shop. What of that? I dare say he soaked fly paper, as I told you at the beginning."

"That is arsenic—not strychnine," said Poirot mildly.

"What does that matter? Arsenic would put poor Emily out of the way just as well as strychnine. If I'm convinced he did it, it doesn't matter a jot to me *how* he did it."

"Exactly. *If* you are convinced he did it," said Poirot quietly. "I will put my question in another form. Did you ever in your heart of hearts believe that Mrs. Inglethorp was poisoned by her husband?"

"Good heavens!" cried Miss Howard. "Haven't I always told you the man is a villain? Haven't I always told you he would murder her in her bed? Haven't I always hated him like poison?"

"Exactly," said Poirot. "That bears out my little idea entirely."

"What little idea?"

"Miss Howard, do you remember a conversation that took place on the day of my friend's arrival here? He repeated it to me, and there is a sentence of yours that has impressed me very much. Do you remember affirming that if a crime had been committed, and anyone you loved had been murdered, you felt certain that you would know by instinct who the criminal was, even if you were quite unable to prove it?"

"Yes, I remember saying that. I believe it too. I suppose you think it nonsense?"

"Not at all."

"And yet you will pay no attention to my instinct against Alfred Inglethorp."

"No," said Poirot curtly. "Because your instinct is not against Mr. Inglethorp."

"What?"

"No. You wish to believe he committed the crime. You believe him capable of committing it. But your instinct tells you he did not commit it. It tells you more—shall I go on?"

She was staring at him, fascinated, and made a slight affirmative movement of the hand.

"Shall I tell you why you have been so vehement against Mr. Inglethorp? It is because you have been trying to believe what you wish to believe. It is because you are trying to drown and stifle your instinct, which tells you another name——"

"No, no, no!" cried Miss Howard wildly, flinging up her hands.

"Don't say it! Oh, don't say it! It isn't true! It can't be true. I don't know what put such a wild—such a dreadful—idea into my head!"

"I am right, am I not?" asked Poirot.

"Yes, yes; you must be a wizard to have guessed. But it can't be so—it's too monstrous, too impossible. It *must* be Alfred Inglethorp."

Poirot shook his head gravely.

"Don't ask me about it," continued Miss Howard, "because I shan't tell you. I won't admit it, even to myself. I must be mad to think of such a thing."

Poirot nodded, as if satisfied.

"I will ask you nothing. It is enough for me that it is as I thought. And I—I, too, have an instinct. We are working together towards a common end."

"Don't ask me to help you, because I won't. I wouldn't lift a finger to—to——" She faltered.

"You will help me in spite of yourself. I ask you nothing—but you will be my ally. You will not be able to help yourself. You will do the only thing that I want of you."

"And that is?"

"You will watch!"

Evelyn Howard bowed her head.

"Yes, I can't help doing that. I am always watching—always hoping I shall be proved wrong."

"If we are wrong, well and good," said Poirot. "No one will be more pleased than I shall. But, if we are right? If we are right, Miss Howard, on whose side are you then?"

"I don't know, I don't know——"

"Come now."

"It could be hushed up."

"There must be no hushing up."

"But Emily herself——" She broke off.

"Miss Howard," said Poirot gravely, "this is unworthy of you."

Suddenly she took her face from her hands.

"Yes," she said quietly, "that was not Evelyn Howard who spoke!" She flung her head up proudly. "*This* is Evelyn Howard! And she is on the side of Justice! Let the cost be what it may." And with these words, she walked firmly out of the room.

"There," said Poirot, looking after her, "goes a very valuable ally. That woman, Hastings, has got brains as well as a heart."

I did not reply.

"Instinct is a marvellous thing," mused Poirot. "It can neither be explained nor ignored."

"You and Miss Howard seem to know what you are talking about," I observed coldly. "Perhaps you don't realize that *I* am still in the dark."

"Really? Is that so, *mon ami?*"

"Yes. Enlighten me, will you?"

Poirot studied me attentively for a moment or two. Then, to my intense surprise, he shook his head decidedly.

"No, my friend."

"Oh, look here, why not?"

"Two is enough for a secret."

"Well, I think it is very unfair to keep back facts from me."

"I am not keeping back facts. Every fact that I know is in your possession. You can draw your own deductions from them. This time it is a question of ideas."

"Still, it would be interesting to know."

Poirot looked at me very earnestly, and again shook his head.

"You see," he said sadly, "*you* have no instincts."

"It was intelligence you were requiring just now," I pointed out.

"The two often go together," said Poirot enigmatically.

The remark seemed so utterly irrelevant that I did not even take the trouble to answer it. But I decided that if I made any interesting and important discoveries—as no doubt I should—I would keep them to myself, and surprise Poirot with the ultimate result.

There are times when it is one's duty to assert oneself.

NINE

Dr. Bauerstein

I had had no opportunity as yet of passing on Poirot's message to Lawrence. But now, as I strolled out on the lawn, still nursing a grudge against my friend's high-handedness, I saw Lawrence on the croquet lawn, aimlessly knocking a couple of very ancient balls about, with a still more ancient mallet.

It struck me that it would be a good opportunity to deliver my message. Otherwise, Poirot himself might relieve me of it. It was true that I did not quite gather its purport, but I flattered myself that by Lawrence's reply, and perhaps a little skillful cross-examination on my part, I should soon perceive its significance. Accordingly I accosted him.

"I've been looking for you," I remarked untruthfully.

"Have you?"

"Yes. The truth is, I've got a message for you—from Poirot."

"Yes?"

"He told me to wait until I was alone with you," I said, dropping my voice significantly, and watching him intently out of the corner of my eye. I have always been rather good at what is called, I believe, creating an atmosphere.

"Well?"

There was no change of expression in the dark melancholic face. Had he any idea of what I was about to say?

"This is the message." I dropped my voice still lower. "'Find the extra coffee-cup, and you can rest in peace.'"

"What on earth does he mean?" Lawrence stared at me in quite unaffected astonishment.

"Don't you know?"

"Not in the least. Do you?"

I was compelled to shake my head.

"What extra coffee-cup?"

"I don't know."

"He'd better ask Dorcas, or one of the maids, if he wants to know about coffee-cups. It's their business, not mine. I don't know anything about the coffee-cups, except that we've got some that are never used, which are a perfect dream! Old Worcester. You're not a connoisseur, are you, Hastings?"

I shook my head.

"You miss a lot. A really perfect bit of old china—it's pure delight to handle it, or even to look at it."

"Well, what am I to tell Poirot?"

"Tell him I don't know what he's talking about. It's double Dutch to me."

"All right."

I was moving off towards the house again when he suddenly called me back.

"I say, what was the end of that message? Say it over again, will you?"

"'Find the extra coffee-cup, and you can rest in peace.' Are you sure you don't know what it means?" I asked him earnestly.

He shook his head.

"No," he said musingly, "I don't. I—I wish I did."

The boom of the gong sounded from the house, and we went in together. Poirot had been asked by John to remain to lunch, and was already seated at the table.

By tacit consent, all mention of the tragedy was barred. We conversed on the war, and other outside topics. But after the cheese and biscuits had been handed round, and Dorcas had left the room, Poirot suddenly leant forward to Mrs. Cavendish.

"Pardon me, madame, for recalling unpleasant memories, but I have a little idea"—Poirot's "little ideas" were becoming a perfect byword—"and would like to ask one or two questions."

"Of me? Certainly."

"You are too amiable, madame. What I want to ask is this: the door leading into Mrs. Inglethorp's room from that of Mademoiselle Cynthia, it was bolted, you say?"

"Certainly it was bolted," replied Mary Cavendish, rather surprised. "I said so at the inquest."

"Bolted?"

"Yes." She looked perplexed.

"I mean," explained Poirot, "you are sure it was bolted, and not merely locked?"

"Oh, I see what you mean. No, I don't know. I said bolted, meaning that it was fastened, and I could not open it, but I believe all the doors were found bolted on the inside."

"Still, as far as you are concerned, the door might equally well have been locked?"

"Oh, yes."

"You yourself did not happen to notice, madame, when you entered Mrs. Inglethorp's room, whether that door was bolted or not?"

"I—I believe it was."

"But you did not see it?"

"No. I—never looked."

"But *I* did," interrupted Lawrence suddenly. "I happened to notice that it *was* bolted."

"Ah, that settles it." And Poirot looked crestfallen.

I could not help rejoicing that, for once, one of his "little ideas" had come to naught.

After lunch Poirot begged me to accompany him home. I consented rather stiffly.

"You are annoyed, is it not so?" he asked anxiously, as we walked through the park.

"Not at all," I said coldly.

"That is well. That lifts a great load from my mind."

This was not quite what I had intended. I had hoped that he would have observed the stiffness of my manner. Still, the fervour of his words went towards the appeasing of my just displeasure. I thawed.

"I gave Lawrence your message," I said.

"And what did he say? He was entirely puzzled?"

"Yes. I am quite sure he had no idea of what you meant."

I had expected Poirot to be disappointed; but, to my surprise, he replied that that was as he had thought, and that he was very glad. My pride forbade me to ask any questions.

Poirot switched off on another tack.

"Mademoiselle Cynthia was not at lunch to-day? How was that?"

"She is at the hospital again. She resumed work to-day."

"Ah, she is an industrious little demoiselle. And pretty too. She is like pictures I have seen in Italy. I would rather like to see that dispensary of hers. Do you think she would show it to me?"

"I am sure she would be delighted. It's an interesting little place."

"Does she go there every day?"

"She has all Wednesdays off, and comes back to lunch on Saturdays. Those are her only times off."

"I will remember. Women are doing great work nowadays, and Mademoiselle Cynthia is clever—oh, yes, she has brains, that little one."

"Yes. I believe she has passed quite a stiff exam."

"Without doubt. After all, it is very responsible work. I suppose they have very strong poisons there?"

"Yes, she showed them to us. They are kept locked up in a little cupboard. I believe they have to be very careful. They always take out the key before leaving the room."

"Indeed. It is near the window, this cupboard?"

124

"No, right the other side of the room. Why?"

Poirot shrugged his shoulders.

"I wondered. That is all. Will you come in?"

We had reached the cottage.

"No. I think I'll be getting back. I shall go round the long way through the woods."

The woods round Styles were very beautiful. After the walk across the open park, it was pleasant to saunter lazily through the cool glades. There was hardly a breath of wind, the very chirp of the birds was faint and subdued. I strolled on a little way, and finally flung myself down at the foot of a grand old beech-tree. My thoughts of mankind were kindly and charitable. I even forgave Poirot for his absurd secrecy. In fact, I was at peace with the world. Then I yawned.

I thought about the crime, and it struck me as being very unreal and far off.

I yawned again.

Probably, I thought, it really never happened. Of course, it was all a bad dream. The truth of the matter was that it was Lawrence who had murdered Alfred Inglethorp with a croquet mallet. But it was absurd of John to make such a fuss about it, and to go shouting out: "I tell you I won't have it!"

I woke up with a start.

At once I realized that I was in a very awkward predicament. For, about twelve feet away from me, John and Mary Cavendish were standing facing each other, and they were evidently quarrelling. And, quite as evidently, they were unaware of my vicinity, for before I could move or speak John repeated the words which had aroused me from my dream.

"I tell you, Mary, I won't have it."

Mary's voice came, cool and liquid:

"Have *you* any right to criticize my actions?"

"It will be the talk of the village! My mother was only buried on Saturday, and here you are gadding about with the fellow."

"Oh," she shrugged her shoulders, "if it is only village gossip that you mind!"

"But it isn't. I've had enough of the fellow hanging about. He's a Polish Jew, anyway."

"A tinge of Jewish blood is not a bad thing. It leavens the"—she looked at him—"stolid stupidity of the ordinary Englishman."

Fire in her eyes, ice in her voice. I did not wonder that the blood rose to John's face in a crimson tide.

"Mary!"

"Well?" Her tone did not change.

The pleading died out of his voice.

"Am I to understand that you will continue to see Bauerstein against my express wishes?"

"If I choose."

"You defy me?"

"No, but I deny your right to criticize my actions. Have *you* no friends of whom I should disapprove?"

John fell back a pace. The colour ebbed slowly from his face.

"What do you mean?" he said, in an unsteady voice.

"You see!" said Mary quietly. "You *do* see, don't you, that *you* have no right to dictate to *me* as to the choice of my friends?"

John glanced at her pleadingly, a stricken look on his face.

"No right? Have I *no* right, Mary?" he said unsteadily. He stretched out his hands. "Mary——"

For a moment, I thought she wavered. A softer expression came over her face, then suddenly she turned almost fiercely away.

"None!"

She was walking away when John sprang after her, and caught her by the arm.

"Mary"—his voice was very quiet now—"are you in love with this fellow Bauerstein?"

She hesitated, and suddenly there swept across her face a strange expression, old as the hills, yet with something eternally young about it. So might some Egyptian sphinx have smiled.

126

She freed herself quietly from his arm, and spoke over her shoulder.

"Perhaps," she said; and then swiftly passed out of the little glade, leaving John standing there as though he had been turned to stone.

Rather ostentatiously, I stepped forward, crackling some dead branches with my feet as I did so. John turned. Luckily, he took it for granted that I had only just come upon the scene.

"Hullo, Hastings. Have you seen the little fellow safely back to his cottage? Quaint little chap! Is he any good, though, really?"

"He was considered one of the finest detectives of his day."

"Oh, well, I suppose there must be something in it, then. What a rotten world it is, though!"

"You find it so?" I asked.

"Good Lord, yes! There's this terrible business to start with. Scotland Yard men in and out of the house like a jack-in-the-box! Never know where they won't turn up next. Screaming headlines in every paper in the country—damn all journalists, I say! Do you know there was a whole crowd staring in at the lodge gates this morning. Sort of Madame Tussaud's chamber of horrors business that can be seen for nothing. Pretty thick, isn't it?"

"Cheer up, John!" I said soothingly. "It can't last for ever."

"Can't it, though? It can last long enough for us never to be able to hold up our heads again."

"No, no, you're getting morbid on the subject."

"Enough to make a man morbid, to be stalked by beastly journalists and stared at by gaping moon-faced idiots, wherever he goes! But there's worse than that."

"What?"

John lowered his voice:

"Have you ever thought, Hastings—it's a nightmare to me—who did it? I can't help feeling sometimes it must have been an accident. Because—because—who could have done it? Now Inglethorp's out of the way, there's no one else; no one, I mean, except—one of us."

Yes, indeed, that was nightmare enough for any man! One of us? Yes, surely it must be so, unless——

A new idea suggested itself to my mind. Rapidly, I considered it. The light increased. Poirot's mysterious doings, his hints—they all fitted in. Fool that I was not to have thought of this possibility before, and what a relief for us all.

"No, John," I said, "it isn't one of us. How could it be?"

"I know, but, still, who else is there?"

"Can't you guess?"

"No."

I looked cautiously round, and lowered my voice.

"Dr. Bauerstein!" I whispered.

"Impossible!"

"Not at all."

"But what earthly interest could he have in my mother's death?"

"That I don't see," I confessed, "but I'll tell you this: Poirot thinks so."

"Poirot? Does he? How do you know?"

I told him of Poirot's intense excitement on hearing that Dr. Bauerstein had been at Styles on the fatal night, and added:

"He said twice: 'That alters everything.' And I've been thinking. You know Inglethorp said he had put down the coffee in the hall? Well, it was just then that Bauerstein arrived. Isn't it possible that, as Inglethorp brought him through the hall, the doctor dropped something into the coffee in passing?"

"H'm," said John. "It would have been very risky."

"Yes, but it was possible."

"And then, how could he know it was her coffee? No, old fellow, I don't think that will wash."

But I had remembered something else.

"You're quite right. That wasn't how it was done. Listen." And I then told him of the cocoa sample which Poirot had taken to be analysed.

John interrupted just as I had done.

"But, look here, Bauerstein had had it analysed already?"

"Yes, yes, that's the point. I didn't see it either until now. Don't you understand? Bauerstein had it analysed—that's just it! If Bauerstein's the murderer, nothing could be simpler than for him to substitute some ordinary cocoa for his sample, and send that to be tested. And of course they would find no strychnine! But no one would dream of suspecting Bauerstein, or think of taking another sample—except Poirot," I added, with belated recognition.

"Yes, but what about the bitter taste that cocoa won't disguise?"

"Well, we've only his word for that. And there are other possibilities. He's admittedly one of the world's greatest toxicologists——"

"One of the world's greatest what? Say it again."

"He knows more about poisons than almost anybody," I explained. "Well, my idea is, that perhaps he's found some way of making strychnine tasteless. Or it may not have been strychnine at all, but some obscure drug no one has ever heard of, which produces much the same symptoms."

"H'm, yes, that might be," said John. "But look here, how could he have got at the cocoa? That wasn't downstairs?"

"No, it wasn't," I admitted reluctantly.

And then, suddenly, a dreadful possibility flashed through my mind. I hoped and prayed it would not occur to John also. I glanced sideways at him. He was frowning perplexedly, and I drew a deep breath of relief, for the terrible thought that had flashed across my mind was this: that Dr. Bauerstein might have had an accomplice.

Yet surely it could not be! Surely no woman as beautiful as Mary Cavendish could be a murderess. Yet beautiful women had been known to poison.

And suddenly I remembered that first conversation at tea on the day of my arrival, and the gleam in her eyes as she had said that poison was a woman's weapon. How agitated she had been on that fatal Tuesday evening! Had Mrs. Inglethorp discovered something between her and Bauerstein, and threatened to tell her husband? Was it to stop that denunciation that the crime had been committed?

Then I remembered that enigmatical conversation between Poirot and Evelyn Howard. Was this what they had meant? Was this the monstrous possibility that Evelyn had tried not to believe?

Yes, it all fitted in.

No wonder Miss Howard had suggested "hushing it up." Now I understood that unfinished sentence of hers: "Emily her-self———." And in my heart I agreed with her. Would not Mrs. Inglethorp have preferred to go unavenged rather than have such terrible dishonour fall upon the name of Cavendish.

"There's another thing," said John suddenly, and the unexpected sound of his voice made me start guiltily. "Something which makes me doubt if what you say can be true."

"What's that?" I asked, thankful that he had gone away from the subject of how the poison could have been introduced into the cocoa.

"Why, the fact that Bauerstein demanded a post-mortem. He needn't have done so. Little Wilkins would have been quite content to let it go at heart disease."

"Yes," I said doubtfully. "But we don't know. Perhaps he thought it safer in the long run. Someone might have talked afterwards. Then the Home Office might have ordered exhumation. The whole thing would have come out, then, and he would have been in an awkward position, for no one would have believed that a man of his reputation could have been deceived into calling it heart disease."

"Yes, that's possible," admitted John. "Still," he added, "I'm blest if I can see what his motive could have been."

I trembled.

"Look here," I said, "I may be altogether wrong. And, remember, all this is in confidence."

"Oh, of course—that goes without saying."

We had walked, as we talked, and now we passed through the little gate into the garden. Voices rose near at hand, for tea was spread out under the sycamore-tree, as it had been on the day of my arrival.

Cynthia was back from the hospital, and I placed my chair beside her, and told her of Poirot's wish to visit the dispensary.

"Of course! I'd love him to see it. He'd better come to tea there one day. I must fix it up with him. He's such a dear little man! But he *is* funny. He made me take the brooch out of my tie the other day, and put it in again, because he said it wasn't straight."

I laughed.

"It's quite a mania with him."

"Yes, isn't it?"

We were silent for a minute or two, and then, glancing in the direction of Mary Cavendish, and dropping her voice, Cynthia said:

"Mr. Hastings."

"Yes?"

"After tea, I want to talk to you."

Her glance at Mary had set me thinking. I fancied that between these two there existed very little sympathy. For the first time, it occurred to me to wonder about the girl's future. Mrs. Inglethorp had made no provisions of any kind for her, but I imagined that John and Mary would probably insist on her making her home with them—at any rate until the end of the war. John, I knew, was very fond of her, and would be sorry to let her go.

John, who had gone into the house, now reappeared. His good-natured face wore an unaccustomed frown of anger.

"Confound those detectives! I can't think what they're after! They've been in every room in the house—turning things inside out, and upside down. It really is too bad! I suppose they took advantage of our all being out. I shall go for that fellow Japp, when I next see him!"

"Lot of Paul Prys," grunted Miss Howard.

Lawrence opined that they had to make a show of doing something.

Mary Cavendish said nothing.

After tea, I invited Cynthia to come for a walk, and we sauntered off into the woods together.

"Well?" I inquired, as soon as we were protected from prying eyes by the leafy screen.

With a sigh, Cynthia flung herself down, and tossed off her hat. The sunlight, piercing through the branches, turned the auburn of her hair to quivering gold.

"Mr. Hastings—you are always so kind, and you know such a lot."

It struck me at this moment that Cynthia was really a very charming girl! Much more charming than Mary, who never said things of that kind.

"Well?" I asked benignantly, as she hesitated.

"I want to ask your advice. What shall I do?"

"Do?"

"Yes. You see, Aunt Emily always told me I should be provided for. I suppose she forgot, or didn't think she was likely to die—anyway, I am *not* provided for! And I don't know what to do. Do you think I ought to go away from here at once?"

"Good heavens, no! They don't want to part with you, I'm sure."

Cynthia hesitated a moment, plucking up the grass with her tiny hands. Then she said: "Mrs. Cavendish does. She hates me."

"Hates you?" I cried, astonished.

Cynthia nodded.

"Yes. I don't know why, but she can't bear me; and *he* can't, either."

"There I know you're wrong," I said warmly. "On the contrary, John is very fond of you."

"Oh, yes—*John*. I meant Lawrence. Not, of course, that I care whether Lawrence hates me or not. Still, it's rather horrid when no one loves you, isn't it?"

"But they do, Cynthia dear," I said earnestly. "I'm sure you are mistaken. Look, there is John—and Miss Howard——"

Cynthia nodded rather gloomily. "Yes, John likes me, I think, and of course Evie, for all her gruff ways, wouldn't be unkind to a fly. But Lawrence never speaks to me if he can help it, and Mary can hardly bring herself to be civil to me. She wants Evie to stay on, is begging her to, but she doesn't want me, and—and—I don't know what to do." Suddenly the poor child burst out crying.

I don't know what possessed me. Her beauty, perhaps, as she sat there, with the sunlight glinting down on her head; perhaps the sense of relief at encountering someone who so obviously could have no connection with the tragedy; perhaps honest pity for her youth and loneliness. Anyway, I leant forward, and taking her little hand, I said awkwardly:

"Marry me, Cynthia."

Unwittingly, I had hit upon a sovereign remedy for her tears. She sat up at once, drew her hand away, and said, with some asperity:

"Don't be silly!"

I was a little annoyed.

"I'm not being silly. I am asking you to do me the honour of becoming my wife."

To my intense surprise, Cynthia burst out laughing, and called me a "funny dear."

"It's perfectly sweet of you," she said, "but you know you don't want to!"

"Yes, I do. I've got——"

"Never mind what you've got. You don't really want to—and I don't either."

"Well, of course, that settles it," I said stiffly. "But I don't see anything to laugh at. There's nothing funny about a proposal."

"No, indeed," said Cynthia. "Somebody might accept you next time. Good-bye, you've cheered me up *very* much."

And, with a final uncontrollable burst of merriment, she vanished through the trees.

Thinking over the interview, it struck me as being profoundly unsatisfactory.

It occurred to me suddenly that I would go down to the village, and look up Bauerstein. Somebody ought to be keeping an eye on the fellow. At the same time, it would be wise to allay any suspicions he might have as to his being suspected. I remembered how Poirot had relied on my diplomacy. Accordingly, I went to the little house with the "Apartments" card inserted in the window, where I knew he lodged, and tapped on the door.

An old woman came and opened it.

"Good afternoon," I said pleasantly. "Is Dr. Bauerstein in?"

She stared at me.

"Haven't you heard?"

"Heard what?"

"About him."

"What about him?"

"He's took."

"Took? Dead?"

"No, took by the perlice."

"By the police!" I gasped. "Do you mean they've arrested him?"

"Yes, that's it, and——"

I waited to hear no more, but tore up the village to find Poirot.

TEN
The Arrest

To my extreme annoyance, Poirot was not in, and the old Belgian who answered my knock informed me that he believed he had gone to London.

I was dumbfounded. What on earth could Poirot be doing in London! Was it a sudden decision on his part, or had he already made up his mind when he parted from me a few hours earlier?

I retraced my steps to Styles in some annoyance. With Poirot away, I was uncertain how to act. Had he foreseen this arrest? Had he not, in all probability, been the cause of it? Those questions I could not resolve. But in the meantime what was I to do? Should I announce the arrest openly at Styles, or not? Though I did not acknowledge it to myself, the thought of Mary Cavendish was weighing on me. Would it not be a terrible shock to her? For the moment, I set aside utterly any suspicions of her. She could not be implicated—otherwise I should have heard some hint of it.

Of course, there was no possibility of being able permanently to conceal Dr. Bauerstein's arrest from her. It would be announced in every newspaper on the morrow. Still, I shrank from blurting it out. If only Poirot had been accessible, I could have asked his advice. What possessed him to go posting off to London in this unaccountable way?

In spite of myself, my opinion of his sagacity was immeasurably heightened. I would never have dreamt of suspecting the doctor, had not Poirot put it into my head. Yes, decidedly, the little man was clever.

After some reflecting, I decided to take John into my confidence, and leave him to make the matter public or not, as he thought fit.

He gave vent to a prodigious whistle, as I imparted the news.

"Great Scott! You *were* right, then. I couldn't believe it at the time."

"No, it is astonishing until you get used to the idea, and see how it makes everything fit in. Now, what are we to do? Of course, it will be generally known to-morrow."

John reflected.

"Never mind," he said at last, "we won't say anything at present. There is no need. As you say, it will be known soon enough."

But to my intense surprise, on getting down early the next morning, and eagerly opening the newspapers, there was not a word about the arrest! There was a column of mere padding about "The Styles Poisoning Case," but nothing further. It was rather inexplicable, but I supposed that, for some reason or other, Japp wished to keep it out of the papers. It worried me just a little, for it suggested the possibility that there might be further arrests to come.

After breakfast, I decided to go down to the village, and see if Poirot had returned yet; but, before I could start, a well-known face blocked one of the windows, and the well-known voice said:

"*Bonjour, mon ami!*"

"Poirot," I exclaimed, with relief, and seizing him by both hands, I dragged him into the room. "I was never so glad to see anyone. Listen, I have said nothing to anybody but John. Is that right?"

"My friend," replied Poirot, "I do not know what you are talking about."

"Dr. Bauerstein's arrest, of course," I answered impatiently.

"Is Bauerstein arrested, then?"

"Did you not know it?"

"Not the least in the world." But, pausing a moment, he added: "Still, it does not surprise me. After all, we are only four miles from the coast."

"The coast?" I asked, puzzled. "What has that got to do with it?"

Poirot shrugged his shoulders.

"Surely, it is obvious!"

"Not to me. No doubt I am very dense, but I cannot see what the proximity of the coast has got to do with the murder of Mrs. Inglethorp."

"Nothing at all, of course," replied Poirot, smiling. "But we were speaking of the arrest of Dr. Bauerstein."

"Well, he is arrested for the murder of Mrs. Inglethorp——"

"What?" cried Poirot, in apparently lively astonishment. "Dr. Bauerstein arrested for the murder of Mrs. Inglethorp?"

"Yes."

"Impossible! That would be too good a farce! Who told you that, my friend?"

"Well, no one exactly told me," I confessed. "But he is arrested."

"Oh, yes, very likely. But for espionage, *mon ami*."

"Espionage?" I gasped.

"Precisely."

"Not for poisoning Mrs. Inglethorp?"

"Not unless our friend Japp has taken leave of his senses," replied Poirot placidly.

"But—but I thought you thought so too?"

Poirot gave me one look, which conveyed a wondering pity, and his full sense of the utter absurdity of such an idea.

"Do you mean to say," I asked, slowly adapting myself to the new idea, "that Dr. Bauerstein is a spy?"

Poirot nodded.

"Have you never suspected it?"

"It never entered my head."

"It did not strike you as peculiar that a famous London doctor should bury himself in a little village like this, and should be in the habit of walking about at all hours of the night, fully dressed?"

"No," I confessed, "I never thought of such a thing."

"He is, of course, a German by birth," said Poirot thoughtfully, "though he has practised so long in this country that nobody thinks of him as anything but an Englishman. He was naturalized about fifteen years ago. A very clever man—a Jew, of course."

"The blackguard!" I cried indignantly.

"Not at all. He is, on the contrary, a patriot. Think what he stands to lose. I admire the man myself."

But I could not look at it in Poirot's philosophical way.

"And this is the man with whom Mrs. Cavendish has been wandering about all over the country!" I cried indignantly.

"Yes. I should fancy he had found her very useful," remarked Poirot. "So long as gossip busied itself in coupling their names together, any other vagaries of the doctor's passed unobserved."

"Then you think he never really cared for her?" I asked eagerly—rather too eagerly, perhaps, under the circumstances.

"That, of course, I cannot say, but—shall I tell you my own private opinion, Hastings?"

"Yes."

"Well, it is this: that Mrs. Cavendish does not care, and never has cared one little jot about Dr. Bauerstein!"

"Do you really think so?" I could not disguise my pleasure.

"I am quite sure of it. And I will tell you why."

"Yes?"

"Because she cares for someone else, *mon ami*."

"Oh!" What did he mean? In spite of myself, an agreeable warmth spread over me. I am not a vain man where women are concerned, but I remembered certain evidences, too lightly thought of at the time, perhaps, but which certainly seemed to indicate——

My pleasing thoughts were interrupted by the sudden

entrance of Miss Howard. She glanced round hastily to make sure there was no one else in the room, and quickly produced an old sheet of brown paper. This she handed to Poirot, murmuring as she did so the cryptic words:

"On top of the wardrobe." Then she hurriedly left the room.

Poirot unfolded the sheet of paper eagerly, and uttered an exclamation of satisfaction. He spread it out on the table.

"Come here, Hastings. Now tell me, what is that initial—J. or L.?"

It was a medium sized sheet of paper, rather dusty, as though it had lain by for some time. But it was the label that was attracting Poirot's attention. At the top, it bore the printed stamp of Messrs. Parkson's, the well-known theatrical costumiers, and it was addressed to "—(the debatable initial) Cavendish, Esq., Styles Court, Styles St. Mary, Essex."

"It might be T., or it might be L.," I said, after studying the thing for a minute or two. "It certainly isn't a J."

"Good," replied Poirot, folding up the paper again. "I, also, am of your way of thinking. It is an L., depend upon it!"

"Where did it come from?" I asked curiously. "Is it important?"

"Moderately so. It confirms a surmise of mine. Having deduced its existence, I set Miss Howard to search for it, and, as you see, she has been successful."

"What did she mean by 'On the top of the wardrobe'?"

"She meant," replied Poirot promptly, "that she found it on top of a wardrobe."

"A funny place for a piece of brown paper," I mused.

"Not at all. The top of a wardrobe is an excellent place for brown paper and cardboard boxes. I have kept them there myself. Neatly arranged, there is nothing to offend the eye."

"Poirot," I asked earnestly, "have you made up your mind about this crime?"

"Yes—that is to say, I believe I know how it was committed."

"Ah!"

"Unfortunately, I have no proof beyond my surmise, unless——" With sudden energy, he caught me by the arm, and whirled me down the hall, calling out in French in his excitement: "Mademoiselle Dorcas, Mademoiselle Dorcas, *un moment, s'il vous plaît!*"

Dorcas, quite flurried by the noise, came hurrying out of the pantry.

"My good Dorcas, I have an idea—a little idea—if it should prove justified, what magnificent chance! Tell me, on Monday, not Tuesday, Dorcas, but Monday, the day before the tragedy, did anything go wrong with Mrs. Inglethorp's bell?"

Dorcas looked very surprised.

"Yes, sir, now you mention it, it did; though I don't know how you came to hear of it. A mouse, or some such, must have nibbled the wire through. The man came and put it right on Tuesday morning."

With a long drawn exclamation of ecstasy, Poirot led the way back to the morning-room.

"See you, one should not ask for outside proof—no, reason should be enough. But the flesh is weak, it is consolation to find that one is on the right track. Ah, my friend, I am like a giant refreshed. I run! I leap!"

And, in very truth, run and leap he did, gambolling wildly down the stretch of lawn outside the long window.

"What is your remarkable little friend doing?" asked a voice behind me, and I turned to find Mary Cavendish at my elbow. She smiled, and so did I. "What is it all about?"

"Really, I can't tell you. He asked Dorcas some question about a bell, and appeared so delighted with her answer that he is capering about as you see!"

Mary laughed.

"How ridiculous! He's going out of the gate. Isn't he coming back to-day?"

"I don't know. I've given up trying to guess what he'll do next."

"Is he quite mad, Mr. Hastings?"

"I honestly don't know. Sometimes, I feel sure he is as mad as a hatter; and then, just as he is at his maddest, I find there is method in his madness."

"I see."

In spite of her laugh, Mary was looking thoughtful this morning. She seemed grave, almost sad.

It occurred to me that it would be a good opportunity to tackle her on the subject of Cynthia. I began rather tactfully, I thought, but I had not gone far before she stopped me authoritatively.

"You are an excellent advocate, I have no doubt, Mr. Hastings, but in this case your talents are quite thrown away. Cynthia will run no risk of encountering any unkindness from me."

I began to stammer feebly that I hoped she hadn't thought—— But again she stopped me, and her words were so unexpected that they quite drove Cynthia, and her troubles, out of my mind.

"Mr. Hastings," she said, "do you think I and my husband are happy together?"

I was considerably taken aback, and murmured something about it's not being my business to think anything of the sort.

"Well," she said quietly, "whether it is your business or not, I will tell you that we are *not* happy."

I said nothing, for I saw that she had not finished.

She began slowly, walking up and down the room, her head a little bent, and that slim, supple figure of hers swaying gently as she walked. She stopped suddenly, and looked up at me.

"You don't know anything about me, do you?" she asked. "Where I come from, who I was before I married John—anything, in fact? Well, I will tell you. I will make a father confessor of you. You are kind, I think—yes, I am sure you are kind."

Somehow, I was not quite as elated as I might have been. I remembered that Cynthia had begun her confidences in much the same way. Besides, a father confessor should be elderly, it is not at all the role for a young man.

"My father was English," said Mrs. Cavendish, "but my mother was a Russian."

"Ah," I said, "now I understand——"

"Understand what?"

"A hint of something foreign—different—that there has always been about you."

"My mother was very beautiful, I believe. I don't know, because I never saw her. She died when I was quite a little child. I believe there was some tragedy connected with her death—she took an overdose of some sleeping draught by mistake. However that may be, my father was broken-hearted. Shortly afterwards, he went into the Consular Service. Everywhere he went, I went with him. When I was twenty-three, I had been nearly all over the world. It was a splendid life—I loved it."

There was a smile on her face, and her head was thrown back. She seemed living in the memory of those old glad days.

"Then my father died. He left me very badly off. I had to go and live with some old aunts in Yorkshire." She shuddered. "You will understand me when I say that it was a deadly life for a girl brought up as I had been. The narrowness, the deadly monotony of it, almost drove me mad." She paused a minute, and added in a different tone: "And then I met John Cavendish."

"Yes?"

"You can imagine that, from my aunts' point of view, it was a very good match for me. But I can honestly say it was not this fact which weighed with me. No, he was simply a way of escape from the insufferable monotony of my life."

I said nothing, and after a moment, she went on:

"Don't misunderstand me. I was quite honest with him. I told him, what was true, that I liked him very much, that I hoped to come to like him more, but that I was not in any way what the world calls 'in love' with him. He declared that that satisfied him, and so—we were married."

She waited a long time, a little frown had gathered on her

142

forehead. She seemed to be looking back earnestly into those past days.

"I think—I am sure—he cared for me at first. But I suppose we were not well matched. Almost at once, we drifted apart. He— it is not a pleasing thing for my pride, but it is the truth—tired of me very soon." I must have made some murmur of dissent, for she went on quickly: "Oh, yes, he did! Not that it matters now—now that we've come to the parting of the ways."

"What do you mean?"

She answered quietly:

"I mean that I am not going to remain at Styles."

"You and John are not going to live here?"

"John may live here, but I shall not."

"You are going to leave him?"

"Yes."

"But why?"

She paused a long time, and said at last:

"Perhaps—because I want to be—free!"

And, as she spoke, I had a sudden vision of broad spaces, virgin tracts of forests, untrodden lands—and a realization of what freedom would mean to such a nature as Mary Cavendish. I seemed to see her for a moment as she was, a proud wild crea- ture, as untamed by civilization as some shy bird of the hills. A little cry broke from her lips:

"You don't know, you don't know, how this hateful place has been prison to me!"

"I understand," I said, "but—but don't do anything rash."

"Oh, rash!" Her voice mocked at my prudence.

Then suddenly I said a thing I could have bitten out my tongue for:

"You know that Dr. Bauerstein has been arrested?"

An instant coldness passed like a mask over her face, blotting out all expression.

"John was so kind as to break that to me this morning."

143

"Well, what do you think?" I asked feebly.

"Of what?"

"Of the arrest?"

"What should I think? Apparently he is a German spy; so the gardener had told John."

Her face and voice were absolutely cold and expressionless. Did she care, or did she not?

She moved away a step or two, and fingered one of the flower vases.

"These are quite dead. I must do them again. Would you mind moving—thank you, Mr. Hastings." And she walked quietly past me out of the window, with a cool little nod of dismissal.

No, surely she could not care for Bauerstein. No woman could act her part with that icy unconcern.

Poirot did not make his appearance the following morning, and there was no sign of the Scotland Yard men.

But, at lunch-time, there arrived a new piece of evidence—or rather lack of evidence. We had vainly tried to trace the fourth letter, which Mrs. Inglethorp had written on the evening preceding her death. Our efforts having been in vain, we had abandoned the matter, hoping that it might turn up of itself one day. And this is just what did happen, in the shape of a communication, which arrived by the second post from a firm of French music publishers, acknowledging Mrs. Inglethorp's cheque, and regretting they had been unable to trace a certain series of Russian folksongs. So the last hope of solving the mystery, by means of Mrs. Inglethorp's correspondence on the fatal evening, had to be abandoned.

Just before tea, I strolled down to tell Poirot of the new disappointment, but found, to my annoyance, that he was once more out.

"Gone to London again?"

"Oh, no, monsieur, he has but taken the train to Tadminster. 'To see a young lady's dispensary,' he said."

"Silly ass!" I ejaculated. "I told him Wednesday was the one day she wasn't there! Well, tell him to look us up to-morrow morning, will you?"

"Certainly, monsieur."

But, on the following day, no sign of Poirot. I was getting angry. He was really treating us in the most cavalier fashion.

After lunch, Lawrence drew me aside, and asked if I was going down to see him.

"No, I don't think I shall. He can come up here if he wants to see us."

"Oh!" Lawrence looked indeterminate. Something unusually nervous and excited in his manner roused my curiosity.

"What is it?" I asked. "I could go if there's anything special."

"It's nothing much, but—well, if you are going, will you tell him——" he dropped his voice to a whisper—"I think I've found the extra coffee-cup!"

I had almost forgotten that enigmatical message of Poirot's, but now my curiosity was aroused afresh.

Lawrence would say no more, so I decided that I would descend from my high horse, and once more seek out Poirot at Leastways Cottage.

This time I was received with a smile. Monsieur Poirot was within. Would I mount? I mounted accordingly.

Poirot was sitting by the table, his head buried in his hands. He sprang up at my entrance.

"What is it?" I asked solicitously. "You are not ill, I trust?"

"No, no, not ill. But I decide an affair of great moment."

"Whether to catch the criminal or not?" I asked facetiously.

But, to my great surprise, Poirot nodded gravely.

"'To speak or not to speak,' as your so great Shakespeare says, 'that is the question.'"

I did not trouble to correct the quotation.

"You are not serious, Poirot?"

"I am of the most serious. For the most serious of all things hangs in the balance."

"And that is?"

"A woman's happiness, *mon ami*," he said gravely.

I did not quite know what to say.

"The moment has come," said Poirot thoughtfully, "and I do not know what to do. For, see you, it is a big stake for which I play. No one but I, Hercule Poirot, would attempt it!" And he tapped himself proudly on the breast.

After pausing a few minutes respectfully, so as not to spoil his effect, I gave him Lawrence's message.

"Aha!" he cried. "So he has found the extra coffee-cup. That is good. He has more intelligence than would appear, this long-faced Monsieur Lawrence of yours!"

I did not myself think very highly of Lawrence's intelligence; but I forebore to contradict Poirot, and gently took him to task for forgetting my instructions as to which were Cynthia's days off.

"It is true. I have the head of a sieve. However, the other young lady was most kind. She was sorry for my disappointment, and showed me everything in the kindest way."

"Oh, well, that's all right, then, and you must go to tea with Cynthia another day."

I told him about the letter.

"I am sorry for that," he said. "I always had hopes of that letter. But no, it was not to be. This affair must all be unravelled from within." He tapped his forehead. "These little grey cells. It is 'up to them'—as you say over here." Then, suddenly, he asked: "Are you a judge of finger-marks, my friend?"

"No," I said, rather surprised, "I know that there are no two finger-marks alike, but that's as far as my science goes."

"Exactly."

He unlocked a little drawer, and took out some photographs which he laid on the table.

"I have numbered them, 1, 2, 3. Will you describe them to me?"

I studied the proofs attentively.

146

"All greatly magnified, I see. No. 1, I should say, are a man's finger-prints; thumb and first finger. No. 2 are a lady's; they are much smaller, and quite different in every way. No. 3"—I paused for some time—"there seem to be a lot of confused finger-marks, but here, very distinctly, are No. 1's."

"Overlapping the others?"

"Yes."

"You recognize them beyond fail?"

"Oh, yes; they are identical."

Poirot nodded, and gently taking the photographs from me locked them up again.

"I suppose," I said, "that as usual, you are not going to explain?"

"On the contrary. No. 1 were the finger-prints of Monsieur Lawrence. No. 2 were those of Mademoiselle Cynthia. They are not important. I merely obtained them for comparison. No. 3 is a little more complicated."

"Yes?"

"It is, as you see, highly magnified. You may have noticed a sort of blur extending all across the picture. I will not describe to you the special apparatus, dusting powder, etc., which I used. It is a well-known process to the police, and by means of it you can obtain a photograph of the finger-prints of any object in a very short space of time. Well, my friend, you have seen the finger-marks—it remains to tell you the particular object on which they had been left."

"Go on—I am really excited."

"*Eh bien!* Photo No. 3 represents the highly magnified surface of a tiny bottle in the top poison cupboard of the dispensary in the Red Cross Hospital at Tadminster—which sounds like the house that Jack built!"

"Good heavens!" I exclaimed. "But what were Lawrence Cavendish's finger-marks doing on it? He never went near the poison cupboard the day we were there!"

"Oh, yes, he did!"

"Impossible! We were all together the whole time."

Poirot shook his head.

"No, my friend, there was a moment when you were not all together. There was a moment when you could not have been all together, or it would not have been necessary to call to Monsieur Lawrence to come and join you on the balcony."

"I'd forgotten that," I admitted. "But it was only for a moment."

"Long enough."

"Long enough for what?"

Poirot's smile became rather enigmatical.

"Long enough for a gentleman who had once studied medicine to gratify a very natural interest and curiosity."

Our eyes met. Poirot's were pleasantly vague. He got up and hummed a little tune. I watched him suspiciously.

"Poirot," I said, "what was in this particular little bottle?"

Poirot looked out of the window.

"Hydro-chloride of strychnine," he said, over his shoulder, continuing to hum.

"Good heavens!" I said it quite quietly. I was not surprised. I had expected that answer.

"They use the pure hydro-chloride of strychnine very little—only occasionally for pills. It is the official solution, Liq. Strychnine Hydro-clor. that is used in most medicines. That is why the finger-marks have remained undisturbed since then."

"How did you manage to take this photograph?"

"I dropped my hat from the balcony," explained Poirot simply. "Visitors were not permitted below at that hour, so, in spite of my many apologies, Mademoiselle Cynthia's colleague had to go down and fetch it for me."

"Then you knew what you were going to find?"

"No, not at all. I merely realized that it was possible, from your story, for Monsieur Lawrence to go to the poison cupboard. The possibility had to be confirmed, or eliminated."

"Poirot," I said, "your gaiety does not deceive me. This is a very important discovery."

"I do not know," said Poirot. "But one thing does strike me. No doubt it has struck you too."

"What is that?"

"Why, that there is altogether too much strychnine about this case. This is the third time we run up against it. There was strychnine in Mrs. Inglethorp's tonic. There is the strychnine sold across the counter at Styles St. Mary by Mace. Now we have more strychnine, handled by one of the household. It is confusing; and, as you know, I do not like confusion."

Before I could reply, one of the other Belgians opened the door and stuck his head in.

"There is a lady below, asking for Mr Hastings."

"A lady?"

I jumped up. Poirot followed me down the narrow stairs. Mary Cavendish was standing in the doorway.

"I have been visiting an old woman in the village," she explained, "and as Lawrence told me you were with Monsieur Poirot I thought I would call for you."

"Alas, madame," said Poirot, "I thought you had come to honour me with a visit!"

"I will some day, if you ask me," she promised him, smiling.

"That is well. If you should need a father confessor, madame"—she started ever so slightly—"remember, Papa Poirot is always at your service."

She stared at him for a few minutes, as though seeking to read some deeper meaning into his words. Then she turned abruptly away.

"Come, will you not walk back with us too, Monsieur Poirot?"

"Enchanted, madame."

All the way to Styles, Mary talked fast and feverishly. It struck me that in some way she was nervous of Poirot's eyes.

The weather had broken, and the sharp wind was almost autumnal in its shrewishness. Mary shivered a little, and buttoned her black sports coat closer. The wind through the trees made a mournful noise, like some great giant sighing.

We walked up to the great door of Styles, and at once the knowledge came to us that something was wrong.

Dorcas came running out to meet us. She was crying and wringing her hands. I was aware of other servants huddled together in the background, all eyes and ears.

"Oh, m'am! Oh, m'am! I don't know how to tell you——"

"What is it, Dorcas?" I asked impatiently. "Tell us at once."

"It's those wicked detectives. They've arrested him—they've arrested Mr. Cavendish!"

"Arrested Lawrence?" I gasped.

I saw a strange look come into Dorcas's eyes.

"No, sir. Not Mr. Lawrence—Mr. John."

Behind me, with a wild cry, Mary Cavendish fell heavily against me, and as I turned to catch her I met the quiet triumph in Poirot's eyes.

ELEVEN

The Case for the Prosecution

The trial of John Cavendish for the murder of his stepmother took place two months later.

Of the intervening weeks I will say little, but my admiration and sympathy went out unfeignedly to Mary Cavendish. She ranged herself passionately on her husband's side, scorning the mere idea of his guilt, and fought for him tooth and nail.

I expressed my admiration to Poirot, and he nodded thoughtfully.

"Yes, she is of those women who show at their best in adversity. It brings out all that is sweetest and truest in them. Her pride and her jealousy have——"

"Jealousy?" I queried.

"Yes. Have you not realized that she is an unusually jealous woman? As I was saying, her pride and jealousy have been laid aside. She thinks of nothing but her husband, and the terrible fate that is hanging over him."

He spoke very feelingly, and I looked at him earnestly, remembering that last afternoon, when he had been deliberating whether or not to speak. With his tenderness for "a woman's happiness," I felt glad that the decision had been taken out of his hands.

"Even now," I said, "I can hardly believe it. You see, up to the very last minute, I thought it was Lawrence!"

Poirot grinned.

151

"I know you did."

"But John! My old friend John!"

"Every murderer is probably somebody's old friend," observed Poirot philosophically. "You cannot mix up sentiment and reason."

"I must say I think you might have given me a hint."

"Perhaps, *mon ami*, I did not do so, just because he *was* your old friend."

I was rather disconcerted by this, remembering how I had busily passed on to John what I believed to be Poirot's views concerning Bauerstein. He, by the way, had been acquitted of the charge brought against him. Nevertheless, although he had been too clever for them this time, and the charge of espionage could not be brought home to him, his wings were pretty well clipped for the future.

I asked Poirot whether he thought John would be condemned. To my intense surprise, he replied that, on the contrary, he was extremely likely to be acquitted.

"But, Poirot——" I protested.

"Oh, my friend, have I not said to you all along that I have no proofs. It is one thing to know that a man is guilty, it is quite another matter to prove him so. And, in this case, there is terribly little evidence. That is the whole trouble. I, Hercule Poirot, know, but I lack the last link in my chain. And unless I can find that missing link——" He shook his head gravely.

"When did you first suspect John Cavendish?" I asked, after a minute or two.

"Did you not suspect him at all?"

"No, indeed."

"Not after that fragment of conversation you overheard between Mrs. Cavendish and her mother-in-law, and her subsequent lack of frankness at the inquest?"

"No."

"Did you not put two and two together, and reflect that if it was not Alfred Inglethorp who was quarrelling with his wife—and you remember, he strenuously denied it at the inquest—it must be either Lawrence or John. Now, if it was Lawrence, Mary Cavendish's conduct was just as inexplicable. But if, on the other hand, it was John, the whole thing was explained quite naturally."

"So," I cried, a light breaking in upon me, "it was John who quarrelled with his mother that afternoon?"

"Exactly."

"And you have known this all along?"

"Certainly. Mrs. Cavendish's behaviour could only be explained that way."

"And yet you say he may be acquitted?"

Poirot shrugged his shoulders.

"Certainly I do. At the police court proceedings, we shall hear the case for the prosecution, but in all probability his solicitors will advise him to reserve his defence. That will be sprung upon us at the trial. And—ah, by the way, I have a word of caution to give you, my friend. I must not appear in the case."

"What?"

"No. Officially, I have nothing to do with it. Until I have found that last link in my chain, I must remain behind the scenes. Mrs. Cavendish must think I am working for her husband, not against him."

"I say, that's playing it a bit low down," I protested.

"Not at all. We have to deal with a most clever and unscrupulous man, and we must use any means in our power—otherwise he will slip through our fingers. That is why I have been careful to remain in the background. All the discoveries have been made by Japp, and Japp will take all the credit. If I am called upon to give evidence at all"—he smiled broadly—"it will probably be as a witness for the defence."

I could hardly believe my ears.

"It is quite *en règle*," continued Poirot. "Strangely enough, I can give evidence that will demolish one contention of the prosecution."

"Which one?"

"The one that relates to the destruction of the will. John Cavendish did not destroy that will."

Poirot was a true prophet. I will not go into the details of the police court proceedings, as it involves many tiresome repetitions. I will merely state baldly that John Cavendish reserved his defence, and was duly committed for trial.

September found us all in London. Mary took a house in Kensington, Poirot being included in the family party.

I myself had been given a job at the War Office, so was able to see them continually.

As the weeks went by, the state of Poirot's nerves grew worse and worse. That "last link" he talked about was still lacking. Privately, I hoped it might remain so, for what happiness could there be for Mary, if John were not acquitted?

On September 15th John Cavendish appeared in the dock at the Old Bailey, charged with "The Wilful Murder of Emily Agnes Inglethorp," and pleaded "Not Guilty."

Sir Ernest Heavywether, the famous K.C., had been engaged to defend him.

Mr. Philips, K.C., opened the case for the Crown.

The murder, he said, was a most premeditated and cold-blooded one. It was neither more nor less than the deliberate poisoning of a fond and trusting woman by the stepson to whom she had been more than a mother. Ever since his boyhood, she had supported him. He and his wife had lived at Styles Court in every luxury, surrounded by her care and attention. She had been their kind and generous benefactress.

He proposed to call witnesses to show how the prisoner, a profligate and spendthrift, had been at the end of his financial tether, and had also been carrying on an intrigue with a certain Mrs. Raikes, a neighbouring farmer's wife. This having come to his stepmother's ears, she taxed him with it on the afternoon before her death, and a quarrel ensued, part of which was overheard.

On the previous day, the prisoner had purchased strychnine at the village chemist's shop, wearing a disguise by means of which he hoped to throw the onus of the crime upon another man—to wit, Mrs. Inglethorp's husband, of whom he had been bitterly jealous. Luckily for Mr. Inglethorp, he had been able to produce an unimpeachable alibi.

On the afternoon of July 17th, continued Counsel, immediately after the quarrel with her son, Mrs. Inglethorp made a new will. This will was found destroyed in the grate of her bedroom the following morning, but evidence had come to light which showed that it had been drawn up in favour of her husband. Deceased had already made a will in his favour before her marriage, but—and Mr. Philips wagged an expressive forefinger—the prisoner was not aware of that. What had induced the deceased to make a fresh will, with the old one still extant, he could not say. She was an old lady, and might possibly have forgotten the former one; or—this seemed to him more likely—she may have had an idea that it was revoked by her marriage, as there had been some conversation on the subject. Ladies were not always very well versed in legal knowledge. She had, about a year before, executed a will in favour of the prisoner. He would call evidence to show that it was the prisoner who ultimately handed his stepmother her coffee on the fatal night. Later in the evening, he had sought admission to her room, on which occasion, no doubt, he found an opportunity of destroying the will which, as far as he knew, would render the one in his favour valid.

The prisoner had been arrested in consequence of the discovery, in his room, by Detective Inspector Japp—a most brilliant officer—of the identical phial of strychnine which had been sold at the village chemist's to the supposed Mr. Inglethorp on the day before the murder. It would be for the jury to decide whether or not these damning facts constituted an overwhelming proof of the prisoner's guilt.

And, subtly implying that a jury which did not so decide, was quite unthinkable, Mr. Philips sat down and wiped his forehead.

The first witnesses for the prosecution were mostly those who had been called at the inquest, the medical evidence being again taken first.

Sir Ernest Heavywether, who was famous all over England for the unscrupulous manner in which he bullied witnesses, only asked two questions.

"I take it, Dr. Bauerstein, that strychnine, as a drug, acts quickly?"

"Yes."

"And that you are unable to account for the delay in this case?"

"Yes."

"Thank you."

Mr. Mace identified the phial handed him by Counsel as that sold by him to "Mr. Inglethorp." Pressed, he admitted that he only knew Mr. Inglethorp by sight. He had never spoken to him. The witness was not cross-examined.

Alfred Inglethorp was called, and denied having purchased the poison. He also denied having quarrelled with his wife. Various witnesses testified to the accuracy of these statements.

The gardeners' evidence, as to the witnessing of the will was taken, and then Dorcas was called.

Dorcas, faithful to her "young gentlemen," denied strenuously that it could have been John's voice she heard, and resolutely declared, in the teeth of everything, that it was Mr. Inglethorp who had been in the boudoir with her mistress. A rather wistful smile passed across the face of the prisoner in the dock. He knew only too well how useless her gallant defiance was, since it was not the object of the defence to deny this point. Mrs. Cavendish, of course, could not be called upon to give evidence against her husband.

After various questions on other matters, Mr. Philips asked:

"In the month of June last, do you remember a parcel arriving for Mr. Lawrence Cavendish from Parkson's?"

Dorcas shook her head.

"I don't remember, sir. It may have done, but Mr. Lawrence was away from home part of June."

"In the event of a parcel arriving for him whilst he was away, what would be done with it?"

"It would either be put in his room or sent on after him."

"By you?"

"No, sir, I should leave it on the hall table. It would be Miss Howard who would attend to anything like that."

Evelyn Howard was called and, after being examined on other points, was questioned as to the parcel.

"Don't remember. Lots of parcels come. Can't remember one special one."

"You do not know if it was sent after Mr. Lawrence Cavendish to Wales, or whether it was put in his room?"

"Don't think it was sent after him. Should have remembered it if it was."

"Supposing a parcel arrived addressed to Mr. Lawrence Cavendish, and afterwards it disappeared, should you remark its absence?"

"No, don't think so. I should think someone had taken charge of it."

"I believe, Miss Howard, that it was you who found this sheet of brown paper?" He held up the same dusty piece which Poirot and I had examined in the morning-room at Styles.

"Yes, I did."

"How did you come to look for it?"

"The Belgian detective who was employed on the case asked me to search for it."

"Where did you eventually discover it?"

"On the top of—of—a wardrobe."

"On top of the prisoner's wardrobe?"

"I—I believe so."

"Did you not find it yourself?"

"Yes."

"Then you must know where you found it?"

"Yes, it was on the prisoner's wardrobe."

"That is better."

An assistant from Parkson's, Theatrical Costumiers, testified that on June 29th, they had supplied a black beard to Mr. L. Cavendish, as requested. It was ordered by letter, and a postal order was enclosed. No, they had not kept the letter. All transactions were entered in their books. They had sent the beard, as directed, to "L. Cavendish, Esq., Styles Court."

Sir Ernest Heavywether rose ponderously.

"Where was the letter written from?"

"From Styles Court."

"The same address to which you sent the parcel?"

"Yes."

"And the letter came from there?"

"Yes."

Like a beast of prey, Heavywether fell upon him:

"How do you know?"

"I—I don't understand."

"How do you know that letter came from Styles? Did you notice the postmark?"

"No—but——"

"Ah, you did *not* notice the postmark! And yet you affirm so confidently that it came from Styles. It might, in fact, have been any postmark?"

"Y—es."

"In fact, the letter, though written on stamped notepaper, might have been posted from anywhere? From Wales, for instance?"

The witness admitted that such might be the case, and Sir Ernest signified that he was satisfied.

Elizabeth Wells, second housemaid at Styles, stated that after she had gone to bed she remembered that she had bolted the front door, instead of leaving it on the latch as Mr. Inglethorp had requested. She had accordingly gone downstairs again to rectify her error. Hearing a slight noise in the West wing, she had peeped along the passage, and had seen Mr. John Cavendish knocking at Mrs. Inglethorp's door.

Sir Ernest Heavywether made short work of her, and under his unmerciful bullying she contradicted herself hopelessly, and Sir Ernest sat down again with a satisfied smile on his face.

With the evidence of Annie, as to the candle grease on the floor, and as to seeing the prisoner take the coffee into the boudoir, the proceedings were adjourned until the following day.

As we went home, Mary Cavendish spoke bitterly against the prosecuting counsel.

"That hateful man! What a net he has drawn around my poor John! How he twisted every little fact until he made it seem what it wasn't!"

"Well," I said consolingly, "it will be the other way about to-morrow."

"Yes," she said meditatively; then suddenly dropped her voice. "Mr. Hastings, you do not think—surely it could not have been Lawrence—Oh, no, that could not be!"

But I myself was puzzled, and as soon as I was alone with Poirot I asked him what he thought Sir Ernest was driving at.

"Ah!" said Poirot appreciatively. "He is a clever man, that Sir Ernest."

"Do you think he believes Lawrence guilty?"

"I do not think he believes or cares anything! No, what he is trying for is to create such confusion in the minds of the jury that they are divided in their opinion as to which brother did it. He is endeavouring to make out that there is quite as much evidence against Lawrence as against John—and I am not at all sure that he will not succeed."

Detective-inspector Japp was the first witness called when the trial was reopened, and gave his evidence succinctly and briefly. After relating the earlier events, he proceeded:

"Acting on information received, Superintendent Summerhaye and myself searched the prisoner's room, during his temporary absence from the house. In his chest of drawers, hidden beneath some underclothing, we found: first, a pair of gold-rimmed pince-nez similar to those worn by Mr. Inglethorp"—these were exhibited—"secondly, this phial."

The phial was that already recognized by the chemist's assistant, a tiny bottle of blue glass, containing a few grains of a white crystalline powder, and labelled: "Strychnine Hydro-chloride. POISON."

A fresh piece of evidence discovered by the detectives since the police court proceedings was a long, almost new piece of blotting-paper. It had been found in Mrs. Inglethorp's cheque book, and on being reversed at a mirror, showed clearly the words: ". . . erything of which I die possessed I leave to my beloved husband Alfred Ing..." This placed beyond question the fact that the destroyed will had been in favour of the deceased lady's husband. Japp then produced the charred fragment of paper recovered from the grate, and this, with the discovery of the beard in the attic, completed his evidence.

But Sir Ernest's cross-examination was yet to come.

"What day was it when you searched the prisoner's room?"

"Tuesday, the 24th of July."

"Exactly a week after the tragedy?"

"Yes."

"You found these two objects, you say, in the chest of drawers. Was the drawer unlocked?"

"Yes."

"Does it not strike you as unlikely that a man who had committed a crime should keep the evidence of it in an unlocked drawer for anyone to find?"

"He might have stowed them there in a hurry."

"But you have just said it was a whole week since the crime. He would have had ample time to remove them and destroy them."

"Perhaps."

160

"There is no perhaps about it. Would he, or would he not have had plenty of time to remove and destroy them?"

"Yes."

"Was the pile of underclothes under which the things were hidden heavy or light?"

"Heavyish."

"In other words, it was winter underclothing. Obviously, the prisoner would not be likely to go to that drawer?"

"Perhaps not."

"Kindly answer my question. Would the prisoner, in the hottest week of a hot summer, be likely to go to a drawer containing winter underclothing. Yes, or no?"

"No."

"In that case, is it not possible that the articles in question might have been put there by a third person, and that the prisoner was quite unaware of their presence?"

"I should not think it likely."

"But it is possible?"

"Yes."

"That is all."

More evidence followed. Evidence as to the financial difficulties in which the prisoner had found himself at the end of July. Evidence as to his intrigue with Mrs. Raikes—poor Mary, that must have been bitter hearing for a woman of her pride. Evelyn Howard had been right in her facts, though her animosity against Alfred Inglethorp had caused her to jump to the conclusion that he was the person concerned.

Lawrence Cavendish was then put into the box. In a low voice, in answer to Mr. Philips' questions, he denied having ordered anything from Parkson's in June. In fact, on June 29th, he had been staying away, in Wales.

Instantly, Sir Ernest's chin was shooting pugnaciously forward.

"You deny having ordered a black beard from Parkson's on June 29th?"

"I do."

"Ah! In the event of anything happening to your brother, who will inherit Styles Court?"

The brutality of the question called a flush to Lawrence's pale face. The judge gave vent to a faint murmur of disapprobation, and the prisoner in the dock leant forward angrily.

Heavywether cared nothing for his client's anger.

"Answer my question, if you please."

"I suppose," said Lawrence quietly, "that I should."

"What do you mean by you 'suppose'? Your brother has no children. You *would* inherit it, wouldn't you?"

"Yes."

"Ah, that's better," said Heavywether, with ferocious geniality. "And you'd inherit a good slice of money too, wouldn't you?"

"Really, Sir Ernest," protested the judge, "these questions are not relevant."

Sir Ernest bowed, and having shot his arrow proceeded.

"On Tuesday, the 17th July, you went, I believe, with another guest, to visit the dispensary at the Red Cross Hospital in Tadminster?"

"Yes."

"Did you—while you happened to be alone for a few seconds—unlock the poison cupboard, and examine some of the bottles?"

"I—I—may have done so."

"I put it to you that you did do so?"

"Yes."

Sir Ernest fairly shot the next question at him.

"Did you examine one bottle in particular?"

"No, I do not think so."

"Be careful, Mr. Cavendish. I am referring to a little bottle of Hydro-chloride of Strychnine."

Lawrence was turning a sickly greenish colour.

"N—o—I am sure I didn't."

"Then how do you account for the fact that you left the unmistakable impress of your finger-prints on it?"

The bullying manner was highly efficacious with a nervous disposition.

"I—I suppose I must have taken up the bottle."

"I suppose so too! Did you abstract any of the contents of the bottle?"

"Certainly not."

"Then why did you take it up?"

"I once studied to be a doctor. Such things naturally interest me."

"Ah! So poisons 'naturally interest' you, do they? Still, you waited to be alone before gratifying that 'interest' of yours?"

"That was pure chance. If the others had been there, I should have done just the same."

"Still, as it happens, the others were not there?"

"No, but——"

"In fact, during the whole afternoon, you were only alone for a couple of minutes, and it happened—I say, it happened—to be during those two minutes that you displayed your 'natural interest' in Hydro-chloride of Strychnine?"

Lawrence stammered pitiably.

"I—I——"

With a satisfied and expressive countenance, Sir Ernest observed:

"I have nothing more to ask you, Mr. Cavendish."

This bit of cross-examination had caused great excitement in court. The heads of the many fashionably attired women present were busily laid together, and their whispers became so loud that the judge angrily threatened to have the court cleared if there was not immediate silence.

There was little more evidence. The hand-writing experts were called upon for their opinion of the signature of "Alfred Inglethorp" in the chemist's poison register. They all declared unanimously that it was certainly not his hand-writing, and gave it as their view that it might be that of the prisoner disguised. Cross-examined, they admitted that it might be the prisoner's hand-writing cleverly counterfeited.

Sir Ernest Heavywether's speech in opening the case for the defence was not a long one, but it was backed by the full force of his emphatic manner. Never, he said, in the course of his long experience, had he known a charge of murder rest on slighter evidence. Not only was it entirely circumstantial, but the greater part of it was practically unproved. Let them take the testimony they had heard and sift it impartially. The strychnine had been found in a drawer in the prisoner's room. That drawer was an unlocked one, as he had pointed out, and he submitted that there was no evidence to prove that it was the prisoner who had concealed the poison there. It was, in fact, a wicked and malicious attempt on the part of some third person to fix the crime on the prisoner. The prosecution had been unable to produce a shred of evidence in support of their contention that it was the prisoner who ordered the black beard from Parkson's. The quarrel which had taken place between prisoner and his stepmother was freely admitted, but both it and his financial embarrassments had been grossly exaggerated.

His learned friend—Sir Ernest nodded carelessly at Mr. Philips—had stated that if the prisoner were an innocent man, he would have come forward at the inquest to explain that it was he, and not Mr. Inglethorp, who had been the participator in the quarrel. He thought the facts had been misrepresented. What had actually occurred was this. The prisoner, returning to the house on Tuesday evening, had been authoritatively told that there had been a violent quarrel between Mr. and Mrs. Inglethorp. No suspicion had entered the prisoner's head that anyone could possibly have mistaken his voice for that of Mr. Inglethorp. He naturally concluded that his stepmother had had two quarrels.

The prosecution averred that on Monday, July 16th, the prisoner had entered the chemist's shop in the village, disguised as

Mr. Inglethorp. The prisoner, on the contrary, was at that time at a lonely spot called Marston's Spinney, where he had been summoned by an anonymous note, couched in blackmailing terms, and threatening to reveal certain matters to his wife unless he complied with its demands. The prisoner had, accordingly, gone to the appointed spot, and after waiting there vainly for half an hour had returned home. Unfortunately, he had met with no one on the way there or back who could vouch for the truth of his story, but luckily he had kept the note, and it would be produced as evidence.

As for the statement relating to the destruction of the will, the prisoner had formerly practised at the Bar, and was perfectly well aware that the will made in his favour a year before was automatically revoked by his stepmother's remarriage. He would call evidence to show who did destroy the will, and it was possible that that might open up quite a new view of the case.

Finally, he would point out to the jury that there was evidence against other people besides John Cavendish. He would direct their attention to the fact that the evidence against Mr. Lawrence Cavendish was quite as strong, if not stronger than that against his brother.

He would now call the prisoner.

John acquitted himself well in the witness-box. Under Sir Ernest's skilful handling, he told his tale credibly and well. The anonymous note received by him was produced, and handed to the jury to examine. The readiness with which he admitted his financial difficulties, and the disagreement with his stepmother, lent value to his denials.

At the close of his examination, he paused, and said:

"I should like to make one thing clear. I utterly reject and disapprove of Sir Ernest Heavywether's insinuations against my brother. My brother, I am convinced, had no more to do with the crime than I have."

Sir Ernest merely smiled, and noted with a sharp eye that John's protest had produced a very favourable impression on the jury.

Then the cross-examination began.

"I understand you to say that it never entered your head that the witnesses at the inquest could possibly have mistaken your voice for that of Mr. Inglethorp. Is not that very surprising?"

"No, I don't think so. I was told there had been a quarrel between my mother and Mr. Inglethorp, and it never occurred to me that such was not really the case."

"Not when the servant Dorcas repeated certain fragments of the conversation—fragments which you must have recognized?"

"I did not recognize them."

"Your memory must be unusually short!"

"No, but we were both angry, and, I think, said more than we meant. I paid very little attention to my mother's actual words."

Mr. Philips' incredulous sniff was a triumph of forensic skill. He passed on to the subject of the note.

"You have produced this note very opportunely. Tell me, is there nothing familiar about the hand-writing of it?"

"Not that I know of."

"Do you not think that it bears a marked resemblance to your own hand-writing—carelessly disguised?"

"No, I do not think so."

"I put it to you that it is your own hand-writing!"

"No."

"I put it to you that, anxious to prove an alibi, you conceived the idea of a fictitious and rather incredible appointment, and wrote this note yourself in order to bear out your statement!"

"No."

"Is it not a fact that, at the time you claim to have been waiting about at a solitary and unfrequented spot, you were really in the chemist's shop in Styles St. Mary, where you purchased strychnine in the name of Alfred Inglethorp?"

"No, that is a lie."

"I put it to you that, wearing a suit of Mr. Inglethorp's clothes, with a black beard trimmed to resemble his, you were there—and signed the register in his name!"

"That is absolutely untrue."

"Then I will leave the remarkable similarity of hand-writing between the note, the register, and your own, to the consideration of the jury," said Mr. Philips, and sat down with the air of a man who has done his duty, but who was nevertheless horrified by such deliberate perjury.

After this, as it was growing late, the case was adjourned till Monday.

Poirot, I noticed, was looking profoundly discouraged. He had that little frown between the eyes that I knew so well.

"What is it, Poirot?" I inquired.

"Ah, *mon ami*, things are going badly, badly."

In spite of myself, my heart gave a leap of relief. Evidently there was a likelihood of John Cavendish being acquitted.

When we reached the house, my little friend waved aside Mary's offer of tea.

"No, I thank you, madame. I will mount to my room."

I followed him. Still frowning, he went across to the desk and took out a small pack of patience cards. Then he drew up a chair to the table, and, to my utter amazement, began solemnly to build card houses!

My jaw dropped involuntarily, and he said at once:

"No, *mon ami*, I am not in my second childhood! I steady my nerves, that is all. This employment requires precision of the fingers. With precision of the fingers goes precision of the brain. And never have I needed that more than now!"

"What is the trouble?" I asked.

With a great thump on the table, Poirot demolished his carefully built up edifice.

"It is this, *mon ami*! That I can build card houses seven stories high, but I cannot"—thump—"find"—thump—" that last link of which I spoke to you."

I could not quite tell what to say, so I held my peace, and he began slowly building up the cards again, speaking in jerks as he did so.

"It is done—so! By placing—one card—on another—with mathematical—precision!"

I watched the card house rising under his hands, story by story. He never hesitated or faltered. It was really almost like a conjuring trick.

"What a steady hand you've got," I remarked. "I believe I've only seen your hand shake once."

"On an occasion when I was enraged, without doubt," observed Poirot, with great placidity.

"Yes indeed! You were in a towering rage. Do you remember? It was when you discovered that the lock of the despatch-case in Mrs. Inglethorp's bedroom had been forced. You stood by the mantelpiece, twiddling the things on it in your usual fashion, and your hand shook like a leaf! I must say——"

But I stopped suddenly. For Poirot, uttering a hoarse and inarticulate cry, again annihilated his masterpiece of cards, and putting his hands over his eyes swayed backwards and forwards, apparently suffering the keenest agony.

"Good heavens, Poirot!" I cried. "What is the matter? Are you taken ill?"

"No, no," he gasped. "It is—it is—that I have an idea!"

"Oh!" I exclaimed, much relieved. "One of your 'little ideas'?"

"Ah, *ma foi*, no!" replied Poirot frankly. "This time it is an idea gigantic! Stupendous! And you—*you*, my friend, have given it to me!"

Suddenly clasping me in his arms, he kissed me warmly on both cheeks, and before I had recovered from my surprise ran headlong from the room.

Mary Cavendish entered at that moment.

"What *is* the matter with Monsieur Poirot? He rushed past me crying out: 'A garage! For the love of Heaven, direct me to a garage, madame!' And, before I could answer, he had dashed out into the street."

I hurried to the window. True enough, there he was, tearing down the street, hatless, and gesticulating as he went. I turned to Mary with a gesture of despair.

"He'll be stopped by a policeman in another minute. There he goes, round the corner!"

Our eyes met, and we stared helplessly at one another.

"What can be the matter?"

I shook my head.

"I don't know. He was building card houses, when suddenly he said he had an idea, and rushed off as you saw."

"Well," said Mary, "I expect he will be back before dinner."

But night fell, and Poirot had not returned.

TWELVE
The Last Link

Poirot's abrupt departure had intrigued us all greatly. Sunday morning wore away, and still he did not reappear. But about three o'clock a ferocious and prolonged hooting outside drove us to the window, to see Poirot alighting from a car, accompanied by Japp and Summerhaye. The little man was transformed. He radiated an absurd complacency. He bowed with exaggerated respect to Mary Cavendish.

"Madame, I have your permission to hold a little *réunion* in the *salon*? It is necessary for everyone to attend."

Mary smiled sadly.

"You know, Monsieur Poirot, that you have *carte blanche* in every way."

"You are too amiable, madame."

Still beaming, Poirot marshalled us all into the drawing-room, bringing forward chairs as he did so.

"Miss Howard—here. Mademoiselle Cynthia. Monsieur Lawrence. The good Dorcas. And Annie. *Bien!* We must delay our proceedings a few minutes until Mr. Inglethorp arrives. I have sent him a note."

Miss Howard rose immediately from her seat.

"If that man comes into the house, I leave it!"

"No, no!" Poirot went up to her and pleaded in a low voice.

Finally Miss Howard consented to return to her chair. A few

minutes later Alfred Inglethorp entered the room.

The company once assembled, Poirot rose from his seat with the air of a popular lecturer, and bowed politely to his audience.

"*Messieurs, mesdames*, as you all know, I was called in by Monsieur John Cavendish to investigate this case. I at once examined the bedroom of the deceased which, by the advice of the doctors, had been kept locked, and was consequently exactly as it had been when the tragedy occurred. I found: first, a fragment of green material; second, a stain on the carpet near the window, still damp; thirdly, an empty box of bromide powders.

"To take the fragment of green material first, I found it caught in the bolt of the communicating door between that room and the adjoining one occupied by Mademoiselle Cynthia. I handed the fragment over to the police who did not consider it of much importance. Nor did they recognize it for what it was—a piece torn from a green land armlet."

There was a little stir of excitement.

"Now there was only one person at Styles who worked on the land—Mrs. Cavendish. Therefore it must have been Mrs. Cavendish who entered the deceased's room through the door communicating with Mademoiselle Cynthia's room."

"But that door was bolted on the inside!" I cried.

"When I examined the room, yes. But in the first place we have only her word for it, since it was she who tried that particular door and reported it fastened. In the ensuing confusion she would have had ample opportunity to shoot the bolt across. I took an early opportunity of verifying my conjectures. To begin with, the fragment corresponds exactly with a tear in Mrs. Cavendish's armlet. Also, at the inquest, Mrs. Cavendish declared that she had heard, from her own room, the fall of the table by the bed. I took an early opportunity of testing that statement by stationing my friend Monsieur Hastings in the left wing of the building, just outside Mrs. Cavendish's door. I myself, in company with the police, went to the deceased's room, and whilst there I, apparently accidentally, knocked over the table in question, but found that, as I had expected, Monsieur Hastings had heard no sound at all. This confirmed my belief that Mrs. Cavendish was not speaking the truth when she declared that she had been dressing in her room at the time of the tragedy. In fact, I was convinced that, far from having been in her own room, Mrs. Cavendish was actually in the deceased's room when the alarm was given."

I shot a quick glance at Mary. She was very pale, but smiling.

"I proceeded to reason on that assumption. Mrs. Cavendish is in her mother-in-law's room. We will say that she is seeking for something and has not yet found it. Suddenly Mrs. Inglethorp awakens and is seized with an alarming paroxysm. She flings out her arm, overturning the bed table, and then pulls desperately at the bell. Mrs. Cavendish, startled, drops her candle, scattering the grease on the carpet. She picks it up, and retreats quickly to Mademoiselle Cynthia's room, closing the door behind her. She hurries out into the passage, for the servants must not find her where she is. But it is too late! Already footsteps are echoing along the gallery which connects the two wings. What can she do? Quick as thought, she hurries back to the young girl's room, and starts shaking her awake. The hastily aroused household come trooping down the passage. They are all busily battering at Mrs. Inglethorp's door. It occurs to nobody that Mrs. Cavendish has not arrived with the rest, but—and this is significant—I can find no one who saw her come from the other wing." He looked at Mary Cavendish. "Am I right, madame?"

She bowed her head.

"Quite right, monsieur. You understand that, if I had thought I would do my husband any good by revealing these facts, I would have done so. But it did not seem to me to bear upon the question of his guilt or innocence."

"In a sense, that is correct, madame. But it cleared my mind of many misconceptions, and left me free to see other facts in their true significance."

"The will!" cried Lawrence. "Then it was you, Mary, who destroyed the will?"

She shook her head, and Poirot shook his also.

"No," he said quietly. "There is only one person who could possibly have destroyed that will—Mrs. Inglethorp herself!"

"Impossible!" I exclaimed. "She had only made it out that very afternoon!"

"Nevertheless, *mon ami*, it was Mrs. Inglethorp. Because, in no other way can you account for the fact that, on one of the hottest days of the year, Mrs. Inglethorp ordered a fire to be lighted in her room."

I gave a gasp. What idiots we had been never to think of that fire as being incongruous! Poirot was continuing:

"The temperature on that day, messieurs, was 80 degrees in the shade. Yet Mrs. Inglethorp ordered a fire! Why? Because she wished to destroy something, and could think of no other way. You will remember that, in consequence of the War economics practiced at Styles, no waste paper was thrown away. There was therefore no means of destroying a thick document such as a will. The moment I heard of a fire being lighted in Mrs. Inglethorp's room, I leaped to the conclusion that it was to destroy some important document—possibly a will. So the discovery of the charred fragment in the grate was no surprise to me. I did not, of course, know at the time that the will in question had only been made this afternoon, and I will admit that, when I learnt that fact, I fell into a grievous error. I came to the conclusion that Mrs. Inglethorp's determination to destroy her will arose as a direct consequence of the quarrel she had that afternoon, and that therefore the quarrel took place after, and not before the making of the will.

"Here, as we know, I was wrong, and I was forced to abandon that idea. I faced the problem from a new standpoint. Now, at four o'clock, Dorcas overheard her mistress saying angrily: 'You need not think that any fear of publicity, or scandal between husband and wife will deter me." I conjectured, and conjectured rightly, that these words were addressed, not to her husband, but to Mr. John Cavendish. At five o'clock, an hour later, she uses almost the same words, but the standpoint is different. She admits to Dorcas, 'I don't know what to do; scandal between husband and wife is a dreadful thing.' At four o'clock she has been angry, but completely mistress of herself. At five o'clock she is in violent distress, and speaks of having had a great shock.

"Looking at the matter psychologically, I drew one deduction which I was convinced was correct. The second 'scandal' she spoke of was not the same as the first—and it concerned herself!

"Let us reconstruct. At four o'clock, Mrs. Inglethorp quarrels with her son, and threatens to denounce him to his wife—who, by the way, overheard the greater part of the conversation. At four-thirty, Mrs. Inglethorp, in consequence of a conversation on the validity of wills, makes a will in favour of her husband, which the two gardeners witness. At five o'clock, Dorcas finds her mistress in a state of considerable agitation, with a slip of paper—'a letter,' Dorcas thinks—in her hand, and it is then that she orders the fire in her room to be lighted. Presumably, then, between four-thirty and five o'clock, something has occurred to occasion a complete revolution of feeling, since she is now as anxious to destroy the will, as she was before to make it. What was that something?

"As far as we know, she was quite alone during that half-hour. Nobody entered or left that boudoir. What then occasioned this sudden change of sentiment?

"One can only guess, but I believe my guess to be correct. Mrs. Inglethorp had no stamps in her desk. We know this, because later she asked Dorcas to bring her some. Now in the opposite corner of the room stood her husband's desk—locked. She was anxious to find some stamps, and, according to my theory, she tried her own keys in the desk. That one of them fitted I know. She therefore opened the desk, and in searching for the stamps she came across something else—that slip of paper which Dorcas saw in her hand, and which assuredly was never meant for Mrs.

Inglethorp's eyes. On the other hand, Mrs. Cavendish believed that the slip of paper to which her mother-in-law clung so tenaciously was a written proof of her own husband's infidelity. She demanded it from Mrs. Inglethorp who assured her, quite truly, that it had nothing to do with that matter. Mrs. Cavendish did not believe her. She thought that Mrs. Inglethorp was shielding her stepson. Now Mrs. Cavendish is a very resolute woman, and, behind her mask of reserve, she was madly jealous of her husband. She determined to get hold of that paper at all costs, and in this resolution chance came to her aid. She happened to pick up the key of Mrs. Inglethorp's despatch-case, which had been lost that morning. She knew that her mother-in-law invariably kept all important papers in this particular case.

"Mrs. Cavendish, therefore, made her plans as only a woman driven desperate through jealousy could have done. Some time in the evening she unbolted the door leading into Mademoiselle Cynthia's room. Possibly she applied oil to the hinges, for I found that it opened quite noiselessly when I tried it. She put off her project until the early hours of the morning as being safer, since the servants were accustomed to hearing her move about her room at that time. She dressed completely in her land kit, and made her way quietly through Mademoiselle Cynthia's room into that of Mrs. Inglethorp."

He paused a moment, and Cynthia interrupted:

"But I should have woken up if anyone had come through my room?"

"Not if you were drugged, mademoiselle."

"Drugged?"

"*Mais, oui!*"

"You remember"—he addressed us collectively again—"that through all the tumult and noise next door Mademoiselle Cynthia slept. That admitted of two possibilities. Either her sleep was feigned—which I did not believe—or her unconsciousness was induced by artificial means.

"With this latter idea in my mind, I examined all the coffee-cups most carefully, remembering that it was Mrs. Cavendish who had brought Mademoiselle Cynthia her coffee the night before. I took a sample from each cup, and had them analysed—with no result. I had counted the cups carefully, in the event of one having been removed. Six persons had taken coffee, and six cups were duly found. I had to confess myself mistaken.

"Then I discovered that I had been guilty of a very grave oversight. Coffee had been brought in for seven persons, not six, for Dr. Bauerstein had been there that evening. This changed the face of the whole affair, for there was now one cup missing. The servants noticed nothing, since Annie, the housemaid, who took in the coffee, brought in seven cups, not knowing that Mr. Inglethorp never drank it, whereas Dorcas, who cleared them away the following morning, found six as usual—or strictly speaking she found five, the sixth being the one found broken in Mrs. Inglethorp's room.

"I was confident that the missing cup was that of Mademoiselle Cynthia. I had an additional reason for that belief in the fact that all the cups found contained sugar, which Mademoiselle Cynthia never took in her coffee. My attention was attracted by the story of Annie about some 'salt' on the tray of cocoa which she took every night to Mrs. Inglethorp's room. I accordingly secured a sample of that cocoa, and sent it to be analysed."

"But that had already been done by Dr. Bauerstein," said Lawrence quickly.

"Not exactly. The analyst was asked by him to report whether strychnine was, or was not, present. He did not have it tested, as I did, for a narcotic."

"For a narcotic?"

"Yes. Here is the analyst's report. Mrs. Cavendish administered a safe, but effectual, narcotic to both Mrs. Inglethorp and Mademoiselle Cynthia. And it is possible that she had a *mauvais quart d'heure* in consequence! Imagine her feelings when her

176

mother-in-law is suddenly taken ill and dies, and immediately after she hears the word 'Poison'! She has believed that the sleeping draught she administered was perfectly harmless, but there is no doubt that for one terrible moment she must have feared that Mrs. Inglethorp's death lay at her door. She is seized with panic, and under its influence she hurries downstairs, and quickly drops the coffee-cup and saucer used by Mademoiselle Cynthia into a large brass vase, where it is discovered later by Monsieur Lawrence. The remains of the cocoa she dare not touch. Too many eyes are upon her. Guess at her relief when strychnine is mentioned, and she discovers that after all the tragedy is not her doing.

"We are now able to account for the symptoms of strychnine poisoning being so long in making their appearance. A narcotic taken with strychnine will delay the action of the poison for some hours."

Poirot paused. Mary looked up at him, the colour slowly rising in her face.

"All you have said is quite true, Monsieur Poirot. It was the most awful hour of my life. I shall never forget it. But you are wonderful. I understand now——"

"What I meant when I told you that you could safely confess to Papa Poirot, eh? But you would not trust me."

"I see everything now," said Lawrence. "The drugged cocoa, taken on top of the poisoned coffee, amply accounts for the delay."

"Exactly. But was the coffee poisoned, or was it not? We come to a little difficulty here, since Mrs. Inglethorp never drank it."

"What?" The cry of surprise was universal.

"No. You will remember my speaking of a stain on the carpet in Mrs. Inglethorp's room? There were some peculiar points about that stain. It was still damp, it exhaled a strong odour of coffee, and imbedded in the nap of the carpet I found some little splinters of china. What had happened was plain to me, for not two minutes before I had placed my little case on the table near the window, and the table, tilting up, had deposited it upon the floor on precisely the identical spot. In exactly the same way, Mrs. Inglethorp had laid down her cup of coffee on reaching her room the night before, and the treacherous table had played her the same trick.

"What happened next is mere guess work on my part, but I should say that Mrs. Inglethorp picked up the broken cup and placed it on the table by the bed. Feeling in need of a stimulant of some kind, she heated up her cocoa, and drank it off then and there. Now we are faced with a new problem. We know the cocoa contained no strychnine. The coffee was never drunk. Yet the strychnine must have been administered between seven and nine o'clock that evening. What third medium was there—a medium so suitable for disguising the taste of strychnine that it is extraordinary no one has thought of it?" Poirot looked round the room, and then answered himself impressively. "Her medicine!"

"Do you mean that the murderer introduced the strychnine into her tonic?" I cried.

"There was no need to introduce it. It was already there—in the mixture. The strychnine that killed Mrs. Inglethorp was the identical strychnine prescribed by Dr. Wilkins. To make that clear to you, I will read you an extract from a book on dispensing which I found in the Dispensary of the Red Cross Hospital at Tadminster:

"'The following prescription has become famous in text books:

Strychninae Sulph.	1 gr.
Potass Bromide	ʒvi
Aqua ad.	ʒviii
Fiat Mistura	

This solution deposits in a few hours the greater part of the strychnine salt as an insoluble bromide in transparent crystals. A lady in England lost her life by taking a similar mixture: the precipitated strychnine collected at the bottom, and in taking the last dose she swallowed nearly all of it!

"Now there was, of course, no bromide in Dr. Wilkins' prescription, but you will remember that I mentioned an empty box of bromide powders. One or two of those powders introduced into the full bottle of medicine would effectually precipitate the strychnine, as the book describes, and cause it to be taken in the last dose. You will learn later that the person who usually poured out Mrs. Inglethorp's medicine was always extremely careful not to shake the bottle, but to leave the sediment at the bottom of it undisturbed.

"Throughout the case, there have been evidences that the tragedy was intended to take place on Monday evening. On that day, Mrs. Inglethorp's bell wire was neatly cut, and on Monday evening Mademoiselle Cynthia was spending the night with friends, so that Mrs. Inglethorp would have been quite alone in the right wing, completely shut off from help of any kind, and would have died, in all probability, before medical aid could have been summoned. But in her hurry to be in time for the village entertainment Mrs. Inglethorp forgot to take her medicine, and the next day she lunched away from home, so that the last—and fatal—dose was actually taken twenty-four hours later than had been anticipated by the murderer; and it is owing to that delay that the final proof—the last link of the chain—is now in my hands."

Amid breathless excitement, he held out three thin strips of paper.

"A letter in the murderer's own hand-writing, *mes amis!* Had it been a little clearer in its terms, it is possible that Mrs. Inglethorp, warned in time, would have escaped. As it was, she realized her danger, but not the manner of it."

In the deathly silence, Poirot pieced together the slips of paper and, clearing his throat, read:

Dearest Evelyn:

'You will be anxious at hearing nothing. It is all right—only it will be to-night instead of last night. You understand. There's a good time coming once the old woman is dead and out of the way. No one can possibly bring home the crime to me. That idea of yours about the

bromides was a stroke of genius! But we must be very circumspect. A false step——'

"Here, my friends, the letter breaks off. Doubtless the writer was interrupted; but there can be no question as to his identity. We all know this hand-writing and——"

A howl that was almost a scream broke the silence.

"You devil! How did you get it?"

A chair was overturned. Poirot skipped nimbly aside. A quick movement on his part, and his assailant fell with a crash.

"Messieurs, mesdames," said Poirot, with a flourish, "let me introduce you to the murderer, Mr. Alfred Inglethorp!"

THIRTEEN
Poirot Explains

P oirot, you old villain," I said, "I've half a mind to strangle
you! What do you mean by deceiving me as you have done?"
We were sitting in the library. Several hectic days lay
behind us. In the room below, John and Mary were together once
more, while Alfred Inglethorp and Miss Howard were in custody.
Now at last, I had Poirot to myself, and could relieve my still
burning curiosity.

Poirot did not answer me for a moment, but at last he said:

"I did not deceive you, *mon ami*. At most, I permitted you to
deceive yourself."

"Yes, but why?"

"Well, it is difficult to explain. You see, my friend, you have a
nature so honest, and a countenance so transparent, that—*enfin*,
to conceal your feelings is impossible! If I had told you my ideas,
the very first time you saw Mr. Alfred Inglethorp that astute gentleman would have—in your so expressive idiom—'smelt a rat'!
And then, *bonjour* to our chances of catching him!"

"I think that I have more diplomacy than you give me credit for."

"My friend," besought Poirot, "I implore you, do not enrage
yourself! Your help has been of the most invaluable. It is but the
extremely beautiful nature that you have, which made me pause."

"Well," I grumbled, a little mollified. "I still think you might
have given me a hint."

"But I did, my friend. Several hints. You would not take them. Think now, did I ever say to you that I believed John Cavendish guilty? Did I not, on the contrary, tell you that he would almost certainly be acquitted?"

"Yes, but——"

"And did I not immediately afterwards speak of the difficulty of bringing the murderer to justice? Was it not plain to you that I was speaking of two entirely different persons?"

"No," I said, "it was not plain to me!"

"Then again," continued Poirot, "at the beginning, did I not repeat to you several times that I didn't want Mr. Inglethorp arrested *now*? That should have conveyed something to you."

"Do you mean to say you suspected him as long ago as that?"

"Yes. To begin with, whoever else might benefit by Mrs. Inglethorp's death, her husband would benefit the most. There was no getting away from that. When I went up to Styles with you that first day, I had no idea as to how the crime had been committed, but from what I knew of Mr. Inglethorp I fancied that it would be very hard to find anything to connect him with it. When I arrived at the château, I realized at once that it was Mrs. Inglethorp who had burnt the will; and there, by the way, you cannot complain, my friend, for I tried my best to force on you the significance of that bedroom fire in midsummer."

"Yes, yes," I said impatiently. "Go on."

"Well, my friend, as I say, my views as to Mr. Inglethorp's guilt were very much shaken. There was, in fact, so much evidence against him that I was inclined to believe that he had not done it."

"When did you change your mind?"

"When I found that the more efforts I made to clear him, the more efforts he made to get himself arrested. Then, when I discovered that Inglethorp had nothing to do with Mrs. Raikes and that in fact it was John Cavendish who was interested in that quarter, I was quite sure."

"But why?"

"Simply this. If it had been Inglethorp who was carrying on an intrigue with Mrs. Raikes, his silence was perfectly comprehensible. But, when I discovered that it was known all over the village that it was John who was attracted by the farmer's pretty wife, his silence bore quite a different interpretation. It was nonsense to pretend that he was afraid of the scandal, as no possible scandal could attach to him. This attitude of his gave me furiously to think, and I was slowly forced to the conclusion that Alfred Inglethorp wanted to be arrested. *Eh bien!* from that moment, I was equally determined that he should not be arrested."

"Wait a minute. I don't see why he wished to be arrested?"

"Because, *mon ami*, it is the law of your country that a man once acquitted can never be tried again for the same offence. Aha! but it was clever—his idea! Assuredly, he is a man of method. See here, he knew that in his position he was bound to be suspected, so he conceived the exceedingly clever idea of preparing a lot of manufactured evidence against himself. He wished to be arrested. He would then produce his irreproachable alibi—and, hey presto, he was safe for life!"

"But I still don't see how he managed to prove his alibi, and yet go to the chemist's shop?"

Poirot stared at me in surprise.

"Is it possible? My poor friend! You have not yet realized that it was Miss Howard who went to the chemist's shop?"

"Miss Howard?"

"But, certainly. Who else? It was most easy for her. She is of a good height, her voice is deep and manly; moreover, remember, she and Inglethorp are cousins, and there is a distinct resemblance between them, especially in their gait and bearing. It was simplicity itself. They are a clever pair!"

"I am still a little fogged as to how exactly the bromide business was done," I remarked.

"*Bon!* I will reconstruct for you as far as possible. I am inclined to think that Miss Howard was the master mind in that affair.

You remember her once mentioning that her father was a doctor? Possibly she dispensed his medicines for him, or she may have taken the idea from one of the many books lying about when Mademoiselle Cynthia was studying for her exam. Anyway, she was familiar with the fact that the addition of a bromide to a mixture containing strychnine would cause the precipitation of the latter. Probably the idea came to her quite suddenly. Mrs. Inglethorp had a box of bromide powders, which she occasionally took at night. What could be easier than quietly to dissolve one or more of those powders in Mrs. Inglethorp's large sized bottle of medicine when it came from Coot's? The risk is practically nil. The tragedy will not take place until nearly a fortnight later. If anyone has seen either of them touching the medicine, they will have forgotten it by that time. Miss Howard will have engineered her quarrel, and departed from the house. The lapse of time, and her absence, will defeat all suspicion. Yes, it was a clever idea! If they had left it alone, it is possible the crime might never have been brought home to them. But they were not satisfied. They tried to be too clever—and that was their undoing."

Poirot puffed at his tiny cigarette, his eyes fixed on the ceiling.

"They arranged a plan to throw suspicion on John Cavendish, by buying strychnine at the village chemist's, and signing the register in his hand-writing.

"On Monday Mrs. Inglethorp will take the last dose of her medicine. On Monday, therefore, at six o'clock, Alfred Inglethorp arranges to be seen by a number of people at a spot far removed from the village. Miss Howard has previously made up a cock and bull story about him and Mrs. Raikes to account for his holding his tongue afterwards. At six o'clock, Miss Howard, disguised as Alfred Inglethorp, enters the chemist's shop, with her story about a dog, obtains the strychnine, and writes the name of Alfred Inglethorp in John's handwriting, which she had previously studied carefully.

"But, as it will never do if John, too, can prove an alibi, she writes him an anonymous note—still copying his hand-writing—which takes him to a remote spot where it is exceedingly unlikely that anyone will see him.

"So far, all goes well. Miss Howard goes back to Middlingham. Alfred Inglethorp returns to Styles. There is nothing that can compromise him in any way, since it is Miss Howard who has the strychnine, which, after all, is only wanted as a blind to throw suspicion on John Cavendish.

"But now a hitch occurs. Mrs. Inglethorp does not take her medicine that night. The broken bell, Cynthia's absence—arranged by Inglethorp through his wife—all these are wasted. And then—he makes his slip.

"Mrs. Inglethorp is out, and he sits down to write to his accomplice, who, he fears, may be in a panic at the non-success of their plan. It is probable that Mrs. Inglethorp returned earlier than he expected. Caught in the act, and somewhat flurried he hastily shuts and locks his desk. He fears that if he remains in the room he may have to open it again, and that Mrs. Inglethorp might catch sight of the letter before he could snatch it up. So he goes out and walks in the woods, little dreaming that Mrs. Inglethorp will open his desk, and discover the incriminating document.

"But this, as we know, is what happened. Mrs. Inglethorp reads it, and becomes aware of the perfidy of her husband and Evelyn Howard, though, unfortunately, the sentence about the bromides conveys no warning to her mind. She knows that she is in danger—but is ignorant of where the danger lies. She decides to say nothing to her husband, but sits down and writes to her solicitor, asking him to come on the morrow, and she also determines to destroy immediately the will which she has just made. She keeps the fatal letter."

"It was to discover that letter, then, that her husband forced the lock of the despatch-case?"

"Yes, and from the enormous risk he ran we can see how fully he realized its importance. That letter excepted, there was absolutely nothing to connect him with the crime."

"There's only one thing I can't make out, why didn't he destroy it at once when he got hold of it?"

"Because he did not dare take the biggest risk of all—that of keeping it on his own person."

"I don't understand."

"Look at it from his point of view. I have discovered that there were only five short minutes in which he could have taken it—the five minutes immediately before our own arrival on the scene, for before that time Annie was brushing the stairs, and would have seen anyone who passed going to the right wing. Figure to yourself the scene! He enters the room, unlocking the door by means of one of the other doorkeys—they were all much alike. He hurries to the despatch-case—it is locked, and the keys are nowhere to be seen. That is a terrible blow to him, for it means that his presence in the room cannot be concealed as he had hoped. But he sees clearly that everything must be risked for the sake of that damning piece of evidence. Quickly, he forces the lock with a penknife, and turns over the papers until he finds what he is looking for.

"But now a fresh dilemma arises: he dare not keep that piece of paper on him. He may be seen leaving the room—he may be searched. If the paper is found on him, it is certain doom. Probably, at this minute, too, he hears the sounds below of Mr. Wells and John leaving the boudoir. He must act quickly. Where can he hide this terrible slip of paper? The contents of the waste-paper-basket are kept and in any case, are sure to be examined. There are no means of destroying it; and he dare not keep it. He looks round, and he sees—what do you think, *mon ami?*"

I shook my head.

"In a moment, he has torn the letter into long thin strips, and rolling them up into spills he thrusts them hurriedly in amongst the other spills in the vase on the mantle-piece."

I uttered an exclamation.

"No one would think of looking there," Poirot continued. "And he will be able, at his leisure, to come back and destroy this solitary piece of evidence against him."

"Then, all the time, it was in the spill vase in Mrs. Inglethorp's bedroom, under our very noses?" I cried.

Poirot nodded.

"Yes, my friend. That is where I discovered my 'last link,' and I owe that very fortunate discovery to you."

"To me?"

"Yes. Do you remember telling me that my hand shook as I was straightening the ornaments on the mantelpiece?"

"Yes, but I don't see——"

"No, but I saw. Do you know, my friend, I remembered that earlier in the morning, when we had been there together, I had straightened all the objects on the mantelpiece. And, if they were already straightened, there would be no need to straighten them again, unless, in the meantime, someone else had touched them."

"Dear me," I murmured, "so that is the explanation of your extraordinary behaviour. You rushed down to Styles, and found it still there?"

"Yes, and it was a race for time."

"But I still can't understand why Inglethorp was such a fool as to leave it there when he had plenty of opportunity to destroy it."

"Ah, but he had no opportunity. *I* saw to that."

"You?"

"Yes. Do you remember reproving me for taking the household into my confidence on the subject?"

"Yes."

"Well, my friend, I saw there was just one chance. I was not sure then if Inglethorp was the criminal or not, but if he was I reasoned that he would not have the paper on him, but would have hidden it somewhere, and by enlisting the sympathy of the household I could effectually prevent his destroying it. He was already under suspicion, and by making the matter public I secured the services of about ten amateur detectives, who would be watching him unceasingly, and being himself aware of their watchfulness he would not dare seek further to destroy the document. He was therefore forced to depart from the house, leaving it in the spill vase."

"But surely Miss Howard had ample opportunities of aiding him."

"Yes, but Miss Howard did not know of the paper's existence. In accordance with their prearranged plan, she never spoke to Alfred Inglethorp. They were supposed to be deadly enemies, and until John Cavendish was safely convicted they neither of them dared risk a meeting. Of course I had a watch kept on Mr. Inglethorp, hoping that sooner or later he would lead me to the hiding-place. But he was too clever to take any chances. The paper was safe where it was; since no one had thought of looking there in the first week, it was not likely they would do so afterwards. But for your lucky remark, we might never have been able to bring him to justice."

"I understand that now; but when did you first begin to suspect Miss Howard?"

"When I discovered that she had told a lie at the inquest about the letter she had received from Mrs. Inglethorp."

"Why, what was there to lie about?"

"You saw that letter? Do you recall its general appearance?"

"Yes—more or less."

"You will recollect, then, that Mrs. Inglethorp wrote a very distinctive hand, and left large clear spaces between her words. But if you look at the date at the top of the letter you will notice that 'July 17th' is quite different in this respect. Do you see what I mean?"

"No," I confessed, "I don't."

"You do not see that that letter was not written on the 17th, but on the 7th—the day after Miss Howard's departure? The '1' was written in before the '7' to turn it into the '17th'."

"But why?"

"That is exactly what I asked myself. Why does Miss Howard

suppress the letter written on the 17th, and produce this faked one instead? Because she did not wish to show the letter of the 17th. Why, again? And at once a suspicion dawned in my mind. You will remember my saying that it was wise to beware of people who were not telling you the truth."

"And yet," I cried indignantly, "after that, you gave me two reasons why Miss Howard could not have committed the crime!"

"And very good reasons too," replied Poirot. "For a long time they were a stumbling-block to me until I remembered a very significant fact: that she and Alfred Inglethorp were cousins. She could not have committed the crime single-handed, but the reasons against that did not debar her from being an accomplice. And, then, there was that rather over-vehement hatred of hers! It concealed a very opposite emotion. There was, undoubtedly, a tie of passion between them long before he came to Styles. They had already arranged their infamous plot—that he should marry this rich, but rather foolish old lady, induce her to make a will leaving her money to him, and then gain their ends by a very cleverly conceived crime. If all had gone as they planned, they would probably have left England, and lived together on their poor victim's money.

"They are a very astute and unscrupulous pair. While suspicion was to be directed against him, she would be making quiet preparations for a very different *dénouement*. She arrives from Middlingham with all the compromising items in her possession. No suspicion attaches to her. No notice is paid to her coming and going in the house. She hides the strychnine and glasses in John's room. She puts the beard in the attic. She will see to it that sooner or later they are duly discovered."

"I don't quite see why they tried to fix the blame on John," I remarked. "It would have been much easier for them to bring the crime home to Lawrence."

"Yes, but that was mere chance. All the evidence against him arose out of pure accident. It must, in fact, have been distinctly annoying to the pair of schemers."

"His manner was unfortunate," I observed thoughtfully.

"Yes. You realize, of course, what was at the back of that?"

"No."

"You did not understand that he believed Mademoiselle Cynthia guilty of the crime?"

"No," I exclaimed, astonished. "Impossible!"

"Not at all. I myself nearly had the same idea. It was in my mind when I asked Mr. Wells that first question about the will. Then there were the bromide powders which she had made up, and her clever male impersonations, as Dorcas recounted them to us. There was really more evidence against her than anyone else."

"You are joking, Poirot!"

"No. Shall I tell you what made Monsieur Lawrence turn so pale when he first entered his mother's room on the fatal night? It was because, whilst his mother lay there, obviously poisoned, he saw, over your shoulder, that the door into Mademoiselle Cynthia's room was unbolted."

"But he declared that he saw it bolted!" I cried.

"Exactly," said Poirot dryly. "And that was just what confirmed my suspicion that it was not. He was shielding Mademoiselle Cynthia."

"But why should he shield her?"

"Because he is in love with her."

I laughed.

"There, Poirot, you are quite wrong! I happen to know for a fact that, far from being in love with her, he positively dislikes her."

"Who told you that, *mon ami?*"

"Cynthia herself."

"*La pauvre petite!* And she was concerned?"

"She said that she did not mind at all."

"Then she certainly did mind very much," remarked Poirot. "They are like that—*les femmes!*"

"What you say about Lawrence is a great surprise to me," I said.

"But why? It was most obvious. Did not Monsieur Lawrence make the sour face every time Mademoiselle Cynthia spoke and laughed with his brother? He had taken it into his long head that Mademoiselle Cynthia was in love with Monsieur John. When he entered his mother's room, and saw her obviously poisoned, he jumped to the conclusion that Mademoiselle Cynthia knew something about the matter. He was nearly driven desperate. First he crushed the coffee-cup to powder under his feet, remembering that *she* had gone up with his mother the night before, and he determined that there should be no chance of testing its contents. Thenceforward, he strenuously, and quite uselessly, upheld the theory of 'Death from natural causes'."

"And what about the 'extra coffee-cup'?"

"I was fairly certain that it was Mrs. Cavendish who had hidden it, but I had to make sure. Monsieur Lawrence did not know at all what I meant; but, on reflection, he came to the conclusion that if he could find an extra coffee-cup anywhere his lady love would be cleared of suspicion. And he was perfectly right."

"One thing more. What did Mrs. Inglethorp mean by her dying words?"

"They were, of course, an accusation against her husband."

"Dear me, Poirot," I said with a sigh, "I think you have explained everything. I am glad it has all ended so happily. Even John and his wife are reconciled."

"Thanks to me."

"How do you mean—thanks to you?"

"My dear friend, do you not realize that it was simply and solely the trial which has brought them together again? That John Cavendish still loved his wife, I was convinced. Also, that she was equally in love with him. But they had drifted very far apart. It all arose from a misunderstanding. She married him without love. He knew it. He is a sensitive man in his way, he would not force himself upon her if she did not want him. And, as he withdrew, her love awoke. But they are both unusually proud, and their pride held them inexorably apart. He drifted into an entanglement with Mrs. Raikes, and she deliberately cultivated the friendship of Dr. Bauerstein. Do you remember the day of John Cavendish's arrest, when you found me deliberating over a big decision?"

"Yes, I quite understood your distress."

"Pardon me, *mon ami*, but you did not understand it in the least. I was trying to decide whether or not I would clear John Cavendish at once. I could have cleared him—though it might have meant a failure to convict the real criminals. They were entirely in the dark as to my real attitude up to the very last moment—which partly accounts for my success."

"Do you mean that you could have saved John Cavendish from being brought to trial?"

"Yes, my friend. But I eventually decided in favour of 'a woman's happiness'. Nothing but the great danger through which they have passed could have brought these two proud souls together again."

I looked at Poirot in silent amazement. The colossal cheek of the little man! Who on earth but Poirot would have thought of a trial for murder as a restorer of conjugal happiness!

"I perceive your thoughts, *mon ami*," said Poirot, smiling at me. "No one but Hercule Poirot would have attempted such a thing! And you are wrong in condemning it. The happiness of one man and one woman is the greatest thing in all the world."

His words took me back to earlier events. I remembered Mary as she lay white and exhausted on the sofa, listening, listening. There had come the sound of the bell below. She had started up. Poirot had opened the door, and meeting her agonized eyes had nodded gently. "Yes, madame," he said. "I have brought him back to you." He had stood aside, and as I went out I had seen the look in Mary's eyes, as John Cavendish had caught his wife in his arms.

"Perhaps you are right, Poirot," I said gently. "Yes, it is the greatest thing in the world."

Suddenly, there was a tap at the door, and Cynthia peeped in.

"I—I only——"

"Come in," I said, springing up.

She came in, but did not sit down.

"I—only wanted to tell you something——"

"Yes?"

Cynthia fidgeted with a little tassel for some moments, then, suddenly exclaiming: "You dears!" kissed first me and then Poirot, and rushed out of the room again.

"What on earth does this mean?" I asked, surprised.

It was very nice to be kissed by Cynthia, but the publicity of the salute rather impaired the pleasure.

"It means that she has discovered Monsieur Lawrence does not dislike her as much as she thought," replied Poirot philosophically.

"But——"

"Here he is."

Lawrence at that moment passed the door.

"Eh! Monsieur Lawrence," called Poirot. "We must congratulate you, is it not so?"

Lawrence blushed, and then smiled awkwardly. A man in love is a sorry spectacle. Now Cynthia had looked charming.

I sighed.

"What is it, *mon ami?*"

"Nothing," I said sadly. "They are two delightful women!"

"And neither of them is for you?" finished Poirot. "Never mind. Console yourself, my friend. We may hunt together again, who knows? And then——"

THE END